"*The Orc King* finds Drizzt's whirling scimitar blades tackling both familiar foes and refreshingly ambiguous moral challenges . . . The story line marks the continuation of Salvatore's maturation as a writer, introducing more complex themes into a frequently black-and-white fantasy landscape."

—*Kirkus*

"(R.A. Salvatore) is not only skilled enough to create fantastic worlds littered with dozens upon dozens of magnificent characters, creatures, landscapes, and wonders, but he has been born with the additional talent of being able to take what appears within the fabric of his mind's eye, and bring it to life with descriptive, colorful, rich, and meaningful verbiage."

—Todd McFarlane

"There's good reason this saga is one of the most popular—and beloved—fantasy series of all time: breakneck pacing, deeply complex characters and nonstop action. If you read just one adventure fantasy saga in your lifetime, let it be this one."

—Paul Goat Allen, *B&N Explorations* on *Streams of Silver*

"When reading . . . the Legend of Drizzt, I believe you will wonder whether (R.A. Salvatore) is writing fiction, or whether he is describing a secret place he's been to, a secret history he's really experienced and is kind enough to reveal to us."

—James Merendino, Director of *SLC Punk*

"Salvatore's fight scenes are probably the best I've ever read. His description, though detailed, is very fast paced. Every time I read one, my heart races and my hands shake. It is pure brilliance . . ."

—SFFWorld on *The Legacy*

"The action sequences are parallel to none and I have discovered what an extraordinary writer R.A. Salvatore is. *Sojourn* is the perfect fantasy novel and Drizzt Do'Urden is the most exceptional fantasy character ever created. Any way you look at it, this book is stupendous, a masterpiece of fantasy that any reader will love."

—*Conan Tigard* f

## THE LEGEND OF DRIZZT®

*Homeland*
*Exile*
*Sojourn*
*The Crystal Shard*
*Streams of Silver*
*The Halfling's Gem*
*The Legacy*
*Starless Night*
*Siege of Darkness*
*Passage to Dawn*
*The Silent Blade*
*The Spine of the World*
*Sea of Swords*

## THE HUNTER'S BLADES

*The Thousand Orcs*
*The Lone Drow*
*The Two Swords*

## TRANSITIONS

*The Orc King*
*The Pirate King*
*The Ghost King*

## THE SELLSWORDS

*Servant of the Shard*
*Promise of the Witch-King*
*Road of the Patriarch*

# THE LEGEND OF DRIZZT

## 25TH ANNIVERSARY EDITION

R.A. SALVATORE

BOOK I : HOMELAND ✦ EXILE ✦ SOJOURN

# THE LEGEND OF DRIZZT®

## 25th Anniversary Edition, Book I



Published by Wizards of the Coast LLC. Manufactured by: Hasbro SA, Rue Emile-Boéchat 31, 2800 Delémont, CH. Represented by Hasbro Europe, 2 Roundwood Ave, Stockley Park, Uxbridge, Middlesex, UB11 1AZ, UK.



Printed in the U.S.A.

Cover art by Todd Lockwood

Hardcover Edition First Printing: February 2008
This Edition First Printing: September 2013

This book collects the complete text from the December 2005 edition of Homeland, the March 2006 edition of Exile, and the June 2006 edition of Sojourn.

9

ISBN: 978-0-7869-6537-3
620A7097000001 EN

For customer service, contact:

U.S., Canada, Asia Pacific, & Latin America: Wizards of the Coast LLC, P.O. Box 707, Renton, WA 98057-0707, +1-800-324-6496, www.wizards.com/customerservice

U.K., Eire, & South Africa: Wizards of the Coast LLC, c/o Hasbro UK Ltd., P.O. Box 43, Newport, NP19 4YD, UK, Tel: +08457 12 55 99, Email: wizards@hasbro.co.uk

All other countries: Wizards of the Coast p/a Hasbro Belgium NV/SA, Industrialaan 1, 1702 Groot-Bijgaarden, Belgium, Tel: +32.70.233.277, Email: wizards@hasbro.be

Visit our web site at www.wizards.com

Dedications

## Homeland

To my best friend,
my brother,
Gary

## Exile

To Diane,
with all my love

## Sojourn

It is time for me to acknowledge the two people whose belief in me and whose creative influence helped to make Drizzt's tales possible.
I dedicate *Sojourn* to
Mary Kirchoff and J. Eric Severson,
editors and friends, with all my thanks

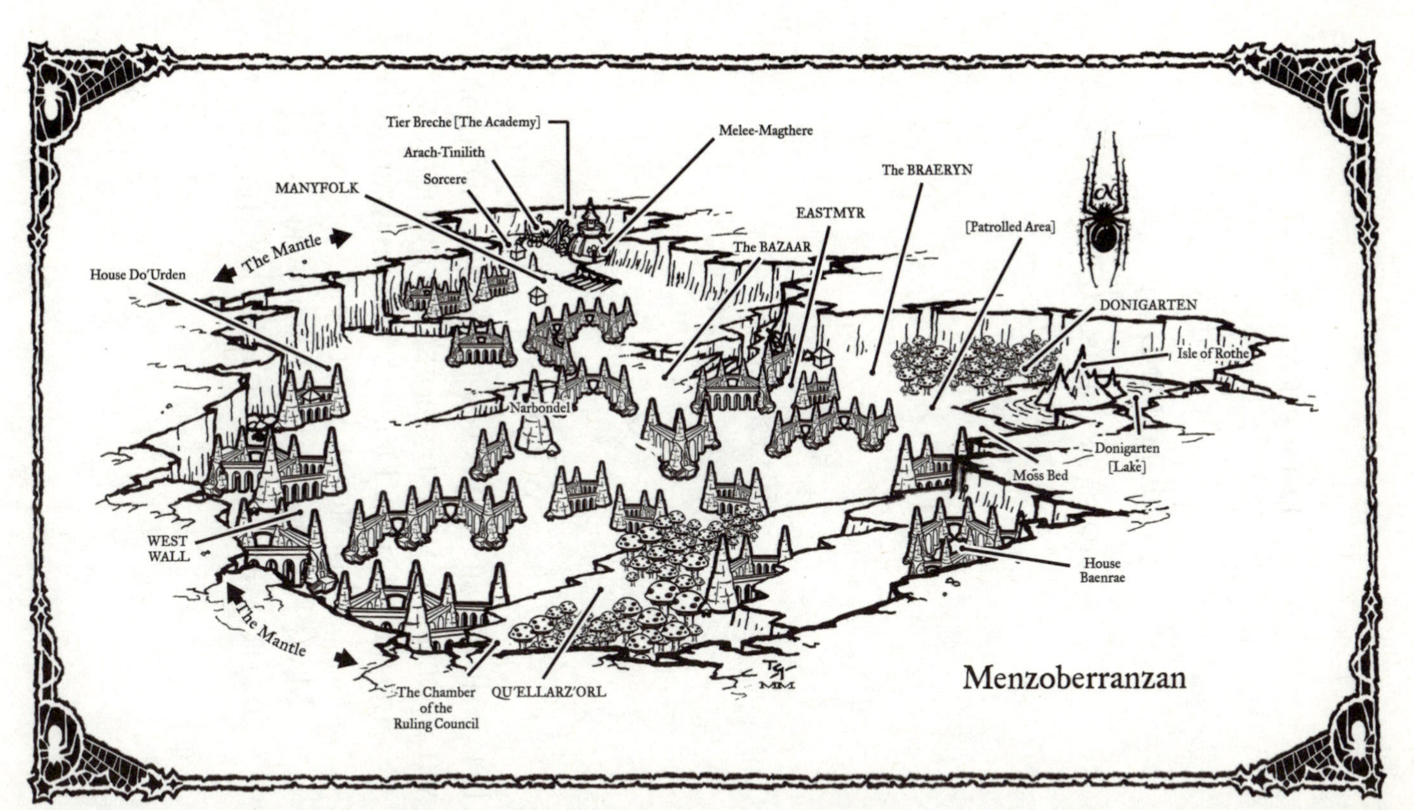
Tier Breche [The Academy]
Melee-Magthere
Arach-Tinilith
Sorcere
MANYFOLK
The BRAERYN
EASTMYR
The BAZAAR
[Patrolled Area]
The Mantle
House Do'Urden
DONIGARTEN
Isle of Rothe
Narbondel
Donigarten
[Lake]
Moss Bed
WEST
WALL
House
Baenrae
The Mantle
The Chamber
of the
Ruling Council
QU'ELLARZ'ORL
Menzoberranzan

HOMELAND
THE LEGEND OF DRIZZT
BOOK I

# Prelude

Never does a star grace this land with a poet's light of twinkling mysteries, nor does the sun send to here its rays of warmth and life. This is the Underdark, the secret world beneath the bustling surface of the Forgotten Realms, whose sky is a ceiling of heartless stone and whose walls show the gray blandness of death in the torchlight of the foolish surface-dwellers that stumble here. This is not their world, not the world of light. Most who come here uninvited do not return.

Those who do escape to the safety of their surface homes return changed. Their eyes have seen the shadows and the gloom, the inevitable doom of the Underdark.

Dark corridors meander throughout the dark realm in winding courses, connecting caverns great and small, with ceilings high and low. Mounds of stone as pointed as the teeth of a sleeping dragon leer down in silent threat or rise up to block the way of intruders.

There is a silence here, profound and foreboding, the crouched hush of a predator at work. Too often the only sound, the only reminder to travelers in the Underdark that they have not lost their sense of hearing altogether, is a distant and echoing drip of water, beating like the heart of a beast, slipping through the silent stones to the deep Underdark pools of chilled water. What lies beneath the still onyx surface of these pools one can only guess. What secrets await the brave, what horrors await the foolish, only the imagination can reveal—until the stillness is disturbed.

This is the Underdark.

⚔ ⚔ ⚔ ⚔ ⚔

There are pockets of life here, cities as great as many of those on the surface. Around any of the countless bends and turns in the gray stone a traveler might stumble suddenly into the perimeter of such a city, a stark contrast to the emptiness of the corridors. These places are not havens, though; only the foolish traveler would assume so. They are the homes of the most evil races in all the Realms, most notably the duergar, the kuo-toa, and the drow.

In one such cavern, two miles wide and a thousand feet high, looms Menzoberranzan, a monument to the other worldly and—ultimately—deadly grace that marks the race of drow elves. Menzoberranzan is not a large city by drow standards; only twenty thousand dark elves reside there. Where, in ages past, there had been an empty cavern of roughly shaped stalactites and stalagmites now stands artistry, row after row of carved castles thrumming in a quiet glow of magic. The city is perfection of form, where not a stone has been left to its natural shape. This sense of order and control, however, is but a cruel facade, a deception hiding the chaos and vileness that rule the dark elves' hearts. Like their cities, they are a beautiful, slender, and delicate people, with features sharp and haunting.

Yet the drow are the rulers of this unruled world, the deadliest of the deadly, and all other races take cautious note of their passing. Beauty itself pales at the end of a dark elf's sword. The drow are the survivors, and this is the Underdark, the valley of death—the land of nameless nightmares.

# Part One

## Station

Station: In all the world of the drow, there is no more important word. It is the calling of their—of our—religion, the incessant pulling of hungering heartstrings. Ambition overrides good sense and compassion is thrown away in its face, all in the name of Lolth, the Spider Queen.

Ascension to power in drow society is a simple process of assassination. The Spider Queen is a deity of chaos, and she and her high priestesses, the true rulers of the drow world, do not look with ill favor upon ambitious individuals wielding poisoned daggers.

Of course, there are rules of behavior; every society must boast of these. To openly commit murder or wage war invites the pretense of justice, and penalties exacted in the name of drow justice are merciless. To stick a dagger in the back of a rival during the chaos of a larger battle or in the quiet shadows of an alley, however, is quite acceptable—even applauded. Investigation is not the forte of drow justice. No one cares enough to bother.

Station is the way of Lolth, the ambition she bestows to further the chaos, to keep her drow "children" along their appointed course of self-imprisonment. Children? Pawns, more likely, dancing dolls for the Spider Queen, puppets on the imperceptible but impervious strands of her web. All climb the Spider Queen's ladders; all hunt for her pleasure; and all fall to the hunters of her pleasure.

Station is the paradox of the world of my people, the limitation of our power within the hunger for power. It is gained through treachery and invites treachery against those who gain it. Those most powerful in Menzoberranzan spend their days watching over their shoulders, defending against the daggers that would find their backs. Their deaths usually come from the front.

—Drizzt Do'Urden

# Menzoberranzan

To a surface dweller, he might have passed undetected only a foot away. The padded footfalls of his lizard mount were too light to be heard, and the pliable and perfectly crafted mesh armor that both rider and mount wore bent and creased with their movements as well as if the suits had grown over their skin.

Dinin's lizard trotted along in an easy but swift gait, floating over the broken floor, up the walls, and even across the long tunnel's ceiling. Subterranean lizards, with their sticky and soft three-toed feet, were preferred mounts for just this ability to scale stone as easily as a spider. Crossing hard ground left no damning tracks in the lighted surface world, but nearly all of the creatures of the Underdark possessed infravision, the ability to see in the infrared spectrum. Footfalls left heat residue that could easily be tracked if they followed a predictable course along a corridor's floor.

Dinin clamped tight to his saddle as the lizard plodded along a stretch of the ceiling, then sprang out in a twisting descent to a point farther along the wall. Dinin did not want to be tracked.

He had no light to guide him, but he needed none. He was a dark elf, a drow, an ebon-skinned cousin of those sylvan folk who danced under the stars on the world's surface. To Dinin's superior eyes, which translated subtle variations of heat into vivid and colorful images, the Underdark was far from a lightless place. Colors all across the spectrum swirled before him in the stone of the walls and the floor, heated by some distant fissure or hot stream. The heat of living things was the most distinctive, letting the dark elf view his enemies in details as intricate as any surface-dweller would find in brilliant daylight.

Normally Dinin would not have left the city alone; the world of the Underdark was too dangerous for solo treks, even for a drow elf. This day was different, though. Dinin had to be certain that no unfriendly drow eyes marked his passage.

A soft blue magical glow beyond a sculpted archway told the drow that he neared the city's entrance, and he slowed the lizard's pace accordingly. Few used this narrow tunnel, which opened into Tier Breche, the northern section of Menzoberranzan devoted to the Academy, and none but the mistresses and masters, the instructors of the Academy, could pass through here without attracting suspicion.

Dinin was always nervous when he came to this point. Of the hundred tunnels that opened off the main cavern of Menzoberranzan, this one was the best guarded. Beyond the archway, twin statues of gigantic spiders sat in quiet defense. If an enemy crossed through, the spiders would animate and attack, and alarms would be sounded throughout the Academy.

Dinin dismounted, leaving his lizard clinging comfortably to a wall at his chest level. He reached under the collar of his *piwafwi*, his magical, shielding cloak, and took out his neck-purse. From this Dinin produced the insignia of House Do'Urden, a spider wielding various weapons in each of its eight legs and emblazoned with the letters "DN," for Daermon N'a'shezbaernon, the ancient and formal name of House Do'Urden.

"You will await my return," Dinin whispered to the lizard as he waved the insignia before it. As with all the drow houses, the insignia of House Do'Urden held several magical dweomers, one of which gave family members absolute control over the house pets. The lizard would obey unfailingly, holding its position as though it were rooted to the stone, even if a scurry rat, its favorite morsel, napped a few feet from its maw.

Dinin took a deep breath and gingerly stepped to the archway. He could see the spiders leering down at him from their fifteen-foot height. He was a drow of the city, not an enemy, and could pass through any other tunnel unconcerned, but the Academy was an unpredictable place; Dinin had heard that the spiders often refused entry—viciously—even to uninvited drow.

He could not be delayed by fears and possibilities, Dinin reminded himself. His business was of the utmost importance to his family's battle plans. Looking straight ahead, away from the towering spiders, he strode between them and onto the floor of Tier Breche.

He moved to the side and paused, first to be certain that no one lurked nearby, and to admire the sweeping view of Menzoberranzan. No one, drow or otherwise, had ever looked out from this spot without a sense of wonder at the drow city. Tier Breche was the highest point on the floor of the two-mile cavern, affording a panoramic view to the rest of Menzoberranzan. The cubby of the Academy was narrow, holding only the three structures that comprised the drow school: Arach-Tinilith, the spider-shaped school of Lolth; Sorcere, the gracefully curving, many-spired tower of wizardry; and Melee-Magthere, the somewhat plain pyramidal structure where male fighters learned their trade.

Beyond Tier Breche, through the ornate stalagmite columns that marked the entrance to the Academy, the cavern dropped away quickly and spread wide, going far beyond Dinin's line of vision to either side and farther back than his keen eyes could possibly see. The colors of Menzoberranzan were threefold to the sensitive eyes of the drow. Heat patterns from various fissures and hot springs swirled about the entire cavern. Purple and red, bright yellow and subtle blue, crossed and merged, climbed the walls and stalagmite mounds, or ran off singularly in cutting lines against the backdrop of dim gray stone. More confined than these generalized and natural gradations of color in the infrared spectrum were the regions of intense magic, like the spiders Dinin had walked between, virtually glowing with energy. Finally there were the actual lights of the city, faerie fire and highlighted sculptures on the houses. The drow were proud of the beauty of their designs, and especially ornate columns or perfectly crafted gargoyles were almost always limned in permanent magical lights.

Even from this distance Dinin could make out House Baenre, First House of Menzoberranzan. It encompassed twenty stalagmite pillars and half again that number of gigantic stalactites. House Baenre had existed for five thousand years, since the founding of Menzoberranzan, and in that time the work to perfect the house's art had never ceased. Practically every inch of the immense structure glowed in faerie fire, blue at the outlying towers and brilliant purple at the huge central dome.

The sharp light of candles, foreign to the Underdark, glared through some of the windows of the distant houses. Only clerics or wizards would light the fires, Dinin knew, as necessary pains in their world of scrolls and parchments.

This was Menzoberranzan, the city of drow. Twenty thousand dark elves lived there, twenty thousand soldiers in the army of evil.

A wicked smile spread across Dinin's thin lips when he thought of some of those soldiers who would fall this night.

Dinin studied Narbondel, the huge central pillar that served as the timeclock of Menzoberranzan. Narbondel was the only way the drow had to mark the passage of time in a world that otherwise knew no days and no seasons. At the end of each day, the city's appointed Archmage cast his magical fires into the base of the stone pillar. There the spell lingered throughout the cycle—a full day on the surface—and gradually spread its warmth up the structure of Narbondel until the whole of it glowed red in the infrared spectrum. The pillar was fully dark now, cooled since the dweomer's fires had expired. The wizard was even now at the base, Dinin reasoned, ready to begin the cycle anew.

It was midnight, the appointed hour.

Dinin moved away from the spiders and the tunnel exit and crept along the side of Tier Breche, seeking the "shadows" of heat patterns in the wall, which would effectively hide the distinct outline of his own body temperature. He came at last to Sorcere, the school of wizardry, and slipped into the narrow alley between the tower's curving base and Tier Breche's outer wall.

"Student or master?" came the expected whisper.

"Only a master may walk out-of-house in Tier Breche in the black death of Narbondel," Dinin responded.

A heavily robed figure moved around the arc of the structure to stand before Dinin. The stranger remained in the customary posture of a master of the drow Academy, his arms out before him and bent at the elbows, his hands tight together, one on top of the other in front of his chest.

That pose was the only thing about this one that seemed normal to Dinin. "Greetings, Faceless One," he signaled in the silent hand code of the drow, a language as detailed as the spoken word. The quiver of Dinin's hands belied his calm face, though, for the sight of this wizard put him as far on the edge of his nerves as he had ever been.

"Secondboy Do'Urden," the wizard replied in the gestured code. "Have you my payment?"

"You will be compensated," Dinin signaled pointedly, regaining his composure in the first swelling bubbles of his temper. "Do you dare to doubt the promise of Malice Do'Urden, Matron Mother of Daermon N'a'shezbaernon, Tenth House of Menzoberranzan?"

The Faceless One slumped back, knowing he had erred. "My apologies, Secondboy of House Do'Urden," he answered, dropping to one knee in a gesture of surrender. Since he had entered this conspiracy, the wizard had feared that his impatience might cost him his life. He had been caught in the violent throes of one of his own magical experiments, the tragedy melting away all of his facial features and leaving behind a blank hot spot of white and green goo. Matron Malice Do'Urden, reputedly as skilled as anyone in all the vast city in mixing potions and salves, had offered him a sliver of hope that he could not pass by.

No pity found its way into Dinin's callous heart, but House Do'Urden needed the wizard. "You will get your salve," Dinin promised calmly, "when Alton DeVir is dead."

"Of course," the wizard agreed. "This night?"

Dinin crossed his arms and considered the question. Matron Malice had instructed him that Alton DeVir should die even as their families' battle commenced. That scenario now seemed too clean, too easy, to Dinin. The Faceless One did not miss the sparkle that suddenly brightened the scarlet glow in the young Do'Urden's heat-sensing eyes.

"Wait for Narbondel's light to approach its zenith," Dinin replied, his hands working through the signals excitedly and his grimace seeming more of a twisted grin.

"Should the doomed boy know of his house's fate before he dies?" the wizard asked, guessing the wicked intentions behind Dinin's instructions.

"As the killing blow falls," answered Dinin. "Let Alton DeVir die without hope."

⚔ ⚔ ⚔ ⚔ ⚔

Dinin retrieved his mount and sped off down the empty corridors, finding an intersecting route that would take him in through a different entrance to the city proper. He came in along the eastern end of the great cavern, Menzoberranzan's produce section, where no drow families would see that he had been outside the city limits and where only a few unremarkable stalagmite pillars rose up from the flat stone. Dinin spurred his mount along the banks of Donigarten, the city's small pond with its moss-covered island that housed a fair-sized herd of cattle-like creatures called rothe. A hundred goblins and orcs looked up from their herding and fishing duties to mark the drow soldier's swift passage. Knowing their restrictions as slaves, they took care not to look Dinin in the eye.

Dinin would have paid them no heed anyway. He was too consumed by the urgency of the moment. He kicked his lizard to even greater speeds when he again was on the flat and curving avenues between the glowing drow castles. He moved toward the south-central region of the city, toward the grove of giant mushrooms that marked the section of the finest houses in Menzoberranzan.

As he came around one blind turn, he nearly ran over a group of four wandering bugbears. The giant hairy goblin things paused a moment to consider the drow, then moved slowly but purposefully out of his way.

The bugbears recognized him as a member of House Do'Urden, Dinin knew. He was a noble, a son of a high priestess, and his surname, Do'Urden, was the name of his house. Of the twenty thousand dark elves in Menzoberranzan, only a thousand or so were nobles, actually the children of the sixty-seven recognized families of the city. The rest were common soldiers.

Bugbears were not stupid creatures. They knew a noble from a commoner, and though drow elves did not carry their family insignia in plain view, the pointed and tailed cut of Dinin's stark white hair and the distinctive pattern of purple and red lines in his black *piwafwi* told them well enough who he was.

The mission's urgency pressed upon Dinin, but he could not ignore the bugbears' slight. How fast would they have scampered away if he had been a member of House Baenre or one of the other seven ruling houses? he wondered.

"You will learn respect of House Do'Urden soon enough!" the dark elf whispered under his breath, as he turned and charged his lizard at the group. The bugbears broke into a run, turning down an alley strewn with stones and debris.

Dinin found his satisfaction by calling on the innate powers of his race. He summoned a globe of darkness—impervious to both infravision and normal sight—in the fleeing creatures' path. He supposed that it was unwise to call such attention to himself, but a moment later, when he heard crashing and sputtered curses as the bugbears stumbled blindly over the stones, he felt it was worth the risk.

His anger sated, he moved off again, picking a more careful route through the heat shadows. As a member of the tenth house of the city, Dinin could go as he pleased within the giant cavern without question, but Matron Malice had made it clear that no one connected to House Do'Urden was to be caught anywhere near the mushroom grove.

Matron Malice, Dinin's mother, was not to be crossed, but it was only a rule, after all. In Menzoberranzan, one rule took precedence over all of the petty others: Don't get caught.

At the mushroom grove's southern end, the impetuous drow found what he was looking for: a cluster of five huge floor-to-ceiling pillars that were hollowed into a network of chambers and connected with metal and stone parapets and bridges. Red-glowing gargoyles, the standard of the house, glared down from a hundred perches like silent sentries. This was House DeVir, Fourth House of Menzoberranzan.

A stockade of tall mushrooms ringed the place, every fifth one a shrieker, a sentient fungus named (and favored as guardians) for the shrill cries of alarm it emitted whenever a living being passed it by. Dinin kept a cautious distance, not wanting to set off one of the shriekers and knowing also that other, more deadly wards protected the fortress. Matron Malice would see to those.

An expectant hush permeated the air of this city section. It was general knowledge throughout Menzoberranzan that Matron Ginafae of House DeVir had fallen out of favor with Lolth, the Spider Queen deity to all drow and the true source of every house's strength. Such circumstances were never openly discussed among the drow, but everyone who knew fully expected that some family lower in the city hierarchy soon would strike out against the crippled House DeVir.

Matron Ginafae and her family had been the last to learn of the Spider Queen's displeasure—ever was that Lolth's devious way—and Dinin could tell just by scanning the outside of House DeVir that the doomed family had not found sufficient time to erect proper defenses. DeVir sported nearly four hundred soldiers, many female, but those that Dinin could now see at their posts along the parapets seemed nervous and unsure.

Dinin's smile spread even wider when he thought of his own house, which grew in power daily under the cunning guidance of Matron Malice. With all three of his sisters rapidly approaching the status of high priestess, his brother an accomplished wizard, and his uncle Zaknafein, the finest weapons master in all of Menzoberranzan, busily training the three hundred soldiers, House Do'Urden was a complete force. And, Matron Malice, unlike Ginafae, was in the Spider Queen's full favor.

"Daermon N'a'shezbaernon," Dinin muttered under his breath, using the formal and ancestral reference to House Do'Urden. "Ninth House of Menzoberranzan!" He liked the sound of it.

⚔ ⚔ ⚔ ⚔ ⚔

Halfway across the city, beyond the silver-glowing balcony and the arched doorway twenty feet up the cavern's west wall, sat the principals of House

Do'Urden, gathered to outline the final plans of the night's work. On the raised dais at the back of the small audience chamber sat venerable Matron Malice, her belly swollen in the final hours of pregnancy. Flanking her in their places of honor were her three daughters, Maya, Vierna, and the eldest, Briza, a newly ordained high priestess of Lolth. Maya and Vierna appeared as younger versions of their mother, slender and deceptively small, though possessing great strength. Briza, though, hardly carried the family resemblance. She was big—huge by drow standards—and rounded in the shoulders and hips. Those who knew Briza well figured that her size was merely a circumstance of her temperament; a smaller body could not have contained the anger and brutal streak of House Do'Urden's newest high priestess.

"Dinin should return soon," remarked Rizzen, the present patron of the family, "to let us know if the time is right for the assault."

"We go before Narbondel finds its morning glow!" Briza snapped at him in her thick but razor-sharp voice. She turned a crooked smile to her mother, seeking approval for putting the male in his place.

"The child comes this night," Matron Malice explained to her anxious husband. "We go no matter what news Dinin bears."

"It will be a boy child," groaned Briza, making no effort to hide her disappointment, "third living son of House Do'Urden."

"To be sacrificed to Lolth," put in Zaknafein, a former patron of the house who now held the important position of weapons master. The skilled drow fighter seemed quite pleased at the thought of sacrifice, as did Nalfein, the family's eldest son, who stood at Zak's side. Nalfein was the elderboy, and he needed no more competition beyond Dinin within the ranks of House Do'Urden.

"In accord with custom," Briza glowered and the red of her eyes brightened. "To aid in our victory!"

Rizzen shifted uncomfortably. "Matron Malice," he dared to speak, "you know well the difficulties of birthing. Might the pain distract you—"

"You dare to question the matron mother?" Briza started sharply, reaching for the snake-headed whip so comfortably strapped—and writhing—on her belt. Matron Malice stopped her with an outstretched hand.

"Attend to the fighting," the matron said to Rizzen. "Let the females of the house see to the important matters of this battle."

Rizzen shifted again and dropped his gaze.

⚔⚔⚔⚔⚔

Dinin came to the magically wrought fence that connected the keep within the city's west wall with the two small stalagmite towers of House Do'Urden, and which formed the courtyard to the compound. The fence was adamantine, the hardest metal in all the world, and adorning it were a hundred weapon-wielding spider carvings, each ensorcelled with deadly glyphs and wards. The mighty gate of House Do'Urden was the envy of many a drow house, but so soon after viewing the spectacular houses in the mushroom grove, Dinin could only find disappointment when looking upon his own abode. The compound was plain and somewhat bare, as was the section of wall, with the notable exception of the mithral-and-adamantine balcony running along the second level, by the arched doorway reserved for the nobility of the family. Each baluster of that balcony sported a thousand carvings, all of which blended into a single piece of art.

House Do'Urden, unlike the great majority of the houses in Menzoberranzan, did not stand free within groves of stalactites and stalagmites. The bulk of the structure was within a cave, and while this setup was indisputably defensible, Dinin found himself wishing that his family could show a bit more grandeur.

An excited soldier rushed to open the gate for the returning secondboy. Dinin swept past him without so much as a word of greeting and moved across the courtyard, conscious of the hundred and more curious glances that fell upon him. The soldiers and slaves knew that Dinin's mission this night had something to do with the anticipated battle.

No stairway led to the silvery balcony of House Do'Urden's second level. This, too, was a precautionary measure designed to segregate the leaders of the house from the rabble and the slaves. Drow nobles needed no stairs; another manifestation of their innate magical abilities allowed them the power of levitation. With hardly a conscious thought to the act, Dinin drifted easily through the air and dropped onto the balcony.

He rushed through the archway and down the house's main central corridor, which was dimly lit in the soft hues of faerie fire, allowing for sight in the normal light spectrum but not bright enough to defeat the use of infravision. The ornate brass door at the corridor's end marked the secondboy's destination, and he paused before it to allow his eyes to shift back to the infrared spectrum. Unlike the corridor, the room beyond the door had no light source. It was the audience hall of the high priestesses, the anteroom to House Do'Urden's grand chapel. The drow clerical rooms, in accord with the dark rites of the Spider Queen, were not places of light.

When he felt he was prepared, Dinin pushed straight through the door, shoving past the two shocked female guards without hesitation and moving boldly to stand before his mother. All three of the family daughters narrowed their eyes at their brash and pretentious brother. To enter without permission! he knew they were thinking. Would that it was he who was to be sacrificed this night!

As much as he enjoyed testing the limitations of his inferior station as a male, Dinin could not ignore the threatening dances of Vierna, Maya, and Briza. Being female, they were bigger and stronger than Dinin and had trained all their lives in the use of wicked drow clerical powers and weapons. Dinin watched as enchanted extensions of the clerics, the dreaded snake-headed whips on his sisters' belts, began writhing in anticipation of the punishment they would exact. The handles were adamantine and ordinary enough, but the whips' lengths and multiple heads were living serpents. Briza's whip, in particular, a wicked six-headed device, danced and squirmed, tying itself into knots around the belt that held it. Briza was always the quickest to punish.

Matron Malice, however, seemed pleased by Dinin's swagger. The secondboy knew his place well enough by her measure and he followed her commands fearlessly and without question.

Dinin took comfort in the calmness of his mother's face, quite the opposite of the shining white-hot faces of his three sisters. "All is ready," he said to her. "House DeVir huddles within its fence—except for Alton, of course, foolishly attending his studies in Sorcere."

"You have met with the Faceless One?" Matron Malice asked.

"The Academy was quiet this night," Dinin replied. "Our meeting went off perfectly."

"He has agreed to our contract?"

"Alton DeVir will be dealt with accordingly," Dinin chuckled. He then remembered the slight alteration he had made in Matron Malice's plans, delaying Alton's execution for the sake of his own lust for added cruelty. Dinin's thought evoked another recollection as well: high priestesses of Lolth had an unnerving talent for reading thoughts.

"Alton will die this night," Dinin quickly completed the answer, assuring the others before they could probe him for more definite details.

"Excellent," Briza growled. Dinin breathed a little easier.

"To the meld," Matron Malice ordered.

The four drow males moved to kneel before the matron and her daughters: Rizzen to Malice, Zaknafein to Briza, Nalfein to Maya, and Dinin to Vierna. The clerics chanted in unison, placing one hand delicately upon the forehead of their respective soldier, tuning in to his passions.

"You know your places," Matron Malice said when the ceremony was completed. She grimaced through the pain of another contraction. "Let our work begin."

⚔ ⚔ ⚔ ⚔ ⚔

Less than an hour later, Zaknafein and Briza stood together on the balcony outside the upper entrance to House Do'Urden. Below them, on the cavern floor, the second and third brigades of the family army, Rizzen's and Nalfein's, bustled about, fitting on heated leather straps and metal patches—camouflage against a distinctive elven form to heat-seeing drow eyes. Dinin's group, the initial strike force that included a hundred goblin slaves, had long since departed.

"We will be known after this night," Briza said. "None would have suspected that a tenth house would dare to move against one as powerful as DeVir. When the whispers ripple out after this night's bloody work, even Baenre will take note of Daermon N'a'shezbaernon!" She leaned out over the balcony to watch as the two brigades formed into lines and started out, silently, along separate paths that would bring them through the winding city to the mushroom grove and the five-pillared structure of House DeVir.

Zaknafein eyed the back of Matron Malice's eldest daughter, wanting nothing more than to put a dagger into her spine. As always, though, good judgment kept Zak's practiced hand in its place.

"Have you the articles?" Briza inquired, showing Zak considerably more respect than she had when Matron Malice sat protectively at her side. Zak was only a male, a commoner allowed to don the family name as his own because he sometimes served Matron Malice in a husbandly manner and had once been the patron of the house. Still, Briza feared to anger him. Zak was the weapons master of House Do'Urden, a tall and muscular male, stronger than most females, and those who had witnessed his fighting wrath considered him among the finest warriors of either sex in all of Menzoberranzan. Besides Briza and her mother, both high priestesses of the Spider Queen, Zaknafein, with his unrivaled swordsmanship, was House Do'Urden's trump.

Zak held up the black hood and opened the small pouch on his belt, revealing several tiny ceramic spheres.

Briza smiled evilly and rubbed her slender hands together. "Matron Ginafae will not be pleased," she whispered.

Zak returned the smile and turned to view the departing soldiers. Nothing gave the weapons master more pleasure than killing drow elves, particularly clerics of Lolth.

"Prepare yourself," Briza said after a few minutes.

Zak shook his thick hair back from his face and stood rigid, eyes tightly closed. Briza drew her wand slowly, beginning the chant that would activate the device. She tapped Zak on one shoulder, then the other, then held the wand motionless over his head.

Zak felt the frosty sprinkles falling down on him, permeating his clothes and armor, even his flesh, until he and all of his possessions had cooled to a uniform temperature and hue. Zak hated the magical chill—it felt as he imagined death would feel—but he knew that under the influence of the wand's sprinkles he was, to the heat-sensing eyes of the creatures of the Underdark, as gray as common stone, unremarkable and undetectable.

Zak opened his eyes and shuddered, flexing his fingers to be sure they could still perform the fine edge of his craft. He looked back to Briza, already in the midst of the second spell, the summoning. This one would take a while, so Zak leaned back against the wall and considered again the pleasant, though dangerous, task before him. How thoughtful of Matron Malice to leave all of House DeVir's clerics to him!

"It is done," Briza announced after a few minutes. She led Zak's gaze upward, to the darkness beneath the unseen ceiling of the immense cavern.

Zak spotted Briza's handiwork first, an approaching current of air, yellow-tinted and warmer than the normal air of the cavern. A living current of air.

The creature, a conjuration from an elemental plane, swirled to hover just beyond the lip of the balcony, obediently awaiting its summoner's commands.

Zak didn't hesitate. He leaped out into the thing's midst, letting it hold him suspended above the floor.

Briza offered him a final salute and motioned her servant away. "Good fighting," she called to Zak, though he was already invisible in the air above her.

Zak chuckled at the irony of her words as the twisting city of Menzoberranzan rolled out below him. She wanted the clerics of House DeVir dead as surely as Zak did, but for very different reasons. All complications aside, Zak would have been just as happy killing clerics of House Do'Urden.

The weapons master took up one of his adamantine swords, a drow weapon magically crafted and unbelievably sharp with the edge of killing dweomers. "Good fighting indeed," he whispered. If only Briza knew how good.

# 2 The Fall of House DeVir

Dinin noted with satisfaction that any of the meandering bugbears, or any other of the multitude of races that composed Menzoberranzan, drow included, now made great haste to scurry out of his way. This time the secondboy of House Do'Urden was not alone. Nearly sixty soldiers of the house walked in tight lines behind him. Behind these, in similar order though with far less enthusiasm for the adventure, came a hundred armed slaves of lesser races—goblins, orcs, and bugbears.

There could be no doubt for onlookers—a drow house was on a march to war. This was not an everyday event in Menzoberranzan but neither was it unexpected. At least once every decade a house decided that its position within the city hierarchy could be improved by another house's elimination. It was a risky proposition, for all of the nobles of the "victim" house had to be disposed of quickly and quietly. If even one survived to lay an accusation upon the perpetrator, the attacking house would be eradicated by Menzoberranzan's merciless system of "justice."

If the raid was executed to devious perfection, though, no recourse would be forthcoming. All of the city, even the ruling council of the top eight matron mothers, would secretly applaud the attackers for their courage and intelligence and no more would ever be said of the incident.

Dinin took a roundabout route, not wanting to lay a direct trail between

House Do'Urden and House DeVir. A half-hour later, for the second time that night, he crept to the mushroom grove's southern end, to the cluster of stalagmites that held House DeVir. His soldiers streamed out behind him eagerly, readying weapons and taking full measure of the structure before them.

The slaves were slower in their movements. Many of them looked about for some escape, for they knew in their hearts that they were doomed in this battle. They feared the wrath of the dark elves more than death itself, though, and would not attempt to flee. With every exit out of Menzoberranzan protected by devious drow magic, where could they possibly go? Every one of them had witnessed the brutal punishments the drow elves exacted on recaptured slaves. At Dinin's command, they jumped into their positions around the mushroom fence.

Dinin reached into his large pouch and pulled out a heated sheet of metal. He flashed the object, brightened in the infrared spectrum, three times behind him to signal the approaching brigades of Nalfein and Rizzen. Then, with his usual cockiness, Dinin spun it quickly into the air, caught it, and replaced it in the secrecy of his heat-shielding pouch. On cue with the twirling signal, Dinin's drow brigade fitted enchanted darts to their tiny hand-held crossbows and took aim on the appointed targets.

Every fifth mushroom was a shrieker, and every dart held a magical dweomer that could silence the roar of a dragon.

". . . two . . . three," Dinin counted, his hand signaling the tempo since no words could be heard within the sphere of magical silence cast about his troops. He imagined the "click" as the drawn string on his little weapon released, loosing the dart into the nearest shrieker. So it went all around the cluster of House DeVir, the first line of alarm systematically silenced by three-dozen enchanted darts.

⚔ ⚔ ⚔ ⚔ ⚔

Halfway across Menzoberranzan, Matron Malice, her daughters, and four of the house's common clerics were gathered in Lolth's unholy circle of eight. They ringed an idol of their wicked deity, a gemstone carving of a drow-faced spider, and called to Lolth for aid in their struggles.

Malice sat at the head, propped in a chair angled for birthing. Briza and Vierna flanked her, Briza clutching her hand.

The select group chanted in unison, combining their energies into a single offensive spell. A moment later, when Vierna, mentally linked to Dinin, understood that the first attack group was in position, the Do'Urden circle of eight sent the first insinuating waves of mental energy into the rival house.

⚔ ⚔ ⚔ ⚔ ⚔

Matron Ginafae, her two daughters, and the five principal clerics of the common troops of House DeVir huddled together in the darkened anteroom of the five-stalagmite house's main chapel. They had gathered there in solemn prayer every night since Matron Ginafae had learned that she had fallen into Lolth's disfavor. Ginafae understood how vulnerable her house remained until she could find a way to appease the Spider Queen. There were sixty-six other houses in Menzoberranzan, fully twenty of which might dare to attack House DeVir at such an obvious disadvantage. The eight clerics were anxious now, somehow suspecting that this night would be eventful.

Ginafae felt it first, a chilling blast of confusing perceptions that caused her to stutter over her prayer of forgiveness. The other clerics of House DeVir glanced nervously at the matron's uncharacteristic slip of words, looking for confirmation.

"We are under attack," Ginafae breathed to them, her head already pounding with a dull ache under the growing assault of the formidable clerics of House Do'Urden.

⚔ ⚔ ⚔ ⚔ ⚔

A second signal from Dinin put the slave troops into motion. Still using stealth as their ally, they quietly rushed to the mushroom fence and cut through with wide-bladed swords. The secondboy of House

Do'Urden watched and enjoyed as the courtyard of House DeVir was easily penetrated. "Not such a prepared guard," he whispered in silent sarcasm to the red-glowing gargoyles on the high walls. The statues had seemed such an ominous guard earlier that night. Now they just watched helplessly.

Dinin recognized the measured but growing anticipation in the soldiers around him; their drow battle-lust was barely contained. Every now and came a killing flash as one of the slaves stumbled over a warding glyph, but the secondboy and the other drow only laughed at the spectacle. The lesser races were the expendable "fodder" of House Do'Urden's army. The only purpose in bringing the goblinoids to House DeVir was to trigger the deadly traps and defenses along the perimeter, to lead the way for the drow elves, the true soldiers.

The fence was now opened and secrecy was thrown away. House DeVir's soldiers met the invading slaves head-on within the compound. Dinin barely had his hand up to begin the attack command when his sixty anxious drow warriors jumped up and charged, their faces twisted in wicked glee and their weapons waving menacingly.

They halted their approach on cue, though, remembering one final task set out to them. Every drow, noble or commoner, possessed certain magical abilities. Bringing forth a globe of darkness, as Dinin had done to the bugbears in the street earlier that night, came easily to even the lowliest of the dark elves. So it went now, with sixty Do'Urden soldiers blotting out the perimeter of House DeVir above the mushroom fence in ball after ball of blackness.

For all of their stealth and precautions, House Do'Urden knew that many eyes were watching the raid. Witnesses were not too much of a problem; they could not, or would not, care enough to identify the attacking house. But custom and rules demanded that certain attempts at secrecy be enacted, the etiquette of drow warfare. In the blink of a red-glowing drow eye, House DeVir became, to the rest of the city, a dark blot on Menzoberranzan's landscape.

Rizzen came up behind his youngest son. "Well done," he signaled in the intricate finger language of the drow. "Nalfein is in through the back."

"An easy victory," the cocky Dinin signaled back, "if Matron Ginafae and her clerics are held at bay."

"Trust in Matron Malice," was Rizzen's response. He clapped his son's shoulder and followed his troops in through the breached mushroom fence.

⚔ ⚔ ⚔ ⚔ ⚔

High above the cluster of House DeVir, Zaknafein rested comfortably in the current-arms of Briza's aerial servant, watching the drama unfold. From this vantage, Zak could see within the ring of darkness and could hear within the ring of magical silence. Dinin's troops, the first drow soldiers in, had met resistance at every door and were being beaten badly.

Nalfein and his brigade, the troops of House Do'Urden most practiced in the ways of wizardry, came through the fence at the rear of the complex. Lightning strikes and magical balls of acid thundered into the courtyard at the base of the DeVir structures, cutting down Do'Urden fodder and DeVir defenses alike.

In the front courtyard, Rizzen and Dinin commanded the finest fighters of House Do'Urden. The blessings of Lolth were with his house, Zak could see when the battle was fully joined, for the strikes of the soldiers of House Do'Urden came faster than those of their enemies, and their aim proved more deadly. In minutes, the battle had been taken fully inside the five pillars.

Zak stretched the incessant chill out of his arms and willed the aerial servant to action. Down he plummeted on his windy bed, and he fell free the last few feet to the terrace along the top chambers of the central pillar. At once, two guards, one a female, rushed out to greet him.

They hesitated in confusion, though, trying to sort out the true form of this unremarkable gray blur—too long.

They had never heard of Zaknafein Do'Urden. They didn't know that death was upon them.

Zak's whip flashed out, catching and gashing the female's throat, while his other hand walked his sword through a series of masterful thrusts and parries that put the male off balance. Zak finished both in a single, blurring movement, snapping the whip-entwined female from the terrace with a twist of his wrist and spinning a kick into the male's face that likewise dropped him to the cavern floor.

Zak was then inside, where another guard rose up to meet him . . . but fell at his feet.

Zak slipped along the curving wall of the stalactite tower, his cooled body blending perfectly with the stone. Soldiers of House DeVir rushed all about him, trying to formulate some defense against the host of intruders who had already won out the lowest level of every structure and had taken two of the pillars completely.

Zak was not concerned with them. He blocked out the clanging ring of adamantine weapons, the cries of command, and the screams of death, concentrating instead on a singular sound that would lead him to his destination: a unified, frantic chant.

He found an empty corridor covered with spider carvings and running into the center of the pillar. As in House Do'Urden, this corridor ended in a large set of ornate double doors, their decorations dominated by arachnid forms. "This must be the place." Zak muttered under his breath, fitting his hood to the top of his head.

A giant spider rushed out of its concealment to his side.

Zak dived to his belly and kicked out under the thing, spinning into a roll that plunged his sword deep into the monster's bulbous body. Sticky fluids gushed out over the weapons master, and the spider shuddered to a quick death.

"Yes," Zak whispered, wiping the spider juices from his face, "this must be the place." He pulled the dead monster back into its hidden cubby and slipped in beside the thing, hoping that no one had noticed the brief struggle.

By the sounds of ringing weapons, Zak could tell that the fighting had almost reached this floor. House DeVir now seemed to have its defenses in place, though, and was finally holding its ground.

"Now, Malice," Zak whispered, hoping that Briza, attuned to him in the meld, would sense his anxiety. "Let us not be late!"

⚔ ⚔ ⚔ ⚔ ⚔

Back in the clerical anteroom of House Do'Urden, Malice and her subordinates continued their brutal mental assault on the clerics of House DeVir. Lolth heard their prayers louder than those of their counterparts, giving the clerics of House Do'Urden the stronger spells in their mental combat. Already they had easily put their enemies into a defensive posture. One of the lesser priestesses in DeVir's circle of eight had been crushed by Briza's mental insinuations and now lay dead on the floor barely inches from Matron Ginafae's feet.

But the momentum had slowed suddenly and the battle seemed to be swinging back to an even level. Matron Malice, struggling with the impending birth, could not hold her concentration, and without her voice, the spells of her unholy circle weakened.

At her mother's side, powerful Briza clutched her mother's hand so tightly that all the blood was squeezed from it, leaving it cool—the only cool spot on the laboring female—to the eyes of the others. Briza studied the contractions and the crowning cap of the coming child's white hair, and calculated the time to the moment of birth. This technique of translating the pain of birth into an offensive spell attack had never been tried before, except in legend, and Briza knew that timing would be the critical factor.

She whispered into her mother's ear, coaxing out the words of a deadly incantation.

Matron Malice echoed back the beginnings of the spell, sublimating her gasps, and transforming her rage of agony into offensive power.

"*Dinnen douward ma brechen tol,*" Briza implored.

"*Dinnen douward. . . maaa . . . brechen tol!*" Malice growled, so determined to focus through the pain that she bit through one of her thin lips.

The baby's head appeared, more fully this time, and this time to stay.

Briza trembled and could barely remember the incantation herself. She whispered the final rune into the matron's ear, almost fearing the consequences.

Malice gathered her breath and her courage. She could feel the tingling of the spell as clearly as the pain of the birth. To her daughters standing around the idol, staring at her in disbelief, she appeared as a red blur of heated fury, streaking sweat lines that shone as brightly as the heat of boiling water.

"*Abec*," the matron began, feeling the pressure building to a crescendo. "*Abec*." She felt the hot tear of her skin, the sudden slippery release as the baby's head pushed through, the sudden ecstacy of birthing. "*Abec di'n'a'BREG DOUWARD!*" Malice screamed, pushing away all of the agony in a final explosion of magical power that knocked even the clerics of her own house from their feet.

⚔ ⚔ ⚔ ⚔ ⚔

Carried on the thrust of Matron Malice's exultation, the dweomer thundered into the chapel of House DeVir, shattered the gemstone idol of Lolth, sundered the double doors into heaps of twisted metal, and threw Matron Ginafae and her overmatched subordinates to the floor.

Zak shook his head in disbelief as the chapel doors flew past him. "Quite a kick, Malice." He chuckled and spun around the entryway, into the chapel. Using his infravision, he took a quick survey and head count of the lightless room's seven living occupants, all struggling back to their feet, their robes tattered. Again shaking his head at the bared power of Matron Malice, Zak pulled his hood down over his face.

A snap of his whip was the only explanation he offered as he smashed a tiny ceramic globe at his feet. The sphere shattered, dropping out a pellet that Briza had enchanted for just such occasions, a pellet glowing with the brightness of daylight.

For eyes accustomed to blackness, tuned in to heat emanations, the intrusion of such radiance came in a blinding flash of agony. The clerics' cries of pain only aided Zak in his systematic trek around the room, and he smiled widely under his hood every time he felt his sword bite into drow flesh.

He heard the beginnings of a spell across the way and knew that one of the DeVirs had recovered enough from the assault to be dangerous. The weapons master did not need his eyes to aim, however, and the crack of his whip took Matron Ginafae's tongue right out of her mouth.

⚔ ⚔ ⚔ ⚔ ⚔

Briza placed the newborn on the back of the spider idol and lifted the ceremonial dagger, pausing to admire its cruel workmanship. Its hilt was a spider's body sporting eight legs, barbed so as to appear furred, but angled down to serve as blades. Briza lifted the instrument above the baby's chest. "Name the child," she implored her mother. "The Spider Queen will not accept the sacrifice until the child is named!"

Matron Malice lolled her head, trying to fathom her daughter's meaning. The matron mother had thrown everything into the moment of the spell and the birth, and she was now barely coherent.

"Name the child!" Briza commanded, anxious to feed her hungry goddess.

⚔ ⚔ ⚔ ⚔ ⚔

"It nears its end," Dinin said to his brother when they met in a lower hall of one of the lesser pillars of House DeVir. "Rizzen is winning through to the top, and it is believed that Zaknafein's dark work has been completed."

"Two score of House DeVir's soldiers have already turned allegiance to us," Nalfein replied.

"They see the end," laughed Dinin. "One house serves them as well as another, and in the eyes of commoners no house is worth dying for. Our task will be finished soon."

"Too quickly for anyone to take note," Nalfein said. "Now Do'Urden, Daermon N'a'shezbaernon, is the Ninth House of Menzoberranzan and DeVir be damned!"

"Alert!" Dinin cried suddenly, eyes widening in feigned horror as he looked over his brother's shoulder.

Nalfein reacted immediately, spinning to face the danger at his back, only to put the true danger at his back. For even as Nalfein realized the deception, Dinin's sword slipped into his spine. Dinin put his head to his brother's shoulder and pressed his cheek to Nalfein's, watching the red sparkle of heat leave his brother's eyes.

"Too quickly for anyone to take note," Dinin teased, echoing his brother's earlier words.

He dropped the lifeless form to his feet. "Now Dinin is elderboy of House Do'Urden, and Nalfein be damned."

⚔ ⚔ ⚔ ⚔ ⚔

"Drizzt," breathed Matron Malice. "The child's name is Drizzt!"

Briza tightened her grip on the knife and began the ritual. "Queen of Spiders, take this babe," she began. She raised the dagger to strike. "Drizzt Do'Urden we give to you in payment for our glorious vic—"

"Wait!" called Maya from the side of the room. Her melding with her brother Nalfein had abruptly ceased. It could only mean one thing. "Nalfein is dead," she announced. "The baby is no longer the third living son."

Vierna glanced curiously at her sister. At the same instant that Maya had sensed Nalfein's death, Vierna, melded with Dinin, had felt a strong emotive surge. Elation? Vierna brought a slender finger up to her pursed lips, wondering if Dinin had successfully pulled off the assassination.

Briza still held the spider-shaped knife over the babe's chest, wanting to give this one to Lolth.

"We promised the Spider Queen the third living son," Maya warned. "And that has been given."

"But not in sacrifice," argued Briza.

Vierna shrugged, at a loss. "If Lolth accepted Nalfein, then he has been given. To give another might evoke the Spider Queen's anger."

"But to not give what we have promised would be worse still!" Briza insisted.

"Then finish the deed," said Maya.

Briza clenched down tight on the dagger and began the ritual again.

"Stay your hand," Matron Malice commanded, propping herself up in the chair. "Lolth is content; our victory is won. Welcome, then, your brother, the newest member of House Do'Urden."

"Just a male," Briza commented in obvious disgust, walking away from the idol and the child.

"Next time we shall do better," Matron Malice chuckled, though she wondered if there would be a next time. She approached the end of her fifth century of life, and drow elves, even young ones, were not a particularly fruitful lot. Briza had been born to Malice at the youthful age of one hundred, but in the almost four centuries since, Malice had produced only five other children. Even this baby, Drizzt, had come as a surprise, and Malice hardly expected that she would ever conceive again.

"Enough of such contemplations," Malice whispered to herself, exhausted. "There will be ample time . . ." She sank back into her chair and fell into fitful, though wickedly pleasant, dreams of heightening power.

⚔ ⚔ ⚔ ⚔ ⚔

Zaknafein walked through the central pillar of the DeVir complex, his hood in his hand and his whip and sword comfortably replaced on his belt. Every now and a ring of battle sounded, only to be quickly ended. House Do'Urden had rolled through to victory, the tenth house had taken the fourth, and now all that remained was to remove evidence and witnesses. One group of lesser female clerics marched through, tending to the wounded Do'Urdens and animating the corpses of those beyond their ability, so that the bodies could walk away from the crime scene. Back at the Do'Urden compound, those corpses not beyond repair would be resurrected and put back to work.

Zak turned away with a visible shudder as the clerics moved from room to room, the marching line of Do'Urden zombies growing ever longer at their backs.

As distasteful as Zaknafein found this troupe, the one that followed was even worse. Two Do'Urden clerics led a contingent of soldiers through the structure, using detection spells to determine hiding places of surviving DeVirs. One stopped in the hallway just a few steps from Zak, her eyes turned inward as she felt the emanations of her spell. She held her fingers out in front of her, tracing a slow line, like some macabre divining rod, toward drow flesh.

"In there!" she declared, pointing to a panel at the base of the wall. The soldiers jumped to it like a pack of ravenous wolves and tore through the secret door. Inside a hidden cubby huddled the children of House DeVir. These were nobles, not commoners, and could not be taken alive.

Zak quickened his pace to get beyond the scene, but he heard vividly the children's helpless screams as the hungry Do'Urden soldiers finished their job. Zak found himself in a run now. He rushed around a bend in the hallway, nearly bowling over Dinin and Rizzen.

"Nalfein is dead," Rizzen declared impassively.

Zak immediately turned a suspicious eye on the younger Do'Urden son.

"I killed the DeVir soldier who committed the deed," Dinin assured him, not even hiding his cocky smile.

Zak had been around for nearly four centuries, and he was certainly not ignorant of the ways of his ambitious race. The brother princes had come in defensively at the back of the lines, with a host of Do'Urden soldiers between them and the enemy. By the time they even encountered a drow that was not of their own house, the majority of the DeVirs' surviving soldiers had already switched allegiance to House Do'Urden. Zak doubted that either of the Do'Urden brothers had even seen action against a DeVir.

"The description of the carnage in the prayer room has been spread throughout the ranks," Rizzen said to the weapons master. "You performed with your usual excellence—as we have come to expect."

Zak shot the patron a glare of contempt and kept on his way, down though the structure's main doors and out beyond the magical darkness and silence into Menzoberranzan's dark dawn. Rizzen was Matron Malice's present partner in a long line of partners, and no more. When Malice was finished with him, she would either relegate him back to the ranks of the common soldiery, stripping him of the name Do'Urden and all the rights that accompanied it, or she would dispose of him. Zak owed him no respect.

Zak moved out beyond the mushroom fence to the highest vantage point he could find, then fell to the ground. He watched, amazed, a few moments later, when the procession of the Do'Urden army, patron and son, soldiers and clerics, and the slow-moving line of two dozen drow zombies, made its way back home. They had lost, and left behind, nearly all of their slave fodder in the attack, but the line leaving the wreckage of House DeVir was longer than the line that had come in earlier that night. The slaves had been replaced twofold by captured DeVir slaves, and fifty or more of the DeVir common troops, showing typical drow loyalty, had willingly joined the attackers. These traitorous drow would be interrogated—magically interrogated—by the Do'Urden clerics to ensure their sincerity.

They would pass the test to a one, Zak knew. Drow elves were creatures of survival, not of principle. The soldiers would be given new identities and would be kept within the privacy of the Do'Urden compound for a few months, until the fall of House DeVir became an old and forgotten tale.

Zak did not follow immediately. Rather, he cut through the rows of mushroom trees and found a secluded dell, where he plopped down on a patch of mossy carpet and raised his gaze to the eternal darkness of the cavern's ceiling—and the eternal darkness of his existence.

It would have been prudent for him to remain silent at that time; he was an invader to the most powerful section of the vast city. He thought of the possible witnesses to his words, the same dark elves who had watched the fall of House DeVir, who had wholeheartedly enjoyed the spectacle. In the face of such behavior and such carnage as this night had seen, Zak could not contain his emotions. His lament came out as a plea to some god beyond his experience.

"What place is this that is my world; what dark coil has my spirit embodied?" he whispered the angry disclaimer that had always been a part of him. "In light, I see my skin as black; in darkness, it glows white in the heat of this rage I cannot dismiss.

"Would that I had the courage to depart, this place or this life, or to stand openly against the wrongness that is the world of these, my kin. To seek an existence that does not run afoul to that which I believe, and to that which I hold dear faith is truth.

"Zaknafein Do'Urden, I am called, yet a drow I am not, by choice or by deed. Let them discover this being that I am, then. Let them rain their wrath on these old shoulders already burdened by the hopelessness of Menzoberranzan."

Ignoring the consequences, the weapons master rose to his feet and yelled, "Menzoberranzan, what hell are you?"

A moment later, when no answer echoed back out of the quiet city, Zak flexed the remaining chill of Briza's wand from his weary muscles. He found some comfort as he patted the whip on his belt—the instrument that had taken the tongue from the mouth of a matron mother.

# 3
# The Eyes of a Child

Masoj, the young apprentice—which at this point in his magic-using career meant that he was no more than a cleaning attendant—leaned on his broom and watched as Alton DeVir moved through the door into the highest chamber of the spire. Masoj almost felt sympathy for the student, who had to go in and face the Faceless One.

Masoj felt excitement as well, though, knowing that the ensuing fireworks between Alton and the faceless master would be well worth the watching. He went back to his sweeping, using the broom as an excuse to get farther around the curve of the room's floor, closer to the door.

⚔ ⚔ ⚔ ⚔ ⚔

"You requested my presence, Master Faceless One," Alton DeVir said again, keeping one hand in front of his face and squinting to fight the brilliant glare of the room's three lighted candles. Alton shifted uncomfortably from one foot to the other just inside the shadowy room's door.

Hunched across the way, the Faceless One kept his back to the young DeVir. Better to be done with this cleanly, the master reminded himself. He knew, though, that the spell he was now preparing would kill Alton before the student could learn his family's fate, before the Faceless One could fully complete Dinin Do'Urden's final instructions. Too much was at stake. Better to be done with this cleanly.

"You . . ." Alton began again, but he prudently held his words and tried to sort out the situation before him. How unusual to be summoned to the private chambers of a master of the Academy before the day's lessons had even begun.

When he had first received the summons, Alton feared that he had somehow failed one of his lessons. That could be a fatal mistake in Sorcere. Alton was close to graduation, but the disdain of a single master could put an end to that.

He had done quite well in his lessons with the Faceless One, had even believed that this mysterious master favored him. Could this call be simply a courtesy of congratulations on his impending graduation? Unlikely, Alton realized against his hopes. Masters of the drow Academy did not often congratulate students.

Alton then heard quiet chanting and noticed that the master was in the midst of spellcasting. Something cried out as very wrong to him now; something about this whole situation did not fit the strict ways of the Academy. Alton set his feet firmly and tensed his muscles, following the advice of the motto that had been drilled into the thoughts of every student at the Academy, the precept that kept drow elves alive in a society so devoted to chaos: Be prepared.

⚔ ⚔ ⚔ ⚔ ⚔

The doors exploded before him, showering the room with stone splinters and throwing Masoj back against the wall. He felt the show well worth both the inconvenience and the new bruise on his shoulder when Alton DeVir scrambled out of the room. The student's back and left arm trailed wisps of smoke, and the most exquisite expression of terror and pain that Masoj had ever seen was etched on the DeVir noble's face.

Alton stumbled to the floor and kicked into a roll, desperate to put some ground between himself and the murderous master. He made it down and around the descending arc of the room's floor and through the door that led into the next lower chamber just as the Faceless One made his appearance at the sundered door.

The master stopped to spit a curse at his misfire, and to consider the best way to replace his door. "Clean it up!" he snapped at Masoj, who was again leaning casually with his hands atop his broomstick and his chin atop his hands.

Masoj obediently dropped his head and started sweeping the stone splinters. He looked up as the Faceless One stalked past, however, and cautiously started after the master.

Alton couldn't possibly escape, and this show would be too good to miss.

* * * * *

The third room, the Faceless One's private library, was the brightest of the four in the spire, with dozens of candles burning on each wall.

"Damn this light!" Alton spat, stumbling his way down through the dizzying blur to the door that led to the Faceless One's entry hall, the lowest room of the master's quarters. If he could get down from this spire and outside of the tower to the courtyard of the Academy, he might be able to turn the momentum against the master.

Alton's world remained the darkness of Menzoberranzan, but the Faceless One, who had spent so many decades in the candlelight of Sorcere, had grown accustomed to using his eyes to see shades of light, not heat.

The entry hall was cluttered with chairs and chests, but only one candle burned there, and Alton could see clearly enough to dodge or leap any obstacles. He rushed to the door and grabbed the heavy latch. It turned easily enough, but when Alton tried to shoulder through, the door did not budge and a burst of sparkling blue energy threw him back to the floor.

"Curse this place," Alton spat. The portal was magically held. He knew a spell to open such enchanted doors but doubted whether his magic would be strong enough to dispel the castings of a master. In his haste and fear, the words of the dweomer floated through Alton's thoughts in an indecipherable jumble.

"Do not run, DeVir," came the Faceless One's call from the previous chamber. "You only lengthen your torment!"

"A curse upon you, too," Alton replied under his breath. Alton forgot about the stupid spell; it would never come to him in time. He glanced around the room for an option.

His eyes found something unusual halfway up the side wall, in an opening between two large cabinets. Alton scrambled back a few steps to get a better angle but found himself caught within the range of the candlelight, within the deceptive field where his eyes registered both heat and light.

He could only discern that this section of the wall showed a uniform glow in the heat spectrum and that its hue was subtly different from the stone of the walls. Another doorway? Alton could only hope his guess to be right. He rushed back to the center of the room, stood directly across from the object, and forced his eyes away from the infrared spectrum, fully back into the world of light.

As his eyes adjusted, what came into view both startled and confused the young DeVir. He saw no doorway, nor any opening with another chamber behind it. What he looked upon was a reflection of himself, and a portion of the room he now stood in. Alton had never, in his fifty-five years of life, witnessed such a spectacle, but he had heard the masters of Sorcere speak of these devices. It was a mirror.

A movement in the upper doorway of the chamber reminded Alton that the Faceless One was almost upon him. He couldn't hesitate to ponder his options. He put his head down and charged the mirror.

Perhaps it was a teleportation door to another section of the city, perhaps a simple door to a room beyond. Or perhaps, Alton dared to imagine in those few desperate seconds, this was some interplanar gate that would bring him into a strange and unknown plane of existence!

He felt the tingling excitement of adventure pulling him on as he neared the wondrous thing—then he felt only the impact, the shattering glass, and the unyielding stone wall behind it.

Perhaps it was just a mirror.

⚔ ⚔ ⚔ ⚔ ⚔

"Look at his eyes," Vierna whispered to Maya as they examined the newest member of House Do'Urden.

Truly the babe's eyes were remarkable. Though the child had been out of the womb for less than an hour, the pupils of his orbs darted back and forth inquisitively. While they showed the expected radiating glow of eyes seeing into the infrared spectrum, the familiar redness was tinted by a shade of blue, giving them a violet hue.

"Blind?" wondered Maya. "Perhaps this one will be given to the Spider Queen still."

Briza looked back to them anxiously. Dark elves did not allow children showing any physical deficiency to live.

"Not blind," replied Vierna, passing her hand over the child and casting an angry glare at both of her eager sisters. "He follows my fingers."

Maya saw that Vierna spoke the truth. She leaned closer to the babe, studying his face and strange eyes. "What do you see, Drizzt Do'Urden?" she asked softly, not in an act of gentleness toward the babe, but so that she would not disturb her mother, resting in the chair at the head of the spider idol. "What do you see that the rest of us cannot?"

⚔ ⚔ ⚔ ⚔ ⚔

Glass crunched under Alton, digging deeper wounds as he shifted his weight in an effort to rise to his feet. What would it matter? he thought. "My mirror!" he heard the Faceless One groan, and he looked up to see the outraged master towering over him.

How huge he seemed to Alton! How great and powerful, fully blocking the candlelight from this little alcove between the cabinets, his form enhanced tenfold to the eyes of the helpless victim by the mere implications of his presence.

Alton then felt a gooey substance floating down around him, detached webbing finding a sticky hold on the cabinets, on the wall, and on Alton. The young DeVir tried to leap up and roll away, but the Faceless One's spell already held him fast, trapped him as a dirgit fly would be trapped in the strands of a spider's home.

"First my door," the Faceless One growled at him, "and now this, my mirror! Do you know the pains I suffered to acquire such a rare device?"

Alton turned his head from side to side, not in answer, but to free at least his face from the binding substance.

"Why did you not just stand still and let the deed be finished cleanly?" the Faceless One roared, thoroughly disgusted.

"Why?" Alton lisped, spitting some of the webbing from his thin lips. "Why would you want to kill me?"

"Because you broke my mirror!" the Faceless One shot back.

It didn't make any sense, of course—the mirror had only been shattered after the initial attack—but to the master, Alton supposed, it didn't have to make sense. Alton knew his cause to be hopeless, but he continued on in his efforts to dissuade his opponent.

"You know of my house, of House DeVir," he said, indignant, "fourth in the city. Matron Ginafae will not be pleased. A high priestess has ways to learn the truth of such situations!"

"House DeVir?" The Faceless One laughed. Perhaps the torments that Dinin Do'Urden had requested would be in line after all. Alton had broken his mirror!

"Fourth house!" Alton spat.

"Foolish youth," the Faceless One cackled. "House DeVir is no more—not fourth, not fifty-fourth, nothing."

Alton slumped, though the webbing did its best to hold his body erect. What could the master be babbling about?

"They all are dead," the Faceless One taunted. "Matron Ginafae sees Lolth more clearly this day." Alton's expression of horror pleased the disfigured master. "All dead," he snarled one more time. "Except for poor Alton, who lives on to hear of his family's misfortune. That oversight shall be remedied now!" The Faceless One raised his hands to cast a spell.

"Who?" Alton cried.

The Faceless One paused and seemed not to understand.

"What house did this?" the doomed student clarified. "Or what conspiracy of houses brought down DeVir?"

"Ah, you should be told," replied the Faceless One, obviously enjoying the situation. "I suppose it is your right to know before you join your kin in the realm of death." A smile widened across the opening where his lips once had been.

"But you broke my mirror!" the master growled. "Die stupid, stupid boy! Find your own answers!"

The Faceless One's chest jerked out suddenly, and he shuddered in convulsions, babbling curses in a tongue far beyond the terrified student's comprehension. What vile spell did this disfigured master have prepared for him, so wretched that its chant sounded in an arcane language foreign to learned Alton's ears, so unspeakably evil that its semantics jerked on the very edge of its caster's control? The Faceless One then fell forward to the floor and expired.

Stunned, Alton followed the line of the master's hood down to his back—to the tail of a protruding dart. Alton watched the poisoned thing as it continued to shudder from the body's impact, then he turned his scan upward to the center of the room, where the young cleaning attendant stood calmly.

"Nice weapon, Faceless One!" Masoj beamed, rolling a two-handed, crafted crossbow over in his hands. He threw a wicked smile at Alton and fitted another dart.

⚔ ⚔ ⚔ ⚔ ⚔

Matron Malice hoisted herself out of her chair and willed herself to her feet. "Out of the way!" she snapped at her daughters.

Maya and Vierna scooted away from the spider idol and the baby. "See his eyes, Matron Mother," Vierna dared to remark. "They are so unusual."

Matron Malice studied the child. Everything seemed in place, and a good thing, too, for Nalfein, elderboy of House Do'Urden, was dead, and this boy, Drizzt, would have a difficult job replacing the valuable son.

"His eyes," Vierna said again.

The matron shot her a venomous look but bent low to see what the fuss was about.

"Purple?" Malice said, startled. Never had she heard of such a thing.

"He is not blind," Maya was quick to put in, seeing the disdain spreading across her mother's face.

"Fetch the candle," Matron Malice ordered. "Let us see how these eyes appear in the world of light."

Maya and Vierna reflexively headed for the sacred cabinet, but Briza cut them off. "Only a high priestess may touch the holy items," she reminded them in a tone that carried the weight of a threat. She spun around haughtily, reached into the cabinet, and produced a single half-used red candle. The clerics hid their eyes and Matron Malice put a prudent hand over the baby's face as Briza lit the sacred candle. It produced only a tiny flame, but to drow eyes it came as a brilliant intrusion.

"Bring it," said Matron Malice after several moments of adjusting. Briza moved the candle near Drizzt, and Malice gradually slid her hand away.

"He does not cry," Briza remarked, amazed that the babe could quietly accept such a stinging light.

"Purple again," whispered the matron, paying no heed to her daughter's rambling. "In both worlds, the child's eyes show as purple."

Vierna gasped audibly when she looked again upon her tiny brother and his striking lavender orbs.

"He is your brother," Matron Malice reminded her, viewing Vierna's gasp as a hint of what might come. "When he grows older and those eyes pierce you so, remember, on your life, that he is your brother."

Vierna turned away, almost blurting a reply she would have regretted making. Matron Malice's exploits with nearly every male soldier of the Do'Urden house—and many others that the seductive matron managed to sneak away from other houses—were almost legendary in Menzoberranzan. Who was she to be spouting reminders of prudent and proper behavior? Vierna bit her lip and hoped that neither Briza nor Malice had been reading her thoughts at that moment.

In Menzoberranzan, thinking such gossip about a high priestess, whether or not it was true, got you painfully executed.

Her mother's eyes narrowed, and Vierna thought she had been discovered. "He is yours to prepare," Matron Malice said to her.

"Maya is younger," Vierna dared to protest. "I could attain the level of high priestess in but a few years if I may keep to my studies."

"Or never," the matron sternly reminded her. "Take the child to the chapel proper. Wean him to words and teach him all that he will need to know to properly serve as a page prince of House Do'Urden."

"I will see to him," Briza offered, one hand subconsciously slipping to her snake-headed whip. "I do so enjoy teaching males their place in our world."

Malice glared at her. "You are a high priestess. You have other duties more important than word-weaning a male child." Then to Vierna, she said, "The babe is yours; do not disappoint me in this! The lessons you teach Drizzt will reinforce your own understanding of our ways. This exercise at 'mothering' will aid you in your quest to become a high priestess." She let Vierna take a moment to view the task in a more positive light, then her tone became unmistakably threatening once again. "It may aid you, but it surely can destroy you!"

Vierna sighed but kept her thoughts silent. The chore that Matron Malice had dropped on her shoulders would consume the bulk of her time for at least ten years. Vierna didn't like the prospects, she and this purple-eyed child together for ten long years. The alternative, however, the wrath of Matron Malice Do'Urden, seemed a worse thing by far.

⚔ ⚔ ⚔ ⚔ ⚔

Alton blew another web from his mouth. "You are just a boy, an apprentice," he stammered. "Why would you—?"

"Kill him?" Masoj finished the thought. "Not to save you, if that is your hope." He spat down at the Faceless One's body. "Look at me, a prince of the sixth house, a cleaning steward for that wretched—"

"Hun'ett," Alton cut in. "House Hun'ett is the sixth house."

The younger drow put a finger to pursed lips. "Wait," he remarked with a widening smile, an evil smile of sarcasm. "We are the fifth house now, I suppose, with DeVir wiped out."

"Not yet!" Alton growled.

"Momentarily," Masoj assured him, fingering the crossbow quarrel.

Alton slumped even farther back in the web. To be killed by a master was bad enough, but the indignity of being shot down by a boy. . . .

"I suppose I should thank you," Masoj said. "I had planned to kill that one for many tendays."

"Why?" Alton pressed his new assailant. "You would dare to kill a master of Sorcere simply because your family put you in servitude to him?"

"Because he would snub me!" Masoj yelled. "Four years I have slaved for him, that back end of a carrion crawler. Cleaned his boots. Prepared salve for his disgusting face! Was it ever enough? Not for that one." He spat at the corpse again and continued, talking more to himself than to the trapped student. "Nobles aspiring to wizardry have the advantage of being trained as apprentices before they reach the proper age for entry into Sorcere."

"Of course," Alton said. "I myself trained under—"

"He meant to keep me out of Sorcere!" Masoj rambled, ignoring Alton altogether. "He would have forced me into Melee-Magthere, the fighters' school, instead. The fighters' school! My twenty-fifth birthday is only two tendays away." Masoj looked up, as though he suddenly remembered that he was not alone in the room.

"I knew I must kill him," he continued, now speaking directly to Alton. "Then you come along and make it all so convenient. A student and master killing each other in a fight? It has happened before. Who would question it? I suppose, then, that I should thank you, Alton DeVir of No House Worth Mentioning," Masoj chided with a low, sweeping bow. "Before I kill you, I mean."

"Wait!" cried Alton. "Kill me to what gain?"

"Alibi."

"But you have your alibi, and we can make it better!"

"Explain," said Masoj, who, admittedly, was in no particular hurry. The Faceless One was a high-level wizard; the webs weren't going anywhere anytime soon.

"Free me," Alton said earnestly.

"Can you be as stupid as the Faceless One proclaimed you?"

Alton took the insult stoically—the kid had the crossbow. "Free me so that I may assume the Faceless One's identity," he explained. "The death of a master arouses suspicion, but if no master is believed dead . . ."

"And what of this?" Masoj asked, kicking the corpse.

"Burn it," said Alton, his desperate plan coming fully into focus. "Let it be Alton DeVir. House DeVir is no more, so there will be no retaliation, no questions."

Masoj seemed skeptical.

"The Faceless One was practically a hermit," Alton reasoned. "And I am near to graduation; certainly I can handle the simple chores of basic teaching after thirty years of study."

"And what is my gain?"

Alton gawked, nearly burying himself in webbing, as if the answer were obvious. "A master in Sorcere to call mentor. One who can ease your way through your years of study."

"And one who can dispose of a witness at his earliest convenience," Masoj added slyly.

"And what then would be my gain?" Alton shot back. "To anger House Hun'ett, fifth in all the city, and I with no family at my back? No, young Masoj, I am not as stupid as the Faceless One named me."

Masoj ticked a long and pointed fingernail against his teeth and considered the possibilities. An ally among the masters of Sorcere? This held possibilities.

Another thought popped into Masoj's mind, and he pulled open the cabinet to Alton's side and began rummaging through the contents. Alton flinched when he heard some ceramic and glass containers crashing together, thinking of the components, possibly even completed potions, that might be lost by the apprentice's carelessness. Perhaps Melee-Magthere would be a better choice for this one, he thought.

A moment later, though, the younger drow reappeared, and Alton remembered that he was in no position to make such judgments.

"This is mine," Masoj demanded, showing Alton a small black object: a remarkably detailed onyx figurine of a hunting panther. "A gift from a denizen of the lower planes for some help I gave to him."

"You aided such a creature?" Alton had to ask, finding it difficult to believe that a mere apprentice had the resources necessary to even survive an encounter with such an unpredictable and mighty foe.

"The Faceless One—" Masoj kicked the corpse again—"took the credit and the statue, but they are mine! Everything else in here will go to you, of course. I know the magical dweomers of most and will show you what is what."

Brightening at the hope that he would indeed survive this dreadful day, Alton cared little about the figurine at that moment. All he wanted was to be freed of the webs so that he could find out the truth of his house's fate. Then Masoj, ever a confusing young drow, turned suddenly and started away.

"Where are you going?" Alton asked.

"To get the acid."

"Acid?" Alton hid his panic well, though he had a terrible feeling that he understood what Masoj meant to do.

"You want the disguise to appear authentic," Masoj explained matter-of-factly. "Otherwise, it would not be much of a disguise. We should take advantage of the web while it lasts. It will hold you still."

"No," Alton started to protest, but Masoj wheeled on him, the evil grin wide on his face.

"It does seem a bit of pain, and a lot of trouble to go through," Masoj admitted. "You have no family and will find no allies in Sorcere, since the Faceless One was so despised by the other masters." He brought the crossbow up level with Alton's eyes and fitted another poisoned dart. "Perhaps you would prefer death."

"Get the acid!" Alton cried.

"To what end?" Masoj teased, waving the crossbow. "What have you to live for, Alton DeVir of No House Worth Mentioning?"

"Revenge," Alton sneered, the sheer wrath of his tone setting the confident Masoj on his heels. "You have not learned this yet—though you will, my young student—but nothing in life gives more purpose than the hunger for revenge!"

Masoj lowered the bow and eyed the trapped drow with respect, almost fear. Still, the apprentice Hun'ett could not appreciate the gravity of Alton's proclamation until Alton reiterated, this time with an eager smile on his face, "Get the acid."

# 4
# The First House

Four cycles of Narbondel—four days—later, a glowing blue disk floated up the mushroom-lined stone path to the spider-covered gate of House Do'Urden. The sentries watched it from the windows of the two outer towers and from the compound as it hovered patiently three feet off the ground. Word came to the ruling family only seconds later.

"What can it be?" Briza asked Zaknafein when she, the weapons master, Dinin, and Maya assembled on the balcony of the upper level.

"A summons?" Zak asked as much as answered. "We will not know until we investigate." He stepped up on the railing and out into the empty air, then levitated down to the compound floor. Briza motioned to Maya, and the youngest Do'Urden daughter followed Zak.

"It bears the standard of House Baenre," Zak called up after he had moved closer. He and Maya opened the large gates, and the disk slipped in, showing no hostile movements.

"Baenre," Briza repeated over her shoulder, down the house's corridor to where Matron Malice and Rizzen waited.

"It seems that you are requested in audience, Matron Mother," Dinin put in nervously.

Malice moved out to the balcony, and her husband obediently followed.

"Do they know of our attack?" Briza asked in the silent code, and every member of House Do'Urden, noble and commoner alike, shared that unpleasant thought. House DeVir had been eliminated only a few days before, and a calling card from the First Matron Mother of Menzoberranzan could hardly be viewed as a coincidence.

"Every house knows," Malice replied aloud, not believing the silence to be a necessary precaution within the boundaries of her own complex. "Is the evidence against us so overwhelming that the ruling council will be forced to action?" She stared hard at Briza, her dark eyes alternating between the red glow of infravision and the deep green they showed in the aura of normal light. "That is the question we must ask." Malice stepped up onto the balcony, but Briza grabbed the back of her heavy black robe to stay her.

"You do not mean to go with the thing?" Briza asked.

Malice's answering look showed even more startlement. "Of course," she replied. "Matron Baenre would not openly call upon me if she meant me harm. Even her power is not so great that she can ignore the tenets of the city."

"You are certain that you will be safe?" Rizzen asked, truly concerned. If Malice was killed, Briza would take over the house, and Rizzen doubted that the eldest daughter would want any male by her side. Even if the vicious female did desire a patron, Rizzen would not want to be the one in that position. He was not Briza's father, was not even as old as Briza. Clearly, the present patron of the house had a lot at stake in Matron Malice's continued good health.

"Your concern touches me," Malice replied, knowing her husband's true fears. She pulled out of Briza's grasp and stepped off the railing, straightening her robes as she slowly descended. Briza shook her head disdainfully and motioned Rizzen to follow her back inside the house, not thinking it wise that the bulk of the family be so exposed to unfriendly eyes.

"Do you want an escort?" Zak asked as Malice sat on the disk.

"I am certain that I will find one as soon as I am beyond the perimeter of our compound," Malice replied. "Matron Baenre would not risk exposing me to any danger while I am in the care of her house."

"Agreed," said Zak, "but do you want an escort from House Do'Urden?"

"If one was wanted, two disks would have floated in," Malice said in a tone of finality. The matron was beginning to find the concerns of those around her stifling. She was the matron mother, after all, the strongest, the oldest, and the wisest, and did not appreciate others second-guessing her. To the disk, Malice said, "Execute your appointed task, and let us be done with it!"

Zak nearly snickered at Malice's choice of words.

"Matron Malice Do'Urden," came a magical voice from the disk, "Matron Baenre offers her greetings. Too long has it been since last you two have sat in audience."

"Never," Malice signaled to Zak. "Then take me to House Baenre!" Malice demanded. "I do not wish to waste my time conversing with a magical mouth!"

Apparently, Matron Baenre had anticipated Malice's impatience, for without another word, the disk floated back out of the Do'Urden compound.

Zak shut the gate as it left, then quickly signaled his soldiers into motion. Malice did not want any open company, but the Do'Urden spy network would covertly track every movement of the Baenre sled, to the very gates of the ruling house's grand compound.

* * * * *

Malice's guess about an escort was correct. As soon as the disk swept down from the pathway to the Do'Urden compound, twenty soldiers of House Baenre, all female, moved out from concealment along the sides of the boulevard. They formed a defensive diamond around the guest matron mother. The guard at each point of the formation wore black robes emblazoned on the back with a large purple-and-red spider design—the robes of a high priestess.

"Baenre's own daughters," Malice mused, for only the daughters of a noble could attain such a rank. How careful the First Matron Mother had been to ensure Malice's safety on the trip!

Slaves and drow commoners tripped over themselves in a frantic effort to get far out of the way of the approaching entourage as the group made its way through the curving streets toward the mushroom grove. The soldiers of House Baenre alone wore their house insignia in open view, and no one wanted to invoke the anger of Matron Baenre in any way.

Malice just rolled her eyes in disbelief and hoped that she might know such power before she died.

She rolled her eyes again a few minutes later, when the group approached the ruling house. House Baenre encompassed twenty tall and majestic stalagmites, all interconnected with gracefully sweeping and arching bridges and parapets. Magic and faerie fire glowed from a thousand separate sculptures and a hundred regally adorned guardsmen paced about in perfect formations.

Even more striking were the inverse structures, the thirty smaller stalactites of House Baenre. They hung down from the ceiling of the cavern, their roots lost in the high darkness. Some of them connected tip-to-tip with the stalagmite mounds, while others hung freely like poised spears. Ringing balconies, curving up like the edging of a screw, had been built along the length of all of these, glowing with an overabundance of magic and highlighted design.

Magic, too, was the fence that connected the bases of the outer stalagmites, encircling the whole of the compound. It was a giant web, silver against the general blue of the rest of the outer compound. Some said it had been a gift from Lolth herself, with iron-strong strands as thick as a drow elf's arm. Anything touching Baenre's fence, even the sharpest of drow weapons, would simply stick fast until the matron mother willed the fence to let it free.

Malice and her escorts moved straight toward a symmetrical and circular section of this fence, between the tallest of the outer towers. As they neared, the gate spiraled and wound out, leaving a gap large enough for the caravan to step through.

Malice sat through it all, trying to appear unimpressed.

Hundreds of curious soldiers watched the procession as it made its way to the central structure of House Baenre, the great purple-glowing chapel dome. The common soldiers left the entourage, leaving only the four high priestesses to escort Matron Malice inside.

The sights beyond the great doors to the chapel did not disappoint her. A central altar dominated the place with a row of benches spiraling out in several dozen circuits to the perimeter of the great hall. Two thousand drow could sit there with room to stretch. Statues and idols too numerous to count stood all about the place, glowing in a quiet black light. In the air high above the altar loomed a gigantic glowing image, a red-and-black illusion that slowly and continually shifted between the forms of a spider and a beautiful drow female.

"A work of Gromph, my principal wizard," Matron Baenre explained from her perch on the altar, guessing that Malice, like everyone else who ever came to Chapel Baenre, was awestruck by the sight. "Even wizards have their place."

"As long as they remember their place," Malice replied, slipping down from the now stationary disk.

"Agreed," said Matron Baenre. "Males can get so presumptuous at times, especially wizards! Still, I wish that I had Gromph at my side more often these days. He has been appointed Archmage of Menzoberranzan, you know, and seems always at work on Narbondel or some other such tasks."

Malice just nodded and held her tongue. Of course, she knew that Baenre's son was the city's chief wizard. Everybody knew. Everybody knew, too, that Baenre's daughter Triel was the Matron Mistress of the Academy, a position of honor in Menzoberranzan second only to the title of matron mother of an individual family. Malice had little doubt that Matron Baenre would somehow work that fact into the conversation before too long.

Before Malice took a step toward the stairs to the altar, her newest escort stepped out from the shadows. Malice scowled openly when she saw the thing, a creature known as an illithid, a mind flayer. It stood about six feet tall, fully a foot taller than Malice, most of the difference being the result of the creature's enormous head. Glistening with slime, the head resembled an octopus with pupil-less, milky white eyes.

Malice composed herself quickly. Mind flayers were not unknown in Menzoberranzan, and rumors said that one had befriended Matron Baenre.

These creatures, though, more intelligent and more evil than even the drow, almost always inspired shudders of revulsion.

"You may call him Methil," Matron Baenre explained. "His true name is beyond my pronunciation. He is a friend."

Before Malice could reply, Baenre added, "Of course, Methil gives me the advantage in our discussion, and you are not accustomed to illithids." Then, as Malice's mouth drooped open in disbelief, Matron Baenre dismissed the illithid.

"You read my thought," Malice protested. Few could insinuate themselves through the mental barriers of a high priestess well enough to read her thoughts, and the practice was a crime of the highest order in drow society.

"No!" Matron Baenre explained, immediately on the defensive. "Your pardon, Matron Malice. Methil reads thoughts, even the thoughts of a high priestess, as easily as you or I hear words. He communicates telepathically. On my word, I did not even realize that you had not yet spoken your thoughts."

Malice waited to watch the creature depart the great hall, then walked up the steps to the altar. In spite of her efforts against the action, she could not help peeking up at the transforming spider-and-drow image every now and.

"How fares House Do'Urden?" Matron Baenre asked, feigning politeness.

"Well enough," replied Malice, more interested at that moment in studying her counterpart than in conversing. They were alone atop the altar, though no doubt a dozen or so clerics wandered through the shadows of the great hall, keeping a watchful eye on the situation.

Malice had all that she could handle in hiding her contempt for Matron Baenre. Malice was old, nearly five hundred, but Matron Baenre was ancient. Her eyes had seen the rise and fall of a millennium, by some accounts, though drow rarely lived past their seventh—and certainly not their eighth—century. While drow normally did not show their age—Malice was as beautiful and vibrant now as she had been on her one-hundredth birthday—Matron Baenre was withered and worn. The wrinkles surrounding her mouth resembled a spider's web, and she could hardly keep the heavy lids of her eyes from dropping altogether. Matron Baenre should be dead, Malice noted, but still she lives.

Matron Baenre, seeming so beyond her time of life, was pregnant, and due in only a few tendays.

In this aspect, too, Matron Baenre defied the norm of the dark elves. She had given birth twenty times, twice as often as any others in Menzoberranzan, and fifteen of those she bore were female, every one a high priestess! Ten of Baenre's children were older than Malice!

"How many soldiers do you now command?" Matron Baenre asked, leaning closer to show her interest.

"Three hundred," Malice replied.

"Oh," mused the withered old drow, pursing a finger to her lips. "I had heard the count at three-hundred fifty."

Malice grimaced in spite of herself. Baenre was teasing her, referring to the soldiers House Do'Urden had added in its raid on House DeVir.

"Three hundred," Malice said again.

"Of course," replied Baenre, resting back.

"And House Baenre holds a thousand?" Malice asked for no better reason than to keep herself on even terms in the discussion.

"That has been our number for many years."

Malice wondered again why this old decrepit thing was still alive. Surely more than one of Baenre's daughters aspired to the position of matron mother. Why hadn't they conspired and finished Matron Baenre off? Or why hadn't any of them, some in the later stages of life, struck out on their own to form separate houses, as was the norm for noble daughters when they passed their fifth century? While they lived under Matron Baenre's rule, their children would not even be considered nobles but would be relegated to the ranks of the commoners.

"You have heard of the fate of House DeVir?" Matron Baenre asked directly, growing as tired of the hesitant small talk as her counterpart.

"Of what house?" Malice asked pointedly. At this time, there was no such thing as House DeVir in Menzoberranzan. To drow reckoning, the house no longer existed; the house never existed.

Matron Baenre cackled. "Of course," she replied. "You are matron mother of the ninth house now. That is quite an honor."

Malice nodded. "But not as great an honor as matron mother of the eighth house."

"Yes," agreed Baenre, "but ninth is only one position away from a seat on the ruling council."

"That would be an honor indeed," Malice replied. She was beginning to understand that Baenre was not simply teasing her, but was congratulating her as well, and prodding her on to greater glories. Malice brightened at the thought. Baenre was in the highest favor of the Spider Queen. If she was pleased with House Do'Urden's ascension, then so was Lolth.

"Not as much of an honor as you would believe," said Baenre. "We are a group of meddling old females, gathering every so often to find new ways to put our hands into places they do not belong."

"The city recognizes your rule."

"Does it have a choice?" Baenre laughed. "Still, drow business is better left to the matron mothers of the individual houses. Lolth would not stand for a presiding council exacting anything that even remotely resembled total rule. Do you not believe that House Baenre would have conquered all of Menzoberranzan long ago if that was the Spider Queen's will?"

Malice shifted proudly in her chair, appalled by such arrogant words.

"Not now, of course," Matron Baenre explained. "The city is too large for such an action in this age. But long ago, before you were even born, House Baenre would not have found such a conquest difficult. But that is not our way. Lolth encourages diversity. She is pleased that houses stand to balance each other, ready to fight beside each other in times of common need." She paused a moment and let a smile appear on her wrinkled lips. "And ready to pounce upon any that fall out of her favor."

Another direct reference to House DeVir, Malice noted, this time directly connected to the Spider Queen's pleasure. Malice eased out of her angry posture and found the rest of her discussion—fully two hours long—with Matron Baenre quite enjoyable.

Still, when she was back on the disk and floating out through the compound, past the grandest and strongest house in all of Menzoberranzan,

Malice was not smiling. In the face of such an open display of power, she could not forget that Matron Baenre's purpose in summoning her had been twofold: to privately and cryptically congratulate her on her perfect coup, and to vividly remind her not to get too ambitious.

# 5 Weaning

For five long years Vierna devoted almost every waking moment to the care of baby Drizzt. In drow society, this was not so much a nurturing time as an indoctrinating time. The child had to learn basic motor and language skills, as did children of all the intelligent races, but a drow elf also had to be grilled on the precepts that bound the chaotic society together.

In the case of a male child such as Drizzt, Vierna spent hour after endless hour reminding him that he was inferior to the drow females. Since almost all of this portion of Drizzt's life was spent in the family chapel, he encountered no males except during times of communal worship. Even when all in the house gathered for the unholy ceremonies, Drizzt remained silent at Vierna's side, with his gaze obediently on the floor.

When Drizzt was old enough to follow commands, Vierna's workload lessened. Still, she spent many hours teaching her younger brother—presently they were working on the intricate facial, hand, and body movements of the silent code. Often, though, she just set Drizzt about the endless task of cleaning the domed chapel. The room was barely a fifth the size of the great hall in House Baenre, but it could hold all the dark elves of House Do'Urden with a hundred seats to spare.

Being a weanmother was not so bad now, Vierna thought, but still she wished that she could devote more of her time to her studies. If Matron Malice had appointed Maya to the task of rearing the child, Vierna might already have been ordained as a high priestess. Vierna still had another five years in her duties with Drizzt; Maya might attain high priestesshood before her!

Vierna dismissed that possibility. She could not afford to worry about such problems. She would finish her tenure as weanmother in just a few short years. On or around his tenth birthday, Drizzt would be appointed page prince of the family and would serve all the household equally. If her work with Drizzt did not disappoint Matron Malice, Vierna knew that she would get her due.

"Go up the wall," Vierna instructed. "Tend to that statue." She pointed to a sculpture of a naked drow female about twenty feet from the floor. Young Drizzt looked up at it, confused. He couldn't possibly climb up to the sculpture and wipe it clean while holding any secure perch. Drizzt knew the high price of disobedience, though—even of hesitation—and he reached up, searching for his first handhold.

"Not like that!" Vierna scolded.

"How?" Drizzt dared to ask, for he had no idea of what his sister was hinting at.

"Will yourself up to the gargoyle," Vierna explained.

Drizzt's small face crinkled in confusion.

"You are a noble of House Do'Urden!" Vierna shouted at him. "Or at least you will one day earn that distinction. In your neck-purse you possess the emblem of the house, an item of considerable magic." Vierna still wasn't certain if Drizzt was ready for such a task; levitation was a high manifestation of innate drow magic, certainly more difficult that limning objects in faerie fire or summoning globes of darkness. The Do'Urden emblem heightened these innate powers of drow elves, magic that usually emerged as a drow matured. Whereas most drow nobles could summon the magical energy to levitate once every day or so, the nobles of House Do'Urden, with their insignia tool, could do so repeatedly.

Normally, Vierna would never have tried this on a male child younger than ten, but Drizzt had shown her so much potential in the last couple of years that she saw no harm in the attempt. "Just put yourself in line with the statue," she explained, "and will yourself to rise."

Drizzt looked up at the female carving, then lined his feet just out in front of the thing's angled and delicate face. He put a hand to his collar, trying to attune himself to the emblem. He had sensed before that the magic coin possessed some type of power, but it was only a raw sensation, a child's intuition. Now that Drizzt had some focus and confirmation to his suspicions, he clearly felt the vibrations of magical energy.

A series of deep breaths cleared distracting thoughts from the young drow's mind. He blocked out the other sights of the room; all he saw was the statue, the destination. He felt himself grow lighter, his heels went up, and he was on one toe, though he felt no weight upon it. Drizzt looked over at Vierna, his smile wide in amazement . . . then he tumbled to a heap.

"Foolish male!" Vierna scolded. "Try again! Try a thousand times if you must!" She reached for the snake-headed whip on her belt. "If you fail . . ."

Drizzt looked away from her, cursing himself. His own elation had caused the spell to falter. He knew that he could do it now, though, and he was not afraid of being beaten. He concentrated again on the sculpture and let the magical energy gather within his body.

Vierna, too, knew that Drizzt would eventually succeed. His mind was keen, as sharp as any Vierna had ever known, including those of the other females of House Do'Urden. The child was stubborn, too; Drizzt would not let the magic defeat him. She knew he would stand under the sculpture until he fainted from hunger if need be.

Vierna watched him go through a series of small successes and failures, the last one dropping Drizzt from a height of nearly ten feet. Vierna flinched, wondering if he was seriously hurt. Drizzt, whatever his wounds, did not even cry out but moved back into position and started concentrating all over again.

"He is young for that," came a comment from behind Vierna. She turned in her seat to see Briza standing over her, a customary scowl on the older sister's face.

"Perhaps," Vierna replied, "but I'll not know until I let him try."

"Whip him when he fails," Briza suggested, pulling her cruel six-headed instrument from her belt. She gave the whip a loving look—as if it were some sort of pet—and let a snake's head writhe about her neck and face. "Inspiration."

"Put it away," Vierna retorted. "Drizzt is mine to rear, and I need no help from you!"

"You should watch how you speak to a high priestess," Briza warned, and all of the snake heads, extensions of her thoughts, turned menacingly toward Vierna.

"As Matron Malice will watch how you interfere with my tasks," Vierna was quick to reply.

Briza put her whip away at the mention of Matron Malice. "Your tasks," she echoed scornfully. "You are too yielding for such a chore. Male children must be disciplined; they must be taught their place." Realizing that Vierna's threat held dire consequences, the older sister turned and left.

Vierna let Briza have the last word. The weanmother looked back to Drizzt, still trying to get up to the statue. "Enough!" she ordered, recognizing that the child was tiring; he could barely get his feet off the ground.

"I will do it!" Drizzt snapped back at her.

Vierna liked his determination, but not the tone of his reply. Perhaps there was some truth to Briza's words. Vierna snapped the snake-headed whip from her belt. A little inspiration might go a long way.

* * * * *

Vierna sat in the chapel the next day, watching Drizzt hard at work polishing the statue of the naked female. He had levitated the full twenty feet in his first attempt this day.

Vierna could not help but be disappointed when Drizzt did not look back to her and smile at the success. She saw him now, hovering up in the air, his hands a blur as they worked the brushes. Most vividly of all, though, Vierna saw the scars on her brother's naked back, the legacy of their "inspirational" discussion. In the infrared spectrum, the whip lines showed clearly, trails of warmth where the insulating layers of skin had been stripped away.

Vierna understood the gain in beating a child, particularly a male child.

Few drow males ever raised a weapon against a female, unless under the order of some other female. "How much do we lose?" Vierna wondered aloud. "What more could one such as Drizzt become?"

When she heard the words spoken aloud, Vierna quickly brushed the blasphemous thoughts from her mind. She aspired to become a high priestess of the Spider Queen, Lolth the Merciless. Such thoughts were not in accord with the rules of her station. She cast an angry glare on her little brother, transferring her guilt, and again took out her instrument of punishment.

She would have to whip Drizzt again this day, for the sacrilegious thoughts he had inspired within her.

⚔ ⚔ ⚔ ⚔ ⚔

So the relationship continued for another five years, with Drizzt learning the basic lessons of life in drow society while endlessly cleaning the chapel of House Do'Urden. Beyond the supremacy of female drow (a lesson always accentuated by the wicked snake-headed whip), the most compelling lessons were those concerning the surface elves, the faeries. Evil empires often bound themselves in webs of hate toward fabricated enemies, and none in the history of the world were better at it than the drow. From the first day they were able to understand the spoken word, drow children were taught that whatever was wrong in their lives could be blamed on the surface elves.

Whenever the fangs of Vierna's whip sliced into Drizzt's back, he cried out for the death of a faerie. Conditioned hatred was rarely a rational emotion.

# Part Two

## The Weapons Master

Empty hours, empty days.

I find that I have few memories of that first period of my life, those first sixteen years when I labored as a servant. Minutes blended into hours, hours into days, and so on, until the whole of it seemed one long and barren moment. Several times I managed to sneak out onto the balcony of House Do'Urden and look out over the magical lights of Menzoberranzan. On all of those secret journeys, I found myself entranced by the growing, and dissipating, heat-light of Narbondel, the timeclock pillar. Looking back on that now, on those long hours watching the glow of the wizard's fire slowly walk its way up and down the pillar I am amazed at the emptiness of my early days.

I clearly remember my excitement, tingling excitement, each time I got out of the house and set myself into position to observe the pillar. Such a simple thing it was, yet so fulfilling compared to the rest of my existence.

Whenever I hear the crack of a whip, another memory—more a sensation than a memory actually—sends a shiver through my spine. The shocking jolt and the ensuing numbness from those snake-headed weapons is not something that any person would soon forget. They bite under your skin, sending waves of magical energy through your body, waves that make your muscles snap and pull beyond their limits.

Yet I was luckier than most. My sister Vierna was near to becoming a high priestess when she was assigned the task of rearing me and was at a period of her life where she possessed far more energy than such a job required. Perhaps, then, there was more to those first ten years under her care than I now recall. Vierna never showed the intense wickedness of our mother—or, more particularly, of our oldest sister, Briza. Perhaps there were good times in the solitude of the house chapel; it is possible that Vierna allowed a more gentle side of herself to show through to her baby brother.

Maybe not. Even though I count Vierna as the kindest of my sisters, her words drip in the venom of Lolth as surely as those of any cleric in Menzoberranzan. It seems unlikely that she would risk her aspirations toward high priesthood for the sake of a mere child, a mere male child.

Whether there were indeed joys in those years, obscured in the unrelenting assault of Menzoberranzan's wickedness, or whether that earliest period of my life was even more painful than the years that followed—so painful that my mind hides the memories—I cannot be certain. For all my efforts, I cannot remember them.

I have more insight into the next six years, but the most prominent recollection of the days I spent serving the court of Matron Malice—aside from the secret trips outside the house—is the image of my own feet.

A page prince is never allowed to raise his gaze.

—Drizzt Do'Urden

# 6

# "Two-Hands"

Drizzt promptly answered the call to his matron mother's side, not needing the whip Briza used to hurry him along. How often he had felt the sting of that dreaded weapon! Drizzt held no thoughts of revenge against his vicious oldest sister. With all of the conditioning he had received, he feared the consequences of striking her—or any female—far too much to entertain such notions.

"Do you know what this day marks?" Malice asked him as he arrived at the side of her great throne in the chapel's darkened anteroom.

"No, Matron Mother," Drizzt answered, unconsciously keeping his gaze on his toes. A resigned sigh rose in his throat as he noticed the unending view of his own feet. There had to be more to life than blank stone and ten wiggling toes, he thought.

He slipped one foot out of his low boot and began doodling on the stone floor. Body heat left discernible tracings in the infrared spectrum, and Drizzt was quick and agile enough to complete simple drawings before the initial lines had cooled.

"Sixteen years," Matron Malice said to him. "You have breathed the air of Menzoberranzan for sixteen years. An important period of your life has passed."

Drizzt did not react, did not see any importance or significance to the declaration. His life was an unending and unchanging routine. One day, sixteen years, what difference did it make? If his mother considered important the things he had been put through since his earliest recollections, Drizzt shuddered to think of what the next decades might hold.

He had nearly completed his picture of a round-shouldered drow—Briza—being bitten on the behind by an enormous viper.

"Look at me," Matron Malice commanded.

Drizzt felt at a loss. His natural tendency once had been to look upon a person with whom he was talking, but Briza had wasted no time in beating that instinct out of him. The place of a page prince was servitude, and the only eyes a page prince's were worthy of meeting were those of the creatures that scurried across the stone floor—except the eyes of a spider, of course; Drizzt had to avert his gaze whenever one of the eight-legged things crawled into his vision. Spiders were too good for the likes of a page prince.

"Look at me," Malice said again, her tone hinting at volatile impatience. Drizzt had witnessed the explosions before, a wrath so incredibly vile that it swept aside anything and everything in its path. Even Briza, so pompous and cruel, ran for hiding when the matron mother grew angry.

Drizzt forced his gaze up tentatively, scanning his mother's black robes, using the familiar spider pattern along the garment's back and sides to judge the angle of his gaze. He fully expected, as every inch passed, a smack on his head, or a lashing on his back—Briza was behind him, always with her snake-headed whip near her anxious hand.

Then he saw her, the mighty Matron Malice Do'Urden, her heat-sensing eyes flashing red and her face cool, not flushed with angry heat. Drizzt kept tense, still expecting a punishing blow.

"Your tenure as page prince is ended," Malice explained. "You are secondboy of House Do'Urden now and are accorded all the . . ."

Drizzt's gaze unconsciously slipped back to the floor.

"Look at me!" his mother screamed in sudden rage.

Terrified, Drizzt snapped his gaze back to her face, which now was glowing a hot red. On the edge of his vision he saw the wavering heat of Malice's swinging hand, though he was not foolish enough to try to dodge the blow. He was on the floor then, the side of his face bruised.

Even in the fall, though, Drizzt was alert and wise enough to keep his gaze locked on to that of Matron Malice.

"No more a servant!" the matron mother roared. "To continue acting like one would bring disgrace to our family." She grabbed Drizzt by the throat and dragged him roughly to his feet.

"If you dishonor House Do'Urden," she promised, her face an inch from his, "I will put needles into your purple eyes."

Drizzt didn't blink. In the six years since Vierna had relinquished care of him, putting him into general servitude to all the family, he had come to know Matron Malice well enough to understand all of the subtle connotations of her threats. She was his mother—for whatever that was worth—but Drizzt did not doubt that she would enjoy sticking needles in his eyes.

⚔ ⚔ ⚔ ⚔ ⚔

"This one is different," Vierna said, "in more than the shade of his eyes."

"In what way, then?" Zaknafein asked, trying to keep his curiosity at a professional level. Zak had always liked Vierna better than the others, but she recently had been ordained a high priestess, and had since become too eager for her own good.

Vierna slowed the pace of her gait—the door to the chapel's antechamber was in sight now. "It is hard to say," she admitted. "Drizzt is as intelligent as any male child I have ever known; he could levitate by the age of five. Yet, after he became the page prince, it took tendays of punishment to teach him the duty of keeping his gaze to the floor, as if such a simple act ran unnaturally counter to his constitution."

Zaknafein paused and let Vierna move ahead of him. "Unnatural?" he whispered under his breath, considering the implications of Vierna's observations. Unusual, perhaps, for a drow, but exactly what Zaknafein would expect—and hope for—from a child of his loins.

He moved behind Vierna into the lightless anteroom. Malice, as always, sat in her throne at the head of the spider idol, but all the other chairs in the room had been moved to the walls, even though the entire family was present. This was to be a formal meeting, Zak realized, for only the matron mother was accorded the comfort of a seat.

"Matron Malice," Vierna began in her most reverent voice, "I present to you Zaknafein, as you requested."

Zak moved up beside Vierna and exchanged nods with Malice, but he was more intent on the youngest Do'Urden, standing naked to the waist at the matron mother's side.

Malice held up one hand to silence the others, then motioned for Briza, holding a house *piwafwi*, to continue.

An expression of elation brightened Drizzt's childish face as Briza, chanting through the appropriate incantations, placed the magical cloak, black and shot with streaks of purple and red, over his shoulders.

"Greetings, Zaknafein Do'Urden," Drizzt said heartily, drawing stunned looks from all in the room. Matron Malice had not granted him privilege to speak; he hadn't even asked her permission!

"I am Drizzt, secondboy of House Do'Urden, no more the page prince. I can look at you now—I mean at your eyes and not your boots. Mother told me so." Drizzt's smile disappeared when he looked up at the burning scowl of Matron Malice.

Vierna stood as if turned to stone, her jaw hanging open and her eyes wide in disbelief.

Zak, too, was amazed, but in a different manner. He brought a hand up to pinch his lips together, to prevent them from spreading into a smile that would have inevitably erupted into belly-shaking laughter. Zak couldn't remember the last time he had seen the matron mother's face so very bright!

Briza, in her customary position behind Malice, fumbled with her whip, too confounded by her young brother's actions to even know what in the Nine Hells she should do.

That was a first, Zak knew, for Malice's eldest daughter rarely hesitated when punishment was in order.

At the matron's side, but now prudently a step farther away, Drizzt quieted and stood perfectly still, biting down on his bottom lip. Zak could see, though, that the smile remained in the young drow's eyes. Drizzt's informality and disrespect of station had been more than an unconscious slip of the tongue and more than the innocence of inexperience.

The weapons master took a long step forward to deflect the matron mother's attention from Drizzt. "Secondboy?" he asked, sounding impressed, both for the sake of Drizzt's swelling pride and to placate and distract Malice. "Then it is time for you to train."

Malice let her anger slip away, a rare event. "Only the basics at your hand, Zaknafein. If Drizzt is to replace Nalfein, his place at the Academy will be in Sorcere. Thus the bulk of his preparation will fall upon Rizzen and his knowledge, limited though it may be, of the magical arts."

"Are you so certain that wizardry is his lot, Matron?" Zak was quick to ask.

"He appears intelligent," Malice replied. She shot an angry glare at Drizzt. "At least, some of the time. Vierna reported great progress with his command of the innate powers. Our house needs a new wizard." Malice snarled reflexively, reminded of Matron Baenre's pride in her wizard son, the Archmage of the city. It had been sixteen years since Malice's meeting with the First Matron Mother of Menzoberranzan, but she had never forgotten even the tiniest detail of that encounter. "Sorcere seems the natural course."

Zak took a flat coin from his neck-purse, flipped it into a spin, and snatched it out of the air. "Might we see?" he asked.

"As you will," Malice agreed, not surprised at Zak's desire to prove her wrong. Zak placed little value in wizardry, preferring the hilt of a blade to the crystal rod component of a lightning bolt.

Zak moved to stand before Drizzt and handed him the coin. "Flip it."

Drizzt shrugged, wondering what this vague conversation between his mother and the weapons master was all about. Until now, he had heard nothing of any future profession being planned for him, or of this place called Sorcere. With a consenting shrug of his shoulders, he slid the coin onto his curled index finger and snapped it into the air with his thumb, easily catching it. He then held it back out to Zak and gave the weapons master a confused look, as if to ask what was so important about such an easy task.

Instead of taking the coin, the weapons master pulled another from his neck-purse. "Try both hands," he said to Drizzt, handing it to him.

Drizzt shrugged again, and in one easy motion, put the coins up and caught them.

Zak turned an eye on Matron Malice. Any drow could have performed that feat, but the ease with which this one executed the catch was a pleasure to observe. Keeping a sly eye on the matron, Zak produced two more coins. "Stack two on each hand and send all four up together," he instructed Drizzt.

Four coins went up. Four coins were caught. The only parts of Drizzt's body that had even flinched were his arms.

"Two-hands," Zak said to Malice. "This one is a fighter. He belongs in Melee-Magthere."

"I have seen wizards perform such feats," Malice retorted, not pleased by the look of satisfaction on the troublesome weapons master's face. Zak once had been Malice's proclaimed husband, and quite often since that distant time she took him as her lover. His skills and agility were not confined to the use of weapons. But along with the pleasures that Zaknafein gave to Malice, sensual skills that had prompted Malice to spare Zak's life on more than a dozen occasions, came a multitude of headaches. He was the finest weapons master in Menzoberranzan, another fact that Malice could not ignore, but his disdain, even contempt, for the Spider Queen had often landed House Do'Urden into trouble.

Zak handed two more coins to Drizzt. Now enjoying the game, Drizzt put them into motion. Six went up. Six came down, the correct three landing in each hand.

"Two-hands," Zak said more emphatically. Matron Malice motioned for him to continue, unable to deny the grace of her youngest son's display.

"Could you do it again?" Zak asked Drizzt.

With each hand working independently, Drizzt soon had the coins stacked atop his index fingers, ready to flip. Zak stopped him there and pulled out four more coins, building each of the piles five high. Zak paused a moment to study the concentration of the young drow (and also to keep his hands over the coins and ensure that they were brightened enough by the warmth of his body heat for Drizzt to properly see them in their flight).

"Catch them all, Secondboy," he said in all seriousness. "Catch them all, or you will land in Sorcere, the school of magic. That is not where you belong!"

Drizzt still had only a vague idea of what Zak was talking about, but he could tell from the weapons master's intensity that it must be important. He took a deep breath to steady himself, then snapped the coins up. He sorted their glow quickly, discerning each individual item. The first two fell easily into his hands, but Drizzt saw that the scattering pattern of the rest would not drop them so readily in line.

Drizzt exploded into action, spinning a complete circle, his hands an indecipherable blur of motion. Then he straightened suddenly and stood before Zak. His hands were in fists at his sides and a grim look lay on his face.

Zak and Matron Malice exchanged glances, neither quite sure of what had happened.

Drizzt held his fists out to Zak and slowly opened them, a confident smile widening across his childish face.

Five coins in each hand.

Zak blew a silent whistle. It had taken him, the weapons master of the house, a dozen tries to complete that maneuver with ten coins. He walked over to Matron Malice.

"Two-hands," he said a third time. "He is a fighter, and I am out of coins."

"How many could he do?" Malice breathed, obviously impressed in spite of herself.

"How many could we stack?" Zaknafein shot back with a triumphant smile.

Matron Malice chuckled out loud and shook her head. She had wanted Drizzt to replace Nalfein as the house wizard, but her stubborn weapons master had, as always, deflected her course. "Very well, Zaknafein," she said, admitting her defeat. "The secondboy is a fighter."

Zak nodded and started back to Drizzt.

"Perhaps one day soon to be the weapons master of House Do'Urden," Matron Malice added to Zak's back. Her sarcasm stopped Zak short, and he eyed her over his shoulder.

"With this one," Matron Malice continued wryly, wrenching back the upper hand with her usual lack of shame, "could we expect anything less?"

Rizzen, the present patron of the family shifted uncomfortably. He knew, and so did everyone—even the slaves of House Do'Urden—that Drizzt was not his child.

⚔ ⚔ ⚔ ⚔ ⚔

"Three rooms?" Drizzt asked when he and Zak entered the large training hall at the southernmost end of the Do'Urden complex. Balls of multicolored magical light had been spaced along the length of the high-ceilinged stone room, basking the entirety in a comfortably dim glow. The hall had only three doors: one to the east, which led to an outer chamber that opened onto the balcony of the house; one directly across from Drizzt, on the south wall, leading into the last room in the house; and the one from the main hallway that they had just passed through. Drizzt knew from the many locks Zak was now fastening behind them that he wouldn't often be going back that way.

"One room," Zak corrected.

"But two more doors," Drizzt reasoned, looking out across the room. "With no locks."

"Ah," Zak corrected, "their locks are made of common sense." Drizzt was beginning to get the picture. "That door," Zak continued, pointing to the south, "opens into my private chambers. You do not ever want me to find you in there. The other one leads to the tactics room, reserved for times of war. When—if—you ever prove yourself to my satisfaction, I might invite you to join me there. That day is years away, so consider this single magnificent hall—" he swept his arm out in a wide arc—"your home."

Drizzt looked around, not overly thrilled. He had dared to hope that he had left this kind of treatment behind him with his page prince days. This setup, though, brought him back even to before his six years of servitude in the house, back to that decade when he had been locked away in the family chapel with Vierna. This room wasn't even as large as the chapel, and was too tight for the likings of the spirited young drow. His next question came out as a growl.

"Where do I sleep?"

"Your home," Zak answered matter-of-factly.

"Where do I take meals?"

"Your home."

Drizzt's eyes narrowed to slits and his face flushed in glowing heat. "Where do I . . ." he began stubbornly, determined to foil the weapons master's logic.

"Your home," Zak replied in the same measured and weighted timbre before Drizzt could finish the thought.

Drizzt planted his feet firmly and crossed his arms over his chest. "It sounds messy," he growled.

"It had better not be," Zak growled back.

"Then what is the purpose?" Drizzt began. "You pull me away from my mother—"

"You will address her as Matron Malice," Zak warned. "You will always address her as Matron Malice."

"From my mother—"

Zak's next interruption came not with words but with the swing of a curled fist.

Drizzt awoke about twenty minutes later.

"First lesson," Zak explained, casually leaning against the wall a few feet away. "For your own good. You will always address her as Matron Malice."

Drizzt rolled to his side and tried to prop himself up on his elbow but found his head reeling as soon as it left the black-rugged floor. Zak grabbed him and hoisted him up.

"Not as easy as catching coins," the weapons master remarked.

"What?"

"Parrying a blow."

"What blow?"

"Just agree, you stubborn child."

"Secondboy!" Drizzt corrected, his voice again a growl, and his arms defiantly back over his chest.

Zak's fist curled at his side, a not-too-subtle point that Drizzt did not miss. "Do you need another nap?" the weapons master asked calmly.

"Secondboys can be children," Drizzt wisely conceded.

Zak shook his head in disbelief. This was going to be interesting. "You may find your time here enjoyable," he said, leading Drizzt over to a long, thick, and colorfully (though most of the colors were somber) decorated curtain. "But only if you can learn some control over that wagging tongue of yours." A sharp tug sent the curtain floating down, revealing the most magnificent weapons rack the young drow (and many older drow as well) had ever seen. Polearms of many sorts, swords, axes, hammers, and every other kind of weapon Drizzt could imagine—and a whole bunch he'd never imagine—sat in an elaborate array.

"Examine them," Zak told him. "Take your time and your pleasure. Learn which ones sit best in your hands, follow most obediently the commands of your will. By the time we have finished, you will know every one of them as a trusted companion."

Wide-eyed, Drizzt wandered along the rack, viewing the whole place and the potential of the whole experience in a completely different light. For his entire young life, sixteen years, his greatest enemy had been boredom. Now, it appeared, Drizzt had found weapons to fight that enemy.

Zak headed for the door to his private chamber, thinking it better that Drizzt be alone in those first awkward moments of handling new weapons.

The weapons master stopped, though, when he reached his door and looked back to the young Do'Urden. Drizzt swung a long and heavy halberd, a polearm more than twice his height, in a slow arc. For all of Drizzt's attempts to keep the weapon under control, its momentum spun his tiny frame right to the ground.

Zak heard himself chuckle, but his laughter only reminded him of the grim reality of his duty. He would train Drizzt, as he had trained a thousand young dark elves before him, to be a warrior, preparing him for the trials of the Academy and life in dangerous Menzoberranzan. He would train Drizzt to be a killer.

How against this one's nature that mantle seemed! thought Zak. Smiles came too easily to Drizzt; the thought of him running a sword through the heart of another living being revolted Zaknafein. That was the way of the drow, though, a way that Zak had been unable to resist for all of his four centuries of life. Pulling his stare from the spectacle of Drizzt at play, Zak moved into his chamber and shut the door.

"Are they all like that?" he asked into his nearly empty room. "Do all drow children possess such innocence, such simple, untainted smiles that cannot survive the ugliness of our world?" Zak started for the small desk to the side of the room, meaning to lift the darkening shade off the continually glowing ceramic globe that served as the chamber's light source. He changed his mind as that image of Drizzt's delight with the weapons refused to diminish, and he headed instead for the large bed across from the door.

"Or are you unique, Drizzt Do'Urden?" he continued as he fell onto the cushioned bed. "And if you are so different, what, then, is the cause? The blood, my blood, that courses through your veins? Or the years you spent with your weanmother?"

Zak threw an arm across his eyes and considered the many questions. Drizzt was different from the norm, he decided at length, but he didn't know whether he should thank Vierna—or himself.

After a while, sleep took him. But it brought the weapons master little comfort. A familiar dream visited him, a vivid memory that would never fade.

Zaknafein heard again the screams of the children of House DeVir as the Do'Urden soldiers—soldiers he himself had trained—slashed at them.

"This one is different!" Zak cried, leaping up from his bed. He wiped the cold sweat from his face.

"This one is different." He had to believe that.

# 7
# Dark Secrets

"Do you truly mean to try?" Masoj asked, his voice condescending and filled with disbelief.

Alton turned his hideous glare on the student.

"Direct your anger elsewhere, Faceless One," Masoj said, averting his gaze from his mentor's scarred visage. "I am not the cause of your frustration. The question was valid."

"For more than a decade, you have been a student of the magical arts," Alton replied. "Still you fear to explore the nether world at the side of a master of Sorcere."

"I would have no fear beside a true master," Masoj dared to whisper.

Alton ignored the comment, as he had with so many others he had accepted from the apprenticing Hun'ett over the last sixteen years. Masoj was Alton's only tie to the outside world, and while Masoj had a powerful family, Alton had only Masoj.

They moved through the door into the uppermost chamber of Alton's four-room complex. A single candle burned there, its light diminished by an abundance of dark-colored tapestries and the black hue of the room's stone and rugs. Alton slid onto his stool at the back of the small, circular table, and placed a heavy book down before him.

"It is a spell better left for clerics," Masoj protested, sitting down across from the faceless master. "Wizards command the lower planes; the dead are for the clerics alone."

Alton looked around curiously, then turned a frown up at Masoj, the master's grotesque features enhanced by the dancing candlelight. "It seems that I have no cleric at my call," the Faceless One explained sarcastically. "Would you rather I try for another denizen of the Nine Hells?"

Masoj rocked back in his chair and shook his head helplessly and emphatically. Alton had a point. A year before, the Faceless One had sought answers to his questions by enlisting the aid of an ice devil. The volatile thing froze the room until it shone black in the infrared spectrum and smashed a matron mother's treasure horde worth of alchemical equipment. If Masoj hadn't summoned his magical cat to distract the ice devil, neither he nor Alton would have gotten out of the room alive.

"Very well, then," Masoj said unconvincingly, crossing his arms in front of him on the table. "Conjure your spirit and find your answers."

Alton did not miss the involuntary shudder belied by the ripple in Masoj's robes. He glared at the student for a moment, then went back to his preparations.

As Alton neared the time of casting, Masoj's hand instinctively went into his pocket, to the onyx figurine of the hunting cat he had acquired on the day Alton had assumed the Faceless One's identity. The little statue was enchanted with a powerful dweomer that enabled its possessor to summon a mighty panther to his side. Masoj had used the cat sparingly, not yet fully understanding the dweomer's limitations and potential dangers. "Only in times of need," Masoj reminded himself quietly when he felt the item in his hand. Why was it that those times kept occurring when he was with Alton? the apprentice wondered.

Despite his bravado, this time Alton privately shared Masoj's trepidation. Spirits of the dead were not as destructive as denizens of the lower planes, but they could be equally cruel and subtler in their torments.

Alton needed his answer, though. For more than a decade and a half he had sought his information through conventional channels, enquiring of masters and students—in a roundabout manner, of course—of the details concerning the fall of House DeVir. Many knew the rumors of that eventful night; some even detailed the battle methods used by the victorious house.

None, though, would name that perpetrating house. In Menzoberranzan, one did not utter anything resembling an accusation, even if the belief was commonly shared, without enough undeniable proof to spur the ruling council into a unified action against the accused. If a house botched a raid and was discovered, the wrath of all Menzoberranzan would descend upon it until the family name had been extinguished. But in the case of a successfully executed attack, such as the one that felled House DeVir, an accuser was the one most likely to wind up at the wrong end of a snake-headed whip.

Public embarrassment, perhaps more than any guidelines of honor, turned the wheels of justice in the city of drow.

Alton now sought other means for the solution to his quest. First he had tried the lower planes, the ice devil, to disastrous effect. Now Alton had in his possession an item that could end his frustrations: a tome penned by a wizard of the surface world. In the drow hierarchy, only the clerics of Lolth dealt with the realm of the dead, but in other societies, wizards also dabbled into the spirit world. Alton had found the book in the library of Sorcere and had managed to translate enough of it, he believed, to make a spiritual contact.

He wrung his hands together, gingerly opened the book to the marked page, and scanned the incantation one final time. "Are you ready?" he asked Masoj.

"No."

Alton ignored the student's unending sarcasm and placed his hands flat on the table. He slowly sunk into his deepest meditative trance.

"*Fey innad* . . ." He paused and cleared his throat at the slip. Masoj, though he hadn't closely examined the spell, recognized the mistake.

"*Fey innunad de-min* . . ." Another pause.

"Lolth be with us," Masoj groaned under his breath.

Alton's eyes popped wide, and he glared at the student. "A translation," he growled. "From the strange language of a human wizard!"

"Gibberish," Masoj retorted.

"I have in front of me the private spellbook of a wizard from the surface world," Alton said evenly. "An archmage, according to the scribbling of the orcan thief who stole it and sold it to our agents." He composed himself again and shook his hairless head, trying to return to the depths of his trance.

"A simple, stupid orc managed to steal a spellbook from an archmage," Masoj whispered rhetorically, letting the absurdity of the statement speak for itself.

"The wizard was dead!" Alton roared. "The book is authentic!"

"Who translated it?" Masoj replied calmly.

Alton refused to listen to any more arguments. Ignoring the smug look on Masoj's face, he began again.

"*Fey innunad de-min de-sul de-ket.*"

Masoj faded out and tried to rehearse a lesson from one of his classes, hoping that his sobs of laughter wouldn't disturb Alton. He didn't believe for a moment that Alton's attempt would prove successful, but he didn't want to screw up the fool's line of babbling again and have to suffer through the ridiculous incantation all the way from the beginning still another time.

A short time later, when Masoj heard Alton's excited whisper, "Matron Ginafae?" he quickly focused his attention back on the events at hand.

Sure enough, an unusual ball of green-hued smoke appeared over the candle's flame and gradually took a more definite shape.

"Matron Ginafae!" Alton gasped again when the summons was complete. Hovering before him was the unmistakable image of his dead mother's face.

The spirit scanned the room, confused. "Who are you?" it asked at length.

"I am Alton. Alton DeVir, your son."

"Son?" the spirit asked.

"Your child."

"I remember no child so very ugly."

"A disguise," Alton replied quickly, looking back at Masoj and expecting a snicker. If Masoj had chided and doubted Alton before, he now showed only sincere respect.

Smiling, Alton continued, "Just a disguise, that I might move about in the city and exact revenge upon our enemies!"

"What city?"

"Menzoberranzan, of course."

Still the spirit seemed not to understand.

"You are Ginafae?" Alton pressed. "Matron Ginafae DeVir?"

The spirit's features contorted into a twisted scowl as it considered the question. "I was . . . I think."

"Matron Mother of House DeVir, Fourth House of Menzoberranzan," Alton prompted, growing more excited. "High priestess of Lolth."

The mention of the Spider Queen sent a spark through the spirit. "Oh, no!" it balked. Ginafae remembered now. "You should not have done this, my ugly son!"

"It is just a disguise," Alton interrupted.

"I must leave you," Ginafae's spirit continued, glancing around nervously. "You must release me!"

"But I need some information from you, Matron Ginafae."

"Do not call me that!" the spirit shrieked. "You do not understand! I am not in Lolth's favor . . ."

"Trouble," whispered Masoj offhandedly, hardly surprised.

"Just one answer!" Alton demanded, refusing to let another opportunity to learn his enemies' identities slip past him.

"Quickly!" the spirit shrieked.

"Name the house that destroyed DeVir."

"The house?" Ginafae pondered. "Yes, I remember that evil night. It was House—"

The ball of smoke puffed and bent out of shape, twisting Ginafae's image and sending her next words out as an indecipherable blurb.

Alton leaped to his feet. "No!" he screamed. "You must tell me! Who are my enemies?"

"Would you count me as one?" the spirit image said in a voice very different from the one it had used earlier, a tone of sheer power that stole the blood from Alton's face. The image twisted and transformed, became something ugly, uglier than Alton. Hideous beyond all experience on the Material Plane.

Alton was not a cleric, of course, and he had never studied the drow religion beyond the basic tenets taught to males of the race. He knew the creature now hovering in the air before him, though, for it appeared as an oozing, slimy stick of melted wax: a yochlol, a handmaiden of Lolth.

"You dare to disturb the torment of Ginafae?" the yochlol snarled.

"Damn!" whispered Masoj, sliding slowly down under the black tablecloth. Even he, with all of his doubts of Alton, had not expected his disfigured mentor to land them in trouble this serious.

"But . . ." Alton stuttered.

"Never again disturb this plane, feeble wizard!" the yochlol roared.

"I did not try for the Abyss," Alton protested meekly. "I only meant to speak with—"

"With Ginafae!" the yochlol snarled. "Fallen priestess of Lolth. Where would you expect to find her spirit, foolish male? Frolicking in Olympus, with the false gods of the surface elves?"

"I did not think . . ."

"Do you ever?" the yochlol growled.

"Nope," Masoj answered silently, careful to keep himself as far out of the way as possible.

"Never again disturb this plane," the yochlol warned a final time. "The Spider Queen is not merciful and has no tolerance for meddling males!" The creature's oozing face puffed and swelled, expanding beyond the limits of the smoky ball. Alton heard gurgling, gagging noises, and he stumbled back over his stool, putting his back flat against the wall and bringing his arms up defensively in front of his face.

The yochlol's mouth opened impossibly wide and spewed forth a hail of small objects. They ricocheted off Alton and tapped against the wall all around him. Stones? the faceless wizard wondered in confusion. One of the objects then answered his unspoken question. It caught hold of Alton's layered black robes and began crawling up toward his exposed neck. Spiders.

A wave of the eight-legged beasts rushed under the little table, sending Masoj tumbling out the other side in a desperate roll. He scrambled to his feet and turned back, to see Alton slapping and stomping wildly, trying to get out of the main host of the crawling things.

"Do not kill them!" Masoj screamed. "To kill spiders is forbidden by the—"

"To the Nine Hells with the clerics and their laws!" Alton shrieked back.

Masoj shrugged in helpless agreement, reached around under the folds of his own robes, and produced the same two-handed crossbow he had used to kill the Faceless One those years ago. He considered the powerful weapon and the tiny spiders scrambling around the room.

"Overkill?" he asked aloud. Hearing no answer, he shrugged again and fired.

The heavy bolt knifed across Alton's shoulder, cutting a deep line. The wizard stared in disbelief, then turned an ugly grimace on Masoj.

"You had one on your shoulder," the student explained.

Alton's scowl did not relent.

"Ungrateful?" Masoj snarled. "Foolish Alton, all of the spiders are on your side of the room. Remember?" Masoj turned to leave and called, "Good hunting," over his shoulder. He reached for the handle to the door, but as his long fingers closed around it, the portal's surface transformed into the image of Matron Ginafae. She smiled widely, too widely, and an impossibly long and wet tongue reached out and licked Masoj across the face.

"Alton!" he cried, spinning back against the wall out of the slimy member's reach. He noticed the wizard in the midst of spellcasting, Alton fighting to hold his concentration as a host of spiders continued their hungry ascent up his flowing robes.

"You are a dead one," Masoj commented matter-of-factly, shaking his head.

Alton fought through the exacting ritual of the spell, ignored his own revulsion of the crawling things, and forced the evocation to completion. In all of his years of study, Alton never would have believed he could do such a thing; he would have laughed at the mere mention of it. Now, however, it seemed a far preferable fate to the yochlol's creeping doom.

He dropped a fireball at his own feet.

⚔ ⚔ ⚔ ⚔ ⚔

Naked and hairless, Masoj stumbled through the door and out of the inferno. The flaming faceless master came next, diving into a roll and stripping his tattered and burning robe from his back as he went.

As he watched Alton patting out the last of the flames, a pleasant memory flashed in Masoj's mind, and he uttered the single lament that dominated his every thought at this disastrous moment.

"I should have killed him when I had him in the web."

⚔ ⚔ ⚔ ⚔ ⚔

A short time later, after Masoj had gone back to his room and his studies, Alton slipped on the ornamental metallic bracers that identified him as a master of the Academy and slipped outside the structure of Sorcere. He moved to the wide and sweeping stairway leading down from Tier Breche and sat down to take in the sights of Menzoberranzan.

Even with this view, though, the city did little to distract Alton from thoughts of his latest failure. For sixteen years he had forsaken all other dreams and ambitions in his desperate search to find the guilty house. For sixteen years he had failed.

He wondered how long he could keep up the charade, and his spirits. Masoj, his only friend—if Masoj could be called a friend—was more than halfway through his studies at Sorcere. What would Alton do when Masoj graduated and returned to House Hun'ett?

"Perhaps I shall carry on my toils for centuries to come," he said aloud, "only to be murdered by a desperate student, as I—as Masoj—murdered the Faceless One. Might that student disfigure himself and take my place?" Alton couldn't stop the ironic chuckle that passed his lipless mouth at the notion of a perpetual "faceless master" of Sorcere. At what point would the Matron

Mistress of the Academy get suspicious? A thousand years? Ten thousand? Or might the Faceless One outlive Menzoberranzan itself? Life as a master was not such a bad lot, Alton supposed. Many drow would sacrifice much to be given such an honor.

Alton dropped his face into the crook of his elbow and forced away such ridiculous thoughts. He was not a real master, nor did the stolen position bring him any measure of satisfaction. Perhaps Masoj should have shot him that day, sixteen years ago, when Alton was trapped in the Faceless One's web.

Alton's despair only deepened when he considered the actual time frame involved. He had just passed his seventieth birthday and was still young by drow standards. The notion that only a tenth of his life was behind him was not a comforting one to Alton DeVir this night.

"How long will I survive?" he asked himself. "How long until this madness that is my existence consumes me?" Alton looked back out over the city. "Better that the Faceless One had killed me," he whispered. "For now I am Alton of No House Worth Mentioning."

Masoj had dubbed him that on the first morning after House DeVir's fall, but way back then, with his life teetering on the edge of a crossbow, Alton had not understood the title's implications. Menzoberranzan was nothing more than a collection of individual houses. A rogue commoner might latch on to one of them to call his own, but a rogue noble wouldn't likely be accepted by any house in the city. He was left with Sorcere and nothing more . . . until his true identity was discovered at last. What punishments would he then face for the crime of killing a master? Masoj may have committed the crime, but Masoj had a house to defend him. Alton was only a rogue noble.

He sat back on his elbows and watched the rising heat-light of Narbondel. As the minutes became hours, Alton's despair and self-pity went through inevitable change. He turned his attention to the individual drow houses now, not to the conglomeration that bound them as a city, and he wondered what dark secrets each harbored. One of them, Alton reminded himself, held the secret he most dearly wanted to know. One of them had wiped out House DeVir.

Forgotten was the night's failure with Matron Ginafae and the yochlol, forgotten was the lament for an early death. Sixteen years was not so long a time, Alton decided. He had perhaps seven centuries of life left within his slender frame. If he had to, Alton was prepared to spend every minute of those long years searching for the perpetrating house.

"Vengeance," he growled aloud, needing, feeding off, that audible reminder of his only reason for continuing to draw breath.

# 8 Kindred

Zak pressed in with a series of low thrusts. Drizzt tried to back away quickly and return to even footing, but the relentless assault followed his every step, and he was forced to keep his movements solely on the defensive. More often than not, Drizzt found the hilts of his weapons closer to Zak than the blades.

Zak then dropped into a low crouch and came up under Drizzt's defense.

Drizzt twirled his scimitars in a masterful cross, but he had to straighten stiffly to dodge the weapons master's equally deft assault. Drizzt knew that he had been set up, and he fully expected the next attack as Zak shifted his weight to his back leg and dived in, both sword tips aimed for Drizzt's loins.

Drizzt spat a silent curse and spun his scimitars into a downward cross, meaning to use the "V" of his blades to catch his teacher's swords. On a sudden impulse, Drizzt hesitated as he intercepted Zak's weapons, and he jumped away instead, taking a painful slap on the inside of one thigh. Disgusted, he threw both of his scimitars to the floor.

Zak, too, leaped back. He held his swords out to his sides, a look of sincere confusion on his face. "You should not have missed that move," he said bluntly.

"The parry is wrong," Drizzt replied.

Awaiting further explanation, Zak lowered one sword tip to the floor and leaned on the weapon. In past years, Zak had wounded, even killed, students for such blatant defiance.

"The cross-down defeats the attack, but to what gain?" Drizzt continued. "When the move is completed, my sword tips remain down too low for any effective attack routine, and you are able to slip back and free."

"But you have defeated my attack."

"Only to face another," Drizzt argued. "The best position I can hope to obtain from the cross-down is an even stance."

"Yes . . . " Zak prompted, not understanding his student's problem with that scenario.

"Remember your own lesson!" Drizzt shouted. "'Every move should bring an advantage you preach to me, but I see no advantage in using the cross-down."

"You recite only one part of that lesson for your own purpose," Zak scolded, now growing equally angry. "Complete the phrase, or use it not at all! 'Every move should bring an advantage or take away a disadvantage.' The cross-down defeats the double thrust low, and your opponent obviously has gained the advantage if he even attempts such a daring offensive maneuver! Returning to an even stance is far preferable at that moment."

"The parry is wrong." Drizzt said stubbornly.

"Pick up your blades," Zak growled at him, taking a threatening step forward. Drizzt hesitated and Zak charged, his swords leading.

Drizzt dropped to a crouch, snatched up the scimitars, and rose to meet the assault while wondering if it was another lesson or a true attack.

The weapons master pressed furiously, snapping off cut after cut and backing Drizzt around in circles. Drizzt defended well enough and began to notice an all-too-familiar pattern as Zak's attacks came consistently lower, again forcing the hilts of Drizzt's weapons up and out over the scimitars' blades.

Drizzt understood that Zak meant to prove his point with actions, not words. Seeing the fury on Zak's face, though, Drizzt wasn't certain how far the weapons master would carry his point. If Zak proved correct in his observations, would he strike again to Drizzt's thigh? Or to his heart? Zak came up and under and Drizzt stiffened and straightened. "Double thrust low!" the weapons master growled, and his swords dived in.

Drizzt was ready for him. He executed the cross-down, smiling smugly at the ring of metal as his scimitars crossed over the thrusting swords. Drizzt then followed through with only one of his blades, thinking he could deflect both of Zak's swords well enough in that manner. Now with one blade free of the parry, Drizzt spun it over in a devious counter.

As soon as Drizzt reversed the one hand, Zak saw the ploy—a ruse he had suspected Drizzt would try. Zak dropped one of his own sword tips—the one nearest to the hilt of Drizzt's single parrying blade—to the ground, and Drizzt, trying to maintain an even resistance and balance along the length of the blocking scimitar, lost his balance. Drizzt was quick enough to catch himself before he had stumbled too far, though his knuckles pinched into the stone of the floor. He still believed that he had Zak caught in his trap, and that he could finish his brilliant counter. He took a short step forward to regain his full balance.

The weapons master dropped straight down to the floor, under the arc of Drizzt's swinging scimitar, and spun a single circuit, driving his booted heel into the back of Drizzt's exposed knee. Before Drizzt had even realized the attack, he found himself lying flat on his back.

Zak abruptly broke his own momentum and threw his feet back under him. Before Drizzt could begin to understand the dizzying counter-counter, he found the weapons master standing over him with the tip of Zak's sword painfully and pointedly drawing a tiny drop of blood from his throat.

"Have you anything more to say?" Zak growled.

"The parry is wrong," Drizzt answered.

Zak's laughter erupted from his belly. He threw his sword to the ground, reached down, and pulled the stubborn young student to his feet. He calmed quickly, his gaze finding that of Drizzt's lavender orbs as he pushed the student out to arm's length. Zak marveled at the ease of Drizzt's stance, the way he held the twin scimitars almost as if they were a natural extension of his arms. Drizzt had been in training only a few months, but already he had mastered the use of nearly every weapon in the vast armory of House Do'Urden.

Those scimitars! Drizzt's chosen weapons, with curving blades that enhanced the dizzying flow of the young fighter's sweeping battle style. With those scimitars in hand, this young drow, barely more than a child, could outfight half the members of the Academy, and a shiver tingled through Zak's spine when he pondered just how magnificent Drizzt would become after years of training.

It was not just the physical abilities and potential of Drizzt Do'Urden that made Zaknafein pause and take note, however. Zak had come to realize that Drizzt's temperament was indeed different from that of the average drow; Drizzt possessed a spirit of innocence and lacked any maliciousness. Zak couldn't help but feel proud when he looked upon Drizzt. In all manners, the young drow held to the same principles—morals so unusual in Menzoberranzan—as Zak.

Drizzt had recognized the connection as well, though he had no idea of how unique his and Zak's shared perceptions were in the evil drow world. He realized that "Uncle Zak" was different from any of the other dark elves he had come to know, though that included only his own family and a few dozen of the house soldiers. Certainly Zak was much different from Briza, Drizzt's oldest sister, with her zealous, almost blind, ambitions in the mysterious religion of Lolth. Certainly Zak was different from Matron Malice, Drizzt's mother, who seemed never to say anything at all to Drizzt unless it was a command for service.

Zak was able to smile at situations that didn't necessarily bring pain to anyone. He was the first drow Drizzt had met who was apparently content with his station in life. Zak was the first drow Drizzt had ever heard laugh.

"A good try," the weapons master conceded of Drizzt's failed counter.

"In a real battle, I would have been dead," Drizzt replied.

"Surely," said Zak, "but that is why we train. Your plan was masterful, your timing perfect. Only the situation was wrong. Still, I will say it was a good try."

"You expected it," said the student.

Zak smiled and nodded. "That is, perhaps, because I had seen the maneuver attempted by another student."

"Against you?" Drizzt asked, feeling a little less special now that he knew his battle insights were not so unique.

"Hardly," Zak replied with a wink. "I watched the counter fail from the same angle as you, to the same result."

Drizzt's face brightened again. "We think alike," he commented.

"We do," said Zak, "but my knowledge has been increased by four centuries of experience, while you have not even lived through a score of years. Trust me, my eager student. The cross-down is the correct parry."

"Perhaps," Drizzt replied.

Zak hid a smile. "When you find a better counter, we shall try it. But until then, trust my word. I have trained more soldiers than I can count, all the army of House Do'Urden and ten times that number when I served as a master in Melee-Magthere. I taught Rizzen, all of your sisters, and both of your brothers."

"Both?"

"I . . ." Zak paused and shot a curious glance at Drizzt. "I see," he said after a moment. "They never bothered to tell you." Zak wondered if it was his place to tell Drizzt the truth. He doubted that Matron Malice would care either way; she probably hadn't told Drizzt simply because she hadn't considered the story of Nalfein's death worth telling.

"Yes, both." Zak decided to explain. "You had two brothers when you were born: Dinin, whom you know, and an older one, Nalfein, a wizard of considerable power. Nalfein was killed in battle on the very night you drew your first breath."

"Against dwarves or vicious gnomes?" Drizzt squeaked, as wide-eyed as a child begging for a frightening bedtime story. "Was he defending the city from evil conquerors or rogue monsters?"

Zak had a hard time reconciling the warped perceptions of Drizzt's innocent beliefs. "Bury the young in lies," he lamented under his breath, but to Drizzt he answered, "No."

"Then against some opponent more foul?" Drizzt pressed. "Wicked elves from the surface?"

"He died at the hands of a drow!" Zak snapped in frustration, stealing the eagerness from Drizzt's shining eyes.

Drizzt slumped back to consider the possibilities, and Zak could hardly bear to watch the confusion that twisted his young face.

"War with another city?" Drizzt asked somberly. "I did not know . . ."

Zak let it go at that. He turned and moved silently toward his private chamber. Let Malice or one of her lackeys destroy Drizzt's innocent logic. Behind him, Drizzt held his next line of questions in check, understanding that the conversation, and the lesson, was at an end. Understanding, too, that something important had just transpired.

⚔ ⚔ ⚔ ⚔ ⚔

The weapons master battled Drizzt through long hours as the days blended into tendays, and the tendays into months. Time became unimportant; they fought until exhaustion overwhelmed them, and went back to the training floor again as soon as they were able.

By the third year, at the age of nineteen, Drizzt was able to hold out for hours against the weapons master, even taking the offensive in many of their contests.

Zak enjoyed these days. For the first time in many years, he had met one with the potential to become his fighting equal. For the first time that Zak could ever remember, laughter often accompanied the clash of adamantine weapons in the training room.

He watched Drizzt grow tall and straight, attentive, eager, and intelligent. The masters of the Academy would be hard put just to hold a stalemate against Drizzt, even in his first year!

That thought thrilled the weapons master only as long as it took him to remember the principles of the Academy, the precepts of drow life, and what they would do to his wonderful student. How they would steal that smile from Drizzt's lavender eyes.

A pointed reminder of that drow world outside the practice room visited them one day in the person of Matron Malice.

"Address her with proper respect," Zak warned Drizzt when Maya announced the matron mother's entrance. The weapons master prudently moved out a few steps to greet the head of House Do'Urden privately.

"My greetings, Matron," he said with a low bow. "To what do I owe the honor of your presence?"

Matron Malice laughed at him, seeing through his facade.

"So much time do you and my son spend in here," she said. "I came to witness the benefit to the boy."

"He is a fine fighter," Zak assured her.

"He will have to be," Malice muttered. "He goes to the Academy in only a year."

Zak narrowed his eyes at her doubting words and growled, "The Academy has never seen a finer swordsman."

The matron walked away from him to stand before Drizzt. "I doubt not your prowess with the blade," she said to Drizzt, though she shot a sly gaze back at Zak as she spoke the words. "You have the proper blood. There are other qualities that make up a drow warrior—qualities of the heart. The attitude of a warrior!"

Drizzt didn't know how to respond to her. He had seen her only a few times in all of the last three years, and they had exchanged no words.

Zak saw the confusion on Drizzt's face and feared that the boy would slip up—precisely what Matron Malice wanted. Then Malice would have an excuse to pull Drizzt out of Zak's tutelage—dishonoring Zak in the process—and give him over to Dinin or some other passionless killer. Zak may have been the finest instructor with the blade, but now that Drizzt had learned the use of weapons, Malice wanted him emotionally hardened.

Zak couldn't risk it; he valued his time with young Drizzt too much. He pulled his swords from their jeweled scabbards and charged right by Matron Malice, yelling, "Show her, young warrior!"

Drizzt's eyes became burning flames at the approach of his wild instructor. His scimitars came into his hands as quickly as if he had willed them to appear.

It was a good thing they had! Zak came in on Drizzt with a fury that the young drow had never before seen, more so even than the time Zak had shown Drizzt the value of the cross-down parry. Sparks flew as sword rang against scimitar, and Drizzt found himself driven back, both of his arms already aching from the thudding force of the heavy blows.

"What are you . . ." Drizzt tried to ask.

"Show her," Zak growled, slamming in again and again.

Drizzt barely dodged one cut that surely would have killed him. Still, confusion kept his moves purely defensive.

Zak slapped one of Drizzt's scimitars, then the other, out wide, and used an unexpected weapon, bringing his foot straight up in front of him and slamming his heel into Drizzt's nose.

Drizzt heard the crackle of cartilage and felt the warmth of his own blood running freely down his face. He dived back into a roll, trying to keep a safe distance from his crazed opponent until he could realign his senses.

From his knees he saw Zak, a short distance away and approaching. "Show her!" Zak growled angrily with every determined step.

The purple flames of faerie fire limned Drizzt's skin, making him an easier target. He responded the only way he could; he dropped a globe of darkness over himself and Zak. Sensing the weapons master's next move, Drizzt dropped to his belly and scrambled out, keeping his head low—a wise choice.

At his first realization of the darkness, Zak had quickly levitated up about ten feet and rolled right over, sweeping his blades down to Drizzt's face level.

When Drizzt came clear of the other side of the darkened globe, he looked back and saw only the lower half of Zak's legs. He didn't need to watch anything more to understand the weapons master's deadly blind attacks. Zak would have cut him apart if he had not dropped low in the blackness.

Anger replaced confusion. When Zak dropped from his magical perch and came rushing back out the front of the globe, Drizzt let his rage lead him back into the fight. He spun a pirouette just before he reached Zak, his lead scimitar cutting a gracefully arcing line and his other following in a deceptively sharp stab straight over that line.

Zak dodged the thrusting point and put a backhand block on the other.

Drizzt wasn't finished. He set his thrusting blade into a series of short, wicked pokes that kept Zak on the retreat for a dozen steps and more, back into the conjured darkness. They now had to rely on their incredibly keen sense of hearing and their instincts. Zak finally managed to regain a foothold, but Drizzt immediately set his own feet into action, kicking away whenever the balance of his swinging blades allowed for it. One foot even slipped through Zak's defenses, blasting the breath from the weapons master's lungs.

They came back out the side of the globe, and Zak, too, glowed in the outline of faerie fire. The weapons master felt sickened by the hatred etched on his young student's face, but he realized that this time, neither he nor Drizzt had been given a choice in the matter. This fight had to be ugly, had to be real. Gradually, Zak settled into an easy rhythm, solely defensive, and let Drizzt, in his explosive fury, wear himself down.

Drizzt played on and on, relentless and tireless. Zak coaxed him by letting him see openings where there were none, and Drizzt was always quick to oblige, launching a thrust, cut, or kick.

Matron Malice watched the spectacle silently. She couldn't deny the measure of training Zak had given her son; Drizzt was—physically—more than ready for battle.

Zak knew that, to Matron Malice, sheer skill with weapons might not be enough. Zak had to keep Malice from conversing with Drizzt for any length of time. She would not approve of her son's attitudes.

Drizzt was tiring now, Zak could see, though he recognized the weariness in his student's arms to be partly deception.

"Go with it," he muttered silently, and he suddenly "twisted" his ankle, his right arm flailing out wide and low as he struggled for balance, opening a hole in his defenses that Drizzt could not resist.

The expected thrust came in a flash, and Zak's left arm streaked in a short crosscut that slapped the scimitar right out of Drizzt's hand.

"Ha!" Drizzt cried, having expected the move and launching his second ruse. His remaining scimitar knifed over Zak's left shoulder, inevitably dipping in the follow-through of the parry.

But by the time Drizzt even launched the second blow, Zak was already down to his knees. As Drizzt's blade cut harmlessly high, Zak sprang to his feet and launched a right cross, hilt first, that caught Drizzt squarely in the face. A stunned Drizzt leaped back a long step and stood perfectly still for a long moment. His remaining scimitar dropped to the ground, and his glossed eyes did not blink.

"A feint within a feint within a feint!" Zak calmly explained.

Drizzt slumped to the floor, unconscious.

Matron Malice nodded her approval as Zak walked back over to her. "He is ready for the Academy," she remarked.

Zak's face turned sour and he did not answer.

"Vierna is there already," Malice continued, "to teach as a mistress in Arach-Tinilith, the School of Lolth. It is a high honor."

A laurel for House Do'Urden, Zak knew, but he was smart enough to keep his thoughts silent.

"Dinin will leave soon," said the matron.

Zak was surprised. Two children serving as masters in the Academy at the same time? "You must have worked hard to get such accommodations," he dared to remark.

Matron Malice smiled. "Favors owed, favors called in."

"To what end?" asked Zak. "Protection for Drizzt?"

Malice laughed aloud. "From what I have just witnessed, Drizzt would more likely protect the other two!"

Zak bit his lip at the comment. Dinin was still twice the fighter and ten times the heartless killer as Drizzt. Zak knew that Malice had other motives.

"Three of the first eight houses will be represented by no fewer than four children in the Academy over the next two decades," Matron Malice admitted. "Matron Baenre's own son will begin in the same class as Drizzt."

"So you have aspirations," Zak said. "How high, then, will House Do'Urden climb under the guidance of Matron Malice?"

"Sarcasm will cost you your tongue," the matron mother warned. "We would be fools to let slip by such an opportunity to learn more of our rivals!"

"The first eight houses," Zak mused. "Be cautious, Matron Malice. Do not forget to watch for rivals among the lesser houses. There once was a house named DeVir that made such a mistake."

"No attack will come from behind," Malice sneered. "We are the ninth house but boast more power than but a handful of others. None will strike at our backs; there are easier targets higher up the line."

"And all to our gain," Zak put in.

"That is the point of it all, is it not?" Malice asked, her evil smile wide on her face.

Zak didn't need to respond; the matron knew his true feelings. That precisely was not the point.

⚔ ⚔ ⚔ ⚔ ⚔

"Speak less and your jaw will heal faster," Zak said later, when he again was alone with Drizzt.

Drizzt cast him a vile glance.

The weapons master shook his head. "We have become great friends," he said.

"So I had thought," mumbled Drizzt.

"Then think clearly," Zak scolded. "Do you believe that Matron Malice would approve of such a bonding between her weapons master and her youngest—her prized youngest—son? You are a drow, Drizzt Do'Urden, and of noble birth. You may have no friends!"

Drizzt straightened as if he had been slapped in the face.

"None openly, at least," Zak conceded, laying a comforting hand on the youngster's shoulder. "Friends equate to vulnerability, inexcusable vulnerability. Matron Malice would never accept . . ." He paused, realizing that he was browbeating his student. "Well," he admitted in quiet conclusion, "at least we two know who we are."

Somehow, to Drizzt, that just didn't seem enough.

# 9
# Families

"Come quickly," Zak instructed Drizzt one evening after they had finished their sparring. By the urgency of the weapons master's tone, and by the fact that Zak didn't even pause to wait for Drizzt, Drizzt knew that something important was happening.

He finally caught up to Zak on the balcony of House Do'Urden, where Maya and Briza already stood.

"What is it?" Drizzt asked.

Zak pulled him close and pointed out across the great cavern, to the northeastern reaches of the city. Lights flashed and faded in sudden bursts, a pillar of fire rose into the air, then disappeared.

"A raid," Briza said of offhandedly. "Minor houses, and of no concern to us."

Zak saw that Drizzt did not understand.

"One house has attacked another," he explained. "Revenge, perhaps, but most likely an attempt to climb to a higher rank in the city."

"The battle has been long," Briza remarked, "and still the lights flash."

Zak continued to clarify the event for the confused secondboy of the house. "The attackers should have blocked the battle within rings of darkness. Their inability to do so might indicate that the defending house was ready for the raid."

"All cannot be going well for the attackers," Maya agreed.

Drizzt could hardly believe what he was hearing. Even more alarming than the news itself was the way his family talked about the event. They were so calm in their descriptions, as if this was an expected occurrence.

"The attackers must leave no witnesses," Zak explained to Drizzt, "else they will face the wrath of the ruling council."

"But we are witnesses," Drizzt reasoned.

"No," Zak replied. "We are onlookers; this battle is none of our affair. Only the nobles of the defending house are awarded the right to place accusations against their attackers."

"If any nobles are left alive," Briza added, obviously enjoying the drama.

At that moment, Drizzt wasn't sure if he liked this new revelation. However he might have felt, he found that he could not tear his gaze from the continuing spectacle of drow battle. All the Do'Urden compound was astir now, soldiers and slaves running about in search of a better vantage point and shouting out descriptions of the action and rumors of the perpetrators.

This was drow society in all its macabre play, and while it seemed ultimately wrong in the heart of the youngest member of House Do'Urden, Drizzt could not deny the excitement of the night. Nor could Drizzt deny the expressions of obvious pleasure stamped upon the faces of the three who shared the balcony with him.

⚔ ⚔ ⚔ ⚔ ⚔

Alton made his way through his private chambers one final time, to make certain that any artifacts or tomes that might seem even the least bit sacrilegious were safely hidden. He was expecting a visit from a matron mother, a rare occasion for a master of the Academy not connected with Arach-Tinilith, the School of Lolth. Alton was more than a little anxious about the motives of this particular visitor, Matron SiNafay Hun'ett, head of the city's fifth house and mother of Masoj, Alton's partner in conspiracy.

A bang on the stone door of the outermost chamber in his complex told Alton that his guest had arrived. He straightened his robes and took yet another glance around the room. The door swung open before Alton could get there, and Matron SiNafay swept into the room. How easily she made the transformation—walking from the absolute dark of the outside corridor into the candlelight of Alton's chamber—without so much as a flinch.

SiNafay was smaller than Alton had imagined, diminutive even by the standards of the drow. She stood barely more than four feet high and weighed, by Alton's estimation, no more than fifty pounds. She was a matron mother, though, and Alton reminded himself that she could strike him dead with a single spell.

Alton averted his gaze obediently and tried to convince himself that there was nothing unusual about this visit. He grew less at ease, however, when Masoj trotted in and to his mother's side, a smug smile on his face.

"Greetings from House Hun'ett, Gelroos," Matron SiNafay said. "Twenty-five years and more it has been since we last talked."

"Gelroos?" Alton mumbled under his breath. He cleared his throat to cover his surprise. "My greetings to you, Matron SiNafay," he managed to stammer. "Has it been so very long?"

"You should come to the house," the matron said. "Your chambers remain empty."

My chambers? Alton began to feel very sick.

SiNafay did not miss the look. A scowl crossed her face and her eyes narrowed evilly.

Alton suspected that his secret was out. If the Faceless One had been a member of the Hun'ett family, how could Alton hope to fool the matron mother of the house? He scanned for the best escape route, or for some way he could at least kill the traitorous Masoj before SiNafay struck him down.

When he looked back toward Matron SiNafay, she had already begun a quiet spell. Her eyes popped wide at its completion, her suspicions confirmed.

"Who are you?" she asked, her voice sounding more curious than concerned.

There was no escape, no way to get at Masoj, standing prudently close to his powerful mother's side.

"Who are you?" SiNafay asked again, taking a three-headed instrument from her belt, the dreaded snake-headed whip that injected the most painful and incapacitating poison known to drow.

"Alton," he stuttered, having no choice but to answer. He knew that since she now was on her guard, SiNafay would use simple magic to detect any lies he might concoct. "I am Alton DeVir."

"DeVir?" Matron SiNafay appeared at least intrigued. "Of the House DeVir that died some years ago?"

"I am the only survivor," Alton admitted.

"And you killed Gelroos—Gelroos Hun'ett—and took his place as master in Sorcere," the matron reasoned, her voice a snarl. Doom closed in all around Alton.

"I did not . . . I could not know his name . . . He would have killed me!" Alton stuttered.

"I killed Gelroos," came a voice from the side.

SiNafay and Alton turned to Masoj, who once again held his favorite two-handed crossbow.

"With this," the young Hun'ett explained. "On the night House DeVir fell. I found my excuse in Gelroos's battle with that one." He pointed to Alton.

"Gelroos was your brother," Matron SiNafay reminded Masoj.

"Damn his bones!" Masoj spat. "For four miserable years I served him—served him as if he were a matron mother! He would have kept me from Sorcere, would have forced me into the Melee-Magthere instead."

The matron looked from Masoj to Alton and back to her son. "And you let this one live," she reasoned, a smile again on her lips. "You killed your enemy and forged an alliance with a new master in a single move."

"As I was taught," Masoj said through clenched teeth, not knowing whether punishment or praise would follow.

"You were just a child," SiNafay remarked, suddenly realizing the timetable involved.

Masoj accepted the compliment silently.

Alton watched it all anxiously. "Then what of me?" he cried. "Is my life forfeit?"

SiNafay turned a glare on him. "Your life as Alton DeVir ended, so it would seem, on the night House DeVir fell. Thus you remain the Faceless One, Gelroos Hun'ett. I can use your eyes in the Academy—to watch over my son and my enemies."

Alton could hardly breathe. To so suddenly find himself allied with one of the most powerful houses in Menzoberranzan. A jumble of possibilities and questions flooded his mind, one in particular, which had haunted him for nearly two decades.

His adopted matron mother recognized his excitement. "Speak your thoughts," she commanded.

"You are a high priestess of Lolth," Alton said boldly, that one notion overpowering all caution. "It is within your power to grant me my fondest desire."

"You dare to ask a favor?" Matron SiNafay balked, though she saw the torment on Alton's face and was intrigued by the apparent importance of this mystery. "Very well"

"What house destroyed my family?" Alton growled. "Ask the nether world, I beg, Matron SiNafay."

SiNafay considered the question carefully, and the possibilities of Alton's apparent thirst for vengeance. Another benefit of allowing this one into the family? SiNafay wondered.

"This is known to me already," she replied. "Perhaps when you have proven your value, I will tell—"

"No!" Alton cried. He stopped short, realizing that he had interrupted a matron mother, a crime that could invoke a punishment of death.

SiNafay held back her angry urges. "This question must be very important for you to act so foolishly," she said.

"Please," Alton begged. "I must know. Kill me if you will, but tell me first who it was."

SiNafay liked his courage, and his obsession could only prove of value to her. "House Do'Urden," she said.

"Do'Urden?" Alton echoed, hardly believing that a house so far back in the city hierarchy could have defeated House DeVir.

"You will take no actions against them," Matron SiNafay warned. "And

I will forgive your insolence—this time. You are a son of House Hun'ett now; remember always your place!" She let it stay at that, knowing that one who had been clever enough to carry out such a deception for the better part of two decades would not be foolish enough to disobey the matron mother of his house.

"Come Masoj," SiNafay said to her son, "let us leave this one alone so that he may consider his new identity."

⚔ ⚔ ⚔ ⚔ ⚔

"I must tell you, Matron SiNafay," Masoj dared to say as he and his mother made their way out of Sorcere, "Alton DeVir is a buffoon. He might bring harm to House Hun'ett."

"He survived the fall of his own house," SiNafay replied, "and has played through the ruse as the Faceless One for nineteen years. A buffoon? Perhaps, but a resourceful buffoon at the least."

Masoj unconsciously rubbed the area of his eyebrow that had never grown back. "I have suffered the antics of Alton DeVir for all these years," he said. "He does have a fair share of luck, I admit, and can get himself out of trouble—though he is usually the one who puts himself into it!"

"Do not fear," SiNafay laughed. "Alton brings value to our house."

"What can we hope to gain?"

"He is a master of the Academy," SiNafay replied. "He gives me eyes where I now need them." She stopped her son and turned him to face her so that he might understand the implications of her every word. "Alton DeVir's claim against House Do'Urden may work in our favor. He was a noble of the house, with rights of accusation."

"You mean to use Alton DeVir's charge to rally the great houses into punishing House Do'Urden?" Masoj asked.

"The great houses would hardly be willing to strike out for an incident that occurred almost twenty years ago," SiNafay replied. "House Do'Urden executed House DeVir's destruction nearly to perfection—a clean kill. To so much as speak an open charge against the Do'Urdens now would be to invite the wrath of the great houses on ourselves."

"What good then is Alton DeVir?" Masoj asked. "His claim is useless to us."

The matron replied, "You are only a male and cannot understand the complexities of the ruling hierarchy. With Alton DeVir's charge whispered into the proper ears, the ruling council might look the other way if a single house took revenge on Alton's behalf."

"To what end?" Masoj remarked, not understanding the importance. "You would risk the losses of such a battle for the destruction of a lesser house?"

"So thought House DeVir of House Do'Urden," explained SiNafay. "In our world, we must be as concerned with the lower houses as with the higher ones. All of the great houses would be wise now to watch closely the moves of Daermon N'a'shezbaernon, the ninth house that is known as Do'Urden. It now has both a master and a mistress serving in the Academy and three high priestesses, with a fourth nearing the goal."

"Four high priestesses?" Masoj pondered. "In a single house." Only three of the top eight houses could claim more than that. Normally, sisters aspiring to such heights inspired rivalries that inevitably thinned the ranks.

"And the legions of House Do'Urden number more than three hundred fifty," SiNafay continued, "all of them trained by perhaps the finest weapons master in all the city."

"Zaknafein Do'Urden, of course!" Masoj recalled.

"You have heard of him?"

"His name is often spoken at the Academy, even in Sorcere."

"Good," SiNafay purred. "Then you will understand the full weight of the mission I have chosen for you."

An eager light came into Masoj's eyes.

"Another Do'Urden is soon to begin there," SiNafay explained. "Not a master, but a student. By the words of those few who have seen this boy, Drizzt, at training, he will be as fine a fighter as Zaknafein. We should not allow this."

"You want me to kill the boy?" Masoj asked eagerly.

"No," SiNafay replied, "not yet. I want you to learn of him, to understand the motivations of his every move. If the time to strike does come, you must be ready."

Masoj liked the devious assignment, but one thing still bothered him more than a little. "We still have Alton to consider," he said. "He is impatient and daring. What are the consequences to House Hun'ett if he strikes House Do'Urden before the proper time? Might we invoke open war in the city, with House Hun'ett viewed as the perpetrator?"

"Do not worry, my son," Matron SiNafay replied. "If Alton DeVir makes a grievous error while in the guise of Gelroos Hun'ett, we expose him as a murderous imposter and no member of our family. He will be an unhoused rogue with an executioner facing him from every direction."

Her casual explanation put Masoj at ease, but Matron SiNafay, so knowledgeable in the ways of drow society, had understood the risk she was taking from the moment she had accepted Alton DeVir into her house. Her plan seemed foolproof, and the possible gain—the elimination of this growing House Do'Urden—was a tempting piece of bait.

But the dangers, too, were very real. While it was perfectly acceptable for one house to covertly destroy another, the consequences of failure could not be ignored. Earlier that very night, a lesser house had struck out against a rival and, if the rumors held true, had failed. The illuminations of the next day would probably force the ruling council to enact a pretense of justice, to make an example of the unsuccessful attackers. In her long life, Matron SiNafay had witnessed this "justice" several times.

Not a single member of any of the aggressor houses—she was not even allowed to remember their names—had ever survived.

⚔ ⚔ ⚔ ⚔ ⚔

Zak awakened Drizzt early the next morning. "Come," he said. "We are bid to go out of the house this day."

All thoughts of sleep washed away from Drizzt at the news. "Outside the house?" he echoed. In all of his nineteen years, Drizzt had never once walked beyond the adamantine fence of the Do'Urden complex. He had only watched that outside world of Menzoberranzan from the balcony.

While Zak waited, Drizzt quickly collected his soft boots and his *piwafwi*. "Will there be no lesson this day?" Drizzt asked.

"We shall see," was all that Zak replied, but in his thoughts, the weapons master figured that Drizzt might be in for one of the most startling revelations of his life. A house had failed in a raid, and the ruling council had requested the presence of all the nobles of the city, to bear witness to the weight of justice.

Briza appeared in the corridor outside the practice room's door. "Hurry," she scolded. "Matron Malice does not wish our house to be among the last groups joining the gathering!"

The matron mother herself, floating atop a blue-glowing disk—for matron mothers rarely walked through the city—led the procession out of House Do'Urden's grand gate. Briza walked at her mother's side, with Maya and Rizzen in the second rank and Drizzt and Zak taking up the rear. Vierna and Dinin, attending to the duties of their positions in the Academy, had gone to the ruling council's summons with a different group.

All the city was astir this morning, rumbling in the rumors of the failed raid. Drizzt walked through the bustle wide-eyed, staring in wonderment at the close-up view of the decorated drow houses. Slaves of every inferior race—goblins, orcs, even giants—scrambled out of the way, recognizing Malice, riding her enchanted carriage, as a matron mother. Drow commoners halted conversations and remained respectfully silent as the noble family passed.

As they made their way toward the northwestern section, the location of the guilty house, they came into a lane blocked by a squabbling caravan of duergar, gray dwarves. A dozen carts had been overturned or locked together—apparently, two groups of duergar had come into the narrow lane together, neither relinquishing the right-of-way.

Briza pulled the snake-headed whip from her belt and chased off a few of the creatures, clearing the way for Malice to float up to the apparent leaders of the two groups.

The dwarves turned on her angrily—until they realized her station.

"Beggin' yer pardon, Madam," one of them stammered. "Un-fortunate accident is all."

Malice eyed the contents of one of the nearest carts, crates of giant crab legs and other delicacies.

"You have slowed my journey," Malice said calmly.

"We have come to your city in hopes of trade," the other duergar explained. He cast an angry glare at his counterpart, and Malice understood that the two were rivals, probably bartering the same goods to the same drow house.

"I will forgive your insolence . . ." she offered graciously, still eyeing the crates.

The two duergar suspected what was forthcoming. So did Zak. "We eat well tonight," he whispered to Drizzt with a sly wink. "Matron Malice would not let such an opportunity slip by without gain."

". . . if you can see your way to deliver half of these carts to the gate of House Do'Urden this night," Malice finished.

The duergar started to protest but quickly dismissed the foolish notion. How they hated dealing with drow elves!

"You will be compensated appropriately," Malice continued. "House Do'Urden is not a poor house. Between both of your caravans, you will still have enough goods to satisfy the house you came to see."

Neither of the duergar could refute the simple logic, but under these trading circumstances, where they had offended a matron mother, they knew the compensation for their valuable foods would hardly be appropriate. Still, the gray dwarves could only accept it all as a risk of doing business in Menzoberranzan. They bowed politely and set their troops to clearing the way for the drow procession.

ЖЖЖЖЖ

House Teken'duis, the unsuccessful raiders of the previous night, had barricaded themselves within their two-stalagmite structure, fully expecting what was to come. Outside their gates, all of the nobles of Menzoberranzan, more than a thousand drow, had gathered, with Matron Baenre and the other seven matron mothers of the ruling council at their head. More disastrous for the guilty house, the entirety of the three schools of the Academy, students and instructors, had surrounded the Teken'duis compound.

Matron Malice led her group to the front line behind the ruling matrons. As she was matron of the ninth house, only one step from the council, other drow nobles readily stepped out of her way.

"House Teken'duis has angered the Spider Queen!" Matron Baenre proclaimed in a voice amplified by magical spells.

"Only because they failed," Zak whispered to Drizzt.

Briza cast both males an angry glare.

Matron Baenre bade three young drow, two females and a male, to her side. "These are all that remain of House Freth," she explained. "Can you tell us, orphans of House Freth," she asked of them, "who it was that attacked your home?"

"House Teken'duis!" they shouted together.

"Rehearsed," Zak commented.

Briza turned around again. "Silence!" she whispered harshly.

Zak slapped Drizzt on the back of the head. "Yes," he agreed. "Do be quiet!"

Drizzt started to protest, but Briza had already turned away and Zak's smile was too wide to argue against.

"Then it is the will of the ruling council," Matron Baenre was saying, "that House Teken'duis suffer the consequences of their actions!"

"What of the orphans of House Freth?" came a call from the crowd.

Matron Baenre stroked the head of the oldest female, a cleric recently finished in her studies at the Academy. "Nobles they were born, and nobles they remain," Baenre said. "House Baenre accepts them into its protection; they bear the name of Baenre now."

Disgruntled whispers filtered through the gathering. Three young nobles, two of them female, was quite a prize. Any house in the city gladly would have taken them in.

"Baenre," Briza whispered to Malice. "Just what the first house needs more clerics!"

"Sixteen high priestesses is not enough, it seems," Malice answered.

"And no doubt, Baenre will take any surviving soldiers of House Freth," Briza reasoned.

Malice was not so certain. Matron Baenre was walking a thin line by taking even the surviving nobles. If House Baenre got too powerful, Lolth surely would take exception. In situations such as this, where a house had been almost eradicated, surviving common soldiers were normally pooled out to bidding houses. Malice would have to watch for such an auction. Soldiers did not come cheaply, but at this time, Malice would welcome the opportunity to add to her forces, particularly if there were any magic-users to be had.

Matron Baenre addressed the guilty house. "House Teken'duis!" she called. "You have broken our laws and have been rightfully caught. Fight if you will, but know that you have brought this doom upon yourself!" With a wave of her hand, she set the Academy, the dispatcher of justice, into motion.

Great braziers had been placed in eight positions around House Teken'duis, attended by mistresses of Arach-Tinilith and the highest-ranking clerical students. Flames roared to life and shot into the air as the high priestesses opened gates to the lower planes. Drizzt watched closely, mesmerized and hoping to catch a glimpse of either Dinin or Vierna.

Denizens of the lower planes, huge, many-armed monsters, slime covered and spitting fire, stepped through the flames. Even the nearest high priestesses backed away from the grotesque horde. The creatures gladly accepted such servitude. When the signal from Matron Baenre came, they eagerly descended upon House Teken'duis.

Glyphs and wards exploded at every corner of the house's feeble gate, but these were mere inconveniences to the summoned creatures.

The wizards and students of Sorcere then went into action, slamming at the top of House Teken'duis with conjured lightning bolts, balls of acid, and fireballs.

Students and masters of Melee-Magthere, the school of fighters, rushed about with heavy crossbows, firing into windows where the doomed family might try to escape.

The horde of monsters bashed through the doors. Lightning flashed and thunder boomed.

Zak looked at Drizzt, and a frown replaced the master's smile. Caught up in the excitement—and it certainly was exciting—Drizzt bore an expression of awe.

The first screams of the doomed family rolled out from the house, screams so terrible and agonized that they stole any macabre pleasure that Drizzt might have been experiencing. He grabbed Zak's shoulder, spinning the weapons master to him, begging for an explanation.

One of the sons of House Teken'duis, fleeing a ten-armed giant monster, stepped out onto the balcony of a high window. A dozen crossbow quarrels struck him simultaneously, and before he even fell dead, three separate lightning bolts alternately lifted him from the balcony, then dropped him back onto it.

Scorched and mutilated, the drow corpse started to tumble from its high perch, but the grotesque monster reached out a huge, clawed hand from the window and pulled it back in to devour it.

"Drow justice," Zak said coldly. He didn't offer Drizzt any consolation; he wanted the brutality of this moment to stick in the young drow's mind for the rest of his life.

The siege went on for more than an hour, and when it was finished, when the denizens of the lower planes were dismissed through the braziers' gates and the students and instructors of the Academy started their march back to Tier Breche, House Teken'duis was no more than a glowing lump of lifeless, molten stone.

Drizzt watched it all, horrified, but too afraid of the consequences to run away. He did not notice the artistry of Menzoberranzan on the return trip to House Do'Urden.

# 10 Stain of Blood

Zaknafein is out of the house?" Malice asked.

"I sent him and Rizzen to the Academy to deliver a message to Vierna," Briza explained. "He shan't return for many hours, not before the light of Narbondel begins its descent."

"That is good," said Malice. "You both understand your duties in this farce?"

Briza and Maya nodded. "I have never heard of such a deception," Maya remarked. "Is it necessary?"

"It was planned for another of the house," Briza answered, looking to Matron Malice for confirmation. "Nearly four centuries ago."

"Yes," agreed Malice. "The same was to be done to Zaknafein, but the unexpected death of Matron Vartha, my mother, disrupted the plans."

"That was when you became the matron mother," Maya said.

"Yes," replied Malice, "though I had not passed my first century of life and was still training in Arach-Tinilith. It was not a pleasant time in the history of House Do'Urden."

"But we survived," said Briza. "With the death of Matron Vartha, Nalfein and I became nobles of the house."

"The test on Zaknafein was never attempted," Maya reasoned.

"Too many other duties preceded it," Malice answered.

"We will try it on Drizzt, though," said Maya.

"The punishment of House Teken'duis convinced me that this action had to be taken," said Malice.

"Yes," Briza agreed. "Did you notice Drizzt's expression throughout the execution?"

"I did," answered Maya. "He was revolted."

"Unfitting for a drow warrior," said Malice, "and so this duty is upon us. Drizzt will leave for the Academy in a short time; we must stain his hands with drow blood and steal his innocence."

"It seems a lot of trouble for a male child," Briza grumbled. "If Drizzt cannot adhere to our ways, then why do we not simply give him to Lolth?"

"I will bear no more children!" Malice growled in response. "Every member of this family is important if we are to gain prominence in the city!" Secretly Malice hoped for another gain in converting Drizzt to the evil ways of the drow. She hated Zaknafein as much as she desired him, and turning Drizzt into a drow warrior, a true heartless drow warrior, would distress the weapons master greatly.

"On with it, then," Malice proclaimed. She clapped her hands, and a large chest walked in, supported by eight animated spider legs. Behind it came a nervous goblin slave.

"Come, Byuchyuch," Malice said in a comforting tone. Anxious to please, the slave bounded up before Malice's throne and held perfectly still as the matron mother went through the incantation of a long and complicated spell.

Briza and Maya watched in admiration at their mother's skills; the little goblin's features bulged and twisted, and its skin darkened. A few minutes later, the slave had assumed the appearance of a male drow. Byuchyuch looked at its features happily, not understanding that the transformation was merely a prelude to death.

"You are a drow soldier now," Maya said to it, "and my champion. You must kill only a single, inferior fighter to take your place as a free commoner of House Do'Urden!"

After ten years as an indentured servant to the wicked dark elves, the goblin was more than eager.

Malice rose and started out of the anteroom. "Come," she ordered, and her two daughters, the goblin, and the animated chest fell in line behind her.

They came upon Drizzt in the practice room, polishing the razor edge of his scimitars. He leaped straight up to silent attention at the sight of the unexpected visitors.

"Greetings, my son," Malice said in a tone more motherly than Drizzt had ever heard. " We have a test for you this day, a simple task necessary for your acceptance into Melee-Magthere."

Maya moved before her brother. "I am the youngest, beside yourself," she declared. "Thus, I am granted the rights of challenge, which I now execute."

Drizzt stood confused. He had never heard of such a thing. Maya called the chest to her side and reverently opened the cover.

"You have your weapons and your *piwafwi*," she explained. "Now it is time for you to don the complete outfit of a noble of House Do'Urden." From the chest she pulled out a pair of high black boots and handed them to Drizzt.

Drizzt eagerly slipped out of his normal boots and put on the new ones. They were incredibly soft, and they magically shifted and adjusted to a perfect fit on his feet. Drizzt knew the magic within them: they would allow him to move in absolute silence. Before he had even finished admiring them, though, Maya gave him the next gift, even more magnificent.

Drizzt dropped his *piwafwi* to the floor as he took a set of silvery chain mail. In all the Realms, there was no armor as supple and finely crafted as drow chain mail. It weighed no more than a heavy shirt and would bend as easily as silken cloth, yet could deflect the tip of a spear as surely as dwarven-crafted plate mail.

"You fight with two weapons," Maya said, "and therefore need no shield. But put your scimitars in this; it is more fitting to a drow noble." She handed Drizzt a black leather belt, its clasp a huge emerald and its two scabbards richly decorated in jewels and gemstones.

"Prepare yourself," Malice said to Drizzt. "The gifts must be earned." As Drizzt started to don the outfit, Malice moved beside the altered goblin, which stood nervously in the growing realization that its fight would be no simple task.

"When you kill him, the items will be yours," Malice promised. The goblin's smile returned tenfold; it could not comprehend that it had no chance against Drizzt.

When Drizzt again fastened his *piwafwi* around his neck, Maya introduced the phony drow soldier. "This is Byuchyuch," she said, "my champion. You must defeat him to earn the gifts . . . and your proper place in the family."

Never doubting his abilities, and thinking the contest to be a simple sparring match, Drizzt readily agreed. "Let it begin, then," he said, drawing his scimitars from their lavish sheaths.

Malice gave Byuchyuch a comforting nod, and the goblin took up the sword and shield that Maya had provided and moved right in at Drizzt.

Drizzt began slowly, trying to take a measure of his opponent before attempting any daring offensive strikes. In only a moment, though, Drizzt realized how badly Byuchyuch handled the sword and shield. Not knowing the truth of the creature's identity, Drizzt could hardly believe that a drow would show such ineptitude with weapons. He wondered if Byuchyuch was baiting him, and with that thought, continued his cautious approach.

After a few more moments of Byuchyuch's wild and off balance swings, however, Drizzt felt compelled to take the initiative. He slapped one scimitar against Byuchyuch's shield. The goblin-drow responded with a lumbering thrust, and Drizzt slapped its sword from its hand with his free blade and executed a simple twist that brought the scimitar's tip to a halt against the hollow of Byuchyuch's chest.

"Too easy," Drizzt muttered under his breath.

But the true test had only begun.

On cue, Briza cast a mind-numbing spell on the goblin, freezing it in its helpless position. Still aware of its predicament, Byuchyuch tried to dive away, but Briza's spell held it still.

"Finish the strike," Malice said to Drizzt. Drizzt looked at his scimitar, then to Malice, unable to believe what he was hearing.

"Maya's champion must be killed," Briza snarled.

"I cannot—" Drizzt began.

"Kill!" Malice roared, and this time the word carried the weight of a magical command.

"Thrust!" Briza likewise commanded.

Drizzt felt their words compelling his hand to action. Thoroughly disgusted with the thought of murdering a helpless foe, he concentrated with all of his mental strength to resist. While he managed to deny the commands for a few seconds, Drizzt found that he could not pull the weapon away.

"Kill!" Malice screamed.

"Strike!" yelled Briza.

It went on for several more agonizing seconds. Sweat beaded on Drizzt's brow. Then the young drow's willpower broke. His scimitar slipped quickly between Byuchyuch's ribs and found the unfortunate creature's heart. Briza released Byuchyuch from her holding spell then, to let Drizzt see the agony on the phony drow's face and hear the gurgles as the dying Byuchyuch slipped to the floor.

Drizzt could not find his breath as he stared at his bloodstained weapon.

It was Maya's turn to act. She clipped Drizzt on the shoulder with her mace, knocking him to the floor.

"You killed my champion!" she growled. "Now you must fight me!"

Drizzt rolled back to his feet, away from the enraged female. He had no intention of fighting, but before he could even drop his weapons, Malice read his thoughts and warned, "If you do not fight, Maya will kill you!"

"This is not the way," Drizzt protested, but his words were lost in the ring of adamantine as he parried a heavy blow with one scimitar.

He was now into it, whether he liked it or not. Maya was a skilled fighter—all females spent many hours training with weapons—and she was stronger than Drizzt. But Drizzt was Zak's son, the prime student, and when he admitted to himself that he had no way out of this predicament, he came in at Maya's mace and shield with every cunning maneuver he had been taught.

Scimitars weaved and dipped in a dance that awed Briza and Maya. Malice hardly noticed, caught in the midst of yet another mighty spell.

Malice never doubted that Drizzt could defeat his sister, and she had incorporated her expectations into the plan.

Drizzt's moves were all defensive as he continued to hope for some semblance of sanity to come over his mother, and that this whole thing would be stopped. He wanted to back Maya up, cause her to stumble, and end the fight by putting her in a helpless position. Drizzt had to believe that Briza and Malice would not compel him to kill Maya as he had killed Byuchyuch.

Finally, Maya did slip. She threw her shield out to deflect an arcing scimitar but became overbalanced in the block, and her arm went wide. Drizzt's other blade knifed in, only to nick at Maya's breast and force her back.

Malice's spell caught the weapon in mid-thrust.

The bloodstained adamantine blade writhed to life and Drizzt found himself holding the tail of a serpent, a fanged viper that turned back against him!

The enchanted snake spat its venom in Drizzt's eyes, blinding him, then he felt the pain of Briza's whip. All six snake heads of the awful weapon bit into Drizzt's back, tearing through his new armor and jolting him in excruciating pain. He crumbled down into a curled position, helpless as Briza snapped the whip in, again and again.

"Never strike at a drow female!" she screamed as she beat Drizzt into unconsciousness.

An hour later, Drizzt opened his eyes. He was in his bed, Matron Malice standing over him. The high priestess had tended to his wounds, but the sting remained, a vivid reminder of the lesson. But it was not nearly as vivid as the blood that still stained Drizzt's scimitar.

"The armor will be replaced," Malice said to him. "You are a drow warrior now. You have earned it." She turned and walked out of the room, leaving Drizzt to his pain and his fallen innocence.

⚔ ⚔ ⚔ ⚔ ⚔

"Do not send him," Zak argued as emphatically as he dared. He stared up at Matron Malice, the smug queen on her high throne of stone and black velvet. As always, Briza and Maya stood obediently by her sides.

"He is a drow fighter," Malice replied, her tone still controlled. "He must go to the Academy. It is our way."

Zak looked around helplessly. He hated this place, the chapel anteroom, with its sculptures of the Spider Queen leering down at him from every angle, and with Malice sitting—towering—above him from her seat of power.

Zak shook the images away and regained his courage, reminding himself that this time he had something worth arguing about.

"Do not send him!" he growled. "They will ruin him!"

Matron Malice's hands clenched down on the rock arms of her great chair.

"Already Drizzt is more skilled than half of those in the Academy," Zak continued quickly, before the matron's anger burst forth. "Allow me two more years, and I will make him the finest swordsman in all of Menzoberranzan!"

Malice eased back on her seat. From what she had seen of her son's progress, she could not deny the possibilities of Zak's claim. "He goes," she said calmly. "There is more to the making of a drow warrior than skill with weapons. Drizzt has other lessons he must learn."

"Lessons of treachery?" Zak spat, too angry to care about the consequences. Drizzt had told him what Malice and her evil daughters had done that day, and Zak was wise enough to understand their actions. Their "lesson" had nearly broken the boy, and had, perhaps, forever stolen from Drizzt the ideals he held so dear. Drizzt would find his morals and principles harder to cling to now that the pedestal of purity had been knocked out from under him.

"Watch your tongue, Zaknafein," Matron Malice warned.

"I fight with passion!" the weapons master snapped. "That is why I win. Your son, too, fights with passion—do not let the conforming ways of the Academy take that from him!"

"Leave us," Malice instructed her daughters. Maya bowed and rushed out through the door. Briza followed more slowly, pausing to cast a suspicious eye upon Zak.

Zak didn't return the glare, but he entertained a fantasy concerning his sword and Briza's smug smile.

"Zaknafein," Malice began, again coming forward in her chair. "I have tolerated your blasphemous beliefs through these many years because of your skill with weapons. You have taught my soldiers well, and your love of killing drow, particularly clerics of the Spider Queen, has aided the ascent of House Do'Urden. I am not, and have not been, ungrateful.

"But I warn you now, one final time, that Drizzt is my son, not his sire's! He will go to the Academy and learn what he must to take his place as a prince of House Do'Urden. If you interfere with what must be, Zaknafein, I will no longer turn my eyes from your actions! Your heart will be given to Lolth."

Zak stamped his heels on the floor and snapped a short bow of his head, then spun about and departed, trying to find some option in this dark and hopeless picture.

As he made his way through the main corridor, he again heard in his mind the screams of the dying children of House DeVir, children who never got the chance to witness the evils of the drow Academy. Perhaps they were better off dead.

# II
# Grim Preference

Zak slid one of his swords from its scabbard and admired the weapon's wondrous detail. This sword, as with most of the drow weapons, had been forged by the gray dwarves, then traded to Menzoberranzan. The duergar workmanship was exquisite, but it was the work done on the weapon after the dark elves had acquired it that made it so very special. None of the races of the surface or Underdark could outdo the dark elves in the art of enchanting weapons. Imbued with the strange emanations of the Underdark, the magical power unique to the lightless world, and blessed by the unholy clerics of Lolth, no blade ever sat in a wielder's hand more ready to kill.

Other races, mostly dwarves and surface elves, also took pride in their crafted weapons. Fine swords and mighty hammers hung over mantles as showpieces, always with a bard nearby to spout the accompanying legend that most often began, "In the days of yore . . ."

Drow weapons were different, never showpieces. They were locked in the necessities of the present, never in reminiscences, and their purpose remained unchanged for as long as they held an edge fine enough for battle—fine enough to kill.

Zak brought the blade up before his eyes. In his hands, the sword had become more than an instrument of battle. It was an extension of his rage, his answer to an existence he could not accept.

It was his answer, too, perhaps, to another problem that seemed to have no resolution.

He walked into the training hall, where Drizzt was hard at work spinning attack routines against a practice dummy. Zak paused to watch the young drow at practice, wondering if Drizzt would ever again consider the dance of weapons a form of play. How the scimitars flowed in Drizzt's hands! Interweaving with uncanny precision, each blade seemed to anticipate the other's moves and whirred about in perfect complement.

This young drow might soon be an unrivaled fighter, a master beyond Zaknafein himself.

"Can you survive?" Zak whispered. "Have you the heart of a drow warrior?" Zak hoped that the answer would be an emphatic "no," but either way, Drizzt was surely doomed.

Zak looked down at his sword again and knew what he must do. He slid its sister blade from its sheath and started a determined walk toward Drizzt.

Drizzt saw him coming and turned at the ready. "A final fight before I leave for the Academy?" He laughed.

Zak paused to take note of Drizzt's smile. A facade? Or had the young drow really forgiven himself for his actions against Maya's champion. It did not matter, Zak reminded himself. Even if Drizzt had recovered from his mother's torments, the Academy would destroy him. The weapons master said nothing; he just came on in a flurry of cuts and stabs that put Drizzt immediately on the defensive. Drizzt took it in stride, not yet realizing that this final encounter with his mentor was much more than their customary sparring.

"I will remember everything you taught me," Drizzt promised, dodging a cut and launching a fierce counter of his own. "I will carve my name in the halls of Melee-Magthere and make you proud."

The scowl on Zak's face surprised Drizzt, and the young drow grew even more confused when the weapons master's next attack sent a sword knifing straight at his heart. Drizzt leaped aside, slapping at the blade in sheer desperation, and narrowly avoided impalement.

"Are you so very sure of yourself?" Zak growled, stubbornly pursuing Drizzt.

Drizzt set himself as their blades met in ringing fury. "I am a fighter," he declared. "A drow warrior!"

"You are a dancer!" Zak shot back in a derisive tone. He slammed his sword onto Drizzt's blocking scimitar so savagely that the young drow's arm tingled.

"An imposter!" Zak cried. "A pretender to a title you cannot begin to understand!"

Drizzt went on the offensive. Fires burned in his lavender eyes and new strength guided his scimitars' sure cuts.

But Zak was relentless. He fended the attacks and continued his lesson. "Do you know the emotions of murder?" he spat. "Have you reconciled yourself to the act you committed?"

Drizzt's only answers were a frustrated growl and a renewed attack.

"Ah, the pleasure of plunging your sword into the bosom of a high priestess," Zak taunted. "To see the light of warmth leave her body while her lips utter silent curses in your face! Or have you ever heard the screams of dying children?"

Drizzt let up his attack, but Zak would not allow a break. The weapons master came back on the offensive, each thrust aimed for a vital area.

"How loud, those screams," Zak continued. "They echo over the centuries in your mind; they chase you down the paths of your entire life."

Zak halted the action so that Drizzt might weigh his every word. "You have never heard them, have you, dancer?" The weapons master stretched his arms out wide, an invitation. "Come, then, and claim your second kill," he said, tapping his stomach. "In the belly, where the pain is greatest, so that my screams may echo in your mind. Prove to me that you are the drow warrior you claim to be."

The tips of Drizzt's scimitars slowly made their way to the stone floor. He wore no smile now.

"You hesitate," Zak laughed at him. "This is your chance to make your name. A single thrust, and you will send a reputation into the Academy before you. Other students, even masters, will whisper your name as you pass. 'Drizzt Do'Urden,' they will say. 'The boy who slew the most honored weapons master in all of Menzoberranzan!' Is this not what you desire?"

"Damn you," Drizzt spat back, but still he made no move to attack.

"Drow warrior?" Zak chided him. "Do not be so quick to claim a title you cannot begin to understand!"

Drizzt came on then, in a fury he had never before known. His purpose was not to kill, but to defeat his teacher, to steal the taunts from Zak's mouth with a fighting display too impressive to be derided.

Drizzt was brilliant. He followed every move with three others and worked Zak low and high, inside and out wide. Zak found his heels under him more often than the balls of his feet, too involved was he in staying away from his student's relentless thrusts to even think of taking the offensive. He allowed Drizzt to continue the initiative for many minutes, dreading its conclusion, the outcome he had already decided to be the most preferable.

Zak then found that he could stand the delay no longer. He sent one sword out in a lazy thrust, and Drizzt promptly slapped the weapon out of his hand.

Even as the young drow came on in anticipation of victory, Zak slipped his empty hand into a pouch and grabbed a magical little ceramic ball—one of those that so often had aided him in battle.

"Not this time, Zaknafein!" Drizzt proclaimed, keeping his attacks under control, remembering well the many occasions that Zak reversed feigned disadvantage into clear advantage.

Zak fingered the ball, unable to come to terms with what he must do.

Drizzt walked him through an attack sequence, then another, measuring the advantage he had gained in stealing a weapon. Confident of his position, Drizzt came in low and hard with a single thrust.

Though Zak was distracted at the time, he still managed to block the attack with his remaining sword. Drizzt's other scimitar slashed down on top of the sword, pinning its tip to the floor. In the same lightning movement, Drizzt slipped his first blade free of Zak's parry and brought it up and around, stopping the thrust barely an inch from Zak's throat.

"I have you!" the young drow cried.

Zak's answer came in an explosion of light beyond anything Drizzt had ever imagined.

Zak had prudently closed his eyes, but Drizzt, surprised, could not accept the sudden change. His head burned in agony, and he reeled backward, trying to get away from the light, away from the weapons master.

Keeping his eyes tightly shut, Zak had already divorced himself from the need of vision. He let his keen ears guide him now, and Drizzt, shuffling and stumbling, was an easy target to discern. In a single motion, the whip came off Zak's belt and he lashed out, catching Drizzt around the ankles and dropping him to the floor.

Methodically, the weapons master came on, dreading every step but knowing his chosen course of action to be correct.

Drizzt realized that he was being stalked, but he could not understand the motive. The light had stunned him, but he was more surprised by Zak's continuation of the battle. Drizzt set himself, unable to escape the trap, and tried to think his way around his loss of sight. He had to feel the flow of battle, to hear the sounds of his attacker and anticipate each coming strike.

He brought his scimitars up just in time to block a sword chop that would have split his skull.

Zak hadn't expected the parry. He recoiled and came in from a different angle. Again he was foiled.

Now more curious than wanting to kill Drizzt, the weapons master went through a series of attacks, sending his sword into motions that would have sliced through the defenses of many who could see him.

Blinded, Drizzt fought him off, putting a scimitar in line with each new thrust.

"Treachery!" Drizzt yelled, painful residual explosions from the bright light still bursting inside his head. He blocked another attack and tried to regain his footing, realizing that he had little chance of continuing to fend off the weapons master from a prone position.

The pain of the stinging light was too great, though, and Drizzt, barely holding the edge of consciousness, stumbled back to the stone, losing one scimitar in the process. He spun over wildly, knowing that Zak was closing in.

The other scimitar was knocked from his hand.

"Treachery," Drizzt growled again. "Do you so hate to lose?"

"Do you not understand?" Zak yelled back at him. "To lose is to die! You may win a thousand fights, but you can only lose one!" He put his sword in line with Drizzt's throat. It would be a single clean blow. He knew that he should do it, mercifully, before the masters of the Academy got hold of his charge.

Zak sent his sword spinning across the room, and he reached out with his empty hands, grabbed Drizzt by the front of his shirt, and hoisted him to his feet.

They stood face-to-face, neither seeing the other very well in the blinding glare, and neither able to break the tense silence. After a long and breathless moment, the dweomer of the enchanted pebble faded and the room became more comfortable. Truly, the two dark elves looked upon each other in a different light.

"A trick of Lolth's clerics," Zak explained. "Always they keep such a spell of light at the ready" A strained smile crossed his face as he tried to ease Drizzt's anger. "Though I daresay that I have turned such light against clerics, even high priestesses, more than a few times."

"Treachery," Drizzt spat a third time.

"It is our way," Zak replied. "You will learn."

"It is your way," snarled Drizzt. "You grin when you speak of murdering clerics of the Spider Queen. Do you so enjoy killing? Killing drow?"

Zak could not find an answer to the accusing question. Drizzt's words hurt him profoundly because they rang of truth, and because Zak had come to view his penchant for killing clerics of Lolth as a cowardly response to his own unanswerable frustrations.

"You would have killed me," Drizzt said bluntly.

"But I did not," Zak retorted. "And now you live to go to the Academy—to take a dagger in the back because you are blind to the realities of our world, because you refuse to acknowledge what your people are.

"Or you will become one of them," Zak growled. "Either way, the Drizzt Do'Urden I have known will surely die."

Drizzt's face twisted, and he couldn't even find the words to dispute the possibilities Zak was spitting at him. He felt the blood drain from his face, though his heart raged. He walked away, letting his glare linger on Zak for many steps.

"Go, then, Drizzt Do'Urden!" Zak cried after him. "Go to the Academy and bask in the glory of your prowess. Remember, though, the consequences of such skills. Always there are consequences!"

Zak retreated to the security of his private chamber. The door to the room closed behind the weapons master with such a sound of finality that it spun Zak back to face its empty stone.

"Go, then, Drizzt Do'Urden," he whispered in quiet lament. "Go to the Academy and learn who you really are."

⚔ ⚔ ⚔ ⚔ ⚔

Dinin came for his brother early the next morning. Drizzt slowly left the training room, looking back over his shoulder every few steps to see if Zak would come out and attack him again or bid him farewell.

He knew in his heart that Zak would not.

Drizzt had thought them friends, had believed that the bond he and Zaknafein had sown went far beyond the simple lessons and swordplay. The young drow had no answers to the many questions spinning in his mind, and the person who had been his teacher for the last five years had nothing left to offer him.

"The heat grows in Narbondel," Dinin remarked when they stepped out onto the balcony. "We must not be late for your first day in the Academy."

Drizzt looked out into the myriad colors and shapes that composed Menzoberranzan. "What is this place?" he whispered, realizing how little he knew of his homeland beyond the walls of his own house. Zak's words—Zak's rage—pressed in on Drizzt as he stood there, reminding him of his ignorance and hinting at a dark path ahead.

"This is the world," Dinin replied, though Drizzt's question had been rhetorical. "Do not worry, Secondboy," he laughed, moving up onto the railing. "You will learn of Menzoberranzan in the Academy. You will learn who you are and who your people are."

The declaration unsettled Drizzt. Perhaps—remembering his last bitter encounter with the drow he had most trusted—that knowledge was exactly what he was afraid of.

He shrugged in resignation and followed Dinin over the balcony in a magical descent to the compound floor: the first steps down that dark path.

Another set of eyes watched intently as Dinin and Drizzt started out from House Do'Urden.

Alton DeVir sat quietly against the side of a gigantic mushroom, as he had every day for the last tenday, staring at the Do'Urden complex.

Daermon N'a'shezbaernon, Ninth House of Menzoberranzan. The house that had murdered his matron, his sisters and brothers, and all there ever was of House DeVir . . . except for Alton.

Alton thought back to the days of House DeVir, when Matron Ginafae had gathered the family members together so that they might discuss their aspirations. Alton, just a student when House DeVir fell, now had a greater insight to those times. Twenty years had brought a wealth of experience.

Ginafae had been the youngest matron among the ruling families, and her potential had seemed unlimited. Then she had aided a gnomish patrol, had used her Lolth-given powers to hinder the drow elves that ambushed the little people in the caverns outside Menzoberranzan—all because Ginafae desired the death of a single member of that attacking drow party, a wizard son of the city's third house, the house labeled as House DeVir's next victim.

The Spider Queen took exception to Ginafae's choice of weapons; deep gnomes were the dark elves' worst enemy in the whole of the Underdark. With Ginafae fallen out of Lolth's favor, House DeVir had been doomed.

Alton had spent twenty years trying to learn of his enemies, trying to discover which drow family had taken advantage of his mother's mistake and had slaughtered his kin. Twenty long years, and his adopted matron, SiNafay Hun'ett, had ended his quest as abruptly as it had begun.

Now, as Alton sat watching the guilty house, he knew only one thing for certain: twenty years had done nothing to diminish his rage.

# Part Three

## The Academy

The Academy.

It is the propagation of the lies that bind drow society together, the ultimate perpetration of falsehoods repeated so many times that they ring true against any contrary evidence. The lessons young drow are taught of truth and justice are so blatantly refuted by everyday life in wicked Menzoberranzan that it is hard to understand how any could believe them. Still they do.

Even now, decades removed, the thought of the place frightens me, not for any physical pain or the ever-present sense of possible death—I have trod down many roads equally dangerous in that way. The Academy of Menzoberranzan frightens me when I think of the survivors, the graduates, existing—reveling—within the evil fabrications that shape their world.

They live with the belief that anything is acceptable if you can get away with it, that self-gratification is the most important aspect of existence, and that power comes only to she or he who is strong enough and cunning enough to snatch it from the failing hands of those who no longer deserve it. Compassion has no place in Menzoberranzan, and yet it is compassion, not fear, that brings harmony to most races. It is harmony, working toward shared goals, that precedes greatness.

Lies engulf the drow in fear and mistrust, refute friendship at the tip of a Lolth-blessed sword The hatred and ambition fostered by these amoral tenets are the doom of my people, a weakness that they perceive as strength. The result is a paralyzing, paranoid existence that the drow call the edge of readiness.

I do not know how I survived the Academy, how I discovered the falsehoods early enough to use them in contrast, and thus strengthen, those ideals I most cherish.

It was Zaknafein, I must believe, my teacher. Through the experiences of Zak's long years, which embittered him and cost him so much, I came to hear the screams: the screams of protest against murderous treachery; the screams of rage from the leaders of drow society, the high priestesses of the Spider Queen, echoing down the paths of my mind, ever to hold a place within my mind. The screams of dying children.

–Drizzt Do'Urden

# 12
# This Enemy, "They"

Wearing the outfit of a noble son, and with a dagger concealed in one boot—a suggestion from Dinin—Drizzt ascended the wide stone stairway that led to Tier Breche, the Academy of the drow. Drizzt reached the top and moved between the giant pillars, under the impassive gazes of two guards, last-year students of Melee-Magthere.

Two dozen other young drow milled about the Academy compound, but Drizzt hardly noticed them. Three structures dominated his vision and his thoughts. To his left stood the pointed stalagmite tower of Sorcere, the school of wizardry. Drizzt would spend the first sixth months of his tenth and last year of study in there.

Before him, at the back of the level, loomed the most impressive structure, Arach-Tinilith, the school of Lolth, carved from the stone into the likeness of a giant spider. By drow reckoning, this was the Academy's most important building and thus was normally reserved for females. Male students were housed within Arach-Tinilith only during their last six months of study.

While Sorcere and Arach-Tinilith were the more graceful structures, the most important building for Drizzt at that tentative moment lined the wall to his right. The pyramidal structure of Melee-Magthere, the school of fighters. This building would be Drizzt's home for the next nine years. His companions, he now realized, were those other dark elves in the compound—fighters, like himself, about to begin their formal training. The class, at twenty-five, was unusually large for the school of fighters.

Even more unusual, several of the novice students were nobles. Drizzt wondered how his skills would measure up against theirs, how his sessions with Zaknafein compared to the battles these others had no doubt fought with the weapons masters of their respective families.

Those thoughts inevitably led Drizzt back to his last encounter with his mentor. He quickly dismissed the memories of that unpleasant duel, and, more pointedly, the disturbing questions Zak's observations had forced him to consider. There was no place for such doubts on this occasion. Melee-Magthere loomed before him, the greatest test and the greatest lesson of his young life.

"My greetings," came a voice behind him. Drizzt turned to face a fellow novice, who wore a sword and dirk uncomfortably on his belt and who appeared even more nervous than Drizzt—a comforting sight.

"Kelnozz of House Kenafin, fifteenth house," the novice said.

"Drizzt Do'Urden of Daermon N'a'shezbaernon, House Do'Urden, Ninth House of Menzoberranzan," Drizzt replied automatically, exactly as Matron Malice had instructed him.

"A noble," remarked Kelnozz, understanding the significance of Drizzt bearing the same surname as his house. Kelnozz dropped into a low bow. "I am honored by your presence."

Drizzt was starting to like this place already. With the treatment he normally received at home, he hardly thought of himself as a noble. Any self-important notions that might have occurred to him at Kelnozz's gracious greeting were dispelled a moment later, though, when the masters came out.

Drizzt saw his brother, Dinin, among them but pretended—as Dinin had warned him to—not to notice, nor to expect any special treatment. Drizzt rushed inside Melee-Magthere along with the rest of the students when the whips began to snap and the masters started shouting of the dire consequences if they tarried. They were herded down a few side corridors and into an oval room.

"Sit or stand as you will!" one of the masters growled. Noticing two of the students whispering off to the side, the master took his whip out and—crack!—took one of the offenders off his feet.

Drizzt couldn't believe how quickly the room then came to order.

"I am Hatch'net," the master began in a resounding voice, "the master of Lore. This room will be your hall of instruction for fifty cycles of Narbondel." He looked around at the adorned belts on every figure. "You will bring no weapons to this place!"

Hatch'net paced the perimeter of the room, making certain that every eye followed his movements attentively. "You are drow," he snapped suddenly. "Do you understand what that means? Do you know where you come from, and the history of our people? Menzoberranzan was not always our home, nor was any other cavern of the Underdark. Once we walked the surface of the world." He spun suddenly and came up right in Drizzt's face.

"Do you know of the surface?" Master Hatch'net snarled.

Drizzt recoiled and shook his head.

"An awful place," Hatch'net continued, turning back to the whole of the group. "Each day, as the glow begins its rise in Narbondel, a great ball of fire rises into the open sky above, bringing hours of a light greater than the punishing spells of the priestesses of Lolth!" He held his arms outstretched, with his eyes turned upward, and an unbelievable grimace spread across his face.

Students' gasps rose up all about him.

"Even in the night, when the ball of fire has gone below the far rim of the world," Hatch'net continued, weaving his words as if he were telling a horror tale, "one cannot escape the uncounted terrors of the surface. Reminders of what the next day will bring, dots of light—and sometimes a lesser ball of silvery fire—mar the sky's blessed darkness.

"Once our people walked the surface of the world," he repeated, his tone now one of lament, "in ages long past, even longer than the lines of the great houses. In that distant age, we walked beside the pale-skinned elves, the faeries!"

"It cannot be true!" one student cried from the side.

Hatch'net looked at him earnestly, considering whether more would be gained by beating the student for his unasked-for interruption or by allowing the group to participate. "It is!" he replied, choosing the latter course. "We thought the faeries our friends; we called them kin! We could not know, in our innocence, that they were the embodiments of deceit and evil. We could not know that they would turn on us suddenly and drive us from them, slaughtering our children and the eldest of our race!

"Without mercy the evil faeries pursued us across the surface world. Always we asked for peace, and always we were answered by swords and killing arrows!"

He paused, his face twisting into a widening, malicious smile. "Then we found the goddess!"

"Praise Lolth!" came one anonymous cry. Again Hatch'net let the slip of tongue go by unpunished, knowing that every accenting comment only drew his audience deeper into his web of rhetoric.

"Indeed," the master replied. "All praise to the Spider Queen. It was she who took our orphaned race to her side and helped us fight off our enemies. It was she who guided the fore-matrons of our race to the paradise of the Underdark. It is she," he roared, a clenched fist rising into the air, "who now gives us the strength and the magic to pay back our enemies.

"We are the drow!" Hatch'net cried. "You are the drow, never again to be downtrodden, rulers of all you desire, conquerors of lands you choose to inhabit!"

"The surface?" came a question.

"The surface?" echoed Hatch'net with a laugh. "Who would want to return to that vile place? Let the faeries have it! Let them burn under the fires of the open sky! We claim the Underdark, where we can feel the core of the world thrumming under our feet, and where the stones of the walls show the heat of the world's power!"

Drizzt sat silent, absorbing every word of the talented orator's often-rehearsed speech. Drizzt was caught, as were all the new students, in Hatch'net's hypnotic variations of inflection and rallying cries. Hatch'net had been the master of Lore at the Academy for more than two centuries, owning more prestige in Menzoberranzan than nearly any other male drow, and many of the females. The matrons of the ruling families understood well the value of his practiced tongue.

So it went every day, an endless stream of hate rhetoric directed against an enemy that none of the students had ever seen. The surface elves were not the only target of Hatch'net's sniping. Dwarves, gnomes, humans, halflings, and all of the surface races—and even subterranean races such as the duergar dwarves, which the drow often traded with and fought beside—each found an unpleasant spot in the master's ranting.

Drizzt came to understand why no weapons were permitted in the oval chamber. When he left his lesson each day, he found his hands clenched by his sides in rage, unconsciously grasping for a scimitar hilt. It was obvious from the commonplace fights among the students that others felt the same way. Always, though, the overriding factor that kept some measure of control was the master's lie of the horrors of the outside world and the comforting bond of the students' common heritage—a heritage, the students would soon come to believe, that gave them enough enemies to battle beyond each other.

The long, draining hours in the oval chamber left little time for the students to mingle. They shared common barracks, but their extensive duties outside of Hatch'net's lessons—serving the older students and masters, preparing meals, and cleaning the building—gave them barely enough time for rest. By the end of the first tenday, they walked on the edge of exhaustion, a condition, Drizzt realized, that only increased the stirring effect of Master Hatch'net's lessons.

Drizzt accepted the existence stoically, considering it far better than the six years he had served his mother and sisters as page prince. Still, there was one great disappointment to Drizzt in his first tendays at Melee-Magthere. He found himself longing for his practice sessions.

He sat on the edge of his bedroll late one night, holding a scimitar up before his shining eyes, remembering those many hours engaged in battle-play with Zaknafein.

"We go to the lesson in two hours," Kelnozz, in the next bunk, reminded him. "Get some rest."

"I feel the edge leaving my hands," Drizzt replied quietly. "The blade feels heavier, unbalanced."

"The grand melee is barely ten cycles of Narbondel away," Kelnozz said. "You will get all the practice you desire there! Fear not, whatever edge has been dulled by the days with the master of Lore will soon be regained. For the next nine years, that fine blade of yours will rarely leave your hands!"

Drizzt slid the scimitar back into its scabbard and reclined on his bunk. As with so many aspects of his life so far—and, he was beginning to fear, with so many aspects of his future in Menzoberranzan—he had no choice but to accept the circumstances of his existence.

⚔ ⚔ ⚔ ⚔ ⚔

"This segment of your training is at an end," Master Hatch'net announced on the morning of the fiftieth day. Another master, Dinin, entered the room, leading a magically suspended iron box filled with meagerly padded wooden poles of every length and design comparable to drow weapons.

"Choose the sparring pole that most resembles your own weapon of choice," Hatch'net explained as Dinin made his way around the room. He came to his brother, and Drizzt's eyes settled at once on his choice: two slightly curving poles about three-and-a-half feet long. Drizzt lifted them out and put them through a simple cut. Their weight and balance closely resembled the scimitars that had become so familiar to his hands.

"For the pride of Daermon N'a'shezbaernon," Dinin whispered, then moved along.

Drizzt twirled the mock weapons again. It was time to measure the value of his sessions with Zak.

"Your class must have an order," Hatch'net was saying as Drizzt turned his attention beyond the scope of his new weapons. "Thus the grand melee. Remember, there can be only one victor!"

Hatch'net and Dinin herded the students out of the oval chamber and out of Melee-Magthere altogether, down the tunnel between the two guardian spider statues at the back of Tier Breche. For all of the students, this was the first time they had ever been out of Menzoberranzan.

"What are the rules?" Drizzt asked Kelnozz, in line at his side.

"If a master calls you out, then you are out," Kelnozz replied.

"The rules of engagement?" asked Drizzt.

Kelnozz cast him an incredulous glance. "Win," he said simply, as though there could be no other answer.

A short time later they came into a fairly large cavern, the arena for the grand melee. Pointed stalactites leered down at them from the ceiling and stalagmite mounds broke the floor into a twisting maze filled with ambush holes and blind corners.

"Choose your strategies and find your starting point," Master Hatch'net said to them. "The grand melee begins in a count of one hundred!"

The twenty-five students set off into action, some pausing to consider the landscape laid out before them, others sprinting off into the gloom of the maze.

Drizzt decided to find a narrow corridor, to ensure that he would fight off one-against-one, and he just started off in his search when he was grabbed from behind.

"A team?" Kelnozz offered.

Drizzt did not respond, unsure of the other's fighting worth and the accepted practices of this traditional encounter.

"Others are forming into teams," Kelnozz pressed. "Some in threes. Together we might have a chance."

"The master said there could be only one victor," Drizzt reasoned.

"Who better than you, if not me," Kelnozz replied with a sly wink. "Let us defeat the others, then we can decide the issue between ourselves."

The reasoning seemed prudent, and with Hatch'net's count already approaching seventy-five, Drizzt had little time to ponder the possibilities. He clapped Kelnozz on the shoulder and led his new ally into the maze.

Catwalks had been constructed all around the room's perimeter, even crossing through the center of the chamber, to give the judging masters a good view of all the action below. A dozen of them were up there now, all eagerly awaiting the first battles so that they might measure the talent of this young class.

"One hundred!" cried Hatch'net from his high perch.

Kelnozz began to move, but Drizzt stopped him, keeping him back in the narrow corridor between two long stalagmite mounds.

"Let them come to us," Drizzt signaled in the silent hand and facial expression code. He crouched in battle readiness. "Let them fight each other to weariness. Patience is our ally!"

Kelnozz relaxed, thinking he had made a good choice in Drizzt.

Their patience was not tested severely, though, for a moment later, a tall and aggressive student burst into their defensive position, wielding a long spear-shaped pole. He came right in on Drizzt, slapping with the butt of his weapon, then spinning it over full in a brutal thrust designed for a quick kill, a strong move perfectly executed.

To Drizzt, though, it seemed the most basic of attack routines—too basic, almost, for Drizzt hardly believed that a trained student would attack another skilled fighter in such a straightforward manner. Drizzt convinced himself in time that this was indeed the chosen method of attack, and no feint, and he launched the proper parry. His scimitar poles spun counter-clockwise in front of him, striking the thrusting spear in succession and driving the weapon's tip harmlessly above the striking line of its wielder's shoulder.

The aggressive attacker, stunned by the advanced parry, found himself open and off balance. Barely a split second later, before the attacker could even begin to recover, Drizzt's counter poked one, then the other scimitar pole into his chest.

A soft blue light appeared on the stunned student's face, and he and Drizzt followed its line up to see a wand-wielding master looking down at them from the catwalk.

"You are defeated," the master said to the tall student. "Fall where you stand!"

The student shot an angry glare at Drizzt and obediently dropped to the stone.

"Come," Drizzt said to Kelnozz, casting a glance up at the master's revealing light. "Any others in the area will know of our position now. We must seek a new defensible area."

Kelnozz paused a moment to watch the graceful hunting strides of his comrade. He had indeed made a good choice in selecting Drizzt, but he knew already, after only a single quick encounter, that if he and this skilled swordsman were the last two standing—a distinct possibility—he would have no chance at all of claiming victory.

Together they rushed around a blind corner, right into two opponents. Kelnozz chased after one, who fled in fright, and Drizzt faced off against the other, who wielded sword and dirk poles.

A wide smile of growing confidence crossed Drizzt's face as his opponent took the offensive, launching routines similarly basic to those of the spear wielder that Drizzt had easily dispatched.

A few deft twists and turns of his scimitars, a few slaps on the inside edges of his opponent's weapons, had the sword and dirk flying wide. Drizzt's attack came right up the middle, where he executed another double-poke into his opponent's chest.

The expected blue light appeared. "You are defeated," came the master's call. "Fall where you stand."

Outraged, the stubborn student chopped viciously at Drizzt. Drizzt blocked with one weapon and snapped the other against his attacker's wrist, sending the sword pole flying to the floor.

The attacker clenched his bruised wrist, but that was the least of his troubles. A blinding flash of lightning exploded from the observing master's wand, catching him full in the chest and hurtling him ten feet backward to crash into a stalagmite mound. He crumpled to the floor, groaning in agony, and a line of glowing heat rose from his scorched body, which lay against the cool gray stone.

"You are defeated!" the master said again.

Drizzt started to the fallen drow's aid, but the master issued an emphatic, "No!"

Then Kelnozz was back at Drizzt's side. "He got away," Kelnozz began, but he broke into a laugh when he saw the downed student. "If a master calls you out, then you are out!" Kelnozz repeated into Drizzt's blank stare.

"Come," Kelnozz continued. "The battle is in full now. Let us find some fun!"

Drizzt thought his companion quite cocky for one who had yet to lift his weapons. He only shrugged and followed.

Their next encounter was not so easy. They came into a double passage turning in and out of several rock formations and found themselves faced off against a group of three—nobles from leading houses, both Drizzt and Kelnozz realized.

Drizzt rushed the two on his left, both of whom wielded single swords, while Kelnozz worked to fend off the third. Drizzt had little experience against multiple opponents, but Zak had taught him the techniques of such a battle quite well. His movements were solely defensive at first, then he settled into a comfortable rhythm and allowed his opponents to tire themselves out, and to make the critical mistakes.

These were cunning foes, though, and familiar with each other's movements. Their attacks complemented each other, slicing in at Drizzt from widely opposing angles.

"Two-hands," Zak had once called Drizzt, and now he lived up to the title. His scimitars worked independently, yet in perfect harmony, foiling every attack.

From a nearby perch on the catwalk, Masters Hatch'net and Dinin looked on, Hatch'net more than a little impressed, and Dinin swelling with pride.

Drizzt saw the frustration mounting on his opponents' faces, and he knew that his opportunity to strike would soon be at hand. Then they crossed up, coming in together with identical thrusts, their sword poles barely inches apart.

Drizzt spun to the side and launched a blinding uppercut slice with his left scimitar, deflecting both attacks. Then he reversed his body's momentum, dropped to one knee, back in line with his opponents, and thrust in low with two snaps of his free right arm. His jabbing scimitar pole caught the first, and the second, squarely in the groin.

They dropped their weapons in unison, clutched their bruised parts, and slumped to their knees. Drizzt leaped up before them, trying to find the words for an apology.

Hatch'net nodded his approval at Dinin as the two masters set their lights on the two losers.

"Help me! " Kelnozz cried from beyond the dividing wall of stalagmites.

Drizzt dived into a roll through a break in the wall, came up quickly, and downed a fourth opponent, who was concealed for a backstab surprise, with a backhand chop to the chest. Drizzt stopped to consider his latest victim. He hadn't even consciously known that the drow was there, but his aim had been perfect!

Hatch'net blew a low whistle as he shifted his light to the most recent loser's face. "He is good!" the master breathed.

Drizzt saw Kelnozz a short distance away, practically forced down to his back by his opponent's skilled maneuvers. Drizzt leaped between the two and deflected an attack that surely would have finished Kelnozz.

This newest opponent, wielding two sword poles, proved Drizzt's toughest challenge yet. He came at Drizzt with complicated feints and twists, forcing him on his heels more than once.

"Berg'inyon of House Baenre," Hatch'net whispered to Dinin. Dinin understood the significance and hoped that his young brother was up to the test.

Berg'inyon was not a disappointment to his distinguished kin. His moves came skilled and measured, and he and Drizzt danced about for many minutes with neither finding any advantage. The daring Berg'inyon then came in with the attack routine perhaps most familiar to Drizzt: the double-thrust low.

Drizzt executed the cross-down to perfection, the appropriate parry as Zaknafein had so pointedly proved to him. Never satisfied, though, Drizzt then reacted on an impulse, agilely snapping a foot up between the hilts of his crossed blades and into his opponent's face. The stunned son of House Baenre fell back against the wall.

"I knew the parry was wrong!" Drizzt cried, already savoring the next time he would get the opportunity to foil the double-thrust low in a session against Zak.

"He is good," Hatch'net gasped again to his glowing companion.

Dazed, Berg'inyon could not fight his way out of the disadvantage. He put a globe of darkness around himself, but Drizzt waded right in, more than willing to fight blindly.

Drizzt put the son of House Baenre through a quick series of attacks, ending with one of Drizzt's scimitar poles against Berg'inyon's exposed neck.

"I am defeated," the young Baenre conceded, feeling the pole. Hearing the call, Master Hatch'net dispelled the darkness. Berg'inyon set both his weapons on the stone and slumped down, and the blue light appeared on his face.

Drizzt couldn't hold back the widening grin. Were there any here that he could not defeat? he wondered.

Drizzt then felt an explosion on the back of his head that dropped him to his knees. He managed to look back in time to see Kelnozz walking away.

"A fool," Hatch'net chuckled, putting his light on Drizzt, then turning his gaze upon Dinin. "A good fool."

Dinin crossed his arms in front of his chest, his face glowing brightly now in a flush of embarrassment and anger.

Drizzt felt the cool stone against his cheek, but his only thoughts at that moment were rooted in the past, locked onto Zaknafein's sarcastic, but painfully accurate, statement: "It is our way!"

# 13
# The Price of Winning

"You deceived me," Drizzt said to Kelnozz that night in the barracks. The room was black around them and no other students stirred in their cots, exhausted from the day's fighting and from their endless duties serving the older students.

Kelnozz fully expected this encounter. He had guessed Drizzt's naiveté early on, when Drizzt had actually queried him about the rules of engagement. An experienced drow warrior, particularly a noble, should have known better, should have understood that the only rule of his existence was the pursuit of victory. Now, Kelnozz knew, this foolish young Do'Urden would not strike at him for his earlier actions—vengeance fueled by anger was not one of Drizzt's traits.

"Why?" Drizzt pressed, finding no answer forthcoming from the smug commoner of House Kenafin.

The volume of Drizzt's voice caused Kelnozz to glance around nervously. They were supposed to be sleeping; if a master heard them arguing . . .

"What is the mystery?" Kelnozz signaled back in the hand code, the warmth of his fingers glowing clearly to Drizzt's heat-sensing eyes. "I acted as I had to act, though I now believe I should have held off a bit longer. Perhaps, if you had defeated a few more, I might have finished higher than third in the class."

"If we had worked together, as we had agreed, you might have won, or finished second at the least," Drizzt signaled back, the sharp movements of his hands reflecting his anger.

"Most assuredly second," Kelnozz replied. "I knew from the beginning that I would be no match for you. You are the finest swordsman I have ever seen."

"Not by the masters standing," Drizzt grumbled aloud.

"Eighth is not so low," Kelnozz, whispered back. "Berg'inyon is only ranked tenth, and he is from the ruling house of Menzoberranzan. You should be glad that your standing is not to be envied by your classmates." A shuffle outside the room's door sent Kelnozz back into the silent code. "Holding a higher rank means only that I have more fighters eyeing my back as a convenient place to rest their daggers."

Drizzt let the implications of Kelnozz's statement slip by; he refused to consider such treachery in the Academy. "Berg'inyon was the finest fighter I saw in the grand melee," he signaled. "He had you beaten until I interceded on your behalf."

Kelnozz smiled the thought away. "Let Berg'inyon serve as a cook in some lowly house for all I care," he whispered even more quietly than before—for the son of House Baenre's bunk was only a few yards away. "He is tenth, yet I, Kelnozz of Kenafin, am third!"

"I am eighth," said Drizzt, an uncharacteristic edge on his voice, more anger than jealousy," but I could defeat you with any weapon."

Kelnozz shrugged, a strangely blurring movement to onlookers seeing in the infrared spectrum. "You did not," he signaled. "I won our encounter."

"Encounter?" Drizzt gasped. "You deceived me, that is all!"

"Who was left standing?" Kelnozz pointedly reminded him. "Who wore the blue light of a master's wand?"

"Honor demands that there be rules of engagement," growled Drizzt.

"There is a rule," Kelnozz snapped back at him. "You may do whatever you can get away with. I won our encounter, Drizzt Do'Urden, and I hold the higher rank! That is all that matters!"

In the heat of the argument, their voices had grown too loud. The door to the room swung wide, and a master stepped onto the threshold, his form vividly outlined by the hallway's blue lights. Both students promptly rolled over and closed their eyes—and their mouths.

The finality of Kelnozz's last statement rocked Drizzt to some prudent observations. He realized then that his friendship with Kelnozz had come to an end—and, perhaps, that he and Kelnozz had never been friends at all.

⚔ ⚔ ⚔ ⚔ ⚔

"You have seen him?" Alton asked, his fingers tapping anxiously on the small table in the highest chamber of his private quarters. Alton had set the younger students of Sorcere to work repairing the blasted place, but the scorch marks on the stone walls remained, a legacy of Alton's fireball.

"I have," replied Masoj. "I have heard of his skill with weapons."

"Eighth in his class after the grand melee," said Alton, "a fine achievement."

"By all accounts, he has the prowess to be first," said Masoj. "One day he will claim that title. I shall be careful around that one."

"He will never live to claim it!" Alton promised. "House Do'Urden puts great pride in this purple-eyed youth, and thus I have decided upon Drizzt as my first target for revenge. His death will bring pain to that treacherous Matron Malice!"

Masoj saw a problem here and decided to put it to rest once and for all. "You will not harm him," he warned Alton. "You will not even go near him."

Alton's tone became no less grim. "I have waited two decades—" he began.

"You can wait a few more," Masoj snapped back. "I remind you that you accepted Matron SiNafay's invitation into House Hun'ett. Such an alliance requires obedience. Matron SiNafay—our matron mother—has placed upon my shoulders the task of handling Drizzt Do'Urden, and I will execute her will."

Alton rested back in his seat across the table and put what was left of his acid-torn chin into a slender palm, carefully weighing the words of his secret partner.

"Matron SiNafay has plans that will bring you all the revenge you could possibly desire," Masoj continued. "I warn you now, Alton DeVir," he snarled, emphasizing the surname that was not Hun'ett, "that if you begin a war with House Do'Urden, or even put them on the defensive with any act of violence unsanctioned by Matron SiNafay, you will incur the wrath of House Hun'ett. Matron SiNafay will expose you as a murderous imposter and will exact every punishment allowable by the ruling council upon your pitiful bones!"

Alton had no way to refute the threat. He was a rogue, without family beyond the adopted Hun'etts. If SiNafay turned against him, he would find no allies. "What plan does SiNafay . . . Matron SiNafay . . . have for House Do'Urden?" he asked calmly. "Tell me of my revenge so that I may survive these torturous years of waiting."

Masoj knew that he had to act carefully at this point. His mother had not forbidden him to tell Alton of the future course of action, but if she had wanted the volatile DeVir to know, Masoj realized, she would have told him herself.

"Let us just say that House Do'Urden's power has grown, and continues to grow, to the point where it has become a very real threat to all the great houses," Masoj purred, loving the intrigue of positioning before a war. "Witness the fall of House DeVir, perfectly executed with no obvious trail. Many of Menzoberranzan's nobles would rest easier if . . ." He let it go at that, deciding that he probably had said too much already.

By the hot glimmer in Alton's eyes, Masoj could tell that the lure had been strong enough to buy Alton's patience.

⚔ ⚔ ⚔ ⚔ ⚔

The Academy held many disappointments for young Drizzt, particularly in that first year, when so many of the dark realities of drow society, realities that Zaknafein had barely hinted at, remained on the edges of Drizzt's cognizance with stubborn resilience. He weighed the masters' lectures of hatred and mistrust in both hands, one side holding the masters' views in the context of the lectures, the other bending those same words into the very different logic assumed by his old mentor. The truth seemed so ambiguous, so hard to define. Through all of the examination, Drizzt found that he could not escape one pervading fact: In his entire young life, the only treachery he had ever witnessed—and so often!—was at the hands of drow elves.

The physical training of the Academy, hours on end of dueling exercises and stealth techniques, was more to Drizzt's liking. Here, with his weapons so readily in his hands, he freed himself of the disturbing questions of truth and perceived truth.

Here he excelled. If Drizzt had come into the Academy with a higher level of training and expertise than that of his classmates, the gap grew only wider as the grueling months passed. He learned to look beyond the accepted defense and attack routines put forth by the masters and create his own methods, innovations that almost always at least equaled—and usually outdid—the standard techniques.

At first, Dinin listened with increasing pride as his peers exalted in his younger brother's fighting prowess. So glowing came the compliments that the eldest son of Matron Malice soon took on a nervous wariness. Dinin was the elderboy of House Do'Urden, a title he had gained by eliminating Nalfein. Drizzt, showing the potential to become one of the finest swordsmen in all of Menzoberranzan, was now the secondboy of the house, eyeing, perhaps, Dinin's title.

Similarly, Drizzt's fellow students did not miss the growing brilliance of his fighting dance. Often they viewed it too close for their liking! They looked upon Drizzt with seething jealousy, wondering if they could ever measure up against his whirling scimitars. Pragmatism was ever a strong trait in drow elves. These young students had spent the bulk of their years observing the elders of their families twisting every situation into a favorable light. Every one of them recognized the value of Drizzt Do'Urden as an ally, and thus, when the grand melee came around the next year, Drizzt was inundated with offers of partnership.

The most surprising query came from Kelnozz of House Kenafin, who had downed Drizzt through deceit the previous year. "Do we join again, this time to the very top of the class?" the haughty young fighter asked as he moved beside Drizzt down the tunnel to the prepared cavern. He moved around and stood before Drizzt easily, as if they were the best of friends, his forearms resting across the hilts of his belted weapons and an overly friendly smile spread across his face.

Drizzt could not even answer. He turned and walked away, pointedly keeping his eye over one shoulder as he left.

"Why are you so amazed?" Kelnozz pressed, stepping quickly to keep up.

Drizzt spun on him. "How could I join again with one who so deceived me?" he snarled. "I have not forgotten your trick!"

"That is the point," Kelnozz argued. "You are more wary this year; certainly I would be a fool to attempt such a move again!"

"How else could you win?" said Drizzt. "You cannot defeat me in open battle." His words were not a boast, just a fact that Kelnozz accepted as readily as Drizzt.

"Second rank is highly honored," Kelnozz reasoned.

Drizzt glared at him. He knew that Kelnozz would not settle for anything less than ultimate victory. "If we meet in the melee," he said with cold finality, "it will be as opponents." He walked off again, and this time Kelnozz did not follow.

⚔ ⚔ ⚔ ⚔ ⚔

Luck bestowed a measure of justice upon Drizzt that day, for his first opponent, and first victim, in the grand melee was none other than his former partner. Drizzt found Kelnozz in the same corridor they had used as a defensible starting point the previous year and took him down with his very first attack combination. Drizzt somehow managed to hold back on his winning thrust, though he truly wanted to jab his scimitar pole into Kelnozz's ribs with all his strength.

Then Drizzt was off into the shadows, picking his way carefully until the numbers of surviving students began to dwindle. With his reputation, Drizzt had to be extra wary, for his classmates recognized a common advantage in eliminating one of his prowess early in the competition. Working alone, Drizzt had to fully scope out every battle before he engaged, to ensure that each opponent had no secret companions lurking nearby.

This was Drizzt's arena, the place where he felt most comfortable, and he was up to the challenge. In two hours, only five competitors remained, and after another two hours of cat and mouse, it came down to only two: Drizzt and Berg'inyon Baenre.

Drizzt moved out into an open stretch of the cavern. "Come out, then, student Baenre!" he called. "Let us settle this challenge openly and with honor!"

Watching from the catwalk, Dinin shook his head in disbelief.

"He has relinquished all advantage," said Master Hatch'net, standing beside the elderboy of House Do'Urden. "As the better swordsman, he had Berg'inyon worried and unsure of his moves. Now your brother stands out in the open, showing his position."

"Still a fool," Dinin muttered.

Hatch'net spotted Berg'inyon slipping behind a stalagmite mound a few yards behind Drizzt. "It should be settled soon."

"Are you afraid?" Drizzt yelled into the gloom. "If you truly deserve the top rank, as you freely boast, then come out and face me openly. Prove your words, Berg'inyon Baenre, or never speak them again!"

The expected rush of motion from behind sent Drizzt into a sidelong roll.

"Fighting is more than swordplay!" the son of House Baenre cried as he came on, his eyes gleaming at the advantage he now seemed to hold.

Berg'inyon stumbled then, tripped up by a wire Drizzt had set out, and fell flat to his face. Drizzt was on him in a flash, scimitar pole tip in at Berg'inyon's throat.

"So I have learned," Drizzt replied grimly.

"Thus a Do'Urden becomes the champion," Hatch'net observed, putting his blue light on the face of House Baenre's defeated son. Hatch'net then stole Dinin's widening smile with a prudent reminder: "Elderboys should beware secondboys with such skills."

⚔ ⚔ ⚔ ⚔ ⚔

While Drizzt took little pride in his victory that second year, he took great satisfaction in the continued growth of his fighting skills. He practiced every waking hour when he was not busy in the many serving duties of a young student. Those duties were reduced as the years passed—the youngest students were worked the hardest—and Drizzt found more and more time in private training. He reveled in the dance of his blades and the harmony of his movements. His scimitars became his only friends, the only things he dared to trust.

He won the grand melee again the third year, and the year after that, despite the conspiracies of many others against him. To the masters, it became obvious that none in Drizzt's class would ever defeat him, and the next year they placed him into the grand melee of students three years his senior. He won that one, too.

The Academy, above anything else in Menzoberranzan, was a structured place, and though Drizzt's advanced skill defied that structure in terms of battle prowess, his tenure as a student would not be lessened. As a fighter, he would spend ten years in the Academy, not such a long time considering the thirty years of study a wizard endured in Sorcere, or the fifty years a budding priestess would spend in Arach-Tinilith. While fighters began their training at the young age of twenty, wizards could not start until their twenty-fifth birthday, and clerics had to wait until the age of forty.

The first four years in Melee-Magthere were devoted to singular combat, the handling of weapons. In this, the masters could teach Drizzt little that Zaknafein had not already shown him.

After that, though, the lessons became more involved. The young drow warriors spent two full years learning group fighting tactics with other warriors, and the subsequent three years incorporated those tactics into warfare techniques beside, and against, wizards and clerics.

The final year of the Academy rounded out the fighters' education. The first six months were spent in Sorcere, learning the basics of magic use, and the last six, the prelude to graduation, saw the fighters in tutelage under the priestesses of Arach-Tinilith.

All the while there remained the rhetoric, the hammering in of those precepts that the Spider Queen held so dear, those lies of hatred that held the drow in a state of controllable chaos.

To Drizzt, the Academy became a personal challenge, a private classroom within the impenetrable womb of his whirling scimitars. Inside the adamantine walls he formed with those blades, Drizzt found he could ignore the many injustices he observed all around him, and could somewhat insulate himself against words that would have poisoned his heart. The Academy was a place of constant ambition and deceit, a breeding ground for the ravenous, consuming hunger for power that marked the life of all the drow.

Drizzt would survive it unscathed, he promised himself.

As the years passed, though, as the battles began to take on the edge of brutal reality, Drizzt found himself caught up time and again in the heated throes of situations he could not so easily brush away.

# 14 Proper Respect

They moved through the winding tunnels as quietly as a whispering breeze, each step measured in stealth and ending in an alert posture. They were ninth-year students working on their last year in Melee-Magthere, and they operated as often outside the cavern of Menzoberranzan as within. No longer did padded poles adorn their belts; adamantine weapons hung there now, finely forged and cruelly edged.

At times, the tunnels closed in around them, barely wide enough for one dark elf to squeeze through. Other times, the students found themselves in huge caverns with walls and ceilings beyond their sight. They were drow warriors, trained to operate in any type of Underdark landscape and learned in the ways of any foe they might encounter.

"Practice patrols," Master Hatch'net had called these drills, though he had warned the students that "practice patrols" often met monsters quite real and unfriendly.

Drizzt, still rated in the top of his class and in the point position, led this group, with Master Hatch'net and ten other students following in formation behind. Only twenty-two of the original twenty-five in Drizzt's class remained. One had been dismissed—and subsequently executed—for a foiled assassination attempt on a high-ranking student, a second had been killed in the practice arena, and a third had died in his bunk of natural causes—for a dagger in the heart quite naturally ends one's life.

In another tunnel a short distance away, Berg'inyon Baenre, holding the class's second rank, led Master Dinin and the other half of the class in a similar exercise.

Day after day, Drizzt and the others had struggled to keep the fine edge of readiness. In three months of these mock patrols, the group had encountered only one monster, a cave fisher, a nasty crablike denizen of the Underdark. Even that conflict had provided only brief excitement, and no practical experience, for the cave fisher had slipped out along the high ledges before the drow patrol could even get a strike at it.

This day, Drizzt sensed something different. Perhaps it was an unusual edge on Master Hatch'net's voice or a tingling in the stones of the cavern, a subtle vibration that hinted to Drizzt's subconscious of other creatures in the maze of tunnels. Whatever the reason, Drizzt knew enough to follow his instincts, and he was not surprised when the telltale glow of a heat source flitted down a side passage on the periphery of his vision. He signaled for the rest of the patrol to halt, then quickly climbed to a perch on a tiny ledge above the side passage's exit.

When the intruder emerged into the main tunnel, he found himself lying back down on the floor with two scimitar blades crossed over his neck. Drizzt backed away immediately when he recognized his victim as another drow student.

"What are you doing down here?" Master Hatch'net demanded of the intruder. "You know that the tunnels outside Menzoberranzan are not to be traveled by any but the patrols!"

"Your pardon, Master," the student pleaded. "I bring news of an alert."

All in the patrol crowded around, but Hatch'net backed them off with a glare and ordered Drizzt to set them out in defensive positions.

"A child is missing," the student went on, "a princess of House Baenre! Monsters have been spotted in the tunnels!"

"What sort of monsters?" Hatch'net asked. A loud clacking noise, like the sound of two stones being chipped together, answered his question.

"Hook horrors!" Hatch'net signaled to Drizzt at his side. Drizzt had never seen such beasts, but he had learned enough about them to understand why

Master Hatch'net had suddenly reverted to the silent hand code. Hook horrors hunted through a sense of hearing more acute than that of any other creature in all the Underdark. Drizzt immediately relayed the signal around to the others, and they held absolutely quiet for instructions from the master. This was the situation they had trained to handle for the last nine years of their lives, and only the sweat on their palms belied the calm readiness of these young drow warriors.

"Spells of darkness will not foil hook horrors," Hatch'net signaled to his troops. "Nor will these." He indicated the pistol crossbow in his hand and the poison-tipped dart it held, a common first-strike weapon of the dark elves. Hatch'net put the crossbow away and drew his slender sword.

"You must find a gap in the creature's bone armor," he reminded the others, "and slip your weapon through to the flesh." He tapped Drizzt on the shoulder, and they started off together, the other students falling into line behind them.

The clacking resounded clearly, but, echoing off the stone walls of the tunnels, it provided a confusing beacon for the hunting drow. Hatch'net let Drizzt steer their course and was impressed by the way the student soon discerned the pattern of the echo riddle. Drizzt's step came in confidence, though many of the others in the patrol glanced about anxiously, unsure of the peril's direction or distance.

Then a singular sound froze them all where they stood, cutting through the din of the clacking monsters and resounding again and again, surrounding the patrol in the echoing madness of a terrifying wail. It was the scream of a child.

"Princess of House Baenre!" Hatch'net signaled to Drizzt. The master started to order his troops into a battle formation, but Drizzt didn't wait to watch the commands. The scream had sent a shudder of revulsion through his spine, and when it sounded again, it lighted angry fires in his lavender eyes.

Drizzt sprinted off down the tunnel, the cold metal of his scimitars leading the way.

Hatch'net organized the patrol into quick pursuit. He hated the thought of losing a student as skilled as Drizzt, but he considered, too, the benefits of Drizzt's rash actions. If the others watched the finest of their class die in an act of stupidity, it would be a lesson they would not soon forget.

Drizzt cut around a sharp corner and down a straight expanse of narrow, broken walls. He heard no echoes now, just the ravenous clacking of the waiting monsters and the muffled cries of the child.

His keen ears caught the slight sounds of his patrol at his back, and he knew that if he was able to hear them, the hook horrors surely could. Drizzt would not relinquish the passion or the immediacy of his quest. He climbed to a ledge ten feet above the floor, hoping it would run the length of the corridor. When he slipped around a final bend, he could barely distinguish the heat of the monsters' forms through the blurring coolness of their bony exoskeletons, shells nearly equal in temperature to the surrounding stone.

He made out five of the giant beasts, two pressed against the stone and guarding the corridor and three others farther back, in a little cul-de-sac, toying with some—crying—object.

Drizzt mustered his nerve and continued along the ledge, using all the stealth he had ever learned to creep by the sentries. Then he saw the child princess, lying in a broken heap at the foot of one of the monstrous bipeds. Her sobs told Drizzt that she was alive. Drizzt had no intention of engaging the monsters if he could help it, hoping that he might perhaps slip in and steal the child away.

Then the patrol came headlong around the bend in the corridor, forcing Drizzt to action.

"Sentries!" he screamed in warning, probably saving the lives of the first four of the group. Drizzt's attention abruptly returned to the wounded child as one of the hook horrors raised its heavy, clawed foot to crush her.

The beast stood nearly twice Drizzt's height and outweighed him more than five times over. It was fully armored in the hard shell of its exoskeleton and adorned with gigantic clawed hands and a long and powerful beak. Three of the monsters stood between Drizzt and the child.

Drizzt couldn't care about any of those details at that horrible, critical moment. His fears for the child outweighed any concern for the danger looming before him. He was a drow warrior, a fighter trained and outfitted for battle, while the child was helpless and defenseless.

Two of the hook horrors rushed at the ledge, just the break Drizzt needed. He rose up to his feet and leaped out over them, coming down in a fighting blur onto the side of the remaining hook horror. The monster lost all thoughts of the child as Drizzt's scimitars snapped in at its beak relentlessly, cracking into its facial armor in a desperate search for an opening.

The hook horror fell back, overwhelmed by its opponent's fury and unable to catch up to the blades' blinding, stinging movements.

Drizzt knew that he had the advantage on this one, but he knew, as well, that two others would soon be at his back. He did not relent. He slid down from his perch on the monster's side and rolled around to block its retreat, dropping between its stalagmite-like legs and tripping it to the stone. Then he was on top of it, poking furiously as it floundered on its belly.

The hook horror desperately tried to respond, but its armored shell was too encumbering for it to twist out from under the assault.

Drizzt knew his own situation was even more desperate. Battle had been joined in the corridor, but Hatch'net and the others couldn't possibly get through the sentries in time to stop the two hook horrors undoubtedly charging his back. Prudence dictated that Drizzt relinquish his position over this one and spin away into a defensive posture.

The child's agonized scream, however, overruled prudence. Rage burned in Drizzt's eyes so blatantly that even the stupid hook horror knew its life was soon to end. Drizzt put the tips of his scimitars together in a V and plunged them down onto the back of the monster's skull with all his might. Seeing a slight crack in the creature's shell, Drizzt crossed the hilts of his weapons, reversed the points, and split a clear opening in the monster's defense. He then snapped the hilts together and plunged the blades straight down, through the soft flesh and into the monster's brain.

A heavy claw sliced a deep line across Drizzt's shoulders, tearing his *piwafwi* and drawing blood. He dived forward into a roll and came up with his wounded back to the far wall. Only one hook horror moved in at him; the other picked up the child.

"No!" Drizzt screamed in protest. He started forward, only to be slapped back by the attacking monster. Then, paralyzed, he watched in horror as the other hook horror put an end to the child's screams.

Rage replaced determination in Drizzt's eyes. The closest hook horror rushed at him, meaning to crush him against the stone. Drizzt recognized its intentions and didn't even try to dodge out of the way. Instead, he reversed his grip on his weapons and locked them against the wall, above his shoulders.

With the momentum of the monster's eight-hundred-pound bulk carrying it on, even the armor of its shell could not protect the hook horror from the adamantine scimitars. It slammed Drizzt up against the wall, but in doing so impaled itself through the belly.

The creature jumped back, trying to wriggle free, but it could not escape the fury of Drizzt Do'Urden. Savagely the young drow twisted the impaled blades. He then shoved off from the wall with the strength of anger, tumbling the giant monster backward.

Two of Drizzt's enemies were dead, and one of the hook horror sentries in the hallway was down, but Drizzt found no relief in those facts. The third hook horror towered over him as he desperately tried to get his blades free from his latest victim. Drizzt had no escape from this one.

The second patrol arrived then, and Dinin and Berg'inyon Baenre rushed into the cul-de-sac, along the same ledge Drizzt had taken. The hook horror turned away from Drizzt just as the two skilled fighters came at it.

Drizzt ignored the painful gash in his back and the cracks he had no doubt suffered in his slender ribs. Breathing came to him in labored gasps, but this, too, was of no consequence. He finally managed to free one of his blades, and he charged at the monster's back. Caught in the middle of the three skilled drow, the hook horror went down in seconds.

The corridor was finally cleared, and the dark elves rushed in all around the cul-de-sac. They had lost only one student in their battle against the monster sentries.

"A princess of House Barrison'del'armgo," remarked one of the students in Dinin's patrol, looking at the child's body.

"House Baenre, we were told," said another student, one from Hatch'net's group. Drizzt did not miss the discrepancy.

Berg'inyon Baenre rushed over to see if the victim was indeed his youngest sister.

"Not of my house," he said with obvious relief after a quick inspection. He then laughed as further examination revealed a few other details about the corpse. "Not even a princess!" he declared.

Drizzt watched it all curiously, noting the impassive, callous attitude of his companions most of all.

Another student confirmed Berg'inyon's observation. "A boy child!" he spouted. "But of what house?"

Master Hatch'net moved over to the tiny body and reached down to take the purse from around the child's neck. He emptied its contents into his hand, revealing the emblem of a lesser house.

"A lost waif," he laughed to his students, tossing the empty purse back to the ground and pocketing its contents," of no consequence."

"A fine fight," Dinin was quick to add, "with only one loss. Go back to Menzoberranzan proud of the work you have accomplished this day."

Drizzt slapped the blades of his scimitars together in a resounding ring of protest.

Master Hatch'net ignored him. "Form up and head back," he told the others. "You all performed well this day." He then glared at Drizzt, stopping the angry student in his tracks.

"Except for you!" Hatch'net snarled. "I cannot ignore the fact that you downed two of the beasts and helped with a third," Hatch'net scolded, "but you endangered the rest of us with your foolish bravado!"

"I warned of the sentries—" Drizzt stuttered.

"Damn your warning!" shouted the master. "You went off without command! You ignored the accepted methods of battle! You led us in here blindly! Look at the corpse of your fallen companion!" Hatch'net raged, pointing to the dead student in the corridor. "His blood is on your hands!"

"I meant to save the child," Drizzt argued.

"We all meant to save the child!" retorted Hatch'net.

Drizzt was not so certain. What would a child be doing out in these corridors all alone? How convenient that a group of hook horrors, a rarely seen beast in the region of Menzoberranzan, just happened by to provide training for this "practice patrol." Too convenient, Drizzt knew, considering that the passages farther from the city teemed with the true patrols of seasoned warriors, wizards, and even clerics.

"You knew what was around the bend in the tunnel," Drizzt said evenly, his eyes narrowing at the master.

The slap of a blade across the wound on his back made Drizzt lurch in pain, and he nearly lost his footing. He turned to find Dinin glaring down at him.

"Keep your foolish words unspoken," Dinin warned in a harsh whisper, "or I will cut out your tongue."

⚔ ⚔ ⚔ ⚔ ⚔

"The child was a plant," Drizzt insisted when he was alone with his brother in Dinin's room.

Dinin's response was a stinging smack across the face.

"They sacrificed him for the purpose of the drill," growled the unrelenting younger Do'Urden.

Dinin launched a second punch, but Drizzt caught it in mid-swing. "You know the truth of my words," Drizzt said. "You knew about it all along."

"Learn your place, Secondboy," Dinin replied in open threat, "in the Academy and in the family." He pulled away from his brother.

"To the Nine Hells with the Academy!" Drizzt spat at Dinin's face. "If the family holds similar . . ." He noticed that Dinin's hands now held sword and dirk.

Drizzt jumped back, his own scimitars coming out at the ready. "I have no desire to fight you, my brother," he said. "Know well that if you attack, I will defend. Only one of us will walk out of here."

Dinin considered his next move carefully. If he attacked and won, the threat to his position in the family would be at an end. Certainly no one, not even Matron Malice, would question the punishment he levied against his impertinent younger brother. Dinin had seen Drizzt in battle, though. Two hook horrors! Even Zaknafein would be hard pressed to attain such a victory. Still, Dinin knew that if he did not carry through with his threat, if he let Drizzt face him down, he might give Drizzt confidence in their future struggles, possibly inciting the treachery he had always expected from the secondboy.

"What is this, then?" came a voice from the room's door way. The brothers turned to see their sister Vierna, a mistress of Arach-Tinilith. "Put your weapons away," she scolded. "House Do'Urden cannot afford such infighting now!"

Realizing that he had been let off the hook, Dinin readily complied with the demands, and Drizzt did likewise.

"Consider yourselves fortunate," said Vierna, "for I'll not tell Matron Malice of this stupidity. She would not be merciful, I promise you."

"Why have you come unannounced to Melee-Magthere?" asked the elderboy, perturbed by his sister's attitude. He, too, was a master of the Academy, even if he was only a male, and deserved some respect.

Vierna glanced up and down the hallway, then closed the door behind her. "To warn my brothers," she explained quietly. "There are rumors of vengeance against our house."

"By what family?" Dinin pressed. Drizzt just stood back in confused silence and let the two continue. "For what deed?"

"For the elimination of House DeVir, I would presume," replied Vierna. "Little is known; the rumors are vague. I wanted to warn you both, though, so that you might keep your guard especially high in the coming months."

"House DeVir fell many years ago," said Dinin. "What penalty could still be enacted?"

Vierna shrugged. "They are just rumors," she said. "Rumors to be listened to!"

"We have been accused of a wrongful deed?" Drizzt asked. "Surely our family must call out this false accuser."

Vierna and Dinin exchanged smiles. "Wrongful?" Vierna laughed.

Drizzt's expression revealed his confusion.

"On the very night you were born," Dinin explained, "House DeVir ceased to exist. An excellent attack, thank you."

"House Do'Urden?" gasped Drizzt, unable to come to terms with the startling news. Of course, Drizzt knew of such battles, but he had held out hope that his own family was above that sort of murderous action.

"One of the finest eliminations ever carried out," Vierna boasted. "Not a witness left alive."

"You . . . our family . . . murdered another family?"

"Watch your words, Secondboy," Dinin warned. "The deed was perfectly executed. In the eyes of Menzoberranzan, therefore, it never happened."

"But House DeVir ceased to exist," said Drizzt.

"To a child," said Dinin with a laugh.

A thousand possibilities assaulted Drizzt at that awful moment, a thousand pressing questions that he needed answered. One in particular stood out vividly, welling like a lump of bile in his throat.

"Where was Zaknafein that night?" he asked.

"In the chapel of House DeVir's clerics, of course," replied Vierna "Zaknafein plays his part in such business so very well."

Drizzt rocked back on his heels, hardly able to believe what he was hearing. He knew that Zak had killed drow before, had killed clerics of Lolth before, but Drizzt had always assumed that the weapons master had acted out of necessity, in self-defense.

"You should show more respect to your brother," Vierna scolded him. "To draw weapons against Dinin! You owe him your life!"

"You know?" Dinin chuckled, casting Vierna a curious glance.

"You and I were melded that night," Vierna reminded him. "Of course I know."

"What are you talking about?" asked Drizzt, almost afraid to hear the reply.

"You were to be the third-born male in the family," Vierna explained, "the third living son."

"I have heard of my brother Nal—" The name stuck in Drizzt's throat as he began to understand. All he had ever been able to learn of Nalfein was that he had been killed by another drow.

"You will learn in your studies at Arach-Tinilith that third living sons are customarily sacrificed to Lolth," Vierna continued. "So were you promised. On the night that you were born, the night that House Do'Urden battled House DeVir, Dinin made his ascent to the position of elderboy." She cast a sly glance at her brother, standing with his arms proudly crossed over his chest.

"I can speak of it now," Vierna smiled at Dinin, who nodded his head in accord. "It happened too long ago for any punishment to be brought against Dinin."

"What are you talking about?" Drizzt demanded. Panic hovered all about him. "What did Dinin do?"

"He put his sword into Nalfein's back," Vierna said calmly.

Drizzt swam on the edge of nausea. Sacrifice? Murder? The annihilation of a family, even the children? What were his siblings talking about?

"Show respect to your brother!" Vierna demanded. "You owe him your life."

"I warn the both of you," she purred, her ominous glare shaking Drizzt and knocking Dinin from his confident pedestal. "House Do'Urden may be on a course of war. If either of you strike out against the other, you will bring the wrath of all your sisters and Matron Malice—four high priestesses—down upon your worthless soul!" Confident that her threat carried sufficient weight, she turned and left the room.

"I will go," Drizzt whispered, wanting only to skulk away to a dark corner.

"You will go when you are dismissed!" Dinin scolded. "Remember your place, Drizzt Do'Urden, in the Academy and in the family."

"As you remembered yours with Nalfein?"

"The battle against DeVir was won," Dinin replied, taking no offense. "The act brought no peril to the family."

Another wave of disgust swept over Drizzt. He felt as if the floor were climbing up to swallow him, and he almost hoped that it would.

"It is a difficult world we inhabit," Dinin said.

"We make it so," Drizzt retorted. He wanted to continue further, to implicate the Spider Queen and the whole amoral religion that would sanction such destructive and treacherous actions. Drizzt wisely held his tongue, though. Dinin wanted him dead; he understood that now. Drizzt understood as well that if he gave his scheming brother the opportunity to turn the females of the family against him, Dinin surely would.

"You must learn," Dinin said, again in a controlled tone, "to accept the realities of your surroundings. You must learn to recognize your enemies and defeat them."

"By whatever means are available," Drizzt concluded.

"The mark of a true warrior!" Dinin replied with a wicked laugh.

"Are our enemies drow elves?"

"We are drow warriors!" Dinin declared sternly. "We do what we must to survive,"

"As you did, on the night of my birth," Drizzt reasoned, though at this point, there was no remaining trace of outrage in his resigned tone. "You were cunning enough to get away cleanly with the deed."

Dinin's reply, though expected, stung the younger drow profoundly. "It never happened."

# 15 On The Dark Side

I am Drizzt—"

"I know who you are," replied the student mage, Drizzt's appointed tutor in Sorcere. "Your reputation precedes you. Most in all the Academy have heard of you and of your prowess with weapons."

Drizzt bowed low, a bit embarrassed.

"That skill will be of little use to you here," the mage went on. "I am to tutor you in the wizardly arts, the dark side of magic, we call them. This is a test of your mind and your heart; meager metal weapons will play no part. Magic is the true power of our people!"

Drizzt accepted the berating without reply. He knew that the traits this young mage was boasting of were also necessary qualities of a true fighter. Physical attributes played only a minor role in Drizzt's style of battle. Strong will and calculated maneuvers, everything the mage apparently believed only wizards could handle, won the duels that Drizzt fought.

"I will show you many marvels in the next few months," the mage went on, "artifacts beyond your belief and spells of a power beyond your experience!"

"May I know your name?" Drizzt asked, trying to sound somewhat impressed by the student's continued stream of self-glorification. Drizzt had already learned quite a lot about wizardry from Zaknafein, mostly of the weaknesses inherent in the profession. Because of magic's usefulness in situations other than battle, drow wizards were accorded a high position in the society, second to the clerics of Lolth. It was a wizard, after all, who lighted the glowing Narbondel, timeclock of the city, and wizards who lighted faerie fires on the sculptures of the decorated houses.

Zaknafein had little respect for wizards. They could kill quickly and from a distance, he had warned Drizzt, but if one could get in close to them, they had little defense against a sword.

"Masoj," replied the mage. "Masoj Hun'ett of House Hun'ett, beginning my thirtieth and final year of study. Soon I will be recognized as a full wizard of Menzoberranzan, with all of the privileges accorded my station."

"Greetings, then, Masoj Hun'ett," Drizzt replied. "I, too, have but a year remaining in my training at the Academy, for a fighter spends only ten years."

"A lesser talent," Masoj was quick to remark. "Wizards study thirty years before they are even considered practiced enough to go out and perform their craft."

Again Drizzt accepted the insult graciously. He wanted to get this phase of his instruction over with, then finish out the year and be rid of the Academy altogether.

⚔ ⚔ ⚔ ⚔ ⚔

Drizzt found his six months under Masoj's tutelage actually the best of his stay at the Academy. Not that he came to care for Masoj; the budding wizard constantly sought ways to remind Drizzt of fighters' inferiority. Drizzt sensed a competition between himself and Masoj, almost as if the mage were setting him up for some future conflict. The young fighter shrugged his way through it, as he always had, and tried to get as much out of the lessons as he could.

Drizzt found that he was quite proficient in the ways of magic. Every drow, the fighters included, possessed a degree of magical talent and certain innate abilities. Even drow children could conjure a globe of darkness or edge their opponents in a glowing outline of harmless colored flames. Drizzt handled these tasks easily, and in a few tendays, he could manage several cantrips and a few lesser spells.

With the innate magical talents of the dark elves also came a resistance to magical attacks, and that is where Zaknafein had recognized the wizards' greatest weakness. A wizard could cast his most powerful spell to perfection, but if his intended victim was a drow elf, the wizard may well have found no results for his efforts. The surety of a well-aimed sword thrust always impressed Zaknafein, and Drizzt, after witnessing the drawbacks of drow magic during those first tendays with Masoj, began to appreciate the course of training he had been given.

He still found great enjoyment in many of the things Masoj showed him, particularly the enchanted items housed in the tower of Sorcere. Drizzt held wands and staves of incredible power and went through several attack routines with a sword so heavily enchanted that his hands tingled from its touch.

Masoj, too, watched Drizzt carefully through it all, studying the young warrior's every move, searching for some weakness that he might exploit if House Hun'ett and House Do'Urden ever did fall into the expected conflict. Several times, Masoj saw an opportunity to eliminate Drizzt, and he felt in his heart that it would be a prudent move. Matron SiNafay's instructions to him, though, had been explicit and unbending.

Masoj's mother had secretly arranged for him to be Drizzt's tutor. This was not an unusual situation; instruction for fighters during their six months in Sorcere was always handled one-on-one by higher-level Sorcere students. When she had told Masoj of the setup, SiNafay quickly reminded him that his sessions with the young Do'Urden remained no more than a scouting mission. He was not to do anything that might even hint of the planned conflict between the two houses. Masoj was not fool enough to disobey.

Still, there was one other wizard lurking in the shadows, who was so desperate that even the warnings of the matron mother did little to deter him.

⚔ ⚔ ⚔ ⚔ ⚔

"My student, Masoj, has informed me of your fine progress," Alton DeVir said to Drizzt one day.

"Thank you, Master Faceless One," Drizzt replied hesitantly, more than a little intimidated that a master of Sorcere had invited him to a private audience.

"How do you perceive magic, young warrior?" Alton asked. "Has Masoj impressed you?"

Drizzt didn't know how to respond. Truly, magic had not impressed him as a profession, but he did not want to insult a master of the craft. "I find the art beyond my abilities," he said tactfully. "For others, it seems a powerful course, but I believe my talents are more closely linked to the sword."

"Could your weapons defeat one of magical power?" Alton snarled. He quickly bit back the sneer, trying not to tip off his intent.

Drizzt shrugged. "Each has its place in battle," he replied. "Who could say which is the mightier? As with every combat, it would depend upon the individuals engaged."

"Well, what of yourself?" Alton teased. "First in your class, I have heard, year after year. The masters of Melee-Magthere speak highly of your talents."

Again Drizzt found himself flushed with embarrassment. More than that, though, he was curious as to why a master and student of Sorcere seemed to know so much about him.

"Could you stand against one of magical powers?" asked Alton. "Against a master of Sorcere, perhaps?"

"I do not—" Drizzt began, but Alton was too enmeshed in his own ranting to hear him.

"Let us learn!" the Faceless One cried. He drew out a thin wand and promptly loosed a bolt of lightning at Drizzt.

Drizzt was down into a dive before the wand even discharged. The lightning bolt sundered the door to Alton's highest chamber and bounced about the adjourning room, breaking items and scorching the walls.

Drizzt came rolling back to his feet at the side of the room, his scimitars drawn and ready. He still was unsure of this master's intent.

"How many can you dodge?" Alton teased, waving the wand in a threatening circle. "What of the other spells I have at my disposal—those that attack the mind, not the body?"

Drizzt tried to understand the purpose of this lesson and the part he was meant to play in it. Was he supposed to attack this master?

"These are not practice blades," he warned, holding his weapons out toward Alton.

Another bolt roared in, forcing Drizzt to dodge back to his original position. "Does this seem like practice to you, foolish Do'Urden?" Alton growled. "Do you know who I am?"

Alton's time of revenge had come—damn the orders of Matron SiNafay!

Just as Alton was about to reveal the truth to Drizzt, a dark form slammed into the master's back, knocking him to the floor. He tried to squirm away but found himself helplessly pinned by a huge black panther.

Drizzt lowered the tips of his blades; he was at a loss to understand any of this.

"Enough, Guenhwyvar!" came a call from behind Alton. Looking past the fallen master and the cat, Drizzt saw Masoj enter the room.

The panther sprang away from Alton obediently and moved to rejoin its master. It paused on its way, to consider Drizzt, who stood ready in the middle of the room.

So enchanted was Drizzt with the beast, the graceful flow of its rippling muscles and the intelligence in its saucer eyes, that he paid little attention to the master who had just attacked him, though Alton, unhurt, was back to his feet and obviously upset.

"My pet," Masoj explained. Drizzt watched in amazement as Masoj dismissed the cat back to its own plane of existence by sending its corporeal form back into the magical onyx statuette he held in his hand.

"Where did you get such a companion?" Drizzt asked.

"Never underestimate the powers of magic," Masoj replied, dropping the figurine into a deep pocket. His beaming smile became a scowl as he looked to Alton.

Drizzt, too, glanced at the faceless master. That a student had dared to attack a master seemed impossibly odd to the young fighter. This situation grew more puzzling each minute.

Alton knew that he had overstepped his bounds, and that he would have to pay a high price for his foolishness if he could not find some way out of this predicament.

"Have you learned your lesson this day?" Masoj asked Drizzt, though Alton realized that the question was also directed his way.

Drizzt shook his head. "I am not certain of the point of all this," he answered honestly.

"A display of the weakness of magic," Masoj explained, trying to disguise the truth of the encounter, "to show you the disadvantage caused by the necessary intensity of a casting wizard; to show you the vulnerability of a mage obsessed—" he eyed Alton directly at this point—"with spellcasting. The complete vulnerability when a wizard's intended prey becomes his overriding concern."

Drizzt recognized the lie for what it was, but he could not understand the motives behind this day's events. Why would a master of Sorcere attack him so? Why would Masoj, still just a student, risk so much to come to his defense?

"Let us bother the master no more," Masoj said, hoping to deflect Drizzt's curiosity further. "Come with me now to our practice hall. I will show you more of Guenhwyvar, my magical pet."

Drizzt looked to Alton, wondering what the unpredictable master would do next.

"Do go," Alton said calmly, knowing the facade Masoj had begun would be his only way around the wrath of his adopted matron mother. "I am confident that this day's lesson was learned," he said, his eyes on Masoj.

Drizzt glanced back to Masoj, then back to Alton again. He let it go at that. He wanted to learn more of Guenhwyvar.

⚔ ⚔ ⚔ ⚔ ⚔

When Masoj had Drizzt back in the privacy of the tutor's own room, he took out the polished onyx figurine in the form of a panther and called

Guenhwyvar back to his side. The mage breathed easier after he had introduced Drizzt to the cat, for Drizzt spoke no more about the incident with Alton.

Never before had Drizzt encountered such a wonderful magical item. He sensed a strength in Guenhwyvar, a dignity, that belied the beast's enchanted nature. Truly, the cat's sleek muscles and graceful moves epitomized the hunting qualities drow elves so dearly desired. Just by watching Guenhwyvar's movements, Drizzt believed, he could improve his own techniques.

Masoj let them play together and spar together for hours, grateful that Guenhwyvar could help him smooth over any damage that foolish Alton had done.

Drizzt had already put his meeting with the faceless master far behind him.

⚔ ⚔ ⚔ ⚔ ⚔

"Matron SiNafay would not understand," Masoj warned Alton when they were alone later that day.

"You will tell her," Alton reasoned matter-of-factly. So frustrated was he with his failure to kill Drizzt that he hardly cared.

Masoj shook his head. "She need not know."

A suspicious smile found its way across Alton's disfigured face. "What do you want?" he asked coyly. "Your tenure here is almost at its end. What more might a master do for Masoj?"

"Nothing," Masoj replied. "I want nothing from you."

"Then why?" Alton demanded. "I desire no debts following my paths. This incident is to be done with here and now!"

"It is done," Masoj replied. Alton didn't seem convinced.

"What could I gain from telling Matron SiNafay of your foolish actions?" Masoj reasoned. "Likely, she would kill you, and the coming war with House Do'Urden would have no basis. You are the link we need to justify the attack. I desire this battle; I'll not risk it for the little pleasure I might find in your tortured demise."

"I was foolish," Alton admitted, more somberly. "I had not planned to kill Drizzt when I summoned him here, just to watch him and learn of him, so that I might savor more when the time to kill him finally arrived. Seeing him before me, though, seeing a cursed Do'Urden standing unprotected before me . . . !"

"I understand," said Masoj sincerely. "I have had those same feelings when looking upon that one."

"You have no grudge against House Do'Urden."

"Not the house," Masoj explained, "that one! I have watched him for nearly a decade, studied his movements and his attitudes."

"You like not what you see?" Alton asked, a hopeful tone in his voice.

"He does not belong," Masoj replied grimly. "After six months by his side, I feel I know him less now than I ever did. He displays no ambition, yet has emerged victorious from his class's grand melee nine years in a row. It's unprecedented! His grasp of magic is strong; he could have been a wizard, a very powerful wizard, if he had chosen that course of study."

Masoj clenched his fist, searching for the words to convey his true emotions about Drizzt. "It is all too easy for him," he snarled. "There is no sacrifice in Drizzt's actions, no scars for the great gains he makes in his chosen profession."

"He is gifted," Alton remarked, "but he trains as hard as any I have ever seen, by all accounts."

"That is not the problem," Masoj groaned in frustration. There was something less tangible about Drizzt Do'Urden's character that truly irked the young Hun'ett. He couldn't recognize it now, because he had never witnessed it in any dark elf before, and because it was so very foreign to his own makeup. What bothered Masoj—and many other students and masters—was the fact that Drizzt excelled in all the fighting skills the drow elves most treasured but hadn't given up his passion in return. Drizzt had not paid the price that the rest of the drow children were made to sacrifice long before they had even entered the Academy.

"It is not important," Masoj said after several fruitless minutes of contemplation. "I will learn more of the young Do'Urden in time."

"His tutelage under you was finished, I had thought," said Alton. "He goes to Arach-Tinilith for the final six months of his training—quite inaccessible to you."

"We both graduate after those six months," Masoj explained. "We will share our indenture time in the patrol forces together."

"Many will share that time," Alton reminded him. "Dozens of groups patrol the corridors of the region. You may never even see Drizzt in all the years of your term."

"I already have arranged for us to serve in the same group," replied Masoj. He reached into his pocket and produced the onyx figurine of the magical panther.

"A mutual agreement between yourself and the young Do'Urden," Alton reasoned with a complimentary smile.

"It appears that Drizzt has become quite fond of my pet," Masoj chuckled.

"Too fond?" Alton warned. "You should watch your back for scimitars."

Masoj laughed aloud. "Perhaps our friend, Do'Urden, should watch his back for panther claws!"

# 16
# SACRILEGE

"Last day," Drizzt breathed in relief as he donned his ceremonial robes. If the first six months of this final year, learning the subtleties of magic in Sorcere, had been the most enjoyable, these last six in the school of Lolth had been the least. Every day, Drizzt and his classmates had been subjected to endless eulogies to the Spider Queen, tales and prophecies of her power and of the rewards she bestowed upon loyal servants.

"Slaves" would have been a better word, Drizzt had come to realize, for nowhere in all this grand school to the drow deity had he heard anything synonymous with, or even hinting at, the word love. His people worshiped Lolth; the females of Menzoberranzan gave over their entire existence in her servitude. Their giving was wholly wrought of selfishness, though; a cleric of the Spider Queen aspired to the position of high priestess solely for the personal power that accompanied the title.

It all seemed so very wrong in Drizzt's heart.

Drizzt had drifted through the six months of Arach-Tinilith with his customary stoicism, keeping his eyes low and his mouth shut. Now, finally, he had come to the last day, the Ceremony of Graduation, an event most holy to the drow, and wherein, Vierna had promised him, he would come to understand the true glory of Lolth.

With tentative steps, Drizzt moved out from the shelter of his tiny, unadorned room. He worried that this ceremony had become his personal trial. Up to now, very little about the society around Drizzt had made any sense to him, and he wondered, despite his sister's assurances, whether the events of this day would allow him to see the world as his kin saw it. Drizzt's fears had taken a spiral twist, one rolling out from the other to surround him in a predicament be could not escape.

Perhaps, he worried, he truly feared that the day's events would fulfill Vierna's promise.

Drizzt shielded his eyes as he entered the circular ceremonial hall of Arach-Tinilith. A fire burned in the center of the room, in an eight-legged brazier that resembled, as everything in this place seemed to resemble, a spider. The headmistress of all the Academy, the matron mistress, and the other twelve high priestesses serving as instructors of Arach-Tinilith, including Drizzt's sister, sat cross-legged in a circle around the brazier. Drizzt and his classmates from the school of fighters stood along the wall behind them.

"*Ma ku!*" the matron mistress commanded, and all was silent save the crackle of the brazier's flames. The door to the room opened again, and a young cleric entered. She was to be the first graduate of Arach-Tinilith this year, Drizzt had been told, the finest student in the school of Lolth. Thus, she had been awarded the highest honors in this ceremony. She shrugged off her robes and walked naked through the ring of sitting priestesses to stand before the flames, her back to the matron mistress.

Drizzt bit his lip, embarrassed and a little excited. He had never seen a female in such a light before, and he suspected that the sweat on his brow was from more than the brazier's heat. A quick glance around the room told him that his classmates entertained similar ideas.

"*Bae-go si'n'ee calamay,*" the matron mistress whispered, and red smoke poured from the brazier, coloring the room in a hazy glow. It carried an aroma with it, rich and sickly sweet. As Drizzt breathed the scented air, he felt himself grow lighter and wondered if he soon would be floating off the floor.

The flames in the brazier suddenly roared higher, causing Drizzt to squint against the brightness and turn away. The clerics began a ritual chant, though the words were unfamiliar to Drizzt. He hardly paid them any heed, though, for he was too intent on holding his own thoughts in the overpowering swoon of the inebriating haze.

"*Glabrezu*," the matron mistress moaned, and Drizzt recognized the tone as a summons, the name of a denizen of the lower planes. He looked back to the events at hand and saw the matron mistress holding a single-tongued snake whip.

"Where did she get that?" Drizzt mumbled, then he realized that he had spoken aloud and hoped he hadn't disturbed the ceremony. He was comforted when he glanced around, for many of his classmates were mumbling to themselves, and some seemed hardly able to hold their balance.

"Call to it," the matron mistress instructed the naked student.

Tentatively, the young cleric spread her arms out wide and whispered, "*Glabrezu*."

The flames danced about the rim of the brazier. The smoke wafted into Drizzt's face, compelling him to inhale it. His legs tingled on the edge of numbness, yet they somehow felt more sensitive, more alive, than they ever had before.

"*Glabrezu*," he heard the student say again louder, and Drizzt heard, too, the roar of the flames. Brightness assaulted him, but somehow he didn't seem to care. His gaze roamed about the room, unable to find a focus, unable to place the strange, dancing sights in accord with the ritual's sounds.

He heard the high priestesses gasping and coaxing the student on, knowing the conjuring to be at hand. He heard the snap of the snake whip—another incentive?—and cries of "*Glabrezu!*" from the student. So primal, so powerful, were these screams that they cut through Drizzt and the other males in the room with an intensity they never would have believed possible.

The flames heard the call. They roared higher and higher and began to take shape. One sight caught the vision of all in the room now—caught it and held it fully. A giant head, a goat-horned dog, appeared within the flames, apparently studying this alluring young drow student who had dared to utter its name.

Somewhere beyond the other-planar form, the snake whip cracked again, and the female student repeated her call, her cry beckoning, praying.

The giant denizen of the lower planes stepped through the flames. The sheer unholy power of the creature stunned Drizzt. Glabrezu towered nine feet and seemed much more, with muscled arms ending in giant pincers instead of hands and a second set of smaller arms, normal arms, protruding from the front of its chest.

Drizzt's instincts told him to attack the monster and rescue the female student, but when he looked around for support, he found the matron mistress and the other teachers of the school back in their ritualistic chanting, this time with an excited edge permeating their every word.

Through all the haze and the daze, the tantalizing, dizzying aroma of the smoky red incense continued its assault on reality. Drizzt trembled, teetered on a narrow ledge of control, his gathering rage fighting the scented smoke's confusing allure. Instinctively, his hands went to the hilts of the scimitars on his belt.

Then a hand brushed against his leg.

He looked down to see a mistress, reclined and asking him to join her—a scene that had suddenly become general around the chamber.

The smoke continued its assault on him.

The mistress beckoned to him, her fingernails lightly scraping the skin of his leg.

Drizzt ran his fingers through his thick hair, trying to find some focal point in the dizziness. He did not like this loss of control, this mental numbness that stole the fine edge of his reflexes and alertness.

He liked even less the scene unfolding before him. The sheer wrongness of it assaulted his soul. He pulled away from the mistress's hopeful grasp and stumbled across the room, tripping over numerous entwined forms too engaged to take note of him. He made the exit as quickly as his wobbly legs could carry him, and he rushed out of the room, pointedly closing the door behind him.

Only the screams of the female student followed him. No stone or mental barricade could block them out.

Drizzt leaned heavily against the cool stone wall, grasping at his stomach.

He hadn't even paused to consider the implications of his actions; he knew only that he had to get out of that foul room.

Vierna then was beside him, her robe opened casually in the front. Drizzt, his head clearing, began to wonder about the price of his actions. The look on his sister's face, he noted with still more confusion, was not one of scorn.

"You prefer privacy," she said, her hand resting easily on Drizzt's shoulder. Vierna made no move to close her robe. "I understand," she said.

Drizzt grabbed her arm and pulled her away. "What insanity is this?" he demanded.

Vierna's face twisted as she came to understand her brother's true intentions in leaving the ceremony. "You refused a high priestess!" she snarled at him. "By the laws, she could kill you for your insolence."

"I do not even know her," Drizzt shot back. "I am expected to—"

"You are expected to do as you are instructed!"

"I care nothing for her," Drizzt stammered. He found he could not hold his hands steady.

"Do you think Zaknafein cared for Matron Malice?" Vierna replied, knowing that the reference to Drizzt's hero would surely sting him. Seeing that she had indeed wounded her brother, Vierna softened her expression and took his arm. "Come back," she purred, "into the room. There is still time."

Drizzt's cold glare stopped her as surely as the point of a scimitar.

"The Spider Queen is the deity of our people," Vierna sternly reminded him. "I am one of those who speaks her will."

"I would not be so proud of that," Drizzt retorted, clinging to his anger against the wave of very real fear that threatened to defeat his principled stand.

Vierna slapped him hard across the face. "Go back to the ceremony!" she demanded.

"Go kiss a spider," Drizzt replied. "And may its pincers tear your cursed tongue from your mouth."

It was Vierna now who could not hold her hands steady. "You should take care when you speak to a high priestess," she warned.

"Damn your Spider Queen!" Drizzt spat. "Though I am certain Lolth found damnation eons ago!"

"She brings us power!" Vierna shrieked.

"She steals everything that makes us worth more than the stone we walk upon!" Drizzt screamed back.

"Sacrilege!" Vierna sneered, the word rolling off her tongue like the whistle of the matron mistress's snake whip.

A climactic, anguished scream erupted from inside the room.

"Evil union," Drizzt muttered, looking away.

"There is a gain," Vierna replied, quickly back in control of her temper.

Drizzt cast an accusing glance her way. "Have you had a similar experience?"

"I am a high priestess," was her simple reply.

Darkness hovered all about Drizzt, outrage so intense that he nearly swooned. "Did it please you?" he spat.

"It brought me power," Vierna growled back. "You cannot understand the value."

"What did it cost you?"

Vierna's slap nearly knocked Drizzt from his feet. "Come with me," she said, grabbing the front of his robe. "There is a place I want to show to you."

They moved out from Arach-Tinilith and across the Academy's courtyard. Drizzt hesitated when they reached the pillars that marked the entrance to Tier Breche.

"I cannot pass between these," he reminded his sister. "I am not yet graduated from Melee-Magthere."

"A formality," Vierna replied, not slowing her pace at all. "I am a mistress of Arach-Tinilith; I have the power to graduate you."

Drizzt wasn't certain of the truth of Vierna's claim, but she was indeed a mistress of Arach-Tinilith. As much as Drizzt feared the edicts of the Academy, he didn't want to anger Vierna again.

He followed her down the wide stone stairs and out into the meandering roadways of the city proper.

"Home?" he dared to ask after a short while.

"Not yet," came the curt reply. Drizzt didn't press the point any further.

They veered off to the eastern end of the great cavern, across from the wall that held House Do'Urden, and came to the entrances of three small tunnels, all guarded by glowing statues of giant scorpions. Vierna paused for just a moment to consider which was the correct course, then led on again, down the smallest of the tunnels.

The minutes became an hour, and still they walked. The passage widened and soon led them into a twisting catacomb of crisscrossing corridors. Drizzt quickly lost track of the path behind them as they made their way through, but Vierna followed a predetermined course that she knew well.

Then, beyond a low archway, the floor suddenly dropped away and they found themselves on a narrow ledge overlooking a wide chasm. Drizzt looked at his sister curiously but held his question when he saw that she was deep in the concentration. She uttered a few simple commands, then tapped herself and Drizzt on the forehead.

"Come," she instructed, and she and Drizzt stepped off the ledge and levitated down to the chasm floor.

A thin mist, from some unseen hot pool or tar pit, hugged the stone. Drizzt could sense the danger here, and the evil. A brooding wickedness hung in the air as tangibly as the mist.

"Do not fear," Vierna signaled to him. "I have put a spell of masking upon us. They cannot see us."

"They?" Drizzt's hands asked, but even as he motioned in the code, he heard a scuttling off to the side. He followed Vierna's gaze down to a distant boulder and the wretched thing perched upon it.

At first, Drizzt thought it was a drow elf, and from the waist up, it was indeed, though bloated and pale. Its lower body, though, resembled a spider, with eight arachnid legs to support its frame. The creature held a bow ready in its hands but seemed confused, as though it could not discern what had entered its lair.

Vierna was pleased by the disgust on her brother's face as he viewed the thing. "Look upon it well, younger brother," she signaled. "Behold the fate of those who anger the Spider Queen."

"What is it?" Drizzt signaled back quickly.

"A drider," Vierna whispered in his ear. Then, back in the silent code, she added, "Lolth is not a merciful deity."

Drizzt watched, mesmerized, as the drider shifted its position on the boulder, searching for the intruders. Drizzt couldn't tell if it was a male or female, so bloated was its torso, but he knew that it didn't matter. The creature was not a natural creation and would leave no descendants behind, whatever its gender. It was a tormented body, nothing more, hating itself, in all probability, more than everything else around it.

"I am merciful," Vierna continued silently, though she knew her brother's attention was fully on the drider. She rested back flat against the stone wall.

Drizzt spun on her, suddenly realizing her intent.

Then Vierna sank into the stone. "Goodbye, little brother," came her final call. "This is a better fate than you deserve."

"No!" Drizzt growled, and he clawed at the empty wall until an arrow sliced into his leg. The scimitars flashed out in his hands as he spun back to face the danger. The drider took aim for a second shot.

Drizzt meant to dive to the side, to the protection of another boulder, but his wounded leg immediately fell numb and useless. Poison.

Drizzt just got one blade up in time to deflect the second arrow, and he dropped to one knee to clutch at his wound. He could feel the cold poison making its way through his limb, but he stubbornly snapped off the arrow shaft and turned his attention back to the attacker. He would have to worry about the wound later, would have to hope that he could tend to it in time. Right now, his only concern was to get out of the chasm.

He turned to flee, to seek a sheltered spot where he could levitate back up to the ledge, but he found himself face-to-face with another drider.

An axe sliced by his shoulder, barely missing its mark. Drizzt blocked the return blow and launched his second scimitar into a thrust, which the drider stopped with a second axe.

Drizzt was composed now, and was confident that he could defeat this foe, even with one leg limiting his mobility—until an arrow cracked into his back.

Drizzt lurched forward under the weight of the blow, but managed to parry another attack from the drider before him. Drizzt dropped to his knees and fell face-down.

When the axe-wielding drider, thinking Drizzt dead, started toward him, Drizzt kicked into a roll that put him squarely under the creature's bulbous belly. He plunged his scimitar up with all his strength, then curled back under the deluge of spidery fluids.

The wounded drider tried to scurry away but fell to the side, its insides draining out onto the stone floor. Still, Drizzt had no hope. His arms, too, were numb now, and when the other wretched creature descended upon him, he could not hope to fight it off. He struggled to cling to consciousness, searching for some way out, battling to the bitter end. His eyelids became heavy. . . .

Then Drizzt felt a hand grab his robe, and he was roughly lifted to his feet and slammed against the stone wall.

He opened his eyes to see his sister's face.

"He lives," Drizzt heard her say. "We must get him back quickly and tend to his wounds"

Another figure moved in front of him.

"I thought this the best way," Vierna apologized.

"We cannot afford to lose him," came an unemotional reply. Drizzt recognized the voice from his past. He fought through the blur and forced his eyes to focus.

"Malice," he whispered. "Mother."

Her enraged punch brought him into a clearer mindset.

"Matron Malice!" she growled, her angry scowl only an inch from Drizzt's face. "Do not ever forget that!"

To Drizzt, her coldness rivaled the poison's, and his relief at seeing her faded away as quickly as it had flooded through him.

"You must learn your place!" Malice roared, reiterating the command that had haunted Drizzt all of his young life. "Hear my words," she demanded, and Drizzt heard them keenly. "Vierna brought you to this place to have you killed. She showed you mercy." Malice cast a disappointed glance at her daughter.

"I understand the will of the Spider Queen better than she," the matron continued, her spittle spraying Drizzt with every word. "If ever you speak ill of Lolth, our goddess, again, I will take you back to this place myself! But not to kill you; that would be too easy." She jerked Drizzt's head to the side so that he could look upon the grotesque remains of the drider he had killed.

"You will come back here," Malice assured him, "to become a drider."

# Part Four

# Guenhwyvar

What eyes are these that see
The pain I know in my innermost soul?
What eyes are these that see
The twisted strides of my kindred,
Led on in the wake of
toys unbridled:
Arrow, bolt, and sword tip?

Yours . . . aye, yours,
Straight run and muscled spring,
Soft on padded paws, sheathed claws,
Weapons rested for their need,
Stained not by frivolous blood
Or murderous deceit.

Face to face, my mirror;
Reflection in a still pool by light.
Would that I might keep that image
Upon this face mine own.

Would that I might keep that heart
Within my breast untainted.

Hold tight to the proud honor of your spirit,
Mighty Guenhwyvar,
And hold tight to my side,
My dearest friend.

–Drizzt Do'Urden

# 17 HOMECOMING

Drizzt was graduated—formally—on schedule and with the highest honors in his class. Perhaps Matron Malice had whispered into the right ears, smoothing over her son's indiscretions, but Drizzt suspected that more likely none of those present at the Ceremony of Graduation even remembered that he had left.

He moved through the decorated gate of House Do'Urden, drawing stares from the common soldiery, and over to the cavern floor below the balcony. "So I am home," he remarked under his breath, "for whatever that means." After what had happened in the drider lair, Drizzt wondered if he would ever view House Do'Urden as his home again. Matron Malice was expecting him. He didn't dare arrive late.

"It is good that you are home," Briza said to him when she saw him rise up over the balcony's railing.

Drizzt stepped tentatively through the entryway beside his oldest sister, trying to get a firm grasp on his surroundings. Home, Briza called it, but to Drizzt, House Do'Urden seemed as unfamiliar as the Academy had on his first day as a student. Ten years was not such a long time in the centuries of life a drow elf might know, but to Drizzt, more than the decade of absence now separated him from this place.

Maya joined them in the great corridor leading to the chapel anteroom.

"Greetings, Prince Drizzt," she said, and Drizzt couldn't tell if she was being sarcastic or not. "We have heard of the honors you achieved at Melee-Magthere. Your skill did House Do'Urden proud." In spite of her words, Maya could not hide a derisive chuckle as she finished the thought. "Glad, I am, that you did not become drider food."

Drizzt's glare stole the smile from her face.

Maya and Briza exchanged concerned glances. They knew of the punishment Vierna had put upon their younger brother, and of the vicious scolding he had received at the hands of Matron Malice. They each cautiously rested a hand on their snake whips, not knowing how foolish their dangerous young brother might have become.

It was not Matron Malice or Drizzt's sisters that now had Drizzt measuring every step before he took it. He knew where he stood with his mother and knew what he had to do to keep her appeased. There was another member of the family, though, that evoked both confusion and anger in Drizzt. Of all his kin, only Zaknafein pretended to be what he was not. As Drizzt made his way to the chapel, he glanced anxiously down every side passage, wondering when Zak would make his appearance.

"How long before you leave for patrol?" Maya asked, pulling Drizzt from his contemplations.

"Two days," Drizzt replied absently, his eyes still darting from shadow to shadow. Then he was at the anteroom door, with no sign of Zak. Perhaps the weapons master was within, standing beside Malice.

"We know of your indiscretions," Briza snapped, suddenly cold, as she placed her hand on the latch to the anteroom's door. Drizzt was not surprised by her outburst. He was beginning to expect such explosions from the high priestesses of the Spider Queen.

"Why could you not just enjoy the pleasures of the ceremony?" Maya added. "We are fortunate that the mistresses and the matron of the Academy were too involved in their own excitement to note your movements. You would have brought shame upon our entire house!"

"You might have placed Matron Malice in Lolth's disfavor," Briza was quick to add.

The best thing I could ever do for her, Drizzt thought. He quickly dismissed the notion, remembering Briza's uncanny proficiency at reading minds.

"Let us hope he did not," Maya said grimly to her sister. "The tides of war hang thick in the air."

"I have learned my place," Drizzt assured them. He bowed low. "Forgive me, my sisters, and know that the truth of the drow world is fast opening before my young eyes. Never will I disappoint House Do'Urden in such a way again."

So pleased were his sisters at the proclamation that the ambiguity of Drizzt's words slipped right past them. Then Drizzt, not wanting to push his luck too far, also slipped past them, making his way through the door, noting with relief that Zaknafein was not in attendance.

"All praises to the Spider Queen!" Briza yelled after him.

Drizzt paused and turned to meet her gaze. He bowed low a second time. "As it should be," he muttered.

⚔ ⚔ ⚔ ⚔ ⚔

Creeping behind the small group, Zak had studied Drizzt's every move, trying to measure the toll a decade at the Academy had exacted on the young fighter.

Gone now was the customary smile that lit Drizzt's face. Gone, too, Zak supposed, was the innocence that had kept this one apart from the rest of Menzoberranzan.

Zak leaned back heavily against the wall in a side passage. He had caught only portions of the conversation at the anteroom door. Most clearly he had heard Drizzt's heartfelt accord with Briza's honoring of Lolth.

"What have I done?" the weapons master asked himself. He looked back around the bend in the main corridor, but the door to the anteroom had already closed.

"Truly, when I look upon the drow—the drow warrior!—that was my most treasured, I shame for my cowardice," Zak lamented. "What has Drizzt lost that I might have saved?"

He drew his smooth sword from its scabbard, his sensitive fingers running the length of the razor edge. "A finer blade you would be had you tasted the blood of Drizzt Do'Urden, to deny this world, our world, another soul for its taking, to free that one from the unending torments of life!" He lowered the weapon's tip to the floor.

"But I am a coward," he said. "I have failed in the one act that could have brought meaning to my pitiful existence. The secondboy of House Do'Urden lives, it would appear, but Drizzt Do'Urden, my Two-hands, is long dead." Zak looked back to the emptiness where Drizzt had been standing, the weapons master's expression suddenly a grimace. "Yet this pretender lives.

"A drow warrior."

Zak's weapon clanged to the stone floor and his head slumped down to be caught by the embrace of his open palms, the only shield Zaknafein Do'Urden had ever found.

⚔ ⚔ ⚔ ⚔ ⚔

Drizzt spent the next day at rest, mostly in his room, trying to keep out of the way of the other members of his immediate family. Malice had dismissed him without a word in their initial meeting, but Drizzt did not want to confront her again. Likewise, he had little to say to Briza and Maya, fearing that sooner or later they would begin to understand the true connotations of his continuing stream of blasphemous responses. Most of all, though, Drizzt did not want to see Zaknafein, the mentor he had once thought of as his salvation against the realities around him, the one glowing light in the darkness that was Menzoberranzan.

That, too, Drizzt believed, had been only a lie.

On his second day home, when Narbondel, the timeclock of the city, had just begun its cycle of light, the door to Drizzt's small chamber swung open and Briza walked in. "An audience with Matron Malice," she said grimly.

A thousand thoughts rushed through Drizzt's mind as he grabbed his boots and followed his oldest sister down the passageways to the house chapel. Had Malice and the others discovered his true feelings toward their evil deity? What punishments did they now have waiting for him?

Unconsciously, Drizzt eyed the spider carvings on the chapel's arched entrance.

"You should be more familiar and more at ease with this place," Briza scolded, noting his discomfort. "It is the place of our people's highest glories."

Drizzt lowered his gaze and did not respond—and was careful not to even think of the many stinging retorts he felt in his heart.

His confusion doubled when they entered the chapel, for Rizzen, Maya, and Zaknafein stood before the matron mother, as expected. Beside them, though, stood Dinin and Vierna.

"We are all present," Briza said, taking her place at her mother's side.

"Kneel," Malice commanded, and the whole family fell to its knees. The matron mother paced slowly around them all, each pointedly dropping his or her eyes in reverence, or just in common sense, as the great lady walked by.

Malice stopped beside Drizzt. "You are confused by the presence of Dinin and Vierna," she said. Drizzt looked up at her. "Do you not yet understand the subtle methods of our survival?"

"I had thought that my brother and sister were to continue on at the Academy," Drizzt explained.

"That would not be to our advantage," Malice replied.

"Does it not bring a house strength to have mistresses and masters seated at the Academy?" Drizzt dared to ask.

"It does," replied Malice, "but it separates the power. You have heard tidings of war?"

"I have heard hinting of trouble," said Drizzt, looking over at Vierna, "though nothing more tangible."

"Hinting?" Malice huffed, angered that her son could not understand the importance. "They are more than most houses ever hear before the blade falls!" She spun away from Drizzt and addressed the whole group. "The rumors hold truth," she declared.

"Who?" asked Briza. "What house conspires against House Do'Urden?"

"None behind us in rank," Dinin replied, though the question had not been asked to him and it was not his place to speak unbidden.

"How do you know this?" Malice asked, letting the oversight pass. Malice understood Dinin's value and knew that his contributions to this discussion would be important.

"We are the ninth house of the city," Dinin reasoned, "but among our ranks we claim four high priestesses, two of them former mistresses of Arach-Tinilith." He looked at Zak. "We have, as well, two former masters of Melee-Magthere, and Drizzt was awarded the highest laurels from the school of fighters. Our soldiers number nearly four hundred, all skilled and battle-tested. Only a few houses claim more."

"What is your point?" Briza asked sharply.

"We are the ninth house," Dinin laughed, "but few above us could defeat us. . . ."

"And none behind," Matron Malice finished for him. "You show good judgment, Elderboy. I have come to the same conclusions."

"One of the great houses fears House Do'Urden," Vierna concluded. "It needs us gone to protect its own position."

"That is my belief," Malice answered. "An uncommon practice, for family wars usually are initiated by the lower-ranking house, desiring a better position within the city hierarchy."

"Then we must take great care," Briza said.

Drizzt listened carefully to their words, trying to make sense of it all. His eyes never left Zaknafein, though, who knelt impassively at the side. What did the callous weapons master think of all this? Drizzt wondered. Did the thought of such a war thrill him, that he might be able to kill more dark elves?

Whatever his feelings, Zak gave no outward clue. He sat quietly and by all appearances was not even listening to the conversation.

"It would not be Baenre," Briza said, her words sounding like a plea for confirmation. "Certainly we have not yet become a threat to them!"

"We must hope you are correct," Malice replied grimly, remembering vividly her tour of the ruling house. "Likely, it is one of the weaker houses above us, fearing its own unsteady position. I have not yet been able to learn any incriminating information against any in particular, so we must prepare for the worst. Thus, I have called Vierna and Dinin back to my side."

"If we learn of our enemies. . . ." Drizzt began impulsively. All eyes snapped upon him. It was bad enough for the elderboy to speak without being addressed, but for the secondboy, just graduated from the Academy, the act could be considered blasphemous.

Wanting all perspectives, Matron Malice again let the oversight pass. "Continue," she prompted.

"If we discover which house plots against us," Drizzt said quietly, "could we not expose it?"

"To what end?" Briza snarled at him. "Conspiracy without action is no crime."

"Then might we use reason?" Drizzt pressed, continuing against the barrage of incredulous glares that came at him from every face in the room—except from Zak's. "If we are the stronger, then let them submit without battle. Rank House Do'Urden as it should be and let the assumed threat to the weaker house be ended."

Malice grabbed Drizzt by the front of his cloak and heaved him to his feet. "I forgive your foolish thoughts," she growled, "this time!" She dropped him back to the floor, and the silent reprimands of his siblings descended upon him.

Again, though, Zak's expression did not match the others in the room. Indeed, Zak put a hand up over his mouth to hide his amusement. Perhaps there remained a bit of the Drizzt Do'Urden he had known, he dared to hope. Perhaps the Academy had not fully tainted the young fighter's spirit.

Malice whirled on the rest of the family, simmering fury and lust glowing in her eyes. "This is not the time to fear. This," she cried, a slender finger pointing out from in front of her face, "is the time to dream! We are House Do'Urden, Daermon N'a'shezbaernon, of power beyond the understanding of the great houses. We are the unknown entity of this war. We hold every advantage!

"Ninth house?" she laughed. "In short time, only seven houses will remain ahead of us!"

"What of the patrol?" Briza cut in. "Are we to allow the secondboy to go off alone, exposed?"

"The patrol will begin our advantage," the conniving matron explained. "Drizzt will go, and included in his group will be a member of at least four of the houses above us."

"One may strike at him," Briza reasoned.

"No," Malice assured her. "Our enemies in the coming war would not reveal themselves so clearly—not yet. The appointed assassin would have to defeat two Do'Urdens in such a confrontation."

"Two?" asked Vierna.

"Again, Lolth has shown us her favor," explained Malice. "Dinin will lead Drizzt's patrol group."

The elderboy's eyes lit up at the news. "Then Drizzt and I might become the assassins in this conflict," he purred.

The smile disappeared from the matron mother's face. "You will not strike without my consent," she warned in a tone so cold that Dinin fully understood the consequences of disobedience, "as you have done in the past."

Drizzt did not miss the reference to Nalfein, his murdered brother. His mother knew! Malice had done nothing to punish her murderous son. Now Drizzt's hand went up to his face, to hide an expression of horror that only could have brought him trouble in this setting.

"You are there to learn," Matron Malice said to Dinin, "to protect your brother, as Drizzt is there to protect you. Do not destroy our advantage for the gain of a single kill." An evil smile found its way back onto her bone-hued face. "But, if you learn of our enemy, . . ." she said.

"If the proper opportunity presents itself, . . ." Briza finished, guessing her mother's wicked thoughts and throwing an equally vile smile the matron's way.

Malice looked upon her eldest daughter with approval. Briza would prove a fine successor for the house!

Dinin's smile became wide and lascivious. Nothing pleased the elderboy of House Do'Urden more than the opportunity for an assassination.

"Go, then, my family," Malice said. "Remember that unfriendly eyes are upon us, watching our every move, waiting for the time to strike."

Zak was the first out of the chapel, as always, this time with an added spring in his step. It wasn't the prospect of fighting another war that guided his moves, though the thought of killing more clerics of the Spider Queen certainly pleased him. Rather, Drizzt's display of naiveté, his continued misconceptions of the common weal of drow existence, brought Zak hope.

Drizzt watched him go, thinking Zak's strides reflected his desire to kill. Drizzt didn't know whether to follow and confront the weapons master here and now or to let it pass, to shrug it away as readily as he had dismissed most of the cruel world around him. The decision was made for him when Matron Malice stepped in front of him and kept him in the chapel.

"To you, I say this," she began when they were alone. "You have heard the mission I placed upon your shoulders. I will not tolerate failure!"

Drizzt shrank back from the power of her voice.

"Protect your brother," came the grim warning, "or I shall give you to Lolth for judgment."

Drizzt understood the implications, but the matron took the pleasure to spell them out anyway.

"You would not enjoy your life as a drider."

A lightning blast cut across the still black waters of the underground lake, searing the heads of the approaching water trolls. Sounds of battle echoed through the cavern.

Drizzt had one monster—scrags, they were called—cornered on a small peninsula, blocking the wretched thing's path back to the water. Normally, a single drow faced off evenly against a water troll would not have the advantage, but as the others of his patrol group had come to see in the past few tendays, Drizzt was no ordinary young drow.

The scrag came on, oblivious to its peril. A single, blinding movement from Drizzt lopped off the creature's reaching arms. Drizzt moved in quickly for the kill, knowing too well the regenerative powers of trolls.

Then another scrag slipped out of the water at his back.

Drizzt had expected this, but he gave no outward indication that he saw the second scrag coming. He kept his concentration ahead of him, driving deep slashes into the maimed and all but defenseless troll's torso.

Just as the monster behind him was about to latch its claws onto him, Drizzt fell to his knees and cried, "Now!"

The concealed panther, crouched in the shadows at the peninsula's base, did not hesitate. One great stride brought Guenhwyvar into position, and it sprang, crashing heavily onto the unsuspecting scrag, tearing the life from the thing before it could respond to the attack.

Drizzt finished off his troll and turned to admire the panther's work. He extended his hand, and the great cat nuzzled it. How well the two fighters had come to know each other! thought Drizzt.

Another blast of lightning thundered in, this one close enough to steal Drizzt's sight.

"Guenhwyvar!" Masoj Hun'ett, the bolt's caster, cried. "To my side!"

The panther managed to brush against Drizzt's leg as it moved to obey. When his vision returned, Drizzt walked off in the other direction, not wanting to view the scolding that Guenhwyvar always seemed to receive when he and the cat worked together.

Masoj watched Drizzt's back as he went, wanting to put a third bolt right between the young Do'Urden's shoulder blades. The wizard of House Hun'ett did not miss the specter of Dinin Do'Urden, off to the side, watching with more than casual glances.

"Learn your loyalties!" Masoj snarled at Guenhwyvar. Too often, the panther left the wizard's side to join in combat with Drizzt. Masoj knew that the cat was better complemented by the moves of a fighter, but he knew, too, the vulnerability of a wizard involved in spellcasting. Masoj wanted Guenhwyvar at his side, protecting him from enemies—he shot another glance at Dinin—and "friends" alike.

He threw the statuette to the ground at his feet. "Begone!" he commanded.

In the distance, Drizzt had engaged another scrag and made short work of it as well. Masoj shook his head as he watched the display of swordsmanship. Every day, Drizzt grew stronger.

"Give the order to kill him soon, Matron SiNafay," Masoj whispered. The young wizard did not know how much longer he would be able to carry out the task. Masoj wondered whether he could win the fight even now.

⚔ ⚔ ⚔ ⚔ ⚔

Drizzt shielded his eyes as he struck a torch to seal a dead troll's wounds. Only fire ensured that trolls would not recuperate, even from the grave.

The other battles had died away as well, Drizzt noted, and he saw the flames of torches springing up all across the bank of the lake. He wondered if all of his twelve drow companions had survived, though he also wondered if he truly cared. Others were more than ready to take their places.

Drizzt knew that the only companion who really mattered—Guenhwyvar—was safely back in its home on the Astral Plane.

"Form a guard!" came Dinin's echoing command as the slaves, goblins, and orcs moved in to search for troll treasure, and to salvage whatever they might of the scrags.

When the fires had consumed the scrag he'd set ablaze, Drizzt dipped his torch in the black water, then paused for a moment to let his eyes readjust to the darkness. "Another day," he said softly, "another enemy defeated."

He liked the excitement of patrolling, the thrill of the edge of danger, and the knowledge that he was now putting his weapons to use against vile monsters.

Even here, though, Drizzt could not escape the lethargy that had come to pervade his life, the general resignation that marked his every step. For, though his battles these days were fought against the horrors of the Underdark, monsters killed of necessity, Drizzt had not forgotten the meeting in the chapel of House Do'Urden.

He knew that his scimitars soon would be put to use against the flesh of drow elves.

⚔ ⚔ ⚔ ⚔ ⚔

Zaknafein looked out over Menzoberranzan, as he so often did when Drizzt's patrol group was out of the city. Zak was torn between wanting to sneak out of the house to fight at Drizzt's side, and hoping that the patrol would return with the news that Drizzt had been slain.

Would Zak ever find the answer to the dilemma of the youngest Do'Urden? he wondered. Zak knew that he could not leave the house; Matron Malice was keeping a very close eye on him. She sensed his anguish over Drizzt, Zak knew, and she most definitely did not approve. Zak was often her lover, but they shared little other than that.

Zak thought back to the battles he and Malice had fought over Vierna, another child of common concern, centuries before. Vierna was a female, her fate sealed from the moment of her birth, and Zak could do nothing to halt the assault of the Spider Queen's overwhelming religion.

Did Malice fear that he might have better luck influencing the actions of a male child? Apparently the matron did, but even Zak was not so certain if her fears were justified; even he couldn't measure his influence over Drizzt.

He peered out over the city now, silently watching for the patrol group's return—waiting, as always, for Drizzt's safe return, but secretly hoping, that his dilemma would be ended by the claws and fangs of a lurking monster.

# 18
# The Back Room

"My greetings, Faceless One," the high priestess said, pushing past Alton into his private chambers in Sorcere.

"And mine to you, Mistress Vierna," Alton replied, trying to keep the fear out of his voice. Vierna Do'Urden coming to see him at this time had to be more than coincidence. "What act has brought me the honor of a visit from a mistress of Arach-Tinilith?"

"No longer a mistress," said Vierna. "I have returned to my home."

Alton paused to consider the news. He knew that Dinin Do'Urden had also resigned his position at the Academy.

"Matron Malice has brought her family back together," Vierna continued. "There are stirrings of war. You have heard them, no doubt?"

"Just rumors," Alton stuttered, now beginning to understand why Vierna had come to call on him. House Do'Urden had used the Faceless One before in its plotting—in its attempt to assassinate Alton! Now, with rumors of war whispered throughout Menzoberranzan, Matron Malice was reestablishing her network of spies and assassins.

"You know of them?" Vierna asked sharply.

"I have heard little," Alton breathed, careful now not to anger the powerful female. "Not enough to report to your house. I did not even suspect that House Do'Urden was involved until now, when you informed me." Alton could only hope that Vierna had no detection spell aimed at his words.

Vierna relaxed, apparently appeased by the explanation. "Listen more carefully to the rumors, Faceless One," she said. "My brother and I have left the Academy; you are to be the eyes and ears of House Do'Urden in this place."

"But . . ." Alton stuttered.

Vierna held up a hand to stop him. "We know of our failure in our last transaction," she said. She bowed low, something a high priestess rarely did to a male. "Matron Malice sends her deepest apologies that the unguent you received for the assassination of Alton DeVir did not restore the features to your face."

Alton nearly choked on the words, now understanding why an unknown messenger had delivered the jar of healing salve some thirty years before. The cloaked figure was an agent of House Do'Urden, come to repay the Faceless One for his assassination of Alton! Of course, Alton had never even tried the unguent. With his luck, it would have worked, and would have restored the features of Alton DeVir.

"This time, your payment cannot fail," Vierna went on, though Alton, too caught up in the irony of it all, hardly listened. "House Do'Urden possesses a wizard's staff but no wizard worthy to wield it. It belonged to Nalfein, my brother, who died in the victory over DeVir."

Alton wanted to strike out at her. Even he wasn't that stupid, though.

"If you can discern which house plots against House Do'Urden," Vierna promised, "the staff will be yours! A treasure indeed for such a small act."

"I will do what I can," Alton replied, having no other response to the incredible offer.

"That is all Matron Malice asks of you," said Vierna, and she left the wizard, quite certain that House Do'Urden had secured a capable agent within the Academy.

⚔ ⚔ ⚔ ⚔ ⚔

"Dinin and Vierna Do'Urden have resigned their positions," said Alton excitedly as the diminutive matron mother came to him later that same evening.

"This is already known to me," replied SiNafay Hun'ett.

She looked around disdainfully at the littered and scorched room, then took a seat at the small table.

"There is more," Alton said quickly, not wanting SiNafay to get upset about being disturbed over old news. "I have had a visitor this day, Mistress Vierna Do'Urden!"

"She suspects?" Matron SiNafay growled.

"No, no!" Alton replied. "Quite the opposite. House Do'Urden wishes to employ me as a spy, as it once employed the Faceless One to assassinate me!"

SiNafay paused for a moment, stunned, then issued a laugh straight from her belly. "Ah, the ironies of our lives!" she roared.

"I had heard that Dinin and Vierna were sent to the Academy only to oversee the education of their younger brother," remarked Alton.

"An excellent cover," SiNafay replied. "Vierna and Dinin were sent as spies for the ambitious Matron Malice. My compliments to her."

"Now they suspect trouble," Alton stated, sitting opposite his matron mother.

"They do," agreed SiNafay. "Masoj patrols with Drizzt, but House Do'Urden has also managed to plant Dinin in the group."

"Then Masoj is in danger," reasoned Alton.

"No," said SiNafay. "House Do'Urden does not know that House Hun'ett perpetrates the threat against it, else it would not have come to you for information. Matron Malice knows your identity."

A look of terror crossed Alton's face.

"Not your true identity," SiNafay laughed at him. "She knows the Faceless One as Gelroos Hun'ett, and she would not have come to a Hun'ett if she suspected our house."

"Then we have an excellent opportunity to throw House Do'Urden into chaos!" Alton cried. "If I implicate another house, even Baenre, perhaps, our position will be strengthened." He chuckled at the possibilities. "Malice will reward me with a staff of great power—a weapon I will turn against her at the proper moment!"

"Matron Malice!" SiNafay corrected sternly. Even though she and Malice were soon to be open enemies, SiNafay would not permit a male to show such disrespect to a matron mother. "Do you really believe that you could carry out such a deception?"

"When Mistress Vierna returns . . ."

"You will not deal with a lesser priestess with such valued information, foolish DeVir. You will face Matron Malice herself, a formidable foe. If she sees through your lies, do you know what she will do to your body?"

Alton gulped audibly. "I am willing to take the risk," he said, crossing his arms resolutely on the table.

"What of House Hun'ett when the biggest lie is revealed?" SiNafay asked. "What advantage will we enjoy when Matron Malice knows the Faceless One's true identity?"

"I understand," Alton answered, crestfallen but unable to refute SiNafay's logic. "Then what are we to do? What am I to do?"

Matron SiNafay was already considering their next moves. "You will resign your tenure," she said at length. "Return to House Hun'ett, within my protection."

"Such an act might also implicate House Hun'ett to Matron Malice," Alton reasoned.

"It may," replied SiNafay, "but it is the safest route. I will go to Matron Malice in feigned anger, telling her to leave House Hun'ett out of her troubles. If she wishes to make an informant of a member of my family, then she should come to me for permission—though I'll not grant it this time!"

SiNafay smiled at the possibilities of such an encounter. "My anger, my fear, alone could implicate a greater house against House Do'Urden, even a conspiracy between more than one house," she said, obviously enjoying the added benefits. "Matron Malice will certainly have much to think about, and much to worry about!"

Alton hadn't even heard SiNafay's last comments. The words about granting her permission "this time" had brought a disturbing notion into his mind. "And did she?" he dared to ask, though his words were barely audible.

"What do you mean?" asked SiNafay, not following his thoughts.

"Did Matron Malice come to you?" Alton continued, frightened but needing an answer. "Thirty years ago. Did Matron SiNafay grant her permission for Gelroos Hun'ett to become an agent, an assassin to complete House DeVir's elimination?"

A wide smile spread across SiNafay's face, but it vanished in the blink of an eye as she threw the table across the room, grabbed Alton by the front of his robes, and pulled him roughly to within an inch of her scowling visage.

"Never confuse personal feelings with politics!" the tiny but obviously strong matron growled, her tone carrying the unmistakable weight of an open threat. "And never ask me such a question again!"

She threw Alton to the floor but didn't release him from her penetrating glare.

Alton had known all along that he was merely a pawn in the intrigue between House Hun'ett and House Do'Urden, a necessary link for Matron SiNafay to carry out her treacherous plans. Every now and, though, Alton's personal grudge against House Do'Urden caused him to forget his lowly place in this conflict. Looking up now at SiNafay's bared power, he realized that he had overstepped the bounds of his position.

⚔ ⚔ ⚔ ⚔ ⚔

At the back end of the mushroom grove, the southern wall of the cavern that housed Menzoberranzan, was a small, heavily guarded cave. Beyond the ironbound doors stood a single room, used only for gatherings of the city's eight ruling matron mothers.

The smoke of a hundred sweet-smelling candles permeated the air; the matron mothers liked it that way. After almost half a century of studying scrolls in the candlelight of Sorcere, Alton did not mind the light, but he was indeed uncomfortable in the chamber. He sat at the back end of a spider-shaped table, in a small, unadorned chair reserved for guests of the council. Between the table's eight hairy legs were the ruling matron mothers' thrones, all jeweled and dazzling in the candlelight.

The matrons filed in, pompous and wicked, casting belittling glares at the male. SiNafay, at Alton's side, put a hand on his knee and gave him a reassuring wink. She would not have dared to request a gathering of the ruling council if she was not certain of the worthiness of her news. The ruling matron mothers viewed their seats as honorary in nature and did not appreciate being brought together except in times of crisis.

At the head of the spider table sat Matron Baenre, the most powerful figure in all of Menzoberranzan, an ancient and withered female with malicious eyes and a mouth unaccustomed to smiles.

"We are gathered, SiNafay," Baenre said when all eight members had found their appointed chairs. "For what reason have you summoned the council?"

"To discuss a punishment," SiNafay replied.

"Punishment?" Matron Baenre echoed, confused. The recent years had been unusually quiet in the drow city, without an incident since the Teken'duis Freth conflict. To the First Matron's knowledge, no acts had been committed that might require a punishment, certainly none so blatant as to force the ruling council to action. "What individual deserves this?"

"Not an individual," explained Matron SiNafay. She glanced around at her peers, measuring their interest. "A house," she said bluntly. "Daermon N'a'shezbaernon, House Do'Urden." Several gasps of disbelief came in reply, as SiNafay had expected.

"House Do'Urden?" Matron Baenre questioned, surprised that any would implicate Matron Malice. By all of Baenre's knowledge, Malice remained in high regard with the Spider Queen, and House Do'Urden had recently placed two instructors in the Academy.

"For what crime do you dare to charge House Do'Urden?" asked one of the other matrons.

"Are these words of fear, SiNafay?" Matron Baenre had to ask. Several of the ruling matrons had expressed concern about House Do'Urden. It was well known that Matron Malice desired a seat on the ruling council, and, by all measures of the power of her house, she seemed destined to get it.

"I have appropriate cause," SiNafay insisted.

"The others seem to doubt you," replied Matron Baenre. "You should explain your accusation—quickly, if you value your reputation."

SiNafay knew that more than her reputation was at stake; in

Menzoberranzan, a false accusation was a crime on par with murder. "We all remember the fall of House DeVir," SiNafay began. "Seven of us now gathered sat upon the ruling council beside Matron Ginafae DeVir."

"House DeVir is no more," Matron Baenre reminded her.

"Because of House Do'Urden," SiNafay said bluntly.

This time the gasps came out as open anger.

"How dare you speak such words?" came one reply.

"Thirty years!" came another. "The issue has been forgotten!"

Matron Baenre quieted them all before the clamor rose into violent action—a not uncommon occurrence in the council chamber. "SiNafay," she said through the dry sneer on her lips. "One cannot make such an accusation; one cannot discuss such beliefs openly so long after the event! You know our ways. If House Do'Urden did indeed commit this act, as you insist, it deserves our compliments, not our punishment, for it carried it through to perfection. House DeVir is no more, I say. It does not exist!"

Alton shifted uneasily, caught somewhere between rage and despair. SiNafay was far from dismayed, though; this was going exactly as she had envisioned and hoped.

"Oh, but it does!" she responded, rising to her feet. She pulled the hood from Alton's head. "In this person!"

"Gelroos?" asked Matron Baenre, not understanding.

"Not Gelroos," SiNafay replied. "Gelroos Hun'ett died the night House DeVir died. This male, Alton DeVir, assumed Gelroos's identity and position, hiding from further attacks by House Do'Urden!"

Baenre whispered some instructions to the matron at her right side, then waited as she went through the semantics of a spell. Baenre motioned for SiNafay to return to her seat then faced Alton.

"Speak your name," Baenre commanded.

"I am Alton DeVir," Alton said, gaining strength from the identity he had waited so very long to proclaim, "son of Matron Ginafae and a student of Sorcere on the night House Do'Urden attacked."

Baenre looked to the matron at her side.

"He speaks the truth," the matron assured her. Whispers sprang up all around the spider table, of amusement more than anything else.

"That is why I summoned the ruling council," SiNafay quickly explained.

"Very well, SiNafay," said Matron Baenre. "My compliments to you, Alton DeVir, on your resourcefulness and ability to survive. For a male, you have shown great courage and wisdom. Surely you both know that the council cannot exact punishment upon a house for a deed committed so long ago. Why would we so desire? Matron Malice Do'Urden sits in the favor of the Spider Queen; her house shows great promise. You must reveal to us greater need if you wish any punishment against House Do'Urden."

"I do not wish such a thing," SiNafay quickly replied. "This matter, thirty years removed, is no longer in the realm of the ruling council. House Do'Urden does indeed show promise, my peers, with four high priestesses and a host of other weapons, not the least of which being their secondboy, Drizzt, first graduate of his class." She had purposely mentioned Drizzt, knowing that the name would strike a wound in Matron Baenre. Baenre's own prized son, Berg'inyon, had spent the last nine years ranked behind the wonderful young Do'Urden.

"Then why have you bothered us?" Matron Baenre demanded, an unmistakable edge in her voice.

"To ask you to close your eyes," SiNafay purred. "Alton is a Hun'ett now, under my protection. He demands vengeance for the act committed against his family, and, as a surviving member of the attacked family, he has the right of accusation."

"House Hun'ett will stand beside him?" Matron Baenre asked, turning curious and amused.

"Indeed," replied SiNafay. "Thus is House Hun'ett bound!"

"Vengeance?" another matron quipped, also now more amused than angered. "Or fear? It would seem to my ears that the matron of House Hun'ett uses this pitiful DeVir creature for her own gain. House Do'Urden aspires to higher ranking, and Matron Malice desires to sit upon the ruling council, a threat to House Hun'ett, perhaps?"

"Be it vengeance or prudence, my claim—Alton DeVir's claim—must be deemed as legitimate," replied SiNafay, "to our mutual gain." She smiled wickedly and looked straight to the First Matron. "To the gain of our sons, perhaps, in their quest for recognition."

"Indeed," replied Matron Baenre in a chuckle that sounded more like a cough. A war between Hun'ett and Do'Urden might be to everyone's gain, but not, Baenre suspected, as SiNafay believed. Malice was a powerful matron, and her family truly deserved a ranking higher than ninth. If the fight did come, Malice probably would get her seat on the council, replacing SiNafay.

Matron Baenre looked around at the other matrons, and guessed from their hopeful expressions that they shared her thoughts. Let Hun'ett and Do'Urden fight it out; whatever the outcome, the threat of Matron Malice would be ended. Perhaps, Baenre hoped, a certain young Do'Urden male would fall in battle, propelling her own son into the position he deserved.

Then the First Matron spoke the words SiNafay had come to hear, the silent permission of Menzoberranzan's ruling council.

"This matter is settled, my sisters," Matron Baenre declared, to the accepting nods of all at the table. "It is good that we never met this day."

# 19
# Promises of Glory

"Have you found the trail?" Drizzt whispered, moving up beside the great panther. He gave Guenhwyvar a pat on the side and knew from the slackness of the cat's muscles that no danger was nearby.

"Gone, then," Drizzt said, staring off into the emptiness of the corridor in front of them. "'Wicked gnomes, my brother called them when we found the tracks by the pool. Wicked and stupid." He sheathed his scimitar and knelt beside the panther, his arm comfortable draped across Guenhwyvar's back. "They're smart enough to elude our patrol."

The cat looked up as if it had understood his every word, and Drizzt rubbed a hand roughly over Guenhwyvar's, his finest friend's, head. Drizzt remembered clearly his elation on the day, a tenday before, when Dinin had announced—to Masoj Hun'ett's outrage—that Guenhwyvar would be deployed at the patrol's point position beside Drizzt.

"The cat is mine!" Masoj had reminded Dinin.

"You are mine!" Dinin, the patrol leader, had replied, ending any further debate. Whenever the figurine's magic would permit, Masoj summoned Guenhwyvar from the Astral Plane and bid the cat to run up in front, bringing Drizzt an added degree of safety and a valued companion.

Drizzt knew from the unfamiliar heat patterns on the wall that they had gone the limit of their patrol route. He had purposely put a lot of ground, more than was advised, between himself and the rest of the patrol. Drizzt had confidence that he and Guenhwyvar could take care of themselves, and with the others far behind, he could relax and enjoy the wait. The minutes Drizzt spent in solitude gave him the time he needed in his endless effort to sort through his confused emotions. Guenhwyvar, seemingly non-judgmental and always approving, offered Drizzt a perfect audience for his audible contemplations.

"I begin to wonder the worth of it all," Drizzt whispered to the cat. "I do not doubt the value of these patrols—this tenday alone, we have defeated a dozen monsters that might have brought great harm to the city—but to what end?"

He looked deeply into the panther's saucer eyes and found sympathy there, and Drizzt knew that Guenhwyvar somehow understood his dilemma.

"Perhaps I still do not know who I am," Drizzt mused, "or who my people are. Every time I find a clue to the truth, it leads me down a path that I dare not continue upon, to conclusions I cannot accept."

"You are drow," came a reply behind them. Drizzt turned abruptly to see Dinin a few feet away, a look of grave concern on his face.

"The gnomes have fled beyond our reach," Drizzt said, trying to deflect his brother's concerns.

"Have you not learned what it means to be a drow?" Dinin asked. "Have you not come to understand the course of our history and the promise of our future?"

"I know of our history as it was taught at the Academy," Drizzt replied. "They were the very first lessons we received. Of our future, and more so of the place we now reside, though, I do not understand."

"You know of our enemies," Dinin prompted.

"Countless enemies," replied Drizzt with a heavy sigh. "They fill the holes of the Underdark, always waiting for us to let down our guard. We will not, and our enemies will fall to our power."

"Ah, but our true enemies do not reside in the lightless caverns of our world," said Dinin with a sly smile. "Theirs is a world strange and evil." Drizzt knew who Dinin was referring to, but he suspected that his brother was hiding something.

"The faeries," Drizzt whispered, and the word prompted a jumble of emotions within him. All of his life, he had been told of his evil cousins, of how they had forced the drow into the bowels of the world. Busily engaged in the duties of his everyday life, Drizzt did not think of them often, but whenever they came to mind, he used their name as a litany against everything he hated in his life. If Drizzt could somehow blame the surface elves—as every other drow seemed to blame them—for the injustices of drow society, he could find hope for the future of his people. Rationally, Drizzt had to dismiss the stirring legends of the elven war as another of the endless stream of lies, but in his heart and hopes, Drizzt clung desperately to those words.

He looked back to Dinin. "The faeries," he said again, "whatever they may be."

Dinin chuckled at his brother's relentless sarcasm; it had become so commonplace. "They are as you have learned," he assured Drizzt. "Without worth and vile beyond your imagination, the tormentors of our people, who banished us in eons past; who forced—"

"I know the tales," Drizzt interrupted, alarmed at the increasing volume of his excited brother's voice. Drizzt glanced over his shoulder. "If the patrol is ended, let us meet the others closer to the city. This place is too dangerous for such discussions." He rose to his feet and started back, Guenhwyvar at his side.

"Not as dangerous as the place I soon will lead you," Dinin replied with that same sly smile.

Drizzt stopped and looked at him curiously.

"I suppose you should know," Dinin teased. "We were selected because we are the finest of the patrol groups, and you have certainly played an important role in our attaining that honor."

"Chosen for what?"

"In a fortnight, we will leave Menzoberranzan," explained Dinin. "Our trail will take us many days and many miles from the city."

"How long?" Drizzt asked, suddenly very curious.

"Two tendays, maybe three," replied Dinin, "but well worth the time. We shall be the ones, my young brother, who enact a measure of revenge upon our most hated foes, who strike a glorious blow for the Spider Queen!"

Drizzt thought that he understood, but the notion was too outrageous for him to be certain.

"The elves!" Dinin beamed. "We have been chosen for a surface raid!"

Drizzt was not as openly excited as his brother, unsure of the implications of such a mission. At last he would get to view the surface elves and face the truth of his heart and hopes. Something more real to Drizzt, the disappointment he had known for so many years, tempered his elation, reminded him that while the truth of the elves might bring an excuse to the dark world of his kin, it might instead take away something more important. He was unsure how to feel.

⚔ ⚔ ⚔ ⚔ ⚔

"The surface," Alton mused. "My sister went there once—on a raid. A most marvelous experience, so she said!" He looked at Masoj, not knowing how to figure the forlorn expression on the young Hun'ett's face. "Now your patrol makes the journey. I envy you."

"I am not going," Masoj declared.

"Why?" Alton gasped. "This is a rare opportunity indeed. Menzoberranzan—to the anger of Lolth, I am certain—has not staged a surface raid in two decades. It may be twenty more years before the next, and by then you will no longer be among the patrols."

Masoj looked out from the small window of Alton's room in House Hun'ett, surveying the compound.

"Besides," Alton continued quietly, "up there, so far from prying eyes, you might find the chance to dispose of two Do'Urden's. Why would you not go?"

"Have you forgotten a ruling that you played a part in?" Masoj asked, whirling on Alton accusingly. "Two decades ago, the masters of Sorcere decided that no wizards are to travel anywhere near the surface!"

"Of course," Alton replied, remembering the meeting. Sorcere seemed so distant to him now, though he had been within the Hun'ett house for only a few tendays. "We concluded that drow magic may work differently—unexpectedly—under the open sky," he explained. "On that raid twenty years ago—"

"I know the story," Masoj growled, and he finished the sentence for Alton. "A wizard's fireball expanded beyond its normal dimensions, killing several drow. Dangerous side effects, you masters called it, though I've a belief that the wizard conveniently disposed of some enemies under the guise of an accident!"

"Yes," Alton agreed. "So said the rumors. In the absence of evidence . . ." He let the thought go, seeing that he was doing little to comfort Masoj. "That was so long ago," he said, trying to offer some hope. "Have you no recourse?"

"None," Masoj replied. "Things move so very slowly in Menzoberranzan; I doubt that the masters have even begun their investigation into the matter."

"A pity," Alton said. "It would have been the perfect opportunity."

"No more of that!" Masoj scolded. "Matron SiNafay has not given me her command to eliminate Drizzt Do'Urden or his brother. You have already been warned to keep your personal desires to yourself. When the matron bids me to strike, I will not fail her. Opportunities can be created."

"You speak as if you already know how Drizzt Do'Urden will die," Alton said.

An smile spread over Masoj's face as he reached into the pocket of his robe and produced the onyx figurine, his unthinking magical slave, which the foolish Drizzt had come to trust so dearly. "Oh, I do," he replied, giving the statuette of Guenhwyvar an easy toss, then catching it and holding it out on display.

"I do."

⚔ ⚔ ⚔ ⚔ ⚔

The members of the chosen raiding party quickly came to realize that this would be no ordinary mission. They did not go out on patrol from Menzoberranzan at all during the next tenday. Rather, they remained, day and night, sequestered within a barrack of Melee-Magthere. Through nearly every waking hour, the raiders huddled around an oval table in a conference room, hearing the detailed plans of their pending adventure, and, over and over again, Master Hatch'net, the master of Lore, spinning his tales of the vile elves.

Drizzt listened intently to the stories, allowing himself, forcing himself, to fall within Hatch'net's hypnotic web. The tales had to be true; Drizzt did not know what he would hold onto to preserve his principles if they were not.

Dinin presided over the raid's tactical preparations, displaying maps of the long tunnels the group would travel, grilling them over and over until they had memorized the route perfectly.

To this, as well, the eager raiders—except for Drizzt—listened intently, all the while fighting to keep their excitement from bursting out in a wild cheer. As the tenday of preparations neared its end, Drizzt took note that one member of the patrol group had not been attending. At first, Drizzt had reasoned that Masoj was learning his duties in the raid in Sorcere, with his old masters. With the departure time fast approaching and the battle plans clearly taking shape, though, Drizzt began to understand that Masoj would not be joining them.

"Where is our wizard?" Drizzt dared to ask in the late hours of one session.

Dinin, not appreciating the interruption, glared at his brother. "Masoj will not be joining us," he answered, knowing that others might now share Drizzt's concern, a distraction they could not afford at such a critical time.

"Sorcere has decreed that no wizards may travel to the surface," Master Hatch'net explained. "Masoj Hun'ett will await your return in the city. It is a great loss to you indeed, for Masoj has proven his worth many times over. Fear not, though, for a cleric of Arach-Tinilith shall accompany you."

"What of . . ." Drizzt began above the approving whispers of the other raiders.

Dinin cut his brother's thoughts short, easily guessing the question. "The cat belongs to Masoj," he said flatly. "The cat stays behind."

"I could talk to Masoj," Drizzt pleaded.

Dinin's stern glance answered the question without the need for words. "Our tactics will be different on the surface," he said to all the group, silencing their whispers. "The surface is a world of distance, not the blind enclosures of bending tunnels. Once our enemies are spotted, our task will be to surround them, to close off the distances." He looked straight at his young brother. "We will have no need of a point guard, and in such a conflict, a spirited cat could well prove more trouble than aid."

Drizzt had to be satisfied with the answer. Arguing would not help, even if he could get Masoj to let him take the panther—which he knew in his heart he could not. He shook the brooding desires out of his head and forced himself to hear his brother's words. This was to be the greatest challenge of Drizzt's young life, and the greatest danger.

Over the final two days, as the battle plan became ingrained into every thought, Drizzt found himself growing more and more agitated. Nervous energy kept his palms moist with sweat, and his eyes darted about, too alert.

Despite his disappointment over Guenhwyvar, Drizzt could not deny the excitement that bubbled within him. This was the adventure he had always wanted, the answer to his questions of the truth of his people. Up there, in the vast strangeness of that foreign world, lurked the surface elves, the unseen nightmare that had become the common enemy, and thus the common bond, of all the drow. Drizzt would discover the glory of battle, exacting proper revenge upon his people's most hated foes. Always before, Drizzt had fought out of necessity, in training gyms or against the stupid monsters that ventured too near his home.

Drizzt knew that this encounter would be different. This time his thrusts and cuts would be carried by the strength of deeper emotions, guided by the honor of his people and their common courage and resolve to strike back against their oppressors. He had to believe that.

Drizzt lay back in his cot the night before the raiding party's departure and brought his scimitars through some slow-motion maneuvers above him.

"This time," he whispered aloud to the blades while marveling at their intricate dance even at such a slow speed. "This time your ring will sound out in the song of justice!"

He placed the scimitars down at the side of his cot and rolled over to find some needed sleep. "This time," he said again, teeth clenched and eyes shining with determination.

Were his proclamations his belief or his hope? Drizzt had dismissed the disturbing question the very first time it had entered his thoughts, having no more room for doubts than he had for brooding. He no longer considered the possibility of disappointment; it had no place in the heart of a drow warrior.

To Dinin, though, studying Drizzt curiously from the shadows of the doorway, it sounded as if his younger brother was trying to convince himself of the truth of his own words.

# 20
# That Foreign World

The fourteen members of the patrol group made their way through twisting tunnels and giant caverns that suddenly opened wide before them. Silent on magical boots and nearly invisible behind their *piwafwis*, they communicated only in their hand code. For the most part, the ground's slope was barely perceptible, though at times the group climbed straight up rocky chimneys, every step and every handhold drawing them nearer their goal. They crossed through the boundaries of claimed territories, of monsters and the other races, but the hated gnomes and even the duergar dwarves wisely kept their heads hidden. Few in all the Underdark would purposely intercept a drow raiding party.

By the end of a tenday, all the drow could sense the difference in their surroundings. The depth still would have seemed stifling to a surface dweller, but the dark elves were accustomed to the constant oppression of a thousand thousand tons of rock hanging over their heads. They turned every corner expecting the stone ceiling to fly away into the vast openness of the surface world.

Breezes wafted past them—not the sulfur-smelling hot winds rising off the magma of deep earth, but moist air, scented with a hundred aromas unknown to the drow. It was springtime above, though the dark elves, in their seasonless environs, knew nothing of that, and the air was full of the scents of new-blossomed flowers and budding trees. In the seductive allure of those tantalizing aromas, Drizzt had to remind himself again and again that the place they approached was wholly evil and dangerous. Perhaps, he thought, the scents were merely a diabolical lure, a bait to an unsuspecting creature to bring it into the surface world's murderous grip.

The cleric of Arach-Tinilith who was traveling with the raiding party walked near to one wall and pressed her face against every crack she encountered. "This one will suffice," she said a short time later. She cast a spell of seeing and looked into the tiny crack, no more than a finger's width, a second time.

"How are we to get through that?" one of the patrol members signaled to another. Dinin caught the gestures and ended the silent conversation with a scowl.

"It is daylight above," the cleric announced. "We shall have to wait here."

"For how long?" Dinin asked, knowing his patrol to be on the edge of readiness with their long-awaited goal so very near.

"I cannot know," the cleric replied. "No more than half a cycle of Narbondel. Let us remove our packs and rest while we may."

Dinin would have preferred to continue, just to keep his troops busy, but he did not dare speak against the priestess. The break did not prove a long one, though, for a couple of hours later, the cleric checked through the crack once more and announced that the time had come.

"You first," Dinin said to Drizzt. Drizzt looked at his brother incredulously, having no idea of how he could pass through such a tiny crack.

"Come," instructed the cleric, who now held a many-holed orb. "Walk past me and continue through."

As Drizzt passed the cleric, she spoke the orb's command word and held it over Drizzt's head. Black flakes, blacker than Drizzt's ebony skin, drifted over him, and he felt a tremendous shudder ripple across his spine.

The others looked on in amazement as Drizzt's body narrowed to the width of a hair and he became a two-dimensional image, a shadow of his former self.

Drizzt did not understand what was happening, but the crack suddenly widened before him. He slipped into it, found movement in his present form merely an enactment of will, and, drifted through the twists, turns, and bends of the tiny channel like a shadow on the broken face of a rocky cliff. He then was in a long cave, standing across from its single exit.

A moonless night had fallen, but even this seemed bright to the deep-dwelling drow. Drizzt felt himself pulled toward the exit, toward the surface world's openness. The other raiders began slipping through the crack and into the cavern then, one by one with the cleric coming in last. Drizzt was the first to feel the shudder as his body resumed its natural state. In a few moments, they all were eagerly checking their weapons.

"I will remain here," the cleric told Dinin. "Hunt well. The Spider Queen is watching."

Dinin warned his troops once again of the dangers of the surface, then he moved to the front of the cave, a small hole on the side of a rocky spur of a tall mountain. "For the Spider Queen," Dinin proclaimed. He took a steadying breath and led them through the exit, under the open sky.

Under the stars! While the others seemed nervous under those revealing lights, Drizzt found his gaze pulled heavenward to the countless points of mystical twinkling. Bathed in the starlight, he felt his heart lift and didn't even notice the joyful singing that rode on the night wind, so fitting it seemed.

Dinin heard the song, and he was experienced enough to recognize it as the eldritch calling of the surface elves. He crouched and surveyed the horizon, picking out the light of a single fire down in the distant expanse of a wooded valley. He nudged his troops to action—and pointedly nudged the wonderment from his brother's eyes—and started them off.

Drizzt could see the anxiety on his companions' faces, so contrasted by his own inexplicable sense of serenity. He suspected at once that something was very wrong with the whole situation. In his heart Drizzt had known from the minute he had stepped out of the tunnel that this was not the vile world the masters at the Academy had taken such pains to describe. He did feel unusual with no stone ceiling above him, but not uncomfortable. If the stars, calling to his heartstrings, were indeed reminders of what the next day might bring, as Master Hatch'net had said, then surely the next day would not be so terrible.

Only confusion dampened the feeling of freedom that Drizzt felt, for either he had somehow fallen into a trap of perception, or his companions, his brother included, viewed their surroundings through tainted eyes.

It fell on Drizzt as another unanswered burden: were his feelings of comfort here weakness or truth of heart?

"They are akin to the mushroom groves of our home," Dinin assured the others as they tentatively moved under the perimeter boughs of a small forest, "neither sentient nor harmful."

Still, the younger dark elves flinched and brought their weapons to the ready whenever a squirrel skipped across a branch overheard or an unseen bird called out to the night. The dark elves' was a silent world, far different from the chattering life of a springtime forest, and in the Underdark, nearly every living thing could, and most certainly would, try to harm anything invading its lair. Even a cricket's chirp sounded ominous to the alert ears of the drow.

Dinin's course was true, and soon the faerie song drowned out every other sound and the light of a fire became visible through the boughs. Surface elves were the most alert of the races, and a human—or even a sneaky halfling—would have had little chance of catching them unawares.

The raiders this night were drow, more skilled in stealth than the most proficient alley thief. Their footfalls went unheard, even across beds of dry, fallen leaves, and their crafted armor, shaped perfectly to the contours of their slender bodies, bent with their movements without a rustle. Unnoticed, they lined the perimeter of the small glade, where a score of faeries danced and sang.

Transfixed by the sheer joy of the elves' play, Drizzt hardly noticed the commands his brother issued then in the silent code. Several children danced among the gathering, marked only by the size of their bodies, and were no freer in spirit than the adults they accompanied. So innocent they all seemed, so full of life and wistfulness, and obviously bonded to each other by friendship more profound than Drizzt had ever known in Menzoberranzan. So unlike the stories Hatch'net had spun of them, tales of vile, hating wretches.

Drizzt sensed more than saw that his group was on the move, fanning out to gain a greater advantage. Still he did not take his eyes from the spectacle before him. Dinin tapped him on the shoulder and pointed to the small crossbow that hung from his belt, then slipped off into position in the brush off to the side.

Drizzt wanted to stop his brother and the others, wanted to make them wait and observe the surface elves that they were so quick to name enemies. Drizzt found his feet rooted to the earth and his tongue weighted heavily in the sudden dryness that had come into his mouth. He looked to Dinin and could only hope that his brother mistakenly thought his labored breaths the exaltations of battlelust.

Then Drizzt's keen ears heard the soft thrum of a dozen tiny bowstrings. The elven song carried on a moment longer, until several of the group dropped to the earth.

"No!" Drizzt screamed in protest, the words torn from his body by a profound rage even he did not understand. The denial sounded like just another war cry to the drow raiders, and before the surface elves could even begin to react, Dinin and the others were upon them.

Drizzt, too, leaped into the glade's lighted ring, his weapons in hand, though he had given no thought to his next move. He wanted only to stop the battle, to put an end to the scene unfolding before him.

Quite at ease in their woodland home, the surface elves weren't even armed. The drow warriors sliced through their ranks mercilessly, cutting them down and hacking at their bodies long after the light of life had flown from their eyes.

One terrified female, dodging this way and that, came before Drizzt. He dipped the tips of his weapons to the earth, searching for some way to give a measure of comfort.

The female then jerked straight as a sword dived into her back, its tip thrusting right through her slender form. Drizzt watched, mesmerized and horrified, as the drow warrior behind her grasped the weapon hilt in both hands and twisted it savagely. The female elf looked straight at Drizzt in the last fleeting seconds of her life, her eyes crying for mercy. Her voice was no more than the sickening gurgle of blood.

His face the exultation of ecstacy, the drow warrior tore his sword free and sliced it across, taking the head from the elven female's shoulders.

"Vengeance!" he cried at Drizzt, his face contorted in furious glee, his eyes burning with a light that shone demonic to the stunned Drizzt. The warrior hacked at the lifeless body one more time, then spun away in search of another kill.

Only a moment later, another elf, this one a young girl, broke free of the massacre and rushed in Drizzt's direction, screaming a single word over and over. Her cry was in the tongue of the surface elves, a dialect foreign to Drizzt, but when he looked upon her fair face, streaked with tears, he understood what she was saying. Her eyes were on the mutilated corpse at his feet; her anguish outweighed even the terror of her own impending doom. She could only be crying, "Mother!"

Rage, horror, anguish, and a dozen other emotions racked Drizzt at that horrible moment. He wanted to escape his feelings, to lose himself in the blind frenzy of his kin and accept the ugly reality. How easy it would have been to throw away the conscience that pained him so.

The elven child rushed up before Drizzt but hardly saw him, her gaze locked upon her dead mother, the back of the child's neck open to a single, clean blow. Drizzt raised his scimitar, unable to distinguish between mercy and murder.

"Yes, my brother!" Dinin cried out to him, a call that cut through his comrades," screams and whoops and echoed in Drizzt's ears like an accusation. Drizzt looked up to see Dinin, covered from head to foot in blood and standing amid a hacked cluster of dead elves.

"Today you know the glory it is to be a drow!" Dinin cried, and he punched a victorious fist into the air. "Today we appease the Spider Queen!"

Drizzt responded in kind, then snarled and reared back for a killing blow.

He almost did it. In his unfocused outrage, Drizzt Do'Urden almost became as his kin. He almost stole the life from that beautiful child's sparkling eyes.

At the last moment, she looked up at him, her eyes shining as a dark mirror into Drizzt's blackening heart. In that reflection, that reverse image of the rage that guided his hand, Drizzt Do'Urden found himself.

He brought the scimitar down in a mighty sweep, watching Dinin out of the corner of his eye as it whisked harmlessly past the child. In the same motion, Drizzt followed with his other hand, catching the girl by the front of her tunic and pulling her face-down to the ground.

She screamed, unharmed but terrified, and Drizzt saw Dinin thrust his fist into the air again and spin away.

Drizzt had to work quickly; the battle was almost at its gruesome end. He sliced his scimitars expertly above the huddled child's back, cuffing her clothing but not so much as scratching her tender skin. Then he used the blood of the headless corpse to mask the trick, taking grim satisfaction that the elven mother would be pleased to know that, in dying, she had saved the life of her daughter.

"Stay down," he whispered in the child's ear. Drizzt knew that she could not understand his language, but he tried to keep his tone comforting enough for her to guess at the deception. He could only hope he had done an adequate job a moment later, when Dinin and several others came over to him.

"Well done!" Dinin said exuberantly, trembling with sheer excitement. "A score of the orc-bait dead and not a one of us even injured! The matrons of Menzoberranzan will be pleased indeed, though we'll get no plunder from this pitiful lot!" He looked down at the pile at Drizzt's feet, then clapped his brother on the shoulder.

"Did they think they could get away?" Dinin roared.

Drizzt fought hard to sublimate his disgust, but Dinin was so entranced by the blood-bath that he wouldn't have noticed anyway.

"Not with you here!" Dinin continued. "Two kills for Drizzt!"

"One kill!" protested another, stepping beside Dinin. Drizzt set his hands firmly on the hilts of his weapons and gathered up his courage. If this approaching drow had guessed the deception, Drizzt would fight to save the elven child. He would kill his companions, even his brother, to save the little girl with the sparkling eyes—until he himself was slain. At least then Drizzt would not have to witness their slaughter of the child.

Luckily, the problem never came up. "Drizzt got the child," the drow said to Dinin, "but I got the elder female. I put my sword right through her back before your brother ever brought his scimitars to bear!"

It came as a reflex, an unconscious strike against the evil all about him. Drizzt didn't even realize the act as it happened, but a moment later, he saw the boasting drow lying on his back, clutching at his face and groaning in agony. Only then did Drizzt notice the burning pain in his hand, and he looked down to see his knuckles, and the scimitar hilt they clutched, spattered with blood.

"What are you about?" Dinin demanded.

Thinking quickly, Drizzt did not even reply to his brother. He looked past Dinin, to the squirming form on the ground, and transferred all the rage in his heart into a curse that the others would accept and respect. "If ever you steal a kill from me again," he spat, sincerity dripping from his false words, "I will replace the head lost from its shoulders with your own!"

Drizzt knew that the elven child at his feet, though doing her best, had begun a slight shudder of sobbing, and he decided not to press his luck. "Come, then," he growled. "Let us leave this place. The stench of the surface world fills my mouth with bile!"

He stormed away, and the others, laughing, picked up their dazed comrade and followed.

"Finally," Dinin whispered as he watched his brother's tense strides. "Finally you have learned what it is to be a drow warrior!"

Dinin, in his blindness, would never understand the irony of his words.

⚔ ⚔ ⚔ ⚔ ⚔

"We have one more duty before we return home," the cleric explained to the group when it reached the cave's entrance. She alone knew of the raid's second purpose. "The matrons of Menzoberranzan have bid us to witness the ultimate horror of the surface world, that we might warn our kindred."

Our kindred? Drizzt mused, his thoughts black with sarcasm. As far as he could see, the raiders had already witnessed the horror of the surface world: themselves!

"There!" Dinin cried, pointing to the eastern horizon.

The tiniest shading of light limned the dark outline of distant mountains. A surface dweller would not even have noticed it, but the dark elves saw it clearly, and all of them, even Drizzt, recoiled instinctively.

"It is beautiful," Drizzt dared to remark after taking a moment to consider the spectacle.

Dinin's glare came at him icy cold, but no colder than the look the cleric cast Drizzt's way. "Remove your cloaks and equipment, even your armor," she instructed the group. "Quickly. Place them within the shadows of the cave so that they will not be affected by the light."

When the task was completed, the cleric led them out into the growing light. "Watch," was her grim command.

The eastern sky assumed a hue of purplish pink, then pink altogether, its brightening causing the dark elves to squint uncomfortably. Drizzt wanted to deny the event, to put it into the same pile of anger that denied the master of Lore's words concerning the surface elves.

Then it happened; the top rim of the sun crested the eastern horizon. The surface world awakened to its warmth, its life-giving energy. Those same rays assaulted the drow elves' eyes with the fury of fire, tearing into orbs unaccustomed to such sights.

"Watch!" the cleric cried at them. "Witness the depth of the horror!"

One by one, the raiders cried out in pain and fell into the cave's darkness, until Drizzt stood alone beside the cleric in the growing daylight. Truly the light assaulted Drizzt as keenly as it had his kin, but he basked in it, accepting it as his purgatory, exposing him for all to view while its stinging fires cleansed his soul.

"Come," the cleric said to him at length, not understanding his actions. "We have borne witness. We may now return to our homeland."

"Homeland?" Drizzt replied, subdued.

"Menzoberranzan!" the cleric cried, thinking the male confused beyond reason. "Come, before the inferno burns the skin from your bones. Let our surface cousins suffer the flames, a fitting punishment for their evil hearts!"

Drizzt chuckled hopelessly. A fitting punishment? He wished that he could pluck a thousand such suns from the sky and set them in every chapel in Menzoberranzan, to shine eternally.

Then Drizzt could take the light no more. He scrambled dizzily back into the cave and donned his outfit. The cleric had the orb in hand, and Drizzt again was the first through the tiny crack. When all the group rejoined in the tunnel beyond, Drizzt took his position at the point and led them back into the descending path's deepening gloom—back down into the darkness of their existence.

# 21

# May It Please the Goddess

Did you please the goddess?" Matron Malice asked, her question as much a threat as an inquiry. At her side, the other females of House Do'Urden, Briza, Vierna, and Maya, looked on impassively, hiding their jealousy.

"Not a single drow was slain," Dinin replied, his voice thick with the sweetness of drow evil. "We cut them and slashed them!" He drooled as his recounting of the elven slaughter brought back the lust of the moment. "Bit them and ripped them!"

"What of you?" the matron mother interrupted, more concerned with the consequences to her own family's standing than with the raid's general success.

"Five," Dinin answered proudly. "I killed five, all of them females!"

The matron's smile thrilled Dinin. Then Malice scowled as she turned her gaze on Drizzt. "And him?" she inquired, not expecting to be pleased with the answer. Malice did not doubt her youngest son's prowess with weapons, but she had come to suspect that Drizzt had too much of Zaknafein's emotional makeup to ever be an attribute in such situations.

Dinin's smile confused her. He walked over to Drizzt and draped an arm comfortably across his brother's shoulders. "Drizzt got only one kill," Dinin began, "but it was a female child."

"Only one?" Malice growled.

From the shadows off to the side, Zaknafein listened in dismay. He wanted to shut out the elderboy Do'Urden's damning words, but they held Zak in their grip. Of all the evils Zak had ever encountered in Menzoberranzan, this surely had to be the most disappointing. Drizzt had killed a child.

"But the way he did it!" Dinin exclaimed. "He hacked her apart; sent all of Lolth's fury slicing into her twitching body! The Spider Queen must have treasured that kill above all the others."

"Only one," Matron Malice said again, her scowl hardly softening.

"He would have had two," Dinin continued. "Shar Nadal of House Maevret stole one from his blade—another female."

"Then Lolth will look with favor on House Maevret," Briza reasoned.

"No," Dinin replied. "Drizzt punished Shar Nadal for his actions. The son of House Maevret would not respond to the challenge."

The memory stuck in Drizzt's thoughts. He wished that Shar Nadal had come back at him, so he could have vented his rage more fully. Even that wish sent pangs of guilt coursing through Drizzt.

"Well done, my children," Malice beamed, now satisfied that both of them had acted properly in the raid. "The Spider Queen will look upon House Do'Urden with favor for this event. She will guide us to victory over this unknown house that seeks to destroy us."

⚔ ⚔ ⚔ ⚔ ⚔

Zaknafein left the audience hall with his eyes down and one hand nervously rubbing his sword's hilt. Zak remembered the time he had deceived Drizzt with the light bomb, when he had Drizzt defenseless and beaten. He could have spared the young innocent from his horrid fate. He could have killed Drizzt then and there, mercifully, and released him from the inevitable circumstances of life in Menzoberranzan.

Zak paused in the long corridor and turned back to watch the chamber. Drizzt and Dinin came out then, Drizzt casting Zak a single, accusatory look and pointedly turning away down a side passage.

The gaze cut through the weapons master. "So it has come to this," Zak murmured to himself. "The youngest warrior of House Do'Urden, so full of the hate that embodies our race, has learned to despise me for what I am."

Zak thought again of that moment in the training gym, that fateful second when Drizzt's life teetered on the edge of a poised sword. It indeed would have been a merciful act to kill Drizzt at that time.

With the sting of the young drow warrior's gaze still cutting so keenly into his heart, Zak couldn't decide whether the deed would have been more merciful to Drizzt or to himself.

⚔ ⚔ ⚔ ⚔ ⚔

"Leave us," Matron SiNafay commanded as she swept into the small room lighted by a candle's glow. Alton gawked at the request; it was, after all, his personal room! Alton prudently reminded himself that SiNafay was the matron mother of the family, the absolute ruler of House Hun'ett. With a few awkward bows and apologies for his hesitation, he backed out of the room.

Masoj watched his mother cautiously as she waited for Alton to move away. From SiNafay's agitated tone, Masoj understood the significance of her visit. Had he done something to anger his mother? Or, more likely, had Alton? When SiNafay spun back on him, her face twisted in evil glee, Masoj realized that her agitation was really excitement.

"House Do'Urden has erred!" she snarled. "It has lost the Spider Queen's favor!"

"How?" Masoj replied. He knew that Dinin and Drizzt had returned from a successful raid, an assault that all of the city was talking about in tones of high praise.

"I do not know the details," Matron SiNafay replied, finding a measure of calmness in her voice. "One of them, perhaps one of the sons, did something to displease Lolth. This was told to me by a handmaiden of the Spider Queen. It must be true!"

"Matron Malice will work quickly to correct the situation," Masoj reasoned. "How long do we have?"

"Lolth's displeasure will not be revealed to Matron Malice," SiNafay replied. "Not soon. The Spider Queen knows all. She knows that we plan to attack House Do'Urden, and only an unfortunate accident will inform Matron Malice of her desperate situation before her house is crushed!

"We must move quickly," Matron SiNafay went on. "Within ten cycles of Narbondel, the first strike must fall! The full battle will begin soon after, before House Do'Urden can link its loss to our wrongdoing."

"What is to be their sudden loss?" Masoj prompted, thinking, hoping, he had already guessed the answer.

His mother's words were like sweet music to his ears. "Drizzt Do'Urden," she purred, "the favored son. Kill him."

Masoj rested back and clasped his slender fingers behind his head, considering the command.

"You will not fail me," SiNafay warned.

"I will not," Masoj assured her. "Drizzt, though young, is already a powerful foe. His brother, a former master of Melee-Magthere, is never far from his side." He looked up at his matron mother, his eyes gleaming. "May I kill the brother, too?"

"Be cautious, my son," SiNafay replied. "Drizzt Do'Urden is your target. Concentrate your efforts toward his death."

"As you command," Masoj replied, bowing low.

SiNafay liked the way her young son heeded to her desires without question. She started out of the room, confident in Masoj's ability to perform the task.

"If Dinin Do'Urden somehow gets in the way," she said, turning back to throw Masoj a gift for his obedience, "you may kill him, too."

Masoj's expression revealed too much eagerness for the second task.

"You will not fail me!" SiNafay said again, this time in an open threat that stole some of the wind out of Masoj's filling sails. "Drizzt Do'Urden must die within ten days!"

Masoj forced any distracting thoughts of Dinin out of his mind. "Drizzt must die," he whispered over and over, long after his mother had gone. He already knew how he wanted to do it. He only had to hope that the opportunity would come soon.

✕ ✕ ✕ ✕ ✕

The awful memory of the surface raid followed Drizzt, haunted him, as he wandered the halls of Daermon N'a'shezbaernon. He had rushed from the audience chamber as soon as Matron Malice had dismissed him, and had slipped away from his brother at the first opportunity, wanting only to be alone.

The images remained: the broken sparkle in the young elven girl's eyes as she knelt over her murdered mother's corpse; the elven woman's horrified expression, twisting in agony as Shar Nadal ripped the life from her body. The surface elves were there in Drizzt's thoughts; he could not dismiss them. They walked beside Drizzt as he wandered, as real as they had been when Drizzt's raiding group had descended upon their joyful song.

Drizzt wondered if he would ever be alone again.

Eyes down, consumed by his empty sense of loss, Drizzt did not mark the path before him. He jumped back, startled, when he turned a corner and bumped into somebody.

He stood facing Zaknafein.

"You are home," the weapons master said absently, his blank face revealing none of the tumultuous emotions swirling through his mind.

Drizzt wondered if he could properly hide his own grimace. "For a day," he replied, equally nonchalant, though his rage with Zaknafein was no less intense. Now that Drizzt had witnessed the wrath of drow elves firsthand, Zak's reputed deeds rang out to Drizzt as even more evil. "My patrol group goes back out at Narbondel's first light."

"So soon?" asked Zak, genuinely surprised.

"We are summoned," Drizzt replied, starting past. Zak caught him by the arm.

"General patrol?" he asked.

"Focused," Drizzt replied. "Activity in the eastern tunnels."

"So the heroes are summoned," chuckled Zak.

Drizzt did not immediately respond. Was there sarcasm in Zak's voice? Jealousy, perhaps, that Drizzt and Dinin were allowed to go out to fight, while Zak had to remain within the House Do'Urden's confines to fulfill his role as the family's fighting instructor? Was Zak's hunger for blood so great that he could not accept the duties thrust upon them all? Zak had trained Drizzt and Dinin, had he not? And hundreds of others; he'd transformed them into living weapons, into murderers.

"How long will you be out?" Zak pressed, more interested in Drizzt's whereabouts.

Drizzt shrugged. "A tenday at the longest."

"And?"

"Home."

"That is good," said Zak. "I will be pleased to see you back within the walls of House Do'Urden." Drizzt didn't believe a word of it.

Zak then slapped him on the shoulder in a sudden, unexpected movement designed to test Drizzt's reflexes. More surprised than threatened, Drizzt accepted the pat without response, not sure of his uncle's intent.

"The gym, perhaps?" asked Zak. "You and l, as it once was."

Impossible! Drizzt wanted to shout. Never again would it be as it once was. Drizzt held those thoughts to himself and nodded his assent. "I would enjoy that," he replied, secretly wondering how much satisfaction he would gain by cutting Zaknafein down. Drizzt knew the truth of his people now, and knew that he was powerless to change anything. Maybe he could make a change in his private life, though. Maybe by destroying Zaknafein, his greatest disappointment, Drizzt could remove himself from the wrongness around him.

"As would I," Zak said, the friendliness of his tone hiding his private thoughts—thoughts identical to Drizzt's.

"In a tenday, then," Drizzt said, and he pulled away, unable to continue the encounter with the drow who once had been his dearest friend, and who, Drizzt had come to learn, was truly as devious and evil as the rest of his kin.

⚔ ⚔ ⚔ ⚔ ⚔

"Please, my matron," Alton whimpered, "it is my right. I beg of you!"

"Rest easy, foolish DeVir," SiNafay replied, and there was pity in her voice, an emotion seldom felt and almost never revealed.

"I have waited—"

"The time is almost upon you," SiNafay countered, her tone growing more threatening. "You have tried for this one before."

Alton's grotesque gawk brought a smile to SiNafay's face.

"Yes," she said, "I know of your bungled attempt on Drizzt Do'Urden's life. If Masoj had not arrived, the young warrior would probably have slain you."

"I would have destroyed him!" Alton growled.

SiNafay did not argue the point. "Perhaps you would have won," she said, "only to be exposed as a murderous imposter, with the wrath of all of Menzoberranzan hanging over your head!"

"I did not care."

"You would have cared, I promise you!" Matron SiNafay sneered. "You would have forfeited your chance to claim a greater revenge. Trust in me, Alton DeVir. Your—our—victory is at hand."

"Masoj will kill Drizzt, and maybe Dinin," Alton grumbled.

"There are other Do'Urdens awaiting the fell hand of Alton DeVir," Matron SiNafay promised. "High priestesses."

Alton could not dismiss the disappointment he felt at not being allowed to go after Drizzt. He badly wanted to kill that one. Drizzt had brought him embarrassment that day in his chambers at Sorcere; the young drow should have died quickly and quietly. Alton wanted to make up for that mistake.

Alton also could not ignore the promise that Matron SiNafay had just made to him. The thought of killing one or more of the high priestesses of House Do'Urden did not displease him at all.

⚔ ⚔ ⚔ ⚔ ⚔

The pillowy softness of the plush bed, so different from the rest of the hard stone world of Menzoberranzan, offered Drizzt no relief from the pain. Another ghost had reared up to overwhelm even the images of carnage on the surface: the specter of Zaknafein.

Dinin and Vierna had told Drizzt the truth of the weapons master, of Zak's role in the fall of House DeVir, and of how Zak so enjoyed slaughtering other drow—other drow who had done nothing to wrong him or deserve his wrath.

So Zaknafein, too, took part in this evil game of drow life, the endless quest to please the Spider Queen.

"As I so pleased her on the surface?" Drizzt couldn't help but mumble, the sarcasm of the spoken words bringing him some small measure of comfort.

The comfort Drizzt felt in saving the life of the elven child seemed such a minor act against the overwhelming wrongs his raiding group had exacted on her people. Matron Malice, his mother, had so enjoyed hearing the bloody recounting. Drizzt remembered the elven child's horror at the sight of her dead mother. Would he, or any dark elf, be so devastated if they looked upon such a sight. Unlikely, he thought. Drizzt hardly shared a loving bond with Malice, and most drow would be too engaged in measuring the consequences of their mother's death to their own station to feel any sense of loss.

Would Malice have cared if either Drizzt or Dinin had fallen in the raid? Again Drizzt knew the answer. All that Malice cared about was how the raid affected her own base of power. She had reveled in the notion that her children had pleased her evil goddess.

What favor would Lolth show to House Do'Urden if she knew the truth of Drizzt's actions? Drizzt had no way to measure how much, if any, interest the Spider Queen had taken in the raid. Lolth remained a mystery to him, one he had no desire to explore. Would she be enraged if she knew the truth of the raid? Or if she knew the truth of Drizzt's thoughts at this moment?

Drizzt shuddered to think of the punishments he might be bringing upon himself, but he had already firmly decided upon his course of action, whatever the consequences. He would return to House Do'Urden in a tenday. He would go then to the practice gym for a reunion with his old teacher.

He would kill Zaknafein in a tenday.

⚔ ⚔ ⚔ ⚔ ⚔

Caught up in the emotions of a dangerous and heartfelt decision, Zaknafein hardly heard the biting scrape as he ran the whetstone along his sword's gleaming edge.

The weapon had to be perfect, with no jags or burrs. This deed had to be executed without malice or anger.

A clean blow, and Zak would rid himself of the demons of his own failures, hide himself once again within the sanctuary of his private chambers, his secret world. A clean blow, and he would do what he should have done a decade before.

"If only I had found the strength then," he lamented. "How much grief might I have spared Drizzt? How much pain did his days at the Academy bring to him, that he is so very changed?" The words rang hollow in the empty room. They were just words, useless now, for Zak had already decided that Drizzt was out of reason's reach. Drizzt was a drow warrior, with all of the wicked connotations carried in such a title.

The choice was gone to Zaknafein if he wished to hold any pretense of value to his wretched existence. This time, he could not stay his sword. He had to kill Drizzt.

# 22

# Gnomes, Wicked Gnomes

Among the twists and turns of the tunnel mazes of the Underdark, slipping about their silent way, went the svirfnebli, the deep gnomes. Neither kind nor evil, and so out of place in this world of pervading wickedness, the deep gnomes survived and thrived. Haughty fighters, skilled in crafting weapons and armor, and more in tune to the songs of the stone than even the evil gray dwarves, the svirfnebli continued their business of plucking gems and precious metals in spite of the perils awaiting them at every turn.

When the news came back to Blingdenstone, the cluster of tunnels and caverns that composed the deep gnomes' city, that a rich vein of gemstones had been discovered twenty miles to the east—as the rockworm, the thoqqua, burrowed—Burrow-warden Belwar Dissengulp had to climb over a dozen others of his rank to be awarded the privilege of leading the mining expedition. Belwar and all of the others knew well that forty miles east—as the rockworm burrowed—would put the expedition dangerously close to Menzoberranzan, and that even getting there would mean a tenday of hiking, probably through the territories of a hundred other enemies. Fear was no measure against the love svirfnebli had for gems, though, and every day in the Underdark was a risk.

When Belwar and his forty miners arrived in the small cavern described by the advance scouts and inscribed with the gnomes' mark of treasure, they found that the claims had not been exaggerated. The burrow-warden took care not to get overly excited, though. He knew that twenty thousand drow elves, the svirfnebli's most hated and feared enemy, lived less than five miles away.

Escape tunnels became the first order of business, winding constructions high enough for a three-foot gnome but not for a taller pursuer. All along the course of these the gnomes placed breaker walls, designed to deflect a lightning bolt or offer some protection from the expanding flames of a fireball.

Then, when the true mining at last began, Belwar kept fully a third of his crew on guard at all times and walked the area of the work with one hand always clutching the magical emerald, the summoning stone, he kept on a chain around his neck.

⚔ ⚔ ⚔ ⚔ ⚔

"Three full patrol groups," Drizzt remarked to Dinin when they arrived at the open "field" on the eastern side of Menzoberranzan. Few stalagmites lined this region of the city, but it did not seem so open now, with dozens of anxious drow milling about.

"Gnomes are not to be taken lightly," Dinin replied. "They are wicked and powerful—"

"As wicked as surface elves?" Drizzt had to interrupt, covering his sarcasm with false exuberance.

"Almost," his brother warned grimly, missing the connotations of Drizzt's question. Dinin pointed off to the side, where a contingent of female drow was coming in to join the group. "Clerics," he said, "and one of them a high priestess. The rumors of activity must have been confirmed."

A shudder coursed through Drizzt, a tingle of prebattle excitement. That excitement was altered and lessened, though, by fear, not of physical harm, or even of the gnomes. Drizzt feared that this encounter might be a repeat of the surface tragedy.

He shook the black thoughts away and reminded himself that this time, unlike the surface expedition, his home was being invaded. The gnomes had crossed the boundaries of the drow realm. If they were as evil as Dinin and all the others claimed, Menzoberranzan had no choice but to respond with force. If.

Drizzt's patrol, the most celebrated group among the males, was selected to lead, and Drizzt, as always, took the point position. Still unsure, he wasn't thrilled with the assignment, and as they started out, Drizzt even contemplated leading the group astray. Or perhaps, Drizzt thought, he could contact the gnomes privately before the others arrived and warn them to flee.

Drizzt realized the absurdity of the notion. He couldn't stop the wheels of Menzoberranzan from turning along their designated course, and he couldn't do anything to hinder the two score drow warriors, excited and impatient, at his back. Again he was trapped and on the edge of despair.

Masoj Hun'ett appeared then and made everything better.

"Guenhwyvar!" the young wizard called, and the great panther came bounding. Masoj left the cat beside Drizzt and headed back toward his place in the line.

Guenhwyvar could no more hide its elation at seeing Drizzt than Drizzt could contain his own smile. With the interruption of the surface raid, and his time back home, he hadn't seen Guenhwyvar in more than a month. Guenhwyvar thumped against Drizzt's side as it passed, nearly knocking the slender drow from his feet. Drizzt responded with a heavy pat, vigorously rubbing a hand over the cat's ear.

They both turned back together, suddenly conscious of the unhappy glare boring into them. There stood Masoj, arms crossed over his chest and a visible scowl heating up his face.

"I shan't use the cat to kill Drizzt," the young wizard muttered to himself. "I want the pleasure for myself!"

Drizzt wondered if jealousy prompted that scowl. Jealousy of Drizzt and the cat, or of everything in general? Masoj had been left behind when Drizzt had gone to the surface. Masoj had been no more than a spectator when the victorious raiding party returned in glory. Drizzt backed away from Guenhwyvar, sensitive to the wizard's pain.

As soon as Masoj had moved away to take his position farther down the line, Drizzt dropped to one knee and threw a headlock on Guenhwyvar.

⚔ ⚔ ⚔ ⚔ ⚔

Drizzt found himself even gladder for Guenhwyvar's companionship when they passed beyond the familiar tunnels of the normal patrol routes. It was a saying in Menzoberranzan that "no one is as alone as the point of a drow patrol," and Drizzt had come to understand this keenly in the last few months. He stopped at the far end of a wide way and held perfectly still, focusing his ears and eyes to the trails behind him. He knew that more than forty drow were approaching his position, fully arrayed for battle and agitated. Still, not a sound could Drizzt detect, and not a motion was discernible in the eerie shadows of cool stone. Drizzt looked down at Guenhwyvar, waiting patiently by his side, and started off again.

He could sense the hot presence of the war party at his back. That intangible sensation was the only thing that disproved Drizzt's feelings that he and Guenhwyvar were quite alone.

Near the end of that day, Drizzt heard the first signs of trouble. As he neared an intersection in the tunnel, cautiously pressed close to one wall, he felt a subtle vibration in the stone. It came again a second later, and then again, and Drizzt recognized it as the rhythmic tapping of a pick or hammer.

He took a magically heated sheet, a small square that fit into the palm of his hand, out of his pack. One side of the item was shielded in heavy leather, but the other shone brightly to eyes seeing in the infrared spectrum. Drizzt flashed it down the tunnel behind him, and a few seconds later Dinin came up to his side.

"Hammer," Drizzt signaled in the silent code, pointing to the wall. Dinin pressed against the stone and nodded in confirmation.

"Fifty yards?" Dinin's hand motions asked.

"Less than one hundred," Drizzt confirmed.

With his own prepared sheet, Dinin flashed the get-ready signal into the gloom behind him, then moved with Drizzt and Guenhwyvar around the intersection toward the tapping.

Only a moment later, Drizzt looked upon svirfnebli gnomes for the very first time. Two guards stood barely twenty feet away, chest-high to a drow and hairless, with skin strangely akin to the stone in both texture and heat radiations. The gnomes' eyes glowed brightly in the telltale red of infravision. One glance at those eyes reminded Drizzt and Dinin that deep gnomes were as much at home in the darkness as were the drow, and they both prudently ducked behind a rocky outcropping in the tunnel.

Dinin promptly signaled to the next drow in line, and so on, until the entire party was alerted. Then he crouched low and peeked out around the bottom of the outcropping. The tunnel continued another thirty feet beyond the gnome guards and around a slight bend, ending in some larger chamber. Dinin couldn't clearly see this area, but the glow of it, from the heat of the work and a cluster of bodies, spilled out into the corridor.

Again Dinin signaled back to his hidden comrades, and then he turned to Drizzt. "Stay here with the cat," he instructed, and he darted back down around the intersection to formulate plans with the other leaders.

Masoj, a few places back in the line, noted Dinin's movements and wondered if the opportunity to deal with Drizzt had suddenly come upon him. If the patrol was discovered with Drizzt all alone in front, was there some way Masoj could secretly blast the young Do'Urden? The opportunity, if ever it was truly there, passed quickly, though, as other drow soldiers came up beside the plotting wizard. Dinin soon returned from the back of the line and headed back to join his brother.

"The chamber has many exits," Dinin signaled to Drizzt when they were together. "The other patrols are moving into position around the gnomes."

"Might we parley with the gnomes?" Drizzt's hands asked in reply, almost subconsciously. He recognized the expression spreading across Dinin's face, but knew that he had already plunged in. "Send them away without conflict?"

Dinin grabbed Drizzt by the front of his *piwafwi* and pulled him close, too close, to that terrible scowl. "I will forget that you asked that question," he whispered, and he dropped Drizzt back to the stone, considering the issue closed.

"You start the fight," Dinin signaled. "When you see the sign from behind, darken the corridor and rush past the guards. Get to the gnome leader; he is the key to their strength with the stone."

Drizzt didn't fully understand what gnomish power his brother hinted at, but the instructions seemed simple enough, if somewhat suicidal.

"Take the cat if the cat will go," Dinin continued. "The entire patrol will be by your side in moments. The remaining groups will come in from the other passages."

Guenhwyvar nuzzled up to Drizzt, more than ready to follow him into battle. Drizzt took comfort in that when Dinin departed, leaving him alone again at the front. Only a few seconds later came the command to attack. Drizzt shook his head in disbelief when he saw the signal; how fast drow warriors found their positions!

He peeked around at the gnomish guards, still holding their silent vigil, completely unaware. Drizzt drew his blades and patted Guenhwyvar for luck, then called upon the innate magic of his race and dropped a globe of darkness in the corridor.

Squeals of alarm sounded throughout the tunnels, and Drizzt charged in, diving right into the darkness between the unseen guards and rolling back to his feet on the other side of his spell, only two running strides from the small chamber. He saw a dozen gnomes scrambling about, trying to prepare their defenses. Few of them paid Drizzt any attention, though, as the sounds of battle erupted from various side corridors.

One gnome chopped a heavy pick at Drizzt's shoulder. Drizzt got a blade up to block the blow but was amazed at the strength in the diminutive gnome's arms. Still, Drizzt could then have killed his attacker with the other scimitar. Too many doubts, and too many memories, though, haunted his actions. He brought a leg up into the gnome's belly, sending the little creature sprawling.

Belwar Dissengulp, next in line for Drizzt, noted how easily the young drow had dispatched one of his finest fighters and knew that the time had already come to use his most powerful magic. He pulled the emerald summoning stone from his neck and threw it to the ground at Drizzt's feet.

Drizzt jumped back, sensing the emanations of magic. Behind him,

Drizzt heard the approach of his companions, overpowering the shocked gnome guards and rushing to join him in the chamber. Then Drizzt's attentions went squarely to the heat patterns of the stone floor in front of him. The grayish lines wavered and swam, as if the stone was somehow coming alive.

The other drow fighters roared in past Drizzt, bearing down on the gnome leader and his charges. Drizzt didn't follow, guessing that the event unfolding at his feet was more critical than the general battle now echoing throughout the complex.

Fifteen feet tall and seven wide, an angry, towering humanoid monster of living stone rose before Drizzt.

"Elemental!" came a scream to the side. Drizzt glanced over to see Masoj, Guenhwyvar at his side, fumbling through a spellbook, apparently in search of some dweomer to battle this unexpected monster. To Drizzt's dismay, the frightened wizard mumbled a couple of words and vanished.

Drizzt set his feet under him, and took a measure of the monster, ready to spring aside in an instant. He could sense the thing's power, the raw strength of the earth embodied in living arms and legs.

A lumbering arm swung out in a wide arc, whooshing above Drizzt's ducking head and slamming into the cavern wall, crushing rocks into dust.

"Do not let it hit me," Drizzt instructed himself in a whisper that came out as a disbelieving gasp. As the elemental recoiled its arm, Drizzt poked a scimitar at it, chipping away a small chunk, barely a scratch. The elemental grimaced in pain—apparently Drizzt could indeed hurt it with his enchanted weapons.

Still standing in the same spot off to the side, the invisible Masoj held his next spell in check, watching the spectacle and waiting for the combatants to weaken each other. Perhaps the elemental would destroy Drizzt altogether. Invisible shoulders gave a resigned shrug. Masoj decided to let the gnomish power do his dirty work for him.

The monster launched another blow, and another, and Drizzt dived forward and scrambled through the thing's stone pillar legs. The elemental reacted quickly and stomped heavily with one foot, barely missing the agile drow, and sending branching cracks in the floor for many feet in either direction.

Drizzt was up in a flash, slicing and thrusting with both his blades into the elemental's backside, then springing back out of reach as the monster swung about, leading with another ferocious blow.

The sounds of battle grew more distant. The gnomes had taken flight—those that were still alive—but the drow warriors were in full pursuit, leaving Drizzt to face the elemental.

The monster stomped again, the thunder of its foot nearly knocking Drizzt from his feet, and it came in hard, falling down at Drizzt, using the tonnage of its body as a weapon. If Drizzt had been even slightly surprised, or if his reflexes had not been honed to such perfection, he surely would have been crushed flat. He managed to get to the side of the monster's bulk, while taking only a glancing blow from a swinging arm.

Dust rushed up from the terrific impact; cavern walls and ceiling cracked and dropped flecks and stones to the floor. As the elemental regained its feet, Drizzt backed away, overwhelmed by such unconquerable strength.

He was all alone against it, or so Drizzt thought. A sudden ball of hot fury enveloped the elemental's head, claws raking deep scratches into its face.

"Guenhwyvar!" Drizzt and Masoj shouted in unison, Drizzt in elation that an ally had been found, and Masoj in rage. The wizard did not want Drizzt to survive this battle, and he dared not launch any magical attacks, at Drizzt or the elemental, with his precious Guenhwyvar in the way.

"Do something, wizard!" Drizzt cried, recognizing the shout and understanding now that Masoj was still around.

The elemental bellowed in pain, its cry sounding as the rumble of huge boulders crashing down a rocky mountain. Even as Drizzt moved back in to help his feline friend, the monster spun, impossibly quick, and dived headfirst to the floor.

"No!" Drizzt cried, realizing that Guenhwyvar would be crushed. Then the cat and the elemental, instead of slamming against the stone, sank down into it!

⚔ ⚔ ⚔ ⚔ ⚔

The purple flames of faerie fire outlined the figures of the gnomes, showing the way for drow arrows and swords. The gnomes countered with magic of their own, illusionists' tricks mostly. "Down here!" one drow soldier cried, only to slam face first into the stone of a wall that had appeared as the entrance to a corridor.

Even though the gnome magic managed to keep the dark elves somewhat confused, Belwar Dissengulp grew frightened. His elemental, his strongest magic and only hope, was taking too long with the single drow warrior far back in the main chamber. The burrow-warden wanted the monster by his side when the main combat began. He ordered his forces into tight defensive formations, hoping that they could hold out.

Then the drow warriors, detained no more by gnomish tricks, were upon them, and fury stole Belwar's fear. He lashed out with his heavy pickaxe, smiling grimly as he felt the mighty weapon bite into drow flesh.

All magic was aside now, all formations and carefully laid battle plans dissolved into the wild frenzy of the brawl. Nothing mattered, except to hit the enemy, to feel the pick head or blade sinking into flesh. Above all others, deep gnomes hated the drow, and in all the Underdark there was nothing a dark elf enjoyed more than slicing a svirfnebli into littler pieces.

⚔ ⚔ ⚔ ⚔ ⚔

Drizzt rushed to the spot, but only the unbroken section of floor remained. "Masoj?" he gasped, looking for some answers from the one schooled in such strange magic.

Before the wizard could answer, the floor erupted behind Drizzt. He spun, weapons ready, to face the towering elemental.

Then Drizzt watched in helpless agony as the broken mist that was the great panther, his dearest companion, rolled off the elemental's shoulders and broke apart as it neared the floor.

Drizzt ducked another blow, though his eyes never left the dissipating dust-and-mist cloud. Was Guenhwyvar no more? Was his only friend gone from him forever? A new light grew in Drizzt lavender eyes, a primal rage that simmered throughout his body. He looked back to the elemental, unafraid.

"You are dead," he promised, and he walked in.

The elemental seemed confused, though of course it could not understand Drizzt's words. It dropped a heavy arm straight down to squash its foolish opponent. Drizzt did not even raise his blades to parry, knowing that every ounce of his strength could not possibly deflect such a blow. Just as the falling arm was about to reach him, he dashed forward, within its range.

The quickness of his move surprised the elemental, and the ensuing flurry of swordplay took Masoj's breath away. The wizard had never seen such grace in battle, such fluidity of motion. Drizzt climbed up and down the elemental's body, hacking and slashing, digging the points of his weapons home and flicking off pieces of the monster's stone skin.

The elemental howled its avalanche howl and spun in circles, trying to catch up to Drizzt and squash him once and for all. Blind anger brought new levels of expertise to the magnificent young swordsman, though, and the elemental caught nothing but air or its own stony body under its heavy slaps.

"Impossible," Masoj muttered when he found his breath. Could the young Do'Urden actually defeat an elemental? Masoj scanned the rest of the area. Several drow and many gnomes lay dead or grievously wounded, but the main fighting was moving even farther away as the gnomes found their tiny escape tunnels and the drow, enraged beyond good sense, followed them.

Guenhwyvar was gone. In this chamber, only Masoj, the elemental, and Drizzt remained as witnesses. The invisible wizard felt his mouth draw up in a smile. Now was the time to strike.

Drizzt had the elemental lurching to one side, nearly beaten, when the bolt roared in, a blast of lightning that blinded the young drow and sent him flying into the chamber's back wall. Drizzt watched the twitch of his hands, the wild dance of his stark white hair before his unmoving eyes. He felt nothing—no pain, no reviving draw of air into his lungs—and heard nothing, as if his life force had been some how suspended.

The attack dispelled Masoj's dweomer of invisibility, and he came back in view, laughing wickedly. The elemental, down in a broken, crumbled mass, slowly slipped back into the security of the stone floor.

"Are you dead?" the wizard asked Drizzt, the voice breaking the hush of Drizzt's deafness in dramatic booms. Drizzt could not answer, didn't really know the answer anyway. "Too easy," he heard Masoj say, and he suspected that the wizard was referring to him and not the elemental.

Then Drizzt felt a tingling in his fingers and bones and his lungs heaved suddenly, grabbing a volume of air. He gasped in rapid succession, then found control of his body and realized that he would survive.

Masoj glanced around for returning witnesses and saw none. "Good," he muttered as he watched Drizzt regain his senses. The wizard was truly glad that Drizzt's death had not been so very painless. He thought of another spell that would make the moment more fun.

A hand—a gigantic stone hand—reached out of the floor just then and grasped Masoj's leg, pulling his feet right into the stone.

The wizard's face twisted in a silent scream.

Drizzt's enemy saved his life. Drizzt snatched up one of the scimitars from the ground and hacked at the elemental's arm. The weapon sliced in, and the monster, its head reappearing between Drizzt and Masoj, howled in rage and pain and pulled the trapped wizard deeper into the stone.

With both hands on the scimitar's hilt, Drizzt struck as hard as he could, splitting the elemental's head right in half. This time the rubble did not sink back into its earthen plane; this time the elemental was destroyed.

"Get me out of here!" Masoj demanded. Drizzt looked at him, hardly believing that Masoj was still alive, for he was waist deep in solid stone.

"How?" Drizzt gasped. "You . . ." He couldn't even find the words to express his amazement.

"Just get me out!" the wizard cried.

Drizzt fumbled about, not knowing where to begin.

"Elementals travel between planes," Masoj explained, knowing that he had to calm Drizzt down if he ever wanted to get out of the floor. Masoj knew, too, that the conversation could go a long way in deflecting Drizzt's obvious suspicions that the lightning bolt had been aimed at him. "The ground an earth elemental traverses becomes a gate between the Plane of Earth and our plane, the Material Plane. The stone parted around me as the monster pulled me in, but it is quite uncomfortable." He twitched in pain as the stone tightened around one foot. "The gate is closing fast!"

"Then Guenhwyvar might be . . ." Drizzt started to reason.

He plucked the statuette right out of Masoj's front pocket and carefully inspected it for any flaws in its perfect design.

"Give me that!" Masoj demanded, embarrassed and angry.

Reluctantly, Drizzt handed the figurine over. Masoj glanced at it quickly and dropped it back into the pocket.

"Is Guenhwyvar unharmed?" Drizzt had to ask.

"It is not your concern," Masoj snapped back. The wizard, too, was worried about the cat, but at this moment, Guenhwyvar was the least of his troubles. "The gate is closing," he said again. "Go get the clerics!"

Before Drizzt could start off, a slab of stone in the wall behind him slid away, and the rock-hard fist of Belwar Dissengulp slammed into the back of his head.

# 23

# A Single Clean Blow

"The gnomes took him," Masoj said to Dinin when the patrol leader returned to the cavern. The wizard lifted his arms over his head to give the high priestess and her assistants a better view of his predicament.

"Where?" Dinin demanded. "Why did they let you live?"

Masoj shrugged. "A secret door," he explained, "somewhere on the wall behind you. I suspect that they would have taken me as well, except . . ." Masoj looked down at the floor, still holding him tightly up to the waist. "The gnomes would have killed me, but for your arrival."

"You are fortunate, wizard," the high priestess said to Masoj. "I have memorized a spell this day that will release the stone's hold on you." She whispered some instructions to her assistants and they took out water skins and pouches of clay and began tracing a ten foot square on the floor around the trapped wizard. The high priestess moved over to the wall of the chamber and prepared for her prayers.

"Some have escaped," Dinin said to her.

The high priestess understood. She whispered a quick detection spell and studied the wall. "Right there," she said. Dinin and another male rushed over to the spot and soon found the almost imperceptible outline to the secret door.

As the high priestess began her incantation, one of her cleric assistants threw the end of a rope to Masoj. "Hold on," the assistant teased, "and hold your breath!"

"Wait—" Masoj began, but the stone floor all around him transformed into mud and the wizard slipped under.

Two clerics, laughing, pulled Masoj out a moment later.

"Nice spell," the wizard remarked, spitting mud.

"It has its purposes," replied the high priestess. "Especially when we fight against the gnomes and their tricks with the stone. I carried it as a safeguard against earth elementals." She looked at a piece of rubble at her feet, unmistakably one eye and the nose of such a creature. "I see that my spell was not needed in that manner."

"I destroyed that one," Masoj lied.

"Indeed," said the high priestess, unconvinced. She could tell by the cut of the rubble that a blade had made the wound. She let the issue drop when the scrape of sliding stone turned them all to the wall.

"A maze," moaned the fighter beside Dinin when he peered into the tunnel. "How will we find them?"

Dinin thought for a moment, then spun on Masoj. "They have my brother," he said, an idea coming to mind. "Where is your cat?"

"About," Masoj stalled, guessing Dinin's plan and not really wanting Drizzt rescued.

"Bring it to me," Dinin ordered. "The cat can smell Drizzt."

"I cannot . . . I mean," Masoj stuttered.

"Now, wizard!" Dinin commanded. "Unless you wish me to tell the ruling council that some of the gnomes escaped because you refused to help!"

Masoj tossed the figurine to the ground and called for Guenhwyvar, not really knowing what would happen next. Had the earth elemental really destroyed Guenhwyvar? The mist appeared, in seconds transforming into the panther's corporeal body.

"Well," Dinin prompted, indicating the tunnel.

"Go find Drizzt!" Masoj commanded the cat. Guenhwyvar sniffed around the area for a moment, then bounded off down the small tunnel, the drow patrol in silent pursuit.

✕✕✕✕✕

"Where . . ." Drizzt started when he finally began the long climb from the depths of unconsciousness. He understood that he was sitting, and knew, too, that his hands were bound in front of him.

A small but undeniably strong hand caught him by the back of the hair and pulled his head back roughly.

"Quiet!" Belwar whispered harshly, and Drizzt was surprised that the creature could speak his language. Belwar let go of Drizzt and turned to join other svirfnebli.

From the chamber's low height and the gnomes' nervous movements, Drizzt realized that this group had taken flight.

The gnomes began a quiet conversation in their own tongue, which Drizzt could not begin to understand. One of them asked the gnome who had ordered Drizzt to be quiet, apparently the leader, a heated question. Another grunted his accord and spoke some harsh words, turning on Drizzt with a dangerous look in his eyes.

The leader slapped the other gnome hard on the back and sent him off through one of the two low exits in the chamber, then put the others into defensive positions. He walked over to Drizzt. "You come with us to Blingdenstone," he said in hesitant words.

"Then?" Drizzt asked.

Belwar shrugged. "The king'll decide. If you cause me no trouble, I'll tell him to let you go."

Drizzt laughed cynically.

"Well, then," said Belwar, "if the king says to kill you, I'll make sure it comes in a single clean blow."

Again Drizzt laughed. "Do you believe that I believe?" he asked. "Torture me now and have your fun. That is your evil way!"

Belwar started to slap him but held his hand in check. "Svirfnebli don't torture!" he declared, louder than he should have. "Drow elves torture!" He turned away but spun back, reiterating his promise. "A single clean blow."

Drizzt found that he believed the sincerity in the gnome's voice, and he had to accept that promise as a measure of mercy far greater than the gnome would have received if Dinin's patrol had captured him. Belwar turned to walk away, but Drizzt, intrigued, had to learn more of the curious creature.

"How have you learned my language?" he asked.

"Gnomes are not stupid," Belwar retorted, unsure of what Drizzt was leading to.

"Nor are drow," Drizzt replied earnestly, "but I have never heard the language of the svirfnebli spoken in my city."

"There once was a drow in Blingdenstone," Belwar explained, now nearly as curious about Drizzt as Drizzt was about him.

"Slave," Drizzt reasoned.

"Guest!" Belwar snapped. "Svirfnebli keep no slaves!"

Again Drizzt found that he could not refute the sincerity in Belwar's voice. "What is your name?" he asked.

The gnome laughed at him. "Do you think me stupid?" Belwar asked. "You desire my name that you might use its power in some dark magic against me!"

"No," Drizzt protested.

"I should kill you now for thinking me stupid!" Belwar growled, ominously lifting his heavy pick. Drizzt shifted uncomfortably, not knowing what the gnome would do next.

"My offer remains," Belwar said, lowering the pick. "No trouble, and I tell the king to let you go." Belwar didn't believe that would happen any more than did Drizzt, so the svirfneblin, with a helpless shrug, offered Drizzt the next best thing. "Or else, a single clean blow."

A commotion from one of the tunnels turned Belwar away. "Belwar," called one of the other gnomes, rushing back into the small chamber. The gnome leader turned a wary eye on Drizzt to see if the drow had caught the mention of his name.

Drizzt wisely kept his head turned away, pretending not to listen. He had indeed heard the name of the gnome leader who had shown him mercy. Belwar, the other svirfneblin had said. Belwar, a name that Drizzt would never forget.

Fighting from down the passageway caught everyone's attention, then, and several svirfnebli scrambled back into the chamber. Drizzt knew from their excitement that the drow patrol was close behind.

Belwar started barking out commands, mostly organizing the retreat down the chamber's other tunnel. Drizzt wondered where he would fit into the gnome's thinking. Certainly Belwar couldn't hope to outrun the drow patrol dragging along a prisoner.

Then the gnome leader suddenly stopped talking and stopped moving. Too suddenly.

The drow clerics had led the way in with their insidious, paralyzing spells. Belwar and another gnome were held fast by the dweomer, and the rest of the gnomes, realizing this, broke into a wild scramble for the rear exit.

The drow warriors, Guenhwyvar leading the way, charged into the room. Any relief Drizzt might have felt at seeing his feline friend unharmed was buried under the ensuing slaughter. Dinin and his troops cut into the disorganized gnomes with typical drow savagery.

In seconds—horrible seconds that seemed like hours to Drizzt—only Belwar and the other gnome caught in the clerical spell remained alive in the chamber. Several of the svirfnebli had managed to flee down the back corridor, but most of the drow patrol was off in pursuit.

Masoj came into the chamber last, looking thoroughly wretched in his mud-covered clothing. He remained at the tunnel exit and did not even look Drizzt's way, except to note that his panther was standing protectively beside the secondboy of House Do'Urden.

"Again you have found your measure of luck, and more," Dinin said to Drizzt as he cut his brother's bonds.

Looking around at the carnage in the chamber, Drizzt wasn't so sure.

Dinin handed him back his scimitars, then turned to the drow standing watch over the two paralyzed gnomes. "Finish them," Dinin instructed.

A wide smile spread over the other drow's face, and he pulled a jagged knife from his belt. He held it up in front of a gnome's face, teasing the helpless creature. "Can they see it?" he asked the high priestess.

"That is the fun of the spell," the high priestess replied. "The svirfneblin understands what is about to happen. Even now he is struggling to break out of the hold."

"Prisoners!" Drizzt blurted.

Dinin and the others turned to him, the drow with the dagger wearing a scowl both angry and disappointed.

"For House Do'Urden?" Drizzt asked Dinin hopefully. "We could benefit from—"

"Svirfnebli do not make good slaves," Dinin replied.

"No," agreed the high priestess, moving beside the dagger-wielding fighter. She nodded to the warrior and his smile returned tenfold. He struck hard. Only Belwar remained.

The warrior waved his bloodstained dagger ominously and moved in front of the gnome leader.

"Not that one!" Drizzt protested, unable to bear anymore. "Let him live!" Drizzt wanted to say that Belwar could do them no harm, and that killing the defenseless gnome would be a cowardly and vile act. Drizzt knew that appealing to his kin for mercy would be a waste of time.

Dinin's expression was more a look of anger than curiosity this time.

"If you kill him, then no gnomes will remain to return to their city and tell of our strength," Drizzt reasoned, grasping at the one slim hope he could find. "We should send him back to his people, send him back to tell them of their folly in entering the domain of the drow!"

Dinin looked back to the high priestess for advice.

"It seems proper reasoning," she said with a nod.

Dinin was not so certain of his brother's motives. Not taking his eyes off Drizzt, he said to the warrior, "Then cut off the gnome's hands."

Drizzt didn't flinch, realizing that if he did, Dinin would surely slaughter Belwar.

The warrior replaced the dagger on his belt and took out his heavy sword.

"Wait," said Dinin, still eyeing Drizzt. "Release him from the spell first; I want to hear his screams."

Several drow moved over to put the tips of their swords at Belwar's neck as the high priestess released her magical hold. Belwar made no moves.

The appointed drow warrior grasped his sword in both hands, and Belwar, brave Belwar, held his arms straight out and motionless in front of him.

Drizzt averted his gaze, unable to watch and awaiting, fearing, the gnome's cry.

Belwar noted Drizzt's reaction. Was it compassion?

The drow warrior then swung his sword. Belwar never took his stare off Drizzt as the sword cut across his wrists, lighting a million fires of agony in his arms.

Neither did Belwar scream. He wouldn't give Dinin the satisfaction. The gnome leader looked back to Drizzt one final time as two drow fighters ushered him out of the chamber, and he recognized the true anguish, and the apology, behind the young drow's feigned impassive facade.

Even as Belwar was leaving, the dark elves who had chased off after the fleeing gnomes returned from the other tunnel. "We could not catch them in these tiny passage ways," one of them complained.

"Damn!" Dinin growled. Sending a handless gnome victim back to Blingdenstone was one thing, but letting healthy members of the gnome expedition escape was quite an other. "I want them caught!"

"Guenhwyvar can catch them," Masoj proclaimed, then he called the cat to his side and eyed Drizzt all the while.

Drizzt's heart raced as the wizard patted the great cat.

"Come, my pet," Masoj said. "There is hunting left to be done!" The wizard watched Drizzt squirm at the words, knowing that Drizzt did not approve of Guenhwyvar engaging in such tactics.

"They are gone?" Drizzt asked Dinin, his voice on the edge of desperation.

"Running all the way back to Blingdenstone," Dinin replied calmly. "If we let them."

"And will they return?"

Dinin's sour scowl reflected the absurdity of his brother's question. "Would you?"

"Our task is complete, then," Drizzt reasoned, trying vainly to find some way out of Masoj's ignoble designs for the panther.

"We have won the day," Dinin agreed, "though our own losses have been great. We may find still more fun, with the help of the wizard's pet."

"Fun," Masoj echoed pointedly at Drizzt. "Be gone, Guenhwyvar, into the tunnels. Let us learn how fast a frightened gnome may run!"

Only a few minutes later, Guenhwyvar came back into the chamber, dragging a dead gnome in its mouth.

"Return!" Masoj commanded as Guenhwyvar dropped the body at his feet. "Bring me more!"

Drizzt's heart dropped at the sound of the corpse flopping to the stone floor. He looked into Guenhwyvar's eyes and saw a sadness as profound as his own. The panther was a hunter, as honorable in its own way as was Drizzt. To the evil Masoj, though, Guenhwyvar was a toy and nothing more, an instrument for his perverted pleasures, killing for no reason other than his master's joy of killing.

In the hands of the wizard, Guenhwyvar was no more than a murderer.

Guenhwyvar paused at the entrance to the small tunnel and looked to Drizzt almost apologetically.

"Return!" Masoj screamed, and he kicked the cat in the rear. Then Masoj, too, turned an eye back on Drizzt, a vindictive eye. Masoj had missed his chance to kill the young Do'Urden; he would have to be careful how he explained such a mistake to his unforgiving mother. Masoj decided to worry about that unpleasant encounter later. For now, at least, he had the satisfaction of watching Drizzt suffer.

Dinin and the others were oblivious to the unfolding drama between Masoj and Drizzt; too engaged in their wait for Guenhwyvar's return; too engaged in their speculations of the expressions of terror the gnomes would cast back at such a perfect killer; too caught up in the macabre humor of the moment, that perverted drow humor that brought laughter when tears were needed.

# Part Five

## Zaknafein

**Zaknafein Do'Urden: mentor, teacher, friend. I, in the blind agony of my own frustrations, more than once came to recognize Zaknafein as none of these. Did I ask of him more than he could give? Did I expect perfection of a tormented soul; hold Zaknafein up to standards beyond his experiences, or standards impossible in the face of his experiences?**

**I might have been him. I might have lived, trapped within the helpless rage, buried under the daily assault of the wickedness that is Menzoberranzan and the pervading evil that is my own family, never in life to find escape.**

**It seems a logical assumption that we learn from the mistakes of our elders. This, I believe, was my salvation. Without the example of Zaknafein, I, too, would have found no escape—not in life.**

Is this course I have chosen a better way than the life Zaknafein knew? I think, yes, though I find despair often enough sometimes to long for that other way. It would have been easier. Truth, though, is nothing in the face of self-falsehood, and principles are of no value if the idealist cannot live up to his own standards.

This, then, is a better way.

I live with many laments, for my people, for myself, but mostly for that weapons master, lost to me now, who showed me how—and why—to use a blade.

There is no pain greater than this; not the cut of a jagged-edged dagger nor the fire of a dragon's breath. Nothing burns in your heart like the emptiness of losing something, someone, before you truly have learned of its value. Often now I lift my cup in a futile toast, an apology to ears that cannot hear:

To Zak, the one who inspired my courage.

—Drizzt Do'Urden

# 24

# To Know Our Enemies

Eight drow dead, and one a cleric," Briza said to Matron Malice on the balcony of House Do'Urden. Briza had rushed back to the compound with the first reports of the encounter, leaving her sisters at the central plaza of Menzoberranzan with the gathered throng, awaiting further information. "But nearly two score of the gnomes died, a clear victory."

"What of your brothers?" asked Malice. "How did House Do'Urden fare in this encounter?"

"As with the surface elves, Dinin's hand slew five," replied Briza. "They say that he led the main assault fearlessly, and he killed the most gnomes."

Matron Malice beamed with the news, though she suspected that Briza, standing patiently behind a smug smile, was holding something dramatic back from her. "What of Drizzt?" the matron demanded, having no patience for her daughter's games. "How many svirfnebli fell at his feet?"

"None," Briza replied, but still the smile remained. "Still the day belonged to Drizzt!" she added quickly, seeing an angry scowl spreading across her volatile mother's face. Malice did not seem amused.

"Drizzt defeated an earth elemental," Briza cried, "all alone, almost, with only minor help from a wizard! The high priestess of the patrol named the kill his!"

Matron Malice gasped and turned away. Drizzt had ever been an enigma to her, as fine with the blade as any but lacking the proper attitude and the proper respect. Now this: an earth elemental! Malice herself had seen such a monster ravage an entire drow raiding party, killing a dozen seasoned warriors before wandering off on its way. Yet her son, her confusing son, had defeated one single-handedly!

"Lolth will favor us this day," Briza commented, not quite understanding her mother's reaction.

Briza's words struck an idea in Malice. "Gather your sisters," she commanded. "We shall meet in the chapel. If House Do'Urden so fully won the day out in the tunnels, perhaps the Spider Queen will grace us with some information."

"Vierna and Maya await the forthcoming news in the city plaza," Briza explained, mistakenly believing her mother to be referring to information about the battle. "Surely we will know the entire story within an hour."

"I care nothing for a battle against gnomes!" Malice scolded. "You have told everything that is important to our family; the rest does not matter. We must parlay your brothers' heroics into gain."

"To learn of our enemies!" Briza blurted as she realized what her mother had in mind.

"Exactly," replied Malice. "To learn which house it is that threatens House Do'Urden. If the Spider Queen truly finds favor with us this day, she may grace us with the knowledge we need to defeat our enemies!"

A short while later, the four high priestesses of House Do'Urden gathered around the spider idol in the chapel anteroom. Before them, in a bowl of the deepest onyx, burned the sacred incense—sweet, deathlike, and favored by the yochlol, the handmaidens of Lolth.

The flame moved through a variety of colors, from orange to green to brilliant red. It then took shape, heard the beckons of the four priestesses and the urgency in the voice of Matron Malice. The top of the fire, no longer dancing, smoothed and rounded, assumed the form of a hairless head, then stretched upward, growing. The flame disappeared, consumed by the yochlol's image, a half melted pile of wax with grotesquely elongated eyes and a drooping mouth.

"Who has summoned me?" the small figure demanded telepathically.

The yochlol's thoughts, too powerful for its diminutive stature, boomed within the heads of the gathered drow.

"I have, handmaiden," Malice replied aloud, wanting her daughters to hear. The matron bowed her head. "I am Malice, loyal servant of the Spider Queen."

In a puff of smoke, the yochlol disappeared, leaving only glowing incense embers in the onyx bowl. A moment later, the handmaiden reappeared, full size, standing behind Matron Malice. Briza, Vierna, and Maya held their breath as the being laid two sickly tentacles on their mother's shoulders.

Matron Malice accepted the tentacles without reply, confident in her cause for summoning the yochlol.

"Explain to me why you dare to disturb me," came the yochlol's insidious thoughts.

"To ask a simple question," Malice replied silently, for no words were necessary to communicate with a handmaiden. "One whose answer you know."

"Does this question interest you so greatly?" the yochlol asked. "You risk such dire consequences."

"It is imperative that I learn the answer," replied Matron Malice. Her three daughters watched curiously, hearing the yochlol's thoughts but only guessing at their mother's unspoken replies.

"If the answer is so important, and it is known to the handmaidens, and thus to the Spider Queen, do you not believe that Lolth would have given it to you if she so chose?"

"Perhaps, before this day, the Spider Queen did not deem me worthy to know," Malice responded. "Things have changed."

The handmaiden paused and rolled its elongated eyes back into its head as if communicating with some distant plane.

"Greetings, Matron Malice Do'Urden," the yochlol said aloud after a few tense moments. The creature's spoken voice was calm and overly smooth for the thing's grotesque appearance.

"My greetings to you, and to your mistress, Queen of Spiders," replied Malice. She shot a wry smile at her daughters and still didn't turn to face the creature behind her. Apparently Malice's guess of Lolth's favor had been correct.

"Daermon N'a'shezbaernon has pleased Lolth," the handmaiden said. "The males of your house have won the day, even above the females that journeyed with them. I must accept Matron Malice Do'Urden's summons." The tentacles slid off Malice's shoulders, and the yochlol stood rigid behind her, awaiting her commands.

"Glad I am to please the Spider Queen," Malice began. She sought the proper way to phrase her question. "For the summons, as I have said, I beg only the answer to a simple question."

"Ask it," prompted the yochlol, and the mocking tone told Malice and her daughters that the monster already knew the question.

"My house is threatened, say the rumors," said Malice.

"Rumors?" The yochlol laughed an evil, grating sound.

"l trust in my sources," Malice replied defensively. "I would not have called upon you if I did not believe the threat."

"Continue," said the yochlol, amused by the whole affair. "They are more than rumors, Matron Malice Do'Urden. Another house plans war upon you."

Maya's immature gasp brought scornful eyes upon her from her mother and her sisters.

"Name this house to me," Malice pleaded. "If Daermon N'a'shezbaernon truly has pleased the Spider Queen this day, then I bid Lolth to reveal our enemies, that we might destroy them!"

"And if this other house also has pleased the Spider Queen?" the handmaiden mused. "Would Lolth then betray it to you?"

"Our enemies hold every advantage," Malice protested. "They know of House Do'Urden. No doubt they watch us every day, laying their plans. We ask Lolth only to give us knowledge equal to that of our enemies. Reveal them and let us prove which house is more worthy of victory."

"What if your enemies are greater than you?" asked the handmaiden. "Would Matron Malice Do'Urden then call upon Lolth to intervene and save her pitiful house?"

"No!" cried Malice. "We would call upon those powers that Lolth has given us to fight our foes. Even if our enemies are the more powerful, let Lolth be assured that they will suffer great pain for their attack on House Do'Urden!"

Again the handmaiden sank back within itself, finding the link to its home plane, a place darker than Menzoberranzan. Malice clenched tightly to Briza's hand, to her right, and Vierna's, to her left. They in turn passed along the confirmation of their bond to Maya, at the foot of the circle.

"The Spider Queen is pleased, Matron Malice Do'Urden," the handmaiden said at length. "Trust that she will favor House Do'Urden more than your enemies when battle rings out—perhaps . . ." Malice flinched at the ambiguity of that final word, grudgingly accepting that Lolth never made any promises, at any time.

"What of my question," Malice dared to protest, "the reason for the summons?"

There came a bright flash that stole the four clerics' vision. When their eyesight returned to them, they saw the yochlol, tiny again, and glaring out at them from the flames of the onyx bowl.

"The Spider Queen does not give an answer that is already known!" The handmaiden proclaimed, the sheer power of its otherworldly voice cutting into the drow ears. The fire erupted in another blinding flash, and the yochlol disappeared, leaving the precious bowl sundered into a dozen pieces.

Matron Malice grabbed a large piece of the shattered onyx and threw it against a wall. "Already known?" she cried in rage. "Known to whom? Who in my family keeps this secret from me?"

"Perhaps the one who knows does not know that she knows," Briza put in, trying to calm her mother. "Or perhaps the information is newly found, and she has not yet had the chance to come to you with it."

"She?" growled Matron Malice. "What 'she' do you speak of, Briza? We are all here. Are any of my daughters stupid enough to miss such an obvious threat to our family?"

"No, Matron!" Vierna and Maya cried together, terrified of Malice's growing wrath, rising beyond control.

"Never have I seen any sign!" said Vierna.

"Nor l! " added Maya. "By your side I have been these many tendays, and I have seen no more than you!"

"Are you implying that I have missed something?" Malice growled, her knuckles white at her sides.

"No, Matron!" Briza shouted above the commotion, loud enough to settle her mother for the moment and turn Malice's attention fully upon her eldest daughter.

"Not she, then," Briza reasoned. "He. One of your sons may have the answer, or Zaknafein or Rizzen, perhaps."

"Yes," agreed Vierna. "They are only males, too stupid to understand the importance of minor details."

"Drizzt and Dinin have been out of the house," added Briza, "out of the city. In their patrol group are children of every powerful house, every house that would dare to threaten us!"

The fires in Malice's eyes glowed, but she relaxed at the reasoning. "Bring them to me when they return to Menzoberranzan," she instructed Vierna and Maya. "You," she said to Briza, "bring Rizzen and Zaknafein. All the family must be present, so that we may learn what we may learn!"

"The cousins, and the soldiers, too?" asked Briza. "Perhaps one beyond the immediate family knows the answer."

"Should we bring them together, as well?" offered Vierna, her voice edged with the rising excitement of the moment. "A gathering of the whole clan, a general war party of House Do'Urden?"

"No," Malice replied, "not the soldiers or the cousins. I do not believe they are involved in this; the handmaiden would have told us the answer if one of my direct family did not know it. It is my embarrassment to ask a question whose answer should be known to me, whose answer someone within the circle of my family knows." She gritted her teeth as she spat out the rest of her thoughts.

"I do not enjoy being embarrassed!"

⚔ ⚔ ⚔ ⚔ ⚔

Drizzt and Dinin came into the house a short while later, exhausted and glad the adventure was over. They had barely passed the entrance and turned down the wide corridor that led to their rooms when they bumped into Zaknafein, coming the other way.

"So the hero has returned," Zak remarked, eyeing Drizzt directly. Drizzt did not miss the sarcasm in his voice.

"We've completed our job—successfully," Dinin shot back, more than a little perturbed at being excluded from Zak's greeting. "I led—"

"I know of the battle," Zak assured him. "It has been endlessly recounted throughout the city. Now leave us, Elderboy. I have unfinished business with your brother."

"I leave when I choose to leave!" Dinin growled.

Zak snapped a glare upon him. "I wish to speak to Drizzt, only to Drizzt, so leave."

Dinin's hand went to his sword hilt, not a smart move. Before he even moved the weapon hilt an inch from the scabbard, Zak had slapped him twice in the face with one hand. The other had somehow produced a dagger and put its tip at Dinin's throat.

Drizzt watched in amazement, certain that Zak would kill Dinin if this continued.

"Leave," Zak said again, "on your life."

Dinin threw his hands up and slowly backed away. "Matron Malice will hear of this!" he warned.

"I will tell her myself," Zak laughed at him. "Do you think she will trouble herself on your behalf, fool? As far as Matron Malice cares, the family males determine their own hierarchy. Go away, Elderboy. Come back when you have found the courage to challenge me."

"Come with me, brother," Dinin said to Drizzt.

"We have business," Zak reminded Drizzt.

Drizzt looked to both of them, once and back again, stunned by their open willingness to kill each other. "I will stay," he decided. "I do indeed have unfinished business with the weapons master."

"As you choose, hero," Dinin spat, and he turned on his heel and stormed away.

"You have made an enemy," Drizzt remarked to Zak.

"I have made many," Zak laughed, "and I will make many more before my day ends! But no mind. Your actions have inspired jealousy in your brother—your older brother. You are the one who should be wary."

"He hates you openly," reasoned Drizzt.

"But would gain nothing from my death," Zak replied. "I am no threat to Dinin, but you . . ." He let the word hang in the air.

"Why would I threaten him?" Drizzt protested. "Dinin has nothing I desire."

"He has power," Zak explained. "He is the elderboy now but was not always."

"He killed Nalfein, the brother I never met."

"You know of this?" said Zak. "Perhaps Dinin suspects that another secondboy will follow the same course he took to become the elderboy of House Do'Urden."

"Enough," Drizzt growled, tired of the whole stupid system of ascension. How well you know it, Zaknafein, he thought. How many did you murder to attain your position?

"An earth elemental," Zak said, blowing a low whistle with the words. "It is a powerful foe that you defeated this day." He bowed low, showing Drizzt mockery beyond any doubt. "What is next for the young hero? A daemon, perhaps? A demigod? Surely there is nothing that can—"

"Never have I heard such senseless words stream from your mouth," Drizzt retorted. Now it was time for some sarcasm of his own. "Is it that I have inspired jealousy in another besides my brother?"

"Jealousy?" Zak cried. "Wipe your nose, sniveling little boy! A dozen earth elementals have fallen to my blade! Daemons, too! Do not overestimate your deeds or your abilities. You are one warrior among a race of warriors. To forget that surely will prove fatal." He ended the line with pointed emphasis, almost in a sneer, and Drizzt began to consider again just how real their appointed "practice" in the gym would become.

"I know my abilities," Drizzt replied, "and my limitations. I have learned to survive."

"As have I," Zak shot back, "for so many centuries!"

"The gym awaits," Drizzt said calmly.

"Your mother awaits," Zak corrected. "She bids us all to the chapel. Fear not, though. There will be time for our meeting."

Drizzt walked past Zak without another word, suspecting that his and Zak's blades would finish the conversation for them. What had become of

Zaknafein? Drizzt wondered. Was this the same teacher who had trained him those years before the Academy? Drizzt could not sort through his feelings. Was he seeing Zak differently because of the things he had learned of Zak's exploits, or was there truly something different, something harder, about the weapons master's demeanor since Drizzt had returned from the Academy?

The sound of a whip brought Drizzt from his contemplations.

"I am your patron!" he heard Rizzen say.

"That's of no consequence!" retorted a female voice, the voice of Briza. Drizzt slipped to the corner of the next intersection and peeked around. Briza and Rizzen faced off, Rizzen unarmed, but Briza holding her snake-headed whip.

"Patron," Briza laughed, "a meaningless title. You are a male lending your seed to the matron and of no more importance."

"Four I have sired," Rizzen said indignantly.

"Three!" Briza corrected, snapping the whip to accentuate the point. "Vierna is Zaknafein's, not yours! Nalfein is dead, leaving only two. One of those is female and above you. Only Dinin is truly under your rank!"

Drizzt sank back against the wall and looked behind him to the empty corridor he had just walked. He had always suspected that Rizzen was not his true father. The male had never paid him any mind, had never scolded him or praised him or offered to him any advice or training. To hear Briza say it, though, . . . and Rizzen not deny it!

Rizzen fumbled about for some retort to Briza's stinging words. "Does Matron Malice know of your desires?" he snarled. "Does she know that her eldest daughter seeks her title?"

"Every eldest daughter seeks the title of matron mother," Briza laughed at him. "Matron Malice would be a fool to suspect otherwise. I assure you that she is not, nor am I. I will get the title from her when she is weak with age. She knows and accepts this as fact."

"You admit that you will kill her?"

"If not I, then Vierna. If not Vierna, then Maya. It is our way, stupid male. It is the word of Lolth."

Rage burned in Drizzt as he heard the evil proclamations, but he remained silent at the corner.

"Briza will not wait for age to steal her mother's power," Rizzen snarled, "not when a dagger will expedite the transfer. Briza hungers for the throne of the house!"

Rizzen's next words came out as an indecipherable scream as the six-headed whip went to work again and again.

Drizzt wanted to intervene, to rush out and cut them both down, but, of course, he could not. Briza acted now as she had been taught, followed the words of the Spider Queen in asserting her dominance over Rizzen. She wouldn't kill him, Drizzt knew.

But what if Briza got carried away in the frenzy? What if she did kill Rizzen? In the empty void that was beginning to grow in his heart, Drizzt wondered if he even cared.

⚔ ⚔ ⚔ ⚔ ⚔

"You let him escape!" Matron SiNafay roared at her son. "You will learn not to disappoint me!"

"No, my matron!" Masoj protested. "I hit him squarely with a lightning bolt. He never even suspected the blow to be aimed at him! I could not finish the deed; the monster had me caught in the gate to its own plane!"

SiNafay bit her lip, forced to accept her son's reasoning. She knew that she had given Masoj a difficult mission. Drizzt was a powerful foe, and to kill him without leaving an obvious trail would not be easy.

"I will get him," Masoj promised, determination showing on his face. "I have the weapon readied; Drizzt will be dead before the tenth cycle, as you commanded."

"Why should I grant you another chance?" SiNafay asked him. "Why should I believe that you will fare better the next time you try?"

"Because I want him dead!" Masoj cried. "More than even you, my matron. I want to tear the life from Drizzt Do'Urden! When he is dead, I want to rip out his heart and display it as a trophy!"

SiNafay could not deny her son's obsession. "Granted," she said. "Get him, Masoj Hun'ett. On your life, strike the first blow against House Do'Urden and kill its secondboy."

Masoj bowed, the grimace never leaving his face, and swept out of the room.

"You heard everything," SiNafay signaled when the door had closed behind her son. She knew that Masoj might well have his ear to the door, and she did not want him to know of this conversation.

"I did," Alton replied in the silent code, stepping out from behind a curtain.

"Do you concur with my decision?" SiNafay's hands asked.

Alton was at a loss. He had no choice but to abide by his matron mother's decisions, but he did not think that SiNafay had been wise in sending Masoj back out after Drizzt. His silence grew long.

"You do not approve," Matron SiNafay bluntly motioned.

"Please, Matron Mother," Alton replied quickly. "I would not . . ."

"You are forgiven," SiNafay assured him. "I am not so certain that I should have allowed Masoj a second opportunity. Too much could go wrong."

"Then why?" Alton dared to ask. "You did not grant me a second chance, though I desire Drizzt Do'Urden's death as fiercely as any."

SiNafay cast him a scornful glare, sending him back on his courageous heels. "You doubt my judgment?"

"No!" Alton cried aloud. He slipped a hand over his mouth and dropped to his knees in terror. "Never, my matron," he signaled silently. "I just do not understand the problem as clearly as you. Forgive me my ignorance."

SiNafay's laughter sounded like the hiss of a hundred angry snakes. "We see together in this matter," she assured Alton. "I would no more give Masoj a second chance than I gave you."

"But—" Alton started to protest.

"Masoj will go back after Drizzt, but this time he will not be alone," SiNafay explained. "You will follow him, Alton DeVir. Keep him safe and finish the deed, on your life."

Alton beamed at the news that he would finally find some taste of vengeance. SiNafay's final threat didn't even concern him. "Could it ever be any other way?" his hands asked casually.

⚔ ⚔ ⚔ ⚔ ⚔

"Think!" Malice growled, her face close, her breath hot on Drizzt's face. "You know something!"

Drizzt slumped back from the overpowering figure and glanced nervously around at his gathered family. Dinin, similarly grilled just a moment ago, kneeled with his chin in hand. He tried vainly to come up with an answer before Matron Malice upped the level of the interrogation techniques. Dinin did not miss Briza's motions toward her snake whip, and the unnerving sight did little to aid his memory.

Malice slapped Drizzt hard across the face and stepped away. "One of you has learned the identity of our enemies," she snapped at her sons. "Out there, on patrol, one of you has seen some hint, some sign."

"Perhaps we saw it but did not know it for what it was," Dinin offered.

"Silence!" Malice screamed, her face bright with rage. "When you know the answer to my question, you may speak! Only then!" She turned to Briza. "Help Dinin find his memory!"

Dinin dropped his head to his arms, folded on the floor in front of him, and arched his back to accept the torture. To do otherwise would only enrage Malice more.

Drizzt closed his eyes and recounted the events of his many patrols. He jerked involuntarily when he heard the snake whip's crack and his brother's soft groan.

"Masoj," Drizzt whispered, almost unconsciously. He looked up at his mother, who held her hand out to halt Briza's attacks—to Briza's dismay.

"Masoj Hun'ett," Drizzt said more loudly. "In the fight against the gnomes, he tried to kill me."

All the family, particularly Malice and Dinin, leaned forward toward Drizzt, hanging on his every word.

"When I battled the elemental," Drizzt explained, spitting out the last word as a curse upon Zaknafein. He cast an angry glare at the weapons master and continued, "Masoj Hun'ett struck me down with a bolt of lightning."

"He may have been shooting for the monster," Vierna insisted. "Masoj insisted that it was he who killed the elemental, but the high priestess of the patrol denied his claim."

"Masoj waited," Drizzt replied. "He did nothing until I began to gain the advantage over the monster. Then he loosed his magic, as much at me as at the elemental. I think he hoped to destroy us both."

"House Hun'ett," Matron Malice whispered.

"Fifth House," Briza remarked, "under Matron SiNafay."

"So that is our enemy," said Malice.

"Perhaps not," said Dinin, wondering even as he spoke the words why he hadn't left well enough alone. To disprove the theory only invited more whipping.

Matron Malice did not like his hesitation as he reconsidered the argument. "Explain!" she commanded.

"Masoj Hun'ett was angry at being excluded from the surface raid," said Dinin. "We left him in the city, only to witness our triumphant return." Dinin fixed his eyes straight on his brother. "Masoj has ever been jealous of Drizzt and all the glories that my brother has found, rightly or wrongly. Many are jealous of Drizzt and would see him dead."

Drizzt shifted uncomfortably in his seat, knowing the last words to be an open threat. He glanced over to Zaknafein and marked the weapons master's smug smile.

"Are you certain of your words?" Malice said to Drizzt, shaking him from his private thoughts.

"There is the cat," Dinin interrupted, "Masoj Hun'ett's magical pet, though it holds closer to Drizzt's side than to the wizard's."

"Guenhwyvar walks the point beside me," Drizzt protested, "a position that you ordered."

"Masoj does not like it," Dinin retorted.

Perhaps that is why you put the cat there, Drizzt thought, but he kept the words to himself. Was he seeing conspiracies in coincidence? Or was his world so truly filled with devious schemes and silent struggles for power?

"Are you certain of your words?" Malice asked Drizzt again, pulling him from his pondering.

"Masoj Hun'ett tried to kill me," he asserted. "I do not know his reasons, but his intent I do not doubt!"

"House Hun'ett, then," Briza remarked, "a mighty foe."

"We must learn of them," Malice said. "Dispatch the scouts! I will know the count of House Hun'ett's soldiers, its wizards, and, particularly, its clerics."

"If we are wrong," Dinin said. "If House Hun'ett is not the conspiring house—"

"We are not wrong!" Malice screamed at him.

"The yochlol said that one of us knows the identity of our enemy," reasoned Vierna. "All we have is Drizzt's tale of Masoj."

"Unless you are hiding something," Matron Malice growled at Dinin, a threat so cold and wicked that it stole the blood from the elderboy's face.

Dinin shook his head emphatically and slumped back, having nothing more to add to the conversation.

"Prepare a communion," Malice said to Briza. "Let us learn of Matron SiNafay's standing with the Spider Queen."

Drizzt watched incredulously as the preparations began at a frantic pace, each command from Matron Malice following a practiced defensive course. It wasn't the precision of Drizzt's family's battle planning that amazed him—he would expect nothing less from this group. It was the eager gleam in every eye.

# 25

# The Weapons Masters

"Impudent!" growled the yochlol. The fire in the brazier puffed, and the creature again stood behind Malice, again draped dangerous tentacles over the matron mother. "You dare to summon me again?"

Malice and her daughters glanced around, on the edge of panic. They knew that the mighty being was not toying with them; the handmaiden truly was enraged this time.

"House Do'Urden pleased the Spider Queen, it is true," the yochlol answered their unspoken thoughts, "but that one act does not dispel the displeasure your family brought upon Lolth in the recent past. Do not think that all is forgiven, Matron Malice Do'Urden!"

How small and vulnerable Matron Malice felt now. Her power paled in the face of the wrath of one of Lolth's personal servants.

"Displeasure?" she dared to whisper. "How has my family brought displeasure to the Spider Queen? By what act?"

The handmaiden's laughter erupted in a spout of flames and flying spiders, but the high priestesses held their positions. They accepted the heat and the crawling things as part of their penance.

"I have told you before, Matron Malice Do'Urden," the yochlol snarled with its droopy mouth, "and I shall tell you one final time. The Spider Queen does not reply to questions whose answers are already known!" In a blast of explosive energy that sent the four females of House Do'Urden tumbling to the floor, the handmaiden was gone.

Briza was the first to recover. She prudently rushed over to the brazier and smothered the remaining flames, thus closing the gate to the Abyss, the yochlol's home plane.

"Who?" screamed Malice, the powerful matriarch once again. "Who in my family has invoked the wrath of Lolth?" Malice appeared small again then, as the implications of the yochlol's warning became all too clear. House Do'Urden was about to go to war with a powerful family. Without Lolth's favor, House Do'Urden likely would cease to exist.

"We must find the perpetrator," Malice instructed her daughters, certain that none of them was involved. They were high priestesses, one and all. If any of them had done some misdeed in the eyes of the Spider Queen, the summoned yochlol surely would have exacted punishment on the spot. By itself, the handmaiden could have leveled House Do'Urden.

Briza pulled the snake whip from her belt. "I will get the information we require!" she promised.

"No!" said Matron Malice. "We must not reveal our search. Be it a soldier or a member of House Do'Urden, the guilty one is trained and hardened against pain. We cannot hope that torture will pull the confession from his lips; not when he knows the consequences of his actions. We must discover the cause of Lolth's displeasure immediately and properly punish the criminal. The Spider Queen must stand behind us in our struggles!"

"How, then, are we to discern the perpetrator?" the eldest daughter complained, reluctantly replacing the snake whip on her belt.

"Vierna and Maya, leave us," Matron Malice instructed. "Say nothing of these revelations and do nothing to hint at our purpose."

The two younger daughters bowed and scurried away, not happy with their secondary roles but unable to do anything about them.

"First we will look," Malice said to Briza. "We will see if we can learn of the guilty one from afar."

Briza understood. "The scrying bowl," she said. She rushed from the anteroom and into the chapel proper. In the central altar she found the valuable item, a wide golden bowl laced throughout with black pearls. Hands trembling,

Briza placed the bowl atop the altar and reached into the most sacred of the many compartments. This was the holding bin for the prized possession of House Do'Urden, a great onyx chalice.

Malice then joined Briza in the chapel proper and took the chalice from her. Moving to the large font at the entrance to the great room, Malice dipped the chalice into a sticky fluid, the unholy water of her religion. She then chanted, "*Spiderae aught icor ven.*" The ritual complete, Malice moved back to the altar and poured the unholy water into the golden bowl.

She and Briza sat down to watch.

⚔ ⚔ ⚔ ⚔ ⚔

Drizzt stepped onto the floor of Zaknafein's training gym for the first time in more than a decade and felt as if he had come home. He'd spent the best years of his young life here—almost wholly here. For all the disappointments he had encountered since—and no doubt would continue to experience throughout his life—Drizzt would never forget that brief sparkle of innocence, that joy, he had known when he was a student in Zaknafein's gym.

Zaknafein entered and walked over to face his former student. Drizzt saw nothing familiar or comforting in the weapons master's face. A perpetual scowl now replaced the once common smile. It was an angry demeanor that hated everything around it, perhaps Drizzt most of all. Or had Zaknafein always worn such a grimace? Drizzt had to wonder. Had nostalgia glossed over Drizzt's memories of those years of early training? Was this mentor, who had so often warmed Drizzt's heart with a lighthearted chuckle, actually the cold, lurking monster that Drizzt now saw before him?

"Which has changed, Zaknafein," Drizzt asked aloud, "you, my memories, or my perceptions?"

Zak seemed not even to hear the whispered question. "Ah, the young hero has returned," he said, "the warrior with exploits beyond his years."

"Why do you mock me?" Drizzt protested.

"He who killed the hook horrors," Zak continued. His swords were out in his hands now, and Drizzt responded by drawing his scimitars. There was no need to ask the rules of engagement in this contest, or the choice of weapons.

Drizzt knew, had known before he had ever come here, that there would be no rules this time. The weapons would be their weapons of preference, the blades that each of them had used to kill so many foes.

"He who killed the earth elemental," Zak snarled derisively. He launched a measured attack, a simple lunge with one blade. Drizzt batted it aside without even thinking of the parry.

Sudden fires erupted in Zak's eyes, as if the first contact had sundered all the emotional bonds that had tempered his thrust. "He who killed the girl child of the surface elves!" he cried, an accusation and no compliment. Now came the second attack, vicious and powerful, an arcing swipe descending at Drizzt's head. "Who cut her apart to appease his own thirst for blood!"

Zak's words knocked Drizzt off his guard emotionally, wrapped his heart in confusion like some devious mental whip. Drizzt was a seasoned warrior, though, and his reflexes did not register the emotional distraction. A scimitar came up to catch the descending sword and deflected it harmlessly aside.

"Murderer! " Zak snarled openly. "Did you enjoy the dying child's screams?" He came at Drizzt in a furious whirl, swords dipping and diving, slicing at every angle.

Drizzt, enraged by the hypocrite's accusations, matched the fury, screaming out for no better reason than to hear the anger of his own voice.

Any watching the battle would have found no breath in the next few blurring moments. Never had the Underdark witnessed such a vicious fight as when these two masters of the blade each attacked the demon possessing the other—and himself.

Adamantine sparked and nicked, droplets of blood spattered both the combatants, though neither felt any pain, and neither knew if he'd injured the other.

Drizzt came with a two blade sidelong swipe that drove Zak's swords out wide. Zak followed the motion quickly, turned a complete circle, and slammed back into Drizzt's thrusting scimitars with enough force to knock the young warrior from his feet. Drizzt fell into a roll and came back up to meet his charging adversary.

A thought came over him.

Drizzt came up high, too high, and Zak drove him back on his heels. Drizzt knew what would soon be coming; he invited it openly. Zak kept Drizzt's weapons high through several combined maneuvers. He then went with the move that had defeated Drizzt in the past, expecting that the best Drizzt could attain would be equal footing: double-thrust low.

Drizzt executed the appropriate cross-down parry, as he had to, and Zak tensed, waiting for his eager opponent to try to improve the move. "Child killer!" he growled, goading on Drizzt.

He didn't know that Drizzt had found the solution.

With all the anger he had ever known, all the disappointments of his young life gathering within his foot, Drizzt focused on Zak. That smug face, feigning smiles and drooling for blood.

Between the hilts, between the eyes, Drizzt kicked, blowing out every ounce of rage in a single blow.

Zak's nose crunched flat. His eyes lolled upward, and blood exploded over his hollow cheeks. Zak knew that he was falling, that the devilish young warrior would be on him in a flash, gaining an advantage that Zak could not hope to overcome.

"What of you, Zaknafein Do'Urden?" he heard Drizzt snarl, distantly, as though he were falling far away. "I have heard of the exploits of House Do'Urden's weapons master! How he so enjoys killing!" The voice was closer now, as Drizzt stalked in, and as the rebounding rage of Zaknafein sent him spiraling back to the battle.

"I have heard how murder comes so very easily to Zaknafein!" Drizzt spat derisively. "The murder of clerics, of other drow! Do you so enjoy it all?" He ended the question with a blow from each scimitar, attacks meant to kill Zak, to kill the demon in them both.

But Zaknafein was now fully back to consciousness, hating himself and Drizzt equally. At the last moment, his swords came up and crossed, lightning fast, throwing Drizzt's arms wide. Then Zak finished with a kick of his own, not so strong from the prone position but accurate in its search for Drizzt's groin.

Drizzt sucked in his breath and twirled away, forcing himself back into composure when he saw Zaknafein, still dazed, rising to his feet. "Do you so enjoy it all?" he managed to ask again.

"Enjoy?" the weapons master echoed.

"Does it bring you pleasure?" Drizzt grimaced.

"Satisfaction!" Zak corrected. "I kill. Yes, I kill."

"You teach others to kill!"

"To kill drow!" Zak roared, and he was back in Drizzt's face, his weapons up but waiting for Drizzt to make the next move.

Zak's words again entwined Drizzt in a mesh of confusion. Who was this drow standing before him?

"Do you think that your mother would let me live if I did not serve her evil designs?" Zak cried.

Drizzt did not understand.

"She hates me," Zak said, more in control as he began to understand Drizzt's confusion, "despises me for what I know." Drizzt cocked his head.

"Are you so blind to the evil around you?" Zak yelled in his face. "Or has it consumed you, as it consumes all of them, in this murderous frenzy that we call life?"

"The frenzy that holds you?" Drizzt retorted, but there was little conviction in his voice now. If he understood Zak's words correctly—if Zak played the killing game simply because of his hatred for the perverted drow—the most Drizzt could blame him for was cowardice.

"No frenzy holds me," Zak replied. "I live as best I can. I survive in a world that is not my own, not my heart." The lament in his words, the droop of his head as he admitted his helplessness, struck a familiar chord in Drizzt. "I kill, kill drow, to serve Matron Malice—to placate the rage, the frustration, that I know in my soul. When I hear the children scream . . ." His gaze snapped up on Drizzt and he rushed in all of a sudden, his fury returned tenfold.

Drizzt tried to get his scimitars up, but Zak knocked one of them across the room and drove the other aside. He rushed in step with Drizzt's awkward retreat until he had Drizzt pinned against a wall. The tip of Zak's sword drew a droplet of blood from Drizzt's throat.

"The child lives!" Drizzt gasped. "I swear, I did not kill the elven child!"

Zak relaxed a bit but still held Drizzt, sword to throat. "Dinin said—"

"Dinin was mistaken," Drizzt replied frantically. "Fooled by me. I knocked the child down—only to spare her—and covered her with the blood of her murdered mother to mask my own cowardice!"

Zak leaped back, overwhelmed.

"I killed no elves that day," Drizzt said to him. "The only ones I desired to kill were my own companions!"

⚔ ⚔ ⚔ ⚔ ⚔

"So now we know," said Briza, staring into the scrying bowl, watching the conclusion of the battle between Drizzt and Zaknafein and hearing their every word. "It was Drizzt who angered the Spider Queen."

"You suspected him all along, as did I," Matron Malice replied, "though we both hoped differently."

"So much promise!" Briza lamented. "How I wish that one had learned his place, his values. Perhaps . . ."

"Mercy?" Matron Malice snapped at her. "Do you show mercy that would further invoke the Spider Queen's displeasure?"

"No, Matron," Briza replied. "I had only hoped that Drizzt could be used in the future, as you have used Zaknafein all these years. Zaknafein is growing older."

"We are about to fight a war, my daughter," Malice reminded her. "Lolth must be appeased. Your brother has brought his fate upon himself; his actions were his own to decide."

"He decided wrongly."

⚔ ⚔ ⚔ ⚔ ⚔

The words hit Zaknafein harder than Drizzt's boot had. The weapons master threw his swords to the ends of the room and rushed in on Drizzt. He buried him in a hug so intense that it took the young drow a long moment to even realize what had happened.

"You have survived!" Zak said, his voice broken by muffled tears. "Survived the Academy, where all the others died!"

Drizzt returned the embrace, tentatively, still not guessing the depth of Zak's elation.

"My son!"

Drizzt nearly fainted, overwhelmed by the admission of what he had always suspected, and even more so by the knowledge that he was not the only one in his dark world angered by the ways of the drow. He was not alone.

"Why?" Drizzt asked, pushing Zak out to arm's length. "Why have you stayed?"

Zak looked at him incredulously. "Where would I go? No one, not even a drow weapons master would survive for long out in the caverns of the Underdark. Too many monsters, and other races, hunger for the sweet blood of dark elves."

"Surely you had options."

"The surface?" Zak replied. "To face the painful inferno every day? No, my son, I am trapped, as you are trapped."

Drizzt had feared that statement, had feared that he would find no solution from his newfound father to the dilemma that was his life. Perhaps there were no answers.

"You will do well in Menzoberranzan," Zak said to comfort him. "You are strong, and Matron Malice will find an appropriate place for your talents, whatever your heart may desire."

"To live a life of assassinations, as you have?" Drizzt asked, trying futilely to keep the rage out of his words.

"What choice is before us?" Zak answered, his eyes seeking the unjudging stone of the floor.

"I will not kill drow," Drizzt declared flatly.

Zak's eyes snapped back on him. "You will," he assured his son. "In Menzoberranzan, you will kill or be killed."

Drizzt looked away, but Zak's words pursued him, could not be blocked out.

"There is no other way," the weapons master continued softly. "Such is our world. Such is our life. You have escaped this long, but you will find that your luck soon will change." He grabbed Drizzt's chin firmly and forced his son to look at him directly.

"I wish that it could be different," Zak said honestly, "but it is not such a bad life. I do not lament killing dark elves. I perceive their deaths as their salvation from this wicked existence. If they care so dearly for their Spider Queen, then let them go and visit her!"

Zak's growing smile washed away suddenly. "Except for the children," he whispered. "Often have I heard the cries of dying children, though never, I promise you, have I caused them. I have always wondered if they, too, are evil, born evil. Or if the weight of our dark world bends them to fit our foul ways."

"The ways of the demon Lolth," Drizzt agreed.

They both paused for many heartbeats, each privately weighing the realities of his own personal dilemma. Zak was next to speak, having long ago come to terms with the life that was offered to him.

"Lolth," he chuckled. "She is a vicious queen, that one. I would sacrifice everything for a chance at her ugly face!"

"I almost believe you would," Drizzt whispered, finding his smile.

Zak jumped back from him. "I would indeed," he laughed heartily. "So would you!"

Drizzt flipped his lone scimitar up into the air, letting it spin over twice before catching it again by the hilt. "True enough!" he cried. "But no longer would I be alone!"

# 26

# Angler of The Underdark

Drizzt wandered alone through the maze of Menzoberranzan, drifting past the stalagmite mounds, under the leering points of the great stone spears that hung from the cavern's high ceiling. Matron Malice had specifically ordered all of the family to remain within the house, fearing an assassination attempt by House Hun'ett. Too much had happened to Drizzt this day for him to obey. He had to think, and contemplating such blasphemous thoughts, even silently, in a house full of nervous clerics might get him into serious trouble.

This was the quiet time of the city; the heat-light of Narbondel was only a sliver at the stone's base, and most of the drow comfortably slept within their stone houses. Soon after he slipped through the adamantine gate of the House Do'Urden compound, Drizzt began to understand the wisdom of Matron Malice's command. The city's quiet now seemed to him like the crouched hush of a predator. It was poised to drop upon him from behind every one of the many blind corners he faced on this trek.

He would find no solace here in which he might truly contemplate the day's events, the revelations of Zaknafein, kindred in more than blood. Drizzt decided to break all the rules—that was the way of the drow, after all—and head out of the city, down the tunnels he knew so well from his tendays of patrol.

An hour later, he was still walking, lost in thought and feeling safe enough, for he was well within the boundaries of the patrol region.

He entered a high corridor, ten paces wide and with broken walls lined in loose rubble and crossed by many ledges. It seemed as though the passage once had been much wider. The ceiling was far beyond sight, but Drizzt had been through here a dozen times, up on the many ledges, and he gave the place no thought.

He envisioned the future, the times that he and Zaknafein, his father, would share now that no secrets separated them. Together they would be unbeatable, a team of weapons masters, bonded by steel and emotions. Did House Hun'ett truly understand what it would be facing? The smile on Drizzt's face disappeared as soon as he considered the implications: he and Zak, together, cutting through House Hun'ett's ranks with deadly ease, through the ranks of drow elves—killing their own people.

Drizzt leaned against the wall for support, understanding firsthand the frustration that had racked his father for many centuries. Drizzt did not want to be like Zaknafein, living only to kill, existing in a protective sphere of violence, but what choices lay before him? Leave the city?

Zak had balked when Drizzt asked him why he had not left. "Where would I go?" Drizzt whispered now, echoing Zak's words. His father had proclaimed them trapped, and so it seemed to Drizzt.

"Where would I go?" he asked again. "Travel the Underdark, where our people are so despised and a single drow would become a target for everything he passed? Or to the surface, perhaps, and let that ball of fire in the sky burn out my eyes so that I may not witness my own death when the elven folk descend upon me?"

The logic of the reasoning trapped Drizzt as it had trapped Zak. Where could a drow elf go? Nowhere in all the Realms would an elf of dark skin be accepted.

Was the choice then to kill? To kill drow?

Drizzt rolled over against the wall, his physical movement an unconscious act, for his mind whirled down the maze of his future. It took him a moment to realize that his back was against something other than stone.

He tried to leap away, alert again now that his surroundings were not as they should be. When he pushed out, his feet came up from the ground and he landed back in his original position. Frantically, before he took the time to consider his predicament, Drizzt reached behind his neck with both hands.

They, too, stuck fast to the translucent cord that held him. Drizzt knew his folly then, and all the tugging in the world would not free his hands from the line of the angler of the Underdark, a cave fisher.

"Fool!" he scolded himself as he felt himself lifted from the ground. He should have suspected this, should have been more careful alone in the caverns. But to reach out barehanded! He looked down at the hilts of his scimitars, useless in their sheaths.

The cave fisher reeled him in, pulled him up the long wall toward its waiting maw.

Masoj Hun'ett smiled smugly to himself as he watched Drizzt depart the city. Time was running short for him, and Matron SiNafay would not be pleased if he failed again in his mission to destroy the secondboy of House Do'Urden. Now Masoj's patience had apparently paid off, for Drizzt had come out alone, had left the city! There were no witnesses. It was too easy.

Eagerly the wizard pulled the onyx figurine from his pouch and dropped it to the ground. "Guenhwyvar!" he called as loudly as he dared, glancing around at the nearest stalagmite house for signs of activity.

The dark smoke appeared and transformed a moment later into Masoj's magical panther. Masoj rubbed his hands together, thinking himself marvelous for having concocted such a devious and ironic end to the heroics of Drizzt Do'Urden.

"I have a job for you," he told the cat, "one that you'll not enjoy!"

Guenhwyvar slumped casually and yawned as though the wizard's words were hardly a revelation.

"Your point companion has gone out on patrol," Masoj explained as he pointed down the tunnel, "by himself. It's too dangerous."

Guenhwyvar stood back up, suddenly very interested.

"Drizzt should not be out there alone," Masoj continued. "He could get killed."

The evil inflections of his voice told the panther his intent before he ever spoke the words.

"Go to him, my pet," Masoj purred. "Find him out there in the gloom and kill him!" He studied Guenhwyvar's reaction, measured the horror he had laid on the cat. Guenhwyvar stood rigid, as unmoving as the statue used to summon it.

"Go!" Masoj ordered. "You cannot resist your master's commands! I am your master, unthinking beast! You seem to forget that fact too often!"

Guenhwyvar resisted for a long moment, a heroic act in itself, but the magic's urges, the incessant pull of the master's command, outweighed any instinctive feelings the great panther might have had. Reluctantly at first, but then pulled by the primordial desires of the hunt, Guenhwyvar sped off between the enchanted statues guarding the tunnel and easily found Drizzt's scent.

⚔ ⚔ ⚔ ⚔ ⚔

Alton DeVir slumped back behind the largest of the stalagmite mounds, disappointed at Masoj's tactics. Masoj would let the cat do his work for him; Alton would not even witness Drizzt Do'Urden's death!

Alton fingered the powerful wand that Matron SiNafay had given to him when he set out after Masoj that night. It seemed that the item would play no role in Drizzt's demise.

Alton took comfort in the item, knowing that he would have ample opportunity to put it to proper use against the remainder of House Do'Urden.

⚔ ⚔ ⚔ ⚔ ⚔

Drizzt fought for the first half of his ascent, kicking and spinning, ducking his shoulders under any outcrop he passed in a futile effort to hold back the pull of the cave fisher. He knew from the outset, though, against those warrior instincts that refused to surrender, that he had no chance to halt the incessant pull.

Halfway up, one shoulder bloodied, the other bruised, and with the floor nearly thirty feet below him, Drizzt resigned himself to his fate. If he would find a chance against the crablike monster that waited at the top of the line, it would be in the last instant of the ascent. For now, he could only watch and wait.

Perhaps death was not so bad an alternative to the life he would find among the drow, trapped within the evil framework of their dark society. Even Zaknafein, so strong and powerful and wise with age, had never been able to come to terms with his existence in Menzoberranzan; what chance did Drizzt have?

When Drizzt had passed through his small bout with self pity, when the angle of his ascent changed, showing him the lip of the final ledge, the fighting spirit within him took over once again. The cave fisher might have him, he decided then, but he'd put a boot or two into the thing's eyes before it got its meal!

He could hear the clacking of the anxious monster's eight crablike legs. Drizzt had seen a cave fisher before, though it had scrambled away before he and his patrol could catch up to it. He had imagined it then, and could imagine it now, in battle. Two of its legs ended in wicked claws, pincers that snipped up prey to fit into the maw.

Drizzt turned himself face-in to the cliff, wanting to view the thing as soon as his head crested the ledge. The anxious clacking grew louder, resounding alongside the thumping of Drizzt's heart. He reached the ledge.

Drizzt peeked over, only a foot or two from the monster's long proboscis, with the maw just inches behind. Pincers reached out to grab him before he could get his footing; he would get no chance to kick out at the thing.

He closed his eyes, hoping again that death would be preferable to his life in Menzoberranzan.

A familiar growl then brought him from his thoughts.

Slipping through the maze of ledges, Guenhwyvar came in sight of the cave fisher and Drizzt just before Drizzt had reached the final ledge. This was a moment of salvation or death for the cat as surely as for Drizzt. Guenhwyvar had traveled here under Masoj's direct command, giving no consideration to its duty and acting only on its own instincts in accord with the compelling magic. Guenhwyvar could not go against that edict, that premise for the cat's very existence . . . until now.

The scene before the panther, with Drizzt only seconds from death, brought to Guenhwyvar a strength unknown to the cat, and unforeseen to the creator of the magical figurine. That instant of terror gave a life to Guenhwyvar beyond the scope of the magic.

By the time Drizzt had opened his eyes, the battle was in full fury. Guenhwyvar leaped atop the cave fisher but nearly went right over, for the monster's six remaining legs were rooted to the stone by the same goo that held Drizzt fast to the long filament. Undaunted, the cat raked and bit, a ball of frenzy trying to find a break in the fisher's armored shell.

The monster retaliated with his pincers, flipping them over its back with surprising agility and finding one of Guenhwyvar's forelegs.

Drizzt was no longer being pulled in; the monster had other business to attend to.

Pincers cut through Guenhwyvar's soft flesh, but the cat's blood was not the only dark fluid staining the cave fisher's back. Powerful feline claws tore up a section of the shell armor, and great teeth plunged beneath it. As the cave fisher's blood splattered to the stone, its legs began to slip.

Watching the goo under the crablike legs dissolve as the blood of the monster struck it, Drizzt understood what would happen as a line of that same blood made its way down the filament, toward him. He would have to strike fast if the opportunity came; he would have to be ready to help Guenhwyvar.

The fisher stumbled to the side, rolling Guenhwyvar away and spinning Drizzt over in a complete bumping circuit.

Still the blood oozed down the line, and Drizzt felt the filament's hold loosen from his top hand as the liquid came in contact.

Guenhwyvar was up again, facing the fisher, looking for an attack route through the waiting pincers.

Drizzt's hand was free. He snapped up a scimitar and dived straight ahead, sinking the tip into the fisher's side. The monster reeled about, the jolt and the continuing blood flow shaking Drizzt from the filament altogether. The drow was agile enough to find a handhold before he had fallen far, though his drawn scimitar tumbled down to the floor.

Drizzt's diversion opened the fisher's defenses for just a moment, and Guenhwyvar did not hesitate. The cat barreled into its foe, teeth finding the same fleshy hold they had already ripped. They went deeper, under the skin, crushing organs as Guenhwyvar's raking claws kept the pincers at bay.

By the time Drizzt climbed back to the level of the battle, the cave fisher shuddered in the throes of death. Drizzt pulled himself up and rushed to his friend's side.

Guenhwyvar retreated step for step, its ears flattened and teeth bared.

At first, Drizzt thought that the pain of a wound blinded the cat, but a quick survey dispelled that theory. Guenhwyvar had only one injury, and that was not serious. Drizzt had seen the cat with worse.

Guenhwyvar continued to retreat, continued to growl, as the incessant pounding of Masoj's command, back again after the instant of terror, hammered at its heart. The cat fought the urges, tried to see Drizzt as an ally, not as prey, but the urges . . .

"What is wrong, my friend?" Drizzt asked softly, resisting the urge to draw his remaining blade in defense. He dropped to one knee. "Do you not recognize me? How often we have fought together!"

Guenhwyvar crouched low and tamped down its hind legs, preparing, Drizzt knew, to spring. Still Drizzt did not draw his weapon, did nothing to threaten the cat. He had to trust that Guenhwyvar was true to his perceptions, that the panther was everything he believed it to be. What now could be guiding these unfamiliar reactions? What had brought Guenhwyvar out here at this late hour?

Drizzt found his answers when he remembered Matron Malice's warnings about leaving House Do'Urden.

"Masoj sent you to kill me!" he said bluntly. His tone confused the cat, and it relaxed a bit, not yet ready to spring. "You saved me, Guenhwyvar. You resisted the command."

Guenhwyvar's growl sounded in protest.

"You could have let the cave fisher do the deed for you," Drizzt retorted, "but you did not! You charged in and saved my life! Fight the urges,

Guenhwyvar! Remember me as your friend, a better companion than Masoj Hun'ett could ever be!"

Guenhwyvar backed away another step, caught in a pull that it could not yet resolve. Drizzt watched the cat's ears come up from its head and knew that he was winning the contest.

"Masoj claims ownership," he went on, confident that the cat, through some intelligence Drizzt could not know, understood the meaning of his words. "I claim friendship. I am your friend, Guenhwyvar, and I'll not fight against you."

He leaped forward, arms unthreateningly wide, face and chest fully exposed. "Even at the cost of my own life!"

Guenhwyvar did not strike. Emotions pulled at the cat stronger than any magical spell, those same emotions that had put Guenhwyvar into action when it first saw Drizzt in the cave fisher's clutches.

Guenhwyvar reared up and leaped out, crashing into Drizzt and knocking him to his back, then burying him in a rush of playful slaps and mock bites.

The two friends had won again; they had defeated two foes this day.

When Drizzt paused from the greeting to consider all that had transpired, though, he realized that one of the victories was not yet complete. Guenhwyvar was his in spirit now but still held by another, one who did not deserve the cat, who enslaved the cat in a life that Drizzt could no longer witness.

None of the confusion that had followed Drizzt Do'Urden out of Menzoberranzan that night remained. For the first time in his life, he saw the road he must follow, the path to his own freedom.

He remembered Zaknafein's warnings, and the same impossible alternatives that he had contemplated, to no resolution.

Where, indeed, could a drow elf go?

"Worse to be trapped within a lie," he whispered absently. The panther cocked its head to the side, sensing again that Drizzt's words carried great importance. Drizzt returned the curious stare with one that came suddenly grim.

"Take me to your master," he demanded, "your false master."

# Untroubled Dreams

Zaknafein sank down into his bed in an easy sleep, the most comfortable rest he had ever known. Dreams did come to him this night, a rush of dreams. Far from tumultuous, they only enhanced his comfort. Zak was free now of his secret, of the lie that had dominated every day of his adult life.

Drizzt had survived! Even the dreaded Academy of Menzoberranzan could not daunt the youth's indomitable spirit and sense of morality. Zaknafein Do'Urden was no longer alone. The dreams that played in his mind showed him the same wonderful possibilities that had followed Drizzt out of the city.

Side by side they would stand, unbeatable, two as one against the perverted foundations of Menzoberranzan.

A stinging pain in his foot brought Zak from his slumbers. He saw Briza immediately, at the bottom of his bed, her snake whip in hand. Instinctively, Zak reached over the side to fetch his sword.

The weapon was gone. Vierna stood at the side of the room, holding it. On the opposite side, Maya held Zak's other sword.

How had they come in so stealthily? Zak wondered. Magical silence, no doubt, but Zak was still surprised that he had not sensed their presence in time. Nothing had ever caught him unawares, awake or asleep.

Never before had he slept so soundly, so peacefully. Perhaps, in Menzoberranzan, such pleasant dreams were dangerous.

"Matron Malice will see you," Briza announced.

"I am not properly dressed," Zak replied casually. "My belt and weapons, if you please."

"We do not please!" Briza snapped, more at her sisters than at Zak. "You will not need the weapons."

Zak thought otherwise.

"Come, now," Briza commanded, and she raised the whip.

"I should be certain of Matron Malice's intentions before I acted so boldly, were I you," Zak warned. Briza, reminded of the power of the male she now threatened, lowered her weapon.

Zak rolled out of bed, putting the same intense glare alternately on Maya and Vierna, watching their reactions to better conclude Malice's reasons for summoning him.

They surrounded him as he left his room, keeping a cautious but ready distance from the deadly weapons master. "Must be serious," Zak remarked quietly, so that only Briza, in front of the troupe, could hear. Briza turned and flashed him a wicked smile that did nothing to dispel his suspicions.

Neither did Matron Malice, who leaned forward in her throne in anticipation even before they entered the room.

"Matron," Zak offered, dipping into a bow and pulling the side of his nightshirt out wide to draw attention to his inappropriate dress. He wanted to let Malice know his feelings of being ridiculed at such a late hour.

The matron offered no return greeting. She rested back in her throne. One slender hand rubbed her sharp chin, while her eyes locked upon Zaknafein.

"Perhaps you could tell me why you've summoned me," Zak dared to say, his voice still holding an edge of sarcasm. "I would prefer to return to my slumbers. We should not give House Hun'ett the advantage of a tired weapons master."

"Drizzt has gone," growled Malice.

The news slapped Zak like a wet rag. He straightened, and the teasing smile disappeared from his face.

"He left the house against my commands," Malice went on. Zak relaxed visibly; when Malice announced that Drizzt was gone, Zak had first thought that she and her devious cohorts had driven him out or killed him.

"A spirited boy," Zak remarked. "Surely he will return soon."

"Spirited," Malice echoed, and her tone did not put the description in a positive light.

"He will return," Zak said again. "There's no need for our alarm, for such extreme measures." He glared at Briza, though he knew well that the matron mother had called him to audience to do more than tell him of Drizzt's departure.

"The secondboy disobeyed the matron mother," Briza snarled, a rehearsed interruption.

"Spirited," Zak said again, trying not to chuckle. "A minor indiscretion."

"How often he seems to have those," Malice commented. "Like another spirited male of House Do'Urden."

Zak bowed again, taking her words as a compliment. Malice already had his punishment decided, if she meant to punish him at all, His actions now, at this trial—if that's what it was—would be of little consequence.

"The boy has displeased the Spider Queen!" Malice growled, openly enraged and tired of Zak's sarcasm. "Even you were not foolish enough to do that!"

A dark cloud passed across Zak's face. This meeting was indeed serious; Drizzt's life could be at stake.

"But you know of his crime," Malice continued, easing back again. She liked that she had Zak concerned and on the defensive. She had found his vulnerable spot. It was her turn to tease.

"Leaving the house?" Zak protested. "A minor error in judgment. Lolth would not be concerned with such a trifle issue."

"Do not feign ignorance, Zaknafein. You know that the elven child lives!"

Zak lost his breath in a sharp gasp. Malice knew! Damn it all, Lolth knew!

"We are about to go to war," Malice continued calmly, "we are not in

Lolth's favor, and we must correct the situation."

She eyed Zak directly. "You are aware of our ways and know that we must do this."

Zak nodded, trapped. Anything he did now to disagree would only make matters worse for Drizzt—if matters could be worse for Drizzt.

"The secondboy must be punished," Briza said.

Another rehearsed interruption, Zak knew. He wondered how many times Briza and Malice had practiced this encounter.

"Am I to punish him, then?" Zak asked. "I'll not whip the boy; that is not my place."

"His punishment is none of your concern," Malice said.

"Then why disturb my slumber?" Zak asked, trying to detach himself from Drizzt's predicament, more for Drizzt's sake than his own.

"I thought that you would wish to know," Malice replied. "You and Drizzt became so close this day in the gym. Father and son."

She saw! Zak realized. Malice, and probably that wretched Briza, had watched the whole encounter! Zak's head drooped as he came to know that he had unwittingly played a part in Drizzt's predicament.

"An elven child lives," Malice began slowly, rolling out each word in dramatic clarity, "and a young drow must die."

"No!" The word came out of Zak before he realized he was speaking. He tried to find some escape. "Drizzt was young. He did not understand . . ."

"He knew exactly what he was doing!" Malice screamed back at him. "He does not regret his actions! He is so like you, Zaknafein! Too like you."

"Then he can learn," Zak reasoned. "I have not been a burden to you, Mali—Matron Malice. You have profited by my presence. Drizzt is no less skilled than I; he can be valuable to us."

"Dangerous to us," Matron Malice corrected. "You and he standing together? The thought does not please me."

"His death will aid House Hun'ett," Zak warned, grabbing at anything he could find to defeat the matron's intent.

"The Spider Queen demands his death," Malice replied sternly. "She must be appeased if Daermon N'a'shezbaernon is to have any hope in its struggles against House Hun'ett."

"I beg you, do not kill the boy."

"Sympathy?" Malice mused. "It does not become a drow warrior, Zaknafein. Have you lost your fighting will?"

"I am old, Malice."

"Matron Malice!" Briza protested, but Zak put a look on her so cold that she lowered her snake whip before she had even begun to put it to use.

"Older still will I become if Drizzt is put to his death."

"I do not desire this either," Malice agreed, but Zak recognized her lie. She didn't care about Drizzt, or about anything else, beyond gaining the Spider Queen's favor.

"Yet I see no alternative. Drizzt has angered Lolth, and she must be appeased before our war."

Zak began to understand. This meeting wasn't about Drizzt at all. "Take me in the boy's stead," he said.

Malice's narrow grin could not hide her feigned surprise. This was what she had desired from the very beginning.

"You are a proven fighter," the matron argued. "Your value, as you yourself have already admitted, cannot be underestimated. To sacrifice you to the Spider Queen would appease her, but what void will be left in House Do'Urden in the wake of your passing?"

"A void that Drizzt can fill," Zak replied. He secretly hoped that Drizzt, unlike he, would find some escape from it all, some way around Matron Malice's evil plots.

"You are certain of this?"

"He is my equal in battle," Zak assured her. "He will grow stronger, too, beyond what Zaknafein has ever attained."

"You are willing to do this for him?" Malice sneered, eager drool edging her mouth.

"You know that I am," Zak replied.

"Ever the fool," Malice put in.

"To your dismay," Zak continued, undaunted, "you know that Drizzt would do the same for me."

"He is young," Malice purred. "He will be taught better."

"As you taught me?" snapped Zak.

Malice's victorious grin became a grimace. "I warn you, Zaknafein," she growled in all her vile rage. "If you do anything to disrupt the ceremony to appease the Spider Queen, if, in the end of your wasted life, you choose to anger me one final time, I will give Drizzt to Briza. She and her torturous toys will give him to Lolth!"

Unafraid, Zak held his head high. "I have offered myself, Malice," he spat. "Have your fun while you may. In the end, Zaknafein will be at peace; Matron Malice Do'Urden will ever be at war!"

Shaking in anger, the moment of triumph stolen by a few simple words, Malice could only whisper, "Take him!"

Zak offered no resistance as Vierna and Maya tied him to the spider-shaped altar in the chapel. He watched Vierna mostly, seeing an edge of sympathy rimming her quiet eyes. She, too, might have been like him, but whatever hope he had for that possibility had been buried long ago under the relentless preaching of the Spider Queen.

"You are sad," Zak remarked to her.

Vierna straightened and tugged tightly on one of Zak's bonds, causing him to grimace in pain. "A pity," she replied as coldly as she could. "House Do'Urden must give much to repay Drizzt's foolish deed. I would have enjoyed watching the two of you together in battle."

"House Hun'ett would not have enjoyed the sight," Zak replied with a wink. "Cry not . . . my daughter."

Vierna slapped him across the face. "Take your lies to your grave!"

"Deny it as you choose, Vierna," was all that Zak cared to reply.

Vierna and Maya backed away from the altar. Vierna fought to hold her scowl and Maya bit back an amused chuckle, as Matron Malice and Briza entered the room. The matron mother wore her greatest ceremonial robe, black and weblike, clinging and floating about her all at once, and Briza carried a sacred coffer.

Zak paid them no heed as they began their ritual, chanting for the Spider Queen, offering their hopes for appeasement. Zak had his own hopes at that moment.

"Beat them all," he whispered under his breath. "Do more than survive, my son, as I have survived. Live! Be true to the callings in your heart."

Braziers roared to life; the room glowed. Zak felt the heat, knew that contact to that darker plane had been achieved.

"Take this . . ." he heard Matron Malice chant, but he put the words out of his thoughts and continued the final prayers of his life.

The spider-shaped dagger hovered over his chest. Malice clenched the instrument in her bony hands, the sheen of her sweat-soaked skin catching the orange reflection of the fires in a surrealistic glow.

Surreal, like the transition from life to death.

# 28

# Rightful Owner

How long had it been? An hour? Two? Masoj paced the length of the gap between the two stalagmite mounds just a few feet from the entrance to the tunnel that Drizzt, and Guenhwyvar, had taken. "The cat should have returned by now," the wizard grumbled, at the end of his patience.

Relief flooded through his face a moment later, when Guenhwyvar's great black head peered around the edge of the tunnel, behind one of the displacer beast statue guardians. The fur around the cat's maw was conspicuously wet with fresh blood.

"It is done?" Masoj asked, barely able to contain a shout of elation. "Drizzt Do'Urden is dead?"

"Hardly," came the reply. Drizzt, for all his idealism, had to admit a tinge of pleasure as a cloud of dread cooled the elated fires in the sinister wizard's cheeks.

"What is this, Guenhwyvar?" Masoj demanded. "Do as I bid you! Kill him now!"

Guenhwyvar stared blankly at Masoj, then lay at Drizzt's feet.

"You admit your attempt on my life?" Drizzt asked.

Masoj measured the distance to his adversary—ten feet. He might be able to get off one spell. Perhaps. Masoj had seen Drizzt move, quick and sure, and had little desire to chance the attack if he could find another way out of this predicament. Drizzt had not yet drawn a weapon, though the young warrior's hands rested easily across the hilts of his deadly blades.

"I understand," Drizzt continued calmly. "House Hun'ett and House Do'Urden are to battle."

"How did you know?" Masoj blurted without thinking, too shocked by the revelation to consider that Drizzt might merely be goading him into a larger admission.

"I know much but care little," Drizzt replied. "House Hun'ett wishes to wage war against my family. For what reason, I cannot guess."

"For the vengeance of House DeVir!" came a reply from a different direction.

Alton, standing on the side of a stalagmite mound, looked down at Drizzt.

A smile spread over Masoj's face. The odds had so quickly changed.

"House Hun'ett cares not at all for House DeVir," Drizzt replied, still composed in the face of this new development. "I have learned enough of the ways of our people to know that the fate of one house is not the concern of another."

"But it is my concern!" Alton cried, and he threw back the cowl of his hood, revealing the hideous face, scarred by acid for the sake of a disguise. "I am Alton DeVir, lone survivor of House DeVir! House Do'Urden will die for its crimes against my family, starting with you."

"I was not even born when the battle took place," Drizzt protested.

"Of little consequence!" Alton snarled. "You are a Do'Urden, a filthy Do'Urden. That is all that matters."

Masoj tossed the onyx figurine to the ground. "Guenhwyvar!" he commanded. "Be gone!"

The cat looked over its shoulder to Drizzt, who nodded his approval.

"Be gone!" Masoj cried again. "I am your master! You cannot disobey me!"

"You do not own the cat," Drizzt said calmly.

"Who does, then?" Masoj snapped. "You?"

"Guenhwyvar," Drizzt replied. "Only Guenhwyvar. I would think that a wizard would have a better understanding of the magic around him."

With a low growl that might have been a mocking laugh, Guenhwyvar loped across the stone to the figurine and dissipated into smoky nothingness.

The cat walked down the length of the planar tunnel, toward its home in the Astral Plane. Ever before had Guenhwyvar been anxious to make this journey, to escape the foul commands of its drow masters. This time, though, the cat hesitated with every stride, looking back over its shoulder to the dot of darkness that was Menzoberranzan.

"Will you deal?" Drizzt offered.

"You are in no position to bargain," Alton laughed, drawing out the slender wand that Matron SiNafay had given him.

Masoj cut him short. "Wait," he said. "Perhaps Drizzt will prove valuable to our struggle against House Do'Urden." He eyed the young warrior directly. "You will betray your family?"

"Hardly," Drizzt snickered. "As I have already said to you, I care little for the coming conflict. Let House Hun'ett and House Do'Urden both be damned, as surely they will! My concerns are personal."

"You must have something to offer us in exchange for your gain," Masoj explained. "Otherwise, what bargain can you hope to make?"

"I do have something to give to you in return," Drizzt replied, his voice calm, "your lives."

Masoj and Alton looked to each other and laughed aloud, but there was a trace of nervousness in their chuckles.

"Give me the figurine, Masoj," Drizzt continued, undaunted. "Guenhwyvar never belonged to you and will serve you no more."

Masoj stopped laughing.

"In return," Drizzt went on before the wizard could reply, "I will leave House Do'Urden and not take part in the battle."

"Corpses do not fight." Alton sneered.

"I will take another Do'Urden with me," Drizzt spat at him. "A weapons master. Surely House Hun'ett will have gained an advantage if both Drizzt and Zaknafein—"

"Silence!" Masoj screamed. "The cat is mine! I do not need any bargains from a pitiful Do'Urden! You are dead, fool, and House Do'Urden's weapons master will follow you to your grave!"

"Guenhwyvar is free!" Drizzt growled.

The scimitars came out in Drizzt's hands. He had never really fought a wizard before, let alone two, but he remembered vividly from past encounters the sting of their spells. Masoj had already begun to cast, but of more concern was Alton, out of quick reach and pointing that slender wand.

Before Drizzt ever decided his course of action, the issue was settled for him. A cloud of smoke engulfed Masoj and he fell back, his spell disrupted with the shock.

Guenhwyvar was back.

Alton was out of Drizzt's reach. Drizzt could not hope to get to the wizard before the wand went off, but to Guenhwyvar's streamlined feline muscles, the distance was not so great. Hind legs tamped a footing and snapped, launching the hunting panther through the air.

Alton brought the wand to bear on this new nemesis in time and released a mighty bolt, scorching Guenhwyvar's chest. Greater strength than a single bolt, though, would be needed to deter the ferocious panther. Stunned but still fighting, Guenhwyvar slammed into the faceless wizard, dropping him off the back side of the stalagmite mound.

The lightning bolt's flash stunned Drizzt as well, but he continued to pursue Masoj and could only hope that Guenhwyvar had survived. He rushed around the base of the other stalagmite mound and came face-to-face with Masoj, once again in the act of spellcasting. Drizzt didn't slow; he ducked his head and barreled into his opponent, his scimitars leading the way.

He slipped right through his opponent—right through the image of his opponent!

Drizzt crashed heavily into the stone and rolled aside, trying to escape the magical attack he knew was coming.

This time, Masoj, standing fully thirty feet behind the projection of his image, was taking no chances with a miss. He launched a volley of magical missiles of energy that veered unerringly to intercept the dodging fighter. They slammed into Drizzt, jolting him, bruising him under his skin.

But Drizzt was able to shake away the numbing pain and regain his footing. He knew where the real Masoj was standing now and had no intention of letting the trickster out of sight again.

A dagger in his hand, Masoj watched Drizzt's stalking approach.

Drizzt didn't understand. Why wasn't the wizard preparing another spell? The fall had reopened the wound in Drizzt's shoulder, and the magical bolts had torn his side and one leg. The wounds were not serious, though, and Masoj had no chance against him in physical combat.

The wizard stood before him, unconcerned, dagger drawn and a wicked smile on his face.

Face down on the hard stone, Alton felt the warmth of his own blood running freely between the melted holes that were his eyes. The cat was higher up the side of the mound, not yet fully recovered from the lightning bolt.

Alton forced himself up and raised his wand for a second strike . . . but the wand had snapped in half.

Frantically Alton recovered the other piece and held it up before his melted, disbelieving eyes. Guenhwyvar was coming again, but Alton didn't notice.

The glowing ends of the wand, a power building within the magical stick, enthralled him. "You cannot do that," Alton whispered in protest.

Guenhwyvar leaped just as the broken wand exploded.

A ball of fire roared up into Menzoberranzan's night, chunks of rubble rocketed off the great cavern's eastern wall and ceiling, and both Drizzt and Masoj were knocked from their feet.

"Now Guenhwyvar belongs to no one," Masoj sneered, tossing the figurine to the ground.

"No DeVir remains to claim vengeance on House Do'Urden," Drizzt growled back, his anger holding off his despair. Masoj became the focus of that anger, and the wizard's mocking laughter led Drizzt toward him in a furious rush. Just as Drizzt got in range, Masoj snapped his fingers and was gone.

"Invisible," Drizzt roared, slicing futilely at the empty air before him. His exertions took the edge from his blind rage and he realized that Masoj was no longer in front of him. How foolish he must seem to the wizard. How vulnerable!

Drizzt crouched to listen. He sensed a distant chanting from up above, on the cavern wall.

Drizzt's instincts told him to dive to the side, but his new understanding of wizards told him that Masoj would anticipate such a move. Drizzt feigned to the left and heard the climactic words of the building spell. As the lightning blast thundered harmlessly to the side, Drizzt sprinted straight ahead, hoping his vision would return in time for him to get to the wizard.

"Damn you!" Masoj cried, understanding the feint as soon as he had errantly fired. Rage became terror in the next instant, as Masoj caught sight of Drizzt, sprinting across the stone, leaping the rubble, and crossing the sides of the mounds with all the grace of a hunting cat.

Masoj fumbled in his pockets for the components to his next spell. He had to be quick. He was fully twenty feet from the cavern floor, perched on a narrow ledge, but Drizzt was moving fast, impossibly fast!

The ground beneath him did not register in Drizzt's conscious thoughts. The cavern wall would have seemed unclimbable to him in a more rational state, but now he gave it not a care. Guenhwyvar was lost to him. Guenhwyvar was gone.

That wicked wizard on the ledge, that embodiment of demonic evil, had caused it. Drizzt sprang to the wall, found one hand free—he must have discarded one scimitar—and caught a tenuous hold. It wasn't enough for a rational drow, but Drizzt's mind ignored the protests of the muscles in his straining fingers. He had only ten feet to go.

Another volley of energy bolts thudded into Drizzt, hammering the top of his head in rapid succession.

"How many spells remain, wizard?" he heard himself defiantly cry as he ignored the pain.

Masoj fell back when Drizzt looked up at him, when the burning light of those lavender orbs fell upon him like a pronouncement of doom. He had seen Drizzt in battle many times, and the sight of the fighting young warrior had haunted him through all the planning of this assassination.

But Masoj had never seen Drizzt enraged before. If he had, he never would have agreed to try to kill Drizzt. If he had, he would have told

Matron SiNafay to go sit on a stalagmite.

What spell was next? What spell could slow the monster that was Drizzt Do'Urden?

A hand, glowing with the heat of anger, grabbed the lip of the ledge. Masoj stomped on it with the heel of his boot. The fingers were broken—the wizard knew that the fingers were broken—but Drizzt, impossibly, was up beside him and the blade of a scimitar was through the wizard's ribs.

"The fingers are broken!" the dying mage gasped in protest.

Drizzt looked down at his hand and realized the pain for the first time. "Perhaps," he said absently, "but they will heal."

---

Drizzt, limping, found his other scimitar and cautiously picked his way over the rubble of one of the mounds. Fighting the fear within his broken heart, he forced himself to peer over the crest at the destruction. The back side of the mound glowed eerily in the residual heat, a beacon for the awakening city.

So much for stealth.

Pieces of Alton DeVir lay scattered at the bottom, around the wizard's smoldering robes. "Have you found peace, Faceless One?" Drizzt whispered, exhaling the last of his anger. He remembered the assault Alton had launched against him those years ago in the Academy. The faceless master and Masoj had explained it away as a test for a budding warrior.

"How long you have carried your hate," Drizzt muttered at the blasted bits of corpse.

But Alton DeVir was not his concern now. He scanned the rest of the rubble, looking for some clue to Guenhwyvar's fate, not certain how a magical creature would fare in such a disaster. Not a sign of the cat remained, nothing that would even hint that Guenhwyvar had ever been there.

Drizzt consciously reminded himself that there was no hope, but the anxious spring in his steps mocked his stern visage. He rushed back down the mound and around the other stalagmite, where Masoj and he had been when the wand exploded. He spotted the onyx figurine immediately.

He lifted it gently in his hands. It was warm, as though it, too, had been caught in the blast, and Drizzt could sense that its magic had diminished. Drizzt wanted to call the cat, then, but he didn't dare, knowing that the travel between the planes heavily taxed Guenhwyvar. If the cat had been injured, Drizzt figured that it would be better to give it some time to recuperate.

"Oh, Guenhwyvar," he moaned, "my friend, my brave friend." He dropped the figurine into his pocket.

He could only hope that Guenhwyvar had survived.

# 29

# Alone

Drizzt walked back around the stalagmite, back to the body of Masoj Hun'ett. He had had no choice but to kill his adversary; Masoj had drawn the battle lines.

That fact did little to dispel the guilt in Drizzt as he looked upon the corpse. He had killed another drow, had taken the life of one of his own people. Was he trapped, as Zaknafein had been trapped for so very many years, in a cycle of violence that would know no end?

"Never again," Drizzt vowed to the corpse. "Never again will I kill a drow elf."

He turned away, disgusted, and knew as soon as he looked back to the silent, sinister mounds of the vast drow city that he would not survive long in Menzoberranzan if he held to that promise.

A thousand possibilities whirled in Drizzt's mind as he made his way through the winding ways of Menzoberranzan. He pushed the thoughts aside, stopped them from dulling his alertness. The light was general now in Narbondel; the drow day was beginning, and activity had started from every corner of the city. In the world of the surface-dwellers, the day was the safer time, when light exposed assassins. In Menzoberranzan's eternal darkness, the daytime of the dark elves was even more dangerous than the night.

Drizzt picked his way carefully, rolling wide from the mushroom fence of the noblest houses, wherein lay House Hun'ett. He encountered no more adversaries and made the safety of the Do'Urden compound a short time later. He rushed through the gate and by the surprised soldiers without a word of explanation and shoved aside the guards below the balcony.

The house was strangely quiet; Drizzt would have expected them all to be up and about with battle imminent. He gave the eerie stillness no more thought, and he cut a straight line to the training gym and Zaknafein's private quarters.

Drizzt paused outside the gym's stone door, his hand tightly clenched on the handle of the portal. What would he propose to his father? That they leave? He and Zaknafein on the perilous trails of the Underdark, fighting when they must and escaping the burdensome guilt of their existence under drow rule? Drizzt liked the thought, but he wasn't so certain now, standing before the door, that he could convince Zak to follow such a course. Zak could have left before, at any time during the centuries of his life, but when Drizzt had asked him why he had remained, the heat had drained from the weapons master's face. Were they indeed trapped in the life offered to them by Matron Malice and her evil cohorts?

Drizzt grimaced away the worries; no sense in arguing to himself with Zak only a few steps away.

The training gym was as quiet as the rest of the house. Too quiet. Drizzt hadn't expected Zak to be there, but something more than his father was absent. The father's presence, too, was gone.

Drizzt knew that something was wrong, and each step he took toward Zak's private door quickened until he was in full flight. He burst in without a knock, not surprised to find the bed empty.

"Malice must have sent him out in search of me," Drizzt reasoned. "Damn, I have caused him trouble!" He turned to leave, but something caught his eye and held him in the room—Zak's sword belt.

Never would the weapons master have left his room, not even for functions within the safety of House Do'Urden, without his swords. "Your weapon is your most trusted companion," Zak had told Drizzt a thousand times. "Keep it ever at your side!"

"House Hun'ett?" Drizzt whispered, wondering if the rival house had magically attacked in the night, while he was out battling Alton and Masoj. The compound, though, was serene; surely the soldiers would have known if anything like that had occurred.

Drizzt picked up the belt for inspection. No blood, and the clasp neatly unbuckled. No enemy had torn this from Zak. The weapons master's pouch lay beside it, also intact.

"What, then?" Drizzt asked aloud. He replaced the sword belt beside the bed, but slung the pouch across his neck, and turned, not knowing where he should go next.

He had to see about the rest of the family, he realized before he had even stepped through the door. Perhaps then this riddle about Zak would become more clear.

Dread grew out of that thought as Drizzt headed down the long and decorated corridor to the chapel anteroom. Had Malice, or any of them, brought Zak harm? For what purpose? The notion seemed illogical to Drizzt, but it nagged him every step, as if some sixth sense were warning him.

There still was no sign of anyone.

The anteroom's ornate doors swung in, magically and silently, even as Drizzt raised his hand to knock on them. He saw the matron mother first, sitting smugly on her throne at the rear of the room, her smile inviting.

Drizzt's discomfort did not diminish when he entered. The whole family was there: Briza, Vierna, and Maya to the sides of their matron, Rizzen and Dinin unobtrusively standing beside the left wall. The whole family. Except for Zak.

Matron Malice studied her son carefully, noting his many wounds. "I instructed you not to leave the house," she said to Drizzt, but she was not scolding him. "Where did your travels take you?"

"Where is Zaknafein?" Drizzt asked in reply.

"Answer the matron mother!" Briza yelled at him, her snake whip prominently displayed on her belt.

Drizzt glared at her and she recoiled, feeling the same bitter chill that Zaknafein had cast over her earlier in the night.

"I instructed you not to leave the house," Malice said again, still holding calm. "Why did you disobey me?"

"I had matters to attend," Drizzt replied, "urgent matters. I did not wish to bother you with them."

"War is upon us, my son," Matron Malice explained. "You are vulnerable out in the city by yourself. House Do'Urden cannot afford to lose you now."

"My business had to be handled alone," Drizzt answered.

"Is it completed?"

"It is."

"Then I trust that you will not disobey me again." The words came calm and even, but Drizzt understood at once the severity of the threat behind them.

"To other matters, then," Malice went on.

"Where is Zaknafein?" Drizzt dared to ask again.

Briza mumbled some curse under her breath and pulled the whip from her belt. Matron Malice threw an outstretched hand in her direction to stay her. They needed tact, not brutality, to bring Drizzt under control at this critical time. There would be ample opportunities for punishment after House Hun'ett was properly defeated.

"Concern yourself not with the fate of the weapons master," Malice replied. "He works for the good of House Do'Urden even as we speak—on a personal mission."

Drizzt didn't believe a word of it. Zak would never have left without his weapons. The truth hovered about Drizzt's thoughts, but he wouldn't let it in.

"Our concern is House Hun'ett," Malice went on, addressing them all. "The war's first strikes may fall this day."

"The first strikes already have fallen," Drizzt interrupted. All eyes came back to him, to his wounds. He wanted to continue the discussion about Zak but knew that he would only get himself, and Zak, if Zak was still alive, into further trouble. Perhaps the conversation would bring him more clues.

"You have seen battle?" Malice asked.

"You know of the Faceless One?" Drizzt asked.

"Master of the Academy," Dinin answered, "of Sorcere. We have dealt with him often."

"He has been of use to us in the past," said Malice, "but no more, I believe. He is a Hun'ett, Gelroos Hun'ett."

"No," Drizzt replied. "Once he may have been, but Alton DeVir is his name . . . was his name."

"The link!" Dinin growled, suddenly comprehending. "Gelroos was to kill Alton on the night of House DeVir's fall!"

"It would seem that Alton DeVir proved the stronger," mused Malice, and all became clear to her. "Matron SiNafay Hun'ett accepted him, used him to her gain," she explained to her family. She looked back to Drizzt. "You battled with him?"

"He is dead," Drizzt answered.

Matron Malice cackled with delight.

"One less wizard to deal with," Briza remarked, replacing the whip on her belt.

"Two," Drizzt corrected, but there was no boasting in his voice. He was not proud of his actions. "Masoj Hun'ett is no more."

"My son!" Matron Malice cried. "You have brought us a great edge in this war!" She glanced all about her family, infecting them, except Drizzt, with her elation. "House Hun'ett may not even choose to strike us now, knowing its disadvantage. We will not let them get away! We will destroy them this day and become the Eighth House of Menzoberranzan! Woe to the enemies of Daermon N'a'shezbaernon!

"We must move at once, my family," Malice reasoned, her hands rubbing over each other in excitement. "We cannot wait for an attack. We must take the offensive! Alton DeVir is gone now; the link that justifies this war is no more. Surely the ruling council knew of Hun'ett's intentions, and with both her wizards dead and the element of surprise lost, Matron SiNafay will move quickly to stop the battle."

Drizzt's hand unconsciously slipped into Zak's pouch as the others joined Malice in her plotting.

"Where is Zak?" Drizzt demanded again, above the chorus.

Silence dropped as quickly as the tumult had begun.

"He is of no concern to you, my son," Malice said to him, still keeping to her tact despite Drizzt's impudence. "You are the weapons master of House Do'Urden now. Lolth has forgiven your insolence; you have no crimes weighing against you. Your career may begin anew, to glorious heights!"

Her words cut through Drizzt as surely as his own scimitar might. "You killed him," he whispered aloud, the truth too awful to be contained in silent thought.

The matron's face suddenly gleamed, hot with rage. "You killed him!" she shot back at Drizzt. "Your insolence demanded repayment to the Spider Queen!"

Drizzt's tongue got all tangled up behind his teeth.

"But you live," Malice went on, relaxing again in her chair, "as the elven child lives."

Dinin was not the only one in the room to gasp audibly.

"Yes, we know of your deception," Malice sneered. "The Spider Queen always knew. She demanded restitution."

"You sacrificed Zaknafein?" Drizzt breathed, hardly able to get the words out of his mouth. "You gave him to that damned Spider Queen?"

"I would watch how I spoke of Queen Lolth," Malice warned. "Forget Zaknafein. He is not your concern. Look to your own life, my warrior son. All glories are offered to you, a station of honor."

Drizzt was indeed looking to his own life at that moment; at the proposed path that offered him a life of battle, a life of killing drow.

"You have no options," Malice said to him, seeing his inward struggle. "I offer to you now your life. In exchange, you must do as I bid, as Zaknafein once did."

"You kept your bargain with him," Drizzt spat sarcastically.

"I did!" Matron Malice protested. "Zaknafein went willingly to the altar, for your sake!"

Her words stung Drizzt for only a moment. He would not accept the guilt for Zaknafein's death! He had followed the only course he could, on the surface against the elves and here in the evil city.

"My offer is a good one," Malice said. "I give it here, before all the family.

Both of us will benefit from the agreement . . . Weapons Master?"

A smile spread across Drizzt's face when he looked into Matron Malice's cold eyes, a grin that Malice took as acceptance.

"Weapons Master?" Drizzt echoed. "Not likely."

Again Malice misunderstood. "I have seen you in battle," she argued. "Two wizards! You underestimate yourself."

Drizzt nearly laughed aloud at the irony of her words. She thought he would fail where Zaknafein had failed, would fall into her trap as the former weapons master had fallen, never to climb back out. "It is you who underestimate me, Malice," Drizzt said with threatening calm.

"Matron!" Briza demanded, but she held back, seeing that Drizzt and everyone else was ignoring her as the drama played out.

"You ask me to serve your evil designs," Drizzt continued. He knew but didn't care that all of them were nervously fingering weapons or preparing spells, were waiting for the proper moment to strike the blasphemous fool dead. Those childhood memories of the agony of snake whips reminded him of the punishment for his actions. Drizzt's fingers closed around a circular object, adding to his courage, though he would have continued in any case.

"They are a lie, as our—no, your—people are a lie!"

"Your skin is as dark as mine," Malice reminded him. "You are a drow, though you have never learned what that means!"

"Oh, I do know what it means."

"Then act by the rules!" Matron Malice demanded.

"Your rules?" Drizzt growled back. "But your rules are a damned lie as well, as great a lie as that filthy spider you claim as a deity!"

"Insolent slug," Briza cried, raising her snake whip.

Drizzt struck first. He pulled the object, the tiny ceramic globe, from Zaknafein's pouch.

"A true god damn you all!" he cried as he slammed the ball to the stone floor. He snapped his eyes shut as the pebble within the ball, enchanted by a powerful light-emanating dweomer, exploded into the room and erupted into his kin's sensitive eyes. "And damn that Spider Queen as well!"

Malice reeled backward, taking her great throne right over in a heavy crash to the hard stone. Cries of agony and rage came from every corner of the room as the sudden light bored into the stunned drow. Finally Vierna managed to launch a countering spell and returned the room to its customary gloom.

"Get him!" Malice growled, still trying to shake off the heavy fall. "I want him dead!"

The others had hardly recovered enough to heed to her commands, and Drizzt was already out of the house.

⚔ ⚔ ⚔ ⚔ ⚔

Carried on the silent winds of the Astral Plane, the call came. The entity of the panther stood up, ignoring its pains, and took note of the voice, a familiar, comforting voice.

The cat was off, then, running with all its heart and strength to answer the summons of its new master.

⚔ ⚔ ⚔ ⚔ ⚔

A short while later, Drizzt crept out of a little tunnel, Guenhwyvar at his side, and moved through the courtyard of the Academy to look down upon Menzoberranzan for the last time.

"What place is this," Drizzt asked the cat quietly, "that I call home? These are my people, by skin and by heritage, but I am no kin to them. They are lost and ever will be.

"How many others are like me, I wonder?" Drizzt whispered, taking one final look. "Doomed souls, as was Zaknafein, poor Zak. I do this for him, Guenhwyvar; I leave as he could not. His life has been my lesson, a dark scroll etched by the heavy price exacted by Matron Malice's evil promises.

"Goodbye, Zak!" he cried, his voice rising in final defiance. "My father. Take heart, as do I, that when we meet again, in a life after this, it will surely not be in the hellfire our kin are doomed to endure!"

Drizzt motioned the cat back into the tunnel, the entrance to the untamed Underdark. Watching the cat's easy movements, Drizzt realized again how fortunate he was to have found a companion of like spirit, a true friend. The way would not be easy for him and Guenhwyvar beyond the guarded borders of Menzoberranzan. They would be unprotected and alone—though better off, by Drizzt's estimation—more than they ever could be amid the evilness of the drow.

Drizzt stepped into the tunnel behind Guenhwyvar and left Menzoberranzan behind.

EXILE
THE LEGEND OF DRIZZT
BOOK II

# Prelude

The monster lumbered along the quiet corridors of the Underdark, its eight scaly legs occasionally scuffing the stone. It did not recoil at its own echoing sounds, fearing the revealing noise. Nor did it scurry for cover, expecting the rush of another predator. For even in the dangers of the Underdark, this creature knew only security, confident of its ability to defeat any foe. Its breath reeked of deadly poison, the hard edges of its claws dug deep gouges into solid stone, and the rows of spearlike teeth that lined its wicked maw could tear through the thickest of hides. But worst of all was the monster's gaze, the gaze of a basilisk, which could transmutate into solid stone any living thing it fell upon.

This creature, huge and terrible, was among the greatest of its kind. It did not know fear.

The hunter watched the basilisk pass as he had watched it earlier that same day. The eight-legged monster was the intruder here, coming into the hunter's domain. He had witnessed the basilisk kill several of his rothé—the small, cattlelike creatures that enhanced his table—with its poison breath, and the rest of the herd had fled blindly down the endless tunnels, perhaps never to return.

The hunter was angry.

He watched now as the monster trudged down the narrow passageway, just the route the hunter had suspected it would take. He slid his weapons from their sheaths, gaining confidence, as always, as soon as he felt their fine balance. The hunter had owned them since his childhood, and even after nearly three decades of almost constant use, they bore only the slightest hints of wear. Now they would be tested again.

The hunter replaced his weapons and waited for the sound that would spur him to motion.

A throaty growl stopped the basilisk in its tracks. The monster peered ahead curiously, though its poor eyes could distinguish little beyond a few feet. Again came the growl, and the basilisk hunched down, waiting for the challenger, its next victim, to spring out and die.

Far behind, the hunter came out of his cubby, running impossibly fast along the tiny cracks and spurs in the corridor walls. In his magical cloak, his *piwafwi*, he was invisible against the stone, and with his agile and practiced movements, he made not a sound.

He came impossibly silent, impossibly fast.

The growl issued again from ahead of the basilisk but had not come any closer. The impatient monster shuffled forward, anxious to get on with the killing. When the basilisk crossed under a low archway, an impenetrable globe of absolute darkness enveloped its head and the monster stopped suddenly and took a step back, as the hunter knew it would.

The hunter was upon it then. He leaped from the passage wall, executing three separate actions before he ever reached his mark. First he cast a simple spell, which lined the basilisk's head in glowing blue and purple flames. Next he pulled his hood down over his face, for he did not need his eyes in battle, and against a basilisk a stray gaze could only bring him doom. Then, drawing his deadly scimitars, he landed on the monster's back and ran up its scales to get to its head.

The basilisk reacted as soon as the dancing flames outlined its head. They did not burn, but their outline made the monster an easy target. The basilisk spun back, but before its head had turned halfway, the first scimitar had dived into one of its eyes. The creature reared and thrashed, trying to get at the hunter. It breathed its noxious fumes and whipped its head about.

The hunter was the faster. He kept behind the maw, out of death's way. His second scimitar found the basilisk's other eye, then the hunter unleashed his fury.

The basilisk was the intruder; it had killed his rothé! Blow after savage blow bashed into the monster's armored head, flecked off scales, and dived for the flesh beneath.

The basilisk understood its peril but still believed that it would win. It had always won. If it could only get its poisonous breath in line with the furious hunter.

The second foe, the growling feline foe, was upon the basilisk then, having sprung toward the flame-lined maw without fear. The great cat latched on and took no notice of the poisonous fumes, for it was a magical beast, impervious to such attacks. Panther claws dug deep lines into the basilisk's gums, letting the monster drink of its own blood.

Behind the huge head, the hunter struck again and

again, a hundred times and more. Savagely, viciously, the scimitars slammed through the scaly armor, through the flesh, and through the skull, battering the basilisk down into the blackness of death.

Long after the monster lay still, the pounding of the bloodied scimitars slowed.

The hunter removed his hood and inspected the broken pile of gore at his feet and the hot stains of blood on his blades. He raised the dripping scimitars into the air and proclaimed his victory with a scream of primal exultation.

He was the hunter and this was his home!

When he had thrown all of his rage out in that scream, though, the hunter looked upon his companion and was ashamed. The panther's saucer eyes judged him, even if the panther did not. The cat was the hunter's only link to the past, to the civilized existence the hunter once had known.

"Come, Guenhwyvar," he whispered as he slid the scimitars back into their sheaths. He reveled in the sound of the words as he spoke them. It was the only voice he had heard for a decade. But every time he spoke now, the words seemed more foreign and came to him with difficulty.

Would he lose that ability, too, as he had lost every other aspect of his former existence? This the hunter feared greatly, for without his voice, he could not summon the panther.

He then truly would be alone.

Down the quiet corridors of the Underdark went the hunter and his cat, making not a sound, disturbing no rubble. Together they had come to know the dangers of this hushed world. Together they had learned to survive. Despite the victory, though, the hunter wore no smile this day. He feared no foes, but was no longer certain whether his courage came from confidence or from apathy about living.

Perhaps survival was not enough.

# Part One

## The Hunter

I remember vividly the day I walked away from the city of my birth, the city of my people. All the Underdark lay before me, a life of adventure and excitement, with possibilities that lifted my heart. More than that, though, I left Menzoberranzan with the belief that I could now live my life in accordance with my principles. I had Guenhwyvar at my side and my scimitars belted on my hips. My future was my own to determine.

But that drow, the young Drizzt Do'Urden who walked out of Menzoberranzan on that fated day, barely into my fourth decade of life, could not begin to understand the truth of time, of how its passage seemed to slow when the moments were not shared with others. In my youthful exuberance, I looked forward to several centuries of life.

How do you measure centuries when a single hour seems a day and a single day seems a year?

Beyond the cities of the Underdark, there is food for those who know how to find it and safety for those who know how to hide. More than anything else, though, beyond the teeming cities of the Underdark, there is solitude.

As I became a creature of the empty tunnels, survival became easier and more difficult all at once. I gained in the physical skills and experience necessary to live on. I could defeat almost anything that wandered into my chosen domain, and those few monsters that I could not defeat, I could surely flee or hide from. It did not take me long, however, to discover one nemesis that I could neither defeat nor flee. It followed me wherever I went—indeed, the farther I ran, the more it closed in around me. My enemy was solitude, the interminable, incessant silence of hushed corridors.

Looking back on it these many years later, I find myself amazed and appalled at the changes I endured under such an existence. The very identity of every reasoning being is defined by the language, the communication, between that being and others around it. Without that link, I was lost. When I left Menzoberranzan, I determined that my life would be based on principles, my strength adhering to unbending beliefs. Yet after only a few months alone in the Underdark, the only purpose for my survival was my survival. I had become a creature of instinct, calculating and cunning but not thinking, not using my mind for anything more than directing the newest kill.

Guenhwyvar saved me, I believe. The same companion that had pulled me from certain death in the clutches of monsters unnumbered rescued me from a death of emptiness—less dramatic, perhaps, but no less fatal. I found myself living for those moments when the cat could walk by my side, when I had another living creature to hear my words, strained though they had become. In addition to every other value, Guenhwyvar became my time clock, for I knew that the cat could come forth from the Astral Plane for a half-day every other day.

Only after my ordeal had ended did I realize how critical that one-quarter of my time actually was. Without Guenhwyvar, I would not have found the resolve to continue. I would never have maintained the strength to survive.

Even when Guenhwyvar stood beside me, I found myself growing more and more ambivalent toward the fighting. I was secretly hoping that some denizen of the Underdark would prove stronger than I. Could the pain of tooth or talon be greater than the emptiness and the silence?

I think not.

—Drizzt Do'Urden

# I
# Anniversary Present

Matron Malice Do'Urden shifted uneasily on the stone throne in the small and darkened anteroom to the great chapel of House Do'Urden. To the dark elves, who measured time's passage in decades, this was a day to be marked in the annals of Malice's house, the tenth anniversary of the ongoing covert conflict between the Do'Urden family and House Hun'ett. Matron Malice, never one to miss a celebration, had a special present prepared for her enemies.

Briza Do'Urden, Malice's eldest daughter, a large and powerful drow female, paced about the anteroom anxiously, a not uncommon sight. "It should be finished by now," she grumbled as she kicked a small three-legged stool. It skidded and tumbled, chipping away a piece of mushroom-stem seat.

"Patience, my daughter," Malice replied somewhat recriminatory, though she shared Briza's sentiments. "Jarlaxle is a careful one." Briza turned away at the mention of the outrageous mercenary and moved to the room's ornately carved stone doors. Malice did not miss the significance of her daughter's actions.

"You do not approve of Jarlaxle and his band," the matron mother stated flatly.

"They are houseless rogues," Briza spat in response, still not turning to face her mother. "There is no place in Menzoberranzan for houseless rogues. They disrupt the natural order of our society. And they are males!"

"They serve us well," Malice reminded her. Briza wanted to argue about the extreme cost of hiring the mercenary band, but she wisely held her tongue. She and Malice had been at odds almost continually since the start of the Do'Urden-Hun'ett war.

"Without Bregan D'aerthe, we could not take action against our enemies," Malice continued. "Using the mercenaries, the houseless rogues, as you have named them, allows us to wage war without implicating our house as the perpetrator."

"Then why not be done with it?" Briza demanded, spinning back toward the throne. "We kill a few of Hun'ett's soldiers, they kill a few of ours. And all the while, both houses continue to recruit replacements! It will not end! The only winners in the conflict are the mercenaries of Bregan D'aerthe—and whatever band Matron SiNafay Hun'ett has hired—feeding off the coffers of both houses!"

"Watch your tone, my daughter," Malice growled as an angry reminder. "You are addressing a matron mother."

Briza turned away again. "We should have attacked House Hun'ett immediately, on the night Zaknafein was sacrificed," she dared to grumble.

"You forget the actions of your youngest brother on that night," Malice replied evenly.

But the matron mother was wrong. If she lived a thousand more years, Briza would not forget Drizzt's actions on the night he had forsaken his family. Trained by Zaknafein, Malice's favorite lover and reputably the finest weapon master in all of Menzoberranzan, Drizzt had achieved a level of fighting ability far beyond the drow norm. But Zak had also given Drizzt the troublesome and blasphemous attitudes that Lolth, the Spider Queen deity of the dark elves, would not tolerate. Finally, Drizzt's sacrilegious ways had invoked Lolth's wrath, and the Spider Queen, in turn, had demanded his death.

Matron Malice, impressed by Drizzt's potential as a warrior, had acted boldly on Drizzt's behalf and had given Zaknafein's heart to Lolth to compensate for Drizzt's sins. She forgave Drizzt in the hope that without

Zaknafein's influences he would amend his ways and replace the deposed weapon master.

In return, though, the ungrateful Drizzt had betrayed them all, had run off into the Underdark—an act that had not only robbed House Do'Urden of its only potential remaining weapon master, but also had placed Matron Malice and the rest of the Do'Urden family out of Lolth's favor. In the disastrous end of all their efforts, House Do'Urden had lost its premier weapon master, the favor of Lolth, and its would-be weapon master. It had not been a good day.

Luckily, House Hun'ett had suffered similar woes on that same day, losing both its wizards in a botched attempt to assassinate Drizzt. With both houses weakened and in Lolth's disfavor, the expected war had been turned into a calculated series of covert raids.

Briza would never forget.

A knock on the anteroom door startled Briza and her mother from their private memories of that fateful time. The door swung open, and Dinin, the elderboy of the house, walked in.

"Greetings, Matron Mother," he said in appropriate manner and dipping into a low bow. Dinin wanted his news to be a surprise, but the grin that found its way onto his face revealed everything.

"Jarlaxle has returned!" Malice snarled in glee. Dinin turned toward the open door, and the mercenary, waiting patiently in the corridor, strode in. Briza, ever amazed at the rogue's unusual mannerisms, shook her head as Jarlaxle walked past her. Nearly every dark elf in Menzoberranzan dressed in a quiet and practical manner, in robes adorned with the symbols of the Spider Queen or in supple chain-link armor under the folds of a magical and camouflaging *piwafwi* cloak.

Jarlaxle, arrogant and brash, followed few of the customs of Menzoberranzan's inhabitants. He was most certainly not the norm of drow society and he flaunted the differences openly, brazenly. He wore not a cloak nor a robe, but a shimmering cape that showed every color of the spectrum both in the glow of light and in the infrared spectrum of heat-sensing eyes. The cape's magic could only be guessed, but those closest to the mercenary leader indicated that it was very valuable indeed.

Jarlaxle's vest was sleeveless and cut so high that his slender and tightly muscled stomach was open for all to view. He kept a patch over one eye, though careful observers would understand it as ornamental, for Jarlaxle often shifted it from one eye to the other.

"My dear Briza," Jarlaxle said over his shoulder, noting the high priestess's disdainful interest in his appearance. He spun about and bowed low, sweeping off the wide-brimmed hat—another oddity, and even more so since the hat was overly plumed in the monstrous feathers of a diatryma, a gigantic Underdark bird—as he stooped.

Briza huffed and turned away at the sight of the mercenary's dipping head. Drow elves wore their thick white hair as a mantle of their station, each cut designed to reveal rank and house affiliation. Jarlaxle the rogue wore no hair at all, and from Briza's angle, his clean-shaven head appeared as a ball of pressed onyx.

Jarlaxle laughed quietly at the continuing disapproval of the eldest Do'Urden daughter and turned back toward Matron Malice, his ample jewelry tinkling and his hard and shiny boots clumping with every step. Briza took note of this as well, for she knew that those boots, and that jewelry, only seemed to make noise when Jarlaxle wished them to do so.

"It is done?" Matron Malice asked before the mercenary could even begin to offer a proper greeting.

"My dear Matron Malice," Jarlaxle replied with a pained sigh, knowing that he could get away with the informalities in light of his grand news. "Did you doubt me? Surely I am wounded to my heart."

Malice leaped from her throne, her fist clenched in victory. "Dipree Hun'ett is dead!" she proclaimed. "The first noble victim of the war!"

"You forget Masoj Hun'ett," remarked Briza, "slain by Drizzt ten years ago. And Zaknafein Do'Urden," Briza had to add, against her better judgment, "killed by your own hand."

"Zaknafein was not noble by birth," Malice sneered at her impertinent daughter. Briza's words stung Malice nonetheless. Malice had decided to sacrifice Zaknafein in Drizzt's stead against Briza's recommendations.

Jarlaxle cleared his throat to deflect the growing tension. The mercenary knew that he had to finish his business and be out of House Do'Urden as quickly as possible. Already he knew—though the Do'Urdens did not—that the appointed hour drew near. "There is the matter of my payment," he reminded Malice.

"Dinin will see to it," Malice replied with a wave of her hand, not turning her eyes from her daughter's pernicious stare.

"I will take my leave," Jarlaxle said, nodding to the elderboy.

Before the mercenary had taken his first step toward the door, Vierna, Malice's second daughter, burst into the room, her face glowing brightly in the infrared spectrum, heated with obvious excitement.

"Damn," Jarlaxle whispered under his breath.

"What is it?" Matron Malice demanded.

"House Hun'ett," Vierna cried. "Soldiers in the compound! We are under attack!"

⚔ ⚔ ⚔ ⚔ ⚔

Out in the courtyard, beyond the cavern complex, nearly five hundred soldiers of House Hun'ett—fully a hundred more than the house reportedly possessed—followed the blast of a lightning bolt through House Do'Urden's adamantite gates. The three hundred fifty soldiers of the Do'Urden household swarmed out of the shaped stalagmite mounds that served as their quarters to meet the attack.

Outnumbered but trained by Zaknafein, the Do'Urden troops formed into proper defensive positions, shielding their wizards and clerics so that they might cast their spells.

An entire contingent of Hun'ett soldiers, empowered with enchantments of flying, swooped down the cavern wall that housed the royal chambers of House Do'Urden. Tiny hand-held crossbows clicked and thinned the ranks of the aerial force with deadly, poison-tipped darts. The aerial invaders' surprise had been achieved, though, and the Do'Urden troops were quickly put into a precarious position.

⚔ ⚔ ⚔ ⚔ ⚔

"Hun'ett has not the favor of Lolth!" Malice screamed. "It would not dare to openly attack!" She flinched at the refuting, thunderous sounds of another, and then still another, bolt of lightning.

"Oh?" Briza snapped.

Malice cast her daughter a threatening glare but didn't have time to continue the argument. The normal method of attack by a drow house would involve the rush of soldiers combined with a mental barrage by the house's highest-ranking clerics. Malice, though, felt no mental attack, which told her beyond any doubt that it was indeed House Hun'ett that had come to her gates. The clerics of Hun'ett, out of the Spider Queen's favor, apparently could not use their Lolth-given powers to launch the mental assault. If they had, Malice and her daughters, also out of the Spider Queen's favor, could not have hoped to counter.

"Why would they dare to attack?" Malice wondered aloud.

Briza understood her mother's reasoning. "They are bold indeed," she said, "to hope that their soldiers alone can eliminate every member of our house." Everyone in the room, every drow in Menzoberranzan, understood the brutal, absolute punishments exacted upon any house that failed to eradicate another house. Such attacks were not frowned upon, but getting caught at the deed most certainly was.

Rizzen, the present patron of House Do'Urden, came into the anteroom then, his face grim. "We are outnumbered and outpositioned," he said. "Our defeat will be swift, I fear."

Malice would not accept the news. She struck Rizzen with a blow that knocked the patron halfway across the floor, then she spun on Jarlaxle. "You must summon your band!" Malice cried at the mercenary. "Quickly!"

"Matron," Jarlaxle stuttered, obviously at a loss. "Bregan D'aerthe is a secretive group. We do not engage in open warfare. To do so could invoke the wrath of the ruling council!"

"I will pay you whatever you desire," the desperate matron mother promised.

"But the cost—"

"Whatever you desire!" Malice snarled again.

"Such action—" Jarlaxle began.

Again, Malice did not let him finish his argument. "Save my house, mercenary," she growled. "Your profits will be great, but I warn you, the cost of your failure will be far greater!"

Jarlaxle did not appreciate being threatened, especially by a lame matron mother whose entire world was fast crumbling around her. But in the mercenary's ears the sweet ring of the word "profits" outweighed the threat a thousand times over. After ten straight years of exorbitant rewards in the Do'Urden-Hun'ett conflict, Jarlaxle did not doubt Malice's willingness or ability to pay as promised, nor did he doubt that this deal would prove even more lucrative than the agreement he had struck with Matron SiNafay Hun'ett earlier that same tenday.

"As you wish," he said to Matron Malice with a bow and a sweep of his garish hat. "I will see what I can do." A wink at Dinin set the elderboy on his heels as he exited the room.

When the two got out on the balcony overlooking the Do'Urden compound, they saw that the situation was even more desperate than Rizzen had described. The soldiers of House Do'Urden—those still alive—were trapped in and around one of the huge stalagmite mounds anchoring the front gate.

One of Hun'ett's flying soldiers dropped onto the balcony at the sight of a Do'Urden noble, but Dinin dispatched the intruder with a single, blurring attack routine.

"Well done," Jarlaxle commented, giving Dinin an approving nod. He moved to pat the elderboy Do'Urden on the shoulder, but Dinin slipped out of reach.

"We have other business," he pointedly reminded Jarlaxle. "Call your troops, and quickly, else I fear that House Hun'ett will win the day."

"Be at ease, my friend Dinin," Jarlaxle laughed. He pulled a small whistle from around his neck and blew into it. Dinin heard not a sound, for the instrument was magically tuned exclusively for the ears of members of Bregan D'aerthe.

The elderboy Do'Urden watched in amazement as Jarlaxle calmly puffed out a specific cadence, then he watched in even greater amazement as more than a hundred of House Hun'ett's soldiers turned against their comrades.

Bregan D'aerthe owed allegiance only to Bregan D'aerthe.

⚔ ⚔ ⚔ ⚔ ⚔

"They could not attack us," Malice said stubbornly, pacing about the chamber. "The Spider Queen would not aid them in their venture."

"They are winning without the Spider Queen's aid," Rizzen reminded her, prudently ducking into the room's farthest corner even as he spoke the unwanted words.

"You said that they would never attack!" Briza growled at her mother. "Even as you explained why we could not dare to attack them!" Briza remembered that conversation vividly, for it was she who had suggested the open attack on House Hun'ett. Malice had scolded her harshly and publicly, and now Briza meant to return the humiliation. Her voice dripped of angry sarcasm as she aimed each word at her mother. "Could it be that Matron Malice Do'Urden has erred?"

Malice's reply came in the form of a glare that wavered somewhere between rage and terror. Briza returned the threatening look without ambiguity and suddenly the matron mother of House Do'Urden did not feel so very invincible and sure of her actions. She started forward nervously a moment later when Maya, the youngest of the Do'Urden daughters, entered the room.

"They have breached the house!" Briza cried, assuming the worst. She grabbed at her snake-headed whip. "And we have not even begun our preparations for defense!"

"No!" Maya quickly corrected. "No enemies have crossed the balcony. The battle has turned against House Hun'ett!"

"As I knew it would," Malice observed, pulling herself straight and speaking pointedly at Briza. "Foolish is the house that moves without the favor of Lolth!" Despite her proclamation, though, Malice guessed that more than the judgment of the Spider Queen had come into play out in the courtyard. Her reasoning led her inescapably to Jarlaxle and his untrustworthy band of rogues.

⚔ ⚔ ⚔ ⚔ ⚔

Jarlaxle stepped off the balcony and used his innate drow abilities to levitate down to the cavern floor. Seeing no need to involve himself in a battle that was obviously under control, Dinin rested back and watched the mercenary go, considering all that had just transpired. Jarlaxle had played both sides off against the other, and once again the mercenary and his band had been the only true winners. Bregan D'aerthe was undeniably unscrupulous, but Dinin had to admit, undeniably effective.

Dinin found that he liked the renegade.

⚔ ⚔ ⚔ ⚔ ⚔

"The accusation has been properly delivered to Matron Baenre?" Malice asked Briza when the light of Narbondel, the magically heated stalagmite mound that served as the time clock of Menzoberranzan, began its steady climb, marking the dawn of the next day.

"The ruling house expected the visit," Briza replied with a smirk. "All of the city whispers of the attack, and of how House Do'Urden repelled the invaders of House Hun'ett."

Malice futilely tried to hide her vain smile. She enjoyed the attention and the glory that she knew would be lavished upon her house.

"The ruling council will be convened this very day," Briza went on. "No doubt to the dismay of Matron SiNafay Hun'ett and her doomed children."

Malice nodded her agreement. To eradicate a rival house in Menzoberranzan was a perfectly acceptable practice among the drow. But to fail in the attempt, to leave even one witness of noble blood alive to make an accusation, invited the judgment of the ruling council, a wrath that wrought absolute destruction in its wake.

A knock turned them both toward the room's ornate door.

"You are summoned, Matron," Rizzen said as he entered. "Matron Baenre has sent a chariot for you."

Malice and Briza exchanged hopeful but nervous glances. When punishment fell upon House Hun'ett, House Do'Urden would move into the eighth rank of the city hierarchy, a most desirable position. Only the matron mothers of the top eight houses were accorded a seat on the city's ruling council.

"Already?" Briza asked her mother.

Malice only shrugged in reply and followed Rizzen out of the room and down to the house's balcony. Rizzen offered her a hand of assistance, which she promptly and stubbornly slapped away. Her pride apparent with every move, Malice stepped over the railing and floated down to the courtyard, where the bulk of her remaining soldiery was gathered. The floating, blue-glowing disk bearing the insignia of House Baenre hovered just outside the blasted adamantite gate of the Do'Urden compound.

Malice proudly strode through the gathered crowd; dark elves fell over each other trying to get out of her way. This was her day, she decided, the day she achieved the seat on the ruling council, the position she so greatly deserved.

"Matron Mother, I will accompany you through the city," offered Dinin, standing at the gate.

"You will remain here with the rest of the family," Malice corrected. "The summons is for me alone."

"How can you know?" Dinin questioned, but he realized he had overstepped his rank as soon as the words had left his mouth.

By the time Malice turned her reprimanding glare toward him, he had already disappeared into the mob of soldiers.

"Proper respect," Malice muttered under her breath, and she instructed the nearest soldiers to remove a section of the propped and tied gate. With a final, victorious glance at her subjects, Malice stepped out and took a seat on the floating disk.

This was not the first time that Malice had accepted such an invitation from Matron Baenre, so she was not the least bit surprised when several Baenre clerics moved out from the shadows to encircle the floating disk in a protective guard. The last time Malice had made this trip, she had been tentative, not really understanding Baenre's intent in summoning her. This time, though, Malice folded her arms defiantly across her chest and let the curious onlookers view her in all the splendor of her victory.

Malice accepted the stares proudly, feeling positively superior. Even when the disk reached the fabulous weblike fence of House Baenre, with its thousand marching guards and towering stalagmite and stalactite structures, Malice's pride had not diminished.

She was of the ruling council now, or soon would be; no longer did she have to feel intimidated anywhere in the city.

Or so she thought.

"Your presence is requested in the chapel," one of Baenre's clerics said to her when the disk came to a stop at the base of the great domed building's sweeping stairs.

Malice stepped down and ascended the polished stones. As soon as she entered, she noticed a figure sitting on one of the chairs atop the raised central altar. The seated drow, the only other person visible in the chapel, apparently did not notice that Malice had entered. She sat back comfortably, watching the huge illusionary image at the top of the dome shift through its forms, first appearing as a gigantic spider, then a beautiful drow female.

As she moved closer, Malice recognized the robes of a matron mother, and she assumed, as she had all along, that it was Matron Baenre herself, the most powerful figure in all of Menzoberranzan, awaiting her. Malice made her way up the altar's stairs, coming up behind the seated drow. Not waiting for an invitation, she boldly walked around to greet the other matron mother.

It was not, however, the ancient and emaciated form of Matron Baenre that Malice Do'Urden encountered on the dais of the Baenre chapel. The seated matron mother was not old beyond the years of a drow and as withered and dried as some bloodless corpse. Indeed, this drow was no older than Malice and quite diminutive. Malice recognized her all too well.

"SiNafay!" she cried, nearly toppling.

"Malice," the other replied calmly.

A thousand troublesome possibilities rolled through Malice's mind. SiNafay Hun'ett should have been huddling in fear in her doomed house, awaiting the annihilation of her family. Yet here SiNafay sat, comfortably, in the hallowed quarters of Menzoberranzan's most important family!

"You do not belong in this place!" Malice protested, her slender fists clenched at her side. She considered the possibilities of attacking her rival there and then, of throttling SiNafay with her own hands.

"Be at ease, Malice," SiNafay remarked casually. "I am here by the invitation of Matron Baenre, as are you."

The mention of Matron Baenre and the reminder of where they were calmed Malice considerably. One did not act out of sorts in the chapel of House Baenre! Malice moved to the opposite end of the circular dais and took a seat, her gaze never leaving the smugly smiling face of SiNafay Hun'ett.

After a few interminable moments of silence, Malice had to speak her mind. "It was House Hun'ett that attacked my family in the last dark of Narbondel," she said. "I have many witnesses to the fact. There can be no doubt!"

"None," SiNafay replied, her agreement catching Malice off her guard.

"You admit the deed?" she balked.

"Indeed," said SiNafay. "Never have I denied it."

"Yet you live," Malice sneered. "The laws of Menzoberranzan demand justice upon you and your house."

"Justice?" SiNafay laughed at the absurd notion. Justice had never been more than a facade and a means of keeping the pretense of order in chaotic Menzoberranzan. "I acted as the Spider Queen demanded of me."

"If the Spider Queen approved of your methods, you would have been victorious," Malice reasoned.

"Not so," interrupted another voice. Malice and SiNafay turned about just as Matron Baenre magically appeared, sitting comfortably in the chair farthest back on the dais.

Malice wanted to scream out at the withered matron mother, both for spying on her conversation and for apparently refuting her claims against SiNafay. Malice had managed to survive the dangers of Menzoberranzan for five hundred years, though, primarily because she understood the implications of angering one such as Matron Baenre.

"I claim the rights of accusation against House Hun'ett," she said calmly.

"Granted," replied Matron Baenre. "As you have said, and as SiNafay agreed, there can be no doubt."

Malice turned triumphantly on SiNafay, but the matron mother of House Hun'ett still sat relaxed and unconcerned.

"Then why is she here?" Malice cried, her tone edged in explosive violence. "SiNafay is an outlaw. She—"

"We have not argued against your words," Matron Baenre interrupted. "House Hun'ett attacked and failed. The penalties for such a deed are well known and agreed upon, and the ruling council will convene this very day to see that justice is carried through."

"Then why is SiNafay here?" Malice demanded.

"Do you doubt the wisdom of my attack?" SiNafay asked Malice, trying to keep a chuckle under her breath.

"You were defeated," Malice reminded her matter-of-factly. "That alone should provide your answer."

"Lolth demanded the attack," said Matron Baenre.

"Why, then, was House Hun'ett defeated?" Malice asked stubbornly. "If the Spider Queen—"

"I did not say that the Spider Queen had imbued her blessings upon House Hun'ett," Matron Baenre interrupted, somewhat crossly. Malice shifted back in her seat, remembering her place and her predicament.

"I said only that Lolth demanded the attack," Matron Baenre continued. "For ten years all of Menzoberranzan has suffered the spectacle of your private war. The intrigue and excitement wore away long ago, let me assure you both. It had to be decided."

"And it was," declared Malice, rising from her seat. "House Do'Urden has proven victorious, and I claim the rights of accusation against SiNafay Hun'ett and her family!"

"Sit down, Malice," SiNafay said. "There is more to this than your simple rights of accusation."

Malice looked to Matron Baenre for confirmation, though, considering the present situation, she could not doubt SiNafay's words.

"It is done," Matron Baenre said to her. "House Do'Urden has won, and House Hun'ett will be no more."

Malice fell back into her seat, smiling smugly at SiNafay. Still, though, the matron mother of House Hun'ett did not seem the least bit concerned.

"I will watch the destruction of your house with great pleasure," Malice assured her rival. She turned to Baenre. "When will punishment be exacted?"

"It is already done," Matron Baenre replied mysteriously.

"SiNafay lives!" Malice cried.

"No," the withered matron mother corrected. "She who was SiNafay Hun'ett lives."

Now Malice was beginning to understand. House Baenre had always been opportunistic. Could it be that Matron Baenre was stealing the high priestesses of House Hun'ett to add to her own collection?

"You will shelter her?" Malice dared to ask.

"No," Matron Baenre replied evenly. "That task will fall to you."

Malice's eyes went wide. Of all the many duties she had ever been appointed in her days as a high priestess of Lolth, she could think of none more distasteful. "She is my enemy! You ask that I give her shelter?"

"She is your daughter," Matron Baenre shot back. Her tone softened and a wry smile cracked her thin lips. "Your oldest daughter, returned from travels to Ched Nasad, or some other city of our kin."

"Why are you doing this?" Malice demanded. "It is unprecedented!"

"Not completely correct," replied Matron Baenre. Her fingers tapped together out in front of her while she sank back within her thoughts, remembering some of the strange consequences of the endless line of battles within the drow city.

"Outwardly, your observations are correct," she continued to explain to Malice. "But surely you are wise enough to know that many things occur behind the appearances in Menzoberranzan. House Hun'ett must be destroyed—that cannot be changed—and all of the nobles of House Hun'ett must be slaughtered. It is, after all, the civilized thing to do." She paused a moment to ensure that Malice was fully comprehending the meaning of her next statement. "They must appear, at least, to be slaughtered."

"And you will arrange this?" Malice asked.

"I already have," Matron Baenre assured her.

"But what is the purpose?"

"When House Hun'ett initiated its attack against you, did you call upon the Spider Queen in your struggles?" Matron Baenre asked bluntly.

The question startled Malice, and the expected answer upset her more than a little.

"And when House Hun'ett was repelled," Matron Baenre went on coldly, "did you give praise to the Spider Queen? Did you call upon a handmaiden of Lolth in your moment of victory, Malice Do'Urden?"

"Am I on trial here?" Malice cried. "You know the answer, Matron Baenre." She looked at SiNafay uncomfortably as she replied, fearing that she might be giving some valued information away. "You are aware of my situation concerning the Spider Queen. I dare not summon a yochlol until I have seen some sign that I have regained Lolth's favor."

"And you have seen no sign," SiNafay remarked.

"None other than the defeat of my rival," Malice growled back at her.

"That was not a sign from the Spider Queen," Matron Baenre assured them both. "Lolth did not involve herself in your struggles. She only demanded that they be finished!"

"Is she pleased at the outcome?" Malice asked bluntly.

"That is yet to be determined," replied Matron Baenre. "Many years ago, Lolth made clear her desires that Malice Do'Urden sit upon the ruling council. Beginning with the next light of Narbondel, it shall be so."

Malice's chin rose with pride.

"But understand your dilemma," Matron Baenre scolded her, rising up out of her chair. Malice slumped back immediately.

"You have lost more than half of your soldiers," Baenre explained. "And you do not have a large family surrounding and supporting you. You rule the eighth house of the city, yet it is known by all that you are not in the Spider Queen's favor. How long do you believe House Do'Urden will hold its position? Your seat on the ruling council is in jeopardy even before you have assumed it!"

Malice could not refute the ancient matron's logic. They both knew the ways of Menzoberranzan. With House Do'Urden so obviously crippled, some lesser house would soon take advantage of the opportunity to better its station. The attack by House Hun'ett would not be the last battle fought in the Do'Urden compound.

"So I give to you SiNafay Hun'ett . . . Shi'nayne Do'Urden . . . a new daughter, a new high priestess," said Matron Baenre. She turned then to SiNafay to continue her explanation, but Malice found herself suddenly distracted as a voice called out to her in her thoughts, a telepathic message.

*Keep her only as long as you need her, Malice Do'Urden,* it said. Malice looked around, guessing the source of the communication. On a previous visit to House Baenre, she had met Matron Baenre's mind flayer, a telepathic beast. The creature was nowhere in sight, but neither had Matron Baenre been when Malice had first entered the chapel. Malice looked around alternately at the remaining empty seats atop the dais, but the stone furniture showed no signs of any occupants.

A second telepathic message left her no doubts.

*You will know when the time is right.*

". . . and the remaining fifty of House Hun'ett's soldiers," Matron Baenre was saying. "Do you agree, Matron Malice?"

Malice looked at SiNafay, an expression that might have been acceptance or wicked irony. "I do," she replied.

"Go, then, Shi'nayne Do'Urden," Matron Baenre instructed SiNafay. "Join your remaining soldiers in the courtyard. My wizards will get you to House Do'Urden in secrecy."

SiNafay cast a suspicious glance Malice's way, then moved out of the great chapel.

"I understand," Malice said to her hostess when SiNafay had gone.

"You understand nothing!" Matron Baenre yelled back at her, suddenly enraged. "I have done all that I may for you, Malice Do'Urden! It was Lolth's wish that you sit upon the ruling council, and I have arranged, at great personal cost, for that to be so."

Malice knew then, beyond any doubt, that House Baenre had prompted House Hun'ett to action. How deep did Matron Baenre's influence go, Malice wondered? Perhaps the withered matron mother also had anticipated, and possibly arranged, the actions of Jarlaxle and the soldiers of Bregan D'aerthe, ultimately the deciding factor in the battle.

She would have to find out about that possibility, Malice promised herself. Jarlaxle had dipped his greedy fingers quite deeply into her purse.

"No more," Matron Baenre continued. "Now you are left to your own wiles. You have not found the favor of Lolth, and that is the only way you, and House Do'Urden, will survive!"

Malice's fist clenched the arm of her chair so tightly that she almost expected to hear the stone cracking beneath it. She had hoped, with the defeat of House Hun'ett, that she had put the blasphemous deeds of her youngest son behind her.

"You know what must be done," said Matron Baenre. "Correct the wrong, Malice. I have put myself forward on your behalf. I will not tolerate continued failure!"

* * * * *

"The arrangements have been explained to us, Matron Mother," Dinin said to Malice when she returned to the adamantite gate of House Do'Urden. He followed Malice across the compound and then levitated up beside her to the balcony outside the noble quarters of the house.

"All of the family is gathered in the anteroom," Dinin went on. "Even the newest member," he added with a wink.

Malice did not respond to her son's feeble attempt at humor. She pushed Dinin aside roughly and stormed down the central corridor, commanding the anteroom door to open with a single powerful word. The family scrambled out of her way as she crossed to her throne, on the far side of the spider-shaped table.

They had anticipated a long meeting, to learn the new situation confronting them and the challenges they must overcome. What they got instead was a brief glimpse at the rage burning within Matron Malice. She glared at them alternately, letting each of them know beyond any doubt that she would not accept anything less than she demanded. Her voice grating as though her mouth were filled with pebbles, she growled, "Find Drizzt and bring him to me!"

Briza started to protest, but Malice shot her a glare so utterly cold and threatening that it stole the words away. The eldest daughter, as stubborn as her mother and always ready for an argument, averted her eyes. And no one else in the anteroom, though they shared Briza's unspoken concerns, made any motion to argue.

Malice then left them to sort out the specifics of how they would accomplish the task. Details were not at all important to Malice.

The only part she meant to play in all of this was the thrust of the ceremonial dagger into her youngest son's chest.

# 2
# Voices in the Dark

Drizzt stretched away his weariness and forced himself to his feet. The efforts of his battle against the basilisk the night before, of slipping fully into that primal state so necessary for survival, had drained him thoroughly. Yet Drizzt knew that he could afford no more rest; his rothé herd, the guaranteed food supply, had been scattered among the maze of tunnels and had to be retrieved.

Drizzt quickly surveyed the small and unremarkable cave that served as his home, ensuring that all was as it should be. His eyes lingered on the onyx statuette of the panther. He was held by a profound longing for Guenhwyvar's companionship. In his ambush of the basilisk, Drizzt had kept the panther by his side for a long period—nearly the entire night—and Guenhwyvar would need to rest back on the Astral Plane. More than a full day would pass before Drizzt could bring a rested Guenhwyvar forth again, and to attempt to use the figurine before then in any but a desperate situation would be foolish. With a resigned shrug, Drizzt dropped the statuette into his pocket and tried vainly to dismiss his loneliness.

After a quick inspection of the rock barricade blocking the entrance to the main corridor, Drizzt moved to the smaller crawl tunnel at the back of the cave. He noticed the scratches on the wall by the tunnel, the notches he had scrawled to mark the passage of the days. Drizzt absently scraped another one now, but realized that it was not important. How many times had he forgotten to scratch the mark? How many days had slipped past him unnoticed, between the hundreds of scratches on that wall?

Somehow, it no longer seemed to matter. Day and night were one, and all the days were one, in the life of the hunter. Drizzt hauled himself up into the tunnel and crawled for many minutes toward the dim light source at the other end. Though the presence of light, the result of the glow of an unusual type of fungus, normally would have been uncomfortable to a dark elf's eyes, Drizzt felt a sincere sense of security as he crossed through the crawl tunnel into the long chamber.

Its floor was broken into two levels, the lower being a moss-filled bed crossed by a small stream, and the upper being a grove of towering mushrooms. Drizzt headed for the grove, though he was not normally welcomed there. He knew that the myconids, the fungus-men, a weird cross between humanoid and toadstool, were watching him anxiously. The basilisk had come in here in its first travels to the region, and the myconids had suffered a great loss. Now they were no doubt scared and dangerous, but Drizzt suspected that they knew, as well, that it was he who had slain the monster. Myconids were not stupid beings; if Drizzt kept his weapons sheathed and made no unexpected moves, the fungus-men probably would accept his passage through their tended grove.

The wall to the upper tier was more than ten feet high and nearly sheer, but Drizzt scaled it as easily and as quickly as if it had sported a wide and flat staircase. A group of myconids fanned out around him as he reached the top, some only half Drizzt's height, but most twice as tall as the drow. Drizzt crossed his arms over his chest, a commonly accepted Underdark signal of peace.

The fungus-men found Drizzt's appearance disgusting—as disgusting as he considered them—but they did indeed understand that Drizzt had destroyed the basilisk. For many years the myconids had lived beside the rogue drow, each protecting the life-filled chamber that served as their mutual sanctuary. An oasis such as this place, with edible plants, a stream full of fish, and a herd of rothé, was not common in the harsh and empty stone caverns of the Underdark, and predators wandering along the outer tunnels invariably found their way in. Then it was left to the fungus-men, and to Drizzt, to defend their domain.

The largest of the myconids moved forward to stand before the dark elf. Drizzt made no move, understanding the importance of establishing an acceptance between himself and the new king of the fungus-man colony. Still, Drizzt tensed his muscles, preparing a spring to the side if things did not go as he expected.

The myconid spewed forth a cloud of spores. Drizzt studied them in the split-second it took them to descend over him, knowing that the mature myconids could emit many different types of spore, some quite dangerous. But Drizzt recognized the hue of this particular cloud and accepted it wholly.

*King dead. Me king,* came the myconid's thoughts through the telepathic bond inspired by the spore cloud.

*You are king,* Drizzt responded mentally. How he wished these fungoids could speak aloud! *As it was?*

*Bottom for dark elf, grove for myconid,* replied the fungus-man.

*Agreed.*

*Grove for myconid!* the fungus-man thought again, this time emphatically.

Drizzt silently dropped down off the ledge. He had accomplished his mission with the fungoid; neither he nor the new king had any desire to continue the meeting.

Off at a swift pace, Drizzt leaped the five-foot-wide stream and padded out across the thick moss. The chamber was longer than it was wide and it rolled back for many yards, turning a slight bend before it reached the larger exit to the twisting maze of Underdark tunnels. Around that bend, Drizzt looked again upon the destruction wreaked by the basilisk. Several half-eaten rothé lay about—Drizzt would have to dispose of those corpses before their stench attracted even more unwelcome visitors—and other rothé stood perfectly still, petrified by the gaze of the dreaded monster. Directly in front of the chamber exit stood the former myconid king, a twelve-foot giant, now no more than an ornamental statue.

Drizzt paused to regard it. He had never learned the fungoid's name, and had never given it his, but Drizzt supposed that the thing had been his ally at least, perhaps even his friend. They had lived side by side for several years, though they had rarely encountered each other, and both had realized a bit more security just by the other's presence. All told, though, Drizzt felt no remorse at the sight of his petrified ally. In the Underdark, only the strongest survived, and this time the myconid king had not been strong enough.

In the wilds of the Underdark, failure allowed for no second chance.

Out in the tunnels again, Drizzt felt his rage beginning to build. He welcomed it fully, focusing his thoughts on the carnage in his domain and accepting the anger as an ally in the wilds. He came through a series of tunnels and turned into the one where he had placed his darkness spell the night before, where Guenhwyvar had crouched, ready to spring upon the basilisk. Drizzt's spell was long gone now and using his infravision, he could make out several warm-glowing forms crawling over the cooling mound that Drizzt knew to be the dead monster.

The sight of the thing only heightened the hunter's rage.

Instinctively, he grasped the hilt of one of his scimitars. As though it moved of its own accord, the weapon shot out as Drizzt passed the basilisk's head, splatting sickeningly into the exposed brains. Several blind cave rats took flight at the sound and Drizzt, again without thinking, snapped off a thrust with his second blade, pinning one to the stone. Without even slowing his pace, he scooped the rat up and dropped it into his pouch. Finding the rothé could be a tedious process, and the hunter would need to eat.

For the remainder of that day and half of the next, the hunter moved out away from his domain. The cave rat was not a particularly enjoyable meal, but it sustained Drizzt, allowing him to continue, allowing him to survive. To the hunter in the Underdark, nothing else mattered.

That second day out, the hunter knew he was closing in on a group of his lost beasts. He summoned Guenhwyvar to his side and with the panther's help, had little trouble finding the rothé. Drizzt had hoped that all of the herd would still be together, but he found only a half-dozen in the area. Six were better than none, though, and Drizzt set Guenhwyvar into motion, herding the rothé back toward the moss cave. Drizzt set a brutal pace, knowing that the task would be much easier and safer with Guenhwyvar by his side. By the time the panther tired and had to return to its home plane, the rothé were comfortably grazing by the familiar stream.

The drow set out again immediately, this time taking two dead rats along for the ride. He called Guenhwyvar again when he was able and dismissed the panther when he had to, then again after that, as the days rolled by without further sign. But the hunter did not surrender his search. Frightened rothé could cover an incredible amount of ground, and in the maze of twisting tunnels and huge caverns, the hunter knew that many more days could pass before he caught up to the beasts.

Drizzt found his food where he could, taking down a bat with a perfect throw of a dagger—after tossing up a deceptive screen of pebbles—and dropping a boulder onto the back of a giant Underdark crab. Eventually, Drizzt grew weary of the search and longed for the security of his small cave. Doubting that the rothé, running blind, could have survived this long out in the tunnels, so far from their water and food, he accepted his herd's loss and decided to return home via a route that would bring him back to the region of the moss cavern from a different direction.

Only the clear tracks of his lost herd would detour him from his set course, Drizzt decided, but as he rounded a bend halfway home, a strange sound caught his attention and held it.

Drizzt pressed his hands against the stone, feeling the subtle, rhythmical vibrations. A short distance away, something banged the stone in succession. Measured hammering.

The hunter drew his scimitars and crept along, using the continuing vibrations to guide him through the winding passageways.

The flickering light of a fire dropped him into a crouch, but he did not flee, drawn by the knowledge that an intelligent being was nearby. Quite possibly the stranger would prove to be a threat, but perhaps, Drizzt hoped in the back of his mind, it could be something more than that.

Then Drizzt saw them, two banging at the stone with crafted pickaxes, another collecting rubble in a wheelbarrow, and two more standing guard. The hunter knew at once that more guards would be about; he probably had penetrated their defenses without even seeing them. Drizzt summoned one of the abilities of his heritage and drifted slowly up into the air, guiding his levitation with his hands along the stone. Luckily, the tunnel was high at this point, so the hunter could observe the mining creatures in relative safety.

They were shorter that Drizzt and hairless, with squat and muscled torsos perfectly designed for the mining that was their calling in life. Drizzt had encountered this race before and had learned much of them during his years at the Academy back in Menzoberranzan. These were svirfnebli, deep gnomes, the most hated enemies of the drow in all the Underdark.

Once, long ago, Drizzt had led a drow patrol into battle against a group of svirfnebli and personally had defeated an earth elemental that the deep gnome leader had summoned. Drizzt remembered that time now, and like all of the memories of his existence, the thoughts pained him. He had been captured by the deep gnomes, roughly tied, and held prisoner in a secret chamber. The svirfnebli had not mistreated him, though they suspected—and explained to Drizzt—that they would eventually have to kill him. The group's leader had promised Drizzt as much mercy as the situation allowed.

Drizzt's comrades, though, led by Dinin, his own brother, had stormed in, showing the deep gnomes no mercy at all. Drizzt had managed to convince his brother to spare the svirfneblin leader's life, but Dinin, showing typical drow cruelty, had ordered the deep gnome's hands severed before releasing him to flee to his homeland.

Drizzt shook himself from the anguishing memories and forced his thoughts back to the situation at hand. Deep gnomes could be formidable adversaries, he reminded himself, and they would not likely welcome a drow elf to their mining operations. He had to keep alert.

The miners apparently had struck a rich vein, for they began talking in excited tones. Drizzt reveled in the sound of those words, though he could not begin to understand the strange gnomish language. A smile not inspired by victory in battle found its way onto Drizzt's face for the first time in years as the svirfnebli scrambled about the stone, tossing huge chunks into their wheelbarrows and calling for other nearby companions to come and join in the fun. As Drizzt had suspected, more than a dozen unseen svirfnebli came in from every direction.

Drizzt found a high perch against the wall and watched the miners long after his levitation spell had expired. When at last their wheelbarrows were overfilled, the deep gnomes formed a column and started away. Drizzt realized that his prudent course at that time would be to let them get far away, then slip back to his home.

But, against the simple logic that guided his survival, Drizzt found that he could not so easily let the sound of the voices get away. He picked his way down the high wall and fell into pace behind the svirfneblin caravan, wondering where it would lead.

For many days Drizzt followed the deep gnomes. He resisted the temptation to summon Guenhwyvar, knowing that the panther could use the extended rest and himself satisfied in the company, however distant, of the deep gnomes' chatter. Every instinct warned the hunter against continuing in his actions, but for the first time in a very long time, Drizzt overruled the instincts of his more primal self. He needed to hear the gnomish voices more than he needed the simple necessities of survival.

The corridors became more worked, less natural, around him, and Drizzt knew that he was approaching the svirfneblin homeland. Again the potential dangers loomed up before him, and again he dismissed them as secondary. He quickened his pace and put the mining caravan in sight, suspecting that the svirfnebli would have some cunning traps set about.

The deep gnomes measured their steps at this point, taking care to avoid certain areas. Drizzt carefully mimicked their movements and nodded knowingly as he noticed a loose stone here and a low trip-wire there. Then Drizzt ducked back behind an outcropping as new voices joined the sound of the miners.

The mining troupe had come to a long and wide stairway, ascending between two walls of absolutely sheer and uncracked stone. To the side of the stair was an opening barely high and wide enough for the wheelbarrows, and Drizzt watched with sincere admiration as the deep gnome miners moved the carts to this opening and fastened the lead one to a chain. A series of taps on the stone sent a signal to an unseen operator, and the chain creaked, drawing the wheelbarrow into the hole. One by one the carts disappeared, and the svirfneblin band thinned as well, taking to the stairs as their load lessened.

As the two remaining deep gnomes hitched the last cart to the chain and tapped out the signal, Drizzt took a gamble borne of desperation. He waited for the deep gnomes to turn their backs and darted to the cart, catching it just as it disappeared into the low tunnel. Drizzt understood the depth of his foolishness when the last deep gnome, still apparently unaware of his presence, replaced a stone at the bottom of the passage, blocking any possible retreat.

The chain pulled on and the cart rolled up at an angle as steep as the paralleling staircase. Drizzt could see nothing ahead, for the wheelbarrow, designed for a perfect fit, took up the entire height and width of the tunnel. Drizzt noticed then that the cart had little wheels along its sides as well, aiding in its passage. It felt so good to be in the presence of such intelligence again, but Drizzt could not ignore the danger surrounding him. The svirfnebli would not take well to an intruding drow elf; it was likely they would strike out with weapons, not questions.

After several minutes, the passage leveled off and widened. A single svirfneblin was there, effortlessly turning the crank that hauled up the wheelbarrows. Intent on his business, the deep gnome did not notice Drizzt's dark form dart from behind the last cart and silently slip through the room's side door.

Drizzt heard voices as soon as he opened the door. He continued ahead, though, having nowhere else to go, and dropped to his belly on a narrow ledge. The deep gnomes, guards and miners, were below him, talking on a landing at the top of the wide stairway. At least a score stood there now, the miners recounting the tales of their rich find.

At the back end of the landing, through two immense and partly ajar metal-bound stone doors, Drizzt caught a glimpse of the svirfneblin city. The drow could see but a fraction of the place, and that not very well from his position on the ledge, but he guessed that the cavern beyond those massive doors was not nearly as large as the chamber housing Menzoberranzan.

Drizzt wanted to go in there! He wanted to jump up and rush through those doors, give himself over to the deep gnomes for whatever judgment they deemed fair. Perhaps they would accept him; perhaps they would see

Drizzt Do'Urden for who he truly was.

The svirfnebli on the landing, laughing and chatting, made their way into the city.

Drizzt had to go now, had to spring up and follow them beyond the massive doors.

But the hunter, the being who had survived a decade in the savage wilds of the Underdark, could not move from the ledge. The hunter, the being who had defeated a basilisk and countless other of this dangerous world's monsters, could not give himself over in the hopes of civilized mercy. The hunter did not understand such concepts.

The massive stone doors closed—and the moment of flickering light in Drizzt's darkening heart died—with a resounding crash.

After a long and tormented moment, Drizzt Do'Urden rolled off the ledge and dropped to the landing at the top of the stairs. His vision blurred suddenly as he made his way down, the path away from the teeming life beyond the doors, and it was only the primal instincts of the hunter that sensed the presence of still more svirfneblin guards. The hunter leaped wildly over the startled deep gnomes and rushed out again into the freedom offered by the wild Underdark's open passageways.

When he had put the svirfneblin city far behind, Drizzt reached into his pocket and took out the statuette, the summons to his only companion. A moment later, though, Drizzt dropped the figurine back, refusing to call the cat, punishing himself for his weakness on the ledge. If he had been stronger on the ledge beside the immense doors, he could have put an end to his torment, one way or another.

The instincts of hunter battled Drizzt for control as he made his way along the passages that would take him back to the moss-filled cavern. As the Underdark and the press of undeniable danger continued to close in around him, those primal, alert instincts took command, denying any further distracting thoughts of the svirfnebli and their city.

Those primal instincts were the salvation and the damnation of Drizzt Do'Urden.

# 3
# Snakes and Swords

"How many tendays has it been?" Dinin signaled to Briza in the silent hand code of the drow. "How many tendays have we hunted through these tunnels for our renegade brother?"

Dinin's expression revealed his sarcasm as he motioned the thoughts. Briza scowled at him and did not reply. She cared for this tedious duty even less than he. She was a high priestess of Lolth and had been the eldest daughter, accorded a high place of honor within the family structure. Never before would Briza have been sent off on such a hunt. But now, for some unexplained reason, SiNafay Hun'ett had joined the family, relegating Briza to a lesser position.

"Five?" Dinin continued, his anger growing with each darting movement of his slender fingers. "Six? How long has it been, sister?" he pressed. "How long has SiNaf—Shi'nayne . . . been sitting at Matron Malice's side?"

Briza's snake-headed whip came off her belt, and she spun angrily on her brother. Dinin, realizing that he had gone too far with his sarcastic prodding, defensively drew his sword, and tried to duck away. Briza's strike came faster, easily defeating Dinin's pitiful attempt at a parry, and three of the six heads connected squarely on the elderboy Do'Urden's chest and shoulder. Cold pain spread through Dinin's body, leaving only a helpless numbness in its wake. His sword arm drooped and he started to topple forward.

Briza's powerful hand shot out and caught him by the throat as he swooned, easily lifting him onto his toes. Then, looking around at the other five members of the hunting party to ensure that none were moving in Dinin's favor, Briza slammed her stunned brother roughly into the stone wall. The high priestess leaned heavily on Dinin, one hand tight against his throat.

"A wise male would measure his gestures more carefully," Briza snarled aloud, though she and the others had been explicitly instructed by Matron Malice not to communicate in any method other than the silent code once they were beyond Menzoberranzan's borders.

It took Dinin a long while to fully appreciate his predicament. As the numbness wore away, he realized that he could not draw breath, and though his hand still held his sword, Briza, outweighing him by a score of pounds, had it pinned close to his side. Even more distressing, his sister's free hand held the dreaded snake-whip aloft. Unlike ordinary whips, that evil instrument needed little room to work its snap. The animated snake heads could coil and strike from close range simply as an extension of their wielder's will.

"Matron Malice would not question your death," Briza whispered harshly. "Her sons have ever been trouble to her!"

Dinin looked past his hulking captor to the common soldiers of the patrol.

"Witnesses?" Briza laughed, guessing his thoughts. "Do you really believe they will speak against a high priestess for the sake of a mere male?" Briza's eyes narrowed and she moved her face right up to Dinin's. "A mere male corpse?" She cackled once again and released Dinin suddenly, and he dropped to his knees, struggling to regain a normal rhythm to his breathing.

"Come," Briza signaled in the silent code to the rest of the patrol. "I sense that my youngest brother is not in this area. We shall return to the city and restock our packs."

Dinin watched his sister's back as she made the preparations for their departure. He wanted nothing more than to put his sword between her shoulder blades. Dinin was smarter than to try such a move, though. Briza had been a high priestess of the Spider Queen for more than three centuries and was now in the favor of Lolth, even if Matron Malice and the rest of House Do'Urden was not. Even if her evil goddess had not been looking over her, Briza was a formidable foe, skilled in spells and with that cruel whip always ready at her side.

"My sister," Dinin called after her as she started away. Briza spun on him, surprised that he would dare to speak aloud to her.

"Accept my apologies," Dinin said. He motioned for the other soldiers to keep moving, then returned to using the hand code, so that the commoners would not know his further conversation with Briza.

"I am not pleased by the addition of SiNafay Hun'ett to the family," Dinin explained.

Briza's lips curled up in one of her typically ambiguous smiles; Dinin couldn't be sure if she was agreeing with him or mocking him. "You think yourself wise enough to question the decisions of Matron Malice?" her fingers asked.

"No!" Dinin signaled back emphatically. "Matron Malice does as she must, and always for the welfare of House Do'Urden. But I do not trust the displaced Hun'ett. SiNafay watched her house smashed into bits of heated rock by the judgment of the ruling council. All of her treasured children were slain; and most of her commoners as well. Can she truly be loyal to House Do'Urden after such a loss?"

"Foolish male," Briza signaled in reply. "Priestesses understand that loyalty is owed only to Lolth. SiNafay's house is no more, thus SiNafay is no more. She is Shi'nayne Do'Urden now, and by the order of the Spider Queen, she will fully accept all of the responsibilities that accompany the name."

"I do not trust her," Dinin reiterated. "Nor am I pleased to see my sisters, the true Do'Urdens, moved down the hierarchy to make room for her. Shi'nayne should have been placed beneath Maya, or housed among the commoners."

Briza snarled at him, though she wholeheartedly agreed. "Shi'nayne's rank in the family is of no concern to you. House Do'Urden is stronger for the addition of another high priestess. That is all a male need care about!"

Dinin nodded his acceptance of her logic and wisely sheathed his sword before beginning to rise from his knees. Briza likewise replaced the snake-whip on her belt but continued to watch her volatile brother out of the corner of her eye.

Dinin would be more careful around Briza now. He knew that his survival depended on his ability to walk beside his sister, for Malice would continue to send Briza out on these hunting patrols beside him. Briza was the strongest of the Do'Urden daughters, with the best chance of finding and capturing Drizzt. And Dinin, having been a patrol leader for the city for more than a decade, was the most familiar of anyone in the house with the tunnels beyond Menzoberranzan.

Dinin shrugged at his rotten luck and followed his sister back down the tunnels to the city. A short respite, no more than a day, and they would be back on the march again, back on the prowl for their elusive and dangerous brother, whom Dinin truly had no desire to find.

⚔ ⚔ ⚔ ⚔ ⚔

Guenhwyvar's head turned abruptly and the great panther froze perfectly still, one paw cocked and ready to move.

"You heard it, too," Drizzt whispered, moving tightly to the panther's side. "Come, my friend. Let us see what new enemy has entered our domain."

They sped off together, equally silent, down corridors they knew so very well. Drizzt stopped suddenly, and Guenhwyvar did likewise, at the echo of a scuffle. It was made by a boot, Drizzt knew, and not by some natural monster of the Underdark. Drizzt pointed up to a broken pile of rubble overlooking a wide and many-tiered cavern on its other side. Guenhwyvar led him there, where they could find a better vantage point.

The drow patrol came into view only a few moments later, a group of seven, though they were too far away for Drizzt to make out any particulars. Drizzt was amazed that he had heard them so easily, for he remembered those days when he had taken the point position on such patrols. How alone he had felt then, up at the lead of more than a dozen dark elves, for they made not a whisper with their practiced movements and they kept to the shadows so well that even Drizzt's keen eyes could not begin to locate them.

And yet, this hunter that Drizzt had become, this primal, instinctive self, had found this group easily.

⚔ ⚔ ⚔ ⚔ ⚔

Briza stopped suddenly and closed her eyes, concentrating on the emanations of her spell of location.

"What is it?" Dinin's fingers asked her when she looked back to him. Her startled and obviously excited expression revealed much.

"Drizzt?" Dinin breathed aloud, hardly able to believe.

"Silence!" Briza's hands cried out at him. She glanced around to survey her surroundings, then signaled to the patrol to follow her to the shadows of the wall in the immense, and exposed, cavern.

Briza nodded her confirmation to Dinin then, confident that their mission would at last be completed.

"Can you be sure it is Drizzt?" Dinin's fingers asked. In his excitement, he could barely keep the movements precise enough to convey his thoughts. "Perhaps some scavenger—"

"We know that our brother lives," Briza motioned quickly. "Matron Malice would no longer be out of Lolth's favor if it were otherwise. And if Drizzt lives, then we can assume that he possesses the item!"

⚔ ⚔ ⚔ ⚔ ⚔

The sudden evasive movement of the patrol caught Drizzt by surprise. The group could not possibly have seen him under the cover of the jutting rocks, and he held faith in the silence of his footfalls, and of Guenhwyvar's. Yet Drizzt felt certain that it was he the patrol was hiding from. Something felt out of place in this whole encounter. Dark elves were rare this far from Menzoberranzan. Perhaps it was no more than the paranoia necessary to survive in the wilds of the Underdark, Drizzt told himself. Still, he suspected that more than chance had brought this group to his domain.

"Go, Guenhwyvar," he whispered to the cat. "View our guests and return to me." The panther sped away through the shadows circumventing the large cavern. Drizzt sank low into the rubble, listened, and waited.

Guenhwyvar returned to him only a minute later, though it seemed an eternity to Drizzt.

"Did you know them?" Drizzt asked. The cat scratched a paw across the stone.

"Of our old patrol?" Drizzt wondered aloud. "The fighters you and I walked beside?"

Guenhwyvar seemed uncertain and made no definite movements.

"A Hun'ett then," Drizzt said, thinking he had solved the riddle. House Hun'ett had at last come looking for him to repay him for the deaths of Alton and Masoj, the two Hun'ett wizards who had died trying to kill Drizzt. Or perhaps the Hun'etts had come in search of Guenhwyvar, the magical item that Masoj once had possessed.

When Drizzt took a moment from his pondering to study Guenhwyvar's reaction, he realized that his assumptions were wrong. The panther had backed away from him a step and seemed agitated by his stream of suppositions.

"Then who?" Drizzt asked. Guenhwyvar reared up on its hind legs and straddled Drizzt's shoulders, one great paw patting Drizzt's neck-purse. Not understanding, Drizzt slipped the item off his neck and emptied its contents into a palm, revealing a few gold coins, a small gemstone, and the emblem of his house, a silvery token engraved with the initials of Daermon N'a'shezbaernon, House Do'Urden. Drizzt realized at once what Guenhwyvar was hinting at.

"My family," he whispered harshly. Guenhwyvar backed away from him and again scratched a paw excitedly across the stone.

A thousand memories flooded through Drizzt at that moment, but all of them, good and bad, led him inescapably to one possibility: Matron Malice had neither forgiven nor forgotten his actions on that fated day. Drizzt had abandoned her and the ways of the Spider Queen, and he knew well enough the ways of Lolth to realize that his actions had not left his mother in good standing.

Drizzt looked back into the gloom of the wide cavern. "Come," he panted to Guenhwyvar, and he ran off down the tunnels. His decision to leave Menzoberranzan had been painful and uncertain, and now Drizzt had no desire to encounter his kin and rekindle all of the doubts and fears.

He and Guenhwyvar ran on for more than an hour, turning down secret passageways and crossing into the most confusing sections of the area's tunnels. Drizzt knew the region intimately and felt certain that he could leave the patrol group far behind with little effort.

But when at last he paused to catch his breath, Drizzt sensed—and he only had to look at Guenhwyvar to confirm his suspicions—that the patrol was still on his trail, perhaps even closer than before.

Drizzt knew then that he was being magically tracked; there could be no other explanation. "But how?" he asked the panther. "I am hardly the drow they knew as a brother, in appearance or in thought. What could they be sensing that would be familiar enough for their magical spells to hold on to?" Drizzt surveyed himself quickly, his eyes first falling upon his crafted weapons.

The scimitars were indeed wondrous, but so were the majority of the drow weapons in Menzoberranzan. And these particular blades had not even been crafted in House Do'Urden and were not of any design favored by Drizzt's family. His cloak then, he wondered? The *piwafwi* was a signpost of a house, bearing the stitch patterns and designs of a single family.

But Drizzt's *piwafwi* had been tattered and torn beyond recognition and he could hardly believe that a location spell would recognize it as belonging to House Do'Urden.

"Belonging to House Do'Urden," Drizzt whispered aloud. He looked at Guenhwyvar and nodded suddenly—he had his answer. He again removed his neck pouch and took out the token, the emblem of Daermon N'a'shezbaernon. Created by magic, it possessed its own magic, a dweomer distinct to that one house. Only a noble of House Do'Urden would carry one.

Drizzt thought for a moment, then replaced the token and slipped the neck-purse over Guenhwyvar's head. "Time for the hunted to become the hunter," he purred to the great cat.

⚔ ⚔ ⚔ ⚔ ⚔

"He knows he is being followed," Dinin's hands flashed to Briza. Briza didn't justify the statement with a reply. Of course Drizzt knew of the pursuit; it was obvious that he was trying to evade them. Briza remained unconcerned. Drizzt's house emblem burned as a distinct directional beacon in her magically enhanced thoughts.

Briza stopped, though, when the party came to a fork in the passage. The signal came from beyond the fork, but not in any definitive way to either side. "Left," Briza signaled to three of the commoner soldiers, then, "Right," to the remaining two. She held her brother back, signaling that she and Dinin would hold their position at the fork to serve as a reserve for both groups.

High above the scattering patrol, hovering in the shadows of the stalactite-covered ceiling, Drizzt smiled at his cunning. The patrol might have kept pace with him, but it would have no chance at all of catching Guenhwyvar.

The plan had been executed and completed to perfection, for Drizzt had only meant to lead the patrol on until it was far from his domain and weary of the hopeless search. But as Drizzt floated there, looking down upon his brother and eldest sister, he found himself longing for something more. A few moments passed, and Drizzt was certain that the dispatched soldiers were a good distance away. He drew out his scimitars, thinking then that a meeting with his siblings might not be so bad after all.

"He moves farther away," Briza spoke to Dinin, not fearing the sound of her own voice, since she felt certain of her renegade brother's distant position. "At great speed."

"Drizzt was always adept in the Underdark," Dinin replied, nodding. "He will prove a difficult catch."

Briza snickered. "He will tire long before my spells expire. We will find him breathless in a dark hole." But Briza's cockiness turned to blank amazement a second later when a dark form dropped right between her and Dinin.

Dinin, too, hardly even registered the shock of it all. He saw Drizzt for just a split second, then his eyes crisscrossed, following the descending arc of a scimitar's rushing hilt. Dinin went down heavily, with the smooth stone of the floor pressing against his cheek, a sensation to which Dinin was oblivious.

Even as one hand did its work on Dinin, Drizzt's other hand shot a scimitar tip close to Briza's throat, meaning to force her surrender. Briza was not as surprised as Dinin, though, and she always kept a hand close to her whip. She danced back from Drizzt's attack, and six snake heads shot up into the air, coiled and searching for an opening.

Drizzt turned full to face her, weaving his scimitars into defensive patterns to keep the stinging vipers at bay. He remembered the bite of those dreaded whips; like every drow male, he had been taught it many times during his childhood.

"Brother Drizzt," Briza said loudly, hoping the patrol would hear her and understand the call back to her side. "Lower your weapons. It does not have to be like this."

The sound of familiar words, of drow words, overwhelmed Drizzt. How good it was to hear them again, to remember that he was more than a single-minded hunter, that his life was more than mere survival.

"Lower your weapons," Briza said again, more pointedly.

"Wh—why are you here?" Drizzt stammered at her.

"For you, of course, my brother," Briza replied, too kindly. "The war with House Hun'ett is, at long last, ended. It is time for you to come home."

A part of Drizzt wanted to believe her, wanted to forget those facts of drow life that had forced him out of the city of his birth. A part of Drizzt wanted to drop the scimitars to the stone and return to the shelter—and the companionship—of his former life. Briza's smile was so inviting.

Briza recognized his weakening resolve. "Come home, dear Drizzt," she purred, her words holding the bindings of a minor magical spell. "You are needed. You are the weapon master of House Do'Urden now."

The sudden change in Drizzt's expression told Briza that she had erred. Zaknafein, Drizzt's mentor and dearest friend, had been the weapon master of House Do'Urden, and Zaknafein had been sacrificed to the Spider

Queen. Drizzt would never forget that fact.

Indeed, Drizzt remembered much more than the comforts of home at that moment. He remembered even more clearly the wrongs of his past life, the wickedness that his principles simply could not tolerate.

"You should not have come," Drizzt said, his voice sounding like a growl. "You must never come this way again!"

"Dear brother," Briza replied, more to buy time than to correct her obvious error. She stood still, her face frozen in that double-edged smile of hers.

Drizzt looked behind Briza's lips, which were thick and full by drow standards. The priestess spoke no words, but Drizzt could clearly see that her mouth was moving behind that frozen smile.

A spell!

Briza had always been skilled at such deceptions. "Go home!" Drizzt cried at her, and he launched an attack.

Briza ducked away from the blow easily enough, for it was not meant to strike, only to disrupt her spellcasting.

"Damn you, Drizzt the rogue," she spat, all pretense of friendship gone. "Lower your weapons at once, on pain of death!" Her snake-whip came up in open threat.

Drizzt set his feet wide apart. Fires burned in his lavender eyes as the hunter within him rose to meet the challenge.

Briza hesitated, taken aback by the sudden ferocity brewing in her brother. This was no ordinary drow warrior standing before her, she knew beyond doubt. Drizzt had become something more than that, something more formidable.

But Briza was a high priestess of Lolth, near the top of the drow hierarchy. She would not be frightened away by a mere male.

"Surrender!" she demanded. Drizzt couldn't even decipher her words, for the hunter standing against Briza was no longer Drizzt Do'Urden. The savage, primal warrior that memories of dead Zaknafein had invoked was impervious to words and lies.

Briza's arm pumped, and the whip's six viper heads whirled in, twisting and weaving of their own volition to gain the best angles of attack.

The hunter's scimitars responded in an indistinguishable blur. Briza couldn't begin to follow their lightning-quick motions, and when her attack routine was ended, she knew only that none of the snakeheads had found a mark, but that only five of the heads remained attached to the whip.

Now in rage that nearly matched her opponent's, Briza charged in, flailing away with her damaged weapon. Snakes and scimitars and slender drow limbs intertwined in a deadly ballet.

A head bit into the hunter's leg, sending a burst of cold pain coursing through his veins. A scimitar defeated another deceptive attack, splitting a head down the middle, right between the fangs.

Another head bit into the hunter. Another head fell free to the stone.

The opponents separated, taking measure of each other. Briza's breath came hard after the few furious minutes, but the hunter's chest moved easily and rhythmically. Briza had not been struck, but Drizzt had taken two hits.

The hunter had learned long ago to ignore pain, though. He stood ready to continue, and Briza, her whip now sporting only three heads, stubbornly came in on him. She hesitated for a split-second when she noticed Dinin still prone on the floor but with his senses apparently returning. Might her brother rise to her aid?

Dinin squirmed and tried to stand but found no strength in his legs to lift him.

"Damn you," Briza growled, her venom aimed at Dinin, or at Drizzt—it didn't matter. Calling on the power of her Spider Queen deity, the high priestess of Lolth lashed out with all of her strength.

Three snake heads dropped to the floor after a single cross of the hunter's blades.

"Damn you!" Briza screamed again, this time pointedly at Drizzt. She grasped the mace from her belt and swung a vicious overhand chop at her defiant brother's head.

Crossed scimitars caught the clumsy blow long before it found its mark, and the hunter's foot came up and kicked once, twice, and then a third time into Briza's face before it went back to the floor.

Briza staggered backward, blood in her eyes and running freely from her nose. She made out the lines of her brother's form beyond the blurring heat of her own blood, and she launched a desperate, wide-arcing hook.

The hunter set one scimitar to parry the mace, turning its blade so that Briza's hand ran down its cruel edge even as the mace swept wide of its mark. Briza screamed in agony and dropped her weapon.

The mace fell to the floor beside two of her fingers.

Dinin was up then, behind Drizzt, with his sword in his hand. Using all of her discipline, Briza kept her eyes locked on Drizzt, holding his attention. If she could distract him long enough . . .

The hunter sensed the danger and spun on Dinin.

All that Dinin saw in his brother's lavender eyes was his own death. He threw his sword to the ground and crossed his arms over his chest in surrender.

The hunter issued a growling command, hardly intelligible, but Dinin fathomed its meaning well enough, and he ran away as fast as his legs could carry him.

Briza started to slip around, meaning to follow Dinin, but a scimitar blade cut her off, locking under her chin and forcing her head so far back that all she could see was the dark stone of the ceiling.

Pain burned in the hunter's limbs, pain inflicted by this one and her evil whip. Now the hunter meant to end the pain and the threat. This was his domain!

Briza uttered a final prayer to Lolth as she felt the razor-sharp edge begin its cut. But then, in the instant of a black blur, she was free. She looked down to see Drizzt pinned to the floor by a huge black panther. Not taking the time to ask questions, Briza sped off down the tunnel after Dinin.

The hunter squirmed away from Guenhwyvar and leaped to his feet. "Guenhwyvar!" he cried, pushing the panther away. "Get her! Kill . . . !"

Guenhwyvar replied by falling into a sitting position and issuing a wide and drawn out yawn. With one lazy movement, the panther brought a paw under the string of the neck-purse and snapped it off to the ground.

The hunter burned with rage. "What are you doing?" he screamed, snatching up the purse. Had Guenhwyvar sided against him? Drizzt backed away a step, hesitantly bringing his scimitars up between him and the panther. Guenhwyvar made no move, but just sat there staring at Drizzt.

A moment later, the click of a crossbow told Drizzt of the absolute absurdity of his line of thinking. The dart would have found him, no doubt, but Guenhwyvar sprang up suddenly and intercepted its flight. Drow poison had no effect on the likes of a magical cat.

Three drow fighters appeared on one side of the fork, two more on the other. All thoughts of revenge on Briza flew from Drizzt then, and he followed Guenhwyvar in full flight down the twisting passageways. Without the guidance of the high priestess and her magic, the commoner fighters did not even attempt to follow.

A long while later, Drizzt and Guenhwyvar turned into a side passage and paused in their flight, listening for any sounds of pursuit.

"Come," Drizzt instructed, and he started slowly away, certain that the threat of Dinin and Briza had been successfully repelled.

Again Guenhwyvar dropped to a sitting position.

Drizzt looked curiously at the panther. "I told you to come," he growled. Guenhwyvar fixed a stare upon him, a look that filled the renegade drow with guilt. Then the cat rose and walked slowly toward its master.

Drizzt nodded his accord, thinking that Guenhwyvar meant to obey him. He turned and started again to walk off, but the panther circled around him, stopping his progress. Guenhwyvar continued the circular pacing and slowly the telltale mist began to appear.

"What are you doing?" Drizzt demanded.

Guenhwyvar did not slow.

"I did not dismiss you!" Drizzt shouted as the panther's corporeal form melted away. Drizzt spun about frantically, trying to catch hold of something.

"I did not dismiss you!" he cried again, helplessly.

Guenhwyvar had gone.

It was a long walk back to Drizzt's sheltered cave. That last image of Guenhwyvar followed his every step, the cat's saucer eyes boring into his back. Guenhwyvar had judged him, he realized beyond any doubt. In his blind rage, Drizzt had almost killed his sister; he surely would have slain Briza if Guenhwyvar had not pounced upon him.

At last, Drizzt crawled into the little stone cubby that served as his bedroom.

His contemplations crawled in with him. A decade before, Drizzt had killed Masoj Hun'ett, and on that occasion had vowed never to kill a drow again. To Drizzt, his word was the core of his principles, those very same principles that had forced him to give up so very much.

Drizzt surely would have forsaken his word this day had it not been for Guenhwyvar's actions. How much better, then, was he from those dark elves he had left behind?

Drizzt clearly had won the encounter against his siblings and was confident that he could continue to hide from Briza—and from all the other enemies that Matron Malice sent against him. But alone in that tiny cave, Drizzt realized something that distressed him greatly.

He couldn't hide from himself.

# 4

# Flight from the Hunter

Drizzt gave no thought at all to his actions as he went about his daily routines over the next few days. He would survive, he knew. The hunter would have it no other way. But the rising price of that survival struck a deep and discordant note in the heart of Drizzt Do'Urden.

If the constant rituals of the day warded away the pain, Drizzt found himself unprotected at day's end. The encounter with his siblings haunted him, stayed in his thoughts as vividly as if it were recurring every night. Inevitably, Drizzt awoke terrified and alone, engulfed by the monsters of his dreams. He understood—and the knowledge heightened his helplessness—that no swordplay, however dazzling, could hope to defeat them.

Drizzt did not fear that his mother would continue her quest to capture and punish him, though he knew beyond any doubt that she certainly would. This was his world, far different from Menzoberranzan's winding avenues, with ways that the drow living in the city could not begin to understand. Out in the wilds, Drizzt held confidence that he could survive against whatever nemeses Matron Malice sent after him.

Drizzt also had managed to release himself from the overwhelming guilt of his actions against Briza. He rationalized that it was his siblings who had forced the dangerous encounter, and it was Briza, in trying to cast a spell, who had initiated the combat. Still, Drizzt realized that he would spend many days finding answers to the questions his actions had raised concerning the nature of his character.

Had he become this savage and merciless hunter because of the harsh conditions imposed on him? Or was this hunter an expression of the being Drizzt had been all along? They were not questions that Drizzt would easily answer, but at this time, they were not foremost among his thoughts.

The thing that Drizzt could not dismiss about the encounter with his siblings was the sound of their voices, the melody of spoken words that he could understand and respond to. In all of his recollections of those few moments with Briza and Dinin, the words, not the blows, stood out most clearly. Drizzt clung to them desperately, listening to them over and over again in his mind and dreading the day when they would fade away. Then, though he might remember them, he would no longer hear them.

He would be alone again.

Drizzt pulled the onyx figurine out of his pocket for the first time since Guenhwyvar had drifted away from him. He placed it on the stone before him and looked at his wall scratches to determine just how long it had been since he had last summoned the panther. Immediately, Drizzt realized the futility of that approach. When was the last time he had scratched that wall? And what use were the markings anyway? How could Drizzt be certain of his count even if he dutifully notched the mark after every one of his sleep periods?

"Time is something of that other world," Drizzt mumbled, his tone clearly a lament. He lifted his dagger toward the stone, an act of denial against his own proclamation.

"What does it matter?" Drizzt asked rhetorically, and he dropped the dagger to the ground. The ring as it struck the stone sent a shiver along Drizzt's spine, as though it was a bell signaling his surrender.

His breathing came hard. Sweat beaded on his ebony brow, and his hands felt suddenly cold. All around him, the walls of his cave, the close stone that had sheltered him for years against the ever-encroaching dangers of the Underdark, now pressed in on him. He imagined leering faces in the lines of cracks and the shapes of rocks. The faces mocked him and laughed at him, belittling his stubborn pride.

He turned to flee but stumbled on a stone and fell to the ground. He scraped a knee in the process and tore yet another hole in his tattered *piwafwi*. Drizzt hardly cared for his knee or his cloak when he looked back to the stumbling stone, for another fact assailed him, leaving him in utter confusion.

The hunter had tripped. For the first time in more than a decade, the hunter had tripped.

"Guenhwyvar!" Drizzt cried frantically. "Come to me! Oh, please, my Guenhwyvar!"

He didn't know if the panther would respond. After their last less-than-friendly parting, Drizzt couldn't be certain that Guenhwyvar would ever walk by his side again. Drizzt clawed his way toward the figurine, every inch seeming a tedious fight in the weakness of his despair.

Presently the swirling mist appeared. The panther would not desert its master, would not hold lasting judgment against the drow who had been its friend.

Drizzt relaxed as the mist took form, using the sight of it to block the evil hallucinations in the stones. Soon Guenhwyvar was sitting beside him and casually licking at one great paw. Drizzt locked the panther's saucer eyes in a stare and saw no judgment there. It was just Guenhwyvar, his friend and his salvation.

Drizzt curled his legs under him, sprang out to the cat, and wrapped the muscled neck in a tight and desperate embrace. Guenhwyvar accepted the hold without response, wiggling loose only enough to continue the paw-licking. If the cat, in its otherworldly intelligence, understood the importance of that hug, it offered no outward signs.

⚔ ⚔ ⚔ ⚔ ⚔

Restlessness marked Drizzt's next days. He kept on the move, running the circuits of the tunnels around his sanctuary. Matron Malice was after him, he continually reminded himself. He could not afford any holes in his defenses.

Deep inside himself, beyond the rationalizations, Drizzt knew the truth of his movements. He could offer himself the excuse of patrolling, but he had, in fact, taken flight. He ran from the voices and the walls of his small cave. He ran from Drizzt Do'Urden and back toward the hunter.

Gradually, his routes took a wider course, often keeping him from his cave for many days at a stretch. Secretly, Drizzt hoped for an encounter with a powerful foe. He needed a tangible reminder of the necessity of his primal existence, a battle against some horrid monster that would place him in a mode of purely instinctive survival.

What Drizzt found instead one day was the vibration of a distant tapping on the wall, the rhythmical, measured tap of a miner's pick.

Drizzt leaned back against the wall and carefully considered his next move. He knew where the sound would lead him; he was in the same tunnels that he had wandered when he went in search of his lost rothé, the same tunnels where he had encountered the svirfneblin mining party a few tendays before. At that time, Drizzt could not admit it to himself, but it was no simple coincidence that he had happened into this region again. His subconscious had brought him to hear the tapping of the svirfneblin hammers, and more particularly, to hear the laughter and chatter of the deep gnomes' voices.

Now Drizzt, leaning heavily against a wall, truly was torn. He knew that going to spy on the svirfneblin miners would only bring him more torment, that in hearing their voices he would become even more vulnerable to the pangs of loneliness. The deep gnomes surely would go back to their city, and Drizzt again would be left empty and alone.

But Drizzt had come to hear the tapping, and now it vibrated in the stone, beckoning him with a pull too great to ignore. His better judgment fought the urges that pulled him toward that sound, but his decision had been made even as he had taken the first steps into this region. He berated himself for his foolishness, shook his head in denial. In spite of his conscious reasoning, his legs were moving, carrying him toward the rhythmic sound of the tapping pickaxes.

The alert instincts of the hunter argued against remaining near the miners even as Drizzt looked down from a high ledge upon the group of svirfnebli. But Drizzt did not leave. For several days, as far as he could measure, he stayed in the vicinity of the deep gnome miners, catching bits of their conversations wherever he could, watching them at work and at play.

When the inevitable day came that the miners began to pack up their wagons, Drizzt understood the depth of his folly. He had been weak in coming to the deep gnomes; he had denied the brutal truth of his existence. Now he would have to go back to his dark and empty hole, all the more lonely for the memories of the last few days.

The wagons rolled out of sight down the tunnels toward the svirfneblin city. Drizzt took the first steps back toward his sanctuary, the moss-covered cave with the fast-running stream and the myconid-tended mushroom grove.

In all the centuries of life he had left to live, Drizzt Do'Urden would never look upon that place again.

He did not later remember when his direction had turned; it had not been a conscious decision. Something pulled at him—the lingering rumble of the ore-filled wagons perhaps—and only when Drizzt heard the slam of Blingdenstone's great outer doors did he realize what he meant to do.

"Guenhwyvar," Drizzt whispered to the figurine, and he flinched at the disturbing volume of his own voice. The svirfneblin guards on the wide staircase were engaged in a conversation of their own, though, and Drizzt was quite safe.

The gray mist swirled around the statuette and the panther came to its master's call. Guenhwyvar's ears flattened and the panther sniffed around cautiously, trying to resolve the unfamiliar setting.

Drizzt took a deep breath and forced the words from his mouth. "I wanted to say good-bye to you, my friend," he whispered. Guenhwyvar's ears came up straight, and the pupils of the cat's shining yellow eyes widened then narrowed again as Guenhwyvar took a quick study of Drizzt.

"In case . . ." Drizzt continued. "I cannot live out there anymore, Guenhwyvar. I fear I am losing everything that gives meaning to life. I fear I am losing my self." He glanced back over his shoulder at the ascending stairway to Blingdenstone. "And that is more precious to me than my life. Can you understand, Guenhwyvar? I need more, more than simple survival. I need a life defined by more than the savage instincts of this creature I have become."

Drizzt slumped back against the passageway's stone wall. His words sounded so logical and simple, yet he knew that every step up that stair to the deep gnome city would be a trial of his courage and his convictions. He remembered the day he'd stood on the ledge outside Blingdenstone's great doors. As much as he wanted to, Drizzt could not bring himself to follow the deep gnomes in. He was fully caught in a very real paralysis that had gripped him and held him firmly when he thought of rushing through the portals into the deep gnome city.

"You have rarely judged me, my friend," Drizzt said to the panther. "And in those times, always you have judged me fairly. Can you understand, Guenhwyvar? In the next few moments, we may become lost from each other forever. Can you understand why I must do this?"

Guenhwyvar padded over to Drizzt's side and nuzzled its great feline head into the drow's ribs.

"My friend," Drizzt whispered into the cat's ear. "Go back now before I lose my courage. Go back to your home and hope that we shall meet again."

Guenhwyvar turned away obediently and paced to the figurine. The transition seemed too fast to Drizzt this time, then only the figurine remained. Drizzt scooped it up and considered it. He considered again the risk before him. Then, driven by the same subconscious needs that had brought him this far, Drizzt rushed to the stair and started up. Above him, the deep gnome conversation had ceased; apparently the guards sensed that someone or something was approaching.

But the svirfnebli guards' surprise was no less when a drow elf walked over the top of the staircase and onto the landing before the doors of their city.

Drizzt crossed his arms over his chest, a defenseless gesture that the drow elves took as a signal of truce. Drizzt could only hope that the svirfnebli were familiar with the motion, for his mere appearance had absolutely unnerved the guards. They fell over each other, scrambling around the small landing, some rushing to protect the doors to the city, others surrounding Drizzt within a ring of weapon tips, and still others rushing frantically to the stairs and down a few, trying to see if this dark elf was just the first of an entire drow war party.

One svirfneblin, the leader of the guard contingent and apparently looking for some explanation, barked out a series of pointed demands at Drizzt. Drizzt shrugged helplessly, and the half-dozen deep gnomes around him jumped back a cautious step at his innocuous movement.

The svirfneblin spoke again, more loudly, and jabbed the very sharp point of his iron spear in Drizzt's direction. Drizzt could not begin to understand or respond to the foreign tongue. Very slowly and in obvious view, he slid one hand down over his stomach to the clasp of his belt buckle. The deep gnome leader's hands wrung tightly over the shaft of his weapon as he watched the dark elf's every movement.

A flick of Drizzt's wrist released the clasp and his scimitars clanged loudly on the stone floor.

The svirfnebli jumped in unison, then recovered quickly and came in on him. On a single word from the leader of the group, two of the guards dropped their weapons and began a complete, and not overly gentle, search of the intruder. Drizzt flinched when they found the dagger he had kept in his boot. He thought himself stupid for forgetting the weapon and not revealing it openly from the beginning.

A moment later, when one of the svirfnebli reached into the deepest pocket of Drizzt's *piwafwi* and pulled out the onyx figurine, Drizzt flinched even more.

Instinctively, Drizzt reached for the panther, a pleading expression on his face.

He received the butt end of a spear in the back for his efforts. Deep gnomes were not an evil race, but they held no love for dark elves. The svirfnebli had survived for centuries untold in the Underdark with few allies but many enemies, and they ever ranked the drow elves as foremost among the latter. Since the founding of the ancient city of Blingdenstone, the majority of all of the many svirfnebli who had been killed in the wilds had fallen at the ends of drow weapons.

Now, inexplicably, one of these same dark elves had walked right up to their city doors and willingly surrendered his weapons.

The deep gnomes bound Drizzt's hands tightly behind his back, and four of the guards kept their weapon tips resting on him, ready to drive them home at Drizzt's slightest threatening movement. The remaining guards returned from their search of the stairway, reporting no other drow elves anywhere in the vicinity. The leader remained suspicious, though, and he posted guards at various strategic positions, then motioned to the two deep gnomes waiting at the city's doors.

The massive portals parted, and Drizzt was led in. He could only hope in that moment of fear and excitement that he had left the hunter out in the wilds of the Underdark.

# Unholy Ally

In no hurry to stand before his outraged mother, Dinin wandered slowly toward the anteroom to House Do'Urden's chapel. Matron Malice had called for him, and he could not refuse the summons. He found Vierna and Maya in the corridor beyond the ornate doors, similarly tentative.

"What is it about?" Dinin asked his sisters in the silent hand code.

"Matron Malice has been with Briza and Shi'nayne all the day," Vierna's hands replied.

"Planning another expedition in search of Drizzt," Dinin motioned half heartedly, not liking the idea that he would no doubt be included in such plans.

The two females did not miss their brother's disdainful scowl. "Was it really so terrible?" Maya asked. "Briza would say little about it."

"Her severed fingers and torn whip revealed much," Vierna put in, a wry smile crossing her face as she motioned. Vierna, like every other sibling of House Do'Urden, had little love for her eldest sister.

No agreeing smile spread on Dinin's face as he remembered his encounter with Drizzt. "You witnessed our brother's prowess when he lived among us," Dinin's hands replied. "His skills have improved tenfold in his years outside the city."

"But what was he like?" Vierna asked, obviously intrigued by Drizzt's ability to survive. Ever since the patrol had returned with the report that Drizzt was still alive, Vierna had secretly hoped that she would see her younger brother again. They had shared a father, so it was said, and Vierna held more sympathy for Drizzt than was wise, given Malice's feelings for him.

Noticing her excited expression, and remembering his own humiliation at Drizzt's hands, Dinin cast a disapproving scowl at her. "Fear not, dear sister," Dinin's hands said quickly. "If Malice sends you out into the wilds this time, as I suspect she will, you will see all of Drizzt you wish to see, and more!" Dinin clapped his hands together for emphasis as he ended, and he strode right between the two females and through the anteroom's door.

"Your brother has forgotten how to knock," Matron Malice said to Briza and Shi'nayne, who stood at her sides.

Rizzen, kneeling before the throne, looked up over his shoulder to see Dinin.

"I did not give you permission to lift your eyes!" Malice screamed at the patron. She pounded her fist on the arm of her great throne, and Rizzen fell down to his belly in fear. Malice's next words carried the strength of a spell.

"Grovel!" she commanded, and Rizzen crawled to her feet. Malice extended her hand to the male, all the while looking straight at Dinin. The elderboy did not miss his mother's point.

"Kiss," she said to Rizzen, and he quickly began lavishing kisses onto her extended hand. "Stand," Malice issued her third command.

Rizzen got about halfway to his feet before the matron punched him squarely in the face, dropping him in a heap to the stone floor.

"If you move, I shall kill you," Malice promised, and Rizzen lay perfectly still, not doubting her in the least.

Dinin knew that the continued show had been more for his benefit than for Rizzen's. Still, unblinking, Malice eyed him.

"You have failed me," she said at length. Dinin accepted the berating without argument, without even daring to breathe until Malice turned sharply on Briza.

"And you!" Malice shouted. "Six trained drow warriors beside you, and you, a high priestess, could not bring Drizzt back to me."

Briza clenched and unclenched the weakened fingers that Malice had magically restored to her hand.

"Seven against one," Malice ranted, "and you come running back here with tales of doom!"

"I will get him, Matron Mother," Maya promised as she took her place beside Shi'nayne. Malice looked to Vierna, but the second daughter was more reluctant to make such grand claims.

"You speak boldly," Dinin said to Maya. Immediately, Malice's disbelieving grimace fell upon him in a harsh reminder that it was not his place to speak.

But Briza promptly completed Dinin's thought. "Too boldly," she growled. Malice's gaze descended upon her on cue, but Briza was a high priestess in the favor of the Spider Queen and was well within her rights to speak. "You know nothing of our young brother," Briza went on, speaking as much to Malice as to Maya.

"He is only a male," Maya retorted. "I would—"

"You would be cut down!" Briza yelled. "Hold your foolish words and empty promises, youngest sister. Out in the tunnels beyond Menzoberranzan, Drizzt would kill you with little effort."

Malice listened intently to it all. She had heard Briza's account of the meeting with Drizzt several times, and she knew enough about her oldest daughter's courage and powers to understand that Briza did not speak falsely.

Maya backed down from the confrontation, not wanting any part of a feud with Briza.

"Could you defeat him?" Malice asked Briza, "now that you better understand what he has become?"

In response, Briza flexed her wounded hand again. It would be several tendays before she regained full use of the replaced fingers.

"Or you?" Malice asked Dinin, understanding Briza's pointed gesture as a conclusive answer.

Dinin fidgeted about, not knowing how to respond to his volatile mother.

The truth might put him at odds with Malice, but a lie surely would land him back in the tunnels against his brother.

"Speak truly with me!" Malice roared. "Do you wish another hunt for Drizzt, so that you may regain my favor?"

"I . . ." Dinin stuttered, then he lowered his eyes defensively. Malice had put a detection spell on his reply, Dinin realized. She would know if he tried to lie to her. "No," he said flatly. "Even at the cost of your favor, Matron Mother, I do not wish to go out after Drizzt again."

Maya and Vierna—even Shi'nayne—started in surprise at the honest response, thinking nothing could be worse than a matron mother's wrath. Briza, though, nodded in agreement, for she, too, had seen as much of Drizzt as she cared to see. Malice did not miss the significance of her daughter's motion.

"Your pardon, Matron Mother," Dinin went on, trying desperately to heal any ill feelings he had stirred. "I have seen Drizzt in combat. He took me down too easily—as I believed that no foe ever could. He defeated Briza fairly, and I have never seen her beaten! I do not wish to hunt my brother again, for I fear that the result would only bring more anger to you and more trouble to House Do'Urden."

"You are afraid?" Malice asked slyly.

Dinin nodded. "And I know that I would only disappoint you again, Matron Mother. In the tunnels that he names as home, Drizzt is beyond my skills. I cannot hope to outdo him."

"I can accept such cowardice in a male," Malice said coldly. Dinin, with no recourse, accepted the insult stoically.

"But you are a high priestess of Lolth!" Malice taunted Briza. "Certainly a rogue male is not beyond the powers that the Spider Queen has given to you!"

"Hear Dinin's words, my matron," Briza replied.

"Lolth is with you!" Shi'nayne shouted at her.

"But Drizzt is beyond the Spider Queen," Briza snapped back. "I fear that Dinin speaks the truth—for all of us. We cannot catch Drizzt out there. The wilds of the Underdark are his domain, where we are only strangers."

"Then what are we to do?" Maya grumbled.

Malice rested back in her throne and put her sharp chin in her palm. She had coaxed Dinin under the weight of a threat, and yet he still declared that he would not willingly venture after Drizzt. Briza, ambitious and powerful, and in the favor of Lolth even if House Do'Urden and Matron Malice were not, came back without her prized whip and the fingers of one hand.

"Jarlaxle and his band of rogues?" Vierna offered, seeing her mother's dilemma. "Bregan D'aerthe has been of value to us for many years."

"The mercenary leader will not agree," Malice replied, for she had tried to hire the soldier of fortune for the endeavor years before. "Every member of Bregan D'aerthe abides by the decisions of Jarlaxle, and all the wealth we possess will not tempt him. I suspect that Jarlaxle is under the strict orders of Matron Baenre. Drizzt is our problem, and we are charged by the Spider Queen with correcting that problem."

"If you command me to go, I shall," Dinin spoke out. "I fear only that I will disappoint you, Matron Mother. I do not fear Drizzt's blades, or death itself if it is in service to you." Dinin had read his mother's dark mood well enough to know that she had no intention of sending him back out after Drizzt, and he thought himself wise in being so generous when it didn't cost him anything.

"I thank you, my son," Malice beamed at him. Dinin had to hold his snicker when he noticed all three of his sisters glaring at him. "Now leave us," Malice continued condescendingly, stealing Dinin's moment. "We have business that does not concern a male."

Dinin bowed low and swept toward the door. His sisters took note of how easily Malice had stolen the proud spring from his step.

"I will remember your words," Malice said wryly, enjoying the power play and the silent applause. Dinin paused, his hand on the handle of the ornate door. "One day you will prove your loyalty to me, do not doubt."

All five of the high priestesses laughed at Dinin's back as he rushed out of the room.

On the floor, Rizzen found himself in quite a dangerous dilemma. Malice had sent Dinin away, saying in essence that males had no right to remain in the room. Yet Malice had not given Rizzen permission to move. He planted his feet and fingers against the stone, ready to spring away in an instant.

"Are you still here?" Malice shrieked at him. Rizzen bolted for the door.

"Hold!" Malice cried at him, her words once again empowered by a magical spell.

Rizzen stopped suddenly, against his better judgment and unable to resist the dweomer of Matron Malice's spell.

"I did not give you permission to move!" Malice screamed behind him.

"But—" Rizzen started to protest.

"Take him!" Malice commanded her two youngest daughters, and Vierna and Maya rushed over and roughly grabbed Rizzen.

"Put him in a dungeon cell," Malice instructed them. "Keep him alive. We will need him later."

Vierna and Maya hauled the trembling male out of the anteroom. Rizzen did not dare offer any resistance.

"You have a plan," Shi'nayne said to Malice. As SiNafay, the matron mother of House Hun'ett, the newest Do'Urden had learned to see purpose in every action. She knew the duties of a matron mother well and understood that Malice's outburst against Rizzen, who had in fact done nothing wrong, was more of calculated design than of true outrage.

"I agree with your assessment," Malice said to Briza. "Drizzt has gone beyond us."

"But by the words of Matron Baenre herself, we must not fail," Briza reminded her mother. "Your seat on the ruling council must be strengthened at all cost."

"We shall not fail," Shi'nayne said to Briza, eyeing Malice all the while. Another wry look came across Malice's face as Shi'nayne continued. "In ten years of battle against House Do'Urden," she said, "I have come to understand the methods of Matron Malice. Your mother will find a way to catch Drizzt." She paused, noting her mother's widening smile. "Or has she, perhaps, already found a way?"

"We shall see," Malice purred, her confidence growing in her former rival's decree of respect. "We shall see."

⚔ ⚔ ⚔ ⚔ ⚔

More than two hundred commoners of House Do'Urden milled about the great chapel, excitedly exchanging rumors of the coming events. Commoners were rarely allowed in this sacred place, only on the high holidays of Lolth or in communal prayer before a battle. Yet there were no expectations among them of any impending war, and this was no holy day on the drow calendar.

Dinin Do'Urden, also anxious and excited, moved about the crowd, settling dark elves into the rows of seats encircling the raised central dais. Being only a male, Dinin would not partake of the ceremony at the altar and Matron Malice had told him nothing of her plans. From the instructions she had given him, though, Dinin knew that the results of this day's events would prove critical to the future of his family. He was the chant leader; he would continually move throughout the assembly, leading the commoners in the appropriate verses to the Spider Queen.

Dinin had played this role often before, but this time Matron Malice had warned him that if a single voice called out incorrectly, Dinin's life would be forfeit. Still another fact disturbed the elderboy of House Do'Urden. He was normally accompanied in his chapel duties by the other male noble of the house, Malice's present mate. Rizzen had not been seen since that day when the whole family had gathered in the anteroom. Dinin suspected that Rizzen's reign as patron soon would come to a crashing end. It was no secret that Matron Malice had given previous mates to Lolth.

When all of the commoners were seated, magical red lights began to glow softly all about the room. The illumination increased gradually, allowing the gathered dark elves to comfortably shift their dual-purpose eyes from the infrared spectrum into the realm of light.

Misty vapors rolled out from under the seats, hugged the floor, and rose in curling wisps. Dinin led the crowd in a low hum, the calling of Matron Malice.

Malice appeared at the top of the room's domed ceiling, her arms outstretched and the folds of her spider-emblazoned black robes whipping about in an enchanted breeze. She descended slowly, turning complete circuits to survey the gathering—and to let them look upon the splendor that was their matron mother.

When Malice alighted on the central dais, Briza and Shi'nayne appeared on the ceiling, floating down in similar fashion. They landed and took their places, Briza at the cloth-covered case off to the side of the spider-shaped sacrificial table and Shi'nayne behind Matron Malice.

Malice clapped her hands and the humming stopped abruptly. Eight braziers lining the central dais roared to life, their flames' brightness less painful to the sensitive drow eyes in the red, mist-enshrouded glow.

"Enter, my daughters!" Malice cried, and all heads turned to the chapel's main doors. Vierna and Maya came in, with Rizzen, sluggish and apparently drugged, supported between them and a casket floating in the air behind them.

Dinin, among others, thought this an odd arrangement. He could assume, he supposed, that Rizzen was to be sacrificed, but he had never heard of a coffin being brought in to the ceremony.

The younger Do'Urden daughters moved up to the central dais and quickly strapped Rizzen down to the sacrificial table. Shi'nayne intercepted the floating casket and guided it to a position off to the side opposite Briza.

"Call to the handmaiden!" Malice cried, and Dinin immediately sent the gathering into the desired chant. The braziers roared higher; Malice and the other high priestesses prodded the crowd on with magically enhanced shouts of key words in the summoning. A sudden wind came up from nowhere, it seemed, and whipped the mist into a frenzied dance.

The flames of all eight braziers shot out in high lines over Malice and the others, joining in a furious burst above the center of the circular platform. The braziers puffed once in a unified explosion, throwing the last of their flames into the summoning, then burned low as the lines of fire rolled together in a gathered ball and became a singular pillar of flame.

The commoners gasped but continued their chanting as the pillar rolled through the colors of the spectrum, gradually cooling until the flames were no more. In their place stood a tentacled creature, taller than a drow elf and resembling a half-melted candle with elongated, drooping facial features. All the crowd recognized the being, though few commoners had ever actually seen one before, except perhaps in illustrations in the clerical books. All in attendance knew well enough the importance of this gathering at that moment, for no drow could possibly miss the significance of the presence of a yochlol, a personal handmaiden of Lolth.

"Greetings, Handmaiden," Malice said loudly. "Blessed is Daermon N'a'shezbaernon for your presence."

The yochlol surveyed the gathering for a long while, surprised that House Do'Urden had issued such a summons. Matron Malice was not in the favor of Lolth.

Only the high priestesses felt the telepathic question. *Why dare you call to me?*

"To right our wrongs!" Malice cried out aloud, drawing the whole of the gathering into the tense moment. "To regain the favor of your Mistress, the favor that is the only purpose of our existence!" Malice looked pointedly at Dinin, and he began the correct song, the highest song of praise to the Spider Queen.

*I am pleased by your display, Matron Malice,* came the yochlol's thoughts, this time directed solely at Malice. *But you know that this gathering does nothing to aid in your peril!*

*This is but the beginning,* Malice answered mentally, confident that the handmaiden could read her every thought. The matron took comfort in that knowledge, for she held faith that her desires to regain the favor of Lolth were sincere. *My youngest son has wronged the Spider Queen. He must pay for his deeds.*

The other high priestesses, excluded from the telepathic conversation, joined in the song to Lolth.

*Drizzt Do'Urden lives,* the yochlol reminded Malice. *And he is not in your custody.*

*That shall soon be corrected,* Malice promised.

*What do you desire of me?*

"Zin-carla!" Malice cried aloud.

The yochlol swayed backward, momentarily stunned by the boldness of the request. Malice held her ground, determined that her plan would not fail. Around her, the other priestesses held their breath, fully realizing that the moment of triumph or disaster was upon them all.

*It is our highest gift,* came the yochlol's thoughts, *given rarely even to matrons in the favor of the Spider Queen. And you, who have not pleased Lolth, dare to ask for Zin-carla?*

*It is right and fitting,* Malice replied. Then aloud, needing the support of her family, she cried, "Let my youngest son learn the folly of his ways and the power of the enemies he has made. Let my son witness the horrible glory of Lolth revealed, so that he will fall to his knees and beg forgiveness!" Malice reverted to telepathic communication. *Only then shall the spirit-wraith drive a sword into his heart!*

The yochlol's eyes went blank as the creature fell into itself, seeking guidance from its home plane of existence. Many minutes—agonizing minutes to Matron Malice and all of the hushed gathering—passed before the yochlol's thoughts came back.

*Have you the corpse?*

Malice signaled to Maya and Vierna, and they rushed over to the casket and removed the stone lid. Dinin understood then that the box was not brought for Rizzen, but was already occupied. An animated corpse crawled out of it and staggered over to Malice's side. It was badly decomposed and many of its features had rotted away altogether, but Dinin and most of the others in the great chapel recognized it immediately: Zaknafein Do'Urden, the legendary weapon master.

*Zin-carla,* the yochlol asked, *so that the weapon master you gave to the Spider Queen might correct the wrongs of your youngest son?*

*It is appropriate,* Malice replied. She sensed that the yochlol was pleased, as she had expected. Zaknafein, Drizzt's tutor, had helped to inspire the blasphemous attitudes that had ruined Drizzt. Lolth, the queen of chaos, enjoyed ironies, and to have this same Zaknafein serve as executioner would inevitably please her.

*Zin-carla requires great sacrifice,* came the yochlol's demand.

The creature looked over to the spider-shaped table, where Rizzen lay oblivious to his surroundings. The yochlol seemed to frown, if such creatures could frown, at the sight of such a pitiful sacrifice. The creature then turned back to Matron Malice and read her thoughts.

*Do continue,* the yochlol prompted, suddenly very interested.

Malice lifted her arms, beginning yet another song to Lolth. She motioned to Shi'nayne, who walked to the case beside Briza and took out the ceremonial dagger, the most precious possession of House Do'Urden. Briza flinched when she saw her newest "sister" handle the item, its hilt the body of a spider with eight blade-like legs reaching down under it. For centuries it had been Briza's place to drive the ceremonial dagger into the hearts of gifts to the Spider Queen.

Shi'nayne smirked at the eldest daughter as she walked away, sensing Briza's anger. She joined Malice at the table beside Rizzen and moved the dagger out over the doomed patron's heart.

Malice grabbed her hands to stop her. "This time I must do it," Malice explained, to Shi'nayne's dismay. Shi'nayne looked back over her shoulder to see Briza returning her smirk tenfold.

Malice waited until the song had ended, and the gathering remained absolutely silent as Malice alone began the proper chant. "*Takken bres duis bres,*" she began, both her hands wringing over the hilt of the deadly instrument.

A moment later, Malice's chant neared completion and the dagger went up high. All the house tensed, awaiting the moment of ecstacy, the savage giving to the foul Spider Queen.

The dagger came down, but Malice turned it abruptly to the side and drove it instead into the heart of Shi'nayne, Matron SiNafay Hun'ett, her most hated rival.

"No!" gasped SiNafay, but the deed was done. Eight blade-legs grasped at her heart. SiNafay tried to speak, to cast a spell of healing on herself or a curse upon Malice, but only blood came out of her mouth. Gasping her last breaths, she fell forward over Rizzen.

All the house erupted in screams of shock and joy as Malice tore the dagger out from under SiNafay Hun'ett, and her enemy's heart along with it.

"Devious!" Briza screamed above the tumult, for even she had not known Malice's plans. Once again, Briza was the eldest daughter of House Do'Urden, back in the position of honor that she so dearly craved.

*Devious!* the yochlol echoed in Malice's mind. *Know that we are pleased!*

Behind the gruesome scene, the animated corpse fell limply to the floor. Malice looked at the handmaiden and understood. "Put Zaknafein on the table! Quickly!" she instructed her younger daughters. They scrambled about, roughly displacing Rizzen and SiNafay and getting Zaknafein's body in place.

Briza, too, went into motion, carefully lining up the many jars of unguents that had been painstakingly prepared for this moment. Matron Malice's reputation as the finest salve maker in the city would be put to the test in this effort.

Malice looked at the yochlol. "Zin-carla?" she asked aloud.

*You have not regained the favor of Lolth!* came the telepathic reply, so powerfully that Malice was driven to her knees. Malice clutched at her head, thinking it would explode from the building pressure.

Gradually the pain eased away. But you have pleased the Spider Queen this day, Malice Do'Urden, the yochlol explained. *And it is agreed that your plans for your sacrilegious son are appropriate. Zin-carla is granted, but know it as your final chance, Matron Malice Do'Urden! Your greatest fears cannot begin to approach the truth of the consequences of failure!*

The yochlol disappeared in an explosive fireball that rocked the chapel of House Do'Urden. Those gathered only rose to a higher frenzy at the bared power of the evil deity, and Dinin led them again in a song of praise to Lolth.

"Ten tendays!" came the final cry of the handmaiden, a voice so mighty that the lesser drow covered their ears and cowered on the floor.

And so for ten tendays, for seventy cycles of Narbondel, the daily time clock of Menzoberranzan, all of House Do'Urden gathered in the great chapel, Dinin and Rizzen leading the commoners in songs to the Spider Queen, while Malice and her daughters worked over Zaknafein's corpse with magical salves and combinations of powerful spells.

The animation of a corpse was a simple spell for a priestess, but Zin-carla went far beyond that feat. Spirit-wraith, the undead result would be called, a zombie imbued with the skills of its former life and controlled by the matron mother appointed by Lolth. It was the most precious of Lolth's gifts, rarely asked for and even more rarely granted, for Zin-carla—returning the spirit to the body—was a risky practice indeed. Only through the sheer willpower of the enchanting priestess were the undead being's desired skills kept separate from the unwanted memories and emotions. The edge of consciousness and control was a fine line to walk, even considering the mental discipline required of a high priestess. Furthermore, Lolth only granted Zin-carla for the completion of specific tasks, and stumbling from that fine line of discipline inevitably would result in failure.

Lolth was not merciful in the face of failure.

# 6
# Blingdenstone

Blingdenstone was different from anything that Drizzt had ever seen. When the svirfneblin guards ushered him in through the immense stone and iron doors, he had expected a sight not unlike Menzoberranzan, though on a lesser scale. His expectations could not have been further from the truth.

While Menzoberranzan sprawled in a single huge cavern, Blingdenstone was composed of a series of chambers interconnected by low tunnels. The largest cavern of the complex, just beyond the iron doors, was the first section Drizzt entered. The city guard was housed there, and the chamber had been shaped and designed solely for defense. Dozens of tiers and twice that number of smooth stairways rose and fell, so that while an attacker might be only ten feet from a defender, he would possibly have to climb down several levels and up several others to get close enough to strike. Low walls of perfectly fitted piled stone defined the walkways and weaved around higher, thicker walls that could keep an invading army bottled up for a painfully long time in the chamber's exposed sections.

Scores of svirfnebli rushed about their posts to confirm the whispers that a drow elf had been brought in through the doors. They leered down at Drizzt from every perch, and he couldn't be certain if their expressions signified curiosity or outrage. In either case, the deep gnomes were certainly prepared against anything he might attempt; every one of them clutched darts or heavy crossbows, cocked and ready.

The svirfnebli led Drizzt through the chamber, up as many stairs as they went down, always within the defined walkways and always with several other deep gnome guards nearby. The path turned and dropped, rose up quickly, and cut back on itself many times, and the only way that Drizzt could keep his bearing was by watching the ceiling, which was visible even from the lowest levels of the chamber. The drow smirked inwardly but dared not show a smile at the thought that even if no deep gnome soldiers were present, an invading army would likely spend hours trying to find its way through this single chamber.

Down at the end of a low and narrow corridor, where the deep gnomes had to travel single file and Drizzt had to crouch with every step, the troupe entered the city proper. Wider but not nearly as long as the first room, this chamber, too, was tiered, though with far fewer levels. Dozens of cave entrances lined the walls to all sides and fires burned in several areas, a rare sight in the Underdark, for fuel was not easily found. Blingdenstone was bright and warm by Underdark standards but not uncomfortable in either case.

Drizzt felt at ease, despite his obvious predicament, as he watched the svirfnebli go about their daily routines all around him. Curious gazes fell on him but did not linger, for the deep gnomes of Blingdenstone were an industrious lot with hardly the time to stand idly and watch.

Again Drizzt was led down clearly defined roadways. These in the city proper were not as twisting and difficult as the ones in the entrance cavern. Here the roads rolled out smoothly and straight, and all apparently led to a large, central stone building.

The leader of the group escorting Drizzt rushed ahead to speak with two pick-wielding guards at this central structure. One of the guards bolted inside, while the other held the iron door open for the patrol and its prisoner. Moving with urgency for the first time since they had entered the city, the svirfnebli rushed Drizzt through a series of bending corridors ending in a circular chamber no more than eight feet in diameter and with an uncomfortably low ceiling. The room was empty except for a single stone chair. As soon as he was placed in this, Drizzt understood its purpose. Iron shackles were built into the chair, and Drizzt was belted down tightly at every joint. The svirfnebli were not overly gentle, but when Drizzt flinched as the chain around his waist doubled up and pinched him, one of the deep gnomes quickly released then reset it, firmly but smoothly.

They left Drizzt alone in the dark and empty room. The stone door closed with a dull thud of finality, and Drizzt could hear not a sound from beyond.

The hours passed.

Drizzt flexed his muscles, seeking some give in the tight shackles. One hand wiggled and pulled, and only the pain of the iron biting into his wrist alerted him to his actions. He was reverting to the hunter again, acting to survive and desiring only to escape.

"No!" Drizzt yelled. He tensed every muscle and forced them back under his rational control. Had the hunter gained that much of a place? Drizzt had come here willingly, and thus far, the meeting had proceeded better than he had expected. This was not the time for desperate action, but was the hunter strong enough to overrule even Drizzt's rational decisions?

Drizzt didn't find the time to answer those questions, for a second later, the stone door banged open and a group of seven elderly—judging from the extraordinary number of wrinkles crossing their faces—svirfnebli entered and fanned out around the stone chair. Drizzt recognized the apparent importance of this group, for where the guards had worn leather jacks set with mithral rings, these deep gnomes wore robes of fine material. They bustled about, inspecting Drizzt closely and chattering in their undecipherable tongue.

One svirfneblin held up Drizzt's house emblem, which had been taken from his neck purse, and uttered, "Menzoberranzan?"

Drizzt nodded as much as his iron collar would allow, eager to strike up some kind of communication with his captors. The deep gnomes had other intentions, however. They went back to their private—and now even more excited—conversation.

It went on for many minutes, and Drizzt could tell by the inflections of their voices that a couple of the svirfnebli were less than thrilled at having a dark elf prisoner from the city of their closest and most-hated enemies. By the angry tone of their arguing, Drizzt almost expected one of them to turn at any moment and slice his throat.

It didn't happen like that, of course; deep gnomes were neither rash nor cruel creatures. One of the group did turn from the others and walk over to face Drizzt squarely. He asked, in halting but unmistakably drow language, "By the stones, dark elf, why have you come?"

Drizzt did not know how to answer that simple question. How could he even begin to explain his years of loneliness in the Underdark? Or the decision to forsake his evil people and live in accordance with his principles?

"Friend," he replied simply, and then he shifted uncomfortably, thinking his response absurd and inadequate.

The svirfneblin, though, apparently thought otherwise. He scratched his hairless chin and considered the answer deeply. "You . . . you came in to us from Menzoberranzan?" he asked, his hawklike nose crinkling as he uttered each word.

"I did," Drizzt replied, gaining confidence.

The deep gnome tilted his head, waiting for Drizzt to extrapolate.

"I left Menzoberranzan many years ago," Drizzt tried to explain. His eyes stared away into the past as he remembered the life he had deserted. "It was never my home."

"Ah, but you lie, dark elf!" the svirfneblin shrieked, holding up the emblem of House Do'Urden and missing the private connotations of Drizzt's words.

"I lived for many years in the city of the drow," he replied quickly. "I am Drizzt Do'Urden, once the secondboy of House Do'Urden." He looked at the emblem the svirfneblin held, stamped with the insignia of his family, and tried to explain. "Daermon N'a'shezbaernon."

The deep gnome turned to his comrades, who began talking all at once. One of them nodded excitedly, apparently recognizing the drow house's ancient name, which surprised Drizzt.

The deep gnome who had been questioning Drizzt tapped his fingers over his wrinkled lips, making annoying little smacking sounds while he contemplating the interrogation's direction. "By all of our information,

House Do'Urden survives," he remarked casually, noting Drizzt's reactions. When Drizzt did not immediately respond, the deep gnome snapped at him accusingly, "You are no rogue!"

How could the svirfnebli know that? Drizzt wondered. "I am a rogue by choice . . ." he started to explain.

"Ah, dark elf," the deep gnome replied, again calmly. "You are here by choice, that much I can believe. But a rogue? By the stones, dark elf—" the deep gnome's face contorted suddenly and fearfully—"you are a spy!" Then, suddenly, the deep gnome once again calmed and relaxed into a comfortable posture.

Drizzt eyed him carefully. Was this svirfneblin adept at such abrupt attitude changes, designed to keep a prisoner off guard? Or was such unpredictability the norm for this race? Drizzt struggled with it for a moment, trying to remember his one previous encounter with deep gnomes. But then his questioner reached into an impossibly deep pocket in his thick robes and produced a familiar figurine.

"Tell me, now tell me true, dark elf, and spare yourself much torment. What is this?" the deep gnome asked quietly.

Drizzt felt his muscles twitching again. The hunter wanted to call to Guenhwyvar, to bring the panther in so that it could tear these wrinkled old svirfnebli apart. One of them might hold the keys to Drizzt's chains—then he would be free . . .

Drizzt shook the thoughts from his head and drove the hunter out of his mind. He knew the desperation of his situation and had known it from the moment he had decided to come to Blingdenstone. If the svirfnebli truly believed him a spy, they surely would execute him. Even if they were not certain of his intent, could they dare to keep him alive?

"It was folly to come here," Drizzt whispered under his breath, realizing the dilemma he had placed upon himself and upon the deep gnomes. The hunter tried to get back into his thoughts. A single word, and the panther would appear.

"No!" Drizzt cried for the second time that day, dismissing that darker side of himself. The deep gnomes jumped back, fearing that the drow was casting a spell. A dart nicked into Drizzt's chest, releasing a puff of gas on impact.

Drizzt swooned as the gas filled his nostrils. He heard the svirfnebli shuffling about him, discussing his fate in their foreign tongue. He saw the form of one, only a shadow, close in on him and grasp at his fingers, searching his hands for possible magical components.

When Drizzt's thoughts and vision had at last cleared, all was as it had been. The onyx figurine came up before his eyes. "What is this?" the same deep gnome asked him again, this time a bit more insistently.

"A companion," Drizzt whispered. "My only friend." Drizzt thought hard about his next actions for a long moment. He really couldn't blame the svirfnebli if they killed him, and Guenhwyvar should be more than a statuette adorning some unknowing deep gnome's mantle.

"Its name is Guenhwyvar," Drizzt explained to the deep gnome. "Call to the panther and it will come, an ally and friend. Keep it safe, for it is very precious and very powerful."

The svirfneblin looked to the figurine and then back to Drizzt, curiously and cautiously. He handed the figurine to one of his companions and sent him out of the room with it, not trusting the drow. If the drow had spoken truly, and the deep gnome did not doubt that he had, Drizzt had just given away the secret to a very valuable magical item. Even more startling, if Drizzt had spoken truly, he might have relinquished his single chance of escape. This svirfneblin had lived for nearly two centuries and was as knowledgeable in the ways of the dark elves as any of his people. When a drow elf acted unpredictably, as this one surely had, it troubled the svirfneblin deeply. Dark elves were cruel and evil by well-earned reputation, and when an individual drow fit that usual pattern, he could be dealt with efficiently and without remorse. But what might the deep gnomes do with a drow who showed a measure of unexpected morals?

The svirfnebli went back to their private conversation, ignoring Drizzt altogether. Then they left, with the exception of the one who could speak the dark elf tongue.

"What will you do?" Drizzt dared to ask.

"Judgment is reserved for the king alone," the deep gnome replied soberly. "He will rule on your fate in several days perhaps, based on the observations of his advising council, the group you have met." The deep gnome bowed low, then looked Drizzt in the eye as he rose and said bluntly, "I suspect, dark elf, that you will be executed."

Drizzt nodded, resigned to the logic that would call for his death.

"But I believe you are different, dark elf," the deep gnome went on. "I suspect, as well, that I will recommend leniency, or at least mercy, in the execution." With a quick shrug of his heavyset shoulders, the svirfneblin turned about and headed for the door.

The tone of the deep gnome's words struck a familiar chord in Drizzt. Another svirfneblin had spoken to Drizzt in a similar manner, with strikingly similar words, many years before.

"Wait," Drizzt called. The svirfneblin paused and turned, and Drizzt fumbled with his thoughts, trying to remember the name of the deep gnome he had saved on that past occasion.

"What is it?" the svirfneblin asked, growing impatient.

"A deep gnome," Drizzt sputtered. "From your city, I believe. Yes, he had to be."

"You know one of my people, dark elf?" the svirfneblin prompted, stepping back to the stone chair. "Name him."

"I do not know," Drizzt replied. "I was a member of a hunting party, years ago, a decade perhaps. We battled a group of svirfnebli that had come into our region." He flinched at the deep gnome's frown but continued on, knowing that the single svirfneblin survivor of that encounter might be his only hope. "Only one deep gnome survived, I think, and returned to Blingdenstone."

"What was this survivor's name?" the svirfneblin demanded angrily, his arms crossed tightly over his chest and his heavy boot tapping on the stone floor.

"I do not remember," Drizzt admitted.

"Why do you tell me this?" the svirfneblin growled. "I had thought you different from—"

"He lost his hands in the battle," Drizzt went on stubbornly. "Please, you must know of him."

"Belwar?" the svirfneblin replied immediately. The name rekindled even more memories in Drizzt.

"Belwar Dissengulp," Drizzt spouted. "Then he is alive! He might remember—"

"He will never forget that evil day, dark elf!" the svirfneblin declared through clenched teeth, an angry edge evident in his voice. "None in Blingdenstone will ever forget that evil day!"

"Get him. Get Belwar Dissengulp," Drizzt pleaded.

The deep gnome backed out of the room, shaking his head at the dark elf's continued surprises.

The stone door slammed shut, leaving Drizzt alone to contemplate his mortality and to push aside hopes he dared not hope.

⚔ ⚔ ⚔ ⚔ ⚔

"Did you think that I would let you go away from me?" Malice was saying to Rizzen when Dinin entered the chapel's anteroom. "It was but a ploy to keep SiNafay Hun'ett's suspicions at ease."

"Thank you, Matron Mother," Rizzen replied in honest relief. Bowing with every step, he backed away from Malice's throne.

Malice looked around at her gathered family. "Our tendays of toil are ended," she proclaimed. "Zin-carla is complete!"

Dinin wrung his hands in anticipation. Only the females of the family had seen the product of their work. On cue from Malice, Vierna moved to a curtain on the side of the room and pulled it away. There stood Zaknafein, the weapon master, no longer a rotting corpse, but showing the vitality he had possessed in life.

Dinin rocked back on his heels as the weapon master came forward to stand before Matron Malice.

"As handsome as you always were, my dear Zaknafein," Malice purred to the spirit-wraith. The undead thing made no response.

"And more obedient," Briza added, drawing chuckles from all the females.

"This . . . he . . . will go after Drizzt?" Dinin dared to ask, though he fully understood that it was not his place to speak. Malice and the others were too absorbed by the spectacle of Zaknafein to punish the elderboy's oversight.

"Zaknafein will exact the punishment that your brother so deeply deserves," Malice promised, her eyes sparkling at the notion.

"But wait," Malice said coyly, looking from the spirit-wraith to Rizzen. "He is too pretty to inspire fear in my impudent son." The others exchanged confused glances, wondering if Malice was further trying to placate Rizzen for the ordeal she had put him through.

"Come, my husband," Malice said to Rizzen. "Take your blade and mark your dead rival's face. It will feel good to you, and it will inspire terror in Drizzt when he looks upon his old mentor!"

Rizzen moved tentatively at first, then gained confidence as he closed on the spirit-wraith. Zaknafein stood perfectly still, not breathing or blinking, seemingly oblivious to the events around him. Rizzen put a hand to his sword, looking back to Malice one final time for confirmation.

Malice nodded. With a snarl, Rizzen brought his sword out of its sheath and thrust it at Zaknafein's face.

But it never got close.

Quicker than the others could follow, the spirit-wraith exploded into motion. Two swords came out and cut away, diving and crossing with perfect precision. The sword went flying from Rizzen's hand and before the doomed patron of House Do'Urden could even speak a word of protest, one of Zaknafein's swords crossed over his throat and the other plunged deep into his heart.

Rizzen was dead before he hit the floor, but the spirit-wraith was not so quickly and cleanly finished with him. Zaknafein's weapons continued their assault, hacking and slicing into Rizzen a dozen times until Malice, satisfied with the display, called him off.

"That one bores me," Malice explained to the disbelieving stares of her children. "I have another patron already selected from among the commoners."

It was not, however, Rizzen's death that inspired the awestruck expressions of Malice's children; they cared nothing for any of the mates that their mother chose as patron of the house, always a temporary position. It was the speed and skill of the spirit-wraith that had stolen their breath.

"As good as in life," Dinin remarked.

"Better!" Malice replied. "Zaknafein is all that he was as a warrior, and now that fighting skill holds his every thought. He will view no distractions from his chosen course. Look upon him, my children. Zin-carla, the gift of Lolth." She turned to Dinin and smiled wickedly.

"I'll not approach the thing," Dinin gasped, thinking his macabre mother might desire a second display.

Malice laughed at him. "Fear not, Elderboy. I have no cause to harm you."

Dinin hardly relaxed at her words. Malice needed no cause; the hacked body of Rizzen showed that fact all too clearly.

"You will lead the spirit-wraith out," Malice said.

"Out?" Dinin replied tentatively.

"Into the region where you encountered your brother," Malice explained.

"I am to stay beside the thing?" Dinin gasped.

"Lead him out and leave him," Malice replied. "Zaknafein knows his prey. He has been imbued with spells to aid him in his hunt."

Off to the side, Briza seemed concerned.

"What is it?" Malice demanded of her, seeing her frown.

"I do not question the spirit-wraith's power, or the magic that you have placed upon it," Briza began tentatively, knowing that Malice would accept no discord regarding this all-important matter.

"You still fear your youngest brother?" Malice asked her.

Briza didn't know how to answer.

"Allay your fears, as valid as you may think them," Malice said calmly. "All of you. Zaknafein is the gift of our queen. Nothing in all the Underdark will stop him!" She looked at the undead monster. "You will not fail me, will you my weapon master?"

Zaknafein stood impassive, bloodied swords back in their scabbards, hands at his sides, and eyes unblinking. A statue, he seemed, not breathing. Unalive.

But any who thought Zaknafein inanimate needed only to look at the spirit-wraith's feet, to the mutilated lump of gore that had been the patron of House Do'Urden.

# Part Two

## Belwar

Friendship: The word has come to mean many different things among the various races and cultures of both the Underdark and the surface of the Realms. In Menzoberranzan, friendship is generally born out of mutual profit. While both parties are better off for the union, it remains secure. But loyalty is not a tenet of drow life, and as soon as a friend believes that he will gain more without the other, the union—and likely the other's life—will come to a swift end.

I have had few friends in my life, and if I live a thousand years, I suspect that this will remain true. There is little to lament in this fact, though, for those who have called me friend have been persons of great character and have enriched my existence, given it worth. First there was Zaknafein, my father and mentor, who showed me that I was not alone and that

I was not incorrect in holding to my beliefs. Zaknafein saved me, from both the blade and the chaotic, evil, fanatic religion that damns my people.

Yet I was no less lost when a handless deep gnome came into my life, a svirfneblin that I had rescued from certain death, many years before, at my brother Dinin's merciless blade. My deed was repaid in full, for when the svirfneblin and I again met, this time in the clutches of his people, I would have been killed—truly would have preferred death—were it not for Belwar Dissengulp.

My time in Blingdenstone, the city of the deep gnomes, was such a short span in the measure of my years. I remember well Belwar's city and his people, and I always shall. Theirs was the first society I came to know that was based on the strengths of community, not the paranoia of selfish individualism. Together the deep gnomes survive against the perils of the hostile Underdark, labor in their endless toils of mining the stone, and play games that are hardly distinguishable from every other aspect of their rich lives.

Greater indeed are pleasures that are shared.

—Drizzt Do'Urden

# 7 Most Honored Burrow-Warden

"Our thanks for your coming, Most Honored Burrow-Warden," said one of the deep gnomes gathered outside the small room holding the drow prisoner. The entire group of svirfneblin elders bowed low at the burrow-warden's approach.

Belwar Dissengulp flinched at the gracious greeting. He had never come to terms with the many laurels his people had mantled upon him since that disastrous day more than a decade before, when the drow elves had discovered his mining troupe in the corridors east of Blingdenstone, near Menzoberranzan. Horribly maimed and nearly dead from loss of blood, Belwar had limped back to Blingdenstone as the only survivor of the expedition.

The gathered svirfnebli parted for Belwar, giving him a clear view of the room and the drow. To prisoners strapped in the chair, the circular chamber seemed solid, unremarkable stone with no opening other than the heavy iron-bound door. There was, however, a single window in the chamber, covered by illusions of both sight and sound, that allowed the svirfneblin captors to view the prisoner at all times.

Belwar studied Drizzt for several moments. "He is a drow," the burrow-warden huffed in his resonant voice, sounding a bit perturbed. Belwar still could not understand why he had been summoned.

"Appearing as any other drow."

"The prisoner claims he met you out in the Underdark," an ancient svirfneblin said to Belwar. His voice was barely a whisper, and he dropped his gaze to the floor as he completed the thought. "On that day of great loss."

Belwar flinched again at the mention of that day. How many times must he relive it?

"He may have," Belwar said with a noncommittal shrug. "Not much can I distinguish between the appearances of drow elves, and not much do I wish to try!"

"Agreed," said the other. "They all look alike."

As the deep gnome spoke, Drizzt turned his face to the side and faced them directly, though he could not see or hear anything beyond the illusion of stone.

"Perhaps you may remember his name, Burrow-Warden," another svirfneblin offered. The speaker paused, seeing Belwar's sudden interest in the drow.

The circular chamber was lightless, and under such conditions, the eyes of a creature seeing in the infrared spectrum shone clearly. Normally, these eyes appeared as dots of red light, but that was not the case with Drizzt Do'Urden. Even in the infrared spectrum, this drow's eyes showed clearly as lavender.

Belwar remembered those eyes.

"*Magga cammara,*" Belwar breathed. "Drizzt," he mumbled in reply to the other deep gnome.

"You do know him!" several of the svirfnebli cried together.

Belwar held up the handless stumps of his arms, one capped with the mithral head of a pickaxe, the other with the head of a hammer. "This drow, this Drizzt," he stammered, trying to explain. "Responsible for my condition, he was!"

Some of the others murmured prayers for the doomed drow, thinking the burrow-warden was angered by the memory. "Then King Schnicktick's decision stands," one of them said. "The drow is to be executed immediately."

"But he, this Drizzt, he saved my life," Belwar interjected loudly. The others, incredulous, turned on him.

"Never was it Drizzt's decision that my hands be severed," the burrow-warden went on. "It was his offering that I be allowed to return to Blingdenstone. 'As an example,' this Drizzt said, but I understood even then that the words were uttered only to placate his cruel kin. The truth behind those words, I know, and that truth was mercy!"

⚔ ⚔ ⚔ ⚔ ⚔

An hour later, a single svirfneblin councilor, the one who had spoken to Drizzt earlier, came to the prisoner. "It was the decision of the king that you be executed," the deep gnome said bluntly as he approached the stone chair.

"I understand," Drizzt replied as calmly as he could. "I will offer no resistance to your verdict." Drizzt considered his shackles for a moment. "Not that I could."

The svirfneblin stopped and considered the unpredictable prisoner, fully believing in Drizzt's sincerity. Before he continued, meaning to expand on the events of the day, Drizzt completed his thought.

"I ask only one favor," Drizzt said. The svirfneblin let him finish, curious of the unusual drow's reasoning.

"The panther," Drizzt went on. "You will find Guenhwyvar to be a valued companion and a dear friend indeed. When I am no more, you must see to it that the panther is given to a deserving master—Belwar Dissengulp perhaps. Promise me this, good gnome, I beg."

The svirfneblin shook his hairless head, not to deny Drizzt's plea, but in simple disbelief. "The king, with much remorse, simply could not allow the risks of keeping you alive," he said somberly. The deep gnome's wide mouth turned up in a smile as he quickly added, "But the situation has changed!"

Drizzt cocked his head, hardly daring to hope.

"The burrow-warden remembers you, dark elf," the svirfneblin proclaimed. "Most Honored Burrow-Warden Belwar Dissengulp has spoken for you and will accept the responsibility of keeping you!"

"Then . . . I am not to die?"

"Not unless you bring death upon yourself."

Drizzt could barely utter the words. "And I am to be allowed to live among your people? In Blingdenstone?"

"That is yet to be determined," replied the svirfneblin. "Belwar Dissengulp has spoken for you, and that is a very great thing. You will go to live with him. Whether the situation will be continued or expanded . . ." He let it hang at that, giving an unanswering shrug.

Following his release, the walk through the caverns of Blingdenstone was truly an exercise in hope for the beleaguered drow. Drizzt saw every sight in the deep gnome city as a contrast to Menzoberranzan. The dark elves had worked the great cavern of their city into shaped artwork, undeniably beautiful. The deep gnome city, too, was beautiful, but its features remained the natural traits of the stone. Where the drow had taken their cavern as their own, cutting it to their designs and tastes, the svirfnebli had fitted themselves into the native designs of their complex.

Menzoberranzan held a vastness, with a ceiling up beyond sight, that Blingdenstone could not approach. The drow city was a series of individual family castles, each a closed fortress and a house unto itself. In the deep gnome city was a general sense of home, as if the entire complex within the mammoth stone-and-metal doors was a singular structure, a community shelter from the ever-present dangers of the Underdark.

The angles of the svirfneblin city, too, were different. Like the features of the diminutive race, Blingdenstone's buttresses and tiers were rounded, smooth, and gracefully curving. Conversely, Menzoberranzan was an angular place, as sharp as the point of a stalactite, a place of alleyways and leering terraces. Drizzt considered the two cities distinctive of the races they housed, sharp and soft like the features—and the hearts, Drizzt dared to imagine—of their respective inhabitants.

Tucked away in a remote corner of one of the outer chambers sat Belwar's dwelling, a tiny structure of stone built around the opening of an even smaller cave. Unlike most of the open-faced svirfneblin dwellings, Belwar's house had a front door.

One of the five guards escorting Drizzt tapped on the door with the butt of his mace. "Greetings, Most Honored Burrow-Warden!" he called. "By orders of King Schnicktick, we have delivered the drow."

Drizzt took note of the respectful tone of the guard's voice. He had feared for Belwar on that day a decade and more ago, and had wondered if Dinin's cutting off the deep gnome's hands wasn't more cruel than simply killing the unfortunate creature. Cripples did not fare well in the savage Underdark.

The stone door swung open and Belwar greeted his guests. Immediately his gaze locked with Drizzt's in a look they had shared ten years before, when they had last parted.

Drizzt saw a somberness in the burrow-warden's eyes, but the stout pride remained, if a bit diminished. Drizzt did not want to look upon the svirfnebli's disfigurement; too many unpleasant memories were tied up in that long-ago deed. But inevitably, the drow's gaze dropped, down Belwar's barrel-like torso to the ends of his arms, which hung by his side.

Far from his fears, Drizzt's eyes widened in wonderment when he looked upon Belwar's "hands." On the right side, wondrously fitted to cap the stub of his arm, was the blocked head of a hammer crafted of mithral and etched with intricate, fabulous runes and carvings of an earth elemental and some other creatures that Drizzt did not know.

Belwar's left appendage was no less spectacular. There the deep gnome wielded a two-headed pickaxe, also of mithral and equally crafted in runes and carvings, most notably a dragon taking flight across the flat surface of the instrument's wider end. Drizzt could sense the magic in Belwar's hands, and he realized that many other svirfnebli, both artisans and magic-users, had played a part in perfecting the items.

"Useful," Belwar remarked after allowing Drizzt to study his mithral hands for a few moments.

"Beautiful," Drizzt whispered in reply, and he was thinking of more than the hammer and pick. The hands themselves were indeed marvelous, but the implications of their crafting seemed even more so to Drizzt. If a dark elf, particularly a drow male, had crawled back into Menzoberranzan in such a disfigured state, he would have been rejected and put out by his family to wander about as a helpless rogue until some slave or other drow finally put an end to his misery. There was no room for apparent weakness in the drow culture. Here, obviously, the svirfnebli had accepted Belwar and had cared for him in the best way they knew how.

Drizzt politely returned his stare to the burrow-warden's eyes. "You remembered me," he said. "I had feared—"

"Later we shall talk, Drizzt Do'Urden," Belwar interrupted. Using the svirfneblin tongue, which Drizzt did not know, the burrow-warden said to the guards, "If your business is completed, then take your leave."

"We are at your command, Most Honored Burrow-Warden," one of the guards replied. Drizzt noticed Belwar's slight shudder at the mention of the title. "The king has sent us as escorts and guards, to remain by your side until the truth of this drow is revealed."

"Be gone, then," Belwar replied, his booming voice rising in obvious ire. He looked directly at Drizzt as he finished. "I know the truth of this one already. I am in no danger."

"Your pardon, Most Honor—"

"You are excused," Belwar said abruptly, seeing that the guard meant to argue. "Be gone. I have spoken for this one. He is in my care, and I fear him not at all."

The svirfneblin guards bowed low and slowly moved away. Belwar took Drizzt inside the door, then turned him back to slyly point out that two of the guards had taken up cautious positions beside nearby structures. "Too much do they worry for my health," he remarked dryly in the drow tongue.

"You should be grateful for such care," Drizzt replied.

"I am not ungrateful!" Belwar shot back, an angry flush coming to his face.

Drizzt read the truth behind those words. Belwar was not ungrateful, that much was correct, but the burrow-warden did not believe that he deserved such attention. Drizzt kept his suspicions private, not wanting to further embarrass the proud svirfneblin.

The inside of Belwar's house was sparsely furnished with a stone table and single stool, several shelves of pots and jugs, and a fire pit with an iron cooking grate. Beyond the rough-hewn entrance to the back room, the room within the small cave, was the deep gnome's sleeping quarters, empty except for a hammock strung from wall to wall. Another hammock, newly acquired for Drizzt, lay in a heap on the floor, and a leather, mithral-ringed jack hung on the back wall, with a pile of sacks and pouches underneath it.

"In the entry room we shall string it," Belwar said, pointing with his hammer-hand to the second hammock. Drizzt moved to get the item, but Belwar caught him with his pick-hand and spun him about.

"Later," the svirfneblin explained. "First you must tell me why you have come." He studied Drizzt's battered clothing and scuffed and dirty face. It was obvious that the drow had been out in the wilds for some time. "And tell me, too, you must, where you have come from."

Drizzt flopped down on the stone floor and put his back against the wall. "I came because I had nowhere else to go," he answered honestly.

"How long have you been out of your city, Drizzt Do'Urden?" Belwar asked him softly. Even in quieter tones, the solid deep gnome's voice rang out with the clarity of a finely tuned bell. Drizzt marveled at its emotive range and how it could convey sincere compassion or inspire fear with subtle changes of volume.

Drizzt shrugged and let his head roll back so that his gaze was raised to the ceiling. His mind already looked down a road to his past. "Years—I have lost count of the time." He looked back to the svirfneblin. "Time has little meaning in the open passages of the Underdark."

From Drizzt's ragged appearance, Belwar could not doubt the truth of his words, but the deep gnome was surprised nonetheless. He moved over to the table in the center of the room and took a seat on a stool. Belwar had witnessed Drizzt in battle, had once seen the drow defeat an earth elemental—no easy feat! But if Drizzt was indeed speaking the truth, if he had survived alone out in the wilds of the Underdark for years, then the burrow-warden's respect for him would be even more considerable.

"Of your adventures, you must tell me, Drizzt Do'Urden," Belwar prompted. "I wish to know everything about you, so that I may better understand your purpose in coming to a city of your racial enemies."

Drizzt paused for a long time, wondering where and how to begin. He trusted Belwar—what other choice did he have?—but he wasn't sure if the svirfneblin could begin to understand the dilemma that had forced him out of the security of Menzoberranzan. Could Belwar, living in a community of such obvious friendship and cooperation, understand the tragedy that was Menzoberranzan? Drizzt doubted it, but again, what choice did he have?

Drizzt quietly recounted to Belwar the story of the last decade of his life; of the impending war between House Do'Urden and House Hun'ett; of his meeting with Masoj and Alton, when he acquired Guenhwyvar; of the sacrifice of Zaknafein, Drizzt's mentor, father, and friend; and of his subsequent decision to forsake his kin and their evil deity, Lolth. Belwar realized that Drizzt was talking about the dark goddess the deep gnomes called Lolth, but he calmly let the regionalism pass. If Belwar had any suspicions at all, not really knowing Drizzt's true intent on that day when they had met many years before, the burrow-warden soon came to believe that his guesses about this drow had been accurate. Belwar found himself shuddering and trembling as Drizzt told of life in the Underdark, of his encounter with the basilisk, and the battle with his brother and sister.

Before Drizzt even mentioned his reason for seeking the svirfnebli—the agony of his loneliness and the fear that he was losing his very identity in the savagery necessary to survive in the wilds—Belwar had guessed it all. When Drizzt came to the final days of his life outside of Blingdenstone, he picked his words carefully. Drizzt had not yet come to terms with his feelings and fears of who he truly was, and he was not yet ready to divulge his thoughts, however much he trusted his new companion.

The burrow-warden sat silently, just looking at Drizzt when the drow had finished his tale. Belwar understood the pain of the recounting. He did not prod for more information or ask for details of personal anguish that Drizzt had not openly shared.

"*Magga cammara,*" the deep gnome whispered soberly.

Drizzt cocked his head.

"By the stones," Belwar explained. "*Magga cammara.*"

"By the stones indeed," Drizzt agreed. A long and uncomfortable silence ensued.

"A fine tale, it is," Belwar said quietly. He patted Drizzt once on the shoulder, then walked into the cave-room to retrieve the spare hammock. Before Drizzt even rose to assist, Belwar had set the hammock in place between hooks on the walls.

"Sleep in peace, Drizzt Do'Urden," Belwar said, as he turned to retire. "No enemies have you here. No monsters lurk beyond the stone of my door."

Then Belwar was gone into the other room and Drizzt was left alone in the undecipherable swirl of his thoughts and emotions. He remained uncomfortable, but surely, his was hope renewed.

# 8

# STRANGERS

Drizzt looked out Belwar's open door at the daily routines of the svirfneblin city, as he had every day for the last few tendays. Drizzt felt as though his life was in a state of limbo, as though everything had been put into stasis. He had not seen or heard of Guenhwyvar since he had come to Belwar's house, nor had he any expectations of getting his *piwafwi* or his weapons and armor back anytime soon. Drizzt accepted it all stoically, figuring that he, and Guenhwyvar, were better off now than they had been in many years and confident that the svirfnebli would not harm the statuette or any of his other possessions. The drow sat and watched, letting events take their due course.

Belwar had gone out this day, one of the rare occasions that the reclusive burrow-warden left his house. Despite the fact that the deep gnome and Drizzt rarely conversed—Belwar was not the type who spoke simply for the sake of hearing his own voice—Drizzt found that he missed the burrow-warden. Their friendship had grown, even if the substance of their conversations had not.

A group of young svirfnebli walked past and shouted a few quick words at the drow within. This had happened many times before, particularly in the first days after Drizzt had entered the city. On those previous occasions, Drizzt had been left wondering if he had been greeted or insulted. This time, though, Drizzt understood the basic friendly meaning of the words, for Belwar had taken the time to instruct him in the basics of the svirfneblin tongue.

The burrow-warden returned hours later to find Drizzt sitting on the stone stool, watching the world slip past.

"Tell me, dark elf," the deep gnome asked in his hearty, melodic voice, "what do you see when you look upon us? Are we so foreign to your ways?"

"I see hope," Drizzt replied. "And I see despair."

Belwar understood. He knew that the svirfneblin society was better suited to the drow's principles, but watching the bustle of Blingdenstone from afar could only evoke painful memories in his new friend.

"King Schnicktick and I met this day," the burrow-warden said. "I tell you in truth that he is very interested in you."

"Curious would seem a better word," Drizzt replied, but he smiled as he did so, and Belwar wondered how much pain was hidden behind the grin.

The burrow-warden dipped into a short, apologetic bow, surrendering to Drizzt's blunt honesty. "Curious, then, as you wish. You must know that you are not as we have come to regard drow elves. I beg that you take no offense."

"None," Drizzt answered honestly. "You and your people have given me more than I dared hope. If I had been killed that first day in the city, I would have accepted the fate without placing blame on the svirfnebli."

Belwar followed Drizzt's gaze out across the cavern, to the group of gathered youngsters. "You should go among them," Belwar offered.

Drizzt looked at him, surprised. In all the time he had spent in Belwar's house, the svirfneblin had never suggested such a thing. Drizzt had assumed that he was to remain the burrow-warden's guest, and that Belwar had been made personally responsible for curtailing his movements.

Belwar nodded toward the door, silently reiterating his suggestion. Drizzt looked out again. Across the cavern, the group of young svirfnebli, a dozen or so, had begun a contest of heaving rather large stones at an effigy of a basilisk, a life-sized likeness built of stones and old suits of armor. Svirfnebli were highly skilled in the magical crafts of illusion, and one such illusionist had placed minor enchantments upon the likeness to smooth out the rough spots and make the effigy appear even more lifelike.

"Dark elf, you must go out sometime," Belwar reasoned. "How long will you find my home's blank walls fulfilling?"

"They suit you," Drizzt retorted, a bit more sharply than he had intended.

Belwar nodded and slowly turned about to survey the room. "So they do," he said quietly, and Drizzt could clearly see his great pain. When Belwar turned back to the drow, his round-featured face held an unmistakably resigned expression. "*Magga cammara*, dark elf. Let that be your lesson."

"Why?" Drizzt asked him. "Why does Belwar Dissengulp, the Most Honored Burrow-Warden—" Belwar flinched again at the title—"remain within the shadows of his own door?"

Belwar's jaw firmed up and his dark eyes narrowed. "Go out," he said in a resonating growl. "Young you are, dark elf, and all the world is before you. Old I am. My day is long past."

"Not so old," Drizzt started to argue, determined this time to press the burrow-warden into revealing what it was that troubled him so. But Belwar simply turned and walked silently into his cave-room, pulling closed behind him the blanket he had strung up as a door.

Drizzt shook his head and banged his fist into his palm in frustration. Belwar had done so much for him, first by saving him from the svirfneblin king's judgment, then by befriending him over the last few tendays and teaching him the svirfneblin tongue and the deep gnomes' ways. Drizzt had been unable to return the favor, though he clearly saw that Belwar carried some great burden. Drizzt wanted to rush through the blanket now, go to the burrow-warden, and make him speak his gloomy thoughts.

Drizzt would not yet be so bold with his new friend, however. He would find the key to the burrow-warden's pain in time, he vowed, but right now he had his own dilemma to overcome. Belwar had given him permission to go out into Blingdenstone!

Drizzt looked back to the group across the cavern. Three of them stood perfectly still before the effigy, as if turned to stone. Curious, Drizzt moved to the doorway, and then, before he realized what he was doing, he was outside and approaching the young deep gnomes.

The game ended as the drow neared, the svirfnebli being more interested in meeting the dark elf they had rumored about for so many tendays. They rushed over to Drizzt and surrounded him, whispering curiously.

Drizzt felt his muscles tense involuntarily as the svirfnebli moved all about him. The primal instincts of the hunter sensed a vulnerability that could not be tolerated. Drizzt fought hard to sublimate his alter ego, silently but firmly reminding himself that the svirfnebli were not his enemies.

"Greetings, drow friend of Belwar Dissengulp," one of the youngsters offered. "I am Seldig, fledgling and pledgling, and to be an expedition miner in but three years hence."

It took Drizzt a long moment to sort out the deep gnome's rapid speech patterns. He did understand the significance of Seldig's future occupation, though, for Belwar had told him that expedition miners, those svirfnebli who went out into the Underdark in search of precious minerals and gems, were among the highest ranking deep gnomes in all the city.

"Greetings, Seldig," Drizzt answered at length. "I am Drizzt Do'Urden." Not really knowing what he should do next, Drizzt crossed his arms over his chest. To the dark elves, this was a gesture of peace, though Drizzt was not certain if the motion was universally accepted throughout the Underdark.

The svirfnebli looked around at each other, returned the gesture, then smiled in unison at the sound of Drizzt's relieved sigh.

"You have been in the Underdark, so it is said," Seldig went on, motioning for Drizzt to follow him back to the area of their game.

"For many years," Drizzt replied, falling into step beside the young svirfneblin. The hunting ego within the drow grew ill at ease at the following deep gnomes' proximity, but Drizzt was in full control of his reflexive paranoia. When the group reached the fabricated basilisk's side, Seldig sat on the stone and bid Drizzt to give them a tale or two of his adventures.

Drizzt hesitated, doubting that his command of the svirfneblin tongue would be sufficient for such a task, but Seldig and the others pressed him. At length, Drizzt nodded and stood. He spent a moment in thought, trying to remember some tale that might interest the youngsters. His gaze unconsciously roamed the cavern, searching for some clue. It fell upon, and locked upon, the illusion-heightened basilisk effigy.

"Basilisk," Seldig explained.

"I know," Drizzt replied. "I have met such a creature." He turned casually back to the group and was startled by its appearance. Seldig and every one of his companions had rocked forward, their mouths hanging open in a mixture of expressed intrigue, terror, and delight.

"Dark elf! You have seen a basilisk?" one of them asked incredulously. "A real, living basilisk?"

Drizzt smiled as he came to decipher their amazement. The svirfnebli, unlike the dark elves, sheltered the younger members of their community. Though these deep gnomes were probably as old as Drizzt, they had rarely, if ever, been out of Blingdenstone. By their age, drow elves would have spent years patrolling the corridors beyond Menzoberranzan. Drizzt's recognition of the basilisk would not have been so unbelievable to the deep gnomes then, though the formidable monsters were rare even in the Underdark.

"You said that basilisks were not real!" one of the svirfnebli shouted to another, and he pushed him hard on the shoulder.

"Never I did!" the other protested, returning the shove.

"My uncle saw one once," offered another.

"Scrapings in the stone was all your uncle saw!" Seldig laughed. "They were the tracks of a basilisk, by his own proclamation."

Drizzt's smile widened. Basilisks were magical creatures, more common on other planes of existence. While drow, particularly the high priestesses, often opened gates to other planes, such monsters obviously were beyond the norm of svirfneblin life. Few were the deep gnomes who had ever looked upon a basilisk. Drizzt chuckled aloud. Fewer still, no doubt, were the deep gnomes who ever returned to tell that they had seen one!

"If your uncle followed the trail and found the monster," Seldig continued, "he would sit to this day as a pile of stone in a passageway! I say to you now that rocks do not tell such tales!"

The berated deep gnome looked around for some rebuttal. "Drizzt Do'Urden has seen one!" he protested. "He is not so much a pile of stone!" All eyes turned back to Drizzt.

"Have you really seen one, dark elf?" Seldig asked. "Answer only in truth, I beg."

"One," Drizzt replied.

"And you escaped from it before it could return the gaze?" Seldig asked, a question he and the other svirfnebli considered rhetorical.

"Escaped?" Drizzt echoed the gnomish word, unsure of its meaning.

"Escape . . . err . . . run away," Seldig explained. He looked to one of the other svirfnebli, who promptly feigned a look of sheer horror, then stumbled and scrambled frantically a few steps away. The other deep gnomes applauded the performance, and Drizzt joined in their laughter.

"You ran from the basilisk before it could return your gaze," Seldig reasoned.

Drizzt shrugged, a bit embarrassed, and Seldig guessed that he was withholding something.

"You did not run away?"

"I could not . . . escape," Drizzt explained. "The basilisk had invaded my home and had killed many of my rothé. Homes," he paused, searching for the correct svirfneblin word. "Sanctuaries," he explained at length, "are not commonplace in the wilds of the Underdark. Once found and secured, they must be defended at all costs."

"You fought it?" came an anonymous cry from the rear of the svirfneblin group.

"With stones from afar?" asked Seldig. "That is the accepted method."

Drizzt looked over at the pile of boulders the deep gnomes had been hurling at the effigy, then considered his own slender frame. "My arms could not even lift such stones." He laughed.

"Then how?" asked Seldig. "You must tell us."

Drizzt now had his story. He paused for a few moments, collecting his thoughts. He realized that his limited skills with his new language would not allow him to weave much of an intricate tale, so he decided to illustrate his words. He found two poles that the svirfnebli had been carrying, explained them as scimitars, then examined the effigy's construction to ensure that it would hold his weight.

The young deep gnomes huddled around anxiously as Drizzt set up the situation, detailing his darkness spell—actually placing one just beyond the basilisk's head—and the positioning of Guenhwyvar, his feline companion. The svirfnebli sat on their hands and leaned forward, gasping at every word. The effigy seemed to come alive in their minds, a lumbering monster, with Drizzt, this stranger to their world, lurking in the shadows behind it.

The drama played out and the time came for Drizzt to enact his movements in the battle. He heard the svirfnebli gasp in unison as he sprang lightly onto the basilisk's back, carefully picking his steps up toward the thing's head. Drizzt became caught up in their excitement, and this only heightened his memories.

It all became so real.

The deep gnomes moved in close, anticipating a dazzling display of swordsmanship from this remarkable drow who had come to them from the wilds of the Underdark.

Then something terrible happened.

One moment he was Drizzt the showman, entertaining his new friends with a tale of courage and weaponry. The next moment, as the drow lifted one of his pole props to strike at the phony monster, he was Drizzt no longer. The hunter stood atop the basilisk, just as he had that day back in the tunnels outside the moss filled cave.

Poles jabbed at the monster's eyes; poles slammed viciously into the stone head.

The svirfnebli backed away, some in fear, others in simple caution. The hunter pounded away, and the stone chipped and cracked. The slab that served as the creature's head broke away and fell, the dark elf tumbling behind. The hunter went down in a precise roll, came back to his feet, and charged right back in, slamming away furiously with his poles. The wooden weapons snapped apart and Drizzt's hands bled, but he—the hunter—would not yield.

Strong deep gnome hands grabbed the drow by the arms, trying to calm him. The hunter spun on his newest adversaries. They were stronger than he, and two held him tightly, but a few deft twists had the svirfnebli off balance. The hunter kicked at their knees and dropped to his own, turning about as he fell and launching the two svirfnebli into headlong rolls.

The hunter was up at once, broken scimitars at the ready as a single foe moved in at him.

Belwar showed no fear, held his arms defenselessly out wide. "Drizzt!" he called over and over. "Drizzt Do'Urden!"

The hunter eyed the svirfnebli's hammer and pick, and the sight of the mithral hands invoked soothing memories. Suddenly, he was Drizzt again. Stunned and ashamed, he dropped the poles and eyed his scraped hands.

Belwar caught the drow as he swooned, hoisted him up in his arms and carried him back to his hammock.

⚔ ⚔ ⚔ ⚔ ⚔

Troubled dreams invaded Drizzt's sleep, memories of the Underdark and of that other, darker self that he could not escape.

"How can I explain?" he asked Belwar when the burrow-warden found him sitting on the edge of the stone table later that night. "How can I possibly offer an apology?"

"None is needed," Belwar said to him.

Drizzt looked at him incredulously. "You do not understand," Drizzt began, wondering how he could possibly make the burrow-warden comprehend the depth of what had come over him.

"Many years you have lived out in the Underdark," Belwar said, "surviving where others could not."

"But have I survived?" Drizzt wondered aloud.

Belwar's hammer-hand patted the drow's shoulder gently, and the burrow-warden sat down on the table beside him. There they remained throughout the night. Drizzt said no more, and Belwar didn't press him. The burrow-warden knew his role that night: a silent support.

Neither knew how many hours had passed when Seldig's voice came in from beyond the door. "Come, Drizzt Do'Urden," the young deep gnome called. "Come and tell us more tales of the Underdark."

Drizzt looked at Belwar curiously, wondering if the request was part of some devious trick or ironic joke.

Belwar's smile dispelled that notion. "*Magga cammara*, dark elf," the deep gnome chuckled. "They'll not let you hide."

"Send them away," Drizzt insisted.

"So willing are you to surrender?" Belwar retorted, a distinct edge to his normally round-toned voice. "You who have survived the trials of the wilds?"

"Too dangerous," Drizzt explained desperately, searching for the words. "I cannot control . . . cannot be rid of . . ."

"Go with them, dark elf," Belwar said. "They will be more cautious this time."

"This . . . beast . . . follows me," Drizzt tried to explain.

"Perhaps for a while," the burrow-warden replied casually. "*Magga cammara*, Drizzt Do'Urden! Five tendays is not such a long time, not measured against the trials you have endured over the last ten years. Your freedom will be gained from this . . . beast."

Drizzt's lavender eyes found only sincerity in Belwar Dissengulp's dark gray orbs.

"But only if you seek it," the burrow-warden finished.

"Come out, Drizzt Do'Urden," Seldig called again from beyond the stone door.

This time, and every time in the days to come, Drizzt, and only Drizzt, answered the call.

⚔ ⚔ ⚔ ⚔ ⚔

The myconid king watched the dark elf prowl across the cavern's moss-covered lower level. It was not the same drow that had left, the fungoid knew, but Drizzt, an ally, had been the king's only previous contact with the dark elves. Oblivious to its peril, the eleven-foot giant crept down to intercept the stranger.

The spirit-wraith of Zaknafein did not even attempt to flee or hide as the animated mushroom-man closed in. Zaknafein's swords were comfortably set in his hands. The myconid king puffed a cloud of spores, seeking a telepathic conversation with the newcomer.

But undead monsters existed on two distinct planes, and their minds were impervious to such attempts. Zaknafein's material body faced the myconid, but the spirit-wraith's mind was far distant, linked to his corporeal form by Matron Malice's will. The spirit-wraith closed over the last few feet to his adversary.

The myconid puffed a second cloud, this one of spores designed to pacify an opponent, and this cloud was equally futile. The spirit-wraith came on steadily, and the giant raised its powerful arms to strike it down.

Zaknafein blocked the swings with quick cuts of his razor-edged swords, severing the myconid's hands. Too fast to follow, the spirit-wraith's weapons slashed at the king's mushroomlike torso, and dug deep wounds that drove the fungoid backward and to the ground.

From the top level, dozens of the older and stronger myconids lumbered down to rescue their injured king. The spirit-wraith saw their approach but did not know fear. Zaknafein finished his business with the giant, then turned calmly to meet the assault.

Fungus-men came on, blasting their various spores. Zaknafein ignored the clouds, none of which could possibly affect him, and concentrated fully on the clubbing arms. Myconids came charging in all around him.

And they died all around him.

They had tended their grove for centuries untold, living in peace and going about their own way. But when the spirit-wraith returned from the crawl-tunnel that led to the now-abandoned small cave that once had served as Drizzt's home, Zak's fury would tolerate no semblance of peace. Zaknafein rushed up the wall to the mushroom grove, hacking at everything in his path.

Giant mushrooms tumbled like cut trees. Below, the small rothé herd, nervous by nature, broke into a frenzied stampede and rushed out into the tunnels of the open Underdark. The few remaining fungus-men, having witnessed the power of this dark elf, scrambled to get out of his thrashing way. But myconids were not fast-moving creatures, and Zaknafein relentlessly chased them down.

Their reign in the moss-covered cave, and the mushroom grove they had tended for so very long, came to a sudden and final end.

# 9 Whispers in the Tunnels

The svirfneblin patrol inched its way around the bends of the broken and twisting tunnel, war hammers and pickaxes held at the ready. The deep gnomes were not far from Blingdenstone—less than a day out—but they had gone into their practiced battle formations usually reserved for the deep Underdark.

The tunnel reeked of death.

The lead deep gnome, knowing that the carnage lay just beyond, gingerly peeked over a boulder. *Goblins!* his senses cried out to his companions, a clear voice in the racial empathy of the svirfnebli. When the dangers of the Underdark closed in on the deep gnomes, they rarely spoke aloud, reverting to a communal empathic bond that could convey basic thoughts.

The other svirfnebli clutched their weapons and began deciphering a battle plan from the excited jumble of their mental communications. The leader, still the only one who had peered over the boulder, halted them with an overriding notion. *Dead goblins!*

The others followed him around the boulder to the grisly scene. A score of goblins lay about, hacked and torn.

"Drow," one of the svirfneblin party whispered, after seeing the precision of the wounds and the obvious ease with which the blades had cut through the unfortunate creatures' hides. Among the Underdark races, only the drow wielded such slender and wicked-edged blades.

*Too close,* another deep gnome responded empathetically, punching the speaker on the shoulder.

"These have been dead for a day and more," another said aloud, refuting his companion's caution. "The dark elves would not lie in wait in the area. It is not their way."

"Nor is it their way to slaughter bands of goblins," the one who had insisted on the silent communications replied. "Not when there are prisoners to be taken!"

"They would take prisoners only if they meant to return directly to Menzoberranzan," remarked the first. He turned to the leader. "Burrow-Warden Krieger, at once we must go back to Blingdenstone and report this carnage!"

"A thin report it would be," Krieger replied. "Dead goblins in the tunnels? It is not such an uncommon sight."

"This is not the first sign of drow activity in the region," the other remarked. The burrow-warden could deny neither the truth of his companion's words nor the wisdom of the suggestion. Two other patrols had returned to Blingdenstone recently with tales of dead monsters—most probably slain by drow elves—lying in the corridors of the Underdark.

"And look," the other deep gnome continued, bending low to scoop a pouch off one of the goblins. He opened it to reveal a handful of gold and silver coins. "What dark elf would be so impatient as to leave such booty behind?"

"Can we be sure that this was the doings of the drow?" Krieger asked, though he himself did not doubt the fact. "Perhaps some other creature has come to our realm. Or possibly some lesser foe, goblin or orc, has found drow weapons."

*Drow!* the thoughts of several of the others agreed immediately.

"The cuts were swift and precise," said one. "And I see nothing to indicate any wounds beyond those suffered by the goblins. Who else but dark elves are so efficient in their killing?"

Burrow-Warden Krieger walked off alone a bit farther down the passage, searching the stone for some clue to this mystery. Deep gnomes possessed an affinity to the rock beyond that of most creatures, but this passage's stone walls told the burrow-warden nothing. The goblins had been killed by weapons, not the clawed hands of monsters, yet they hadn't been looted. All of the kills were confined to a small area, showing that the unfortunate goblins hadn't even found the time to flee. That twenty goblins were cut down so quickly implicated a drow patrol of some size, and even if there had been only a handful of the dark elves, one of them, at least, would have pillaged the bodies.

"Where shall we go, Burrow-Warden?" one of the deep gnomes asked at Krieger's back. "Onward to scout out the reported mineral cache or back to Blingdenstone to report this?"

Krieger was a wily old svirfneblin who thought that he knew every trick of the Underdark. He wasn't fond of mysteries, but this scene had him scratching his bald head without a clue. Back, he relayed to the others, reverting to the silent empathic method. He found no arguments among his kin; deep gnomes always took great care to avoid drow elves whenever possible.

The patrol promptly shifted into a tight defensive formation and began its trek back home.

Levitating off to the side, in the shadows of the high ceiling's stalactites, the spirit-wraith of Zaknafein Do'Urden watched their progress and marked well their path.

⚔ ⚔ ⚔ ⚔ ⚔

King Schnicktick leaned forward in his stone throne and considered the burrow-warden's words carefully. Schnicktick's councilors, seated around him, were equally curious and nervous, for this report only confirmed the two previous tales of potential drow activity in the eastern tunnels.

"Why would Menzoberranzan be edging in on our borders?" one of the councilors asked when Krieger had finished. "Our agents have made no mention of any intent of war. Surely we would have had some indications if Menzoberranzan's ruling council planned something dramatic."

"We would," King Schnicktick agreed, to silence the nervous chatter that sprang up in the wake of the councilor's grim words. "To all of you I offer the reminder that we do not know if the perpetrators of these reported kills were drow elves at all."

"Your pardon, my King," Krieger began tentatively.

"Yes, Burrow-Warden," Schnicktick replied immediately, slowly waving one stubby hand before his craggy face to prevent any protests. "You are quite certain of your observations. And well enough do I know you to trust in your judgments. Until this drow patrol has been seen, however, no assumptions will I make."

"Then we may agree only that something dangerous has invaded our eastern region," another of the councilors put in.

"Yes," answered the svirfneblin king. "We must set about discovering the truth of the matter. The eastern tunnels are therefore sealed from further mining expeditions." Schnicktick again waved his hands to calm the ensuing groans. "I know that several promising veins of ore have been reported—we will get to them as soon as we may. But for the present, the east, northeast, and southeast regions are hereby declared war patrol exclusive. The patrols will be doubled, both in the number of groups and in the size of each, and their range will be extended to encompass all the region within a three-day march of Blingdenstone. Quickly must this mystery be resolved."

"What of our agents in the drow city?" asked a councilor. "Should we make contact?"

Schnicktick held his palms out. "Be at ease," he explained. "We will keep our ears open wide, but let us not inform our enemies that we suspect their movements." The svirfneblin king did not have to express his concerns that their agents within Menzoberranzan could not be entirely relied upon. The informants might readily accept svirfneblin gemstones in exchange for minor information, but if the powers of Menzoberranzan were planning something drastic in Blingdenstone's direction, agents would quite likely work double-deals against the deep gnomes.

"If we hear any unusual reports from Menzoberranzan," the king continued, "or if we discover that the intruders are indeed drow elves, then we will increase our network's actions. Until then, let the patrols learn what they may."

The king dismissed his council then, preferring to remain alone in his throne room to consider the grim news. Earlier that same tenday, Schnicktick had heard of Drizzt's savage attack on the basilisk effigy.

Lately, it seemed, King Schnicktick of Blingdenstone had heard too much of dark elves' exploits.

⚔ ⚔ ⚔ ⚔ ⚔

The svirfneblin scouting patrols moved farther out into the eastern tunnels. Even those groups that found nothing came back to Blingdenstone full of suspicions, for they had sensed a stillness in the Underdark beyond the quiet norm. Not a single svirfneblin had been injured so far, but none seemed anxious to travel out on the patrols. There was something evil in the tunnels, they knew instinctively, something that killed without question and without mercy.

One patrol found the moss-covered cavern that once had served as Drizzt's sanctuary. King Schnicktick was saddened when he heard that the peaceable myconids and their treasured mushroom grove were destroyed.

Yet, for all of the endless hours the svirfnebli spent wandering the tunnels, not an enemy did they spot. They continued with their assumption that dark elves, so secretive and brutal, were involved.

"And we now have a drow living in our city," a deep gnome councilor reminded the king during one of their daily sessions.

"Has he caused any trouble?" Schnicktick asked.

"Minor," replied the councilor. "And Belwar Dissengulp, the Most Honored Burrow-Warden, speaks for him still and keeps him in his house as guest, not prisoner. Burrow-Warden Dissengulp will accept no guards around the drow."

"Have the drow watched," the king said after a moment of consideration. "But from a distance. If he is a friend, as Master Dissengulp most obviously believes, then he should not suffer our intrusions."

"And what of the patrols?" asked another councilor, this one a representative from the entrance cavern that housed the city guard. "My soldiers grow weary. They have seen nothing beyond a few signs of battle, have heard nothing but the scrape of their own tired feet."

"We must be alert," King Schnicktick reminded him. "If the dark elves are massing . . ."

"They are not," the councilor replied firmly. "We have found no camp, nor any trace of a camp. This patrol from Menzoberranzan, if it is a patrol, attacks and then retreats to some sanctuary we cannot locate, possibly magically inspired."

"And if the dark elves truly meant to attack Blingdenstone," offered another, "would they leave so many signs of their activity? The first slaughter, the goblins found by Burrow-Warden Krieger's expedition, occurred nearly a tenday ago, and the tragedy of the myconids was some time before that. I have never heard of dark elves wandering about an enemy city, and leaving signs such as slaughtered goblins, for days before they execute their full attack."

The king had been thinking along the same lines for some time. When he awoke each day and found Blingdenstone intact, the threat of a war with Menzoberranzan seemed more distant. but though Schnicktick took comfort in the similar reasoning of his councilor, he could not ignore the gruesome scenes his soldiers had been finding in the eastern tunnels. Something, probably drow, was down there, too close for his liking.

"Let us assume that Menzoberranzan does not plan war against us at this time," Schnicktick offered. "Then why are drow elves so close to our doorway? Why would drow elves haunt the eastern tunnels of Blingdenstone, so far from home?"

"Expansion?" replied one councilor.

"Renegade raiders?" questioned another. Neither possibility seemed very likely. Then a third councilor chirped in a suggestion, so simple that it caught the others off guard.

"They are looking for something."

The king of the svirfnebli dropped his dimpled chin heavily into his hands, thinking he had just heard a possible solution to the puzzle and feeling foolish that he had not thought of it before.

"But what?" asked one of the councilors, obviously feeling the same. "Dark elves rarely mine the stone—they do not do it very well when they try, I must add—and they would not have to go so far from Menzoberranzan to find precious minerals. What, so near to Blingdenstone, might the dark elves be looking for?"

"Something they have lost," replied the king. Immediately his thoughts went to the drow that had come to live among his people. It all seemed too much of a coincidence to be ignored. "Or someone," Schnicktick added, and the others did not miss his point.

"Perhaps we should invite our drow guest to sit with us in council?"

"No," the king replied. "But perhaps our distant surveillance of this Drizzt is not enough. Get orders to Belwar Dissengulp that the drow is to be monitored every minute. and Firble," he said to the councilor nearest him. "Since we have reasonably concluded that no war is imminent with the dark elves, set the spy network into motion. Get me information from Menzoberranzan, and quickly. I like not the prospect of dark elves wandering about my front door. It does so diminish the neighborhood."

Councilor Firble, the chief of covert security in Blingdenstone, nodded in agreement, though he wasn't pleased by the request. Information from Menzoberranzan was not cheaply gained, and it as often turned out to be a calculated deception as the truth. Firble did not like dealing with anyone or anything that could outsmart him, and he numbered dark elves as first on that ill-favored list.

⚔ ⚔ ⚔ ⚔ ⚔

The spirit-wraith watched as yet another svirfneblin patrol made its way down the twisting tunnel. The tactical wisdom of the being that once had been the finest weapon master in all of Menzoberranzan had kept the undead monster and his anxious sword arm in check for the last few days. Zaknafein did not truly understand the significance of the increasing number of deep gnome patrols, but he sensed that his mission would be put into jeopardy if he struck out against one of them. At the very least, his attack against so organized a foe would send alarms ringing throughout the corridors, alarms that the elusive Drizzt surely would hear.

Similarly, the spirit-wraith had sublimated his vicious urges against other living things and had left the svirfneblin patrols nothing to find in the last few days, purposely avoiding conflicts with the many denizens of the region. Matron Malice Do'Urden's evil will followed Zaknafein's every move, pounding relentlessly at his thoughts, urging him on with a great vengeance. Any killing that Zaknafein did sated that insidious will temporarily, but the undead thing's tactical wisdom overruled the savage summons. The slight flicker that was Zaknafein's remaining reasoning knew that he would only find his return to the peace of death when Drizzt Do'Urden joined him in his eternal sleep.

The spirit-wraith kept his swords in their sheaths as he watched the deep gnomes pass by.

Then, as still another group of weary svirfnebli made its way back to the west, another flicker of cognition stirred within the spirit-wraith. If these deep gnomes were so prominent in this region, it seemed likely that Drizzt Do'Urden would have encountered them.

This time, Zaknafein did not let the deep gnomes wander out beyond his sight. He floated down from the concealment of the stalactite-strewn ceiling and fell into pace behind the patrol. The name of Blingdenstone bobbed at the edge of his conscious grasp, a memory of his past life.

"Blingdenstone," the spirit-wraith tried to speak aloud, the first word Matron Malice's undead monster had tried to utter. But the name came out as no more than an undecipherable snarl.

# 10
# Belwar's Guilt

Drizzt went out with Seldig and his new friends many times during the passing days. The young deep gnomes, on advice from Belwar, kept their time with the drow elf in calm and unobtrusive games; no more did they press Drizzt for re-enactments of exciting battles he had fought in the wilds.

For the first few times Drizzt went out, Belwar watched him from the door. The burrow-warden did trust Drizzt, but he also understood the trials the drow had endured. A life of savagery and brutality such as the one Drizzt had known could not so easily be dismissed.

Soon, though, it became apparent to Belwar, and to all the others who observed Drizzt, that the drow had settled into a comfortable rhythm with the young deep gnomes and posed little threat to any of the svirfnebli of Blingdenstone. Even King Schnicktick, worried of the events beyond the city's borders, came to agree that Drizzt could be trusted.

"You have a visitor," Belwar said to Drizzt one morning. Drizzt followed the burrow-warden's movements to the stone door, thinking Seldig had come to call on him early this day. When Belwar opened the door, though, Drizzt nearly toppled over in surprise, for it was no svirfneblin that bounded into the stone structure. Rather, it was a huge and black feline form.

"Guenhwyvar!" Drizzt cried out, dropping into a low crouch to catch the rushing panther. Guenhwyvar bowled him over, playfully swatting him with a great paw.

When at last Drizzt managed to get out from under the panther and into a sitting position, Belwar walked over to him and handed him the onyx figurine. "Surely the councilor charged with examining the panther was sorry to part with it," the burrow-warden said. "But Guenhwyvar is your friend, first and most."

Drizzt could not find the words to reply. Even before the panther's return, the deep gnomes of Blingdenstone had treated him better than he deserved, or so he believed. Now for the svirfnebli to return so powerful a magical item, to show him such absolute trust, touched him deeply.

"At your leisure you may return to the House Center, the building in which you were detained when first you came to us," Belwar went on, "and retrieve your weapons and armor."

Drizzt was a bit tentative at the notion, remembering the incident at the mock-up of the basilisk. What damage might he have wrought that day if he had been armed, not with poles, but with fine drow scimitars?

"We will keep them here and keep them safe," Belwar said, understanding his friend's sudden distress. "If you need them, you will have them."

"I am in your debt," Drizzt replied. "In the debt of all Blingdenstone."

"We do not consider friendship a debt," the burrow-warden replied with a wink. He left Drizzt and Guenhwyvar then and went back into the cave-room of his house, allowing the two dear friends a private reunion.

Seldig and the other young deep gnomes were in for quite a treat that day when Drizzt came out to join them with Guenhwyvar by his side. Seeing the cat at play with the svirfnebli, Drizzt could not help but remember that tragic day, a decade before, when Masoj had used Guenhwyvar to hunt down the last of Belwar's fleeing miners. Apparently, Guenhwyvar had dismissed that awful memory altogether, for the panther and the young deep gnomes frolicked together for the entire day.

Drizzt wished only that he could so readily dismiss the errors of his past.

⚔ ⚔ ⚔ ⚔ ⚔

"Most Honored Burrow-Warden," came a call a couple of days later, while Belwar and Drizzt were enjoying their morning meal. Belwar paused and sat perfectly still, and Drizzt did not miss the unexpected cloud of pain that crossed his host's broad features. Drizzt had come to know the svirfneblin so very well, and when Belwar's long, hawklike nose turned up in a certain way, it inevitably signaled the burrow-warden's distress.

"The king has reopened the eastern tunnels," the voice continued. "There are rumors of a thick vein of ore only a day's march. It would do honor to my expedition if Belwar Dissengulp would find his way to accompany us."

A hopeful smile widened on Drizzt's face, not for any thoughts he had of venturing out, but because he had noticed that Belwar seemed a bit too reclusive in the otherwise open svirfneblin community.

"Burrow-Warden Brickers," Belwar explained to Drizzt grimly, not sharing the drow's budding enthusiasm in the least. "One of those who comes to my door before every expedition, bidding me to join in the journey."

"And you never go," Drizzt reasoned.

Belwar shrugged. "A courtesy call, nothing more," he said, his nose twitching and his wide teeth grating together.

"You are not worthy to march beside them," Drizzt added, his tone dripping with sarcasm. At last, he believed, he had found the source of his friend's frustration.

Again Belwar shrugged.

Drizzt scowled at him. "I have seen you at work with your mithral hands," he said. "You would be no detriment to any party! Indeed, far more! Do you so quickly consider yourself crippled, when those about you do not?"

Belwar slammed his hammer-hand down on the table, sending a fair-sized crack running through the stone. "I can cut rock faster than the lot of them!" the burrow-warden growled fiercely. "And if monsters descended upon us . . ." He waved his pickaxe-hand in a menacing way, and Drizzt did not doubt that the barrel-chested deep gnome could put the instrument to good use.

"Enjoy the day, Most Honored Burrow-Warden," came a final cry from outside the door. "As ever, we shall respect your decision, but as ever, we also shall lament your absence."

Drizzt stared curiously at Belwar. "Why, then?" he asked at length. "If you are as competent as all—yourself included—agree, why do you remain behind? I know the love svirfnebli have for such expeditions, yet you are not interested. Nor do you ever speak of your own adventures outside Blingdenstone. Is it my presence that holds you at home? Are you bound to watch over me?"

"No," Belwar replied, his booming voice echoing back several times in Drizzt's keen ears. "You have been granted the return of your weapons, dark elf. Do not doubt our trust."

"But . . ." Drizzt began, but he stopped short, suddenly realizing the truth of the deep gnome's reluctance. "The fight," he said softly, almost apologetically. "That evil day more than a decade ago."

Belwar's nose verily rolled up over itself, and he briskly turned away.

"You blame yourself for the loss of your kin!" Drizzt continued, gaining volume as he gained confidence in his reasoning. Still, the drow could hardly believe his words as he spoke them.

But when Belwar turned back on him, the burrow-warden's eyes were rimmed with wetness and Drizzt knew that the words had struck home.

Drizzt ran a hand through his thick white mane, not really knowing how to respond to Belwar's dilemma. Drizzt personally had led the drow party against the svirfnebli mining group, and he knew that no blame for the disaster could rightly be placed on any of the deep gnomes. Yet, how could Drizzt possibly explain that to Belwar?

"I remember that fated day," Drizzt began tentatively. "Vividly I remember it, as if that evil moment will be frozen in my thoughts, never to recede."

"No more than in mine," the burrow-warden whispered. Drizzt nodded his accord. "Equally, though," he said, "for I find myself caught within the very same web of guilt that entraps you."

Belwar looked at him curiously, not really understanding.

"It was I who led the drow patrol," Drizzt explained. "I found your troupe, errantly believing you to be marauders intending to descend upon Menzoberranzan."

"If not you, then another," Belwar replied.

"But none could have led them as well as I," Drizzt said. "Out there—" he glanced at the door—"in the wilds, I was at home. That was my domain."

Belwar was listening to his every word now, just as Drizzt had hoped.

"And it was I who defeated the earth elemental," Drizzt continued, speaking matter-of-factly, not cockily. "Had it not been for my presence, the battle would have proved equal. Many svirfnebli would have survived to return to Blingdenstone."

Belwar could not hide his smile. There was a measure of truth in Drizzt's words, for Drizzt had indeed been a major factor in the drow attack's success. But Belwar found Drizzt's attempt to dispel his guilt a bit of a stretch of the truth.

"I do not understand how you can blame yourself," Drizzt said, now smiling and hoping that his levity would bring some measure of comfort to his friend. "With Drizzt Do'Urden at the lead of the drow party, you never had a chance"

"*Magga cammara*! It is a painful subject to jest of," Belwar replied, though he chuckled in spite of himself even as he spoke the words.

"Agreed," said Drizzt, his tone suddenly serious. "But dismissing the tragedy in a jest is no more ridiculous than living mired in guilt for a blameless incident. No, not blameless," Drizzt quickly corrected himself. "The blame lies on the shoulders of Menzoberranzan and its inhabitants. It is the way of the drow that caused the tragedy. It is the wicked existence they live, every day, that doomed your expedition's peaceable miners."

"Charged with the responsibility of his group is a burrow-warden," Belwar retorted. "Only a burrow-warden may call an expedition. He must then accept the responsibility of his decision."

"You chose to lead the deep gnomes so close to Menzoberranzan?" Drizzt asked.

"I did."

"Of your own volition?" Drizzt pressed. He believed that he understood the ways of the deep gnomes well enough to know that most, if not all, of their important decisions were democratically resolved. "Without the word of Belwar Dissengulp, the mining party would never have come into that region?"

"We knew of the find," Belwar explained. "A rich cache of ore. It was decided in council that we should risk the nearness to Menzoberranzan. I led the appointed party."

"If not you, then another," Drizzt said pointedly, mimicking Belwar's earlier words.

"A burrow-warden must accept the respons—" Belwar began, his gaze drifting away from Drizzt.

"They do not blame you," Drizzt said, following Belwar's empty stare to the blank stone door. "They honor you and care for you."

"They pity me!" Belwar snarled.

"Do you need their pity?" Drizzt cried back. "Are you less than they? A helpless cripple?"

"Never I was!"

"Then go out with them!" Drizzt yelled at him. "See if they truly pity you. I do not believe that at all, but if your assumptions prove true, if your people do pity their 'Most Honored Burrow-Warden,' then show them the truth of Belwar Dissengulp! If your companions mantle upon you neither pity nor blame, then do not place either burden upon your own shoulders!"

Belwar stared at his friend for a very long moment, but he did not reply.

"All the miners who accompanied you knew the risk of venturing so close to Menzoberranzan," Drizzt reminded him. A smile widened on Drizzt's face. "None of them, yourself included, knew that Drizzt Do'Urden would lead your drow opponents against you. If you had, you certainly would have stayed at home."

"*Magga cammara*," Belwar mumbled. He shook his head in disbelief, both at Drizzt's joking attitude and at the fact that, for the first time in over a decade, he did feel better about those tragic memories. He rose up from the stone table, flashed a grin at Drizzt, and headed for the inner room of his house.

"Where are you going?" Drizzt asked.

"To rest," replied the burrow-warden. "The events of this day have already wearied me."

"The mining expedition will depart without you."

Belwar turned back and cast an incredulous stare at Drizzt. Did the drow really expect that Belwar would so easily refute years of guilt and just go bounding off with the miners?

"I had thought Belwar Dissengulp possessed more courage," Drizzt said to him. The scowl that crossed the burrow-warden's face was genuine, and Drizzt knew that he had found a weakness in Belwar's armor of self-pity.

"Boldly do you speak," Belwar growled through a grimace.

"Boldly to a coward," Drizzt replied. The mithral-handed svirfneblin stalked in, his breathing coming in great heaves of his densely muscled chest.

"If you do not like the title, then cast it away!" Drizzt growled in his face. "Go with the miners. Show them the truth of Belwar Dissengulp, and learn it for yourself!"

Belwar banged his mithral hands together. "Run out then and get your weapons!" he commanded. Drizzt hesitated. Had he just been challenged? Had he gone too far in his attempt to shake the burrow-warden loose of his guilty bonds?

"Get your weapons, Drizzt Do'Urden," Belwar growled again, "for if I am to go with the miners, then so are you!"

Elated, Drizzt clasped the deep gnome's head between his long, slender hands and banged his forehead softly into Belwar's, the two exchanging stares of deep admiration and affection. In an instant, Drizzt rushed away, scrambling to the House Central to retrieve his suit of finely meshed chain mail, his *piwafwi*, and his scimitars.

Belwar just banged a hand against his head in disbelief, nearly knocking himself from his feet, and watched Drizzt's wild dash out of the front door.

It would prove an interesting trip.

⚔ ⚔ ⚔ ⚔ ⚔

Burrow-Warden Brickers accepted Belwar and Drizzt readily, though he gave Belwar a curious look behind Drizzt's back, inquiring as to the drow's respectability. Even the doubting burrow-warden could not deny the value of a dark elf ally out in the wilds of the Underdark, particularly if the whispers of drow activity in the eastern tunnels proved to be true.

But the patrol saw no activity, or carnage, as they proceeded to the region named by the scouts. The rumors of a thick vein of ore were not exaggerated in the least, and the twenty-five miners of the expedition went to work with an eagerness unlike any the drow had ever witnessed. Drizzt was especially pleased for Belwar, for the burrow-warden's hammer and pickaxe hands chopped away at the stone with a precision and power that outdid any of the others. It didn't take long for Belwar to realize that he was not being pitied by his comrades in any way. He was a member of the expedition—an honored member and no detriment—who filled the wagons with more ore than any of his companions.

Through the days they spent in the twisting tunnels, Drizzt, and Guenhwyvar, when the cat was available, kept a watchful guard around the camp. After the first day of mining, Burrow-Warden Brickers assigned a third companion guard for the drow and panther, and Drizzt suspected correctly that his new svirfneblin companion had been appointed as much to watch him as to look for dangers from beyond. As the time passed, though, and the svirfneblin troupe became more accustomed to their ebon-skinned companion, Drizzt was left to roam about as he chose.

It was an uneventful and profitable trip, just the way the svirfnebli liked it, and soon, having encountered not a single monster, their wagons were filled with precious minerals. Clapping each other on the backs—Belwar being careful not to pat too hard—they gathered up their equipment, formed their pull-carts into a line, and set off for home, a journey that would take them two days bearing the heavy wagons.

After only a few hours of travel, one of the scouts ahead of the caravan returned, his face grim.

"What is it?" Burrow-Warden Brickers prompted, suspecting that their good fortune had ended.

"Goblin tribe," the svirfneblin scout replied. "Two score at the least. They have put up in a small chamber ahead—to the west and up a sloping passage."

Burrow-Warden Brickers banged a fist into a wagon. He did not doubt that his miners could handle the goblin band, but he wanted no trouble. Yet with the heavy wagons rumbling along noisily, avoiding the goblins would be no easy feat. "Pass the word back that we sit quiet," he decided at length. "If a fight there will be, let the goblins come to us."

"What is the trouble?" Drizzt asked Belwar as he came in at the back of the caravan. He had kept a rear guard since the troupe had broken camp.

"Band of goblins," Belwar replied. "Brickers says we stay low and hope they pass us by."

"And if they do not?" Drizzt had to ask.

Belwar tapped his hands together. "They're only goblins," he muttered grimly, "but I, and all my kin, wish the path had stayed clear."

It pleased Drizzt that his new companions were not so anxious for battle, even against an enemy they knew they could easily defeat. If Drizzt had been traveling beside a drow party, the whole of the goblin tribe probably would be dead or captured already.

"Come with me," Drizzt said to Belwar. "I need you to help Burrow-Warden Brickers understand me. I have a plan, but I fear that my limited command of your language will not allow me to explain its subtleties."

Belwar hooked Drizzt with his pickaxe-hand, spinning the slender drow about more roughly than he had intended. "No conflicts do we desire," he explained. "Better that the goblins go their own way."

"I wish for no fight," Drizzt assured him with a wink. Satisfied, the deep gnome fell into step behind Drizzt.

Brickers smiled widely as Belwar translated Drizzt's plan. "The expressions on the goblins' faces will be well worth seeing," Brickers laughed to Drizzt. "I should like to accompany you myself!"

"Better left for me," Belwar said. "Both the goblin and drow languages are known to me, and you have responsibilities back here, in case things do not go as we hope."

"The goblin tongue is known to me as well," Brickers replied. "And I can understand our dark elf companion well enough. As for my duties with the caravan, they are not as great as you believe, for another burrow-warden accompanies us this day."

"One who has not seen the wilds of the Underdark for many years," Belwar reminded him.

"Ah, but he was the finest of his trade," retorted Brickers. "The caravan is under your command, Burrow-Warden Belwar. I choose to go and meet with the goblins beside the drow."

Drizzt had understood enough of the words to fathom Brickers's general course of action. Before Belwar could argue, Drizzt put a hand on his shoulder and nodded. "If the goblins are not fooled and we need you, come in fast and hard," he said.

Then Brickers removed his gear and weapons, and Drizzt led him away. Belwar turned to the others cautiously, not knowing how they would feel about the decision. His first glance at the caravan's miners told him that they stood firmly behind him, every one, waiting and willing to carry out his commands.

Burrow-Warden Brickers was not the least disappointed with the expressions on the goblins' toothy and twisted faces when he and Drizzt walked into their midst. One goblin let out a shriek and lifted a spear to throw, but Drizzt, using his innate magical abilities, dropped a globe of darkness over its head, blinding it fully. The spear came out anyway and Drizzt snapped out a scimitar and sliced it from the air as it flew by.

Brickers, his hands bound, for he was emulating a prisoner in this farce, dropped his jaw open at the speed and ease with which the drow took down the flying spear. The svirfneblin then looked to the band of goblins and saw that they were similarly impressed.

"One more step and they are dead," Drizzt promised in the goblin tongue, a guttural language of grunts and whimpers. Brickers came to understand a moment later when he heard a wild shuffle of boots and a whimper from behind. The deep gnome turned to see two goblins, limned by the dancing purplish flames of the drow's faerie fire, scrambling away as fast as their floppy feet could carry them.

Again the svirfneblin looked at Drizzt in amazement. How had Drizzt even known that the sneaky goblins were back there?

Brickers, of course, could not know of the hunter, that other self of Drizzt Do'Urden that gave this drow a distinct edge in encounters such as this. Nor could the burrow-warden know that at that moment Drizzt was engaged in yet another struggle to control that dangerous alter ego.

Drizzt looked at the scimitar in his hand and back to the crowd of goblins. At least three dozen of them stood ready, yet the hunter beckoned Drizzt to attack, to bite hard into the cowardly monsters and send them fleeing down every passageway leading out of the room. One look at his bound svirfneblin companion, though, reminded Drizzt of his plan in coming here and allowed him to put the hunter to rest.

"Who is the leader?" he asked in guttural goblin.

The goblin chieftain was not so anxious to single itself out to a drow elf, but a dozen of its subordinates, showing typical goblin courage and loyalty, spun on their heels and poked their stubby fingers in its direction.

With no other choice, the goblin chieftain puffed out its chest, straightened its bony shoulders, and strode forward to face the drow. "Bruck!" the chieftain named itself, thumping a fist into its chest.

"Why are you here?" Drizzt sneered as he said it.

Bruck simply did not know how to answer such a question. Never before had the goblin thought to ask permission for its tribe's movements.

"This region belongs to the drow!" Drizzt growled. "You do not belong here!"

"Drow city many walks," Bruck complained, pointing over Drizzt's head—the wrong way to Menzoberranzan, Drizzt noted, but he let the error pass. "This svirfneblin land."

"For now," replied Drizzt, prodding Brickers with the butt of his scimitar. "But my people have decided to claim the region as our own." A small flame flickered in Drizzt's lavender eyes and a devious smile spread across his face. "Will Bruck and the goblin tribe oppose us?"

Bruck held its long-fingered hands out helplessly.

"Be gone!" Drizzt demanded. "We have no need of slaves now, nor do we wish the revealing sound of battle echoing down the tunnels! Name yourself as lucky, Bruck. Your tribe will flee and live . . . this time!"

Bruck turned to the others, looking for some assistance. Only one drow elf had come against them, while more than three dozen goblins stood ready with their weapons. The odds were promising if not overwhelming.

"Be gone!" Drizzt commanded, pointing his scimitar at a side passage. "Run until your feet grow too weary to carry you!"

The goblin chieftain defiantly hooked its fingers into the piece of rope holding up its loincloth.

A cacophonous banging sounded all around the small chamber then, showing the tempo of purposeful drumming on the stone. Bruck and the other goblins looked around nervously, and Drizzt did not miss the opportunity.

"You dare defy us?" the drow cried, causing Bruck to be edged by the purple-glowing flames. "Then let stupid Bruck be the first to die!"

Before Drizzt even finished the sentence, the goblin chieftain was gone, running with all speed down the passage Drizzt had indicated. Justifying the flight as loyalty to their chieftain, the whole lot of the goblin tribe set off in quick pursuit. The swiftest even passed Bruck by.

A few moments later, Belwar and the other svirfneblin miners appeared at every passage. "Thought you might need some support," the mithral-handed burrow-warden explained, tapping his hammer hand on the stone.

"Perfect was your timing and your judgment, Most Honored Burrow-Warden," Brickers said to his peer when he managed to stop laughing. "Perfect, as we have come to expect from Belwar Dissengulp!"

A short while later, the svirfneblin caravan started on its way again, the whole troupe excited and elated by the events of the last few days. The deep gnomes thought themselves very clever in the way they had avoided trouble. The gaiety turned into a full-fledged party when they arrived in Blingdenstone—and svirfnebli, though usually a serious, work-minded people, threw parties as well as any race in all the Realms.

Drizzt Do'Urden, for all of his physical differences with the svirfnebli, felt more at home and at ease than he had ever felt in all the four decades of his life.

And never again did Belwar Dissengulp flinch when a fellow svirfneblin addressed him as "Most Honored Burrow-Warden."

The spirit-wraith was confused. Just as Zaknafein had begun to believe that his prey was within the svirfneblin city, the magical spells that Malice had placed upon him sensed Drizzt's presence in the tunnels. Luckily for Drizzt and the svirfneblin miners, the spirit-wraith had been far away when he caught the scent. Zaknafein worked his way back through the tunnels, dodging deep gnome patrols. Every potential encounter he avoided proved a struggle for Zaknafein, for Matron Malice, back on her throne in Menzoberranzan, grew increasingly impatient and agitated.

Malice wanted the taste of blood, but Zaknafein kept to his purpose, closing in on Drizzt. But then, suddenly, the scent was gone.

⚔ ⚔ ⚔ ⚔ ⚔

Bruck groaned aloud when another solitary dark elf wandered into his encampment the next day. No spears were hoisted and no goblins even attempted to sneak up behind this one.

"We went as we were ordered!" Bruck complained, moving to the front of the group before he was called upon. The goblin chieftain knew now that his underlings would point him out anyway.

If the spirit-wraith even understood the goblin's words, he did not show it in any way. Zaknafein kept walking straight at the goblin chieftain, his swords in his hands.

"But we—" Bruck began, but the rest of his words came out as gurgles of blood. Zaknafein tore his sword out of the goblin's throat and rushed at the rest of the group.

Goblins scattered in all directions. A few, trapped between the crazed drow and the stone wall, raised crude spears in defense. The spirit wraith waded through them, hacking away weapons and limbs with every slice. One goblin poked through the spinning swords, the tip of its spear burying deep into Zaknafein's hip.

The undead monster didn't even flinch. Zak turned on the goblin and struck it with a series of lightning-fast, perfectly aimed blows that took its head and both of its arms from its body.

In the end, fifteen goblins lay dead in the chamber and the tribe was scattered and still running down every passage in the region. The spirit-wraith, covered in the blood of his enemies, exited the chamber through the passage opposite from the one in which he had entered, continuing his frustrated search for the elusive Drizzt Do'Urden.

⚔ ⚔ ⚔ ⚔ ⚔

Back in Menzoberranzan, in the anteroom to the chapel of House Do'Urden, Matron Malice rested, thoroughly exhausted and momentarily sated. She had felt every kill as Zaknafein made it, had felt a burst of ecstacy every time her spirit-wraith's sword had plunged into another victim.

Malice pushed away her frustrations and her impatience, her confidence renewed by the pleasures of Zaknafein's cruel slaughter. How great Malice's ecstacy would be when the spirit-wraith at last encountered her traitorous son!

# II
# The Informant

Councilor Firble of Blingdenstone moved tentatively into the small rough-hewn cavern, the appointed meeting place. An army of svirfnebli, including several deep gnome enchanters holding stones that could summon earth elemental allies, moved into defensive positions all along the corridors to the west of the room. Despite this, Firble was not at ease. He looked down the eastern tunnel, the only other entrance into the chamber, wondering what information his agent would have for him and worrying over how much it would cost.

Then the drow made his swaggering entrance, his high black boots kicking loudly on the stone. His gaze darted about quickly to ensure that Firble was the only svirfneblin in the chamber—their usual deal—then strode up to the deep gnome councilor and dropped into a low bow.

"Greetings, little friend with the big purse," the drow said with a laugh. His command of the svirfneblin language and dialect, with the perfect inflections and pauses of a deep gnome who had lived a century in Blingdenstone, always amazed Firble.

"You could exercise some caution," Firble retorted, again glancing around anxiously.

"Bah," the drow snorted, clicking the hard heels of his boots together. "You have an army of deep gnome fighters and wizards behind you, and I . . . well, let us just agree that I am well protected as well."

"That fact I do not doubt, Jarlaxle," Firble replied. "Still, I would prefer that our business remain as private and as secretive as possible."

"All of the business of Bregan D'aerthe is private, my dear Firble," Jarlaxle answered, and again he bowed low, sweeping his wide-brimmed hat in a long and graceful arc.

"Enough of that," said Firble. "Let us be done with our business, so that I may return to my home."

"Then ask," said Jarlaxle.

"There has been an increase in drow activity near Blingdenstone," explained the deep gnome.

"Has there?" Jarlaxle asked, appearing surprised. The drow's smirk revealed his true emotions, though. This would be an easy profit for Jarlaxle, for the very same matron mother in Menzoberranzan who had recently employed him was undoubtedly connected with the Blingdenstone's distress. Jarlaxle liked coincidences that made the profits come easy.

Firble knew the ploy of feigned surprise all too well. "There has," he said firmly.

"And you wish to know why?" Jarlaxle reasoned, still holding a facade of ignorance.

"It would seem prudent, from our vantage point," huffed the councilor, tired of Jarlaxle's unending game. Firble knew without any doubts that Jarlaxle was aware of the drow activity near Blingdenstone, and of the purpose behind it. Jarlaxle was a rogue without house, normally an unhealthy position in the world of the dark elves. Yet this resourceful mercenary survived—even thrived—in his renegade position. Through it all, Jarlaxle's greatest advantage was knowledge—knowledge of every stirring within Menzoberranzan and the regions surrounding the city.

"How long will you require?" Firble asked. "My king wishes to complete this business as swiftly as possible."

"Have you my payment?" the drow asked, holding out a hand.

"Payment when you bring me the information," Firble protested. "That has always been our agreement."

"So it has," agreed Jarlaxle. "This time, though, I need no time to gather your information. If you have my gems, we can be done with our business right now."

Firble pulled the pouch of gems from his belt and tossed them to the drow. "Fifty agates, finely cut," he said with a growl, never pleased by the price. He had hoped to avoid using Jarlaxle this time; like any deep gnome, Firble did not easily part with such sums.

Jarlaxle quickly glanced into the pouch, then dropped it into a deep pocket. "Rest easy, little deep gnome," he began, "for the powers who rule Menzoberranzan plan no actions against your city. A single drow house has an interest in the region, nothing more."

"Why?" Firble asked after a long moment of silence had passed. The svirfneblin hated having to ask, knowing the inevitable consequence.

Jarlaxle held out his hand. Ten more finely cut agates passed over.

"The house searches for one of its own," Jarlaxle explained. "A renegade whose actions have put his family out of the favor of the Spider Queen."

Again a few interminable moments of silence passed. Firble could guess easily enough the identity of this hunted drow, but King Schnicktick would roar until the ceiling fell in if he didn't make certain. He pulled ten more gemstones from his belt pouch. "Name the house," he said.

"Daermon N'a'shezbaernon," replied Jarlaxle, casually dropping the gems into his deep pocket. Firble crossed his arms over his chest and scowled. The unscrupulous drow had caught him once again.

"Not the ancestral name!" the councilor growled, grudgingly pulling out another ten gems.

"Really, Firble," Jarlaxle teased. "You must learn to be more specific in your questioning. Such errors do cost you so much!"

"Name the house in terms that I might understand," Firble instructed. "And name the hunted renegade. No more will I pay you this day, Jarlaxle."

Jarlaxle held his hand up and smiled to silence the deep gnome. "Agreed," he laughed, more than satisfied with his take. "House Do'Urden, Eighth House of Menzoberranzan searches for its secondboy." The mercenary noted a hint of recognition in Firble's expression. Might this little meeting provide Jarlaxle with information that he could turn into further profit at the coffers of Matron Malice?

"Drizzt is his name," the drow continued, carefully studying the svirfneblin's reaction. Slyly, he added, "Information of his whereabouts would bring a high profit in Menzoberranzan."

Firble stared at the brash drow for a long time. Had he given away too much when the renegade's identity had been revealed? If Jarlaxle had guessed that Drizzt was in the deep gnome city, the implications could be grim. Now Firble was in a predicament. Should he admit his mistake and try to correct it? But how much would it cost Firble to buy Jarlaxle's promise of silence? And no matter how great the payment, could Firble really trust the unscrupulous mercenary?

"Our business is at its end," Firble announced, deciding to trust that Jarlaxle had not guessed enough to bargain with House Do'Urden. The councilor turned on his heel and started out of the chamber.

Jarlaxle secretly applauded Firble's decision. He had always believed the svirfneblin councilor a worthy bargaining adversary and was not now disappointed. Firble had revealed little information, too little to take to Matron Malice, and if the deep gnome had more to give, his decision to abruptly end the meeting was a wise one. In spite of their racial differences, Jarlaxle had to admit that he actually liked Firble. "Little gnome," he called out after the departing figure. "I offer you a warning."

Firble spun back, his hand defensively covering his closed gem pouch.

"Free of charge," Jarlaxle said with a laugh and a shake of his bald head. But then the mercenary's visage turned suddenly serious, even grim. "If you know of Drizzt Do'Urden," Jarlaxle continued, "keep him far away. Lolth herself has charged Matron Malice Do'Urden with Drizzt's death, and Malice will do whatever she must to accomplish the task. And even if Malice fails, others will take up the hunt, knowing that the Do'Urden's death will bring great pleasure to the Spider Queen. He is doomed, Firble, and so doomed will be any foolish enough to stand beside him."

"An unnecessary warning," Firble replied, trying to keep his expression calm. "For none in Blingdenstone know or care anything for this renegade dark elf. Nor, I assure you, do any in Blingdenstone hold any desire to find the favor of the dark elves' Spider Queen deity!"

Jarlaxle smiled knowingly at the svirfneblin's bluff. "Of course," he replied, and he swept off his grand hat, dropping into yet another bow.

Firble paused a moment to consider the words and the bow, wondering again if he should try to buy the mercenary's silence.

Before he came to any decision, though, Jarlaxle was gone, clomping his hard boots loudly with every departing step. Poor Firble was left to wonder.

He needn't have. Jarlaxle did indeed like little Firble, the mercenary admitted to himself as he departed, and he would not divulge his suspicions of Drizzt's whereabouts to Matron Malice.

Unless, of course, the offer was simply too tempting.

Firble just stood and watched the empty chamber for many minutes, wondering and worrying.

⚔ ⚔ ⚔ ⚔ ⚔

For Drizzt, the days had been filled with friendship and fun. He was somewhat of a hero with the svirfneblin miners who had gone out into the tunnels beside him, and the story of his clever deception against the goblin tribe grew with every telling. Drizzt and Belwar went out often, now, and whenever they entered a tavern or meeting house, they were greeted by cheers and offers of free food and drink. Both the friends were glad for the other, for together they had found their place and their peace.

Already Burrow-Warden Brickers and Belwar were busily planning another mining expedition. Their biggest task was narrowing the list of volunteers, for svirfnebli from every corner of the city had contacted them, eager to travel beside the dark elf and the most honored burrow-warden.

When a loud and insistent knock came one morning on Belwar's door, both Drizzt and the deep gnome figured it to be more recruits looking for a place in the expedition. They were indeed surprised to find the city guard waiting for them, bidding Drizzt, at the point of a dozen spears, to go with them to an audience with the king.

Belwar appeared unconcerned. "A precaution," he assured Drizzt, pushing away his breakfast plate of mushrooms and moss sauce. Belwar went to the wall to grab his cloak, and if Drizzt, concentrating on the spears, had noticed Belwar's jerking and unsure movements, the drow most certainly would not have been assured.

The journey through the deep gnome city was quick indeed, with the anxious guards prodding the drow and the burrow-warden along. Belwar continued to brush the whole thing off as a "precaution" with every step, and in truth, Belwar did a fine job keeping a measure of calm in his round-toned voice. But Drizzt carried no illusions with him into the king's chambers. All of his life had been filled with crashing ends to promising beginnings.

King Schnicktick sat uncomfortably on his stone throne, his councilors standing equally ill at ease around him. He did not like this duty that had been placed upon his shoulders—the svirfnebli considered themselves loyal friends—but in light of councilor Firble's revelations, the threat to Blingdenstone could not be ignored.

Especially not for the likes of a dark elf.

Drizzt and Belwar moved to stand before the king, Drizzt curious, though ready to accept whatever might come of this, but Belwar on the edge of anger.

"My thanks in your prompt arrival," King Schnicktick greeted them, and he cleared his throat and looked around to his councilors for support.

"Spears do keep one in motion," Belwar snarled sarcastically.

The svirfneblin king cleared his throat again, noticeably uncomfortable, and shifted in his seat. "My guard does get a bit excited," he apologized. "Please take no offense."

"None taken," Drizzt assured him.

"Your time in our city you have enjoyed?" Schnicktick asked, managing a bit of a smile.

Drizzt nodded. "Your people have been gracious beyond anything I could have asked for or expected," he replied.

"And you have proven yourself a worthy friend, Drizzt Do'Urden," Schnicktick said. "Truly our lives have been enriched by your presence."

Drizzt bowed low, full of gratitude for the svirfneblin king's kind words. But Belwar narrowed his dark gray eyes and crinkled his hooked nose, beginning to understand what the king was leading up to.

"Unfortunately," King Schnicktick began, looking around pleadingly to his councilors, and not directly at Drizzt, "a situation has come upon us . . ."

"*Magga cammara*!" shouted Belwar, startling everyone in attendance. "No!" King Schnicktick and Drizzt looked at the burrow-warden in disbelief.

"You mean to put him out," Belwar snarled accusingly at Schnicktick.

"Belwar!" Drizzt began to protest.

"Most Honored Burrow-Warden," the svirfneblin king said sternly. "It is not your place to interrupt. If again you do so, I will be forced to have you removed from this chamber."

"It is true then," Belwar groaned softly. He looked away.

Drizzt glanced from the king to Belwar and back again, confused as to the purpose behind this whole encounter.

"You have heard of the suspected drow activity in the tunnels near our eastern borders?" the king asked Drizzt.

Drizzt nodded.

"We have learned the purpose of this activity," Schnicktick explained. The pause as the svirfneblin king looked yet another time to his councilors sent shivers through Drizzt's spine. He knew beyond any doubts what was coming next, but the words wounded him deeply anyway. "You, Drizzt Do'Urden, are that purpose."

"My mother searches for me," Drizzt replied flatly.

"But she will not find you!" Belwar snarled in defiance aimed at both Schnicktick and this unknown mother of his new friend. "Not while you remain a guest of the deep gnomes of Blingdenstone!"

"Belwar, hold!" King Schnicktick scolded. He looked back to Drizzt and his visage softened. "Please, friend Drizzt, you must understand. I cannot risk war with Menzoberranzan."

"I do understand," Drizzt assured him with sincerity. "I will gather my things."

"No!" Belwar protested. He rushed up to the throne. "We are svirfnebli. We do not put out friends in the face of any danger!" The burrow-warden ran from councilor to councilor, pleading for justice. "Only friendship has Drizzt Do'Urden shown us, and we would put him out! *Magga cammara*! If our loyalties are so fragile, are we any better than the drow of Menzoberranzan?"

"Enough, Most Honored Burrow-Warden!" King Schnicktick cried out in a tone of finality that even stubborn Belwar could not ignore. "Our decision did not come easily to us, but it is final! I will not put Blingdenstone in jeopardy for the sake of a dark elf, no matter that he has shown himself to be a friend." Schnicktick looked to Drizzt. "I am truly sorry."

"Do not be," Drizzt replied. "You do only as you must, as I did on that long-ago day when I chose to forsake my people. That decision I made alone, and I have never asked any for approval or aid. You, good svirfneblin king, and your people have given me back so much that I had lost. Believe that I have no desire to invoke the wrath of Menzoberranzan against Blingdenstone. I would never forgive myself if I played any part in that tragedy. I will be gone from your fair city within the hour. And in parting I offer only gratitude."

The svirfneblin king was touched by the words, but his position remained unbending. He motioned for his guardsmen to accompany Drizzt, who accepted the armed escort with a resigned sigh. He looked once to Belwar, standing helplessly beside the svirfneblin councilors, then left the king's halls.

⚔ ⚔ ⚔ ⚔ ⚔

A hundred deep gnomes, particularly Burrow-Warden Krieger and the other miners of the single expedition Drizzt had accompanied, said their farewells to the drow as he walked out of Blingdenstone's huge doors. Conspicuously absent was Belwar Dissengulp; Drizzt had not seen the burrow-warden at all in the hour since he had left the throne room. Still, Drizzt was grateful for the send-off these svirfnebli gave him. Their kind words comforted him and gave him the strength that he knew he would need in the trials of the coming years. Of all the memories Drizzt would take out of Blingdenstone, he vowed to hold onto those parting words.

Still, when Drizzt moved away from the gathering, across the small platform and down the wide staircase, he heard only the resounding echoes of the enormous doors slamming shut behind him. Drizzt trembled as he looked down the tunnels of the wild Underdark, wondering how he could possibly survive the trials this time. Blingdenstone had been his salvation from the hunter; how long would it take that darker side to rear up again and steal his identity?

But what choice did Drizzt have? Leaving Menzoberranzan had been his decision, the right decision. Now, though, knowing better the consequences of his choice, Drizzt wondered about his resolve. Given the opportunity to do it all over again, would he now find the strength to walk away from his life among his people?

He hoped that he would.

A shuffle off to the side brought Drizzt alert. He crouched and drew his scimitars, thinking that Matron Malice had agents waiting for him who had expected him to be expelled from Blingdenstone. A shadow moved a moment later, but it was no drow assassin that came in at Drizzt.

"Belwar!" he cried in relief. "I feared that you would not say farewell."

"And so I will not," replied the svirfneblin.

Drizzt studied the burrow-warden, noticing the full pack that Belwar wore. "No, Belwar, I cannot allow—"

"I do not remember asking for your permission," the deep gnome interrupted. "I have been looking for some excitement in my life. Thought I might venture out and see what the wide world has to offer."

"It is not as grand as you expect," Drizzt replied grimly. "You have your people, Belwar. They accept you and care for you. That is a greater gift than anything you can imagine."

"Agreed," replied the burrow-warden. "And you, Drizzt Do'Urden, have your friend, who accepts you and cares for you. And stands beside you. Now, are we going to be on with this adventure, or are we going to stand here and wait for that wicked mother of yours to walk up and cut us down?"

"You cannot begin to imagine the dangers," Drizzt warned, but Belwar could see that the drow's resolve was already starting to wear away.

Belwar banged his mithral hands together. "And you, dark elf cannot begin to imagine the ways I can deal with such dangers! I am not letting you walk off alone into the wilds. Understand that as fact—*magga cammara*—and we can get on with things."

Drizzt shrugged helplessly, looked once more to the stubborn determination stamped openly on Belwar's face, and started off down the tunnel, the deep gnome falling into step at his side. This time, at least, Drizzt had a companion he could talk to, a weapon against the intrusions of the hunter. He put his hand in his pocket and fingered the Guenhwyvar's onyx figurine. Perhaps, Drizzt dared to hope, the three of them would have a chance to find more than simple survival in the Underdark.

For a long time afterward, Drizzt wondered if he had acted selfishly in giving in so easily to Belwar. Whatever guilt he felt, however, could not begin to compare with the profound sense of relief Drizzt knew whenever he looked down at his side, to the most honored burrow-warden's bald, bobbing head.

# Part Three

## Friends and Foes

To live or to survive? Until my second time out in the wilds of the Underdark, after my stay in Blingdenstone, I never would have understood the significance of such a simple question.

When first I left Menzoberranzan, I thought survival enough; I thought that I could fall within myself, within my principles, and be satisfied that I had followed the only course open to me. The alternative was the grim reality of Menzoberranzan and compliance with the wicked ways that guided my people. If that was life, I believed, simply surviving would be far preferable.

And yet, that "simple survival" nearly killed me. Worse, it nearly stole everything that I held dear.

The svirfnebli of Blingdenstone showed me a different way. Svirfneblin society, structured and nurtured on communal values and unity, proved to be everything that I had always hoped Menzoberranzan would be. The svirfnebli did much more than merely survive. They lived and laughed and worked, and the gains they made were shared by the whole, as was the pain of the losses they inevitably suffered in the hostile subsurface world.

Joy multiplies when it is shared among friends, but grief diminishes with every division. That is life.

And so, when I walked back out of Blingdenstone, back into the empty Underdark's lonely chambers, I walked with hope. At my side went Belwar, my new friend, and in my pocket went the magical figurine that could summon Guenhwyvar, my proven friend. In my brief stay with the deep gnomes, I had witnessed life as I always had hoped it would be—I could not return to simply surviving.

With my friends beside me, I dared to believe that I would not have to.

—Drizzt Do'Urden

# 12 Wilds, Wilds, Wilds

"Did you set it?" Drizzt asked Belwar when the burrow-warden returned to his side in the winding passage.

"The fire pit is cut," Belwar replied, tapping his mithral hands triumphantly—but not too loudly—together. "And I rumpled the extra bedroll off in a corner. Scraped my boots all over the stone and put your neck-purse in a place where it will be easily found. I even left a few silver coins under the blanket—I figure I'll not be needing them anytime soon, anyway." Belwar managed a chuckle, but despite the disclaimer, Drizzt could see that the svirfneblin did not so easily part with valuables.

"A fine deception," Drizzt offered, to take away the sting of the cost.

"And what of you, dark elf?" Belwar asked. "Have you seen or heard anything?"

"Nothing," Drizzt replied. He pointed down a side corridor. "I sent Guenhwyvar away on a wide circuit. If anyone is near, we will soon know."

Belwar nodded. "Good plan," he remarked. "Setting the false camp this far from Blingdenstone should keep your troublesome mother from my kinfolk."

"And perhaps it will lead my family to believe that I am still in the region and plan to remain," Drizzt added hopefully. "Have you given any thought to our destination?"

"One way is as good as another," remarked Belwar, hoisting his hands out wide. "No cities are there, beyond our own, anywhere close. None to my knowledge, at least."

"West, then," offered Drizzt. "Around Blingdenstone and off into the wilds, straight away from Menzoberranzan."

"A wise course, it would seem," agreed the burrow-warden. Belwar closed his eyes and attuned his thoughts to the emanations of the stone. Like many Underdark races, deep gnomes possessed the ability to recognize magnetic variations in the rock, an ability that allowed them to judge direction as accurately as a surface dweller might follow the sun's trail. A moment later, Belwar nodded and pointed down the appropriate tunnel.

"West," Belwar said. "And quickly. The more distance you put between yourself and that mother of yours, the safer we all shall be." He paused to consider Drizzt for a long moment, wondering if he might be prodding his new friend a bit too deeply with his next question.

"What is it?" Drizzt asked him, recognizing his apprehension.

Belwar decided to risk it, to see just how close he and Drizzt had become. "When first you learned that you were the reason for the drow activity in the eastern tunnels," the deep gnome began bluntly, "you seemed a bit weak in the knees, if you understand me. They are your family, dark elf. Are they so terrible?"

Drizzt's chuckle put Belwar at ease, told the deep gnome that he had not pressed too far. "Come," Drizzt said, seeing Guenhwyvar return from the scouting trek. "If the deception of the camp is complete, then let us take our first steps into our new life. Our road should be long enough for tales of my home and family."

"Hold," said Belwar. He reached into his pouch and produced a small coffer. "A gift from King Schnicktick," he explained as he lifted the lid and removed a glowing brooch, its quiet illumination bathing the area around them.

Drizzt stared at the burrow-warden in disbelief. "It will mark you as a fine target," the drow remarked.

Belwar corrected him. "It will mark us as fine targets," he said with a sly snort. "But fear not, dark elf, the light will keep more enemies at bay than it will bring. I am not so fond of tripping on crags and chips in the floor!"

"How long will it glow?" Drizzt asked, and Belwar gathered from his tone that the drow hoped it would fade soon.

"Forever is the dweomer," Belwar replied with a wide smirk. "Unless some priest or wizard counters it. Stop your worrying. What creatures of the Underdark would willingly walk into an illuminated area?"

Drizzt shrugged and trusted in the experienced burrow-warden's judgment. "Very well," he said, shaking his white mane helplessly. "Then off for the road."

"The road and the tales," replied Belwar, falling into step beside Drizzt, his stout little legs rolling along to keep up with the drow's long and graceful strides.

They walked for many hours, stopped for a meal, then walked for many more. Sometimes Belwar used his illuminating brooch; other times the friends walked in darkness, depending on whether or not they perceived danger in the area. Guenhwyvar was frequently about yet rarely seen, the panther eagerly taking up its appointed duties as a perimeter guard.

For a tenday straight, the companions stopped only when weariness or hunger forced a break in the march, for they were anxious to be as far from Blingdenstone—and from those hunting Drizzt—as possible. Still, another full tenday would pass before the companions moved out into tunnels that Belwar did not know. The deep gnome had been a burrow-warden for almost fifty years, and he had led many of Blingdenstone's farthest-reaching mining expeditions.

"This place is known to me," Belwar often remarked when they entered a cavern. "Took a wagon of iron," he would say, or mithral, or a multitude of other precious minerals that Drizzt had never even heard of. And though the burrow-warden's extended tales of those mining expeditions all ran in basically the same direction—how many ways can a deep gnome chop stone?—Drizzt always listened intently, savoring every word.

He knew the alternative.

For his part in the storytelling, Drizzt recounted his adventures in Menzoberranzan's Academy and his many fond memories of Zaknafein and the training gym. He showed Belwar the double-thrust low and how the pupil had discovered a parry to counter the attack, to his mentor's surprise and pain. Drizzt displayed the intricate hand and facial combinations of the silent drow code, and he briefly entertained the notion of teaching the language to Belwar. The deep gnome promptly burst into loud and rolling laughter. His dark eyes looked incredulously at Drizzt, and he led the drow's gaze down to the ends of his arms. With a hammer and pickaxe for hands, the svirfneblin could hardly muster enough gestures to make the effort worthwhile. Still, Belwar appreciated that Drizzt had offered to teach him the silent code. The absurdity of it all gave them both a fine laugh.

Guenhwyvar and the deep gnome also became friends during those first couple of tendays on the trail. Often, Belwar would fall into a deep slumber only to be awakened by prickling in his legs, fast asleep under the weight of six hundred pounds of panther. Belwar always grumbled and swatted Guenhwyvar on the rump with his hammer-hand—it became a game between the two—but Belwar truly didn't mind the panther being so close. In fact, Guenhwyvar's mere presence made sleep—which always left one so vulnerable in the wilds—much easier to come by.

"Do you understand?" Drizzt whispered to Guenhwyvar one day. Off to the side, Belwar was fast asleep, flat on his back on the stone, using a rock for a pillow. Drizzt shook his head in continued amazement when he studied the little figure. He was beginning to suspect that the deep gnomes carried their affinity with the earth a bit too far.

"Go get him," he prompted the cat

Guenhwyvar lumbered over and plopped across the burrow-warden's legs. Drizzt moved away into the shielding entrance of a tunnel to watch.

Only a few minutes later, Belwar awoke with a snarl. "*Magga cammara*, panther!" the deep gnome growled. "Why must you always bed down on me, instead of beside me?" Guenhwyvar shifted slightly but let out only a deep sigh in response.

"*Magga cammara*, cat!" Belwar roared again. He wiggled his toes frantically, trying futilely to keep the circulation going and dismiss the tingles that had already begun. "Away with you!" The burrow-warden propped himself up on one elbow and swung his hammer-hand at Guenhwyvar's backside.

Guenhwyvar sprang away in feigned flight, quicker than Belwar's swat. But just as the burrow-warden relaxed, the panther cut back on its tracks, pivoted completely, and leaped atop Belwar, burying him and pinning him flat to the stone.

After a few moments of struggling, Belwar managed to get his face out from under Guenhwyvar's muscled chest.

"Get yourself off me or suffer the consequences!" the deep gnome growled, obviously an empty threat. Guenhwyvar shifted, getting a bit more comfortable in its perch.

"Dark elf!" Belwar called as loudly as he dared. "Dark elf, take your panther away. Dark elf!"

"Greetings," Drizzt answered, walking in from the tunnel as though he had only just arrived. "Are you two playing again? I had thought my time as sentry near to its end."

"Your time has passed," replied Belwar, but the svirfneblin's words were mulled by thick black fur as Guenhwyvar shifted again. Drizzt could see Belwar's long, hooked nose, though, crinkle up in irritation.

"Oh, no, no," said Drizzt. "I am not so tired. I would not think of interrupting your game. I know that you both enjoy it so." He walked by, giving Guenhwyvar a complimentary pat on the head and a sly wink as he passed.

"Dark elf!" Belwar grumbled at his back as Drizzt departed. But the drow kept going, and Guenhwyvar, with Drizzt's blessings, soon fell fast asleep.

⚔ ⚔ ⚔ ⚔ ⚔

Drizzt crouched low and held very still, letting his eyes go through the dramatic shift from infravision—viewing the heat of objects in the infrared spectrum—to normal vision in the realm of light. Even before the transformation was completed, Drizzt could tell that his guess had been correct. Ahead, beyond a low natural archway, came a red glow. The drow held his position, deciding to let Belwar catch up to him before he went to investigate. Only a moment later, the dimmer glow of the deep gnome's enchanted brooch came into view.

"Put out the light," Drizzt whispered, and the brooch's glow disappeared.

Belwar crept along the tunnel to join his companion. He, too, saw the red glow beyond the archway and understood Drizzt's caution. "Can you bring the panther?" the burrow-warden asked quietly.

Drizzt shook his head. "The magic is limited by spans of time. Walking the material plane tires Guenhwyvar. The panther needs to rest."

"Back the way we came, we could go," Belwar suggested. "Perhaps there is another tunnel around."

"Five miles," replied Drizzt, considering the length of the unbroken passageway behind them. "Too long."

"Then let us see what is ahead," the burrow-warden reasoned, and he started boldly off. Drizzt liked Belwar's straightforward attitude and quickly joined him.

Beyond the archway, which Drizzt had to crouch nearly double to get under, they found a wide and high cavern, its floor and walls covered in a mosslike growth that emitted the red light. Drizzt pulled up short, at a loss, but Belwar recognized the stuff well enough.

"Baruchies!" the burrow-warden blurted, the word turning into a chuckle. He turned to Drizzt and not seeing any reaction to his smile, explained. "Crimson spitters, dark elf. Not for decades have I seen such a patch of the stuff. Quite a rare sight they are, you know."

Drizzt, still at a loss, shook the tenseness out of his muscles and shrugged, then started forward. Belwar's pick hand hooked him under the arm, and the powerful deep gnome spun him back abruptly.

"Crimson spitters," the burrow-warden said again, pointedly emphasizing the latter of the words. "*Magga cammara*, dark elf, how did you get along through the years?"

Belwar turned to the side and slammed his hammer-hand into the wall of the archway, taking off a fair-sized chunk of stone. He scooped this up in the flat of his pick-hand and flipped it off to the side of the cavern. The stone hit the red-glowing fungus with a soft thud, then a burst of smoke and spores blasted into the air.

"Spit," explained Belwar, "and choke you to death will the spore! If you plan to cross here, walk lightly, my brave, foolish friend."

Drizzt scratched his unkempt white locks and considered the predicament. He had no desire to return the five miles down the tunnel, but neither did he plan to go plodding through this field of red death. He stood tall just inside the archway and looked around for some solution. Several stones, a possible walkway, rose up out of the baruchies, and beyond them lay a trail of clear stone about ten feet wide running perpendicular to the archway across the chasm.

"We can make it through," he told Belwar. "There is a clear path."

"There always is in a field of baruchies," the burrow-warden replied under his breath.

Drizzt's keen ears caught the comment. "What do you mean?" he asked, springing agilely out to the first of the raised stones.

"A grubber is about," the deep gnome explained. "Or has been."

"A grubber?" Drizzt prudently hopped back to stand beside the burrow-warden.

"Big caterpillar," Belwar explained. "Grubbers love baruchies. They are the only things the crimson spitters do not seem to bother."

"How big?"

"How wide was the clear path?" Belwar asked him.

"Ten feet, perhaps," Drizzt answered, hopping back out to the first stepping stone to view it again.

Belwar considered the answer for a moment. "One pass for a big grubber, two for most."

Drizzt hopped back to the side of the burrow-warden again, giving a cautious look over his shoulder. "Big caterpillar," he remarked.

"But with a little mouth," Belwar explained. "Grubbers eat only moss and molds—and baruchies, if they can find them. Peaceful enough creatures, all in all."

For the third time, Drizzt sprang out to the stone. "Is there anything else I should know before I continue?" he asked in exasperation.

Belwar shook his head.

Drizzt led the way across the stones, and soon the two companions stood in the middle of the ten-foot path. It traversed the cavern and ended with the entrance to a passage on either side. Drizzt pointed both ways, wondering which direction Belwar would prefer.

The deep gnome started to the left, then stopped abruptly and peered ahead. Drizzt understood Belwar's hesitation, for he, too, felt the vibrations in the stone under his feet.

"Grubber," said Belwar. "Stand quiet and watch, my friend. They are quite a sight."

Drizzt smiled wide and crouched low, eager for the entertainment. When he heard a quick shuffle behind him, though, Drizzt began to suspect that something was out of sorts.

"Where . . ." Drizzt began to ask when he turned about and saw Belwar in full flight toward the other exit.

Drizzt stopped speaking abruptly when an explosion like the crash of a cave-in erupted from the other way, the way he had been watching.

"Quite a sight!" he heard Belwar call, and he couldn't deny the truth of the deep gnome's words when the grubber made its appearance. It was huge—bigger than the basilisk Drizzt had killed—and looked like a gigantic pale gray worm, except for the multitude of little feet pumping along beside its massive torso. Drizzt saw that Belwar had not lied, for the thing had no mouth to speak of, and no talons or other apparent weapons. But the giant was coming straight at Drizzt with a vengeance now, and Drizzt couldn't get the image of a flattened dark elf, stretched from one end of the cavern to the other, out of his mind. He reached for his scimitars, then realized the absurdity of that plan. Where would he hit the thing to slow it? Throwing his hands helplessly out wide, Drizzt spun on his heel and fled after the departing burrow-warden.

The ground shook under Drizzt's feet so violently that he wondered if he might topple to the side and be blasted by the baruchies. But then the tunnel entrance was just ahead and Drizzt could see a smaller side passage, too small for the grubber, just outside the baruchie cavern. He darted ahead the last few strides, then cut swiftly into the small tunnel, diving into a roll to break his momentum. Still, he ricocheted hard off the wall, then the grubber slammed in behind, smashing at the tunnel entrance and dropping pieces of stone all about.

When the dust finally cleared, the grubber remained outside the passage, humming a low, growling moan and every so often, banging its head against the stone. Belwar stood just a few feet farther in than Drizzt, the deep gnome's arms crossed over his chest and a satisfied grin on his face.

"Peaceful enough?" Drizzt asked him, rising to his feet and shaking off the dust.

"They are indeed," replied Belwar with a nod. "But grubbers do love their baruchies and have no mind to share the things!"

"You almost got me crushed!" Drizzt snarled at him.

Again Belwar nodded. "Mark it well, dark elf, for the next time you set your panther to sleep on me, I will surely do worse!"

Drizzt fought hard to hide his smile. His heart still pumped wildly under the influence of the adrenaline burst, but Drizzt held no anger toward his companion. He thought back to encounters he had suffered just a few months before, when he was out alone in the wilds. How different life would be with Belwar Dissengulp by his side! How much more enjoyable! Drizzt glanced back over his shoulder to the angry and stubborn grubber.

And how much more interesting!

"Come along," the smug svirfneblin continued, starting off down the passage. "We are only making the grubber angrier by loitering in its sight."

The passageway narrowed and turned a sharp bend just a few feet farther in. Around the bend, the companions found even more trouble, for the corridor ended in a blank stone wall. Belwar moved right up to inspect it, and it was Drizzt's turn to cross his arms over his chest and gloat.

"You have put us in a dangerous spot, little friend" the drow said. "An angry grubber behind, trapping us in a box corridor!"

Pressing his ear to the stone, Belwar waved Drizzt off with his hammer-hand. "Merely an inconvenience," the deep gnome assured him. "There is another tunnel beyond—not more than seven feet."

"Seven feet of stone," Drizzt reminded him.

But Belwar didn't seem concerned. "A day," he said. "Perhaps two." Belwar held his arms out wide and began a chant too low for Drizzt to hear clearly, though the drow realized that Belwar was engaged in some sort of spellcasting.

*"Bivrip!"* Belwar cried.

Nothing happened.

The burrow-warden turned back on Drizzt and did not seem disappointed. "A day," he proclaimed again.

"What did you do?" Drizzt asked him.

"Set my hands a humming," replied the deep gnome. Seeing that Drizzt was completely at a loss, Belwar turned on his heel and slammed his hammer hand into the wall. An explosion of sparks brightened the small passage, blinding Drizzt. By the time the drow's eyes could adjust to the continuing burst of Belwar's punching and hacking, he saw that his svirfneblin companion already had ground several inches of rock into fine dust at his feet.

"*Magga cammara*, dark elf," Belwar cried with a wink. "You did not believe that my people would go to all the trouble of crafting such fine hands for me without puffing a bit of magic into them, did you?"

Drizzt moved to the side of the passage and sat. "You are full of surprises, little friend," he answered with a sigh of surrender.

"I am indeed!" Belwar roared, and he pounded the stone again, sending flecks flying in every direction.

They were out of the box corridor in a day, as Belwar had promised, and they set off again, traveling now—by the deep gnome's estimation—generally north. Luck had followed them so far, and they both knew it, for they had spent two tendays in the wilds and had encountered nothing more hostile than a grubber protecting its baruchies.

A few days later, their luck changed.

"Summon the panther," Belwar bade Drizzt as they crouched in the wide tunnel they had been traveling. Drizzt did not argue the wisdom of the burrow-warden's request; he didn't like the green glow ahead any more than Belwar did. A moment later, the black mist swirled and took shape, and Guenhwyvar stood beside them.

"I go first," Drizzt said. "You both follow together, twenty steps behind." Belwar nodded and Drizzt turned and started away. Drizzt almost expected the movement when the svirfneblin's pickaxe-hand hooked him and turned him about.

"Be careful," Belwar said. Drizzt only smiled in reply, touched at the sincerity in his friend's voice and thinking again how much better it was to have a companion by his side. Then Drizzt dismissed his thoughts and moved away, letting his instincts and experience guide him.

He found the glow to be emanating from a hole in the corridor floor. Beyond it, the corridor continued but bent sharply, nearly doubling back on itself. Drizzt fell to his belly and peered down the hole. Another passage, about ten feet below him, ran perpendicular to the one he was in, opening a short way ahead into what appeared to be a large cavern.

"What is it?" Belwar whispered, coming up behind.

"Another corridor to a chamber," Drizzt replied. "The glow comes from there." He lifted his head and looked down into the ensuing darkness of the higher corridor. "Our tunnel continues," Drizzt reasoned. "We can go right by it."

Belwar looked down the passageway they had been traveling, noting the turn. "Doubles back," he reasoned. "And probably comes right out at that side passage we passed an hour ago." The deep gnome dropped to the dirt and looked into the hole.

"What would make such a glow?" Drizzt asked him, easily guessing that Belwar's curiosity was as keen as his own. "Another form of moss?"

"None that I know," Belwar replied.

"Shall we find out?"

Belwar smiled at him, then hooked his pick-hand on the ledge and swung over and in, dropping down to the lower tunnel. Drizzt and Guenhwyvar followed silently, the drow, scimitars in hand, again taking the lead as they moved toward the glow.

They came into a wide and high chamber, its ceiling far beyond their sight and a lake of green-glowing foul-smelling liquid bubbling and hissing twenty feet below them. Dozens of interconnected narrow stone walkways, varying from one to ten feet wide, crisscrossed the gorge, most ending at exits leading into more side corridors.

"*Magga cammara*," whispered the stunned svirfneblin, and Drizzt shared that thought.

"It appears as though the floor was blasted away," Drizzt remarked when he again found his voice.

"Melted away," replied Belwar, guessing the liquid's nature. He hacked off a chunk of stone at his side and tapping Drizzt to get his attention, dropped it into the green lake. The liquid hissed as if in anger where the rock hit, eating away at the stone before it even sank from sight.

"Acid," Belwar explained.

Drizzt looked at him curiously. He knew of acid from his days of training under the wizards of Sorcere in the Academy. Wizards often concocted such vile liquids for use in their magical experiments, but Drizzt did not figure that acid would appear naturally, or in such quantities.

"Some wizard's working, I would guess," said Belwar. "An experiment out of control. It has probably been here for a hundred years, eating away at the floor, sinking down inch by inch."

"But what remains of the floor seems secure enough," observed Drizzt, pointing to the walkways. "And we have a score of tunnels to choose from."

"Then let us begin at once," said Belwar. "I do not like this place. We are exposed in the light, and I would not care to take quick flight along such narrow bridges—not with a lake of acid below me!"

Drizzt agreed and took a cautious step out on the walkway, but Guenhwyvar quickly moved past him. Drizzt understood the panther's logic and wholeheartedly agreed. "Guenhwyvar will lead us," he explained to Belwar. "The panther is the heaviest and quick enough to spring away if a section begins to fall."

The burrow-warden was not completely satisfied. "What if Guenhwyvar does not make it to safety?" he asked, truly concerned. "What will the acid do to a magical creature?"

Drizzt wasn't certain of the answer. "Guenhwyvar should be safe," he reasoned, pulling the onyx figurine from his pocket. "I hold the gateway to the panther's home plane."

Guenhwyvar was a dozen strides away by then—the walkway seemed sturdy enough—and Drizzt set out to follow. "*Magga cammara*, I pray you are right," he heard Belwar mumble at his back as he took the first steps out from the ledge.

The chamber was huge, several hundred feet across even to the nearest exit. The companions neared the halfway point—Guenhwyvar had already passed it—when they heard a strange chanting sound. They stopped and glanced about, searching for the source.

A weird-looking creature stepped out from one of the numerous side passages. It was bipedal and black skinned, with a beaked bird's head and the torso of a man, featherless and wingless. Both of its powerful-looking arms ended in hooked, wicked claws, and its legs ended in three-toed feet. Another creature stepped out from behind it, and another from behind them.

"Relatives?" Belwar asked Drizzt, for the creatures did indeed resemble some weird cross between a dark elf and a bird.

"Hardly," Drizzt replied. "In all of my life, I have never heard of such creatures."

"Doom! Doom!" came the continuing chant, and the friends looked around to see more of the bird-men stepping out from other passages. They were dire corbies, an ancient race more common to the southern reaches of the Underdark—though rare even there—and almost unknown in this part of the world. Corbies had never been of much concern to any of the Underdark races, for the bird-men's methods were crude and their numbers were small. To a passing band of adventurers, however, a flock of savage dire corbies meant trouble indeed.

"Nor have I ever encountered such creatures," Belwar agreed. "But I do not believe that they are pleased to see us."

The chant became a series of horrifying shrieks as the corbies began to disperse out onto the walkways, walking at first, but occasionally breaking into quick trots, their anxiety obviously increasing.

"You are wrong, my little friend," Drizzt remarked. "I believe that they are quite pleased to have their dinner delivered to them."

Belwar looked around helplessly. Nearly all of their escape routes were already cut off, and they couldn't hope to get out without a fight. "Dark elf, I can think of a thousand places I would rather do battle," the burrow-warden said with a resigned shrug and a shudder as he took another look down into the acid lake. Taking a deep breath to calm himself, Belwar began his ritual to enchant his magical hands.

"Move while you chant," Drizzt instructed him, leading him on. "Let us get as close to an exit as we can before the fighting begins."

One group of corbies closed rapidly at the party's side, but Guenhwyvar, with a mighty spring that spanned two of the walkways, cut the bird-men off.

*"Bivrip!"* Belwar cried, completing his spell, and he turned toward the impending battle.

"Guenhwyvar can take care of that group," Drizzt assured him, quickening his steps toward the nearest wall. Belwar saw the drow's reasoning; still another group of enemies had come out of the exit they were making for.

The momentum of Guenhwyvar's leap carried the panther straight into the pack of corbies, bowling two of them right off the walkway. The bird men shrieked horribly as they fell to their deaths, but their remaining companions seemed unbothered by the loss. Drooling and chanting, "Doom! Doom!" they tore in at Guenhwyvar with their sharp talons.

The panther had formidable weapons of its own. Each swat of a great claw tore the life from a corby or sent it tumbling from the walkway to the acid lake. But while the cat continued to slash into the birdmen's ranks, the fearless corbies continued to fight back, and more rushed in eagerly to join. A second group came from the opposite direction and surrounded Guenhwyvar.

⚔ ⚔ ⚔ ⚔ ⚔

Belwar set himself on a narrow section of the walkway and let the line of corbies come to him. Drizzt, taking a parallel route along a walkway fifteen feet to his friend's side, did likewise, drawing his scimitars somewhat reluctantly. The drow could feel the savage instincts of the hunter welling up within him as the battle drew near, and he fought back with all of his willpower to sublimate the wild urges. He was Drizzt Do'Urden, no more the hunter, and he would face his foes fully in control of his every movement.

Then the corbies were upon him, flailing away, shrieking their frenzied chants. Drizzt did little more than parry in those first seconds, the flats of his blades working marvelously to deflect each attempted strike. The scimitars spun and whirled, but the drow, refusing to loose the killer within him, made little headway in his fight. After several minutes, he still faced off against the first corby that had come at him.

Belwar was not so reserved. Corby after corby rushed in at the little svirfneblin, only to be pounded to a sudden halt by the burrow-warden's explosive hammer-hand. The electrical jolt and the sheer force of the blow often killed the corby where it stood, but Belwar never waited long enough to find out. Following each hammer blow, the deep gnome's pickaxe-hand came across in a roundhouse arc, sweeping the latest victim from the walkway.

The svirfneblin had dropped a half-dozen of the bird-men before he got the chance to look over at Drizzt. He recognized at once the inner struggle the drow was fighting.

"*Magga cammara*!" Belwar screamed. "Fight them, dark elf, and fight to win! They will show no mercy! There can be no truce! Kill them—cut them down—or surely they shall kill you!"

Drizzt hardly heard Belwar's words. Tears rimmed his lavender eyes, though even in that blur, the almost magical rhythm of his weaving blades did not slow. He caught his opponent off balance and reversed the motion of a thrust, slamming the bird-man in the head with the pommel of his scimitar. The corby dropped like a stone and rolled. It would have fallen from the ledge, but Drizzt stepped across it and held it in place.

Belwar shook his head and belted another adversary. The corby hopped backward, its chest smoking and charred by the jarring impact of the enchanted hammer-hand. The corby looked at Belwar in blank disbelief, but uttered not a sound, nor made any move at all, as the pickaxe hooked in, catching it in the shoulder and launching it out over the acid lake.

⚔ ⚔ ⚔ ⚔ ⚔

Guenhwyvar flustered the hungry attackers. As the corbies closed in on the panther's back, thinking the kill at hand, Guenhwyvar crouched and sprang. The panther soared through the green light as though it had taken flight, landing on yet another of the walkways fully thirty feet away. Skidding on the smooth stone, Guenhwyvar just managed to halt before toppling over the ledge into the acid pool.

The corbies glanced around in stunned amazement for just a moment, then took up their shrieks and wails and set off along the walkways in pursuit.

A single corby, near where Guenhwyvar had landed, ran fearlessly to battle the cat. Guenhwyvar's teeth found its neck in an instant and squeezed the life from it.

But while the panther was so engaged, the corbies' devilish trap showed another twist. From far above in the high-ceilinged cavern, a corby at last saw a victim in position. The bird-man wrapped its arms around the heavy boulder on the ledge beside it and pushed out, dropping with the stone.

At the last second, Guenhwyvar saw the plummeting monster and scrambled out of its path. The corby, in its suicidal ecstacy, didn't even care. The bird-man slammed into the walkway, the momentum of the heavy boulder shattering the narrow bridge to pieces.

The great panther tried to spring out again, but the stone underneath Guenhwyvar's feet disintegrated before they could set and spring. Claws scratching futilely at the crumbling bridge, Guenhwyvar followed the corby and its boulder down into the acid lake.

Hearing the elated shouts of the bird-men behind him, Belwar spun about just in time to see Guenhwyvar's fall. Drizzt, too engaged at the time—for another corby flailed away at him and the one he had dropped was stirring back to consciousness between his feet—did not see. But the drow did not have to see. The figurine in Drizzt's pocket heated suddenly, wisps of smoke rising ominously from Drizzt's *piwafwi* cloak. Drizzt could guess easily enough what had happened to his dear Guenhwyvar. The drow's eyes narrowed, their sudden fire melting away his tears.

He welcomed the hunter.

Corbies fought with fury. The highest honor of their existence was to die in battle. And those closest to Drizzt Do'Urden soon realized that the moment of their highest honor was upon them.

The drow thrust both his scimitars straight out, each finding an eye of the corby facing him. The hunter pulled out the blades, spun them over in his hands, and plunged them down into the bird-man at his feet. He snapped the scimitars up immediately and plunged them down again, taking grim satisfaction in the sound of their smooth cut.

Then the drow dived headlong into the corbies ahead of him, his blades cutting in from every possible angle.

Hit a dozen times before it ever launched a single swing, the first corby was quite dead before it even fell. Then the second, then the third. Drizzt backed them up to a wider section of the walkway. They came at him three at a time.

They died at his feet three at a time.

"Get them, dark elf," mumbled Belwar, seeing his friend explode into action. The corby coming to meet the burrow-warden turned its head to see what had caught Belwar's attention. When it turned back, it was met squarely in the face by the deep gnome's hammer-hand. Pieces of beak flew in every direction, and that unfortunate corby was the first of its species to take flight in several millennium of evolution. Its short airborne excursion pushed its companions back from the deep gnome, and the corby landed, dead on its back, many feet from Belwar.

The enraged deep gnome wasn't finished with this one. He raced up, bowling from the walkway the single corby who managed to get back to intercept him. When he arrived at last at his beakless victim, Belwar drove his pickaxe-hand deep into its chest. With that single muscled arm, the burrow-warden hoisted the dead corby high into the air and let out a horrifying shriek of his own.

The other corbies hesitated. Belwar looked to Drizzt and was dismayed.

A score of corbies crowded in on the wide section of the walkway where the drow made his stand. Another dozen lay dead at Drizzt feet, their blood running off the ledge and dripping into the acid lake in rhythmic hissing *plops*. But it wasn't the odds that Belwar feared; with his precise movements and measured thrusts, Drizzt was undeniably winning. High above the drow, though, another suicidal corby and his pet rock took a dive.

Belwar believed that Drizzt's life had come to a crashing end.

But the hunter sensed the peril.

A corby reached for Drizzt. With a flash of the drow's scimitars, both its arms flew free of their respective shoulders. In the same dazzling movement, Drizzt snapped his bloodied scimitars into their sheaths and bolted for the edge of the platform. He reached the lip and leaped out toward Belwar just as the suicidal boulder-riding corby crashed down, taking the platform and a score of its kin with it into the acid pool.

Belwar heaved his beakless trophy into the corbies facing him and dropped to his knees, reaching out with his pickaxe-hand to try to aid his soaring friend. Drizzt caught the burrow-warden's hand and the ledge at the same time, slamming his face into the stone but finding a hold.

The jolt ripped the drow's *piwafwi*, though, and Belwar watched helplessly as the onyx figurine rolled out and dropped toward the acid.

Drizzt caught it between his feet.

Belwar nearly laughed aloud at the futility and hopelessness of it all. He looked over his shoulder to see the corbies resuming their advance.

"Dark elf, surely it has been fun," the svirfneblin said resignedly to Drizzt, but the drow's response stole the levity from Belwar as surely as it stole the blood from the deep gnome's face.

"Swing me!" Drizzt growled so powerfully that Belwar obeyed before he even realized what he was doing.

Drizzt rolled out and came swinging back toward the walkway, and when he bounced into the stone, every muscle in his body jerked violently to aid his momentum.

He rolled right around the bottom of the walkway, scrambling and clawing with his arms and legs to gain a footing back up behind the crouching deep gnome. By the time Belwar realized what Drizzt had done and thought to turn around, Drizzt had his scimitars out and slicing across the face of the first approaching corby.

"Hold this," Drizzt bade his friend, flicking the onyx figurine to Belwar with his toe. Belwar caught the item between his arms and fumbled it into a pocket. Then the deep gnome stood back and watched, taking up a rear guard, as Drizzt cut a devastating path to the nearest exit.

Five minutes later, to Belwar's absolute amazement, they were running free down a darkened tunnel, the frustrated shrieks of "Doom! Doom!" fast fading behind them.

# 13
# A Little Place to Call Home

Enough. Enough!" the winded burrow-warden gasped at Drizzt, trying to slow his companion. "*Magga cammara*, dark elf. We have left them far behind."

Drizzt spun on the burrow-warden, scimitars ready in hand and angry fires burning still in his lavender eyes. Belwar backed away quickly and cautiously.

"Calm, my friend," the svirfneblin said quietly, but despite the reassurance, the burrow-warden's mithral hands came defensively in front of him. "The threat to us is ended."

Drizzt breathed deeply to steady himself, then, realizing that he had not put his scimitars away, promptly slipped them into their sheaths.

"Are you all right?" Belwar asked, moving back to Drizzt's side. Blood smeared the drow's face from where he had slammed into the side of the walkway.

Drizzt nodded. "It was the fight," he tried vainly to explain. "The excitement. I had to let go of—"

"You need not explain," Belwar cut him short. "You did fine, dark elf. Better than fine. Had it not been for your actions, we, all three, surely would have fallen."

"It came back to me," Drizzt groaned, searching for the words that could explain. "That darker part of me. I had thought it gone."

"It is," the burrow-warden said.

"No," argued Drizzt. "That cruel beast that I have become possessed me fully against those bird-men. It guided my blades, savagely and without mercy."

"You guided your own blades," Belwar assured him.

"But the rage," replied Drizzt. "The unthinking rage. All I wanted to do was kill them and hack them down."

"If that was the truth, we would be there still," reasoned the svirfneblin. "By your actions, we escaped. There are many more of the bird-men back there to be killed, yet you led the way from the chamber. Rage? Perhaps, but surely not unthinking rage. You did as you had to do, and you did it well, dark elf. Better than anyone I have ever seen. Do not apologize, to me or to yourself!"

Drizzt leaned back against the wall to consider the words. He was comforted by the deep gnome's reasoning and appreciated Belwar's efforts. Still, though, the burning fires of rage he had felt when Guenhwyvar fell into the acid lake haunted him, an emotion so overwhelming that Drizzt had not yet come to terms with it. He wondered if he ever would.

In spite of his uneasiness, though, Drizzt felt comforted by the presence of his svirfneblin friend. He remembered other encounters of the last years, battles he had been forced to fight alone. Then, like now, the hunter had welled within him, had come to the fore and guided the deadly strikes of his blades. But there was a difference this time that Drizzt could not deny. Before, when he was alone, the hunter did not so readily depart. Now, with Belwar by his side, Drizzt was fully back in control.

Drizzt shook his thick white mane, trying to dismiss any last remnants of the hunter. He thought himself foolish now for the way he had begun the battle against the bird-men, slapping with the flat of his blades. He and Belwar might be in the cavern still if Drizzt's instinctive side had not emerged, if he had not learned of Guenhwyvar's fall.

He looked at Belwar suddenly, remembering the inspiration of his anger. "The statuette!" he cried. "You have it."

Belwar scooped the item out of his pocket. "*Magga cammara*!" Belwar exclaimed, his round toned voice edged with panic. "Might the panther be wounded? What effect would the acid have against Guenhwyvar? Might the panther have escaped to the Astral Plane?"

Drizzt took the figurine and examined it in trembling hands, taking comfort in the fact that it was not marred in any way. Drizzt believed that he should wait before calling Guenhwyvar; if the panther was injured, it surely would heal better at rest in its own plane of existence. But Drizzt could not wait to learn of Guenhwyvar's fate. He placed the figurine down on the ground at his feet and called out softly.

Both the drow and the svirfneblin sighed audibly when the mist began to swirl around the onyx statue. Belwar took out his enchanted brooch to better observe the cat.

A dreadful sight awaited them. Obediently, faithfully, Guenhwyvar came to Drizzt's summons, but as soon as the drow saw the panther, he knew that he should have left Guenhwyvar alone so that it might lick its wounds. Guenhwyvar's silken black coat was burned and showing more patches of scalded skin than fur. Once-sleek muscles hung ragged, burned from the bone, and one eye remained closed and horribly scarred.

Guenhwyvar stumbled, trying to get to Drizzt's side. Drizzt rushed to Guenhwyvar instead, dropping to his knees and throwing a gentle hug around the panther's huge neck.

"Guen," he mumbled.

"Will it heal?" Belwar asked softly, his voice nearly breaking apart on every word.

Drizzt shook his head, at a loss. Truly, he knew very little about the panther beyond its abilities as his companion. Drizzt had seen Guenhwyvar wounded before, but never seriously. Now he could only hope that the magical extra-planar properties would allow Guenhwyvar to recover fully.

"Go back home," Drizzt said. "Rest and get well, my friend. I will call for you in a few days."

"Perhaps we can give some aid now," Belwar offered.

Drizzt knew the futility of that suggestion. "Guenhwyvar will better heal at rest," he explained as the cat dissipated into the mist again. "We can do nothing for Guenhwyvar that will carry over to the other plane. Being here in our world taxes the panther's strength. Every minute takes a toll."

Guenhwyvar was gone and only the figurine remained. Drizzt picked it up and studied it for a very long time before he could bear to drop it back into a pocket.

⚔ ⚔ ⚔ ⚔ ⚔

A sword flicked the bedroll up into the air, then slashed and cut beside its sister blade until the blanket was no more than a tattered rag. Zaknafein glanced down at the silver coins on the floor. Such an obvious dupe, but the camp, and the prospect of Drizzt returning to it, had kept Zaknafein at bay for several days!

Drizzt Do'Urden was gone, and he had taken great pains to announce his departure from Blingdenstone. The spirit-wraith paused to consider this new bit of information, and the necessity of thought, of tapping into the rational being that Zaknafein had been on more than an instinctive level, brought the inevitable conflict between this undead animation and the spirit of the being it held captive.

⚔ ⚔ ⚔ ⚔ ⚔

Back in her anteroom, Matron Malice Do'Urden felt the struggle within her creation. In Zin-carla, control of the spirit-wraith remained the responsibility of the matron mother that the Spider Queen graced with the gift. Malice had to work hard at the appointed task, had to spit off a succession of chants and spells to insinuate herself between the thought processes of the spirit wraith and the emotions and soul of Zaknafein Do'Urden.

⚔ ⚔ ⚔ ⚔ ⚔

The spirit-wraith lurched as he felt the intrusions of Malice's powerful will. It proved to be no contest; in barely a second, the spirit-wraith was studying the small chamber Drizzt and one other being, probably a deep gnome, had disguised as a campsite. They were gone now, tendays out, and no doubt moving away from Blingdenstone with all speed. Probably, the spirit-wraith reasoned, moving away from Menzoberranzan as well.

Zaknafein moved outside the chamber into the main tunnel. He sniffed one way, back east toward Menzoberranzan, then turned and dropped to a crouch and sniffed again. The location spells Malice had imbued upon Zaknafein could not cover such distances, but the minute sensations the spirit wraith received from his inspection only confirmed his suspicions. Drizzt had gone west.

Zaknafein walked off down the tunnel, not the slightest limp evident from the wound he had received at the end of a goblin's spear, a wound that would have crippled a mortal being. He was more than a tenday behind Drizzt, maybe two, but the spirit-wraith was not concerned. His prey had to sleep, had to rest and eat. His prey was flesh, and mortal—and weak.

⚔ ⚔ ⚔ ⚔ ⚔

"What manner of being is it?" Drizzt whispered to Belwar as they watched the curious bipedal creature filling buckets in a fast-running stream. This entire area of the tunnels was magically lighted, but Drizzt and Belwar felt safe enough in the shadows of a rocky outcropping a few dozen yards from the stooping robed figure.

"A man," Belwar replied. "Human, from the surface."

"He is a long way from home," Drizzt remarked. "Yet he seems comfortable in his surroundings. I would not believe that a surface-dweller could survive in the Underdark. It goes against the teachings I received in the Academy."

"Probably a wizard," Belwar reasoned. "That would account for the light in this region. And it would account for his being here."

Drizzt looked at the svirfneblin curiously.

"A strange lot are wizards," Belwar explained, as though the truth was self-evident. "Human wizards, even more than any others, so I've heard tell. Drow wizards practice for power. Svirfneblin wizards practice the arts to better know the stone. But human wizards," the deep gnome went on, obvious disdain in his tone. "*Magga cammara*, dark elf, human wizards are a different lot altogether!"

"Why do human wizards practice the art of magic at all?" Drizzt asked.

Belwar shook his head. "I do not believe that any scholars have yet discovered the reason," he replied in all sincerity. "A strange and dangerously unpredictable race are the humans, and better to be left alone."

"You have met some?"

"A few." Belwar shuddered, as though the memory was not a pleasant one. "Traders from the surface. Ugly things, and arrogant. The whole of the world is only for them, by their thinking."

The resonant voice rang out a bit more loudly than Belwar had intended, and the robed figure by the stream cocked his head in the companions' direction.

"Comen out, leetle rodents," the human called in a language that the companions could not understand. The wizard reiterated the request in another tongue, then in drow, and then in two more unknown tongues, and then in svirfneblin. He continued on for many minutes, Drizzt and Belwar looking at each other in disbelief.

"He is a learned man," Drizzt whispered to the deep gnome.

"Rats, probibably," the human muttered to himself. He glanced around, seeking some way to flush out the unseen noisemakers, thinking that the creatures might provide a fine meal.

"Let us learn if he is friend or foe," Drizzt whispered, and he started to move out from the concealment. Belwar stopped him and looked at him doubtfully, but then, with no recourse other than his own instincts, he shrugged and let Drizzt move on.

"Greetings, human so far from home," Drizzt said in his native language, stepping out from behind the outcropping.

The human's eyes went hysterically wide and he pulled roughly on his scraggly white beard. "You ist notten a rat!" he shrieked in strained but understandable drow.

"No," Drizzt said. He looked back to Belwar, who was moving out to join him.

"Thieves!" the human cried. "Comen to shteal my home, ist you?"

"No," Drizzt said again.

"Go avay!" the human yelled, waving his hands as a farmer would to shoo chickens. "Getten. Go on, qvickly now!"

Drizzt and Belwar exchanged curious glances.

"No," Drizzt said a third time.

"Thees ist my home, stupit dark elven!" the human spat. "Did I asket you to comen here? Did I sent a letter invititing you to join me in my home? Or perhapst you and your oogly little friend simply consider it your duty to velcome me to the neighborhood!"

"Careful, drow," Belwar whispered as the human rambled on. "He's a wizard, for sure, and a shaky one, even by human standards."

"Oren maybe bot the drow ant deep gnome races fear of me?" the human mused, more to himself than to the intruders. "Yes, of course. They have heard that I, Brister Fendlestick, decided to take to the corridors of the Underdark and have joined forces to protecket themselvens against me! Yes, yes, it all seems so clear, and so pititiful, to me now!"

"I have fought wizards before," Drizzt replied to Belwar under his breath. "Let us hope that we can settle this without blows. Whatever must happen, though, know that I have no desire to return the way we came." Belwar nodded his grim agreement as Drizzt turned back to the human. "Perhaps we can convince him simply to let us pass," Drizzt whispered.

The human trembled on the verge of an explosion. "Fine!" he screamed suddenly. "Then do not getten away!" Drizzt saw his error in thinking that he might reason with this one. The drow started forward, meaning to close in before the wizard could launch any attacks.

But the human had learned to survive in the Underdark, and his defenses were in place long before Drizzt and Belwar ever appeared around the rocky outcropping. He waved his hands and uttered a single word that the companions could not understand. A ring on his finger glowed brightly and loosed a tiny ball of fire up into the air between him and the intruders.

"Velcome to my home, then!" the wizard yelled triumphantly. "Play with this!" He snapped his fingers and vanished.

Drizzt and Belwar could feel the explosive energy gathering around the glowing orb.

"Run!" the burrow-warden cried, and he turned to flee. In Blingdenstone, most of the magic was illusionary, designed for defense. But in Menzoberranzan, where Drizzt had learned of magic, the spells were undeniably offensive. Drizzt knew the wizard's attack, and he knew that in these narrow and low corridors, flight would not be an option.

"No!" he cried, and he grabbed the back of Belwar's leather jack and pulled the deep gnome along, straight toward the glowing orb. Belwar knew to trust in Drizzt, and he turned and ran willingly beside his friend. The burrow-warden understood the drow's plan as soon as his eyes managed to tear away from the spectacle of the orb. Drizzt was making for the stream.

The friends dived headlong into the water, bouncing and scraping on the stones, just as the fireball exploded.

A moment later, they rose up from the steaming water, wisps of smoke rising from the back of their clothing, which had not been submerged. They coughed and sputtered, for the flames had temporarily stolen the air from the chamber, and the residual heat from the glowing stones nearly overwhelmed them.

"Humans," Belwar muttered grimly. He pulled himself from the water and shook vigorously. Drizzt came out beside him and couldn't hide his laughter.

The deep gnome, though, found no levity at all in the situation. "The wizard," he pointedly reminded Drizzt. Drizzt dropped into a crouch and glanced nervously all around. They set off at once.

⚔ ⚔ ⚔ ⚔ ⚔

"Home!" Belwar proclaimed a couple of days later. The two friends looked down from a narrow ledge at a wide and high cavern that housed an underground lake. Behind them was a three-chambered cave with only a single tiny entrance, easily defensible.

Drizzt climbed the ten or so feet to stand by his friend on the topmost ledge. "Possibly," he tentatively agreed, "though we left the wizard only a few days' walk from here."

"Forget the human," Belwar snarled, glancing over at the burn mark on his precious jack.

"And I am not so fond of having so large a pool only a few feet from our door," Drizzt continued.

"With fish it is filled!" the burrow-warden argued. "And with mosses and plants that will keep our bellies full, and water that seems clean enough!"

"But such an oasis will attract visitors," reasoned Drizzt. We would find little rest, I fear."

Belwar looked down the sheer wall to the floor of the large cavern. "Never a problem," he said with a snicker. "The bigger ones cannot get up here, and the smaller ones . . . well, I have seen the cut of your blades, and you have seen the strength of my hands. About the smaller ones I shall not worry!"

Drizzt liked the svirfneblin's confidence, and he had to agree that they had found no other place suitable for use as a dwelling. Water, hard to find and more often than not, undrinkable, was a precious commodity in the dry Underdark. With the lake and the growth about it, Drizzt and Belwar would never have to travel far to find a meal.

Drizzt was about to agree, but then a movement down by the water caught his and Belwar's attention.

"And crabs!" spouted the svirfneblin, obviously not having the same reaction to the sight as the drow. "*Magga cammara*, dark elf! Crabs! As fine a meal as ever you will find!"

Indeed it was a crab that had slipped out of the lake, a gigantic, twelve-foot monster with pincers that could snap a human—or an elf or a gnome—fully in half. Drizzt looked at Belwar incredulously. "A meal?" he asked.

Belwar's smile rolled right up around his crinkled nose as he banged his hammer and pick hands together.

They ate crab meat that night, and the day after that, and the day after that, and the day after that, and Drizzt soon was quite willing to agree that the three-chambered cave by the underground lake made a fine home.

⚔ ⚔ ⚔ ⚔ ⚔

The spirit-wraith paused to consider the red-glowing field. In life, Zaknafein Do'Urden would have avoided such a patch, respecting the inherent dangers of odd-glowing rooms and luminous mosses. But to the spirit-wraith the trail was clear; Drizzt had come this way.

The spirit-wraith waded in, ignoring the noxious puffs of deadly spores that shot up at him with every step, choking spores that filled the lungs of unfortunate creatures.

But Zaknafein did not draw breath.

Then came the rumbling as the grubber rushed to protect its domain. Zaknafein fell into a defensive crouch, the instincts of the being he once had been sensing the danger. The grubber rolled into the glowing moss patch but noticed no intruder to chase away. It moved in anyway, thinking that a meal of baruchies might not be such a bad thing.

When the grubber reached the center of the chamber, the spirit-wraith let his levitation spell dissipate. Zaknafein landed on the monster's back, locking his legs fast. The grubber thrashed and thundered about the room, but Zaknafein's balance did not waver.

The grubber's hide was thick and tough, able to repel all but the finest of weapons, which Zaknafein possessed.

⚔ ⚔ ⚔ ⚔ ⚔

"What was that?" Belwar asked one day, stopping his work on the new door blocking their cave opening. Down by the pool, Drizzt apparently had heard the sound as well, for he had dropped the helmet he was using to fetch some water and had drawn both scimitars. He held a hand up to keep the burrow-warden silent, then picked his way back to the ledge for a quiet conversation.

The sound, a loud clacking noise, came again.

"You know it, dark elf?" Belwar asked softly.

Drizzt nodded. "Hook horrors," he replied, "possessing the keenest hearing in all the Underdark." Drizzt kept his recollections of his sole encounter with this type of monster to himself. It had occurred during a patrol exercise, with Drizzt leading his Academy class through the tunnels outside Menzoberranzan. The patrol came upon a group of the giant, bipedal creatures with exoskeletons as hard as plated metal armor and powerful beaks and claws. The drow patrol, mostly through Drizzt's exploits, had won the day, but what Drizzt remembered most keenly was his belief that the encounter had been an exercise planned by the masters of the Academy, and that they had sacrificed an innocent drow child to the hook horrors for the sake of realism.

"Let us find them," Drizzt said quietly but grimly. Belwar paused to catch his breath when he saw the dangerous simmer in the drow's lavender eyes.

"Hook horrors are dangerous rivals," Drizzt explained, noticing the deep gnome's hesitation. "We cannot allow them to roam the region."

Following the clacking noises, Drizzt had little trouble closing in. He silently picked his way around a final bend with Belwar close by his side. In a wider section of the corridor stood a single hook horror, banging its heavy claws rhythmically against the stone as a svirfneblin miner might use his pickaxe.

Drizzt held Belwar back, indicating that he could dispatch the monster quickly if he could sneak in on it without being noticed. Belwar agreed but remained poised to join in at the first opportunity or need.

The hook horror, obviously engaged in its game with the stone wall, did not hear or see the approaching stealthy drow. Drizzt came right in beside the monster, looking for the easiest and fastest way to dispatch it. He saw only one opening in the exoskeleton, a slit between the creature's breastplate and its wide neck. Getting a blade in there could be a bit of a problem, though, for the hook horror was nearly ten feet tall.

But the hunter found the solution. He came in hard and fast at the hook horror's knee, butting with both his shoulders and bringing his blades up into the creature's crotch. The hook horror's legs buckled, and it tumbled back over the drow. As agile as any cat, Drizzt rolled out and sprang on top of the felled monster, both his blades coming tip in at the slit in the armor.

He could have finished the hook horror at once; his scimitars easily could have slipped through the bony defenses. But Drizzt saw something—terror?—on the hook horror's face, something in the creature's expression that should not have been there. He forced the hunter back inside, took control of his swords, and hesitated for just a second—long enough for the hook horror, to Drizzt's absolute amazement, to speak in clear and proper drow language, "Please . . . do . . . not . . . kill . . . me!"

# 14
# Clacker

The scimitars slowly eased away from the hook horror's neck.

"Not . . . as I . . . ap-appear," the monster tried to explain in its halting speech. With each uttered word, the hook horror seemed to become more comfortable with the language. "I am . . . pech."

"Pech?" Belwar gawked, moving up to Drizzt's side. The svirfneblin looked down at the trapped monster with understandable confusion. "A bit big you are for a pech," he remarked.

Drizzt looked from the monster to Belwar, seeking some explanation. The drow had never heard the word before.

"Rock children," Belwar explained to him. "Strange little creatures. Hard as the stone and living for no other reason than to work it."

"Sounds like a svirfneblin," Drizzt replied.

Belwar paused a moment to figure out if he had been complimented or insulted. Unable to discern, the burrow-warden continued somewhat cautiously. "There are not many pech about, and fewer still that look like this one!" He cast a doubting eye at the hook horror, then gave Drizzt a look that told the drow to keep his scimitars at the ready.

"Pech . . . n-n-no more," the hook horror stammered, clear remorse evident in its throaty voice. "Pech no more."

"What is your name?" Drizzt asked it, hoping to find some clues to the truth.

The hook horror thought for a long moment, then shook its great head helplessly. "Pech . . . n-n-no more," the monster said again, and it purposely tilted its beaked face backward, widening the crack in its exoskeleton armor and inviting Drizzt to finish the strike.

"You cannot remember your name?" Drizzt asked, not so anxious to kill the creature. The hook horror neither moved nor replied. Drizzt looked to Belwar for advice, but the burrow-warden only shrugged helplessly.

"What happened?" Drizzt pressed the monster. "You must tell me what happened to you."

"W-w-w . . ." The hook horror struggled to reply. "W-wi-wizard. Evil wi-zard."

Somewhat schooled in the ways of magic and in the unscrupulous uses its practitioners often put it to, Drizzt began to understand the possibilities and began to believe this strange creature. "A wizard changed you?" he asked, already guessing the answer. He and Belwar exchanging amazed expressions. "I have heard of such spells."

"As have I," agreed the burrow-warden. "*Magga cammara*, dark elf, I have seen the wizards of Blingdenstone use similar magic when we needed to infiltrate . . ." The deep gnome paused suddenly, remembering the heritage of the elf he was addressing.

"Menzoberranzan," Drizzt finished with a chuckle.

Belwar cleared his throat, a bit embarrassed, and turned back to the monster. "A pech you once were," he said, needing to hear the whole explanation spelled out in one clear thought, "and some wizard changed you into a hook horror."

"True," the monster replied. "Pech no more."

"Where are your companions?" the svirfneblin asked. "If what I have heard of your people is true, pech do not often travel alone."

"D-d-d-dead," said the monster. "Evil w-w-w—"

"Human wizard?" Drizzt prompted.

The great beak bobbed in an excited nod. "Yes, m-m-man."

"And the wizard then left you to your pains as a hook horror," Belwar said. He and Drizzt looked long and hard at each other, and then the drow stepped away, allowing the hook horror to rise.

"I w-w-w-wish you w-w-w-would k-k-kill me," the monster then said, twisting up into a sitting position. It looked at its clawed hands with obvious disgust. "The s-stone, the stone . . . lost to me."

Belwar raised his own crafted hands in response. "So had I once believed," he said. "You are alive, and no longer are you alone. Come with us to the lake, where we can talk some more."

Presently the hook horror agreed and began, with much effort, to raise its quarter-ton bulk from the floor. Amid the scraping and shuffling of the creature's hard exoskeleton, Belwar prudently whispered to Drizzt, "Keep your blades at the ready!"

The hook horror finally stood, towering to its imposing ten-foot height, and the drow did not argue Belwar's logic.

For many hours, the hook horror recounted its adventures to the two friends. As amazing as the story was the monster's growing acclimation to the use of language. This fact, and the monster's descriptions of its previous existence—of a life tapping and shaping the stone in an almost holy reverence—further convinced Belwar and Drizzt of the truth of its bizarre tale.

"It feels g-g-good to speak again, though the language is not my own," the creature said after a while. "It feels as if I have f-found again a part of what I once w-w-was."

With his own similar experiences so clear in his mind, Drizzt understood the sentiments completely.

"How long have you been this way?" Belwar asked.

The hook horror shrugged, its huge chest and shoulders rattling through the movement. "Tendays, m-months," it said. "I cannot remember. The time is l-lost to me."

Drizzt put his face in his hands and exhaled a deep sigh, in full empathy and sympathy with the unfortunate creature. Drizzt, too, had felt so lost and alone out in the wilds. He, too, knew the grim truth of such a fate. Belwar patted the drow softly with his hammer-hand.

"And where now are you going?" the burrow-warden asked the hook horror. "Or where were you coming from?"

"Chasing the w-w-w—" the hook horror replied, fumbling helplessly over that last word as though the mere mention of the evil wizard pained the creature greatly. "But so much is l-lost to me. I would find him with l-little effort if I was still p-p-pech. The stones would tell me where to l-look. But I cannot talk to them very often anymore." The monster rose from its seat on the stone. "I will go," it said determinedly. "You are not safe with me around."

"You will stay," Drizzt said suddenly and with a tone of finality that could not be denied.

"I c-cannot control," the hook horror tried to explain.

"You've no need to worry," said Belwar. He pointed to the doorway up on the ledge at the side of the cavern. "Our home is up there, with a door too small for you to get through. Down here by the lake you must rest until we all decide our best course of action."

The hook horror was exhausted, and the svirfneblin's reasoning seemed sound enough. The monster dropped heavily back to the stone and curled up as much as its bulky body would allow. Drizzt and Belwar took their leave, glancing back at their strange new companion with every step.

"Clacker," Belwar said suddenly, stopping Drizzt beside him. With great effort, the hook horror rolled over to consider the deep gnome, understanding that Belwar had uttered the word in its direction.

"That is what we shall call you, if you have no objections," the svirfneblin explained to the creature and to Drizzt. "Clacker!"

"A fitting name," Drizzt remarked.

"It is a g-good name," agreed the hook horror, but silently the creature wished that it could remember its pech name, the name that rolled on and on like a rounded boulder in a sloping passage and spoke prayers to the stone with each growling syllable.

"We will widen the door," Drizzt said when he and Belwar got inside their cave complex. "So that Clacker may enter and rest beside us in safety."

"No, dark elf," argued the burrow-warden. "That we shall not do."

"He is not safe out there beside the water," Drizzt replied. "Monsters will find him."

"Safe enough he is!" snorted Belwar. "What monster would willingly attack a hook horror?" Belwar understood Drizzt's sincere concern, but he understood, too, the danger in Drizzt's suggestion. "I have witnessed such spells," the svirfneblin said somberly. "They are called polymorph. Immediately comes the change of the body, but the change of the mind can take time."

"What are you saying?" Drizzt's voice edged on panic.

"Clacker is still a pech," replied Belwar, "trapped though he is in the body of a hook horror. But soon, I fear, Clacker will be a pech no more. A hook horror he will become, mind and body, and however friendly we might be, Clacker will come to think of us as no more than another meal."

Drizzt started to argue, but Belwar silenced him with one sobering thought. "Would you enjoy having to kill him, dark elf?"

Drizzt turned away. "His tale is familiar to me."

"Not as much as you believe," replied Belwar.

"I, too, was lost," Drizzt reminded the burrow-warden.

"So you believe," Belwar answered. "But that which was essentially Drizzt Do'Urden remained within you, my friend. You were as you had to be, as the situation around you forced you to be. This is different. Not just in body, but in very essence will Clacker become a hook horror. His thoughts will be the thoughts of a hook horror and *Magga cammara*, he will not return your grant of mercy when you are the one on the ground."

Drizzt could not be satisfied, though he could not refute the deep gnome's blunt logic. He moved into the complex's left-hand chamber, the one he had claimed as his bedroom, and fell into his hammock.

"Alas for you, Drizzt Do'Urden," Belwar mumbled under his breath as he watched the drow's heavy movements, laden with sorrow. "And alas for our doomed pech friend." The burrow-warden went into his own chamber and crawled into his hammock, feeling terrible about the whole situation but determined to remain coldly logical and practical, whatever the pain. For Belwar understood that Drizzt felt a kinship to the unfortunate creature, a potentially fatal bond founded in empathy for Clacker's loss of self.

Later that night, an excited Drizzt shook the svirfneblin from his slumber. "We must help him," Drizzt whispered harshly.

Belwar wiped an arm across his face and tried to orient himself. His sleep had been uneasy, filled with dreams in which he had cried *"Bivrip!"*

in an impossibly loud voice, then had proceeded to bash the life out of his newest companion.

"We must help him!" Drizzt said again, even more forcefully. Belwar could tell by the drow's haggard appearance that Drizzt had found no sleep this night.

"I am no wizard," the burrow-warden said. "Neither are—"

"Then we will find one." Drizzt growled. "We will find the human who cursed Clacker and force him to reverse the dweomer! We saw him by the stream only a few days ago. He cannot be so far away!"

"A mage capable of such magic will prove no easy foe," Belwar was quick to reply. "Have you so quickly forgotten the fireball?" Belwar glanced to the wall, to where his scorched leather jack hung on a peg, as if to convince himself. "The wizard is beyond us, I fear," Belwar mumbled, but Drizzt could see the lack of conviction in the burrow-warden's expression as he spoke the words.

"Are you so quick to condemn Clacker?" Drizzt asked bluntly. A wide smile began to spread over Drizzt's face as he saw the svirfneblin weakening. "Is this the same Belwar Dissengulp who took in a lost drow? That most honored burrow-warden who would not give up hope for a dark elf that everyone else considered dangerous and beyond help?"

"Go to sleep, dark elf," Belwar retorted, pushing Drizzt away with his hammer-hand.

"Wise advice, my friend," said Drizzt. "And you sleep well. We may have a long road ahead of us."

"*Magga cammara*," huffed the taciturn svirfneblin, stubbornly holding to his facade of gruff practicality. He rolled away from Drizzt and soon was snoring.

Drizzt noted that Belwar's snores now sounded from the depths of a deep and contented sleep.

⚔ ⚔ ⚔ ⚔ ⚔

Clacker beat against the wall with his clawed hands, tap- tapping the stone relentlessly.

"Not again," a flustered Belwar whispered to Drizzt. "Not out here!"

Drizzt sped along the winding corridor, homing in on the monotonous sound. "Clacker!" he called softly when the hook horror was in sight.

The hook horror turned to face the approaching drow, clawed hands wide and ready and a growing hiss slipping through his great beak. A moment later, Clacker realized what he was doing and abruptly stopped.

"Why must you continue that banging?" Drizzt asked him, trying to pretend, even to himself, that he had not seen Clacker's battle stance. "We are out in the wilds, my friend. Such sounds invite visitors."

The giant monster's head drooped. "You should not have c-c-come out with m-me," Clacker said. "I c-c-cannot—t-too many things will happen that I cannot c-control."

Drizzt reached up and put a comforting hand on Clacker's bony elbow. "It was my fault," the drow said, understanding the hook horror's meaning. Clacker had apologized for turning dangerously on Drizzt. "We should not have gone off in different directions," Drizzt continued, "and I should not have approached you so quickly and without warning. We will all stay together now, though our search may prove longer, and Belwar and I will help you to maintain control."

Clacker's beaked face brightened. "It does feel so very g-good to t-t-tap the stone," he proclaimed. Clacker banged a claw on the rock as if to jolt his memory. His voice and his gaze trailed away as he thought of his past life, the one that the wizard had stolen from him. All the pech's days had been spent tapping the stone, shaping the stone, talking to the precious stone.

"You will be pech again," Drizzt promised.

Belwar, approaching from the tunnel, heard the drow's words and was not so certain. They had been out in the tunnels for more than a tenday and had found not a sign of the wizard. The burrow-warden took some comfort in the fact that Clacker seemed to be winning back part of himself from his monstrous state, seemed to be regaining a measure of his pech personality. Belwar had watched the same transformation in Drizzt just a few tendays before, and beneath the survivalistic barriers of the hunter that Drizzt had become, Belwar had discovered his closest friend.

But the burrow-warden took care not to assume the same results with

Clacker. The hook horror's condition was the result of powerful magic, and no amount of friendship could reverse the workings of the wizard's dweomer. In finding Drizzt and Belwar, Clacker had been granted a temporary—and only temporary—reprieve from a miserable and undeniable fate.

They moved on through the tunnels of the Underdark for several more days without any luck. Clacker's personality still did not deteriorate, but even Drizzt, who had left the cave complex beside the lake so full of hope, began to feel the weight of increasing reality.

Then, just as Drizzt and Belwar had begun discussing returning to their home, the group came into a fair-sized cavern littered with rubble from a recent collapse of the ceiling.

"He has been here!" Clacker cried, and he offhandedly lifted a huge boulder and tossed it against a distant wall, where it shattered into so much rubble. "He has been here!" The hook horror rushed about, smashing stone and throwing boulders with growing, explosive rage.

"How can you know?" Belwar demanded, trying to stop his giant friend's tirade.

Clacker pointed up at the ceiling. "He d-did this. The w-w-w—he did this!"

Drizzt and Belwar exchanged concerned glances. The chamber's ceiling, which had been about fifteen feet up, was gouged and blasted, and in its center loomed a massive hole that extended up to twice the ceiling's former height. If magic had caused that devastation, it was powerful magic indeed!

"The wizard did this?" Belwar echoed. He cast that stubbornly practical look he had perfected toward Drizzt one more time.

"His t-t-tower," Clacker replied, and rushed off about the chamber to see if he could discern which exit the wizard had taken.

Now Drizzt and Belwar were completely at a loss, and Clacker, when he finally took the time to look at them, realized their confusion.

"The w-w-w—"

"Wizard," Belwar put in impatiently.

Clacker took no offense, even appreciated the assistance. "The w-wizard has a t-tower," the excited hook horror tried to explain. "A g-great iron t-tower that he takes with him, setting it up wherever it is c-c-convenient." Clacker looked up at the ruined ceiling. "Even if it does not always fit."

"He carries a tower?" Belwar asked, his long nose crinkling right up over itself.

Clacker nodded excitedly, but then didn't take the time to explain further, for he had found the wizard's trail, a clear boot print in a bed of moss leading down another of the corridors.

Drizzt and Belwar had to be satisfied with their friend's incomplete explanation, for the chase was on. Drizzt took up the lead, using all the skills he had learned in the drow Academy and had heightened during his decade alone in the Underdark. Belwar, with his innate racial understanding of the Underdark and his magically lighted brooch, kept track of their direction, and Clacker, in those instances when he fell more completely back into his former self, asked the stones for guidance. The three of them passed another blasted chamber, and another chamber that showed clear signs of the tower's presence, though its ceiling was high enough to accommodate the structure.

A few days later, the three companions turned into a wide and high cavern, and far back from them, beside a rushing stream, loomed the wizard's home. Again Drizzt and Belwar looked at each other helplessly, for the tower stood fully thirty feet high and twenty across, its smooth metallic walls mocking their plans. They took separate and cautious routes to the structure and were even more amazed, for the tower's walls were pure adamantite, the hardest metal in all the world.

They found only a single door, small and barely showing its outline in the perfection of the tower's craftsmanship. They didn't have to test it to know that it was secure against unwelcome visitors.

"The w-w-w—he is in there," Clacker snarled, running his claws over the door in desperation.

"Then he will have to come out," Drizzt reasoned. "And when he does, we will be waiting for him."

The plan did not satisfy the pech. With a rumbling roar that echoed throughout the region, Clacker threw his huge body against the tower door, then jumped back and slammed it again. The door didn't even shudder under the pounding, and it quickly became obvious to the deep gnome and the drow that Clacker's body would certainly lose the battle.

Drizzt tried vainly to calm his giant friend, while Belwar moved off to the side and began a familiar chant.

Finally, Clacker tumbled down in a heap, sobbing in exhaustion and pain and helpless rage. Then Belwar, his mithral hands sparking whenever they touched, waded in.

"Move aside!" the burrow-warden demanded. "I have come too far to be stopped by a single door!" Belwar moved directly in front of the small door and slammed his enchanted hammer-hand at it with all his strength. A blinding flash of blue sparks burst out in every direction. The deep gnome's muscled arms worked furiously, scraping and bashing, but when Belwar had exhausted his energy, the tower door showed only the slightest of scratches and superficial burns.

Belwar banged his hands together in disgust, showering himself in harmless sparks, and Clacker agreed wholeheartedly with his frustrated sentiments. Drizzt, though, was more angry and concerned than his friends. Not only had the wizard's tower stopped them, but the wizard inside undoubtedly knew of their presence. Drizzt moved about the structure cautiously, noting the many arrow slits. Creeping below one, he heard a soft chant, and though he couldn't understand the wizard's words, he could guess easily enough the human's intent.

"Run!" he yelled to his companions, and then, in sheer desperation, he grabbed a nearby stone and hauled it up into the opening of the arrow slit. Luck was with the drow, for the wizard completed his spell just as the rock slammed against the opening. A lightning bolt roared out, shattered the stone, and sent Drizzt flying, but it reflected back into the tower.

"Damnation! Damnation!" came a squeal from inside the tower. "I hate vhen that hoppens!"

Belwar and Clacker rushed over to help their fallen friend. The drow was only stunned, and he was up and ready before they ever got there.

"Oh, you ist going to pay dearly for that one, yest you ist!" came a cry from within.

"Run away!" cried the burrow-warden, and even the outraged hook horror was in full agreement. But as soon as Belwar looked into the drow's lavender eyes, he knew that Drizzt would not flee. Clacker, too, backed away a step from the fires gathering within Drizzt Do'Urden.

"*Magga cammara*, dark elf, we cannot get in," the svirfneblin prudently reminded Drizzt.

Drizzt pulled out the onyx figurine and held it against the arrow slit, blocking it with his body. "We shall see," he growled, and then he called to Guenhwyvar.

The black mist swirled about and found only one empty path clear from the figurine.

"I vill keell you all!" cried the unseen wizard.

The next sound from within the tower was a low panther's growl, and then the wizard's voice rang out again. "I cood be wrong!"

"Open the door!" Drizzt screamed. "On your life, foul wizard!"

"Never!"

Guenhwyvar roared again, then the wizard screamed and the door swung wide.

Drizzt led the way. They entered a circular room, the tower's bottom level. An iron ladder ran up its center to a trap door, the wizard's attempted escape route. The human hadn't quite made it, however, and he hung upside-down off the back side of the ladder, one leg hooked at the knee through a rung. Guenhwyvar, appearing fully healed from the ordeal in the acid lake and looking again like the most magnificent of panthers, perched on the other side of the ladder, casually mouthing the wizard's calf and foot.

"Do come een!" the wizard cried, throwing his arms out wide, then drawing them back to pull his drooping robe up from his face. Wisps of smoke rose from the remaining tatters of the lightning-blackened robe. "I am Brister Fendlestick. Velcome to my hoomble home!"

Belwar kept Clacker at the door, holding his dangerous friend back with his hammer-hand, while Drizzt moved up to take charge of the prisoner. The drow paused long enough to regard his dear feline companion, for he hadn't summoned Guenhwyvar since that day when he had sent the panther away to heal.

"You speak drow," Drizzt remarked, grabbing the wizard by the collar and agilely spinning him down to his feet. Drizzt eyed the man suspiciously; he had never seen a human before the encounter in the corridor by the stream. To this point, the drow wasn't overly impressed.

"Many tongues ist known to me," replied the wizard, brushing himself off. And then, as if his proclamation was meant to carry some great importance, he added, "I am Brister Fendlestick!"

"Do you name pech among your languages?" Belwar growled from the door.

"Pech?" the wizard replied, spitting the word with apparent distaste.

"Pech," Drizzt snarled, emphasizing his response by snapping the edge of a scimitar to within an inch of the wizard's neck.

Clacker took a step forward, easily sliding the blocking svirfneblin across the smooth floor.

"My large friend was once a pech," Drizzt explained. "You should know that."

"Pech," the wizard spat. "Useless leetle things, and always they ist in the way" Clacker took another long stride forward.

"Be on with it, drow," Belwar begged, futilely leaning against the huge hook horror.

"Give him back his identity," Drizzt demanded. "Make our friend a pech again. And be quick about it."

"Bah!" snorted the wizard. "He ist better off as he ist!" the unpredictable human replied. "Why would anyone weesh to remain a pech?"

Clacker's breath came in a loud gasp. The sheer strength of his third stride sent Belwar skidding off to the side.

"Now, wizard," Drizzt warned. From the ladder, Guenhwyvar issued a long and hungry growl.

"Oh, very vell, very vell!" the wizard spouted, throwing up his hands in disgust. "Wretched pech!" He pulled an immense book from of a pocket much too small to hold it. Drizzt and Belwar smiled to each other, thinking victory at hand. But then the wizard made a fatal mistake.

"I shood have killed him as I killed the others," he mumbled under his breath, too low for even Drizzt, standing right beside him, to make out the words.

But hook horrors had the keenest hearing of any creature in the Underdark.

A swipe of Clacker's enormous claw sent Belwar spiraling across the room. Drizzt, spinning about at the sound of heavy steps, was thrown aside by the momentum of the rushing giant, the drow's scimitars flying from his hands. And the wizard, the foolish wizard, padded Clacker's impact with the iron ladder, a jolt so vicious that it bowed the ladder and sent Guenhwyvar flying off the other side.

Whether the initial crushing blow of the hook horror's five-hundred-pound body had killed the wizard was academic by the time either Drizzt or Belwar had recovered enough to call out to their friend. Clacker's hooks and beak slashed and snapped relentlessly, tearing and crushing. Every now and then came a sudden flash and a puff of smoke as another of the many magical items that the wizard carried snapped apart.

And when the hook horror had played out his rage and looked around at his three companions, surrounding him in battle-ready stances, the lump of gore at Clacker's feet was no longer recognizable.

Belwar started to remark that the wizard had agreed to change Clacker back, but he didn't see the point. Clacker fell to his knees and dropped his face into his claws, hardly believing what he had done.

"Let us be gone from this place," Drizzt said, sheathing his blades.

"Search it," Belwar suggested, thinking that marvelous treasures might be hidden within. But Drizzt could not remain for another moment. He had seen too much of himself in the unbridled rage of his giant companion, and the smell of the bloodied heap filled him with frustrations and fears that he could not tolerate. With Guenhwyvar in tow, he walked from the tower.

Belwar moved over and helped Clacker to his feet, then guided the trembling giant from the structure. Stubbornly practical, though, the burrow-warden made his companions wait around while he scoured the tower, searching for items that might aid them, or for the command word that would allow him to carry the tower along. But either the wizard was a poor man—which Belwar doubted—or he had his treasures safely hidden away, possibly in some other plane of existence, for the svirfneblin found nothing beyond a simple water skin and a pair of worn boots. If the marvelous adamantite tower had a command word, it had gone to the grave with the wizard.

Their journey home was a quiet one, lost in private concerns, regrets, and memories. Drizzt and Belwar did not have to speak their most pressing fear. In their discussions with Clacker, they both had learned enough of the normally peaceable race of pech to know that Clacker's murderous outburst was far removed from the creature he once had been.

But, the deep gnome and the drow had to admit to themselves, Clacker's actions were not so far removed from the creature he was fast becoming.

# 15
# Pointed Reminders

"What do you know?" Matron Malice demanded of Jarlaxle, walking at her side across the compound of House Do'Urden. Malice normally would not have been so conspicuous with the infamous mercenary, but she was worried and impatient. Reported stirring within the hierarchy of Menzoberranzan's ruling families did not bode well for House Do'Urden.

"Know?" Jarlaxle echoed, feigning surprise.

Malice scowled at him, as did Briza, walking on the other side of the brash mercenary.

Jarlaxle cleared his throat, though it sounded more like a laugh. He couldn't supply Malice with the details of the rumblings; he was not so foolish as to betray the more powerful houses of the city. But Jarlaxle could tease Malice with a simple statement of logic that only confirmed what she already had assumed. "Zin-carla, the spirit-wraith, has been in use for a very long time."

Malice struggled to keep her breathing inconspicuously smooth. She realized that Jarlaxle knew more than he would say, and the fact that the calculating mercenary had so coolly stated the obvious told her that her fears were justified. The spirit-wraith of Zaknafein had indeed been searching for Drizzt for a very long time. Malice did not need to be reminded that the Spider Queen was not known for her patience.

"Have you any more to tell me?" Malice asked.

Jarlaxle shrugged noncommittally.

"Then be gone from my house," the matron mother snarled.

Jarlaxle hesitated for a moment, wondering if he should demand payment for the little information he had provided. Then he dipped into one of his well-known low, hat-sweeping bows and turned for the gate.

He would find his payment soon enough.

In the anteroom to the house chapel an hour later, Matron Malice rested back in her throne and let her thoughts roll out into the winding tunnels of the wild Underdark. Her telepathy with the spirit-wraith was limited, usually a passing of strong emotions, nothing more. But from those internal struggles of Zaknafein, who had been Drizzt's father and closest friend in life and was now Drizzt's deadliest enemy, Malice could learn much of her spirit-wraith's progress. Anxieties caused by Zaknafein's inner struggle inevitably would increase whenever the spirit-wraith got close to Drizzt.

Now, after the disturbing meeting with Jarlaxle, Malice had to learn of Zaknafein's progress. A short time later, her efforts were rewarded.

⚔ ⚔ ⚔ ⚔ ⚔

"Matron Malice insists that the spirit-wraith has gone west, beyond the svirfneblin city," Jarlaxle explained to Matron Baenre. The mercenary had set out straight from House Do'Urden to the mushroom grove in the southern end of Menzoberranzan, to where the greatest of the drow families were housed.

"The spirit-wraith keeps to the trail," Matron Baenre mused, more to herself than to her informant. "That is good."

"But Matron Malice believes that Drizzt has a lead of many days, even tendays," Jarlaxle went on.

"She told you this?" Matron Baenre asked incredulously, amazed that Malice would reveal such damaging information.

"Some information can be gathered without words," the mercenary replied slyly. "Matron Malice's tone inferred much that she did not wish me to know."

Matron Baenre nodded and closed her wrinkled eyes, wearied by the whole experience. She had played a role in getting Matron Malice onto the ruling council, but now she could only sit and wait to see if Malice would remain.

"We must trust in Matron Malice," Matron Baenre said at length.

Across the room from Baenre and Jarlaxle, El-viddinvelp, Matron Baenre's companion mind flayer, turned its thoughts away from the conversation. The drow mercenary had reported that Drizzt had gone west, far out from Blingdenstone, and that news carried potential importance that could not be ignored.

The mind flayer projected its thoughts far out to the west, issued a clear warning down the corridors that were not as empty as they might appear.

⚔ ⚔ ⚔ ⚔ ⚔

Zaknafein knew as soon as he looked upon the still lake that he had caught up to his quarry. He dropped low into the crooks and crags along the wide cavern's wall and made his way about. Then he found the unnatural door and the cave complex beyond.

Old feelings stirred within the spirit-wraith, feelings of the kinship he once had known with Drizzt. New, savage emotions were quick to overwhelm them, though, as Matron Malice came into Zaknafein's mind in a wild fury. The spirit-wraith burst through the door, swords drawn, and tore through the complex. A blanket flew into the air and came down in pieces as Zaknafein's swords sliced across it a dozen times.

When the fit of rage had played itself out, Matron Malice's monster settled back into a crouch to examine the situation.

Drizzt was not at home.

It took the hunting spirit-wraith only a short time to determine that Drizzt, and a companion, or perhaps even two, had set out from the cavern a few days before. Zaknafein's tactical instincts told him to lie in wait, for surely this was no phony campsite, as had been the one outside the deep gnome city. Surely Zaknafein's prey meant to return.

The spirit-wraith sensed that Matron Malice, back on her throne in the drow city, would endure no delays. Time was running short for her—the dangerous whispers were growing louder every day—and Malice's fears and impatience cost her dearly this time.

⚔ ⚔ ⚔ ⚔ ⚔

Only a few hours after Malice had driven the spirit-wraith into the tunnels in pursuit of her renegade son, Drizzt, Belwar, and Clacker returned to the cavern by a different route.

Drizzt sensed at once that something was very wrong. He drew his blades and rushed across to the ledge, springing up to the door of the cave complex before Belwar and Clacker could even begin to question him.

When they arrived at the cave, they understood Drizzt's alarm. The place was destroyed, hammocks and bedrolls torn apart, bowls and a small box that had been stuffed with gathered foods smashed and thrown to every corner. Clacker, who could not fit inside the complex, spun from the door and moved away, ensuring that no enemy was lurking in the far reaches of the large cavern.

"*Magga cammara*!" Belwar roared. "What monster did this?"

Drizzt held up a blanket and pointed out the clean cuts in the fabric. Belwar did not miss the drow's meaning.

"Blades," the burrow-warden said grimly. "Fine and crafted blades."

"The blades of a drow," Drizzt finished for him.

"Far are we from Menzoberranzan," Belwar reminded him. "Far out in the wilds, beyond the knowledge and sight of your kin."

Drizzt knew better than to agree with such an assumption. For the bulk of his young life, Drizzt had witnessed the fanaticism that guided the lives of Lolth's foul priestesses. Drizzt himself had traveled on a raid many miles to the surface of the Realms, a raid that suited no better purpose than to give the Spider Queen a sweet taste of the blood of surface elves. "Do not underestimate Matron Malice," he said grimly.

"If it is indeed your mother come to call," Belwar growled, clapping his hands together, "she will find more than she expected waiting for her. We shall lie for her," the svirfneblin promised, "the three of us."

"Do not underestimate Matron Malice," Drizzt said again. "This encounter was no coincidence, and Matron Malice will be prepared for whatever we have to offer."

"You cannot know that," Belwar reasoned, but when the burrow-warden recognized the sincere dread in the drow's lavender eyes, all conviction drifted out of his voice.

They gathered what few usable items remained and set out only a short while later, again going west to put even more distance between themselves and Menzoberranzan.

Clacker took up the lead, for few monsters would willingly put themselves in the path of a hook horror. Belwar walked in the middle, the solid anchor of the party, and Drizzt floated along silently far to the rear, taking it upon himself to protect his friends if his mother's agents should catch up to them. Belwar had reasoned that they might have a good lead on whoever ruined their home. If the perpetrators had set off in pursuit of them from the cave complex, following their trail to the tower of the dead wizard, many days would pass before the enemy even returned to the cavern of the lake. Drizzt was not so secure in the burrow-warden's reasoning.

He knew his mother too well.

After several interminable days, the troupe came into a region of broken floors, jagged walls, and ceilings filled with stalactites that leered down at them like poised monsters. They closed in their ranks, needing the comfort of companionship. Despite the attention it might draw, Belwar took out his magically lighted brooch and pinned it on his leather jack. Even in the glow, the shadows thrown by sharp-edged mounds promised only peril.

This region seemed more hushed than the Underdark's usual stillness. Rarely did travelers in the subterranean world of the Realms hear the sounds of other creatures, but here the quiet felt more profound, as though all life somehow had been stolen from the place. Clacker's heavy steps and the scrape of Belwar's boots echoed unnervingly off the many stone faces.

Belwar was the first to sense approaching danger. Subtle vibrations in the stone called out to the svirfneblin that he and his friends were not alone. He stopped Clacker with his pick-hand, then looked back to Drizzt to see if the drow shared his uneasy feelings.

Drizzt signaled to the ceiling, then levitated up into the darkness, seeking an ambush spot among the many stalactites. The drow drew one of his scimitars as he ascended and put his other hand on the onyx figurine in his pocket.

Belwar and Clacker set up behind a ridge of stone, the deep gnome mumbling through the refrain that would enchant his mithral hands. Both felt better in the knowledge that the drow warrior was above them, looking over them.

But Drizzt was not the only one who figured the stalactites as an ambush spot. As soon as he entered the layer of jagged, spearlike stones, the drow knew he was not alone.

A form, slightly larger than Drizzt but obviously humanoid, drifted out around a nearby stalactite. Drizzt kicked off a stone to propel himself at it, drawing his other scimitar as he went. He knew his peril a moment later, for his enemy's head resembled a four-tentacled octopus. Drizzt had never actually viewed such a creature before, but he knew what it was: an illithid, a mind flayer, the most evil and most feared monster in all the Underdark.

The mind flayer struck first, long before Drizzt had closed within his scimitar's limited range. The monster's tentacles wiggled and waved, and—*fwoop!*—a cone of mental energy rolled over Drizzt. The drow fought back against the impending blackness with all of his willpower. He tried to concentrate on his target, tried to focus his anger, but the illithid blasted again. Another mind flayer appeared and fired its stunning force at Drizzt from the side.

Belwar and Clacker could see nothing of the encounter, for Drizzt was above the radius of the deep gnome's illuminating brooch. Both sensed that something was going on above them, though, and the burrow-warden risked a whispered call to his friend.

"Drizzt?"

His answer came only a moment later, when two scimitars clanged to the stone. Belwar and Clacker started toward the weapons in surprise, then fell back. Before them the air shimmered and wavered, as if an invisible door to some other plane of existence was being opened.

An illithid stepped through, appearing right before the surprised friends and letting out its mental blast before either of them even had time to cry out. Belwar reeled and stumbled to the floor, but Clacker, his mind already in conflict between hook horror and pech, was not so adversely affected.

The mind flayer loosed its force again, but the hook horror stepped right through the stunning cone and smashed the illithid with a single blow of his enormous clawed hand.

Clacker looked all around, and then up. Other mind flayers were drifting down from the ceiling, two holding Drizzt by the ankles. More invisible doors opened. In an instant, blast after blast came at Clacker from every angle, and the defense of his dual personalities' inner turmoil quickly began to wear away. Desperation and welling outrage took over Clacker's actions.

Clacker was solely a hook horror at that moment, acting on the instinctive rage and ferocity of the monstrous breed.

But even the hard shell of a hook horror proved no defense against the mind flayers' continuing insidious blasts. Clacker rushed at the two holding Drizzt.

The darkness caught him halfway there.

He was kneeling on the stone—he knew that much. Clacker crawled on, refusing to surrender, refusing to relinquish the sheer anger.

Then he lay on the floor, with no thoughts of Drizzt or Belwar or rage.

There was only darkness.

# Part Four

## Helpless

There have been many times in my life when I have felt helpless. It is perhaps the most acute pain a person can know, founded in frustration and ventless rage. The nick of a sword upon a battling soldier's arm cannot compare to the anguish a prisoner feels at the crack of a whip. Even if the whip does not strike the helpless prisoner's body, it surely cuts deeply at his soul.

We all are prisoners at one time or another in our lives, prisoners to ourselves or to the expectations of those around us. It is a burden that all people endure, that all people despise, and that few people ever learn to escape. I consider myself fortunate in this respect, for my life has traveled along a fairly straight-running path of improvement. Beginning in Menzoberranzan, under the relentless scrutiny of the evil Spider Queen's high priestesses, I suppose that my situation could only have improved.

In my stubborn youth, I believed that I could stand alone, that I was strong enough to conquer my enemies with sword and with principles. Arrogance convinced me that by sheer determination, I could conquer helplessness itself. Stubborn and foolish youth, I must admit, for when I look back on those years now, I see quite clearly that rarely did I stand alone and rarely did I have to stand alone. Always there were friends, true and dear, lending me support even when I believed I did not want it, and even when I did not realize they were doing it.

Zaknafein, Belwar, Clacker, Mooshie, Bruenor, Regis, Catti-brie, Wulfgar, and of course, Guenhwyvar, dear Guenhwyvar. These were the companions who justified my principles, who gave me the strength to continue against any foe, real or imagined. These were the companions who fought the helplessness, the rage, and frustration.

These were the friends who gave me my life.

—Drizzt Do'Urden

# 16
# Insidious Chains

Clacker looked down to the far end of the long and narrow cavern, to the many-towered structure that served as a castle to the illithid community. Though his vision was poor, the hook horror could make out the squat forms crawling about on the rock castle, and he could plainly hear the chiming of their tools. They were slaves, Clacker knew—duergar, goblins, deep gnomes, and several other races that Clacker did not know—serving their illithid masters with their skills in stonework, helping to continue the improvement and design on the huge lump of rock that the mind flayers had claimed as their home.

Perhaps Belwar, so obviously suited to such endeavors, was already at work on the massive building.

The thoughts fluttered through Clacker's mind and were forgotten, replaced by the hook horror's less involved instincts. The mind flayers' stunning blasts had reduced Clacker's mental resistance and the wizard's polymorph spell had taken more of him, so much so that he could not even realize the lapse. Now his twin identities battled evenly, leaving poor Clacker in a state of simple confusion.

If he understood his dilemma, and if he had known the fate of his friends, he might have considered himself fortunate.

The mind flayers suspected that there was more to Clacker than his hook horror body would indicate. The illithid community's survival was based on knowledge and by reading thoughts, and though they could not penetrate the jumble that was Clacker's mind, they saw clearly that the mental workings within the bony exoskeleton were decidedly unlike those expected from a simple Underdark monster.

The mind flayers were not foolish masters, and they knew, too, the dangers of trying to decipher and control an armed and armored quarter-ton killing monster. Clacker was simply too dangerous and unpredictable to be kept in close quarters. In the illithids' slave society, however, there was a place for everyone.

Clacker stood upon an island of stone, a slab of rock perhaps fifty yards in diameter and surrounded by a deep and wide chasm. With him were assorted other creatures, including a small herd of rothé and several battered duergar who obviously had spent too long under the illithids' mind-melting influences. The gray dwarves sat or stood, blank-faced, staring out at nothing at all and awaiting, Clacker soon came to understand, their turn on the supper table of their cruel masters.

Clacker paced the island's perimeter, searching for some escape, though the pech part of him would have recognized the futility of it all. Only a single bridge spanned the warding chasm, a magical and mechanical thing that recoiled tightly against the chasm's other side when not in use.

A group of mind flayers with a single burly ogre slave approached the lever that controlled the bridge. Immediately, Clacker was assaulted by their telepathic suggestions. A single course of action cut through the jumble of his thoughts, and at that moment, he learned of his purpose on the island. He was to be the shepherd for the mind flayers' flock. They wanted a gray dwarf and a rothé, and the shepherd slave obediently went to work.

Neither victim offered any resistance. Clacker neatly twisted the gray dwarf's neck, then, not so neatly, bashed in the rothé's skull. He sensed that the illithids were pleased, and this notion brought some curious emotions to him, satisfaction being the most prevalent.

Hoisting both creatures, Clacker moved to the gorge to stand opposite the group of illithids.

An illithid pulled back on the bridge's waist-high lever. Clacker noted that the action of the trigger was away from him; an important fact, though the hook horror did not exactly understand why at that time. The stone-and-metal bridge grumbled and shook and shot out from the cliff opposite Clacker. It rolled out toward the island until it caught securely on the stone at Clacker's feet.

*Come to me,* came one illithid's command. Clacker might have managed to resist the command if he had seen any point in it. He stepped out onto the bridge, which groaned considerably under his bulk.

*Halt! Drop the kills,* came another suggestion when the hook horror was halfway across. *Drop the kills!* the telepathic voice cried again. *And get back to your island!*

Clacker considered his alternatives. The rage of the hook horror welled within him, and his thoughts that were pech, angered by the loss of his friends, were in complete agreement. A few strides would take him to his enemies.

On command from the mind flayers, the ogre moved up to the lip of the bridge. It stood a bit taller than Clacker and was nearly as wide, but it was unarmed and would not be able to stop him. Off to the side of the burly guard, though, Clacker recognized a more serious defense. The illithid who had pulled the lever to activate the bridge stood by it still, one hand, a curious four-fingered appendage, eagerly clenching and unclenching it.

Clacker would not get across the remaining portion and past the blocking ogre before the bridge rolled away from under him, dropping him into the depths of the chasm. Reluctantly, the hook horror placed his kills on the bridge and stepped back to his stone island. The ogre came out immediately and retrieved the dead dwarf and rothé for its masters.

The illithid then pulled the lever, and in the blink of an eye, the magical bridge snapped back across the gorge, leaving Clacker stranded once more.

*Eat,* one of the illithids instructed. An unfortunate rothé wandered by the hook horror as the command came surging into his thoughts, and Clacker absently dropped a heavy claw onto its head.

As the illithids departed, Clacker sat down to his meal, reveling in the taste of blood and meat. His hook horror side won over completely during the raw feast, but every time Clacker looked back across the gorge and down the narrow cavern to the illithid castle, a tiny pech voice within him piped out its concern for a svirfneblin and a drow.

⚔ ⚔ ⚔ ⚔ ⚔

Of all the slaves recently captured in the tunnels outside the illithid castle, Belwar Dissengulp was the most sought after. Aside from the curiosity factor of the svirfneblin's mithral hands, Belwar was perfectly suited for the two duties most desired in an illithid slave: working the stone and fighting in the gladiatorial arena.

The illithid slave auction went into an uproar when the deep gnome was marched forward. Bids of gold and magic items, private spells and tomes of knowledge, were thrown about with abandon. In the end, the burrow-warden was sold to a group of three mind flayers, the three who had led the party that had captured him. Belwar, of course, had no knowledge of the transaction; before it was ever completed, the deep gnome was ushered away down a dark and narrow tunnel and placed in a small, unremarkable room.

A short while later, three voices echoed in his mind, three unique telepathic voices that the deep gnome understood and would not forget—the voices of his new masters.

An iron portcullis rose before Belwar, revealing a well-lighted circular room with high walls and rows of audience seats above them.

*Do come out,* one of the masters bade him, and the burrow-warden, fully desiring only to please his master, did not hesitate. When he exited the short passageway, he saw that several dozen mind flayers had gathered all about on stone benches. Those strange four-fingered illithid hands pointed down at him from every direction, all backed by the same expressionless octopus face. Following the telepathic link, though, Belwar had no trouble finding his master among the crowd, busily arguing odds and antes with a small group.

Across the way, a similar portcullis opened and a huge ogre stepped out. Immediately the creature's eyes went up into the crowd as it sought its own master, the focal point of its existence.

*This evil ogre beast has threatened me, my brave svirfneblin champion,* came the telepathic encouragement of Belwar's master a short while later, after all of the betting had been settled. *Do destroy it for me.*

Belwar needed no further prompting, nor did the ogre, having received a similar message from its master. The gladiators rushed each other furiously, but while the ogre was young and rather stupid, Belwar was a crafty old veteran. He slowed at the last moment and rolled to the side.

The ogre, trying desperately to kick at him as it ended its charge, stumbled for just a moment.

Too long.

Belwar's hammer-hand crunched into the ogre's knee with a crack that resounded as powerfully as a wizard's lightning bolt. The ogre lurched forward, nearly doubling over, and Belwar drove his pickaxe-hand into the ogre's meaty backside. As the giant monster stumbled off balance to the side, Belwar threw himself at its feet, tripping it to the stone.

The burrow-warden was up in an instant, leaping onto the prone giant and running right up it toward its head. The ogre recovered quickly enough to catch the svirfneblin by the front of his jack, but even as the monster started to hurl the nasty little opponent away, Belwar dug his pickaxe-hand deep into its chest. Howling in rage and pain, the stupid ogre continued its throw, and Belwar was jerked out straight.

The sharp tip of the pickaxe held its grip and the deep gnome's momentum tore a wide gash in the ogre's chest. The ogre rolled and flailed, finally freeing itself from the cruel mithral hand. A huge knee caught Belwar in the rump, launching him to the stone many feet away. The burrow-warden came back up to his feet after a few short bounces, dazed and smarting but still desiring nothing but to please his master.

He heard the silent cheering and telepathic shouting of every illithid in the room, but one call cut through the mental din with precise clarity.

*Kill it!* Belwar's master commanded.

Belwar didn't hesitate. Still flat on its back, the ogre clutched at its chest, trying vainly to stop its lifeblood from flowing away. The wounds it already had suffered probably would have proved fatal, but Belwar was far from satisfied. This wretched thing had threatened his master! The burrow-warden charged straight at the top of the ogre's head, his hammer-hand leading the way. Three quick punches softened the monster's skull, then the pickaxe dived in for the killing blow.

The doomed ogre jerked wildly in the last spasms of its life, but Belwar felt no pity. He had pleased his master; nothing else in all the world mattered to the burrow-warden at that moment.

Up in the stands, the proud owner of the svirfneblin champion collected his due of gold and potion bottles. Contented that it had done well in selecting this one, the illithid looked back to Belwar, who still chopped and bashed at the corpse. Though it enjoyed watching its new champion at savage play, the illithid quickly sent out a message to cease. The dead ogre, after all, was also part of the bet.

No sense in ruining dinner.

⚔ ⚔ ⚔ ⚔ ⚔

At the heart of the illithid castle stood a huge tower, a gigantic stalagmite hollowed and sculpted to house the most important members of the strange community. The inside of the giant stone structure was ringed by balconies and spiraling stairways, each level housing several of the mind flayers. But it was the bottom chamber, unadorned and circular, that held the most important being of all, the central brain.

Fully twenty feet in diameter, this boneless lump of pulsating flesh tied the mind flayer community together in telepathic symbiosis. The central brain was the composite of their knowledge, the mental eye that guarded their outside chambers and which had heard the warning cries of the illithid from the drow city many miles to the east. To the illithids of the community, the central brain was the coordinator of their entire existence and nothing short of their god. Thus, only a very few slaves were allowed within this special tower, captives with sensitive and delicate fingers that could massage the illithid god-thing and soothe it with tender brushes and warm fluids.

Drizzt Do'Urden was among this group.

The drow knelt on the wide walkway that ringed the room, reaching out to stroke the amorphous mass, feeling keenly its pleasures and displeasures. When the brain became upset, Drizzt felt the sharp tingles and the tenseness in the veined tissues. He would massage more forcefully, easing his beloved master back to serenity.

When the brain was pleased, Drizzt was pleased. Nothing else in all the world mattered; the renegade drow had found his purpose in life. Drizzt Do'Urden had come home.

⚔ ⚔ ⚔ ⚔ ⚔

"A most profitable capture, that one," said the mind flayer in its watery, otherworldly voice. The creature held up the potions it had won in the arena.

The other two illithids wiggled their four-fingered hands, indicating their agreement.

*Arena champion,* one of them remarked telepathically.

"And tooled to dig," the third added aloud. A notion entered its mind and thus, the minds of the others. *Perhaps to carve?*

The three illithids looked over to the far side of the chamber, where the work had begun on a new cubby area.

The first illithid wiggled its fingers and gurgled, "In time the svirfneblin will be put to such menial tasks. Now he must win for me more potions, more gold. A most profitable capture!"

"As were all taken in the ambush," said the second.

"The hook horror tends the herd," explained the third.

"And the drow tends the brain," gurgled the first. "I noticed him as I ascended to our chamber. That one will prove a proficient masseuse, to the pleasure of the brain and to the benefit of us all."

"And there is this," said the second, one of its tentacles snapping out to nudge the third. The third illithid held up an onyx figurine.

*Magic?* wondered the first.

Indeed, the second mentally responded. *Linked to the Astral Plane. An entity stone, I believe.*

"Have you called to it?" the first asked aloud.

Together, the other illithids clenched their hands, the mind flayer signal for no. "A dangerous foe, mayhaps," explained the third. "We thought it prudent to observe the beast on its own plane before summoning it."

"A wise choice," agreed the first. "When will you be going?"

"At once," said the second. "And will you accompany us?"

The first illithid clenched its fists, then held out the potion bottle. "Profits to be won," it explained.

The other two wiggled their fingers excitedly. Then, as their companion retired to another room to count its winnings, they sat down in comfortable, overstuffed chairs and prepared themselves for their journey.

They floated together, leaving their corporeal bodies at rest on the chairs. They ascended beside the figurine's link to the Astral Plane, visible to them in their astral state as a thin silvery cord. They were beyond their companions' cavern now, beyond the stones and noises of the Material Plane, floating into the vast serenity of the astral world. Here, there were few sounds other than the continuous chanting of the astral wind. Here, too, there was no solid structure—none in terms of the material world—with matter being defined in gradations of light.

The illithids veered away from the figurine's silver cord as they neared the completion of their astral ascent. They would come into the plane near to the entity of the great panther, but not so close as to make it aware of their presence. Illithids were not normally welcome guests, being despised by nearly every creature on every plane they traveled.

They came fully into their astral state without incident and had little trouble locating the entity represented by the figurine.

Guenhwyvar romped through a forest of starlight in pursuit of the entity of the elk, continuing the endless cycle. The elk, no less magnificent than the panther, leaped and sprang in perfect balance and unmistakable grace. The elk and Guenhwyvar had played out this scenario a million times and would play it out a million, million more. This was the order and harmony that ruled the panther's existence, that ultimately ruled the planes of all the universe.

Some creatures, though, like the denizens of the lower planes, and like the mind flayers that now observed the panther from afar, could not accept the simple perfection of this harmony and could not recognize the beauty of this eternal hunt. As they watched the wondrous panther in its life's play, the illithids' only thoughts centered on how they might use the cat to their best advantage.

# 17 A Delicate Balance

Belwar studied his latest foe carefully, sensing some familiarity with the armored beast's appearance. Had he befriended such a creature before? he wondered. Whatever doubts the svirfneblin gladiator might have had, though, could not break into the deep gnome's consciousness, for Belwar's illithid master continued its insidious stream of telepathic deceptions.

*Kill it, my brave champion,* the illithid pleaded from its perch in the stands. *It is your enemy, most assuredly, and it shall bring harm to me if you do not kill it!*

The hook horror, much larger than Belwar's lost friend, charged the svirfneblin, having no reservations about making a meal of the deep gnome.

Belwar coiled his stubby legs under him and waited for the precise moment. As the hook horror bore down on him, its clawed hands wide to prevent him from dodging to the side, Belwar sprang straight ahead, his hammer-hand leading the way right up into the monster's chest. Cracks ran all through the hook horror's exoskeleton from the sheer force of the blow, and the monster swooned as it continued forward.

Belwar's flight made a quick reversal, for the hook horror's weight and momentum was much greater than the svirfneblin's. He felt his shoulder snap out of joint, and he, too, nearly fainted from the sudden agony. Again the callings of Belwar's illithid master overruled his thoughts, and even the pain.

The gladiators crashed together in a heap, Belwar buried beneath the monster's bulk. The hook horror's encumbering size prevented it from getting its arms at the burrow-warden, but it had other weapons. A wicked beak dived at Belwar. The deep gnome managed to get his pickaxe-hand in its path, but still the hook horror's giant head pushed on, twisting Belwar's arm backward. The hungry beak snapped and twisted barely an inch from the burrow-warden's face.

Throughout the stands of the large arena, illithids jumped about and chatted excitedly, both in their telepathic mode and in their gurgling, watery voices. Fingers wiggled in opposition to clenched fists as the mind flayers prematurely tried to collect on bets.

Belwar's master, fearing the loss of its champion, called out to the hook horror's master. *Do you yield?* it asked, trying to make the thoughts appear confident.

The other illithid turned away smugly and shut down its telepathic receptacles. Belwar's master could only watch.

The hook horror could not drive any closer; the svirfneblin's arm was locked against the stone at the elbow, the mithral pickaxe firmly holding back the monster's deadly beak. The hook horror reverted to a different tactic, raising its head free of Belwar's hand in a sudden jerking movement.

Belwar's warrior intuition saved him at that moment, for the hook horror reversed suddenly and the deadly beak dived back in. The normal reaction and expected defense would have been to swipe the monster's head to the side with the pickaxe-hand. The hook horror anticipated such a counter, and Belwar anticipated that it would.

Belwar threw his arm across in front of him, but shortened his reach so that the pickaxe passed well below the hook horror's plunging beak. The monster, meanwhile, believing that Belwar was attempting to strike a blow, stopped its dive exactly as it had planned.

But the mithral pickaxe reversed its direction much quicker than the monster anticipated. Belwar's backhand caught the hook horror right behind the beak and snapped its head to the side. Then, ignoring the searing pain from his injured shoulder, Belwar curled his other arm at the elbow and punched out. There was no strength behind the blow, but at that moment, the hook horror came back around the pickaxe and opened its beak for a bite at the deep gnome's exposed face.

Just in time to catch a mithral hammer instead.

Belwar's hand wedged far back in the hook horror's mouth, opening the beak more than it was designed to open. The monster jerked wildly, trying to free itself, each sudden twist sending waves of pain down the burrow-warden's wounded arm.

Belwar responded with equal fury, whacking again and again at the side of the hook horror's head with his free hand. Blood oozed down the giant beak as the pickaxe dug in.

"Do you yield?" Belwar's master now shouted in its watery voice at the hook horror's master.

The question was premature again, however, for down in the arena, the armored hook horror was far from defeated. It used another weapon: its sheer weight. The monster ground its chest into the lying deep gnome, trying simply to crush the life out of him.

"Do *you* yield?" the hook horror's master retorted, seeing the unexpected turn of events.

Belwar's pickaxe caught the hook horror's eye, and the monster howled in agony. Illithids jumped and pointed, wiggling their fingers and clenching and unclenching their fists.

Both masters of the gladiators understood how much they had to lose. Would either participant ever be fit to fight again if the battle was allowed to continue?

*Mayhaps we should consider a draw?* Belwar's master offered telepathically. The other illithid readily agreed. Both masters sent messages down to their champions. It took several brutal moments to calm the fires of rage and end the contest, but eventually, the illithid suggestions overruled the gladiators' savage instincts of survival. Suddenly, both the deep gnome and the hook horror felt an affinity for each other, and when the hook horror rose, it lent a claw to the svirfneblin to help him to his feet.

A short while later, Belwar sat on the single stone bench in his tiny, unadorned cell, just inside the tunnel to the circular arena. The burrow-warden's hammer-wielding arm had gone completely numb and a gruesome purplish blue bruise covered his entire shoulder. Many days would pass before Belwar would be able to compete in the arena again, and it troubled him deeply that he would not soon please his master.

The illithid came to him to inspect the damage. It had potions that could help heal the wound, but even with the magical aid, Belwar obviously needed time to rest. The mind flayer had other uses for the svirfneblin, though. A cubby in its private quarters needed completing.

*Come,* the illithid bade Belwar, and the burrow-warden jumped to his feet and rushed out, respectfully remaining a stride behind his master.

A kneeling drow caught Belwar's attention as the mind flayer led him through the bottom level of the central tower. How fortunate the dark elf was to be able to touch and bring pleasure to the central brain of the community! Belwar then thought no more of it, though, as he made the ascent to the structure's third level and to the suite of rooms that his three masters shared.

The other two illithids sat in their chairs, motionless and apparently lifeless. Belwar's master paid little heed to the spectacle; it knew that its companions were far away in their astral travels and that their corporeal bodies were quite safe. The mind flayer did pause to wonder, for just a moment, how its companions fared in that distant plane. Like all illithids, Belwar's master enjoyed astral travel, but pragmatism, a definite illithid trait, kept the creature's thoughts on the business at hand. It had made a large investment in buying Belwar, an investment it was not willing to lose.

The mind flayer led Belwar into a back room and sat him down on an unremarkable stone table. Then, suddenly, the illithid bombarded Belwar with telepathic suggestions and questions, probing as it roughly set the injured shoulder and applied wrappings. Mind flayers could invade a creature's thoughts on first contact, either with their stunning blow or with telepathic communications, but it could take tendays, even months, for an illithid to fully dominate its slave. Each encounter broke down more of the slave's natural resistance to the illithid's mental insinuations, revealed more of the slave's memories and emotions.

Belwar's master was determined to know everything about this curious svirfneblin, about his strange, crafted hands and about the unusual company he chose to keep. This time during the telepathic exchange, the illithid focused on the mithral hands, for it sensed that Belwar was not performing up to his capabilities.

The illithid's thoughts probed and prodded, and sometime later fell into a deep corner of Belwar's mind and learned a curious chant.

*Bivrip?* it questioned Belwar. Simply on reflex, the burrow-warden banged his hands together, then winced in pain from the shock of the blow.

The illithid's fingers and tentacles wiggled eagerly. It had touched upon something important, it knew, something that could make its champion stronger. If the mind flayer allowed Belwar the memory of the chant, however, it would give back to the svirfneblin a part of himself, a conscious memory of his days before slavery.

The illithid handed Belwar still another healing potion, then glanced around to inspect its wares. If Belwar was to continue as a gladiator, he would have to face the hook horror again in the arena; by illithid rules, a rematch was required after a draw. Belwar's master doubted that the svirfneblin would survive another battle against that armored champion.

Unless . . .

⚔ ⚔ ⚔ ⚔ ⚔

Dinin Do'Urden paced his lizard mount through the region of Menzoberranzan's lesser houses, the most congested section of the city. He kept the cowl of his *piwafwi* pulled low about his face and bore no insignia revealing him as a noble of a ruling house. Secrecy was Dinin's ally, both from the watching eyes of this dangerous section of the city, and from the disapproving glares of his mother and sister. Dinin had survived long enough to understand the dangers of complacency. He lived in a state that bordered on paranoia; he never knew when Malice and Briza might be watching.

A group of bugbears sauntered out of the walking lizard's way. Fury swept through the proud elderboy of House Do'Urden at the slaves' casual manner. Dinin's hand went instinctively to the whip on his belt.

Dinin wisely checked his rage, though, reminding himself of the possible consequences of being revealed. He turned another of the many sharp corners and moved down through a row of connected stalagmite mounds.

"So you have found me," came a familiar voice from behind and to the side. Surprised and afraid, Dinin stopped his mount and froze in his saddle. He knew that a dozen tiny crossbows—at least—were trained on him.

Slowly, Dinin turned his head to watch Jarlaxle's approach. Out here in the shadows, the mercenary seemed much different from the overly polite and compliant drow Dinin had known in House Do'Urden. Or perhaps it was just the specter of the two sword-wielding drow guards standing by Jarlaxle's sides and Dinin's own realization that he didn't have Matron Malice around to protect him.

"One should ask permission before entering another's house," Jarlaxle said calmly but with definite threatening undertones. "Common courtesy."

"I am out in the open streets," Dinin reminded him.

Jarlaxle's smile denied the logic. "My house."

Dinin remembered his station, and the thoughts inspired some courage. "Should a noble of a ruling house, then, ask Jarlaxle's permission before leaving his front gate?" the elderboy growled. "And what of Matron Baenre, who would not enter the least of Menzoberranzan's houses without seeking permission from the appropriate matron mother? Should Matron Baenre, too, ask permission of Jarlaxle, the houseless rogue?" Dinin realized that he might be carrying the insult a bit too far, but his pride demanded the words.

Jarlaxle relaxed visibly and the smile that came to his face almost appeared sincere. "So you have found me," he said again, this time dipping into his customary bow. "State your purpose and be done with it."

Dinin crossed his arms over his chest belligerently, gaining confidence at the mercenary's apparent concessions. "Are you so certain that I was looking for you?"

Jarlaxle exchanged grins with his two guards. Snickers from unseen soldiers in the shadows of the lane stole a good measure of Dinin's budding confidence.

"State your business, Elderboy," Jarlaxle said more pointedly, "and be done with it."

Dinin was more than willing to complete this encounter as quickly as possible. "I require information concerning Zin-carla," he said bluntly. "The spirit-wraith of Zaknafein has walked the Underdark for many days. Too many, perhaps?"

Jarlaxle's eyes narrowed as he followed the elderboy's reasoning. "Matron Malice sent you to me?" he stated as much as asked.

Dinin shook his head and Jarlaxle did not doubt his sincerity. "You are as wise as you are skilled in the blade," the mercenary offered graciously, slipping into a second bow, one that seemed somehow ambiguous out here in Jarlaxle's dark world.

"I have come of my own initiative," Dinin said firmly. "I must find some answers."

"Are you afraid, Elderboy?"

"Concerned," Dinin replied sincerely, ignoring the mercenary's taunting tone. "I never make the error of underestimating my enemies, or my allies."

Jarlaxle cast him a confused glance.

"I know what my brother has become," Dinin explained. "And I know who Zaknafein once was."

"Zaknafein is a spirit-wraith now," Jarlaxle replied, "under the control of Matron Malice."

"Many days," Dinin said quietly, believing the implications of his words spoke loudly enough.

"Your mother asked for Zin-carla," Jarlaxle retorted, a bit sharply. "It is Lolth's greatest gift, given only so that the Spider Queen is pleased in return. Matron Malice knew the risk when she requested Zin-carla. Surely you understand, Elderboy, that spirit-wraiths are given for the completion of a specific task."

"And what are the consequences of failure?" Dinin asked bluntly, matching Jarlaxle's perturbed attitude.

The mercenary's incredulous stare was all the answer Dinin needed. "How long does Zaknafein have?" Dinin asked.

Jarlaxle shrugged noncommittally and answered with a question of his own. "Who can guess at Lolth's plans?" he asked. "The Spider Queen can be a patient one—if the gain is great enough to justify the wait. Is Drizzt's value such?" Again the mercenary shrugged. "That is for Lolth, and for Lolth alone, to decide."

Dinin studied Jarlaxle for a long moment, until he was certain that the mercenary had nothing left to offer him. Then he turned back to his lizard mount and pulled the cowl of his *piwafwi* low. When he regained his saddle, Dinin spun about, thinking to issue one final comment, but the mercenary and his guards were nowhere to be found.

⚔ ⚔ ⚔ ⚔ ⚔

*"Bivrip!"* Belwar cried, completing the spell. The burrow-warden banged his hands together again, and this time did not wince, for the pain was not so intense. Sparks flew when the mithral hands crashed together, and Belwar's master clapped its four-fingered hands in absolute glee.

The illithid simply had to see its gladiator in action now. It looked about for a target and spotted the partially cut cubby. A whole set of telepathic instructions roared into the burrow-warden's mind as the illithid imparted mental images of the design and depth it wanted for the cubby.

Belwar moved right in. Unsure of the strength in his wounded shoulder, the one guiding the hammer-hand, he led with the pickaxe. The stone exploded into dust under the enchanted hand's blow, and the illithid sent a clear message of its pleasure flooding into Belwar's thoughts. Even the armor of a hook horror would not stand against such a blow!

Belwar's master reinforced the instructions it had given to the deep gnome, then moved into an adjoining chamber to study. Left alone to his work, so very similar to the tasks he had worked at for all of his century of life, Belwar found himself wondering.

Nothing in particular crossed the burrow-warden's few coherent thoughts; the need to please his illithid master remained the foremost guidance of his movements. For the first time since his capture, though, Belwar wondered.

Identity? Purpose?

The enchanting spell-song of his mithral hands ran through his mind again, became a focus of his unconscious determination to sort through the blur of his captors' insinuations. *"Bivrip?"* he muttered again, and the word triggered a more recent memory, an image of a drow elf, kneeling and massaging the god-thing of the illithid community.

"Drizzt?" Belwar muttered under his breath, but the name was forgotten in the next bang of his pick-hand, obliterated by the svirfneblin's continuing desire to please his illithid master.

The cubby had to be perfect.

A lump of flesh rippled under an ebon-skinned hand and a wave of anxiety flooded through Drizzt, imparted by the central brain of the mind flayer community. The drow's only emotional response was sadness, for he could not bear to see the brain in distress. Slender fingers kneaded and rubbed; Drizzt lifted a bowl of warm water and poured it slowly over the flesh. Then Drizzt was happy, for the flesh smoothed out under his skilled touch, and the brain's anxious emotions soon were replaced by a teasing hint of gratitude.

Behind the kneeling drow, across the wide walkway, two illithids watched it all and nodded approvingly. Drow elves always had proved skilled at this task, and this latest captive was one of the finest so far.

The illithids wiggled their fingers eagerly at the implications of that shared thought. The central brain had detected another drow intruder in the illithid webs that were the tunnels beyond the long and narrow cavern—another slave to massage and sooth.

So the central brain believed.

Four illithids moved out from the cavern, guided by the images imparted by the central brain. A single drow had entered their domain, an easy capture for four illithids.

So the mind flayers believed.

# 18
# The Element of Surprise

The spirit-wraith picked his silent way through the broken and twisting corridors, traveling with the light and practiced steps of a veteran drow warrior. But the mind flayers, guided by their central brain, anticipated Zaknafein's course perfectly and were waiting for him.

As Zaknafein came beside the same stone ridge where Belwar and Clacker had fallen, an illithid jumped out at him and—*fwoop!*—blasted its stunning energy.

At that close range, few creatures could have resisted such a powerful blow, but Zaknafein was an undead thing, a being not of this world. The proximity of Zaknafein's mind, linked to another plane of existence, could not be measured in steps. Impervious to such mental attacks, the spirit-wraith's swords dived straight in, each taking the startled illithid in one of its milky, pupil-less eyes.

The three other mind flayers floated down from the ceiling, loosing their stunning blasts as they came. Swords in hand, Zaknafein waited confidently for them, but the mind flayers continued their descent. Never before had their mental attacks failed them; they could not believe that the incapacitating cones of energy would prove futile now.

*Fwoop!* A dozen times the illithids fired, but the spirit-wraith seemed not to notice. The illithids, beginning to worry, tried to reach inside Zaknafein's thoughts to understand how he had possibly avoided the effects. What they found was a barrier beyond their penetrating capabilities, a barrier that transcended their present plane of existence.

They had witnessed Zaknafein's swordplay against their unfortunate companion and had no intention of engaging this skilled drow in melee combat. Telepathically, they promptly agreed to reverse their direction.

But they had descended too far.

Zaknafein cared nothing for the illithids and would have walked contentedly off on his way. To the illithid's misfortune, though, the spirit-wraith's instincts, and Zaknafein's past-life knowledge of mind flayers, led him to a simple conclusion: If Drizzt had traveled this way—and Zaknafein knew that he had—he most likely had encountered the mind flayers. An undead being could defeat them, but a mortal drow, even Drizzt, would find himself at a sorry disadvantage.

Zaknafein sheathed one sword and sprang up to the ridge of stone. In the blur of a second fast leap, the spirit-wraith caught one of the rising illithids by the ankle.

*Fwoop!* The creature blasted again, but it was a doomed thing with little defense against Zaknafein's slashing sword. With incredible strength, the spirit-wraith heaved himself straight up, his sword leading the way. The illithid slapped down at the blade vainly, but its empty hands could not defeat the spirit-wraith's aim. Zaknafein's sword sliced up through the mind flayer's belly and into its heart and lungs.

Gasping and clutching at the huge wound, the illithid could only watch helplessly as Zaknafein found his footing and kicked off the mind flayer's chest. The dying illithid tumbled away, head over heels, and slammed into the wall, then hung grotesquely in midair even after death, its blood spattering the floor below.

Zaknafein's leap sent him crashing into the next floating illithid, and the momentum took both of them into the last of the group. Arms flailed and tentacles waved wildly, seeking some hold on the drow warrior's flesh. More deadly, though, was the blade, and a moment later, the spirit-wraith pulled free of his latest two victims, enacted a levitation spell of his own, and floated gently back to the stone floor. Zaknafein walked calmly away, leaving three illithids hanging dead in the air for the duration of their levitation spells, and a fourth dead on the floor.

The spirit-wraith did not bother to wipe the blood from his swords; he realized that very soon there would be more killing.

⚔ ⚔ ⚔ ⚔ ⚔

The two mind flayers continued observing the panther's entity. They did not know it, but Guenhwyvar was aware of their presence. In the Astral Plane, where material senses such as smell and taste had no meaning, the panther substituted other subtle senses. Here, Guenhwyvar hunted through a sense that translated the emanations of energy into clear mental images, and the panther could readily distinguish between the aura of an elk and a rabbit without ever seeing the particular creature. Illithids were not so uncommon on the Astral Plane, and Guenhwyvar recognized their emanations.

The panther had not yet decided whether their presence was mere coincidence or was in some way connected to the fact that Drizzt had not called in many days. The apparent interest the mind flayers showed in Guenhwyvar suggested the latter, a most disturbing notion to the panther.

Still, Guenhwyvar did not want to make the first move against so dangerous an enemy. The panther continued its daily routines, keeping a wary eye on the unwanted audience.

Guenhwyvar noticed the shift in the mind flayers' emanations as the creatures began a rapid descent back to the Material Plane. The panther could wait no longer.

Springing through the stars, Guenhwyvar charged upon the mind flayers. Occupied in their efforts to begin their return journey, the illithids did not react until it was too late. The panther dived in below one, catching its silvery cord in fangs of sharp light. Guenhwyvar's neck flexed and twisted, and the silvery cord snapped. The helpless illithid drifted away, a castaway on the Astral Plane.

The other mind flayer, more concerned with saving itself, ignored its companion's frenzied pleas and continued its descent toward the planar tunnel that would return it to its corporeal body. The illithid almost slipped beyond Guenhwyvar's reach, but the panther's claws latched on firmly just as it entered the planar tunnel. Guenhwyvar rode along.

From his little stone island, Clacker saw the commotion growing all through the long and narrow cavern. Illithids rushed all about, telepathically commanding slaves into defensive formations. Lookouts disappeared through every exit, while other mind flayers floated up into the air to keep a general watch on the situation.

Clacker recognized that some crisis had come upon the community, and a single logical thought forced its way through the hook horror's base thinking: If the mind flayers became preoccupied with some new enemy, this might be his chance to escape. With a new focus to his thinking, Clacker's pech side found a firm footing. His largest problem would be the chasm, for he certainly could not leap across it. He figured that he could toss a gray dwarf or a rothé the distance, but that would hardly aid his own escape.

Clacker's gaze fell on the lever of the bridge, then back to his companions on the stone island. The bridge was retracted; the high lever leaned toward the island. A well-aimed projectile might push it back. Clacker banged his huge claws together—an action that reminded him of Belwar—and hoisted a gray dwarf high into the air. The unfortunate creature soared toward the lever but came up short, instead slamming into the chasm wall and plummeting to its death.

Clacker stamped an angry foot and turned to find another missile. He had no idea of how he would get to Drizzt and Belwar, and at that moment, he didn't pause to worry about them. Clacker's problem right now was getting off his prison island.

This time a young rothé went high into the air.

There was no subtlety, no secrecy, to Zaknafein's entrance. Having no fear of the mind flayers' primary attack methods, the spirit-wraith walked straight into the long and narrow cavern, right out into the open. A group of three illithids descended on him immediately, loosing their stunning blasts.

Again the spirit-wraith walked through the mental energy without a flinch, and the three illithids found the same fate as the four that had stood against Zaknafein out in the tunnels.

Then came the slaves. Desiring only to please their masters, goblins, gray dwarves, orcs, and even a few ogres, charged at the drow invader. Some brandished weapons, but most had only their hands and teeth, thinking to bury the lone drow under their sheer numbers.

Zaknafein's swords and feet were too quick for such straightforward tactics. The spirit-wraith danced and slashed, darting in one direction then reversing his motion suddenly and hacking down his closest pursuers.

Behind the action, the illithids formed their own defensive lines, reconsidering the wisdom of their tactics. Their tentacles wiggled wildly as their mental communications flooded forth, trying to make some sense of this unexpected turn. They had not trusted enough in their slaves to hand them all weapons, but as slave after slave fell to the stone, clawing at mortal wounds, the mind flayers came to regret their mounting losses. Still, the illithids believed they would win out. Behind them, more groups of slaves were being herded down to join the fray. The lone invader would tire, his steps would slow, and their horde would crush him.

The mind flayers could not know the truth of Zaknafein. They could not know that he was an undead thing, a magically animated thing that would not tire and would not slow.

* * * * *

Belwar and his master watched the spasmodic jerking of one of the illithid bodies, a telltale sign that the host spirit was returning from its astral journey. Belwar did not understand the implications of the convulsive movements, but he sensed that his master was glad, and that, in turn, pleased him.

But Belwar's master was also a bit concerned that only one of its companions was returning, for the central brain's summons took the highest priority and could not be ignored. The mind flayer watched as its companion's spasms settled into a pattern, and then was even more confused, for a dark mist appeared around the body.

At the same instant the illithid returned to the Material Plane, Belwar's master telepathically shared in its pain and terror. Before Belwar's master could begin to react, though, Guenhwyvar materialized atop the seated illithid, tearing and slashing at the body.

Belwar froze as a flicker of recognition coursed through him. *"Bivrip?"* he whispered under his breath, and then, "Drizzt?" and the image of the kneeling drow came clearly into his mind.

*Kill it my brave champion! Do kill it!* Belwar's master implored, but it was already too late for the illithid's unfortunate companion. The seated mind flayer flailed away frantically; its tentacles wiggled and latched onto the cat in an attempt to get at Guenhwyvar's brain. Guenhwyvar swiped across with a mighty claw, a single blow that tore the illithid's octopus head from its shoulders.

Belwar, his hands still enchanted from his work on the cubby, advanced slowly toward the panther, his steps bound not by fear, but by confusion. The burrow-warden turned to his master and asked, "Guenhwyvar?"

The mind flayer knew that it had given too much back to the svirfneblin. The recall of the enchanting spell had inspired other, dangerous memories in this slave. No longer could Belwar be relied upon.

Guenhwyvar sensed the illithid's intent and sprang out from the dead mind flayer only an instant before the remaining creature blasted at Belwar.

Guenhwyvar hit the burrow-warden squarely, sending him sprawling to the floor. Feline muscles flexed and strained as the cat landed, turning Guenhwyvar on the spot at an angle for the room's exit.

*Fwoop!* The mind flayer's assault clipped Belwar as he tumbled, but the deep gnome's confusion and his mounting rage held off the insidious attack. For that one moment, Belwar was free, and he rolled to his feet, viewing the illithid as the wretched and evil thing that it was.

"Go, Guenhwyvar!" the burrow-warden cried, and the cat needed no prodding. As an astral being, Guenhwyvar understood much about illithid society and knew the key to any battle against a lair of such creatures. The panther flew against the door with all its weight, bursting out onto the balcony high above the chamber that held the central brain.

Belwar's master, fearing for its god-thing, tried to follow, but the deep gnome's strength had returned tenfold with his anger, and his wounded arm felt no pain as he smashed his enchanted hammer-hand into the squishy flesh of the illithid's head. Sparks flew and scorched the illithid's face, and the creature slammed back into the wall, its milky, pupil-less eyes staring at Belwar in disbelief.

Then it slid, ever so slowly, to the floor, down into the darkness of death.

Forty feet below the room, the kneeling drow sensed his revered master's fear and outrage and looked up just as the black panther sprang out into the air. Fully entranced by the central brain, Drizzt did not recognize Guenhwyvar as his former companion and dearest friend; he saw at that moment only a threat to the being he most loved. But Drizzt and the other massaging slaves could only watch helplessly as the mighty panther, teeth bared and paws wide, plummeted down onto the middle of the bulbous mass of veined flesh that ruled the illithid community.

# 19
# Headaches

Approximately one hundred twenty illithids resided in and around the stone castle in the long and narrow cavern, and every one of them felt the same searing headache when Guenhwyvar dived into the community's central brain.

Guenhwyvar plowed through the mass of defenseless flesh, the cat's great claws tearing and slashing a path through the gore. The central brain imparted emotions of absolute terror, trying to inspire its servants. Understanding that help would not soon arrive, the thing reverted to pleading with the panther.

Guenhwyvar's primal ferocity, however, allowed for no mental intrusions. The panther dug on savagely and was buried in the spurting slime.

Drizzt shouted in outrage and ran all about the walkway, trying to find some way to get at the intruding panther. Drizzt felt his beloved master's anguish keenly and pleaded for somebody—anybody—to do something. Other slaves jumped and cried, and mind flayers ran about in a frenzy, but Guenhwyvar was out in the center of the huge mass, beyond the reach of any weapons the mind flayers could use.

A few moments later, Drizzt stopped his jumping and shouting. He wondered where and who he was, and what in the Nine Hells this great disgusting lump in front of him possibly could be. He looked around the walkway and caught similar confused expressions on the faces of several duergar dwarves, another dark elf, two goblins, and a tall and wickedly scarred bugbear. The mind flayers still rushed about, looking for some attack angle on the panther, the primary threat, and paid no heed to the confused slaves. Guenhwyvar made a sudden appearance from behind the folds of brain. The cat came up over a fleshy ridge for just a moment, then disappeared back into the gore. Several mind flayers fired their mind blasts at the fleeting target, but Guenhwyvar was out of sight too quickly for their energy cones to strike—but not too quickly for Drizzt to catch a glimpse.

"Guenhwyvar?" the drow cried as a multitude of thoughts rushed back into his mind. The last thing he remembered was floating up among the stalactites in a broken corridor, up to where other sinister shapes lurked.

An illithid moved right beside the drow, too intent on the action within the brain to realize that Drizzt was a slave no longer. Drizzt had no weapons other than his own body, but he hardly cared in that moment of sheer anger. He leaped high into the air behind the unsuspecting monster and kicked his foot into the back of the thing's octopus head. The illithid tumbled forward onto the central brain and bounced along the rubbery folds several times before it could find any hold.

All about the walkway, the slaves realized their freedom. The gray dwarves banded together immediately and took down two illithids in a wild rush, pummeling the creatures and stomping on them with their heavy boots.

*Fwoop!* A blast came from the side, and Drizzt turned to see the other dark elf reeling from the stunning blow. A mind flayer rushed in on the drow and grabbed him in a tight hug. Four tentacles latched on to the doomed dark elf's face, clamping on, then digging in toward his brain.

Drizzt wanted to go to the drow's aid, but a second illithid moved between them and took aim. Drizzt dived to the side as another attack sounded. *Fwoop!* He came up running, desperately trying to put more ground between himself and the illithid. The other drow's scream held Drizzt for a moment, though, and he glanced back over his shoulder.

Grotesque, bulging lines crossed up the drow's face, a visage contorted by more anguish than Drizzt had ever before witnessed. Drizzt saw the illithid's head jerk, and the tentacles, buried beneath the drow's skin and reaching and sucking at his brain, pulsed and bulged. The doomed drow screamed again, one final time, then he fell limp in the illithid's arms and the creature finished its gruesome feast.

The scarred bugbear unwittingly saved Drizzt from a similar fate. In its flight, the seven-foot-tall creature crossed right between Drizzt and the pursuing mind flayer just as the illithid fired again. The blow stunned the bugbear for the moment it took the illithid to close in. As the mind flayer reached for its supposedly helpless victim, the bugbear swung a huge arm and knocked the pursuer to the stone.

More mind flayers rushed out onto the balconies overlooking the circular chamber. Drizzt had no idea where his friends might be, or how he might escape, but the single door he spotted beside the walkway seemed his only chance. He charged straight at it, but it burst open just before he arrived.

Drizzt crashed into the waiting arms of yet another illithid.

⚔ ⚔ ⚔ ⚔ ⚔

If the inside of the stone castle was a tumult of confusion, the outside was chaos. No slaves charged at Zaknafein now. The wounding of the central brain had freed them from the mind flayers' suggestions, and now the goblins, gray dwarves, and all the others were more concerned with their own escape. Those closest to the cavern exits rushed out; others ran about wildly, trying to keep out of range of the continuing illithid mind blasts.

Hardly giving his actions a thought, Zaknafein whipped across with a sword, taking out a goblin as it ran screaming past. Then the spirit-wraith closed in on the creature that had been pursuing the goblin. Walking through yet another stunning blast, Zaknafein chopped the mind flayer down.

In the stone castle, Drizzt had regained his identity, and the magical spells imbued upon the spirit-wraith honed in on the target's thought patterns. With a gutteral growl, Zaknafein made a straight course toward the castle, leaving a host of dead and wounded, slave and illithid alike, in his wake.

⚔⚔⚔⚔⚔

Another rothé bleated out in surprise as it soared through the air. Three of the beasts limped about across the way; a fourth had followed the duergar to the bottom of the chasm. This time, though, Clacker's aim was true, and the small cowlike creature slammed into the lever, throwing it back. At once, the enchanted bridge rolled out and secured itself at Clacker's feet. The hook horror scooped up another gray dwarf, just for luck, and started out across the bridge.

He was nearly halfway across when the first mind flayer appeared, rushing toward the lever. Clacker knew that he couldn't possibly get all the way across before the illithid disengaged the bridge.

He had only one shot.

The gray dwarf, oblivious to its surroundings, went high into the air above the hook horror's head. Clacker held his throw and continued across, letting the illithid close in as much as possible. As the mind flayer reached a four-fingered hand toward the lever, the duergar missile crashed into its chest, throwing it to the stone.

Clacker ran for his life. The illithid recovered and pushed the lever forward. The bridge snapped back, opening the deep chasm.

A final leap just as the metal-and-stone bridge zipped out from under his feet sent Clacker crashing into the side of the chasm. He got his arms and shoulders over the lip of the gorge and kept enough wits about him to quickly scramble over to the side.

The illithid pulled back on the lever, and the bridge shot out again, clipping Clacker. The hook horror had moved far enough to the side, though, and Clacker's grip was strong enough to hold against the force as the rushing bridge scraped across his armored chest.

The illithid cursed and pulled the lever back, then rushed to meet the hook horror. Weary and wounded, Clacker had not yet begun to pull himself up when the illithid arrived. Waves of stunning energy rolled over him. His head drooped and he slid back several inches before his claws found another hold.

The mind flayer's greed cost it dearly. Instead of simply blasting and kicking Clacker from the ledge, it thought it could make a quick meal of the helpless hook horror's brain. It knelt before Clacker, four tentacles diving in eagerly to find an opening in his facial armor.

Clacker's dual entities had resisted the illithid blasts out in the tunnels, and now, too, the stunning mental energy had only a minimal effect. When the illithid's octopus head appeared right in front of his face, it shocked Clacker back to awareness.

A snap of a beak removed two of the probing tentacles, then a desperate lunge of a claw caught the illithid's knee. Bones crushed into dust under the mighty grip, and the illithid cried in agony, both telepathically and in its watery, otherworldly voice.

A moment later, its cries faded as it plummeted down the deep chasm. A levitation spell might have saved the falling illithid, but such spellcasting required concentration and the pain of a torn face and crushed knee delayed such actions. The illithid thought of levitating at the same moment that the point of a stalagmite drove through its backbone.

⚔ ⚔ ⚔ ⚔ ⚔

The hammer-hand crashed through the door of another stone chest. "Damn!" Belwar spat, seeing that this one, too, contained nothing more than illithid clothing. The burrow-warden was certain that his equipment would be nearby, but already half of his former masters' rooms lay in ruin with nothing to show for the effort.

Belwar moved back into the main chamber and over to the stone seats. Between the two chairs, he spotted the figurine of the panther. He scooped it into a pouch, then squashed the head of the remaining illithid, the astral castaway, with his pickaxe-hand almost as an afterthought; in the confusion, the svirfneblin had nearly forgotten that one monster remained. Belwar heaved the body away, sending it down in a heap on the floor.

"*Magga cammara*," the svirfneblin muttered when he looked back to the stone chair and saw the outline of a trap door where the creature had been sitting. Never putting finesse above efficiency, Belwar's hammer-hand quickly reduced the door to rubble, and the burrow-warden looked upon the welcome sight of familiar backpacks.

Belwar shrugged and followed the course of the logic, swiping across at the other illithid, the one Guenhwyvar had decapitated. The headless monster fell away, revealing another trap door.

"The drow shall find need of these," Belwar remarked when he cleared away the chunks of broken stone and lifted out a belt that held two sheathed scimitars. He darted for the exit and met an illithid right in the doorway.

More particularly, Belwar's humming hammer-hand met the illithid's chest. The monster flew backward, spinning over the balcony's metal railing.

Belwar rushed out and charged to the side, having no time to check if the illithid had somehow caught a handhold and having no time to stay and play in any case. He could hear the commotion below, the mental attacks and the screams, and the continuing growls of a panther that sounded like music in the burrow-warden's ears.

⚔ ⚔ ⚔ ⚔ ⚔

His arms pinned to his sides by the illithid's unexpectedly powerful hug, Drizzt could only twist and jerk his head about to slow the tentacles' progress. One found a hold, then another, and began burrowing under the drow's ebony skin.

Drizzt knew little of mind flayer anatomy, but it was a bipedal creature and he allowed himself some assumptions. Wiggling a bit to the side, so that he was not directly facing the horrid thing, he brought a knee slamming up into the creature's groin. By the sudden loosening of the illithid's grip, and by the way its milky eyes seemed to widen, Drizzt guessed that his assumptions had been correct. His knee slammed up again, then a third time.

Drizzt heaved with all his strength and broke free of the weakened illithid's hug. The stubborn tentacles continued their climb up the sides of Drizzt's face, though, reaching for his brain. Explosions of burning pain racked Drizzt and he nearly fainted, his head drooping forward limply.

But the hunter would not surrender.

When Drizzt looked up again, the fire in his lavender eyes fell upon the illithid like a damning curse. The hunter grasped the tentacles and tore them out savagely, pulling them straight down to bow the illithid's head.

The monster fired its mind blast, but the angle was wrong and the energy did nothing to slow the hunter. One hand held tightly to the tentacles while the other slammed in with the frenzy of a dwarven hammer at a mithral strike on the monster's soft head.

Blue-black bruises welled in the fleshy skin; one pupil-less eye swelled and closed. A tentacle dug into the drow's wrist; the frantic illithid raked and punched with its arms, but the hunter didn't notice. He pounded away at the head, pounded the creature down to the stone floor. Drizzt tore his arm away from the tentacle's grasp, then both fists flailed away until the illithid's eyes closed forever.

The ring of metal spun the drow about. Lying on the floor just a few feet away was a familiar and welcome sight.

⚔ ⚔ ⚔ ⚔ ⚔

Satisfied that the scimitars had landed near his friend, Belwar charged down a stone stairway at the nearest illithid. The monster turned and loosed its blast. Belwar answered with a scream of sheer rage—a scream that partially blocked the stunning effect—and he hurled himself through the air, meeting the waves of energy head on.

Though dazed from the mental assault, the deep gnome crashed into the illithid and they fell over into a second monster that had been rushing up to help. Belwar could hardly find his bearings, but he clearly understood that the jumble of arms and legs all about him were not the limbs of friends. The burrow-warden's mithral hands slashed and punched, and he scrambled away along the second balcony in search of another stair. By the time the two wounded illithids recovered enough to respond, the wild svirfneblin was long gone.

Belwar caught another illithid by surprise, splatting its fleshy head flat against the wall as he came down onto the next level. A dozen other mind flayers roamed all about this balcony, though, most of them guarding the two stairways down to the tower's bottom chamber. Belwar took a quick detour by springing up to the top of the metal railing, then dropping the fifteen feet to the floor.

⚔ ⚔ ⚔ ⚔ ⚔

A blast of stunning energy rolled over Drizzt as he reached for his weapons. The hunter resisted, though, his thoughts simply too primitive for such a sophisticated attack form. In a single movement too quick for his latest adversary to respond to, he snapped one scimitar from its sheath and spun about, slicing the blade at an upward angle. The scimitar buried itself halfway through the pursuing mind flayer's head.

The hunter knew that the monster was already dead, but he tore out the scimitar and whacked the illithid one more time as it fell, for no particular reason at all.

Then the drow was up and running, both blades drawn, one dripping illithid blood and the other hungry for more. Drizzt should have been looking for an escape route—that part that was Drizzt Do'Urden *would* have looked—but the hunter wanted more. His hunter-self demanded revenge on the brain mass that had enslaved him.

A single cry saved the drow then, brought him back from the spiraling depths of his blind, instinctive rage.

"Drizzt!" Belwar shouted, limping over to his friend. "Help me, dark elf! My ankle twisted in the fall!" All thoughts of revenge suddenly thrown away, Drizzt Do'Urden rushed to his svirfneblin companion's side.

Arm in arm, the two friends left the circular chamber. A moment later, Guenhwyvar, sleek from the blood and gore of the central brain, bounded up to join them.

"Lead us out," Drizzt begged the panther, and Guenhwyvar willingly took up a point position.

They ran down winding, rough-hewn corridors. "Not made by any svirfneblin," Belwar was quick to point out, throwing his friend a wink.

"I believe they were," Drizzt retorted easily, returning the wink. "Under the charms of a mind flayer, I mean," he quickly added.

"Never!" Belwar insisted. "Never the work of a svirfneblin is this, not even if his mind had been melted away!" In spite of their dire peril, the deep gnome managed a belly laugh, and Drizzt joined him.

Sounds of battle sounded from the side passages of every intersection they crossed. Guenhwyvar's keen senses kept them along the clearest route, though the panther had no way of knowing which way was out. Still, whatever lay in any direction could only be an improvement over the horrors they had left.

A mind flayer jumped out into their corridor just after Guenhwyvar crossed an intersection. The creature hadn't seen the panther and faced Drizzt and Belwar fully. Drizzt threw the svirfneblin down and dived into a headlong roll toward his adversary, expecting to be blasted before he ever got close.

But when the drow came out of the roll and looked up, his breath came back in a profound sigh of relief. The mind flayer lay face down on the stone, Guenhwyvar comfortably perched atop its back.

Drizzt moved to his feline companion as Guenhwyvar casually finished the grim business, and Belwar soon joined them.

"Anger, dark elf," the svirfneblin remarked. Drizzt looked at him curiously.

"I believe anger can fight back against their blasts," Belwar explained. "One got me up on the stairs, but I was so mad, I hardly noticed. Perhaps I am mistaken, but—"

"No," Drizzt interrupted, remembering how little he had been affected, even at close range, when he had gone to retrieve his scimitars. He had been in the thralls of his alter ego then, that darker, maniacal side he so desperately had tried to leave behind. The illithid's mental assault had been all but useless against the hunter. "You are not mistaken," Drizzt assured his friend. "Anger can beat them, or at least slow the effects of their mind assaults."

"Then get mad!" Belwar growled as he signaled Guenhwyvar ahead.

Drizzt threw his supporting arm back under the burrow-warden's shoulder and nodded his agreement with Belwar's suggestion. The drow

realized, though, that blind rage such as Belwar was speaking of could not be consciously created. Instinctive fear and anger might defeat the illithids, but Drizzt, from his experiences with his alter ego, knew those were emotions brought on by nothing short of desperation and panic.

The small party crossed through several more corridors, through a large, empty room, and down yet another passage. Slowed by the limping svirfneblin, they soon heard heavy footsteps closing in from behind.

"Too heavy for illithids," Drizzt remarked, looking back over his shoulder.

"Slaves," Belwar reasoned.

*Fwoop!* An attack sounded behind them. *Fwoop! Fwoop!* The sounds came to them, followed by several thuds and groans.

"Slaves once again," Drizzt said grimly. The pursuing footsteps came on again, this time sounding more like a light shuffle.

"Faster!" Drizzt cried, and Belwar needed no prompting. They ran on, thankful for every turn in the passage, for they feared that the illithids were only steps behind.

They then came into a large and high hall. Several possible exits came into view, but one, a set of large iron doors, held their attention keenly. Between them and the doors was a spiraling iron stairway, and on a balcony not so far above loomed a mind flayer.

"He'll cut us off!" Belwar reasoned. The footsteps came louder from behind. Belwar looked back toward the waiting illithid curiously when he saw a wide smile cross the drow's face. The deep gnome, too, grinned widely.

Guenhwyvar took the spiraling stairs in three mighty bounds. The illithid wisely fled along the balcony and off into the shadows of adjoining corridors. The panther did not pursue, but held a high, guarding position above Drizzt and Belwar.

Both the drow and the svirfneblin called their thanks as they passed, but their elation turned sour when they arrived at the doors. Drizzt pushed hard, but the portals would not budge.

"Locked!" he cried.

"Not for long!" growled Belwar. The enchantment had expired in the deep gnome's mithral hands, but he charged ahead anyway, pounding his hammer-hand against the metal.

Drizzt moved behind the deep gnome, keeping a rear guard and expecting the illithids to enter the hall at any moment. "Hurry, Belwar," he begged.

Both mithral hands worked furiously on the doors. Gradually, the lock began to loosen and the doors opened just an inch. "*Magga cammara*, dark elf!" the burrow-warden cried. "A bar it is that holds them! On the other side!"

"Damn!" Drizzt spat, and across the way, a group of several mind flayers entered the hall.

Belwar didn't relent. His hammer-hand smashed at the door again and again.

The illithids crossed the stairway and Guenhwyvar sprang into their midst, bringing the whole group tumbling down. At that horrible moment, Drizzt realized that he did not have the onyx figurine.

The hammer-hand banged the metal in rapid succession, widening the gap between the doors. Belwar pushed his pickaxe-hand through in an uppercut motion and lifted the bar from its locking clasps. The doors swung wide.

"Come quickly!" the deep gnome yelled to Drizzt. He hooked his pickaxe-hand under the drow's shoulder to pull him along, but Drizzt shrugged away the hold.

"Guenhwyvar!" Drizzt cried.

*Fwoop!* The evil sound came repeatedly from the pile of bodies. Guenhwyvar's reply came as more of a helpless wail than a growl.

Drizzt's lavender eyes burned with rage. He took a single stride back toward the stairway before Belwar figured out a solution.

"Wait!" the svirfneblin called, and he was truly relieved when Drizzt turned about to hear him. Belwar thrust his hip toward the drow and tore open his belt pouch. "Use this!"

Drizzt pulled out the onyx figurine and dropped it at his feet. "Be gone, Guenhwyvar!" he shouted. "Go back to the safety of your home!"

Drizzt and Belwar couldn't even see the panther amid the throng of illithids, but they sensed the mind flayers' sudden distress even before the telltale black mist appeared around the onyx figurine.

As a group, the illithids spun toward them and charged.

"Get the other door!" Belwar cried. Drizzt had grabbed the figurine and was already moving in that direction. The iron portals slammed shut and Drizzt worked to replace the locking bar. Several clasps on the outside of the door had been broken under the burrow-warden's ferocious assault, and the bar was bent, but Drizzt managed to set it in place securely enough to at least slow the illithids.

"The other slaves are trapped," Drizzt remarked.

"Goblins and gray dwarves mostly," Belwar replied.

"And Clacker?"

Belwar threw his arms out helplessly.

"I pity them all," groaned Drizzt, sincerely horrified at the prospect. "Nothing in all the world can torture more than the mental clutches of mind flayers."

"Aye, dark elf," whispered Belwar.

The illithids slammed into the doors, and Drizzt pushed back, further securing the lock.

"Where do we go?" Belwar asked behind him, and when Drizzt turned and surveyed the long and narrow cavern, he certainly understood the burrow-warden's confusion. They spotted at least a dozen exits, but between them and every one rushed a crowd of terrified slaves or a group of illithids.

Behind them came another heavy thud, and the doors creaked open several inches.

"Just go!" Drizzt shouted, pushing Belwar along. They charged down a wide stairway, then out across the broken floor, picking a route that would get them as far from the stone castle as possible.

"Ware danger on all sides!" Belwar cried. "Slave and flayer alike!"

"Let them beware!" Drizzt retorted, his scimitars leading the way. He slammed a goblin down with the hilt of one blade as it stumbled into his way, and a moment later, sliced the tentacles from the face of an illithid as it began to suck the brain from a recaptured duergar.

Then another former slave, a bigger one, jumped in front of Drizzt. The drow rushed it headlong, but this time he stayed his scimitars.

"Clacker!" Belwar yelled behind Drizzt.

"B-b-back of . . . the . . . cavern," the hook horror panted, its grumbled words barely decipherable. "The b-b-best exit."

"Lead on," Belwar replied excitedly, his hopes returning. Nothing would stand against the three of them united. When the burrow-warden started after his giant hook horror friend, however, he noticed that Drizzt wasn't following. At first Belwar feared that a mind blast had caught the drow, but when he returned to Drizzt's side, he realized otherwise.

Atop another of the many wide stairways that ran through the many-tiered cavern, a single slender figure mowed through a group of slaves and illithids alike.

"By the gods," Belwar muttered in disbelief, for the devastating movements of this single figure truly frightened the deep gnome.

The precise cuts and deft twists of the twin swords were not at all frightening to Drizzt Do'Urden. Indeed, to the young dark elf, they rang with a familiarity that brought an old ache to his heart. He looked at Belwar blankly and spoke the name of the single warrior who could fit those maneuvers, the only name that could accompany such magnificent swordplay.

"Zaknafein."

# 20

# Father, My Father

How many lies had Matron Malice told him? What truth could Drizzt ever find in the web of deceptions that marked drow society? His father had not been sacrificed to the Spider Queen! Zaknafein was here, fighting before him, wielding his swords as finely as Drizzt had ever seen.

"What is it?" Belwar demanded.

"The drow warrior," Drizzt was barely able to whisper.

"From your city, dark elf?" Belwar asked." Sent after you?"

"From Menzoberranzan," Drizzt replied. Belwar waited for more information, but Drizzt was too enthralled by Zak's appearance to go into much detail.

"We must go," the burrow-warden said at length.

"Quickly," agreed Clacker, returning to his friends. The hook horror's voice sounded more controlled now, as though the mere appearance of Clacker's friends had aided his pech side in its continuing internal struggle. "The mind flayers are organizing defenses. Many slaves are down."

Drizzt spun out of the reach of Belwar's pick-hand. "No," he said firmly. "I'll not leave him!"

"*Magga cammara*, dark elf!" Belwar shouted at him. "Who is it?"

"Zaknafein Do'Urden," Drizzt yelled back, more than matching the burrow-warden's rising ire. Drizzt's volume dropped considerably as he finished the thought, though, and he nearly choked on the words, "My father."

By the time Belwar and Clacker exchanged disbelieving stares, Drizzt was gone, running to and then up the wide stairway. Atop it, the spirit-wraith stood among a mound of victims, mind flayers and slaves alike, who had found the great misfortune of getting in his way. Farther along the higher tier, several illithids had taken flight from the undead monster.

Zaknafein started to pursue them, for they were running toward the stone castle, following the course the spirit-wraith had determined from the beginning. A thousand magical alarms sounded within the spirit-wraith, though, and abruptly turned him back to the stair.

Drizzt was coming. Zin-carla's moment of fulfillment, the purpose of Zaknafein's animation, at last had arrived!

"Weapon master!" Drizzt cried, springing up lightly to stand by his father's side. The younger drow bubbled with elation, not realizing the truth of the monster standing before him. When Drizzt got near Zak, though, he sensed that something was wrong. Perhaps it was the strange light in the spirit-wraith's eyes that slowed Drizzt's rush. Perhaps it was the fact that Zaknafein did not return his joyful call.

A moment later, it was the downward slice of a sword.

Drizzt somehow managed to get a blocking scimitar up in time. Confused, he still believed that Zaknafein simply had not recognized him.

"Father!" he shouted. "I am Drizzt!"

One sword dived ahead, while the second started in a wide slice, then rushed suddenly toward Drizzt's side. Matching the spirit-wraith's speed, Drizzt came down with one scimitar to parry the first attack and sliced across with the other to foil the second.

"Who are you?" Drizzt demanded desperately, furiously.

A flurry of blows came straight in. Drizzt worked frantically to keep them at bay, but then Zaknafein came across with a backhand and managed to sweep both of Drizzt's blades out to the same side. The spirit-wraith's second sword followed closely, a cut aimed straight at Drizzt's heart, one that Drizzt could not possibly block.

Back down at the bottom of the stairway, Belwar and Clacker cried out, thinking their friend doomed.

Zaknafein's moment of victory was stolen from him, though, by the instincts of the hunter. Drizzt sprang to the side ahead of the plunging blade, then twisted and ducked under Zaknafein's deadly cut. The sword nicked him under his jawbone, leaving a painful gash. When Drizzt completed his roll and found his footing despite the angles of the stair, he showed no sign of acknowledging the injury. When Drizzt again faced his father's imposter, simmering fires burned in his lavender eyes.

Drizzt's agility amazed even his friends, who had seen him before in battle. Zaknafein rushed out immediately after completing his swing, but Drizzt was up and ready before the spirit-wraith caught up to him.

"Who are you?" Drizzt demanded again. This time his voice was deathly calm. "What are you?"

The spirit-wraith snarled and charged recklessly. Believing beyond any doubt that this was not Zaknafein, Drizzt did not miss the opening. He rushed back toward his original position, knocked a sword aside, and slipped a scimitar through as he passed his charging adversary. Drizzt's blade cut through the fine mesh armor and dug deeply into Zaknafein's lung, a wound that would have stopped any mortal opponent.

But Zaknafein did not stop. The spirit-wraith did not draw breath and did not feel pain. Zak turned back on Drizzt and flashed a smile so evil that it would have made Matron Malice stand up and applaud.

Back now on the top step of the stairway, Drizzt stood wide-eyed in amazement. He saw the gruesome wound and saw, against all possibility, Zaknafein steadily advancing, not even flinching.

"Get away!" Belwar cried from the bottom of the stairs. An ogre rushed at the deep gnome, but Clacker intercepted and immediately crushed the thing's head in a claw.

"We must leave," Clacker said to Belwar, the clarity of his voice turning the burrow-warden on his heel.

Belwar could see it clearly in the hook horror's eyes; in that critical moment, Clacker was more a pech than he had been since before the wizard's polymorph spell.

"The stones tell me of illithids gathering within the castle," Clacker explained, and the deep gnome was not surprised that Clacker had heard the voices of the stones. "The illithids will rush out soon," Clacker continued, "to the certain demise of every slave left in the cavern!"

Belwar did not doubt a word of it, but to the svirfneblin, loyalty far outweighed personal safety. "We cannot leave the drow," he replied through clenched teeth.

Clacker nodded in full agreement and charged out to chase away a group of gray dwarves that had come too close.

"Run, dark elf!" Belwar cried. "We have no time!"

Drizzt didn't hear his svirfneblin friend. He focused on the approaching weapon master, the monster impersonating his father, even as Zaknafein focused on him. Of all the many evils perpetrated by Matron Malice, none, by Drizzt's estimation, were greater than this abomination. Malice somehow had perverted the one thing in Drizzt's world that had given him pleasure. Drizzt had believed Zaknafein dead, and that thought was painful enough.

But now this.

It was more than the young drow could bear. He wanted to fight this monster with all his heart and soul, and the spirit-wraith, created for no other reason than this very battle, wholly concurred.

Neither noticed the illithid descending from the darkness above, farther back on the platform, behind Zaknafein.

"Come, monster of Matron Malice," Drizzt growled, sliding his weapons together. "Come and feel my blades."

Zaknafein paused only a few steps away and flashed his wicked smile again. The swords came up; the spirit-wraith took another step.

*Fwoop!*

The illithid's blast rolled over both of them. Zaknafein remained unaffected, but Drizzt caught the force fully. Darkness rolled over him; his eyelids drooped with undeniable weight. He heard his scimitars fall to the stone, but he was beyond any other comprehension.

Zaknafein snarled in gleeful victory, banged his swords together, and stepped toward the falling drow.

Belwar screamed, but it was Clacker's monstrous cry of protest that sounded loudest, rising above the din of the battle-filled cavern. Everything Clacker had ever known as a pech rushed back to him when he saw the drow who had befriended him fall, doomed. That pech identity surged back more keenly, perhaps, than Clacker had even known in his former life.

Zaknafein lunged, seeing his helpless victim in range, but then smashed headfirst into a stone wall that had appeared from nothingness. The spirit-wraith bounced back, his eyes wide in frustration. He clawed at the wall and pounded on it, but it was quite real and sturdy. The stone blocked Zaknafein fully from the stairway and his intended prey.

Back down the stairway, Belwar turned his stunned gaze on Clacker. The svirfneblin had heard that some pech could conjure such stone walls. "Did you . . . ?" the burrow-warden gasped.

The pech in a hook horror's body did not pause long enough to answer. Clacker leaped the stairs four at a stride and gently hoisted Drizzt in his huge arms. He even thought to retrieve the drow's scimitars, then came pounding back down the flight.

"Run!" Clacker commanded the burrow-warden. "For all of your life, run, Belwar Dissengulp!"

The deep gnome, scratching his head with his pickaxe-hand, did indeed run. Clacker cleared a wide path to the cavern's rear exit—none dared stand before his enraged charge—and the burrow-warden, with his short svirfneblin legs, one of which was sprained, had a difficult time keeping up.

Back up the stairs, behind the wall, Zaknafein could only assume that the floating illithid, the same one that had blasted Drizzt, had blocked his charge. Zaknafein whirled about on the monster and screamed in sheer hatred.

*Fwoop!* Another blast came.

Zaknafein leaped up and sliced off both of the illithid's feet with a single stroke. The illithid levitated higher, sending mental cries of anguish and distress to its companions.

Zaknafein couldn't reach the thing, and with other illithids rushing in from every angle, the spirit-wraith didn't have time to enact his own levitation spell. Zaknafein blamed this illithid for his failure; he would not let it escape. He hurled a sword as precisely as any spear.

The illithid looked down at Zaknafein in disbelief, then to the blade buried half to the hilt in its chest and knew that its life was at an end.

Mind flayers rushed toward Zaknafein, firing their stunning blasts as they came. The spirit-wraith had only one sword remaining, but he smashed his opponents down anyway, venting his frustrations on their ugly octopus heads.

Drizzt had escaped . . . for now.

# 21
# Lost and Found

"Praise Lolth," Matron Malice stammered, sensing the distant elation of her spirit-wraith. "He has Drizzt!" The matron mother snapped her gaze to one side, then the other, and her three daughters backed away at the sheer power of the emotions contorting her visage.

"Zaknafein has found your brother!"

Maya and Vierna smiled at each other, glad that this whole ordeal might finally be coming to a conclusion. Since the enactment of Zin-carla, the normal and necessary routines of House Do'Urden had virtually ceased, and every day their nervous mother had turned further and further inward, absorbed by the spirit-wraith's hunt.

Across the anteroom, Briza's smile would have shown a different light to any who took the time to notice, an almost disappointed light.

Fortunately for the first-born daughter, Matron Malice was too absorbed by distant events to take note. The matron mother fell deeper into her meditative trance, savoring every morsel of rage the spirit-wraith threw out, in the knowledge that her blasphemous son was on the receiving end of that anger. Malice's breathing came in excited gasps as Zaknafein and Drizzt played through their sword fight, then the matron mother nearly lost her breath altogether.

Something had stopped Zaknafein.

"No!" Malice screamed, leaping out of her decorated throne. She glanced around, looking for someone to strike or something to throw. "No!" she cried again. "It cannot be!"

"Drizzt has escaped?" Briza asked, trying to keep the smugness out of her voice. Malice's subsequent glare told Briza that her tone might have revealed too much of her thoughts.

"Is the spirit-wraith destroyed?" Maya cried in sincere distress.

"Not destroyed," Malice replied, an obvious tremor in her usually firm voice. "But once more, your brother runs free!"

"Zin-carla has not yet failed," Vierna reasoned, trying to console her excited mother.

"The spirit-wraith is very close," Maya added, picking up Vierna's cue.

Malice dropped back into her seat and wiped the sweat out of her eyes. "Leave me," she commanded her daughters, not wanting them to observe her in such a sorry state. Zin-carla was stealing her life away, Malice knew, for every thought, every hope, of her existence hinged on the spirit-wraith's success.

When the others had gone, Malice lit a candle and took out a tiny, precious mirror. What a wretched thing she had become in the last few tendays. She had hardly eaten, and deep lines of worry creased her formerly glass-smooth, ebony skin. By appearances, Matron Malice had aged more in the last few tendays than in the century before that.

"I will become as Matron Baenre," she whispered in disgust, "withered and ugly." For perhaps the very first time in her long life, Malice began to wonder of the value of her continual quest for power and the merciless Spider Queen's favor. The thoughts disappeared as quickly as they had come, though. Matron Malice had gone too far for such silly regrets. By her strength and devotion, Malice had taken her house to the status of a ruling family and had secured a seat for herself on the prestigious ruling council.

She remained on the verge of despair, though, nearly broken by the strains of the last years. Again she wiped the sweat from her eyes and looked into the little mirror.

What a wretched thing she had become.

Drizzt had done this to her, she reminded herself. Her youngest son's actions had angered the Spider Queen; his sacrilege had put Malice on the edge of doom.

"Get him, my spirit-wraith," Malice whispered with a sneer. At that moment of anger, she hardly cared what future the Spider Queen would lay out for her.

More than anything else in all the world, Matron Malice Do'Urden wanted Drizzt dead.

They ran through the winding tunnels blindly, hoping that no monsters would rear up suddenly before them. With the danger so very real at their backs, the three companions could not afford the usual caution.

Hours passed and still they ran. Belwar, older than his friends and with little legs working two strides for every one of Drizzt's and three strides for each of Clacker's, tired first, but that didn't slow the group. Clacker hoisted the burrow-warden onto a shoulder and ran on.

How many miles they had covered they could not know when they at last broke for their first rest. Drizzt, silent and melancholy through all the trek, took up a guard position at the entrance to the small alcove they had chosen as a temporary camp. Recognizing his drow friend's deep pain, Belwar moved over to offer comfort.

"Not what you expected, dark elf?" the burrow-warden asked softly. With no answer forthcoming, but with Drizzt obviously needing to talk, Belwar pressed on. "The drow in the cavern you knew. Did you claim that he was your father?"

Drizzt snapped an angry glare on the svirfneblin, but his visage softened considerably when he took the moment to realize Belwar's concern.

"Zaknafein," Drizzt explained. "Zaknafein Do'Urden, my father and mentor. It was he who trained me with the blade and who instructed me in all my life. Zaknafein was my only friend in Menzoberranzan, the only drow I have ever known who shared my beliefs."

"He meant to kill you," Belwar stated flatly. Drizzt winced, and the burrow-warden quickly tried to offer him some hope. "Did he not recognize you, perhaps?"

"He was my father," Drizzt said again, "my closest companion for two decades."

"Then why, dark elf?"

"That was not Zaknafein," replied Drizzt. "Zaknafein is dead, sacrificed by my mother to the Spider Queen."

"*Magga cammara*," Belwar whispered, horrified at the revelation concerning Drizzt's parents. The straightforwardness with which Drizzt explained the heinous deed led the burrow-warden to believe that Malice's sacrifice was not so very unusual in the drow city. A shudder coursed through Belwar's spine, but he sublimated his revulsion for the sake of his tormented friend.

"I do not yet know what monster Matron Malice has put in Zaknafein's guise," Drizzt went on, not even noticing Belwar's discomfort.

"A formidable foe, whatever it may be," the deep gnome remarked.

That was exactly what troubled Drizzt. The drow warrior he had battled in the illithid cavern moved with the precision and unmistakable style of Zaknafein Do'Urden. Drizzt's rationale could deny that Zaknafein would turn against him, but his heart told him that the monster he had crossed swords with was indeed his father.

"How did it end?" Drizzt asked after a long pause.

Belwar looked at him curiously.

"The fight," Drizzt explained. "I remember the illithid but nothing more."

Belwar shrugged and looked to Clacker. "Ask him," the burrow-warden replied. "A stone wall appeared between you and your enemies, but how it got there I can only guess."

Clacker heard the conversation and moved over to his friends. "I put it there," he said, his voice still perfectly clear.

"Powers of a pech?" Belwar asked. The deep gnome knew the reputation of pech powers with the stone, but not in enough detail to fully understand what Clacker had done.

"We are a peaceful race," Clacker began, realizing that this might be his only chance to tell his friends of his people. He remained more pechlike than he had since the polymorph, but already he felt the base urges of a hook horror creeping back in. "We desire only to work the stone. It is our calling and our love. And with this symbiosis with the earth comes a measure of power. The stones speak to us and aid us in our toils."

Drizzt looked wryly at Belwar. "Like the earth elemental you once raised against me."

Belwar snorted an embarrassed laugh.

"No," Clacker said soberly, determined not to get sidetracked. "Deep gnomes, too, can call upon the powers of the earth, but theirs is a different relationship. The svirfnebli's love of the earth is only one of their varied definitions of happiness." Clacker looked away from his companions, to the rock wall. "Pech are brothers with the earth. It aids us as we aid it, out of affection."

"You speak of the earth as though it is some sentient being," Drizzt remarked, not sarcastically, just out of curiosity.

"It is, dark elf," replied Belwar, imagining Clacker as he must have appeared before his encounter with the wizard, "for those who can hear it."

Clacker's huge beaked head nodded in accord. "Svirfnebli can hear the earth's distant song," he said. "Pech can speak to it directly."

This was all quite beyond Drizzt's understanding. He knew the sincerity in his companions' words, but drow elves were not nearly as connected to the rocks of the Underdark as the svirfnebli and the pech. Still, if Drizzt needed any proof of what Belwar and Clacker were hinting at, he had only to recall his battle against Belwar's earth elemental that decade ago, or imagine the wall that had somehow appeared out of nowhere to block his enemies in the illithid cavern.

"What do the stones tell you now?" Drizzt asked Clacker. "Have we outdistanced our enemies?"

Clacker moved over and put his ear to the wall. "The words are vague now," he said with obvious lament in his voice. His companions understood the connotation of his tone. The earth was speaking no less clearly; it was Clacker's hearing, impeded by the impending return of the hook horror, that had begun to fade.

"I hear no others in pursuit," Clacker went on, "but I am not so sure as to trust my ears." He snarled suddenly, spun away, and walked back to the far side of the alcove.

Drizzt and Belwar exchanged concerned looks, then moved to follow.

"What is it?" the burrow-warden dared to ask the hook horror, though he could guess readily enough.

"I am falling," Clacker replied, and the grating that had returned to his voice only emphasized the point. "In the illithid cavern, I was pech—more pech than ever before. I was pech in narrow focus. I was the earth." Belwar and Drizzt seemed not to understand.

"The w-w-wall," Clacker tried to explain. "Bringing up such a wall is a task that only a g-g-group of pech elders could accomplish, working together through painstaking rituals." Clacker paused and shook his head violently, as though he was trying to throw out the hook horror side. He slammed a heavy claw into the wall and forced himself to continue. "Yet I did it. I became the stone and merely lifted my hand to block Drizzt's enemies!"

"And now it is leaving," Drizzt said softly. "The pech is falling away from your grasp once again, buried under the instincts of a hook horror."

Clacker looked away and again banged a hook against the wall in reply. Something in the motion brought him comfort, and he repeated it, over and over, rhythmically tap-tapping as if trying to hold on to a piece of his former self.

Drizzt and Belwar walked out of the alcove and back into the corridor to give their giant friend his privacy. A short time later, they noticed that the tapping had ceased, and Clacker stuck his head out, his huge, birdlike eyes filled with sorrow. His stuttered words sent shivers through the spines of his friends, for they found that they could not deny his logic or his desire.

"P-please k-k-kill me."

# Part Five

## Spirit

Spirit. It cannot be broken and it cannot be stolen away. A victim in the throes of despair might feel otherwise, and certainly the victim's "master" would like to believe it so. But in truth, the spirit remains, sometimes buried but never fully removed.

That is the false assumption of Zin-carla and the danger of such sentient animation. The priestesses, I have come to learn, claim it as the highest gift of the Spider Queen deity who rules the drow. I think not. Better to call Zin-carla Lolth's greatest lie.

The physical powers of the body cannot be separated from the rationale of the mind and the emotions of the heart. They are one and the same, a compilation of a singular being. It is in the harmony of these three—body, mind, and heart—that we find spirit.

How many tyrants have tried? How many

rulers have sought to reduce their subjects to simple, unthinking instruments of profit and gain? They steal the loves, the religions, of their people; they seek to steal the spirit.

Ultimately and inevitably, they fail. This I must believe. If the flame of the spirit's candle is extinguished, there is only death, and the tyrant finds no gain in a kingdom littered with corpses.

But it is a resilient thing, this flame of spirit, indomitable and ever-striving. In some, at least, it will survive, to the tyrant's demise.

Where, then, was Zaknafein, my father, when he set out purposefully to destroy me? Where was I in my years alone in the wilds, when this hunter that I had become blinded my heart and guided my sword hand often against my conscious wishes?

We both were there all along, I came to know, buried but never stolen.

Spirit. In every language in all the Realms, surface and Underdark, in every time and every place, the word has a ring of strength and determination. It is the hero's strength, the mother's resilience, and the poor man's armor. It cannot be broken, and it cannot be taken away.

This I must believe.

–Drizzt Do'Urden

# 22
# Without Direction

The sword cut came too swiftly for the goblin slave to even cry out in terror. It toppled forward, quite dead before it ever hit the floor. Zaknafein stepped on its back and continued on; the path to the narrow cavern's rear exit lay open before the spirit-wraith, barely ten yards away.

Even as the undead warrior moved beyond his latest kill, a group of illithids came into the cavern in front of him. Zaknafein snarled and did not turn away or slow in the least. His logic and his strides were direct; Drizzt had gone through this exit, and he would follow.

Anything in his way would fall to his blade.

*Let this one go on its way!* came a telepathic cry from several points in the cavern, from other mind flayers who had witnessed Zaknafein in action. *You cannot defeat him! Let the drow leave!*

The mind flayers had seen enough of the spirit-wraith's deadly blades; more than a dozen of their comrades had died at Zaknafein's hand already.

This new group standing in Zaknafein's way did not miss the urgency of the telepathic pleas. They parted to either side with all speed—except for one.

The illithid race based its existence on pragmatism founded in vast volumes of communal knowledge. Mind flayers considered base emotions such as pride fatal flaws. It proved to be true again on this occasion.

*Fwoop!* The single illithid blasted the spirit-wraith, determined that none should be allowed to escape.

An instant later, the time of a single, precise swipe of a sword, Zaknafein stepped on the fallen illithid's chest and continued on his way out into the wilds of the Underdark.

No other illithids made any move to stop him.

Zaknafein crouched and carefully picked his path. Drizzt had traveled down this tunnel; the scent was fresh and clear. Even so, in his careful pursuit, where he would often have to pause and check the trail, Zaknafein could not move as swiftly as his intended prey.

But, unlike Zaknafein, Drizzt had to rest.

⚔ ⚔ ⚔ ⚔ ⚔

"Hold!" The tone of Belwar's command left no room for debate. Drizzt and Clacker froze in their tracks, wondering what had put the burrow-warden on sudden alert.

Belwar moved over and put his ear to the rock wall. "Boots," he whispered, pointing to the stone. "Parallel tunnel."

Drizzt joined his friend by the wall and listened intently, but though his senses were keener than almost any other dark elf, he was not nearly as adept at reading the vibrations of the stone as the deep gnome.

"How many?" he asked.

"A few," replied Belwar, but his shrug told Drizzt that he was only making a hopeful approximation.

"Seven," said Clacker from a few paces down the wall, his voice clear and sure. "Duergar—gray dwarves—fleeing from the illithids, as are we."

"How can you . . ." Drizzt started to ask, but he stopped, remembering what Clacker had told him concerning the powers of the pech.

"Do the tunnels cross?" Belwar asked the hook horror. "Can we avoid the duergar?"

Clacker turned back to the stone for the answers. "The tunnels join a short way ahead," he replied, "then continue on as one."

"Then if we stay here, the gray dwarves will probably pass us by," Belwar reasoned.

Drizzt was not so certain of the deep gnome's reasoning.

"We and the duergar share a common enemy," Drizzt remarked, then his eyes widened as a thought came to him suddenly. "Allies?"

"Though often the duergar and drow travel together, gray dwarves do not usually ally with svirfnebli," Belwar reminded him. "Or hook horrors, I would guess!"

"This situation is far from usual," Drizzt was quick to retort. "If the duergar are in flight from the mind flayers, then they are probably ill-equipped and unarmed. They might welcome such an alliance, to the gain of both groups."

"I do not believe they will be as friendly as you assume," Belwar replied with a sarcastic snicker, "but concede I will that this narrow tunnel is not a defensible region, more suited to the size of a duergar than to the long blades of a drow and the longer-still arms of a hook horror. If the duergar double back at the crossroad and head toward us, we may have to do battle in an area that will favor them."

"Then to the place where the tunnels join," said Drizzt, "and let us learn what we may."

The three companions soon came into a small, oval-shaped chamber. Another tunnel, the one in which the duergar were traveling, entered the area right beside the companions' tunnel, and a third passage ran out from the back of the room. The friends moved across into the shadows of this farthest tunnel even as the shuffling of boots echoed in their ears.

A moment later, the seven duergar came into the oval chamber. They were haggard, as Drizzt had suspected, but they were not unarmed. Three carried clubs, another a dagger, two held swords, and the last sported two large rocks.

Drizzt held his friends back and stepped out to meet the strangers. Though neither race held much love for the other, drow and duergar often formed mutually gainful alliances. Drizzt guessed that the chances of forming a peaceful alliance would be greater if he went out alone.

His sudden appearance startled the weary gray dwarves. They rushed all about frantically, trying to form some defensive posture. Swords and clubs came up at the ready, and the dwarf holding the rocks cocked his arm back for a throw.

"Greetings, duergar," Drizzt said hoping that the gray dwarves would understand the drow tongue. His hand rested easily on the hilts of his sheathed scimitars; he knew he could get to them quickly enough if he needed them.

"Who might ye be?" one of the sword-wielding gray dwarves asked in shaky but understandable drow.

"A refugee, as yourselves," replied Drizzt, "fleeing from the slavery of the cruel mind flayers."

"Then ye know our hurry," snarled the duergar, "so be standin' outa our way!"

"I offer to you an alliance," said Drizzt. "Surely greater numbers will only aid us when the illithids come."

"Seven's as good as eight," the duergar stubbornly replied. Behind the speaker, the rock thrower pumped his arm threateningly.

"But not as good as ten," Drizzt reasoned calmly.

"Ye got friends?" asked the duergar, his tone noticeably softening. He glanced about nervously, looking for a possible ambush. "More drow?"

"Hardly," Drizzt answered.

"I seen him!" cried another of the group, also in the drow tongue, before Drizzt could begin to explain. "He runned out with the beaked monster an' the svirfneblin!"

"Deep gnome!" The leader of the duegar spat at Drizzt's feet. "Not a friend o' the duergar or the drow!"

Drizzt would have been willing to let the failed offer go at that, when he and his friends moving on their way and the gray dwarves going their own. But the well-earned reputation of the duergar labeled them as neither peaceful nor overly intelligent. With the illithids not far behind, this band of gray dwarves hardly needed more enemies.

A rock sailed at Drizzt's head. A scimitar flashed out and deflected it harmlessly aside.

*"Bivrip!"* came the burrow-warden's cry from the tunnel, Belwar and

Clacker rushed out, not surprised in the least by the sudden turn of events.

In the drow Academy, Drizzt, like all dark elves, had spent months learning the ways and tricks of the gray dwarves. That training saved him now, for he was the first to strike, lining all seven of his diminutive opponents in the harmless purple flames of faerie fire.

Almost at the same time, three of the duergar faded from view, exercising their innate talents of invisibility. The purple flames remained, though, clearly outlining the disappearing dwarves.

A second rock flew through the air, slamming into Clacker's chest. The armored monster would have smiled at the pitiful attack if a beak could smile, and Clacker continued his charge straight ahead into the duergar's midst.

The rock thrower and the dagger wielder fled out of the hook horror's way, having no weapons that could possibly hurt the armored giant. With other foes readily available, Clacker let them go. They came around the side of the chamber, bearing straight in at Belwar, thinking the svirfneblin the easiest of the targets.

The swipe of a pickaxe abruptly stopped their charge. The unarmed duergar lunged forward, trying to grab the arm before it could launch a backswing. Belwar anticipated the attempt and crossed over with his hammer-hand, slamming the duergar squarely in the face. Sparks flew, bones crumbled, and gray skin burned and splattered. The duergar flew to his back and writhed about frantically, clutching his broken face.

The dagger wielder was not so anxious anymore.

Two invisible duergar came at Drizzt. With the outline of purple flames, Drizzt could see their general movement, and he had prudently marked these two as the sword-wielders. But Drizzt was at a clear disadvantage, for he could not distinguish subtle thrusts and cuts. He backed away, putting distance between himself and his companions.

He sensed an attack and threw out a blocking scimitar, smiling at his luck when he heard the ring of weapons. The gray dwarf came into view for just a moment, to show Drizzt his wicked smile, then faded quickly away.

"How many does ye think ye can block?" the other invisible duergar asked smugly.

"More than you, I suspect," Drizzt replied, and then it was the drow's turn to smile. His enchanted globe of absolute darkness descended over all three of the combatants, stealing the duergar advantage.

In the wild rush of the battle, Clacker's savage hook horror instincts took full control of his actions. The giant did not understand the significance of the empty purple flames that marked the third invisible duergar, and he charged instead at the two remaining gray dwarves, both holding clubs.

Before the hook horror ever got there, a club smashed into his knee, and the invisible duergar chuckled in glee. The other two began to fade from sight, but Clacker now paid them no heed. The invisible club struck again, this time smashing into the hook horror's thigh.

Possessed by the instincts of a race that had never been concerned with finesse, the hook horror howled and fell forward, burying the purple flames under his massive chest. Clacker hopped and dropped several times, until he was satisfied that the unseen enemy was crushed to death.

But then a flurry of clubbing blows rained down upon the back of the hook horror's head.

The dagger-wielding duergar was no novice to battle. His attacks came in measured thrusts, forcing Belwar, wielding heavier weapons, to take the initiative. Deep gnomes hated duergar as profoundly as duergar hated deep gnomes, but Belwar was no fool. His pickaxe waved about only to keep his opponent at bay, while his hammer-hand remained cocked and ready.

Thus, the two sparred without gain for several moments, both content to let the other make the first error. When the hook horror cried out in pain, and with Drizzt out of sight, Belwar was forced to act. He stumbled forward, feigning a trip, and lurched ahead with his hammer-hand as his pickaxe dipped low.

The duergar recognized the ploy, but could not ignore the obvious opening in the svirfneblin's defense. The dagger came in over the pickaxe, diving straight at Belwar's throat.

The burrow-warden threw himself backward with equal speed and lifted a leg as he went, his boot clipping the duergar's chin. The gray dwarf kept coming, though, diving down atop the falling deep gnome, his dagger's point leading the way.

Belwar got his pickaxe up only a split second before the jagged weapon found his throat. The burrow-warden managed to move the duergar's arm out wide, but the gray dwarf's considerable weight pressed them together, their faces barely an inch apart.

"Got ye now!" the duergar cried.

"Get this!" Belwar snarled back, and he freed up his hammer-hand enough to launch a short but heavy punch into the duergar's ribs. The duergar slammed his forehead into Belwar's face, and Belwar bit him on the nose in response. The two rolled about, spitting and snarling, and using whatever weapons they could find.

By the sound of ringing blades, any observers outside Drizzt's darkness globe would have sworn that a dozen warriors battled within. The frenzied tempo of swordplay was solely the doing of Drizzt Do'Urden. In such a situation, fighting blindly, the drow reasoned that the best battle method would be to keep all the blades as far away from his body as possible. His scimitars charged out relentlessly and in perfect harmony, pressing the two gray dwarves back on their heels.

Each arm worked its own opponent, keeping the gray dwarves rooted in place squarely in front of Drizzt. If one of his enemies managed to get around to his side, the drow knew, he would be in serious trouble.

Each scimitar swipe brought a ring of metal, and each passing second gave Drizzt more understanding of his opponents' abilities and attack strategies. Out in the Underdark, Drizzt had fought blindly many times, once even donning a hood against the basilisk he'd met.

Overwhelmed by the sheer speed of the drow's attacks, the duergar could only work their swords back and forth and hope that a scimitar didn't slide through.

The blades sang and rang as the two duergar frantically parried and dodged. Then came a sound that Drizzt had hoped for, the sound of a scimitar digging into flesh. A moment later, one sword clanged to the stone and its wounded wielder made the fatal mistake of crying out in pain.

Drizzt's hunter-self rose to the surface at that moment and focused on that cry, and his scimitar shot straight ahead, smashing into the gray dwarf's teeth and on through the back of its head.

The hunter turned on the remaining duergar in fury. Around and around his blades spun in swirling circular motions. Around and around, then one shot out in a sudden straightforward thrust, too quickly for a blocking response. It caught the duergar in the shoulder, gashing a deep wound.

"Give! Give!" the gray dwarf cried, not desiring the same fate as its companion. Drizzt heard another sword drop to the floor. "Please, drow elf!"

At the duergar's words, the drow buried his instinctive urges. "I accept your surrender," Drizzt replied, and he moved close to his opponent, putting the tip of his scimitar to the gray dwarf's chest. Together, they walked out of the area darkened by Drizzt's spell.

Searing agony ripped through Clacker's head, every blow sending waves of pain. The hook horror gurgled out an animal's growl and exploded into furious motion, heaving up from the crushed duergar and spinning over at the newest foes.

A duergar club smashed in again, but Clacker was beyond any sensation of pain. A heavy claw bashed through the purple outline, through the invisible duergar's skull. The gray dwarf came back into view suddenly, the concentration needed to maintain a state of invisibility stolen by death, the greatest thief of all.

The remaining duergar turned to flee, but the enraged hook horror moved faster. Clacker caught the gray dwarf in a claw and hoisted him into the air. Screeching like a frenzied bird, the hook horror hurled the unseen opponent into the wall. The duergar came back into sight, broken and crumbled at the base of the stone wall.

No opponents stood to face the hook horror, but Clacker's savage hunger was far from satiated. Drizzt and the wounded duergar emerged from the darkness then, and the hook horror barreled in.

With the specter of Belwar's combat taking his attention, Drizzt did not realize Clacker's intent until the duergar prisoner screamed in terror.

By then, it was too late.

Drizzt watched his prisoner's head go flying back into the globe of darkness.

"Clacker!" the drow screamed in protest. Then Drizzt ducked and dived backward for his own life as the other claw came viciously swinging across.

Spotting new prey nearby, the hook horror didn't follow the drow into the globe. Belwar and the dagger-wielding duergar were too engaged in their own struggles to notice the approaching crazed giant. Clacker bent low, collected the prone combatants in his huge arms, and heaved them both straight up into the air. The duergar had the misfortune of coming down first, and Clacker promptly batted it across the chamber. Belwar would have found a similar fate, but crossed scimitars intercepted the hook horror's next blow.

The giant's strength slid Drizzt back several feet, but the parry softened the blow enough for Belwar to fall by. Still, the burrow-warden crashed heavily into the floor and spent a long moment too dazed to react.

"Clacker!" Drizzt cried again, as a giant foot came up with the obvious intent of squashing Belwar flat. Needing all his speed and agility, Drizzt dived around to the back of the hook horror, dropped to the floor, and went for Clacker's knees, as he had in their first encounter. Trying to stomp on the prone svirfneblin, Clacker was already a bit off balance, and Drizzt easily tripped him to the stone. In the blink of an eye, the drow warrior sprang atop the monster's chest and slipped a scimitar tip between the armored folds of Clacker's neck.

Drizzt dodged a clumsy swing as Clacker continued to struggle. The drow hated what he had to do, but then the hook horror calmed suddenly and looked up at him with sincere understanding.

"D-d-do . . . it," came a garbled demand. Drizzt, horrified, glanced over to Belwar for support. Back on his feet, the burrow-warden just looked away.

"Clacker?" Drizzt asked the hook horror. "Are you Clacker once again?"

The monster hesitated, then the beaked head nodded slightly.

Drizzt sprang away and looked at the carnage in the chamber. "Let us leave," he said.

Clacker remained prone a moment longer, considering the grim implications of his reprieve. With the battle's conclusion, the hook horror side backed out of its full control of Clacker's consciousness. Those savage instincts lurked, Clacker knew, not far from the surface, waiting for another opportunity to find a firm hold. How many times would the faltering pech side be able to fight those instincts?

Clacker slammed the stone, a mighty blow that sent cracks running through the chamber's floor. With great effort, the weary giant climbed to his feet. In his embarrassment, Clacker didn't look at his companions, but just stormed away down the tunnel, each banging footstep falling like a hammer on a nail in Drizzt Do'Urden's heart.

"Perhaps you should have finished it, dark elf," Belwar suggested, moving beside his drow friend.

"He saved my life in the illithid cavern," Drizzt retorted sharply. "And has been a loyal friend."

"He tried to kill me, and you," the deep gnome said grimly. "*Magga cammara*."

"I am his friend!" Drizzt growled, grabbing the svirfneblin's shoulder. "You ask me to kill him?"

"I ask you to act as his friend," retorted Belwar, and he pulled free of the grasp and started away down the tunnel after Clacker.

Drizzt grabbed the burrow-warden's shoulder again and roughly spun him around.

"It will only get worse, dark elf," Belwar said calmly into Drizzt's grimace. "A firmer hold does the wizard's spell gain with every passing day. Clacker will try to kill us again, I fear, and if he succeeds, the realization of the act will destroy him more fully than your blades ever could!"

"I cannot kill him," Drizzt said, and he was no longer angry. "Nor can you."

"Then we must leave him," the deep gnome replied. "We must let Clacker go free in the Underdark, to live his life as a hook horror. That surely is what he will become, body and spirit."

"No," said Drizzt. "We must not leave him. We are his only chance. We must help him."

"The wizard is dead," Belwar reminded him, and the deep gnome turned away and started again after Clacker.

"There are other wizards," Drizzt replied under his breath, this time making no move to impede the burrow-warden. The drow's eyes narrowed and he snapped his scimitars back into their sheaths. Drizzt knew what he must do, what price his friendship with Clacker demanded, but he found the thought too disturbing to accept.

There were indeed other wizards in the Underdark, but chance meetings were far from common, and wizards capable of dispelling Clacker's polymorphed state would be fewer still. Drizzt knew where such wizards could be found, though.

The thought of returning to his homeland haunted Drizzt with every step he and his companions took that day. Having viewed the consequences of his decision to leave Menzoberranzan, Drizzt never wanted to see the place again, never wanted to look upon the dark world that had so damned him.

But if he chose now not to return, Drizzt knew that he would soon witness a more wicked sight than Menzoberranzan. He would watch Clacker, a friend who had saved him from certain death, degenerate fully into a hook horror. Belwar had suggested abandoning Clacker, and that course seemed preferable to the battle that Drizzt and the deep gnome surely must fight if they were near Clacker when the degeneration became complete.

Even if Clacker were far removed, though, Drizzt knew that he would witness the degeneration. His thoughts would stay on Clacker, the friend he had abandoned, for the rest of his days, just one more pain for the tormented drow.

In all the world, Drizzt could think of nothing he desired less than viewing the sights of Menzoberranzan or conversing with his former people. Given the choice, he would prefer death over returning to the drow city, but the choice was not so simple. It hinged on more than Drizzt's personal desires. He had founded his life on principles, and those principles now demanded loyalty. They demanded that he put Clacker's needs above his own desires, because Clacker had befriended him and because the concept of true friendship far outweighed personal desires.

Later on, when the friends had set camp for a short rest, Belwar noticed that Drizzt was engaged in some inner conflict. Leaving Clacker, who once again was tap-tapping at the stone wall, the svirfneblin moved cautiously by the drow's side.

Belwar cocked his head curiously. "What are you thinking, dark elf?"

Drizzt, too caught up in his emotional turbulence, did not return Belwar's gaze. "My homeland boasts a school of wizardry," Drizzt replied with steadfast determination.

At first the burrow-warden didn't understand what Drizzt hinted at, but then, when Drizzt glanced over to Clacker, Belwar realized the implications of Drizzt's simple statement.

"Menzoberranzan?" the svirfneblin cried. "You would return there, hoping that some dark elf wizard would show mercy upon our pech friend?"

"I would return there because Clacker has no other chance," Drizzt retorted angrily.

"Then no chance at all has Clacker," Belwar roared. "*Magga cammara*, dark elf. Menzoberranzan will not be so quick to welcome you!"

"Perhaps your pessimism will prove valid," said Drizzt. "Dark elves are not moved by mercy, I agree, but there may be other options."

"You are hunted," Belwar said. His tone showed that he hoped his simple words would shake some sense into his drow companion.

"By Matron Malice," Drizzt retorted. "Menzoberranzan is a large place, my little friend, and loyalties to my mother will play no part in any encounter we find beyond those with my own family. I assure you that I have no plans to meet anyone from my own family!"

"And what, dark elf, might we offer in exchange for dispelling Clacker's curse?" Belwar replied sarcastically. "What have we to offer that any dark elf wizard of Menzoberranzan would value?"

Drizzt's reply started with a blurring cut of a scimitar, was heightened by a familiar simmering fire in the drow's lavender eyes, and ended with a simple statement that even stubborn Belwar could not find the words to refute.

"The wizard's life."

# 23

# Ripples

Matron Baenre took a long and careful scan of Malice Do'Urden, measuring how greatly the trials of Zin-carla had weighed on the matron mother. Deep lines of worry creased Malice's once smooth face, and her stark white hair, which had been the envy of her generation, was, for one of the very few times in five centuries, frazzled and unkempt. Most striking, though, were Malice's eyes, once radiant and alert but now dark with weariness and sunken in the sockets of her dark skin.

"Zaknafein almost had him," Malice explained, her voice an uncharacteristic whine. "Drizzt was in his grasp, and yet somehow, my son managed to escape!

"But the spirit-wraith is close on his trail again," Malice quickly added, seeing Matron Baenre's disapproving frown. In addition to being the most powerful figure in all of Menzoberranzan, the withered matron mother of House Baenre was considered Lolth's personal representative in the city. Matron Baenre's approval was Lolth's approval, and by the same logic, Matron Baenre's disapproval most often spelled disaster for a house.

"Zin-carla requires patience, Matron Malice," Matron Baenre said calmly. "It has not been so long."

Malice relaxed a bit, until she looked again at her surroundings. She hated the chapel of House Baenre, so huge and demeaning. The entire

Do'Urden complex could fit within this single chamber, and if Malice's family and soldiers were multiplied ten times over, they still would not fill the rows of benches. Directly above the central altar, directly above Matron Malice, loomed the illusionary image of the gigantic spider, shifting into the form of a beautiful drow female, then back again into an arachnid. Sitting here alone with Matron Baenre under that overpowering image made Malice feel even more insignificant.

Matron Baenre sensed her guest's uneasiness and moved to comfort her. "You have been given a great gift," she said sincerely. "The Spider Queen would not bestow Zin-carla, and would not have accepted the sacrifice of SiNafay Hun'ett, a matron mother, if she did not approve of your methods and your intent."

"It is a trial," Malice replied offhandedly.

"A trial you will not fail!" Matron Baenre retorted. "And then the glories you will know, Malice Do'Urden! When the spirit-wraith of he who was Zaknafein has completed his task and your renegade son is dead, you will sit in honor on the ruling council. Many years, I promise you, will pass before any house will dare to threaten House Do'Urden. The Spider Queen will shine her favor upon you for the proper completion of Zin-carla. She will hold your house in the highest regard and will defend you against rivals."

"What if Zin-carla fails?" Malice dared to ask. "Let us suppose . . ." Her voice trailed away as Matron Baenre's eyes widened in shock.

"Speak not the words!" Baenre scolded. "And think not of such impossibilities! You grow distracted by fear, and that alone will spell your doom. Zin-carla is an exercise of willpower and a test of your devotion to the Spider Queen. The spirit-wraith is an extension of your faith and your strength. If you falter in your trust, then the spirit-wraith of Zaknafein will falter in his quest!"

"I will not falter!" Malice roared, her hands clenched around the armrests of her chair. "I accept the responsibility of my son's sacrilege, and with Lolth's help and blessings, I will enact the appropriate punishment upon Drizzt."

Matron Baenre relaxed back in her seat and nodded her approval. She had to support Malice in this endeavor, by the command of Lolth, and she knew enough of Zin-carla to understand that confidence and determination were two of the primary ingredients for success. A matron mother involved in Zin-carla had to proclaim her trust in Lolth and her desire to please Lolth often and sincerely.

Now, though, Malice had another problem, a distraction she could ill afford. She had come to House Baenre of her own volition, seeking aid.

"Then of this other matter," Matron Baenre prompted, fast growing tired of the meeting.

"I am vulnerable," Malice explained. "Zin-carla steals my energy and attention. I fear that another house may seize the opportunity."

"No house has ever attacked a matron mother in the thralls of Zin-carla," Matron Baenre pointed out, and Malice realized that the withered old drow spoke from experience.

"Zin-carla is a rare gift," Malice replied, "given to powerful matrons with powerful houses, almost assuredly in the highest favor of the Spider Queen. Who would attack under such circumstances? But House Do'Urden is far different. We have just suffered the consequences of war. Even with the addition of some of House Hun'ett's soldiers, we are crippled. It is well known that I have not yet regained Lolth's favor but that my house is eighth in the city, putting me on the ruling council, an enviable position."

"Your fears are misplaced," Matron Baenre assured her, but Malice slumped back in frustration in spite of the words. Matron Baenre shook her head helplessly. "I see that my words alone cannot soothe. Your attention must be on Zin-carla. Understand that, Malice Do'Urden. You have no time for such petty worries."

"They remain," said Malice.

"Then I will end them," offered Matron Baenre. "Return to your house now, in the company of two hundred Baenre soldiers. The numbers will secure your battlements, and my soldiers shall wear the house emblem of Baenre. None in the city will dare to strike with such allies."

A wide smile rolled across Malice's face, a grin that diminished a few of those worry lines. She accepted Matron Baenre's generous gift as a signal that perhaps Lolth still did favor House Do'Urden.

"Go back to your home and concentrate on the task at hand," Matron

Baenre continued. "Zaknafein must find Drizzt again and kill him. That is the deal you offered to the Spider Queen. But fear not for the spirit-wraith's last failure or the time lost. A few days, or tendays, is not very long in Lolth's eyes. The proper conclusion of Zin-carla is all that matters."

"You will arrange for my escort?" Malice asked, rising from her chair.

"It is already waiting," Matron Baenre assured her.

Malice walked down from the raised central dais and out through the many rows of the giant chapel. The huge room was dimly lit, and Malice could barely see, as she exited, another figure moving toward the central dais from the opposite direction. She assumed it to be Matron Baenre's companion illithid, a common figure in the great chapel. If Malice had known that Matron Baenre's mind flayer had left the city on some private business in the west, she might have paid more heed to the distant figure.

Her worry lines would have increased tenfold.

"Pitiful," Jarlaxle remarked as he ascended to sit beside Matron Baenre. "This is not the same Matron Malice Do'Urden that I knew only a few short months ago."

"Zin-carla is not cheaply given," Matron Baenre replied.

"The toll is great," Jarlaxle agreed. He looked straight at Matron Baenre, reading her eyes as well as her forthcoming reply. "Will she fail?"

Matron Baenre chuckled aloud, a laugh that sounded more like a wheeze. "Even the Spider Queen could only guess at the answer. My—our—soldiers should lend Matron Malice enough comfort to complete the task. That is my hope at least. Malice Do'Urden once was in Lolth's highest regard, you know. Her seat on the ruling council was demanded by the Spider Queen."

"Events do seem to lead to the completion of Lolth's will," Jarlaxle snickered, remembering the battle between House Do'Urden and House Hun'ett, in which Bregan D'aerthe had played the pivotal role. The consequences of that victory, the elimination of House Hun'ett, had put House Do'Urden in the city's eighth position and thus, had placed Matron Malice on the ruling council.

"Fortunes smile on the favored," Matron Baenre remarked.

Jarlaxle's grin was replaced by a suddenly serious look. "And is

Malice—Matron Malice," he quickly corrected, seeing Baenre's immediate glower, "now in the Spider Queen's favor? Will fortunes smile on House Do'Urden?"

"The gift of Zin-carla removed both favor and disfavor, I would assume," Matron Baenre explained. "Matron Malice's fortunes are for her and her spirit-wraith to determine."

"Or, for her son—this infamous Drizzt Do'Urden—to destroy," Jarlaxle completed. "Is this young warrior so very powerful? Why has Lolth not simply crushed him?"

"He has forsaken the Spider Queen," Baenre replied, "fully and with all his heart. Lolth has no power over Drizzt and has determined him to be Matron Malice's problem."

"A rather large problem, it would seem," Jarlaxle chuckled with a quick shake of his bald head. The mercenary noticed immediately that Matron Baenre did not share his mirth.

"Indeed," she replied somberly, and her voice trailed off on the word as she sank back for some private thoughts. She knew the dangers, and the possible profits, of Zin-carla better than anyone in the city. Twice before Matron Baenre had asked for the Spider Queen's greatest gift, and twice before she had seen Zin-carla through to successful completion. With the unrivaled grandeur of House Baenre all about her, Matron Baenre could not forget the gains of Zin-carla's success. But every time she saw her withered reflection in a pool or a mirror, she was vividly reminded of the heavy price.

Jarlaxle did not intrude on the matron mother's reflections. The mercenary contemplated on his own at that moment. In a time of trial and confusion such as this, a skilled opportunist would find only gain. By Jarlaxle's reckoning, Bregan D'aerthe could only profit from the granting of Zin-carla to Matron Malice. If Malice proved successful and reinforced her seat on the ruling council, Jarlaxle would have another very powerful ally within the city. If the spirit-wraith failed, to the ruin of House Do'Urden, the price on this young Drizzt's head certainly would escalate to a level that might tempt the mercenary band.

⚔⚔⚔⚔⚔

As she had on her journey to the first house of the city, Malice imagined ambitious gazes following her return through the winding streets of Menzoberranzan. Matron Baenre had been quite generous and gracious. Accepting the premise that the withered old matron mother was indeed Lolth's voice in the city, Malice could barely contain her smile.

Undeniably, though, the fears still remained. How readily would Matron Baenre come to Malice's aid if Drizzt continued to elude Zaknafein, if Zincarla ultimately failed? Malice's position on the ruling council would be tenuous then—as would the continued existence of House Do'Urden.

The caravan passed House Fey-Branche, ninth house of the city and most probably the greatest threat to a weakened House Do'Urden. Matron Halavin Fey-Branche was no doubt watching the procession beyond her adamantite gates, watching the matron mother who now held the coveted eighth seat on the ruling council.

Malice looked at Dinin and the ten soldiers of House Do'Urden, walking by her side as she sat atop the floating magical disc. She let her gaze wander to the two hundred soldiers, warriors openly bearing the proud emblem of House Baenre, marching with disciplined precision behind her modest troupe.

What must Matron Halavin Fey-Branche be thinking at such a sight? Malice wondered. She could not contain her ensuing smile.

"Our greatest glories are soon to come," Malice assured her warrior son. Dinin nodded and returned the wide smile, wisely not daring to steal any of the joy from his volatile mother.

Privately, though, Dinin couldn't ignore his disturbing suspicions that many of the Baenre soldiers, drow warriors he had never had the occasion to meet before, looked vaguely familiar. One of them even shot a sly wink at the elderboy of House Do'Urden.

Jarlaxle's magical whistle being blown on the balcony of House Do'Urden came vividly to Dinin's mind.

# 24

# Faith

Drizzt and Belwar did not have to remind each other of the significance of the green glow that appeared far ahead up the tunnel. Together they quickened their pace to catch up with and warn Clacker, who continued his approach with strides quickened by curiosity. The hook horror always led the party now; Clacker simply had become too dangerous for Drizzt and Belwar to allow him to walk behind.

Clacker turned abruptly at their sudden approach, waved a claw menacingly, and hissed.

"Pech," Belwar whispered, speaking the word he had been using to strike a recollection in his friend's fast-fading consciousness. The troupe had turned back toward the east, toward Menzoberranzan, as soon as Drizzt had convinced the burrow-warden of his determination to aid Clacker. Belwar, having no other options, had finally agreed with the drow's plan as Clacker's only hope, but though they had turned immediately and had quickened their march, both now feared that they would not arrive in time. The transformation in Clacker had been dramatic since the confrontation with the duergar. The hook horror could barely speak and often turned threateningly on his friends.

"Pech," Belwar said again as he and Drizzt neared the anxious monster. The hook horror paused, confused.

"Pech!" Belwar growled a third time, and he tapped his hammer-hand against the stone wall.

As if a light of recognition had suddenly gone on within the turmoil that was his consciousness, Clacker relaxed and dropped his heavy arms to his sides.

Drizzt and Belwar looked past the hook horror to the green glow and exchanged concerned glances. They had committed themselves fully to this course and had little choice in their actions now.

"Corbies live in the chamber beyond," Drizzt began quietly, speaking each word slowly and distinctly to ensure that Clacker understood. "We have to get directly across and out the other side swiftly, for if we hope to avoid a battle, we have no time for delays. Take care in your steps. The only walkways are narrow and treacherous."

"C-C-Clac—" the hook horror stammered futilely.

"Clacker," Belwar offered.

"L-l-l—" Clacker stopped suddenly and threw a claw out in the direction of the green-glowing chamber.

"Clacker lead?" Drizzt said, unable to bear the hook horror's struggling. "Clacker lead," Drizzt said again, seeing the great head bobbing in accord.

Belwar didn't seem so sure of the wisdom of that suggestion. "We have fought the bird-men before and have seen their tricks," the svirfneblin reasoned. "But Clacker has not."

"The sheer bulk of the hook horror should deter them," Drizzt argued. "Clacker's mere presence may allow us to avoid a fight."

"Not against the corbies, dark elf," said the burrow-warden. "They will attack anything without fear. You witnessed their frenzy, their disregard for their own lives. Even your panther did not deter them."

"Perhaps you are right," Drizzt agreed, "but even if the corbies do attack, what weapons do they possess that could defeat a hook horror's armor? What defense could the birdmen offer against Clacker's great claws. Our giant friend will sweep them aside."

"You forget the stone-riders up above," the burrow-warden pointedly reminded him. "They will be quick to take a ledge down, and take Clacker with it!"

Clacker turned away from the conversation and stared into the stone of the walls in a futile effort to recapture a portion of his former self. He felt a slight urge to begin tap-tapping on the stone, but it was no greater than his continuing urge to smash a claw into the face of either the svirfneblin or the drow.

"I will deal with any corbies waiting above the ledges," Drizzt replied. "You just follow Clacker across—a dozen paces behind."

Belwar glanced over and noticed the mounting tension in the hook horror. The burrow-warden realized that they could not afford any delays, so he shrugged and pushed Clacker off, motioning down the passage toward the green glow. Clacker started away, and Drizzt and Belwar fell into step behind.

"The panther?" Belwar whispered to Drizzt as they rounded the last bend in the tunnel.

Drizzt shook his head briskly, and Belwar, remembering Guenhwyvar's last painful episode in the corby chamber, did not question him further.

Drizzt patted the deep gnome on the shoulder for luck, then moved up past Clacker and was the first to enter the quiet chamber. With a few simple motions, the drow stepped into a levitation spell and floated silently up. Clacker, amazed by this strange place with the glowing lake of acid below him, hardly noticed Drizzt's movements. The hook horror stood perfectly still, glancing all about the chamber and using his keen sense of hearing to locate any possible enemies.

"Move," Belwar whispered behind him. "Delay will bring disaster!"

Clacker started out tentatively, then picked up speed as he gained confidence in the strength of the narrow, unsupported walkway. He took the straightest course he could discern, though even this meandered about before it reached the exiting archway opposite the one they had entered.

"Do you see anything, dark elf?" Belwar called as loudly as he dared a few uneventful moments later. Clacker had passed the midpoint of the chamber without incident and the burrow-warden could not contain his mounting anxiety. No corbies had shown themselves; not a sound had been made beyond the heavy thumping of Clacker's feet and the shuffling of Belwar's worn boots.

Drizzt floated back down to the ledge, far behind his companions. "Nothing," he replied. The drow shared Belwar's suspicions that no dire corbies were about. The hush of the acid-filled cavern was absolute and unnerving. Drizzt ran out toward the center of the chamber, then lifted off again in his levitation, trying to get a better angle on all of the walls.

"What do you see?" Belwar asked him a moment later. Drizzt looked down to the burrow-warden and shrugged.

"Nothing at all."

"*Magga cammara*," grumbled Belwar, almost wishing that a corby would step out and attack.

Clacker had nearly reached the targeted exit by this time, though Belwar, in his conversation with Drizzt, had lagged behind and remained near the center of the huge room. When the burrow-warden finally turned back to the path ahead, the hook horror had disappeared under the arch of the exit.

"Anything?" Belwar called out to both of his companions. Drizzt shook his head and continued to rise. He rotated slowly about, scanning the walls, unable to believe that no corbies lurked in ambush.

Belwar looked back to the exit. "We must have chased them out," he muttered to himself, but in spite of his words, the burrow-warden knew better. When he and Drizzt had taken flight from this room a couple of tendays before, they had left several dozen of the bird-men behind them. Certainly the toll of a few dead corbies would not have chased away the rest of the fearless clan.

For some unknown reason, no corbies had come out to stand against them.

Belwar started off at a quick pace, thinking it best not to question their good fortune. He was about to call out to Clacker, to confirm that the hook horror had indeed moved to safety, when a sharp, terror-filled squeal rolled out from the exit, followed by a heavy crash. A moment later, Belwar and Drizzt had their answers.

The spirit-wraith of Zaknafein Do'Urden stepped under the arch and out onto the ledge.

"Dark elf!" the burrow-warden called sharply.

Drizzt had already seen the spirit-wraith and was descending as rapidly as he could toward the walkway near the middle of the chamber.

"Clacker," Belwar called, but he expected no answer, and received none, from the shadows beyond the archway. The spirit-wraith steadily advanced.

"You murderous beast!" the burrow-warden cursed, setting his feet wide apart and slamming his mithral hands together. "Come out and get your due!" Belwar fell into his chant to empower his hands, but Drizzt interrupted him.

"No!" the drow cried out high above. "Zaknafein is here for me, not you. Move out of his way!"

"Was he here for Clacker?" Belwar yelled back. "A murderous beast, he is, and I have a score to settle!"

"You do not know that," Drizzt replied, increasing his descent as fast as he dared to catch up to the fearless burrow-warden. Drizzt knew that Zaknafein would get to Belwar first, and he could guess easily enough the grim consequences.

"Trust me now, I beg," Drizzt pleaded. "This drow warrior is far beyond your abilities."

Belwar banged his hands together again, but he could not honestly refute Drizzt's words. Belwar had seen Zaknafein in battle only that one time in the illithid cavern, but the monster's blurring movements had stolen his breath. The deep gnome backed away a few steps and turned down a side walkway, seeking another route to the arched exit so that he might learn Clacker's fate.

With Drizzt so plainly in sight, the spirit-wraith paid the little svirfneblin no heed. Zaknafein charged right past the side walkway and continued on to fulfill the purpose of his existence.

Belwar thought to pursue the strange drow, to close from behind and help Drizzt in the battle, but another cry issued from under the archway, a cry so pain-filled and pitiful that the burrow-warden could not ignore it. He stopped as soon as he got back on the main walkway, then looked both ways, torn in his loyalties.

"Go!" Drizzt shouted at him. "See to Clacker. This is Zaknafein, my father." Drizzt noticed a slight hesitation in the spirit-wraith's charge at the mention of those words, a hesitation that brought Drizzt a flicker of understanding.

"Your father? *Magga cammara*, dark elf!" Belwar protested. "Back in the illithid cavern—"

"I am safe enough," Drizzt interjected.

Belwar did not believe that Drizzt was safe at all, but against the protests of his own stubborn pride, the burrow-warden realized that the battle that was about to begin was far beyond his abilities. He would be of little help against this mighty drow warrior, and his presence in the battle might actually prove detrimental to his friend. Drizzt would have a difficult enough time without worrying about Belwar's safety.

Belwar banged his mithral hands together in frustration and rushed toward the archway and the continuing moans of his fallen hook horror companion.

⚔ ⚔ ⚔ ⚔ ⚔

Matron Malice's eyes widened and she uttered a sound so primal that her daughters, gathered by her side in the anteroom, knew immediately that the spirit-wraith had found Drizzt. Briza glanced over at the younger Do'Urden priestesses and dismissed them. Maya obeyed immediately, but Vierna hesitated.

"Go," Briza snarled, one hand dropping to the snakeheaded whip on her belt. "Now."

Vierna looked to her matron mother for support, but Malice was quite lost in the spectacle of the distant events. This was the moment of triumph for Zin-carla and for Matron Malice Do'Urden; she would not be distracted by the petty squabbling of her inferiors.

Briza then was alone with her mother, standing behind the throne and studying Malice as intently as Malice watched Zaknafein.

⚔ ⚔ ⚔ ⚔ ⚔

As soon as he entered the small chamber beyond the archway, Belwar knew that Clacker was dead, or soon would be. The giant hook horror body lay on the floor, bleeding from a single but wickedly precise wound across the neck. Belwar began to turn away, then realized that he owed comfort, at least, to his fallen friend. He dropped to one knee and forced himself to watch as Clacker went into a series of violent convulsions.

Death terminated the polymorph spell, and Clacker gradually reverted to his former self. The huge, clawed arms trembled and jerked, twisted and popped into the long and spindly, yellow-skinned arms of a pech. Hair sprouted through the cracking armor of Clacker's head and the great beak split apart and dissipated. The massive chest, too, fell away, and the whole body compacted with a grinding sound that sent shivers up and down the hardy burrow-warden's spine.

The hook horror was no more, and in death, Clacker was as he had been. He was a bit taller than Belwar, though not nearly as wide, and his features were broad and strange, with pupil-less eyes and a flattened nose.

"What was your name, my friend?" the burrow-warden whispered, though he knew that Clacker would never answer. He bent down and lifted the pech's head in his arms, taking some comfort in the peace that finally had come to the tormented creature's face.

⚔ ⚔ ⚔ ⚔ ⚔

"Who are you that takes the guise of my father?" Drizzt asked as the spirit-wraith stalked across the last few paces.

Zaknafein's snarl was indecipherable, and his response came more clearly in the hacking slice of a sword.

Drizzt parried the attack and jumped back. "Who are you?" he demanded again. "You are not my father!"

A wide smile spread over the spirit-wraith's face. "No," Zaknafein replied in a shaky voice, an answer that was inspired from an anteroom many miles away.

"I am your . . . mother!" The swords came on again in a blinding flurry.

Drizzt, confused by the response, met the charge with equal ferocity and the many sudden hits of sword on scimitar sounded like a single ring.

⚔ ⚔ ⚔ ⚔ ⚔

Briza watched her mother's every movement. Sweat poured down Malice's brow and her clenched fists pounded on the arms of her stone throne even after they had begun to bleed. Malice had hoped that it would be like this, that the final moment of her triumph would shine clearly in her thoughts from across the miles. She heard Drizzt's every frantic word and felt his distress so very keenly. Never had Malice known such pleasure!

Then she felt a slight twinge as Zaknafein's consciousness struggled against her control. Malice pushed Zaknafein aside with a guttural snarl; his animated corpse was her tool!

Briza noted her mother's sudden snarl with more than a passing interest.

⚔ ⚔ ⚔ ⚔ ⚔

Drizzt knew beyond any doubts that this was not Zaknafein Do'Urden who stood before him, yet he could not deny the unique fighting style of his former mentor. Zaknafein was in there—somewhere—and Drizzt would have to reach him if he hoped to get any answers.

The battle quickly settled into a comfortable, measured rhythm, both opponents launching cautious attack routines and paying careful attention to their tenuous footing on the narrow walkway.

Belwar entered the room then, bearing Clacker's broken body. "Kill him, Drizzt!" the burrow-warden cried. "*Magga . . .*" Belwar stopped and was afraid when he witnessed the battle. Drizzt and Zaknafein seemed to intertwine, their weapons spinning and darting, only to be parried away. They seemed as one, these two dark elves that Belwar had considered distinctly different, and that notion unnerved the deep gnome.

When the next break came in the struggle, Drizzt glanced over to the burrow-warden and his gaze locked on the dead pech. "Damn you!" he spat, and he rushed back in, scimitars diving and chopping at the monster who had murdered Clacker.

The spirit-wraith parried the foolishly bold assault easily and worked Drizzt's blades up high, rocking Drizzt back on his heels. This, too, seemed so very familiar to the young drow, a fighting approach that Zaknafein had used against him many times in their sparring matches back in Menzoberranzan. Zaknafein would force Drizzt high, then come in suddenly low with both of his swords. In their early contests, Zaknafein had often defeated Drizzt with this maneuver, the double-thrust low, but in their last encounter in the drow city, Drizzt had found the answering parry and had turned the attack against his mentor.

Now Drizzt wondered if this opponent would follow through with the expected attack routine, and he wondered, too, how Zaknafein would react to his counter. Were any of Zak's memories within the monster he now faced?

Still the spirit-wraith kept Drizzt's blades working defensively high. Zaknafein then took a quick step back and came in low with both blades.

Drizzt dropped his scimitars into a downward X, the appropriate cross-down parry that pinned the attacking swords low. Drizzt kicked his foot up between the hilts of his blades and straight at his opponent's face.

The spirit-wraith somehow anticipated the countering attack and was out of reach before the boot could connect. Drizzt believed that he had an answer, for only Zaknafein Do'Urden could have known.

"You *are* Zaknafein!" Drizzt cried. "What has Malice done to you?"

The spirit-wraith's hands trembled visibly in their hold on the swords and his mouth twisted as though he was trying to say something.

⚔ ⚔ ⚔ ⚔ ⚔

"No!" Malice screamed, and she violently tore back the control of her monster, walking the delicate and dangerous line between Zaknafein's physical abilities and the consciousness of the being he once had been.

"You are mine, wraith," Malice bellowed, "and by the will of Lolth, you shall complete the task!"

⚔ ⚔ ⚔ ⚔ ⚔

Drizzt saw the sudden regression of the murderous spirit-wraith. Zaknafein's hands no longer trembled and his mouth locked into a thin and determined grimace once again.

"What is it, dark elf?" Belwar demanded, confused by the strange encounter. Drizzt noticed that the deep gnome had placed Clacker's body on a ledge and was steadily approaching. Sparks flew from Belwar's mithral hands whenever they bumped together.

"Stay back!" Drizzt called to him. The presence of an unknown enemy could ruin the plans that were beginning to formulate in Drizzt's mind. "It is Zaknafein," he tried to explain to Belwar. "Or at least a part of it is!"

In a voice too low for the burrow-warden to hear, Drizzt added, "And I believe I know how to get to that part." Drizzt came on in a flurry of measured attacks that he knew Zaknafein could easily deflect. He did not want to destroy his opponent, but rather he sought to inspire other memories of fighting routines that would be familiar to Zaknafein.

He put Zaknafein through the paces of a typical training session, talking all the while in the same way that he and the weapon master used to talk back in Menzoberranzan. Malice's spirit-wraith countered Drizzt's familiarity with savagery, and matched Drizzt's friendly words with animal-like snarls. If Drizzt thought he could lull his opponent with complacency, he was badly mistaken.

Swords rushed at Drizzt inside and out, seeking a hole in his expert defenses. Scimitars matched their speed and precision, catching and stopping each arcing cut and deflecting every straightforward thrust harmlessly wide.

A sword slipped through and nicked Drizzt in the ribs. His fine armor held back the weapon's razor edge, but the weight of the blow would leave a deep bruise. Rocked back on his heels, Drizzt saw that his plan would not be so easily executed.

"You are my father!" he shouted at the monster. "Matron Malice is your enemy, not I!"

The spirit-wraith mocked the words with an evil laugh and came on wildly. From the very beginning of the battle, Drizzt had feared this moment, but now he stubbornly reminded himself that this was not really his father that stood before him.

Zaknafein's careless offensive charge inevitably left gaps in his defenses, and Drizzt found them, once and then again, with his scimitars. One blade gashed a hole in the spirit-wraith's belly, another slashed deeply into the side of his neck.

Zaknafein only laughed again, louder, and came on.

Drizzt fought in sheer panic, his confidence faltering. Zaknafein was nearly his equal, and Drizzt's blades barely hurt the thing! Another problem quickly became evident as well, for time was against Drizzt. He did not know exactly what it was that he faced, but he suspected that it would not tire.

Drizzt pressed with all his skill and speed. Desperation drove him to new heights of swordsmanship. Belwar started out again to join in, but he stopped a moment later, stunned by the display.

Drizzt hit Zaknafein several more times, but the spirit-wraith seemed not to notice, and as Drizzt stepped up the tempo, the spirit-wraith's intensity grew to match his own. Drizzt could hardly believe that this was not Zaknafein Do'Urden fighting against him; he could recognize the moves of his father and former mentor so very clearly. No other soul could move that perfectly muscled drow body with such precision and skill.

Drizzt was backing away again, giving ground and waiting patiently for his opportunities. He reminded himself over and over that it was not Zaknafein that he faced, but some monster created by Matron Malice for the sole purpose of destroying him. Drizzt had to be ready; his only chance of surviving this encounter was to trip his opponent from the ledge. With the spirit-wraith fighting so brilliantly, though, that chance seemed remote indeed.

The walkway turned slightly around a short bend, and Drizzt felt it carefully with one foot, sliding it along. Then a rock right under Drizzt's foot broke free from the side of the walkway.

Drizzt stumbled, and his leg, to the knee, slipped down beside the bridge. Zaknafein came upon him in a rush. The whirling swords soon had Drizzt down on his back across the narrow walkway, his head hanging precariously over the lake of acid.

"Drizzt!" Belwar screamed helplessly. The deep gnome rushed out, though he could not hope to arrive in time or defeat Drizzt's killer. "Drizzt!"

Perhaps it was that call of Drizzt's name, or maybe it was just the moment of the kill, but the former consciousness of Zaknafein flickered to life in that instant and the sword arm, readied for a killing plunge that Drizzt could not have deflected, hesitated.

Drizzt didn't wait for any explanations. He punched out with a scimitar hilt, then the other, both connecting squarely on Zaknafein's jaw and moving the spirit-wraith back. Drizzt was up again, panting and favoring a twisted ankle.

"Zaknafein!" Confused and frustrated by the hesitation, Drizzt screamed at his opponent.

"Driz—" the spirit-wraith's mouth struggled to reply. Then Malice's monster rushed back in, swords leading.

Drizzt defeated the attack and slipped away again. He could sense his father's presence; he knew that the true Zaknafein lurked just below the surface of this creature, but how could he free that spirit? Clearly, he could not hope to continue this struggle much longer.

"It is you," Drizzt whispered. "No one else could fight so. Zaknafein is there, and Zaknafein will not kill me." Another thought came to Drizzt then, a notion he had to believe.

Once again, the truth of Drizzt's convictions became the test.

Drizzt slipped his scimitars back into their sheaths.

The spirit-wraith snarled; his swords danced about in the air and cut viciously, but Zaknafein did not come on.

⚔ ⚔ ⚔ ⚔ ⚔

"Kill him!" Malice squealed in glee, thinking her moment of victory at hand. The images of the combat, though, flitted away from her suddenly, and she was left with only darkness. She had given too much back to

Zaknafein when Drizzt had stepped up the tempo of the combat. She had been forced to allow more of Zak's consciousness back into her animation, needing all of Zaknafein's fighting skills to defeat her warrior son.

Now Malice was left with blackness, and with the weight of impending doom hanging precariously over her head. She glanced back at her too-curious daughter, then sank back within her trance, fighting to regain control.

⚔ ⚔ ⚔ ⚔ ⚔

"Drizzt," Zaknafein said, and the word felt so very good indeed to the animation. Zak's swords went into their sheaths, though his hands had to struggle against the demands of Matron Malice every inch of the way.

Drizzt started toward him, wanting nothing more than to hug his father and dearest friend, but Zaknafein put out a hand to keep him back.

"No," the spirit-wraith explained. "I do not know how long I can resist. The body is hers, I fear," Zaknafein replied.

Drizzt did not understand at first. "Then you are—?"

"I am dead," Zaknafein stated bluntly. "At peace, be assured. Malice has repaired my body for her own vile purposes."

"But you defeated her," Drizzt said, daring to hope. "We are together again"

"A temporary stay, and no more." As if to accentuate the point, Zaknafein's hand involuntarily shot to his sword hilt. He grimaced and snarled, and stubbornly fought back, gradually loosening his grip on the weapon. "She is coming back, my son. That one is always coming back!"

"I cannot bear to lose you again," Drizzt said. "When I saw you in the illithid cavern—"

"It was not me that you saw," Zaknafein tried to explain. "It was the zombie of Malice's evil will. I am gone, my son. I have been gone for many years."

"You are here," Drizzt reasoned.

"By Malice's will, not . . . my own." Zaknafein growled, and his face contorted as he struggled to push Malice away for just a moment longer.

Back in control, Zaknafein studied the warrior that his son had become. "You fight well," he remarked. "Better than I had ever imagined. That is good, and it is good that you had the courage to run—" Zaknafein's face contorted again suddenly, stealing the words. This time, both of his hands went to his swords, and this time, both weapons came flashing out.

"No!" Drizzt pleaded as a mist welled in his lavender eyes. "Fight her."

"I . . . cannot," the spirit-wraith replied. "Flee from this place, Drizzt. Flee to the very . . . ends of the world! Malice will never forgive. She . . . will never stop—"

The spirit-wraith leaped forward, and Drizzt had no choice but to draw his weapons. But Zaknafein jerked suddenly before he got within reach of Drizzt.

"For us!" Zak cried in startling clarity, a call that pealed like a trumpet of victory in the green-glowing chamber and echoed across the miles to Matron Malice's heart like the final toll of a drum signaling the onset of doom. Zaknafein had wrested control again, for just a fleeting instant—one that allowed the charging spirit-wraith to veer off the walkway.

# 25

# Consequences

Matron Malice could not even scream her denial. A thousand explosions pounded her brain when Zaknafein went into the acid lake, a thousand realizations of impending and unavoidable disaster. She leaped from her stone throne, her slender hands twisting and clenching in the air as though she were trying to find something tangible to grasp, something that wasn't there.

Her breath rasped in labored gasps and wordless snarls issued from her gulping mouth. After a moment in which she could not calm herself, Malice heard one sound more clearly than the din of her own contortions. Behind her came the slight hiss of the small, wicked snake heads of a high priestess's whip.

Malice spun about, and there stood Briza, her face grimly and determinedly set and her whip's six living snake heads waving in the air.

"I had hoped that my time of ascension would be many years away," the eldest daughter said calmly. "But you are weak, Malice, too weak to hold House Do'Urden together in the trials that will follow our—your—failure."

Malice wanted to laugh in the face of her daughter's foolishness; snake-headed whips were personal gifts from the Spider Queen and could not be used against matron mothers. For some reason, though, Malice could not find the courage or conviction to refute her daughter at that moment. She watched, mesmerized, as Briza's arm slowly reared back and then shot forward.

The six snake heads uncoiled toward Malice. It was impossible! It went against all tenets of Lolth's doctrine! The fanged heads came on eagerly and dived into Malice's flesh with all the Spider Queen's fury behind them. Searing agony coursed through Malice's body, jolting and racking her and leaving an icy numbness in its wake.

Malice teetered on the brink of consciousness, trying to hold firmly against her daughter, trying to show Briza the futility and stupidity of continuing the attack.

The snake-whip snapped again and the floor rushed up to swallow Malice. Briza muttered something, Malice heard, some curse or chant to the Spider Queen.

Then came a third crack, and Malice knew nothing more. She was dead before the fifth strike, but Briza pounded on for many minutes, venting her fury to let the Spider Queen be assured that House Do'Urden truly had forsaken its failing matron mother.

By the time Dinin, unexpectedly and unannounced, burst into the room, Briza had settled comfortably into the stone throne. The elderboy glanced over at his mother's battered body, then back to Briza, his head shaking in disbelief, and a wide, knowing grin splayed across his face.

"What have you done, sis—Matron Briza?" Dinin asked, catching his slip of the tongue before Briza could react to it.

"Zin-carla has failed," Briza growled as she glared at him. "Lolth would no longer accept Malice."

Dinin's laughter, which seemed founded in sarcasm, cut to the marrow of Briza's bones. Her eyes narrowed further and she let Dinin see her hand clearly as it moved down to the hilt of her whip.

"You have chosen the perfect moment for ascension," the elderboy explained calmly, apparently not at all worried that Briza would punish him. "We are under attack."

"Fey-Branche?" Briza cried, springing excitedly from her seat. Five minutes in the throne as matron mother, and already Briza faced her first test. She would prove herself to the Spider Queen and redeem House Do'Urden from much of the damage that Malice's failures had caused.

"No, sister," Dinin said quickly, without pretense. "Not House Fey-Branche."

Her brother's cool response put Briza back in the throne and twisted her grin of excitement into a grimace of pure dread.

"Baenre." Dinin, too, no longer smiled.

⚔ ⚔ ⚔ ⚔ ⚔

Vierna and Maya looked out from House Do'Urden's balcony to the approaching forces beyond the adamantite gate. The sisters did not know their enemy, as Dinin had, but they understood from the sheer size of the force that some great house was involved. Still, House Do'Urden boasted two hundred fifty soldiers, many trained by Zaknafein himself. With two hundred more well-trained and well-armed troops on loan from Matron Baenre, both Vierna and Maya figured that their chances were not so bad. They quickly outlined defense strategies, and Maya swung one leg over the balcony railing, meaning to descend to the courtyard and relay the plans to her captains.

Of course, when she and Vierna suddenly realized that they had two hundred enemies already within their gates—enemies they had accepted on loan from Matron Baenre—their plans meant little.

Maya still straddled the railing when the first Baenre soldiers came up on the balcony. Vierna drew her whip and cried for Maya to do the same. But Maya was not moving, and Vierna, on closer inspection, noticed several tiny darts protruding from her sister's body.

Vierna's own snake-headed whip turned on her then, its fangs slicing across her delicate face. Vierna understood at once that House Do'Urden's downfall had been decreed by Lolth herself. "Zin-carla," Vierna mumbled, realizing the source of the disaster. Blood blurred her vision and a wave of dizziness overtook her as darkness closed in all about her.

⚔ ⚔ ⚔ ⚔ ⚔

"This cannot be!" Briza cried. "House Baenre attacks? Lolth has not given me—"

"We had our chance!" Dinin yelled at her. "Zaknafein was our chance—" Dinin looked to his mother's torn body—"and the wraith has failed, I would assume."

Briza growled and lashed out with her whip. Dinin expected the strike, though—he knew Briza so very well—and he darted beyond the weapon's range. Briza took a step toward him.

"Does your anger require more enemies?" Dinin asked, swords in hand. "Go out to the balcony, dear sister, where you will find a thousand awaiting you!"

Briza cried out in frustration but turned away from Dinin and rushed from the room, hoping to salvage something out of this terrible predicament.

Dinin did not follow. He stooped over Matron Malice and looked one final time into the eyes of the tyrant who had ruled his entire life. Malice had been a powerful figure, confident and wicked, but how fragile her rule had proved, broken by the antics of a renegade child.

Dinin heard a commotion out in the corridor, then the anteroom door swung open again. The elderboy did not have to look to know that enemies were in the room. He continued to stare at his dead mother, knowing that he soon would share the same fate.

The expected blow did not fall, however, and several agonizing moments later, Dinin dared to glance back over his shoulder.

Jarlaxle sat comfortably on the stone throne.

"You are not surprised?" the mercenary asked, noting that Dinin's expression did not change.

"Bregan D'aerthe was among the Baenre troops, perhaps all of the Baenre troops," Dinin said casually. He covertly glanced around the room at the dozen or so soldiers who had followed Jarlaxle in. If only he could get to the mercenary leader before they killed him! Dinin thought. Watching the death of the treacherous Jarlaxle might bring some measure of satisfaction to this whole disaster.

"Observant," Jarlaxle said to him. "I hold to my suspicions that you knew all along that your house was doomed."

"If Zin-carla failed," Dinin replied.

"And you knew it would?" the mercenary asked, almost rhetorically.

Dinin nodded. "Ten years ago," he began, wondering why he was telling all this to Jarlaxle, "I watched as Zaknafein was sacrificed to the Spider Queen. Rarely has any house in all of Menzoberranzan seen a greater waste."

"The weapon master of House Do'Urden had a mighty reputation," the mercenary put in.

"Well earned, do not doubt," replied Dinin. "Then Drizzt, my brother—"

"Another mighty warrior."

Again Dinin nodded. "Drizzt deserted us, with war at our gates. Matron Malice's miscalculation could not be ignored. I knew then that House Do'Urden was doomed."

"Your house defeated House Hun'ett, no small feat," reasoned Jarlaxle.

"Only with the help of Bregan D'aerthe," Dinin corrected. "For most of my life, I have watched House Do'Urden, under Matron Malice's steady guidance, ascend through the city hierarchy. Every year, our power and influence grew. For the last decade, though, I have seen us spiral down. I have watched the foundations of House Do'Urden crumble. The structure had to follow the descent."

"As wise as you are skilled with the blade," the mercenary remarked. "I have said that before of Dinin Do'Urden, and it seems that I am proved correct once again."

"If I have pleased you, I ask one favor," Dinin said, rising to his feet. "Grant it if you will."

"Kill you quickly and without pain?" Jarlaxle asked through a widening smile.

Dinin nodded for the third time.

"No," Jarlaxle said simply.

Not understanding, Dinin brought his sword flashing up and ready.

"I'll not kill you at all," Jarlaxle explained.

Dinin kept his sword up high and studied the mercenary's face, looking for some hint as to his intent. "I am a noble of the house," Dinin said. "A witness to the attack. No house elimination is complete if nobles remain alive."

"A witness?" Jarlaxle laughed. "Against House Baenre? To what gain?"

Dinin's sword dropped low.

"Then what is my fate?" he asked. "Will Matron Baenre take me in?" Dinin's tone showed that he was not excited about that possibility.

"Matron Baenre has little use for males," Jarlaxle replied. "If any of your sisters survive—and I believe the one named Vierna has—they may find themselves in Matron Baenre's chapel. But the withered old mother of House Baenre would never see the value of a male such as Dinin, I fear."

"Then what?" Dinin demanded.

"I know your value," Jarlaxle stated casually. He led Dinin's gaze around to the concurring grins of his troops.

"Bregan D'aerthe?" Dinin balked. "Me, a noble, to become a rogue?"

Quicker than Dinin's eye could follow, Jarlaxle whipped a dagger into the body at his feet. The blade buried itself up to the hilt in Malice's back.

"A rogue or a corpse," Jarlaxle casually explained.

It was not so difficult a choice.

⚔ ⚔ ⚔ ⚔ ⚔

A few days later, Jarlaxle and Dinin looked back on the ruined adamantite gate of House Do'Urden. Once it had stood so proud and strong, with its intricate carvings of spiders and the two formidable stalagmite pillars that served as guard towers.

"How fast it changed," Dinin remarked. "I see all my former life before me, yet it is all gone."

"Forget what has gone before," Jarlaxle suggested. The mercenary's sly wink told Dinin that he had something specific in mind as he completed the thought. "Except that which may aid in your future."

Dinin did a quick visual inspection of himself and the ruins. "My battle gear?" he asked, fishing for Jarlaxle's intent. "My training."

"Your brother."

"Drizzt?" Again the cursed name reared up to bring anguish to Dinin!

"It would seem that there is still the matter of Drizzt Do'Urden to be reconciled," Jarlaxle explained. "He's a high prize in the eyes of the Spider Queen."

"Drizzt?" Dinin asked again, hardy believing Jarlaxle's words.

"Why are you so surprised?" Jarlaxle asked. "Your brother is still alive, else why was Matron Malice brought down?"

"What house could be interested in him?" Dinin asked bluntly. "Another mission for Matron Baenre?"

Jarlaxle's laugh belittled him. "Bregan D'aerthe may act without the guidance—or the purse—of a recognized house," he replied.

"You plan to go after my brother?"

"It may be the perfect opportunity for Dinin to show his value to my little family," said Jarlaxle to no one in particular. "Who better to catch the renegade that brought down House Do'Urden? Your brother's value increased many times over with the failure of Zin-carla."

"I have seen what Drizzt has become," said Dinin. "The cost will be great."

"My resources are limitless," Jarlaxle answered smugly, "and no cost is too high if the gain is higher." The eccentric mercenary went silent for a short while, allowing Dinin's gaze to linger over the ruins of his once proud house.

"No," Dinin said suddenly.

Jarlaxle turned a wary eye on him.

"I'll not go after Drizzt," Dinin explained.

"You serve Jarlaxle, the master of Bregan D'aerthe," the mercenary calmly reminded him.

"As I once served Malice, the matron of House Do'Urden," Dinin replied with equal calm. "I would not venture out again after Drizzt for my mother—" He looked at Jarlaxle squarely, unafraid of the consequences—"and I shall not do it again for you."

Jarlaxle spent a long moment studying his companion. Normally the mercenary leader would not tolerate such brazen insubordination, but Dinin was sincere and adamant, beyond doubt. Jarlaxle had accepted Dinin into Bregan D'aerthe because he valued the elderboy's experience and skill; he could not now readily dismiss Dinin's judgment.

"I could have you put to a slow death," Jarlaxle replied, more to see Dinin's reaction than to make any promises. He had no intention of destroying one as valuable as Dinin.

"No worse than the death and disgrace I would find at Drizzt's hands," Dinin answered calmly.

Another long moment passed as Jarlaxle considered the implications of Dinin's words. Perhaps Bregan D'aerthe should rethink its plans for hunting the renegade; perhaps the price would prove too high.

"Come, my soldier," Jarlaxle said at length. "Let us return to our home, to the streets, where we might learn what adventures our futures hold."

# 26 Lights in the Ceiling

Belwar ran along the walkways to get to his friend. Drizzt did not watch the svirfneblin's approach. He kneeled on the narrow bridge, looking down to the bubbling spot in the green lake where Zaknafein had fallen. The acid sputtered and rolled, the scorched hilt of a sword came up into view, then disappeared under the opaque veil of green.

"He was there all along," Drizzt whispered to Belwar. "My father!"

"A mighty chance you took, dark elf," the burrow-warden replied. "*Magga cammara*! When you put your blades away, I thought he would surely strike you down."

"He was there all along," Drizzt said again. He looked up at his svirfneblin friend. "You showed me that."

Belwar screwed up his face in confusion.

"The spirit cannot be separated from the body," Drizzt tried to explain. "Not in life." He looked back to the ripples in the acid lake. "And not in undeath. In my years alone in the wilds, I had lost myself, so I believed. But you showed me the truth. The heart of Drizzt was never gone from this body, and so I knew it to be true with Zaknafein."

"Other forces were involved this time," remarked Belwar. "I would not have been so certain."

"You did not know Zaknafein," Drizzt retorted. He rose to his feet,

the moisture rimming his lavender eyes diminished by the sincere smile that widened across his face. "I did. Spirit, not muscles, guides a warrior's blades, and only he who was truly Zaknafein could move with such grace. The moment of crisis gave Zaknafein the strength to resist my mother's will."

"And you gave him the moment of crisis," reasoned Belwar. "Defeat Matron Malice or kill his own son." Belwar shook his bald head and crinkled up his nose. "*Magga cammara*, but you are brave, dark elf." He shot Drizzt a wink. "Or stupid."

"Neither," replied Drizzt. "I only trusted in Zaknafein." He looked back to the acid lake and said no more.

Belwar fell silent and waited patiently while Drizzt finished his private eulogy. When Drizzt finally looked away from the lake, Belwar motioned for the drow to follow and started off along the walkway. "Come," the burrow-warden said over his shoulder. "Witness the truth of our slain friend."

Drizzt thought the pech a beautiful thing, a beauty inspired by the peaceful smile that at last had found its way onto his tormented friend's face. He and Belwar said a few words, mumbled a few hopes to whatever gods might be listening, and gave Clacker to the acid lake, thinking it a preferable fate to the bellies of the carrion eaters that roamed the Underdark corridors.

Drizzt and Belwar set off again alone, as they had been when they first departed the svirfneblin city, and arrived in Blingdenstone a few days later.

The guards at the city's mammoth gates, though obviously thrilled, seemed confused at their return. They allowed the two companions entrance on the burrow-warden's promise that he would go straight off and inform King Schnicktick.

"This time, he will let you stay, dark elf," Belwar said to Drizzt. "You beat the monster." He left Drizzt at his house, vowing that he would return soon with welcome news.

Drizzt wasn't so sure of any of it. Zaknafein's final warning that Matron Malice would never give up her hunt remained clearly in his thoughts, and he could not deny the truth. Much had happened in the tendays that he and Belwar had been out of Blingdenstone, but none of it, as far as Drizzt knew, diminished the very real threat to the svirfneblin city. Drizzt had only agreed to follow the Belwar back to Blingdenstone because it seemed a proper first step to the plan he had decided upon.

"How long shall we battle, Matron Malice?" Drizzt asked the blank stone when the burrow-warden had gone. He needed to hear his reasoning spoken aloud, to convince himself beyond doubt that his decision had been a wise one. "Neither gains in the conflict, but that is the way of the drow, is it not?" Drizzt fell back onto one of the stools beside the little table and considered the truth of his words.

"You will hunt me, to your ruin or to mine, blinded by the hatred that rules your life. There can be no forgiveness in Menzoberranzan. That would go against the edict of your foul Spider Queen.

"And this is the Underdark, your world of shadows and gloom, but it is not all the world, Matron Malice, and I shall see how long your evil arms can reach!"

Drizzt sat silent for many minutes, remembering his first lessons at the drow Academy. He tried to find some clue that would lead him to believe that the stories of the surface world were no more than lies. The masters' deceptions at the drow Academy had been perfected over centuries and were infallibly complete. Drizzt soon came to realize that he simply would have to trust his feelings.

When Belwar returned, grim-faced, a few hours later, Drizzt's resolve was firm.

"Stubborn, orc-brained . . ." the burrow-warden gnashed through his teeth as he crossed through the stone door.

Drizzt stopped him with a heartfelt laugh.

"They will not hear of your staying!" Belwar yelled at him, trying to steal his mirth.

"Did you truly expect otherwise?" Drizzt asked him. "My fight is not over, dear Belwar. Do you believe that my family could be so easily defeated?"

"We will go back out," Belwar growled, moving over to take the stool near Drizzt. "My generous—" the word dripped of sarcasm—"king agreed that you could remain in the city for a tenday. A single tenday!"

"When I leave, I leave alone," Drizzt interrupted. He pulled the onyx figurine out of his pouch and reconsidered his words. "Almost alone."

"We had this argument before, dark elf," Belwar reminded him.

"That was different."

"Was it?" retorted the burrow-warden. "Will you survive any better alone in the wilds of the Underdark now than you did before? Have you forgotten the burdens of loneliness?"

"I'll not be in the Underdark," Drizzt replied.

"Back to your homeland you mean to go?" Belwar cried, leaping to his feet and sending his stool skidding across the stone.

"No, never!" Drizzt laughed. "Never will I return to Menzoberranzan, unless it is at the end of Matron Malice's chains."

The burrow-warden retrieved his seat and eased back into it, curious.

"Neither will I remain in the Underdark," Drizzt explained. "This is Malice's world, more fitting to the dark heart of a true drow."

Belwar began to understand, but he couldn't believe what he was hearing. "What are you saying?" he demanded. "Where do you mean to go?"

"The surface," Drizzt replied evenly. Belwar leaped up again, sending his stone stool bouncing even farther across the floor.

"I was up there once," Drizzt continued, undaunted by the reaction. He calmed the svirfneblin with a determined gaze. "I partook of a drow massacre. Only the actions of my companions bring pain to my memories of that journey. The scents of the wide world and the cool feel of the wind bring no dread to my heart."

"The surface," Belwar muttered, his head lowered and his voice almost a groan. "*Magga cammara*. Never did I plan to travel there—it is not the place of a svirfneblin." Belwar pounded the table suddenly and looked up, a determined smile on his face. "But if Drizzt will go, then Belwar will go by his side!"

"Drizzt will go alone," the drow replied. "As you just said, the surface is not the place of a svirfneblin."

"Nor a drow," the deep gnome added pointedly.

"I do not fit the usual expectations of drow," Drizzt retorted. "My heart is not their heart, and their home is not mine. How far must I walk through the endless tunnels to be free of my family's hatred? And if, in fleeing Menzoberranzan, I chance upon another of the great dark elf cities, Ched Nasad or some similar place, will those drow, too, take up the hunt to fulfill the Spider Queen's desires that I be slain? No, Belwar, I will find no peace in the close ceilings of this world. You, I fear, would never be content removed from the stone of the Underdark. Your place is here, a place of deserved honor among your people."

Belwar sat quietly for a long time, digesting all that Drizzt had said. He would follow Drizzt willingly if Drizzt desired it so, but he truly did not wish to leave the Underdark. Belwar could raise no argument against Drizzt's desires to go. A dark elf would find many trials up on the surface, Belwar knew, but would they outweigh the pains Drizzt would ever experience in the Underdark?

Belwar reached into a deep pocket and took out the light-giving brooch. "Take this, dark elf," he said softly, flipping it to Drizzt, "and do not forget me."

"Never for a single day in all the centuries of my future," Drizzt promised. "Never once."

⚔ ⚔ ⚔ ⚔ ⚔

The tenday passed all too quickly for Belwar, who was reluctant to see his friend go. The burrow-warden knew that he would never look upon Drizzt again, but he knew also that Drizzt's decision was a sound one. As a friend, Belwar took it upon himself to see that Drizzt had the best chance of success. He took the drow to the finest provisioners in all of Blingdenstone and paid for the supplies out of his own pocket.

Belwar then procured an even greater gift for Drizzt. Deep gnomes had traveled to the surface on occasion, and King Schnicktick possessed several copies of rough maps leading out of the Underdark tunnels.

"The journey will take you many tendays," Belwar said to Drizzt when he handed him the rolled parchment, "but I fear that never would you find your way at all without this."

Drizzt's hands trembled as he unrolled the map. It was true, he now dared to believe. He was indeed going to the surface. He wanted to tell Belwar at that moment to come along; how could he say good-bye to so dear a friend?

But principles had carried Drizzt this far in his travels, and principles demanded that he not be selfish now.

He walked out of Blingdenstone the next day, promising Belwar that if he ever came this way again, he would return to visit. Both of them knew he would never return.

⚔ ⚔ ⚔ ⚔ ⚔

Miles and days passed uneventfully. Sometimes Drizzt held the magical brooch Belwar had given to him high; sometimes he walked in the quiet darkness. Whether coincidence or kind fate, he met no monsters along the course laid out on the rough map. Few things had changed in the Underdark, and though the parchment was old, even ancient, the trail was easily followed.

Shortly after breaking camp on his thirty-third day out of Blingdenstone, Drizzt felt a lightening of the air, a sensation of that cold and vast wind he so vividly remembered.

He pulled the onyx figurine from his pouch and summoned Guenhwyvar to his side. Together they walked on anxiously, expecting the ceiling to disappear around every bend.

They came into a small cave, and the darkness beyond the distant archway was not nearly as gloomy as the darkness behind them. Drizzt held his breath and led Guenhwyvar out.

Stars twinkled through the broken clouds of the night sky, the moon's silvery light splayed out in a duller glow behind one large cloud, and the wind howled a mountain song. Drizzt was high up in the Realms, perched on the side of a tall mountain in the midst of a mighty range.

He minded not at all the bite of the breeze, but stood very still for a long time and watched the meandering clouds pass him on their slow aerial trek to the moon.

Guenhwyvar stood beside him, unjudging, and Drizzt knew the panther always would.

# SOJOURN

THE LEGEND OF DRIZZT® BOOK III

# Prelude

The dark elf sat on the barren mountainside, watching anxiously as the line of red grew above the eastern horizon. This would be perhaps his hundredth dawn, and he knew well the sting the searing light would bring to his lavender eyes—eyes that had known only the darkness of the Underdark for more than four decades.

The drow did not turn away, though, when the upper rim of the flaming sun crested the horizon. He accepted the light as his purgatory, a pain necessary if he was to follow his chosen path, to become a creature of the surface world.

Gray smoke wafted up before the drow's dark-skinned face. He knew what it meant without even looking down. His *piwafwi*, the magical drow-made cloak that had so many times in the Underdark shielded him from probing enemy eyes, had finally succumbed to the daylight. The magic in the cloak had begun fading tendays before, and the fabric itself was simply melting away. Wide holes appeared as patches of the garment dissolved, and the drow pulled his arms in tightly to salvage as much as he could.

It wouldn't make any difference, he knew; the cloak was doomed to waste away in this world so different from where it had been created. The drow clung to it desperately, somehow viewing it as an analogy to his own fate.

The sun climbed higher and tears rolled out of the drow's squinting lavender eyes. He could not see the smoke anymore, could see nothing beyond the blinding glare of that terrible ball of fire. Still he sat and watched, right through the dawn.

To survive, he had to adapt.

He pushed his toe painfully down against a jag in the stone and focused his attention away from his eyes, from the dizziness that threatened to overcome him. He thought of how thin his finely woven boots had become and knew that they, too, would soon dissipate into nothingness.

Then his scimitars, perhaps? Would those magnificent drow weapons, which had sustained him through so many trials, be no more? What fate awaited Guenhwyvar, his magical panther companion? Unconsciously the drow dropped a hand into his pouch to feel the marvelous figurine, so perfect in every detail, which he used to summon the cat. Its solidity reassured him in that moment of doubt, but if it, too, had been crafted by the dark elves, imbued with the magic so particular to their domain, would Guenhwyvar soon be lost?

"What a pitiful creature I will become," the drow lamented in his native tongue. He wondered, not for the first time and certainly not for the last, about the wisdom of his decision to leave the Underdark, to forsake the world of his evil people.

His head pounded; sweat rolled into his eyes, heightening the sting. The sun continued its ascent and the drow could not endure. He rose and turned toward the small cave he had taken as his home, and he again put a hand absently on the panther figurine.

His *piwafwi* hung in tatters about him, serving as

meager protection from the mountain winds' chill bite. There was no wind in the Underdark except for slight currents rising off pools of magma, and no chill except for the icy touch of an undead monster. This surface world, which the drow had known for several months, showed him many differences, many variables—too many, he often believed.

Drizzt Do'Urden would not surrender. The Underdark was the world of his kin, of his family, and in that darkness he would find no rest. Following the demands of his principles, he had struck out against Lolth, the Spider Queen, the evil deity his people revered above life itself. The dark elves, Drizzt's family, would not forgive his blasphemy, and the Underdark had no holes deep enough to escape their long reach.

Even if Drizzt believed that the sun would burn him away, as it burned away his boots and his precious *piwafwi*, even if he became no more than insubstantial, gray smoke blowing away in the chill mountain breeze, he would retain his principles and dignity, those elements that made his life worthwhile.

Drizzt pulled off his cloak's remains and tossed them down a deep chasm. The chilly wind nipped against his sweat-beaded brow, but the drow walked straight and proud, his jaw firm and his lavender eyes wide open.

This was the fate he preferred.

⚔ ⚔ ⚔ ⚔ ⚔

Along the side of a different mountain, not so far away, another creature watched the rising sun. Ulgulu, too, had left his birthplace, the filthy, smoking rifts that marked the plane of Gehenna, but this monster had not come of his own accord. It was Ulgulu's fate, his penance, to grow in this world until he attained sufficient strength to return to his home.

Ulgulu's lot was murder, feeding on the life force of the weak mortals around him. He was close now to attaining his maturity: huge and strong and terrible.

Every kill made him stronger.

# Part One

## Sunrise

It burned at my eyes and pained every part of my body. It destroyed my piwafwi and boots, stole the magic from my armor, and weakened my trusted scimitars. Still, every day, without fail, I was there, sitting upon my perch, my judgment seat, to await the arrival of the sunrise.

It came to me each day in a paradoxical way. The sting could not be denied, but neither could I deny the beauty of the spectacle. The colors just before the sun's appearance grabbed my soul in a way that no patterns of heat emanations in the Underdark ever could. At first, I thought my entrancement a result of the strangeness of the scene, but even now, many years later, I feel my heart leap at the subtle brightening that heralds the dawn.

I know now that my time in the sun—my daily penance—was more than mere desire to adapt to the ways of the surface world. The sun became the symbol of the difference between the Underdark and my new home. The society that I had run away from, a world of secret dealings and treacherous conspiracies, could not exist in the open spaces under the light of day.

This sun, for all the anguish it brought me physically, came to represent my denial of that other, darker world. Those rays of revealing light reinforced my principles as surely as they weakened the drow-made magical items.

In the sunlight the piwafwi, the shielding cloak that defeated probing eyes, the garment of thieves and assassins, became no more than a worthless rag of tattered cloth.

–Drizzt Do'Urden

# I
# Poignant Lessons

Drizzt crept past the shielding shrubs and over the flat and bare stone that led to the cave now serving as his home. He knew that something had crossed this way recently—very recently. There were no tracks to be seen, but the scent was strong.

Guenhwyvar circled on the rocks up above the hillside cave. Sight of the panther gave the drow a measure of comfort. Drizzt had come to trust Guenhwyvar implicitly and knew that the cat would flush out any enemies hiding in ambush. Drizzt disappeared into the dark opening and smiled as he heard the panther come down behind, watching over him.

Drizzt paused behind a stone just inside the entrance, letting his eyes adjust to the gloom. The sun was still bright, though it was fast dipping into the western sky, but the cave was much darker—dark enough for Drizzt to let his vision slip into the infrared spectrum. As soon as the adjustment was completed, Drizzt located the intruder. The clear glow of a heat source, a living creature, emanated from behind another rock deeper in the one-chambered cave. Drizzt relaxed considerably. Guenhwyvar was only a few steps away now, and considering the size of the rock, the intruder could not be a large beast.

Still, Drizzt had been raised in the Underdark, where every living creature, regardless of its size, was respected and considered dangerous.

He signaled for Guenhwyvar to remain in position near the exit and crept around to get a better angle on the intruder.

Drizzt had never seen such an animal before. It appeared almost cat-like, but its head was much smaller and more sharply pointed. The whole of it could not have weighed more than a few pounds. This fact, and the creature's bushy tail and thick fur, indicated that it was more a forager than a predator. It rummaged now through a pack of food, apparently oblivious to the drow's presence.

"Take ease, Guenhwyvar," Drizzt called softly, slipping his scimitars into their sheaths. He took a step toward the intruder for a better look, though he kept a cautious distance so as not to startle it, thinking that he might have found another companion. If he could only gain the animal's trust . . .

The small animal turned abruptly at Drizzt's call, its short front legs quickly backing it against the wall.

"Take ease," Drizzt said quietly, this time to the intruder. "I'll not harm you." Drizzt took another step in and the creature hissed and spun about, its small hind feet stamping down on the stone floor.

Drizzt nearly laughed aloud, thinking that the creature meant to push itself straight through the cave's back wall. Guenhwyvar bounded over then, and the panther's immediate distress stole the mirth from the drow's face.

The animal's tail came up high; Drizzt noticed in the faint light that the beast had distinctive stripes running down its back. Guenhwyvar whimpered and turned to flee, but it was too late. . . .

About an hour later Drizzt and Guenhwyvar walked along the lower trails of the mountain in search of a new home. They had salvaged what they could, though that wasn't very much. Guenhwyvar kept a good distance to the side of Drizzt. Proximity made the stink only worse.

Drizzt took it all in stride, though the stench of his own body made the lesson a bit more poignant than he would have liked. He didn't know the little animal's name, of course, but he had marked its appearance keenly. He would know better the next time he encountered a skunk.

"What of my other companions in this strange world?" Drizzt whispered to himself. It was not the first time the drow had voiced such concerns. He knew very little of the surface and even less of the creatures that lived here. His months had been spent in and about the cave, with only occasional forays down to the lower, more populated regions. There, in his foraging, he had seen some animals, usually at a distance, and had even observed some humans. He had not yet found the courage to come out of hiding, though, to greet his neighbors, fearing potential rejection and knowing that he had nowhere left to run.

The sound of rushing water led the reeking drow and panther to a fast-running brook. Drizzt immediately found some protective shade and began stripping away his armor and clothing, while Guenhwyvar moved downstream to do some fishing. The sound of the panther fumbling around in the water brought a smile to the drow's severe features. They would eat well this night.

Drizzt gingerly flipped the clasp of his belt and laid his crafted weapons beside his mesh chain mail. Truly, he felt vulnerable without the armor and weapons—he never would have put them so far from his reach in the Underdark—but many months had passed since Drizzt had found any need for them. He looked to his scimitars and was flooded by the bittersweet memories of the last time he had put them to use.

He had battled Zaknafein then, his father and mentor and dearest friend. Only Drizzt had survived the encounter. The legendary weapon master was gone now, but the triumph in that fight belonged as much to Zak as it did to Drizzt, for it was not really Zaknafein who had come after Drizzt on the bridges of an acid-filled cavern. Rather, it was Zaknafein's wraith, under the control of Drizzt's evil mother, Matron Malice. She had sought revenge upon her son for his denouncement of Lolth and of the chaotic drow society in general. Drizzt had spent more than thirty years in Menzoberranzan but had never accepted the malicious and cruel ways that were the norm in the drow city. He had been a constant embarrassment to House Do'Urden despite his considerable skill with weapons. When he ran from the city to live a life of exile in the wilds of the Underdark, he had placed his high priestess mother out of Lolth's favor.

Thus, Matron Malice Do'Urden had raised the spirit of Zaknafein, the weapon master she had sacrificed to Lolth, and sent the undead thing after her son. Malice had miscalculated, though, for there remained enough of Zak's soul within the body to deny the attack on Drizzt. In the instant that Zak managed to wrest control from Malice, he had cried out in triumph and leaped into the lake of acid.

"My father," Drizzt whispered, drawing strength from the simple words. He had succeeded where Zaknafein had failed; he had forsaken the evil ways of the drow where Zak had been trapped for centuries, acting as a pawn in Matron Malice's power games. From Zaknafein's failure and ultimate demise, young Drizzt had found strength; from Zak's victory in the acid cavern, Drizzt had found determination. Drizzt had ignored the web of lies his former teachers at the Academy in Menzoberranzan had tried to spin, and he had come to the surface to begin a new life.

Drizzt shuddered as he stepped into the icy stream. In the Underdark he had known fairly constant temperatures and unvarying darkness. Here, though, the world surprised him at every turn. Already he had noticed that the periods of daylight and darkness were not constant; the sun set earlier every day and the temperature—changing from hour to hour, it seemed—had steadily dipped during the last few tendays. Even within those periods of light and dark loomed inconsistencies. Some nights were visited by a silver-glowing orb and some days held a pall of gray instead of a dome of shining blue.

In spite of it all, Drizzt most often felt comfortable with his decision to come to this unknown world. Looking at his weapons and armor now, lying in the shadows a dozen feet from where he bathed, Drizzt had to admit that the surface, for all of its strangeness, offered more peace than anywhere in the Underdark ever could.

Drizzt was in the wilds now, despite his calm. He had spent four months on the surface and was still alone, except when he was able to summon his magical feline companion. Now, stripped bare except for his ragged pants, with his eyes stinging from the skunk spray, his sense of smell lost within the cloud of his own pungent aroma, and his keen sense of hearing dulled by the din of rushing water, the drow was indeed vulnerable.

"What a mess I must appear," Drizzt mused, roughly running his slender fingers through the mat of his thick, white hair. When he glanced back to his equipment, though, the thought was washed quickly from Drizzt's mind. Five hulking forms straddled his belongings and undoubtedly cared little for the dark elf's ragged appearance.

Drizzt considered the grayish skin and dark muzzles of the dog-faced, seven-foot-tall humanoids, but more particularly, he watched the spears and swords that they now leveled his way. He knew this type of monster, for he had seen similar creatures serving as slaves back in Menzoberranzan. In this situation, however, the gnolls appeared much different, more ominous, than Drizzt remembered them.

He briefly considered a rush to his scimitars but dismissed the notion, knowing that a spear would skewer him before he ever got close. The largest of the gnoll band an eight-foot giant with striking red hair, looked at Drizzt for a long moment, eyed the drow's equipment, then looked back to him.

"What are you thinking?" Drizzt muttered under his breath. Drizzt really knew very little about gnolls. At Menzoberranzan's Academy he had been taught that gnolls were of a goblinoid race, evil, unpredictable, and quite dangerous. He had been told that of the surface elves and humans as well, though—and he now realized, of nearly every race that was not drow. Drizzt almost laughed aloud despite his predicament. Ironically, the race that most deserved that mantle of evil unpredictability was the drow themselves!

The gnolls made no other moves and uttered no commands. Drizzt understood their hesitancy at the sight of a dark elf, and he knew that he must seize that natural fear if he was to have any chance at all. Calling upon the innate abilities of his magical heritage, Drizzt waved his dark hand and outlined all five gnolls in harmless purple-glowing flames.

One of the beasts dropped immediately to the ground, as Drizzt had hoped, but the others halted at a signal from their more experienced leader's outstretched hand. They looked around nervously, apparently wondering about the wisdom of continuing this meeting. The gnoll chieftain, though, had seen harmless faerie fire before, in a fight with an unfortunate—now deceased—ranger, and knew it for what it was.

Drizzt tensed in anticipation and tried to determine his next move.

The gnoll chieftain glanced around at its companions, as if studying how fully they were limned by the dancing flames. Judging by the completeness of the spell, this was no ordinary drow peasant standing in the stream—or so Drizzt hoped the chieftain was thinking.

Drizzt relaxed a bit as the leader dipped its spear and signaled for the others to do likewise. The gnoll then barked a jumble of words that sounded like gibberish to the drow. Seeing Drizzt's obvious confusion, the gnoll called something in the guttural tongue of goblins.

Drizzt understood the goblin language, but the gnoll's dialect was so very strange that he managed to decipher only a few words, "friend" and "leader" being among them.

Cautiously, Drizzt took a step toward the bank. The gnolls gave ground, opening a path to his belongings. Drizzt took another tentative step, then grew more at ease when he noticed a black feline form crouched in the bushes a short distance away. At his command Guenhwyvar, in one great spring, would come crashing into the gnoll band.

"You and I to walk together?" Drizzt asked the gnoll leader, using the goblin tongue and trying to simulate the creature's dialect.

The gnoll replied in a hurried shout, and the only thing that Drizzt thought he understood was the last word of the question: ". . . ally?"

Drizzt nodded slowly, hoping he understood the creature's full meaning.

"Ally!" the gnoll croaked, and all of its companions smiled and laughed in relief and patted each other on the back. Drizzt reached his equipment then, and immediately strapped on his scimitars. Seeing the gnolls distracted, the drow glanced at Guenhwyvar and nodded to the thick growth along the trail ahead. Swiftly and silently, Guenhwyvar took up a new position. No need to give all of his secrets away, Drizzt figured, not until he truly understood his new companions' intentions.

Drizzt walked along with the gnolls down the mountain's lower, winding passes. The gnolls kept far to the drow's sides, whether out of respect for Drizzt and the reputation of his race or for some other reason, he could not know. More likely, Drizzt suspected, they kept their distance simply because of his odor, which the bath had done little to diminish.

The gnoll leader addressed Drizzt every so often, accentuating its excited words with a sly wink or a sudden rub of its thick, padded hands. Drizzt had no idea of what the gnoll was talking about, but he assumed from the creature's eager lip-smacking that it was leading him to some sort of feast.

Drizzt soon guessed the band's destination, for he had often watched from jutting peaks high in the mountains, the lights of a small human farming community in the valley. Drizzt could only guess at the relationship between the gnolls and the human farmers, but he sensed that it was not a friendly one. When they neared the village, the gnolls dropped into defensive positions, followed lines of shrubs, and kept to the shadows as much as possible. Twilight was fast approaching as the troupe made its way around the village's central area to look down upon a secluded farmhouse off to the west.

The gnoll chieftain whispered to Drizzt, slowly rolling out each word so that the drow might understand. "One family," it croaked. "Three men, two women . . ."

"One young woman," another added eagerly.

The gnoll chieftain gave a snarl. "And three young males," it concluded.

Drizzt thought he now understood the journey's purpose, and the surprised and questioning look on his face prompted the gnoll to confirm it beyond doubt.

"Enemies," the leader declared.

Drizzt, knowing next to nothing of the two races, was in a dilemma. The gnolls were raiders—that much was clear—and they meant to swoop down upon the farmhouse as soon as the last daylight faded away. Drizzt had no intention of joining them in their fight until he had a lot more information concerning the nature of the conflict.

"Enemies?" he asked.

The gnoll leader crinkled its brow in apparent consternation. It spouted a line of gibberish in which Drizzt thought he heard "human . . . weakling . . . slave." All the gnolls sensed the drow's sudden uneasiness, and they began fingering their weapons and glancing to each other nervously.

"Three men," Drizzt said.

The gnoll jabbed its spear savagely toward the ground. "Kill oldest! Catch two!"

"Women?"

The evil smile that spread over the gnoll's face answered the question beyond doubt, and Drizzt was beginning to understand where he stood in the conflict.

"What of the children?" He eyed the gnoll leader squarely and spoke each word distinctly. There could be no misunderstanding. His final question confirmed it all, for while Drizzt could accept the typical savagery concerning mortal enemies, he could never forget the one time he had participated in such a raid. He had saved an elven child on that day, had hidden the girl under her mother's body to keep her from the wrath of his drow companions. Of all the many evils Drizzt had ever witnessed, the murder of children had been the worst.

The gnoll thrust its spear toward the ground, its dog-face contorted in wicked glee.

"I think not," Drizzt said simply, fires springing up in his lavender eyes. Somehow, the gnolls noticed, his scimitars had appeared in his hands.

Again the gnoll's snout crinkled, this time in confusion. It tried to get its spear up in defense, not knowing what this strange drow would do next, but was too late.

Drizzt's rush was too quick. Before the gnoll's spear tip even moved, the drow waded in, scimitars leading. The other four gnolls watched in amazement as Drizzt's blades snapped twice, tearing the throat from their powerful leader. The giant gnoll fell backward silently, grasping futilely at its throat.

A gnoll to the side reacted first, leveling its spear and charging at Drizzt. The agile drow easily deflected the straightforward attack but was careful not to slow the gnoll's momentum. As the huge creature lumbered past, Drizzt rolled around beside it and kicked at its ankles. Off balance, the gnoll stumbled on, plunging its spear deep into the chest of a startled companion.

The gnoll tugged at the weapon, but it was firmly embedded, its barbed head hooked around the other gnoll's backbone. The gnoll had no concern for its dying companion; all it wanted was its weapon. It tugged and twisted and cursed and spat into the agonized expressions crossing its companion's face—until a scimitar bashed in the beast's skull.

Another gnoll, seeing the drow distracted and thinking it wiser to engage the foe from a distance, raised its spear to throw. Its arm went up high, but before the weapon ever started forward, Guenhwyvar crashed in, and the gnoll and panther tumbled away. The gnoll smashed heavy punches into the panther's muscled side, but Guenhwyvar's raking claws were more effective by far. In the split second it took Drizzt to turn from the three dead gnolls at his feet, the fourth of the band lay dead beneath the great panther. The fifth had taken flight.

Guenhwyvar tore free of the dead gnoll's stubborn grasp. The cat's sleek muscles rippled anxiously as it awaited the expected command. Drizzt considered the carnage around him, the blood on his scimitars, and the horrible expressions on the faces of the dead. He wanted to let it end, for he realized that he had stepped into a situation beyond his experience, had crossed the paths of two races that he knew very little about. After a moment of consideration, though, the single notion that stood out in the drow's mind was the gnoll leader's gleeful promise of death to the human children. Too much was at stake.

Drizzt turned to Guenhwyvar, his voice more determined than resigned. "Go get him."

⚔ ⚔ ⚔ ⚔ ⚔

The gnoll scrambled along the trails, its eyes darting back and forth as it imagined dark forms behind every tree or stone.

"Drow!" it rasped over and over, using the word itself as encouragement during its flight. "Drow! Drow!"

Huffing and panting, the gnoll came into a copse of trees stretching between two steep walls of bare stone. It tumbled over a fallen log, slipped, and bruised its ribs on the angled slope of a moss-covered stone. Minor pains would not slow the frightened creature, though, not in the least. The gnoll knew it was being pursued, sensed a presence slipping in and out of the shadows just beyond the edges of its vision.

As it neared the end of the copse, the evening gloom thick about it, the gnoll spotted a set of yellow-glowing eyes peering back at it. The gnoll had seen its companion taken down by the panther and could make a guess as to what now blocked its path.

Gnolls were cowardly monsters, but they could fight with amazing tenacity when cornered. So it was now. Realizing that it had no escape—it certainly couldn't turn back in the direction of the dark elf—the gnoll snarled and heaved its heavy spear.

The gnoll heard a shuffle, a thump, and a squeal of pain as the spear connected. The yellow eyes went away for a moment, then a form scurried off toward a tree. It moved low to the ground, almost catlike, but the gnoll realized at once that his mark had been no panther. When the wounded animal got to the tree, it looked back and the gnoll recognized it clearly.

"Raccoon," the gnoll blurted, and it laughed. "I run from raccoon!" The gnoll shook its head and blew away all of its mirth in a deep breath. The sight of the raccoon had brought a measure of relief, but the gnoll could not forget what had happened back down the path. It had to get back to its lair now, back to report to Ulgulu, its gigantic goblin master, its god-thing, about the drow.

It took a step to retrieve the spear, then stopped suddenly, sensing a movement from behind. Slowly the gnoll turned its head. It could see its own shoulder and the moss-covered rock behind.

The gnoll froze. Nothing moved behind it, not a sound issued from anywhere in the copse, but the beast knew that something was back there. The goblinoid's breath came in short rasps; its fat hands clenched and opened at its sides.

The gnoll spun quickly and roared, but the shout of rage became a cry of terror as six hundred pounds of panther leaped down upon it from a low branch.

The impact laid the gnoll out flat, but it was not a weak creature. Ignoring the burning pains of the panther's cruel claws, the gnoll grasped Guenhwyvar's plunging head, held on desperately to keep the deadly maw from finding a hold on its neck.

For nearly a minute the gnoll struggled, its arms quivering under the pressure of the powerful muscles in the panther's neck. The head came down then and Guenhwyvar found a hold. Great teeth locked onto the gnoll's neck and squeezed away the doomed creature's breath.

The gnoll flailed and thrashed wildly; somehow it managed to roll back over the panther. Guenhwyvar remained viselike, unconcerned. The maw held firm.

In a few minutes, the thrashing stopped.

# 2

# Questions of Conscience

Drizzt let his vision slip into the infrared spectrum, the night vision that could see gradations of heat as clearly as he viewed objects in the light. To his eyes, his scimitars now shone brightly with the heat of fresh blood and the torn gnoll bodies spilled their warmth into the open air.

Drizzt tried to look away, tried to observe the trail where Guenhwyvar had gone in pursuit of the fifth gnoll, but every time, his gaze fell back to the dead gnolls and the blood on his weapons.

"What have I done?" Drizzt wondered aloud. Truly, he did not know. The gnolls had spoken of slaughtering children, a thought that had evoked rage within Drizzt, but what did Drizzt know of the conflict between the gnolls and the humans of the village? Might the humans, even the human children, be monsters? Perhaps they had raided the gnolls' village and killed without mercy. Perhaps the gnolls meant to strike back because they had no choice, because they had to defend themselves.

Drizzt ran from the grizzly scene in search of Guenhwyvar, hoping he could get to the panther before the fifth gnoll was dead. If he could find the gnoll and capture it, he might be able to learn some of the answers that he desperately needed to know.

He moved with swift and graceful strides, making barely a rustle as he slipped through the brush along the trail. He found signs of the gnoll's passing easily enough, and he saw, to his fear, that Guenhwyvar had also discovered the trail. When he came at last to the narrow copse of trees, he fully expected that his search was at its end. Still, Drizzt's heart sank when he saw the cat, reclined beside the final kill.

Guenhwyvar looked at Drizzt curiously as he approached, the drow's stride obviously agitated.

"What have we done, Guenhwyvar?" Drizzt whispered. The panther tilted its head as though it did not understand.

"Who am I to pass such judgment?" Drizzt went on, talking to himself more than to the cat. He turned from Guenhwyvar and the dead gnoll and moved to a leafy bush, where he could wipe the blood from his blades. "The gnolls did not attack me, but they had me at their mercy when they first found me in the stream. And I repay them by spilling their blood!"

Drizzt spun back on Guenhwyvar with the proclamation, as if he expected, even hoped, that the panther would somehow berate him, somehow condemn him and justify his guilt. Guenhwyvar hadn't moved an inch and did not now, and the panther's saucer eyes, shining greenish yellow in the night, did not bore into Drizzt, did not incriminate him for his actions in any way.

Drizzt started to protest, wanting to wallow in his guilt, but Guenhwyvar's calm acceptance would not be shaken. When they had lived out alone in the wilds of the Underdark, when Drizzt had lost himself to savage urges that relished killing, Guenhwyvar had sometimes disobeyed him, had even returned to the Astral Plane once without being dismissed. Now, though, the panther showed no signs of leaving or of disappointment. Guenhwyvar rose to its feet, shook the dirt and twigs from its sleek, black coat, and walked over to nuzzle against Drizzt.

Gradually Drizzt relaxed. He wiped his scimitars once more, this time on the thick grass, and slipped them back into their sheaths, then he dropped a thankful hand onto Guenhwyvar's huge head.

"Their words marked them as evil," the drow whispered to reassure himself. "Their intentions forced my action." His own words lacked conviction, but at that moment, Drizzt had to believe them. He took a deep breath to steady himself and looked inward to find the strength he knew he would need. Realizing then that Guenhwyvar had been at his side for a long time and needed to return to the Astral Plane to rest, he reached into the small pouch at his side.

Before Drizzt ever got the onyx figurine out of his pouch, though, the panther's paw came up and batted it from his grasp. Drizzt looked at Guenhwyvar curiously, and the cat leaned heavily into him, nearly taking him from his feet.

"My loyal friend," Drizzt said, realizing that the weary panther meant to stay beside him. He pulled his hand from the pouch and dropped to one knee, locking Guenhwyvar in a great hug. The two of them, side by side, then walked from the copse.

Drizzt slept not at all that night, but watched the stars and wondered. Guenhwyvar sensed his anxiety and stayed close throughout the rise and set of the moon, and when Drizzt moved out to greet the next dawn, Guenhwyvar plodded along, drawn and tired, at his side. They found a rocky crest in the foothills and sat back to watch the coming spectacle.

Below them the last lights faded from the windows of the farming village. The eastern sky turned to pink, then crimson, but Drizzt found himself distracted. His gaze lingered on the farmhouses far below; his mind tried to piece together the routines of this unknown community and tried to find in that some justification for the previous day's events.

The humans were farmers, that much Drizzt knew, and diligent workers, too, for many of them were already out tending their fields. While those facts brought promise, however, Drizzt could not begin to make sweeping assumptions as to the human race's overall demeanor.

Drizzt came to a decision then, as the daylight stretched wide, illuminating the wooden structures of the town and the wide fields of grain. "I must learn more, Guenhwyvar," he said softly. "If I—if we—are to remain in this world, we must come to understand the ways of our neighbors."

Drizzt nodded as he considered his own words. It had already been proven, painfully proven, that he could not remain a neutral observer to the goings-on of the surface world. Drizzt was often called to action by his conscience, a force he had no power to deny. Yet with so little knowledge of the races sharing this region, his conscience could easily lead him astray.

It could wreak damage against the innocent, thereby defeating the very principles Drizzt meant to champion.

Drizzt squinted through the morning light, eyeing the distant village for some hint of an answer. "I will go there," he told the panther. "I will go and watch and learn."

Guenhwyvar sat silently through it all. If the panther approved or disapproved, or even understood Drizzt's intent, Drizzt could not tell. This time, though, Guenhwyvar made no move of protest when Drizzt reached for the onyx figurine. A few moments later, the great panther was running off through the planar tunnel to its astral home, and Drizzt moved along the trails leading to the human village and his answers. He stopped only once, at the body of the lone gnoll, to take the creature's cloak. Drizzt winced at his own thievery, but the chill night had reminded him that the loss of his *piwafwi* could prove serious.

To this point, Drizzt's knowledge of humans and their society was severely limited. Deep in the bowels of the Underdark, the dark elves had little communication with, or interest in, those of the surface world. The one time in Menzoberranzan that Drizzt had heard anything of humans at all was during his tenure in the Academy, the six months he had spent in Sorcere, the school of wizards. The drow masters had warned the students against using magic "like a human would," implying a dangerous recklessness generally associated with the shorter-lived race.

"Human wizards," the masters had said, "have no fewer ambitions than drow wizards, but while a drow may take five centuries accomplishing those goals, a human has only a few short decades."

Drizzt had carried the implications of that statement with him for a score of years, particularly over the last few months, when he had looked down upon the human village almost daily. If all humans, not just wizards, were as ambitious as so many of the drow—fanatics who might spend the better part of a millennium accomplishing their goals—would they be consumed by a single-mindedness that bordered on hysteria? Or perhaps, Drizzt hoped, the stories he had heard of humans at the Academy were just more of the typical lies that bound his society in a web of intrigue and paranoia. Perhaps humans set their goals at more reasonable levels and found enjoyment and satisfaction in the small pleasures of the short days of their existence.

Drizzt had met a human only once during his travels through the Underdark. That man, a wizard, had behaved irrationally, unpredictably, and ultimately dangerously. The wizard had transformed Drizzt's friend from a pech, a harmless little humanoid creature, into a horrible monster. When Drizzt and his companions went to set things aright at the wizard's tower, they were greeted by a roaring blast of lightning. In the end, the human was killed and Drizzt's friend, Clacker, had been left to his torment.

Drizzt had been left with a bitter emptiness, an example of a man who seemed to confirm the truth of the drow masters' warnings. So it was with cautious steps that Drizzt now traveled toward the human settlement, his steps weighted by the growing fear that he had erred in killing the gnolls.

Drizzt chose to observe the same secluded farmhouse on the western edge of town that the gnolls had selected for their raid. It was a long and low log structure with a single door and several shuttered windows. An open-sided, roofed porch ran the length of the front. Beside it stood a barn, two stories high, with wide and high doors that would admit a huge wagon. Fences of various makes and sizes dotted the immediate yard, many holding chickens or pigs, one corralling a goat, and others encircling straight rows of leafy plants that Drizzt did not recognize.

The yard was bordered by fields on three sides, but the back of the house was near the mountain slopes' thick brush and boulders. Drizzt dug in under the low branches of a pine tree to the side of the house's rear corner, affording him a view of most of the yard.

The three adult men of the house—three generations, Drizzt guessed by their appearances—worked the fields, too far from the trees for Drizzt to discern many details. Closer to the house, though, four children, a daughter just coming into womanhood and three younger boys, quietly went about their chores, tending to the hens and pigs and pulling weeds from a vegetable garden. They worked separately and with minimum interaction for most of the morning, and Drizzt learned little of their family relationships. When a sturdy woman with the same wheat-colored hair as all five children came out on the porch and rang a giant bell, it seemed as if all the spirit that had been cooped up within the workers burst beyond control.

With hoots and shouts, the three boys sprinted for the house, pausing just long enough to toss rotted vegetables at their older sister. At first, Drizzt thought the bombing a prelude to a more serious conflict, but when the young woman retaliated in kind, all four howled with laughter and he recognized the game for what it was.

A moment later, the youngest of the men in the field, probably an older brother, charged into the yard, shouting and waving an iron hoe. The young woman cried encouragement to this new ally and the three boys broke for the porch. The man was quicker, though, and he scooped up the trailing imp in one strong arm and promptly dropped him into the pig trough.

And all the while, the woman with the bell shook her head helplessly and issued an unending stream of exasperated grumbling. An older woman, gray-haired and stick-thin, came out to stand next to her, waving a wooden spoon ominously. Apparently satisfied, the young man draped one arm over the young woman's shoulders and they followed the first two boys into the house. The remaining youngster pulled himself from the murky water and moved to follow, but the wooden spoon kept him at bay.

Drizzt couldn't understand a word of what they were saying, of course, but he figured that the women would not let the little one into the house until he had dried off. The rambunctious youngster mumbled something at the spoon-wielder's back as she turned to enter the house, but his timing was not so great.

The other two men, one sporting a thick, gray beard and the other clean-shaven, came in from the field and sneaked up behind the boy as he grumbled. Up into the air the boy went again and landed with a *splash!* back in the trough. Congratulating themselves heartily, the men went into the house to the cheers of all the others. The soaking boy merely groaned again and splashed some water into the face of a sow that had come over to investigate.

Drizzt watched it all with growing wonderment. He had seen nothing conclusive, but the family's playful manner and the resigned acceptance of even the loser of the game gave him encouragement. Drizzt sensed a common spirit in this group, with all members working toward a common goal. If this single farm proved a reflection of the whole village, then the place surely resembled Blingdenstone, a communal city of the deep gnomes, far more than it resembled Menzoberranzan.

The afternoon went much the same way as the morning, with a mixture of work and play evident throughout the farm. The family retired early, turning down their lamps soon after sunset, and Drizzt slipped deeper into the thicket of the mountainside to consider his observations.

He still couldn't be certain of anything, but he slept more peacefully that night, untroubled by nagging doubts concerning the dead gnolls.

---

For three days the drow crouched in the shadows behind the farm, watching the family at work and at play. The closeness of the group became more and more evident, and whenever a true fight did erupt among the children, the nearest adult quickly stepped in and mediated it to a level of reasonableness. Invariably, the combatants were back at play together within a short span.

All doubts had flown from Drizzt. "Ware my blades, rogues," he whispered to the quiet mountains one night. The young drow renegade had decided that if any gnolls or goblins—or creatures of any other race at all—tried to swoop down upon this particular farming family, they first would have to contend with the whirling scimitars of Drizzt Do'Urden.

Drizzt understood the risk he was taking by observing the farm family. If the farmer-folk noticed him—a distinct possibility—they surely would panic. At this point in his life, though, Drizzt was willing to take that chance. A part of him may even have hoped to be discovered.

Early on the morning of the fourth day, before the sun had found its way into the eastern sky, Drizzt set out on his daily patrol, circumventing the hills and woodlands surrounding the lone farmhouse. By the time the drow returned to his perch, the work day on the farm was in full swing. Drizzt sat comfortably on a bed of moss and peered from the shadows into the brightness of the cloudless day.

Less than an hour later, a solitary figure crept from the farmhouse and in Drizzt's direction. It was the youngest of the children, the sandy-haired lad who seemed to spend nearly as much time in the trough as out of it, usually not of his own volition.

Drizzt rolled around the trunk of a nearby tree, uncertain of the lad's intent. He soon realized that the youngster hadn't seen him, for the boy slipped into the thicket, gave a snort over his shoulder, back toward the farmhouse, and headed off into the hilly woodland whistling all the while. Drizzt understood then that the lad was avoiding his chores, and Drizzt almost applauded the boy's carefree attitude. In spite of that, though, Drizzt wasn't convinced of the small child's wisdom in wandering away from home in such dangerous terrain. The boy couldn't have been more than ten years old; he looked thin and delicate, with innocent, blue eyes peering out from under his amber locks.

Drizzt waited a few moments, to let the boy get a lead and to see if anyone would be following, then he took up the trail, letting the whistling guide him.

The boy moved unerringly away from the farmhouse, up into the mountains, and Drizzt moved behind him by a hundred paces or so, determined to keep the boy out of danger.

In the dark tunnels of the Underdark Drizzt could have crept right up behind the boy—or behind a goblin or practically anything else—and patted him on the rump before being discovered. But after only a half-hour or so of this pursuit, the movements and erratic speed changes along the trail, coupled with the fact that the whistling had ceased, told Drizzt that the boy knew he was being followed.

Wondering if the boy had sensed a third party, Drizzt summoned Guenhwyvar from the onyx figurine and sent the panther off on a flanking maneuver. Drizzt started ahead again at a cautious pace.

A moment later, when the child's voice cried out in distress, the drow drew his scimitars and threw out all caution. Drizzt couldn't understand any of the boy's words, but the desperate tone rang clearly enough.

"Guenhwyvar!" the drow called, trying to bring the distant panther back to his side. Drizzt couldn't stop and wait for the cat, though, and he charged on.

The trail wound up a steep climb, came out of the trees suddenly, and ended on the lip of a wide gorge, fully twenty feet across. A single log spanned the crevasse, and hanging from it near the other side was the boy. His eyes widened considerably at the sight of the ebony-skinned elf, scimitars in hand. He stammered a few words that Drizzt could not begin to decipher.

A wave of guilt flooded through Drizzt at the sight of the imperiled child; the boy had only landed in this predicament because of Drizzt's pursuit. The gorge was only about as deep as it was wide, but the fall ended on jagged rocks and brambles. At first, Drizzt hesitated, caught off guard by the sudden meeting and its inevitable implications, then the drow quickly put his own problems out of mind. He snapped his scimitars back into their sheaths and folding his arms across his chest in a drow signal for peace, he put one foot out on the log.

The boy had other ideas. As soon as he recovered from the shock of seeing the strange elf, he swung himself to a ledge on the stone bank opposite Drizzt and pushed the log from its perch. Drizzt quickly backed off the log as it tumbled down into the crevasse. The drow understood then that the boy had never been in real danger but had pretended distress to flush out his pursuer. And Drizzt presumed, if the pursuer had been one of the boy's family, as the boy no doubt had suspected, the peril might have deflected any thoughts of punishment.

Now Drizzt was the one in the predicament. He had been discovered. He tried to think of a way to communicate with the boy, to explain his presence and stave off panic. The boy didn't wait for any explanations, though. Wide-eyed and terror-stricken, he scaled the bank—via a path he obviously knew well—and darted off into the shrubbery.

Drizzt looked around helplessly. "Wait!" he cried in the drow tongue, though he knew the boy would not understand and would not have stopped even if he could.

A black feline form rushed out beside the drow and sprang into the air, easily clearing the crevasse. Guenhwyvar padded down softly on the other side and disappeared into the thicket.

"Guenhwyvar!" Drizzt cried, trying to halt the panther. Drizzt had no idea how Guenhwyvar would react to the child. To Drizzt's knowledge, the panther had only encountered one human before, the wizard that Drizzt's companions had subsequently killed. Drizzt looked around for some way to follow. He could scale down the side of the gorge, cross at the bottom, and climb back up, but that would take too long.

Drizzt ran back a few steps, then charged the gorge and leaped into the air, calling on his innate powers of levitation as he went. Drizzt was truly relieved when he felt his body pull free of the ground's gravity. He hadn't used his levitation spell since he had come to the surface. The spell served no purpose for a drow hiding under the open sky. Gradually, Drizzt's initial momentum carried him near the far bank. He began to concentrate on drifting down to the stone, but the spell ended abruptly and Drizzt plopped down hard. He ignored the bruises on his knee, and the questions of why his spell had faltered, and came up running, calling desperately for Guenhwyvar to stop.

Drizzt was relieved when he found the cat. Guenhwyvar sat calmly in a clearing, one paw casually pinning the boy facedown to the ground. The child was calling out again—for help, Drizzt assumed—but appeared unharmed.

"Come, Guenhwyvar," Drizzt said quietly, calmly. "Leave the child alone." Guenhwyvar yawned lazily and complied, padding across the clearing to stand at its master's side.

The boy remained down for a long moment. Then, summoning his courage, he moved suddenly, leaping to his feet and spinning to face the dark elf and the panther. His eyes seemed wider still, almost a caricature of terror, peeking out from his now dirty face.

"What are you?" the boy asked in the common human language.

Drizzt held his arms out to the sides to indicate that he did not understand. On impulse, he poked a finger into his chest and replied, "Drizzt Do'Urden." He noticed that the boy was moving slightly, secretly dropping one foot behind the other and sliding the other back into place. Drizzt was not surprised—and he made certain that he kept Guenhwyvar in check this time—when the boy turned on his heel and sprinted away, screaming "Help! It's a drizzit!" with every stride.

Drizzt looked at Guenhwyvar and shrugged, and the cat seemed to shrug back.

# 3
# The Whelps

Nathak, a spindle-armed goblin, made his way slowly up the steep, rocky incline, every step weighted with dread. The goblin had to report his findings—five dead gnolls could not be ignored—but the unfortunate creature seriously doubted that either Ulgulu or Kempfana would willingly accept the news. Still, what options did Nathak have? He could run away, flee down the other side of the mountain, and off into the wilderness. That seemed an even more desperate course, though, for the goblin knew well Ulgulu's taste for vengeance. The great purple-skinned master could tear a tree from the ground with his bare hands, could tear handfuls of stone from the cave wall, and could readily tear the throat from a deserting goblin.

Every step brought a shudder as Nathak moved beyond the concealing scrub into the small entry room of his master's cave complex.

"Bouts time yez isses back," one of the other two goblins in the room snorted. "Yez been gone fer two days!"

Nathak just nodded and took a deep breath.

"What're ye fer?" the third goblin asked. "Did ye finded the gnolls?"

Nathak's face blanched, and no amount of deep breathing could relieve the fit that came over the goblin. "Ulgulu in there?" he asked squeamishly.

The two goblin guards looked curiously at each other, then back to

Nathak. "He finded the gnolls," one of them remarked, guessing the problem. "Dead gnolls."

"Ulgulu won'ts be glad," the other piped in, and they moved apart, one of them lifting the heavy curtain that separated the entry room from the audience chamber.

Nathak hesitated and started to look back, as though reconsidering this whole course. Perhaps flight would be preferable, he thought. The goblin guards grabbed their spindly companion and roughly shoved him into the audience chamber, crossing their spears behind Nathak to prevent any retreat.

Nathak managed to find a measure of composure when he saw that it was Kempfana, not Ulgulu, sitting in the huge chair across the room. Kempfana had earned a reputation among the goblin ranks as the calmer of the ruling brothers, though Kempfana, too, had impulsively devoured enough of his minions to earn their healthy respect. Kempfana hardly took note of the goblin's entrance, instead busily conversing with Lagerbottoms, the fat hill giant that formerly claimed the cave complex as his own.

Nathak shuffled across the room, drawing the gazes of both the hill giant and the huge—nearly as large as the hill giant—scarlet-skinned goblinoid.

"Yes, Nathak," Kempfana prompted, silencing the hill giant's forthcoming protest with a simple wave of the hand. "What have you to report?"

"Me . . . me," Nathak stuttered.

Kempfana's large eyes suddenly glowed orange, a clear sign of dangerous excitement.

"Me finded the gnolls!" Nathak blurted. "Dead. Killded."

Lagerbottoms issued a low and threatening growl, but Kempfana clutched the hill giant's arm tightly, reminding him of who was in charge.

"Dead?" the scarlet-skinned goblin asked quietly.

Nathak nodded.

Kempfana lamented the loss of such reliable slaves, but the barghest whelp's thoughts at that moment were more centered on his brother's inevitably volatile reaction to the news. Kempfana didn't have long to wait.

*"Dead!"* came a roar that nearly split the stone. All three monsters in the room instinctively ducked and turned to the side, just in time to see a huge boulder, the crude door to another room, burst out and go skipping off to the side.

"Ulgulu!" Nathak squealed, and the little goblin fell face-down to the floor, not daring to look.

The huge, purple-skinned goblinlike creature stormed into the audience chamber, his eyes seething in orange-glowing rage. Three great strides took Ulgulu right up beside the hill giant, and Lagerbottoms suddenly seemed very small and vulnerable.

"Dead!" Ulgulu roared again in rage. As his goblin tribe had diminished, killed either by the humans of the village or by other monsters—or eaten by Ulgulu during his customary fits of anger—the small gnoll band had become the primary capturing force for the lair.

Kempfana cast an ugly glare at his larger sibling. They had come to the Material Plane together, two barghest whelps, to eat and grow. Ulgulu had promptly claimed dominance, devouring the strongest of their victims and thus, growing larger and stronger. By the color of Ulgulu's skin, and by his sheer size and strength, it was apparent that the whelp would soon be able to return to the reeking valley rifts of Gehenna.

Kempfana hoped that day was near. When Ulgulu was gone, he would rule; he would eat and grow stronger. Then Kempfana, too, could escape his interminable weaning period on this cursed plane, could return to compete among the barghests on their rightful plane of existence.

"Dead," Ulgulu growled again. "Get up, wretched goblin, and tell me how! What did this to my gnolls?"

Nathak groveled a minute longer, then managed to rise to his knees. "Me no know," the goblin whimpered. "Gnolls dead, slashed and ripped."

Ulgulu rocked back on the heels of his floppy, oversized feet. The gnolls had gone off to raid a farmhouse, with orders to return with the farmer and his oldest son. Those two hardy human meals would have strengthened the great barghest considerably, perhaps even bringing Ulgulu to the level of maturation he needed to return to Gehenna.

Now, in light of Nathak's report, Ulgulu would have to send Lagerbottoms, or perhaps even go himself, and the sight of either the giant or the purple-skinned monstrosity could prompt the human settlement to dangerous, organized action. "Tephanis!" Ulgulu roared suddenly.

Over on the far wall, across from where Ulgulu had made his crashing entrance, a small pebble dislodged and fell. The drop was only a few feet, but by the time the pebble hit the floor, a slender sprite had zipped out of the small cubby he used as a bedroom, crossed the twenty feet of the audience hall, and run right up Ulgulu's side to sit comfortably atop the barghest's immense shoulder.

"You-called-for-me, yes-you-did, my-master," Tephanis buzzed, too quickly. The others hadn't even realized that the two-foot-tall sprite had entered the room. Kempfana turned away, shaking his head in amazement.

Ulgulu roared with laughter; he so loved to witness the spectacle of Tephanis, his most prized servant. Tephanis was a quickling, a diminutive sprite that moved in a dimension that transcended the normal concept of time. Possessing boundless energy and an agility that would shame the most proficient halfling thief, quicklings could perform many tasks that no other race could even attempt. Ulgulu had befriended Tephanis early in his tenure on the Material Plane—Tephanis was the only member of the lair's diverse tenants that the barghest did not claim rulership over—and that bond had given the young whelp a distinct advantage over his sibling. With Tephanis scouting out potential victims, Ulgulu knew exactly which ones to devour and which ones to leave to Kempfana, and knew exactly how to win against those adventurers more powerful than he.

"Dear Tephanis," Ulgulu purred in an odd sort of grating sound. "Nathak, poor Nathak,"—The goblin didn't miss the implications of that reference—"has informed me that my gnolls have met with disaster."

"And-you-want-me-to-go-and-see-what-happened-to-them, my-master," Tephanis replied. Ulgulu took a moment to decipher the nearly unintelligible string of words, then nodded eagerly.

"Right-away, my-master. Be-back-soon."

Ulgulu felt a slight shiver on his shoulder, but by the time he, or any of the others, realized what Tephanis had said, the heavy drape separating the chamber from the entry room was floating back to its hanging position. One of the goblins poked its head in for just a moment, to see if Kempfana or Ulgulu had summoned it, then returned to its station, thinking the drape's movement a trick of the wind.

Ulgulu roared in laughter again; Kempfana cast him a disgusted glare. Kempfana hated the sprite and would have killed it long ago, except that he couldn't ignore the potential benefits, assuming that Tephanis would work for him once Ulgulu had returned to Gehenna.

Nathak slipped one foot behind the other, meaning to silently retreat from the room. Ulgulu stopped the goblin with a look.

"Your report served me well," the barghest started.

Nathak relaxed, but only for the moment it took Ulgulu's great hand to shoot out, catch the goblin by the throat, and lift Nathak from the floor.

"But it would have served me better if you had taken the time to find out what happened to my gnolls!"

Nathak swooned and nearly fainted, and by the time half of his body had been stuffed into Ulgulu's eager mouth, the spindle-armed goblin wished he had.

* * * * *

"Rub the behind, ease the pain. Switch it brings it back again. Rub the behind, ease the pain. Switch it brings it back again," Liam Thistledown repeated over and over, a litany to take his concentration from the burning sensation beneath his britches, a litany that mischievous Liam knew all too well. This time was different, though, with Liam actually admitting to himself, after a while, that he had indeed run out on his chores.

"But the drizzit was true," Liam growled defiantly.

As if in answer to his statement, the shed's door opened just a crack and Shawno, the second youngest to Liam, and Eleni, the only sister, slipped in.

"Got yourself into it this time," Eleni scolded in her best big-sister voice. "Bad enough you run off when there's work to be done, but coming home with such tales!"

"The drizzit was true," Liam protested, not appreciating Eleni's pseudomothering. Liam could get into enough trouble with just his parents scolding him; he didn't need Eleni's ever-sharp hindsight. "Black as Connor's anvil and with a lion just as black!"

"Quiet, you both," Shawno warned. "If dad's to learn that we're out here talking such, he'll whip the lot of us."

"Drizzit," Eleni huffed doubtfully.

"True!" Liam protested too loudly, bringing a stinging slap from Shawno. The three turned, faces ashen, when the door swung open.

"Get in here!" Eleni whispered harshly, grabbing Flanny, who was a bit older than Shawno but three years Eleni's junior, by the collar and hoisting him into the woodshed. Shawno, always the worrier of the group, quickly poked his head outside to see that no one was watching, then softly closed the door.

"You should not be spying on us!" Eleni protested.

"How'd I know you was in here?" Flanny shot back. "I just came to tease the little one." He looked at Liam, twisted his mouth, and waved his fingers menacingly in the air. "Ware, ware," Flanny crooned. "I am the drizzit, come to eat little boys!"

Liam turned away, but Shawno was not so impressed. "Aw, shut up!" he growled at Flanny, emphasizing his point with a slap on the back of his brother's head. Flanny turned to retaliate, but Eleni stepped between them.

"Stop it!" Eleni cried, so loudly that all four Thistledown children slapped a finger over their lips and said, "Ssssh!"

"The drizzit was true," Liam protested again. "I can prove it—if you're not too scared!"

Liam's three siblings eyed him curiously. He was a notorious fibber, they all knew, but what now would be the gain? Their father hadn't believed Liam, and that was all that mattered as far as the punishment was concerned. Yet Liam was adamant, and his tone told them all that there was substance behind the proclamation.

"How can you prove the drizzit?" Flanny asked.

"We've no chores tomorrow," Liam replied. "We'll go blueberry picking in the mountains."

"Ma and Daddy'd never let us," Eleni put in.

"They would if we can get Connor to go along," said Liam, referring to their oldest brother.

"Connor'd not believe you," Eleni argued.

"But he'd believe you!" Liam replied sharply, drawing another communal "Ssssh!"

"I don't believe you," Eleni retorted quietly. "You're always making things up, always causing trouble and lying to get out of it!"

Liam crossed his little arms over his chest and stamped one foot impatiently at his sister's continuing stream of logic. "But you will believe me," Liam growled, "if you get Connor to go!"

"Aw, do it," Flanny pleaded to Eleni, though Shawno, thinking of the potential consequences, shook his head.

"So we go up into the mountains," Eleni said to Liam, prompting him to continue and thus revealing her agreement.

Liam smiled widely and dropped to one knee, collecting a pile of sawdust in which to draw a rough map of the area where he had encountered the drizzit. His plan was a simple one, using Eleni, casually picking blueberries, as bait. The four brothers would follow secretly and watch as she feigned a twisted ankle or some other injury. Distress had brought the drizzit before; surely with a pretty young girl as bait, it would bring the drizzit again.

Eleni balked at the idea, not thrilled at being planted as a worm on a hook.

"But you don't believe me anyway," Liam quickly pointed out. His inevitable smile, complete with a gaping hole where a tooth had been knocked out, showed that her own stubbornness had cornered her.

"So I'll do it, then!" Eleni huffed. "And I don't believe in your drizzit, Liam Thistledown! But if the lion is real, and I get chewed, I'll tan you good!" With that, Eleni turned and stormed out of the woodshed.

Liam and Flanny spit in their hands, then turned daring glares on Shawno until he overcame his fears. Then the three brothers brought their palms together in a triumphant, wet slap. Any disagreements between them always seemed to vanish whenever one of them found a way to bother Eleni.

None of them told Connor about their planned hunt for the drizzit. Rather, Eleni reminded him of the many favors he owed her and promised that she would consider the debt paid in full—but only after Liam had agreed to take on Connor's debt if they didn't find the drizzit—if Connor would only take her and the boys blueberry picking.

Connor grumbled and balked, complaining about some shoeing that needed to be done to one of the mares, but he could never resist his little sister's batting blue eyes and wide, bright smile, and Eleni's promise of erasing his considerable debt had sealed his fate. With his parents' blessing, Connor led the Thistledown children up into the mountains, buckets in the children's hands and a crude sword belted on his hip.

⚔ ⚔ ⚔ ⚔ ⚔

Drizzt saw the ruse coming long before the farmer's young daughter moved out alone in the blueberry patch. He saw, too, the four Thistledown boys, crouched in the shadows of a nearby grove of maple trees, Connor, somewhat less than expertly, brandishing the crude sword.

The youngest had led them here, Drizzt knew. The day before, the drow had witnessed the boy being pulled out into the woodshed. Cries of "drizzit!" had issued forth after every switch, at least at the beginning. Now the stubborn lad wanted to prove his outrageous story.

The blueberry picker jerked suddenly, then fell to the ground and cried out. Drizzt recognized "Help!" as the same distress call the sandy-haired boy had used, and a smile widened across his dark face. By the ridiculous way the girl had fallen, Drizzt saw the game for what it was. The girl was not injured now; she was simply calling out for the drizzit.

With an incredulous shake of his thick white mane, Drizzt started away, but an impulse grabbed at him. He looked back to the blueberry patch, where the girl sat rubbing her ankle, all the while glancing nervously around or back toward her concealed brothers. Something pulled at Drizzt's heartstrings at that moment, an urge he could not resist. How long had he been alone, wandering without companionship? He longed for Belwar at that moment, the svirfneblin who had accompanied him through many trials in the wilds of the Underdark. He longed for Zaknafein, his father and friend. Seeing the interplay between the caring siblings was more than Drizzt Do'Urden could bear.

The time had come for Drizzt to meet his neighbors.

Drizzt hiked the hood of his oversized gnoll cloak up over his head, though the ragged garment did little to hide the truth of his heritage, and bounded across the field. He hoped that if he could at least deflect the girl's initial reaction to seeing him, he might find some way to communicate with her. The hopes were farfetched at best.

"The drizzit!" Eleni gasped under her breath when she saw him coming. She wanted to cry out loud but found no breath; she wanted to run, but her terror held her firmly.

From the copse of trees, Liam spoke for her. "The drizzit!" the boy cried. "I told you so! I told you so!" He looked to his brothers, and Flanny and Shawno were having the expected excited reactions. Connor's face, though, was locked into a look of dread so profound that one glance at it stole the joy from Liam.

"By the gods," the eldest Thistledown son muttered. Connor had adventured with his father and had been trained to spot enemies. He looked now to his three confused brothers and muttered a single word that explained nothing to the inexperienced boys. "Drow."

Drizzt stopped a dozen paces from the frightened girl, the first human woman he had seen up close, and studied her. Eleni was pretty by any race's standards, with huge, soft eyes, dimpled cheeks, and smooth, golden skin. Drizzt knew there would be no fight here. He smiled at Eleni and crossed his arms gently over his chest. "Drizzt," he corrected, pointing to his chest. A movement to the side turned him away from the girl.

"Run, Eleni!" Connor Thistledown cried, waving his sword and bearing down on the drow. "It is a dark elf! A drow! Run for your life!"

Of all that Connor had cried, Drizzt only understood the word "drow." The young man's attitude and intent could not be mistaken, though, for Connor charged straight between Drizzt and Eleni, his sword tip pointed Drizzt's way. Eleni managed to get to her feet behind her brother, but she did not flee as he had instructed. She, too, had heard of the evil dark elves, and she would not leave Connor to face one alone.

"Turn away, dark elf," Connor growled. "I am an expert swordsman and much stronger than you."

Drizzt held his hands out helplessly, not understanding a word.

"Turn away!" Connor yelled.

On an impulse, Drizzt tried to reply in the drow silent code, an intricate language of hand and facial gestures.

"He's casting a spell!" Eleni cried, and she dived down into the blueberries. Connor shrieked and charged.

Before Connor even knew of the counter, Drizzt grabbed him by the forearm, used his other hand to twist the boy's wrist and take away the sword, spun the crude weapon three times over Connor's head, flipped it in his slender hand then handed it, hilt first, back to the boy.

Drizzt held his arms out wide and smiled. In drow custom, such a show of superiority without injuring the opponent invariably signaled a desire for friendship. To the oldest son of farmer Bartholemew Thistledown, the drow's blinding display brought only awe-inspired terror.

Connor stood, mouth agape, for a long moment. His sword fell from his hand but he didn't notice; his pants, soiled, clung to his thighs, but he didn't notice.

A scream erupted from somewhere within Connor. He grabbed Eleni, who joined in his scream, and they fled back to the grove to collect the others, then farther, running until they crossed the threshold of their own home.

Drizzt was left, his smile fast fading and his arms out wide, standing all alone in the blueberry patch.

⚔ ⚔ ⚔ ⚔ ⚔

A set of dizzily darting eyes had watched the exchange in the blueberry patch with more than a casual interest. The unexpected appearance of a dark elf, particularly one wearing a gnoll cloak, had answered many questions for Tephanis. The quickling sleuth had already examined the gnoll corpses but simply could not reconcile the gnolls' fatal wounds with the crude weapons usually wielded by the simple village farmers. Seeing the magnificent twin scimitars so casually belted on the dark elf's hips and the ease with which the dark elf had dispatched the farm boy, Tephanis knew the truth.

The dust trail left by the quickling would have confused the best rangers in the Realms. Tephanis, never a straightforward sprite, zipped up the mountain trails, spinning circuits around some trees, running up and down the sides of others, and generally doubling, even tripling, his route. Distance never bothered Tephanis; he stood before the purple-skinned barghest whelp even before Drizzt, considering the implications of the disastrous meeting, had left the blueberry patch.

# 4 Worries

Farmer Bartholemew Thistledown's perspective changed considerably when Connor, his oldest son, renamed Liam's "drizzit" a dark elf. Farmer Thistledown had spent his entire forty-five years in Maldobar, a village fifty miles up the Dead Orc River north of Sundabar. Bartholemew's father had lived here, and his father's father before him. In all that time, the only news any Farmer Thistledown had ever heard of dark elves was the tale of a suspected drow raid on a small settlement of wild elves a hundred miles to the north, in Coldwood. That raid, if it was even perpetrated by the drow, had occurred more than a decade before.

Lack of personal experience with the drow race did not diminish Farmer Thistledown's fears at hearing his children's tale of the encounter in the blueberry patch. Connor and Eleni, two trusted sources old enough to keep their wits about them in a time of crisis, had viewed the elf up close, and they held no doubts about the color of his skin.

"The only thing I can't rightly figure," Bartholemew told Benson Delmo, the fat and cheerful mayor of Maldobar and several other farmers gathered at his house that night, "is why this drow let the children go free. I'm no expert on the ways of dark elves, but I've heard tell enough about them to expect a different sort of action."

"Perhaps Connor fared better in his attack than he believed," Delmo piped in tactfully. They had all heard the tale of Connor's disarming; Liam and the other Thistledown children, except for poor Connor, of course, particularly enjoyed retelling that part.

As much as he appreciated the mayor's vote of confidence, though, Connor shook his head emphatically at the suggestion. "He took me," Connor admitted. "Maybe I was too surprised at the sight of him, but he took me—clean."

"And no easy feat," Bartholemew put in, deflecting any forthcoming snickers from the gruff crowd. "We've all seen Connor at fighting. Just last winter, he took down three goblins and the wolves they were riding!"

"Calm, good Farmer Thistledown," the mayor offered. "We've no doubts of your son's prowess."

"I've my doubts about the truth o' the foe!" put in Roddy McGristle, a bear-sized and bear-hairy man, the most battle-seasoned of the group. Roddy spent more time up in the mountains than tending his farm, a recent endeavor he didn't particularly enjoy, and whenever someone offered a bounty on orc ears, Roddy invariably collected the largest portion of the coffers, often larger than the rest of the town combined.

"Put yer neck hairs down," Roddy said to Connor as the boy began to rise, a sharp protest obviously forthcoming. "I know what ye says ye seen, and I believe that ye seen what ye says. But ye called it a drow, an' that title carries more than ye can begin to know. If it was a drow ye found, my guess's that yerself an' yer kin'd be lying dead right now in that there blueberry patch. No, not a drow, by my guess, but there's other things in them mountains could do what ye says this thing did."

"Name them," Bartholemew said crossly, not appreciating the doubts Roddy had cast over his son's story. Bartholemew didn't much like Roddy anyway. Farmer Thistledown kept a respectable family, and every time crude and loud Roddy McGristle came to pay a visit, it took Bartholemew and his wife many days to remind the children, particularly Liam, about proper behavior.

Roddy just shrugged, taking no offense at Bartholemew's tone. "Goblin, troll—might be a wood elf that's seen too much o' the sun." His laughter, erupting after the last statement, rolled over the group, belittling their seriousness.

"Then how do we know for sure," said Delmo.

"We find out by finding it," Roddy offered. "Tomorrow mornin',"—he pointed around at each man sitting at Bartholemew's table—"we go out an' see what we can see." Considering the impromptu meeting at an end, Roddy slammed his hands down on the table and pushed himself to his feet. He looked back before he got to the farmhouse door, though, and cast an exaggerated wink and a nearly toothless smile back at the group. "And boys," he said, "don't be forgettin' yer weapons!"

Roddy's cackle rolled back in on the group long after the rough-edged mountain man had departed.

"We could call in a ranger," one of the other farmers offered hopefully as the dispirited group began to depart. "I heard there's one in Sundabar, one of Lady Alustriel's sisters."

"A bit too early for that," Mayor Delmo answered, defeating any optimistic smiles.

"Is it ever too early when drow are involved?" Bartholemew quickly put in.

The mayor shrugged. "Let us go with McGristle," he replied. "If anyone can find some truth up in the mountains, it's him." He tactfully turned to Connor. "I believe your tale, Connor. Truly I do. But we've got to know for sure before we put out a call for such distinguished assistance as a sister of the Lady of Silverymoon."

The mayor and the rest of the visiting farmers departed, leaving Bartholemew, his father, Markhe, and Connor alone in the Thistledown kitchen.

"Wasn't no goblin or wood elf," Connor said in a low tone that hinted at both anger and embarrassment.

Bartholemew patted his son on the back, never doubting him.

⚔ ⚔ ⚔ ⚔ ⚔

Up in a cave in the mountains, Ulgulu and Kempfana, too, spent a night of worry over the appearance of a dark elf.

"If he's a drow, then he's an experienced adventurer," Kempfana offered to his larger brother. "Experienced enough, perhaps, to send Ulgulu into maturity."

"And back to Gehenna!" Ulgulu finished for his conniving brother. "You do so dearly desire to see me depart."

"You, too, hope for the day when you may return to the smoking rifts," Kempfana reminded him.

Ulgulu snarled and did not reply. The appearance of a dark elf prompted many considerations and fears beyond Kempfana's simple statement of logic. The barghests, like all intelligent creatures on nearly every plane of existence, knew of the drow and maintained a healthy respect for the race. While one drow might not be too much of a problem, Ulgulu knew that a dark elf war party, perhaps even an army, could prove disastrous. The whelps were not invulnerable. The human village had provided easy pickings for the barghest whelps and might continue to do so for some time if Ulgulu and Kempfana were careful about their attacks. But if a band of dark elves showed up, those easy kills could disappear quite suddenly.

"This drow must be dealt with," Kempfana remarked. "If he is a scout, then he must not return to report."

Ulgulu snapped a cold glare on his brother, then called to his quickling. "Tephanis," he cried, and the quickling was upon his shoulder before he had even finished the word.

"You-need-me-to-go-and-kill-the-drow, my-master," the quickling replied. "I-understand-what-you-need-me-to-do!"

"No!" Ulgulu shouted immediately, sensing that the quickling intended to go right out. Tephanis was halfway to the door by the time Ulgulu finished the syllable, but the quickling returned to Ulgulu's shoulder before the last note of the shout had died away.

"No," Ulgulu said again, more easily. "There may be a gain in the drow's appearance."

Kempfana read Ulgulu's evil grin and understood his brother's intent. "A new enemy for the townspeople," the smaller whelp reasoned. "A new enemy to cover Ulgulu's murders?"

"All things can be turned to advantage," the big, purple-skinned barghest replied wickedly, "even the appearance of a dark elf." Ulgulu turned back to Tephanis.

"You-wish-to-learn-more-of-the-drow, my-master," Tephanis spouted excitedly.

"Is he alone?" Ulgulu asked. "Is he a forward scout to a larger group, as we fear, or a lone warrior? What are his intentions toward the townspeople?"

"He-could-have-killed-the-children," Tephanis reiterated. "I-guess-him-to-desire-friendship."

"I know," Ulgulu snarled. "You have made those points before. Go now and learn more! I need more than your guess, Tephanis, and by all accounts, a drow's actions rarely hint at his true intent!"

Tephanis skipped down from Ulgulu's shoulder and paused, expecting further instructions.

"Indeed, dear Tephanis," Ulgulu purred. "Do see if you can appropriate one of the drow's weapons for me. It would prove usef—" Ulgulu stopped when he noticed the flutter in the heavy curtain blocking the entry room.

"An excitable little sprite," Kempfana noted.

"But with his uses," Ulgulu replied, and Kempfana had to nod in agreement.

⚔ ⚔ ⚔ ⚔ ⚔

Drizzt saw them coming from a mile away. Ten armed farmers followed the young man he had met in the blueberry patch on the previous day. Though they talked and joked, the set of their stride was determined and their weapons were prominently displayed, obviously ready to be put to use. Even more insidious, walking to the side of the main band came a barrel-chested, grim-faced man wrapped in thick skins, brandishing a finely crafted axe and leading two large and snarling yellow dogs on thick chains.

Drizzt wanted to make further contact with the villagers, wanted dearly to continue the events he had set in motion the previous day and learn if he might have, at long last, found a place he could call home, but this coming encounter, he realized, was not the place to make such gains. If the farmers found him, there would surely be trouble, and while Drizzt wasn't too worried for his own safety against the ragged band even considering the grim-faced fighter, he did fear that one of the farmers might get hurt.

Drizzt decided that his mission this day was to avoid the group and to deflect their curiosity. The drow knew the perfect diversion to accomplish those goals. He set the onyx figurine on the ground before him and called to Guenhwyvar.

A buzzing noise off to the side, followed by the sudden rustle of brush, distracted the drow for just a moment as the customary mist swirled around the figurine. Drizzt saw nothing ominous approaching, though, and quickly dismissed it. He had more pressing problems, he thought.

When Guenhwyvar arrived, Drizzt and the cat moved down the trail beyond the blueberry patch, where Drizzt guessed that the farmers would begin their hunt. His plan was simple: He would let the farmers mill about the area for a while, let the farmer's son retell his story of the encounter. Guenhwyvar then would make an appearance along the edge of the patch and lead the group on a futile chase. The black-furred panther might cast some doubts on the farm boy's tale; possibly the older men would assume that the children had encountered the cat and not a dark elf and that their imaginations had supplied the rest of the details. It was a gamble, Drizzt knew, but at the very least, Guenhwyvar would cast some doubts about the existence of the dark elf and would get this hunting party away from Drizzt for a while.

The farmers arrived at the blueberry patch on schedule, a few grim-faced and battle-ready but the majority of the group talking casually in conversations filled with laughter. They found the discarded sword, and Drizzt watched, nodding his head, as the farmer's son played through the events of the previous day. Drizzt noticed, too, that the large axe-wielder, listening to the story halfheartedly, circled the group with his dogs, pointing at various spots in the patch and coaxing the dogs to sniff about. Drizzt had no practical experience with dogs, but he knew that many creatures had superior senses and could be used to aid in a hunt.

"Go, Guenhwyvar," the drow whispered, not waiting for the dogs to get a clear scent.

The great panther loped silently down the trail and took up a position in one of the trees in the same grove where the boys had hidden the previous day. Guenhwyvar's sudden roar silenced the group's growing conversation in an instant, all heads spinning to the trees.

The panther leaped out into the patch, shot right past the stunned humans, and darted across the rising rocks of the mountain slopes. The farmers hooted and took up pursuit, calling for the man with the dogs to take the lead. Soon the whole group, dogs baying wildly, moved off and Drizzt went down into the grove near the blueberry patch to consider the day's events and his best course of action.

He thought that a buzzing noise followed him, but he passed it off as the hum of an insect.

⚔ ⚔ ⚔ ⚔ ⚔

By his dogs' confused actions, it didn't take Roddy McGristle long to figure out that the panther was not the same creature that had left the scent in the blueberry patch. Furthermore, Roddy realized that his ragged companions, particularly the obese mayor, even with his aid, had little chance of catching the great cat; the panther could spring across ravines that would take the farmers many minutes to circumvent.

"Go on!" Roddy told the rest of the group. "Chase the thing along this course. I'll take my dogs'n go far to the side and cut the thing off, turn it back to ye!" The farmers hooted their accord and bounded away, and Roddy pulled back the chains and turned his dogs aside.

The dogs, trained for the hunt, wanted to go on, but their master had another route in mind. Several thoughts bothered Roddy at that moment. He had been in these mountains for thirty years but had never seen, or even heard of, such a cat. Also, though the panther easily could have left its pursuers far behind, it always seemed to appear out in the open not too far away, as though it was leading the farmers on. Roddy knew a diversion when he saw it, and he had a good guess of where the perpetrator might be hiding. He muzzled the dogs to keep them silent and headed back the way he had come, back to the blueberry patch.

⚔⚔⚔⚔⚔

Drizzt rested against a tree in the shadows of the thick copse and wondered how he might further his exposure to the farmers without causing any more panic among them. In his days of watching the single farm family, Drizzt had become convinced that he could find a place among the humans, of this or of some other settlement, if only he could convince them that his intentions were not dangerous.

A buzz to Drizzt's left brought him abruptly from his contemplations. Quickly he drew his scimitars, then something flashed by him, too fast for him to react. He cried out at a sudden pain in his wrist, and his scimitar was pulled from his grasp. Confused, Drizzt looked down to his wound, expecting to see an arrow or crossbow bolt stuck deep into his arm.

The wound was clean and empty. A high-pitched laughter spun Drizzt to the right. There stood the sprite, Drizzt's scimitar casually slung over one shoulder, nearly touching the ground behind the diminutive creature, and a dagger, dripping blood, in his other hand.

Drizzt stayed very still, trying to guess the thing's next move. He had never seen a quickling, or even heard of the uncommon creatures, but he already had a good idea of his speedy opponent's advantage. Before the drow could form any plan to defeat the quickling, though, another nemesis showed itself.

Drizzt knew as soon as he heard the howl that his cry of pain had revealed him. The first of Roddy McGristle's snarling hounds crashed through the brush, charging in low at the drow. The second, a few running strides behind the first, came in high, leaping toward Drizzt's throat.

This time, though, Drizzt was the quicker. He slashed down with his remaining scimitar, cutting the first dog's head and bashing its skull. Without hesitation, Drizzt threw himself backward, reversing his grip on the blade and bringing it up above his face, in line with the leaping dog. The scimitar's hilt locked fast against the tree trunk, and the dog, unable to turn in its flight, drove hard into the set weapon's other end, impaling itself through the throat and chest. The wrenching impact tore the scimitar from Drizzt's hand and dog and blade bounced away into some scrub to the side of the tree.

Drizzt had barely recovered when Roddy McGristle burst in.

"Ye killed my dogs!" the huge mountain man roared, chopping Bleeder, his large, battle-worn axe, down at the drow's head. The cut came deceptively swiftly, but Drizzt managed to dodge to the side. The drow couldn't understand a word of McGristle's continuing stream of expletives, and he knew that the burly man would not understand a word of any explanations Drizzt might try to offer.

Wounded and unarmed, Drizzt's only defense was to continue to dodge away. Another swipe nearly caught him, cutting through his gnoll cloak, but he sucked in his stomach, and the axe skipped off his fine chain mail. Drizzt danced to the side, toward a tight cluster of smaller trees, where he believed his greater agility might give him some advantage. He had to try to tire the enraged human, or at least make the man reconsider his brutal attack. McGristle's ire did not lessen, though. He charged right after Drizzt, snarling and swinging with every step.

Drizzt now saw the shortcomings of his plan. While he might keep away from the large human's bulky body in the tightly packed trees, McGristle's axe could dive between them quite deftly.

The mighty weapon came in from the side at shoulder level. Drizzt dropped flat down on the ground desperately, narrowly avoiding death. McGristle couldn't slow his swing in time, and the heavy—and heavily ensorceled—weapon smashed into the four-inch trunk of a young maple, felling the tree.

The tightening angle of the buckling trunk held Roddy's axe fast. Roddy grunted and tried to tear the weapon free, and did not realize his peril until the last minute. He managed to jump away from the main weight of the trunk but was buried under the maple's canopy. Branches ripped across his face and the side of his head forming a web around him and pinning him tightly to the ground. "Damn ye, drow!" McGristle roared, shaking futilely at his natural prison.

Drizzt crawled away, still clutching his wounded wrist. He found his remaining scimitar, buried to the hilt in the unfortunate dog. The sight pained Drizzt; he knew the value of animal companions. It took him several heartsick moments to pull the blade free, moments made even more dramatic by the other dog, which, merely stunned, was beginning to stir once again.

"Damn ye, drow!" McGristle roared again.

Drizzt understood the reference to his heritage, and he could guess the rest. He wanted to help the fallen man, thinking that he might make some inroads on opening some more civilized communication, but he didn't think that the awakening dog would be so ready to lend a paw. With a final glance around for the sprite that had started this whole thing, Drizzt dragged himself out of the grove and fled into the mountains.

⚔ ⚔ ⚔ ⚔ ⚔

"We should've got the thing!" Bartholemew Thistledown grumbled as the troupe returned to the blueberry patch. "If McGristle had come in where he said he would, we'd've gotten the cat for sure! Where is that dog pack leader, anyhow?"

An ensuing roar of "Drow! Drow!" from the maple grove answered Bartholemew's question. The farmers rushed over to find Roddy still helplessly pinned by the felled maple tree.

"Damned drow!" Roddy bellowed. "Killed my dog! Damned drow!" He reached for his left ear when his arm was free but found that the ear was no longer attached. "Damned drow!" he roared again.

Connor Thistledown let everyone see the return of his pride at the confirmation of his oft-doubted tale, but the eldest Thistledown child was the only one pleased at Roddy's unexpected proclamation. The other farmers were older than Connor; they realized the grim implications of having a dark elf haunting the region.

Benson Delmo, wiping sweat from his forehead, made little secret of how he stood on the news. He turned immediately to the farmer by his side, a younger man known for his prowess in raising and riding horses. "Get to Sundabar," the mayor ordered. "Find us a ranger straightaway!"

In a few minutes, Roddy was pulled free. By this time, his wounded dog had rejoined him, but the knowledge that one of his prized pets had survived did little to calm the rough man.

"Damned drow!" Roddy roared for perhaps the thousandth time, wiping the blood from his cheek. "I'm gonna get me a damned drow!" He emphasized his point by slamming Bleeder, one-handed, into the trunk of another nearby maple, nearly felling that one as well.

# 5 The Stalk of Doom

The goblin guards dived to the side as mighty Ulgulu tore through the curtain and exited the cave complex. The open, crisp air of the chill mountain night felt good to the barghest, better still when Ulgulu thought of the task before him. He looked to the scimitar that Tephanis had delivered, the crafted weapon appearing tiny in Ulgulu's huge, dark-skinned hand.

Ulgulu unconsciously dropped the weapon to the ground. He didn't want to use it this night; the barghest wanted to put his own deadly weapons—claws and teeth—to use, to taste his victims and devour their life essence so that he could become stronger. Ulgulu was an intelligent creature, though, and his rationale quickly overruled the base instincts that so desired the taste of blood. There was purpose in this night's work, a method that promised greater gains and the elimination of the very real threat that the dark elf's unexpected appearance posed.

With a guttural snarl, a small protest from Ulgulu's base urges, the barghest grabbed the scimitar again and pounded down the mountainside, covering long distances with each stride. The beast stopped on the edge of a ravine, where a single narrow trail wound down along the sheer facing of the cliff. It would take him many minutes to scale down the dangerous trail.

But Ulgulu was hungry.

Ulgulu's consciousness fell back into itself, focusing on that spot of his being that fluctuated with magical energy. He was not a creature of the Material Plane, and extra-planar creatures inevitably brought with them powers that would seem magical to creatures of the host plane. Ulgulu's eyes glowed orange with excitement when he emerged from his trance just a few moments later. He peered down the cliff, visualizing a spot on the flat ground below, perhaps a quarter of a mile away.

A shimmering, multicolored door appeared before Ulgulu, hanging in the air beyond the lip of the ravine. His laughter sounding more like a roar, Ulgulu pushed open the door and found, just beyond its threshold, the spot he had visualized. He moved through, circumventing the material distance to the ravine's floor with a single extradimensional step.

Ulgulu ran on, down the mountain and toward the human village, ran on eagerly to set the gears of his cruel plan turning.

As the barghest approached the lowest mountain slopes, he again found that magical corner of his mind. Ulgulu's strides slowed, then the creature stopped altogether, jerking spasmodically and gurgling indecipherably. Bones ground together with popping noises, skin ripped and reformed, darkening nearly to black.

When Ulgulu started away again, his strides—the strides of a dark elf—were not so long.

⚔ ⚔ ⚔ ⚔ ⚔

Bartholemew Thistledown sat with his father, Markhe, and his oldest son that evening in the kitchen of the lone farmhouse on the western outskirts of Maldobar. Bartholemew's wife and mother had gone out to the barn to settle the animals for the night, and the four youngest children were safely tucked into their beds in the small room off the kitchen.

On a normal night the rest of the Thistledown family, all three generations, would also be snugly snoring in their beds, but Bartholemew feared that many nights would pass before any semblance of normalcy returned to the quiet farm. A dark elf had been spotted in the area, and while Bartholemew wasn't convinced that this stranger meant harm—

the drow easily could have killed Connor and the other children—he knew that the drow's appearance would cause a stir in Maldobar for quite some time.

"We could get back to the town proper," Connor offered. "They'd find us a place, and all of Maldobar'd stand behind us then."

"Stand behind us?" Bartholemew responded with sarcasm. "And would they be leaving their farms each day to come out here and help us keep up with our work? Which of them, do ye think, might ride out here each night to tend to the animals?"

Connor's head drooped at his father's berating. He slipped one hand to the hilt of his sword, reminding himself that he was no child. Still, Connor was silently grateful for the supporting hand his grandfather casually dropped on his shoulder.

"Ye've got to think, boy, before ye make such calls," Bartholemew continued, his tone mellowing as he began to realize the profound effect his harsh words had on his son. "The farm's yer lifeblood, the only thing that matters."

"We could send the little ones," Markhe put in. "The boy's got a right to be fearing, with a dark elf about and all."

Bartholemew turned away and resignedly dropped his chin into his palm. He hated the thought of breaking apart the family. Family was their source of strength, as it had been through five generations of Thistledowns and beyond. Yet, here Bartholemew was berating Connor, even though the boy had spoken only for the good of the family.

"I should have thought better, Dad," he heard Connor whisper, and he knew that his own pride could not hold out against the realization of Connor's pain. "I am sorry."

"Ye needn't be," Bartholemew replied, turning back to the others. "I'm the one should apologize. All of us got our neck hairs up with this dark elf about. Ye're right in yer thinking, Connor. We're too far out here to be safe."

As if in answer came a sharp crack of breaking wood and a muffled cry from outside the house, from the direction of the barn. In that single horrible moment, Bartholemew Thistledown realized that he should have come to his decision earlier, when the revealing light of day still offered his family some measure of protection.

Connor reacted first, running to the door and throwing it open. The farmyard was deathly quiet; not the chirp of a cricket disturbed the surrealistic scene. A silent moon loomed low in the sky, throwing long and devious shadows from every fence post and tree. Connor watched, not daring to breathe, through the passing of a second that seemed like an hour.

The barn door creaked and toppled from its hinges. A dark elf walked out into the farmyard.

Connor shut the door and fell back against it, needing its tangible support. "Ma," he breathed to the startled faces of his father and grandfather. "Drow."

The older Thistledown men hesitated, their minds whirling through the tumult of a thousand horrible notions. They simultaneously leaped from their seats, Bartholemew going for a weapon and Markhe moving toward Connor and the door.

Their sudden action freed Connor from his paralysis. He pulled the sword from his belt and swung the door open, meaning to rush out and face the intruder.

A single spring of his powerful legs had brought Ulgulu right up to the farmhouse door. Connor charged over the threshold blindly, slammed into the creature—which only appeared like a slender drow—and bounced back, stunned, into the kitchen. Before any of the men could react, the scimitar slammed down onto the top of Connor's head with all the strength of the barghest behind it, nearly splitting the young man in half.

Ulgulu stepped unhindered into the kitchen. He saw the old man—the lesser remaining enemy—reaching out for him, and called upon his magical nature to defeat the attack. A wave of imparted emotion swept over Markhe Thistledown, a wave of despair and terror so great that he could not combat it. His wrinkled mouth shot open in a silent scream and he staggered backward, crashing into a wall and clutching helplessly at his chest.

Bartholemew Thistledown's charge carried the weight of unbridled rage behind it. The farmer growled and gasped unintelligible sounds as he lowered his pitchfork and bore down on the intruder that had murdered his son.

The slender, assumed frame that held the barghest did not diminish Ulgulu's gigantic strength. As the pitchfork's tips closed the last inches to the creature's chest, Ulgulu slapped a single hand on the weapon's shaft. Bartholemew stopped in his tracks, the butt end of the pitchfork driving hard into his belly, blowing away his breath.

Ulgulu raised his arm quickly, lifting Bartholemew clear off the floor and slamming the farmer's head into a ceiling beam with enough force to break his neck. The barghest casually tossed Bartholemew and his pitiful weapon across the kitchen and stalked over to the old man.

Perhaps Markhe saw him coming; perhaps the old man was too torn by pain and anguish to register any events in the room. Ulgulu moved to him and opened his mouth wide. He wanted to devour the old man, to feast on this one's life force as he had with the younger woman out in the barn. Ulgulu had lamented his actions in the barn as soon as the ecstacy of the kill had faded. Again the barghest's rationale displaced his base urges. With a frustrated snarl, Ulgulu drove the scimitar into Markhe's chest, ending the old man's pain.

Ulgulu looked around at his gruesome work, lamenting that he had not feasted on the strong young farmers but reminding himself of the greater gains his actions this night would yield. A confused cry led him to the side room, where the children slept.

⚔ ⚔ ⚔ ⚔ ⚔

Drizzt came down from the mountains tentatively the next day. His wrist, where the sprite had stabbed him, throbbed, but the wound was clean and Drizzt was confident that it would heal. He crouched in the brush on the hillside behind the Thistledown farm, ready to try another meeting with the children. Drizzt had seen too much of the human community, and had spent too much time alone, to give up. This was where he intended to make his home if he could get beyond the obvious prejudicial barriers, personified most keenly by the large man with the snarling dogs.

From this angle, Drizzt couldn't see the blasted barn door, and all appeared as it should on the farm in the predawn glow.

The farmers did not come out with the sun, however, and always before they had been out no later than its arrival. A rooster crowed and several animals shuffled around the barnyard, but the house remained silent. Drizzt knew this was unusual, but he figured that the encounter in the mountains on the previous day had sent the farmers into hiding. Possibly the family had left the farm altogether, seeking the shelter of the larger cluster of houses in the village proper. The thoughts weighed heavily on Drizzt; again he had disrupted the lives of those around him simply by showing his face. He remembered Blingdenstone, the city of svirfneblin gnomes, and the tumult and potential danger his appearance had brought to them.

The sunny day brightened, but a chill breeze blew down off the mountains. Still not a person stirred in the farmyard or within the house, as far as Drizzt could tell. The drow watched it all, growing more concerned with each passing second.

A familiar buzzing noise shook Drizzt from his contemplations. He drew his lone scimitar and glanced around. He wished he could call Guenhwyvar, but not enough time had passed since the cat's last visit. The panther needed to rest in its astral home for another day before it would be strong enough to walk beside Drizzt. Seeing nothing in his immediate area, Drizzt moved between the trunks of two large trees, a more defensible position against the sprite's blinding speed.

The buzzing was gone an instant later, and the sprite was nowhere to be seen. Drizzt spent the rest of that day moving about the brush, setting trip wires and digging shallow pits. If he and the sprite were to battle again, the drow was determined to change the outcome.

The lengthening shadows and crimson western sky brought Drizzt's attention back to the Thistledown farm. No candles were lighted within the farmhouse to defeat the deepening gloom.

Drizzt grew ever more concerned. The return of the nasty sprite had poignantly reminded him of the dangers in the region, and with the continuing inactivity in the farmyard, a fear budded within him, took root, and quickly grew into a sense of dread.

Twilight darkened into night. The moon rose and climbed steadily into the eastern sky.

Still not a candle burned in the house, and not a sound came through the darkened windows.

Drizzt slipped out of the brush and darted across the short back field. He had no intentions of getting close to the house; he just wanted to see what he might learn. Perhaps the horses and the farmer's small wagon would be gone, lending evidence to Drizzt's earlier suspicion that the farmers had taken refuge in the village.

When he came around the side of the barn and saw the broken door, Drizzt knew instinctively that this was not the case. His fears grew with every step. He peered through the barn door and was not surprised to see the wagon sitting in the middle of the barn and the stalls full of horses.

To the side of the wagon, though, lay the older woman, crumbled and covered in her own dried blood. Drizzt went to her and knew at once that she was dead, killed by some sharp-edged weapon. Immediately his thoughts went to the evil sprite and his own missing scimitar. When he found the other corpse, behind the wagon, he knew that some other monster, something more vicious and powerful, had been involved. Drizzt couldn't even identify this second, half-eaten body.

Drizzt ran from the barn to the farmhouse, throwing out all caution. He found the bodies of the Thistledown men in the kitchen and to his ultimate horror, the children lying too still in their beds. Waves of revulsion and guilt rolled over the drow when he looked upon the young bodies. The word "drizzit" chimed painfully in his mind at the sight of the sandy-haired lad.

The tumult of Drizzt's emotions were too much for him. He covered his ears against that damning word, "drizzit!" but it echoed endlessly, haunting him, reminding him.

Unable to find his breath, Drizzt ran from the house. If he had searched the room more carefully, he would have found, under the bed, his missing scimitar, snapped in half and left for the villagers.

# Part Two

# The Ranger

Does anything in all the world force a heavier weight upon one's shoulders than guilt? I have felt the burden often, have carried it over many steps, on long roads.

Guilt resembles a sword with two edges. On the one hand it cuts for justice, imposing practical morality upon those who fear it. Guilt, the consequence of conscience, is what separates the goodly persons from the evil. Given a situation that promises gain, most drow can kill another, kin or otherwise, and walk away carrying no emotional burden at all. The drow assassin might fear retribution but will shed no tears for his victim.

To humans—and to surface elves, and to all of the other goodly races—the suffering imposed by conscience will usually far outweigh any external threats. Some would conclude that guilt—conscience—is the primary difference between the varied races of the Realms. In this regard, guilt must be considered a positive force.

But there is another side to that weighted emotion. Conscience does not always adhere to rational judgment. Guilt is always a self-imposed burden, but is not always rightly imposed. So it was for me along the road from Menzoberranzan to Icewind Dale. I carried out of Menzoberranzan guilt for Zaknafein, my father, sacrificed on my behalf. I carried into Blingdenstone guilt for Belwar Dissengulp, the svirfneblin my brother had maimed. Along the many roads there came many other burdens: Clacker, killed by the monster that hunted for me; the gnolls, slain by my own hand; and the farmers—most painfully—that simple farm family murdered by the barghest whelp.

Rationally I knew that I was not to blame, that the actions were beyond my influence, or in some cases, as with the gnolls, that I had acted properly. But rationale is little defense against the weight of guilt.

In time, bolstered by the confidence of trusted friends, I came to throw off many of those burdens. Others remain and always shall. I accept this as inevitable, and use the weight to guide my future steps.

This, I believe, is the true purpose of conscience.

—Drizzt Do'Urden

# 6
# Sundabar

Oh, enough, Fret," the tall woman said to the white-robed, white-bearded dwarf, batting his hands away. She ran her fingers through her thick, brown hair, messing it considerably.

"Tsk, tsk," the dwarf replied, immediately moving his hands back to the dirty spot on the woman's cloak. He brushed frantically, but the ranger's continual shifting kept him from accomplishing much. "Why, Mistress Falconhand I do believe that you would do well to consult a few books on proper behavior."

"I just rode in from Silverymoon," Dove Falconhand replied indignantly, tossing a wink to Gabriel, the other fighter in the room, a tall and stern-faced man. "One tends to collect some dirt on the road."

"Nearly a tenday ago!" the dwarf protested. "You attended the banquet last night in this very cloak!" The dwarf then noticed that in his fuss over Dove's cloak he had smudged his silken robes, and that catastrophe turned his attention from the ranger.

"Dear Fret," Dove went on, licking a finger and casually rubbing it over the spot on her cloak, "you are the most unusual of attendants."

The dwarf's face went beet red, and he stamped a shiny slipper on the tiled floor. "Attendant?" he huffed. "I should say . . ."

"Then do!" Dove laughed.

"I am the most—one of the most—accomplished sages in the north! My thesis concerning the proper etiquette of racial banquets—"

"Or lack of proper etiquette—" Gabriel couldn't help but interrupt. The dwarf turned on him sourly—"at least where dwarves are concerned," the tall fighter finished with an innocent shrug.

The dwarf trembled visibly and his slippers played a respectable beat on the hard floor.

"Oh, dear Fret," Dove offered, dropping a comforting hand on the dwarf's shoulder and running it along the length of his perfectly trimmed, yellow beard.

"Fred!" the dwarf retorted sharply, pushing the ranger's hand away. "Fredegar!"

Dove and Gabriel looked at each other for one brief, knowing moment, then cried out the dwarf's surname in an explosion of laughter. "Rockcrusher!"

"Fredegar Quilldipper would be more to the point!" Gabriel added. One look at the fuming dwarf told the man that the time had passed for leaving, so he scooped up his pack and darted from the room, pausing only to slip one final wink Dove's way.

"I only desired to help." The dwarf dropped his hands into impossibly deep pockets and his head drooped low.

"So you have!" Dove cried to comfort him.

"I mean, you do have an audience with Helm Dwarf-friend," Fret went on, regaining some pride. "One should be proper when seeing the Master of Sundabar."

"Indeed one should," Dove readily agreed. "Yet all I have to wear you see before you, dear Fret, stained and dirtied from the road. I am afraid that I shall not cut a very fine figure in the eyes of Sundabar's master. He and my sister have become such friends." It was Dove's turn to feign a vulnerable pout, and though her sword had turned many a giant into vulture food, the strong ranger could play this game better than most.

"Whatever shall I do?" She cocked her head curiously as she glanced at the dwarf. "Perhaps," she teased. "If only . . ."

Fret's face began to brighten at the hint.

"No," Dove said with a heavy sigh. "I could never impose so upon you."

Fret verily bounced with glee, clapping his thick hands together. "Indeed you could, Mistress Falconhand! Indeed you could!"

Dove bit her lip to forestall any further demeaning laughter as the excited dwarf skipped out of the room. While she often teased Fret, Dove would readily admit that she loved the little dwarf. Fret had spent many years in Silverymoon, where Dove's sister ruled, and had made many contributions to the famed library there. Fret really was a noted sage, known for his extensive research into the customs of various races, both good and evil, and he was an expert on issues demihuman. He also was a fine composer. How many times, Dove wondered with sincere humility, had she ridden along a mountain trail, whistling a cheery melody composed by this very same dwarf?

"Dear Fret," the ranger whispered under her breath when the dwarf returned, a silken gown draped over one arm—but carefully folded so that it would not drag across the floor!—assorted jewelry and a pair of stylish shoes in his other hand a dozen pins sticking out from between his pursed lips, and a measuring string looped over one ear. Dove hid her smile and decided to give the dwarf this one battle. She would tiptoe into Helm Dwarf-friend's audience hall in a silken gown, the picture of Ladydom, with the diminutive sage huffing proudly by her side.

All the while, Dove knew, the shoes would pinch and bite at her feet and the gown would find some place to itch where she could not reach. Alas for the duties of station, Dove thought as she stared at the gown and accessories. She looked into Fret's beaming face then and realized that it was worth all the trouble.

Alas for the duties of friendship, she mused.

⚔ ⚔ ⚔ ⚔ ⚔

The farmer had ridden straight through for more than a day; the sighting of a dark elf often had such effects on simple villagers. He had taken two horses out of Maldobar; one he had left a score of miles behind, halfway between the two towns. If he was lucky, he'd find the animal unharmed on the return trip. The second horse, the farmer's prized stallion, was beginning to tire. Still the farmer bent low in the saddle, spurring the steed on. The torches of Sundabar's night watch, high up on the city's thick stone walls, were in sight.

"Stop and speak your name!" came the formal cry from the captain of the gate guards when the rider approached, half an hour later.

⚔ ⚔ ⚔ ⚔ ⚔

Dove leaned on Fret for support as they followed Helm's attendant down the long and decorated corridor to the audience room. The ranger could cross a rope bridge without handrails, could fire her bow with deadly accuracy atop a charging steed, could scramble up a tree in full chain armor, sword and shield in hand. But she could not, for all of her experience and agility, manage the fancy shoes that Fret had squeezed her feet into.

"And this gown," Dove whispered in exasperation, knowing that the impractical garment would split in six or seven places if she had occasion to swing her sword while wearing it, let alone inhaled too abruptly.

Fret looked up at her, wounded.

"This gown is surely the most beautiful . . ." Dove stuttered, careful not to send the tidy dwarf into a tantrum. "Truly I can find no words suitable to my gratitude, dear Fret."

The dwarf's gray eyes shone brightly, though he wasn't sure that he believed a word of it. Either way, Fret figured that Dove cared enough about him to go along with his suggestions, and that fact was all that really mattered to him.

"I beg a thousand pardons, my lady," came a voice from behind. The whole entourage turned to see the captain of the night watch, a farmer by his side, trotting down the somber hallway.

"Good captain!" Fret protested at the violation of protocol. "If you desire an audience with the lady, you must make an introduction in the hall. Then, and only then, and only if the master allows, you may . . ."

Dove dropped a hand on the dwarf's shoulder to silence him. She recognized the urgency etched onto the men's faces, a look the adventuring heroine had seen many times. "Do go on, Captain," she prompted. To placate Fret, she added, "We have a few moments before our audience is set to begin. Master Helm will not be kept waiting."

The farmer stepped forward boldly. "A thousand pardons for myself, my lady," he began, fingering his cap nervously in his hands. "I am but a farmer from Maldobar, a small village north . . ."

"I know of Maldobar," Dove assured him. "Many times I have viewed the place from the mountains. A fine and sturdy community." The farmer brightened at her description. "No harm has befallen Maldobar, I pray."

"Not as yet, my lady," the farmer replied, "but we've sighted trouble, we're not to doubting." He paused and looked to the captain for support. "Drow."

Dove's eyes widened at the news. Even Fret, tapping his foot impatiently throughout the conversation, stopped and took note.

"How many?" Dove asked.

"Only one, as we have seen. We're fearing he's a scout or spy, and up to no good."

Dove nodded her agreement. "Who has seen the drow?"

"Children first," the farmer replied, drawing a sigh from Fret and setting the dwarf's foot impatiently tapping once again.

"Children?" the dwarf huffed.

The farmer's determination did not waver. "Then McGristle saw him," he said, eyeing Dove directly, "and McGristle's seen a lot!"

"What is a McGristle?" Fret huffed.

"Roddy McGristle," Dove answered, somewhat sourly, before the farmer could explain. "A noted bounty hunter and fur trapper."

"The drow killed one of Roddy's dogs," the farmer put in excitedly, "and nearly cut down Roddy! Dropped a tree right on him! He's lost an ear for the experience."

Dove didn't quite understand what the farmer was talking about, but she really didn't need to. A dark elf had been seen and confirmed in the region, and that fact alone set the ranger into motion. She flipped off her fancy shoes and handed them to Fret, then told one of the attendants to go straight off and find her traveling companions and told the other to deliver her regrets to the Master of Sundabar.

"But Lady Falconhand!" Fret cried.

"No time for pleasantries," Dove replied, and Fret could tell by her obvious excitement that she was not too disappointed at canceling her audience with Helm. Already she was wiggling about, trying to open the catch on the back of her magnificent gown.

"Your sister will not be pleased," Fret growled loudly over the tapping of his boot.

"My sister hung up her backpack long ago," Dove retorted, "but mine still wears the fresh dirt of the road!"

"Indeed," the dwarf mumbled, not in a complimentary way.

"Ye mean to come, then?" the farmer asked hopefully.

"Of course," Dove replied. "No reputable ranger could ignore the sighting of a dark elf! My three companions and I will set out for Maldobar this very night, though I beg that you remain here, good farmer. You have ridden hard—it is obvious—and need sleep." Dove glanced around curiously for a moment, then put a finger to her pursed lips.

"What?" the annoyed dwarf asked her.

Dove's face brightened as her gaze dropped down to Fret. "I have little experience with dark elves," she began, "and my companions, to my knowledge, have never dealt with one." Her widening smile set Fret back on his heels.

"Come, dear Fret," Dove purred at the dwarf. Her bare feet slapping conspicuously on the tiled floor, she led Fret, the captain, and the farmer from Maldobar down the hallway to Helm's audience room.

Fret was confused—and hopeful—for a moment by Dove's sudden change of direction. As soon as Dove began talking to Helm, Fret's master, apologizing for the unexpected inconvenience and asking Helm to send along one who might aid in the mission to Maldobar, the dwarf began to understand.

⚔ ⚔ ⚔ ⚔ ⚔

By the time the sun found its way above the eastern horizon the next morning, Dove's party, which included an elf archer and two powerful human fighters, had ridden more than ten miles from Sundabar's heavy gate.

"Ugh!" Fret groaned when the light increased. He rode a sturdy Adbar pony at Dove's side. "See how the mud has soiled my fine clothes! Surely it will be the end of us all! To die filthy on a gods-forsaken road!"

"Pen a song about it," Dove suggested, returning the widening smiles of her other three companions. "The Ballad of the Five Choked Adventurers, it shall be named."

Fret's angry glare lasted only the moment it took Dove to remind him that Helm Dwarf-friend, the Master of Sundabar himself, had commissioned Fret to travel along.

# 7
# Simmering Rage

On the same morning that Dove's party left on the road to Maldobar, Drizzt set out on a journey of his own. The initial horror of his gruesome discovery the previous night had not diminished, and the drow feared that it never would, but another emotion had also entered Drizzt's thinking. He could do nothing for the innocent farmers and their children, nothing except avenge their deaths. That thought was not so pleasing to Drizzt; he had left the Underdark behind, and the savagery as well, he had hoped. With the images of the carnage still so horribly clear in his mind, and all alone as he was, Drizzt could look only to his scimitar for justice.

Drizzt took two precautions before he set out on the murderer's trail. First, he crept back down to the farmyard, to the back of the house, where the farmers had placed a broken plowshare. The metal blade was heavy, but the determined drow hoisted it and carried it away without a thought to the discomfort.

Drizzt then called Guenhwyvar. As soon as the panther arrived and took note of Drizzt's scowl, it dropped into an alert crouch. Guenhwyvar had been around Drizzt long enough to recognize that expression and to believe that they would see battle before it returned to its astral home.

They moved off before dawn, Guenhwyvar easily following the barghest's clear trail, as Ulgulu had hoped. Their pace was slow, with Drizzt hindered by the plowshare, but steady, and as soon as Drizzt caught the sound of a distant buzzing noise, he knew he had done right in collecting the cumbersome item.

Still, the remainder of the morning passed without incident. The trail led the companions into a rocky ravine and to the base of a high, uneven cliff. Drizzt feared that he might have to scale the cliff face—and leave the plowshare behind—but soon he spotted a single narrow trail winding up along the wall. The ascending path remained smooth as it wound around sheer bends in the cliff face, blind and dangerous turns. Wanting to use the terrain to his advantage, Drizzt sent Guenhwyvar far ahead and moved along by himself, dragging the plowshare and feeling vulnerable on the open cliff.

That feeling did nothing to quench the simmering fires in Drizzt's lavender eyes, though, which burned clearly from under the low-pulled cowl of his oversized gnoll cloak. If the sight of the ravine looming just to the side unnerved the drow, he needed only to remember the farmers. A short while later, when Drizzt heard the expected buzzing noise from somewhere lower on the narrow trail, he only smiled.

The buzz quickly closed from behind. Drizzt fell back against the cliff wall and snapped out his scimitar, carefully monitoring the time it took the sprite to close.

Tephanis flashed beside the drow, the quickling's little dagger darting and prodding for an opening in the defensive twists of the waving scimitar. The sprite was gone in an instant, moving up ahead of Drizzt, but Tephanis had scored a hit, nicking Drizzt on one shoulder.

Drizzt inspected the wound and nodded gravely, accepting it as a minor inconvenience. He knew he could not defeat the blinding attack, and he knew, too, that allowing this first strike had been necessary for his ultimate victory. A growl on the path up ahead put Drizzt quickly back on alert. Guenhwyvar had met the sprite, and the panther, with flashing paws that could match the quickling's speed, no doubt had turned the thing back around.

Again Drizzt put his back to the wall, monitoring the buzzing approach. Just as the sprite came around the corner, Drizzt jumped out onto the narrow path, his scimitar at the ready. The drow's other hand was less conspicuous and held steady a metal object, ready to tilt it out to block the opening.

The speeding sprite cut back in toward the wall, easily able, as Drizzt realized, to avoid the scimitar. But in his narrow focus on his target, the sprite failed to notice Drizzt's other hand.

Drizzt hardly registered the sprite's movements, but the sudden "Bong!" and the sharp vibrations in his hand as the creature smacked into the plowshare brought a satisfied grin to his lips. He let the plowshare drop and scooped up the unconscious sprite by the throat, holding it clear of the ground. Guenhwyvar bounded around the bend about the same time the sprite shook the dizziness from his sharp-featured head, his long and pointed ears nearly flopping right over the other side of his head with each movement.

"What creature are you?" Drizzt asked in the goblin tongue, the language that had worked for him with the gnoll band. To his surprise, he found that the sprite understood, though his high-pitched, blurred response came too quickly for Drizzt to even begin to understand.

He gave the sprite a quick jerk to silence him, then growled, "One word at a time! What is your name?"

"Tephanis," the sprite said indignantly. Tephanis could move his legs a hundred times a second, but they didn't do him much good while he was suspended in the air. The sprite glanced down to the narrow ledge and saw his small dagger lying next to the dented plowshare.

Drizzt's scimitar moved in dangerously. "Did you kill the farmers?" he asked bluntly. He almost struck in response to the sprite's ensuing chuckle.

"No," Tephanis said quickly.

"Who did?"

"Ulgulu!" the sprite proclaimed. Tephanis pointed up the path and blurted out a stream of excited words. Drizzt managed to make out a few, "Ulgulu . . . waiting . . . dinner," being the most disturbing of them.

Drizzt really didn't know what he would do with the captured sprite. Tephanis was simply too fast for Drizzt to safely handle. He looked to

Guenhwyvar, sitting casually a few feet up the path, but the panther only yawned and stretched.

Drizzt was about to come back with another question, to try to figure out where Tephanis fit into the whole scenario, but the cocky sprite decided that he had suffered enough of the encounter. His hands moving too fast for Drizzt to react, Tephanis reached down into his boot, produced another knife, and slashed at Drizzt's already injured wrist.

This time, the cocky sprite had underestimated his opponent. Drizzt could not match the sprite's speed, could not even follow the tiny, darting dagger. As painful as the wounds were, though, Drizzt was too filled with rage to take note. He only tightened his grip on the sprite's collar and thrust his scimitar ahead. Even with such limited mobility, Tephanis was quick enough and nimble enough to dodge, laughing wildly all the while.

The sprite struck back, digging a deeper cut into Drizzt's forearm. Finally Drizzt chose a tactic that Tephanis could not counter, one that took the sprite's advantage away. He slammed Tephanis into the wall, then tossed the stunned creature off the cliff.

⚔ ⚔ ⚔ ⚔ ⚔

Some time later, Drizzt and Guenhwyvar crouched in the brush at the base of a steep, rocky slope. At the top, behind carefully placed bushes and branches, lay a cave, and every so often, goblin voices rolled out.

Beside the cave, to the side of the sloping ground was a steep drop. Beyond the cave, the mountain climbed on at an even greater angle. The tracks, though they were sometimes scarce on the bare stone, had led Drizzt and Guenhwyvar to this spot; there could be no doubt that the monster who slaughtered the farmers was in the cave.

Drizzt again fought with his decision to avenge the farmers' deaths. He would have preferred a more civilized justice, a lawful court, but what was he to do? He certainly could not go to the human villagers with his suspicions, nor to anyone else. Crouching in the bush, Drizzt thought again of the farmers, of the sandy-haired boy, of the pretty girl, barely a woman, and of the young man he had disarmed in the blueberry patch. Drizzt fought hard to keep his breathing steady. In the wild Underdark he had sometimes given in to his instinctive urges, a darker side of himself that fought with brutal and deadly efficiency, and Drizzt could feel that alter-ego welling within him once again. At first, he tried to sublimate the rage, but then he remembered the lessons he had learned. This darker side was a part of him, a tool for survival, and was not altogether evil.

It was necessary.

Drizzt understood his disadvantage in the situation, however. He had no idea how many enemies he would encounter, or even what type of monsters they might be. He heard goblins, but the carnage at the farmhouse indicated that something much more powerful was involved. Drizzt's good judgment told him to sit and watch, to learn more of his enemies.

Another fleeting instant of remembrance, the scene at the farmhouse, threw that good judgment aside. Scimitar in one hand the sprite's dagger in another, Drizzt stalked up the stony hill. He didn't slow when he neared the cave, but merely ripped the brush aside and walked straight in.

Guenhwyvar hesitated and watched from behind, confused by the drow's straightforward tactics.

⚔ ⚔ ⚔ ⚔ ⚔

Tephanis felt cool air brushing by his face and thought for a moment that he was enjoying some pleasant dream. The sprite came out of his delusion quickly, though, and realized that he was fast approaching the ground. Fortunately, Tephanis was not far from the cliff. He sent his hands and feet spinning rapidly enough to produce a constant humming sound and clawed and kicked at the cliff in an effort to slow his descent. In the meantime, he began the incantations to a levitation spell, possibly the only thing that could save him.

A few agonizingly slow seconds passed before the sprite felt his body buoyed by the spell. He still hit the ground hard, but he realized that his wounds were minor.

Tephanis stood relatively slowly and dusted himself off. His first thought was to go and warn Ulgulu of the approaching drow, but he reconsidered at once. He could not levitate up to the cave complex in time to warn the barghest, and there was only one path up the cliff face—which the drow was on.

Tephanis had no desire to face that one again.

⚔ ⚔ ⚔ ⚔ ⚔

Ulgulu had not tried to cover his tracks at all. The dark elf had served the barghest's needs; now he planned to make a meal of Drizzt, one that might bring him into maturity and allow him to return to Gehenna.

Ulgulu's two goblin guards were not too surprised at Drizzt's entrance. Ulgulu had told them to expect the drow and to simply delay him out in the entry room until the barghest could come and attend to him. The goblins halted their conversation abruptly, dropped their spears in a blocking cross over the curtain, and puffed out their scrawny chests, foolishly following their boss's instructions as Drizzt approached.

"None can go in—" one of them began, but then, in a single swipe of Drizzt's scimitar, both the goblin and its companion staggered down, clutching at their opened throats. The spear barrier fell away and Drizzt never even slowed as he stalked through the curtain.

In the middle of the inner room, the drow saw his enemy. Scarlet-skinned and giant-sized, the barghest waited with crossed arms and a wicked, confident grin.

Drizzt threw the dagger and charged right in behind it. That throw saved the drow's life, for when the dagger passed harmlessly through his enemy's body, Drizzt recognized the trap. He came in anyway, unable to break his momentum, and his scimitar entered the image without finding anything tangible to cut into.

The real barghest was behind the stone throne at the back of the room. Using another power of his considerable magical repertoire, Kempfana had sent an image of himself into the middle of the room to hold the drow in place.

Immediately Drizzt's instincts told him that he had been set up. This was no real monster he faced but an apparition meant to keep him in the open and vulnerable. The room was sparsely furnished; nothing nearby offered any cover.

Ulgulu, levitating above the drow, came down quickly, lighting softly behind him. The plan was perfect and the target was right in place.

Drizzt, his reflexes and muscles trained and honed to fighting perfection, sensed the presence and dived forward into the image as Ulgulu launched a heavy blow. The barghest's huge hand only clipped Drizzt's flowing hair, but that alone nearly ripped the drow's head to the side.

Drizzt half-turned his body as he dived, rolling back to his feet facing Ulgulu. He met a monster even larger than the giant image, but that fact did nothing to intimidate the enraged drow. Like a stretched cord, Drizzt snapped straight back at the barghest. By the time Ulgulu even recovered from his unexpected miss, Drizzt's lone scimitar had poked him three times in the belly and had dug a neat little hole under his chin.

The barghest roared in rage but was not too badly hurt, for Drizzt's drow-made weapon had lost most of its magic in the drow's time on the surface and only magical weapons—such as Guenhwyvar's claws and teeth—could truly harm a creature from Gehenna's rifts.

The huge panther slammed onto the back of Ulgulu's head with enough force to drop the barghest facedown on the floor. Never had Ulgulu felt such pain as Guenhwyvar's claws raked across his head.

Drizzt moved to join in, when he heard a shuffle from the back of the room. Kempfana came charging out from behind the throne, bellowing in protest.

It was Drizzt's turn to utilize some magic. He threw a globe of darkness in the scarlet-skinned barghest's path, then dived into it himself, crouching on his hands and knees. Unable to slow, Kempfana roared in, stumbled over the braced drow—kicking Drizzt with enough force to blast the air from his lungs—and fell heavily out the other side of the darkness.

Kempfana shook his head to clear it and planted his huge hands to rise. Drizzt was on the barghest's back in no time, hacking away wildly with his vicious scimitar. Blood matted Kempfana's hair by the time he was able to brace himself enough to throw the drow off. He staggered to his feet dizzily and turned to face the drow.

Across the room, Ulgulu crawled and tumbled, rolled and twisted. The panther was too quick and too sleek for the giant's lumbering counters. A dozen gashes scarred Ulgulu's face and now Guenhwyvar had its teeth clamped on the back of the giant's neck and all four paws raking at the giant's back.

Ulgulu had another option, though. Bones crackled and reformed. Ulgulu's scarred face became an elongated snout filled with wicked canine teeth. Thick hair sprouted from all over the giant, fending off Guenhwyvar's claw attacks. Flailing arms became kicking paws.

Guenhwyvar battled a gigantic wolf, and the panther's advantage was short-lived.

Kempfana stalked in slowly, showing Drizzt new respect.

"You killed them all," Drizzt said in the goblin tongue, his voice so utterly cold that it stopped the scarlet-skinned barghest in his tracks.

Kempfana was not a stupid creature. The barghest recognized the explosive rage in this drow and had felt the sharp bite of the scimitar. Kempfana knew better than to walk straight in, so again he called upon his otherworldly skills. In the blink of an orange-burning eye, the scarlet-skinned barghest was gone, stepping through an extradimensional door and reappearing right behind Drizzt.

As soon as Kempfana disappeared, Drizzt instinctively broke to the side. The blow from behind came quicker, though, landing squarely on Drizzt's back and launching him across the room. Drizzt crashed into the base of one wall and came up into a kneel, gasping for his breath.

Kempfana did stalk straight in this time; the drow had dropped his scimitar halfway to the wall, too far away for Drizzt to grasp.

The great barghest-wolf, nearly twice Guenhwyvar's size, rolled over and straddled the panther. Great jaws snapped near Guenhwyvar's throat and face, the panther batting wildly to hold them at bay. Guenhwyvar could not hope to win an even fight against the wolf. The only advantage the panther retained was mobility. Like a black-shafted arrow, Guenhwyvar darted out from under the wolf and toward the curtain.

Ulgulu howled and gave chase, ripping the curtain down and charging on, toward the waning daylight.

Guenhwyvar came out of the cave as Ulgulu tore through the curtain, pivoted instantly, and leaped straight up to the slopes above the entrance. When the great wolf came out, the panther again crashed down on Ulgulu's back and resumed its raking and slashing.

⚔ ⚔ ⚔ ⚔ ⚔

"Ulgulu killed the farmers, not I," Kempfana growled as he approached. He kicked Drizzt's scimitar across to the other side of the room. "Ulgulu wants you—you who killed his gnolls. But I shall kill you, drow warrior. I shall feast on your life force so that I may gain in strength!"

Drizzt, still trying to find his breath, hardly heard the words. The only thoughts that occurred to him were the images of the dead farmers, images that gave Drizzt courage. The barghest drew near and Drizzt snapped a vile gaze upon him, a determined gaze not lessened in the least by the drow's obviously desperate situation.

Kempfana hesitated at the sight of those narrowed, burning eyes, and the barghest's delay brought Drizzt all the time he needed. He had fought giant monsters before, most notably hook horrors. Always Drizzt's scimitars had ended those battles, but for his initial strikes, he had, every time, used only his own body. The pain in his back was no match for his mounting rage. He rushed out from the wall, remaining in a crouch, and dived through Kempfana's legs, spinning and catching a hold behind the barghest's knee.

Kempfana, unconcerned, lurched down to grab the squirming drow. Drizzt eluded the giant's grasp long enough to find some leverage. Still,

Kempfana accepted the attacks as a mere inconvenience. When Drizzt put the barghest off balance, Kempfana willingly toppled, meaning to crush the wiry little elf. Again Drizzt was too quick for the barghest. He twisted out from under the falling giant, put his feet back under him, and sprinted for the opposite end of the chamber.

"No, you shall not!" Kempfana bellowed, crawling then running in pursuit. Just as Drizzt scooped up his scimitar, giant arms wrapped around him and easily lifted him off the ground.

"Crush you and bite you!" Kempfana roared, and indeed, Drizzt heard one of his ribs crack. He tried to wiggle around to face his foe, then gave up on the notion, concentrating instead on freeing his sword arm.

Another rib snapped; Kempfana's huge arms tightened. The barghest did not want to simply kill the drow, though, realizing the great gains toward maturity he could make by devouring so powerful an enemy, by feeding on Drizzt's life force.

"Bite you, drow." The giant laughed. "Feast!"

Drizzt grasped his scimitar in both hands with strength inspired by the images of the farmhouse. He tore the weapon loose and snapped it straight back over his head. The blade entered Kempfana's open, eager mouth and dived down the monster's throat.

Drizzt twisted it and turned it.

Kempfana whipped about wildly and Drizzt's muscles and joints nearly ripped apart under the strain. The drow had found his focus, though, the scimitar hilt, and he continued to twist and turn.

Kempfana went down heavily, gurgling, and rolled onto Drizzt, trying to squash the life out of him. Pain began to seep into Drizzt's consciousness.

"No!" he cried, grabbing at the image of the sandy-haired boy, slain in his bed. Still Drizzt twisted and turned the blade. The gurgling continued, a wheezing sound of air rising through choking blood. Drizzt knew that this battle was won when the creature above him no longer moved.

Drizzt wanted only to curl up and find his breath but told himself that he was not yet finished. He crawled out from under Kempfana, wiped the blood, his own blood, from his lips, unceremoniously ripped his scimitar free of Kempfana's mouth, and retrieved his dagger.

He knew that his wounds were serious, could prove fatal if he didn't attend to them immediately. His breath continued to come in forced, bloodied gasps. It didn't concern him, though, for Ulgulu, the monster who had killed the farmers, still lived.

⚔ ⚔ ⚔ ⚔ ⚔

Guenhwyvar sprang from the giant wolf's back, again finding a tenuous footing on the steep slope above the cave entrance. Ulgulu spun, snarling, and leaped up at the panther, clawing and raking at the stones in an effort to get higher.

Guenhwyvar leaped out over the barghest-wolf, pivoted immediately, and slashed at Ulgulu's backside. The wolf spun but Guenhwyvar leaped by, again to the slope.

The game of hit-and-run went on for several moments, Guenhwyvar striking, then darting away. Finally, though, the wolf anticipated the panther's dodge. Ulgulu brought the leaping panther down in his massive jaws. Guenhwyvar squirmed and tore free, but came up near the steep gorge. Ulgulu hovered over the cat, blocking any escape.

Drizzt exited the cave as the great wolf bore down, pushing Guenhwyvar back. Pebbles rolled out into the gorge; the panther's back legs slipped and clawed back, trying to find a hold. Even mighty Guenhwyvar could not hold out against the weight and strength of the barghest-wolf, Drizzt knew.

Drizzt saw immediately that he could not get the great wolf off Guenhwyvar in time. He pulled out the onyx figurine and tossed it near the combatants. "Be gone, Guenhwyvar!" he commanded.

Guenhwyvar normally would not desert its master in a time of such danger, but the panther understood what Drizzt had in mind. Ulgulu bore in powerfully, determinedly driving Guenhwyvar from the ledge.

Then the beast was pushing only intangible vapors. Ulgulu lurched forward and scrambled wildly, kicking more stones and the onyx figurine into the gorge. Overbalanced, the wolf could not find a hold, and Ulgulu was falling.

Bones popped again, and the canine fur thinned; Ulgulu could not enact a levitation spell in his canine form. Desperate, the barghest concentrated, reaching for his goblinoid form. The wolf maw shortened into a flat-featured face; paws thickened and reformed into arms.

The half-transformed creature didn't make it, but instead cracked into the stone.

Drizzt stepped off the ledge and into a levitation spell, moving down slowly and close to the rocky wall. As it had before, the spell soon died away. Drizzt bounced and clawed through the last twenty feet of the fall, coming to a hard stop at the rocky bottom. He saw the barghest twitching only a few feet away and tried to rise in defense, but darkness overwhelmed him.

⚔ ⚔ ⚔ ⚔ ⚔

Drizzt could not know how many hours had passed when a thunderous roar awakened him some time later. It was dark now and a cloudy night. Slowly the memories of the encounter came back to the dazed and injured drow. To his relief, he saw that Ulgulu lay still on the stone beside him, half a goblin and half a wolf, obviously quite dead.

A second roar, back up by the cave, turned the drow toward the ledge high above him. There stood Lagerbottoms, the hill giant, returned from a hunting trip and outraged by the carnage he had found.

Drizzt knew as soon as he managed to crawl to his feet that he could not fight another battle this day. He searched around for a moment, found the onyx figurine, and dropped it into his pouch. He wasn't too concerned for Guenhwyvar. He had seen the panther through worse calamities—caught in the explosion of a magical wand pulled into the Plane of Earth by an enraged elemental, even dropped into a lake of hissing acid. The figurine appeared undamaged, and Drizzt was certain that Guenhwyvar was now comfortably at rest in its astral home.

Drizzt, however, could afford no such rest. Already the giant had begun picking its way down the rocky slope. With a final look to Ulgulu, Drizzt felt a sense of vengeance that did little to defeat the agonizing, bitter memories of the slaughtered farmers. He set off, moving farther into the wild mountains, running from the giant and from the guilt.

# 8

# Clues and Riddles

More than a day had passed since the massacre when the first of the Thistledowns' neighbors rode out to their secluded farm. The stench of death alerted the visiting farmer to the carnage even before he looked in the house or barn.

He returned an hour later with Mayor Delmo and several other armed farmers at his side. They crawled through the Thistledown house and across the grounds cautiously, putting cloth over their faces to combat the terrible smell.

"Who could have done this?" the mayor demanded. "What monster?" As if in answer, one of the farmers walked out of the bedroom and into the kitchen, holding a broken scimitar in his hands.

"A drow weapon?" the farmer asked. "We should be getting McGristle."

Delmo hesitated. He expected the party from Sundabar to arrive any day and felt that the famed ranger Dove Falconhand would be better able to handle the situation than the volatile and uncontrollable mountain man.

The debate never really began, though, for the snarl of a dog alerted all in the house that McGristle had arrived. The burly, dirty man stalked into the kitchen, the side of his face horribly scarred and caked with brown, dried blood.

"Drow weapon!" he spat, recognizing the scimitar all too clearly. "Same as he used agin me!"

"The ranger will be in soon," Delmo began, but McGristle hardly listened. He stalked about the room and into the adjoining bedroom, gruffly tapping bodies with his foot and bending low to inspect some minor details.

"Saw the tracks outside," McGristle stated suddenly. "Two sets, I make 'em."

"The drow has an ally," the mayor reasoned. "More cause for us to wait for the party from Sundabar."

"Bah, ye hardly know if they're even comin'!" McGristle snorted. "Got to get after the drow now, while the trail's fine for my dog's nose!"

Several of the gathered farmers nodded their accord—until Delmo prudently reminded them of exactly what they might be facing.

"A single drow took you down, McGristle," the mayor said. "Now you think there's two of them, maybe more, and you want us to go and hunt them?"

"Bad fortune, it was, that took me down!" Roddy snapped back. He looked around, appealing to the now less-than-eager farmers. "I had that drow, had him cleaned an' dressed!"

The farmers milled nervously and whispered to each other as the mayor took Roddy by the arm and led him to the side of the room.

"Wait a day," Delmo begged. "Our chances will be much greater if the ranger comes."

Roddy didn't seem convinced. "My battle's my own to fight," he snarled. "He killed my dog an' left me ugly."

"You want him, and you'll have him," the mayor promised, "but there might be more on the table here than your dog or your pride."

Roddy's face contorted ominously, but the mayor was adamant. If a drow war party was indeed operating in the area, all of Maldobar was in imminent danger. The small group's greatest defense until help could arrive from Sundabar was unity, and that defense would fail if Roddy led a group of men—fighters who were scarce enough already—on a chase through the mountains. Benson Delmo was astute enough to know that he could not appeal to Roddy on those terms, though. While the mountain man had remained in Maldobar for a couple of years, he was, in essence, a drifter and owed no allegiance to the town.

Roddy turned away, deciding that the meeting was at its end, but the mayor boldly grabbed his arm and turned him back around. Roddy's dog bared its teeth and growled, but that threat was a small consideration to the fat man in light of the awful scowl that Roddy shot him.

"You'll have the drow," the mayor said quickly, "but wait for the help from Sundabar, I beg." He switched to terms that Roddy could truly appreciate. "I am a man of no small means, McGristle, and you were a bounty hunter before you got here, and still are, I'd expect."

Roddy's expression quickly changed from outrage to curiosity.

"Wait for the help, then go get the drow." The mayor paused, considering his forthcoming offer. He really had no experience in this sort of thing and while he didn't want to come in too low and spoil the interest he had sparked, he didn't want to tax his own purse strings any more than was necessary. "A thousand gold for the drow's head."

Roddy had played this pricing game many times. He hid his delight well; the mayor's offer was five times his normal fee and he would have gone after the drow in any case, with or without payment.

"Two thousand!" the mountain man grumbled without missing a beat, suspecting that more could be exacted for his troubles. The mayor rocked back on his heels but reminded himself several times that the town's very existence might be at stake.

"And not a copper less!" Roddy added, crossing his burly arms over his chest.

"Wait for Mistress Falconhand" Delmo said meekly, "and you shall have your two thousand."

⚔ ⚔ ⚔ ⚔ ⚔

All through the night, Lagerbottoms followed the wounded drow's trail. The bulky hill giant was not yet certain how it felt about the death of Ulgulu and Kempfana, the unasked for masters who had taken over his lair and his life. While Lagerbottoms feared any enemy who could defeat those two, the giant knew that the drow was sorely wounded.

Drizzt realized he was being followed but could do little to hide his tracks. One leg, injured in his bouncing descent into the ravine, dragged painfully and Drizzt had all he could do to keep ahead of the giant. When dawn came, bright and clear, Drizzt knew that his disadvantage had increased. He could not hope to escape the hill giant through the long and revealing light of day.

The trail dipped into a small grouping of variously sized trees, sprouting up wherever they could find cracks between the numerous boulders. Drizzt meant to go straight through—he saw no option other than continuing his flight—but while he leaned on one of the larger trees for support to catch his breath, a thought came to him. The tree's branches hung limply, supple and cordlike.

Drizzt glanced back along the trail. Higher up and crossing a bare expanse of rock, the relentless hill giant plodded along. Drizzt drew his scimitar with the one arm that still seemed to work and hacked down the longest branch he could find. Then he looked for a suitable boulder.

The giant crashed into the copse about a half-hour later, its huge club swinging at the end of one massive arm. Lagerbottoms stopped abruptly when the drow appeared from behind a tree, blocking the path.

Drizzt nearly sighed aloud when the giant stopped, exactly at the appointed area. He had feared that the huge monster would just continue on and swat him down, for Drizzt, injured as he was, could have offered little resistance. Seizing the moment of the monster's hesitation, Drizzt shouted "Halt!" in the goblin language and enacted a simple spell, limning the giant in blue-glowing, harmless flames.

Lagerbottoms shifted uncomfortably but made no advance toward this strange and dangerous enemy. Drizzt eyed the giant's shuffling feet with more than a casual interest.

"Why do you follow me?" Drizzt demanded. "Do you desire to join the others in the sleep of death?"

Lagerbottoms ran his plump tongue over dry lips. So far, this encounter hadn't gone as expected. Now the giant thought past those first instinctual urges that had led him out here and tried to consider the options. Ulgulu and Kempfana were dead; Lagerbottoms had his cave back. But the gnolls and goblins, too, were gone, and that pesky little quickling sprite hadn't been around for a while. A sudden thought came to the giant.

"Friends?" Lagerbottoms asked hopefully.

Though he was relieved to find that combat might be avoided, Drizzt was more than a little skeptical at the offer. The gnoll band had given him a similar offer, to disastrous ends, and this giant was obviously connected to those other monsters that Drizzt had just killed, those who had slaughtered the farm family.

"Friends to what end?" Drizzt asked tentatively, hoping against all reason that he might find this creature to be motivated by some principles, and not just by blood lust.

"To kill," Lagerbottoms replied, as though the answer had been obvious.

Drizzt snarled and jerked his head about in angry denial, his white mane flying wildly. He snapped the scimitar out of its sheath, hardly caring if the giant's foot had found the loop of his snare.

"Kill you!" Lagerbottoms cried, seeing the sudden turn, and the giant lifted his club and took a huge stride forward, a stride shortened by the vinelike branch pulling tightly around his ankle.

Drizzt checked his desire to rush in, reminding himself that the trap had been set into motion, and reminding himself, too, that in his present condition he would be hard put to survive against the formidable giant.

Lagerbottoms looked down at the noose and roared in outrage. The branch wasn't really a proper cord and the noose wasn't so tight. If Lagerbottoms had simply reached down, the giant easily could have slipped the noose off his foot. Hill giants, however, were never known for their intelligence.

"Kill you!" the giant cried again, and it kicked hard against the strain of the branch. Propelled by the considerable force of the kick, the large rock tied to the branch's other end, behind the giant, pelted forward through the underbrush and sailed into Lagerbottoms's back.

Lagerbottoms had started to cry out a third time, but the menacing threat came out as a *whoosh!* of forced air. The heavy club dropped to the ground and the giant, clutching its kidney area, dropped to one knee.

Drizzt hesitated a moment, not knowing whether to run or finish the kill. He didn't fear for himself; the giant would not be coming after him anytime soon, but he could not forget the lurid expression on the giant's face when the monster had said that they might kill together.

"How many other families will you slaughter?" Drizzt asked in the drow tongue.

Lagerbottoms could not begin to understand the language. He just grunted and snarled through the burning pain.

"How many?" Drizzt asked again, his hand wrenching over the scimitar's pommel and his eyes narrowing menacingly.

He came in fast and hard.

⚔ ⚔ ⚔ ⚔ ⚔

To Benson Delmo's absolute relief, the party from Sundabar—Dove Falconhand her three fighting companions, and Fret, the dwarven sage—came in later that day. The mayor offered the troupe food and rest, but as soon as Dove heard of the massacre at the Thistledown farm, she and her companions set straight out, with the mayor, Roddy McGristle, and several curious farmers close behind.

Dove was openly disappointed when they arrived at the secluded farm. A hundred sets of tracks obscured critical clues, and many of the items in the house, even the bodies, had been handled and moved. Still, Dove and her seasoned company moved about methodically, trying to decipher what they could of the gruesome scene.

"Foolish people!" Fret scolded the farmers when Dove and the others had completed their investigation. "You have aided our enemies!"

Several of the farmer-folk, even the mayor, looked around uncomfortably at the berating, but Roddy snarled and towered over the tidy dwarf. Dove quickly interceded.

"Your earlier presence here has marred some of the clues," Dove explained calmly, disarmingly, to the mayor as she prudently stepped between Fret and the burly mountain man. Dove had heard many tales of McGristle before, and his reputation was not one of predictability or calm.

"We didn't know," the mayor tried to explain.

"Of course not," Dove replied. "You reacted as anyone would have."

"Any novice," Fret remarked.

"Shut yer mouth!" McGristle growled, and so did his dog.

"Be at ease, good sir," Dove bade him. "We have too many enemies beyond the town to need some within."

"Novice?" McGristle barked at her. "I've hunted down a hundred men, an' I know enough o' this damned drow to find him."

"Do we know it was the drow?" Dove asked, genuinely doubting.

On a nod from Roddy, a farmer standing on the side of the room produced the broken scimitar.

"Drow weapon," Roddy said harshly, pointing to his scarred face. "I seen it up close!"

One look at the mountain man's jagged wound told Dove that the fine-edged scimitar had not caused it, but the ranger conceded the point, seeing no gain in further argument.

"And drow tracks," Roddy insisted. "The boot prints match close to the ones by the blueberry patch, where we seen the drow!"

Dove's gaze led all eyes to the barn. "Something powerful broke that door," she reasoned. "And the younger woman inside was not killed by any dark elf."

Roddy remained undaunted. "Drow's got a pet," he insisted. "Big, black panther. Damned big cat!"

Dove remained suspicious. She had seen no prints to match a panther's paws, and the way that a portion of the woman had been devoured, bones and all, did not fit any knowledge that she had of great cats. She kept her thoughts to herself, though, realizing that the gruff mountain man wanted no mysteries clouding his already-drawn conclusions.

"Now, if ye've had enough o' this place, let's get onto the trail," Roddy boomed. "My dog's got a scent, and the drow's got a lead big enough already!"

Dove flashed a concerned glance at the mayor, who turned away, embarrassed, under her penetrating gaze.

"Roddy McGristle's to go with you," Delmo explained, barely able to spit out the words, wishing that he had not made his emotionally inspired deal with Roddy. Seeing the cool-headedness of the woman ranger and her party, so drastically different from Roddy's violent temper, the mayor now thought it better that Dove and her companions handle the situation in their own way. But a deal was a deal.

"He'll be the only one from Maldobar joining your troupe," Delmo continued. "He is a seasoned hunter and knows this area better than any."

Again Dove, to Fret's disbelief, conceded the point.

"The day is fast on the wane," Dove said. She added pointedly to McGristle, "We go at first light."

"Drow's got too much of a lead already!" Roddy protested. "We should get after him now!"

"You assume that the drow is running," Dove replied, again calmly, but this time with a stern edge to her voice. "How many dead men once assumed the same of enemies?" This time, Roddy, perplexed, did not shout back. "The drow, or drow band could be holed up nearby. Would you like to come upon them unexpectedly, McGristle? Would it please you to battle dark elves in the dark of night?"

Roddy just threw up his hands, growled, and stalked away, his dog close on his heels.

The mayor offered Dove and her troupe lodging at his own house, but the ranger and her companions preferred to remain behind at the Thistledown farm. Dove smiled as the farmers departed, and Roddy set up camp just a short distance away, obviously to keep an eye on her. She wondered just how much a stake McGristle had in all of this and suspected that there was more to it than revenge for a scarred face and a lost ear.

"Are you really to let that beastly man come with us?" Fret asked later on, as the dwarf, Dove, and Gabriel sat around the blazing fire in the farmyard. The elven archer and the other member of the troupe were out on perimeter guard.

"It is their town, dear Fret," Dove explained. "And I cannot refute McGristle's knowledge of the region."

"But he is so dirty," the dwarf grumbled. Dove and Gabriel exchanged smiles, and Fret, realizing that he would get nowhere with his argument, turned down his bedroll and slipped in, purposefully spinning away from the others.

"Good old Quilldipper," mumbled Gabriel, but he noted that Dove's ensuing smile did little to diminish the sincere concern on her face.

"You've a problem, Lady Falconhand?" he asked.

Dove shrugged. "Some things do not fit properly in the order of things here," she began.

" 'Twas no panther that killed the woman in the barn," Gabriel remarked, for he, too, had noted some discrepancies.

"Nor did any drow kill the farmer, the one they named Bartholemew, in the kitchen," said Dove. "The beam that broke his neck was nearly snapped itself. Only a giant possesses such strength."

"Magic?" Gabriel asked.

Again Dove shrugged. "Drow magic is usually more subtle, according to our sage," she said, looking to Fret, who was already snoring quite loudly. "And more complete. Fret does not believe that drow magic killed Bartholemew or the woman, or destroyed the barn door. And there is another mystery on the matter of the tracks."

"Two sets," Gabriel said, "and made nearly a day apart."

"And of differing depths," added Dove. "One set, the second, might indeed have been those of a dark elf, but the other, the set of the killer, went too deep for an elf's light steps."

"An agent of the drow?" Gabriel offered. "Conjured denizen of the lower planes, perhaps? Might it be that the dark elf came down the next day to inspect its monster's work?" This time, Gabriel joined Dove in her confused shrug.

"So we shall learn," Dove said. Gabriel lit a pipe then, and Dove drifted off into slumber.

* * * * *

"Oh-master, my-master," Tephanis crooned, seeing the grotesque form of the broken, half-transformed barghest. The quickling didn't really care all that much for Ulgulu or the barghest's brother, but their deaths left some severe implications for the sprite's future path. Tephanis had joined Ulgulu's group for mutual gain. Before the barghests came along, the little sprite had spent his days in solitude, stealing whenever he could from nearby villages. He had done all right for himself, but his life had been a lonely and unexciting existence.

Ulgulu had changed all of that. The barghest army offered protection and companionship, and Ulgulu, always scheming for new and more devious kills, had provided Tephanis with unending important missions.

Now the quickling had to walk away from it all, for Ulgulu was dead and Kempfana was dead, and nothing Tephanis could do would change those simple facts.

"Lagerbottoms?" the quickling asked himself suddenly. He thought that the hill giant, the only member missing from the lair, might prove a fine companion. Tephanis saw the giant's tracks clearly enough, heading away from the cave area and out into the deeper mountains. He clapped his hands excitedly, perhaps a hundred times in the next second, then was off, speeding away to find a new friend.

⚔ ⚔ ⚔ ⚔ ⚔

Far up in the mountains, Drizzt Do'Urden looked upon the lights of Maldobar for the last time. Since he had come down from the high peaks after his unpleasant encounter with the skunk, the drow had found a world of savagery nearly equal to the dark realm he had left behind. Whatever hopes Drizzt had realized in his days watching the farming family were lost to him now, buried under the weight of guilt and the awful images of carnage that he knew would haunt him forever.

The drow's physical pain had lessened a bit; he could draw his breath fully now, though the effort sorely stung, and the cuts on his arms and legs had closed. He would survive.

Looking down at Maldobar, another place that he could never call home, Drizzt wondered if that might be a good thing.

# 9 The Chase

"What is it?" Fret asked, cautiously moving behind the folds of Dove's forest-green cape.

Dove, and even Roddy, also moved tentatively, for while the creature seemed dead, they had never seen anything quite like it. It appeared to be some strange, giant-sized mutation between a goblin and a wolf.

They gained in courage as they neared the body, convinced that it was truly dead. Dove bent low and tapped it with her sword.

"It has been dead for more than a day, by my guess," she announced.

"But what is it?" Fret asked again.

"Half-breed," Roddy muttered.

Dove closely inspected the creature's strange joints. She noted, too, the many wounds inflicted upon the thing—tearing wounds, like those caused by the scratching of a great cat.

"Shape-changer," guessed Gabriel, keeping watch at the side of the rocky area.

Dove nodded. "Killed halfway through."

"I never heared of any goblin wizards," Roddy protested.

"Oh, yes," Fret began, smoothing the sleeves of his soft-clothed tunic. "There was, of course, Grubby the Wiseless, pretended archmage, who . . ."

A whistle from high above stopped the dwarf. Up on the ledge stood

Kellindil, the elven archer, waving his arms about. "More up here," the elf called when he had their attention. "Two goblins and a red-skinned giant, the likes of which I have never seen!"

Dove scanned the cliff. She figured that she could scale it, but one look at poor Fret told her that they would have to go back to the trail, a journey of more than a mile. "You remain here," she said to Gabriel. The stern-faced man nodded and moved off to a defensive position among some boulders, while Dove, Roddy, and Fret headed back along the ravine.

Halfway up the single winding path that moved along the cliff, they met Darda, the remaining fighter of the troupe. A short and heavily muscled man, he scratched his stubbly beard and examined what looked to be a plowshare.

"That's Thistledown's!" Roddy cried. "I seen it out back of his farm, set for fixing!"

"Why is it up here?" Dove asked.

"And why might it be bloodied?" added Darda, showing them the stains on the concave side. The fighter looked over the ledge into the ravine, then back to the plowshare. "Some unfortunate creature hit this hard," Darda mused, "then probably went into the ravine."

All eyes focused on Dove as the ranger pulled her thick hair back from her face, put her chin in her delicate but calloused hand and tried to sort through this newest puzzle. The clues were too few, though, and a moment later, Dove threw her hands up in exasperation and headed off along the trail. The path wound in and left the cliff as it leveled near the top, but Dove walked back over to the edge, right above where they had left Gabriel. The fighter spotted her immediately and his wave told the ranger that all was calm below.

"Come," Kellindil bade them, and he led the group into the cave. Some answers came clear to Dove as soon as she glanced upon the carnage in the inner room.

"Barghest whelp!" exclaimed Fret, looking upon the scarlet-skinned, giant corpse.

"Barghest?" Roddy asked, perplexed.

"Of course," piped in Fret. "That does explain the wolf-giant in the gorge."

"Caught in the change," Darda reasoned. "Its many wounds and the stone floor took it before it could complete the transition."

"Barghest?" Roddy asked again, this time angrily, not appreciating being left out of a discussion he could not understand.

"A creature from another plane of existence," Fret explained. "Gehenna, it is rumored. Barghests send their whelps to other planes, sometimes to our own, to feed and to grow." He paused a moment in thought. "To feed," he said again, his tone leading the others.

"The woman in the barn!" Dove said evenly.

The members of Dove's troupe nodded their heads at the sudden revelation, but grim-faced McGristle held stubbornly to his original theory. "Drow killed 'em!" he growled.

"Have you the broken scimitar?" Dove asked. Roddy produced the weapon from beneath one of the many folds in his layered skin garments.

Dove took the weapon and bent low to examine the dead barghest. The blade unmistakably matched the beast's wounds, especially the fatal wound in the barghest's throat.

"You said that the drow wielded two of these," Dove remarked to Roddy as she held up the scimitar.

"The mayor said that," Roddy corrected, "on account of the story Thistledown's son told. When I seen the drow—" he took back the weapon—"he had just the one—the one he used to kill the Thistledown clan!" Roddy purposely didn't mention that the drow, while wielding just the one weapon, had scabbards for two scimitars on his belt.

Dove shook her head, doubting the theory. "The drow killed this barghest," she said. "The wounds match the blade, the sister blade to the one you hold, I would guess. And if you check the goblins in the front room, you will find that their throats were slashed by a similar curving scimitar."

"Like the wounds on the Thistledowns!" Roddy snarled.

Dove thought it best to keep her budding hypothesis quiet, but Fret, disliking the big man, echoed the thoughts of all but McGristle. "Killed by the barghest," the dwarf proclaimed, remembering the two sets of footprints at the farmyard. "In the form of the drow!"

Roddy glowered at him and Dove cast Fret a leading look, wanting the dwarf to remain silent. Fret misinterpreted the ranger's stare, though, thinking it astonishment of his reasoning power, and he proudly continued. "That explains the two sets of tracks, the heavier, earlier set for the bar—"

"But what of the creature in the gorge?" Darda asked Dove, understanding his leader's desire to shut Fret up. "Might its wounds, too, match the curving blade?"

Dove thought for a moment and managed to subtly nod her thanks to Darda. "Some, perhaps," she answered. "More likely, that barghest was killed by the panther—" she looked directly at Roddy—"the cat you claimed the drow kept as a pet."

Roddy kicked the dead barghest. "Drow killed the Thistledown clan!" he growled. Roddy had lost a dog and an ear to the dark elf and would not accept any conclusions that lessened his chances of claiming the two thousand gold piece bounty that the mayor had levied.

A call from outside the cave ended the debate—both Dove and Roddy were glad of that. After leading the troupe into the lair, Kellindil had returned outside, following up on some further clues he had discovered.

"A boot print," the elf explained, pointing to a small, mossy patch, when the others came out. "And here," he showed them scratches in the stone, a clear sign of a scuffle.

"My belief is that the drow went to the ledge," Kellindil explained. "And over, perhaps in pursuit of the barghest and the panther, though on that point I am merely assuming."

After a moment of following the trail Kellindil had reconstructed, Dove and Darda, and even Roddy, agreed with the assumption.

"We should go back into the ravine," Dove suggested. "Perhaps we will find a trail beyond the stony gorge that will lead us toward some clearer answers."

Roddy scratched at the scabs on his head and flashed Dove a disdainful look that showed her his emotions. Roddy cared not a bit for any of the ranger's promised "clearer answers," having drawn all of the conclusions that he needed long ago. Roddy was determined—beyond anything else, Dove knew—to bring back the dark elf's head.

Dove Falconhand was not so certain about the murderer's identity.

Many questions remained for both the ranger and for the other members of her troupe. Why hadn't the drow killed the Thistledown children when they had met earlier in the mountains? If Connor's tale to the mayor had been true, then why had the drow given the boy back his weapon? Dove was firmly convinced that the barghest, and not the drow, had slaughtered the Thistledown family, but why had the drow apparently gone after the barghest lair?

Was the drow in league with the barghests, a communion that fast soured? Even more intriguing to the ranger—whose very creed was to protect civilians in the unending war between the good races and monsters—had the drow sought out the barghest to avenge the slaughter at the farm? Dove suspected the latter was the truth, but she couldn't understand the drow's motives. Had the barghest, in killing the family, put the farmers of Maldobar on alert, thereby ruining a planned drow raid?

Again the pieces didn't fit properly. If the dark elves planned a raid on Maldobar, then certainly none of them would have revealed themselves beforehand. Something inside Dove told her that this single drow had acted alone, had come out and avenged the slain farmers. She shrugged it off as a trick of her own optimism and reminded herself that dark elves were rarely known for such rangerlike acts.

By the time the five got down the narrow path and returned to the sight of the largest corpse, Gabriel had already found the trail, heading deeper into the mountains. Two sets of tracks were evident, the drow's and fresher ones belonging to a giant, bipedal creature, possibly a third barghest.

"What happened to the panther?" Fret asked, growing a bit overwhelmed by his first field expedition in many years.

Dove laughed aloud and shook her head helplessly. Every answer seemed to bring so many more questions.

Drizzt kept on the move at night, running, as he had for so many years, from yet another grim reality. He had not killed the farmers—he had actually saved them from the gnoll band—but now they were dead. Drizzt could not escape that fact. He had entered their lives, quite of his own will, and now they were dead.

On the second night after his encounter with the hill giant, Drizzt saw a distant campfire far down the winding mountain trails, back in the direction of the barghest's lair. Knowing this sight to be more than coincidence, the drow summoned Guenhwyvar to his side, then sent the panther down for a closer look.

Tirelessly the great cat ran, its sleek, black form invisible in the evening shadows as it rapidly closed the distance to the camp.

⚔ ⚔ ⚔ ⚔ ⚔

Dove and Gabriel rested easily by their campfire, amused by the continuing antics of Fret, who busily cleaned his soft jerkin with a stiff brush and grumbled all the while.

Roddy kept to himself across the way, securely tucked into a niche between a fallen tree and a large rock, his dog curled up at his feet.

"Oh, bother for this dirt!" Fret groaned. "Never, never will I get this outfit clean! I shall have to buy a new one." He looked at Dove, who was futilely trying to hold a straight face. "Laugh if you will, Mistress Falconhand" the dwarf admonished. "The price will come out of your purse, do not doubt!"

"A sorry day it is when one must buy fineries for a dwarf," Gabriel put in, and at his words, Dove burst into laughter.

"Laugh if you will!" Fret said again, and he rubbed harder with the brush, wearing a hole right through the garment. "Drat and bebother!" he cursed, then he threw the brush to the ground.

"Shut yer mouth!" Roddy groused at them, stealing the mirth. "Do ye mean to bring the drow down upon us?"

Gabriel's ensuing glare was uncompromising, but Dove realized that the mountain man's advice, though rudely given, was appropriate. "Let us rest, Gabriel," the ranger said to her fighting companion. "Darda and Kellindil will be in soon and our turn shall come for watch. I expect that tomorrow's road will be no less wearisome—" She looked at Fret and winked—"and no less dirty, than today's."

Gabriel shrugged, hung his pipe in his mouth, and clasped his hands behind his head. This was the life that he and all of the adventuring companions enjoyed, camping under the stars with the song of the mountain wind in their ears.

Fret, though, tossed and turned on the hard ground, grumbling and growling as he moved through each uncomfortable position.

Gabriel didn't need to look at Dove to know that she shared his smile. Nor did he have to glance over at Roddy to know that the mountain man fumed at the continuing noise. It no doubt seemed negligible to the ears of a city-living dwarf but rang out conspicuously to those more accustomed to the road.

A whistle from the darkness sounded at the same time Roddy's dog put its fur up and growled.

Dove and Gabriel were up and over to the side of the camp in a second, moving to the perimeter of the firelight in the direction of Darda's call. Likewise, Roddy, pulling his dog along, slipped around the large rock, out of the direct light so that their eyes could adjust to the gloom.

Fret, too involved with his own discomfort, finally noticed the movements. "What?" the dwarf asked curiously. "What?"

After a brief and whispered conversation with Darda, Dove and Gabriel split up, circling the camp in opposite directions to ensure the integrity of the perimeter.

"The tree," came a soft whisper, and Dove dropped into a crouch. In a moment, she sorted out Roddy, cleverly concealed between the rock and some brush. The big man, too, had his weapon readied, and his other hand held his dog's muzzle tightly, keeping the animal silent.

Dove followed Roddy's nod to the widespread branches of a solitary elm. At first, the ranger could discern nothing unusual among the leafy branches, but then came the yellow flash of feline eyes.

"Drow's panther," Dove whispered. Roddy nodded his agreement. They sat very still and watched, knowing that the slightest movement could alert the cat. A few seconds later, Gabriel joined them, falling into a silent position and following their eyes to the same darker spot on the elm. All three understood that time was their ally; even now, Darda and Kellindil were no doubt moving into position.

Their trap would surely have had Guenhwyvar, but a moment later, the dwarf crashed out of the campsite, stumbling right into Roddy. The mountain man nearly fell over, and when he reflexively threw his weaponless hand out to catch himself, his dog rushed out, baying wildly.

Like a black-shafted arrow, the panther bolted from the tree and flew off into the night. Fortune was not with Guenhwyvar, though, for it crossed straight by Kellindil's position, and the keen-visioned elven archer saw it clearly.

Kellindil heard the barking and shouting in the distance, back by the camp, but had no way of knowing what had transpired. Any hesitation the elf had, however, was quickly dispelled when one voice called out clearly.

"Kill the murdering thing!" Roddy cried.

Thinking then that the panther or its drow companion must have attacked the campsite, Kellindil let his arrow fly. The enchanted dart buried itself deeply into Guenhwyvar's flank as the panther rushed by.

Then came Dove's call, berating Roddy. "Do not!" the ranger shouted. "The panther has done nothing to deserve our ire!"

Kellindil rushed out to the panther's trail. With his sensitive elven eyes viewing in the infrared spectrum, he clearly saw the heat of blood dotting the area of the hit and trailing off away from the camp.

Dove and the others came upon him a moment later. Kellindil's elven features, always angular and beautiful, seemed sharp as his angry glare fell over Roddy.

"You have misguided my shot, McGristle," he said angrily. "On your words, I shot a creature undeserving of an arrow! I warn you once, and once alone, to never do so again." After a final glare to show the mountain man how much he meant his words, Kellindil stalked off along the blood trail.

Angry fires welled in Roddy, but he sublimated them, understanding that he stood alone against the formidable foursome and the tidy dwarf. Roddy did let his glare drop upon Fret, though, knowing that none of the others could disagree with his judgment.

"Keep yer tongue in yer mouth when danger nears!" Roddy growled. "And keep yer stinkin' boots off my back!"

Fret looked around incredulously as the group began to move off after Kellindil. "Stinking," the dwarf asked aloud. He looked down, wounded, to his finely polished boots. "Stinking," he said to Dove, who paused to offer a comforting smile. "Dirtied by that one's back, more likely!"

* * * * *

Guenhwyvar limped back to Drizzt soon after the first rays of dawn peeked through the eastern mountains. Drizzt shook his head helplessly, almost unsurprised by the arrow protruding from Guenhwyvar's flank. Reluctantly, but knowing it a wise course, Drizzt drew out the dagger he had taken from the quickling and cut the bolt free.

Guenhwyvar growled softly through the procedure but lay still and offered no resistance. Then Drizzt, though he wanted to keep Guenhwyvar by his side, allowed the panther to return to its astral home, where the wound would heal faster. The arrow had told the drow all he needed to know about his pursuers, and Drizzt believed that he would need the panther again all too soon. He stood out on a rocky outcropping and peered through the growing brightness to the lower trails to the expected approach of yet another enemy.

He saw nothing, of course; even wounded, Guenhwyvar had easily outdistanced the pursuit and for a man or similar being, the campfire was many hours' travel.

But they would come, Drizzt knew, forcing him into yet another battle he did not want. Drizzt looked all around, wondering what devious traps he could set for them, what advantages he could gain when the encounter came to blows, as every encounter seemed to.

Memories of his last meeting with humans, of the man with the dogs and the other farmers, abruptly altered Drizzt's thinking. On that occasion, the battle had been inspired by misunderstanding, a barrier that Drizzt doubted he could ever overcome. Drizzt had fostered no desire then to fight against the humans and fostered none now, despite Guenhwyvar's wound.

The light was growing and the still-injured drow, though he had rested through the night, wanted to find a dark and comfortable hole. But Drizzt could afford no delays, not if he wanted to keep ahead of the coming battle.

"How far will you follow me?" Drizzt whispered into the morning breeze. He vowed in a somber but determined tone, "We shall see."

# 10
# A Question of Honor

"The panther found the drow," Dove concluded after she and her companions had spent some time inspecting the region near the rocky outcropping. Kellindil's arrow lay broken on the ground, at about the same spot where the panther tracks ended. "And the panther disappeared."

"So it would seem," Gabriel agreed, scratching his head and looking down at the confusing trail.

"Hell cat," Roddy McGristle growled. "Gone back to its filthy home!"

Fret wanted to ask, "Your house?" but he wisely held the sarcastic thought to himself.

The others, too, let the mountain man's proclamation slip by. They had no answers to this riddle, and Roddy's guess was as good as any of them could manage. The wounded panther and the fresh blood trail were gone, but Roddy's dog soon had Drizzt's scent. Baying excitedly, the dog led them on, and Dove and Kellindil, both skilled trackers, often discovered other evidence that confirmed the direction.

The trail lay along the side of the mountain, dipped through some thickly packed trees, and continued on across an expanse of bare stone, ending abruptly at yet another ravine. Roddy's dog moved right to the lip and even down to the first step on a rocky and treacherous descent.

"Damned drow magic," Roddy grumbled. He looked around and

bounced a fist off his thigh, guessing that it would take him many hours to circumvent the steep wall.

"The daylight wanes," Dove offered. "Let us set camp here and find our way down in the morn."

Gabriel and Fret nodded their accord, but Roddy disagreed. "The trail's fresh now!" the mountain man argued. "We should get the dog down there and back on it, at least, before we're taking to our beds."

"That could take hours . . ." Fret began to protest, but Dove hushed the tidy dwarf.

"Come," the ranger bade the others, and she walked off to the west, to where the ground sloped at a steep, but climbable decline.

Dove did not agree with Roddy's reasoning, but she wanted no further arguments with Maldobar's appointed representative.

At the bottom of the ravine they found only more riddles. Roddy spurred his dog off in every direction but could find no trace of the elusive drow. After many minutes of contemplation, the truth sparked in Dove's mind and her smile revealed everything to her other seasoned companions.

"He doubled us!" Gabriel laughed, guessing the source of Dove's mirth. "He led us right to the cliff, knowing we would assume he used some magic to get down!"

"What're ye talkin' about?" Roddy demanded angrily, though the experienced bounty hunter understood exactly what had happened.

"You mean that we have to climb all the way back up there?" Fret asked, his voice a whine.

Dove laughed again but sobered quickly as she looked to Roddy and said, "In the morning."

This time the mountain man offered no objections.

By the time the next dawn had broken, the group had hiked to the top of the ravine and Roddy had his dog back on Drizzt's scent, backtracking the trail in the direction of the rocky outcropping where they had first picked it up. The trick had been simple enough, but the same question nagged at all of the experienced trackers: how had the drow broken away from his track cleanly enough to so completely fool the dog. When they came again into the thickly packed trees, Dove knew that they had their answer.

She nodded to Kellindil, who was already dropping off his heavy pack. The nimble elf picked a low-hanging branch and swung up into the trees, searching for possible routes that the climbing drow might have followed. The branches of many trees twined together, so the options seemed many, but after a while, Kellindil correctly guided Roddy and his dog to the new trail, breaking off to the side of the copse and circling back down the side of the mountain, back in the direction of Maldobar.

"The town!" cried a distressed Fret, but the others didn't seem concerned.

"Not the town," offered Roddy, too intrigued to hold his angry edge. As a bounty hunter, Roddy always enjoyed a worthy opponent, at least during the chase. "The stream," Roddy explained, thinking that now he had figured out the drow's mind-set. "Drow's headed for the stream, to follow it along an' break off clean, back out to the wilder land."

"The drow is a crafty adversary," Darda remarked, wholeheartedly agreeing with Roddy's conclusions.

"And now he has at least a day's lead over us," Gabriel remarked.

After Fret's disgusted sigh finally died away, Dove offered the dwarf some hope. "Fear not," she said. "We are well stocked, but the drow is not. He must pause to hunt or forage, but we can continue on."

"We sleep only when need be!" Roddy put in, determined to not be slowed by the group's other members. "And only for short times!"

Fret sighed heavily again.

"And we begin rationing our supplies immediately," Dove added, both to placate Roddy and because she thought it prudent. "We shall be put to it hard enough just to close on the drow. I do not want any delays."

"Rationing," Fret mumbled under his breath. He sighed for the third time and placed a comforting hand on his belly. How badly the tidy dwarf wished that he could be back in his neat little room in Helm's castle in Sundabar!

⚔ ⚔ ⚔ ⚔ ⚔

Drizzt's every intention was to continue deeper into the mountains until the pursuing party had lost its heart for the chase. He kept up his misdirecting tactics, often doubling back and taking to the trees to begin a second trail in an entirely different direction. Many mountain streams provided further barriers to the scent, but Drizzt's pursuers were not novices, and Roddy's dog was as fine a hunting hound as had ever been bred. Not only did the party keep true to Drizzt's trail, but they actually closed the gap over the next few days.

Drizzt still believed that he could elude them, but their continuing proximity brought other, more subtle, concerns to the drow. He had done nothing to deserve such dogged pursuit; he had even avenged the deaths of the farming family. And despite Drizzt's angry vow that he would go off alone, that he would bring no more danger to anyone, he had known loneliness as too close a companion for too many years. He could not help but look over his shoulder, out of curiosity and not fear, and the longing did not diminish.

At last, Drizzt could not deny his curiosity for the pursuing party. That curiosity, Drizzt realized as he studied the figures moving about the campfire one dark night, might prove to be his downfall. Still, the realization, and the second-guessing, came too late for the drow to do anything about it. His needs had dragged him back, and now the campsite of his pursuers loomed barely twenty yards away.

The banter between Dove, Fret, and Gabriel tugged at Drizzt's heartstrings, though he could not understand their words. Any desire the drow felt to walk into the camp was tempered, though, whenever Roddy and his mean-tempered dog strolled by the light. Those two would never pause to hear any explanations, Drizzt knew.

The party had set two guards, one an elf and one a tall human. Drizzt had sneaked past the human, guessing correctly that the man would not be as adept as the elf in the darkness. Now, though, the drow, again against all caution, picked his way around to the other side of the camp, toward the elven sentry.

Only once before had Drizzt encountered his surface cousins. It had been a disastrous occasion. The raiding party for which Drizzt was a scout had slaughtered every member of a surface elf gathering, except for a single elven girl, whom Drizzt had managed to conceal. Driven by those haunting memories, Drizzt needed to see an elf again, a living and vital elf.

The first indication Kellindil had that someone else was in the area came when a tiny dagger whistled past his chest, neatly severing his bowstring. The elf spun about immediately and looked into the drow's lavender eyes. Drizzt stood only a few paces away.

The red glow of Kellindil's eyes showed that he was viewing Drizzt in the infrared spectrum. The drow crossed his hands over his chest in an Underdark signal of peace.

"At last we have met, my dark cousin," Kellindil whispered harshly in the drow tongue, his voice edged in obvious anger and his glowing eyes narrowing dangerously. Quick as a cat, Kellindil snapped a finely crafted sword, its blade glowing in a fiery red flame, from his belt.

Drizzt was amazed and hopeful when he learned that the elf could speak his language, and in the simple fact that the elf had not spoken loudly enough to alert the camp. The surface elf was Drizzt's size and similarly sharp-featured, but his eyes were narrower and his golden hair wasn't as long or thick as Drizzt's white mane.

"I am Drizzt Do'Urden," Drizzt began tentatively.

"I care nothing for what you are called!" Kellindil shot back. "You are drow. That is all I need to know! Come then, drow. Come and let us learn who is the stronger!"

Drizzt had not yet drawn his blade and had no intention of doing so. "I have no desire to battle with you . . ." Drizzt's voice trailed away, as he realized his words were futile against the intense hatred the surface elf held for him.

Drizzt wanted to explain everything to the elf, to tell his tale completely and be vindicated by some voice other than his own. If only another—particularly a surface elf—would learn of his trials and agree with his decisions, agree that he had acted properly through the course of his life in the face of such horrors, then the guilt would fly from Drizzt's shoulders. If only he could find acceptance among those who so hated—as he himself hated—the ways of his dark people, then Drizzt Do'Urden would be at peace.

But the elf's sword tip did not slip an inch toward the ground, nor did the grimace diminish on his fair elven face, a face more accustomed to smiles.

Drizzt would find no acceptance here, not now and probably not ever. Was he forever to be misjudged? he wondered. Or was he, perhaps, misjudging those around him, giving the humans and this elf more credit for fairness than they deserved?

Those were two disturbing notions that Drizzt would have to deal with another day, for Kellindil's patience had reached its end. The elf came at the drow with his sword tip leading the way.

Drizzt was not surprised—how could he have been? He hopped back, out of immediate reach, and called upon his innate magic, dropping a globe of impenetrable blackness over the advancing elf.

No novice to magic, Kellindil understood the drow's trick. The elf reversed direction, diving out the back side of the globe and coming up, sword at the ready.

The lavender eyes were gone.

"Drow!" Kellindil called out loudly, and those in the camp immediately exploded into motion. Roddy's dog started howling, and that excited and threatening yelp followed Drizzt back into the mountains, damning him to his continuing exile.

Kellindil leaned back against a tree, alert but not too concerned that the drow was still in the area. Drizzt could not know it at that time, but his words and ensuing actions—fleeing instead of fighting—had indeed put a bit of doubt in the kindly elf's not-so-closed mind.

⚔ ⚔ ⚔ ⚔ ⚔

"He will lose his advantage in the dawn's light," Dove said hopefully after several fruitless hours of trying to keep up with the drow. They were in a bowl-shaped, rocky vale now, and the drow's trail led up the far side in a high and fairly steep climb.

Fret, nearly stumbling with exhaustion at her side, was quick to reply. "Advantage?" The dwarf groaned. He looked at the next mountain wall and shook his head. "We shall all fall dead of weariness before we find this infernal drow!"

"If ye can't keep up, then fall an' die!" Roddy snarled. "We're not to be lettin' the stinking drow get away this time!"

It was not Fret, however, but another member of the troupe who unexpectedly went down. A large rock soared into the group suddenly, clipping Darda's shoulder with enough force to lift the man from the ground and spin him right over in the air. He never even got the chance to cry out before he fell facedown in the dust.

Dove grabbed Fret and rolled for a nearby boulder, Roddy and Gabriel doing likewise. Another stone, and several more, thundered into the region.

"Avalanche?" the stunned dwarf asked when he recovered from the shock.

Dove, too concerned with Darda, didn't bother to answer, though she knew the truth of their situation and knew that it was no avalanche.

"He is alive," Gabriel called from behind his protective rock, a dozen feet across from Dove's. Another stone skipped through the area, narrowly missing Darda's head.

"Damn," Dove mumbled. She peeked up over the lip of her boulder, scanning both the mountainside and the lower crags at its base. "Now, Kellindil," she whispered to herself. "Get us some time."

As if in answer came the distant twang of the elf's re-strung bow, followed by an angry roar. Dove and Gabriel glanced over to each other and smiled grimly.

"Stone giants!" Roddy cried, recognizing the deep, grating timbre of the roaring voice.

Dove crouched and waited, her back to the boulder and her open pack in her hand. No more stones bounced into the area; rather, thunderous crashes began up ahead of them, near Kellindil's position. Dove rushed out to Darda and gently turned the man over.

"That hurt," Darda whispered, straining to smile at his obvious understatement.

"Do not speak," Dove replied, fumbling for a potion bottle in her pack. But the ranger ran out of time. The giants, seeing her out in the open, resumed their attack on the lower area.

"Get back to the stone!" Gabriel cried. Dove slipped her arm under the fallen man's shoulder to support Darda as, stumbling with every movement, he crawled for the rock.

"Hurry! Hurry!" Fret cried, watching them anxiously with his back flat against the large stone.

Dove leaned over Darda suddenly, flattening him down to the ground as another rock zipped by just above their ducking heads.

Fret started to bite his fingernails, then realized what he was doing and stopped, a disgusted look on his face. "Do hurry!" he cried again to his friends. Another rock bounced by, too close.

Just before Dove and Darda got to Fret, a stone landed squarely on the backside of the boulder. Fret, his back tight against the rock barrier, flew out wildly, easily clearing his crawling companions. Dove placed Darda down behind the boulder, then turned, thinking she would have to go out again and retrieve the fallen dwarf.

But Fret was already back up, cursing and grumbling, and more concerned with a new hole in his fine garment than in any bodily injury.

"Get back here!" Dove screamed at him.

"Drat and bebother these stupid giants!" was all that Fret replied, stomping purposefully back to the boulder, his fists clenched angrily against his hips.

The barrage continued, both up ahead of the pinned companions and in their area. Then Kellindil came diving in, slipping to the rock beside Roddy and his dog.

"Stone giants," the elf explained. "A dozen at the least." He pointed up to a ridge halfway up the mountainside.

"Drow set us up," Roddy growled, banging his fist on the stone.

Kellindil wasn't convinced, but he held his tongue.

⚔ ⚔ ⚔ ⚔ ⚔

Up on the peak of the rocky rise, Drizzt watched the battle unfolding. He had passed through the lower paths an hour earlier, before the dawn. In the dark, the waiting giants had been no obstacle for the stealthy drow; Drizzt had slipped through their line with little trouble.

Now, squinting through the morning light, Drizzt wondered about his course of action. When he had passed the giants, he fully expected that his pursuers would fall into trouble. Should he have somehow tried to warn them? he wondered. Or should he have veered away from the region, leading the humans and the elf out of the giants' path?

Again Drizzt did not understand where he fit in with the ways of this strange and brutal world. "Let them fight among themselves," he said harshly, as though trying to convince himself. Drizzt purposefully recalled his encounter of the previous night. The elf had attacked despite his proclamation that he did not want to fight. He recalled, too, the arrow he had dug out of Guenhwyvar's flank.

"Let them all kill each other," Drizzt said and he turned to leave. He glanced back over his shoulder one final time and noticed that some of the giants were on the move. One group remained at the ridge, showering the valley floor with a seemingly endless supply of rocks while two other groups, one to the left and one to the right, had fanned out, moving to encircle the trapped party.

Drizzt knew then that his pursuers would not escape. Once the giants had them flanked, they would find no protection against the cross fire.

Something stirred within the drow at that moment, the same emotions that had set him into action against the gnoll band. He couldn't know for certain, but as with the gnolls and their plans to attack the farmhouse, Drizzt suspected that the giants were the evil ones in this fight.

Other thoughts softened Drizzt's determined grimace, memories of the human children at play on the farm, of the sandy-haired boy going into the water trough.

Drizzt dropped the onyx figurine to the ground. "Come, Guenhwyvar," he commanded. "We are needed."

⚔ ⚔ ⚔ ⚔ ⚔

"We're being flanked!" Roddy McGristle snarled, seeing the giant bands moving along the higher trails.

Dove, Gabriel, and Kellindil all glanced around and to each other, searching for some way out. They had battled giants many times in their travels, together and with other parties. Always before, they had gone into the fight eagerly, happy to relieve the world of a few troublesome monsters. This time, though, they all suspected that the result might be different. Stone giants were reputably the best rock-throwers in all the realms and a single hit could kill the hardiest of men. Also, Darda, though alive, could not possibly run away, and none of the others had any intentions of leaving him behind.

"Flee, mountain man," Kellindil said to Roddy. "You owe us nothing."

Roddy looked at the archer incredulously. "I don't run away, elf," he growled. "Not from nothin'!"

Kellindil nodded and fitted an arrow to his bow.

"If they get to the side, we're doomed," Dove explained to Fret. "I beg your forgiveness, dear Fret. I should not have taken you from your home."

Fret shrugged the thought away. He reached under his robes and produced a small but sturdy silver hammer. Dove smiled at the sight, thinking how odd the hammer seemed in the dwarf's soft hands, more accustomed to holding a quill.

⚔ ⚔ ⚔ ⚔ ⚔

On the top ridge, Drizzt and Guenhwyvar shadowed the movements of the stone giant band circling to the trapped party's left flank. Drizzt was determined to help the humans, but he wasn't certain of how effective he could be against the likes of four armed giants. Still, he figured that with Guenhwyvar by his side, he could find some way to disrupt the giant group long enough for the trapped party to make a break.

The valley rolled out wider across the way and Drizzt realized that the giant band circling in the other direction, to the trapped party's right flank, was probably out of rock-throwing range.

"Come, my friend," Drizzt whispered to the panther, and he drew his scimitar and started down a descent of broken and jagged stone. A moment later, though, as soon as he noticed the terrain a short distance ahead of the giant band Drizzt grabbed Guenhwyvar by the scruff and led the panther back up to the top ridge.

Here the ground was jagged and cracked but undeniably stable. Just ahead, however, great boulders and hundreds of loose smaller rocks lay strewn about the steeply sloping ground. Drizzt was not so experienced in the dynamics of a mountainside, but even he could see that the steep and loose landscape verged on collapse.

The drow and the cat rushed ahead, again getting above the giant band. The giants were nearly in position; some of them had even begun to launch rocks at the pinned party. Drizzt crept down to a large boulder and heaved against it, setting it into motion. Guenhwyvar's tactics were far less subtle. The panther charged down the mountainside, dislodging stones with every great stride, leaping onto the back side of rocks and springing away as they began tumbling.

Boulders bounced and bounded. Smaller rocks skipped between them, building the momentum. Drizzt, committed to the action, ran down into the midst of the budding avalanche, throwing stones, pushing against others—whatever he could do to add to the rush. Soon the very ground beneath the drow's feet was sliding and the whole section of the mountainside seemed to be coming down.

Guenhwyvar sped along ahead of the avalanche, a beacon of doom for the surprised giants. The panther sprang out over them, but they took note of the great cat only momentarily, as tons of bouncing rocks slammed into them.

Drizzt knew that he was in trouble; he was not nearly as quick and agile as Guenhwyvar and could not hope to outrun the slide, or to get out of its way. He leaped high into the air from the crest of a small ridge and called upon a levitation spell as he went.

Drizzt fought hard to hold his concentration on the effort. The spell had failed him twice before, and if he couldn't hold it now, if he dropped back into the rush of stones, he knew he would surely die.

Despite his determination, Drizzt felt increasingly heavy on the air. He waved his arms futilely, sought that magical energy within his drow body—but he was coming down.

⚔ ⚔ ⚔ ⚔ ⚔

"Th'only ones that can hit us are up in front!" Roddy cried as a thrown boulder bounced harmlessly short of the right flank. "The ones on the right're too far for throwing, and the ones on the left . . . !"

Dove followed Roddy's logic and his gaze to the rising dust cloud on their left flank. She stared hard and long at the cascading rocks, and at what might have been a dark-cloaked elven form. When she looked back at Gabriel, she knew that he, too, had seen the drow.

"We have to go now," Dove called to the elf.

Kellindil nodded and spun to the side of his barrier boulder, his bowstring taut.

"Quickly," Gabriel added, "before the group to the right gets back in range."

Kellindil's bow twanged once and again. Ahead, a giant howled in pain.

"Stay here with Darda," Dove bade Fret, then she, Gabriel, and Roddy—holding his dog on a tight leash—darted out from their cover and charged the giants straight ahead. They rolled from rock to rock, cutting their course in confusing zigzags to prevent the giants from anticipating their movements. All the while, Kellindil's arrows soared above them, keeping the giants more concerned with ducking than with throwing.

Deep crags marked the mountainside's lower slopes, crags that offered cover but that also split the three fighters apart. Neither could they see the giants, but they knew the general direction and picked their separate ways as best they could.

Rounding a sharp bend between two walls of stone, Roddy came upon one of the giants. Immediately the mountain man freed his dog, and the vicious canine charged fearlessly and leaped high, barely reaching the twenty-foot-tall behemoth's waist.

Surprised by the sudden attack, the giant dropped its huge club and caught the dog in midflight. It would have crushed the troublesome mutt in an instant, except that Bleeder, Roddy's wicked axe, sliced into its thigh with all the force the burly mountain man could muster. The giant lurched and Roddy's dog squirmed loose, climbing and clawing, then snapping at the giant's face and neck. Below, Roddy hacked away, chopping the monster down as he would a tree.

⚔ ⚔ ⚔ ⚔ ⚔

Half-floating and half-dancing atop the bouncing stones, Drizzt rode the rock slide. He saw one giant emerge, stumbling, from the tumult, only to be met by Guenhwyvar. Wounded and stunned, the giant went down in a heap.

Drizzt had no time to savor his desperate plan's success. His levitation spell continued somewhat, keeping him light enough so that he could ride along. Even above the main slide, though, rocks bounced heavily into the drow and dust choked him and stung his sensitive eyes. Nearly blinded, he managed to spot a ridge that could provide some shelter, but the only way he could get to it would be to release his levitation spell and scramble.

Another rock nicked into Drizzt, nearly spinning him over in midair. He could sense the spell failing and knew that he had only that one chance. He regained his equilibrium, released his spell, and hit the ground running.

He rolled and scrambled, coming up in a dead run. A rock skipped into the knee of his already wounded leg, forcing him parallel to the ground. Drizzt was rolling again, trying however he could to get to the safety of the ridge.

His momentum ended far short. He came back up to his feet, meaning to thrust ahead over the final distance, but Drizzt's leg had no strength and it buckled immediately, leaving him stranded and exposed.

He felt the impact on his back and thought his life was at its end. A moment later, dazed, Drizzt realized only that he somehow had landed behind the ridge and that he was buried by something, but not by stones or dirt.

Guenhwyvar stayed on top of its master, shielding Drizzt until the last of the bouncing rocks had rolled to a stop.

⚔ ⚔ ⚔ ⚔ ⚔

As the crags gave way to more open ground, Dove and Gabriel came back in sight of each other. They noticed movement directly ahead, behind a loose-fitted wall of piled boulders a dozen feet high and about fifty feet long.

A giant appeared atop the wall, roaring in rage and holding a rock above its head, readied to throw. The monster had several arrows protruding from its neck and chest, but it seemed not to care.

Kellindil's next shot surely caught the giant's attention, though, for the elf put an arrow squarely into the monster's elbow. The giant howled and clutched at its arm, apparently forgetting about its rock, which promptly dropped with a thud upon its head. The giant stood very still, dazed, and two more arrows knocked into its face. It teetered for a moment, then crashed into the dust.

Dove and Gabriel exchanged quick smiles, sharing their appreciation for the skilled elven archer, then continued their charge, going for opposite ends of the wall.

Dove caught one giant by surprise just around her corner. The monster reached for its club, but Dove's sword beat it to the spot and cleanly severed its hand. Stone giants were formidable foes, with fists that could drive a person straight into the ground and a hide nearly as hard as the rock that gave them their name. But wounded, surprised, and without its cudgel, the giant was no match for the skilled ranger. She sprang atop the wall, which put her even with the giant's face, and set her sword to methodical work.

In two thrusts, the giant was blinded. The third, a deft, sidelong swipe, cut a smile into the monster's throat. Then Dove went on the defensive, neatly dodging and parrying the dying monster's last desperate swings.

Gabriel was not as lucky as his companion. The remaining giant was not close to the corner of the piled rock wall. Though Gabriel surprised the monster when he came charging around, the giant had enough time—and a stone in hand—to react.

Gabriel got his sword up to deflect the missile, and the act saved his life. The stone blew the fighter's sword from his hands and still came on with enough force to throw Gabriel to the ground. Gabriel was a seasoned veteran, and the primary reason he was still alive after so very many battles was the fact that he knew when to retreat. He forced himself through that moment of blurring pain and found his footing, then bolted back around the wall.

The giant, with its heavy club in hand came right behind. An arrow greeted the monster as it turned into the open, but it brushed the pesky dart away as no more than an inconvenience and bore down on the fighter.

Gabriel soon ran out of room. He tried to make it back to the broken paths, but the giant cut him off, trapping him in a small box canyon of huge boulders. Gabriel drew his dagger and cursed his ill luck.

Dove had dispatched her giant by this time and rushed out around the stone wall, immediately catching sight of Gabriel and the giant.

Gabriel saw the ranger, too, but he only shrugged, almost apologetically, knowing that Dove couldn't possibly get to him in time to save him.

The snarling giant took a step in, meaning to finish the puny man, but then came a sharp *crack!* and the monster halted abruptly. Its eyes darted about weirdly for a moment or two, then it toppled at Gabriel's feet, quite dead.

Gabriel looked up to the side, to the top of the boulder wall, and nearly laughed out loud.

Fret's hammer was not a large weapon—its head being only two inches across—but it was a solid thing, and in a single swing, the dwarf had driven it clean through the stone giant's thick skull.

Dove approached, sheathing her sword, equally at a loss.

Looking upon their amazed expressions, Fret was not amused.

"I am a dwarf, after all!" he blurted at them, crossing his arms indignantly. The action brought the brain-stained hammer in contact with Fret's tunic, and the dwarf lost his bluster in a fit of panic. He licked his stubby fingers and wiped at the gruesome stain, then regarded the gore on his hand with even greater horror.

Dove and Gabriel did laugh aloud.

"Know that you are paying for the tunic!" Fret railed at Dove. "Oh, you most certainly are!"

A shout to the side brought them from their momentary relief. The four remaining giants, having seen one group of their companions buried in an avalanche and another group cut down so very efficiently, had lost interest in the ambush and had taken flight.

Right behind them went Roddy McGristle and his howling dog.

⚔ ⚔ ⚔ ⚔ ⚔

A single giant had escaped both the avalanche's thunder and the panther's terrible claws. It ran wildly now across the mountainside, seeking the top ridge.

Drizzt set Guenhwyvar in quick pursuit, then found a stick to use as a cane and managed to get to his feet. Bruised, dusty, and still nursing wounds from the barghest battle—and now a dozen more from his mountain ride—Drizzt started away. A movement at the bottom of the slope caught his attention and held him, though. He turned to face the elf and more pointedly, the arrow nocked in the elf's drawn bow.

Drizzt looked around but had nowhere to duck. He could place a globe of darkness somewhere between himself and the elf, possibly, but he realized that the skilled archer, having drawn a bead on him, would not miss him even with that obstacle. Drizzt steadied his shoulders and turned about slowly, facing the elf squarely and proudly.

Kellindil eased his bowstring back and pulled the arrow from its nock. Kellindil, too, had seen the dark-cloaked form floating above the rock slide.

"The others are back with Darda," Dove said, coming upon the elf at that moment, "and McGristle is chasing . . ."

Kellindil neither answered nor looked to the ranger. He nodded curtly, leading Dove's gaze up the slope to the dark form, which moved again up the mountainside.

"Let him go," Dove offered. "That one was never our enemy."

"I fear to let a drow walk free," Kellindil replied.

"As do I," Dove answered, "but I fear the consequences more if McGristle finds the drow."

"We will return to Maldobar and rid ourselves of that man," Kellindil offered, "then you and the others may return to Sundabar for your appointment. I have kin in these mountains; together they and I will watch out for our dark-skinned friend and see that he causes no harm."

"Agreed," said Dove. She turned and started away, and Kellindil, needing no further convincing, turned to follow.

The elf paused and looked back one final time. He reached into his backpack and produced a flask, then laid it out in the open on the ground. Almost as an afterthought, Kellindil produced a second item, this one from his belt, and dropped it to the ground next to the flask. Satisfied, he turned and followed the ranger.

---

By the time Roddy McGristle returned from his wild, fruitless chase, Dove and the others had packed everything together and were prepared to leave.

"Back after the drow," Roddy proclaimed. "He's gained a bit o' time, but we'll close on him fast."

"The drow is gone," Dove said sharply. "We shall pursue him no more."

Roddy's face crinkled in disbelief and he seemed on the verge of exploding.

"Darda is badly in need of rest!" Dove growled at him, not backing down a bit. "Kellindil's arrows are nearly exhausted, as are our supplies."

"I'll not so easily forget the Thistledowns!" Roddy declared.

"Neither did the drow," Kellindil put in.

"The Thistledowns have already been avenged," Dove added, "and you know it is true, McGristle. The drow did not kill them, but he most definitely slew their killers!"

Roddy snarled and turned away. He was an experienced bounty hunter and thus, an experienced investigator. He had, of course, figured out the truth long ago, but Roddy couldn't ignore the scar on his face or the loss of his ear—or the heavy bounty on the drow's head.

Dove anticipated and understood his silent reasoning. "The people of

Maldobar will not be so anxious to see the drow brought in when they learn the truth of the massacre," she said, "and not so willing to pay, I would guess."

Roddy snapped a glare at her, but again he could not dispute her logic. When Dove's party set out on the trail back to Maldobar, Roddy McGristle went with them.

⚔ ⚔ ⚔ ⚔ ⚔

Drizzt came back down the mountainside later that day, searching for something that would tell him his pursuers' whereabouts. He found Kellindil's flask and approached it tentatively, then relaxed when he noticed the other item lying next to it, the tiny dagger he had taken from the sprite, the same one he had used to sever the elf's bowstring on their first meeting.

The liquid within the flask smelled sweet, and the drow, his throat still parched from the rock dust, gladly took a quaff. Tingling chills ran through Drizzt's body, refreshing him and revitalizing him. He had barely eaten for several days, but the strength that had seeped from his now-frail form came rushing back in a sudden burst. His torn leg went numb for a moment, and Drizzt felt that, too, grow stronger.

A wave of dizziness washed over Drizzt then, and he shuffled over to the shade of a nearby boulder and sat down to rest.

When he awoke, the sky was dark and filled with stars, and he felt much better. Even his leg, so torn in the ride down the avalanche, would once again support his weight. Drizzt knew who had left the flask and dagger for him, and now that he understood the nature of the healing potion, his confusion and indecision only grew.

# Part Three

## Montolio

To all the varied peoples of the world nothing is so out of reach, yet so deeply personal and controlling, as the concept of god. My experience in my homeland showed me little of these supernatural beings beyond the influences of the vile drow deity, the Spider Queen, Lolth.

After witnessing the carnage of Lolth's workings, I was not so quick to embrace the concept of any god, of any being that could so dictate, codes of behavior and precepts of an entire society. Is morality not an internal force, and if it is, are principles then to be dictated or felt?

So follows the question of the gods themselves: Are these named entities, in truth, actual beings, or are they manifestations of shared beliefs? Are the dark elves evil because they follow the precepts of the Spider Queen, or is Lolth a culmination of the drow's natural evil conduct?

Likewise, when the barbarians of Icewind Dale charge across the tundra to war, shouting the name of Tempus, Lord of Battles, are they following the precepts of Tempus, or is Tempus merely the idealized name they give to their actions?

This I cannot answer, nor, I have come to realize, can any one else, no matter how loudly they—particularly priests of certain gods—might argue otherwise. In the end, to a preacher's ultimate sorrow, the choice of a god is a personal one, and the alignment to a being is in accord with one's internal code of principles. A missionary might coerce and trick would-be disciples, but no rational being can truly follow the determined orders of any god-figure if those orders run contrary to his own tenets. Neither I, Drizzt Do'Urden, nor my father, Zaknafein, could ever have become disciples of the Spider Queen. And Wulfgar of Icewind Dale, my friend of later years, though he still might yell out to the battle god, does not please this entity called Tempus except on those occasions when he puts his mighty war hammer to use.

The gods of the realms are many and varied—or they are the many and varied names and identities tagged onto the same being.

I know not—and care not—which.

—Drizzt Do'Urden

# Winter

Drizzt picked his way through the rocky, towering mountains for many days, putting as much ground between himself and the farm village—and the awful memories—as he could. The decision to flee had not been a conscious one; if Drizzt had been less out of sorts, he might have seen the charity in the elf's gifts, the healing potion and the returned dagger, as a possible lead to a future relationship.

But the memories of Maldobar and the guilt that bowed the drow's shoulders would not be so easily dismissed. The farming village had become simply one more stopover on the search to find a home, a search that he increasingly believed was futile. Drizzt wondered how he could even go down to the next village that he came upon. The potential for tragedy had been played out all too clearly for him. He didn't stop to consider that the presence of the barghests might have been an unusual circumstance, and that, perhaps, in the absence of such fiends, his encounter might have turned out differently.

At this low point in his life, Drizzt's entire thoughts focused around a single word that echoed interminably in his head and pierced him to his heart: "drizzit."

Drizzt's trail eventually led him to a wide pass in the mountains and to a steep and rocky-gorge filled by the mist of some roaring river far below.

The air had been getting colder, something that Drizzt did not understand and the moist vapor felt good to the drow. He picked his way down the rocky cliff, a journey that took him the better part of the day, and found the bank of the cascading river.

Drizzt had seen rivers in the Underdark, but none to rival this. The Rauvin leaped across stones, throwing spray high into the air. It swarmed around great boulders, did a white-faced skip over fields of smaller stones, and dived suddenly into falls five times the drow's height. Drizzt was enchanted by the sight and the sound, but more than that, he also saw the possibilities of this place as a sanctuary. Many culverts edged the river, still pools where water had deflected from the pull of the main stream. Here, too, gathered the fish, resting from their struggles against the strong current.

The sight brought a grumble from Drizzt's belly. He knelt down over one pool, his hand poised to strike. It took him many tries to understand the refraction of sunlight through the water, but the drow was quick enough and smart enough to learn this game. Drizzt's hand plunged down suddenly and came back up firmly grasping a foot-long trout.

Drizzt tossed the fish away from the water, letting it bounce about on the stones, and soon had caught another. He would eat well this night, for the first time since he had fled the region of the farm village, and he had enough clear and cold water to satisfy any thirst.

This place was called Dead Orc Pass by those who knew the region. The title was somewhat of a misnomer, however, for while hundreds of orcs had indeed died in this rocky valley in numerous battles against human legions, thousands more lived here still, lurking in the many mountain caves, poised to strike against intruders. Few people came here, and none of them wisely.

To naive Drizzt, with the easy supply of food and water and the comfortable mist to battle the surprisingly chilling air, this gorge seemed the perfect retreat.

The drow spent his days huddled in the sheltering shadows of the many rocks and small caves, preferring to fish and forage in the dark hours of night. He didn't view this nocturnal style as a reversion to anything he had once been. When he had first stepped out of the Underdark, he had determined that he would live among the surface dwellers as a surface dweller, and thus, he had taken great pains to acclimate himself to the daytime sun. Drizzt held no such illusions now. He chose the nights for his activities because they were less painful to his sensitive eyes and because he knew that the less exposure his scimitar had to the sun, the longer it would retain its edge of magic.

It didn't take Drizzt very long, however, to understand why the surface dwellers seemed to prefer the daylight. Under the sun's warming rays, the air was still tolerable, if a bit chill. During the night, Drizzt found that he often had to take shelter from the biting breeze that whipped down over the steep edges of the mist-filled gorge. Winter was fast approaching the northland but the drow, raised in the seasonless world of the Underdark, couldn't know that.

On one of these nights, with the wind driving a brutal northern blast that numbed the drow's hands, Drizzt came to an important understanding. Even with Guenhwyvar beside him, huddled beneath a low overhang, Drizzt felt the severe pain growing in his extremities. Dawn was many hours away, and Drizzt seriously wondered if he would survive to see the sunrise.

"Too cold, Guenhwyvar," he stuttered through his chattering teeth. "Too cold."

He flexed his muscles and moved vigorously, trying to restore lost circulation. Then he mentally prepared himself, thinking of times past when he was warm, trying to defeat the despair and trick his own body into forgetting the cold. A single thought stood out clearly, a memory of the kitchens in Menzoberranzan's Academy. In the ever-warm Underdark, Drizzt had never even considered fire as a source of warmth. Always before, Drizzt had seen fire as merely a method of cooking, a means of producing light, and an offensive weapon. Now it took on even greater importance for the drow. As the winds continued to blow colder and colder, Drizzt realized, to his horror, that a fire's heat alone could keep him alive.

He looked about for kindling. In the Underdark, he had burned mushroom stalks, but no mushrooms grew large enough on the surface. There were plants, though, trees that grew even larger than the Underdark's fungus.

"Get me . . . limb," Drizzt stuttered to Guenhwyvar, not knowing any words for wood or tree. The panther regarded him curiously.

"Fire," Drizzt begged. He tried to rise but found his legs and feet numb.

Then the panther did understand. Guenhwyvar growled once and sprinted out into the night. The great cat nearly tripped over a pile of branches and twigs that had been set—by whom, Guenhwyvar did not know—just outside the doorway. Drizzt, too concerned with his survival at the time, did not even question the cat's sudden return.

Drizzt tried unsuccessfully to strike a fire for many minutes, smacking his dagger against a stone. Finally he understood that the wind prevented the sparks from catching, so he moved the setup to a more sheltered area. His legs ached now, and his own saliva froze along his lips and chin.

Then a spark took hold in the dry pile. Drizzt carefully fanned the tiny flame, cupping his hands to prevent the wind from coming in too strongly.

⚔ ⚔ ⚔ ⚔ ⚔

"The flames are up," an elf said to his companion.

Kellindil nodded gravely, still not certain if he and his fellow elves had done right in aiding the drow. Kellindil had come right back out from Maldobar, while Dove and the others had set off for Sundabar, and had met with a small elven family, kinfolk of his, who lived in the mountains near Dead Orc Pass. With their expert aid, the elf had little trouble locating the drow, and together he and his kin had watched, curiously, over the last few tendays.

Drizzt's innocuous lifestyle had not dispelled all of the wary elf's doubts, though. Drizzt was a drow, after all, dark-skinned to view and dark-hearted by reputation.

Still, Kellindil's sigh was one of relief when he, too, noted the slight, distant glow. The drow would not freeze; Kellindil believed that this drow did not deserve such a fate.

⚔ ⚔ ⚔ ⚔ ⚔

After his meal later that night, Drizzt leaned on Guenhwyvar—and the panther gladly accepting the shared body heat—and looked up at the stars, twinkling brightly in the cold air. "Do you remember Menzoberranzan?" he asked the panther. "Do you remember when we first met?"

If Guenhwyvar understood him, the cat gave no indication. With a yawn, Guenhwyvar rolled against Drizzt and dropped its head between two outstretched paws.

Drizzt smiled and roughly rubbed the panther's ear. He had met Guenhwyvar in Sorcere, the wizard school of the Academy, when the panther was in the possession of Masoj Hun'ett, the only drow that Drizzt had ever killed. Drizzt purposely tried not to think of that incident now; with the fire burning brightly, warming his toes, this was no night for unpleasant memories. Despite the many horrors he had faced in the city of his birth, Drizzt had found some pleasures there and had learned many useful lessons. Even Masoj had taught him things that now aided him more than he ever would have believed. Looking back to the crackling flames, Drizzt mused that if it had not been for his apprenticeship duties of lighting candles, he would not even have known how to build a fire. Undeniably, that knowledge had saved him from a chilling death.

Drizzt's smile was short-lived as his thoughts continued along those lines. Not so many months after that particularly useful lesson, Drizzt had been forced to kill Masoj.

Drizzt lay back again and sighed. With neither danger nor confusing companionship apparently imminent, this was perhaps the most simple time of his life, but never had the complexities of his existence so fully overwhelmed him.

He was brought from his tranquillity a moment later, when a large bird, an owl with tufted, hornlike feathers on its rounded head, rushed suddenly overhead. Drizzt laughed at his own inability to relax; in the second it had taken him to recognize the bird as no threat, he had leaped to his feet and drawn his scimitar and dagger. Guenhwyvar, too, had reacted to the startling bird, but in a far different manner. With Drizzt suddenly up and out of the way, the panther rolled closer to the heat of the fire, stretched languidly, and yawned again.

⚔ ⚔ ⚔ ⚔ ⚔

The owl drifted silently on unseen breezes, rising with the mist out of the river valley opposite the wall that Drizzt had originally descended. The bird rushed on through the night to a thick grove of evergreens on the side of a mountain, coming to rest on a wood-and-rope bridge constructed across the higher boughs of three of the trees. After a few moments preening itself, the bird rang a little silver bell, attached to the bridge for just such occasions.

A moment later, the bird rang the bell again.

"I am coming," came a voice from below. "Patience, Hooter. Let a blind man move at a pace that best suits him!" As if it understood, and enjoyed, the game, the owl rang the bell a third time.

An old man with a huge and bristling gray mustache and white eyes appeared on the bridge. He hopped and skipped his way toward the bird. Montolio was formerly a ranger of great renown, who now lived out his final years—by his own choice—secluded in the mountains and surrounded by the creatures he loved best (and he did not consider humans, elves, dwarves, or any of the other intelligent races among them). Despite his considerable age, Montolio remained tall and straight, though the years had taken their toll on the hermit, crinkling one hand up so that it resembled the claw of the bird he now approached.

"Patience, Hooter," he mumbled over and over. Anyone watching him nimbly pick his way across the somewhat treacherous bridge never would have guessed that he was blind, and those who knew Montolio certainly would not describe him that way. Rather, they might have said that his eyes did not function, but they quickly would have added that he did not need them to function. With his skills and knowledge, and with his many animal friends, the old ranger "saw" more of the world around him than most of those with normal sight.

Montolio held out his arm, and the great owl promptly hopped onto it, carefully finding its footing on the man's heavy leather sleeve.

"You have seen the drow?" Montolio asked.

The owl responded with a whoo, then went off into a complicated series of chattering hoots and whoos Montolio took it all in, weighing every detail. With the help of his friends, particularly this rather talkative owl, the ranger had monitored the drow for several days, curious as to why a dark elf had wandered into the valley. At first, Montolio had assumed that the drow was somehow connected to Graul, the chief orc of the region, but as time went on, the ranger began to suspect differently.

"A good sign," Montolio remarked when the owl had assured him that the drow had not yet made contact with the orc tribes Graul was bad enough without having any allies as powerful as dark elves!

Still, the ranger could not figure out why the orcs had not sought out the drow. Possibly they had not caught sight of him; the drow had gone out of his way to remain inconspicuous, setting no fires (before this very night) and only coming out after sunset. More likely, Montolio mused as he gave the matter more thought, the orcs had seen the drow but had not yet found the courage to make contact.

Either way, the whole episode was proving a welcome diversion for the ranger as he went about the daily routines of setting up his house for the coming winter. He did not fear the drow's appearance. Montolio did not fear much of anything—and if the drow and the orcs were not allies, the resulting conflict might well be worth the watching.

"By my leave," the ranger said to placate the complaining owl. "Go and hunt some mice!" The owl swooped off immediately, circled once under then back over the bridge, and headed out into the night.

"Just take care not to eat any of the mice I have set to watching the drow!" Montolio called after the bird, and he chuckled, shook his wild-grown gray locks, and turned back toward the ladder at the end of the bridge. He vowed, as he descended, that he would soon strap on his sword and find out what business this particular dark elf might have in the region.

The old ranger made many such vows.

⚔⚔⚔⚔⚔

Autumn's warning blasts gave way quickly to the onslaught of winter. It hadn't taken Drizzt long to figure out the significance of gray clouds, but when the storm broke this time, in the form of snow instead of rain, the drow was truly amazed. He had seen the whiteness along the tops of the mountains but had never gone high enough to inspect it and had merely assumed that it was a coloration of the rocks. Now Drizzt watched the white flakes descend on the valley; they disappeared in the rush of the river but gathered on the rocks.

As the snow began to mount and the clouds hung ever lower in the sky, Drizzt came to a dreadful realization. Quickly he summoned Guenhwyvar to his side.

"We must find better shelter," he explained to the weary panther. Guenhwyvar had only been released to its astral home the previous day. "And we must stock it with wood for our fires."

Several caves dotted the valley wall on this side of the river. Drizzt found one, not only deep and dark but sheltered from the blowing wind by a high stone ridge. He entered, pausing just inside to let his eyes adapt from the snow's glaring brightness.

The cave floor was uneven and its ceiling was not high. Large boulders were scattered randomly about, and off to the side, near one of these, Drizzt noticed a darker gloom, indicating a second chamber. He placed his armful of kindling down and started toward it, then halted suddenly, both he and Guenhwyvar sensing another presence.

Drizzt drew his scimitar, slipped to the boulder, and peered around it. With his infravision, the cave's other inhabitant, a warm-glowing ball considerably larger than the drow, was not hard to spot. Drizzt knew at once what it was, though he had no name for it. He had seen this creature from afar several times, watching it as it deftly—and with amazing speed, considering its bulk—snatched fish from the river.

Whatever it might be called, Drizzt had no desire to fight with it over the cave; there were other holes in the area, more easily attainable.

The great brown bear, though, seemed to have different ideas. The creature stirred suddenly and came up to its rear legs, its avalanche growl echoing throughout the cave and its claws and teeth all too noticeable.

Guenhwyvar, the astral entity of the panther, knew the bear as an ancient rival, and one that wise cats took great care to avoid. Still the brave panther sprang right in front of Drizzt, willing to take on the larger creature so that its master might escape.

"No, Guenhwyvar!" Drizzt commanded, and he grabbed the cat and pulled himself back in front.

The bear, another of Montolio's many friends, made no move to attack, but it held its position fiercely, not appreciating the interruption of its long-awaited slumber.

Drizzt sensed something here that he could not explain—not a friendship with the bear, but an eerie understanding of the creature's viewpoint. He thought himself foolish as he sheathed his blade, yet he could not deny the empathy he felt, almost as though he was viewing the situation through the bear's eyes.

Cautiously, Drizzt stepped closer, drawing the bear fully into his gaze. The bear seemed almost surprised, but gradually it lowered its claws and its snarling grimace became an expression that Drizzt understood as curiosity.

Drizzt slowly reached into his pouch and took out a fish that he had been saving for his own supper. He tossed it over to the bear, which sniffed it once, then swallowed it down with hardly a chew.

Another long moment of staring ensued, but the tension was gone. The bear belched once, rolled back down, and was soon snoring contentedly.

Drizzt looked at Guenhwyvar and shrugged helplessly, having no idea of how he had just communicated so profoundly with the animal. The panther had apparently understood the connotations of the exchange, too, for Guenhwyvar's fur was no longer ruffled.

For the rest of the time that Drizzt spent in that cave, he took care, whenever he had spare food, to drop a morsel by the slumbering bear. Sometimes, particularly if Drizzt had dropped fish, the bear sniffed and awakened just long enough to gobble the meal. More often, though, the animal ignored the food altogether, rhythmically snoring and dreaming about honey and berries and female bears, and whatever else sleeping bears dreamed about.

⚔ ⚔ ⚔ ⚔ ⚔

"He took up his home with Bluster?" Montolio gasped when he learned from Hooter that the drow and the ornery bear were sharing the two-chambered cave. Montolio nearly fell over—and would have if he hadn't been so close to the supporting tree trunk. The old ranger leaned there, stunned, scratching at the stubble on his face and pulling at his moustache. He had known the bear for several years, and even he wasn't certain that he would be willing to share quarters with it. Bluster was an easily riled creature, as many of Graul's stupid orcs had learned over the years.

"I guess Bluster is too tired to argue," Montolio rationalized, but he knew that something more was brewing here. If an orc or a goblin had gone into that cave, Bluster would have swatted it dead without a second thought. Yet the drow and his panther were in there, day after day, setting their fires in the outer chamber while Bluster snored contentedly in the inner.

As a ranger, and knowing many other rangers, Montolio had seen and heard of stranger things. Up to now, though, he had always considered that innate ability to mentally connect with wild animals the exclusive domain of those surface elves, sprites, halflings, gnomes, and humans who had trained in the woodland way.

"How would a dark elf know of a bear?" Montolio asked aloud, still scratching at his beard. The ranger considered two possibilities: Either there was more to the drow race than he knew, or this particular dark elf was not akin to his kin. Given the elf's already strange behavior, Montolio assumed the latter, though he greatly wanted to find out for sure. His investigation would have to wait, though. The first snow had already fallen, and the ranger knew the second, and the third, and many more, would not be far behind. In the mountains around Dead Orc Pass, little moved once the snows had begun.

⚔ ⚔ ⚔ ⚔ ⚔

Guenhwyvar proved to be Drizzt's salvation through the coming tendays. On those occasions when the panther walked the Material Plane, Guenhwyvar went out into the frigid, deep snows continually, hunting and more importantly, bringing back wood for the life-giving fire.

Still, things were not easy for the displaced drow. Every day Drizzt had to go down to the river and break up the ice that formed in the slower pools, Drizzt's fishing pools, along its bank. It was not a far walk, but the snow was soon deep and treacherous, often sliding down the slope behind Drizzt to bury him in a chilling embrace. Several times, Drizzt stumbled back to his cave, all feeling gone from his hands and legs. He learned quickly to get the fires blazing before he went out, for on his return, he had no strength to hold the dagger and stone to strike a spark.

Even when Drizzt's belly was full and he was surrounded by the glow of the fire and Guenhwyvar's fur, he was cold and utterly miserable. For the first time in many tendays, the drow questioned his decision to leave the Underdark, and as his desperation grew, he questioned his decision to leave Menzoberranzan.

"Surely I am a homeless wretch," he often complained in those no-longer-so-rare moments of self-pity. "And surely I will die here, cold and alone."

Drizzt had no idea of what was going on in the strange world around him. Would the warmth that he found when he first came to the surface world ever return to the land? Or was this some vile curse, perhaps aimed at him by his mighty enemies back in Menzoberranzan? This confusion led Drizzt to a troublesome dilemma: Should he remain in the cave and try to wait out the storm (for what else could he call the wintry season)? Or should he set out from the river valley and seek a warmer climate?

He would have left, and the trek through the mountains most assuredly would have killed him, but he noticed another event coinciding with the harsh weather. The hours of daylight had lessened and the hours of night had increased. Would the sun disappear completely, engulfing the surface in an eternal darkness and eternal cold? Drizzt doubted that possibility, so, using some sand and an empty flask that he had in his pack, he began measuring the time of light and of darkness.

His hopes sank every time his calculations showed an earlier sunset, and as the season deepened, so did Drizzt's despair. His health diminished as well. He was a wretched thing indeed, thin and shivering, when he first noticed the seasonal turn-around, the winter solstice. He hardly believed his findings—his measurements were not so precise—but after the next few days, Drizzt could not deny what the falling sand told him.

The days were growing longer.

Drizzt's hope returned. He had suspected a seasonal variance since the first cool winds had begun to blow months before. He had watched the bear fishing more diligently as the weather worsened, and now he believed that the creature had anticipated the cold and had stored up its fat to sleep it out.

That belief, and his findings about the daylight, convinced Drizzt that this frozen desolation would not endure.

The solstice did not bring any immediate relief, though. The winds blew harder and the snow continued to pile. But Drizzt grew determined again, and more than a winter would be needed to defeat the indomitable drow.

Then it happened—almost overnight, it seemed. The snows lessened, the river ran freer of ice, and the wind shifted to bring in warmer air. Drizzt felt a surge of vitality and hope, a release from grief and from guilt that he could not explain. Drizzt could not realize what urges gripped him, had no name or concept for it, but he was as fully caught up in the timeless spring as all of the natural creatures of the surface world.

One morning, as Drizzt finished his meal and prepared for bed, his long-dormant roommate plodded out of the side chamber, noticeably more slender but still quite formidable. Drizzt watched the ambling bear carefully, wondering if he should summon Guenhwyvar or draw his scimitar. The bear paid him no heed, though. It shuffled right by him, stopped to sniff at and lick the flat stone Drizzt had used as a plate, and ambled out into the warm sunlight, stopping at the cave exit to give a yawn and a stretch so profound that Drizzt understood that its winter nap was at an end. Drizzt understood, too, that the cave would grow crowded very quickly with the dangerous animal up and about, and he decided that perhaps, with the more hospitable weather, the cave might not be worth fighting for.

Drizzt was gone before the bear returned, but to the bear's delight, he had left one final fish meal. Soon Drizzt was setting up in a more shallow and less protected cave a few hundred yards down the valley wall.

# 12
# To Know Your Enemies

Winter gave way as quickly as it had come. The snows lessened daily and the southern wind brought air that had no chill. Drizzt soon settled into a comfortable routine; the biggest problem he faced was the daytime glare of the sun off the still snow-covered ground. The drow had adapted quite well to the sun in his first few months on the surface, moving about—even fighting—in the daylight. Now, though, with the white snow throwing the glaring reflection back in his face, Drizzt could hardly venture out.

He came out only at night and left the daytime to the bear and other such creatures. Drizzt was not too concerned; the snow would be gone soon, he believed, and he could return to the easy life that had marked the last days before winter.

Well fed, well rested, and under the soft light of a shining, alluring moon one night, Drizzt glanced across the river, to the far wall of the valley.

"What is up there?" the drow whispered to himself. Though the river ran strong with the spring melt, earlier that night Drizzt had found a possible way across it, a series of large and closely spaced rocks poking up above the rushing water.

The night was still young; the moon was not halfway up in the sky. Filled with the wanderlust and spirit so typical of the season, Drizzt decided to have a look. He skipped down to the riverbank and jumped lightly and nimbly out onto the stones. To a man or an orc—or most of the other races of the world—crossing on the wet, unevenly spaced, and often rounded stones might have seemed too difficult and treacherous to even make the attempt, but the agile drow managed it quite easily.

He came down on the other bank running, springing over or around the many rocks and crags without a thought or care. How different his demeanor might have been if he had known that he was now on the side of the valley belonging to Graul, the great orc chieftain!

⚔ ⚔ ⚔ ⚔ ⚔

An orc patrol spotted the prancing drow before he was halfway up the valley wall. The orcs had seen the drow before, on occasions when Drizzt was fishing out at the river. Fearful of dark elves, Graul had ordered its minions to keep their distance, thinking the snows would drive the intruder away. But the winter had passed and this lone drow remained, and now he had crossed the river.

Graul wrung his fat-fingered hands nervously when he was told the news. The big orc was comforted a bit by the belief that this drow was alone and not a member of a larger band. He might be a scout or a renegade; Graul could not know for sure, and the implications of either did not please the orc chieftain. If the drow was a scout, more dark elves might follow, and if the drow was a renegade, he might look upon the orcs as possible allies.

Graul had been chieftain for many years, an unusually long tenure for the chaotic orcs. The big orc had survived by taking no chances, and Graul meant to take none now. A dark elf could usurp the leadership of the tribe, a position Graul coveted dearly. This, Graul would not permit. Two orc patrols slipped out of dark holes shortly thereafter, with explicit orders to kill the drow.

⚔ ⚔ ⚔ ⚔ ⚔

A chill wind blew above the valley wall, and the snow was deeper up here, but Drizzt didn't care. Great patches of evergreens rolled out before him, darkening the mountainous valleys and inviting him, after a winter cooped up in the cave, to come and explore.

He had put nearly a mile behind him when he first realized that he was being pursued. He never actually saw anything, except perhaps a fleeting shadow out of the corner of his eye, but those intangible warrior senses told Drizzt the truth beyond doubt. He moved up the side of a steep incline, climbed above a copse of thick trees, and sprinted for the high ridge. When he got there, he slipped behind a boulder and turned to watch.

Seven dark forms, six humanoid and one large canine, came out of the trees behind him, following his trail carefully and methodically. From this distance, Drizzt couldn't tell their race, though he suspected that they were humans. He looked all about, searching for his best course of retreat, or the best defensible area.

Drizzt hardly noticed that his scimitar was in one hand his dagger in the other. When he realized fully that he had drawn the weapons, and that the pursuing party was getting uncomfortably close, he paused and pondered.

He could face the pursuers right here and hit them as they scaled the last few treacherous feet of the slippery climb.

"No," Drizzt growled, dismissing that possibility as soon as it came to him. He could attack, and probably win, but then what burden would he carry away from the encounter? Drizzt wanted no fight, nor did he desire any contact at all. He already carried all the guilt he could handle.

He heard his pursuers' voices, guttural strains similar to the goblin tongue. "Orcs," the drow mouthed silently, matching the language with the creatures' human size.

The recognition did nothing to change the drow's attitudes, though. Drizzt had no love for orcs—he had seen enough of the smelly things back in Menzoberranzan—but neither did he have any reason, any justification, for battling this band. He turned and picked a path and sped off into the night.

The pursuit was dogged; the orcs were too close behind for Drizzt to shake them. He saw a problem developing, for if the orcs were hostile, and by their shouts and snarls, Drizzt believed that to be the case, then Drizzt had missed his opportunity to fight them on favorable ground. The moon had set long ago and the sky had taken on the blue tint of predawn. Orcs did not favor sunlight, but with the glare of the snow all about him, Drizzt would be nearly helpless in it.

Stubbornly the drow ignored the battle option and tried to outrun the pursuit, circling back toward the valley. Here Drizzt made his second error, for another orc band this one accompanied by both a wolf and a much larger form, a stone giant, lay in wait.

The path ran fairly level, one side of it dropping steeply down a rocky slope to the drow's left and the other climbing just as steeply and over ground just as rocky to his right. Drizzt knew his pursuers would have little trouble following him over such a predetermined course, but he relied solely on speed now, trying to get back to his defensible cave before the blinding sun came up.

A snarl warned him a moment before a huge bristle-haired wolf, called a worg, bounded around the boulders just above him and cut him off. The worg sprang at him, its jaws snapping for his head. Drizzt dipped low, under the assault, and his scimitar came out in a flash, slashing across to further widen the beast's huge maw. The worg tumbled down heavily behind the turning drow, its tongue lapping widely at its own gushing blood.

Drizzt whacked it again, dropping it, but the six orcs came rushing in, brandishing spears and clubs. Drizzt turned to flee, then ducked again, just in time, as a hurled boulder flew past, skipping down the rocky decline.

Without a second thought, Drizzt brought a globe of darkness down over his own head.

The four leading orcs plunged into the globe without realizing it. Their remaining two comrades held back, clutching spears and glancing nervously about. They could see nothing inside the magical darkness, but from the rushing thumps of blades and clubs and the wild shouting, it sounded as if an entire army battled in there. Then another sound issued from the darkness, a growling, feline sound.

The two orcs backed away, looking over their shoulders and wishing the stone giant would hurry up and get down to them. One of their orc comrades, and another, came tearing out of the blackness, screaming in terror. The first sped past its startled kin, but the second never made it.

Guenhwyvar latched on to the unfortunate orc and drove it to the ground, tearing the life from it. The panther hardly slowed, leaping out and taking down one of the waiting two as it frantically stumbled to get away. Those remaining outside the globe scrambled and tripped over the rocks, and Guenhwyvar, having finished the second kill, leaped off in pursuit.

Drizzt came out the other side of the globe unscathed, with both his scimitar and dagger dripping orc blood. The giant, huge and square-shouldered, with legs as large as tree trunks, stepped out to face him, and Drizzt never hesitated. He sprang to a large stone, then leaped off, his scimitar leading the way.

His agility and speed surprised the stone giant; the monster never even got its club or its free hand up to block. But luck was not with the drow this time. His scimitar, enchanted in the magic of the Underdark, had seen too much of the surface light. It drove against the stonelike skin of the fifteen-foot giant, bent nearly in half, and snapped at the hilt.

Drizzt bounced back, betrayed for the first time by his trusted weapon.

The giant howled and lifted its club, grinning evilly until a black form soared over its intended victim and crashed into its chest, raking with four cruel claws.

Guenhwyvar had saved Drizzt again, but the giant was hardly finished. It clubbed and thrashed until the panther flew free. Guenhwyvar tried to pivot and come right back in, but the panther landed on the down slope and its momentum broke away the sheet of snow. The cat slid and tumbled, and finally broke free of the slide, unharmed, but far down the mountainside from Drizzt and the battle.

The giant offered no smile this time. Blood seeped from a dozen deep scratches across its chest and face. Behind it, down the trail, the other orc group, led by a second howling worg, was quickly closing.

Like any wise warrior so obviously outnumbered, Drizzt turned and ran.

If the two orcs who had fled from Guenhwyvar had come right back down the slope, they could have cut the drow off. Orcs had never been known for bravery, though, and those two had already crested the ridge of the slope and were still running, not even looking back.

Drizzt sped along the trail, searching for some way he might descend and rejoin the panther. Nowhere on the slope seemed promising, though, for he would have to pick his way slowly and carefully, and no doubt with a giant raining boulders down at him. Going up seemed just as futile with the monster so close behind, so the drow just ran on, along the trail, hoping it wouldn't end anytime soon.

The sun peeked over the eastern horizon then, just another problem—suddenly one of many—for the desperate drow.

Understanding that fortune had turned against him, Drizzt somehow knew, even before he turned the trail's latest sharp corner, that he had come to the end of the road. A rock slide had long ago blocked the trail. Drizzt skidded to a halt and pulled off his pack, knowing that time was against him.

The worg-led orc band caught up to the giant, both gaining confidence in the presence of the other. Together they charged on, with the vicious worg sprinting out to take the lead.

Around a sharp bend the creature sped, stumbling and trying to stop when it tangled suddenly in a looped rope. Worgs were not stupid creatures, but this one didn't fully comprehend the terrible implications as the drow pushed a rounded stone over the ledge. The worg didn't understand that is, until the rope snapped taut and the stone pulled the beast, flying, down behind.

The simple trap had worked to perfection, but it was the only advantage Drizzt could hope to gain. Behind him, the trail was fully blocked, and to the sides, the slopes climbed and dropped too abruptly for him to flee. When the orcs and the giant came around the corner, tentatively after watching their worg go for a rather bumpy ride, Drizzt stood to face them with only a dagger in his hand.

The drow tried to parlay, using the goblin tongue, but the orcs would hear nothing of it. Before the first word left Drizzt's mouth, one of them had launched its spear.

The weapon came in a blur at the sun-blinded drow, but it was a curving shaft thrown by a clumsy creature. Drizzt easily sidestepped and returned the throw with his dagger. The orc could see better than the drow, but it was not as quick. It caught the dagger cleanly, right in the throat. Gurgling, the orc went down, and its closest comrade grabbed at the knife and tore it free, not to save the other orc, but merely to get its hands on so fine a weapon.

Drizzt scooped up the crude spear and planted his feet firmly as the stone giant stalked in.

An owl swooped down above the giant suddenly and gave a hoot, hardly distracting the determined monster. A moment later, though, the giant jerked forward, moved by the weight of an arrow that had suddenly thudded into its back.

Drizzt saw the quivering, black-feathered shaft as the angry giant spun about. The drow didn't question the unexpected aid. He drove his spear with all his strength right into the monster's backside.

The giant would have turned to respond, but the owl swooped in again and hooted and on cue, another arrow whistled in, this one digging into the giant's chest. Another hoot, and another arrow found the mark.

The stunned orcs looked all about for the unseen assailant, but the glaring brightness of the morning sun on the snow offered little assistance to the nocturnal beasts. The giant, struck through the heart, only stood and stared blankly, not even realizing that its life was at an end. The drow drove his spear in again from behind, but that action only served to tumble the monster away from Drizzt.

The orcs looked to each other and all around, wondering which way they could flee.

The strange owl dived in again, this time above an orc, and gave a fourth hoot. The orc, understanding the implications, waved its arms and shrieked, then fell silent with an arrow protruding from its face.

The four remaining orcs broke ranks and fled, one up the slope, another running back the way it had come, and two rushing toward Drizzt.

A deft spin of the spear sent its butt end slamming into the face of one orc, then Drizzt fully completed the spinning motion to deflect the other orc's spear tip toward the ground. The orc dropped the weapon, realizing that it could not get it back in line in time to stop the drow.

⚔ ⚔ ⚔ ⚔ ⚔

The orc climbing the slope understood its doom as the signaling owl closed on it. The terrified creature dived behind a rock upon hearing one hoot, but if it had been a smarter thing, it would have realized its error. By the angle of the shots that had felled the giant, the archer had to be somewhere up on this slope.

An arrow knocked into its thigh as it crouched, dropping it, writhing, to its back. With the orc's growling and thrashing, the unseen and unseeing archer hardly needed the owl's next hoot to place his second shot, this one catching the orc squarely in the chest and silencing it forever.

⚔ ⚔ ⚔ ⚔ ⚔

Drizzt reversed his direction immediately, clipping the second orc with the spear's butt end. In the blink of an eye, the drow reversed his grip a third time and drove the spear tip into the creature's throat, digging upward into its brain. The first orc that Drizzt had hit reeled and shook its head violently, trying to reorient itself to the battle. It felt the drow's hands grab at the front of its dirty bearskin tunic, then it felt a rush of air as it flew out over the ledge, taking the same route as the previously trapped worg.

⚔ ⚔ ⚔ ⚔ ⚔

Hearing the screams of its dying companions, the orc on the trail put its head down and sped on, thinking itself quite clever in taking this route. It changed its mind abruptly, though, when it turned a bend and ran straight into the waiting paws of a huge black panther.

⚔ ⚔ ⚔ ⚔ ⚔

Drizzt leaned back, exhausted, against the stone, holding his spear ready for a throw as the strange owl floated back down the mountainside. The owl kept its distance, though, alighting on the outcropping that forced the trail's sharp bend a dozen steps away.

Movement up above caught the drow's attention. He could hardly see in the blinding light, but he did make out a humanlike form picking a careful path down toward him.

The owl set off again, circling above the drow and calling, and Drizzt crouched, alert and unnerved, as the man slipped down to a position behind the rocky spur. No arrow whistled out to the owl's hooting, though. Instead came the archer.

He was tall, straight, and very old, with a huge gray moustache and wild gray hair. Most curious of all were his milky white and pupilless eyes. If Drizzt had not witnessed the man's archery display, he would have believed the man blind. The old man's limbs seemed quite frail, too, but Drizzt did not let appearances deceive him. The expert archer kept his heavy longbow bowed and ready, an arrow firmly nocked, with hardly any effort. The drow did not have to look far to see the deadly efficiency with which the human could put the powerful weapon to use.

The old man said something in a language that Drizzt could not understand then in a second tongue, then in goblin, which Drizzt understood. "Who are you?"

"Drizzt Do'Urden," the drow replied evenly, taking some hope in the fact that he could at least communicate with this adversary.

"Is that a name?" the old man asked. He chuckled and shrugged. "Whatever it is, and whoever you might be, and whyever you might be here, is of minor consequence."

The owl, noticing movement, started hooting and swooping widely, but it was too late for the old man. Behind him, Guenhwyvar slunk around the bend and closed to within an easy spring, ears flattened and teeth bared.

Seemingly oblivious to the peril, the old man finished his thought. "You are my prisoner now."

Guenhwyvar issued a low, throaty growl and the drow grinned broadly.

"I think not," Drizzt replied.

# 13
# Montolio

"Friend of yours?" the old man asked calmly.

"Guenhwyvar," Drizzt explained.

"Big cat?"

"Oh, yes," Drizzt answered.

The old man eased his bowstring straight and let the arrow slowly slip, point down. He closed his eyes, tilted his head back, and seemed to fall within himself. A moment later, Drizzt noticed that Guenhwyvar's ears came up suddenly, and the drow understood that this strange human was somehow making a telepathic link to the panther.

"Good cat, too," the old man said a moment later. Guenhwyvar walked out from around the outcropping—sending the owl flapping away in a frenzy—and casually stalked past the old man, moving to stand beside Drizzt. Apparently, the panther had relinquished all concerns that the old man was an enemy.

Drizzt considered Guenhwyvar's actions curious, viewing them in the same manner as he had his own empathic agreement with the bear in the cave a season ago.

"Good cat," the old man said again.

Drizzt leaned back against the stone and relaxed his grip on the spear.

"I am Montolio," the old man explained proudly, as though the name should carry some weight with the drow. "Montolio DeBrouchee."

"Well met and fare well," Drizzt said flatly. "If we are done with our meeting, then we may go our own ways."

"We may," Montolio agreed, "if we both choose to."

"Am I to be your . . . prisoner . . . once more?" Drizzt asked with a bit of sarcasm in his voice.

The sincerity of Montolio's ensuing laughter brought a smile to the drow's face despite his cynicism. "Mine?" the old man asked incredulously. "No, no, I believe we have settled that issue. But you have killed some minions of Graul this day, a deed that the orc king will want punished. Let me offer you a room at my castle. The orcs will not approach the place." He showed a wry smile and bent over toward Drizzt to whisper, as if to keep his next words a secret between them. "They will not come near me, you know." Montolio pointed to his strange eyes. "They believe me to be bad magic because of my . . ." Montolio struggled for the word that would convey the thought, but the guttural language was limited and he soon grew frustrated.

Drizzt silently recounted the course of the battle, then his jaw drooped open in undeniable amazement as he realized the truth of what had transpired. The old man was indeed blind! The owl, circling over enemies and hooting, had led his shots. Drizzt looked around at the slain giant and orc and his jaw did not close; the old man hadn't missed.

"Will you come?" Montolio asked. "I would like to gain the—" again he had to search for an appropriate term—"purposes . . . a dark elf would have to live a winter in a cave with Bluster the bear."

Montolio cringed at his own inability to converse with the drow, but from the context, Drizzt could pretty much understand what the old man meant, even figuring out unfamiliar terms such as "winter" and "bear."

"Orc king Graul has ten hundred more fighters to send against you," Montolio remarked, sensing that the drow was having a difficult time considering the offer.

"I will not come with you," Drizzt declared at length. The drow truly wanted to go, wanted to learn a few things about this remarkable man, but too many tragedies had befallen those who had crossed Drizzt's path.

Guenhwyvar's low growl told Drizzt that the panther did not approve of his decision.

"I bring trouble," Drizzt tried to explain to the old man, to the panther, and to himself. "You would be better served, Montolio DeBrouchee, to keep away from me."

"Is this a threat?"

"A warning," Drizzt replied. "If you take me in, if you even allow me to remain near to you, then you will be doomed, as were the farmers in the village."

Montolio perked his ears up at the mention of the distant farming village. He had heard that one family in Maldobar had been brutally killed and that a ranger, Dove Falconhand had been called in to help.

"I do not fear doom," Montolio said, forcing a smile. "I have lived through many . . . fights, Drizzt Do'Urden. I have fought in a dozen bloody wars and spent an entire winter trapped on the side of a mountain with a broken leg. I have killed a giant with only a dagger and . . . befriended every animal for five thousand steps in any direction. Do not fear for me." Again came that wry, knowing smile. "But then," Montolio said slowly, "It is not for me that you fear."

Drizzt felt confused and a bit insulted.

"You fear for yourself," Montolio continued, undaunted. "Self-pity? It does not fit one of your prowess. Dismiss and come along with me."

If Montolio had seen Drizzt's scowl, he would have guessed the forthcoming answer. Guenhwyvar did notice it, and the panther bumped hard into Drizzt's leg.

From Guenhwyvar's reaction, Montolio understood the drow's intent. "The cat wants you to come along," he remarked. "It'll be better than a cave," he promised, "and better food than half-cooked fish."

Drizzt looked down at Guenhwyvar and again the panther bumped him, this time voicing a louder and more insistent growl with the action.

Drizzt remained adamant, reminding himself pointedly by conjuring an image of carnage in a farmhouse far away. "I will not come," he said firmly.

"Then I must name you as an enemy, and a prisoner!" Montolio roared, snapping his bow back to a ready position. "Your cat will not aid you this time, Drizzt Do'Urden!" Montolio leaned in and flashed his smile and whispered, "The cat agrees with me."

It was too much for Drizzt. He knew that the old man wouldn't shoot him, but Montolio's flaky charm soon wore away the drow's mental defenses, considerable though they were.

What Montolio had described as a castle turned out to be a series of wooden caves dug around the roots of huge and tightly packed evergreens. Lean-tos of woven sticks furthered the protection and somewhat linked the caves together, and a low wall of stacked rocks ringed the whole complex. As Drizzt neared the place, he noticed several rope-and-wood bridges crossing from tree to tree at various heights, with rope ladders leading up to them from the ground level and with crossbows securely mounted at fairly regular intervals.

The drow didn't complain that the castle was of wood and dirt, though. Drizzt had spent three decades in Menzoberranzan living in a wondrous castle of stone and surrounded by many more breathtakingly beautiful structures, but none of them seemed as welcoming as Montolio's home.

Birds chittered their welcome at the old ranger's approach. Squirrels, even a raccoon, hopped excitedly among the tree branches to get near him—though they kept their distance when they noticed that a huge panther accompanied Montolio.

"I have many rooms," Montolio explained to Drizzt. "Many blankets and much food." Montolio hated the limited goblin tongue. He had so many things he wanted to say to the drow, and so many things he wanted to learn from the drow. This seemed impossible, if not overly tedious, in a language so base and negative in nature, not designed for complex thoughts or notions. The goblin tongue sported more than a hundred words for killing and for hatred, but not a one for higher emotions such as compassion. The goblin word for friendship could be translated to mean either a temporary military alliance or servitude to a stronger goblin, and neither definition fit Montolio's intentions toward the lone dark elf.

The first task then, the ranger decided, was to teach this drow the common tongue.

"We cannot speak"—There was no word for "properly" in Goblin, so Montolio had to improvise ". . . well . . . in this language," he explained to Drizzt, "but it will serve us as I teach you the tongue of humans—if you wish to learn."

Drizzt remained tentative in his acceptance. When he had walked away from the farming village, he had decided that his lot in life would be as a hermit, and thus far he had done pretty well—better than he had expected. The offer was tempting, though, and on a practical level, Drizzt knew that knowing the common language of the region might keep him out of trouble. Montolio's smile nearly took in the ranger's ears when the drow accepted.

Hooter, the owl, however, seemed not so pleased. With the drow—or, more particularly, with the drow's panther—about, the owl would be spending less time in the comforts of the evergreens' lower boughs.

⚔ ⚔ ⚔ ⚔ ⚔

"Cousin, Montolio DeBrouchee has taken the drow in!" an elf cried excitedly to Kellindil. All the group had been out searching for Drizzt's trail since the winter had broken. With the drow gone from Dead Orc Pass, the elves, particularly Kellindil, had feared trouble, had feared that the drow had perhaps taken in with Graul and his orc minions.

Kellindil jumped to his feet, hardly able to grasp the startling news. He knew of Montolio, the legendary if somewhat eccentric ranger, and he knew, too, that Montolio, with all of his animal contacts, could judge intruders quite accurately.

"When? How?" Kellindil asked, barely knowing where to begin. If the drow had confused him through the previous months, the surface elf was thoroughly flustered now.

"A tenday ago," the other elf answered. "I know not how it came about, but the drow now walks in Montolio's grove, openly and with his panther beside him."

"Is Montolio . . ."

The other elf interrupted Kellindil, seeing where his line of concern was heading. "Montolio is unharmed and in control," he assured Kellindil. "He has taken in the drow of his own accord, it would seem, and now it appears that the old ranger is teaching the dark elf the common tongue."

"Amazing," was all that Kellindil could reply.

"We could set a watch over Montolio's grove," the other elf offered. "If you fear for the old ranger's safety—"

"No," Kellindil replied. "No, the drow once again has proven himself no enemy. I have suspected his friendly intentions since I encountered him near Maldobar. Now I am satisfied. Let us get on with our business and leave the drow and the ranger to theirs."

The other elf nodded his agreement, but a diminutive creature listening outside Kellindil's tent was not so certain.

Tephanis came into the elven camp nightly, to steal food and other items that would make him more comfortable. The sprite had heard of the dark elf a few days earlier, when the elves had resumed their search for Drizzt, and he had taken great pains to listen to their conversation ever since, as curious as any about the whereabouts of the one who had destroyed Ulgulu and Kempfana.

Tephanis shook his floppy-eared head violently. "Drat-the-day-that-that-one-returned!" he whispered, sounding somewhat like an excited bumblebee. Then he ran off, his little feet barely touching the ground. Tephanis had made another connection in the months since Ulgulu's demise, another powerful ally that he did not want to lose.

Within minutes he found Caroak, the great, silver-haired winter wolf, on the high peak that they called their home.

"The-drow-is-with-the-ranger," Tephanis spouted, and the canine beast seemed to understand. "Beware-of-that-one-I-say! It-was-he-who-killed-my-former-masters. Dead!"

Caroak looked down the wide expanse to the mountain that held Montolio's grove. The winter wolf knew that place well, and he knew well enough to stay away from it. Montolio DeBrouchee was friends with all sorts of animals, but winter wolves were more monster than animal, and no friend of rangers.

Tephanis, too, looked Montolio's way, worried that he might again have to face the sneaky drow. The mere thought of encountering that one again made the little sprite's head ache (and the bruise from the plowshare had never completely gone away).

⚔ ⚔ ⚔ ⚔ ⚔

As winter eased into spring over the next few tendays, so did Drizzt and Montolio ease into their friendship. The common tongue of the region was not so very different from the goblin tongue, more a shift of inflection than an alteration of complete words, and Drizzt caught on to it quickly, even learning how to read and write. Montolio proved a fine teacher, and by the third tenday, he spoke to Drizzt exclusively in the common tongue and scowled impatiently every time Drizzt reverted to using goblin to get a point across.

For Drizzt, this was a fun time, a time of easy living and shared pleasures. Montolio's collection of books was extensive, and the drow found himself absorbed in adventures of the imagination, in dragon lore, and accounts of epic battles. Any doubts Drizzt might have had were long gone, as were his doubts about Montolio. The shelter in the evergreens was indeed a castle, and the old man as fine a host as Drizzt had ever known.

Drizzt learned many other things from Montolio during those first tendays, practical lessons that would aid him for the rest of his life. Montolio confirmed Drizzt's suspicions about a seasonal weather change, and he even taught Drizzt how to anticipate the weather from day to day by watching the animals, the sky, and the wind.

In this, too, Drizzt caught on quickly, as Montolio had suspected he would. Montolio never would have believed it until he had witnessed it personally, but this unusual drow possessed the demeanor of a surface elf, perhaps even the heart of a ranger.

"How did you calm the bear?" Montolio asked one day, a question that had nagged at him since the very first day he had learned that Drizzt and Bluster were sharing a cave.

Drizzt honestly did not know how to answer, for he still did not understand what had transpired in that meeting. "The same way you calmed Guenhwyvar when first we met," the drow offered at length.

Montolio's grin told Drizzt that the old man understood better than he. "Heart of a ranger," Montolio whispered as he turned away. With his exceptional ears, Drizzt heard the comment, but he didn't fully comprehend.

Drizzt's lessons came faster as the days rolled along. Now Montolio concentrated on the life around them, the animals and the plants. He showed Drizzt how to forage and how to understand the emotions of an animal simply by watching its movements. The first real test came soon after, when Drizzt, shifting the outward branches of a berry bush, found the entrance to a small den and was promptly confronted by an angry badger.

Hooter, in the sky above, issued a series of cries to alert Montolio, and the ranger's first instinct was to go and help his drow friend. Badgers were possibly the meanest creatures in the region, even above the orcs, quicker to anger than Bluster the bear and quite willing to take the offensive against any opponent, no matter how large. Montolio stayed back, though, listening to Hooter's continuing descriptions of the scene.

Drizzt's first instinct sent his hand flashing to his dagger. The badger reared and showed its wicked teeth and claws, hissing and sputtering a thousand complaints.

Drizzt eased back, even put his dagger back in its sheath. Suddenly, he viewed the encounter from the badger's point of view, knew that the animal felt overly threatened. Somehow, Drizzt then further realized that the badger had chosen this den as a place to raise its soon-coming litter of pups.

The badger seemed confused by the drow's deliberate motions. Late in term, the expectant mother did not want a fight, and as Drizzt carefully slipped the berry bush back in place to conceal the den, the badger eased down to all fours, sniffed the air so that it could remember the dark elf's scent, and went back into its hole.

When Drizzt turned around, he found Montolio smiling and clapping. "Even a ranger would be hard put to calm a riled badger," the old man explained.

"The badger was with pups," Drizzt replied. "She wanted to fight less than I."

"How do you know that?" Montolio asked, though he did not doubt the drow's perceptions.

Drizzt started to answer, then realized that he could not. He looked back to the berry bush, then to Montolio helplessly.

Montolio laughed loudly and returned to his work. He, who had followed the ways of the goddess Mielikki for so many years, knew what was happening, even if Drizzt did not.

"The badger could have ripped you, you do know," the ranger said wryly when Drizzt moved beside him.

"She was with pups," Drizzt reminded him, "and not so large a foe."

Montolio's laughter mocked him. "Not so large?" the ranger echoed. "Trust me, Drizzt, you would rather tangle with Bluster than with a mother badger!"

Drizzt only shrugged in response, having no arguments for the more experienced man.

"Do you really believe that puny knife would have been any defense against her?" Montolio asked, now wanting to take the discussion in a different direction.

Drizzt regarded the dagger, the one he had taken from the sprite. Again he could not argue; the knife was indeed puny. He laughed both to and at himself. "It is all that I have, I fear," he replied.

"We shall see about that," the ranger promised, then said no more about it. Montolio, for all his calm and confidence, knew well the dangers of the wild, mountainous region.

The ranger had come to trust in Drizzt without reservations.

⚔ ⚔ ⚔ ⚔ ⚔

Montolio roused Drizzt shortly before sunset and led the drow to a wide tree in the northern end of the grove. A large hole, almost a cave, lay at the base of the tree, cunningly concealed by shrubs and a blanket colored to resemble the tree trunk. As soon as Montolio pushed this aside, Drizzt understood the secrecy.

"An armory?" the drow asked in amazement.

"You fancy the scimitar," Montolio replied, remembering the weapon Drizzt had broken on the stone giant. "I have a good one, too." He crawled inside and fished about for a while, then returned with a fine, curving blade. Drizzt moved in to the hole to survey the marvelous display of weapons as the ranger exited. Montolio possessed a huge variety of weapons, from ornamental daggers to great bardiche axes to crossbows, light and heavy, all polished and cared for meticulously. Set against the back of the inner tree trunk, running right up into the tree, were a variety of spears, including one metal-shafted ranseur, a ten-foot-long pike with a long and pointed head and two smaller barbs sticking out to the sides near the tip.

"Do you prefer a shield, or perhaps a dirk, for your other hand?" Montolio asked when the drow, muttering to himself in sincere admiration, reappeared. "You may have any but those bearing the taloned owl. That shield, sword, and helmet are my own."

Drizzt hesitated a moment, trying to imagine the blind ranger so outfitted for close melee. "A sword," he said at length, "or another scimitar if you have one."

Montolio looked at him curiously. "Two long blades for fighting," he remarked. "You would likely tangle yourself up in them, I would guess."

"It is not so uncommon a fighting style among the drow," Drizzt said.

Montolio shrugged, not doubting, and went back in. "This one is more for show, I fear," he said as he returned, bearing an overly ornamented blade. "You may use it if you choose, or take a sword. I've a number of those."

Drizzt took the scimitar to measure its balance. It was a bit too light and perhaps a bit too fragile. The drow decided to keep it, though, thinking its curving blade a better compliment to his other scimitar than a straight and cumbersome sword.

"I will care for these as well as you have," Drizzt promised, realizing how great a gift the human had given him. "And I will use them," he added, knowing what Montolio truly wanted to hear, "only when I must."

"Then pray that you may never need them, Drizzt Do'Urden," Montolio replied. "I have seen peace and I have seen war, and I can tell you that I prefer the former! Come now, friend. There are so many more things I wish to show you."

Drizzt regarded the scimitars one final time, then slipped them into the sheaths on his belt and followed Montolio.

With summer fast approaching and with such fine and exciting companionship, both the teacher and his unusual student were in high spirits, anticipating a season of valuable lessons and wondrous events.

⚔ ⚔ ⚔ ⚔ ⚔

How diminished their smiles would have been if they had known that a certain orc king, angered at the loss of ten soldiers, two worgs, and a valued giant ally, had its yellow, bloodshot eyes scanning the region, searching for the drow. The big orc was beginning to wonder if Drizzt had gone back to the Underdark or had taken in with some other group, perhaps with the small elven bands known to be in the region, or with the damnable blind ranger, Montolio. If the drow was still in the area, Graul meant to find him. The orc chieftain took no chances, and the mere presence of the drow constituted a risk.

# 14
# Montolio's Test

"Well, I have waited long enough!" Montolio said sternly late one afternoon. He gave the drow another shake.

"Waited?" Drizzt asked, wiping the sleep from his eyes.

"Are you a fighter or a wizard?" Montolio went on. "Or both? One of those multitalented types? The elves of the surface are known for that."

Drizzt's expression twisted in confusion. "I am no wizard," he said with a laugh.

"Keeping secrets, are you?" Montolio scolded, though his continuing smirk lessened his gruff facade. He pointedly straightened himself outside of Drizzt's bedroom hole and folded his arms over his chest. "That will not do. I have taken you in, and if you are a wizard, I must be told!"

"Why do you say that?" asked the perplexed drow. "Wherever did you—"

"Hooter told me!" Montolio blurted. Drizzt was truly confused. "In the fight when first we met," Montolio explained, "you darkened the area around yourself and some orcs. Do not deny it, wizard. Hooter told me!"

"That was no wizard's spell," Drizzt protested helplessly, "and I am no wizard."

"No spell?" echoed Montolio. "A device then? Well, let me see it!"

"Not a device," Drizzt replied, "an ability. All drow, even the lowest ranking, can create globes of darkness. It is not such a difficult task."

Montolio considered the revelation for a moment. He had no experience with dark elves before Drizzt had come into his life. "What other 'abilities' do you possess?"

"Faerie fire," Drizzt replied. "It is a line of—"

"I know of the spell," Montolio said to him. "It is commonly used by woodland priests. Can all drow create this as well?"

"I do not know," Drizzt answered honestly. "Also, I am—or was—able to levitate. Only drow nobles can accomplish that feat. I fear that the power is lost to me, or soon shall be. That ability has begun to fail me since I came to the surface, as my *piwafwi*, my boots, and my drow-crafted scimitars have failed me."

"Try it," Montolio offered.

Drizzt concentrated for a long moment. He felt himself growing lighter, then he lifted off the ground. As soon as he got up, though, his weight returned and he settled back to his feet. He rose no more than three inches.

"Impressive," Montolio muttered.

Drizzt only laughed and shook his white mane. "May I go back to sleep now?" he asked, turning back to his bedroll.

Montolio had other ideas. He had come to further feel out his companion, to find the limits of Drizzt's abilities, wizardly and otherwise. A new plan came to the ranger, but he had to set it into motion before the sun went down.

"Wait," he bade Drizzt. "You can rest later, after sunset. I need you now, and your 'abilities.' Could you summon a globe of darkness, or must you take time to contemplate the spell?"

"A few seconds," Drizzt replied.

"Then get your armor and weapons," Montolio said, "and come with me. Be quick about it. I do not want to lose the advantage of daylight."

Drizzt shrugged and got dressed, then followed the ranger to the grove's northern end, a little used section of the woodland complex.

Montolio dropped to his knees and pulled Drizzt down beside him, pointing out a small hole on the side of a grassy mound.

"A wild boar has taken to living in there," the old ranger explained. "I do not wish to harm it, but I fear to get close enough to make contact with the thing. Boars are unpredictable at best."

A long moment of silence passed. Drizzt wondered if Montolio simply meant to wait for the boar to emerge.

"Go ahead then," the ranger prompted.

Drizzt turned on him incredulously, thinking that Montolio expected him to walk right up and greet their uninvited and unpredictable guest.

"Do it," the ranger continued. "Enact your darkness globe—right in front of the hole—if you please."

Drizzt understood, and his relieved sigh made Montolio bite his lip to hide his revealing chuckle. A moment later, the area before the grassy mound disappeared in blackness. Montolio motioned for Drizzt to wait behind and headed in.

Drizzt tensed, watching and listening. Several high-pitched squeals issued forth suddenly, then Montolio cried out in distress. Drizzt leaped up and charged in headlong, nearly tripping over his friend's prostrate form.

The old ranger groaned and squirmed and did not answer any of the drow's quiet calls. With no boar to be heard anywhere about, Drizzt dropped down to find out what had happened and recoiled when he found Montolio curled up, clutching at his chest.

"Montolio," Drizzt breathed, thinking the old man seriously wounded. He leaned over to speak directly into the ranger's face, then straightened quicker than he had intended as Montolio's shield slammed into the side of his head.

"It is Drizzt!" the drow cried, rubbing his developing bruise. He heard Montolio jump up before him, then heard the ranger's sword come out of its scabbard.

"Of course it is!" Montolio cackled.

"But what of the boar?"

"Boar?" Montolio echoed. "There is no boar, you silly drow. There never was one. We are the opponents here. The time has come for some fun!"

Now Drizzt fully understood. Montolio had manipulated him to use his darkness merely to take away his advantage of sight. Montolio was challenging him, on even terms. "Flat of the blade!" Drizzt replied, quite willing to play along. How Drizzt had loved such tests of skill back in Menzoberranzan with Zaknafein!

"For the sake of your life!" Montolio retorted with a laugh that came straight from his belly. The ranger sent his sword arcing in, and Drizzt's scimitar drove it harmlessly wide.

Drizzt countered with two rapid and short strokes straight up the middle, an attack that would have defeated most foes but did no more than play a two-note tune on Montolio's well-positioned shield. Certain of Drizzt's location, the ranger shield-rushed straight ahead.

Drizzt was pushed back on his heels before he managed to get out of the way. Montolio's sword came in again from the side, and Drizzt blocked it. The old man's shield slammed straight ahead again, and Drizzt deflected its momentum, digging his heels in stubbornly.

The crafty old ranger thrust the shield up high then, taking one of Drizzt's blades, and a good measure of the drow's balance, along with it, then sent his sword screaming across at Drizzt's midsection.

Drizzt somehow sensed the attack. He leaped back on his toes, sucked in his gut, and threw his rump out behind him. For all his desperation, he still felt the rush as the sword whisked past.

Drizzt went to the offensive, launching several cunning and intricate routines that he believed would end this contest. Montolio anticipated each one, though, for all of Drizzt's efforts were rewarded with the same sound of scimitar on shield. The ranger came on then and Drizzt was sorely pressed. The drow was no novice to blind-fighting, but Montolio lived every hour of every day as a blind man and functioned as well and as easily as most men with perfect vision.

Soon Drizzt realized that he could not win in the globe. He thought of moving the ranger out of the spell's area, but then the situation changed suddenly as the darkness expired. Thinking the game over, Drizzt backed up several steps, feeling his way with his feet up a rising tree root.

Montolio regarded his opponent curiously for a moment, noting the change in fighting attitude, then came on, hard and low.

Drizzt thought himself very clever as he dived headlong over the ranger, meaning to roll to his feet behind Montolio and come back in from one side or the other as the confused human spun about, disoriented.

Drizzt didn't get what he expected, though. Montolio's shield met the drow's face as he was halfway over, and Drizzt groaned and fell heavily to the ground. By the time he shook the dizziness away, he became aware that Montolio was sitting comfortably on his back, sword resting across Drizzt's shoulders.

"How . . ." Drizzt started to ask.

Montolio's voice was as sharp-edged as Drizzt had ever heard it. "You underestimated me, drow. You considered me blind and helpless. Never do that again!"

Drizzt honestly wondered, for just a split second, if Montolio meant to kill him, so angry was the ranger. He knew that his condescension had wounded the man, and he realized then that Montolio DeBrouchee, so confident and able, carried his own weight upon his old shoulders. For the first time since he had met the ranger, Drizzt considered how painful it must have been for the man to lose his sight. What else, Drizzt wondered, had Montolio lost?

"So obvious," Montolio said after a short pause. His voice had softened again. "With me charging in low, as I did."

"Obvious only if you sensed that the darkness spell had ended," Drizzt replied, wondering how disabled Montolio truly was. "I would never have attempted the diving maneuver in the darkness, without my eyes to guide me, yet how could a blind man know that the spell was no more?"

"You told me yourself!" Montolio protested, still making no move to get off Drizzt's back. "In attitude! The sudden shuffle of your feet—too lightly to be made in absolute blackness—and your sigh, drow! That sigh belied your relief, though you knew by then that you could not best me without your sight."

Montolio got up from Drizzt, but the drow remained prone, digesting the revelations. He realized how little he knew about his companion, how much he had taken for granted where Montolio was concerned.

"Come along, then," Montolio said. "This night's first lesson is ended. It was a valuable one, but there are other things we must accomplish."

"You said that I could sleep," Drizzt reminded him.

"I had thought you more competent," Montolio replied immediately, casting a smirk the prone drow's way.

⚔ ⚔ ⚔ ⚔ ⚔

While Drizzt eagerly absorbed the many lessons Montolio set out for him, that night and in the days that followed, the old ranger gathered his own information about the drow. Their work was most concerned with the present, Montolio teaching Drizzt about the world around him and how to survive in it. Invariably one or the other, usually Drizzt, would slip in some comment about his past. It became almost a game between the two, remarking on some distant event, more to measure the shocked expression of the other than to make any relevant point. Montolio had some fine anecdotes about his many years on the road, tales of valorous battles against goblins and humorous pranks that the usually serious-minded rangers often played on one another. Drizzt remained a bit guarded about his own past, but still his tales of Menzoberranzan, of the sinister and insidious Academy and the savage wars pitting family against family, went far beyond anything Montolio had ever imagined.

As great as the drow's tales were, though, Montolio knew that Drizzt was holding back, was carrying some great burden on his shoulders. The ranger didn't press Drizzt at first. He kept his patience, satisfied that he and Drizzt shared principles and—as he came to know with the drastic improvement of Drizzt's ranger skills—a similar way of viewing the world.

One night, beneath the moon's silvery light, Drizzt and Montolio rested back in wooden chairs that the ranger had constructed high in the boughs of a large evergreen. The brightness of the waning moon, as it dipped and dodged behind fast-moving, scattered clouds, enchanted the drow.

Montolio couldn't see the moon, of course, but the old ranger, with Guenhwyvar comfortably draped across his lap, enjoyed the brisk night no less. He rubbed a hand absently through the thick fur on Guenhwyvar's muscled neck and listened to the many sounds carried on the breeze, the chatter of a thousand creatures that the drow never even noticed, even though Drizzt's hearing was superior to Montolio's. Montolio chuckled every now and again, once when he heard a field mouse squealing angrily at an owl—Hooter probably—for interrupting its meal and forcing it to flee into its hole.

Looking at the ranger and Guenhwyvar, so at ease and accepting of one another, Drizzt felt the pangs of friendship and guilt. "Perhaps I should never have come," he whispered, turning his gaze back to the moon.

"Why?" Montolio asked quietly. "You do not like my food?" His smile disarmed Drizzt as the drow turned back to him somberly.

"To the surface, I mean," Drizzt explained, managing a laugh in spite of his melancholy. "Sometimes I think my choice a selfish act."

"Survival usually is," Montolio replied. "I have felt that way myself on some occasions. I was once forced to drive my sword into a man's heart. The harshness of the world brings great remorse, but mercifully it is a passing lament and certainly not one to carry into battle."

"How I wish it would pass," Drizzt remarked, more to himself or to the moon than to Montolio.

But the remark hit Montolio squarely. The closer he and Drizzt had become, the more the ranger shared Drizzt's unknown burden. The drow was young by elf standards but was already world-wise and skilled in battle beyond most professional soldiers. Undeniably one of Drizzt's dark heritage would find barriers in an unaccepting surface world. By Montolio's estimation, though, Drizzt should be able to get through these prejudices and live a long and prosperous life, given his considerable talents. What was it, Montolio wondered, that so burdens this elf? Drizzt suffered more than he smiled and punished himself more than he should.

"Is yours an honest lament?" Montolio asked him. "Most are not, you know. Most self-imposed burdens are founded on misperceptions. We—at least we of sincere character—always judge ourselves by stricter standards than we expect others to abide by. It is a curse, I suppose, or a blessing, depending on how one views it." He cast his sightless gaze Drizzt's way. "Take it as a blessing, my friend, an inner calling that forces you to strive to unattainable heights."

"A frustrating blessing," Drizzt replied casually.

"Only when you do not pause to consider the advances that the striving has brought to you," Montolio was quick to reply, as though he had expected the drow's words. "Those who aspire to less accomplish less. There can be no doubt. It is better, I think, to grab at the stars than to sit flustered because you know you cannot reach them." He shot Drizzt his typical wry smile. "At least he who reaches will get a good stretch, a good view, and perhaps even a low-hanging apple for his effort!"

"And perhaps also a low-flying arrow fired by some unseen assailant," Drizzt remarked sourly.

Montolio tilted his head helplessly against Drizzt's unending stream of pessimism. It pained him deeply to see the good-hearted drow so scarred. "He might indeed," Montolio said, a bit more harshly than he had intended, "but the loss of life is only great to those who chance to live it! Let your arrow come in low and catch the huddler on the ground, I say. His death would not be so tragic!"

Drizzt could not deny the logic, nor the comfort the old ranger gave to him. Over the last few tendays, Montolio's offhanded philosophies and way of looking at the world—pragmatically yet heavily edged with youthful exuberance, put Drizzt more at ease than he had been since his earliest training days in Zaknafein's gymnasium. But Drizzt also could not deny the inevitably short life span of that comfort. Words could soothe, but they could not erase the haunting memories of Drizzt's past, the distant voices of dead Zaknafein, dead Clacker, and the dead farmers. A single mental echo of "drizzit" vanquished hours of Montolio's well-intended advice.

"Enough of this cockeyed banter," Montolio went on, seeming perturbed. "I call you friend, Drizzt Do'Urden, and I hope you call me the same. What sort of friend might I be against this weight that stoops your shoulders unless I know more of it? I am your friend, or I am not. The decision is yours, but if I am not, then I see no purpose in sharing nights as wondrous as this beside you. Tell me, Drizzt, or be gone from my home!"

Drizzt could hardly believe that Montolio, normally so patient and relaxed, had put him on such a spot. The drow's first reaction was to recoil, to build a wall of anger in the face of the old man's presumptions and cling to that which he considered personal. As the moments passed, though, and Drizzt got beyond his initial surprise and took the time to sift through

Montolio's statement, he came to understand one basic truth that excused those presumptions: He and Montolio had indeed become friends, mostly through the ranger's efforts.

Montolio wanted to share in Drizzt's past, so that he might better understand and comfort his new friend.

"Do you know of Menzoberranzan, the city of my birth and of my kin?" Drizzt asked softly. Even speaking the name pained him. "And do you know the ways of my people, or the Spider Queen's edicts?"

Montolio's voice was somber as he replied. "Tell me all of it, I beg."

Drizzt nodded—Montolio sensed the motion even if he could not see it—and relaxed against the tree. He stared at the moon but actually looked right past it. His mind wandered back through his adventures, back down that road to Menzoberranzan, to the Academy, and to House Do'Urden. He held his thoughts there for a while, lingering on the complexities of drow family life and on the welcomed simplicity of his times in the training room with Zaknafein.

Montolio watched patiently, guessing that Drizzt was looking for a place to begin. From what he had learned from Drizzt's passing remarks, Drizzt's life had been filled with adventure and turbulent times, and Montolio knew that it would be no easy feat for Drizzt, with his still limited command of the common tongue, to accurately recount all of it. Also, given the burdens, the guilt and the sorrow, the drow obviously carried, Montolio suspected that Drizzt might be hesitant.

"I was born on an important day in the history of my family," Drizzt began. "On that day, House Do'Urden eliminated House DeVir."

"Eliminated?"

"Massacred," Drizzt explained. Montolio's blind eyes revealed nothing, but the ranger's expression was clearly one of revulsion, as Drizzt had expected. Drizzt wanted his companion to understand the horrible depths of drow society, so he pointedly added, "And on that day, too, my brother Dinin drove his sword through the heart of our other brother, Nalfein."

A shudder coursed up Montolio's spine and he shook his head. He realized that he was only just beginning to understand the burdens Drizzt carried.

"It is the drow way," Drizzt said calmly, matter-of-factly, trying to impart the dark elves' casual attitude toward murder. "There is a strict structure of rank in Menzoberranzan. To climb it, to attain a higher rank, whether as an individual or a family, you simply eliminate those above you."

A slight quiver in his voice betrayed Drizzt to the ranger. Montolio clearly understood that Drizzt did not accept the evil practices, and never had.

Drizzt went on with his story, telling it completely and accurately, at least for the more than forty years he had spent in the Underdark. He told of his days under the strict tutelage of his sister Vierna, cleaning the house chapel endlessly and learning of his innate powers and his place in drow society. Drizzt spent a long time explaining that peculiar social structure to Montolio, the hierarchies based on strict rank, and the hypocrisy of drow "law," a cruel facade screening a city of utter chaos. The ranger cringed as he heard of the family wars. They were brutal conflicts that allowed for no noble survivors, not even children. Montolio cringed even more when Drizzt told him of drow "justice," of the destruction wreaked upon a house that had failed in its attempt to eradicate another family.

The tale was less grim when Drizzt told of Zaknafein, his father and dearest friend. Of course, Drizzt's happy memories of his father became only a short reprieve, a prelude to the horrors of Zaknafein's demise. "My mother killed my father," Drizzt explained soberly, his deep pain evident, "sacrificed him to Lolth for my crimes, then animated his corpse and sent it out to kill me, to punish me for betraying the family and the Spider Queen."

It took a while for Drizzt to resume, but when he did, he again spoke truthfully, even revealing his own failures in his days alone in the wilds of the Underdark. "I feared that I had lost myself and my principles to some instinctive, savage monster," Drizzt said, verging on despair. But then the emotional wave that had been his existence rose again, and a smile found his face as he recounted his time beside Belwar, the most honored svirfneblin burrow-warden, and Clacker, the pech who had been polymorphed into a hook horror. Expectedly, the smile proved short lived, for Drizzt's tale eventually led him to where Clacker fell to Matron Malice's undead monster. Another friend had died on Drizzt's behalf.

Appropriately, by the time Drizzt came to his exit from the Underdark, the dawn peeked through the eastern mountains. Now Drizzt picked his words more carefully, not ready to divulge the tragedy of the farming family for fear that Montolio would judge him and blame him, destroying their newfound bond. Rationally, Drizzt could remind himself that he had not killed the farmers, had even avenged their deaths, but guilt was rarely a rational emotion, and Drizzt simply could not find the words—not yet.

Montolio, aged and wise and with animal scouts throughout the region, knew that Drizzt was concealing something. When they had first met, the drow had mentioned a doomed farming family, and Montolio had heard of a family slaughtered in the village of Maldobar. Montolio didn't believe for a minute that Drizzt could have done it, but he suspected that the drow was somehow involved. He didn't press Drizzt, though. Drizzt had been more honest, and more complete, than Montolio had expected, and the ranger was confident that the drow would fill in the obvious holes in his own time.

"It is a good tale," Montolio said at length. "You have been through more in your few decades than most elves will know in three hundred years. But the scars are few, and they will heal."

Drizzt, not so certain, put a lamenting look upon him, and Montolio could only offer a comforting pat on the shoulder as he rose and headed off for bed.

Drizzt was still asleep when Montolio roused Hooter and tied a thick note to the owl's leg. Hooter wasn't so pleased at the ranger's instructions; the journey could take a tenday, valuable and enjoyable time at this height of the mousing and mating season. For all its whining hoots, however, the owl would not disobey.

Hooter ruffled its feathers, caught the first gust of wind, and soared effortlessly across the snow-covered range to the passes that would take it to Maldobar—and beyond that to Sundabar, if need be. A certain ranger of no small fame, a sister of the Lady of Silverymoon, was still in the region, Montolio knew through his animal connections, and he charged Hooter with seeking her out.

⚔ ⚔ ⚔ ⚔ ⚔

"Will-there-be-no-end-to-it?" the sprite whined, watching the burly human pass along the trail. "First-the-nasty-drow-and-now-this-brute! Am-I-never-to-be-rid-of-these-troublemakers?" Tephanis slapped his head and stamped his feet so rapidly that he dug himself a little hole.

Down on the trail, the big, scarred yellow dog growled and bared its teeth, and Tephanis, realizing that his pouting had been too loud, zipped in a wide semicircle, crossing the trail far behind the traveler and coming up on the other flank. The yellow dog, still looking in the opposite direction, cocked its head and whimpered in confusion.

# 15
# A Shadow Over Sanctuary

Drizzt and Montolio said nothing of the drow's tale over the next couple of days. Drizzt brooded over painfully rekindled memories, and Montolio tactfully gave him the room he needed. They went about their daily business methodically, farther apart, and with less enthusiasm, but the distance was a passing thing, which they both realized.

Gradually they came closer together, leaving Drizzt with hopes that he had found a friend as true as Belwar or even Zaknafein. One morning, though, the drow was awakened by a voice that he recognized all too well, and Drizzt thought at once that his time with Montolio had come to a crashing end.

He crawled to the wooden wall that protected his dugout chamber and peered through.

"Drow elf, Mooshie," Roddy McGristle was saying, holding a broken scimitar out for the old ranger to see. The burly mountain man, looming even larger in the many layers of furs he wore, sat atop a small but muscled horse just outside of the rock wall surrounding the grove. "Ye seen him?"

"Seen?" Montolio echoed sarcastically, giving an exaggerated wink of his milky-white eyes. Roddy was not amused.

"Ye know what I mean!" he growled. "Ye see more'n the rest of us, so don't ye be playin' dumb!" Roddy's dog, showing a wicked scar from where

Drizzt had struck it, caught a familiar scent then and started sniffing excitedly and darting back and forth along the paths of the grove.

Drizzt crouched at the ready, a scimitar in one hand and a look of dread and confusion on his face. He had no desire to fight—he did not even want to strike the dog again.

"Get your dog back to your side!" Montolio huffed.

McGristle's curiosity was obvious. "Seen the dark elf, Mooshie?" he asked again, this time suspiciously.

"Might that I have," Montolio replied. He turned and let out a shrill, barely audible whistle. Immediately, Roddy's dog, hearing the ranger's clear ire in no uncertain terms, dropped its tail between its legs and slunk back to stand beside its master's horse.

"I've a brood of fox pups in there," the ranger lied angrily. "If your dog sets on them . . ." Montolio let the threat hang at that, and apparently Roddy was impressed. He dropped a noose down over the dog's head and pulled it tight to his side.

"A drow, must be the same one, came through here before the first snows," Montolio went on. "You will have a hard hunt for that one, bounty hunter." He laughed. "He had some trouble with Graul, by my knowledge, then set out again, back for his dark home, I would guess. Do you mean to follow the drow down into the Underdark? Certainly your reputation would grow considerably, bounty hunter, though your very life might prove the cost!"

Drizzt relaxed at the words; Montolio had lied for him! He could see that the ranger did not hold McGristle in high regard, and that fact, too, brought comfort to Drizzt. Then Roddy came back forcefully, laying out the story of the tragedy in Maldobar in a blunt and warped way that put Drizzt and Montolio's friendship to a tough test.

"The drow killed the Thistledowns!" Roddy roared at the ranger's smug smile, which vanished in the blink of an eye. "Slaughtered them, and his panther ate one o' them. Ye knew Bartholemew Thistledown, ranger. Shame on ye for talkin' lightly on his murderer!"

"Drow killed them?" Montolio asked grimly.

Roddy held out the broken scimitar once more. "Cut 'em down," he growled. "There's two thousand gold pieces on that one's head—I'll give ye back five hunnerd if ye can find out more for me."

"I have no need of your gold," Montolio quickly replied.

"But do ye have need to see the killer brought in?" Roddy shot back. "Do ye mourn for the deaths o' the Thistledown clan, as fine a family as any?"

Montolio's ensuing pause led Drizzt to believe that the ranger might turn him in. Drizzt decided then that he would not run, whatever Montolio's decision. He could deny the bounty hunter's anger, but not Montolio's. If the ranger accused him, Drizzt would have to face him and be judged.

"Sad day," Montolio muttered. "Fine family, indeed. Catch the drow, McGristle. It would be the best bounty you ever earned."

"Where to start?" Roddy asked calmly, apparently thinking he had won Montolio over. Drizzt thought so, too, especially when Montolio turned and looked back toward the grove.

"You have heard of Morueme's Cave?" Montolio asked.

Roddy's expression visibly dropped at the question. Morueme's Cave, on the edge of the great desert Anauroch, was so named for the family of blue dragons that lived there. "Hunnerd an' fifty miles," McGristle groaned. "Through the Nethers—a tough range."

"The drow went there, or about there, early in the winter," Montolio lied.

"Drow went to the dragons?" Roddy asked, surprised.

"More likely, the drow went to some other hole in that region," Montolio replied. "The dragons of Morueme could possibly know of him. You should inquire there."

"I'm not so quick to bargain with dragons," Roddy said somberly. "Too risky, and even goin', well, it costs too much!"

"Then it seems that Roddy McGristle has missed his first catch," Montolio said. "A good try, though, against the likes of a dark elf."

Roddy reined in his horse and spun the beast about. "Don't ye put yer bets against me, Mooshie!" he roared back over his shoulder. "I'll not let this one get away, if I have to search every hole in the Nethers myself."

"Seems a bit of trouble for two thousand gold," Montolio remarked, not impressed.

"Drow took my dog, my ear, and give me this scar!" Roddy countered, pointing to his torn face. The bounty hunter realized the absurdity of his actions—of course, the blind ranger could not see him—and spun back, setting his horse charging out of the grove.

Montolio waved a hand disgustedly at McGristle's back, then turned to find the drow. Drizzt met him on the edge of the grove, hardly knowing how to thank Montolio.

"Never liked that one," Montolio explained.

"The Thistledown family was murdered," Drizzt admitted bluntly.

Montolio nodded.

"You knew?"

"I knew before you came here," the ranger answered. "Honestly, I wondered if you did it, at first."

"I did not," Drizzt said.

Again Montolio nodded.

The time had come for Drizzt to fill in the details of his first few months on the surface. All the guilt came back to him when he recounted his battle with the gnoll group, and all the pain came rushing back, focused on the word "drizzit," when he told of the Thistledowns and his gruesome discovery. Montolio identified the speedy sprite as a quickling but was quite at a loss to explain the giant goblin and wolf creatures that Drizzt had battled in the cave.

"You did right in killing the gnolls," Montolio said when Drizzt had finished. "Release your guilt for that act and let it fall to nothingness."

"How could I know?" Drizzt asked honestly. "All of my learning ties to Menzoberranzan and still I have not sorted the truth from the lies."

"It has been a confusing journey," Montolio said, and his sincere smile relieved the tension considerably. "Come along, and let me tell you of the races, and of why your scimitars struck for justice when they felled the gnolls."

As a ranger, Montolio had dedicated his life to the unending struggle between the good races—humans, elves, dwarves, gnomes, and halflings being the most prominent members—and the evil goblinoids and giantkind, who lived only to destroy as a bane to the innocent.

"Orcs are my particular unfavorites," Montolio explained. "So now I content myself with keeping an eye—an owl's eye, that is—on Graul and his smelly kin."

So much fell into perspective for Drizzt then. Comfort flooded through the drow, for Drizzt's instincts had proven correct and he could now, for a while and to some measure at least, be free from the guilt.

"What of the bounty hunter and those like him?" Drizzt asked. "They do not seem to fit so well into your descriptions of the races."

"There is good and bad in every race," Montolio explained. "I spoke only of the general conduct, and do not doubt that the general conduct of goblinoids and giantkind is an evil one!"

"How can we know?" Drizzt pressed.

"Just watch the children," Montolio answered. He went on to explain the not-so-subtle differences between children of the goodly races and children of the evil races. Drizzt heard him, but distantly, needing no clarification. Always it seemed to come down to the children. Drizzt had felt better concerning his actions against the gnolls when he had looked upon the Thistledown children at play. And back in Menzoberranzan, what seemed like only a day ago and a thousand years ago at the same time, Drizzt's father had expressed similar beliefs. "Are all drow children evil?" Zaknafein had wondered, and through all of his beleaguered life, Zaknafein had been haunted by the screams of dying children, drow nobles caught in the fire between warring families.

A long, silent moment ensued when Montolio finished, both friends taking the time to digest the day's many revelations. Montolio knew that Drizzt was comforted when the drow, quite unexpectedly, turned to him, smiled widely, and abruptly changed the grim subject.

"Mooshie?" Drizzt asked, recalling the name McGristle had tagged on Montolio at the rock wall.

"Montolio DeBrouchee." The old ranger cackled, tossing a grotesque wink Drizzt's way. "Mooshie, to my friends, and to those like McGristle, who struggle so with any words bigger than 'spit,' 'bear,' or 'kill!' "

"Mooshie," Drizzt mumbled under his breath, taking some mirth at Montolio's expense.

"Have you no chores to do, Drizzit?" the old ranger huffed.

Drizzt nodded and started boisterously away. This time, the ring of "drizzit" did not sting so very badly.

⚔ ⚔ ⚔ ⚔ ⚔

"Morueme's Cave," Roddy griped. "Damned Morueme's Cave!" A split second later, a small sprite sat atop Roddy's horse, staring the stunned bounty hunter in the face. Tephanis had watched the exchange at Montolio's grove and had cursed his luck when the ranger had turned the bounty hunter away. If Roddy could catch Drizzt, the quickling figured, they'd both be out of his way, a fact that did not alarm Tephanis.

"Surely-you-are-not-so-stupid-as-to-believe-that-old-Car?" Tephanis blurted.

"Here!" Roddy cried, grabbing clumsily at the sprite, who merely hopped down, darted back, past the startled dog, and climbed up to sit behind Roddy.

"What in the Nine Hells are you?" the bounty hunter roared. "And sit still!"

"I am a friend," Tephanis said as slowly as he could.

Roddy eyed him cautiously over one shoulder.

"If-you-want-the-drow, you-are-going-the-wrong-way," the sprite said smugly.

A short while later, Roddy crouched in the high bluffs south of Montolio's grove and watched the ranger and his dark-skinned guest going about their chores.

"Good-hunting!" Tephanis offered, then he was gone, back to Caroak, the great wolf that smelled better than this particular human.

Roddy, his eyes fixed upon the distant scene, hardly noticed the quickling's departure. "Ye'll pay for yer lies, ranger," he muttered under his breath. An evil smile spread over his face as he thought of a way to get at the companions. It would be a delicate feat. But then, dealing with Graul always was.

⚔ ⚔ ⚔ ⚔ ⚔

Montolio's messenger returned two days later with a note from Dove Falconhand. Hooter tried to recount the ranger's response, but the excitable owl was completely inept at conveying such long and intricate tales. Flustered and having no other option, Montolio handed the letter to Drizzt and told the drow to read it aloud, and quickly. Not yet a skilled reader, Drizzt was several lines through the creased paper before he realized what it was. The note detailed Dove's accounts of what had happened in Maldobar and along the subsequent chase. Dove's version struck near to the truth, vindicating Drizzt and naming the barghest whelps as the murderers.

Drizzt's relief was so great that he could hardly utter the words as the letter went on to express Dove's pleasure and gratitude that the "deserving drow" had taken in with the old ranger.

"You get your due in the end, my friend," was all that Montolio needed to say.

# Part Four

# Resolutions

I now view my long road as a search for truth—truth in my own heart, in the world around me, and in the larger questions of purpose and of existence. How does one define good and evil?

I carried an internal code of morals with me on my trek, though whether I was born with it or it was imparted to me by Zaknafein—or whether it simply developed from my perceptions—I cannot ever know. This code forced me to leave Menzoberranzan, for though I was not certain of what those truths might have been, I knew beyond doubt that they would not be found in the domain of Lolth.

After many years in the Underdark outside of Menzoberranzan and after my first awful experiences on the surface, I came to doubt the existence of any universal truth, came to wonder if there was, after all, any purpose to life. In the world of drow, ambition was the only purpose, the seeking of material gains that came with increased rank. Even then, that seemed a little thing to me, hardly a reason to exist.

I thank you, Montolio DeBrouchee, for confirming my suspicions. I have learned that the ambition of those who follow selfish precepts is no more than a chaotic waste, a finite gain that must be followed by infinite loss. For there is indeed a harmony in the universe, a concordant singing of common weal. To join that song, one must find inner harmony, must find the notes that ring true.

There is one other point to be made about that truth: Evil creatures cannot sing.

–Drizzt Do'Urden

# 16
# Of Gods and Purpose

The lessons continued to go quite well. The old ranger had lessened the drow's considerable emotional burden, and Drizzt picked up on the ways of the natural world better than anyone Montolio had ever seen. But Montolio sensed that something still bothered the drow, though he had no idea of what it might be.

"Do all humans possess such fine hearing?" Drizzt asked him suddenly as they dragged a huge fallen branch out of the grove. "Or is yours a blessing, perhaps, to make up for your blindness?"

The bluntness of the question surprised Montolio for just the moment it took him to recognize the drow's frustration, an uneasiness caused by Drizzt's failure to understand the man's abilities.

"Or is your blindness, perhaps, a ruse, a deception you use to gain the advantage?" Drizzt pressed relentlessly.

"If it is?" Montolio replied offhandedly.

"Then it is a good one, Montolio DeBrouchee," Drizzt replied. "Surely it aids you against enemies . . . and friends alike." The words tasted bitter to Drizzt, and he suspected that he was letting his pride get the best of him.

"You have not often been bested in battle," Montolio replied, recognizing the source of Drizzt's frustrations as their sparring match. If he could have seen the drow then, Drizzt's expression would have revealed much.

"You take it too hard," Montolio continued after an uneasy silence. "I did not truly defeat you."

"You had me down and helpless."

"You beat yourself," Montolio explained. "I am indeed blind, but not as helpless as you seem to think. You underestimated me. I knew that you would, too, though I hardly believed that you could be so blind."

Drizzt stopped abruptly, and Montolio stopped on cue as the drag on the branch suddenly increased. The old ranger shook his head and cackled. He then pulled out a dagger, spun it high into the air, caught it, and yelling, "Birch!" heaved it squarely into one of the few birch trees by the evergreen grove.

"Could a blind man do that?" Montolio asked rhetorically.

"Then you can see," Drizzt stated.

"Of course not," Montolio retorted sharply. "My eyes have not functioned for five years. But neither am I blind, Drizzt, especially in this place I call my home!

"Yet you thought me blind," the ranger went on, his voice calm again. "In our sparring, when your spell of darkness expired, you believed that you had gained the edge. Did you think that all of my actions—effective actions, I must say—both in the battle against the orcs and in our fight were simply prepared and rehearsed? If I were as crippled as Drizzt Do'Urden believes me, how should I survive another day in these mountains?"

"I did not . . ." Drizzt began, but his embarrassment silenced him. Montolio spoke the truth, and Drizzt knew it. He had, at least on an unconscious level, thought the ranger less than whole since their very first meeting. Drizzt felt he showed his friend no disrespect—indeed, he thought highly of the man—but he had taken Montolio for granted and thought the ranger's limitations greater than his own.

"You did," Montolio corrected, "and I forgive you that. To your credit, you treated me more fairly than any who knew me before, even those who had traveled beside me through uncounted campaigns. Sit now," he bade Drizzt. "It is my turn to tell my tale, as you have told yours.

"Where to begin?" Montolio mused, scratching at his chin. It all seemed so distant to him now, another life that he had left behind. He retained one link to his past, though: his training as a ranger of the goddess Mielikki. Drizzt, similarly instructed by Montolio, would understand.

"I gave my life to the forest, to the natural order, at a very young age," Montolio began. "I learned, as I have begun to teach you, the ways of the wild world and decided soon enough that I would defend that perfection, that harmony of cycles too vast and wonderful to be understood. That is why I so enjoy battling orcs and the like. As I have told you before, they are the enemies of natural order, the enemies of trees and animals as much as of men and the goodly races. Wretched things, all in all, and I feel no guilt in cutting them down!"

Montolio then spent many hours recounting some of his campaigns, expeditions in which he acted singly or as a scout for huge armies. He told Drizzt of his own teacher, Dilamon, a ranger so skilled with a bow that he had never seen her miss, not once in ten thousand shots. "She died in battle," Montolio explained, "defending a farmhouse from a raiding band of giants. Weep not for Mistress Dilamon, though, for not a single farmer was injured and not one of the few giants who crawled away ever showed its ugly face in that region again!"

Montolio's voice dropped noticeably when he came to his more recent past. He told of the Rangewatchers, his last adventuring company, and of how they came to battle a red dragon that had been marauding the villages. The dragon was slain, as were three of the Rangewatchers, and Montolio had his face burned away.

"The clerics fixed me up well," Montolio said somberly. "Hardly a scar to show for my pain." He paused, and Drizzt saw, for the first time since he had met the old ranger, a cloud of pain cross Montolio's face. "They could do nothing for my eyes, though. The wounds were beyond their abilities."

"You came out here to die," Drizzt said, more accusingly than he intended.

Montolio did not refute the claim. "I have suffered the breath of dragons, the spears of orcs, the anger of evil men, and the greed of those who would rape the land for their own gain," the ranger said. "None of those things wounded as deeply as pity. Even my Rangewatcher companions, who had fought beside me so many times pitied me. Even you."

"I did not . . ." Drizzt tried to interject.

"You did indeed," Montolio retorted. "In our battle, you thought yourself superior. That is why you lost! The strength of any ranger is wisdom, Drizzt. A ranger understands himself, his enemies, and his friends. You thought me impaired, else you never would have attempted so brash a maneuver as to jump over me. But I understood you and anticipated the move." That sly smile flashed wickedly. "Does your head still hurt?"

"It does," Drizzt admitted, rubbing the bruise, "though my thoughts seem to be clearing."

"As to your original question," Montolio said, satisfied that his point had been made, "there is nothing exceptional about my hearing, or any of my other senses. I just pay more attention to what they tell than do other folks, and they guide me quite well, as you now understand. Truly, I did not know of their abilities myself when I first came out here, and you are correct in your guess as to why I did. Without my eyes, I thought myself a dead man, and I wanted to die here, in this grove that I had come to know and love in my earlier travels.

"Perhaps it was due to Mielikki, the Mistress of the Forest—though more likely it was Graul, an enemy so close at hand—but it did not take me long to change my intentions concerning my own life. I found a purpose out here, alone and crippled—and I was crippled in those first days. With that purpose came a renewal of meaning in my life, and that in turn led me to realize again my limits. I am old now, and weary, and blind. If I had died five years ago, as I had intended, I would have died with my life incomplete. I never would have known how far I could go. Only in adversity, beyond anything Montolio DeBrouchee had ever imagined, could I have come to know myself and my goddess so well."

Montolio stopped to consider Drizzt. He heard a shuffle at the mention of his goddess, and he took it to be an uncomfortable movement. Wanting to explore this revelation, Montolio reached inside his chain mail and tunic and produced a pendant shaped like a unicorn's head.

"Is it not beautiful?" he pointedly asked.

Drizzt hesitated. The unicorn was perfectly crafted and marvelous in design, but the connotations of such a pendant did not sit easily with the drow. Back in Menzoberranzan Drizzt had witnessed the folly of following the commands of deities, and he liked not at all what he had seen.

"Who is your god, drow?" Montolio asked. In all the tendays he and Drizzt had been together, they had not really discussed religion.

"I have no god," Drizzt answered boldly, "and neither do I want one."

It was Montolio's turn to pause.

Drizzt rose and walked off a few paces.

"My people follow Lolth," he began. "She, if not the cause, is surely the continuation of their wickedness, as this Gruumsh is to the orcs, and as other gods are to other peoples. To follow a god is folly. I shall follow my heart instead."

Montolio's quiet chuckle stole the power from Drizzt's proclamation. "You have a god, Drizzt Do'Urden," he said.

"My god is my heart," Drizzt declared, turning back to him.

"As is mine."

"You named your god as Mielikki," Drizzt protested.

"And you have not found a name for your god yet," Montolio shot back. "That does not mean that you have no god. Your god is your heart, and what does your heart tell you?"

"I do not know," Drizzt admitted after considering the troubling question.

"Think then!" Montolio cried. "What did your instincts tell you of the gnoll band or of the farmers in Maldobar? Lolth is not your deity—that much is certain. What god or goddess then fits that which is in Drizzt Do'Urden's heart?"

Montolio could almost hear Drizzt's continuing shrugs. "You do not know?" the old ranger asked. "But I do."

"You presume much," Drizzt replied, still not convinced.

"I observe much," Montolio said with a laugh. "Are you of like heart with Guenhwyvar?"

"I have never doubted that fact," Drizzt answered honestly.

"Guenhwyvar follows Mielikki."

"How can you know?" Drizzt argued, growing a bit perturbed. He didn't mind Montolio's presumptions about him, but Drizzt considered such labeling an attack on the panther. Somehow to Drizzt, Guenhwyvar seemed to be above gods and all the implications of following one.

"How can I know?" Montolio echoed incredulously. "The cat told me, of course! Guenhwyvar is the entity of the panther, a creature of Mielikki's domain."

"Guenhwyvar does not need your labels," Drizzt retorted angrily, moving briskly to sit again beside the ranger.

"Of course not," Montolio agreed. "But that does not change the fact of it. You do not understand Drizzt Do'Urden. You grew up among the perversion of a deity."

"And yours is the true one?" Drizzt asked sarcastically.

"They are all true, and they are all one, I fear," Montolio replied. Drizzt had to agree with Montolio's earlier observation: He did not understand.

"You view the gods as entities without," Montolio tried to explain. "You see them as physical beings trying to control our actions for their own ends, and thus you, in your stubborn independence, reject them. The gods are within, I say, whether one has named his own or not. You have followed Mielikki all of your life, Drizzt. You merely never had a name to put on your heart."

Suddenly Drizzt was more intrigued than skeptical.

"What did you feel when you first walked out of the Underdark?" Montolio asked. "What did your heart tell you when first you looked upon the sun or the stars, or the forest green?"

Drizzt thought back to that distant day, when he and his drow patrol had come out of the Underdark to raid an elven gathering. Those were painful memories, but within them loomed one sense of comfort, one memory of wondrous elation at the feel of the wind and the scents of newly bloomed flowers.

"And how did you talk to Bluster?" Montolio continued. "No easy feat, sharing a cave with that bear! Admit it or not, you've the heart of a ranger. And the heart of a ranger is a heart of Mielikki."

So formal a conclusion brought back a measure of Drizzt's doubts. "And what does your goddess require?" he asked, the angry edge returned to his voice. He began to stand again, but Montolio slapped a hand over his legs and held him down.

"Require?" The ranger laughed. "I am no missionary spreading a fine word and imposing rules of behavior! Did I not just tell you that gods are within? You know Mielikki's rules as well as I. You have been following them all of your life. I offer you a name for it, that is all, and an ideal of behavior personified, an example that you might follow in times that you stray from what you know is true." With that, Montolio took up the branch and Drizzt followed.

Drizzt considered the words for a long time. He did not sleep that day, though he remained in his den, thinking.

"I wish to know more of your . . . our . . . goddess," Drizzt admitted that next night, when he found Montolio cooking their supper.

"And I wish to teach you," Montolio replied.

⚔ ⚔ ⚔ ⚔ ⚔

A hundred sets of yellow, bloodshot eyes settled to stare at the burly human as he made his way through the encampment, reining his yellow dog tightly to his side. Roddy didn't enjoy coming here, to the fort of the orc king, Graul, but he had no intentions of letting the drow get away this time. Roddy had dealt with Graul several times over the last few years; the orc king, with so many eyes in the wild mountains had proven an invaluable, though expensive, ally in hunting bounties.

Several large orcs purposely crossed Roddy's path, jostling him and angering his dog. Roddy wisely kept his pet still, though he, too, wanted to set upon the smelly orcs. They played this game every time he came in, bumping him, spitting at him, anything to provoke a fight. Orcs were always brave when they outnumbered opponents a hundred to one.

The whole group swept up behind McGristle and followed him closely as he covered the last fifty yards, up a rocky slope, to the entrance of Graul's cave. Two large orcs jumped out of the entrance, brandishing spears, to intercept the intruder.

"Why has yous come?" one of them asked in their native tongue. The other held out its hand as if expecting payment.

"No pay this time," Roddy replied, imitating their dialect perfectly. "This time Graul pay!"

The orcs looked to each other in disbelief, then turned on Roddy and issued snarls that were suddenly cut short when an even larger orc emerged from the cave.

Graul stormed out and threw his guards aside, striding right up to put his oozing snout only an inch from Roddy's nose. "Graul pay?" he snorted, his breath nearly overwhelming Roddy.

Roddy's chuckle was purely for the sake of those excited orc commoners closest to him. He couldn't show any weakness here; like vicious dogs, orcs were quick to attack anyone who did not stand firm against them.

"I have information, King Graul," the bounty hunter said firmly. "Information that Graul would wish to know."

"Speak," Graul commanded.

"Pay?" Roddy asked, though he suspected that he was pushing his luck.

"Speak!" Graul growled again. "If yous wordses has value, Graul will let yous live."

Roddy silently lamented that it always seemed to work this way with Graul. It was difficult to strike any favorable bargain with the smelly chieftain when he was surrounded by a hundred armed warriors. Roddy remained undaunted, though. He hadn't come here for coin—though he had hoped he might extract some—but for revenge. Roddy wouldn't openly strike against Drizzt while the drow was with Mooshie. In these mountains, surrounded by his animal friends, Mooshie was a formidable force, and even if Roddy managed to get past him to the drow, Mooshie's many allies, veterans such as Dove Falconhand would surely avenge the action.

"There be a dark elf in yer domain, mighty orc king!" Roddy proclaimed. He didn't get the shock he had hoped for.

"Rogue," Graul clarified.

"Ye know?" Roddy's wide eyes betrayed his disbelief.

"Drow killed Graul's fighters," the orc chieftain said grimly. All the gathered orcs began stamping and spitting, cursing the dark elf.

"Then why does the drow live?" Roddy asked bluntly. The bounty hunter's eyes narrowed as he came to suspect that Graul did not now know the drow's location. Perhaps he still had something to bargain with.

"Me scouts cannot finds him!" Graul roared, and it was true enough. But any frustration the orc king showed was a finely crafted piece of acting. Graul knew where Drizzt was, even if his scouts did not.

"I have found him!" Roddy roared, and all the orcs jumped and cried in hungry glee. Graul raised his arms to quiet them. This was the critical part, the orc king knew. He scanned the gathering to locate the tribe's shaman, the spiritual leader of the tribe, and found the red-robed orc watching and listening intently, as Graul had hoped.

On advice from that shaman, Graul had avoided any action against Montolio for all these years. The shaman thought the cripple who was not so crippled to be an omen of bad magic, and with their religious leader's warnings, all the orc tribe cowered whenever Montolio was near. But in allying with the drow, and if Graul's suspicions were correct, in helping the drow to win the battle on the high ridge, Montolio had struck where he had no business, had violated Graul's domain as surely as had the renegade drow. Now convinced that the drow was indeed a rogue—for no other dark elves were in the region—the orc king only awaited some excuse that might spur his minions to action against the grove. Roddy, Graul had been informed, might now provide that excuse.

"Speak!" Graul shouted in Roddy's face, to intercept any forthcoming attempts for payment.

"The drow isses with the ranger," Roddy replied. "He sits in the blind ranger's grove!" If Roddy had hoped that his proclamation would inspire another eruption of cursing, jumping, and spitting, he was surely disappointed. The mention of the blind ranger cast a heavy pall over the gathering, and now all the common orcs looked from the shaman to Graul and back again for some guidance.

It was time for Roddy to weave a tale of conspiracy, as Graul had been told he would.

"Ye must goes and gets them!" Roddy cried. "They're not fer . . ."

Graul raised his arms to silence both the muttering and Roddy. "Was it the blind ranger who killded the giant?" the orc king asked Roddy slyly. "And helped the drow to kill me fighters?"

Roddy, of course, had no idea what Graul was talking about, but he was quick enough to catch on to the orc king's intent.

"It was!" he declared loudly. "And now the drow and the ranger plot against ye all! Ye must bash them and smash them before they come and bash yerselves! The ranger'll be bringing his animals, and elveses—lots an' lots of elveses—and dwarveses, too, against Graul!"

The mention of Montolio's friends, particularly the elves and dwarves, which Graul's people hated above everything else in all the world, brought sour expressions on every face and caused more than one orc to look nervously over its shoulder, as if expecting the ranger's army to be encircling the camp even then.

Graul stared squarely at the shaman.

"He-Who-Watches must bless the attack," the shaman replied to the silent question. "On the new moon!" Graul nodded, and the red-robed orc turned about, summoned a score of commoners to his side, and set out to begin the preparations.

Graul reached into a pouch and produced a handful of silver coins for Roddy. Roddy hadn't provided any real information that the king did not already know, but the bounty hunter's declaration of a conspiracy against the orc tribe gave Graul considerable assistance in his attempt to rouse his superstitious shaman against the blind ranger.

Roddy took the pitiful payment without complaint, thinking it well enough that he had achieved his purpose, and turned to leave.

"Yous is to stay," Graul said suddenly at his back. On a motion from the orc king, several orc guards stepped up beside the bounty hunter. Roddy looked suspiciously at Graul.

"Guest," the orc king explained calmly. "Join in the fight."

Roddy wasn't left with many options.

Graul waved his guards aside and went alone back into his cave. The orc guards only shrugged and smiled at each other, having no desire to go back in and face the king's guests, particularly the huge silver-furred wolf.

When Graul had returned to his place within, he turned to speak to his other guest. "Yous was right," Graul said to the diminutive sprite.

"I-am-quite-good-at-getting-information." Tephanis beamed, and silently he added, and-creating-favorable-situations!

Tephanis thought himself clever at that moment, for not only had he informed Roddy that the drow was in Montolio's grove, but he had then arranged with King Graul for Roddy to aid them both. Graul had no love for the blind ranger, Tephanis knew, and with the drow's presence serving as an excuse, Graul could finally persuade his shaman to bless the attack.

"Caroak will help in the fight?" Graul asked, looking suspiciously at the huge and unpredictable silver wolf.

"Of-course," Tephanis said immediately. "It-is-in-our-interest-too-to-see-those-enemies-destroyed!"

Caroak, understanding every word the two exchanged, rose up and sauntered out of the cave. The guards at the entrance did not try to block his way.

"Caroak-will-rouse-the-worgs," Tephanis explained. "A-mighty-force-will-assemble-against-the-blind-ranger. Too-long-has-he-been-an-enemy-of-Caroak."

Graul nodded and mused privately about the coming tendays. If he could get rid of both the ranger and the drow, his valley would be more secure than it had been in many years—since before Montolio's arrival. The ranger rarely engaged the orcs personally, but Graul knew that it was the ranger's animal spies that always alerted the passing caravans. Graul could not remember the last time his warriors had caught a caravan unawares, the preferred orc method. If the ranger was gone, however . . .

With summer, the height of the trading season, fast approaching, the orcs would prey well this year.

All that Graul needed now was confirmation from the shaman, that He-Who-Watches, the orc god Gruumsh One-eye, would bless the attack.

The new moon, a holy time for the orcs and a time when the shaman believed he could learn of the god's pleasures, was more than two tendays away. Eager and impatient, Graul grumbled at the delay, but he knew that he would simply have to wait. Graul, far less religious than others believed, meant to attack no matter the shaman's decision, but the crafty orc king would not openly defy the tribe's spiritual leader unless it was absolutely necessary.

The new moon was not so far away, Graul told himself. Then he would be rid of both the blind ranger and the mysterious drow.

# 17
# OUTNUMBERED

"You seem troubled," Drizzt said to Montolio when he saw the ranger standing on a rope bridge the next morning. Hooter sat in a branch above him.

Montolio, lost in thought, did not immediately answer. Drizzt thought nothing of it. He shrugged and turned away, respecting the ranger's privacy, and took the onyx figurine out of his pocket.

"Guenhwyvar and I will go out for a short hunt," Drizzt explained over his shoulder, "before the sun gets too high. Then I will take my rest and the panther will share the day with you."

Still Montolio hardly heard the drow, but when the ranger noticed Drizzt placing the onyx figurine on the rope bridge, the drow's words registered more clearly and he came out of his contemplations.

"Hold," Montolio said, reaching a hand out. "Let the panther remain at rest."

Drizzt did not understand. "Guenhwyvar has been gone a day and more," he said.

"We may need Guenhwyvar for more than hunting before too long," Montolio began to explain. "Let the panther remain at rest."

"What is the trouble?" Drizzt asked, suddenly serious. "What has Hooter seen?"

"Last night marked the new moon," Montolio said. Drizzt, with his new understanding of the lunar cycles, nodded.

"A holy day for the orcs," Montolio continued. "Their camp is miles away, but I heard their cries last night."

Again Drizzt nodded in recognition. "I heard the strains of their song, but I wondered if it might be no more than the quiet voice of the wind."

"It was the wail of orcs," Montolio assured him. "Every month they gather and grunt and dance wildly in their typical stupor—orcs need no potions to induce it, you know. I thought nothing of it, though they seemed overly loud. Usually they cannot be heard from here. A favorable . . . unfavorable . . . wind carried the tune in, I supposed."

"You have since learned that there was more to the song?" Drizzt assumed.

"Hooter heard them, too," Montolio explained. "Always watching out for me, that one." He glanced at the owl. "He flew off to get a look."

Drizzt also looked up at the marvelous bird, sitting puffed and proud as though it understood Montolio's compliments. Despite the ranger's grave concerns, though, Drizzt had to wonder just how completely Montolio could understand Hooter, and just how completely the owl could comprehend the events around it.

"The orcs have formed a war party," Montolio said, scratching at his bristled beard. "Graul has awakened from the long winter with a vengeance, it seems."

"How can you know?" Drizzt asked. "Can Hooter understand their words?"

"No, no, of course not!" Montolio replied, amused at the notion.

"Then how can you know?"

"A pack of worgs came in, that much Hooter did tell me," Montolio explained. "Orcs and worgs are not the best of friends, but they do get together when trouble is brewing. The orc celebration was a wild one last night, and with the presence of worgs, there can be little doubt."

"Is there a village nearby?" Drizzt asked.

"None closer than Maldobar," Montolio replied. "I doubt the orcs would go that far, but the melt is about done and caravans will be rolling through the pass, from Sundabar to Citadel Adbar and the other way around, mostly. There must be one coming from Sundabar, though I do not believe Graul would be bold enough, or stupid enough, to attack a caravan of heavily armed dwarves coming from Adbar."

"How many warriors has the orc king?"

"Graul could collect thousands if he took the time and had the mind to do it," Montolio said, "but that would take tendays, and Graul has never been known for his patience. Also, he wouldn't have brought the worgs in so soon if he meant to hold off while collecting his legions. Orcs have a way of disappearing while worgs are around, and the worgs have a way of getting lazy and fat with so many orcs around, if you understand my meaning."

Drizzt's shudder showed that he did indeed.

"I would guess that Graul has about a hundred fighters," Montolio went on, "maybe a dozen to a score worgs, by Hooter's count, and probably a giant or two."

"A considerable force to strike at a caravan," Drizzt said, but both the drow and the ranger had other suspicions in mind. When they had first met, two months before, it had been at Graul's expense.

"It will take them a day or two to get ready," Montolio said after an uncomfortable pause. "Hooter will watch them more closely tonight, and I shall call on other spies as well."

"I will go to scout on the orcs," Drizzt added. He saw concern cross Montolio's face but quickly dismissed it. "Many were the times that such duties fell on me as a patrol scout in Menzoberranzan," he said. "It is a task that I feel quite secure in performing. Fear not."

"That was in the Underdark," Montolio reminded him.

"Is the night so different?" Drizzt replied slyly, throwing a wink and a comforting smile Montolio's way. "We shall have our answers."

Drizzt said his "good days" then and headed off to take his rest. Montolio listened to his friend's retreating steps, barely a swish through the thickly packed trees, with sincere admiration and thought it a good plan.

The day passed slowly and uneventfully for the ranger. He busied himself as best he could in considering his defense plans for the grove. Montolio had never defended the place before, except once when a band of foolish thieves had stumbled in, but he had spent many hours formulating and testing different strategies, thinking it inevitable that one day Graul would grow weary of the ranger's meddling and find the nerve to attack.

If that day had come, Montolio was confident that he would be ready.

Little could be done now, though—the defenses could not be put in place before Montolio was certain of Graul's intent—and the ranger found the waiting interminable. Finally, Hooter informed Montolio that the drow was stirring.

"I will set off, then," Drizzt remarked as soon as he found the ranger, noting the sun riding low in the west. "Let us learn what our unfriendly neighbors are planning."

"Have a care, Drizzt," Montolio said, and the genuine concern in his voice touched the drow. "Graul may be an orc, but he is a crafty one. He may well be expecting one of us to come and look in on him."

Drizzt drew his still-unfamiliar scimitars and spun them about to gain confidence in their movement. Then he snapped them back to his belt and dropped a hand into his pocket, taking further comfort in the presence of the onyx figurine. With a final pat on the ranger's back, the scout started off.

"Hooter will be about!" Montolio cried after him. "And other friends you might not expect. Give a shout if you find more trouble than you can handle!"

⚔ ⚔ ⚔ ⚔ ⚔

The orc camp was not difficult to locate, marked as it was by a huge bonfire blazing into the night sky. Drizzt saw the forms, including one of a giant, dancing around the flames, and he heard the snarls and yips of large wolves, worgs, Montolio had called them. The camp was in a small dale, in a clearing surrounded by huge maples and rock walls. Drizzt could hear the orc voices fairly well in the quiet night, so he decided not to get in too close. He selected one massive tree and focused on a lower branch, summoning his innate levitation ability to get him up.

The spell failed utterly, so Drizzt, hardly surprised, slipped his scimitars into his belt and climbed. The trunk branched several times, down low and as high as twenty feet. Drizzt made for the highest break and was just about to start out on a long and winding branch when he heard an intake of breath. Cautiously, Drizzt slipped his head around the large trunk.

On the side opposite him, nestled comfortably in the nook of the trunk and another branch, reclined an orc sentry with its hands clasped behind its head and a blank, bored expression on its face. Apparently the creature was oblivious to the silent-moving dark elf perched less than two feet away.

Drizzt grasped the hilt of a scimitar, then gaining confidence that the stupid creature was too comfortable to even look around, changed his mind and ignored the orc. He focused instead on the events down in the clearing.

The orc language was similar to the goblin tongue in structure and inflection, but Drizzt, no master even at goblin, could only make out a few scattered words. Orcs were ever a rather demonstrative race, though. Two models, effigies of a dark elf and a thin, moustached human, soon showed Drizzt the clan's intent. The largest orc of the gathering, King Graul, probably, sputtered and cursed at the models. Then the orc soldiers and the worgs took turns tearing into them, to the glee of the frenzied onlookers, a glee that turned to sheer ecstacy when the stone giant walked over and flattened the fake dark elf to the ground.

It went on for hours, and Drizzt suspected it would continue until the dawn. Graul and several other large orcs moved away from the main host and began drawing in the dirt, apparently laying battle plans. Drizzt could not hope to get close enough to make out their huddled conversations and he had no intention of staying in the tree with the dawn's revealing light fast approaching.

He considered the orc sentry on the other side of the trunk, now breathing deeply in slumber, before he started down. The orcs meant to attack Montolio's home, Drizzt knew; shouldn't he now strike the first blow?

Drizzt's conscience betrayed him. He came down from the huge maple and fled from the camp, leaving the orc to its snooze in the comfortable nook.

✕✕✕✕✕

Montolio, Hooter on his shoulder, sat on one of the rope bridges, waiting for Drizzt's return. "They are coming for us," the old ranger declared when the drow finally came in. "Graul has his neck up about something, probably a little incident at Rogee's Bluff." Montolio pointed to the west, toward the high ridge where he and Drizzt had met.

"Do you have a sanctuary secured for times such as this?" Drizzt asked. "The orcs will come this very night, I believe, nearly a hundred strong and with powerful allies."

"Run?" Montolio cried. He grabbed a nearby rope and swung down to stand by the drow, Hooter clutching his tunic and rolling along for the ride. "Run from orcs? Did I not tell you that orcs are my special bane? Nothing in all the world sounds sweeter than a blade opening an orc's belly!"

"Should I even bother to remind you of the odds?" Drizzt said, smiling in spite of his concern.

"You should remind Graul!" Montolio laughed. "The old orc has lost his wits, or grown an oversized set of fortitude, to come on when he is so obviously outnumbered!"

Drizzt's only reply, the only possible reply to such an outrageous statement, came as a burst of laughter.

"But then," Montolio continued, not slowing a beat, "I will wager a bucket of freshly caught trout and three fine stallions that old Graul won't come along for the fight. He will stay back by the trees, watching and wringing his fat hands, and when we blast his forces apart, he will be the first to flee! He never did have the nerve for the real fighting, not since he became king anyway. He's too comfortable, I would guess, with too much to lose. Well, we'll take away a bit of his bluster!"

Again Drizzt could not find the words to reply, and he couldn't have stopped laughing at the absurdity anyway. Still, Drizzt had to admit the rousing and comforting effect Montolio's rambling imparted to him.

"You go and get some rest," Montolio said, scratching his stubbly chin and turning all about, again considering his surroundings. "I will begin the preparations—you will be amazed, I promise—and rouse you in a few hours."

The last mumblings the drow heard as he crawled into his blanket in a dark den put it all in perspective. "Yes, Hooter, I've been waiting for this for a long time," Montolio said excitedly, and Drizzt did not doubt a word of it.

⚔⚔⚔⚔⚔

It had been a peaceful spring for Kellindil and his elven kin. They were a nomadic group, ranging throughout the region and taking up shelter where they found it, in trees or in caves. Their love was the open world, dancing under the stars, singing in tune with rushing mountain rivers, hunting harts and wild boar in the thick trees of the mountainsides.

Kellindil recognized the dread, a rarely seen emotion among the carefree group, on his cousin's face as soon as the other elf walked into camp late one night.

All the others gathered about.

"The orcs are stirring," the elf explained.

"Graul has found a caravan?" Kellindil asked.

His cousin shook his head and seemed confused. "It is too early for the traders," he replied. "Graul has other prey in mind."

"The grove," several of the elves said together. The whole group turned to Kellindil then, apparently considering the drow his responsibility.

"I do not believe that the drow was in league with Graul," Kellindil answered their unspoken question. "With all of his scouts, Montolio would have known. If the drow is a friend to the ranger, then he is no enemy to us."

"The grove is many miles from here," one of the others offered. "If we wish to look more closely at the orc king's stirrings, and to arrive in time to aid the old ranger, then we must start out at once."

Without a word of dissent, the wandering elves gathered the necessary supplies, mostly their great long bows and extra arrows. Just a few minutes later, they set off, running through the woods and across the mountain trails, making no more noise than a gentle breeze.

⚔ ⚔ ⚔ ⚔ ⚔

Drizzt awakened early in the afternoon to a startling sight. The day had darkened with gray clouds but still seemed bright to the drow as he crawled out of his den and stretched. High above him he saw the ranger, crawling about the top boughs of a tall pine. Drizzt's curiosity turned to horror, when Montolio, howling like a wild wolf, leaped spread-eagled out of the tree.

Montolio wore a rope harness attached to the pine's thin trunk. As he soared out, his momentum bent the tree, and the ranger came down lightly, bending the pine nearly in two. As soon as he hit the ground, he scrambled to his feet and set the rope harness around some thick roots.

As the scene fully unfolded to Drizzt, he realized that several pines had been bent this way, all pointing to the west and all tied by interconnected ropes. As he carefully picked his way over to Montolio, Drizzt passed a net, several trip wires, and one particularly nasty rope set with a dozen or more double-bladed knives. When the trap was sprung and the trees snapped back up, so would this rope, to the peril of any creatures standing beside it.

"Drizzt?" Montolio asked, hearing the light footsteps. "Ware your steps, now. I would not want to have to rebend all these trees, though I will admit it is a bit of fun."

"You seem to have the preparations well under way," Drizzt said as he came to stand near the ranger.

"I have been expecting this day for a long time," Montolio replied. "I have played through this battle a hundred times in my mind and know the course it will take." He crouched and drew an elongated oval on the ground, roughly the shape of the pine grove. "Let me show you," he explained, and he proceeded to draw the landscape around the grove with such detail and accuracy that Drizzt shook his head and looked again to make sure the ranger was blind.

The grove consisted of several dozen trees, running north-south for about fifty yards and less than half that in width. The ground sloped at a gentle but noticeable incline, with the northern end of the grove being half a tree's height lower than the southern end. Farther to the north the ground was broken and boulder-strewn, with scraggly patches of grass and sudden drops, and crossed by sharply twisting trails.

"Their main force will come from the west," Montolio explained, pointing beyond the rock wall and across the small meadow to a pair of dense copses packed between the many rock ledges and cliff facings. "That is the only way they could come in together."

Drizzt took a quick survey of the surrounding area and did not disagree. Across the grove to the east, the ground was rough and uneven. An army charging from that direction would come into the field of tall grass nearly single-file, straight between two high mounds of stone, and would make an easy target for Montolio's deadly bow. South, beyond the grove, the incline grew steeper, a perfect place for orc spear-throwers and archers, except for the fact that just over the nearest ridge loomed a deep ravine with a nearly unclimbable wall.

"We'll not see any trouble from the south," Montolio piped in, almost as though he had read Drizzt's thoughts. "And if they come from the north, they'll be running uphill to get at us. I know Graul better than that. With such favorable odds, he will charge his host straight in from the west, trying to overrun us."

"Thus the trees," Drizzt remarked in admiration. "And the net and knife-set rope."

"Cunning," Montolio congratulated himself. "But remember, I have had five years to prepare for this. Come along now. The trees are just the beginning. I have duties for you while I finish with the tree trap."

Montolio led Drizzt to another secret, blanket-shielded den. Inside hung lines of strange iron items, resembling animal jaws with a strong chain connected to their bases.

"Traps," Montolio explained. "Pelt hunters set them in the mountains. Wicked things. I find them—Hooter is particularly skilled at spotting them—and take them away. I wish I had eyes to see the hunter scratching his head when he comes for them a tenday later!

"This one belonged to Roddy McGristle," Montolio continued, pulling down the closest of the contraptions. The ranger set it on the ground and carefully maneuvered his feet to pull the jaws apart until they set. "This should slow an orc," Montolio said, grabbing a nearby stick and patting around until he hit the plunger.

The trap's iron jaws snapped shut, the force of the blow breaking the stick cleanly and wrenching the remaining half right out of Montolio's hand. "I have collected more than a score of them," Montolio said grimly, wincing at the evil sound of the iron jaws. "I never thought to put them to use—evil things—but against Graul and his clan the traps might just amend some of the damage they have wrought."

Drizzt needed no further instructions. He brought the traps out into the western meadow, set and concealed them, and staked down the chains several feet away. He put a few just inside the rock wall, too, thinking that the pain they might cause to the first orcs coming over would surely slow those behind.

Montolio was done with the trees by this time; he had bent and tied off more than a dozen of them. Now the ranger was up on a rope bridge that ran north-south, fastening a line of crossbows along the western supports. Once set and loaded, either Montolio or Drizzt could merely trot down the line, firing as he went.

Drizzt planned to go and help, but first he had another trick in mind. He went back to the weapons cache and got the tall and heavy ranseur he had seen earlier. He found a sturdy root in the area where he planned to make his stand and dug a small hole out behind it. He laid the metal-shafted weapon down across this root, with only a foot or so of the butt sticking out over the hole, then covered the whole of it with grass and leaves.

He had just finished when the ranger called to him again.

"Here is the best yet," Montolio said, flashing his sly smile. He brought Drizzt to a split log, hollowed and burned smooth, and pitched to seal any cracks. "Good boat for when the river is high and slow," Montolio explained. "And good for holding Adbar brandy," he added with another smile.

Drizzt, not understanding, eyed him curiously. Montolio had shown Drizzt his kegs of the strong drink more than a tenday before, a gift the ranger had received for warning a Sundabar caravan of Graul's ambush intent, but the dark elf saw no purpose in pouring the drink into a hollowed log.

"Adbar brandy is powerful stuff," Montolio explained. "It burns brighter than all but the finest oil."

Now Drizzt understood. Together, he and Montolio carried the log out and placed it at the end of the only pass from the east. They poured in some brandy, then covered it with leaves and grass.

When they got back to the rope bridge, Drizzt saw that Montolio had already made the preparations on this end. A single crossbow was set facing east, its loaded quarrel headed by a wrapped, oil-soaked rag and a flint and steel resting nearby.

"You will have to sight it in," Montolio explained. "Without Hooter, I cannot be sure, and even with the bird, sometimes the height of my aim is off."

The daylight was almost fully gone now, and Drizzt's keen night vision soon located the split log. Montolio had built the supports along the rope bridge quite well and with just this purpose in mind, and with a few minor adjustments, Drizzt had the weapon locked on its target.

All of the major defenses were in place, and Drizzt and Montolio busied themselves finalizing their strategies. Every so often, Hooter or some other owl would rush in, chattering with news. One came in with the expected confirmation: King Graul and his band were on the march.

"You can call Guenhwyvar now," Montolio said. "They will come in this night."

"Foolish," said Drizzt. "The night favors us. You are blind anyway and in no need of daylight and I surely prefer the darkness."

The owl hooted again.

"The main host will come in from the west," Montolio told Drizzt smugly. "As I said they would. Scores of orcs and a giant besides! Hooter's watching another smaller group that split from the first."

The mention of the giant sent a shudder along Drizzt's spine, but he had every intention and a plan already set, for fighting this one. "I want to draw the giant to me," he said.

Montolio turned to him curiously. "Let us see how the battle goes," the ranger offered. "There is only one giant—you or I will get it."

"I want to draw the giant to me," Drizzt said again, more firmly. Montolio couldn't see the set of the drow's jaw or the seething fires in Drizzt's lavender eyes, but the ranger couldn't deny the determination in Drizzt's voice.

*"Mangura bok woklok,"* he said, and he smiled again, knowing that the strange utterance had caught the drow unaware.

*"Mangura bok woklok,"* Montolio declared again. "'Stupid blockhead: translated word by word. Stone giants hate that phrase—brings them charging in every timed."

*"Mangura bok woklok,"* Drizzt mouthed quietly. He'd have to remember that.

# 18 The Battle of Mooshie's Grove

Drizzt noticed that Montolio looked more than a little troubled after Hooter, back with more news, departed.

"The split of Graul's forces?" he inquired.

Montolio nodded, his expression grim. "Worg-riding orcs—just a handful—circling around to the west."

Drizzt looked out beyond the rock wall, to the pass secured by their brandy trough. "We can stop them," he said.

Still the ranger's expression told of doom. "Another group of worgs—a score or more—is coming from the south." Drizzt did not miss the ranger's fear, as Montolio added, "Caroak is leading them. I never thought that one would fall in with Graul."

"A giant?" Drizzt asked.

"No, winter wolf," Montolio replied. At the words, Guenhwyvar flattened its ears and growled angrily.

"The panther knows," Montolio said as Drizzt looked on in amazement. "A winter wolf is a perversion of nature, a blight against creatures following the natural order, and thus, Guenhwyvar's enemy."

The black panther growled again.

"It's a large creature," Montolio went on, "and too smart for a wolf. I have fought Caroak before. Alone he could give us a time of it! With the worgs around him, and us busy fighting orcs, he might have his way."

Guenhwyvar growled a third time and tore the ground with great claws.

"Guenhwyvar will deal with Caroak," Drizzt remarked.

Montolio moved over and grabbed the panther by the ears, holding Guenhwyvar's gaze with his own sightless expression. "Ware the wolf's breath," the ranger said. "A cone of frost, it is, that will freeze your muscles to your bones. I have seen a giant felled by it!" Montolio turned to Drizzt and knew that the drow wore a concerned expression.

"Guenhwyvar has to keep them away from us until we can chase off Graul and his group," the ranger said, "then we can make arrangements for Caroak." He released his hold on the panther's ears and swatted Guenhwyvar hard on the scruff of the neck.

Guenhwyvar roared a fourth time and darted off through the grove, a black arrow aimed at the heart of doom.

⚔ ⚔ ⚔ ⚔ ⚔

Graul's main attack force came, as expected, from the west, whooping and hollering and trampling the brush in its path. The troops approached in two groups, one through each of the dense copses.

"Aim for the group on the south!" Montolio called up to Drizzt, in position on the crossbow-laden rope bridge. "We've friends in the other!"

As if in confirmation of the ranger's decree, the northern copse erupted suddenly in orc cries that sounded more like terrified shrieks than battle calls. A chorus of throaty growls accompanied the screams. Bluster the bear had come to Montolio's call, Drizzt knew, and by the sounds in the copse, he had brought a number of friends.

Drizzt wasn't about to question their good fortune. He positioned himself behind the closest crossbow and let the quarrel fly as the first orcs emerged from the southern copse. Right down the line the drow ran, clicking off his shots in rapid succession. From down below, Montolio arced a few arrows over the wall.

In the sudden swarm of orcs, Drizzt couldn't tell how many of their shots actually hit, but the buzzing bolts did slow the orc charge and scattered their ranks. Several orcs dropped to their bellies; a few turned and headed straight back into the trees. The bulk of the group, though, and some running to join from the other copse, came on.

Montolio fired one last time, then felt his way back into a sheltered run behind the center of his bent tree traps, where he would be protected on three sides by walls of wood and trees. His bow in one hand he checked his sword and reached around to touch a rope at his other side.

Drizzt noticed the ranger moving into position twenty feet below him and to the side, and he figured that this might be his last free opportunity. He sorted out an object hanging above Montolio's head and dropped a spell over it.

The quarrels had brought minimum chaos to the field of charging orcs, but the traps proved more effective. First one, then another, orc stepped in, their cries rising over the din of the charge. As other orcs saw their companions' pain and peril, they slowed considerably or stopped altogether.

With the commotion growing in the field, Drizzt paused and carefully considered his final shot. He noticed a large, finely outfitted orc watching from the closest boughs of the northern copse. Drizzt knew this was Graul, but his attention shifted immediately to the figure standing next to the orc king. "Damn," the drow muttered, recognizing McGristle. Now he was torn, and he moved the crossbow back and forth between the adversaries. Drizzt wanted to shoot at Roddy, wanted to end his personal torment then and there. But Roddy was not an orc, and Drizzt found himself repulsed by the thought of killing a human.

"Graul is the more important target," the drow told himself, more to distract his inner torment than for any other reason. Quickly, before he could find any more arguments, he took aim and fired. The quarrel whistled long and far, knocking into the trunk of a tree just inches above Graul's head. Roddy promptly grabbed the orc king and pulled him back into the deeper shadows. In their stead came a roaring stone giant, rock in hand.

The boulder clipped the trees beside Drizzt, shaking the branches and bridge alike. A second shot followed at once, this one taking a supporting post squarely and dropping the front half of the bridge.

Drizzt had seen it coming, though he was amazed and horrified by the uncanny accuracy at so far a range. As the front half of the bridge fell away beneath him, Drizzt leaped out, catching a hold in a tangle of branches. When he finally sorted himself out, he was faced by a new problem. From the east came the worg-riders, brandishing torches.

Drizzt looked to the log trap, then to the crossbow. It and the post securing it had survived the boulder hit, but the drow could not hope to cross to it on the faltering bridge.

⚔ ⚔ ⚔ ⚔ ⚔

The leaders of the main host, now behind Drizzt, reached the rock wall then. Fortunately, the first orc leaping over landed squarely into another of the wicked jaw traps, and its companions were not so quick to follow.

Guenhwyvar leaped around and between the many broken crags of stone marking the descent to the north. The panther caught the distant first cries of battle back at the grove, but more intently, Guenhwyvar heard the ensuing howls of the approaching wolf pack. The panther sprang up to a low ledge and waited.

Caroak, the huge silver canine beast, led the charge. Focused on the distant grove, the winter wolf's surprise was complete when Guenhwyvar dropped upon it, scratching and raking wildly.

Clumps of silver fur flew about under the assault. Yelping, Caroak dived into a sidelong roll. Guenhwyvar rode the wolf as a lumberjack might foot-roll a log in a pool, slashing and kicking with each step. But Caroak was a wizened old wolf, a veteran of a hundred battles. As the monster rolled about to its back, a blast of icy frost came at the panther.

Guenhwyvar dodged aside, both from the frost and the onslaught of several worgs. The frost got the panther on the side of the face, though, numbing Guenhwyvar's jaw. Then the chase was on, with Guenhwyvar leaping and tumbling right around the wolf pack, and the worgs, and angry Caroak, nipping at the panther's heels.

⚔ ⚔ ⚔ ⚔ ⚔

Time was running out for Drizzt and Montolio. Above all else, the drow knew that he must protect their rear flank. In synchronous movements, Drizzt kicked off his boots, took the flint in one hand and put a piece of steel in his mouth, and leaped up to a branch that would take him out over the lone crossbow.

He got above it a moment later. Holding with one hand he struck the flint hard. Sparks rolled down, close to the mark. Drizzt struck again and again, and finally, a spark hit the oil-soaked rags tipping the loaded quarrel squarely enough to ignite them.

Now the drow was not so lucky. He rocked and twisted but could not get his foot close enough to the trigger.

Montolio could see nothing, of course, but he knew well enough the general situation. He heard the approaching worgs at the back of the grove and knew that those in front had breached the wall. He sent another bow shot through the thick canopy of bent trees, just for good measure, and hooted loudly three times.

In answer, a group of owls swooped down from the pines, bearing down on the orcs along the rock wall. Like the traps, the birds could only cause minimal real damage, but the confusion bought the defenders a little more time.

⚔ ⚔ ⚔ ⚔ ⚔

To this point, the only clear advantage for the grove's defenders came in the northernmost copse, where Bluster and three of his closest and largest bear buddies had a dozen orcs down and a score more running about blindly.

One orc, in flight from a bear, came around a tree and nearly crashed into Bluster. The orc kept its wits enough to thrust its spear ahead, but the creature hadn't the strength to drive the crude weapon through Bluster's thick hide.

Bluster responded with a heavy swipe that sent the orc's head flying through the trees.

Another great bear ambled by, its huge arms wrapped in front of it. The only clue that the bear held an orc in the crushing hug was the orc's feet, which hung out and kicked wildly below the engulfing fur.

Bluster caught sight of another enemy, smaller and quicker than an orc. The bear roared and charged, but the diminutive creature was long gone before he ever got close.

Tephanis had no intentions of joining the battle. He had come with the northernmost group mostly to keep out of Graul's sight, and had planned all along to remain in the trees and wait out the fighting. The trees didn't seem so safe anymore, so the sprite lighted out, meaning to get into the southern copse.

About halfway to the other woods, the sprite's plans were foiled again. Sheer speed nearly got him past the trap before the iron jaws snapped closed, but the wicked teeth just caught the end his foot. The ensuing jolt blasted the breath from him and left him dazed, facedown in the grass.

⚔ ⚔ ⚔ ⚔ ⚔

Drizzt knew how revealing that little fire on the quarrel would prove, so he was hardly surprised when another giant-hurled rock thundered in. It struck Drizzt's bending branch, and with a series of cracks, the limb swung down.

Drizzt hooked the crossbow with his foot as he dropped, and he hit the trigger immediately, before the weapon was deflected too far aside. Then he stubbornly held his position and watched.

The fiery quarrel reached out into the darkness beyond the eastern rock wall. It skidded in low, sending sparks up through the tall grass, then thudded into the side—the outside—of the brandy-filled trough.

The first half of the worg-riders got across the trap, but the remaining three were not so lucky, bearing in just as flames licked over the side of the dugout. The brandy and kindling roared to life as the riders plunged through. Worgs and orcs thrashed about in the tall grass, setting other pockets of fire.

Those who had already come through spun about abruptly at the sudden conflagration. One orc rider was thrown heavily, landing on its own torch, and the other two barely kept their seats. Above all else, worgs hated fire, and the sight of three of their kin rolling about, furry balls of flame, did little to strengthen their resolve for this battle.

* * *

Guenhwyvar came to a small, level area dominated by a single maple. Onlookers to the panther's rush would have blinked incredulously, wondering if the vertical tree trunk was really a log lying on its side, so fast did Guenhwyvar run up it.

The worg pack came in soon after, sniffing and milling about, certain that the cat was up the tree but unable to pick out Guenhwyvar's black form among the dark boughs.

The panther showed itself soon enough, though, again dropping heavily to the back of the winter wolf, and this time taking care to lock its jaws onto Caroak's ear.

The winter wolf thrashed and yelped as Guenhwyvar's claws did their work. Caroak managed to turn about and Guenhwyvar heard the sharp intake of breath, the same as the one preceding the previous chilling blast.

Guenhwyvar's huge neck muscles flexed, forcing Caroak's open jaws to the side. The foul breath came anyway, blasting three charging worgs right in the face.

Guenhwyvar's muscles reversed and flexed again suddenly, and the panther heard Caroak's neck snap. The winter wolf plopped straight down, Guenhwyvar still atop it.

Those three worgs closest to Guenhwyvar, the three who had caught Caroak's icy breath, posed no threat. One lay on its side, gasping for air that would not move through its frozen lungs, another turned tight circles, fully blinded, and the last stood perfectly still, staring down at its forelegs, which, for some reason, would not answer its call to move.

The rest of the pack, though, nearly a score strong, came in methodically, surrounding the panther in a deadly ring. Guenhwyvar looked all about for some escape, but the worgs did not rush frantically, leaving openings.

They worked in harmony, shoulder to shoulder, tightening the ring.

✕ ✕ ✕ ✕ ✕

The leading orcs milled about the tangle of bent trees, looking for some way through. Some had begun to make progress, but the whole of the trap was interconnected, and any one of a dozen trip wires would send all the pines springing up.

One of the orcs found Montolio's net, then, the hard way. It stumbled over a rope, fell facedown on the net, then went high into the air, one of its companions caught beside it. Neither of them could have imagined how much better off they were than those they had left behind, particularly the orc unsuspectingly straddling the knife-set rope. When the trees sprang up, so did this devilish trap, gutting the creature and lifting it head over heels into the air.

Even those orcs not caught by the secondary traps did not fare well. Tangled branches, bristling with prickly pine needles, shot up all about them, sending a few on a pretty fair ride and scratching and disorienting the others.

Even worse for the orcs, Montolio used the sound of the rushing trees as his signal to open fire. Arrow after arrow whistled down the sheltered run, more hitting the mark than not. One orc lifted its spear to throw, then caught one arrow in the face and another in the chest. Another beast turned and fled, crying "Bad magic!" frantically.

To those crossing the rock wall, the screamer seemed to fly, its feet kicking above the ground. Its startled companions understood when the orc came back down in a heap, a quivering arrow shaft protruding from its back.

Drizzt, still on his tenuous perch, didn't have time to marvel at the efficient execution of Montolio's well-laid plans. From the west, the giant was now on the move and back the other way, the two remaining worg-riders had settled enough to resume their charges, torches held high.

✕ ✕ ✕ ✕ ✕

The ring of snarling worgs tightened. Guenhwyvar could smell their stinking breath. The panther could not hope to charge through the thick ranks, nor could the cat get over them quickly enough to flee.

Guenhwyvar found another route. Hind paws tamped down on Caroak's still-twitching body and the panther arrowed straight up into the air, twenty feet and more. Guenhwyvar caught the maple's lowest branch with long front claws, hooked on, and pulled itself up. Then the panther disappeared into the boughs, leaving the frustrated pack howling and growling.

Guenhwyvar reappeared quickly though, out from the side and back to the ground, and the pack took up the pursuit. The panther had come to know this terrain quite well over the last few tendays and now Guenhwyvar had figured out exactly where to lead the wolves.

They ran along a ridge, with a dark and brooding emptiness on their left flank. Guenhwyvar marked well the boulders and the few scattered trees. The panther couldn't see the chasm's opposite bank and had to trust fully in its memory. Incredibly fast, Guenhwyvar pivoted suddenly and sprang out into the night, touching down lightly across the wide way and speeding off toward the grove. The worgs would have a long jump—too long for most of them—or a long way back around if they meant to follow.

They inched up snarling and scratching at the ground. One poised on the lip and meant to try the leap, but an arrow exploded into its side and destroyed its determination.

Worgs were not stupid creatures, and the sight of the arrow put them on the defensive. The ensuing shower by Kellindil and his kin was more than they expected. Dozens of arrows whistled in, dropping the worgs where they stood. Only a few escaped that barrage, and they promptly scattered to the corners of the night.

⚔ ⚔ ⚔ ⚔ ⚔

Drizzt called upon another magical trick to stop the torch-bearers. Faerie fire, harmless dancing flames, appeared suddenly below the torch fires, rolling down the wooden instrument to lick at the orcs' hands. Faerie fire did not burn—was not even warm—but when the orcs saw the flames engulfing their hands, they were far from rational.

One of them threw its torch out wide, and the jerking motion cost it its seat. It tumbled down in the grass, and the worg turned yet another time and snarled in frustration.

The other orc simply dropped its torch, which fell on top of its mount's head. Sparks and flames erupted from the worg's thick coat, stinging its eyes and ears, and the beast went crazy. It dropped into a headlong roll, bouncing right over the startled orc.

The orc staggered back to its feet, dazed and bruised and holding its arms out wide as if in apology. The singed worg wasn't interested in hearing any, however. It sprang straight in and clamped its powerful jaws on the orc's face.

Drizzt didn't see any of it. The drow could only hope that his trick had worked, for as soon as he had cast the spell, he released his foothold on the crossbow and let the torn branch carry him down to the ground.

Two orcs, finally seeing a target, rushed at the drow as he landed, but as soon as Drizzt's hands were free of the branch, they held his scimitars. The orcs came in, oblivious, and Drizzt slapped their weapons aside and cut them down. The drow waded through more scattered resistance as he made his way to his prepared spot. A grim smile found his face when at last he felt the ranseur's metal shaft under his bare feet. He remembered the giants back in Maldobar that had slain the innocent family, and he took comfort that now he would kill another of their evil kin.

*"Mangura bok woklok!"* Drizzt cried, placing one foot on the root fulcrum and the other on the butt of the hidden weapon.

⚔ ⚔ ⚔ ⚔ ⚔

Montolio smiled when he heard the drow's call, gaining confidence in the proximity of his powerful ally. His bow sang out a few more times, but the ranger sensed that the orcs were coming in at him in a roundabout way, using the thick trees as cover. The ranger waited, baiting them in. Then, just before they closed, Montolio dropped his bow, whipped out his sword and slashed the rope at his side, right below a huge knot. The severed rope rolled up into the air, the knot catching on a fork in the lowest branch, and Montolio's shield, empowered with one of Drizzt's darkness spells, dropped down to hang at precisely the right height for the ranger's waiting arm.

Darkness held little influence over the blind ranger, but the few orcs that had come in at Montolio found themselves in a precarious position. They jostled and swung wildly—one cut down its own brother—while Montolio calmly sorted out the melee and went to methodical work. In the matter of a minute, four of the five who had come in were dead or dying and the fifth had taken flight.

Far from sated, the ranger and his portable ball of darkness followed, searching for voices or sounds that would lead him to more orcs. Again came the cry that made Montolio smile.

⚔ ⚔ ⚔ ⚔ ⚔

*"Mangura bok woklok."* Drizzt yelled again. An orc tossed a spear at the drow, which Drizzt promptly swatted aside. The distant orc was now unarmed, but Drizzt would not pursue, determinedly holding his position.

*"Mangura bok woklok!"* Drizzt cried again. "Come in, stupid blockhead!" This time the giant, approaching the wall in Montolio's direction, heard the words. The great monster hesitated a moment, regarding the drow curiously.

Drizzt didn't miss the opportunity. *"Mangura bok woklok!"*

With a howl and a stamp that shook the earth, the giant kicked a hole in the rock wall and strode toward Drizzt.

*"Mangura bok woklok!"* Drizzt said for good measure, angling his feet properly.

The giant broke into a dead run, scattering terrified orcs before it and slamming its stone and its club together angrily. It sputtered a thousand curses at Drizzt in those few seconds, words that the drow would never decipher. Three times the drow's height and many times his weight, the giant loomed over Drizzt, and its rush seemed as though it would surely bury Drizzt where he calmly stood.

When the giant got only two long strides from Drizzt, committed fully to its collision course, Drizzt dropped all of his weight onto his back foot. The ranseur's butt dropped into the hole. Its tip angled up.

Drizzt leaped back at the moment the giant plowed into the ranseur. The weapon's tip and hooked barbs disappeared into the giant's belly, drove upward through its diaphragm and into its heart and lungs. The metal shaft bowed and seemed as if it would break as its butt end was driven a foot and more into the ground.

The ranseur held, and the giant was stopped cold. It dropped its club and rock, reached helplessly for the metal shaft with hands that had not the strength to even close around it. Huge eyes bulged in denial, in terror, and in absolute surprise. The great mouth opened wide and contorted weirdly, but could not even find the wind to scream.

Drizzt, too, almost cried out, but caught the words before he uttered them. "Amazing," he said, looking back to where Montolio was fighting, for the cry he nearly shouted was a praise to the goddess Mielikki. Drizzt shook his head helplessly and smiled, stunned by the acute perceptions of his not-so-blind companion.

With those thoughts in mind and a sense of righteousness in his heart, Drizzt ran up the shaft and slashed at the giant's throat with both weapons. He continued on, stepping right on the giant's shoulder and head and leaping off toward a group of watching orcs, whooping as he went.

The sight of the giant, their bully, quivering and gasping, had already unnerved the orcs, but when this ebony-skinned and wild-eyed drow monster leaped at them, they broke rank altogether. Drizzt's charge got him to the closest two, and he promptly cut them down and charged on.

Twenty feet to the drow's left, a ball of blackness rolled out of the trees, leading a dozen frightened orcs before it. The orcs knew that to fall within that impenetrable globe was to fall within the blind hermit's reach and to die.

⚔ ⚔ ⚔ ⚔ ⚔

Two orcs and three worgs, all that remained of the torch bearers, regrouped and slipped quietly toward the grove's eastern edge. If they could get in behind the enemy, they believed the battle still could be won.

The orc farthest to the north never even saw the rushing black form. Guenhwyvar plowed it down and charged on, confident that that one would never rise again.

A worg was next in line. Quicker to react than the orc, the worg spun and faced the panther, its teeth bared and jaws snapping.

Guenhwyvar snarled, pulling up short right before it. Great claws came in alternately in a series of slaps. The worg could not match the cat's speed. It swung its jaws from side to side, always a moment too late to catch up to the darting paws. After only five slaps, the worg was defeated. One eye had closed forever, its tongue, half torn, lolled helplessly out one side of its mouth, and its lower jaw was no longer in line with its upper. Only the presence of other targets saved the worg, for when it turned and fled the way it had come, Guenhwyvar, seeing closer prey, did not follow.

Drizzt and Montolio had flushed most of the invading force back out over the rock wall. "Bad magic!" came the general orc cry, voices edged on desperation. Hooter and his owl companions aided the growing frenzy, flapping down all of a sudden in orc faces, nipping with a talon or beak, then rushing off again into the sky. Still another orc discovered one of the traps as it tried to flee. It went down howling and shrieking, its cries only heightening its companions' terror.

"No!" Roddy McGristle cried in disbelief. "Ye've let two beat up yer whole force!"

Graul's glare settled on the burly man.

"We can turn 'em back," Roddy said. "If they see ye, they'll go back to the fight." The mountain man's appraisal was not off the mark. If Graul and Roddy had made their entrance then, the orcs, still numbering more than fifty, might have regrouped. With most of their traps exhausted, Drizzt and Montolio would have been in a sore position indeed! But the orc king had seen another brewing problem to the north and had decided, despite Roddy's protests, that the old man and the dark elf simply weren't worth the effort.

Most of the orcs in the field heard the newest danger before they saw it, for Bluster and his friends were a noisy lot. The largest obstacle the bears found as they rolled through the orc ranks was picking out a single target in the mad rush. They swatted orcs as they passed, then chased them into the copse and beyond, all the way back to their holes by the river. It was high spring; the air was charged with energy and excitement, and how these playful bears loved to swat orcs!

⚔ ⚔ ⚔ ⚔ ⚔

The whole horde of rushing bodies swarmed right past the fallen quickling. When Tephanis awoke, he found that he was the only one alive on the blood-soaked field. Growls and shouts wafted in from the west, the fleeing band and sounds of battle still sounded in the ranger's grove. Tephanis knew that his part in the battle, minor though it had been, was over. Tremendous pain rolled up the sprite's leg, more pain than he had ever known. He looked down to his torn foot and to his horror realized that the only way out of the wicked trap was to complete the gruesome cut, losing the end of his foot and all five of his toes in the process. It was not a difficult job—the foot was hanging by a thin piece of skin—and Tephanis did not hesitate, fearing that the drow would come out at any moment and find him.

The quickling stifled his scream and covered the wound with his torn shirt, then ambled—slowly—off into the trees.

⚔ ⚔ ⚔ ⚔ ⚔

The orc crept along silently, glad for the covering noises of the fight between the panther and a worg. All thoughts of killing the old man or the drow had flown from this orc now; it had seen its comrades chased away by a pack of bears. Now the orc only wanted to find a way out, not an easy feat in the thick, low tangle of pine branches.

It stepped on some dry leaves as it came into one clear area and froze at the resounding crackle. The orc glanced to the left, then slowly brought its head back around to the right. All of a sudden, it jumped and spun, expecting an attack from the rear. But all was clear as far as it could tell and all, except for the distant panther growls and worg yelps, was quiet. The orc let out a profound sigh of relief and sought the trail once again.

It stopped suddenly on instinct and threw its head way back to look up. A dark form crouched on a branch just above the orc's head, and the silvery flash shot down before the orc could begin to react. The curve of the scimitar's blade proved perfect for slipping around the orc's chin and diving into its throat.

The orc stood very still, arms wide and twitching, and tried to scream, but the whole length of its larynx was torn apart. The scimitar came out in a rush and the orc fell backward into death.

Not so far away, another orc finally extracted itself from the hanging net and quickly cut free its buddy. The two of them, enraged and not as anxious to run away without a fight, crept in quietly.

"In the dark," the first explained as they came through one thicket and found the landscape blotted out by an impenetrable globe. "Deep."

Together, the orcs raised their spears and threw, grunting savagely with the effort. The spears disappeared into the dark globe, dead center, one banging into a metallic object but the other striking something softer.

The orcs' cries of victory were cut short by two twangs of a bowstring. One of the creatures lurched forward, dead before it hit the ground, but the other, stubbornly holding its footing, managed to look down to its chest, to the protruding point of an arrowhead. It lived long enough to see Montolio casually stride past and disappear into the darkness to retrieve his shield.

Drizzt watched the old man from a distance, shaking his head and wondering.

* * * * *

"It is ended," the elven scout told the others when they caught up to him among the boulders just south of Mooshie's Grove.

"I am not so certain," Kellindil replied, looking curiously back to the west and hearing the echoes of bear growls and orc screams. Kellindil suspected that something beyond Graul was behind this attack and feeling somewhat responsible for the drow, he wanted to know what it might be.

"The ranger and drow have won the grove," the scout explained.

"Agreed," said Kellindil, "and so your part is ended. Go back, all of you, to the campsite."

"And will you join us?" one of the elves asked, though he had already guessed the answer.

"If the fates decree it," Kellindil replied. "For now, I have other business to attend."

The others did not question Kellindil further. Rarely did he come to their realm and never did he remain with them for long. Kellindil was an adventurer; the road was his home. He set off at once, running to catch up to the fleeing orcs, then paralleling their movements just south of them.

⚔ ⚔ ⚔ ⚔ ⚔

"Ye let just two of them beat ye!" Roddy griped when he and Graul had a moment to stop and catch their breath. "Two of them!"

Graul's answer came in the swing of a heavy club. Roddy partially blocked the blow, but its weight knocked him backward.

"Ye're to pay for that!" the mountain man growled, tearing Bleeder from his belt. A dozen of Graul's minions appeared beside the orc king then and immediately understood the situation.

"Yous has brought ruin to us!" Graul snapped at Roddy. Then to his orcs, he shouted, "Kill him!"

Roddy's dog tripped the closest of the group and Roddy didn't wait for the others to catch up. He turned and sprinted off into the night, using every trick he knew to get ahead of the pursuing band.

His efforts were quickly successful—the orcs really didn't want any more battles this night—and Roddy would have been wise to stop looking over his shoulder.

He heard a rustle up ahead and turned just in time to catch the pommel of a swinging sword squarely in the face. The weight of the blow, multiplied by Roddy's own momentum, dropped the mountain man straight to the ground and into unconsciousness.

"I am not surprised," Kellindil said over the writhing body.

# 19
# Separate Ways

Eight days had done nothing to ease the pain in Tephanis's foot. The sprite ambled about as best he could, but whenever he broke into a sprint, he inevitably veered to one side and more often than not crashed into a bush or, worse, the unbending trunk of a tree.

"Will-you-please-quit-growling-at-me, stupid-dog!" Tephanis snapped at the yellow canine he had been with since the day after the battle. Neither had become comfortable around the other. Tephanis often lamented that this ugly mutt was in no way akin to Caroak.

But Caroak was dead; the quickling had found the winter wolf's torn body. Another companion gone, and now the sprite was alone again. "Alone-except-for-you, stupid-dog," he lamented.

The dog bared its teeth and growled.

Tephanis wanted to slice its throat, wanted to run up and down the length of the mangy animal, cutting and slashing at every inch. He saw the sun riding low in the sky, though, and knew that the beast might soon prove valuable.

"Time-for-me-to-go!" the quickling spouted. Faster than the dog could react, Tephanis darted by it, grabbed at the rope he had hung about the dog's neck, and zipped three complete circuits of a nearby tree. The dog went after him, but Tephanis easily kept out of its reach until the leash snapped taut, flipping the dog right over. "Be-back-soon, you-stupid-thing!"

Tephanis sped along the mountain paths, knowing that this night might be his last chance. The lights of Maldobar burned in the far distance, but it was a different light, a campfire, that guided the quickling. He came upon the small camp just a few minutes later, glad to see that the elf was not around.

He found Roddy McGristle sitting at the base of a huge tree, his arms pulled behind him and tied at the wrists around the trunk. The mountain man seemed a wretched thing—as wretched as the dog—but Tephanis was out of options. Ulgulu and Kempfana were dead, Caroak was dead, and Graul, after the disaster at the grove, had actually placed a bounty on the quickling's head.

That left only Roddy—not much of a choice, but Tephanis had no desire to survive on his own ever again. He sped, unnoticed, to the back of the tree and whispered in the mountain man's ear. "You-will-be-in-Maldobar-tomorrow."

Roddy froze at the unexpected, squeaky voice.

"You will be in Maldobar tomorrow," Tephanis said again, as slowly as he could.

"Go away," Roddy growled at him, thinking that the sprite was teasing him.

"You-should-be-kinder-to-me, oh-you-should!" Tephanis snapped right back. "The-elf-means-to-imprison-you, you-know. For-crimes-against-the-blind-ranger."

"Shut yer mouth," McGristle growled, louder than he had intended.

"What are you about?" came Kellindil's call from not so far away.

"There, you-have-done-it-now, silly-man!" Tephanis whispered.

"I told ye to go away!" Roddy replied.

"I-might, and-then-where-would-you-be? In-prison?" Tephanis said angrily. "I-can-help-you-now, if-you-want-my-help."

Roddy was beginning to understand. "Untie my hands," he ordered.

"They-already-are-untied," Tephanis replied, and Roddy found the sprite's words to be true. He started to rise but changed his mind abruptly as Kellindil entered the camp.

"Keep-still," Tephanis advised. "I-will-distract-your-captor." Tephanis had moved as he spoke the words and Roddy heard only an unintelligible murmur. He kept his hands behind him, though, seeing no other course available with the heavily armed elf approaching.

"Our last night on the road," Kellindil remarked, dropping by the fire the coney he had shot for a meal. He moved in front of Roddy and bent low. "I will send for Lady Falconhand once we have arrived in Maldobar," he said. "She names Montolio DeBrouchee as a friend and will be interested to learn of the events in the grove."

"What do ye know?" Roddy spat at him. "The ranger was a friend o' mine, too!"

"If you are a friend of orc king Graul, then you are no friend of the ranger in the grove," Kellindil retorted.

Roddy had no immediate rebuttal, but Tephanis supplied one. A buzzing noise came from behind the elf and Kellindil, dropping a hand to his sword, spun about.

"What manner of being are you?" he asked the quickling, his eyes wide in amazement.

Kellindil never learned the answer, for Roddy came up suddenly behind him and slammed him to the ground. Kellindil was a seasoned fighter, but in close he was no match for the sheer brawn of Roddy McGristle. Roddy's huge and dirty hands closed on the slender elf's throat.

"I-have-your-dog," Tephanis said to Roddy when the foul business was done. "Tied-it-to-a-tree."

"Who are ye?" Roddy asked, trying to hide his elation, both for his freedom and for the knowledge that his dog still lived. "And what do ye want with me?"

"I-am-a-little-thing, you-can-see-that-to-be-true," Tephanis explained. "I-like-keeping-big-friends."

Roddy considered the offer for a moment. "Well, ye've earned it, he said with a laugh. He found Bleeder, his trusted axe, among the dead elf's belongings and rose up huge and grim-faced. "Come on then, let's get back to the mountains. I've a drow to deal with."

A sour expression crossed the quickling's delicate features, but Tephanis hid it before Roddy could notice. Tephanis had no desire to go anywhere near the blind ranger's grove. Aside from the fact that the orc king had placed a bounty on his head, he knew that the other elves might get suspicious if Roddy showed up without Kellindil. More than that, Tephanis found the pain in his head and foot even more acute at the mere thought of facing the dark elf again.

"No!" the sprite blurted. Roddy, not used to being disobeyed, eyed him dangerously.

"No-need," Tephanis lied. "The-drow-is-dead, killed-by-a-worg."

Roddy didn't seem convinced.

"I-led-you-to-the-drow-once," Tephanis reminded him.

Truly Roddy was disappointed, but he no longer doubted the quickling. If it hadn't been for Tephanis, Roddy knew, he never would have located Drizzt. He would be more than a hundred miles away, sniffing around Morueme's Cave and spending all of his gold on dragon lies. "What about the blind ranger?" Roddy asked.

"He-lives, but-let-him-live," Tephanis replied. "Many-powerful-friends-have-joined-him." He led Roddy's gaze to Kellindil's body. "Elves, many-elves."

Roddy nodded his assent. He had no real grudge against Mooshie and had no desire to face Kellindil's kin.

They buried Kellindil and all of the supplies they couldn't take with them, found Roddy's dog, and set out later that same night for the wide lands to the west.

⚔ ⚔ ⚔ ⚔ ⚔

Back at Mooshie's grove, the summer passed peacefully and productively, with Drizzt coming into the ways and methods of a ranger even more easily than optimistic Montolio had believed. Drizzt learned the name for every tree or bush in the region, and every animal, and more importantly, he learned how to learn, how to observe the clues that Mielikki gave him. When he came upon an animal that he had not encountered before, he found that simply by watching its movements and actions he could quickly discern its intent, demeanor, and mood.

"Go and feel its coat," Montolio whispered to him one day in the gray and blustery twilight. The old ranger pointed across a field, to the tree line and the white flicking of a deer's tail. Even in the dim light, Drizzt had trouble seeing the deer, but he sensed its presence, as Montolio obviously had.

"Will it let me?" Drizzt whispered back. Montolio smiled and shrugged.

Drizzt crept out silently and carefully, following the shadows along the edge of the meadow. He chose a northern, downwind approach, but to get north of the deer, he had to come around from the east. He knew his error when he was still two dozen yards from the deer. It lifted its head suddenly, sniffed, and flicked its white tail.

Drizzt froze and waited for a long moment while the deer resumed its grazing. The skittish creature was on the alert now, and as soon as Drizzt took another measured step, the deer bolted away.

But not before Montolio, taking the southern approach, had gotten close enough to pat its rump as it ran past.

Drizzt blinked in amazement. "The wind favored me!" he protested to the smug ranger.

Montolio shook his head. "Only over the last twenty yards, when you came north of the deer," he explained. "West was better than east until then."

"But you could not get north of the deer from the west," Drizzt said.

"I did not have to," Montolio replied. "There is a high bluff back there," he pointed to the south. "It cuts the wind at this angle—swirls it back around."

"I did not know."

"You have to know," Montolio said lightly. "That is the trick of it. You have to see as a bird might and look down upon all the region before you choose your course "

"I have not learned to fly," Drizzt replied sarcastically.

"Nor have I!" roared the old ranger. "Look above you."

Drizzt squinted as he turned his eyes to the gray sky. He made out a solitary form, gliding easily with great wings held wide to catch the breeze.

"A hawk," the drow said.

"Rode the breeze from the south," Montolio explained, "then banked west on the breaking currents around the bluff. If you had observed its flight, you might have suspected the change in terrain."

"That is impossible," Drizzt said helplessly.

"Is it?" Montolio asked, and he started away—to hide his smile. Of course the drow was correct; one could not tell the topography of the terrain by the flight patterns of a hawk. Montolio had learned of the shifting wind from a certain sneaky owl who had slipped in at the ranger's bidding right after Drizzt had started out across the meadow, but Drizzt didn't have to know that. Let the drow consider the fib for a while, the old ranger decided. The contemplation, recounting all he had learned, would be a valuable lesson.

"Hooter told you," Drizzt said a half-hour later, on the trail back to the grove. "Hooter told you of the wind and told you of the hawk."

"You seem sure of yourself."

"I am," Drizzt said firmly. "The hawk did not cry—I have become aware enough to know that. You could not see the bird, and I know that you did not hear the rush of wind over its wings, whatever you may say!"

Montolio's laughter brought a smile of confirmation to the drow's face.

"You have done well this day," the old ranger said.

"I did not get near the deer," Drizzt reminded him.

"That was not the test," Montolio replied. "You trusted in your knowledge to dispute my claims. You are sure of the lessons you have learned. Now hear some more. Let me tell you a few tricks when approaching a skittish deer."

They talked all the way back to the grove and far into the night after that. Drizzt listened eagerly, absorbing every word as he was let in on still more of the world's wondrous secrets.

A tenday later, in a different field, Drizzt placed one hand on the rump of a doe, the other on the rump of its speckle-coated fawn. Both animals lit out at the unexpected touch, but Montolio "saw" Drizzt's smile from a hundred yards away.

Drizzt's lessons were far from complete when the summer waned, but

Montolio no longer spent much time instructing the drow. Drizzt had learned enough to go out and learn on his own, listening and watching the quiet voices and subtle signs of the trees and the animals. So caught up was Drizzt in his unending revelations that he hardly noticed the profound changes in Montolio. The ranger felt much older now. His back would hardly straighten on chill mornings and his hands often went numb. Montolio remained stoic about it all, hardly one for self-pity and hardly lamenting what he knew was to come.

He had lived long and fully, had accomplished much, and had experienced life more vividly than most men ever would.

"What are your plans?" he said unexpectedly to Drizzt one night as they ate their dinner, a vegetable stew that Drizzt had concocted.

The question hit Drizzt hard. He had no plans beyond the present, and why should he, with life so easy and enjoyable—more so than it had ever been for the beleaguered drow renegade? Drizzt really didn't want to think about the question, so he threw a biscuit at Guenhwyvar to change the subject. The panther was getting a bit too comfortable on Drizzt's bedroll, wrapping up in the blankets to the point where Drizzt worried that the only way to get Guenhwyvar out of the tangle would be to send it back to the astral plane.

Montolio was persistent. "What are your plans, Drizzt Do'Urden?" the old ranger said again firmly. "Where and how will you live?"

"Are you throwing me out?" Drizzt asked.

"Of course not."

"Then I will live with you," Drizzt replied calmly.

"I mean after," Montolio said, growing flustered.

"After what?" Drizzt asked, thinking that Mooshie knew something he did not.

Montolio's laughter mocked his suspicions. "I am an old man," the ranger explained, "and you are a young elf. I am older than you, but even if I were a babe, your years would far outdistance my own. Where will Drizzt Do'Urden go when Montolio DeBrouchee is no more?"

Drizzt turned away. "l do not . . ." he began tentatively. "I will stay here."

"No," Montolio replied soberly. "You have much more before you than this, I hope. This life would not do."

"It has suited you," Drizzt snapped back, more forcefully than he had intended.

"For five years," Montolio said calmly, taking no offense. "Five years after a life of adventure and excitement."

"My life has not been so quiet," Drizzt reminded him.

"But you are still a child," Montolio said. "Five years is not five hundred, and five hundred is what you have remaining. Promise me now that you will reconsider your course when I am no more. There is a wide world out there, my friend, full of pain, but filled with joy as well. The former keeps you on the path of growth, and the latter makes the journey tolerable.

"Promise me now," Montolio said, "that when Mooshie is no more, Drizzt will go and find his place."

Drizzt wanted to argue, to ask the ranger how he was so certain that this grove was not Drizzt's 'place.' A mental scale dipped and leveled, then dipped again within Drizzt at that moment. He weighed the memories of Maldobar, the farmers' deaths, and all the memories before that of the trials he had faced and the evils that had so persistently followed him. Against this, Drizzt considered his heartfelt desire to go back out in the world. How many other Mooshies might he find? How many friends? And how empty would be this grove when he and Guenhwyvar had it to themselves?

Montolio accepted the silence, knowing the drow's confusion. "Promise me that when the time is upon you, you will at least consider what I have said."

Trusting in Drizzt, Montolio did not have to see his friend's affirming nod.

⚔ ⚔ ⚔ ⚔ ⚔

The first snow came early that year, just a light dusting from broken clouds that played hide-and-seek with a full moon. Drizzt, out with Guenhwyvar, reveled in the seasonal change, enjoyed the reaffirmation of the endless cycle. He was in high spirits when he bounded back to the grove, shaking the snow from the thick pine branches as he picked his way in.

The campfire burned low; Hooter sat still on a low branch and even the wind seemed not to make a sound. Drizzt looked to Guenhwyvar for some explanation, but the panther only sat by the fire, somber and still.

Dread is a strange emotion, a culmination of too-subtle clues that brings as much confusion as fear.

"Mooshie?" Drizzt called softly, approaching the old ranger's den. He pushed aside the blanket and used it to screen the light from the embers of the dying campfire, letting his eyes slip into the infrared spectrum.

He remained there for a very long time, watching the last wisps of heat depart from the ranger's body. But if Mooshie was cold, his contented smile emanated warmth.

Drizzt fought back many tears over the next few days, but whenever he remembered that last smile, the final peace that had come over the aged man, he reminded himself that the tears were for his own loss and not for Mooshie.

Drizzt buried the ranger in a cairn beside the grove, then spent the winter quietly, tending to his daily chores and wondering. Hooter came by less and less frequently, and on one occasion the departing look Hooter cast at Drizzt told the drow beyond doubt that the owl would never return to the grove.

In the spring, Drizzt came to understand Hooter's sentiments. For more than a decade, he had been searching for a home, and he had found one with Montolio. But with the ranger gone, the grove no longer seemed so hospitable. This was Mooshie's place, not Drizzt's.

"As I promised," Drizzt mumbled one morning. Montolio had asked him to consider his course carefully when the ranger was no more, and Drizzt now held to his word. He had become comfortable in the grove and was still accepted here, but the grove was no longer his home. His home was out there, he knew, out in that wide world that Montolio had assured him was "full of pain, but filled with joy as well."

Drizzt packed a few items—practical supplies and some of the ranger's more interesting books—belted on his scimitars, and slung the longbow over his shoulder. Then he took a final walk around the grove, viewing one last time the rope bridges, the armory, the brandy barrel and trough, the tree root where he had stopped the charging giant, the sheltered run where Mooshie had made his stand. He called Guenhwyvar, and the panther understood as soon as it arrived.

They never looked back as they moved down the mountain trail, toward the wide world of pains and joys.

# Part Five

## Sojourn

How different the trail seemed as I departed Mooshie's Grove from the road that had led me there. Again I was alone, except when Guenhwyvar came to my call. On this road, though, I was alone only in body. In my mind I carried a name, the embodiment of my valued principles. Mooshie had called Mielikki a goddess; to me she was a way of life.

She walked beside me always along the many surface roads I traversed. She led me out to safety and fought off my despair when I was chased away and hunted by the dwarves of Citadel Adbar, a fortress northeast of Mooshie's Grove. Mielikki, and my belief in my own value, gave me the courage to approach town after town throughout the northland. The receptions were always the same: shock and fear that quickly turned to anger. The more generous of those I encountered told me simply to go away; others chased me with weapons bared. On two occasions I was forced to fight, though I managed to escape without anyone being badly injured.

The minor nicks and scratches were a small price to pay. Mooshie had bidden me not to live as he had, and the old ranger's perceptions, as always, proved true. On my journeys throughout the northland I retained something—hope—that I never would have held if I had remained a hermit in the evergreen grove. As each new village showed on the horizon, a tingle of anticipation quickened my steps. One day, I was determined, I would find acceptance and find my home.

It would happen suddenly, I imagined. I would approach a gate, speak a formal greeting, then reveal myself as a dark elf. Even my fantasy was tempered by reality, for the gate would not swing wide at my approach. Rather, I would be allowed guarded entry, a trial period much like the one I endured in Blingdenstone, the svirfneblin city. Suspicions would linger about me for many months, but in the end, principles would be seen and accepted for what they were; the character of the person would outweigh the color of his skin and the reputation of his heritage.

I replayed that fantasy countless times over the years. Every word of every meeting in my imagined town became a litany against the continued rejections. It would not have been enough, but always there was Guenhwyvar, and now there was Mielikki.

—Drizzt Do'Urden

# 20
# Years and Miles

The Harvest Inn in Westbridge was a favorite gathering place for travelers along the Long Road that stretched between the two great northern cities of Waterdeep and Mirabar. Aside from comfortable bedding at reasonable rates, the Harvest offered Derry's Tavern and Eatery, a renowned story-swapping bar where on any night of any tenday a guest might find adventurers from regions as varied as Luskan and Sundabar. The hearth was bright and warm, the drinks were plentiful, and the yarns woven in Derry's were ones that would be told and retold all across the realms.

Roddy kept the cowl of his worn traveling cloak pulled low about him, hiding his scarred face, as he tore into his mutton and biscuits. The old yellow dog sat on the floor beside him, growling, and every now and Roddy absently dropped it a piece of meat.

The ravenous bounty hunter rarely lifted his head from the plate, but Roddy's bloodshot eyes peered suspiciously from the shadows of his cowl. He knew some of the ruffians gathered in Derry's this night, personally or by reputation, and he wouldn't trust them any more than they, if they were wise, would trust him.

One tall man recognized Roddy's dog as he passed the table and stopped, thinking to greet the bounty hunter. The tall man walked away silently, though, realizing that miserable McGristle wasn't really worth the effort. No one knew exactly what had happened those years before in the mountains near Maldobar, but Roddy had come out of that region deeply scarred, physically and emotionally. Always a surly one, McGristle now spent more time growling than talking.

Roddy gnawed a bit longer then dropped the thick bone down to his dog and wiped his greasy hands on his cloak, inadvertently brushing back the side of his cowl that hid his gruesome scars. Roddy quickly pulled the cowl back down, his gaze darting about for anyone who might have noticed. A single disgusted glance had cost several men their lives where Roddy's scars were concerned.

No one seemed to notice, though, not this time. Most of those who weren't busily eating were over at the bar, arguing loudly.

"Never was it!" one man growled.

"I told you what I saw!" another shot back. "And I told you right!"

"To yer eyes!" the first shouted back, and still another put in, "Ye'd not know one if ye seen one!" Several of the men closed in, bumping chest to chest.

"Stand quiet!" came a voice. A man pushed out of the throng and pointed straight at Roddy, who, not recognizing the man, instinctively dropped his hand to Bleeder, his well-worn axe.

"Ask McGristle!" the man cried. "Roddy McGristle. He knows about dark elves better than any."

A dozen conversations sprouted up at once as the whole group, looking like some amorphous rolling blob, slid over toward Roddy. Roddy's hand was off Bleeder again, crossing fingers with the other one on the table in front of him.

"Ye're McGristle, are ye?" the man asked Roddy, showing the bounty hunter a good measure of respect.

"Might that I am," Roddy replied calmly, enjoying the attention. He hadn't been surrounded by a group so interested in what he had to say since the Thistledown clan had been found murdered.

"Aw," a disgruntled voice piped in from somewhere in the back, "what's he know about dark elves."

Roddy's glare sent those in front back a step, and he noticed the movement. He liked the feeling, liked being important again, respected.

"Drow elf killed my dog," he said gruffly. He reached down and yanked up the old yellow hound's head, displaying the scar. "And dented this one's head. Damned dark elf—" he said deliberately, easing the cowl back from his face—"gave me this." Normally Roddy hid the hideous scars, but the crowd's gasps and mumbles sounded immensely satisfying to the wretched bounty hunter. He turned to the side, gave them a full view, and savored the reaction for as long as he could.

"Black-skinned and white-haired?" asked a short, fat-bellied man, the one who had begun the debate back at the bar with his own tale of a dark elf.

"Would have to be if he was a dark elf," Roddy huffed back. The man looked about triumphantly.

"That is what I tried to tell them," he said to Roddy. "They claim that I saw a dirty elf, or an orc maybe, but I knew it was a drow!"

"If ye see a drow," Roddy said grimly and deliberately, weighing every word with importance, "then ye know ye seen a drow. And ye'll not forget that ye seen a drow! And let any man that doubts yer words go and find a drow for himself. He'll come back to ye with a word of bein' sorry!"

"Well, I seen a dark elf," the man proclaimed. "I was camping in Lurkwood, north of Grunwald. Peaceful enough night, I thought, so I let the fire up a bit to beat the cold wind. Well, in walked this stranger without a warning, without a word!"

Every man in the group hung on the words now, hearing them in a different light now that the drow-scarred stranger had somewhat confirmed the tale.

"Without a word, or a bird call, or nothing!" the fat-bellied man went on. "He had his cloak pulled low, suspicious, so I said to him, 'What are you about?'"

"'Searching for a place that my companions and I may camp the night,' " he answered, calm as you may. Seemed reasonable enough to me, but I still did not like that low cowl."

"'Pull back your hood then,," I told him. 'I share nothing without seeing a man's face.' He considered my words a minute, then he moved his hands up, real slow,"—the man imitated the movement dramatically, glancing around to ensure that he had everyone's attention.

"I needed to see nothing more!" the man cried suddenly, and everyone, though they had heard the same tale told the same way only a moment before, jumped back in surprise. "His hands were as black as coal and as slender as an elf's. I knew then, but I know not how I knew so surely, that it was a drow before me. A drow, I say, and let any man who doubts my words go and find a dark elf for himself!"

Roddy nodded his approval as the fat-bellied man stared down his former doubters. "Seems I've heard too much about dark elves lately," the bounty hunter grumbled.

"I've heared of just the one," another man piped in. "Until we spoke to you, I mean, and heard of your battle. That makes two drow in six years."

"As I said," Roddy remarked grimly, "seems I've heard too much about dark—" Roddy never finished as the group exploded into exaggerated laughter around him. It seemed like the grand old times to the bounty hunter, the days when everyone about him hung tense on his every word.

The only man who wasn't laughing was the fat-bellied storyteller, too shook up from his own recounting of his meeting with the drow. "Still," he said above the commotion, "when I think of those purple eyes staring out at me from under that cowl!"

Roddy's smile disappeared in the blink of an eye. "Purple eyes?" he barely managed to gasp. Roddy had encountered many creatures that used infravision, the heat-sensing sight most common among denizens of the Underdark, and he knew that normally, such eyes showed as dots of red. Roddy still remembered vividly the purple eyes looking down at him when he was trapped under the maple tree. He knew then, and he knew now, that those strange-hued orbs were a rarity even among the dark elves.

Those in the group closest to Roddy stopped their laughing, thinking that Roddy's question shed doubt on the truth of the man's tale.

"They were purple," the fat-bellied man insisted, though there was little conviction in his shaky voice. The men around him waited for Roddy's agreement or rebuttal, not knowing whether or not to laugh at the storyteller.

"What weapons did the drow wield?" Roddy asked grimly, rising ominously to his feet.

The man thought for a moment. "Curved swords," he blurted.

"Scimitars?"

"Scimitars," the other agreed.

"Did the drow say his name?" Roddy asked, and when the man hesitated, Roddy grabbed him by the collar and pulled him over the table. "Did the drow say his name?" the bounty hunter said again, his breath hot on the fat-bellied man's face.

"No . . . er, uh, Driz . . ."

"Drizzit?"

The man shrugged helplessly, and Roddy threw him back to his feet. "Where?" the bounty hunter roared. "And when?"

"Lurkwood," the quivering, full-bellied man said again. "Three tendays ago. Drow's going to Mirabar with the Weeping Friars, I would guess." Most of the crowd groaned at the mention of the fanatic religious group. The Weeping Friars were a ragged band of begging sufferers who believed—or claimed to believe—that there was a finite amount of pain in the world. The more suffering they took on themselves, the friars said, the less remained for the rest of world to endure. Nearly everyone scorned the order. Some were sincere, but some begged for trinkets, promising to suffer horribly for the good of the giver.

"Those were the drow's companions," the fat-bellied man continued. "They always go to Mirabar, go to find the cold, as winter comes on."

"Long way," someone remarked.

"Longer," said another. "The Weeping Friars always take the tunnel route."

"Three hundred miles," the first man who had recognized Roddy put in, trying to calm the agitated bounty hunter. But Roddy never even heard him. His dog in tow, he spun away and stormed out of Derry's, slamming the door behind him and leaving the whole group mumbling to each other in absolute surprise.

"It was Drizzit that took Roddy's dog and ear," the man went on, now turning his attention to the group. He had no previous knowledge of the strange drow's name; he merely had made an assumption based on Roddy's reaction. Now the group flowed around him, holding their collective breath for him to tell them of the tale of Roddy McGristle and the purple-eyed drow. Like any proper patron of Derry's, the man didn't let lack of real knowledge deter him from telling the tale. He hooked his thumbs into his belt and began, filling in the considerable blanks with whatever sounded appropriate.

A hundred more gasps and claps of appreciation and startled delight echoed on the street outside of Derry's that night, but Roddy McGristle and his yellow dog, their wagon wheels already thick in the mud of the Long Road, heard none of them.

"Hey, what-are-you-doing?" came a weary complaint from a sack behind Roddy's bench. Tephanis crawled out. "Why-are-we-leaving?"

Roddy twisted about and took a swipe, but Tephanis, even sleepy-eyed, had no trouble darting out of harm's way.

"Ye lied to me, ye cousin to a kobold!" Roddy growled. "Ye telled me that the drow was dead. But he's not! He's on the road to Mirabar, and I mean to catch him!"

"Mirabar?" Tephanis cried. "Too-far, too-far!" The quickling and Roddy had passed through Mirabar the previous spring. Tephanis thought it a perfectly miserable place, full of grim-faced dwarves, sharp-eyed men, and a wind much too cold for his liking. "We-must-go-south-for-the-winter. South-where-it-is-warm!"

Roddy's ensuing glare silenced the sprite. "I'll forget what ye did to me," he snarled, then he added an ominous warning, "if we get the drow." He turned from Tephanis then, and the sprite crawled back into his sack, feeling miserable and wondering if Roddy McGristle was worth the trouble.

Roddy drove through the night, bending low to urge his horse onward and muttering "Six years!" over and over.

⚔ ⚔ ⚔ ⚔ ⚔

Drizzt huddled close to the fire that roared out of an old ore barrel the group had found. This would be the drow's seventh winter on the surface, but still he remained uncomfortable in the chill. He had spent decades, and his people had lived for many millennia, in the seasonless and warm Underdark. Though winter was still months away, its approach was evident in the chill winds blowing down from the Spine of the World Mountains. Drizzt wore only an old blanket, thin and torn, over his clothes, chain mail, and weapon belt.

The drow smiled when he noticed his companions fidgeting and huffing over who got the next draw on a bottle of wine they had begged and how much the last drinker had taken. Drizzt was alone at the barrel now; the Weeping Friars, while not actually shunning the drow, didn't often go near him. Drizzt accepted this and knew that the fanatics appreciated his companionship for practical, if not aesthetic, reasons. Some of the band actually enjoyed attacks by the various monsters of the land viewing them as opportunities for some true suffering, but the more pragmatic of the group appreciated having the armed and skilled drow around for protection.

The relationship was acceptable to Drizzt, if not fulfilling. He had left Mooshie's Grove years ago filled with hope, but hope tempered by the realities of his existence. Time after time, Drizzt had approached a village only to be put out behind a wall of harsh words, curses, and drawn weapons. Every time, Drizzt shrugged away the snubbing. True to his ranger spirit—for Drizzt was indeed a ranger now, in training as well as in heart—he accepted his lot stoically.

The last rejection had shown Drizzt that his resolve was wearing thin, though. He had been turned away from Luskan, on the Sword Coast, but not by any guards, for he had never even approached the place. Drizzt's own fears had kept him away, and that fact had frightened him more than any swords he had ever faced. On the road outside the city, Drizzt had met up with this handful of Weeping Friars, and the outcasts had tentatively accepted him, as much because they had no means to keep him out as because they were too full of their own wretchedness to care about any racial differences. Two of the group had even thrown themselves at Drizzt's feet, begging him to unleash his "dark elf terrors" and make them suffer.

Through the spring and summer, the relationship had evolved with Drizzt serving as silent guardian while the friars went about their begging and suffering ways. All in all, it was quite distasteful, even sometimes deceitful, to the principled drow, but Drizzt had found no other options.

Drizzt stared into the leaping flames and considered his fate. He still had Guenhwyvar at his call and had put his scimitars and bow to gainful use many times. Every day he told himself that beside the somewhat helpless fanatics, he was serving Mielikki, and his own heart, well. Still, he did not hold the friars in high regard and did not call them friends. Watching the five men now, drunk and slobbering all over each other, Drizzt suspected that he never would.

"Beat me! Slash me!" one of the friars cried suddenly, and he ran over toward the barrel, stumbling into Drizzt. Drizzt caught him and steadied him, but only for a moment.

"Loosh your dwow whickedniss on me head!" the dirty, unshaven friar sputtered, and his lanky frame tumbled down in an angular heap.

Drizzt turned away, shook his head, and unconsciously dropped a hand into his pouch to feel the onyx figurine, needing the touch to remind him that he was not truly alone. He was surviving, fighting an endless and lonely battle, but was far from contented. He had found a place, perhaps, but not a home.

"Like the grove without Montolio," the drow mused. "Never a home."

"Did you say something?" asked a portly friar, Brother Mateus, coming over to collect his drunken companion. "Please excuse Brother Jankin, friend. He has imbibed too much, I fear."

Drizzt's helpless smile told that he had taken no offense, but his next words caught Brother Mateus, the leader and most rational member—if not the most honest—of the group, off guard.

"I will complete the trip to Mirabar with you," Drizzt explained, "then I will leave."

"Leave?" asked Mateus, concerned.

"This is not my place," Drizzt explained.

"Ten-Towns ish the place!" Jankin blurted.

"If anyone has offended you . . ." Mateus said to Drizzt, taking no heed of the drunken man.

"No one," Drizzt said and smiled again. "There is more for me in this life, Brother Mateus. Do not be angry, I beg, but I am leaving. It was not a decision I came to lightly."

Mateus took a moment to consider the words. "As you choose," he said, "but might you at least escort us through the tunnel into Mirabar?"

"Ten-Towns!" Jankin insisted. "Thast the place fer sufferin'! You'd like it, too, drow. Land o' rogues, where a rogue might find hish place!"

"Often there are rakes in the shadows who would prey on unarmed friars," Mateus interrupted, giving Jankin a rough shake.

Drizzt paused a moment, transfixed on Jankin's words. Jankin had collapsed, though, and the drow looked up to Mateus. "Is that not why you take the tunnel route into the city?" Drizzt asked the portly friar. The tunnel was normally reserved for mine carts, rolling down from the Spine of the World, but the friars always went through it, even in situations such as this, when they had to make a complete circuit of the city just to get to the long route's entrance. "To fall victim and suffer?" Drizzt continued. "Surely the road is clear and more convenient with winter still months away." Drizzt did not like the tunnel to Mirabar. Any wanderers they met on that road would be too close for the drow to hide his identity. Drizzt had been accosted there on both his previous trips through.

"The others insist that we go through the tunnel, though it is many miles out of our way," replied Mateus, a sharp edge to his tone. "But I prefer more personal forms of suffering and would appreciate your company through to Mirabar."

Drizzt wanted to scream at the phony friar. Mateus considered missing a single meal a harsh suffering and only used his facade because many gullible people handed coins to the cloaked fanatics, more often than not just to be rid of the smelly men.

Drizzt nodded and watched as Mateus hauled Jankin away. "Then I leave," he whispered under his breath. He could tell himself over and over that he was serving his goddess and his heart by protecting the seemingly helpless band but their behavior often flew in the face of those words.

"Dwow! Dwow!" Brother Jankin slobbered as Mateus dragged him back to the others.

# 21 Hephaestus

Tephanis watched the party of six—the five friars and Drizzt—make their slow way toward the tunnel on the western approach to Mirabar. Roddy had sent the quickling ahead to scout out the region, telling Tephanis to turn the drow, if he found the drow, back toward Roddy. "Bleeder'll be taking care of that one," Roddy had snarled, slapping his formidable axe across his palm.

Tephanis wasn't so sure. The sprite had watched Ulgulu, a master arguably more powerful than Roddy McGristle, dispatched by the drow, and another mighty master, Caroak, had been torn apart by the drow's black panther. If Roddy got his wish and met the drow in battle, Tephanis might soon be searching for yet another master.

"Not-this-time, drow," the sprite whispered suddenly, an idea coming to mind. "This-time-I-get-you!" Tephanis knew the tunnel to Mirabar—he and Roddy had used it the winter before last, when snow had buried the western road—and had learned many of its secrets, including one that the sprite now planned to use to his advantage.

He made a wide circuit around the group, not wanting to alert the sharp-eared drow, and still made the tunnel entrance long before the others. A few minutes later, the sprite was more than a mile in, picking at an intricate lock, one that seemed clumsy to the skilled quickling, on a portcullis crank.

⚔ ⚔ ⚔ ⚔ ⚔

Brother Mateus led the way into the tunnel, with another friar at his side and the remaining three completing a shielding circle around Drizzt. Drizzt had requested this so that he could remain inconspicuous if anyone happened by. He kept his cloak pulled up tightly and his shoulders hunched. He stayed low in the middle of the group.

They met no other travelers and moved along the torch-lit passage at a steady pace. They came to an intersection and Mateus stopped abruptly, seeing the raised portcullis to a passage on the right side. A dozen steps in, an iron door swung wide, and the passage beyond that was pitch black, not torch-lit like the main tunnel.

"How curious," Mateus remarked.

"Careless," another corrected. "Let us pray that no other travelers, who might not know the way as well as we, happen by here and take the wrong path!"

"Perhaps we should close the door," still another offered.

"No," Mateus quickly interjected. "There may be some down there, merchants perhaps, who would not be so pleased if we followed that plan."

"No!" Brother Jankin cried suddenly and ran to the front of the group. "It is a sign! A sign from God! We are beckoned, my brethren, to Phaestus, the ultimate suffering!"

Jankin turned to charge down the tunnel, but Mateus and one other, hardly surprised by Jankin's customarily wild outburst, immediately sprang upon him and bore him to the ground.

"Phaestus!" Jankin cried wildly, his long and shaggy black hair flying all about his face. "I am coming!"

"What is it?" Drizzt had to ask, having no idea of what the friars were talking about, though he thought he recognized the reference. "Who, or what, is Phaestus?"

"Hephaestus," Brother Mateus corrected.

Drizzt did know the name. One of the books he had taken from Mooshie's Grove was of dragon lore, and Hephaestus, a venerable red dragon living in the mountains northwest of Mirabar, had an entry.

"That is not the dragon's real name, of course," Mateus went on between grunts as he struggled with Jankin. "I do not know that, nor does anyone else anymore." Jankin twisted suddenly, throwing the other monk aside, and promptly stomped down on Mateus's sandal.

"Hephaestus is an old red dragon who has lived in the caves west of Mirabar for as long as anyone, even the dwarves, can remember," explained another friar, Brother Herschel, one less engaged than Mateus. "The city tolerates him because he is a lazy one and a stupid one, though I would not tell him so. Most cities, I presume, would choose to tolerate a red if it meant not fighting the thing! But Hephaestus is not much for pillaging—none can recall the last time he even came out of his hole—and he even does some ore-melting for hire, though the fee is steep."

"Some pay it, though," added Mateus, having Jankin back under control, "especially late in the season, looking to make the last caravan south. Nothing can separate metal like a red dragon's breath!" His laughter disappeared quickly as Jankin slugged him, dropping him to the ground.

Jankin bolted free, for just a moment. Quicker than anyone could react, Drizzt threw off his cloak and rushed after the fleeing monk, catching him just inside the heavy iron door. A single step and twisting maneuver put Jankin down hard on his back and took the wild-eyed friar's breath away.

"Let us get by this region at once," the drow offered, staring down at the stunned friar. "I grow tired of Jankin's antics—I might just allow him to run down to the dragon!"

Two of the others came over and gathered Jankin up, then the whole troupe turned to depart.

"Help!" came a cry from farther down the dark tunnel.

Drizzt's scimitars came out in his hands. The friars all gathered around him, peering down into the gloom.

"Do you see anything?" Mateus asked the drow, knowing that Drizzt's night vision was much keener than his own.

"No, but the tunnel turns a short way from here," Drizzt replied.

"Help!" came the cry again. Behind the group, around the corner in the main tunnel, Tephanis had to suppress his laughter. Quicklings were adept ventriloquists, and the biggest problem Tephanis had in deceiving the group was keeping his cries slow enough to be understood.

Drizzt took a cautious step in, and the friars, even Jankin, sobered by the distress call, followed right behind. Drizzt motioned for them to go back, even as he suddenly realized the potential for a trap.

But Tephanis was too quick. The door slammed with a resounding thud and before the drow, two steps away, could push through the startled friars, the sprite already had the door locked. A moment later, Drizzt and the friars heard a second crash as the portcullis came down.

Tephanis was back out in the daylight a few minutes later, thinking himself quite clever and reminding himself to keep a puzzled expression when he explained to Roddy that the drow's party was nowhere to be found.

⚔ ⚔ ⚔ ⚔ ⚔

The friars grew tired of yelling as soon as Drizzt reminded them that their screams might arouse the occupant at the other end of the tunnel. "Even if someone happens by the portcullis, he will not hear you through this door," the drow said, inspecting the heavy portal with the single candle Mateus had lit. A combination of iron, stone, and leather, and perfectly fitted, the door had been crafted by dwarves. Drizzt tried pounding on it with the pommel of a scimitar, but that produced only a dull thud that went no farther than the screams.

"We are lost," groaned Mateus. "We have no way out, and our stores are not too plentiful."

"Another sign!" Jankin blurted suddenly, but two of the friars knocked him down and sat on him before he could run off toward the dragon's den.

"Perhaps there is something to Brother Jankin's thinking," Drizzt said after a long pause.

Mateus looked at him suspiciously. "Are you thinking that our stores would last longer if Brother Jankin went to meet Hephaestus?" he asked.

Drizzt could not hold his laughter. "I have no intention of sacrificing anyone," he said and looked at Jankin struggling under the friars. "No matter how willing! But we have only one way out, it would seem."

Mateus followed Drizzt's gaze down the dark tunnel. "If you plan no sacrifices, then you are looking the wrong way," the portly friar huffed. "Surely you are not thinking to get past the dragon!"

"We shall see," was all that the drow answered. He lit another candle from the first one and moved a short distance down the tunnel. Drizzt's good sense argued against the undeniable excitement he felt at the prospect of facing Hephaestus, but it was an argument that he expected simple necessity to overrule. Montolio had fought a dragon, Drizzt remembered, had lost his eyes to a red. The ranger's memories of the battle, aside from his wounds, were not so terrible. Drizzt was beginning to understand what the blind ranger had told him about the differences between survival and fulfillment. How valuable would be the five hundred years Drizzt might have left to live?

For the friar's sake, Drizzt did hope that someone would come along and open the portcullis and door. The drow's fingers tingled with promised thrills, though, when he reached into his sack and pulled out a book on dragon lore he had taken from the grove.

The drow's sensitive eyes needed little light, and he could make out the script with only minor difficulty. As he suspected, there was an entry for the venerable red who lived west of Mirabar. The book confirmed that Hephaestus was not the dragon's real name, rather the name given to it in reference to some obscure god of blacksmiths.

The entry was not extensive, mostly tales from the merchants who went in to hire the dragon for its breath, and other tales of merchants who apparently said the wrong thing or haggled too much about the cost—or perhaps the dragon was merely hungry or in a foul mood—for they never came back out. Most importantly to Drizzt, the entry confirmed the friar's description of the beast as lazy and somewhat stupid. According to the notes, Hephaestus was overly proud, as dragons usually were, and able to speak the common tongue, but "lacking in the area of suspicious insight normally associated with the breed, particularly with venerable reds."

"Brother Herschel is attempting to pick the lock," Mateus said, coming over to Drizzt. "Your fingers are nimble. Would you give it a try?"

"Neither Herschel nor I could get through that lock," Drizzt said absently, not looking up from the book.

"At least Herschel is trying," Mateus growled, "and not huddled off by himself wasting candles and reading some worthless tome!"

"Not so worthless to any of us who mean to get out of here alive," Drizzt said, still not looking up. He had the portly friar's attention.

"What is it?" Mateus asked, leaning closely over Drizzt's shoulder, even though he could not read.

"It tells of vanity," Drizzt replied.

"Vanity? What does vanity have to do . . ."

"Dragon vanity," Drizzt explained. "A very important point, perhaps. All dragons possess it in excess, evil ones more than good ones."

"Wielding claws as long as swords and breath that can melt a stone, well they should," grumbled Mateus.

"Perhaps," Drizzt conceded, "but vanity is a weakness—do not doubt—even to a dragon. Several heroes have exploited this trait to a dragon's demise."

"Now you're thinking of killing the thing," Mateus gawked.

"If I must," Drizzt said, again absently. Mateus threw up his hands and walked away, shaking his head to answer the questioning stares of the others.

Drizzt smiled privately and returned to his reading. His plans were taking definite form now. He read the entire entry several times, committing every word of it to memory.

Three candles later, Drizzt was still reading and the friars were growing impatient and hungry. They prodded Mateus, who stood, hiked his belt up over his belly, and strode toward Drizzt.

"More vanity?" he asked sarcastically.

"Done with that part," Drizzt answered. He held up the book, showing Mateus a sketch of a huge black dragon curled up around several fallen trees in a thick swamp. "I am learning now of the dragon that may aid our cause."

"Hephaestus is a red," Mateus remarked scornfully, "not a black."

"This is a different dragon," Drizzt explained. "Mergandevinasander of Chult, possibly a visitor to converse with Hephaestus."

Brother Mateus was at a complete loss. "Reds and blacks do not get on well," he snipped, his skepticism obvious. "Every fool knows that."

"Rarely do I listen to fools," Drizzt replied, and again the friar turned and walked away, shaking his head.

"There is something more that you do not know, but Hephaestus most probably will," Drizzt said quietly, too low for anyone to hear. "Mergandevinasander has purple eyes!" Drizzt closed the book, confident that it had given him enough understanding to make his attempt. If he had ever witnessed the terrible splendor of a venerable red before, he would not have been smiling at that moment. But both ignorance and memories of Montolio bred courage in the young drow warrior who had so little to lose, and Drizzt had no intention of giving in to starvation for fear of some unknown danger. He wouldn't go forward either, not yet.

Not until he had time to practice his best dragon voice.

⚔ ⚔ ⚔ ⚔ ⚔

Of all the splendors Drizzt had seen in his adventurous life, none—not the great houses of Menzoberranzan, the cavern of the illithids, even the lake of acid—began to approach the awe-inspiring spectacle of the dragon's lair. Mounds of gold and gems filled the huge chamber in rolling waves, like the wake of some giant ship on the sea. Weapons and armor, gleaming magnificently, were piled all about, and the abundance of crafted items—chalices, goblets and the like—could have fully stocked the treasure rooms of a hundred rich kings.

Drizzt had to remind himself to breathe when he looked upon the splendor. It wasn't the riches that held him so—he cared little for material things—but the adventures that such wondrous items and wealth hinted at tugged Drizzt in a hundred different directions. Looking at the dragon's lair belittled his simple survival on the road with the Weeping Friars and his simple desire to find a peaceful and quiet place to call his home. He thought again of Montolio's dragon tale, and of all the other adventurous tales the blind ranger had told him. Suddenly he needed those adventures for himself.

Drizzt wanted a home, and he wanted to find acceptance, but he realized then, looking at the spoils, that he also desired a place in the books of the bards. He hoped to travel roads dangerous and exciting and even write his own tales.

The chamber itself was immense and uneven, rolling back around blind corners. The whole of it was dimly lit in a smoky, reddish golden glow. It was warm, uncomfortably so when Drizzt and the others took the time to consider the source of that heat.

Drizzt turned back to the waiting friars and winked, then pointed down to his left, to the single exit. "You know the signal," he mouthed silently.

Mateus nodded tentatively, still wondering if it had been wise to trust the drow. Drizzt had been a valuable ally to the pragmatic friar on the road these last few months, but a dragon was a dragon.

Drizzt surveyed the room again, this time looking past the treasures. Between two piles of gold he spotted his target, and that was no less splendid than the jewels and gems. Lying in the valley of those mounds was a huge, scaled tail, red-gold like the hue of the light, swishing slightly and rhythmically back and forth, each swipe piling the gold deeper around it.

Drizzt had seen pictures of dragons before; one of the wizard masters in the Academy had even created illusions of the various dragon types for the students to inspect. Nothing, though, could have prepared the drow for this moment, his first view of a living dragon. In all the known realms there was nothing more impressive, and of all the dragon types, huge reds were perhaps the most imposing.

When Drizzt finally managed to tear his gaze from the tail, he sorted out his path into the chamber. The tunnel exited high on the side of a wall, but a clear trail led down to the floor. Drizzt studied this for a long moment, memorizing every step. Then he scooped two handfuls of dirt into his pockets, removed an arrow from his quiver, and placed a darkness spell over it. Carefully and quietly, Drizzt picked his blind steps down the trail, guided by the continuing swish of the scaly tail. He nearly stumbled when he reached the first pile of gems and heard the tail come to an abrupt stop.

"Adventure," Drizzt reminded himself quietly, and he went on, concentrating on his mental image of his surroundings. He imagined the dragon rearing up before him, seeing through his darkness-globe disguise. He winced instinctively, expecting a burst of flame to engulf him and shrivel him where he stood. But he pressed on, and when he at last came over the gold pile, he was glad to hear the easy, thunderlike, breathing of the slumbering dragon.

Drizzt started up the second mound slowly, letting a spell of levitation form in his thoughts. He didn't really expect the spell to work very well—it had been failing more completely each time he attempted it. Any help he could get would add to the effect of his deception. Halfway up the mound, Drizzt broke into a run, spraying coins and gems with every step. He heard the dragon rouse, but didn't slow, drawing his bow as he went.

When he reached the ridge, he leaped out and enacted the levitation, hanging motionless in the air for a split second before the spell failed. Then Drizzt dropped, firing the bow and sending the darkness globe soaring across the chamber.

He never would have believed that a monster of such size could be so nimble, but when he crashed heavily onto a pile of goblets and jeweled trinkets, he found himself staring into the face of a very angry beast.

Those eyes! Like twin beams of damnation, their gaze latched onto Drizzt, bored right through him, impelled him to fall on his belly and grovel for mercy, and to reveal every deception, to confess every sin to Hephaestus, this god-thing. The dragon's great, serpentine neck angled slightly to the side, but the gaze never let go of the drow, holding him as firmly as one of Bluster the bear's hugs.

A voice sounded faintly but firmly in Drizzt's thoughts, the voice of a blind ranger spinning tales of battle and heroism. At first, Drizzt hardly heard it, but it was an insistent voice, reminding Drizzt in its own special way that five other men depended on him now. If he failed, the friars would die.

This part of the plan was not too difficult for Drizzt, for he truly believed in his words. "Hephaestus!" he cried in the common tongue. "Can it be, at long last? Oh, most magnificent! More magnificent than the tales, by far."

The dragon's head rolled back a dozen feet from Drizzt, and a confused expression came into those all-knowing eyes, revealing the facade. "You know of me?" Hephaestus boomed, the dragon's hot breath blowing Drizzt's white mane behind him.

"All know of you, mighty Hephaestus!" Drizzt cried, scrambling to his knees but not daring to stand. "It was you whom I sought, and now I have found you and am not disappointed!"

The dragon's terrible eyes narrowed suspiciously. "Why would a dark elf seek Hephaestus, Destroyer of Cockleby, Devourer of Ten Thousand Cattle, He Who Crushed Angalander the Stupid Silver, He Who . . ." It went on for many minutes, with Drizzt bearing the foul breath stoically, all the while feigning enchantment with the dragon's listing of his many wicked accomplishments. When Hephaestus was done, Drizzt had to pause a moment to remember the initial question.

His real confusion only added to the deception at the time. "Dark elf?" he asked as if he didn't understand. He looked up at the dragon and repeated the words, even more confused. "Dark elf?"

The dragon looked all around, his gaze falling like twin beacons across the treasure mounds, then lingering for some time on Drizzt's blackness globe, halfway across the room. "I mean you!" Hephaestus roared suddenly, and the force of the yell knocked Drizzt over backward. "Dark elf!"

"Drow?" Drizzt said, recovering quickly and daring now to stand. "No, not I." He surveyed himself and nodded in sudden recognition. "Yes, of course," he said. "So often do I forget this mantle I wear!"

Hephaestus issued a long, low, increasingly impatient growl and Drizzt knew he had better move quickly.

"Not a drow," he said. "Though soon I might be if Hephaestus cannot help me!" Drizzt could only hope that he had piqued the dragon's curiosity. "You have heard of me, I am sure, mighty Hephaestus. I am, or was and hope to be again, Mergandevinasander of Chult, an old black of no small fame."

"Mergandevin . . . ?" Hephaestus began, but the dragon let the word trail away. Hephaestus had heard of the black, of course; dragons knew the names of most of the other dragons in all the world. Hephaestus knew, too, as Drizzt had hoped he would, that Mergandevinasander had purple eyes.

To aid him through the explanation, Drizzt recalled his experiences with Clacker, the unfortunate pech who had been transformed by a wizard into the form of a hook horror. "A wizard defeated me," he began somberly. "A party of adventurers entered my lair. Thieves! I got one of them, though, a paladin!"

Hephaestus seemed to like this little detail, and Drizzt, who had just thought of it, congratulated himself silently.

"How his silvery armor sizzled under the acid of my breath!"

"Pity to so waste him," Hephaestus interjected. "Paladins do make such fine meals!"

Drizzt smiled to hide his uneasiness at the thought. How would a dark elf taste? he could not help but wonder with the dragon's mouth so very near. "I would have killed them all—and a fine treasure take it would have been—but for that wretched wizard! It was he that did this terrible thing to me!" Drizzt looked at his drow form reprovingly.

"Polymorph?" Hephaestus asked, and Drizzt noted a bit of sympathy—he prayed—in the voice.

Drizzt nodded solemnly. "An evil spell. Took my form, my wings, and my breath. Yet I remained Mergandevinasander in thought, though . . ." Hephaestus widened his eyes at the pause, and the pitiful, confused look that Drizzt gave actually backed the dragon up.

"I have found this sudden affinity to spiders," Drizzt muttered. "To pet them and kiss them . . ." So that is what a disgusted red dragon looks like, Drizzt thought when he glanced back up at the beast. Coins and trinkets tinkled all throughout the room as an involuntary shudder coursed through the dragon's spine.

⚔ ⚔ ⚔ ⚔ ⚔

The friars in the low tunnel couldn't see the exchange, but they could make out the conversation well enough and understood what the drow had in mind. For the first time that any of them could recall, Brother Jankin was stricken speechless, but Mateus managed to whisper a few words, echoing their shared sentiments.

"He has got a measure of fortitude, that one!" The portly friar chuckled, and he slapped a hand across his own mouth, fearing that he had spoken too loudly.

⚔ ⚔ ⚔ ⚔ ⚔

"Why have you come to me?" Hephaestus roared angrily. Drizzt skidded backward under the force but managed to hold his balance this time.

"I beg, mighty Hephaestus!" Drizzt pleaded. "I have no choice. I traveled to Menzoberranzan, the city of drow, but this wizard's spell was powerful, they told me, and they could do nothing to dispel it. So I come to you, great and powerful Hephaestus, renowned for your abilities with spells of transmutation. Perhaps one of my own kind . . ."

"A black?" came the thunderous roar, and this time, Drizzt did fall. "Your own kind?"

"No, no, a dragon," Drizzt said quickly, retracting the apparent insult and hopping back to his feet—thinking that he might be running soon. Hephaestus's continuing growl told Drizzt that he needed a diversion, and he found it behind the dragon, in the deep scorch marks along the walls and back of a rectangular alcove. Drizzt figured this was where Hephaestus earned his considerable pay melting ores. The drow couldn't help but shudder as he wondered how many unfortunate merchants or adventurers might have found their end between those blasted walls.

"What caused such a cataclysm?" Drizzt cried in awe. Hephaestus dared not turn away, suspecting treachery. A moment later, though, the dragon realized what the dark elf had noticed and the growl disappeared.

"What god has come down to you, mighty Hephaestus, and blessed you with such a spectacle of power? Nowhere in all the realms is there stone so torn! Not since the fires that formed the world . . ."

"Enough!" Hephaestus boomed. "You who are so learned does not know the breath of a red?"

"Surely fire is the means of a red," Drizzt replied, never taking his gaze from the alcove, "but how intense might the flames be? Surely not so as to wreak such devastation!"

"Would you like to see?" came the dragon's answer in a sinister, smoking hiss.

"Yes!" Drizzt cried, then, "No!" he said, dropping into a fetal curl. He knew he was walking a tentative line here, but he knew it was a necessary gamble. "Truly I would desire to witness such a blast, but truly I fear to feel its heat."

"Then watch, Mergandevinasander of Chult!" Hephaestus roared. "See your better!" The sharp intake of the dragon's breath pulled Drizzt two steps forward, brought his white hair stinging around into his eyes, and nearly tore the blanket-cloak from his back. On the mound behind him, coins toppled forward in a noisy rush.

Then the dragon's serpentine neck swung about in a long and wide arc, putting the great red's head in line with the alcove.

The ensuing blast stole the air from the chamber; Drizzt's lungs burned and his eyes stung, both from the heat and the brightness. He continued to watch, though, as the dragon fire consumed the alcove in a roaring, thunderous blaze. Drizzt noted, too, that Hephaestus closed his eyes tightly when he breathed his fire.

When the conflagration was finished, Hephaestus swung back triumphantly. Drizzt, still looking at the alcove, at the molten rock running down the walls and dripping from the ceiling, did not have to feign his awe.

"By the gods!" he whispered harshly. He managed to look back at the dragon's smug expression. "By the gods," he said again. "Mergandevinasander of Chult, who thought himself supreme, is humbled."

"And well he should be!" Hephaestus boomed. "No black is the equal of a red! Know that now, Mergandevinasander. It is a fact that could save your life if ever a red comes to your door!"

"Indeed," Drizzt promptly agreed. "But I fear that I shall have no door." Again he looked down at his form and scowled with disdain. "No door beyond one in the city of dark elves!"

"That is your fate, not mine," Hephaestus said. "But I shall take pity on you. I shall let you depart alive, though that is more than you deserve for disturbing my slumber!"

This was the critical moment, Drizzt knew. He could have taken

Hephaestus up on the offer; at that moment, he wanted nothing more than to be out of there. But his principles and Mooshie's memory wouldn't let him go. What of his companions in the tunnel? he reminded himself. And what of the adventures for the bards' books?

"Devour me then," he said to the dragon, though he could hardly believe the words as he spoke them. "I who have known the glory of dragonkind cannot be content with life as a dark elf."

Hephaestus's huge maw inched forward.

"Alas for all the dragonkind!" Drizzt wailed. "Our numbers ever decreasing, while the humans multiply like vermin. Alas for the treasures of dragons, to be stolen by wizards and paladins!" The way he spat that last word gave Hephaestus pause.

"And alas for Mergandevinasander," Drizzt continued dramatically, "to be struck down thus by a human wizard whose power outshines even that of Hephaestus, mightiest of dragonkind!"

"Outshines!" Hephaestus cried, and the whole chamber trembled under the power of that roar.

"What am I to believe?" Drizzt yelled back, somewhat pitifully compared to the dragon's volume. "Would Hephaestus not aid one of his own diminishing kind? Nay, that I cannot believe, that the world shall not believe!" Drizzt aimed a pointed finger at the ceiling above him, preaching for all he was worth. He did not have to be reminded of the price of failure. "They will say, one and all from all the wide realms, that Hephaestus dared not try to dispel the wizard's magic, that the great red dared not reveal his weakness against so powerful a spell for fear that his weakness would invite that same wizard-led party to come north for another haul of dragon plunder!

"Ah!" Drizzt shouted, wide-eyed. "But will not Hephaestus's perceived surrender also give the wizard and his nasty thieving friends hope of such plunder? And what dragon possesses more to steal than Hephaestus, the red of rich Mirabar?"

The dragon was at a loss. Hephaestus liked his way of life, sleeping on treasures ever-growing from high-paying merchants. He didn't need the likes of heroic adventurers poking around in his lair! Those were the exact sentiments Drizzt had been counting on.

"Tomorrow!" the dragon roared. "This day I contemplate the spell and tomorrow Mergandevinasander shall be a black once more! Then he shall depart, his tail aflame, if he dares utter one more blasphemous word! Now I must take my rest to recall the spell. You shall not move, dragon in drow form. I smell you where you are and hear as well as anything in all the world. I am not as sound a sleeper as many thieves have wished!"

Drizzt did not doubt a word of it, of course, so while things had gone as well as he had hoped, he found himself in a bit of a mess. He couldn't wait a day to resume his conversation with the red, nor could his friends. How would proud Hephaestus react, Drizzt wondered, when the dragon tried to counter a spell that didn't even exist? And what, Drizzt told himself as he neared panic, would he do if Hephaestus actually did change him into a black dragon?

"Of course, the breath of a black has advantages over a red's," Drizzt blurted as Hephaestus swung away.

The red came back at him in a frightening flash and with frightening fury.

"Would you like to feel my breath?" Hephaestus snarled. "How great would come your boasts then, I must wonder?"

"No, not that," Drizzt replied. "Take no insult, mighty Hephaestus. Truly the spectacle of your fires stole my pride! But the breath of a black cannot be underestimated. It has qualities beyond even the power of a red's fire!"

"How say you?"

"Acid, O Hephaestus the Incredible, Devourer of Ten Thousand Cattle," Drizzt replied. "Acid clings to a knight's armor, digs through in lasting torment."

"As dripping metal might?" Hephaestus asked sarcastically. "Metal melted by a red's fire?"

"Longer, I fear," Drizzt admitted, dropping his gaze. "A red's breath comes in a burst of destruction, but a black's lingers, to the enemy's dismay."

"A burst?" Hephaestus growled. "How long can your breath last, pitiful black? Longer can I breathe, I know!"

"But . . ." Drizzt began, indicating the alcove. This time, the dragon's sudden intake pulled Drizzt several steps forward and nearly whipped him from his feet. The drow kept his wits enough to cry out the appointed signal, "Fires of the Nine Hells!" as Hephaestus swung his head back in line with the alcove.

⚔ ⚔ ⚔ ⚔ ⚔

"The signal!" Mateus said above the tumult. "Run for your lives! Run!"

"Never!" cried the terrified Brother Herschel, and the others, except for Jankin, didn't disagree.

"Oh, to suffer so!" the shaggy-haired fanatic wailed, stepping from the tunnel.

"We have to! On our lives!" Mateus reminded them, catching Jankin by the hair to keep him from going the wrong way.

They struggled at the tunnel exit for several seconds and the other friars, realizing that perhaps their only hope soon would pass them by, burst out of the tunnel and the whole group tumbled out and down the sloping path from the wall. When they recovered, they were surely in a fix, and they danced about aimlessly, not sure of whether to climb back up to the tunnel or light out for the exit. Their desperate scrambling hardly made any headway up the slope, especially with Mateus still trying to rein in Jankin, so the exit was the only way. Tripping all over themselves, the friars fled across the room.

Even their terror did not prevent each of them, even Jankin, from scooping up a pocketful of baubles as he passed.

⚔ ⚔ ⚔ ⚔ ⚔

Never had there been such a blast of dragon fire! Hephaestus, eyes closed, roared on and on, disintegrating the stone in the alcove. Great gouts of flame burst out into the room—Drizzt was nearly overcome by the heat—but the angry dragon did not relent, determined to humble the annoying visitor once and for all.

The dragon peeked once, to witness the effects of his display. Dragons knew their treasure rooms better than anything in the world, and Hephaestus did not miss the image of five fleeting figures darting across the main chamber toward the exit.

The breath stopped abruptly and the dragon swung about. "Thieves!" he roared, splitting stone with his thunderous voice.

Drizzt knew that the game was up.

The great, spear-filled maw snapped at the drow. Drizzt stepped to the side and leaped, having nowhere else to go. He caught one of the dragon's horns and rode up with the beast's head. Drizzt managed to scramble on top of it and held on for all his life as the outraged dragon tried to shake him free. Drizzt reached for a scimitar but found a pocket instead, and he pulled out a handful of dirt. Without the slightest hesitation, the drow flung the dirt down into the dragon's evil eye.

Hephaestus went berserk, snapping his head violently, up and down and all about. Drizzt held on stubbornly, and the devious dragon discerned a better method.

Drizzt understood Hephaestus's intent as the head shot up into the air at full speed. The ceiling was not so high—not compared with Hephaestus's serpentine neck. It was a long fall, but a preferable fate by far, and Drizzt dropped off just before the dragon's head slammed into the rock.

Drizzt dizzily regained his feet as Hephaestus, hardly slowed by the crushing impact, sucked in his breath. Luck saved the drow, and not for the first or the last time, as a considerable chunk of stone fell from the battered ceiling and crashed into the dragon's head. Hephaestus's breath blurted out in a harmless puff and Drizzt darted with all speed over the treasure mound, diving down behind.

Hephaestus roared in rage and loosed the rest of his breath, without thinking, straight for the mound. Gold coins melted together; enormous gemstones cracked under the pressure. The mound was fully twenty feet thick and tightly packed, but Drizzt, against the opposite side, felt his back aflame. He jumped out from the pile, leaving his cloak smoking and meshed with molten gold.

Out came Drizzt, scimitars drawn, as the dragon reared. The drow rushed straight in bravely, stupidly, whacking away with all his strength. He stopped, stunned, after only two blows, both scimitars ringing painfully in his hands; he might as well have banged them against a stone wall!

Hephaestus, head high, had paid the attack no heed. "My gold!" the dragon wailed. Then the beast looked down, his lamplight gaze boring through the drow once more. "My gold!" Hephaestus said again, wickedly.

Drizzt shrugged sheepishly, then he ran.

Hephaestus snapped his tail about, slamming it into yet another mound of treasure and showering the room in flying gold and silver coins and gemstones. "My gold!" the dragon roared over and over as he slammed his way through the tight piles.

Drizzt fell behind another mound. "Help me, Guenhwyvar," he begged, dropping the figurine.

"I smell you, thief!" The dragon purred—as if a thunder storm could purr—not far from Drizzt's mound.

In response, the panther came to the top of the mound, roared in defiance, then sprang away. Drizzt, down at the bottom, listened carefully, measuring the steps, as Hephaestus rushed forward.

"I shall chew you apart, shape-changer!" the dragon bellowed, and his gaping mouth snapped down at Guenhwyvar.

But teeth, even dragon teeth, had little effect on the insubstantial mist that Guenhwyvar suddenly became.

Drizzt managed to pocket a few baubles as he rushed out, his retreat covered by the din of the frustrated dragon's tantrum. The chamber was large and Drizzt was not quite gone when Hephaestus recovered and spotted him. Confused but no less enraged, the dragon roared and started after Drizzt.

In the goblin tongue, knowing from the book that Hephaestus spoke it but hoping that the dragon wouldn't know he knew, Drizzt yelled, "When the stupid beast follows me out, come out and get the rest!"

Hephaestus skidded to a stop and spun about, eyeing the low tunnel that led to the mines. The stupid dragon was in a frightful fit, wanting to munch on the imposing drow but fearing a robbery from behind. Hephaestus stalked over to the tunnel and slammed his scaly head into the wall above it, for good measure, then moved back to think things over.

The thieves had made the exit by now, the dragon knew; he would have to go out under the wide sky if he wanted to catch them—not a wise proposition at this time of year, considering the dragon's lucrative business. In the end, Hephaestus settled the dilemma as he settled every problem: He vowed to thoroughly eat the next merchant party that came his way. His pride restored in that resolution, one that he undoubtedly would forget as soon as he returned to his sleep, the dragon moved back about his chamber, repiling the gold and salvaging what he could from the mounds he inadvertently had melted.

# 22
# Homeward Bound

"You got us through!" Brother Herschel cried. All of the friars except Jankin threw a great hug on Drizzt as soon as the drow caught up to them in a rocky vale west of the dragon lair's entrance.

"If ever there is a way that we can repay you . . . !"

Drizzt emptied his pockets in response, and five sets of eager eyes widened as gold trinkets and baubles rolled forth, glittering in the afternoon sun. One gem in particular, a two-inch ruby, promised wealth beyond anything the friars had ever known.

"For you," Drizzt explained. "All of it. I have no need of treasures."

The friars looked about guiltily, none of them willing to reveal the booty stored in his own pockets. "Perhaps you should keep a bit," Mateus offered, "if you still plan to strike out on your own."

"I do," Drizzt said firmly.

"You cannot stay here," reasoned Mateus. "Where will you go?"

Drizzt really hadn't given it much thought. All he really knew was that his place was not among the Weeping Friars. He pondered a while, recalling the many dead-end roads he had traveled. A thought popped into his head.

"You said it," Drizzt remarked to Jankin. "You named the place a tenday before we entered the tunnel."

Jankin looked at him curiously, hardly remembering.

"Ten-Towns," Drizzt said. "Land of rogues, where a rogue might find his place."

"Ten-Towns?" Mateus balked. "Surely you should reconsider your course, friend. Icewind Dale is not a welcoming place, nor are the hardy killers of Ten-Towns."

"The wind is ever blowing," Jankin added with a wistful look in his dark and hollow eyes, "filled with stinging sand and an icy bite. I will go with you!"

"And the monsters!" added one of the others, slapping Jankin on the back of the head. "Tundra yeti and white bears, and fierce barbarians! No, I would not go to Ten-Towns if Hephaestus himself tried to chase me there!"

"Well the dragon might," said Herschel, glancing nervously back toward the not-so-distant lair. "There are some farmhouses nearby. Perhaps we could stay there the night and get back to the tunnel tomorrow."

"I'll not go with you," Drizzt said again. "You name Ten-Towns an unwelcoming place, but would I find any warmer reception in Mirabar?"

"We will go to the farmers this night," Mateus replied, reconsidering his words. "We will buy you a horse there, and the supplies you will need. I do not wish you to go away at all," he said, "but Ten-Towns seems a good choice—" He looked pointedly at Jankin—"for a drow. Many have found their place there. Truly it is a home for he who has none."

Drizzt understood the sincerity in the friar's voice and appreciated Mateus's graciousness. "How do I find it?" he asked.

"Follow the mountains," Mateus replied. "Keep them always at your right hand's reach. When you get around the range, you have entered Icewind Dale. Only a single peak marks the flat land north of the Spine of the World. The towns are built around it. May they be all that you hope!"

With that, the friars prepared to leave. Drizzt clasped his hands behind his head and leaned back against the valley wall. It was indeed time for his parting with the friars, he knew, but he could not deny both the guilt and loneliness that the prospect offered. The small riches they had taken from the dragon's lair would greatly change his companions' lives, would give them shelter and all the necessities, but wealth could do nothing to alter the barriers that Drizzt faced.

Ten-Towns, the land that Jankin had named a house for the homeless, a gathering ground for those who had nowhere else to go, brought the drow a measure of hope. How many times had fate kicked him? How many gates had he approached hopefully only to be turned away at the tip of a spear? This time will be different, Drizzt told himself, for if he could not find a place in the land of rogues, where then might he turn?

For the beleaguered drow, who had spent so very long running from tragedy, guilt, and prejudices he could not escape, hope was not a comfortable emotion.

⚔ ⚔ ⚔ ⚔ ⚔

Drizzt camped in a small copse that night while the friars went into the small farming village. They returned the next morning leading a fine horse, but with one of their group conspicuously absent.

"Where is Jankin?" Drizzt asked, concerned.

"Tied up in a barn," Mateus replied. "He tried to get away last night, to go back . . ."

"To Hephaestus," Drizzt finished for him.

"If he is still in a mind for it this day, we might just let him go," added a disgusted Herschel.

"Here is your horse," Mateus said, "if the night has not changed your mind."

"And here is a new wrap," offered Herschel. He handed Drizzt a fine, fur-lined cloak. Drizzt knew how uncharacteristically generous the friars were being, and he almost changed his mind. He could not dismiss his other needs, though, and he would not satisfy them among this group.

To display his resolve, the drow moved straight to the animal, meaning to climb right on. Drizzt had seen a horse before, but never so close. He was amazed by the beast's sheer strength, the muscles rippling along the animal's neck, and he was amazed, too, by the height of the animal's back.

He spent a moment staring into the horse's eyes, communicating his intent as best he could. Then, to everyone's shock, even Drizzt's, the horse bent low, allowing the drow to climb easily into the saddle.

"You have a way with horses," remarked Mateus. "Never did you mention that you were a skilled rider."

Drizzt only nodded and did his very best to remain in the saddle when the horse started into a trot. It took the drow many moments to figure out how to control the beast and he had circled far to the east—the wrong way—before he managed to turn about. Throughout the circuit, Drizzt tried hard to keep up his facade, and the friars, never ones for horses themselves, merely nodded and smiled.

Hours later, Drizzt was riding hard to the west, following the southern edge of the Spine of the World.

⚔ ⚔ ⚔ ⚔ ⚔

"The Weeping Friars," Roddy McGristle whispered, looking down from a stony bluff at the band as they made their way back toward Mirabar's tunnel later that same tenday.

"What?" Tephanis gawked, rushing from his sack to join Roddy. For the very first time, the sprite's speed proved a liability. Before he even realized what he was saying, Tephanis blurted, "It-cannot-be! The-dragon . . ."

Roddy's glare fell over Tephanis like the shadow of a thundercloud.

"I-mean-I-assumed . . ." Tephanis sputtered, but he realized that Roddy, who knew the tunnel better than he and knew, too, the sprite's ways with locks, had pretty much guessed the indiscretion.

"Ye took it on yerself to kill the drow," Roddy said calmly.

"Please, my-master," Tephanis replied. "I-did-not-mean . . . I-feared-for-you. The-drow-is-a-devil, I-say! I-sent-them-down-the-dragon's-tunnel. I-thought-that-you . . ."

"Forget it," Roddy growled. "Ye did what ye did, and no more about it. Now get in yer sack. Mighten that we can fix what ye done, if the drow's not dead."

Tephanis nodded, relieved, and zipped back into the sack. Roddy scooped it up and called his dog to his side.

"I'll get the friars talking," the bounty hunter vowed, "but first . . ." Roddy whipped the sack about, slamming it into the stone wall.

"Master!" came the sprite's muffled cry.

"Ye drow-stealin . . ." Roddy huffed, and he beat the sack mercilessly against the unyielding stone. Tephanis squirmed for the first few whacks, even managed to begin a tear with his little dagger. But then the sack darkened with wetness and the sprite struggled no more.

"Drow-stealing mutant," Roddy mumbled, tossing the gory package away. "Come on, dog. If the drow's alive, the friars'll know where to find him."

The Weeping Friars were an order dedicated to suffering, and a couple of them, particularly Jankin, had indeed suffered much in their lives. None of them, though, had ever imagined the level of cruelty they found at the hands of wild-eyed Roddy McGristle, and before an hour had passed, Roddy, too, was driving hard to the west along the southern edge of the mountain range.

The cold eastern wind filled his ears with its endless song. Drizzt had heard it every second since he had rounded the western edge of the Spine of the World and turned north and east, into the barren stretch of land named for this wind, Icewind Dale. He accepted the mournful groan and the wind's freezing bite willingly, for to Drizzt the rush of air came as a gust of freedom.

Another symbol of that freedom, the sight of the wide sea, came as the drow rounded the mountain range. Drizzt had visited the shoreline once, on his passage to Luskan, and now he wanted to pause and go the few miles to its shores again. But the cold wind reminded him of the impending winter, and he understood the difficulty he would find in traveling the dale once the first snows had fallen.

Drizzt spotted Kelvin's Cairn, the solitary mountain on the tundra north of the great range, the first day after he had turned into the dale. He made for it anxiously, visualizing its singular peak as the marking post to the land he would call home. Tentative hope filled him whenever he focused on that mountain.

He passed several small groups, solitary wagons or a handful of men on horseback, as he neared the region of Ten-Towns along the caravan route, a southwestern approach. The sun was low in the west and dim, and Drizzt kept the cowl of his fine cloak pulled low, hiding his ebony skin. He nodded curtly as each traveler passed.

Three lakes dominated the region, along with the peak of rocky Kelvin's Cairn, which rose a thousand feet above the broken plain and was capped with snow even through the short summer. Of the ten towns that gave the area its name, only the principle city, Bryn Shander, stood apart from the lakes. It sat above the plain, on a short hill, its flag whipping defiantly against the stiff wind. The caravan route, Drizzt's trail, led to this city, the region's principle marketplace.

Drizzt could tell from the rising smoke of distant fires that several other communities were within a few miles of the city on the hill. He considered his course for a moment, wondering if he should go to one of these smaller, more secluded towns instead of continuing straight on to the principle city.

"No," the drow said firmly, dropping a hand into his pouch to feel the onyx figurine. Drizzt kicked his horse ahead, up the hill to the walled city's forbidding gates.

"Merchant?" asked one of the two guards standing bored before the iron-bound portal. "Ye're a bit late in the year for trading."

"No merchant," Drizzt replied softly, losing a good measure of his nerve now that the hour was upon him. He reached up slowly to his hood, trying to keep his trembling hand moving.

"From what town, then?" the other guard asked. Drizzt dropped his hand back, his courage deflected by the blunt question.

"From Mirabar," he answered honestly, and before he could stop himself and before the guards posed another distracting question, he reached up and pulled back his hood.

Four eyes popped wide and hands immediately dropped to belted swords.

"No!" Drizzt retorted suddenly. "No, please." A weariness came into both his voice and his posture that the guards could not understand. Drizzt had no strength left for senseless battles of misunderstanding. Against a goblin horde or a marauding giant, the drow's scimitars came easily into his hands, but against one who only battled him because of misperceptions, his blades weighed heavily indeed.

"I have come from Mirabar," Drizzt continued, his voice growing steadier with each syllable, "to Ten-Towns to reside in peace." He held his hands out wide, offering no threat.

The guards hardly knew how to react. Neither of them had ever seen a dark elf—though they knew beyond doubt that Drizzt was one—or knew more about the race than fireside tales of the ancient war that had split the elven peoples apart.

"Wait here," one of the guards breathed to the other, who didn't seem to appreciate the order. "I will go inform Spokesman Cassius." He banged on the iron-bound gate and slipped inside as soon as it was opened wide enough to let him through. The remaining guard eyed Drizzt unblinking, his hand never leaving his sword hilt.

"If you kill me, a hundred crossbows will cut you down," he declared, trying but utterly failing to sound confident.

"Why would I?" Drizzt asked innocently, keeping his hands wide apart and his posture unthreatening. This encounter had gone well so far, he believed. In every other village he had dared approach, those first seeing him had fled in terror or chased him with bared weapons.

The other guard returned a short time later with a small and slender man, clean-shaven and with bright blue eyes that scanned continuously, taking in every detail. He wore fine clothes, and from the respect the two guards showed the man, Drizzt knew at once that he was of high rank.

He studied Drizzt for a long while, considering every move and every feature. "I am Cassius," he said at length, "Spokesman of Bryn Shander and Principle Spokesman of Ten-Towns' Ruling Council."

Drizzt dipped a short bow. "I am Drizzt Do'Urden," he said, "of Mirabar and points beyond, now come to Ten-Towns."

"Why?" Cassius asked sharply, trying to catch him off guard.

Drizzt shrugged. "Is a reason required?"

"For a dark elf, perhaps," Cassius replied honestly.

Drizzt's accepting smile disarmed the spokesman and quieted the two guards, who now stood protectively close to his sides. "I can offer no reason for coming, beyond my desire to come," Drizzt continued. "Long has been my road, Spokesman Cassius. I am weary and in need of rest. Ten-Towns is the place of rogues, I have been told, and do not doubt that a dark elf is a rogue among the dwellers of the surface."

It seemed logical enough, and Drizzt's sincerity came through clearly to the observant spokesman. Cassius dropped his chin in his palm and thought for a long while. He didn't fear the drow, or doubt the elf's words, but he had no intention of allowing the stir that a drow would cause in his city.

"Bryn Shander is not your place," Cassius said bluntly, and Drizzt's lavender eyes narrowed at the unfair proclamation. Undaunted, Cassius pointed to the north. "Go to Lonelywood, in the forest on the northern banks of Maer Dualdon," he offered. He swung his gaze to the southeast. "Or to Good Mead or Dougan's Hole on the southern lake, Redwaters. These are smaller towns, where you will cause less stir and find less trouble."

"And when they refuse my entry?" Drizzt asked. "Where then, fair spokesman? Out in the wind to die on the empty plain?"

"You do not know—"

"I know," Drizzt interrupted. "I have played this game many times. Who will welcome a drow, even one who has forsaken his people and their ways and who desires nothing more than peace?" Drizzt's voice was stern and showed no self-pity, and Cassius again understood the words to be true.

Truly Cassius sympathized. He himself had been a rogue once and had been forced to the ends of the world, to forlorn Icewind Dale, to find a home. There were no ends farther than this; Icewind Dale was a rogue's last stop. Another thought came to Cassius then, a possible solution to the dilemma that would not nag at his conscience.

"How long have you lived on the surface?" Cassius asked, sincerely interested.

Drizzt considered the question for a moment, wondering what point the spokesman meant to make. "Seven years," he replied.

"In the northland?"

"Yes."

"Yet you have found no home, no village to take you in," Cassius said. "You have survived hostile winters and doubtless, more direct enemies. Are you skilled with those blades you hang on your belt?"

"I am a ranger," Drizzt said evenly.

"An unusual profession for a drow," Cassius remarked.

"I am a ranger," Drizzt said again, more forcefully, "well trained in the ways of nature and in the use of my weapons."

"I do not doubt," Cassius mused. He paused, then said, "There is a place offering shelter and seclusion." The spokesman led Drizzt's gaze to the north, to the rocky slopes of Kelvin's Cairn. "Beyond the dwarven vale lies the mountain," Cassius explained, "and beyond that the open tundra. It would do Ten-Towns well to have a scout on the mountain's northern slopes. Danger always seems to come from that direction."

"I came to find my home," Drizzt interrupted. "You offer me a hole in a pile of rock and a duty to those whom I owe nothing." In truth, the suggestion appealed to Drizzt's ranger spirit.

"Would you have me tell you that things are different?" Cassius replied. "I'll not let a wandering drow into Bryn Shander."

"Would a man have to prove himself worthy?"

"A man does not carry so grim a reputation," Cassius replied evenly, without hesitation. "If I were so magnanimous, if I welcomed you on your words alone and threw my gates wide, would you enter and find your home? We both know better than that, drow. Not everyone in Bryn Shander would be so open-hearted, I promise. You would cause an uproar wherever you went and whatever your demeanor and intent, you would be forced into battles.

"It would be the same in any of the towns," Cassius went on, guessing that his words had struck a chord of truth in the homeless drow. "I offer you a hole in a pile of rock, within the borders of Ten-Towns, where your actions, good or bad, will become your reputation beyond the color of your skin. Does my offer seem so shallow now?"

"I shall need supplies," Drizzt said, accepting the truth of Cassius's words. "And what of my horse? I do not think the slopes of a mountain are a proper place for such a beast."

"Trade your horse then," Cassius offered. "My guard will get a fair price and return here with the supplies you will need."

Drizzt thought about the suggestion for a moment, then handed the reins to Cassius.

The spokesman left then, thinking himself quite clever. Not only had he averted any immediate trouble, he had convinced Drizzt to guard his borders, all in a place where Bruenor Battlehammer and his clan of grim-faced dwarves could certainly keep the drow from causing any trouble.

⚔ ⚔ ⚔ ⚔ ⚔

Roddy McGristle pulled his wagon into a small village nestled in the shadows of the mountain range's western end. Snow would come soon, the bounty hunter knew, and he had no desire to be caught halfway up the dale when it began. He'd stay here with the farmers and wait out the winter. Nothing could leave the dale without passing this area, and if Drizzt had gone there, as the friars had revealed, he had nowhere left to run.

⚔ ⚔ ⚔ ⚔ ⚔

Drizzt set out from the gates that night, preferring the darkness for his journey, despite the cold. His direct approach to the mountain took him along the eastern rim of the rocky gorge that the dwarves had claimed as their home. Drizzt took extra care to avoid any guards the bearded folk might have set. He had encountered dwarves only once before, when he had passed Citadel Adbar on his earliest wanderings out of Mooshie's Grove, and it had not been a pleasant experience. Dwarven patrols had chased him off without waiting for any explanations, and they had dogged him through the mountains for many days.

For all his prudence in getting past the valley, though, Drizzt could not ignore a high mound of rocks he came upon, a climb with steps cut into the piled stones. He was less than halfway to the mountain, with several miles and hours of night still to go, but Drizzt moved up the detour, step over step, enchanted by the widening panorama of town lights about him.

The climb was not high, only fifty feet or so, but with the flat tundra and clear night Drizzt was afforded a view of five cities: two on the banks of the lake to the east, two to the west on the largest lake, and Bryn Shander, on its hillock a few miles to the south.

How many minutes passed Drizzt did not know, for the sights sparked too many hopes and fantasies for him to notice. He had been in Ten-Towns for barely a day, but already he was feeling comfortable with the sights, with knowing that thousands of people about the mountain would hear of him and possibly come to accept him.

A grumbling, gravelly voice shook Drizzt from his contemplations. He dropped into a defensive crouch and circled behind a rock. The stream of complaints marked the coming figure clearly. He was wide-shouldered and about a foot shorter than Drizzt, though obviously heavier than the drow. Drizzt knew it was a dwarf even before the figure paused to adjust its helmet—by slamming its head into a stone.

"Dagnaggit blasted," the dwarf muttered, "adjusting" the helmet a second time.

Drizzt was certainly intrigued, but he was also smart enough to realize that a grumbling dwarf wouldn't likely welcome an uninvited drow in the middle of a dark night. As the dwarf moved for yet another adjustment, Drizzt skipped off, running lightly and silently along the side of the trail. He passed close by the dwarf but then was gone with no more rustle than the shadow of a cloud.

"Eh?" the dwarf mumbled when he came back up, this time satisfied with his headgear's fit. "Who's that? What're ye about?" He went into a series of short, spinning hops, eyes darting alertly all about.

There was only the darkness, the stones, and the wind.

# 23
# A Memory Come To Life

The season's first snow fell lazily over Icewind Dale, large flakes drifting down in mesmerizing zigzag dances, so different from the wind-whipped blizzards most common to the region. The young girl, Catti-brie, watched it with obvious enchantment from the doorway of her cavern home, the hue of her deep-blue eyes seeming even purer in the reflection of the ground's white blanket.

"Late in comin', but hard when it gets here," grumbled Bruenor Battlehammer, a red-bearded dwarf, as he came up behind Catti-brie, his adopted daughter. "Suren to be a hard season, as are all in this place for white dragons!"

"Oh, me Daddy!" replied Catti-brie sternly. "Stop yer whining! Suren 'tis a beautiful fall, and harmless enough without the wind to drive it."

"Humans," huffed the dwarf derisively, still behind the girl. Catti-brie could not see his expression, tender toward her even as he grumbled, but she didn't need to. Bruenor was nine parts bluster and one part grouch, by Catti-brie's estimation.

Catti-brie spun on the dwarf suddenly, her shoulder-length, auburn locks twirling about her face. "Can I go out to play?" she asked, a hopeful smile on her face. "Oh, please, me Daddy!"

Bruenor forced on his best grimace. "Go out!" he roared. "None but a fool'd look for an Icewind Dale winter as a place for playin'! Show some sense, girl! The season'd freeze yer bones! "

Catti-brie's smile disappeared, but she refused to surrender so easily. "Well said for a dwarf," she retorted, to Bruenor's horror. "Ye're well enough fit for the holes and the less ye see o' the sky, the more ye're smiling. But I've a long winter ahead, and this might be me last chance to see the sky. Please, Daddy?"

Bruenor could not hold his snarling visage against his daughter's charm, but he did not want her to go out. "I'm fearing there's something prowlin' out there," he explained, trying to sound authoritative. "Sensed it on the climb a few nights back, though I never seen it. Mighten be a white lion, or a white bear. Best to . . ." Bruenor never finished, for Catti-brie's disheartened look more than destroyed the dwarf's imagined fears.

Catti-brie was no novice to the dangers of the region. She had lived with Bruenor and his dwarven clan for more than seven years. A raiding goblin band had killed Catti-brie's parents when she was only a toddler, and though she was human, Bruenor had taken her in as his own.

"Ye're a hard one, me girl," Bruenor said in answer to Catti-brie's relentless, sorrow-filled expression. "Go out and find yer play, then, but don't ye be goin' too far! On yer word, ye spirited filly, keep the caves in sight and a sword and horn on yer belt."

Catti-brie rushed over and planted a wet kiss on Bruenor's cheek, which the taciturn dwarf promptly wiped away, grumbling at the girl's back as she disappeared into the tunnel. Bruenor was the leader of the clan, as tough as the stone they mined. But every time Catti-brie planted an appreciative kiss on his cheek, the dwarf realized he had given in to her.

"Humans!" the dwarf growled again, and he stomped down the tunnel to the mine, thinking to batter a few pieces of iron, just to remind himself of his toughness.

⚔ ⚔ ⚔ ⚔ ⚔

It was easy for the spirited young girl to rationalize her disobedience when she looked back across the valley from the lower slopes of Kelvin's Cairn, more than three miles from Bruenor's front door. Bruenor had told

Catti-brie to keep the caves in sight, and they were, or at least the wider terrain around them was, from this high vantage point.

But Catti-brie, happily sliding down one bumpy expanse, soon found a flaw in not heeding to her experienced father's warnings. She had come to the bottom, a delightful ride, and was briskly rubbing the stinging chill out of her hands, when she heard a low and ominous growl.

"White lion," Catti-brie mouthed silently, remembering Bruenor's suspicion. When she looked up, she saw that her father's guess had not quite hit the mark. It was indeed a great feline the girl saw looking down at her from a bare, stony mound, but the cat was black, not white, and a huge panther, not a lion.

Defiantly, Catti-brie pulled her knife from its sheath. "Keep yerself back, cat!" she said, only the slightest tremor in her voice, for she knew that fear invited attack from wild animals.

Guenhwyvar flattened its ears and plopped to its belly, then issued a long and resounding roar that echoed throughout the stony region.

Catti-brie could not respond to the power in that roar, or to the very long and abundant teeth the panther showed. She searched around for some escape but knew that no matter which way she ran she could not get beyond the panther's first mighty spring.

"Guenhwyvar!" came a call from above. Catti-brie looked back up the snowy expanse to see a slender, cloaked form picking a careful route toward her. "Guenhwyvar!" the newcomer called again. "Be gone from here!"

The panther growled a throaty reply, then bounded away, leaping the snow-covered boulders and springing up small cliffs as easily as if it were running across a smooth and flat field.

Despite her continuing fears, Catti-brie watched the departing panther with sincere admiration. She had always loved animals and had often studied them, but the interplay of Guenhwyvar's sleek muscles was more majestic than anything she had ever imagined. When she at last came out of her trance, she realized that the slender figure was right behind her. She whirled about, knife still in hand.

The blade dropped from her grasp and her breathing halted abruptly as soon as she looked upon the drow.

Drizzt, too, found himself stunned by the encounter. He wanted to make certain that the girl was all right, but when he looked upon Catti-brie, all thoughts of his purpose faded away in a flood of memories.

She was about the same age as the sandy-haired boy on the farm, Drizzt noted initially, and that thought inevitably brought back the agonizing memories of Maldobar. When Drizzt looked more closely, though, into Catti-brie's eyes, his thoughts were sent flying back further into his past, to his days marching alongside his dark kin. Catti-brie's eyes possessed that same joyful and innocent sparkle that Drizzt had seen in the eyes of an elven child, a girl he had rescued from the savage blades of his raiding kin. The memory overwhelmed Drizzt, sent him whirling back to that bloody glade in the elven wood, where his brother and fellow drow had brutally slaughtered an elven gathering. In the frenzy, Drizzt had almost killed the elven child, had almost put himself forever on that same dark road that his kin so willingly followed.

Drizzt shook himself free of the recollection and reminded himself that this was a different child of a different race. He meant to speak a greeting, but the girl was gone.

That damning word, "drizzit," echoed in the drow's thoughts several times as he made his way back to the cave he had set up as his home on the mountain's northern face.

⚔ ⚔ ⚔ ⚔ ⚔

That same night, the onslaught of the season began in full. The cold eastern wind blowing off the Reghed Glacier drove the snow into high, impassable drifts.

Catti-brie watched the snow forlornly, fearing that many tendays might pass before she could again go to Kelvin's Cairn. She hadn't told Bruenor or any of the other dwarves about the drow, for fear of punishment and that Bruenor would drive the drow away. Looking at the piling snow, Catti-brie wished that she had been braver, had remained and talked to the strange elf. Every howl of the wind heightened that wish and made the girl wonder if she had lost her only chance.

⚔ ⚔ ⚔ ⚔ ⚔

"I'm off to Bryn Shander," Bruenor announced one morning more than two months later. An unexpected break had come in Icewind Dale's normal seven-month winter, a rare January thaw. Bruenor eyed his daughter suspiciously for a long moment. "Ye're meanin' to go out yerself this day?" he asked.

"If I may," Catti-brie answered. "The caves're tight around me and the wind's not so cold."

"I'll get a dwarf or two to go with ye," Bruenor offered.

Catti-brie, thinking that now might be her chance to go back to investigate the drow, balked at the notion. "They're all for mendin' their doors!" she retorted, more sharply than she intended. "Don't ye be botherin' them for the likes of meself!"

Bruenor's eyes narrowed. "Ye've too much stubbornness in ye."

"I get it from me dad," Catti-brie said with a wink that shot down any more forthcoming arguments.

"Take care, then," Bruenor began, "and keep—"

". . . the caves in sight!" Catti-brie finished for him. Bruenor spun about and stomped out of the cave, grumbling helplessly and cursing the day he had ever taken a human in for a daughter. Catti-brie only laughed at the unending facade.

Once again it was Guenhwyvar who first encountered the auburn-haired girl. Catti-brie had set straight out for the mountain and was making her way around its western most trails when she spotted the black panther above her, watching her from a rock spur.

"Guenhwyvar," the girl called, remembering the name the drow had used. The panther growled lowly and dropped from the spur, moving closer.

"Guenhwyvar?" Catti-brie said again, less certain, for the panther was only a few dozen strides away. Guenhwyvar's ears came up at the second mention of the name and the cat's taut muscles visibly relaxed.

Catti-brie approached slowly, one deliberate step at a time. "Where's the dark elf, Guenhwyvar?" she asked quietly. "Can ye take me to him?"

"And why would you want to go to him?" came a question from behind.

Catti-brie froze in her tracks, remembering the smooth-toned, melodic voice, then turned slowly to face the drow. He was only three steps behind her, his lavender-eyed gaze locking onto hers as soon as they met. Catti-brie had no idea of what to say, and Drizzt, absorbed again by memories, stood quiet, watching and waiting.

"Be ye a drow?" Catti-brie asked after the silence became unbearable. As soon as she heard her own words, she privately berated herself for asking such a stupid question.

"I am," Drizzt replied. "What does that mean to you?"

Catti-brie shrugged at the strange response. "I've heard that drow be evil, but ye don't seem so to me."

"Then you have taken a great risk in coming out here all by yourself," Drizzt remarked. "But fear not," he quickly added, seeing the girl's sudden uneasiness, "for I am not evil and will bring no harm to you." After the months alone in his comfortable but empty cave, Drizzt did not want this meeting to end quickly.

Catti-brie nodded, believing his words. "Me name's Catti-brie," she said. "Me dad is Bruenor, King o' Clan Battlehammer."

Drizzt cocked his head curiously.

"The dwarves," Catti-brie explained, pointing back to the valley. She understood Drizzt's confusion as soon as she spoke the words. "He's not me real dad," she said. "Bruenor took me in when I was just a babe, when me real parents were . . ."

She couldn't finish, and Drizzt didn't need her to, understanding her pained expression.

"I am Drizzt Do'Urden," the drow interjected. "Well met, Catti-brie, daughter of Bruenor. It is good to have another to talk with. For all these tendays of winter, I have had only Guenhwyvar, there, when the cat is around, and my friend does not say much, of course!"

Catti-brie's smile nearly took in her ears. She glanced over her shoulder to the panther, now reclining lazily in the path. "She's a beautiful cat," Catti-brie remarked.

Drizzt did not doubt the sincerity in the girl's tone, or in the admiring gaze she dropped on Guenhwyvar. "Come here, Guenhwyvar," Drizzt said, and the panther stretched and slowly rose. Guenhwyvar walked right beside Catti-brie, and Drizzt nodded to answer her unspoken but obvious desire. Tentatively at first, but then firmly, Catti-brie stroked the panther's sleek coat, feeling the beast's power and perfection. Guenhwyvar accepted the petting without complaint, even bumped into Catti-brie's side when she stopped for a moment, prodding her to continue.

"Are you alone?" Drizzt asked.

Catti-brie nodded. "Me dad said to keep the caves in sight." She laughed. "I can see them well enough, by me thinkin'!"

Drizzt looked back into the valley, to the far rock wall several miles away. "Your father would not be pleased. This land is not so tame. I have been on the mountain for only two months, and I have fought twice already shaggy white beasts I do not know."

"Tundra yeti," Catti-brie replied. "Ye must be on the northern side. Tundra yeti don't come around the mountain."

"Are you so certain?" Drizzt asked sarcastically.

"I've not ever seen one," Catti-brie replied, "but I'm not fearing them. I came to find yerself, and now I have."

"You have," said Drizzt, "and now what?"

Catti-brie shrugged and went back to petting Guenhwyvar's sleek coat.

"Come," Drizzt offered. "Let us find a more comfortable place to talk. The glare off the snow stings my eyes."

"Ye're used to the dark tunnels?" Catti-brie asked hopefully, eager to hear tales of lands beyond the borders of Ten-Towns, the only place Catti-brie had ever known.

Drizzt and the girl spent a marvelous day together. Drizzt told Catti-brie of Menzoberranzan and Catti-brie answered his tales with stories of Icewind Dale, of her life with the dwarves. Drizzt was especially interested in hearing about Bruenor and his kin, since the dwarves were his closest, and most-feared, neighbors.

"Bruenor talks rough as stone, but I'm knowin' him better than all that!" Catti-brie assured the drow. "He's a right fine one, and so's the rest o' the clan."

Drizzt was glad to hear it, and glad, too, that he had made this connection, both for the implications of having such a friend and even more so because he truly enjoyed the charming and spirited lass's company. Catti-brie's energy and zest for life verily bubbled over. In her presence, the drow could not recall his haunting memories, could only feel good about his decision to save the elven child those many years before. Catti-brie's singsong voice and the careless way she flipped her flowing hair about her shoulders lifted the burden of guilt from Drizzt's back as surely as a giant could have hoisted a rock.

Their tales could have gone on all that day and night, and for many tendays afterward, but when Drizzt noticed the sun riding low along the western horizon, he realized that the time had come for the girl to head back to her home.

"I will take you," Drizzt offered.

"No," Catti-brie replied. "Ye best not. Bruenor'd not understand and ye'd get me in a mountain o' trouble. I can get back, don't ye be worrying! I know these trails better'n yerself, Drizzt Do'Urden, and ye couldn't keep up to me if ye tried!"

Drizzt laughed at the boast but almost believed it. He and the girl set out at once, moving to the mountain's southern most spur and saying their good-byes with promises that they would meet again during the next thaw, or in the spring if none came sooner.

Truly the girl was skipping lightly when she entered the dwarven complex, but one look at her surly father stole a measure of her delight. Bruenor had gone to Bryn Shander that morning on business with Cassius. The dwarf wasn't thrilled to learn that a dark elf had made a home so close to his door, but he guessed that his curious—too curious—daughter would think it a grand thing.

"Keep yerself away from the mountain," Bruenor said as soon as he noticed Catti-brie, and she was in despair.

"But me Dad—" she tried to protest.

"On yer word, girl!" the dwarf demanded. "Ye'll not set foot on that mountain again without me permission! There's a dark elf there, by Cassius's telling. On yer word!"

Catti-brie nodded helplessly, then followed Bruenor back to the dwarven complex, knowing she would have a hard time changing her father's mind, but knowing, too, Bruenor held views far from justified where Drizzt Do'Urden was concerned.

⚔ ⚔ ⚔ ⚔ ⚔

Another thaw came a month later and Catti-brie heeded her promise. She never put one foot on Kelvin's Cairn, but from the valley trails around it, she called out to Drizzt and to Guenhwyvar. Drizzt and the panther, looking for the girl with the break in the weather, were soon beside her, in the valley this time, sharing more tales and a picnic lunch that Catti-brie had packed.

When Catti-brie got back to the dwarven mines that evening, Bruenor suspected much and asked her only once if she had kept her word. The dwarf had always trusted his daughter, but when Catti-brie answered that she had not been on Kelvin's Cairn, his suspicions did not diminish.

# 24
# Revelations

Bruenor ambled along the lower slopes of Kelvin's Cairn for the better part of the morning. Most of the snow was melted now with spring thick in the air, but stubborn pockets still made the trails difficult. Axe in one hand and shield, emblazoned with the foaming mug standard of Clan Battlehammer, in the other, Bruenor trudged on, spitting curses at every slick spot, at every boulder obstacle, and at dark elves in general.

He rounded the northwesternmost spur of the mountain, his long, pointed nose cherry-red from the biting wind and his breath coming hard. "Time for a rest," the dwarf muttered, spotting a stone alcove sheltered by high walls from the relentless wind.

Bruenor wasn't the only one who had noticed the comfortable spot. Just before he reached the ten-foot-wide break in the rock wall, a sudden flap of leathery wings brought a huge, insectlike head rising up before him. The dwarf fell back, startled and wary. He recognized the beast as a remorhaz, a polar worm, and was not so eager to jump in against it.

The remorhaz came out of the cubby in pursuit, its snakelike, forty-foot-long body rolling out like an ice-blue ribbon behind it. Multifaceted bug eyes, shining bright white, honed in on the dwarf. Short, leathery wings kept the creature's front half reared and ready to strike while dozens of scrambling legs propelled the remainder of the long torso.

Bruenor felt the increasing heat as the agitated creature's back began to glow, first to a dull brown, then brightening to red.

"That'll stop the wind for a bit!" the dwarf chuckled, realizing that he could not outrun the beast. He stopped his retreat and waved his axe threateningly.

The remorhaz came straight in, its formidable maw, large enough to swallow the diminutive target whole, snapping down hungrily.

Bruenor jumped aside and angled his shield and body to keep the maw from snapping off his legs, while slamming his axe right between the monster's horns.

The wings beat ferociously, lifting the head back up. The remorhaz, hardly injured, poised to strike again quickly, but Bruenor beat it to the spot. He snatched his bulky axe with his shield hand drew a long dagger, and dived forward, right between the monster's first set of legs.

The great head came down in a rush, but Bruenor had already slipped under the low belly, the beast's most vulnerable spot. "Ye get me point?" Bruenor chided, driving the dagger up between the scale ridge.

Bruenor was too tough and too well armored to be seriously injured by the worm's thrashing, but then the creature began to roll, meaning to put its glowing-hot back on the dwarf.

"No, ye don't, ye confused dragon-worm-bird-bug!" Bruenor howled, scrambling to keep away from the heat. He came to the creature's side and heaved with all his strength, tumbling the off-balance remorhaz right over.

Snow sputtered and sizzled when the fiery back touched down. Bruenor kicked and swatted his way past the thrashing legs to get to the vulnerable underside. The dwarf's many-notched axe smashed in, opening a wide and deep gash.

The remorhaz coiled and snapped its long body to and fro, throwing Bruenor to the side. The dwarf was up in an instant, but not quickly enough, as the polar worm rolled at him. The searing back caught Bruenor on the thigh as he tried to leap away, and the dwarf came out limping, grabbing at his smoking leather leggings.

Then they faced off again, both showing considerably more respect for the other.

The maw gaped; with a quick snap, Bruenor's axe took a tooth from it and deflected it aside. The dwarf's wounded leg buckled with the blow, though, and a stumbling Bruenor could not get out of the way. A long horn hooked Bruenor under the arm and hurled him far to the side.

He crashed amid a small field of rocks, recovered, and purposely banged his head against a large stone to adjust his helmet and knock the dizziness away.

The remorhaz left a trail of blood, but it did not relent. The huge maw opened and the creature hissed, and Bruenor promptly chucked a stone down its gullet.

⚔ ⚔ ⚔ ⚔ ⚔

Guenhwyvar alerted Drizzt to the trouble down at the northwestern spur. The drow had never seen a polar worm before, but as soon as he spotted the combatants, from a ridge high above, he knew that the dwarf was in trouble. Lamenting that he had left his bow back in the cave, Drizzt drew his scimitars and followed the panther down the mountainside as quickly as the slippery trails would allow.

⚔ ⚔ ⚔ ⚔ ⚔

"Come on, then!" the stubborn dwarf roared at the remorhaz, and indeed the monster did charge. Bruenor braced himself, meaning to get in at least one good shot before becoming worm food.

The great head came down at him, but then the remorhaz, hearing a roar from behind, hesitated and looked away.

"Fool move!" the dwarf cried in glee, and Bruenor slashed with his axe at the monster's lower jaw, splitting it cleanly between two great incisors. The remorhaz screeched in pain; its leathery wings flapped wildly, trying to get the head out of the wicked dwarf's reach.

Bruenor hit it again, and a third time, each blow cutting huge creases in the maw and driving the head down.

"Think ye're to bite at me, eh?" the dwarf cried. He lashed out with his shield hand and grabbed at a horn as the remorhaz head began to rise again. A quick jerk turned the monster's head at a vulnerable angle and the knotted muscles in Bruenor's arm snapped viciously, cleaving his mighty axe into the polar worm's skull.

The creature shuddered and thrashed for a second longer, then lay still, its back still glowing hotly.

A second roar from Guenhwyvar took the proud dwarf's eyes from his kill. Bruenor, injured and tentative, looked up to see Drizzt and the panther fast approaching, the drow with both scimitars drawn.

"Come on!" Bruenor roared at them both, misunderstanding their charge. He banged his axe against his heavy shield. "Come on and feel me blade!"

Drizzt stopped abruptly and called for Guenhwyvar to do the same. The panther continued to stalk, though, ears flattened.

"Be gone, Guenhwyvar!" Drizzt commanded.

The panther growled indignantly one final time and sprang away.

Satisfied that the cat was gone, Bruenor snapped his glare on Drizzt, standing at the other end of the fallen polar worm.

"Yerself and me, then?" the dwarf spat. "Ye got the belly to face me axe, drow, or do little girls be more to yer liken'?"

The obvious reference to Catti-brie brought an angry light to Drizzt's eyes, and his grasp on his weapons tightened.

Bruenor swung his axe easily. "Come on," he chided derisively. "Ye got the belly to come and play with a dwarf?"

Drizzt wanted to scream out for all the world to hear. He wanted to spring over the dead monster and smash the dwarf, deny the dwarf's words with sheer and brutal force, but he couldn't. Drizzt couldn't deny Mielikki and couldn't betray Mooshie. He had to sublimate his rage once again, had to take the insults stoically and with the realization that he, and his goddess, knew the truth of what lay in his heart.

The scimitars spun into their sheaths and Drizzt walked away, Guenhwyvar coming up beside him.

Bruenor watched the pair go curiously. At first he thought the drow a coward, but then, as the excitement of the battle gradually diminished,

Bruenor came to wonder about the drow's intent. Had he come down to finish off both combatants, as Bruenor had first assumed? Or had he, possibly, come down to Bruenor's aid?

"Nah," the dwarf muttered, dismissing the possibility. "Not a dark elf!"

The walk back was long for the limping dwarf, giving Bruenor many opportunities to replay the events around the northwestern spur. When he finally arrived back at the mines, the sun had long set and Catti-brie and several dwarves were gathered, ready to go out to look for him.

"Ye're hurt," one of the dwarves remarked. Catti-brie immediately imagined a fight between Drizzt and her father.

"Polar worm," the dwarf explained casually. "Got him good, but got a bit of a burn for me effort."

The other dwarves nodded admiringly at their leader's battle prowess—a polar worm was no easy kill—and Catti-brie sighed audibly.

"I saw the drow!" Bruenor growled at her, suspecting the source of that sigh. The dwarf remained confused about his meeting with the dark elf, and confused, too, about where Catti-brie fit into all of this. Had Catti-brie actually met the dark elf? he wondered.

"I seen him, I did!" Bruenor continued, now speaking more to the other dwarves. "Drow and the biggest an' blackest cat me eyes ever set on. He came down for me, just as I dropped the worm."

"Drizzt would not!" Catti-brie interrupted before her father could get into his customary story-telling roll.

"Drizzt?" Bruenor asked, and the girl turned away, realizing that her lie was up. Bruenor let it go—for the moment.

"He did, I say!" the dwarf continued. "Came in at me with both his blades drawn! I chased that one an' the cat off!"

"We could hunt him down," offered one of the dwarves. "Run him off the mountain!" The others nodded and mumbled their agreement, but Bruenor, still struggling with the drow's intent, cut them short.

"He's got the mountain," Bruenor told them. "Cassius gave it to him, and we need no trouble with Bryn Shander. As long as the drow stays put and stays outa our way, we'll leave him be.

"But" Bruenor continued, eyeing Catti-brie directly, "ye're not to speak to, ye're not to go near, that one again!"

"But—" Catti-brie started futilely.

"Never!" Bruenor roared. "I'll have yer word now, girl, or by Moradin, I'll have that dark elf's head!"

Catti-brie hesitated, horribly trapped.

"Tell me!" Bruenor demanded.

"Ye have me word," the girl mumbled, and she fled back to the dark shelter of the cave.

⚔ ⚔ ⚔ ⚔ ⚔

"Cassius, Spokesman o' Bryn Shander, sent me yer way," the gruff man explained. "Says ye'd know the drow if any would."

Bruenor glanced around his formal audience hall to the many other dwarves in attendance, none of them overly impressed by the rude stranger. Bruenor dropped his bearded chin into his palm and yawned widely, determined to remain outside this apparent conflict. He might have bluffed the crude man and his smelly dog out of the halls without further bother, but Catti-brie, sitting at her father's side, shuffled uneasily.

Roddy McGristle did not miss her revealing movement. "Cassius says ye must've seen the drow, him bein' so close."

"If any of me people have," Bruenor replied absently, "they've spoke not a bit of it. If yer drow's about, he's been no bother."

Catti-brie looked curiously at her father and breathed easier.

"No bother?" Roddy muttered, a sly look coming into his eye. "Never is, that one." Slowly and dramatically, the mountain man peeled back his hood, revealing his scars. "Never a bother, until ye don't expect what ye get!"

"Drow give ye that?" Bruenor asked, not overly alarmed or impressed. "Fancy scars—better'n most I seen."

"He killed my dog!" Roddy growled.

"Don't look dead to me," Bruenor quipped, drawing chuckles from every corner.

"My other dog," Roddy snarled, understanding where he stood with this stubborn dwarf. "Ye care not a thing for me, and well ye shouldn't. But it's not for myself that I'm hunting this one, and not for any bounty on his head. Ye ever heared o' Maldobar?"

Bruenor shrugged.

"North o' Sundabar," Roddy explained. "Small, peaceable place. Farmers all. One family, the Thistledowns, lived on the side o' town, three generations in a single house, as good families will. Bartholemew Thistledown was a good man, I tell ye, as his pa afore him, an' his children, four lads and a filly—much like yer own—standing tall and straight with a heart of spirit and a love o' the world."

Bruenor suspected where the burly man was leading, and by Catti-brie's uncomfortable shifting beside him, he figured that his perceptive daughter knew as well.

"Good family," Roddy mused, feigning a wispy, distant expression. "Nine in the house." The mountain man's visage hardened suddenly and he glared straight at Bruenor. "Nine died in the house," he declared. "Hacked by yer drow, and one ate up by his devil cat!"

Catti-brie tried to respond, but her words came out in a garbled shriek. Bruenor was glad of her confusion, for if she had spoken clearly, her argument would have given the mountain man more than Bruenor wanted him to know. The dwarf laid a hand across his daughter's shoulders, then answered Roddy calmly. "Ye've come to us with a dark tale. Ye shook me daughter, and I'm not for liking me daughter shook!"

"I beg yer forgivings kingly dwarf," Roddy said with a bow, "but ye must be told of the danger on yer door. Drow's a bad one, and so's his devil cat! I want no repeating o' the Maldobar tragedy."

"And ye'll get none in me halls," Bruenor assured him. "We're not simple farmers, take to yer heart. Drow won't be botherin' us any more'n ye've bothered us already."

Roddy wasn't surprised that Bruenor wouldn't help him, but he knew well that the dwarf, or at least the girl, knew more about Drizzt's whereabouts than they had let on. "If not for me, then for Bartholemew Thistledown, I beg ye, good dwarf. Tell me if ye know where I might find the black demon. Or if ye don't know, then give me some soldiers to help me sniff him out."

"Me dwarves've much to do with the melt," Bruenor explained. "Can't be spared chasin' another's fiends." Bruenor really didn't care one way or another for Roddy's gripe with the drow, but the mountain man's story did confirm the dwarf's belief that the dark elf should be avoided, particularly by his daughter. Bruenor actually might have helped Roddy and been done with it, more to get them both out of his valley than for any moral reasons, but he couldn't ignore Catti-brie's obvious distress.

Roddy unsuccessfully tried to hide his anger, looking for some other option. "Where would ye go if ye was runnin', King Bruenor?" he asked. "Ye know the mountain better'n any living, so Cassius telled me. Where should I look?"

Bruenor found that he liked seeing the unpleasant human so distressed. "Big valley," he said cryptically. "Wide mountain. Lot o' holes." He sat quiet for a long moment, shaking his head.

Roddy's facade blew away altogether. "Ye'd help the murderin' drow?" he roared. "Ye call yerself a king, but ye'd . . ."

Bruenor leaped up from his stone throne, and Roddy backed away a cautious step and dropped a hand to Bleeder's handle.

"I've the word o' one rogue against another rogue!" Bruenor growled at him. "One's as good—as bad!—as the other, by me guess!"

"Not by a Thistledown's guess!" Roddy cried, and his dog, sensing his outrage, bared its teeth and growled menacingly.

Bruenor looked at the strange, yellow beast curiously. It was getting near dinnertime and arguments did so make Bruenor hungry! How might a yellow dog fill his belly? he wondered.

"Have ye nothing more to give to me?" Roddy demanded.

"I could give ye me boot," Bruenor growled back. Several well-armed dwarf soldiers moved in close to make certain that the volatile human didn't do anything foolish. "I'd offer ye supper," Bruenor continued, "but ye smell too bad for me table, and ye don't seem the type what'd be takin' a bath."

Roddy yanked his dog's rope and stormed away, banging his heavy boots and slamming through each door he came upon. At Bruenor's nod, four soldiers followed the mountain man to make certain that he left without any unfortunate incidents. In the formal audience hall, the others laughed and howled about the way their king had handled the human.

Catti-brie didn't join in on the mirth, Bruenor noted, and the dwarf thought he knew why. Roddy's tale, true or not, had instilled some doubts in the girl.

"So now ye have it," Bruenor said to her roughly, trying to push her over the edge in their running argument. "The drow's a hunted killer. Now ye'll take me warnings to heart, girl!"

Catti-brie's lips disappeared in a bitter bite. Drizzt had not told her much about his life on the surface, but she could not believe that this drow whom she had come to know would be capable of murder. Neither could Catti-brie deny the obvious: Drizzt was a dark elf, and to her more experienced father, at least, that fact alone gave credence to McGristle's tale.

"Ye hear me, girl?" Bruenor growled.

"Ye've got to get them all together," Catti-brie said suddenly. "The drow and Cassius, and ugly Roddy McGristle. Ye've got to—"

"Not me problem!" Bruenor roared, cutting her short. Tears came quickly to Catti-brie's soft eyes in the face of her father's sudden rage. All the world seemed to turn over before her. Drizzt was in danger, and more so was the truth about his past. Just as stinging to Catti-brie, her father, whom she had loved and admired for all her remembered life, seemed now to turn a deaf ear to the calls for justice.

In that horrible moment, Catti-brie did the only thing an eleven-year-old could do against such odds—she turned from Bruenor and fled.

⚔ ⚔ ⚔ ⚔ ⚔

Catti-brie didn't really know what she meant to accomplish when she found herself running along the lower trails of Kelvin's Cairn, breaking her promise to Bruenor. Catti-brie could not refuse her desire to come, though she had little to offer Drizzt beyond a warning that McGristle was looking for him.

She couldn't sort through all the worries, but then she stood before the drow and understood the real reason she had ventured out. It was not for Drizzt that she had come, though she wanted him safe. It was for her own peace.

"Ye never speaked o' the Thistledowns of Maldobar," she said icily in greeting, stealing the drow's smile. The dark expression that crossed Drizzt's face clearly showed his pain.

Thinking that Drizzt, by his melancholy, had accepted blame for the tragedy, the wounded girl spun and tried to flee. Drizzt caught her by the shoulder, though, turned her about, and held her close. He would be a damned thing indeed if this girl, who had accepted him with all her heart, came to believe the lies.

"I killed no one," Drizzt whispered above Catti-brie's sobs, "except the monsters that slew the Thistledowns. On my word!" He recounted the tale then, in full, even telling of his flight from Dove Falconhand's party.

"And now I am here," he concluded, "wishing to put the experience behind me, though never, on my word, shall I ever forget it!"

"Ye weave two tales apart," Catti-brie replied. "Yerself an' McGristle, I mean."

"McGristle?" Drizzt gasped as though his breath had been blasted from his body. Drizzt hadn't seen the burly man in years and had thought Roddy to be a thing of his distant past.

"Came in today," Catti-brie explained. "Big man with a yellow dog. He's hunting ye."

The confirmation overwhelmed Drizzt. Would he ever escape his past? he wondered. If not, how could he ever hope to find acceptance?

"McGristle said ye killed them," Catti-brie continued.

"Then you have our words alone," Drizzt reasoned, "and there is no evidence to prove either tale." The ensuing silence seemed to go for hours.

"Never did like that ugly brute." Catti-brie sniffed, and she managed her first smile since she had met McGristle.

The affirmation of their friendship struck Drizzt profoundly, but he could not forget the trouble that was now hovering all about him. He would have to fight Roddy, and maybe others if the bounty hunter could stir up resentment—not a difficult task considering Drizzt's heritage. Or Drizzt would have to run away, again accept the road as his home.

"What'll ye do?" Catti-brie asked, sensing his distress.

"Do not fear for me," Drizzt assured her, and he gave her a hug as he spoke, one that he knew might be his way of saying good-bye. "The day grows long. You must get back to your home."

"He'll find ye," Catti-brie replied grimly.

"No," Drizzt said calmly. "Not soon anyway. With Guenhwyvar by my side, we will keep Roddy McGristle away until I can figure my best course. Now, be off! The night comes swiftly and I do not believe that your father would appreciate your coming here."

The reminder that she would have to face Bruenor again set Catti-brie in motion. She bid Drizzt farewell and turned away, then rushed back up to the drow and threw a hug around him. Her step was lighter as she moved back down the mountain. She hadn't resolved anything for Drizzt, at least as far as she knew, but the drow's troubles seemed a distant second compared to her own relief that her friend was not the monster some claimed him to be.

The night would be dark indeed for Drizzt Do'Urden. He had thought McGristle a long-distant problem, but the menace was here now, and none save Catti-brie had jumped to his defense.

He would have to stand alone—again—if he meant to stand at all. He had no allies beyond Guenhwyvar and his own scimitars, and the prospects of battling McGristle—win or lose—did not appeal to him.

"This is no home," Drizzt muttered to the frosty wind. He pulled out the onyx figurine and called to his panther companion. "Come, my friend," he said to the cat. "Let us be away before our adversary is upon us."

Guenhwyvar kept an alert guard while Drizzt packed up his possessions, while the road-weary drow emptied his home.

# 25
# Dwarven Banter

Catti-brie heard the growling dog, but she had no time to react when the huge man leaped out from behind a boulder and grabbed her roughly by the arm. "I knowed ye knowed!" McGristle cried, putting his foul breath right in the girl's face.

Catti-brie kicked him in the shin. "Ye let me go!" she retorted. Roddy was surprised that she had no trace of fear in her voice. He gave her a good shake when she tried to kick him again.

"Ye came to the mountain for a reason," Roddy said evenly, not relaxing his grip. "Ye came to see the drow—I knowed that ye was friends with that one. Seen it in yer eyes! "

"Ye know not a thing!" Catti-brie spat in his face. "Ye talk in lies."

"So the drow told ye his story o' the Thistledowns, eh?" Roddy replied, easily guessing the girl's meaning. Catti-brie knew then that she had erred in her anger, had given the wretch confirmation of her destination.

"The drow?" Catti-brie said absently. "I'm not for guessing what ye're speaking about."

Roddy's laughter mocked her. "Ye been with the drow, girl. Ye've said it plain enough. And now ye're goin' to take me to see him."

Catti-brie sneered at him, drawing another rough shake.

Roddy's grimace softened then, suddenly, and Catti-brie liked even less the look that came into his eye. "Ye're a spirited girl, ain't ye?" Roddy purred, grabbing Catti-brie's other shoulder and turning her to face him squarely. "Full o' life, eh? Ye'll take me to the drow, girl, don't ye doubt. But mighten be there's other things we can do first, things to show ye not to cross the likes o' Roddy McGristle." His caress on Catti-brie's cheek seemed ridiculously grotesque, but horribly and undeniably threatening, and Catti-brie thought she would gag.

It took every bit of Catti-brie's fortitude to face up to Roddy at that moment. She was only a young girl but had been raised among the grim-faced dwarves of Clan Battlehammer, a proud and rugged group. Bruenor was a fighter, and so was his daughter. Catti-brie's knee found Roddy's groin, and as his grip suddenly relaxed, the girl brought one hand up to claw at his face. She kneed him a second time, with less effect, but Roddy's defensive twist allowed her to pull away, almost free.

Roddy's iron grip tightened suddenly around her wrist, and they struggled for just a moment. Then Catti-brie felt an equally rough grab at her free hand and before she could understand what had happened, she was pulled from Roddy's grasp and a dark form stepped by her.

"So ye come to face yer fate," Roddy snarled delightedly at Drizzt.

"Run off," Drizzt told Catti-brie. "This is not your affair." Catti-brie, shaken and terribly afraid, did not argue.

Roddy's gnarled hands clenched Bleeder's handle. The bounty hunter had faced the drow in battle before and had no intention of trying to keep up with that one's agile steps and twists. With a nod, he loosed his dog.

The dog got halfway to Drizzt, was just about to leap at him, when Guenhwyvar buried it, rolling it far to the side. The dog came back to its feet, not seriously wounded but backing off several steps every time the panther roared in its face.

"Enough of this," Drizzt said, suddenly serious. "You have pursued me through years and leagues. I salute your resilience, but your anger is misplaced, I tell you. I did not kill the Thistledowns. Never would I have raised a blade against them!"

"To Nine Hells with the Thistledowns!" Roddy roared back. "Ye think that's what this is about?"

"My head would not bring you your bounty," Drizzt retorted.

"To Nine Hells with the gold!" Roddy yelled. "Ye took my dog, drow, an' my ear!" He banged a dirty finger against the side of his scarred face.

Drizzt wanted to argue, wanted to remind Roddy that it was he who had initiated the fight, and that his own axe swing had felled the tree that had torn his face. But Drizzt understood Roddy's motivation and knew that mere words would not soothe. Drizzt had wounded Roddy's pride, and to a man like Roddy that injury far outweighed any physical pain.

"I want no fight," Drizzt offered firmly. "Take your dog and be gone, on your word alone that you'll pursue me no longer."

Roddy's mocking laughter sent a shudder up Drizzt's spine. "I'll chase ye to the ends o' the world, drow!" Roddy roared. "And I'll find ye every time. No hole's deep enough to keep me from ye. No sea's wide enough! I'll have ye, drow. I'll have ye now or, if ye run, I'll have ye later!"

Roddy flashed a yellow-toothed smile and cautiously stalked toward Drizzt. "I'll have ye drow," the bounty hunter growled again quietly. A sudden rush brought him close and Bleeder swiped across wildly. Drizzt hopped back.

A second strike promised similar results, but Roddy, instead of following through, came with a deceptively quick backhand that glanced Drizzt's chin.

He was on Drizzt in an instant, his axe whipping furiously every which way. "Stand still!" Roddy cried as Drizzt deftly sidestepped, hopped over, or ducked under each blow. Drizzt knew that he was taking a dangerous chance in not countering the wicked blows, but he hoped that if he could tire the burly man, he might still find a more peaceful solution.

Roddy was agile and quick for a big man, but Drizzt was far quicker, and the drow believed that he could play the game a good while longer.

Bleeder came in a side swipe, diving across at Drizzt's chest. The attack was a feint, with Roddy wanting Drizzt to duck under so that he might kick the drow in the face.

Drizzt saw through the deception. He leaped instead of ducked, turned a somersault above the cutting axe, and came down lightly, even closer to Roddy. Now Drizzt did wade in, punching with both scimitar hilts straight into Roddy's face. The bounty hunter staggered backward, feeling warm blood rolling out of his nose.

"Go away," Drizzt said sincerely. "Take your dog back to Maldobar, or wherever it is that you call home."

If Drizzt believed that Roddy would surrender in the face of further humiliation, he was badly mistaken. Roddy bellowed in rage and charged straight in, dipping his shoulder in an attempt to bury the drow.

Drizzt pounded his weapon hilts down onto Roddy's dipped head and launched himself into a forward roll right over Roddy's back. The bounty hunter went down hard but came quickly to his knees, drawing and firing a dagger at Drizzt even as the drow turned back.

Drizzt saw the silvery flicker at the last instant and snapped a blade down to deflect the weapon. Another dagger followed, and another after that, and each time, Roddy advanced a step on the distracted drow.

"I'm knowing yer tricks, drow," Roddy said with an evil grin. Two quick steps brought him right up to Drizzt and Bleeder again sliced in.

Drizzt dived into a sidelong roll and came up a few feet away. Roddy's continuing confidence began to unnerve Drizzt; he had hit the bounty hunter with blows that would have dropped most men, and he wondered how much damage the burly human could withstand. That thought led Drizzt to the inevitable conclusion that he might have to start hitting Roddy with more than his scimitar hilts.

Again Bleeder came from the side. This time, Drizzt did not dodge. He stepped within the arc of the axe blade and blocked with one weapon, leaving Roddy open for a strike with the other scimitar. Three quick right jabs closed one of Roddy's eyes, but the bounty hunter only grinned and charged, catching hold of Drizzt and bearing the lighter combatant to the ground.

Drizzt squirmed and slapped, understanding that his conscience had betrayed him. In such close quarters, he could not match Roddy's strength, and his limited movements destroyed his advantage of speed. Roddy held his position on top and maneuvered one arm to chop down with Bleeder.

A yelp from his yellow dog was the only warning he got, and that didn't register enough for him to avoid the panther's rush. Guenhwyvar bowled Roddy off Drizzt, slamming him to the ground. The burly man kept his wits enough to swipe at the panther as it continued past, nicking Guenhwyvar on the rear flank.

The stubborn dog came rushing in, but Guenhwyvar recovered, pivoted right around Roddy, and drove it away.

When Roddy turned back to Drizzt, he was met by a savage flurry of scimitar blows that he could not follow and could not counter. Drizzt had seen the strike on the panther and the fires in his lavender eyes no longer indicated compromise. A hilt smashed Roddy's face, followed by the flat of the other blade. A foot kicked his stomach, his chest, and his groin in what seemed a single motion. Impervious, Roddy accepted it all with a snarl, but the enraged drow pressed on. One scimitar caught again under the axe head, and Roddy moved to charge, thinking to bear Drizzt to the ground once more.

Drizzt's second weapon struck first, though, slicing across Roddy's forearm. The bounty hunter recoiled, grasping at his wounded limb as Bleeder fell to the ground.

Drizzt never slowed. His rush caught Roddy off guard and several kicks and punches left the man reeling. Drizzt then leaped high into the air and kicked straight out with both feet, connecting squarely on Roddy's jaw and dropping him heavily to the ground. Still Roddy shrugged it off and tried to rise, but this time, the bounty hunter felt the edges of two scimitars come to rest on opposite sides of his throat.

"I told you to be on your way," Drizzt said grimly, not moving his blades an inch but letting Roddy feel the cold metal acutely.

"Kill me," Roddy said calmly, sensing a weakness in his opponent, "if ye got the belly for it!"

Drizzt hesitated, but his scowl did not soften. "Be on your way," he said with as much calm as he could muster, calm that denied the coming trial he knew he would face.

Roddy laughed at him. "Kill me, ye black-skinned devil!" he roared, bulling his way, though he remained on his knees, toward Drizzt. "Kill me or I'll catch ye! Not for doubtin', drow. I'll hunt ye to the corners o' the world and under it if need!"

Drizzt blanched and glanced at Guenhwyvar for support.

"Kill me!" Roddy cried, bordering on hysteria. He grabbed Drizzt's wrists and pulled them forward. Lines of bright blood appeared on both sides of the man's neck. "Kill me as ye killed my dog!"

Horrified, Drizzt tried to pull away, but Roddy's grip was like iron.

"Ye got not the belly for it?" the bounty hunter bellowed. "Then I'll help ye!" He jerked the wrists sharply against Drizzt's pull, cutting deeper lines, and if the crazed man felt pain, it did not show through his unyielding grin.

Waves of jumbled emotions assaulted Drizzt. He wanted to kill Roddy at that moment, more out of stupefied frustration than vengeance, and yet he knew that he could not. As far as Drizzt knew, Roddy's only crime was an unwarranted hunt against him and that was not reason enough. For all that he held dear, Drizzt had to respect a human life, even one as wretched as Roddy McGristle's.

"Kill me!" Roddy shouted over and over, taking lewd pleasure in the drow's growing disgust.

"No!" Drizzt screamed in Roddy's face with enough force to silence the bounty hunter. Enraged to a point where he could not contain his trembling, Drizzt did not wait to see if Roddy would resume his insane cry. He drove a knee into Roddy's chin, pulled his wrists free of Roddy's grasp, then slammed his weapon hilts simultaneously into the bounty hunter's temples.

Roddy's eyes crossed, but he did not swoon, stubbornly shaking the blow away. Drizzt slammed him again and again, finally beating him down, horrified at his own actions and at the bounty hunter's continuing defiance.

When the rage had played itself out, Drizzt stood over the burly man, trembling and with tears rimming his lavender eyes. "Drive that dog far away!" he yelled to Guenhwyvar. Then he dropped his bloodied blades in horror and bent down to make sure that Roddy was not dead.

⚔ ⚔ ⚔ ⚔ ⚔

Roddy awoke to find his yellow dog standing over him. Night was fast falling and the wind had picked up again. His head and arm ached, but he dismissed the pain, wanting only to resume his hunt, confident now that

Drizzt would never find the strength to kill him. His dog caught the scent at once, leading back to the south, and they set off. Roddy's nerve dissipated only a little when they came around a rocky outcropping and found a red-bearded dwarf and a girl waiting for him.

"Ye don't be touchin' me girl, McGristle," Bruenor said evenly. "Ye just shouldn't be touchin' me girl."

"She's in league with the drow!" Roddy protested. "She told the murdering devil of my comin'!"

"Drizzt's not a murderer!" Catti-brie yelled back. "He never did kill the farmers! He says ye're saying that just so others'll help ye to catch him!" Catti-brie realized suddenly that she had just admitted to her father that she had met with the drow. When Catti-brie had found Bruenor, she had told him only of McGristle's rough handling.

"Ye went to him," Bruenor said, obviously wounded. "Ye lied to me, an' ye went to the drow! I telled ye not to. Ye said ye wouldn't . . ."

Bruenor's lament stung Catti-brie profoundly, but she held fast to her beliefs. Bruenor had raised her to be honest, but that included being honest to what she knew was right. "Once ye said to me that everyone gets his due," Catti-brie retorted. "Ye telled me that each is different and each should be seen for what he is. I've seen Drizzt, and seen him true, I tell ye. He's no killer! And he's—" She pointed accusingly at McGristle—"a liar! I take no pride in me own lie, but never could I let Drizzt get caught by this one!"

Bruenor considered her words for a moment, then wrapped one arm about her waist and hugged her tightly. His daughter's deception still stung, but the dwarf was proud that his girl had stood up for what she believed. In truth, Bruenor had come out here, not looking for Catti-brie, whom he believed was sulking in the mines, but to find the drow. The more he recounted his fight with the remorhaz, the more Bruenor became convinced that Drizzt had come down to help him, not to fight him. Now, in light of recent events, few doubts remained.

"Drizzt came and pulled me free of that one," Catti-brie went on. "He saved me."

"Drow's got her mixed," Roddy said, sensing Bruenor's growing attitude and wanting no fight with the dangerous dwarf. "He's a murderin' dog, I say, and so would Bartholemew Thistledown if a dead man could!"

"Bah!" Bruenor snorted. "Ye don't know me girl or ye'd be thinking the better than to call her a liar. And I telled ye before, McGristle, that I don't like me daughter shook! Me thinkin's that ye should be gettin' outa me valley. Me thinkin's that ye should be goin' now."

Roddy growled and so did his dog, which sprung between the mountain man and the dwarf and bared its teeth at Bruenor. Bruenor shrugged, unconcerned, and growled back at the beast, provoking it further.

The dog lurched at the dwarf's ankle, and Bruenor promptly put a heavy boot in its mouth and pinned its bottom jaw to the ground. "And take yer stinkin' dog with ye!"

Bruenor roared, though in admiring the dog's meaty flank, he was thinking again that he might have better use for the surly beast.

"I go where I choose, dwarf!" Roddy retorted. "I'm gonna get me a drow, and if the drow's in yer valley, then so am I!"

Bruenor recognized the clear frustration in the man's voice, and he took closer note then of the bruises on Roddy's face and the gash on his arm. "The drow got away from ye," the dwarf said, and his chuckle stung Roddy acutely.

"Not for long," Roddy promised. "And no dwarf'll stand in my way!"

"Get along back to the mines," Bruenor said to Catti-brie. "Tell the others I mighten be a bit late for dinner." The axe came down from Bruenor's shoulder.

"Get him good," Catti-brie mumbled under her breath, not doubting her father's prowess in the least. She kissed Bruenor atop his helmet, then rushed off happily. Her father had trusted her; nothing in all the world could be wrong.

⚔ ⚔ ⚔ ⚔ ⚔

Roddy McGristle and his three-legged dog left the valley a short while later. Roddy had seen a weakness in Drizzt and thought he could win against the drow, but he saw no such signs in Bruenor Battlehammer. When Bruenor had Roddy down, a feat that hadn't taken very long, Roddy did not doubt for a second that if he had asked the dwarf to kill him, Bruenor gladly would have complied.

From the top of the southern climb, where he had gone for his last look at Ten-Towns, Drizzt watched the wagon roll out of the vale, suspecting that it was the bounty hunter's. Not knowing what it all meant, but hardly believing that Roddy had undergone a change of heart, Drizzt looked down at his packed belongings and wondered where he should turn next.

The lights of the towns were coming on now, and Drizzt watched them with mixed emotions. He had been on this climb several times, enchanted by his surroundings and thinking he had found his home. How different now was this view! McGristle's appearance had given Drizzt pause and reminded him that he was still an outcast, and ever to be one.

"Drizzit," he mumbled to himself, a damning word indeed. At that moment, Drizzt did not believe he would ever find a home, did not believe that a drow who was not in heart a drow had a place in all the realms, surface or Underdark. The hope, ever fleeting in Drizzt's weary heart, had flown altogether.

"Bruenor's Climb, this place is called," said a gruff voice behind Drizzt. He spun about, thinking to flee, but the red-bearded dwarf was too close for him to slip by. Guenhwyvar rushed to the drow's side, teeth bared.

"Put yer pet away, elf," Bruenor said. "If cat tastes as bad as dog, I'll want none of it!

"My place, this is," the dwarf went on, "me bein' Bruenor and this bein' Bruenor's Climb!"

"I saw no sign of ownership," Drizzt replied indignantly, his patience exhausted from the long road that now seemed to grow longer. "I know your claim now, and so I will leave. Take heart, dwarf. I shall not return."

Bruenor put a hand up, both to silence the drow and to stop him from leaving. "Just a pile o' rocks," he said, as close to an apology as Bruenor had ever given. "I named it as me own, but does that make it so? Just a damned piled o' rocks!"

Drizzt cocked his head at the dwarf's unexpected rambling.

"Nothin's what it seems, drow!" Bruenor declared. "Nothin'! Ye try to follow what ye know, ye know? But then ye find that ye know not what ye thought ye knowed! Thought a dog'd be tastin' good—looked good enough—but now me belly's cursing me every move!"

The second mention of the dog sparked a sudden revelation concerning Roddy McGristle's departure. "You sent him away," Drizzt said, pointing down to the route out of the vale. "You drove McGristle off my trail."

Bruenor hardly heard him, and certainly wouldn't have admitted the kind-hearted deed, in any case. "Never trusted humans," he said evenly. "Never know what one's about, and when ye find out, too many's the time it's too late for fixin'! But always had me thoughts straight about other folks. An elf's an elf, after all, and so's a gnome. And orcs are straight-out stupid and ugly. Never knew one to be otherways, an' I known a few!" Bruenor patted his axe, and Drizzt did not miss his meaning.

"So was me thoughts about the drow," Bruenor continued. "Never met one—never wanted to. Who would, I ask? Drow're bad, mean-hearted, so I been telled by me dad an' by me dad's dad, an' by any who's ever telled me." He looked out to the lights of Termalaine on Maer Dualdon in the west, shook his head, and kicked a stone. "Now I heared a drow's prowlin' about me valley, and what's a king to do? Then me daughter goes to him!" A sudden fire came into Bruenor's eyes, but it mellowed quickly, almost as if in embarrassment, as soon as he looked at Drizzt. "She lies in me face—never has she done that afore, and never again if she's a smart one!"

"It was not her fault," Drizzt began, but Bruenor waved his hands about wildly to dismiss the whole thing.

"Thought I knowed what I knowed," Bruenor continued after a short pause, his voice almost a lament. "Had the world figured, sure enough. Easy to do when ye stay in yer own hole."

He looked back to Drizzt, straight into the dim shine of the drow's lavender eyes. "Bruenor's Climb?" the dwarf asked with a resigned shrug. "What's it mean, drow, to put a name on a pile o' rocks? Thought I knowed, I did, an' thought a dog'd taste good." Bruenor rubbed a hand over his belly and frowned. "Call it a pile o' rocks then, an' I've no claim on it more'n yerself! Call it Drizzt's Climb then, an' ye'd be kicking me out!"

"I would not," Drizzt replied quietly. "I do not know that I could if I wished to!"

"Call it what ye will!" Bruenor cried, suddenly distressed. "And call a dog a cow—that don't change the way the thing'll taste!" Bruenor threw up his hands, flustered, and turned away, stomping down the rock path, grumbling with every step.

"And ye be keepin' yer eyes on me girl," Drizzt heard Bruenor snarl above his general grumbles, "if she's so orc-headed as to keep goin' to the stinkin' yeti an' worm-filled mountain! Be knowin' that I hold yerself . . ." The rest faded away as Bruenor disappeared around a bend.

Drizzt couldn't begin to dig his way through that rambling dialogue, but he didn't need to put Bruenor's speech in perfect order. He dropped a hand on Guenhwyvar, hoping that the panther shared the suddenly wondrous panoramic view. Drizzt knew then that he would sit up on the climb, Bruenor's Climb, many times and watch the lights flicker to life, for, adding up all that the dwarf had said, Drizzt surmised one phrase clearly, words he had waited so many years to hear:

Welcome home.

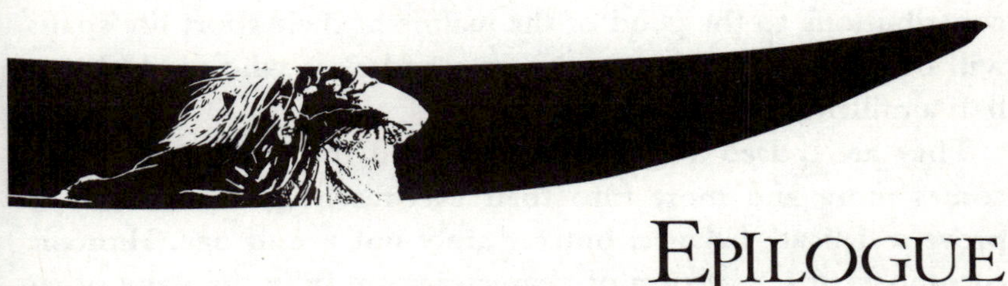

# EPILOGUE

Of all the races in the known realms, none is more confusing, or more confused, than humans. Mooshie convinced me that gods, rather than being outside entities, are personifications of what lies in our hearts. If this is true, then the many, varied gods of the human sects–deities of vastly different demeanors–reveal much about the race.

If you approach a halfling, or an elf, or a dwarf, or any of the other races, good and bad, you have a fair idea of what to expect. There are exceptions, of course; I name myself as one most fervently! But a dwarf is likely to be gruff, though fair, and I have never met an elf, or even heard of one, that preferred a cave to the open sky. A human's preference, though, is his own to know–if even he can sort it out.

In terms of good and evil, then, the human race must be judged most carefully. I have battled vile human assassins, witnessed human wizards so caught up in their power that they mercilessly destroyed all other beings in their paths, and seen cities where groups of humans preyed upon the unfortunate of their own race, living in kingly palaces while other men and women, and even children, starved and died in the gutters of the muddy streets. But

I have met other humans—Catti-brie, Mooshie, Wulfgar, Agorwal of Termalaine—whose honor could not be questioned and whose contributions to the good of the realms in their short life spans will outweigh that of most dwarves and elves who might live a half a millennium and more.

They are indeed a confusing race, and the fate of the world comes more and more into their ever-reaching hands. It may prove a delicate balance, but certainly not a dull one. Humans encompass the spectrum of character more fully than any other beings; they are the only "goodly" race that wages war upon itself—with alarming frequency.

The surface elves hold out hope in the end. They who have lived the longest and seen the birth of many centuries take faith that the human race will mature to goodness, that the evil in it will crush itself to nothingness, leaving the world to those who remain.

In the city of my birth I witnessed the limitations of evil, the self-destruction and inability to achieve higher goals, even goals based upon the acquisition of power. For this reason, I, too, will hold out hope for the humans, and for the realms. As they are the most varied, so too are humans the most malleable, the most able to disagree with that within themselves that they learn to be false.

My very survival has been based upon my belief that there is a higher purpose to this life: that principles are a reward in and of themselves. I cannot, therefore, look forward in despair, but rather with higher hopes for all in mind and with the determination that I might help to reach those heights.

This is my tale, then, told as completely as I can recall and as completely as I choose to divulge. Mine has been a long road filled with ruts and barriers, and only now that I have put so much so far behind me am I able to recount it honestly.

I will never look back on those days and laugh; the toll was too great for humor to seep through. I do often remember Zaknafein, though, and Belwar and Mooshie, and all the other friends I have left behind.

I have often wondered, too, of the many enemies I have faced, of the many lives my blades have ended. Mine has been a violent life in a violent world, full of enemies to myself and to all that I hold dear. I have been praised for the perfect cut of my scimitars, for my abilities in battle, and I must admit that I have many times allowed myself to feel pride in those hard-earned skills.

Whenever I remove myself from the excitement and consider the whole more fully, though, I lament that things could not have been different. It pains me to remember Masoj Hun'ett, the only drow I ever killed; it was he who initiated our battle and he certainly would have killed me if I had not proven the stronger. I can justify my actions on that fated day, but never will I be comfortable with their necessity. There should be a better way than the sword.

In a world so filled with danger, where orcs and trolls loom, seemingly, around every bend in the road, he who can fight is most often hailed as the hero and given generous applause. There is more to the mantle of "hero," I say, than strength of arm or prowess in battle. Mooshie was a hero, truly, because he overcame adversity, because he never blinked at unfavorable odds, and mostly because he acted within a code of clearly defined principles. Can less be said of Belwar Dissengulp, the handless deep gnome who befriended a renegade drow? Or of Clacker, who offered his own life rather than bring danger to his friends?

Similarly, I name Wulfgar of Icewind Dale a hero, who adhered to principle above battle lust. Wulfgar overcame the misperceptions of his savage boyhood, learned to see the world as a place of hope rather than a field of potential conquests. And Bruenor, the dwarf who taught Wulfgar that important difference, is as rightful a king as ever there was in all the realms. He embodies those tenets that his people hold most dear, and they will gladly defend Bruenor with their very lives, singing a song to him even with their dying breaths.

In the end, when he found the strength to deny Matron Malice,

**my father, too, was a hero. Zaknafein, who had lost his battle for principles and identity throughout most of his life, won in the end.**

**None of these warriors, though, outshines a young girl I came to know when I first traveled across Ten-Towns. Of all the people I have ever met, none has held themselves to higher standards of honor and decency than Catti-brie. She has seen many battles, yet her eyes sparkle clearly with innocence and her smile shines untainted. Sad will be the day, and let all the world lament, when a discordant tone of cynicism spoils the harmony of her melodic voice.**

**Often those who call me a hero speak solely of my battle prowess and know nothing of the principles that guide my blades. I accept their mantle for what it is worth, for their satisfaction and not my own. When Catti-brie names me so, then will I allow my heart to swell with the satisfaction of knowing that I have been judged for my heart and not my sword arm; then will I dare to believe that the mantle is justified.**

**And so my tale ends—do I dare to say? I sit now in comfort beside my friend, the rightful king of Mithral Hall, and all is quiet and peaceful and prosperous. Indeed this drow has found his home and his place. But I am young, I must remind myself. I may have ten times the years remaining as those that have already passed. And for all my present contentment, the world remains a dangerous place, where a ranger must hold to his principles, but also to his weapons.**

**Do I dare to believe that my story is fully told?**

**I think not.**

**—Drizzt Do'Urden**

# FIELDING'S VIETNAM

# Fielding Titles

Fielding's Alaska Cruises/Inside Passage
Fielding's Amazon
Fielding's Australia
Fielding's Bahamas
Fielding's Belgium
Fielding's Bermuda
Fielding's Borneo
Fielding's Brazil
Fielding's Britain
Fielding's Budget Europe
Fielding's Caribbean
Fielding's Caribbean Cruises
Fielding's Caribbean East
Fielding's Caribbean West
Fielding's Europe
Fielding's European Cruises
Fielding's Far East
Fielding's France
Fielding's Freewheelin' USA
Fielding's Guide to the World's Most Dangerous Places
Fielding's Guide to Kenya's Best Hotels, Lodges & Homestays
Fielding's Hawaii
Fielding's Holland
Fielding's Italy
Fielding's Las Vegas Agenda
Fielding's London Agenda
Fielding's Los Angeles Agenda
Fielding's Malaysia and Singapore
Fielding's Mexico
Fielding's New York Agenda
Fielding's New Zealand
Fielding's Paris Agenda
Fielding's Portugal
Fielding's Rome Agenda
Fielding's San Diego Agenda
Fielding's Scandinavia
Fielding's Southeast Asia
Fielding's Southern Vietnam on Two Wheels
*Fielding's Spain*
*Fielding's Thailand Including Cambodia, Laos, Myanmar*
Fielding's Vacation Places Rated
Fielding's Vietnam
Fielding's Worldwide Cruises
The Indiana Jones Survival Guide

# FIELDING'S VIETNAM

## The Adventurous Up-to-the-Minute Guide

by

**Wink Dulles**

Fielding Worldwide, Inc.

308 South Catalina Avenue

Redondo Beach, California 90277 U.S.A.

Fielding's Vietnam
Published by Fielding Worldwide, Inc.


**FIELDING WORLDWIDE INC.**

PUBLISHER AND CEO **Robert Young Pelton**
GENERAL MANAGER **John Guillebeaux**
MARKETING DIRECTOR **Paul T. Snapp**
ELECTRONIC PUBLISHING DIRECTOR **Larry E. Hart**
PUBLIC RELATIONS DIRECTOR **Beverly Riess**
ACCOUNT SERVICES MANAGER **Christy Harp**
PROJECT MANAGER **Chris Snyder**
DATABASE PUBLISHING MANAGER **Jacki VanderVoort**

**EDITORS**

**Kathy Knoles** **Linda Charlton**

**PRODUCTION**

**Ron Franco** **Martin Mancha**
**Gini Sardo-Martin** **Ramses Reynoso**
**Craig South** **Janice Whitby**

COVER DESIGNED BY **Digital Artists**
COVER PHOTOGRAPHERS — Front Cover **Mike Yamashita**
Background Photo, Front Cover **Mike Yamashita**
Back Cover **Mike Yamashita**
INSIDE PHOTOS **Wink Dulles, Mike Yamashita**



Inquiries should be addressed to: Fielding Worldwide, Inc., 308 South Catalina Ave., Redondo Beach, California 90277 U.S.A., ☎ *(310) 372-4474*, Facsimile *(310) 376-8064*, 8:30 a.m.–5:30 p.m. Pacific Standard Time.

ISBN 1-56952-095-X

Printed in the United States of America

# Letter from the Publisher

In 1946, Temple Fielding began the first of what would be a remarkable new series of well-written, highly personalized guidebooks for independent travelers. Temple's opinionated, witty, and oft-imitated books have assisted travelers ever since we guided tourists through postwar Europe. More important to some was Fielding's humorous and direct method of steering travelers away from the dull and the insipid. Today, Fielding Travel Guides are still written by experienced travelers for experienced travelers. Our authors carry on Fielding's reputation for creating travel experiences that deliver insight with a sense of discovery and style.

Wink Dulles personifies the Fielding attitude: seasoned, bright, obsessed with detail, and born to seek out new experiences for travelers. He has created the most enlightening travel guide available on post-embargo Vietnam. Wink bought a beat up 500cc motorcycle and drove down muddy roads and cow paths looking for the real Vietnam.

We are working with the Vietnamese government and local tour operators to build tourism from the ground up. Working closely with the only Vietnamese company based in the U.S., we have set up a selection of tours all custom-designed for the adventurous traveler. We have gained permission for access to old battlefields and set up military tours for Vietnam Vets, diving tours from Vietnamese junks that will impress even the most jaded and more. Just look in the back of the book for the selection of tours and give us a call.

Fielding Nam Hai is the name of our Vietnamese office based in Ho Chi Minh City. From there, we cover the Far East to keep our books up to date and relevant. When you are in Vietnam don't be shy about looking Wink up and telling him about your experiences. Write us and tell us what you think should be in subsequent updates.

Welcome to the new Fielding.

RYP

Robert Young Pelton

Publisher and C.E.O.

Fielding Worldwide, Inc.

# Letter from the Publisher

# ABOUT THE AUTHOR

**Wink Dulles**

Wink Dulles is the Southeast Asia correspondent for Fielding Worldwide. His articles have appeared in numerous national publications and his travel writings on Southeast Asia have been published in newspapers across the U.S. including *New York Newsday*, the *Salt Lake Tribune* and the *Santa Barbara News-Press.* Additionally, Dulles is a contributing editor for *AAA World* magazine, *Escape* magazine, and was Asia editor for *UFM* magazine. His travels through Cambodia, Thailand and Vietnam will continue to provide Fielding with an invaluable prospective on this burgeoning region of the world.

Ironically, Dulles, now a welcome part-time inhabitant of Vietnam, is the cousin of the late CIA Director Allen Dulles and former Secretary of State John Foster Dulles, who sent the first American military advisors into Vietnam in the 1950s after the French defeat in the First Indochina War. John Foster Dulles was considered "an enemy of the state," by Hanoi during his eight-year tenure as Secretary of State under President Dwight D. Eisenhower.

Dulles likes to think he lives in Bangkok, Thailand but he's usually somewhere in Southeast Asia faced with the grueling job of keeping Fielding's *Far East*, *Southeast Asia* and *Vietnam* the most up-to-date guides on the market.

# Fielding Rating Icons

**The Fielding Rating Icons are highly personal and awarded to help the besieged traveler choose from among the dizzying array of activities, attractions, hotels, restaurants and sights. The awarding of an icon denotes unusual or exceptional qualities in the relevant category.**

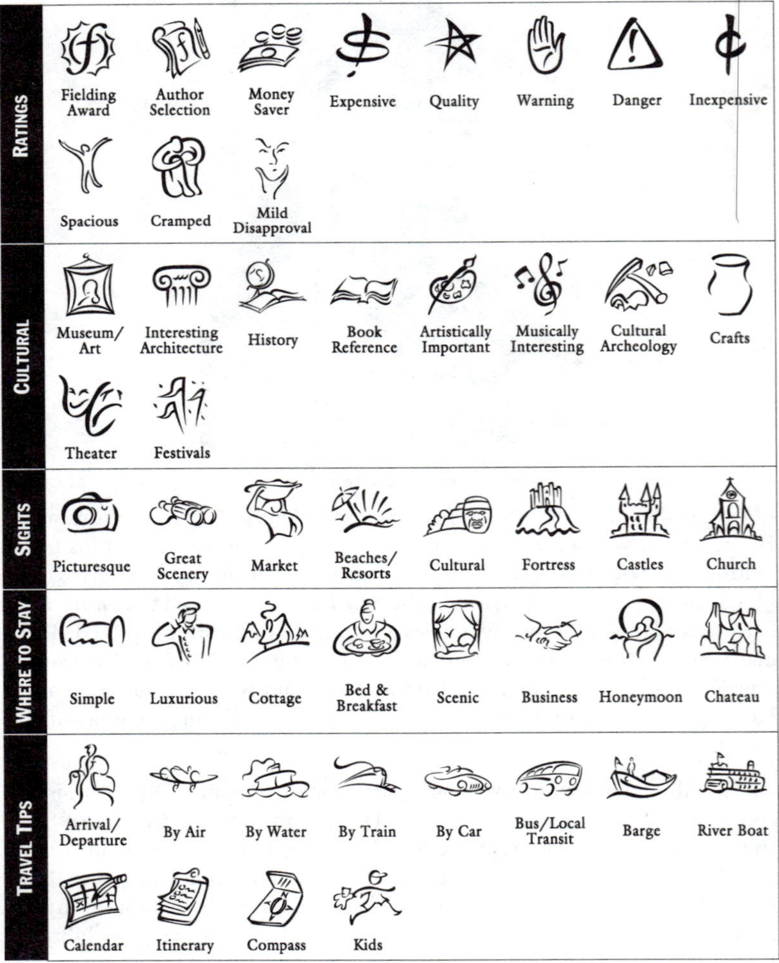

Activities
Downhill Skiing
X-country Skiing
Water Sports
Sailing
Scuba Diving
Snorkeling/ Diving
Deep-sea Fishing
Freshwater Fishing
Swimming
Hiking
Walking
Relaxing
Golf
Tennis
Horseback Riding
General Sports
Cycling
Workout
Special Interest
Nightlife
Singles
Romantic
Nude Beaches
Lecture
Spectacular Cuisine
Wine Tasting
Shopping
Cafe Stops
Gardening
Pro Sports
Mystery

# Legend

## Essentials

Hotel
Youth Hostel
Restaurant
Bank
Telephone
Tourist Info.
Hospital
Pub/Bar
Post Office
Parking
Taxi
Subway
Metro
Market
Cinema
Theatre
Int'l Airport
Regional Airport
Police Station
Courthouse
Gov't. Building

Attraction
Military Airbase
Army Base
Naval base
Fort
University
School

## Historical

Archeological Site
Battleground
Castle
Monument
Museum
Ruin
Shipwreck

## Religious

Church
Buddhist Temple
Hindu Temple
Mosque
Pagoda
Synagogue

## Activities

Beach
Campground
Picnic Area
Golf Course
Boat Launch
Diving
Fishing
Water Skiing
Snow Skiing
Bird Sanctuary
Wildlife Sanctuary
Park
Park Headquarters
Mine
Lighthouse
Windmill
Cruise Port
View
Stadium
Building
Zoo

## Phyisical

International Boundary
County/Regional Boundary
**PARIS** National Capital
**Montego Bay** State/Parish Capital
**Los Angeles** Major City
**Quy Nhon** Town/Village
5 Motorway/Freeway
163 Highway
Primary Road
Secondary Road
Subway

Biking Route
Hiking Trail
Dirt Road
Railroad
RR Railroad Station
Ferry Route
Mountain Peak
Lake
River
Cave
Coral Reef

# ACKNOWLEDGEMENTS

***Fielding guide "Johnny" Do Trong Tu has been in some dangerous places.***

The number of people I wish to thank for the preparation of Fielding's *Vietnam* in the countries of Vietnam, the U.S. and Thailand is vast, but they all deserve to be included in these pages. First and foremost I wish to thank Do Trong Tu, now the operations manager at Ho Chi Minh City's South Sea Travel, and formerly with Saigon Railway Tourist Company. Known by his American-given name "Johnny" during the Vietnam War, Tu provided an invaluable amount of time and expertise in the preparation of this publication. He is a guide of unequaled abilities in this large nation of more than 70 million people. His knowledge of all areas of Vietnam is unsurpassed by Vietnamese guides. By motorcycle, we explored the deepest regions of the Mekong Delta and traversed the coastal route National Highway 1 from

Saigon to Hue. It seemed that every kilometer he wanted to stop and explain the cultural customs, topography and history of the area. We crossed rivers on tiny, dilapidated ferries unknown to tourists during monsoons. I dumped my Honda motorcycle on several occasions in the muddy delta without complaint from him. He was able to secure Vietnamese prices at hotels and restaurants each place we stopped for food or rest (as a foreigner I would have been required to pay at least twice the amount that Tu was able to negotiate). This man knows personally two-thirds of the people living south of Saigon. The other one third are members of his extended family. Money was never an issue. He was simply in nirvana to travel with me. (Traveling without such a man in Vietnam is like crawling through the old Viet Cong Tunnels without light.) He was able to renew visas at a fraction of the cost of conventional travel agents. His life is traveling in his beloved homeland. The years he spent in the States during the 1960s gave him such an acute ability for the English language that the vast majority of Vietnamese he meets believe he is "Viet Khieu," an overseas Vietnamese from the United States. Tu was my guide and is now my trusted friend.

Trust is the first thing that needs to be established in working with the Vietnamese people. With Tu the trust came quickly, and our friendship negated any suspicions of selfishness I might have encountered with men of lesser human qualities. This is a man who is a true Vietnamese. Vietnam is not a war, but a country of friendly inhabitants who wish namely for the best fortune to be bestowed on their friends. Tu's human and professional qualities and qualifications transcend even the typically hospitable intentions and sentiments the Vietnamese have for visiting Americans. The war is over, and Tu is perhaps the man in Vietnam who truly knows this. Thank you *(com on)* Johnny. Tu can be reached at *FAX: 84-8-231071.* Or write him at his home: *322 Pham Van Hai Street, Ward 3, Tan Binh District, Ho Chi Minh City, Vietnam.* He'd love to hear from you if you're planning a visit to Vietnam and will enable you to get the most out of your visit.

For this second edition of Fielding's *Vietnam,* I am especially indebted to Miss Hoanh (you know who you are), who allowed me to tag along on a trip to the boonies.

I'd also like to thank Mr. Yellow River of the Hai Van Hotel in Saigon. His gracious hospitality and help in allowing me to communicate with the U.S. were essential to the success of this project. Also greatly helpful here were Miss Mai, Miss Lien and Mr. Kong. Also thanks to Khan, who introduced me to the sights of Ho Chi Minh City. Especially, I'd like also to thank Mr. Tran Phan Ngoc Hue and his lovely wife Hue, whose help in allowing me to utilize his computer equipment at both his shop and home in Saigon while my own was being repaired in Bangkok saved weeks of time in preparing this manuscript. Also thanks to Nguyen My Chau and Mamason Miss Long of Saigon.

There are countless others in Vietnam I'd like to mention, but the list would constitute a book in itself. In Thailand, I'd like to thank Mr. Pham Manh Hai, press attache at the Vietnamese embassy in Bangkok, as well as the staff at the 27 Hotel, a brothel on Sukhumvit Soi 22, that permitted me to keep mega-kilograms of luggage at the hotel for nearly six months at no cost.

In the U.S., I'd particularly like to thank Robert Young Pelton, an adventurer and the publisher of the Fielding guidebooks, who gave me the lifetime opportunity of preparing Fielding's *Vietnam*. Although his deadlines rival that of a major newspaper's city desk editor, he is a man of the world, who fully realizes the future connections that all nations of the globe will eventually share. Also at Fielding (in Redondo Beach, California), I received major support from Paul Snapp, director of marketing, as well as from editor Kathy Knoles, who handles my American affairs while I'm away from the country. I'd also like to especially thank Beverly Riess. If it wasn't for her, I'd still be driving a beer truck around Santa Barbara County. Also at Fielding, thanks to Larry Hart and Chris Snyder, the computer wizards (i.e., propeller heads) who, have helped make Fielding's *Vietnam* the best guidebook to Vietnam. To the countless others that have helped prepare this book, I say *Yo*!

And special thanks to my parents, Win and Patsy—who were there without being there.

# AUTHOR'S PREFACE

The day U.S. President Bill Clinton lifted the nation's debilitating trade embargo against Vietnam, I was scouring Ho Chi Minh City's dark alleys and market stalls in search of an elusive pair of earplugs in an effort to mute the din of progress, celebration and hope that was emitting from this bustling city of more than 5 million people. The cacophony of building construction swirling in the same audio cocktail with the ceaseless blasts of millions of deafening firecrackers marking the Tet New Year had become too much. Sleep had become merely brief, unrewarding windows of semiconsciousness; the Vietnamese were winning this Tet offensive.

Occasionally, I'd feel a tug on my sleeve. *"Hoa Ky?"* the passersby would inquire, usually adorned in a Chicago Bulls ball cap or an American flag covered T-shirt.

"*Toi la nguoi Hoa Ky,*" I'd respond. "Yes, I'm an American."

"Did you hear? America, Vietnam friends. President Clinton dropped the embargo I heard. Is this true?" Boom! Another fusillade of fireworks.

"I'm not sure," I'd say. "I've heard it, too."

The news stayed only a rumor, and derivatives of, for almost a full day. A cyclo driver approached me, said the embargo had been dropped, but that Clinton had only moments before rescinded the order after it was learned some tattered American POWs were still being held captive in caves in northwestern Vietnam. Then a motorcade whooshed down Central Saigon's Le Loi Blvd., past the Rex Hotel, accompanied by a dozen policemen on siren-spewing motorcycles. "See, they're still negotiating," another man said. "The man in the limousine, that was Premier Vo Van Kiet."

***There's no shortage of subjects for photo buffs throughout Vietnam.***

It hadn't been Vo, but rather the mayor of Saigon, more than likely on his way to dinner. But the Vietnamese on the street were caught up in the moment. This was historic, and suddenly the bursting of the firecrackers in the street took on a different context, and more than a few Saigonese were aware of it.

It was the next day at a computer store when I received confirmed information about the dropping of the embargo. It wasn't from the television. Nor the newspaper. Rather it was in the form of a huge sign that had been posted above the store, which hadn't been there the day before, and it was no less conclusive of the embargo's lifting than the opening of a U.S. embassy in Hanoi. The three letters beamed in a deep, freshly-painted lake blue, and they read "IBM."

The beggars still held their bowls in front of me, and the pickpockets continued to clamor for a better angle at my watch. Babies glazed with the milky, sickening white of advanced cataracts still groveled naked in the slick brown sludge on the sidewalk.

Yet, somehow, things were different. Not with the instantaneousness of a bomb, but rather with the expectancy of comfort that ensues after taking a time release medication. In Vietnam, that incubancy has persevered and festered through 15 years of war and another 20 of economic and social isolation and depravity.

## Guerillas in the Midst

Any world leader who chooses to self exile himself in New Jersey, as did Vietnam's Ngo Dinh Diem during the First Indochina War between 1945 and 1954, has left a place that has a real problem.

Conscripted Americans and soldiers of other aligned nationalities such as Australia, South Korea and Thailand—as well the Viet Cong and the untold millions of civilians—had probably the most gut-wrenching experiences ever confronted by those mentally and physically displaced by war. Armed men in this culturally and topographically idyllic Southeast Asian nation were ordered to burn, napalm, bulldoze and otherwise raze an area three times the size of Montana.

Yet there is not a lot of evidence left of the war in Vietnam. There are the craters left by B-52s near Cu Chi. Scrap metal shops line portions of National Highway 1 in the south near the shells of former U.S. military installations—still offering for sale rusted drivetrains and wheels scavenged from discarded American trucks and personnel carriers. Occasionally, one can spot bunkers in the sand dunes and gun turrets on the beach. There are Viet Cong tunnels in the south and near Quang Tri in central Vietnam.

Surprisingly, there is little testament left to the carnage, both on the ground and in the hearts of the Vietnamese people. What had been defoliated 30 years ago is now lush and verdant. North of Phan Thiet, the visitor notices a drastic change in the countryside—which turns from electric green to sunbaked brown—and often asks if the area had been defoliated. No, it hadn't been. It's simply an arid part of the country. The evidence of Agent Orange (nearly two tons were used during the war), is contained in the people rather than in the topography—children born in the south tend to be smaller than those in the north. The horrors of this pesticide seem to have seeped as deep into the soil as has Vietnamese animosity toward Americans.

Do we owe the Vietnamese a debt? It's a question most Americans to this day struggle with. But suffice it to say that each year dozens of Vietnamese are killed in search of mortar shells and dud grenades and other petty war materiel to sell to American tourists for the equivalent of a stick of gum. I don't see a lot of sodbusters from Lawrence, Kansas crawling around on their hands and knees in corn fields looking for Chinese or Russian shell casings to hawk at their produce stands.

Though I've spent the first few pages of this book outlining a war that has polarized the populace even to this day, Vietnam should be perceived as a country, not a war. There is no war in Vietnam, save that which is happening behind Windsor knots and Waterman pens. The new aggressor in Vietnam is the fusillade of foreign investment poised to transform the nation as no B-52s could hope to do. It is an inner war between an antiquated and isolated ideology and the magnetlike pull of a free market destiny, a balancing act between socialism and capitalism.

Most of Vietnam's population of around 70 million is under 30. An Irish woman in Saigon remarked that she was amazed at the age disparity of the Vietnamese people. People seemed very young or very old, she said. And she was mostly correct in that observation. While much the same scenario can be seen in neighboring Cambodia's Phnom Penh, it is for two very different reasons. Whereas Cambodia's missing generation ended up in shallow, pungent graves outside Phnom Penh after being bludgeoned by the axes of Pol Pot's heinous henchmen, Vietnam's missing generation ended up in Southern California, Minnesota, Virginia and Australia after the capitulation of Saigon to NVA troops in 1975.

They left in droves, some 280,000 alone in 1979. Many died at sea under abhorrent conditions, including cannibalism and subsistence on human waste. Pirates combed the seas for the refugees' dilapidated vessels, raping the women and murdering entire boatloads of Vietnamese. Many of the fleeing Vietnamese vessels were ordered back out to sea by the nations they were adrift to. Malaysia turned 40,000 refugees back to sea in one six-month period alone in the late '70s. By the end of that decade, there were nearly 350,000 Vietnamese in detainment camps in East Asia. Even today, under the United Nations' Orderly Departure Program, an estimated 100,000 Vietnamese leave their homeland each year.

The collapse of the former Soviet Union and the tumbling of Eastern blocs worsened the situation for Vietnam. Vietnamese exports went to hell in a handbasket. Although real growth continued to inch upward at a six-percent clip by 1989, inflation soared to a staggering 75 percent. The former USSR was the recipient of nearly 60 percent of Vietnamese trade. Conversely Vietnam received nearly 75 percent of its imports from the former Soviet Union.

Vietnam today remains one of the most deeply impoverished nations in the world. Its per capita income still fails to exceed US$200 per year. Policemen, the watchdogs of the communist streets, rarely make in excess of $100 per month; they can be seen on the outskirts of every population center stopping bus drivers for kickbacks. In 1991, child malnutrition stood at 60 percent. The monthly rice ration was a mere 13 kgs.

Gratefully, this is all beginning to change. Countries such as Singapore, Hong Kong, Taiwan and Japan have pumped more than US$5 billion into the economy since 1989, a figure that is bound to soar with the lifting of the U.S. embargo and the normalization of U.S.-Vietnam ties.

The demise of the Cold War and the breakup of the former USSR has had a tremendous impact in the thawing of Washington-Hanoi relations. Hanoi began a limited move to a free trade system in 1966 and, by 1989, she opened her doors to relatively unrestricted tourism in the hope of luring desperately needed hard currency. Additionally, the 1991 Paris Peace accords and the subsequent May 1993 free elections in Cambodia have played major roles in reducing tension in the Indochina region.

These events, as well as Hanoi's largely detailed accounting for missing American servicemen (no previous American foe in war has been as thorough), have helped American businesses succeed in pushing the Clinton administration to establish ties with Hanoi. American companies will no doubt realize enormous profits in helping Vietnam to establish a viable communications, transportation and public utilities infrastructure once they transcend the growing pains of the red tape so endemic in communist administrations.

The negative effects of the impending overcommercialization of Vietnam will be profound—the annihilation of offshore reefs, the inevitable extinction of perhaps hundreds of species of both land and sea creatures. There will be the enormous cranes atop the skeletons of skycrapers turning them into hotel rooms and conference centers.

But neither the Vietnamese nor others should fool themselves into thinking that normalized relations between Washington and Hanoi will be the savior of Vietnam. There are many who have beaten the Americans to Hanoi and Saigon. Although the Vietnamese welcome the return of Americans, their welfare is no longer as dependent on that return as many have believed.

Japanese motorbikes and consumer goods, everything from televisions to toothpaste, are satiating the Vietnamese. "American dollars don't necessarily need to come from America," one Thai writer noted. Many believe the embargo, in its latter stages, was no longer significantly impacting the Vietnamese. Land prices, which as recently as 1993 were skyrocketing in anticipation of the lifting of the embargo, have largely stabilized—and even dropped to some extent. Japanese products face no real threat with the introduction of American consumer goods into Vietnam, save for perhaps the legitimate entry of Coca-Cola. Recent surveys indicate that most Vietnamese believe the Japanese make the best household products in the world. The Americans will have to work hard to create a campaign to change that impression.

It would be tempting to call it Hearts and Minds, wouldn't it?

**Wink Dulles**

**Ho Chi Minh City**

## Postscript

As these words are penned to paper, U.S. President Bill Clinton has just normalized relations with Hanoi. I didn't find out about it for three days later as I was trapped with my motorcycle by monsoon floods in remote northeastern Vietnam.

I've had the unique and historic opportunity of being in Vietnam on both the days that the trade embargo was lifted in February 1994 and when Clinton normalized ties with Vietnam on July 11, 1995. For me, they were two utterly distinct experiences. When the trade embargo was lifted I was in the city, and watched in wonder—as did other Saigonese—as workers erected enormous signs bearing the logos of U.S. computer firms and inflated giant balloons announcing American soft drink companies. It was almost laughable. More than a societal milestone, it was a commercial event—a capitalist's circus of banners, bright lights and beautiful women dressed in sexy American liquor company T-shirts moving from table to table at Saigon's bars pouring sample shots of Tennessee whiskey.

Office buildings were being erected—balloons, signs, banners, billboards. You name it, and it was headed for the sky. And it was all new.

On the day the U.S. president normalized ties with Hanoi I was in a far distant place watching an entirely different group of people erect something entirely different, something very old. In Tha Co, a tiny beachside village near the Chinese border, a group of peasants was rebuilding at a snail's pace an old Catholic church that had been razed and gutted as a result of the decades of conflict in Vietnam. Like the yuppies-to-be of Hanoi and Saigon, this tiny, ragtag collection of farmers was also reacting to the normalization of U.S.-Vietnam relations—although, of course, they had no idea this had taken place.

First, the North Vietnamese Army had dismantled the old cathedral for its materials in their war effort against the Americans; then the Chinese further razed it during their invasion of northern Vietnam in 1979. But, over the years, in the middle of this desolate alluvial plain in Vietnam's remotest corner, these Christian peasants—working without wages and without the aid of the Catholic Church—had come to a realization.

"There has been no war here for a while," a village elder told me. "I do not know why, but we haven't seen guns here for quite some time. And we have not had to hide. I think the fighting has stopped. We figured this would be a good time to start rebuilding."

Which is the same thing being said by smartly-clad Vietnamese yuppies with newly-signed joint venture contracts at Saigon's trendiest nightspots.

# TABLE OF CONTENTS

# LIST OF MAPS

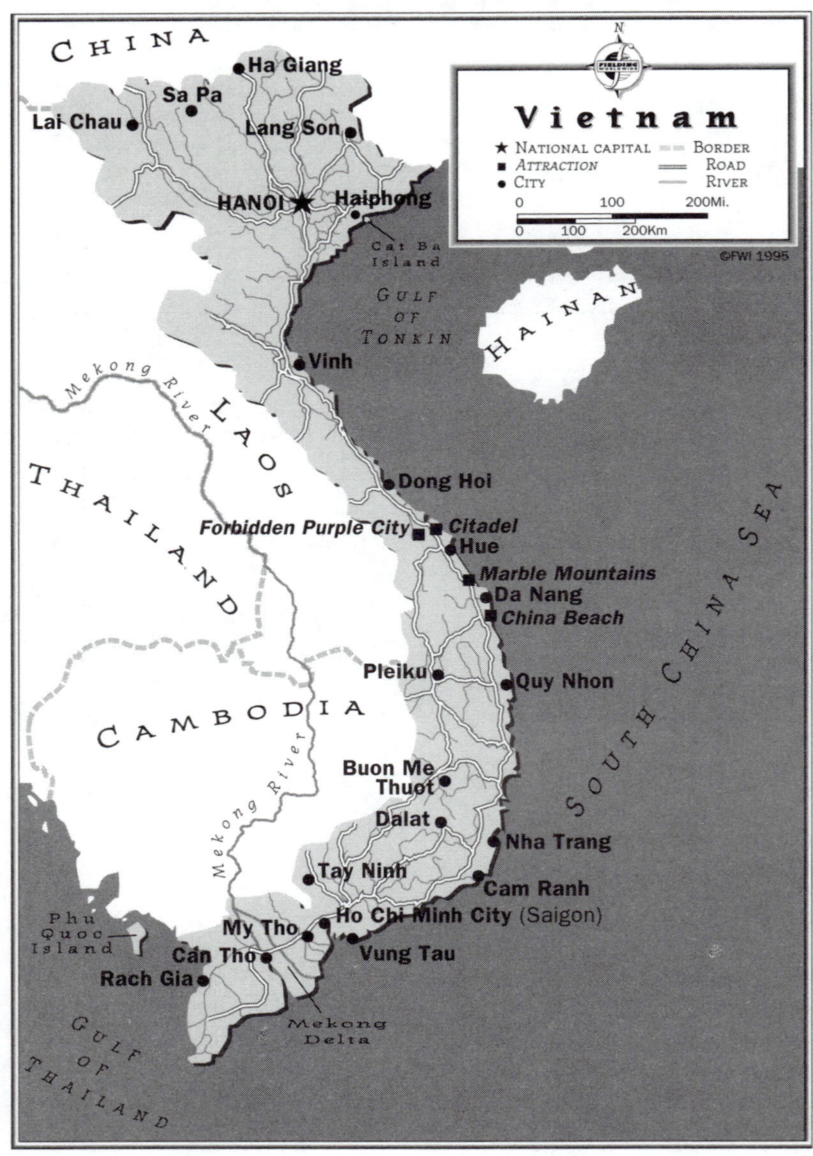

Vietnam
National capital
Attraction
City
Border
Road
River
0 100 200Mi.
0 100 200Km
©FWI 1995
CHINA
Ha Giang
Sa Pa
Lai Chau
Lang Son
HANOI
Haiphong
Cat Ba Island
Gulf of Tonkin
HAINAN
Vinh
Mekong River
LAOS
THAILAND
Dong Hoi
Forbidden Purple City
Citadel
Hue
Marble Mountains
Da Nang
China Beach
SOUTH CHINA SEA
Pleiku
Quy Nhon
CAMBODIA
Mekong River
Buon Me Thuot
Dalat
Nha Trang
Tay Ninh
Cam Ranh
Ho Chi Minh City (Saigon)
Phu Quoc Island
My Tho
Vung Tau
Can Tho
Rach Gia
Mekong Delta
Gulf of Thailand

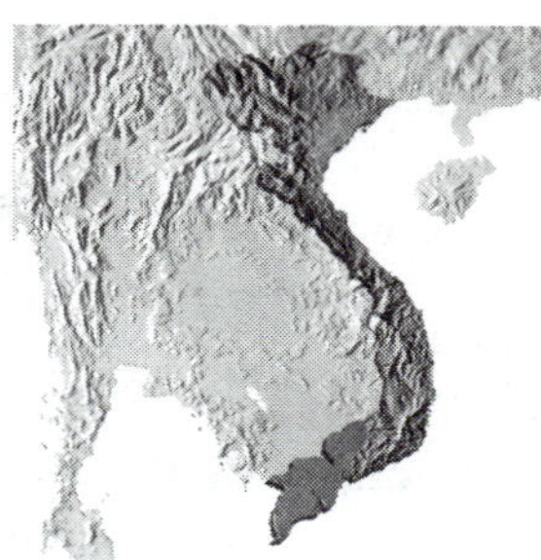

# INTRODUCTION

***Traditional Vietnamese dance and theatre depicts Vietnam's history.***

If any books in the Fielding series of world travel guides require constant updating they are the ones that are written about Southeast Asia.

The Far East, particularly Southeast Asia, is the world's fastest changing region. From Myanmar to Mindanao, from Telukbetung to Na Trang, Southeast Asia is exploding. Economic prosperity is rapidly transforming the face of countries such as Vietnam, as it makes the transition from an agrarian-based, Soviet-aided litany of economic failure to a manufacturing and export giant.

So it is with some trepidation that we prepare this intro to Fielding's *Vietnam*, because as these words are committed to paper, they become out of date. Asia has a maddeningly invigorating habit of doing exactly what you expect the least. Gentle people stage bloody uprisings. Nations hurl themselves from capitalism to religious fanaticism overnight—and vice versa. If one thing is the same in Asia it is change.

For 50 years, Fielding has been renowned for our expertise of the globe's less strife-torn regions—such as Europe, Hawaii and the Caribbean. But now our pioneering books also explore the remote cultures of Borneo, Kenya, Mexico and Brazil. And, of course, the Far East.

## Who Is This Guide For?

Fielding's *Vietnam* is designed to be more fun than the penurious tones and dull squeaking of the backpacking guides, with less air-conditioned sterility of the business guides. It's more exciting than the white bread guides, and more opinionated than all of them combined. Fielding's *Vietnam* is for the person with a lust for the foreign but with a healthy fear of the unknown. You're college educated, have traveled before and really want to get into Vietnam, not just surf. This is the guide to lean on when you get confused, tired or hurried—and the one to ignore when you're on a roll.

## A Word About Guidebooks

Guidebooks, even this one, aren't the end-all for managing your Vietnam adventure. Southeast Asia is a highly dynamic and constantly changing environment. Although Fielding's *Vietnam* listings are up-to-date right up to press time, businesses, eateries, hotels and tour companies both in and pertaining to Vietnam are in a constant state of flux. Phone numbers change. Faxes are installed. Businesses boom and bust. Tour companies come and go on the scene as fast as lip-synching pop stars.

## Where the Heck Is Vietnam?

For most Westerners it's on the other side of the world. Twenty-four hours aboard a plane or two or three and you're there. Sure it's a haul. But while Aunt Tess and Uncle Bill are getting toured to death on a bus in Belgium, you're checking out shrines built before there *was* a Europe—cultures and monuments so old they predate written history.

## What's It Like?

Vietnam offers some of the world's most mysterious and exotic attractions. It possesses a beautiful topography—ranging from rainforests not unlike those found in the deepest jungles of Central and South America and vast deltas to boulder strewn mesas of the variety found in Mexico's Baja peninsula. If the country has had its fill of Western colonialism and domination, it is still very much the virgin for economic exploitation. (But to its credit, Vietnam has been planting 120,000 hectares of new forest-nursing 260,000 hectares of young forest in 1995.)

Vietnam's new riches have made more evident an astoundingly impoverished societal undercarriage, which really can only be called such because there are now other hugely-rich stratas for comparison. The average Vietnamese makes $198 a year. Any trip to this strange land will open your eyes to extremes you have never encountered before, from economic to religious.

## Tourism In Vietnam

Vietnamese cities and the provinces have become the destinations for the 1990s. In a word, Vietnam is hot. For instance, travel is becoming one of Vietnam's single biggest earners of foreign exchange. During the late 80s, these revenues multiplied many times over. Americans and others are descending upon this paradisiacal nation in droves—some to reflect on and make amends with past tragedy, others to see what Hawaii might have been like a couple of hundred years ago or so.

**THE FOREIGN TOURIST FORECAST**

| YEAR | TO VIETNAM (MILLIONS) | TO HCMC (MILLIONS) |
|---|---|---|
| **1995** | *1.40* | *1.0* |
| **1996** | *1.80* | *1.26* |
| **1997** | *2.30* | *1.56* |
| **1998** | *2.80* | *1.80* |
| **1999** | *3.33* | *1.90* |
| **2000** | *3.80* | *2.00* |
| **2005** | *6.20* | *3.10* |
| **2010** | *8.70* | *4.35* |

*Source: Ho Chi Minh City Tourism Department*

Whereas Europe has served as the traditional target of foreign jaunts by North Americans, travelers these days are tossing around names like Danang, Ha Long Bay, Hue and Dalat like they once spoke of Amsterdam and Paris.

**PURPOSES FOR ARRIVALS (%)**

| YEAR | HOLIDAY | BUSINESS | VISIT RELATIVES | OTHER PURPOSES |
|---|---|---|---|---|
| **1992** | *65.1* | *20.4* | *8.0* | *6.5* |
| **1993** | *56.0* | *21.3* | *23.0* | *11.7* |
| **1994** | *44.0* | *22.0* | *29.0* | *5.0* |

*Source: Ho Chi Minh City Tourism Department*

The annual growth rate of arrivals in Vietnam has been between 40 percent and 50 percent for three years running. The number of foreign tourists entering the country surged from 92,500 in 1988 to 1,018,000 in 1994—a tenfold increase in a mere seven years. Fifty-two percent of the new arrivals in 1994 were from China, Hong Kong, Japan, Taiwan, France, the UK, Canada and the United States.

## PLANS FOR THE CONSTRUCTION OF INTERNATIONAL STANDARD HOTELS IN THE SOUTHERN TOURIST ZONES

| YEAR | NUMBER OF FOREIGN TOURISTS | NUMBER OF INTERNATIONAL STANDARD ROOMS | NUMBER OF ADDITIONAL ROOMS NEEDED |
|---|---|---|---|
| **1995** | *1,120,000* | *11,490* | *930* |
| **2000** | *2,750,000* | *29,760* | *18,270* |
| **2005** | *3,900,000* | *44,130* | *14,370* |
| **2010** | *5,300,000* | *60,800* | *16,670* |

*Source: Tourism Development Research Institute*

The number of hotel rooms in the country has also shot up. At press time, there were 674 state-run hotels and 312 private hotels in Vietnam, with a total of 36,000 rooms—compared to 18,000 rooms in 1988. Today, there are at least 18,000 rooms up to international standards. Seven thousand rooms were added in 1994 alone. Foreign hotel investment is now nearly US$2 billion—one-fifth of all the foreign investment in Vietnam. There are at least 125 new projects in the works, including 10 five-star, 24 four-star and 46 three-star caravansaries, projects that will add 13,500 international-standard rooms. It's projected that there will be 31,500 international-standard rooms in Vietnam by 1997.

And they're not just going up in Ho Chi Minh City and Hanoi. The provinces are getting their share. Resorts are springing up in Quang Nam, Ha Long Bay, Van Phong Bay and Ba Ria. Golf courses have been built in Ho Chi Minh City (two, actually), Dalat and Ha Tay Province. Vietnam's first casino has opened.

On the down side, only 10 percent of all tourists to Vietnam return to the country. Reasons for the low figure include a shortage of tourism representative offices in other countries, a poor infrastructure, insufficient investment in tourist sites and underqualified staff at tour companies, restaurants, hotels and tourist attractions. Let's face it—for many, beggars and touts are a turn-off. This is bound to change in the future. But in the meantime, keep in mind that if you're coming from Beverly Hills to see Beverly Hills, stay in Beverly Hills.

And, of course the real Vietnam lies beyond the cities. It's found on the rice terraces of the Central Highlands and the coffee plantations of Dac Lac province, around the spectacular stretches of sand like China Beach, and in the incense-laced temples of Hue. It's found along the banks of the bountiful mouths of the Mekong. It's found in longhouses in the deepest jungles of northern Vietnam and aboard junks anchored in the Gulf of Tonkin. It's chronicled in the works of Somerset Maugham and Graham Greene.

Vietnam, for all its part proud, part shameful—and certainly lengthy—heritage, is just being born in many ways, and is most assuredly an embryonic host to the seasoned traveler.

Some say Vietnam has lost its lure as a frontier destination and to some extent, they're right. You see foreigners all about Saigon, Hanoi, Hue, Ha Long Bay and Danang these days. A lot of them with money, looking to be catered to the same way they would be at the Hyatt in Orlando. But there is still so much of Vietnam left to be explored, so many places the tour buses and vans don't reach. So many places where foreigners have rarely or never been. Besides, if you've never been somewhere, it's a frontier.

**VIETNAM AT A GLANCE**

| *The place* | *Square miles* | *Population* | *Languages* | *Religions* |
|---|---|---|---|---|
| **Vietnam** | **127,330** | **72.1 million** | **Vietnamese, French, Chinese, Khmer** | **Buddhism. Hao Hao, Cao Dai, Christianity, Islam** |
| *Adult literacy rate* | *Life expectancy* | *Pop. growth rate* | *Per capita income* | *Mean years of schooling* |
| **88%** | **63 years** | **2.5%** | **US$198** | **4.5 years** |
| *% labor force in agriculture* | *Arable land as% of total* | *Rural pop.* | *Annual rate of deforestation* | *Growth of urban pop.* |
| **67%** | **17.5%** | **78%** | **0.6%** | **3.6% per annum** |

# Before You Leave

## Travel Documents & Visas

Before you even schedule your trip, you'll need to get a passport. Check to find the closest passport agency in your area. Passport agencies are located in most large cities and selected post offices across the country. Passports cost $65 ($55 to renew). You'll need two passport photos (most photo shops can shoot them for you) and an original birth certificate. No copies. Allow about 30 days for processing, or pay an added fee for a rush turnaround. You'll need visas to visit some countries in Asia (Vietnam is one of them), although many nations will stamp U.S. and Canadian passports with stays from two weeks up to 90 days free of charge (such as Thailand and Malaysia, respectively). Visas are necessary for Vietnam and are good for 30 days. Extensions (I've seen up to 30 days) can be applied for and are usually granted when you're in-country though a travel agent. (Creative travel agents in Vietnam have the means to extend your visa even longer; check around.)

At the time of this writing, the U.S. has recently established normalized relations with Vietnam. Although this will eventually permit travelers to obtain visas directly from the Vietnamese embassy in Washington, Vietnam and the U.S. have not opened new embassies to date, so visas still must be procured through a third party. You can contact one of the Asian tour companies listed in this chapter. They can generally provide visas for about US$100-150; they're so pricey because the tour operators usually arrange for them through their contacts in either Mexico or Canada. Expect a wait of up to 10 days. A more prudent and cheaper way is to get to a place such as Bangkok first. There, most of the travel agencies that line Khao San and Sukhumvit Roads like a muster of slot machines at Las Vegas McCarran Airport might get away with taking about $60-80 from you. You'll think you got a deal—but you didn't. Instead, go right to the Vietnam Embassy at *83/1 Wireless Road, Bangkok* (☎ *251-5835* or *251-5838*, FAX: *(662) 251-7201* or *251-7203*), fill out an application and give them about US$48, a couple of passport-sized photos and 24 hours and, presto, you're in.

**INSIDER TIP**

*It is best to secure airline tickets in and out of Vietnam–or at least confirmed reservations–before you apply for your visa. A Vietnamese visa, unlike a Thai visa, is valid only for the days printed on it. In other words, you must enter Vietnam on the entry date inscribed on the visa, not the day before. (Sometimes you can get away with coming in the day after.). The Vietnamese visa–for Americans–is still a separate document, not a stamp in your passport, even though Washington and Hanoi have full diplomatic relations. This is bound to change in the near future.*

I also recommend heading just a half block down Wireless to **M.K. Ways** (*57/11 Wireless Rd., Patumwan, Bangkok 1033*; ☎ *254-7770*, *255-3390*, *254-4765*, or *255-2892*; FAX: *(662) 254-5583*). If you're nice, they won't charge you much more than the 1200 baht you stood in the long line at the Vietnamese embassy to pay. They'll get you as cheap a fare into either Saigon or Hanoi as you'll find anywhere along Khao San Road. (My first visa only took a couple of days to get back to me from Hanoi, but it seems the capital is being besieged with visa applications and really doesn't appear as capable of handling the surging popularity of its country as quickly as it was only a year ago.) M.K. Ways has been known to pull some hemp-taut strings in Hanoi, but even they now make you wait seven days for the visa.

### INSIDER TIP

*On arrival in Vietnam, two copies of a customs declaration form must be completed, as well as a single arrival/departure card. You will be given one copy of the customs form and a portion of your arrival/departure card. Hold on to these documents as you would your passport. Do not lose them. You'll need to present them both when leaving the country. You'll most likely be fined if you've lost one form or both. And, for godsakes, don't lose your visa. Make a number of photocopies of it, as well as your departure card and customs declaration form.*

### RENTING AN APARTMENT IN VIETNAM

*Some "experts" say Americans are permitted to rent an apartment during the first 30 day visa–others say you're not. Nonetheless, if the authorities discover that you're renting a flat rather than staying at a hotel when you apply for a visa extension, you're in trouble, pal. Tourists are expected to be lodging in Vietnam's hotels (of course because of the additional money it costs to stay in a hotel). When applying for an extension, your exit card must be stamped by a hotel showing the hotel as your lodgings in the country. If you are living in an apartment, make arrangements to stay in a hotel a few days prior to applying for your extension. The hotel will stamp your exit card and the authorities will be happy. If you don't, expect your apartment to be raided during the middle of the night by the immigration police. Not only will you have to pay an extensive fine yourself, but so will your landlord. You may even be asked (ordered, actually) to leave the country. When applying for an extension, you'll need to go through a sponsor (i.e. travel agent). Their prices for the extension will vary from between US$20-40. Shop around. If you've got a good guide, usually he'll have the contacts to get the lower fee.*

## Who Should Travel to Vietnam?

Although Vietnam is becoming a travel destination at almost a fanatical rate, it's important to realize the country's infrastructure isn't close to having the ability of accommodating mass travel. Le Thieu Hung, Saigontourist's general manager recently said that the country has yet to "meet the needs of mass tourism for pleasure and entertainment. Vietnam is still primarily a destination of business people and culturally-minded travelers." At this time, Le Xuan Hien, manager of the operation department of Vietnamtourism said,

"We're rather interested in intellectuals, educated people who come here to see the specific cultural heritage and way of life in our country. We have to be very cautious with mass tourism so that we don't spoil our beautiful country."

## Solo and Group Travel

Solo wandering is probably the purest form of adventure travel, while group or paired travel offers its own rewards. Wandering alone in faraway places takes on a romantic and nomadic aura. Getting from point A to B can become like a pilgrimage. This type of travel courts disaster but is also the most rewarding. It's exploration at its purest, with little to curb adventure except physical stamina and funds. In only a month or two, you will meet more people, do more things and experience more of life's ups and downs than in a year's worth of group or paired travel. If you travel in remote regions of Vietnam, prepare to be arrested, detained, celebrated, attacked, seduced and tricked. It's all part of the experience. But, remember, if you are a woman traveling alone, you're setting yourself up for thieves, thugs and worse. Men certainly aren't immune but are less likely targets.

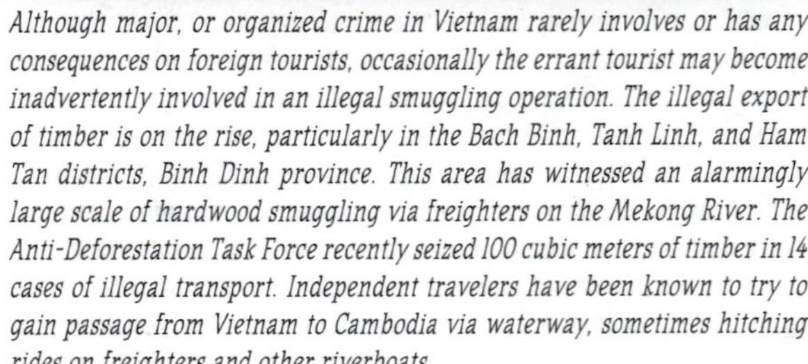

**AUTHOR'S WARNING**

*Although major, or organized crime in Vietnam rarely involves or has any consequences on foreign tourists, occasionally the errant tourist may become inadvertently involved in an illegal smuggling operation. The illegal export of timber is on the rise, particularly in the Bach Binh, Tanh Linh, and Ham Tan districts, Binh Dinh province. This area has witnessed an alarmingly large scale of hardwood smuggling via freighters on the Mekong River. The Anti-Deforestation Task Force recently seized 100 cubic meters of timber in 14 cases of illegal transport. Independent travelers have been known to try to gain passage from Vietnam to Cambodia via waterway, sometimes hitching rides on freighters and other riverboats.*

The next best scenario is traveling with a single friend. The big drawback is the unintended barrier you'll create between yourselves and the locals. You will use the language less, be invited into fewer homes. But this is a better way for women from a security standpoint. Additionally, you won't get as lonely traveling in a pair—and you *will* get lonely traveling solo. A good way is to split up for portions of the trip, arranging to meet at a preset time and place.

Group travel has its rewards if you've only got a week. But that's about it. Essentially, group travel is like relying on the weakest link in a chain. You can never travel faster than the slowest person; accommodations are always full; tables are too small; the prices are always higher—you name it. Group travel turns a simple pleasure into a military exercise.

## What to Pack

Vietnam lies in tropical latitudes. This doesn't mean a prescription of Bain de Soleil and thongs. In the highlands of south and central Vietnam, and throughout the north, temperatures can get quite cold, especially in winter. Jungle areas can be so hot your brain turns to jerky. You'll want as much skin area covered as possible to ward off leeches, malarial mosquitoes and the fatal bites of scared, hungry, pissed off or playful cobras, vipers, hanumans and kraits. (Lions and tigers and bears, oh my!) Ladies, remember where you're going. The Vietnamese on the whole are a tolerant lot and Western fashion has permeated urban areas, but a show of too much skin is taboo. Female lib hasn't gotten to Danang yet. And neither has Madonna's look. Longer dresses, pants and bras are *de rigueur* in most places other than the beach and other heavily touristed areas, especially in religious temples. Pretty Vietnamese girls who may wear the shortest, sexiest dresses and high heels on the street wear very modest swimwear at the beach.

Both sexes should bring along light cotton clothing and not a lot of it. You'll probably—and should—get a lot of what you need where you're going. For starters, a few pairs of trousers and a couple of pairs of shorts will do. Take two or three short-sleeved shirts max, and a single dress shirt. You determine the underwear. Sandals are a good way of getting around; the Asians seem to think so. Walking or hiking boots are a must for the jungle and the mountains. Sneakers are the best all-around bet. Slip-ons will be good if you'll be seeing a lot of temples; laced shoes are not a good idea if you've got a lot of pagodas on your itinerary. A small towel will also come in handy. Other good ideas are a day pack and a fanny pack. Don't bring things you probably won't need: sleeping bag, heavy outerwear, air mattress and such. Unless, of course, the nature of your journey requires this kind of bulk.

Take along a sewing kit, electrical current adapters, and a good Swiss Army knife. Bring contraceptives and condoms. Yeah, condoms. You can get them there, but Asian condoms break like soap bubbles in a pine forest. A *great* insect repellent is essential—like Deet. Some folks swear by preparations such as Avon's Skin So Soft to keep the little buggers away. Keep a marginal supply of duty-free liquor and American cigarettes handy to pay off officials and impress your friends. Johnnie Walker Black Label whiskey is generally the East Asian poison of choice, as are 555 or Marlboro cigarettes. In-country, carry a roll or two of toilet paper. In a lot of places, you won't find it; just a bucket of water. It's why there's not a lot of social grace in the left hand.

## Medical/Health Certificates

You should receive inoculations against **yellow fever**, **hepatitis B**, **tetanus**, **typhoid**, **cholera** and **tuberculosis**. An **influenza** shot couldn't hurt either. (See the "Medical Problems in Vietnam" sidebar in the "Planning Ahead" section of the "Vietnam Today" chapter for a description of Vietnam's maladies.)

Some countries will require that you have, under International Health Regulations adopted by the World Health Organization, an International Certificate of Vaccination against yellow fever. Travelers arriving from infected areas will be required to show proof of vaccination against yellow fever. The certificate will also be stamped with the other inoculations that you have received. Any general practice will be able to provide this service.

### A Word About AIDS (SIDA)

A local guide recently, on a trip in the Mekong Delta, decided he needed a rest at a truck stop (read that as whore house), where Vietnamese women obligingly take in weary travelers for some tea and a little "sympathy." Apparently, the man was not in the habit of using condoms during these little sojourns. He explained to me that, to avoid contracting the HIV virus, he had sex only with Vietnamese girls. "These girls don't have sex with foreigners," he said, his reasoning that the disease could only be spread by foreigners. Although government estimates of the spread of HIV in Vietnam are seriously lacking a firm data gathering procedure, AIDS in Vietnam is very real. At least the Vietnamese are becoming more aware of its dangers. While the general awareness of HIV/AIDS has risen from 2.9 percent of the population in 1991, now more than 40 percent of the population is aware of the danger and the spread of the disease. As of August, 1995, the National Prevention Committee reported 2777 people in Vietnam had contracted the HIV virus, 230 had AIDS and 69 of those with AIDS had died. HCMC has the highest number of people infected with HIV (1356). That using condoms prevents the spread of AIDS was known by 31 percent of the respondents in 1991, that figure jumped to 44 percent by the end of 1993 and 50 percent by 1995.

## International Drivers License

These can be obtained at your state's department of motor vehicles offices or through AAA and other automobile associations. The fee is approximately US$7. If you're planning on driving in Asia, get one. Foreigners who have national or international drivers licenses are required to exchange them for Vietnam drivers licenses if they are planning on driving in Vietnam. In Vietnam, an international drivers license is required to rent a motorbike over 50 cc, although few rental firms will ask to see it. They're more interested in your passport. But don't allow that to make you lazy. The cops may ask to see it from time to time. And if you get into an accident over here, and don't have an international drivers permit, you're in trouble.

## International Student Identity Card

The ISIC card can help with discounts on air tickets and lodging. There's been a surge in bogus cards, which have been readily available in Thailand and Malaysia.To get a real one, contact the Council on International Educational Exchange (CIEE) at *205 E. 42nd. Street, New York, NY 10017-5706;* ☎ *(212) 661-1414.*

## International Youth Hostel Card

This will help you in the expensive places such as Japan but may be totally unrecognized in Indochina. You can get this card through any youth hostel office. Or write *733 15th Street N.W., Suite 840, Washington, DC 20005;* ☎ *(202) 783-6161.*

## Air Travel

There are now myriad airlines that call on the Pacific Rim from the U.S. and a growing number that serve both Ho Chi Minh City and Hanoi. With the lifting of the embargo in February 1994, United Airlines was the first American airline to announce that it would link the U.S. and Vietnam directly. Service to both Ho Chi Minh City and Hanoi may have started on United and Delta by the time you read this.

Take heed that some of the airlines offer better service than the others. It's a long way around to the other side of the globe so you might want to pay the extra bucks for more comfort and better service. Not in terms of upgrading your class, but in choosing an airline. For overall service, comfort, friendliness of the flight crew, food and all the amenities, our hats are tipped to Singapore Airlines. For the feeling of entering Asia the moment you step aboard, these are the folks to fly. Not far behind is Thai Airways. Cathay Pacific and British Airways are in the next league, followed by also-rans Northwest, Korean, Air New Zealand, MAS, Garuda Indonesia, JAL, and Philippines.

When choosing an airline, comfort may be as high a priority as price. Some Asian airlines, such as Singapore, Thai and Cathay Pacific realize this and take extra pains to make the 15–25 hour flights enjoyable. Others, such as MAS and Garuda Indonesia, employ seat configurations and meal strategies designed for a maximum number of Asian travelers.

## Flying to Vietnam

Flights to Vietnam from the United States in economy class with advance purchase cost between $1000 and $1500 return, although you may be able to get a cheaper fare through a ticket broker.

For many travelers to the region, Vietnam is not the only stop and is part of an itinerary that may include a number of other Southeast Asian destinations. Few travelers (especially those on extended journeys) book directly to

Vietnam from their original points of departure. That's why it'll help to know approximately what the fares are to Vietnam from other cities/countries in the region.

## THE STORY OF VIETNAM AIRLINES

*Vietnam Airlines was formed in 1989, but its history dates back to 1954 with the takeover of Hanoi's Gia Lam Airport–now its headquarters–from the French. Then called the Civil Aviation Department, the airline went into service with a limited network of communications, meteorological information, fuel, cargo, and only five aircraft. It launched its first international service–to Beijing–in April 1956. Over the next two years, the domestic service from Hanoi was extended to Vinh, Dong Hoi and Dien Bien Phu.*

*Unification of the country in 1975 brought about a boom in air services due to the dramatic increase in economic, political, cultural and social activities. As a result, the airline expanded its operations under a new organization formed in February 1976–the General Department of Civil Aviation.At the time, it had a modest fleet, many say a damned dangerous modest fleet of ailing IL-14s, Antonov-24s, LI-2s, Yak-40s, dilapidated DC-3s, DC-4s and then later a couple of Boeing 707s.The aircraft were poorly maintained, and safety procedures and equipment were all but nonexistent. The airline was considered, along with China's flagship carrier, perhaps the scariest airline on the planet. Many foreigners simply refused to fly VN altogether.*

*The GDCA also ran a network of aviation departments and airports throughout the country. In 1977, as Vietnam Civil Aviation, the airline carried 21,000 frightened passengers, of whom 7000 were even more frightened foreigners–3000 tons of cargo was also flown during this period. How frightened the freight was flying VN isn't known.*

*By the time it became Vietnam Airlines in 1989, the airline and its blue and white livery, lettering, and precariously fluttering stork logo had become widely known to Vietnamese, foreign passengers, and morticians alike.*

*On April 20, 1993, VN became a company under the Civil Aviation Administration of Vietnam. CAAV is a state-run organization controlling the entire aviation industry of Vietnam. The establishment of the Vietnam Airlines Company is part of the reorganization of Vietnam's aviation industry to meet the growth in air services to and from the country.It marks a significant stage in the development of the airline, namely because it's been forced to purchase newer and safer aircraft as well as seriously update its safety standards.*

## THE STORY OF VIETNAM AIRLINES

*The new VN fleet now stands at 28 aircraft, including the likes of more modern and comfortable Boeing 737-300s and 767s, the Airbus 310 and 320, and ATR-72s. The old Soviet aircraft are being phased out of their remaining domestic flights—but they're still being flown. The airline began utilizing the Gabriel II reservation system in 1991 and is now planning to join Abacus and other global distribution systems to improve its sales system worldwide. Its computer system is also being upgraded to facilitate document management (which had previously been performed by surly, disgruntled bureaucrats), ticketing and check-in services. Phone bookings are now accepted.The number of passengers has been steadily increasing since 1976 at an average of 36 percent. In 1992, VN achieved 150 percent of its passenger and cargo targets—800,000 foreign and domestic passengers and 10,000 tons of cargo. In 1993, VN began scheduled services to Taipei, Moscow and Seoul using aircraft like the 737, A-310 and 320. In October of 1994, daily service was initiated to Singapore.*

*VN now flies to 16 destinations overseas and operates 12 domestic routes. Not surprisingly, the domestic flights are still occasionally aboard the aging and paint-flaked Soviet-era aircraft that dot the tarmacs of Hanoi and Ho Chi Minh airports like exhibits at a Charles Lindberg museum. But even domestic service is changing. I've flown a number of domestic flights within Vietnam and have felt relatively safe (with the aid of 20 mg. of Valium) and only vomited twice.*

*VN's market share of passenger aircraft to and from Vietnam in 1992 was 35 percent—a significant growth from 1990's 12 percent and 1991's 27 percent. Its international passenger load grew by more than 70 percent.*

*VN now operates joint services with Cathay Pacific, Malaysian Airlines, Korean Air, Singapore Airlines and China Airlines—to name a few—on some international routes.*

*With the support of the International Civil Aviation Organization and the United Nations Development program, VN has invested tens of millions of US dollars in upgrading its services as well as ground facilities. To meet new traffic demand to and from the country, VN has inaugurated scheduled services to Japan, France, and Germany in 1994. Could the U.S. be far behind? With President Clinton's lifting of the trade embargo last February, it's a distinct possibility. What remains to be seen, of course, is how far American flyers' stomachs will lift aboard a VN flight.*

Not surprisingly, the place to get the cheapest airfares into Vietnam is Bangkok. The cheapest carrier to fly in and out of Vietnam is Vietnam Airlines (VN). At presstime, VN's one-way fare into Ho Chi Minh City was US$150, and US$160 into Hanoi. Advance purchase isn't required, and there isn't a discount for booking round-trip. To avoid the delays and hassles of running all around Khao San (or the equivalent in other Asian cities) looking for the cheapest airfares, simply contact and book through VN's representative offices charted later in this section.

## AUTHOR'S NOTE: VN PRICE HIKES AND EXPANSION PLANS

*Passengers departing on domestic flights from Hanoi, Hai Phong, Da nang, and HCMC are now required to pay an airport service charge of 15,000 dong (about US$1.50). The fees are said to be used to improve the airports' facilities. Vietnam Airlines has plans to more than double its fleet within the next six years. The airline said it needs an additional 30 to 40 of all types of aircraft by the end of the century. Boeing and McDonnell-Douglas are considered the primary contenders for supplying the new fleet. Currently VN utilizes aging Soviet-built Tupolev and Yak-40 aircraft on domestic routes, although Boeing 767s and A320s have been making the Hanoi-Saigon runs recently. Additionally, the airline flies nine other aircraft on international routes–five Airbus A-320s leased from Air France, two Boeing 767s leased from Ansett Airlines, and the two ATR-72s which the airline owns. Taking advantage of the growing number of travelers to Vietnam, VN hiked its fares in 1995 on domestic routes. Currently, foreigners pay about US$320 return fare between HCMC and Hanoi, an excessive amount that presumably subsidizes the current Vietnamese national fare of about US$64 each way. Pacific Airlines, a recent upstart that marginally competes with VN has announced it will match the fares. Pacific Airlines currently has two aircraft which started a daily shuttle route between HCMC and Hanoi in April 1994 and also flies from HCMC to Panang. Pacific also flies from HCMC to Taipei and Kaohsiung. For reservations and flight information* ☎ 84.8.200978.

## PASSENGER SALES AGENTS FOR VIETNAM AIRLINES

### VIETNAM

**Cantho Tourist**
☎ *88.7.21853*
*FAX: 84.7.122719, 21804*
*27 Chau Van Liem, Cantho*

**Cat Bi Airport**
☎ *0131.48309, 01381.45217*
*Cat Bi Airport, Haiphong*

**FujiCap**
☎ *84.4.260158*
*86 Nguyen Du, Hanoi*

**Vinexad**
☎ *84.4.256662*
*FAX: 84.4.255556*
*14 Ngo Quyen, Hanoi*

**Art Tourist Services**
☎ *84.8.230234*
*FAX: 84.8.298947*
*63 Ly Tu Trong Street, HCMC*

**Peace Tours**
☎ *84.8.294416*
*FAX: 84.8.294416*
*60 Vo Van Tan, 3rd Dist. HCMC*

## PASSENGER SALES AGENTS FOR VIETNAM AIRLINES

**FPT**
☎ *84.4.267312*
*FAX: 84.4.26706*
*25 Ly Thuong Kiet, Ha Noi*

**Nasco**
☎ *84.4.266602*
*FAX: 84.4.266666*
*Noibai Int'l Airport, Hanoi*

**Trade Services Co.**
☎ *84.4.264259*
*FAX: 84.4.256446*
*79 Ba Trieu, Hanoi*

**Vietnamtourism**
☎ *84.4.264319*
*FAX: 84.4.257583*
*30A Ly Thuong Kiet, Hanoi*

**Vinatour**
☎ *84.4.239190*
*54 Nguyen Du, Hanoi*

**New Global Co.**
☎ *84.8.292287*
*108 Ly Tu Trong, 1rst Dist., HCMC*

**Saigontourist**
☎ *84.8.298914*
*FAX: 84.8.224987*
*49 Le Thanh Ton, 1rst Dist., HCMC*

**Vietlink Trading, Travel & Tour Co.**
☎ *84.8.555849*
*FAX: 84.8.555852*
*43-45 Chau Van Liem, 5th Dist., HCMC*

**Vietnamtourism**
☎ *84.8.290776*
*FAX: 84.8.290775*
*234 Nam Ky Khoi Nghia, 3rd Dist., HCMC*

### CHINA

**China Int'l Travel Service Guangzhou**
☎ *86.2.6671453*
*FAX: 86.2.6678048*
*179 Huanshi Rd, 510010 Guangzhou*

**China Travel Service Guangzhou**
☎ *86.2.3331862*
*FAX: 86.2.333247*
*10 Qiao Guang Rd, Guangzhou 510115*

### HONG KONG

**China Travel Air Service**
☎ *85.2.8533888*
*FAX: 85.2.5446174*
*5th Floor, CST House*
*78-83 Connaught Rd., Central*

**HKVN Ltd. (GSA)**
☎ *85.2.8106680*
*FAX: 85.2.8698915*
*1206A Peregrine Tower, Uppo Ctr.*
*89 Queensway, Admiralty*

**Skyvale Ltd.**
☎ *85.2.7656552*
*FAX: 85.2.7657166*
*Twr. A, Room 603*
*Hunghom Commercial Centre*
*37-39 Ma Tau Wai Rt., Kowloon*

**Vietlink Int'l Co. Ltd.**
☎ *85.2.3678113*
*FAX: 85.2.3122735*
*Unit A, 13F Wardley Centre No. 9-11*
*Part Aver, Kowloon*

## PASSENGER SALES AGENTS FOR VIETNAM AIRLINES

**On Chit Travel Service Ltd.**
☎ *85.2.5247819*
*FAX: 85.2.8454713*
*Rm. 801, Lap Fai Bldg.*
*6-8, Pottinger Street C*

**Waylock Travel Ltd.**
☎ *85.2.3328961*
*FAX: 85.2.3859291*
*Rm. 1003, Tai Shing Commercial Bldg.*
*498-500 Nathan Rd., Kowloon*

### LAOS

**Lao Air Booking Co. Ltd.**
☎ *5351*
*38-40 Setthathirath Rd., Box 3080*
*Vientiane*

### MALAYSIA

**Desk Air (Malaysia) SDN BHD**
☎ *60.3.248-7500*
*FAX: 60.3.248-5362*
*MUI Plaza, Ground Floor*
*Japan P. Ramlee, Kuala Lumpur 50250*

**Pelancongan Abadisdn BHD**
☎ *60.3.241-2212*
*FAX: 60.3. 241-2322*
*1rst Floor Wisma Abadi 79, Japan Bukit Bintang 55100, Kuala Lumpur*

**Forefrank Travel**
☎ *60.3.627-7260*
*FAX: 60.3.621-0112*
*Japan Murai Dua, Batu Kompleks*
*Batu Tiga, Japan Ipoh*
*5110 Kuala Lumpur*
*Forefrank*

**Vietlink Group**
☎ *60.3.443-1972*
*FAX: 60.3.441-7008*
*34A Japan Lumut, Damaicompes*
*(off Japan Ipoh)*
*50400 Kuala Lumpur*

**Maple Travel**
☎ *60.3.244-3101*
*FAX: 60.3.242-9392*
*2.46-2.49, 2nd Floor*
*Wisma's Stephen's 88*
*Japan Raja Chulan*
*Kuala Lumpur 50200*

### PHILIPPINES

**Imex Pan Pacific**
☎ *63.2.8125.623*
*FAX: 63.2.8125.625*
*120 G/F Anson Arcade Bldg.*
*Pasay Rd.*
*Makati*
*Metro Manila*

**Far Travel, Inc.**
☎ *63.2.8164072*
*FAX: 63.2.8156203*
*Asian Plaza, 1 De La Costa Street*
*Salcedo Village*
*Metro Manila*

## PASSENGER SALES AGENTS FOR VIETNAM AIRLINES

**Sampuguita Travel Corp.**
☎ *63.2.8180608*
*Fax:63.2.8185037*
*Ground Floor, Mareic Building*
*Tordesillas Street, Salcedo Village, Makati*
*Metro Manila*

**Expertravel & Tours, Inc.**
☎ *63.2.509360*
*FAX: 63.2. 5211785*
*1971-1973 Mabini Street*
*Malate, Metro Manila*

**Ootomo Saia Travel Service**
☎ *63.2.8312441*
*FAX: 63.2.8334361*
*R. 510, Sunset View Towers*
*2230 Roxas Blvd. Pasay*
*Metro 2 Manila*

**Trans Pacific Air Service Corp.**
☎ *879666*
*FAX: 8176902*
*Ground Floor, SGV Building*
*6760 Ayala Ave.*
*Makati, Metro Manila*

### SINGAPORE

**Desk Air (Singapore) PTE Ltd. (GSA)**
☎ *65.3888988*
*FAX: 65.3387810*
*15 Beach Rd. #03-01/11*
*Beach Centre, Singapore*

**Maple Aviation**
☎ *65. 5383787*
*FAX: 5383183*
*133 New Bridge Rd. #14-04/05*
*Chinatown Point, Singapore*

**Region Air Ltd.**
☎ *65.2356277*
*FAX: 65.7361662*
*50 Cuscaden Rd. #06-01 HPL House*
*Singapore*

**Vietlink International (Singapore) Ltd.**
☎ *65.5382050*
*FAX: 65.5386202*
*60 Eu Tong Sen Street #01-07*
*Furama Hotel Shopping Centre*
*Singapore*

**Robelle Tours & Travel Corp.**
☎ *63.2.5219168*
*FAX: 63.2.5217358*
*Ground Floor, L&S Building*
*1414 Roxas Blvd.*
*Ermita, Manila, Philippines*

### TAIWAN

**Hong Yi Travel Service**
☎ *88.6.2.5059212*
*FAX: 88.6.2.5023763*
*Rm. 602. 6-F*
*185 Sung Chiang Rd., Taipei*

**Stone International Development**
☎ *88.6..2.5016521*
*FAX: 88.6.2.5014348*
*6th Floor 1. Min Sheng East Rd.*
*Sec 3 Taipei*

**Uncle Travel Service Ltd.**
☎ *88.6.2.5236204*
*FAX: 88.6.2.5236203*
*3F, No. 67 Cahng Chun Rd. Taipei*

**Worldwide Travel Service**
☎ *88.6.2.5152185*
*FAX: 88.6.2.5091892*
*No. 99 Sung Chiang Rd. Taipei*

## PASSENGER SALES AGENTS FOR VIETNAM AIRLINES

**Vietlink International**
☎ *8662.5683828*
*FAX: 8662.5683820*
*Rm. 1401, #206*
*Sungchiang Rd., Taipei*

**Deks Air Taiwan**
☎ *88.6.2.5061388*
*FAX: 88.6.2.5072581*
*Rms. 3-1 Int'l Nanking Bldg., 3F*
*NO. 103, SEC 3, Nanking East Rd. Taipei*

### THAILAND

**Air People Tour & Travel**
☎ *66.2.2543921-4*
*FAX: 66.2.2553750*
*Regent House Bldg.*
*183 Rajdamri Rd.*
*Bangkok 10330*

**SMI Travel**
☎ *66.2.2511936 or 2525435*
*FAX: 66.2.2511785*
*578-580 Ploenchit Rd., Putumwan*
*Bangkok 10330*

**Desk Air Thailand**
☎ *66.2.2360030*
*FAX: 66.2.2366796*
*Yada Bldg. Ground Floor*
*56 Silom Rd.*
*Bangkok 10500*

**Vietlink Int'l**
☎ *66.2.2214614*
*FAX: 66.2.2256389*
*719 Mahachai Rd., Kwaeng Burapapirom*
*Khet Pranakarn*
*Bangkok 10200*

**OnTime Co.**
☎ *66.2.2520080*
*FAX: 66.2.2512173*
*564-572 Ploenchit Rd.*
*Bangkok 10330*

**Vietnam Tour Services**
☎ *66.2.5802632/3*
*FAX: 66.2.5802631*
*Park Inn Hotel*
*30/11 Rantanathket Rd.*
*Nonthaburi, Bangkok 11000*

**Maple Aviation**
☎ *66.2.2376145-7*
*FAX: 66.2.2376148*
*5th Floor Chan Issara Tower 942/137*
*D.1 Rama 4 Rd.*
*Bangkok 10500*

### UNITED STATES

**Discount Travel & Tours**
☎ *1-714-892-8829*
*FAX: 1-714-892-0688*
*9191 Bolsa Ave, #129*
*Westminster, CA 92683*

**Tokyo Travel Service**
☎ *1-714-434-7136*
*FAX: 1-714-434-0767*
*17220 New Hope Street, #114*
*Fountain Valley, CA 92708*

**C&H International**
☎ *1-213-387-2284*
*FAX: 1-213-387-8442*
*2500 Wilshire Blvd., #1000*
*Los Angeles, CA 90057*

**Vina USA Travel Center**
☎ *1-212-545-7474*
*FAX: 1-212-545-7698*
*373 Fifth Ave.*
*New York, NY 10016*

## PASSENGER SALES AGENTS FOR VIETNAM AIRLINES

**Group Systems Int'l**
☎ *1-310-377-5096*
*FAX: 1-310-544-3532*
*655 Deep Valley Rd., #375*
*Rolling Hills Estates, CA 90274*

**Minh Travel & Tours**
☎ *1-818-281-1088*
*FAX: 1-818-281-2208*
*412 West Valley Blvd.*
*San Gabriel, CA 91766*

**Sunrise Travel Inc.**
☎ *1-617-963-1840*
*FAX: 1-617-963-1843*
*1134 N. Main Street*
*Randolph, MA 02368*

**Vietlink Int'l Travel & Tours**
☎ *1-714-531-9828*
*FAX: 1-714-531-9867*
*9950 Bolsa Ave., Unit D*
*Westminster, CA 92683*

**IMEX Pan-Pacific Inc.**
☎ *1-714-531-2255*
*FAX: 1-714-775-6948*
*14541 Brookhurst Street, #A1*
*Westminster, CA 92683*

The cheapest places to get to are Tokyo, Seoul, Taipei and Hong Kong (because these are typically non-stop). The more isolated the destination, the more expensive. But tickets to the Far East can be had for a lot cheaper through the proliferation of ticket brokers in major cities. Flights that typically cost in the $900 to $1000 range at airline ticket counters and through travel agents can be had for as low as $725 through some brokers. But beware of these guys. Some of them are as fly-by-night as a red-eye to Seoul flanked by Soviet fighters. Don't give them your credit card number over the phone. Instead, try to pick up your ticket and render payment simultaneously at their offices. Many a traveler has made telephone arrangements only to watch their departure date come and go without having received their ticket in the mail. Look in the Sunday travel sections of big papers, such as the *Los Angeles Times* or the *New York Times.*

You can also obtain discounted multidestination airline tickets for about twice the usual return fare to a single destination. These tickets may permit you three or four additional destinations but, of course, restrict you to the cities where the carrier flies. Advance Purchase Excursion tickets are also discounted, but you'll be as equally limited in your choice of destinations. Cancellation penalties can also be enormous.

Another cheap source of airline tickets into Vietnam is Asia itself. One-way fares, for instance, from Bangkok–Hanoi or Kuala Lumpur–Ho Chi Minh City are much cheaper when the tickets are purchased in Bangkok or Kuala Lumpur rather than in the U.S.—even aboard the same carrier. There are hundreds of travel agencies in most East Asian cities and, if you're looking for the cheapest fares, shop around. Once in Kuala Lumpur, I was comparing one-way fares from Singapore to Bangkok and, after having called at least a dozen KL travel agents, I couldn't find anything better than Korean's US$225 offering. Finally a last call I almost didn't make gave me an agent who put me on an almost empty Air New Zealand flight for a hundred bucks. It pays to shop around.

| DISCOUNT TICKET BROKERS | |
|---|---|
| **American Travel Ventures** | ☎ *(310) 274-7061* |
| **Angels International Travel** | ☎ *(800) 400-4150* |
| **Bi-Coastal Travel** | ☎ *(800) 9-COASTAL* |
| **Discover Wholesale Travel** | ☎ *(800) 576-7770* |
| **Eros Travel** | ☎ *(213) 955-9695* |
| **Falcon Wings Travel** | ☎ *(310) 417-3590* |
| **Moon Travel & Tours** | ☎ *(800) 352-2899* |
| **Sky Service Travel** | ☎ *(800) 700-1222* |
| **Silver Wings Travel** | ☎ *(800) 488-9002* |
| **South Sea Tour & Travel** | ☎ *(800) 546-7890* |
| **Supertrip Travel** | ☎ *(800) 338-1898* |
| **Travel Mate** | ☎ *(818) 507-6283* |

## Tours

Taking a tour isn't the cop-out you might think it is. Tours can actually be a better alternative to independent travel if you have only a week or two. You won't experience the delays, language problems or other time-consuming idiosyncracies inherent in the culture you're visiting. Of course you won't be truly experiencing the culture with a few of the tours. Others, though, give you a surprising amount of freedom. Many of the "new breed" of tour operators are themselves formerly—and even currently—independent travelers themselves. Young, and perhaps only entrepreneurial by default, their tours represent not only the spirit of independent travel, but the nuances as well. These days, you can spend a couple of weeks pedaling a bicycle up the coast of Vietnam from Ho Chi Minh City to Hue (courtesy of Velo Asia), while immersing yourself in the hospitality of rural Vietnamese, Khmer and Cham villagers. It's a tour only in the sense that you're sharing your experiences with a handful of other foreigners.

Experienced travelers will tell you that bigger things come in small packages. If you have only a couple of weeks it doesn't make sense to bounce around East Asia like a good pinball shot. Limit your destinations so you can get more out of them.

Hanoi has a slew of plans for both improving and expanding tourist areas throughout the country to attract more foreign visitors. In the Mekong River Delta region, the floating markets Phong Dien and An Binh are targeted for greater accessibility. The remarkable "Great Supermarket" of Phung Hiep (the markets distinctly dissimilar to the floating markets found in and around Bangkok), where seven of the Mekong's waterways converge, is an absolutely impressive sight; during the fruit season, hundreds of boats carrying rambutan, mango and other assorted fruit move in and out of the market areas. Visitors to the area can take an early morning coach from HCMC, eat breakfast at Tan An, and then cross the two ferries (at My Thuan and Hau Giang) to arrive at Can Tho, about 170 km from Saigon. There visitors can take a bus to Soc Trang in the afternoon, visit a Khmer museum and bat pagoda, and then return to Can Tho to view performances of "reformation" music.

The next morning, it's then off to the Ninh Kieu wharf for a steamboat ride of about 25 km to reach the Phung Hiep market. There you can take a steamboat ride through the canals flanked by curious villagers, most of whom will insist that you stay at their homes for a meal of freshly-slaughtered poultry and Vietnamese whiskey the villagers distill under the earth in their backyards. If you're part of the tour, the steamboat ride will probably prevent you from fraternizing with the villagers, as you'll have to go back to Saigon that evening, a ride which won't be a lot of fun if you've imbibed on too much rice whiskey.

Vietnam War vets and their families can take advantage of a visit to the former battlefield at Tay Nguyen on the Central High Plateau. Currently, there are very few tourists enjoying this ecological paradise, which has environmentally recovered completely since the end of the hostilities in 1975. In addition to Khe Sanh, Dien Bien Phu and the Ho Chi Minh Trail, there are a number of barely-visited areas of the Central High Plateau. Interesting locals that see few, if any, tourists in the area include An Khe, Pleime and Dakto, as well as the mountain path to Lak Lake. A number of tourist agencies have combined their resources to make tours to the area viable.

The Central High Plateau has a number of attractions that tourists are infrequently aware of. There's the village of Bien Ho, and in the Lak district you can rent a canoe or ride on the back of an elephant. Hunting is also available for the outdoorsman.

Tourist agencies in HCMC may be able to cut out some of the more expensive portions of the tour, i.e. the airfares. You may be able to get from Da Lat to Buon Ma Thuot or from Buon Ma Thuot to Nha Trang through the

Phoenix Pass (Phuong Hoang)—or take Highway 19 from Quy Nhon to Pleiku via the An Khe Pass. Ask around at the travel agencies spread across HCMC. Some of the better ones are listed in the "Directory" section of the "Ho Chi Minh City" chapter.

There are a lot of operators out there, and a lot of new ones trying to cash in on Vietnam's growing popularity. Get to know as much as possible about a firm before selecting it. Ideally, talk to some other people who've employed the company before. Remember, there are as many different types of tour companies as there are genres of travel. To simplify your tour selection Fielding has organized package tours through a number of recommended tour operators. See "Package Tours" guide on page 479 or ☎ *(800) FW-2-GUIDE* for more information.

## Tours for Vietnam War Veterans

With improving Vietnam/U.S. relations, a few agencies now offer tours of Vietnam through areas where American soldiers fought, were based, and sent on R&R. As Saigontourist phrases it, "As understood by its appellation, war veteran tours have been set up by Vietnamese veterans for their foreign counterparts of the two Indochina Wars." These are special programs for those who served in Vietnam and would like to revisit former locations and areas of combat activities of their military units, of the Viet Cong war zones, and especially former battlefields. There are also more extensive programs for veterans from all countries (U.S., Australia, South Korea, Thailand, France and the Philippines) to visit the sites of former bases and areas of fire-fights. Vietnamtourism says these programs are designed to "promote understanding and friendship, thus helping to heal war wounds." Although the tours will have special appeal to returning American soldiers, all visitors to Vietnam are welcome who share an interest in visiting former battlefields as well as experiencing "the new Vietnam." Highlights of the tours consist of visits to the DMZ, Ben Hai River, Dong Ha, Quang Tri, the former U.S. base at Khe Sanh, Ashau-Aluoi valleys, "Hamburger Hill" (south of Ashau Valley), and the Ho Chi Minh Trail.

Some of the areas visited include:

### BEN HAI RIVER, THE DMZ

*From 1954 to 1975, The Ben Hai River served as the demarcation between the Republic of Vietnam (South Vietnam) and the Democratic Republic of North Vietnam. The Demilitarized Zone consisted of an area 5 km on each side of the river, or demarcation line.*

## HO CHI MINH TRAIL

*Initially, this was only a small trail in the mountainous range of Truong Son only for foot soldiers. But it later developed into an intricate, intertwined road network along the majestic Truong Son range–consisting of a trail for foot messengers and guides, and a larger road for big trucks. For more than a decade, the Ho Chi Minh Trail was a special supply and communication line from North Vietnam to battle sites in South Vietnam.*

For more information, see "Package Tours," page 479.

## Traveling by Road in Vietnam: National Highway 1

Totaling a distance of more than 1700 km, Vietnam's National Highway 1 (in its various stretches of smooth pavement and barely negotiable, dilapidated cattle trails) is the longest and most important roadway in the country. Including Highway 1A, it links Rach Gia in the far south all the way to Hanoi. For most of the route north of HCMC it is flanked by the gorgeous Truong Son mountains on the left and by the clear waters of the South China Sea on the right.

Between villages and cities, the route deteriorates from paved scenic pavement to pothole-ridden trenches meaning that bus drivers, and others who frequent the highway, need backsides of lead to endure. Rarely can you reach speeds of more than 50 mph (78 kph), except on a fast motorcycle where far greater speeds are possible but dangerous due to the vast amount of pedestrian, bicycle and ox cart traffic. At times the shoulder of the highway will be in better shape than the roadway itself, and you'll constantly see motorbikers using the well-worn, but relatively smooth shoulders of the road rather than the highway itself. Roadworkers can be occasionally seen throwing large rocks into the deepest trenches, but there is, amazingly enough, little work that is done to improve NH1. Some of the bridges that were destroyed during the Vietnam War have yet to be repaired, many only crossable by planks and/or railway ties that have been placed over the crumbling grid foundations.

Women line the route toting astoundingly heavy baskets supported by bamboo poles with produce going to market, perhaps many kilometers. They seem to totally ignore the speeding motorbikes and dust- and exhaust-spewing buses and freight trucks that proceed along the highway as if they were its only users. Oxen and horse carts plod the highway, pulling their loads of sugarcane and rice. Bicycles may have as many as three passengers; I've seen as many as six individuals, entire families and maybe some of their friends, astride small Honda 50 cc motorbikes. You'll come across Lambrettas, motorcycles attached with a covered cart with benches running along the sides. They're slow moving and usually packed with at least two dozen people and as many chickens or ducks. It's an unbelievably unsafe way to travel, but is the most popular form of short-distance trips.

***Ornate Vietnamese pagodas flank National Highway 1 in virtually uninhabited areas.***

The most useful device on your own mode of transportation is the horn. If it isn't working, it may as well be the steering that isn't functioning. You'll see hundreds of the brightly colored Ford and Desoto buses packed with passengers like sardines in oil plowing their way to places such as Danang, Hue, Quy Nhon, Vinh, Phan Thiet, Saigon and the likes. Water spews from small pipes in front of the vehicles near the undercarriages. The water is from the large drums attached to the roofs of the vehicles—and they must stop every 100 km or so to have these refilled, as they serve as the vehicles' cooling systems. The occupants don't seem to mind the cramped conditions aboard the buses—perhaps because most are entirely accustomed to such travel. For the average Westerner, a long bus ride is intolerable and doesn't give the traveler the opportunity to really "be on the road," as the driver will stop every couple or so hours at a roadside cafe of his own choosing so the weary passengers can refill their own cooling systems. On the buses, you'll see two young men straddling straps on the stairs of the open doors, yelling at pedestrians and motorists in the bus path to move the hell out of the way.

The few cars you'll see along Highway 1 are usually hired by tourists or are government vehicles. You'll see, though, a number of microbuses of the various Vietnamese tourist agencies bouncing along the roadway usually carrying Viet Kieu (Overseas Vietnamese) tourists up and down the coast. The big trucks are usually relatively recently built Soviet heavy duty trucks, although you'll also see a number of American- and French-made trucks left over from both Indochina wars that are still quite operational, the result of primitive, but ingenious maintenance.

### INSIDER TIP

*Because tourism is expanding so rapidly in Vietnam, some of the sites where locals rarely laid eyes on foreigners are becoming inundated with white-skinned Anglos with funny green eyes, cameras, and Deet. Battle sites from the Vietnam War are particularly becoming popular with foreign tourists. The village of My Lai and Son My village, where American soldiers massacred hundreds of Vietnamese civilians have become hot spots to visit. Since the 25th anniversary of the massacre a couple of years ago, more than 7000 people have visited Son My. More than half the visitors were foreigners, whose number visiting the site increased four-fold between 1993 and 1994. The number of Vietnamese visitors has doubled. So if My Lai is on your itinerary, expect some company.*

Frequently, you'll come across unhusked rice drying in the sun that may spread halfway across the highway. The larger vehicles will roll right over the grain—curiously, the farmers say it helps speed the drying process. The rice is left untended except for the occasional spreading of the path to even the terrain of the grain. Sugarcane and rice paper are also spread across the road at various points, although vehicles aren't meant to drive over the chips and (markers in the form of stones or carts are placed in front of the piles to keep drivers off them). Think of the carbon monoxide and Michelin tire ingredients in your cuisine the next time you're dining.

At various points in the villages along NH1 the road narrows to a mere fly strip as motorcycles, bicycles and heavy trucks barge through the local markets that bulge out into the road like non-ticket holders at a Grateful Dead concert. Additionally spilling out onto the highway are large groups of schoolchildren and other surrounding card games, again, totally oblivious to the traffic. NH1 is as much a social center as it is a thoroughfare.

Of course, there are accidents—many of them. The sites where motorists or pedestrians have died are usually marked with a Buddhist-like shrine, and many drivers stop at these points to pay their respects. It is supposed to be good luck to do so. Near Ca Na, there's even a memorial where a busload of passengers died some years ago.

All along Highway 1 food stalls and cafes abound, their owners dangerously sprinting into the middle of the roadway as if there was an emergency to flag down motorists into their eateries. Usually the cafes are in clumps, so the competition for business, although friendly, is ruthless. In a way, customers at these stalls are a remedy to an emergency, as the stall owners are all quite poor. Wherever you stop, you will be swarmed by children, beggars and such, selling everything from lighter fluid to chewing gum.

Perhaps the great advantage of Highway 1, as well as other routes spread acrosss Vietnam, is the number of Honda repair shops. Every few hundred meters you are bound to see a sign saying "Honda (spelled in various configurations such as 'Hun Da, Honza, Hon Daa', etc.) Xe Dap," the latter meaning the shop also works on bicycles. At virtually any point along Highway 1 if you break down, there will be a Honda repair hootch within rolling distance. Vietnamese, mechanics or not, will instantly try to determine and remedy your bike's malady. Most are quite adept, although they tend to smoke cigarettes so close to gasoline, it's amazing the country hasn't completely defoliated itself without the aid of hostile aggressors.

You'll find that after passing several kilometers through a village or town, a team of policemen will have set up roadblocks. Their purpose is usually to stop buses and trucks for bribes. Tourists are rarely stopped by the police (unless you're traveling independently by motorcycle—then expect to be stopped frequently), although you may find yourself on a microbus whose driver doesn't possess the proper credentials to be transporting tourists. Some of these drivers employ imaginative ways of bypassing the roadblocks. One driver I met near Phan Thiet, before reaching a roadblock, unloaded his tourists and placed them on buses a kilometer before the checkpoint. He picked them back up again on the other side. Police, when they see a large motorcycle approaching, may step out into the road to flag you down with their batons—but upon realizing you're a foreigner will usually allow you to pass (Vietnamese are not allowed to operate motorcycles over 175 cc unless they're in "high positions," usually in the government—or they're police officers themselves).

NH1 is continually surrounded by rice fields, the workers under their conical hats stooped tending to the crop. You'll see statues of the Virgin Mary and ancient Cham towers perched on hilltops or right beside the roadway.

Near Cam Ranh, salt factories flank the roadside, and salt paddies extend out into the deep blue mountain-ringed bay.

Going north, after passing through Danang, you make a journey over one of the most spectacular passes in Vietnam, Hai Van Pass, which reaches an altitude of nearly 500 meters in the Truong Son Mountain Range. The views of both ocean and lush green mountains are unsurpassed anywhere in the world. This pass, many times shrouded in dense fog, is so dangerous and steep that ascending turn-off ramps on downgrades have been constructed for trucks and buses which lose their brakes, which happens constantly on this stretch of roadway. This is the ribbon of NH1 that drivers fear the most, and is perhaps the most dangerous stretch of NH1 in Vietnam. Hai Van Pass, during the 15th century, marked the border between the Kingdom of Champa and Vietnam. On top of the pass, there is an old fort that was built by the French and then later used by the Americans and the South Vietnamese Army.

Between Danang and Lang Co Beach the Vietnamese climate changes dramatically—from sunny, hot and humid to damp, gray and cloud covered—and cold. From this point to Ha Long Bay and Hanoi, you'll think you're in a different country. The fog straddling the mountainsides of Hai Van Pass creates some of the best photo opportunities in Vietnam, but you'll soon become depressed by the lack of sunlight and heat which you despised only hours earlier. Villagers and farmers are dressed in winter clothing.

The one thing to watch out for on NH1 is that it forks frequently, the most confusing fingers of the road being in Quy Nhon and Phan Rang. You may travel several kilometers before you realize you screwed up.

Now that the Friendship Bridge has been completed linking Thailand and Laos, there's a lot of talk about linking Thailand and Vietnam through Laos at other points. Some of the projects seriously being considered are Highway 8, which would link Thailand's northeastern Nakhon Phanom Province with Vietnam's Cua Lo Port, near Vinh, via Khammouan Province in central Laos. Also being considered is Highway 12, which would link Thailand's Nakhon Phanom Province with the Vietnamese port of Hon La. This route is farther south than Highway 8. Highway 9 already links Danang and Hue with Laos and Thailand.

The government is interested in all three roads but particular attention is paid to upgrading Route 9. This is to the benefit of Thailand's Mukdahan Province.There would be less investment involved, and the road traverses relatively flat terrain. Additionally, a new port would not have to be built. But Nakhon Phanom has the edge in that Highway 12 through Khammouan to the Vietnamese coast is only 270 km, as opposed to the 570 km stretch along Highway 9 linking Vietnam with Laos and Thailand. One of the carrots being held out, on the part of the Thais is that construction of Highway 12 would help reduce the pressure of population growth in Bangkok, and would more evenly distribute Thai manufacturing facilities. Laos favors construction of Highway 8, because it would be the shortest way of reaching its capital, Vientiane. Whichever route is chosen, the three countries will still have a modern roadway of international standards that will eventually become a major international transportation link.

**AUTHOR'S NOTE**

*A little advice for travelers in Vietnam: There are 10,000 km of roads, 40 percent of which are rated "poor" or "very poor." There are 8280 road bridges, 50 percent of which are considered dilapidated. There are 2600 km of railways, seven major seaports, three international airports, and 10 domestic airports.*

## Books

The following are some of the best historical and contemporary works on Vietnam:

Browne, Malcombe, *Red Socks and Muddy Boots* (New York Times Press, 1993); this is an excellent, fast-paced accounting of the famous journalist's observations of the Vietnam War based on his 11 years in-country during the 1960s and 70s. It's a humorous and depressing no punches-pulled analysis of the political and military blunders both sides struggled with in justifying both their moral, political and military ambitions in Indochina. Browne, journalist Peter Arnett (now at CNN) and Neil Sheehan were primarily blackballed by US and ARVN forces as traitors, so this makes for fascinating reading of life in a Huey and a suitcase.

Along the same lines is Sheehan's definitive work, *A Bright Shining Lie* (Jonathan Cape, London, 1989). This is a huge account of the war based around the life of John Paul Vann. Well researched and as eye-opening as they come. This was a Pulitzer Prize winner. Sheehan also wrote *Two Cities: Hanoi and Saigon* (Jonathan Cape, London, 1992).

Another colleague of Sheehan's and Browne's was David Halberstram, whose *The Making of A Quagmire* (Ballantine Books, New York) is considered a gem in outlining U.S. participation in the war.

Also check out *The Real War* by Jonathan Shell (Pantheon Books, New York, 1987.

*The Bamboo Cage* by Leo Cooper (Cawthorne, Nigel, 1992). A tear-jerking account of POWs and MIAs in Vietnam during the war.

Francis Fitzgerald's *Fire in the Lake* (Vintage Books, New York, 1972) was also a Pulitzer Prize winner about U.S. involvement during the war.

*Why Vietnam?*, Archimedes Patti (University of California Press, Berkeley, 1980) is a compelling history of OSS (pre CIA) attempts to funnel weapons to Ho Chi Minh at the end of WWII. Patti was with the OSS during this time and was close to Ho when he claimed North Vietnamese independence in 1945.

*A Death in November* by Ellen Hammer (EP Dutton & Sons, New York, 1987) is the story of Diem's overthrow and execution in 1963.

*One Crowded Hour*, Tim Bowden (Angus and Robertson, 1988) chonicles the work of Australian film journalist Neil Davis, who shot footage of the NVA tank crashing through the gates of the presidential palace in April 1975.

*The Tunnels of Cu Chi*, Tom Mangold and John Pennycate (1985). A look at the hardships the Viet Cong faced in building and living in the famed tunnels west of Saigon.

*The Fall of Saigon*, David Butler (Simon & Schuster, 1985) is a look at the events and the chaos surrounding takeover of the South's capital in 1975, as is *55 Days; The Fall of Saigon*, by Alan Dawson (Prentice Hall, Englewood Cliffs, NJ, 1977).

Michael Herr's *Dispatches* (Knopf, New York, 1987) is a journalist's first-hand look at the bloody conflict.

Stanley Karnow's highly respected *Vietnam: A History* (Viking Press, New York, 1983) is one of the most respected works on Vietnam in the last two decades.

*Chickenhawk*, by Robert Mason (Penguin, 1984) is the recollections of a chopper pilot. Fast paced, edge-of-the-seat reading.

*The Pentagon Papers* (Bantam Books, Toronto, 1971) were published by the *New York Times* and had the same effect, if not more, on America's sentiments toward the war as did the 1968 Tet Offensive.

*Born on the Fourth of July*, Ron Kovic (Pocket Books, New York, 1976). This grisly, heart-wrenching account of a soldier maimed during the war was made into a blockbuster movie starring Tom Cruise in an unforgettable role as the author.

*The 13th Valley*. It was written years before the motion picture *Platoon* hit the big screen and is easily the more horrific of the two in describing the terror of being a grunt in the jungle.

*Brothers in Arms* (Avon Books, New York, 1986), by William Broyles Jr. is a mildly interesting account of a former GI-turned-journalist returning to Vietnam some years after the war.

*Portrait of the Vietnamese Soldier* (Red River Press, Hanoi) is a provocative account of the North Vietnamese struggle against the Americans.

William Turley's *The Second Indochina War: A Short Political and Military History, 1954–1975* (Westview, Boulder, 1976), can be hard reading, but it's comprehensive and highly detailed.

Bungling military strategy is examined in *On Strategy*, by Colonel Harry Summers (Presidio Press, Navato, Calif., 1982).

*Bloods: An Oral History of the Vietnam War by Black Veterans*, by Wallace Terry (Ballentine Books, 1984).

*Chained Eagle* is a gripping account of the lives of American POWs by Everett Alverez (Dell, New York, 1989).

*Viet Cong Memoir*, by Truong Nhu Tang, is about the life of a former Viet Cong soldier who later rejected post-1975 Vietnamese politics. (Harcourt Brace Jovanovich, San Diego, 1985).

*Ecological Consequences of the Vietnam War*, SIPRI (Almqvist & Wiksell, Stockholm, 1976). An account of the environmental devastation of the war.

### Other Books of Interest

*The Quiet American*, Graham Greene (Heinemann, London, 1954). Most of us read this highly accurate fictionalized account of the impending American involvement in the Indochinese conflict in university. As relevant today as it was then. Some say it's a masterpiece.

*A Dragon Apparent: Travels in Cambodia, Laos and Vietnam*, by Norman Lewis (Eland Books, 1951). A superb travelogue.

Charles Fenn's *Ho Chi Minh: A Biographical Introduction* (Charles Tutteland Rutland Vermont, 1973).

*Saigon*, Anthony Grey (Pan, London, 1983).

*The Birth of Vietnam*, Keith Taylor (University of California Press, Berkeley, 1983).

J. Helzar, *The Art of Vietnam* (Hanlyn, London, 1973).

Elizabeth Kemp, *Month of Pure Light; The Regreening of Vietnam* (The Women's Press, London, 1990).

Gerald Hickey, *Village in Vietnam* (Yale University Press, New Haven, 1964).

*Vietnamese Anticolonialism: 1885–1925*, by David G. Marr (University of Berkeley, Los Angeles, 1971).

*The Rise of Nationalism in Vietnam: 1900–1941* (Cornell University Press, Ithica, New York, 1976).

*Australia's War in Vietnam* by Frank Frost (Allen and Unwin, Sydney, Boston, and London, 1987).

*All the Way: Australia's Road to Vietnam* by Gregory Pemberton (Allen and Unwin, Sydney, Boston, and London, 1987).

Robert F. Turner, *Vietnamese Communism: Its Origins and Development* (Hoover Institution Press, Stanford, 1975).

### Contemporary Vietnamese-Language Titles

The following are Vietnamese titles that can be obtained at the dealers listed in parantheses.

#### Dealers

**Dainam Co.**, *P.O. Box 4279, 551 W. Arden Ave., Glendale, CA 91203*

**Lang Van**, *P.O. Box 310, Station W, Toronto, Ontario, Canada M6M 5B9*

**Pan Asian**, *P.O. Box 131, Agincourt Station, Scarborough, Ontario, Canada M1S 3B4*

**Tan Lac**, *P.O. Box 680797, Orlando, FL 32868-0797*

**Van Nghe**, *10891 Oak Street, Stanton, CA 90680*

**Vietnamese Book Store**, *P.O. Box 97, Los Alamitos, CA 90720*

**Zien Hong**, *11215 Sageland, Houston, TX 77089*

Ai Khanh's *Mot thoi de nho* (Tan Lac, 1994) is a book of short stories looking at how Overseas Vietnamese have adapted to life in America.

*Nhung moi uu tu cua nguoi Viet doi bo*, by Buu Sao (Tan Lac, 1994), is a tale of the Vietnamese search for social, economic and political solutions to the country's poverty.

*Thep den*, by Dang Chi Binh (Chuong Viet, 1991), is a bitter but moving account of a former spy for the south's imprisonment and "reeducation" during the Vietnam War.

Dao Quoc Ho's *Cuoi ra nuoc mat* (Zien Hong, 1993) is a biting satire of post-reunification Saigon.

The ancient rituals and customs of the Vietnamese Royal Court are examined in *Nhung dai le va vu khuc cua vua chua Viet Nam* (Tan Lac, 1992)

*Anh Hung nuoc toi*, by Dong Tien (Tan Lac, 1993), is a rosy biography of Vietnam's movers and shakers, from Le Loi to Bao Dai to Ho Chi Minh.

In 1993, Duong Thu Huong penned *Tieu thuyet vo de* (Van Nghe, 1993), a war novel set during the Vietnam War starring a female Communist soldier. Duong herself was a Communist fighter during the conflict and is now one of Vietnam's best-known authors.

*Bai gio con trang* (Lang Van, 1994) is Ho Truong An's series of ghost stories set amidst the small villages of southern Vietnam.

*Choi chu* (Zien Hong, 1993) is a guide for helping Vietnamese understand local patois. By Lang Nhan. Also by Lang are *Chuyen ca ke* (Zien Hong, 1993), a humerous look at everyday life in Vietnam; *Giai thoai nha nho* (Zien Hong, 1993), an account of the teaching methods of rural Confucian scholars, and *Truoc den* (Zien Hong, 1993), which are excerpts from the great writers of Vietnam.

Le Ba Kong looks at how well Overseas Vietnamese entrepreneurs are faring in the U.S. and elsewhere in *Nguoi Viet ly huong* (Zien Hong, 1993).

*Dong song sua me*, by Le Hong Hung (Tan Lac, 1994), is a collection of short stories about the author's birthplace.

Le Trung Hoa's *Ho va ten nguoi Viet Nam* (Tan Lac, 1992) is a how-to for parents banging their brains for names for their unborn children. Le also traces family roots and the origins of Vietnamese family names. Plenty of Nguyens are buying.

Le Van Hoe was Vietnamese ambassador to China during the 1805-1820 reign of King Gia Long. His novel, *Truyen kieu chu giai* (Zien Hong, 1993), about 19th-century Vietnamese nobility and gentry, is immensely popular.

The poems of dissident of the Communist regime Nguyen Chi Tien were penned during 20 years of imprisonment in a volume entitled *Tieng vong tu day vuc* (Tan Lac, 1994). Text is in Vietnamese and German.

Kiss-and-tell of the private lives of the Vietnamese courts under the Kings Thieu Tri and Minh Mang can be found in *Truyen cac ong hoang trieu nguyen*, by Nguyen Dac Xuan (Tan Lac, 1994).

Nguyen Huy's description of Vietnamese culture can be found in *Van hoa Viet* (Tan Lac, 1994).

*Ngay buon cung qua mau*, by Nguyen Ngoc Ngan (Xuan Thu, 1990), is an account of how Overseas Vietnamese have assimmilated into Canadian culture. His novel *Quay trong con loc* (Lang Van, 1994) is a look into the changes in Vietnamese society in the modern age of reform in Vietnam.

Nguyen Quoc Thang's *Tien trinh van nghe mien nam* (Tan Lac, 1994) examines the changes in art and literature in post-war Vietnam.

The lives of Overseas Vietnamese who settled in Norway are depicted in *Nguyen Thi Vanh's Na uy va toi* (Tan Lac, 1994).

Popular Vietnamese folktales are told by Nguyen Van Ngoc in *Truyen co nuoc nam* (Tan Lac, 1993).

*Viet Nam nhin tu ben trong va ben ngoai*, by Nguyen Xuan Nghia (Lang Van, 1994) is a personal look at trends and events in Vietnamese society.

Crime in Vietnam is the focus of Tran Hong's *Mang luoi* (Dainam Co., 1994).

Trong Minh's *Ve vang dan Viet* (1991-93) is a two-volume set of biographical sketches of successful Overseas Vietnamese. Rich Murphy has translated the work into English. Text also in Vietnamese.

Nguyen Tu writes about a young girl of a Vietnamese refugee family living in Paris as a guide helping Overseas Vietnamese parents raise their children in foreign cultures. *Chuyen be Kim* (Tan Lac, 1992-94; 2 vol.).

Samples from Vietnamese writers living in Europe can be found in *Van but Viet Nam hai ngoai* (Tan Lac, 1993).

Irina Zisman's *But ky Irina* (Alpha, 1993-94, 2 vol.) is a collection of the author's memories of her experiences in Vietnam including socio/political commentary.

## When You Arrive

Vietnam is a surprisingly easy country to enter these days. The formalities are no more arduous than, say, entering Thailand. Frankly, it's more of a hassle entering Singapore than either Saigon or Hanoi. The infamous scams pulled by Vietnamese customs officials and policemen that were prevalent only a short time ago are all but nonexistent now. Foreigners, who are legitimate tourists of course, have little fear of being harassed or detained while an "illegal entry" fine is negotiated. Be warned, however, that a lot less English is spoken in Hanoi than in Saigon and, that if there is a problem, it probably will be both more expensive and time consuming to solve it. It appears, however, that customs officials in both cities are under instructions in no uncertain terms that each and every stamp on a foreigner's passport is synonymous with much-needed hard currency; the likelihood of you being afforded the opportunity to tell your friends and other potential visitors of the hardships you encountered entering or leaving Vietnam are these days, fortunately, minimal. Even though Vietnam is a communist country, you will be surprised at how much freedom you're afforded.

## SOME ADVICE FOR RETURNING VIET KIEU

*If you're an overseas Vietnamese, or "Viet Kieu," returning to Vietnam, here's a tip: don't show your bucks. Vietnamese can instantly spot an overseas Vietnamese, usually by their behavior and attire. Many Vietnamese are wary of returning "Viet Kieu," and suspicious of their intentions. You may be only a tourist, but many Vietnamese will suspect you've returned to your home country to make a fast buck, especially if you dress flashy and exhibit the behavior and social customs you've acquired in your new home country.*

*Curiously, although they fanatically vie for it, the Vietnamese do not trust wealth, especially the display of it. Additionally, you may face criticism from your anti-communist friends at home, who may accuse you of supporting Marxism. Don't be surprised if many at home call you a VC (Viet Cong). Although relations between Vietnam and the U.S. have normalized, it is still very difficult for overseas Vietnamese to reintegrate with their people. You may feel like a stranger in your own country. The Vietnamese government will welcome your money, of course. Overseas Vietnamese send or bring into the country perhaps US$1 billion each year.*

*If you're an overseas Vietnamese wishing to return permanently to your homeland (as a growing number are), it may not be so easy.*

*Decision No. 59/TTg (implemented the day after U.S. President lifted the embargo in Feb. 1994) is somewhat complicated but essentially limits applicants to three categories of consideration: 1) elderly persons aged 60 or more and children under the age of 16 if they are sponsored by close relatives living in Vietnam; 2) applicants with a post-graduate degree or professional skills needed by the government; 3) management directors of companies associated with investment projects in Vietnam as prioritized by the Law on Foreign Investment.*

*If you hold a foreign passport, forget it. If you hold no passport, forget it. If you left Vietnam illegally in the first place, forget it. In other words, the Vietnamese Vietnam will take back shouldn't have been tainted by counter-revolutionary lifestyles, or should be too old to do anything about it.*

On the plane you will have filled out a customs declaration form. Those items you have declared will be inspected in all likelihood. And even though the idea of having your belongings displayed is unappealing (and downright frightening if you've got on your person anything marginally to highly suspicious, such as gems, figurines, poached animal parts, Chinese elixirs or heroin paste), remember that what you don't declare doesn't exist. Say you're traveling with a laptop computer and don't declare it upon entry. If you're searched upon leaving and it's discovered, you may end up paying a duty on it, if not worse.

## Language and Culture

There are a lot of nuances that differ among the peoples of the Far East. But for every contrast, there are 10 commonalities. Asians, as tolerant as most are, will behave in ways and speak with a body language that will fluster you at first. You'll be tempted to be amused by gestures and customs that seem everything from banal to compulsive. But don't be.

Just use good judgement. Knowing how to dress, present and compose yourself will dispel a ton of potential problems. Remember, it's better to blend in in Asia than to stand out. Dress coolly but conservatively. Shorts, but not short ones are okay in informal environments. Ladies should cover as much of their bodies as reasonably possible. You don't have to look like a nun, but it wouldn't hurt. No short dresses, except perhaps in Hong Kong. Anything you consider sexy will be taken as offensive by your Asian hosts. And try not to look like a hippie. That sarong and the beads you bought in Ko Samui are fine on Ko Samui, but now you're in a land of pith helmets, business suits and olive drab uniforms. Take heed.

Displays of emotion—from affection to anger—are considered crass and rude. Never show anger, regardless of the situation. Most Southeast Asians abhor conflict. Smile even to the man you'd rather kick than converse with. Equally as offensive, in most places, are public displays of sexual affection. Kissing and even holding hands are discouraged in most Asian communities. Save it for the hotel.

When entering an individual's home, in some cases, you'll need to remove your shoes. However, unlike other predominantly Buddhist countries in the region, the Vietnamese are generally not inclined to follow this practice, even inside temples. If you're not sure, your host will not be offended if you politely inquire. Never will you be expected to remove your shoes at hotels and public structures other than some religious temples.

Don't pat anyone on the head, including children. It's a sign of disrespect. And what you do with your hands, do with both hands or your right hand only.The left hand is considered unclean. This includes for eating and passing objects to other people. It's a pain in the rear if you're left-handed, but try and follow the rule at least when it's most appropriate, as in ceremonial occasions, toasts in your honor, etc.

The feet are considered unclean as well. When seated, don't point them in anyone's direction. (A lot of people do it, anyway—it's no big deal unless you appear to be doing it on purpose.)

If eating with chopsticks, place them horizontally across your bowl or on the table when finished.

Finally, be especially careful of the gestures you make. Symbols that are considered innocent or even complimentary in the U.S. are construed differently abroad. However, it's only truthful to say that, as a foreigner, you won't be expected to understand proper gestures and behavior of the Vietnamese. Rather, you'll be expected not to understand. And, in most cases, violations will be dismissed with a smile, if they are even noticed. One reason the Vietnamese are more tolerant of Western idiosyncracies than other East Asian societies is the fact that 5 million Americans and a few hundred thousand other Westerners essentially occupied the southern half of the country for more than 10 years in the 1960s and '70s. Things are changing very rapidly here.

## BEHAVING WITH THE VIETNAMESE SOCIALLY AND IN BUSINESS

*A few notes on how to deal with Vietnamese customs, whether you're in the country on business or pleasure. Simply reading about the "customs" in Asian nations won't be enough to learn the idiosyncrasies of Vietnamese customs and behavior. In terms of business or official meetings, get a good interpreter. That person should teach you correct pronunciation for the individuals you'll be meeting with. Learn Vietnamese greetings (the Crash Course in Speaking Vietnamese in this book will help).*

*Learn now to recognize the individual you'll be meeting before the meeting, either through an interpreter's description or by seeing a photograph. That way, you'll immediately know who to address when entering the room. And do not greet an assistant first! When you shake hands, do so at arm's length rather than up close. Most Westerners are quite a bit taller than their Vietnamese hosts.*

*Sitting at a table during a business meeting, do not cross your legs or show the soles of your feet (this is really not even acceptable in social situations, although the increasing influx of naive Westerners into Vietnam has made the Vietnamese more accustomed to this—but only in social environs). Although the custom of giving and receiving with both hands is common in Southeast Asia, it is not necessary in Vietnam.*

*When handing out business cards, start with the most important person you are with. But give cards to everyone! You never know where the mailroom clerk will be in a few years. If you're short on business cards and have to make photocopies, never mix the two when you're handing out cards. Either hand out a photocopy or the original.*

## BEHAVING WITH THE VIETNAMESE SOCIALLY AND IN BUSINESS

*One of the life threatening habits I've acquired since being in Vietnam is that I've started smoking cigarettes. This was mainly due to the fact that I was incessantly offered them as gifts. Most Vietnamese men smoke, though few women do. Simply, if you're offered a cigarette, take it. Not doing so is somewhat of an insult (although this is changing rapidly as the Vietnamese become more accustomed to non-smoking foreigners), even if you don't smoke. Either smoke it or place it on the table in front of you (in which case you will not be offered another).*

*One of the traditional tips offered to business people doing business with the Vietnamese has been this: If you're employing a translator, address the person you're speaking with, not the translator. When the Vietnamese is speaking with you, look at him and acknowledge him occasionally with a nod of the head. Again, don't look at the interpreter. He is only the conduit of your conversation with the person you are meeting with.*

*In reality, it usually doesn't work this way, and you'll find that many Vietnamese look and speak directly toward the interpreter, rather than at you. It's best when both talking and listening to divide your attention between the interpreter and your audience. It's more interactive and less a charade—as is the nature of all conversations between two people who can't understand a word each other says.*

*Vietnamese love to drink.If you do, too, you've come to the right place. There are different forms of toasting in Vietnam. One of them, which is used frequently, is called "Tram Phan Tram." It means you are required to empty the entire contents of your glass. If you don't drink alcohol, a soft drink or tea will do. But if you do enjoy an occasional whiskey or beer, be prepared to enjoy your imbibement excessively. In Vietnam, you should never refuse hospitality when it's offered.*

## AUTHOR'S OBSERVATION

*The liberalization of the Vietnamese economy has spawned the influx of other Western influences or "extravagances" that would have been unheard of, or in this case, unseen, 10 years ago. A point in case is the rise in cosmetic sales. Just a short time ago, even lipstick was seen as a luxury for the very wealthy, models and actresses. Now Vietnamese are looking to the West for beauty aids, and companies such as Max Factor, Chanel, and Christian Dior couldn't be more ecstatic. Whereas once only Thai-made cosmetic products made poor girls even poorer, now beauty products from firms such as Chanel, Lancome and Revlon can be found in shops lining the boulevards of Hanoi and Saigon. A recent look at some of the shops found that a Suntory gift purse can be had for about US$25, while a bottle of Poison perfume fetches US$80.*

*Although there has existed a counterfeit market for such "brands" from Singapore, Thailand and China for years, it is dwindling quickly, as Vietnamese women are now insisting on the real McCoy. The cosmetic market though, according to most observers is still wide open, and will become increasingly lucrative as more Vietnamese women have the means to look "beautiful"—or use their meager means for beauty at the expense of food. Hopefully, we won't see the "Pepsi Generation" also become the Karen Carpenter generation.*

## Behaving in Temples

The rule of always removing your shoes before entering an Asian temple of worship is not always observed in Vietnam. It depends entirely upon the temple, the lifestyle of its hosts and local custom. As mentioned above, inquire first. At many temples, especially those frequented by tourists, a sign in English will be posted regarding the rule.

If seated before a Buddha, sit on your knees, thigh and hip, with your feet extending behind you. Do not sit in the lotus position (cross-legged). No shorts in temples, although some guides will tell you that it's okay. (They just don't want to offend you.) Cameras may or may not be permitted. Usually they're not in other East Asian temples, but in many Vietnamese temples, they are permitted—especially in those with connections to the state. They charge an additional camera admission fee! And remember, customs and behavior in the south are a lot more relaxed than in the north. It's like the difference between Venice, California and Newport, Rhode Island.

## A Word About Language

We'll admit it; the tongues of the Far East make the languages of Europe seem like dialects of English. Learning Mandarin Chinese, Japanese, Thai, Cambodian, Malay and Vietnamese virtually requires surgery. But a little effort on your part to pick up some rudimentary Vietnamese phrases will go a long way. Unlike many huffy Parisians, Vietnamese people are honored when you make an attempt to speak their language, as futile and unintelligible as the resulting utterance may be.

It's an old phrase, but not without relevance. When overseas, you are an ambassador of your country. How you treat your Vietnamese hosts will be reciprocated to those who follow in your footsteps.

## A Word About Illegal Drugs

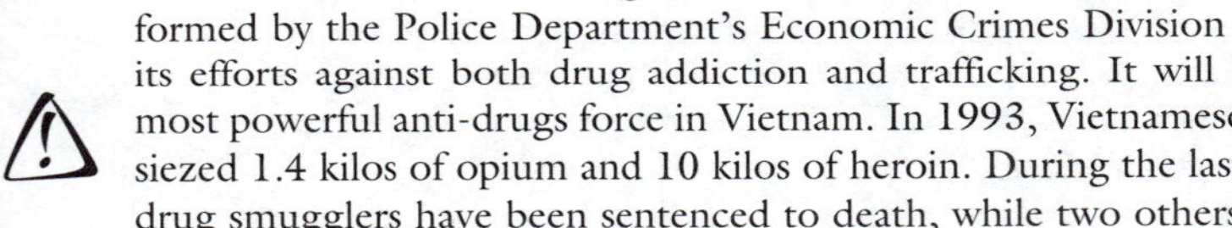

Leave them at home. Drug users and traffickers beware. A special squad formed by the Police Department's Economic Crimes Division will step up its efforts against both drug addiction and trafficking. It will become the most powerful anti-drugs force in Vietnam. In 1993, Vietnamese authorities siezed 1.4 kilos of opium and 10 kilos of heroin. During the last year, three drug smugglers have been sentenced to death, while two others were jailed for life.

In June 1995, a British national born in Hong Kong became the first foreigner executed in Vietnam for drug trafficking. In July, an American was sentenced to 20 years imprisonment and fined US$200,000 for his role in attempting to bring 1600 kg of heroin into the country.

He got off light. Very light.

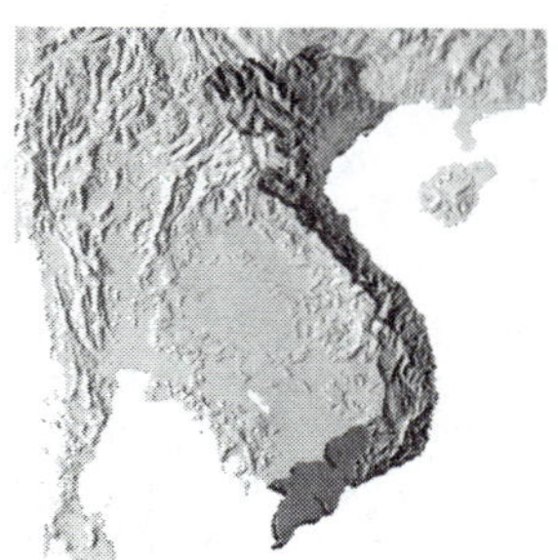

# VIETNAM TODAY

***Barbie, Barbwire and billiards. As Vietnam's economy becomes influenced by the West, so do its artists.***

Two decades after U.S. troops pulled out of Vietnam, Americans are returning to this still-battle-scarred country, only this time, they're coming as tourists and business people.

Thanks to the U.S. government's removal of restrictions against travel to Vietnam in 1992, followed by President Clinton's lifting of the trade embargo in February 1994 and subsequent normalizing of relations in July 1995, a growing slew of tour operators now offer group and individual tour packages to Vietnam. Their numbers—and travelers' options—are expanding at a jackrabbit's pace.

Tours from the U.S. usually fly into Bangkok, Singapore or Hong Kong, convenient gateways for air connections into Vietnam. Although operators say most of their inquiries are for tours that combine Vietnam with Cambodia and Laos, you probably won't see many all-Indochina tours advertised until Cambodia's on-again/off-again political problems are resolved. You will, however, be able to choose from a fairly good selection of tour packages that combine Vietnam with other Asian destinations, including China. (There are good flight connections from Nanning, China into Vietnam.) And soon, maybe by the time you read this, you may be able to fly directly to Vietnam from the U.S. (Look for Delta Airlines and United to be the companies to first offer these routes.)

## VIETNAM IN A NUTSHELL

*One of the most overwhelmingly beautiful countries in the world...with a people to match...71-plus million of them...of the 5 million Americans who fought here during the Vietnam War, 58,000 died and more than 2,200 are still MIA in Indochina—more than 1600 in Vietnam alone...the subsequent international economic embargo of Vietnam crippled the country...it has one of the lowest standards of living in the world...certainly in SE Asia...however, the thawing of relations between the U.S. and Vietnam has spawned a surge in tourism...lifting of the embargo and the normalization of relations is now allowing American businesses to operate aggressively in Vietnam...there are more than 3200 km of coastline...more than the state of California...and most of it pristine...the U.S. dollar is accepted throughout most of the country...Hanoi is moving markedly toward a market economy...it's best to visit now, before the inevitable commercialism suffocates this country's innocence.*

| | |
|---|---|
| **Ho Chi Minh City (Saigon)** | *Although at one time on par with Bangkok, but now eclipsed by the Thai capital, Saigon is still one of the most thriving cities in all of Southeast Asia, certainly the most bustling in Indochina. Vibrant. Entrepreneurial. With the exception of the revolutionary posters and hammer and sickle flags swirling about, you'd never know you were in a communist country. Population about 5 million. Natural attractions include the nearby Mekong Delta. Man-made wonders include the nearby Cu Chi tunnel network.* |
| **Nha Trang** | *This coastal area features beautiful beaches which are popular with both locals and tourists. There's great snorkeling and scuba diving as well as fishing and great seafood.* |

## VIETNAM IN A NUTSHELL

| | |
|---|---|
| **Danang** | *This is a historic city and one of Vietnam's major seaports. And although it bustles with shipping activity, the water is remarkably clean and the area boasts some good beaches. Some of the attractions include the local Cham architecture.* |
| **The Central Highlands** | *Generally known for the great scenery, cooler climate and the Montegnard tribespeople. The verdant mountain scenery is unmatched in Vietnam save perhaps for some areas in the northern part of the country. There are waterfalls and many beautiful, clear lakes.* |
| **Hue** | *This city, although devastated during the war, retains a great deal of its historical charm. Hue is really the traditional cultural, art, educational, and religious capital of Vietnam. There are all kinds of pagodas, palaces and museums to visit here. The royal tombs are just south of the city.* |
| **Ha Long Bay** | *Beautiful beach area with thousands of islands and spectacular grottos rising from the Gulf of Tonkin southeast of Hanoi. The area is targeted by the government to become a major tourist area it says will rival those of Thailand and the Eastern peninsula of Malaysia. Visit this area now, while it is still absolutely pristine.* |
| **Hanoi** | *The charming capital of Vietnam but not nearly as colorful as its onetime rival in the south–Saigon. The people here are more reserved than their neighbors to the south. But it is a charming colonial city if charm is your thing. The Old Quarter, is rapidly becoming transformed by weird-looking add-on building additions and satellite dishes, but the "gingerbread" style architecture and tree-lined boulevards make the capital worth a visit of moderate length.* |

Americans who have already gone to Vietnam say they're amazed by the friendliness the people show toward U.S. visitors, given the recent history of the two countries. They're also surprised to find that just about everything is priced in U.S. dollars, rather than in Vietnamese currency, the dong (about 10,900 dong equals US$1), especially in the larger population centers. Even the departure tax of US$8 is paid in U.S. currency. Hotels and other businesses now accept U.S. issued credit cards, and Vietcom Bank has also started issuing cash advances on U.S.-issued credit cards.

**INSIDER TIP**

*If you're an American, it would be wise for you to make absolutely sure you have enough cash and/or traveler's checks to make it through the entirety of your stay in Vietnam. And I mean the entirety. Even though you may be able to, don't expect it as a given that you'll be able to wire cash in from abroad. Some things are changing very rapidly in Vietnam. Many other things aren't. One is the amount of red tape and paper stamping that is required for any formal transaction or document. Don't assume your American-issued credit card will be accepted in Vinh, even though you were able to take a cash advance out on it in Saigon. One American idiot, whom I won't name, started a bank account in Thailand and, knowing there were branches of the bank throughout Vietnam, brought along just enough traveler's checks to get by for "about a week or two." He just figured that if the cash ran out (it always does), he'd simply drop into the local branch of his bank for a withdrawal from a kindly Vietnamese teller. She told him he was bookoo American and was bookoo dumb for not bookooing enough bookoo to the Saigon branch from the Bangkok bank in the first place. "No biggy," my buddy said, "I'll just take an advance out on my VISA card." She said, "Yes, biggy. No can do." After only five days into a 30-day Vietnam tour, my buddy had to bookoo back to Bangkok for more buckeroos. However, it is worth starting a Thai bank account if you're going to be spending time in the region. You can even start an account and earn interest on it in Vietnam (if you do, we recommend it be with Vietcom Bank). And if you select a Thai bank (and start the account in Thailand) choose the bank carefully. For instance, an account with Bangkok Bank in Thailand won't give you access to your account at a Bangkok Bank branch of the bank in Saigon, unless you've made prior wire arrangements in Thailand. However, an account with Thai Military Bank, I'm informed, will allow you access to your money at a company branch in Vietnam.*

Despite poverty and a Third-World infrastructure, Vietnam—and particularly Ho Chi Minh City (which most people here still refer to as Saigon; in fact, the central part of the city is still officially called Saigon)—still retains its haughty, aggressive air. Rickshaws (called cyclos in Vietnam) buzz around town; street vendors hawk everything from lacquerware to old tires and city boulevards are graced by beautiful, newly restored colonial-era mansions built by the French.

The average hotel leaves something to be desired, although those frequented by monied tourists and business people are overall surprisingly comfortable, if not downright luxurious. The townlike squares around the

Rex and the Continental have the feel of Boston or New Orleans. There are currently about 10 or 12 hotels under construction in Ho Chi Minh City (which will be located in Saigon, Cu Chi, which saw heavy action during the Vietnam War, and Cholon, the city's Chinatown). Among those recently finished are the 260-room Omni Saigon Hotel, which opened in 1993, and the 600-room New World Hotel, which opened in downtown Saigon in 1994. (Hong Kong-based New World is also building a hotel in Pnomh Penh, Cambodia). Also, Club Med plans to build a vacation village some time soon in Vietnam, but is first testing the waters by including the country in the schedules of its cruise vessel, Club Med 2.

Of the hotels already in operation in Ho Chi Minh City, the most luxurious (after the New World)—and the most intriguing—is the Saigon Floating Hotel. Operated by Australia's Southern Pacific Hotel Corporation, the boat-hotel was once a fixture on the Great Barrier Reef. It has about 200 air-conditioned rooms with all the modern amenities, including hairdryers in the bathrooms and a swimming pool on the mainland. If you can't afford to stay there, few can, you can always grab an easy chair at one of the small hostess bars on the other side of the square and watch its bright lines of yellow lights twinkle in the balmy Saigon night.

Other good hotels in Ho Chi Minh City where tourists are accommodated include the century-old, but newly refurbished Continental Hotel, a favorite of W. Somerset Maugham, and the Century Saigon, which is operated by a Hong Kong firm and occupies the site of the former Oscar Hotel.

In Hanoi, the capital, the lovely former Metropole Hotel has gotten a new lease on life, thanks to Pullman/ Sofitel, which restored this *grande dame* of the French colonial era. The Hotel Pullman Metropole has a superb French restaurant and a swimming pool.

## Flora and Fauna

Vietnam's flora and fauna are something to behold, although the forests have been extensively denuded in the last century—particularly by warfare. But compared to other regions of Southeast Asia, Vietnam is Eden. The forests contain as many as 12,000 species of plants. Just more than half of them have been identified.

## AUTHOR'S OBSERVATION

*Peoples' Committees throughout Vietnam have recently received documents from the Vietnamese Ministry of Forestry banning the sale of wild animals, the products of wild animals (including food), skins, stuffed birds and animals, horns, antlers, bones, claws, elephant tusks and gazelle horns, tortoise shells and the skin of leopards and tigers. Additionally, interestingly enough, the husbandry of wild animals was approved in the Forestry Ministry decree for domestic use and export.*

More than 250 species of mammals trod or trapeze the topography; 770 bird species traverse its skies. Nearly 200 species of reptiles slither about, hundreds of species of fish swim in its lakes and coastal waters, and 80 species of amphibians do both. The discoveries of new species continue. But, in sad contrast, hundreds more are expected to soon become extinct. Among those threatened are the tapir (which some believe is already extinct), the Javan rhino, and the kouprey. The Sumatran rhino is already extinct in Vietnam.

Vietnam, like virtually all Southeast Asian countries, has been mired by an abysmal record of protecting threatened wildlife species. Although there's been growing pressure by international wildlife organizations on Vietnam to get its act together—and there have been many strides made in the last few years to eradicate the poaching and/or sale for private use of endangered species—it's still a major problem here.

A little side trip I took recently to Saigon's Cho Cau Mong animal market on Chuong Duong Street was evidence enough. The sign was marked "Exhibition and Sales of Birds and Animals." And we're not talking about canaries, angelfish and cute little poodles. This dilapidated "pet shop" is nothing short of a concentration camp for animals. Here, nearly extinct concolor gibbons and a myriad of other exotic species live packed in cages the size of toothpaste boxes; they're stacked upon each other like pallets in a warehouse with no platforms between them to prevent the excrement of the animals lucky enough to be imprisoned on the top level from dropping their waste onto the animals interred below.

Infant rhesus macaques monkeys, separated from their parents at birth, huddle in fear or insanely leap back and forth in their cages like screaming balls in a short racquetball court—if there is enough room. Many of the species here are protected under the Convention of International Trade of Endangered Species, Flora, and Fauna (CITES)—but obviously not at this market. There are 113 signatories to the CITES measure. Vietnam isn't one of them. The animals here all suffered from scabies, mange and a host of other maladies. Prosemian slow lores groveled in feces, their tiny heads buried into their remaining fur, in cages beside workers pounding the concrete with iron rods and hammers. A pair of CITIES-protected pangolins had been killed and stuffed, and were on display in glass counters. A magnificent 20-foot Indian python was coiled like a mammoth black firehose inside a cage the size of a suitcase. One animal, the douc langur (a monkey indigenous to Vietnam), I saw for sale even though it is officially protected in Vietnam.

Admittedly, this "pet shop" and others like it have been substantially cleaned up by the government in the last few years. Previously, the conditions at the market were even more primitive and inhumane, nothing short of a landfill. And the market offered a greater array of threatened species than it does now. But the trade in exotic animals in Vietnam is still highly lucrative. Additionally, at the market, you can purchase ivory, snake and tiger skins, and the remains of other nearly extinct creatures but don't expect to get them through customs. If you choose to take pictures here (and can get away with it), be careful.

## ELEPHANTS ON THE WANE

*Although the number of elephants in Vietnam stands at between 5000–7000, according to the World Wildlife Fund–mainly living in the Central Highlands–the beasts have been rapidly disappearing in the last decade. The decrease in the last 10 years has been termed only as "substantial." Dumbo's demise has been mainly attributed to poaching tusks and the rapid loss of the elephants' natural habitat, due to farming extension and deforestation.*

As the demise of millennia-old species proceeds unabated, on a brighter note, the discovery of new species of animals and plants continues. Apparently Dr. John MacKinnon, British-born ecologist, has discovered a fascinating new mammal species that resembles a goat, but is more closely related to the cow. DNA samples taken from the horns of the beast, believed inhabiting an area near Vietnam's 350-square-mile Vu Quang Nature Reserve, about 175 miles southwest of Hanoi near the border with Laos, have shown that the animal is nothing like scientists have ever seen. This is indeed the discovery of a large mammal previously unknown to science. The last time something happened of this magnitude was the 1937 discovery of the kouprey, a now nearly extinct species of wild cattle, in the forests of Cambodia.

The new creature is called *Pseudoryx nghetinhensis*—meaning the false oryx of Nghe Tinh (the former name of the province where it was found)—or the Vu Quang Ox. The villagers call the animal a spindlehorn. It's believed that until people began populating the region around 1950, the *Pseudoryx* had no natural enemies. The animal is horned and can weigh in excess of 200 lbs. It sports a brown coat with black-and-white markings and a scent gland used to stake its territory. MacKinnon argues that its existence suggests that cows may have come from the forests, and not from grassy plains and savannahs, as is most commonly believed. Two specimens have been captured alive, but have died in captivity. Scientists say that perhaps 300 of the creatures exist at most.

## UPDATE ON THE RARE VU QUANG OX

*During an expedition in June 1995, scientists discovered the remains of a rare Vu Quang Ox in an area of central Vietnam that was previously thought to be outside of the species' range. Consequently, researchers believe the nearly extinct ox may inhabit areas of the country where it wasn't previously thought to exist. The animal may have crossed north of the Song Ca River into other regions of Nghe An province. Return expeditions will focus on the forests of Bu Huong, Quy Cha district, Nghe An province. Since its discovery last year, the Vu Quang Ox has been thought to live in the highland forests of Vu Quang in Ha Tinh province and Pu Mat in Nghe An. The dead specimen was found about 60 km outside of the forest area which was previously thought to be the perimeter of the animal's habitat. Scientists from a British-based environmental NGO–Frontier–and the Xuan Mai Forestry College first witnessed the capture of a live animal by local Bu Huong hunters before coming across the carcass. Remains of the Vu Quang Ox were first discovered by Vietnamese scientists and MacKinnon during a survey of the Vu Quang forest in May 1992. But it wasn't until May 1993, that an ox was captured alive. Another was captured a short time later and both were sent to Hanoi, where they later died in captivity. The Vu Quang Ox is only one of seven new species of mammal to have been discovered this century.*

Although the first-time visitor would hardly know it, huge parcels of Vietnamese topography were ruined during the Vietnam War. It's estimated that more than 70 million liters of defoliant were used on this country's forests during the war, resulting in a loss most experts put at close to 2.5 million hectares. Whereas nearly half the country was heavily forested during World War II, the figure has dropped to under 20 percent today. It is estimated that by the end of the decade, Vietnam will be virtually entirely denuded of its forests.

Traveling up National Highway 1, these estimates seem slightly exaggerated. The mountains as far as the eye can see appear immensely forested, save for areas where banana groves form columns on the hillsides. However, in the Central Highlands, one can see for miles deforested mountains and hillsides. But in defense of the Vietnamese naturalists' doomsday prediction, I think it's accurate to say that Vietnam's banning of the exporting of raw hardwood had more impetus than simply protecting the nation's forests. The move, many environmentalists believe, was a ploy to lure foreign investment in Vietnam's ability to produce its own wood processing facilities.

Quite simply, the amount of trees felled every year hasn't declined. Instead they're now processed inside Vietnam rather than Taiwan or Singapore; the exporting of processed wood from Vietnam (i.e., paper, cabinetry, furniture, etc.) is still quite legal.

## Vietnam's Geography & People

The terrain in Vietnam varies quite dramatically, from verdant mountainous edifices and dense jungle to coastal plains and delta. The climate is generally considered tropical monsoon although it can actually get quite cool in the north, especially in the mountainous regions in northwestern Vietnam near Laos. Its 127,000,330 square miles (329,707 square kilometers) is roughly equal to that of South Carolina, Virginia, and North Carolina together. Vietnam stretches some 2600 kilometers from tip to tip, but very little of the country is any more than 200 km at any given point, except in the far north. At it's narrowest, Vietnam is barely 60 km wide. But Vietnam's remarkable coastline is nearly 3000 km long, offering miles and miles of virtually deserted white sand beaches.

The largest population centers are Hanoi (pop. 4 million), Haiphong (pop. 1.5 million), and bustling and relatively cosmopolitan Ho Chi Minh City (pop. 5 million).

The estuary of the Mekong Delta, extremely marshy, dominates the lower quarter of the country. The area is low and flat and perfect for the cultivation of rice in this rich soil. The area around Saigon to the north and the east changes—there is low-lying tropical rainforest and the rugged yet verdant chain of the Annamite Mountains.

The climate around Saigon and in the south of the country is year-round tropical, with sometimes intense heat and unbearable humidity, although it never seems to get quite as bad as Bangkok.

**TEMPERATURE AND RAINFALL**

| The place | Annual rainfall (mm) | Mean annual temperature (°C) | Mean annual variation (°C) |
|---|---|---|---|
| **Hanoi** | **1680** | **23.5** | **12.4** |
| **Hue** | **3250** | **25.1** | **—** |
| **Danang** | **2130** | **25.4** | **7.8** |
| **Nha Trang** | **1562** | **26.4** | **4.2** |
| **Dalat** | **1600** | **19.1** | **3.4** |
| **Saigon** | **1960** | **26.9** | **3.1** |

Although never cold, the central highlands and the mountainous regions of the central part of Vietnam can become quite cool, with temperatures dipping as low as 50° F at night. During its northern hemispheric summer, the rainfall in the region can be quite heavy around the delta region—whereas the central highlands experiences the crux of its precipitation during the winter.

**MONTHLY AVERAGE TEMPERATURES AND RAINFALL IN SAIGON AND HANOI**

| *CITY* | *Jan.* | *Feb.* | *Mar.* | *Apr.* | *May* | *Jun.* | *Jul.* | *Aug.* | *Sep.* | *Oct.* | *Nov.* | *Dec.* |
|---|---|---|---|---|---|---|---|---|---|---|---|---|
| **SAIGON** | | | | | | | | | | | | |
| **Avg High (°C/°F)** | **32/ 89** | **33/ 91** | **34/ 93** | **35/ 95** | **33/ 92** | **32/ 89** | **31/ 88** | **31/ 88** | **31/ 88** | **31/ 88** | **31/ 87** | **31/ 87** |
| **Avg Low (°C/°F)** | **21/ 70** | **22/ 71** | **23/ 74** | **24/ 76** | **24/ 76** | **24/ 75** | **24/ 75** | **24/ 75** | **23/ 74** | **23/ 74** | **23/ 74** | **22/ 71** |
| **Rainfall (mm/in.)** | **15/ 0.6** | **3/ 0.1** | **13/ 0.5** | **43/ 1.7** | **221/ 8.1** | **330/ 13.0** | **315/ 12.4** | **269/ 10.6** | **335/ 13.2** | **269/ 10.6** | **114/ 4.5** | **56/ 2.2** |
| **HANOI** | | | | | | | | | | | | |
| **Avg High (°C/°F)** | **20/ 68** | **21/ 69** | **23/ 74** | **28/ 82** | **32/ 90** | **33/ 92** | **33/ 91** | **32/ 90** | **31/ 88** | **29/ 84** | **26/ 78** | **22/ 72** |
| **Avg Low (°C/°F)** | **13/ 56** | **14/ 58** | **17/ 63** | **20/ 69** | **23/ 74** | **26/ 78** | **26/ 78** | **26/ 78** | **24/ 76** | **22/ 71** | **18/ 64** | **15/ 59** |
| **Rainfall (mm/in.)** | **18/ 0.7** | **28/ 1.1** | **38/ 1.5** | **81/ 3.2** | **196/ 7.7** | **239/ 9.4** | **323/ 12.7** | **343/ 13.5** | **254/ 10.0** | **99/ 3.9** | **43/ 1.7** | **20/ 0.8** |

With the exception of the Red River delta, northern Vietnam is heavily mountainous and not flat at all. The southwest monsoon climate means a hot, muggy period from mid-May to mid-September, while a cooler northeast monsoon from the middle of October to mid-March brings less rain. The jungle in the north is immensely thick in some areas and the canopy acts as a dome over much of the northern half of the country. There are, of course, lowlands in the north—referred to commonly as the Red River Delta Plain. This is a coastal plain which extends both south and north from the delta and is seasonally flooded. There is a complex dyke and levee system that prevents serious damage to the rich dark soil.

***Waves gently roll onto the rocky beaches south of Nha Trang.***

Rice fields cover much of the area and the region is densely populated with rice farmers and others who have something to do with its production and distribution.

The Vietnamese, with a 3-percent population growth rate, are comprised primarily of ethnic Vietnamese with a smattering of Chinese, Khmer, Thai, Cham, Muong, Hmong and Meo—among other ethnic minorities. The major religions include Buddhism, Cao Daism, Christianity (brought in by the French and the subsequent arrival of American troops in the early 1960s), two forms of Islam (a variant of Middle Eastern Islam practiced by the Chams and the more traditional practices of ethnic Malays), and Animism.

The Vietnamese originally began their centuries-long migration southward around the year AD 940 from what is now southern China. The migration was part politically forced and part economically forced.They would eventually preside over the entire area known today as the eastern seacoast of the Indochinese peninsula. Pushed on by the promises of independence, a strong national identity of the Vietnamese people formed quickly although their associations with Chinese culture weren't entirely discarded. Even today, Chinese culture plays a vast role in the identity of the typical Vietnamese. Although the 96-year French rule of the region (1858–1954) had a significant impact on Vietnamese life and culture, the Vietnamese still retain milleniums-old family and societal values that have remained unblemished by colonialism and other forays by both the East and the West.

Today, more than a million Chinese make up the total Vietnamese population, and these people are mostly concentrated in the southern half of the country, and in particular the region of Ho Chi Minh City called Cholon. The Chinese make up the largest minority in the country. Although scorned by many ethnic Vietnamese, the Chinese population is largely to be credited with Vietnam's financial success, and particularly with the economic strides made since the end of the 1980s, when the Hanoi government recognized that opening up its economy was an absolute necessity in participating and harvesting gains in world markets.

**WHAT THE VIETNAMESE OWN (%)**

| *HOUSEHOLD WITH* | *HANOI* | *SAIGON* |
|---|---|---|
| **AT LEAST 1 CAR** | **1** | **3** |
| **AT LEAST 1 MOTORBIKE** | **54** | **73** |
| **AIR CONDITIONER** | **2** | **3** |
| **REFRIGERATOR** | **6** | **40** |
| **WASHING MACHINE** | **-** | **7** |
| **STEREO** | **3** | **64** |
| **VIDEO RECORDER** | **3** | **65** |
| **VIDEO CAMERA** | **-** | **2** |
| **COMPUTER** | **-** | **1** |
| **TELEPHONE** | **4** | **5** |
| **TELEVISION** | **90** | **80** |
| **RADIO** | **69** | **82** |

*Source: SGR Vietnam*

The Chinese are most involved with real estate, banking and rice trading in the south, and milling, shopkeeping and mining in the north. After the reunification of the country, the Chinese community was ostracized by the Communist Party, leaving many Chinese with little choice but to flee the country, as they did in droves as boat people—perhaps as many as half a million in the mid and late '70s.

Today, though the Chinese community in Vietnam thrives on Hanoi's reforms. Many thousands have returned to land they once fled and, officially at least, are welcomed with the open arms (and no doubt profit-twinkling eyes) of their one-time adversaries.

The next largest minority in Vietnam are the two main ethnolinguistic groups of Montagnards, mountain people of the Malayo-Polynesian and

Mon-Khmer groups. These people generally occupy the highlands areas and speak so many tongues, no two of which seem to be mutually intelligible, that it's a small miracle that babies grow to speak the same languages as their parents. Perhaps 30 such groups of mountain tribes occupy these highland territories.

And last but not least are the Khmers of Cambodian descent of whom perhaps half a million reside in Vietnam. As expected, most are rice farmers and they're primarily to be found in the southern half of Vietnam near its border with Cambodia as well as along the mouths of the Mekong.

One other small minority in Vietnam of note are the Chams, who once were part of the powerful Champa Kingdom which was annihilated by the Vietnamese in the 16th century.

***Most Vietnamese are usually busier than this produce cart driver.***

There are also the Tai who live in the extreme north of the country near the border with China. They speak a language called Tai-Kadai.

Other groups are the Nung, the Muong and Hmong, who reside generally to the south, north and west of Hanoi and have been largely assimilated into mainstream Vietnamese culture, save for the hill people of the extreme north of the country. There is also a small group of people called the Meo, who live high in the mountains and cultivate livestock, grain and profitable opium. Not surprisingly, this group of people can also be found in the opium poppy growing areas of Laos, Thailand and Myanmar—the infamous Golden Triangle area.

Amerasians—those of Vietnamese mothers and American GI fathers—are perhaps the least regarded of all the peoples of Vietnam. Generally, they're treated as scum and are often found in the streets—mostly in Saigon—looking for handouts. Many of the fortunate ones have emigrated to the United States.

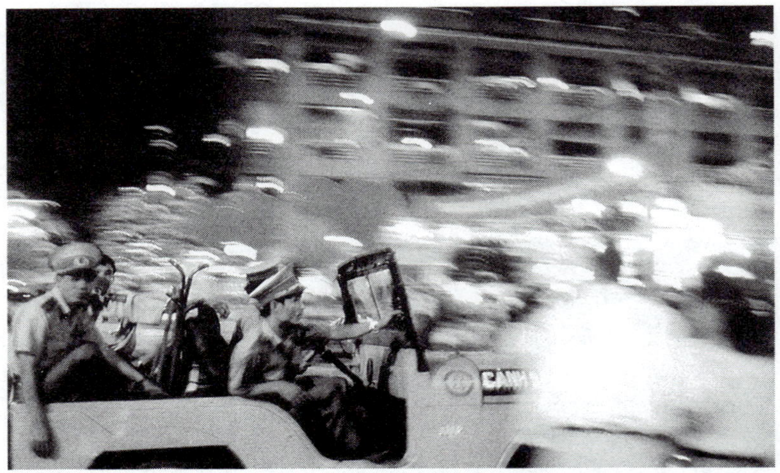

***HCMC police eye the author during a festival celebrating the Tet New Year.***

Vietnamese of all ethnicities speak a surprising array of languages, helped in part by their remaining unscathed by the purges of Pol Pot in Cambodia, who effectively eliminated foreign-language speaking Khmers and ethnic Vietnamese in Cambodia during the late 1970s. Although Vietnamese remains the official language in Vietnam, don't be surprised to hear a fair amount of French being spoken, as well as Chinese and Khmer. English, however, seems to be making the biggest strides in Vietnam, as the language is universally considered the language of international business, and Vietnam is desperately seeking to align itself with the international business community. And don't be surprised to hear a 12-year-old girl speak better English than her 18-year-old brother. It's happening that quickly.

Literacy in the country stands at a remarkable 85 percent according to the latest estimates, and is at its highest among groups save for the Montagnards. Education is provided entirely free by the government, but is difficult to administer due to the continued high birth rate of Vietnamese children and a still largely undeveloped infrastructure. Vocational training is still most rigorously pursued by Vietnamese students, although with the demise of the Soviet educational style structure in Vietnam, liberal arts studies as found in the West are quickly making their way into Vietnam's educational system.

No longer are Vietnamese students being sent by the thousands to school systems in the former Soviet Union and other Eastern European countries that have witnessed their own educational systems collapse. Additionally, Vietnam sends skilled laborers to parts of the world including the Middle East and North Africa.

The average male in Vietnam can expect to live to 62 years, while a woman's average life expectancy hovers around 66 years. However, despite vast improvements in medicine in Vietnam, the infant mortality rate is just a little over 50/1000.

## Vietnam's Religions

Vietnam possesses some of the most numerous and diverse religions in Asia if not all the world, including a number of different forms of Buddhism, Catholicism, Protestantism, Confucianism, numerous hilltribe hybrids of the above, Islam, Tam Giaoism, Hoa Hao, Hinduism, Taoism and the indigenous Cao Daism.

After the fall of Saigon in April 1975, the government made meticulous efforts to eliminate—or at least severely limit—the practice of most religions in the reunified country. Many outspoken clergy and their followers were sent to "reeducation camps" or simply thrown in jail. Religion had no place in the Marxist-Leninist scheme of the collective society. Those religions, Mahayana Buddhism in particular, that were permitted to function to some degree or less were strictly controlled by the state, as were those individuals permitted to become clergy.

Over the years, and especially since the latter 1980s, most doctrines have started to again become integrated into mainstream Vietnamese life, and the government has actually started to play a public relations role, albeit limited in scope, in appearing to associate itself with the importance of spirituality in Vietnam. Descriptions of the major religions practiced in Vietnam are as follows.

### Mahayana and Theravada Buddhism

Mahayana Buddhism is the most extensively practiced religion in Vietnam. Theravada Buddhism is practiced mainly in the south in the Mekong Delta area by the country's inhabitants of Khmer descent. There are some fundamental differences in the two strains of Buddhism.

Mahayana Buddhism means "From the North," and the largest Mahayana sect in Vietnam is Zen. Dao Trang is the second largest school.

*Mahayana Buddhism is Vietnam's largest religion.*

The Chinese monk Mau Tu is usually attributed with introducing Mahayana Buddhism in the second century AD. While Indian Buddhists came in from the sea with their teachings of Theravada Buddhism, Mahayana Buddhism went to the north by way of Nepal, China, Tibet, Mongolia, Korea, Japan and Vietnam (thus it's called the Northern School). It wasn't until nearly 1000 years after Buddhism was introduced into Vietnam that it became the state religion (with the 1138–1175 reign of Emperor Ly Anh Ton). But even Buddhist teachings had become intertwined with the teachings of Confucianism, Taoism and Animism. By the 15th century, it had become so convoluted that Confucianism emerged as the dominant religion of the state. It wasn't until the first two decades of this century that Buddhism once again found a strong foothold in Vietnam; it came in the form of Mahayana Buddhism, which was spread from the north.

There are critical differences between Mahayana Buddhism and Theravada Buddhism, although all Buddhists believe in rebirth, which is common with Hinduism. Buddhists believe their action in this life will determine their manifestations in the next life. Acts in this life will govern those in the next. It's what's commonly called Karma, and it's not a concept looked lightly upon even by Christians, Muslims and others the world over.

Nirvana, or the ultimate enlightenment, is the goal of all Buddhists, and a life of chastity, fasting, and minimal possessions is one of the keys to obtaining this state. Most monks own no more than three sets of clothing, a razor, a food bowl, and a needle. Food cannot be consumed after noon and can only be procured by begging.

Mahayana Buddhists, centered mainly in the north and the central part of Vietnam believe only Gautama Buddha to be the one manifestation of Buddha. The Mahayana Buddhist believes in striving to achieve perfect ideals in the form of generosity, wisdom and patience. Perhaps the fundamental difference between Mahayana and Theravada Buddhists is that the former don't simply believe in enlightenment for themselves. The goal is to reach Bodhissatvahood, the state which allows the monk to stay on earth and help others attain nirvana.

Mahayana Buddhism rose primarily for the reason of making the religion more accessible and attractive to lay people. It was a response to the vast number of followers Hinduism was attracting. Monks began becoming more accessible solely for the purpose of helping others in the quest for enlightenment. As the number of Mahayana Buddhists began to swell, so were expanded the principles of the Mahayana doctrine. However, today, most Mahayana Buddhists also consolidate the teachings of Confucius and other Chinese religions, such as Taoism.

Theravada Buddhism, which came directly from India, more closely conforms to the original doctrines as they were developed in India, and is frequently called by Mahayana Buddhists as the "Lesser Vehicle," a mainly derogatory name that is indicative of the Vietnamese presdisposal to think of the Khmer people as a lower form of humanity. Theravada Buddhism is the most prevalent religion in Cambodia, Thailand and Laos.

The historic Buddha (Sakyumuni) is the Buddha most worshipped by Theravadans. For Theravadans, in theory Buddha images represent not supernatural gods, but shrines to aid in meditation. However, recently these images have been worshipped themselves, which is indicative of the influence Mahayanas are having on Theravada practices.

However, for their part, Theravada Buddhists consider their religion to be a less corrupt form of Buddhism.

### Hoa Hao Buddhism (Dao Hoa Hao)

Huynh Phu So, an occultist who was miraculously cured of a serious disease, founded Hoa Hao sect of Buddhism in 1939. The religion is a type of reformed Buddhism which contends that elaborate rituals are not needed to honor Buddha, but merely a private, simple and unelaborate faith. He did not believe that intermediaries were needed between human beings and God, or the Supreme Being. There are perhaps more than a million followers of the religion today in Vietnam.

The French weren't fond of Huynh—they called him the "Mad Monk"—and suppressed his activities. He was thrown into an insane asylum after jailing him did little to affect his influence (he even converted the psychiatrist who was treating him to the Hoa Hao sect). The sect continued to grow, despite the monk's internment. During World War II, the sect formed its own army with the help of the Japanese. After the war, the sect fought the Viet Minh, and Huynh was assassinated by the Viet Minh. By this time, his army had grown rather strong in the Mekong Delta, particularly in the Chau Doc area. The Hoa Hao army disintegrated after one of its leading commanders was publicly executed by the South Vietnamese Diem regime. Much of the Hoa Hao then joined the Viet Cong.

### Confucianism (Dao Khong)

Confucianism isn't really a religion in the traditional sense. The teachings of Confucius (551–479 BC) are more patterns of social behavior that have become entwined in the daily lives of most Vietnamese, more than an organized religion.

Confucius (Khong Tu in Vietnamese), born before 550 BC in China, saw human beings as both shaped by their society as well as having the ability to shape it themselves. It was social interaction that formed the basis of society. He devised a code of social interaction that specified an individual's obligation to his or her family, government, and community. Hierarchy and sense of duty are principle ingredients of Confucianism.

Confucianism arrived in Vietnam via the Chinese 1000-year rule of the country, between 111 BC and 938 AD. Its philosophy stated that only the emperor could be the intermediary between Earth and Heaven. Virtue through education gave one the right to political power. In this form, there was some degree of equality among individuals, as education rather than birth, determined hierarchy. Virtue could only be acquired through education. As a consequence, education was widespread among the "religion's" followers. Young people were taught about duty, hierarchy, and their responsibilities to both the family and the community at an early age. Each person would know his place in the community hierarchy.

A government-administered test was then given to the students to ascertain those with the greatest amount of education and virtue and it was these individuals who were selected as mandarins, members of the ruling class. Education was seen not only as a tool to acquire education but political status as well.

But only the emperor could establish this mandate between the secular and the spiritual. If virture was lost, it was believed that rebellion was just, and that until virtue was restored natural calamities in the form of floods, earthquakes and typhoons would devastate the land.

Confucianism slowly met its demise in Vietnam during the 1400s as it became more regimented, and as kings became more arrogant and recognized themselves as divine rulers rather than intermediaries between the people and the gods. The Divine Mandate crumbled.

### Cao Daism (Dao Cao Dai)

This is the one indigenous religion to Vietnam, and a strange one at that. It involves the worship of human beings as well as the worship of deities. It was founded to create the perfect religion—a blend of both secular and spiritual devotion. It was founded by Ngo Minh Chieu in the early 1920s and became so popular—gaining millions of followers—areas of southern Vietnam became a virtual political state, particularly in the Mekong Delta region and Tay Ninh, the religion's headquarters nearly 100 km from Saigon. This infuriated the South Vietnamese government to such an extent they broke up the religion and conscripted many of its followers into the South Vietnamese Army. But after reunification of the country and relaxed religious mandates on the part of the Vietnamese government, Cao Daism flourishes again, but this time as a religion only. Cao Dai temples dot the southern Vietnamese landscape from the Mekong Delta to Hue. Above Cao Dai altars is an inscription which translates into "All Religions Have the Same Reason." Today, it's believed that as many as two million Vietnamese are Cao Dai followers. (For more on Cao Daism, see the chapter on "Tay Ninh.")

### Taoism (Dao Lao)

Taoism is another religion whose origins are in China. It's based on the philosophy of Laotse, or Thai Thuong Lao Quan, who lived during the sixth century, although the formal religion of Taoism was actually started by Chang Ling around 143 BC. Although there is some question as to whether or not Laotse actually ever existed (the debate continues today), legend has it that he was consulted by Confucius and was the custodian of the Chinese government's Imperial Archives. Sometime after 143 BC, the religion split into two branches: "The Way of the Heavenly Teacher" and the "Cult of the Immortals."

Taoists believe in the simplicity of life and eventually returning to what is called "The Way," the source of all things. Taoism is so complicated, few Vietnamese understand the religion—even Taoists themselves. But the essence of Taoism, namely its emphasis on contemplation and simplicity, has found its way into the various forms of Buddhism in Indochina. Taoism is a blend of superstitions, sorcery, magic and other mystical beliefs that are reflected in the architecture of Buddhist temples, which are adorned with dragons, snakes and other mythical beasts.

### Christianity and Catholicism

Missionaries from France, Spain and Portugal brought Catholicism to Vietnam in the 16th century—mainly Portuguese Dominicans and French Jesuit priests. The first bishops to be sent to Vietnam were assigned by Pope Alexander VII in 1659, and the first Vietnamese priests were ordained in 1668. There were as many as a million Catholics in Vietnam by the end of the 17th century—and today, behind the Philippines, Vietnam possesses the greatest number of Catholics in Asia. Nearly one million Catholic Vietnamese were part of the hordes of boat people who fled Vietnam after the reunification of the country in 1975. (South Vietnamese President Ngo Dinh Diem was a Catholic.)

Over the centuries, Catholics suffered a tremendous amount of persecution in Vietnam. At many times during the 17th and 18th centuries, the religion was outlawed. After 1975, the practice of Catholicism was virtually untolerated by the new government.

**INSIDER TIP**

*Although the government has become a lot more tolerant of religious practice in Vietnam, it once in a while lets religious hierarchies know in no uncertain terms that it is the state who's boss in Vietnam–that, yes, there's a degree of religious tolerance, but any clergy who had any previous association with the varying regimes of preunification Vietnam will not be tolerated, nor will they be allowed congregations. A case in point is Hanoi's recent falling out with the Vatican over a compromise that would have permitted the appointments of priests with ties to previous South Vietnamese regimes. Hanoi insists that the government must be consulted in the selection of clergy. Vietnamese Prime Minister Vo Van Kiet has said that the issue is one of "national sovereignty," as Vietnam has not signed any agreements with the Vatican allowing them to make "unfettered" decisions in their appointments. "Each country has the right to ensure stability and order through its own rules," Vo said. Things have heated up between the Vatican and Hanoi since September 1993 when authorities in Ho Chi Minh City said "no way" to the appointment of Bishop Huynh Van Nghi as a "supervisor" of the church instead of deputy archbishop. Saigon officials charged that the appointment was part of a "Vatican plot" to place an exiled nephew of former South Vietnamese President Ngo Dinh Diem as successor to the current archbishop. Hanoi, it appears, is taking very cautious steps in permitting a potential element of dissent, the church–which the government has always viewed as a hot bed for antistate activities–to return to its previous, prewar levels of influence.*

But Catholicism flourished during French rule of Vietnam—as it did with the American presence in South Vietnam during the Vietnam War. Under French rule, Catholics were given high positions in the government and preferential treatment in general. From 1954 to 1989 in the north, and from 1975 to 1989 in the south Catholic religious activities were heavily curtailed and monitored by the government. There were restrictions placed on the number of priests and the type of education Catholics could receive. Even today, the Catholic churches you see in both Hanoi and HCMC have become somewhat dilapidated, as the government still looks upon the religion as a capitalist poison.

Protestantism has flourished mainly among about a quarter of a million Montagnards in the Central Highlands. The religion first came to Vietnam in 1910 or 1911. The Montagnards have been harassed by the government for a number of years, and the introduction of Christianity into the populace didn't help matters any. After 1975, Protestant ministers, especially those trained by the Americans, were imprisoned for a number of years. Although you are free to practice the religion in Vietnam today, the state keeps a close watch on Christian activities.

### Hinduism

Originally, Hinduism had its roots in Vietnam with the Cham people, and its influence can be seen in many of the early Cham towers in the southern half of Vietnam, which contain the phallic symbols of Shiva. When the Champa Empire fell in Vietnam in the 15th century, so did much of Hinduism's influence on the Cham people, who then absorbed Muslim ideas into their religious practices. But evidence of Hinduism is still evident even in today's Cham Muslim religious practices.

### Islam

If you want to be a Muslim, but still want to partake in some of life's more secular vices, become a Cham in Vietnam. Although there are small communities of Muslims (such as ethnic Malays, Indonesians and Indians) that practice Islam, the Chams aren't so strict. They're permitted to drink alcohol and they don't make pilgrimages to Mecca. Rather than praying five times a day as do their traditional counterparts, Cham Muslims pray only on Friday and celebrate Ramadan for only three days. Traditional Muslims celebrate Ramadan (which requires dawn-to-dusk fasting) for an entire month.

In fact, Cham Muslims aren't entirely clear about the Islam concept. There are very few copies of the Koran in Cham villages and most of the villagers can't read it. Even the Cham Muslim religious leaders, who wear a white robe and an elaborate turban with colored tassels, can't read the Arabic script, or at least much of it. They've taken common expressions from the Koran and turned them into deities. Their religious services include only a few minutes of reading passages from the Koran, much of them decisively altered in meaning through a lack of understanding of the passages. They're also into animism and Hinduism, as they worship Hindu deities in addition to Mohammed.

The more traditional Muslims in Vietnam essentially fled the country after 1975, but there are still small pockets of Malay and Indian Muslim communities centered mainly in Saigon.

### Worship of Ancestors

Introduced even before Confucianism in Vietnam, ancestor worship is the belief many Vietnamese have that their ancestors watch over and protect them. A person without descendants is doomed to have no home when they die. Ancestors play a role in all important events, including everything from tragedies to success in school to childbirth—and there are ancestor worship holidays on the dates of the ancestors' deaths. Sacrifices are offered to the ancestor. Families have altars in their homes devoted to their ancestors. Some pagodas feature pictures and other items ancestors once possessed on the altars. Usually the pictures depict the ancestors as young people. Ancestor worshippers usually also have plots of land which derive income for the ancestors. The cult also designates a male as the central figure to worship when he dies.

## Vietnam's Government

The Vietnamese government is a socialist peoples' republic, a somewhat cantankerous hybrid of Marxism and Leninism. What this really means, however, depends upon who you talk to. An official in Hanoi may tell you something entirely different than a prosperous Chinese merchant in Saigon's Cholon district, whose perception of "socialism" may be afternoon tea with some neighbors. However, officially, there is one political party, called the Vietnam Communist Party, which was previously referred to as the Vietnamese Workers Party, a title which remained in effect from 1951–1976. This in itself was the offshoot of the Indochinese Workers Party which was formed in the early 1930s by Ho Chi Minh. Vietnam's current constitution was ratified December 18, 1980.

In Vietnam, there are 50 provinces which are centrally controlled under the auspices of three municipalities (Hanoi, Ho Chi Minh City, and Haiphong)—all under central government control.

In the north are Ha Bac, Cao Bang, Hoa Binh, Tuyen Quang, Lao Cai, Yen Bai, Bac Thai, Son La, Quang Ninh, Vinh Phu, Lang Son, Ha Giang, and Lai Chau.

The Red River Delta Area has Ninh Binh, Ha Tay, Nam Ha, Thai Binh, and Hai Hung.

North Central Vietnam includes Nghe An, Thanh Hoa, Quang Tri, Thua Thien-Hue, Ha Tinh, and Quang Binh.

The Central Highlands is composed of Gia Lai, Dac Lac, Kontum, and Lam Dong.

On the South Central Coast lies Quang Nam-Danang, Binh Dinh, Phu Yen, Quang Ngai, Khanh Hoa, Binh Thuan, and Ninh Thuan.

In the South are Song Be, Tay Ninh, Dong Nai, Ba Ria-Vung Tau, Long An, Dong Thap, An Giang, Ben Tre, Kien Giang, Soc Trang, Can Tho, Minh Hai, Tien Giang, Tra Vinh, and Vinh Long

Vietnamese independence from the French occurred in September, 1945, and the reunification of the north and the south officially took place in July of 1976. Some say the real unification took place with the temporary occupation of the United States embassy building during the Tet Offensive of 1968. Some venture to go back even further in time to 1963 when then AP correspondent Malcolm Brown shot his historic photos of a Buddhist monk from Hue self immolating himself on a Saigon street in protest of the policies of the Ngo Dinh Diem government, a series of pictures that ultimately found their way to Washington's Oval Office and JFK's desk who, after gazing in horror at the human pyre in the street orchestrated the roots of Diem's ouster.

Today's facets of the Vietnamese government consist of the executive branch, which is comprised of the Council of Ministers; the State Council (or the Collective Chief of State), people's committees that have jurisdiction over local affairs; the Legislative branch; which is also called the National Assembly (locally there are Peoples' Councils, and the Judicial branch, which is comprised of the Supreme People's Court).

As far as defense goes, it's said that anywhere from 40–50 percent of the central government budget goes into the procurement and maintenance of defense related technology and manpower—which explains why the Vietnamese are some of the poorest souls on the planet. But this is changing rapidly since the government's integration into the world community.

## Vietnam's Language

As you might expect, the Vietnamese language is difficult both to speak and understand. It can be traced to Sino-Tibetan as well as to Austro-Asiatic and Mon-Khmer origins. Under 9th-century Chinese domination, the ideograms the Chinese used were adopted for use with Vietnamese (although gratefully, a Latin-style based script was adopted during the early portion of this century, making the reading of maps and signs possible for hapless Westerners). The original *chu nho* ideograms were utilized as the only form of communication up until the 20th century.

Vietnamese seeking to sever ties with the Chinese in the 13th century further complicated matters by taking the Chinese ideograms and adapting them for their own purposes. This was called *chu nom*, considered a "vulgar" or gutter form of *chu nho*.

In the 17th century, European missionary Alexandre-de-Rhodes mastered the Vietnamese language and actually created the first Romanized Vietnamese dictionary.

The biggest problem in understanding the Vietnamese language is the fundamental barrier that prevents Westerners from becoming proficient with other East Asian tongues—tonal usage. The same "word" can be used with a number of different tones and possess an equally different number of meanings.

The Vietnamese alphabet has 17 consonants, 12 vowels and nearly 20 double consonants. There are no prefixes and no suffixes. There is no use of plurals with nouns and there are double negatives that must be used to accomplish what Westerners can simply do with a simple positive. In other words, if you ask someone in Vietnamese, "Will you have dinner at my house tonight?" the actual translation is something like this: "You'll have dinner at my house tonight, will you not?" Instead of simply replying, "Yes, I will," an affirmative response goes something like this: "No, I will not." If you say the former, you're telling your host that "Yes, I will not be having dinner at your house tonight."

Ay!

As anywhere you travel where the locals speak a different tongue, it can never hurt to pick up on a bit of the language. Simple greetings, phrases and requests in the local language can open a lot of doors. The Vietnamese, like the Thais, the Cambodians, and most peoples of Asia, are impressed and even honored when even the slightest attempt by a foreigner is made to speak the host country's language, no matter how bad the result is (within parameters, of course. You don't want to tell a man that his wife looks like a swollen sow with udders for fingers when you've simply requested a glass of milk). Let the following serve as the briefest of guides to making your Vietnamese visit a little more intelligible.

## A CRASH COURSE IN VIETNAMESE

### GREETINGS AND FORMALITIES

| | |
|---|---|
| Hello<br>Good morning<br>Good afternoon | *Chao* |
| Good night | *Chao* **or** *Chuc ngu ngon* |
| Good bye | *Tam biet* |
| the above formal to older men | *Chao ong* |
| the above formal to older women | *Chao ba* |
| the above informal to men | *Chao anh* |
| the above informal to women | *Chao chi* |
| How are you? | *Có khoe khong?* |
| I am doing well, thank you | *Khoe, cam on* |
| Thank you | *Cam on* |
| Yes | *Vang (in the north)*<br>*Co, phai (in the south)*<br>*Da* |
| No | *Khong* |
| Excuse me | *Xin loi* |
| I am tired | *Toi met* |

### PRONOUNS

| | | | |
|---|---|---|---|
| You | *On* | I | *Toi* |
| to an older man | *Ong* | He | *Cau ay, anh ay* |
| to an older woman | *Ba* | She | *Co ay* |
| to a man of own age | *Anh* | We | *Chung toi* |
| to a woman of own age | *Co* | | |

### NUMBERS

| | | | |
|---|---|---|---|
| 1 | *Mot* | 6 | *Sau* |
| 2 | *Hai* | 7 | *Bay* |
| 3 | *Ba* | 8 | *Tam* |
| 4 | *Bon* | 9 | *Chin* |
| 5 | *Nam* | 10 | *Muoi* |

## A CRASH COURSE IN VIETNAMESE

| | | | |
|---|---|---|---|
| 11 | *Muoi mot* | 16 | *Muoi sau* |
| 12 | *Muoi hai* | 17 | *Muoi bay* |
| 13 | *Muoi ba* | 18 | *Muoi tam* |
| 14 | *Muoi bon* | 19 | *Muoi chin* |
| 15 | *Muoi nam* | 20 | *Hai muoi* |
| 21 | *Hai muoi mot* | 1000 | *Mot nghin* |
| 30 | *Ba muoi* | 10,000 | *Muoi ngan* |
| 90 | *Chin muoi* | 100,000 | *Mot tram nghin* |
| 100 | *Mot tram* | 1 million | *Mot trieu* |
| 110 | *Mot tram muoi* | First | *Thu nhat* |
| 200 | *Hai tram* | Second | *Thu nhi* |

### DAYS OF THE WEEK

| | | | |
|---|---|---|---|
| Sunday | *Thu hai* | Today | *Ngay mai* |
| Monday | *Thu ba* | Yesterday | *Hom qua* |
| Tuesday | *Thu tu* | Tomorrow | *Buoi sang* |
| Wednesday | *Thu nam* | Morning | *Buoi chieu* |
| Thursday | *Thu sau* | Afternoon | *Buoi toi* |
| Friday | *Thu bay* | Evening | *Bay gio* |
| Saturday | *Hom nay* | Right now | *Chu nhat* |

### MONTHS OF THE YEAR

| | | | |
|---|---|---|---|
| January | *Thang gieng* | July | *Thang bay* |
| February | *Thang hai* | August | *Thang tam* |
| March | *Thang ba* | September | *Thang chin* |
| April | *Thang tu* | October | *Thang muoi* |
| May | *Thang nam* | November | *Thang muoi mot* |
| June | *Thang sau* | December | *Thang chap* |
| Year | *Nam* | Month | *Thang* |
| This year | *Nam nay* | Next year | *Nam sau* |
| Last year | *Nam ngoai* | | |

## A CRASH COURSE IN VIETNAMESE

### USEFUL WORDS AND PHRASES

| | | | |
|---|---|---|---|
| My name is… | *Ten toi la…* | What is your name? | *Ten (your) la gi? (see "you")* |
| I would like… | *Toi muon…* | I would not like… | *Toi khong muon…* |
| I like… | *Toi thich…* | I would not like… | *Toi khong muon…* |
| I want… | *Toi can…* | I do not want… | *Toi khong can…* |
| I understand | *Toi hieu* | I do not understand | *Toi khong hieu* |
| I need… | *Toi can* | I am hungry | *Toi doi* |
| To eat | *An* | To drink | *Uong* |
| Thank you | *Cam on* | Please | *Xin* |
| Yes | *Da* | No | *Khong* |
| Come | *Toi* | Go | *Di* |
| Cheap | *Re* | Expensive | *Dat* |
| Man | *Nam* | Woman | *Nu* |
| Give | *Cho* | | |
| Fast | *Nhanh (in the north) Mau (in the south)* | Slow | *Cham* |
| Old | *Cu* | New | *Moi* |
| Clean | *Sach* | Dirty | *Ban* |
| Hot | *Nong* | Cold | *Lanh* |
| Far away | *Xa* | Close by | *Gan* |
| Market | *Cho* | Office | *Van phong* |
| Post office | *Nha buu dien* | Museum | *Bao Tang Vien* |
| Pagoda | *Chua* | Church | *Nha tho* |
| Bank | *Ngan hang* | Tourism office | *Van phong du lich* |
| Telephone | *Dien thoai* | Mosquito net | *Man (in the north) Mung (in the south)* |
| East | *Dong* | West | *Tay* |
| North | *Bac* | South | *Nam* |

## A CRASH COURSE IN VIETNAMESE

### ACCOMMODATIONS

| | | | |
|---|---|---|---|
| Hotel | *Khach san*<br>*Nha khach (guest house)* | Restaurant | *Tiem an* |
| Room | *Phong* | Room key | *Chia khoa phong* |
| Bathroom | *Nha tam*<br>*Phong tam* | | |
| Toilet | *Cau tieu*<br>*Nha ve sinh* | Toilet paper | *Giay ve sinh* |
| I would like an inexpensive room. | *Toi thich mot phong loai re.* | How much does the room cost? | *Gia mot phong bao nhieu?* |
| Where is there a hotel? | *O dau co khach san?* | Air conditioning | *May lanh* |
| Fan | *Quat* | Hot water | *Nuoc nong* |
| Blanket | *Chan (in the north)*<br>*Men (in the south)* | Laundry | *Tiem giat quan do* |
| Sheet | *Ra trai guiong* | Towel | *Khan tam* |

### FOOD AND DRINK

| | | | |
|---|---|---|---|
| Water | *Nuoc* | Beer | *Bia* |
| Coffee | *Ca phe* | Tea | *Nuoc che* |
| Sugar | *Duong* | Beef | *Thit bo* |
| Chicken | *Thit ga* | Pork | *Thit heo* |
| Bat | *Con doi* | Snake | *Ran ho mang (Cobra)*<br>*Con tran (Python)* |
| Goat | *Con de* | Venison | *Thit Nai* |
| Turtle | *Con rua* | Wild pig | *Heo rung* |
| Noodle soup | *Pho* | Rice | *Com* |
| Bread | *Banh mi* | Vegetables | *Rau* |
| Fish | *Ca* | Shrimp | *Tom* |
| Crab | *Cua* | Eel | *Luon* |
| Frog | *Ech* | Oyster | *So* |

## A CRASH COURSE IN VIETNAMESE

| | | | |
|---|---|---|---|
| Fish and vegetable soup | *Lau* | Vegetable soup | *Xup rau* |
| White rice noodles | *Banh Pho* | Eel and vermicelli soup | *Mien Luon* |
| Yellow wheat noodles | *Mi* | Broth | *Nuoc Leo* |
| Dry noodles | *Kho* | Sweet rolls | *Nem*<br>*Cha gio* |
| Apple | *Bom*<br>*Tao* | Apricot | *Le* |
| Avocado | *Trai bo* | Banana | *Trai chuoi* |
| Cherry | *Trai se ri* | Chinese date | *Trai tao ta* |
| Coconut | *Trai dua* | Durian | *Trai sau rieng* |
| Grapes | *Nho* | Grapefruit | *Trai buoi* |
| Green dragon fruit | *Trai thanh long* | Guava | *Trai oi* |
| Jackfruit | *Trai Mit* | Khaki | *Hong xiem* |
| Lemon | *Chanh* | Longan | *Trai nhan* |
| Lychee | *Trai vai* | Mandarin Orange | *Trai quit* |
| Mango | *Trai mang cut* | Orange | *Trai cam* |
| Papaya | *Trai du du*<br>*Qua du du* | Peach | *Trai dao* |
| Pineapple | *Trai khom*<br>*Trai dua* | Plum | *Man*<br>*Mo* |
| Pomelo | *Trai buoi*<br>*Trai doi* | Rambutan | *Chom chom* |
| Starfruit | *Trai khe* | Strawberry | *Trai dau* |
| Tangerine | *Trai quit* | Tomato | *Ca chua* |
| Water apple | *Roi duong (Man)* | Watermelon | *Dua hau* |

### TRAVEL

| | |
|---|---|
| Bus | *Xe buyt* |
| Bus station | *Ben xe buyt* |
| Train | *Xe lua* |
| Train station | *Ga xe lua* |

## A CRASH COURSE IN VIETNAMESE

| | |
|---|---|
| Airport | *San bay* |
| Cyclo (Trishaw) | *Xe xich lo* |
| Map | *Ban do* |
| Schedule | *Bang gio giac*<br>*Thoi bieu* |
| I want to hire a car. | *Toi muon xe hoi.* |
| I want to go to... | *Toi muon di...* |
| Highway | *Xa lo* |
| How long does the trip take? | *Chuyen di se mat bao lau?* |
| How far is it to...? (kilometers) | *Cach xa day bao nhieu kilomet?* |
| What time does the bus leave? | *Xe buyt se chay luc may gio?* |
| What time does the train leave? | *Xe lua se chay luc may gio?* |
| What time does it arrive? | *Xe se den luc may gio?* |
| What time does the first bus leave? | *Chuyen xe buyt som nhat se chay luc may gio?* |
| What times does the last bus leave? | *Chuyen xe buyt cuoi cung se chay luc may gio?* |
| What time does the first train leave? | *Chuyen xe lua som nhat se chay luc may gio?* |
| What time does the last train leave? | *Chuyen xe lua cuoi cung ce chay luc may goi?* |
| I would like a receipt. | *Toi muon bien lai.* |
| I would like a sleeping berth. | *Toi muon giuong ngu.* |

### GEOGRAPHY

| | | | |
|---|---|---|---|
| Mountain | *Nui* | Island | *Hon dao* |
| River | *Song* | Boulevard | *Dai lo* |
| National Highway | *Quoc lo* | City square | *Cong truong* |
| Street | *Duong*<br>*Pho* | Bridge | *Cau* |

### AT THE MARKET

| | | | |
|---|---|---|---|
| Expensive | *Dat tien* | Cheap | *Re tien* |
| Buy | *Mua* | Sell | *Ban* |

## A CRASH COURSE IN VIETNAMESE

| | | | |
|---|---|---|---|
| Market | *Cho* | How much does this cost? | *Cai nay gia bao nhieu?* |
| **EMERGENCIES** | | | |
| Help | *Cuu toi voi* | Police | *Cong an* |
| Thief | *Cuop*<br>*Cap* | Pickpocket | *Moc tui* |
| **MEDICAL** | | | |
| Doctor | *Bac si* | Dentist | *Nha si* |
| Hospital | *Benh vien* | Pharmacy | *Nha thuoc tay.* |
| I am sick. | *Toi bi benh. (in the north)*<br>*Toi bi om. (in he south)* | | |
| Please call me a doctor. | *Lam on goi bac si.* | Please get me to a hospital. | *Lam on dua toi den benh vien.* |
| Diarrhea | *Ia chay* | Stomachache | *Dau bung* |
| Malaria | *Sot ret* | Feverish | *Cam*<br>*Cum* |
| Vomiting | *Oi*<br>*Mua* | Toothache | *Nhuc rang* |
| Headache | *Nhuc dau* | Backache | *Dau lung* |

### SOME OTHER USEFUL PHRASES IN VIETNAMESE

| | |
|---|---|
| Where do I collect my visa? | *Toi nhan visa o dau?* |
| One of my bags is missing. Where do I make a report? | *Toi bi mat moy tui. Toi phai bao o dau?* |
| I bought this camera/video camera in ... | *Toi mua may anh/may quay phim nay o...* |
| I have had this camera/video camera for ...years. | *Toi mua may anh/may quay phim nay...nam roi.* |
| My flight number is... | *So chuyen bay cua toi la...* |
| What is your flight number? | *Chuyen bay cua ong/ba so bao nhieu?* |
| Have they called my flight? | *Ho da thong bao chuyen bay cua toi chua?* |
| Can I carry this as hand luggage? | *Toi co the xach tay tui nay duroc khong?* |
| Where do I pay the airport tax? | *Toi phai dong le phi san bay o dau?* |
| Over there, to the right/left. | *O dang kia, ben Phai/trai.* |
| How much is the airport tax? | *Le phi san bay la bao nhieu?* |

**A CRASH COURSE IN VIETNAMESE**

| | |
|---|---|
| Where is the transit lounge? | *Phong cho di noi chuyen o dau?* |
| Where can I get a taxi? | *Toi co the don taxi o dau?* |

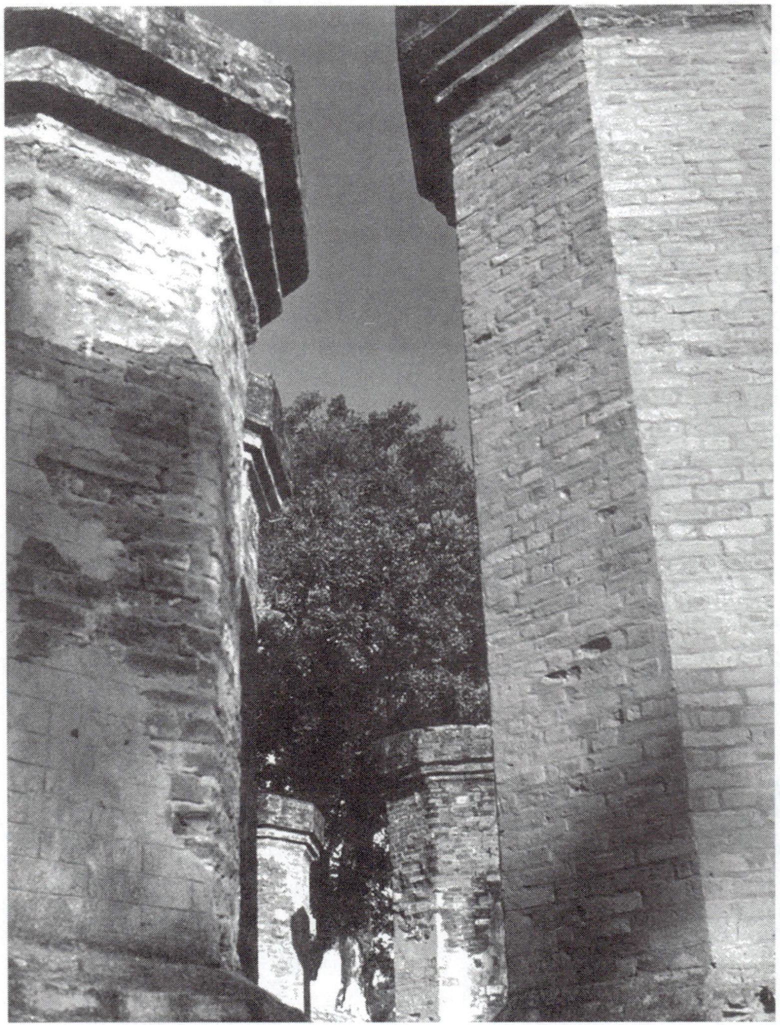

***Cham brick columns at the Po Nagar Cham Towers in Nha Trang.***

# Vietnam's Food

Vietnamese food isn't cuisine that you either love or hate. There are as many as 500 traditional Vietnamese dishes. There's bound to be something you'll sink your teeth into.

The staple food in Vietnam is, of course, rice. Few meals are served without it. Seafood, beef, chicken, pork and other more exotic delicacies such as cobra, rat, dog, deer, bat, gecko, python, turtle, porcupine and the endangered pangolin round out the typical (and not so typical) Vietnamese meal.

Vietnamese food served in roadside stalls and restaurants is remarkably cheap. It's quite easy to consume three full meals a day for under US$3. On the other hand, it's equally as effortless to spend US$20 on a Vietnamese meal at an elegant restaurant.

Rice is served in a large bowl. You'll be given another small bowl for your portion and the meat, vegetables and condiments to mix with it. Rice is dished out with a large spoon, but you'll consume your meal with chopsticks. After adding rice and other ingredients, you hold the small bowl close to your mouth as you consume the contents.

Almost all Vietnamese meals consist of the staple *nuoc mam* (fish sauce), a fermented, odiferous concoction that takes some getting accustomed to. But it tastes a lot better than it smells. A more potent preparation is shrimp sauce (*mam tom*), a fiery liquid that fewer foreigners find palatable.

*Pho* is the Vietnamese staple. It consists of soup (a broth brewed from bones, ginger, *nuoc mam* and prawns), noodles and shredded beef, chicken or pork. Vietnamese rarely consume the leftover broth after finishing the meat and noodles. You can add lemon, chiles or chile sauce to the concoction—I've seen some even add sugar, in the Thai style of garnishing dishes. The noodles served with *pho* and other noodle dishes are of three varieties: yellow wheat noodles (*mi*), white rice noodles (*banh pho*) and rice noodles made with manioc powder (*mien*) that appear more like slimy strands of jelly.

Other popular dishes include *xup rau*, a vegetable soup; *lau*, a fish and vegetable soup; *cha ca*, filleted fish broiled over charcoal; *com tay cam*, gingered chicken or pork served with rice and mushrooms, and *bun thang*, rice noodles with shredded chicken and a fried egg—as well as some other "special" toppings.

Spring rolls (*cha gio*) are a popular appetizer. A sheet of rice paper is filled with sausage, shredded pork or other meat, as well as vermicelli, mushrooms and other ingredients, and then deep fried. Additionally, you can create your own spring rolls using the above ingredients and different vegetables and eat them without first frying them.

Vietnamese meals are typically served with complimentary iced tea—but not the type you're accustomed to back home. The Vietnamese variety is much weaker and is more akin to ice water than tea.

## Western Food

Western food can be found in the cities these days, and even hotels in the boonies will offer an American-style breakfast. In Ho Chi Minh City and Hanoi, there has been a proliferation in recent years of upscale eateries offering all kinds of American and European offerings, using imported steaks from the U.S. and Australia, pasta and oils from Italy, cheeses from France, sausage from Germany, and so on. At some of the finer establishments, you'd never guess you're away from home. However, the Western food served at many of the cheaper Vietnamese restaurants is simply awful.

Additionally, dishes from the non-Western world can be found in the tourists centers. Some of the best Malaysian and Thai food I've tasted I've had in Vietnam. There are restaurants for Indian food, Russian food—even Algerian cuisine. But if you're going strictly native, be prepared to lose some weight. When you think you're full, you may not be, as noodles weigh you down with their liquid content. No one has ever gotten fat on a diet of rice.

### GODS OF THE KITCHEN

*Most Vietnamese houses are quite small and don't have a separate kitchen. Kitchens are typically located in an area of the house close to an opening to the outdoors. Today, the Vietnamese cook on a brazier over an open hearth. The brazier has three grills, or supports, above it to place pans and pots.*

*Before the introduction of braziers, Vietnamese cooks used to rely on three clay blocks as the hearth. These blocks, or stones, became known as the Kitchen Gods. In the mythology of Vietnam, the three blocks represent family fidelity and are based on an old fable that tells of a sailor and his wife.*

*The sailor spent a number of years at sea and the wife assumed that he had died, so she remarried. Then, of, course, the sailor came home. She was overcome with joy and bewilderment and hid her former husband beneath a layer of twigs so that her new mate wouldn't find out. The new husband came home with a freshly-killed deer and decided to cook it on the stack of twigs. He set fire to the twigs, killing the sailor. The wife felt such guilt she threw herself into the flames. At a loss for seeing why his wife would kill herself, the new husband realized he couldn't live without her and immolated himself as well. All three were killed by the fire and martyred as the three stones. What some folks will do for a Whopper and fries.*

### Overcharging

The Vietnamese overcharge Western tourists frequently at restaurants. Even in the boonies, most places are clip-joints and may charge you as much as twice what a Vietnamese would pay for the same dish. Many restaurants charge for some of the condiments they set out before you, although you didn't ask for them. There is even typically a charge for cold cloth that serves as your napkin. If you don't want something, ask the waiter/waitress to take it away. He or she will do so without a fuss.

Examine your bill very carefully. The writing will be in Vietnamese at most places, and it pays to have a Vietnamese with you. If not, go over the bill with the waiter. Ask what each item is and the cost.

Finally, when requesting your check, simply say "*Tinh tien.*"

#### Restaurant Prices

The "Where to Eat" listings in this book use a quick reference rating for the price category of the establishment. They are categorized as follows:

| | |
|---|---|
| **$$$** | **$6 and up** |
| **$$** | **$3–$6** |
| **$** | **Less than $3** |

## History of Vietnam

As Americans, we're all too aware of the recent history of Vietnam. For the last 30 years, its past has been entwined with our own. As Vietnam crippled the U.S. spiritually, we ravaged Vietnam economically. As Vietnam reshaped our own awareness of the world by repelling and finally bursting the bubble of the infallibility of American intervention abroad, we regrouped as a nation, only to witness the crumbling of an impotent strain of Southeast Asian Marxism. Nearly 60,000 young Americans paid for this social rebirth—both America's and Vietnam's—with their lives, along with perhaps 3 million Vietnamese.

Of course, Vietnamese history predates this conflict by centuries, if not milleniums. Not surprisingly, much of the country's culturally rich history has been marred by conflicts.

The early Ly Dynasty seemed to be at war with everyone, and at the same time. There were the Chinese. And there were the Chams. And the Khmers. The list goes on. However, the ancient Vietnamese were a resilient lot. They pushed south toward the Gulf of Thailand and virtually annihilated the retreating Chams.

The Tran Dynasty ruled Vietnam in 1225 and faced its most potent threat from the north. The 300,000-plus Mongol soldiers of Kublai Khan attacked the nation and were repelled. But the dynasty would eventually crumble by 1400, when the Chinese again attempted to gain control. After a largely successful 20-year effort to eradicate Vietnamese culture, Le Loi emerged as the new leader of a free Vietnam. He was phenomenally wealthy and used his riches to help the poor, which made him extraordinarily popular. His family rule included the annexing of Laos and basically ended in 1524, but not until after a significant amount of reforms had been initiated, including civil rights for women. But it was also a time when China culturally dominated Vietnam.

## The Split Between North & South

Soon after Le's demise, conflict again interceded. Vietnam was split between north and south, under the rule of two factions, the Nguyen and the Trinh. Fortified by Portuguese arms, the Nguyen lords prevailed and eventually conquered all of what is present-day Cambodia.

Various factions continued to battle each other and they intermittently ruled Vietnam. Finally, a rebellion in 1771 spread to the south and Nguyen Lu became king of the south, while Nguyen Nhac became king of the central part of the country and Nguyen Hue became king in the north. The Chinese, again seeking to take advantage of the internal turmoil in Vietnam, attacked in the north, but were defeated in 1789.

Nguyen Anh, an exiled prince, managed to gain the support of French traders in India and, with the help of French mercenaries, captured Vietnam in 1802. The Nguyen Dynasty lasted until 1945, at least on paper. But the Vietnamese, on the whole, began rejecting Western influences in the 19th century, in particular those transplanted via religious missionaries. Many of these missionaries' converts were executed by the Vietnamese, prompting the French to capture and control three southern provinces in 1862.

After a French merchant was killed in 1872 by pirates, French retaliation sent the north into anarchy. The emperor, Tu Duc, sought Chinese, English, as well as American assistance in repelling the French, to no avail. Soon, the French were in control of all of what is known today as Indochina. The Indochinese Union was formed in 1887.

The French are generally thought to have controlled the region poorly. There were heavy taxes. Bandits prospered. The opium trade flourished. A growing sense of Vietnamese nationalism then helped fuel the emergence of the Communist Party, led by Ho Chi Minh. After World War II had severely exhausted France's colonial resources and influence, the communists began emerging as the strongest political party in Vietnam. Incidentally, this group, which became known as the Viet Minh during WWII, were supported by both the Chinese and the Americans when they fought the Japanese.

| DYNASTIES IN VIETNAM | | |
|---|---|---|
| **DYNASTY** | **DATES** | **CAPITAL** |
| **Hong Bang Dynasty** | *2876–258 BC* | *Phong Chau* |
| **Thuc Dynasty** | *257–208 BC* | *Loa Thanh* |
| **Trieu Dynasty** | *207–111 BC* | *Phien Ngung* |
| **Trung Sisters** | *AD 40–43* | *Me Linh* |
| **Early Ly Dynasty** | *544–602* | *Around Hanoi* |
| **Ngo Dynasty** | *939–965* | *Co Loa* |
| **Dinh Dynasty** | *968–990* | *Hoa Lu* |
| **Early Le Dynasty** | *980–1009* | *Hoa Lu* |
| **Ly Dynasty** | *1010–1225* | *Thang Long* |
| **Tran Dynasty** | *1225–1400* | *Thang Long* |
| **Ho Dynasty** | *1400–1407* | *Dong Do* |
| **Post Tran Dynasty** | *1407–1413* | |
| **Le Dynasty** | *1427–1788* | *Thang Long* |
| **Mac Dynasty** | *1527–1592* | |
| **Northern Trinh** | *1539–1787* | *Hanoi* |
| **Southern Nguyen** | *1558–1778* | *Hue* |
| **Quang Trung** | *1787–1797* | |
| **Nguyen of Tay Son** | *1788–1802* | *Saigon* |
| **Nguyen Dynasty** | *1802–1945* | *Hue* |

The Japanese overthrew the French Vichy-appointed government in Vietnam in 1945. During their short reign, an estimated 10 million people starved to death due to Japanese requisitions of rice that year.

After the atomic bombs had been dropped on Japan by the Americans later that year, the Viet Minh assumed full control of the north. Other non-communist groups wrestled for power in the south. The Democratic Republic of Vietnam was formed in Hanoi on September 2, 1945.

## Return of the French

Because of further Chinese incursions in the North and a volatile situation in the South (which, incidentally, the British sought to control with both French and Japanese support), the North was forced to bargain with the

French to purge Vietnam of the pesky Chinese. French rule of Vietnam was the price Ho Chi Minh had to pay.

But less than a year later, Vietnamese opposition to the French had risen again. With France foundering in Indochina on American aid, Vietnam again became independent, but still divided north and south. The government in South Vietnam, bolstered by Western support, lost support among the Buddhists as it sought to implement pro-Catholic policies. Protesters hit the streets and a U.S. backed coup in 1963 installed the first of a number of puppet military regimes.

### The Ultimate Backpacker: Uncle Ho's Early Years

*Few know that Ho Chi Minh (the name means "he who enlightens") left Vietnam in 1911 at the age of 21 on an odyssey that wouldn't see him return to his native land for 30 years. Ho was the ultimate backpacker, a world hitchhiker, brimming with passion and wanderlust.*

*Shortly before leaving Saigon for France in June 1911, Ho was a schoolteacher in the boonies. He was born and grew up in the central Vietnamese province of Nghe An, in the village of Hoang Tru. His father, a low-level Mandarin who had studied the Confucian classics and did a short stint behind the walls of Hue's Imperial City, left his wife and three children shortly after dropping out of his imperial posting. Ho, who had changed his name to Nguyen Tat Thanh (Ho was born Nguyen Sinh Cung in May 1890), followed suit and left home at the age of 19. He moved to bustling Saigon and changed his name yet again to Nguyen Van Ba. Sort of like changing your name to John Smith or Bob Jones. Inconspicuous. The perfect name for someone signing on as a coolie aboard a French freighter, which he did—the steamship* Admiral Latouche Treville.

*When the* Treville *arrived in Marseilles, Ho applied to get into the School of Colonies in Paris and was turned down. He became a gardener for awhile before hopping aboard another freighter and spending the next two years (1912 and 1913) traversing the seas and outposts of Europe and North Africa. He spent time in the Belgian Congo, Algeria, Spain and Portugal before arriving in the promised land of America.*

*Ho was enamored with New York and its mish-mash of ethnicities. He remained in the U.S. for a year, intermittently employed in menial labor.*

*Ho got his first taste of underground socialist thinking after he left for London in 1914. There he ran into a number of Irish nationalists and Fabian socialists. He became an apprentice under master pastry chef Georges Aguste Escoffier.*

*Ho rode out World War I in London and then took off again for Paris in 1917 where he came into contact with more leftist intellectuals and expat political dissidents from Africa and Asia. He also came into contact with Vietnamese socialists Phan Van Truong and Phan Tru Trinh, political refugees from the 1908 Hue uprisings and the defacto leaders of Paris' more than 100,000 politically restless Vietnamese expats. Ho ended up joining the Phan's secret nationalist group. He changed his name once again, this time to Nguyen Ai Quoc, meaning "the patriot."*

*It was in Paris where Ho began to create pamphlets and authored letters denouncing the French rule of Vietnam. He joined the French Socialist Party.*

## The Ultimate Backpacker: Uncle Ho's Early Years

*Disgruntled with the impotence of his efforts in Paris, Ho set out for Moscow in 1924. There he joined the Comintern, the Soviet agency tasked with spreading communism around the globe. Again Ho changed his name, to Ly Thuy, and as an assistant to Comintern's agent in Canton, China, formed the Revolutionary Youth League (RYL) for Vietnamese nationalists and revolutionaries in 1925.*

*Swept up in the communist tide that was surging through China, Ho was convinced Vietnam would follow suit and spent his time consolidating Vietnamese opposition to the French. Ho's movement gathered steam quickly until a trusted ally, Chiang Kai-shek, broke from the Moscow-backed communists, forcing Ho to flee back to the Soviet capital.*

*Realizing that his efforts to muster Vietnamese nationalists in Europe was pointless, Ho again returned to East Asia–this time to Thailand disguised as a Buddhist monk. He reignited the RYL in the northern Thai city of Udon, but left for Hong Kong shortly after to unite bickering elements of dissident Vietnamese.*

*In 1930, his efforts were successful and the Indochinese Communist Party was formed. But misfortune struck soon after as a French Comintern agent was arrested in Singapore, the authorities discovering his "black book" of Vietnamese and other dissidents. Ho was busted and ended up in a Hong Kong jail cell for the next two years.*

*In 1933 Ho was to leave Hong Kong for London after coming down with tuberculosis. But he never made it to the British capital, instead ending up back in Moscow, where he'd spend the next five years.*

*Comintern sent him back to China in 1939 at the brink of WWII after the Japanese conquered Manchuria. In the spring of 1941, Ho, now frail at 51, led a group of Vietnamese activists on a week-long trek into Vietnam from China–the first time he had been back to Vietnam in 30 years.*

*He met up with some of his former buddies in Cao Bang province and formed the Viet Minh (officially called the Vietnam Independence League–or Viet Nam Doc Lap Dong Minh). It was at this time Ho finally assumed the moniker Ho Chi Minh.*

*Ho returned to China disguised as a blind beggar to consolidate other revolutionaries, but was caught by a warlord in China's Guangxi province and imprisoned for a year.*

*By the time he got out, the Japanese had taken Vietnam. Realizing the Japanese would have little sympathy for his efforts to create an independent Vietnam, Ho instead made the bold move of contacting the U.S. intelligence organization OSS. He offered the services of the Viet Minh to assist in locating and rescuing downed American flyers in Southeast Asian jungles. Ho's motive was clear: in return for their assistance Ho was gambling that the U.S. government would assist the Viet Minh in preventing the return of the French to recolonize Vietnam after the Japanese defeat–support that would never come. In fact, the U.S. provided massive aid to the French to retake Indochina.*

## The Ultimate Backpacker: Uncle Ho's Early Years

*So when the Americans defeated the Japanese in August 1945, Ho and his supporters moved toward Hanoi and took the capital on August 16.*

*In front of thousands of supporters in a speech given in Hanoi on September 2, 1945, Ho declared in the empyreal paradox of U.S.-Vietnamese relations: "We hold the truth that all men are created equal, and that they are endowed by their Creator with certain unalienable rights. Among them life, liberty and the pursuit of happiness," words very familiar to the Americans, who would 20 years later use their own interpretation of them to wage war against the ultimate backpacker for 10 years.*

## The War in Vietnam

Meanwhile, minds in the north were thinking unification. The Viet Cong was formed in 1960 to force the withdrawal of all foreign troops on Vietnamese soil. In 1964, North Vietnamese troops were making forays into the south. The rickety regime in Saigon was becoming weaker through mass desertions and disillusioned peasants.

The Americans, who had actually had troops inside Vietnam as early as 1955, made a full-scale military commitment to the preservation of the South Vietnamese government.

The turning point in the war came with the Tet (Chinese New Year) Offensive of 1968. Saigon was attacked by the Viet Cong. Mass devastation took place in the countryside. In one three-week period, more than 165,000 civilians were killed in the fighting.

***On April 30, 1975, a North Vietnamese Army tank smashed through this gate to Saigon's Presidential Palace, symbolizing the fall of South Vietnam.***

Growing resistance to the war by Americans helped form the American policy of "Vietnamization," which marked the first efforts toward sending American troops home. But shortly afterwards, the U.S. began its massive carpet bombing of Cambodia. The public outcry in the U.S., combined with the phenomenal and unexpected perseverance and resiliency of the communist troops, ultimately forced the U.S. to negotiate with Hanoi. The withdrawal of all U.S. troops from Vietnam was ceded for Hanoi's recognition of the South's independence. But on April 30, 1975, North Vietnamese troops rolled into Saigon after a massive offensive and South Vietnam fell.

## Post-War Vietnam

The country then began the painful process of reunification and "reeducation." Hundreds of thousands of Vietnamese fled their country for the U.S. and Europe. Cut off from the West economically, Vietnam suffered greatly.

In 1977, Vietnam entered the United Nations. At the end of the following year, the army invaded Cambodia and deposed Pol Pot's murderous Khmer Rouge regime in January of 1979, installing a pro-Hanoi government. But not without tremendous consequences.

By invading Cambodia, Hanoi had overextended itself, and the Cambodian conflict became what many call "Vietnam's Vietnam." While other Southeast Asian countries were tasting a degree of prosperity for the first time, Vietnam was sinking the vast crux of its economic resources into its war machine, impoverishing its people to the lowest levels on the globe. Even though Hanoi's forces had taken Phnom Penh, it spent the next 10 years failing to crush the Khmer Rouge's perpetual insurgency. The war drained Vietnam's already shaky centralized economy.

The Vietnamese government began withdrawing their troops from Cambodia in 1989 and agreed in October, 1991 to the Paris Peace Agreement that paved the way to the first free elections in Cambodia.

The Bill Clinton administration in the U.S. dropped the trade embargo on February 4, 1994 and liaison offices were established in Hanoi and Washington by the end of the year.

On July 11, 1995, President Clinton announced normalized relations between Washington and Hanoi, a bold and controversial move welcomed by the Vietnamese. Clinton has insisted that normalization will speed up the process of resolving the POW/MIA issue. (See the "U.S. & Vietnam: Normalization" chapter.)

### INSIDER TIP

*At presstime, the U.S. and Vietnamese governments have established full diplomatic ties. When liaison offices were exchanged between the two countries in the beginning of 1995, the agreement marked the first major talks between the two countries since the Paris Peace Agreement in 1973 that technically ended U.S. involvement in the Vietnam War. The U.S. office in Hanoi has primarily functioned to assess and aid trade improvements between the two countries and also to continue to monitor human rights issues and American MIA cases. America already maintains an office in Hanoi solely for the purpose of locating MIAs. Vietnam's only official presence in the U.S. up to the liaison/normalization announcements consisted of its delegation to the United Nations in New York. The liaison offices have also been dealing with financial claims made by the two countries following the seizure of American assets by the Communists after the fall of South Vietnam in 1975, and Hanoi's claims of some US$290 million in frozen assets in the United States. American claims are approximately US$230,000, the crux of that being U.S. investments in the south, including seized properties and buildings and enormous assets in South Vietnam once held by Occidental Petroleum Corp (see below). On August 6, 1995, the U.S. Embassy opened at 7 A Lang Ha street, Dong Da District, Hanoi. The opening of the embassy will provide travelers with access to embassy/consular support and services should they get into trouble, lose their passport, etc. in Vietnam.*

## The Peace Process Is Complete

Settling financial and MIA claims have been the keys to achieving normalization. Although there are still a number of issues to be resolved between Vietnamese and American negotiators. Part of the disagreement that remains between the two nations revolves around U.S. and Vietnamese assets left behind in Vietnam after the war. Some estimates put the number of U.S. assets lost after the fall of Saigon in 1975 at $230 million. U.S. government claims include the former U.S. Embassy in Saigon, which is currently being used by a Vietnamese oil company. The Vietnamese, in their behalf, claim that the U.S. maintains frozen Vietnamese assets totalling more than $290 million. U.S. oil companies were big losers with the U.S. withdrawl from Vietnam in 1973. Simply, American companies would prefer to have their old real estate back once they move back into Vietnam rather than having to be forced to procure new land and offices.

The MIA probe will imminently end in 1995 or 1996. Vietnam is opening up its borders and military bases to the Americans to expedite the determination of the fate of the 1647 Americans still unaccounted for in Vietnam. Additionally, 505 Americans are still missing in Laos, 78 in Cambodia, and eight in China. The largest joint search with Vietnamese since the end of the war in 1975 was completed in January 1994. Five more operations, even larger in scope, occurred before the end of the year. U.S. guidelines for a "full accounting" of all U.S. war dead include bringing back those who are still alive, which is unilaterally agreed as highly unlikely, as well as all remains. If the remains cannot be brought home, it must be demonstrated by the Vietnamese why this isn't possible. Groups, including families of missing veterans charge that Hanoi "calculatedly withholds" MIA information.

With the establishment of full ties between Washington and Hanoi, the investigation into these claims should accelerate.

## U.S.-VIETNAM RELATIONS

| | |
|---|---|
| **March 8, 1965** | *The first U.S. combat troops reach Vietnam* |
| **January 27, 1973** | *The United States and North Vietnam sign the Paris cease-fire agreements, essentially ending the American combat role in the war.* |
| **March 29, 1973** | *The last U.S. combat troops leave Vietnam.* |
| **April 1, 1973** | *Hanoi releases the last 591 acknowledged U.S. POWs.* |
| **April 30, 1975** | *Saigon falls to communist troops. Vietnam is reunified. The American trade embargo is extended to all of Vietnam.* |
| **February 1982** | *The Vietnamese government agrees to talks with Washington on Americans still missing from the war.* |
| **September-October 1988** | *The United States and Vietnam conduct the first joint field investigations for American soldiers missing in action.* |
| **April 21, 1991** | *The U.S. and Vietnam agree to open an office in Hanoi to investigate the fate of American MIAs.* |
| **April 29, 1992** | *U.S. President George Bush eases the trade embargo by permitting American sales to Vietnam for humanitarian projects.* |
| **December 14, 1992** | *President Bush permits U.S. companies to open offices to do business feasibility studies and sign contracts in Vietnam.* |
| **July 2, 1993** | *President Bill Clinton ends opposition to settlement of Vietnam's US$140 million arrears to the International Monetary Fund, opening the way for Vietnam to acquire new loans.* |

| U.S.-VIETNAM RELATIONS | |
|---|---|
| **September 13, 1993** | *Clinton permits American businesses to bid on projects financed by international banks.* |
| **January 27, 1994** | *The U.S. Senate approves a nonbinding resolution urging Clinton to lift the embargo.* |
| **February 3, 1994 (Feb. 4 in VN)** | *Clinton announces the lifting of the trade embargo against Vietnam.* |
| **October 5, 1994** | *The House passes a bill saying MIA accounting should remain central to U.S. policy in Vietnam and the principle function of a U.S. liaison office in Hanoi.* |
| **January 27, 1995** | *The United States and Vietnam sign an agreement to open liaison offices in Washington and Hanoi.* |
| **May 23, 1995** | *U.S. Senators John Kerry and John McCain, both Vietnam war veterans, urge Clinton to normalize relations with Vietnam.* |
| **May 31, 1995** | *Vietnam turns over 100 pages of maps and reports about U.S. servicemen killed or captured during the war. An American veteran's map helps locate a mass grave of communist soldiers killed during the war.* |
| **June 1995** | *U.S. Secretary of State Warren Christopher reccomends to Clinton that the U.S. establish formal diplomatic relations with Vietnam.* |
| **July 1995** | *Clinton's national security advisers draft a decision memo for him to approve full relations.* |
| **July 10, 1995** | *White House officials say Clinton will move to establish relations in a Rose Garden announcement.* |
| **July 11, 1995** | *Clinton establishes normalized relations with Vietnam.* |
| **August 6, 1995** | *U.S. Embassy in Hanoi opens.* |

## Planning Ahead

### Vietnamtourism and Saigontourist

VT, Vietnam's official tourist information office, doesn't yet maintain an office in the U.S. (although this is bound to change shortly with the normalization of relations), but you can obtain informative brochures from the U.S. representative, (Ms.) Hont Nguyen, *200 Waterside Plaza, New York, NY 10010* (☎ *(212) 685-8001*). In Saigon, check out SAIGONTOURIST Travel Service at *49 Le Thanh Ton Street*; ☎ *298-914* or *295-834*. Or fax them at *84-8-224987*. In all frankness, though, I didn't find these people particularly helpful save for all but the usual tourist package trips like three-hour expensive (US$15) city tours aboard buses that have to fight off thousands of bicycles and cyclos that swarm Saigon streets like bees in search of tulips to pollinate. Some of their offerings weren't so bad, though. For instance, I recommend the day trip to Bien Hoa, an area in the Mekong River Delta with green rolling hills, for about $35. But you gotta like those buses. If you're simply not into buses, forget it.

## A NOTE ON TOURIST OFFICES, MAPS AND ROADS

*Although tourist offices exist in most major Vietnamese destinations (and even some minor ones—although I couldn't locate one in Tay Ninh), they are often of little use to the independent traveler—this includes especially the major offices of Saigontourist and Vietnamtourism in HCMC.*

*Rather they cater more toward organized tours, providing guides (usually individuals with limited English capabilities at exorbitant prices), renting vehicles (also often at ridiculous rates) and providing little if any information on sites that aren't regularly visited by tourists—sights, regardless of their lack of scenic or cultural appeal, that independent travelers intuitively seek out. Their primary function is to procure dollars, and tour packages comprise the best means of doing so. Even obtaining local maps at the tourist offices can be difficult if not impossible.*

*Saigon is the best place to obtain reasonably detailed maps of areas in southern Vietnam. And the best map stalls line Le Loi Blvd, generally across from the Rex Hotel. Maps cost usually between US$1-2, depending on the area. Hanoi is the best place to find maps to areas in the north.*

*Curiously enough, the least detailed maps seem to fetch the higher prices, and some of them seem virtually useless for ground travel. Many maps depict road routes but do not number them. If you're traveling by surface, before you depart, find someone who knows the numerical identifications of major Vietnamese roads and mark the maps at intervals, as route numbers have a tendency to change at times. In many cities, towns and villages where major routes pass through, the route numbers will become names, such as Le Loi Street, Nguyen Hue Blvd., etc.*

*If you're not bringing a guide with you on independent travel along Vietnamese roadways, have someone mark on the map(s) where road conditions are particularly dismal. This is particularly important if you are drafting an itinerary and expect to reach specific locations at the end of the day.*

## A NOTE ON TOURIST OFFICES, MAPS AND ROADS

*A 150-km trek between Nha Trang and Danang is going to take a considerably shorter period of time than the same distance between Ben Tre and Soc Trang in the south. And the roads in the north, traditionally known for their resemblance to cratered cattle paths rather than vehicle highways, are improving.*

*Tourists traveling north in Vietnam from HCMC to Hanoi have traditionally gone only as far as Hue, at which point they opt to take the train or fly to points north. This still seems to be the case, even though the roads in the north are now in acceptable enough shape to be negotiated by means more sophisticated than a sow.*

### Visas

Individuals and tour operators can obtain visas for travelers, and the processing period doesn't take as long as a month as a lot of other guides claim. Visas are currently procured from the Vietnam Embassy in Washington D.C. Usually it's just a matter of a week or 10 days before it's in your hands.

## INSIDER TIP

*Tour companies and travel agencies are extremely competitive and part of any particular company's lure is its ability to get you a visa quickly. With some companies, it might just take a couple of days, others as long as 10. But remember, that in order for a tour company to get your visa quickly it has to press Vietnamese immigration officials to push the paper like a used-car salesman, some of whom don't like to be shoved around, even when tourist dollars are involved. A travel or tour agency known for its expediency in delivering your visa may ironically not be in such good favor with the Vietnamese authorities because they're such a pain in the rear to the Vietnamese. If you've got the time, settle for the longer visa processing time if your tour operator can compensate in other areas—and believe me, they can. Even so, never wait until the last minute to book.*

The best way to get a visa, as it is with all of the restricted countries in the region, is to get to Bangkok first. There you can pick up a visa in just a few days for around US$60–90 at the travel agencies or for US$48 at the Vietnamese Embassy at *83/1 Wireless Rd.*, directly across from the U.S. Embassy. They're usually open from 9–11 or 11:30 in the morning and 1–4 or so in the afternoon. Show up with a couple of passport photos. If you do use a travel agency, SHOP AROUND! In fact rather than stand on line at the embassy for my visa, I just walked half a block down Wireless Rd. to M.K. Ways. They won't charge you more than the embassy for the visa (almost unheard of in travel agency circles). They also specialize in Indochina tours and bookings and, frankly, they'll probably save you a lot of time prowling around Khao San Road for an airline bargain.

One of the increasingly popular ways of getting to Vietnam is through Cambodia. Again, arrange for your Vietnamese visa in Bangkok, not Phnom Penh. If you do it this way, you can expect to pay as little as US$40 for the single-entry tourist visa. Making Vietnamese visa arrangements in Cambodia is both expensive and time consuming, as it is in Vientiane. In Bangkok, you'll need to get three passport-type photos.

From the U.S., you will need two photos and a copy of your passport. The cost is $65 per person. The application, photos and copy of passport should be mailed to: **Viet Nam Embassy**, *1233 20th Street N.W., Washington, D.C. 20036,* ☎ *(202) 861-0694 or (202) 861-0737.*

#### Business Visas

Business visas are available for up to six months and extendable on a multi-entry basis. The policy seems to change as my business visa was valid for three months, extendable twice—allowing me to stay in the country for nine months before making a "visa run." The best thing to do is to check with your sponsor, as you'll need one in Vietnam to procure a business visa.

Ask your Vietnamese sponsor to submit an application to the Ministry of the Interior. You'll need to give your full name, date and place of birth, profession, passport number (as well the date of issue and expiration), address, nationality, and time and place of entry into Vietnam.

The Ministry will fax or telex the Vietnamese embassy or consulate in your country with an approval number usually between seven and 10 days. Remain in contact with your sponsor to determine when the Ministry has approved your application. Ask the Vietnamese sponsor to give you the visa approval number and the date it was issued in order to track it down in the event that it is delayed.

The Vietnamese embassy or consulate will inform you when your application has been processed and the visa is ready. Show up with four passport photos and a copy of the approval stamp, which you can get faxed to you from your sponsor. You'll need to fill out an application form and pay the requested fee.

### Inoculations and Medical Advice

Arrival within six days after leaving or transiting a yellow fever zone requires an inoculation. But you should have all the proper vaccinations before coming to Vietnam. Disease is rife here. One source told me that Vietnam is the only country in the world where you can still get bubonic plague. Even if it isn't true, just the rumor itself is an indication that you would no more walk around Vietnam without inoculations than you would the surface of the moon without a space suit.

There is pneumonia here of every variety, malaria, diarrheal diseases, tetanus, tuberculosis, cholera, hepatitis, polio, rabies, leprosy, diptheria, dysentery, typhoid and rickets. You should be vaccinated for meningitis, hepatitis A and B, tuberculosis, typhoid, tetenus and diphtheria. Remember to have these performed well in advance of your trip as some will require boosters before you begin your journey. Also note that the period of efficacy differs by vaccination. Some will give you protection longer than others. And all of your vaccinations should be recorded in an International Health Certificate that you should carry with your passport.

Malaria is another story. Of course, you should obtain a larium prescription which you should begin taking about seven days before entering malarial zones. But the problem with this little monster of a disease is that it has this nasty tendency to become immune to virtually every medicine developed to fight it. Malaria mutates like Wolfgang Puck restaurants.

Also essential is a good first-aid kit with all the trimmings. And add to your booty when you get to Asia. A lot of the drugs you need a prescription for in North America, you can get over the counter in East Asia. And if you're going remote, painkillers are a great idea. You'll be thankful if you take a fall. We don't know too many docs Stateside who will write a downer "scrip" simply because you've said you'll be running in a road rally in HCMC for a month. But bring with you anti-diarrheal drugs such as codeine, Imodium or Lomotil along with an antiseptic and a laxative.

### Medical Problems in Vietnam

Food and waterborne diseases are the biggest causes of illness in Vietnam. Diarrhea is the most common problem. Diarrhea is caused by ingesting contaminated food or water, as are other diseases such as parasites, typhoid fever, hepatitis, polio and cholera.

**Cholera** is caused by bacteria and is an acute intestinal infection transmitted though feces-contaminated food or water. Symptoms include vomiting, dehydration, massive diarrhea attacks and muscle cramps. These days, the risk of cholera infection in Vietnam is low if you stick to the usual tourist itineraries. Should you wander off the beaten track, drink only bottled or boiled water and eat only thoroughly cooked food. Peel vegetables before consuming them. You should be vaccinated against cholera if you're going to be spending significant time in rural and unhygienic places, or if you have stomach ulcers, use anti-acid therapy or will be visiting areas known to have cholera outbreaks—in short, anywhere unsanitary or where floods occur, causing sewage to mix with drinking water. The available vaccine is only about 50 percent effective, and really isn't recommended for most travelers. If you decide to be vaccinated, you'll first receive two injections, and boosters every six months if you live in a high-risk area.

**Typhoid fever** is caused by a bacteria either consumed or transmitted between people. The symptoms include headaches, fever, constipation, lack of appetite and sluggishness. Typhoid fever can be treated effectively with antibiotics. The risks associated with typhoid fever are travel to rural areas and unhygienic places. Current vaccines are about 70 percent to 90 percent effective. A single injection of Typhim provides three years protection and doesn't conflict with other inoculations and treatments (such as anti-malarial drugs, antibiotics, etc.) You should get inoculated against typhoid fever if you plan travel in remote parts of Vietnam or will be in the country a month or longer. To avoid risks, drink only bottled water (it's preferable over boiled water) and consume only thoroughly cooked food.

**Dysentery** is the worst diarrhea you've ever had, and more. It's accompanied by a high fever; you believe you are going to die. Bacillary dysentery is relatively easy to treat. Antibiotics will do the trick in only a couple of days. Even without treatment, bacillary dysentery will disappear after a few days. Amoebic dysentery is far more dangerous. Medical attention is usually necessary, as the disease will not disappear like the bacillary variety. If amoebic dysentery isn't treated promptly, liver damage is more than likely.

**Hepatitis** has three strains: A, B, and non-A/non B. Hepatitis A can be contracted in areas where there is poor hygiene and a lack of sanitation. It is spread through contaminated food and water and attacks the liver. Symptoms include fever, vomiting, loss of energy and acute depression—not unlike the symptoms of bacillary dysentery—which appear within three to eight weeks after infection. The disease will run its course after a few weeks of hell—there is no cure. Bedrest and a high-calorie diet are the recommended treatment.

**Hepatitis B** is far more dangerous and is spread though sexual contact, blood transfusions, contaminated needles—the same channels through which AIDS is spread. In Vietnam, don't even consider getting a tattoo or an ear pierced. If you get hepatitis B, you'll have it for the rest of your life. Non A/non B strains are simply other variations of the original. To avoid contracting hepatitis B, take the same precautions as you would to avoid AIDS. If you must have sex, do so only with a condom. Stay away from intravenous drugs, and insist that necessary injections be done with a sterile (preferably new) needle. In many areas of Vietnam, needles are reused and not properly sterilized. The other strains of hepatitis can be avoided by taking the same precautions outlined earlier to prevent contracting food- and water-borne diseases.

**Malaria** is also caused by a parasite, but one that is spread through the Anopheles mosquito rather than through food or water. There are four different types of malaria, although only two strains represent most cases. The deadlier of the two is the P faciparum strain, found widely in the southeastern Mekong Delta. Symptoms usually develop about two weeks after being bitten. They include an intense fever, severe headaches, vomiting, shivering and sweating. The risks are greatest at lower altitudes in the south of Vietnam. Medical attention is a necessity.

Unfortunately, malaria has a tendancy to mutate into other vaccine-resistant strains when confronted with anti-malarial preventatives such as chloroquine, the most prescribed anti-malarial which has become largely ineffective if you're bitten by bugs carrying the P falciparum strain. You can't be innoculated against malaria, but are usually instructed instead to ingest chloroquine (one 500 mg tablet a week), starting two weeks prior to a trip into risk areas. The dosage must then be continued for 4-6 weeks after the trip is finished. Other malaria preventatives include maloprim—which is most effective when taken with chloroquine, but shouldn't be used long-term—and doxycycline, which also has dangerous, long-term effects. It particularly shouldn't be used by pregnant women.

The best advice to prevent malaria is stay away from high-risk areas. Cover exposed skin with a deet mosquito repellant and expose as little shin as possible in malarial areas. At night, sleep under a mosquito net. It would help if you had a fan blowing in your direction.

**Dengue fever** is also a mosquito-borne disease, but not nearly as severe as malaria, although you couldn't imagine anything more severe when you've contracted it. Symptoms are similar to malaria, but usually subside after a few days, before returning to torture you for a couple of weeks.) But then it's gone. There is no vaccine, and antimalarial treatments and preventatives are ineffective against dengue fever. Take the same precautions as you would with malaria.

### Entry By Air

Entry by air is by regularly scheduled flights into Hanoi and Ho Chi Minh City. Both cities are served by a variety of airlines, including Thai, Cathay Pacific, JAL, Korean Air, Garuda Indonesia, Philippine Airlines, MAS, Air France, and others depending on your departure point. There's also, of course, the infamous Vietnam Airlines, which has been likened by more than a few travelers to a fleet of coffins with wings. But I'll be honest, I've survived a number of smooth trips aboard a Vietnam Airlines Boeing 767 and Airbus 320, as well as the Aerospatiale ATR-72, and I figure any British pilot working for a Vietnamese airline had to have done something to get canned at British Airways, such as planting a 747 on a German autobahn. But we made it each time, and he sounded as if he was having a jolly good time of it. I had to admit it, though, it was a little unnerving to board a plane with absolutely no markings. The international fleet up until 1995 was painted white. A couple of numbers on the fantails, that was it. No logo or anything. I can think of a bunch of airspace in areas of the world where that would go over real well. But that's all changed now; the fleet is painted, save for its recent aquisitions from other airlines. One recent trip I took to Hanoi on Vietnam Airlines was aboard a Boeing 767, still wearing the colors and lettering of Royal Brunei Airlines. For a brief moment as we boarded, I did indeed think I was being deported. But the service was great.

There have been reports by Westerners of having to bribe Vietnamese immigration officials both in Hanoi and Ho Chi Minh City after arrival, even with all documentation in order. And it can be expensive—upwards of US$100. But these instances have become virtually extinct, especially since the lifting of America's trade embargo and Vietnam's joining of ASEAN in July 1995.

## READ THIS: PREPARE FOR WHAT TO DECLARE

*When entering Vietnam, be prepared to declare everything of value you're bringing along with you. Whereas you may be accustomed to flying into Bangkok, Manila or KL and taking a leisurely stroll through the Green Line with pounds of photographic equipment and the portable atom splitter your daughter bought you out of a Sharper Image catalog, don't expect such a smooth ride through Saigon's Tan Son Nhat Airport or Hanoi's Noi Bai Airport.*

*To keep the delay at customs to a minimum, write down the serial number and model name of all your electronic and photographic devices, etc. This includes the serial number of each of your lenses. The same goes for laptop computers and peripherals, even electronic datebooks.*

*You'll be required to do so on the customs declaration form–so it makes sense to have the numbers already handy in your wallet, rather than having to fumble through all your gear at the customs officer's desk.*

*On another note, foreigners have traditionally had to declare any amount of foreign currency more than US$5000 when entering Vietnam. By the time you read this, the amount will have risen to US$7000. The State Bank of Vietnam is planning to further increase that amount to US$10,000 in the near future.*

*According to the bank's Foreign Currency Control Department, the illegal transfer of foreign currency is principally executed through the banking system, while illegal transfer through entry and exit ports is rare.*

### Entry By Land

From Cambodia, the border crossing at Moc Bai is currently open to Westerners, who usually are on a bus from Phnom Penh to Ho Chi Minh City. There have been reports of Westerners being detained by Vietnamese border guards trying to solicit bribes. Be cool. The best bet is to pick up your visa (a 15-day transit visa has recently been lowered from US$20 to US$10) at the Cambodian consulate in Saigon (see Ho Chi Minh City "Directory" for the address and phone number).

The border between Vietnam and Laos has recently been opened to foreign tourists at Lao Ebbao. There's a little confusion about the costs of these visas. There is a free 3–5 day transit visa which can be issued at the border at Lao Ebbao, I was told. Another official at the Lao consulate in HCMC said that transit visas lasting a week cost US$25 and can be picked up at the Laos embassy in Hanoi and at both the Laos consulates in Ho Chi Minh City and Danang (Danang, I was told by the Lao consulate in HCMC, is your best bet). From north of Danang, National Highway 9 crosses Vietnam into Laos and finally into Thailand. This route can be traversed by foreign tourists by land. But the road in Laos is in dismal condition, and officials at the consulate said that foreigners should attempt a crossing into and through Laos from Vietnam in the dry season only—which runs from November through April. The roads in Laos west of Vietnam are not navigable during the rainy season between May and October. If you really want to get stuck somewhere for an extended period of time, say six months, in an area where there is virtually nothing that allows human beings to survive, I'd strongly suggest traveling into Laos from Vietnam by road during the rainy season.

The Chinese border to the north is becoming increasingly easier to cross for both Vietnamese and Westerners alike. Most travelers now say it's a piece of cake. Areas that were previously closed to foreigners, such as the border posts at Mong Cai and Dong Dang (20 km northwest of Lang Son), are now open for foreigners with the proper visa documentation. But if you are leaving Vietnam into China via these routes, your Vietnamese visa must specify these border gates as points of departure. You can easily change the departure point stamped on your current Vietnamese visa by paying a visit to the immigration offices in Hanoi or Ho Chi Minh City. Some travel agents in both these cities will also be in a position to do it for you.

### Entry By Sea

Entering Vietnam by sea is legal only by freighter or cruise ship. It would be dangerous to attempt a landing in Vietnam by any other means. It could mean months in jail. Keep your yacht and jet skis in Singapore.

### Currency

The official currency in Vietnam is the dong, although U.S. dollars are accepted, even preferred, in the population centers. Bank notes come in the denominations of 200d, 500d, 1000d, 2000d, 5000d, 10,000d, 20,000d and 50,000d. Most travelers today are using the dollars over the dong for transactions worth more than US$20, and many upscale hotels require payment in dollars, even though an October 1994 law mandated that all major transactions in Vietnam must be made in dong. Carry a good amount of U.S. money in small denominations. Up until 1995, many travelers would use dong for all of their purchases. However, the dollar has gotten marginally stronger against the dong in the last year and, today, most travelers convert large U.S. bills into dong for the best exchange rate (11,000 to the dollar). You could get away using dollars entirely while you're in Vietnam, but it doesn't make a lot of sense these days. But if you must know, 10,900 dong is equal to a buck.

### Tipping

Tipping is becoming increasingly expected in Vietnam, although it certainly isn't required. Some establishments add a 10 percent surcharge. Keeping some duty-free booze and foreign cigarettes on you is always a good idea. Marlboros and 555s are the best bets for the butts, Johnnie Walker Black Label whiskey for the booze. And remember, most waitresses in Vietnam make a salary of US$20 per month. Nearly all help support their families on this amount.

### Official Language

The official language is Vietnamese, which is a combination of Chinese, Tai, Cham and Mon-Khmer. English is spoken by the many Vietnamese who worked with Americans during the Vietnam War as well as a number of schoolchildren and students. There's been an escalating interest in English since the country began opening itself to tourism in 1989. Many in the older set can speak French, and there are a lot of French tourists to practice with.

### Business Hours

Most businesses open between 7 and 8 in the morning, shut down for a couple of hours around 11–12 noon, and open again until 4 or 5 p.m. Government offices are generally open a half-day on Saturday. Museums are generally closed Mondays.

### Telephone, Telex and Fax

These services are actually quite good, especially in Ho Chi Minh City, Hanoi and other tourist and business destinations. They used to be outrageously expensive, but prices are coming down. Faxing is your best bet. In fact, faxing from many places in Vietnam is cheaper than doing so from Thailand, Malaysia and Singapore, even from hotels. Most institutions with faxes in Vietnam charge by the page rather than by a three-minute minimum. It's a better deal if you're only faxing a single page. Expect to pay anywhere from US$6.75 to US$8.50 per page (compared to the 3-minute minimum prices of around US$8-9 in Thailand). And beware. If you're faxing overseas from a hotel, ask to see the hotel's rate chart in print. Opportunistic clerks frequently pad the costs by a dollar or two per page. I've caught a few of them at it. International faxing and phoning is generally cheaper at post offices than at hotels.

#### AUTHOR'S NOTE: TELECOMMUNICATIONS

*The official line is this: Calls to Singapore cost US$3.80 for the first minute and $2.95 for each subsequent minute. Calls to France cost US$4.60/ $3.82 for each subsequent minute. To Indonesia, the rates are US$4.55/$3.50, and to the US, US$4.50/US$3.82. In practice, I found these rates to be higher, not significantly, but high enough so that a business call that might take a certain amount of time adds up. Hotels are generally more expensive than going though a GPO, but don't count on it. Ironically, I've found it cheaper to fax the US from small hotels in the middle of the boonies than to make the "less expensive" calls though the general post offices in the major urban centers. Who knows, you may be getting ripped off. But what the hell are you going to do about it? Interestingly enough, it's a lot cheaper to call into Vietnam than from Vietnam.*

A phone call to the U.S. usually runs around US$5.50 for the first minute and a few pennies less than that for each minute thereafter. It's not cheap. Faxing is a better deal. The influx of foreign business into both Hanoi and Ho Chi Minh City should soon bring these costs down as the country's communications infrastructure develops. Telexes aren't of much use any longer as the West has mostly discarded them in favor of the fax.

## INSIDER TIP

*Vietnam is a communist country. When faxing, avoid including information and/or opinions of a political nature. In some hotels, especially in the provinces, you can fax internationally direct–from hotel fax to destination fax–so there's little to be concerned about. This might be a little paranoid, but beware. In places like Saigon, your fax is first transmitted to the general post office or other fax ccenter before it is refaxed onto your destination. Usually, there's no hassle with this–and I have yet to experience a problem–i.e., state police battering down my hotel door at three in the morning. But just know that other eyes will see your communication before it's sent out of the country. Before you fax overseas, ask the fax operator (i.e. hotel clerk) if your message will be transmitted directly rather than through a middle source. As a rule of thumb, avoid sending anything even remotely controversial that could potentially raise a red flag. Literally. Foreign businesses in Vietnam generally can fax directly out of the country.*

## REACH OUT AND TOUCH SOMEONE

*It's a lot easier to make a phone call in Vietnam. The number of telephone lines in the country has increased by 200,000 to a total of more than 460,000 lines as of the end of 1994–40,000 lines have been installed in Hanoi, 60,000 in HCMC and the remaining 100,000 in the provinces around the country.*

*The total project is expected to cost in the US$275 million range. Most of the investment has come from overseas. Vietnam currently (at presstime) has only three lines for each 1000 people in this country with a population of more than 71 million. The government expects to have 750,000 lines in operation by the end of 1995, bringing the rate to about 10 lines per 1000 people.*

*Most major cities provide relatively easy access to IDD (International Direct Dial) lines, most of them in the better hotels. Most budget travelers make overseas calls from GPOs in Vietnam's cities, and virtually all clerks at these post offices will tell you (seeing that you're a foreigner) that making collect calls overseas cannot be done. However, there is a way to make a collect call overseas. Get to know a Vietnamese local and have him do it for you. In some areas it's more difficult than in others, but generally it can be done.*

### REACH OUT AND TOUCH SOMEONE

*Have an English-speaking Vietnamese friend explain to the clerk that he wants to make an overseas call, say to the U.S. (Vietnamese are given vast preferences over foreigners whenever trying to conduct any type of communications, accommodations, restaurant or utility-related business.) The Vietnamese person will have to give the operator his or her name, of course. Tell the Vietnamese friend to add your name to his when giving his own name to the operator.*

*For instance, if you're calling your parents in Georgia and the Vietnamese's name is Nguyen Tu, tell him to add your name to his. You can use your first name or surname depending upon whom you're calling (and the name the party will recognize you by).*

*If your name is Franklin Beethoven, have the Vietnamese say to the operator that his name is Nguyen Beethoven Tu. Your party in the States will probably recognize the situation and accept the charges. The operator may ask the Vietnamese how the hell he got the name Beethoven, but he simply needs to say it's a nickname. (In this case he might say his music teacher gave it to him, that it's a stupid one, but one that stuck.)*

*There is no guarantee that this will work, but it has worked for me on a number of occasions. A tip should be in order for the Vietnamese helping you. (It'll be a hell of a lot cheaper than paying for the call yourself.)*

#### What to Wear

Vietnam has a sticky, tropical climate. Light cotton clothing is a must, particularly in the south. In the north (especially the mountainous north), it can become quite cool on winter evenings. A sweater or wrap would be appropriate. And places like Ha Long Bay can get darn cold in January. Bring a coat. Jackets and ties for doing business only. (See the "Packing" section in the "Introduction.")

#### Local Time

Vietnam is seven hours ahead of Greenwich mean time. It's in the same time zone as Bangkok and Phnom Penh.

#### Newspapers and Magazines

Vietnamese English-language periodicals in Vietnam include *Vietnam Weekly*, *Vietnam Economic Times*, *Saigon Times*, the highly regarded *Vietnam Investment Review* and *New Vietnam*—all geared toward foreign business travelers, but most contain useful travel information on interesting destinations, some off the trodden path. Best bets in Ho Chi Minh City and Hanoi are the *Bangkok Post*, *The Nation*, *The Asian Wall Street Journal*, *USA Today* and the *International Herald Tribune* for newspapers and *Time* or *Newsweek* for magazines. There are a host of other foreign language publications. In addition, since the lifting of the American embargo, you can pick up even current issues of *People* magazine.Things are *really* changing here. Both the newspapers and the magazines are current. Expect foreign newspapers such as the *Bangkok Post* to be a day late. Although, if you're lucky, you can get the same day's edition in the late afternoon.

**INSIDER TIP**

*Obtaining periodicals and newspapers dealing with the outside world used to be a hassle in Saigon–and an expensive one at that. This seems to be changing. American publications such as the* Wall Street Journal, USA Today, TIME, People *and* Newsweek *are readily available, especially around the Rex and Continental Hotels. Swarms of children scour the streets hawking English-language rags to foreigners, but still, unfortunately, at inflated prices. Be aware that you may be able to bargain for many of the magazines and newspapers the kids are touting, namely because they've been pilfered from the hotels after the guests have finished with them. The bookstore across the square from the Rex has an especially well-endowed newsstand, selling current newspapers and magazines from all over the world. The biggest disappointment is that the best locally produced periodicals, including the* Saigon Times, *the* Vietnam Investment Review *(highly recommended for business travelers) and* Vietnam Today*–all extremely useful and remarkably well-done publications–still fetch exorbitantly high prices. US$4-5 is the norm. (The Saigon Times is only 5000 dong–and only worth 5000 dong.) For many travelers, though, the publications are an investment rather than a way to pass time in the toilet.*

### Electrical Current

Since Vietnam's infrastructure is still rudimentary, and power outages occur without warning, be sure to bring a flashlight. The electric current is 220V/50 cycles in most places. Take along adapter plugs and a converter.

**AUTHOR'S NOTE**

*Vietnam's 500 kilovolt north-south power transmission line has started operation from Hoa Binh, about 75 km west of Hanoi, to Ho Chi Minh City. The line will supply 2.5 billion kwh for the southern cities and is currently the country's biggest infrastructure project. The goal is to provide power to southern cities that chronically suffer from seasonal shortages of power.*

### Local Transportation

**Buses** are one of the best ways to get around because they're so cheap and they get to so many places within the country. And they're even better if you've got a lot of time—because they take a lot of time. Oh, yeah—they break down a lot, too. There are more runs during the night now that curfew restrictions have been relaxed.

**Cars** are a better way to get around than buses but are usually quite expensive, at least 25 cents a km on top of a day charge. And you can't rent them yourself yet, at least to drive. Alas, yours will have to come with a driver. It's better that way anyhow. There's right-side-drive in Vietnam and, although the cops are tough, one of the most common infractions is driving on the left. There are a lot of companies that hire out cars and drivers in Ho Chi Minh City.

You can rent a **moped** (50 cc) without a special license in Vietnam for about US$6 per day, or hire a moped driver. You can even now rent a **motorcycle** in Ho Chi Minh City for about US$10 per day. You will need an international drivers license with a motorcycle certificate, although few rental firms will ask to see it.

**Trains** are also a great way of getting around along the coast. They're slower than the buses, but are a helluva lot more comfy if you shell out enough dollars (you'll be required to pay in dollars) for anything more than a hard seat. The only problem is that the government slaps a surcharge on rail travel that makes it virtually as expensive as flying the same route (at least between Ho Chi Minh City and Hanoi).

**Hitchhiking** can be a piece of cake in Vietnam and not nearly as risky as in Cambodia, but expect to pay for your ride.Other travelers, however, report waiting hours for rides. It pays to look neat.

**Cyclos** are also a cheap way to get around, especially the cities. And they're everywhere where tourists hang out. Bargain shrewdly.

**Bicycles** are perhaps the best and cheapest way to get around in the towns and cities. They rent for no more than a dollar per day and they can be had many places, including hotels, restaurants and sidewalk stalls. Some operators will ask for a deposit sometimes as high as US$20. Outside Saigon and Hanoi, most don't require any.

### INSIDER TIP: TAXIS AND CAR HIRE IN VIETNAM

*A service is available from Tan Son Nhat airport to Saigon. The 20 or so minute ride costs about US$8-15 depending on your negotiating abilities. Taxis are also available from Noi Bai Airport in Hanoi, costing anywhere from US$20-25. The trip is a long one, sometimes taking up to an hour. Within the cities, taxis don't normally cruise the streets looking for a fare. Instead they can be found at taxi stalls, or they can be arranged through hotels or by simply calling them. Some officials say that you can arrange for a car and a driver for about US$35 in both major cities a day, but I haven't found this to be true. Usually the rate,especially if you're considering excursions to the Mekong Delta and Cu Chi Tunnels in Saigon, or Ha Long Bay in Hanoi, can be considerably more expensive.In Saigon, for instance, expect to pay upwards of US$70-90 a day (for a car and a driver in Saigon) and even more in Hanoi. Travel agents will do their best to make you think you're getting the deal of the century. But remember, the only deal of the century that can be found in Vietnam is drinking fresh beer (Bia Hoi). Metered taxis in Saigon and Hanoi are expensive, about US$2 just to get into the car and another US70 cents for every kilometer. Availability depends upon the bookings, so plan your excursions from your hotel well in advance.*

### Tour Operators

The following is a partial listing of the ever-growing number of tour operators jumping on the Vietnam tour package wagon. Call around. Check out the prices and the itineraries that suit your budget and level of intrepidity. Some will merely bus your buns around the beaten track. Others will put you on a bicycle odyssey where you've got a decent chance of doing some pretty outrageous things or getting slammed head-on by a Russian-built freight truck.

(Note: Local numbers are for information; toll-free numbers are for reservations). In the U.S., you can contact:

**Absolute Asia**

*155 W. 68 Street, Suite 525*
*New York, NY 10023*
☎ *(212) 595-5782; (800) 736-8187*

**Adventure Center**

*1311 63rd Street, Ste. 200*
*Emeryville, CA 94608*
☎ *(510) 654-1879; (800) 227-8747*
*FAX: (510) 654-4200*

**All Adventure Travel**

*5589 Rapahoe, Ste. 208*
*Boulder, CO 80303*

☎ *(800) 537-4025*
*FAX: (303) 4404160*

**Apex World Travel**
*4620 West Commercial Way, Ste. 3*
*Pamarac, FL 33319*
☎ *(305) 733-4144; (800) 666-0025*
*FAX: (305) 733-4456*

**Archaeological Tours**
*271 Madison Avenue, Ste. 904*
*New York, NY 10016*
☎ *(212) 986-3054*

**Asian Pacific Adventures**
*826 South Sierra Bonita Avenue*
*Los Angeles, CA 90036*
☎ *(213) 935-3156*
*FAX: (213) 935-2691*

**Bolder Adventures**
*P.O. Box 1279*
*Boulder, CO 80306*
☎ *(303) 443-6789; (800) 642-2742*
*FAX: (303) 443-7078*

**Chinasmith**
*330 West 42nd Street*
*New York, NY 10036*
☎ *(212) 239-2410; (800) US-CHINA*
*FAX: (212) 643-1598*

**Creative Adventures Club**
*3007 Royce Lane*
*Costa Mesa, CA 92626*
☎ *(714) 545-5888; (800) 544-5088*
*FAX: (714) 545-5898*

**Cycle Vietnam**
*P.O. Box 4481*
*Portland, OR 97208*
☎ *(503) 282-8499; (800) 661-1458*
*FAX: (503) 331-1458*

**Diva Worldwide**
☎ *415-777-5351*
*FAX: (415) 334-6365*

**EastQuest**
*1 Beekman Street, #607*
*New York, NY 10038*
☎ *(212) 406-2224; (800) 638-3449*

**Express Travel**
*1050 S. Jackson Street*
*Seattle, WA 98104*
☎ *(206) 324-6530*
*FAX: (206) 328-6334*

**Far East Destinations**
*1001 4th Avenue Plaza, Ste. 2401*
*Seattle, WA 98154*
☎ *(206) 224-0117; (800) 879-2976*
*FAX: (206) 467-9186*

**Gannon Tours**
*11495 Sunset Hills Road*
*Reston, VA 22090*
☎ *(703) 471-9700; (800) GAN-TRVL*
*FAX: (703) 742-0063*

**Himalayan Travel**
*112 Prospect Street*
*Stamford, CT 06901*
☎ *(203) 359-3711; (800) 225-2380*
*FAX: (203) 359-3669*

**InterNation**
*620 Kearny Street*
*San Francisco, CA 94108*
☎ *(415) 392-0244; (800) 553-3533*
*FAX: (415) 392-3369*

**IPI/InterPacific Tours International**
*111 E. 15th Street*
*New York, NY 10003*
☎ *(212) 953-6010; (800) 221-3594*

**Here Today, There Tomorrow**
*1901 Pennsylvania Avenue, N.W., #204*
*Washington, D.C. 20006*
☎ *(202) 296-6373; (800) 368-5965*

**Intrepid Tours**
*315 Post Road West*
*Westport, CT 06880*
☎ *(203) 221-0332; (800) 558-2522*
*FAX: (203) 221-0816*

**Lotus Tours**
*2 Mott Street*
*New York, NY 10013*
☎ *(212) 267-5414*
*FAX: (212) 608-6007*

**Mountain Travel Sobek**
*6420 Fairmount Avenue*
*El Cerrito, CA 94530*
☎ *(510) 527-8100; (800) 227-2384*
*FAX: (510) 525-7710*

**Myths and Mountains**
*976 Tee Court*
*Incline Village, NV 89451*

*☎ (800) 670-6984*
*FAX: (702) 832-4454*

**Natrabu Indo-American Travel**

*433 California Street*
*San Francisco, CA 94104*
*☎ (800) 628-7228*
*FAX: (415) 362-0531*

**Overseas Adventure Travel**

*349 Broadway*
*Cambridge, MA 02139*
*☎ (800) 221-0814*
*FAX: (617) 876-0455*

**Pacific Holidays**

*2 West 45th Street, Ste. 1102*
*New York, NY 10036*
*☎ (212) 764-1977; (800) 355-8025*
*FAX: (212) 764-2396*

**Sino-American Tours**

*37 Bowery*
*New York, N.Y. 10002*
*☎ (212) 966-5866; (800) 221-7982*

**South Sea Tour & Travel**

*210 Post Street Ste 910,*
*San Francisco, CA 94108*
*☎ (415) 397-4644; (800) 546-7890*

**TBI Tours**

*787 Seventh Avenue, Ste. 1101*
*New York, NY 10019*
*☎ (212) 489-1919; (800) 223-0266*
*FAX: (212) 307-0612*

**The Global Spectrum**

*1901 Pennsylvania Avenue NW*
*Washington, DC 20006*
*☎ (202) 293-2065; (800) 419-4446*
*FAX: (202) 296-0815*

**Top Guides**

*1825 San Lorenzo Avenue*
*Berkeley, CA 94707*
*☎ (510) 527-9884; (800) 867-6777*
*FAX: (510) 527-9885*

**Trade Services Co.**

*565 5th Avenue*
*New York, NY 10017*
*☎ (212) 697-1558; (800) 872-3386*
*FAX: (212) 697-2609*

**Travcoa**

*2350 SE Bristol Street*
*Newport Beach, CA 92660*
*☎ (714) 476-2800; (800) 992-2003*
*FAX: (714) 476-2538*

**Vietnam Tours**

*1121 East Missouri, Ste. 115*
*Phoenix, AZ 85014*
*☎ (602) 230-1122*
*FAX: (602) 230-1029*

**Velo Asia**

*1412 MLK Jr. Way*
*Berkeley, CA 94709*
*☎ (800) 884-ASIA*

**Abercrombie & Kent International**

*1520 Kensington Road*
*Oak Brook, IL 60521-2106*
*☎ (708) 954-2944; (800) 323-7308*

**Viva USA**

*1840 W. 17th St.*
*Santa Ana, CA 92706*
*☎ (714) 972-2248*
*FAX: (714) 972-2034*

Or in Bangkok, Thailand, you can contact (country code, 66—city code, 2):

**MK Ways**

*57/11 Wireless Road*
*Patumwan, Bangkok 10330*
*☎ 254-4765, 254-7770, 255-2892, 255-3390*
*FAX: 254-5583*

**Exotissimo Travel**

*21/17 Sukhumvit Soi 4*
*Bangkok 10110*
*☎ 253-5240/1, 255-2747*
*FAX: 254-7683.*

**Lam Son International Ltd.**

*23/1 Sukhumvit Soi 4,*
*Bangkok 10110*
*☎ 255-6692/3/4/5*
*FAX: 255-8859*

**Red Carpet Service & Tour**

*459 New Rama 6 Road*
*Phayathai, Bangkok 10400*
*☎ 215-9951, 215-3331*
*FAX: 662-215-3331*

**Viet Tour Holidays**

*1717 Lard Prao Road*

*Samsennok, Huay- Kwang, Bangkok 10310*
☎ *511-3272*
*FAX: 511-3357*

**Vikamla Tours**

*Room 401 Nana Condo, 23/11 Sukhumvit Soi 4*
*Bangkok 10110*
☎ *252-2340, 255-8859*

## FESTIVALS AND HOLIDAYS

*Like the rest of Southeast Asia, Vietnam enjoys its holidays and festivals.*

| | | |
|---|---|---|
| **January 1** | New Year's Day | *Public Holiday* |
| **February (moveable)** | Tet (Traditional New Year) | *This is the big celebration of the year. It's the time that people forget their grievances; they pay off debts, kiss and make up—that sort of thing. Interestingly enough, Tet also marks everyone's birthday. The Vietnamese don't celebrate individual birthdays. On Tet, everyone's a full year older! The celebration is marked with a tremendous amount of eating. It's believed that the first full week of the year determines how the rest of it will go.* |
| **February 3** | Founding of the Communist Party Day | *Public holiday.* |
| **March (moveable)** | Hai Ba Trung Day | *Marks the revolt the Trung sisters led against the Chinese in A.D. 41.* |
| **April 30** | Liberation Day of South Vietnam | *Public Holiday. Marks the toppling of the Saigon government in 1975.* |
| **April (moveable)** | Thanh Minh, Holiday of the Dead | *Feast of the Pure Light. Vietnamese walk outdoors to contact spirits of the dead. Shrines and tombs are cleaned.* |
| **May 1** | May Day | *Public holiday.* |
| **May 19** | Birthday of Ho Chi Minh | *Public holiday.* |
| **May 28** | Celebration of the birth, death and enlightenment of Buddha | *Public holiday.* |

## FESTIVALS AND HOLIDAYS

| | | |
|---|---|---|
| **August (moveable)** | Wandering Souls Day | *After Tet, this is the second most important festival. By praying for the dead, their sins can be absolved. They can leave hell hungry and naked to their loved ones. Celebrations in temples and homes. Money is burned.* |
| **September 2** | National Day | *Public holiday.* |
| **September 3** | President Ho's Anniversary | *Public holiday.* |
| **September (moveable)** | Mid-Autumn Festival | *A children's holiday that features parades.* |
| **November (moveable)** | Confucious' Birthday | |

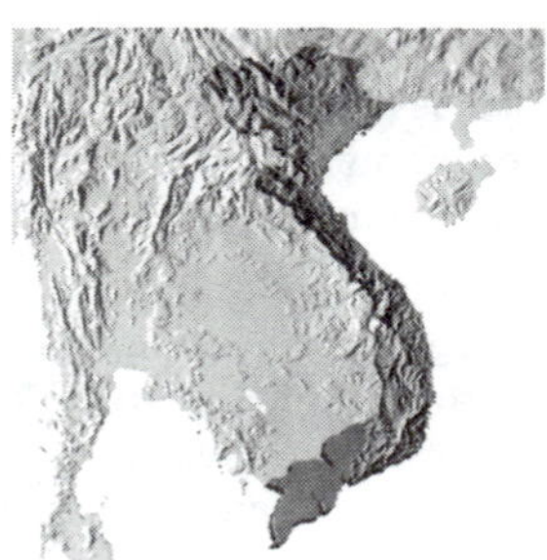

# VIETNAM'S ECONOMY AND DOING BUSINESS IN VIETNAM

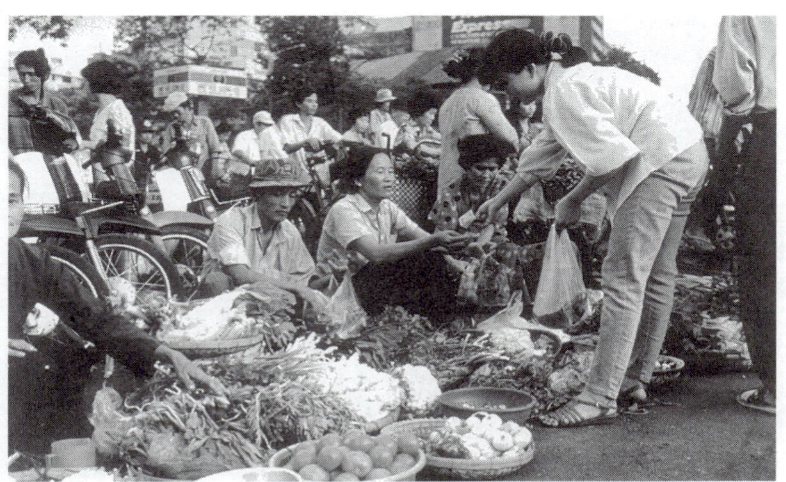

*Vietnam's markets are crammed with vendors and buyers alike during the early morning hours.*

Back in the 1980s, the real growth rate in the Vietnamese economy was estimated to be in the six percent range, but that would hardly be accurate today, as the country is courting foreign investment like a queen bee in heat. The drones of Japan, South Korea, Taiwan, Singapore, Malaysia, Indonesia, Canada, France and Australia have been more than happy to pollinate Vietnam's fertile embryo. Since the lifting of the American trade embargo in February, 1994, U.S. companies have shoveled in more than US$520 million into the Vietnamese economy, according to the U.S.-Vietnam Trade Council. Other estimates put the figure closer to US$550 million.

Vietnam enjoys an abundance of natural resources, including coal, phosphates, hardwoods, gems, manganese, chromate, bauxite, rubber, palm oil, marine products and—of particular interest to American oil interests—vast deposits of offshore oil reserves just waiting to heat every home from Anchorage and Albany—and perhaps even more important, from Quito to Asunscion.

Spices, coffee and tea accounted for 85 percent of all imports from Vietnam into the U.S. in the first three months of 1995. Vietnam is the fifth largest supplier of coffee to the U.S. ranked behind Mexico, Columbia, Brazil and Guatemala. Food processing, chemical fertilizers, cement, textiles, steel and electric power make up the crux of the country's exports, as does a US$900 million trade involving primarily agriculture, seafood, rubber, wood flooring and coal.

***The owner of this hootch is considered prosperous by his peers.***

Exports of seafood, oil and apparel to Japan are substantial and expected to exceed $300 million by the end of 1995.

Nevertheless, Vietnam is poor, perhaps the most impoverished nation on earth—certainly one of the 10 poorest. We've already mentioned the typical American can spend on a pair of mediocre shoes what the average Vietnamese makes in a year. And Vietnam owes the International Monetary Fund some $1.5 billion in debts that its creditors are not likely to recoup. Perhaps the only plus in the whole scenario is that a lot of the cash is owed to the former Soviet Union, whose own crumbling monetary system makes the Vietnamese dong seem as solid as a Michael Milken junk bond investment of the mid 1980s. And this perhaps reveals one of the most ironic economic paradoxes of the nation—Vietnam as a single unique country sharing the same economic woes and monetary cemetery plots. This simply is without foundation. The two halves of the nation have evolved independently of each other, for all intents and purposes, for more than 40 years—and even the fall of Saigon to the north has done little to imperil the entrepreneurialism of the residents of the southern half of the country. Although the party virtually retains a brutal Stalin-like grip on its people, it also covertly encourages perhaps the most liberal of all economic principles in Asia to function unabated. Some call the ideology schizophrenic, others believe it's just plain economic sense in dealing with a communist world that is collapsing around the last bastions of Marxist-Leninism like a ficus in an ice storm. Despite the loss of more than 58,000 American soldiers during the Vietnam War, Vietnam clearly remains two distinct countries.

The south is aggressive, outspoken, even pompous. The north, although tolerant—apparently for the gains it stands to realize—is more suspicious of the wave of Westerners (although first-time American tourists may be stunned on how warmly they're received). Hanoi, although charming enough, is void of the filigree of dissent, of muted protest—of diversity, in other words. It lacks an "edge," where youth and the free-spirited are thwarted from pushing the envelope of thought and art. Ho Chi Minh City makes no such pretense of Marxist piety. A curb may be built for keeping pedestrians from traffic, but they're also a lot of fun for bounding with skateboards and strolling on while donning headsets pounding with the likes of Metallica and Guns 'N Roses.

### AUTHOR'S OBSERVATION: FYI FOR 'VIET KIEU'

*Overseas Vietnamese, or "Viet Kieu" may or may not become a major component of foreign investment in Vietnam. Many analysts think their impact on the economy will be relatively marginal. Others are far more optimistic. FDI (Foreign Direct Investment) in Vietnam in 1994 was in the US$4 billion range. The government is implementing incentive programs for overseas Vietnamese investors. A corporate income tax reduction of 20 percent may be the carrot overseas Vietnamese are looking for but, to date, only a few overseas companies have made any formal contact or inquiries with Vietnam's SCCI (State Committee for Cooperation and Investment).*

Both the north and the south can be considered hard working, and it's one of the reasons Cambodians are so resentful of the ethnic Vietnamese that reside in their country, simply for their work ethic. The Vietnamese are educated, as mentioned earlier, but are beset with the problems of centralized government that continually results in grave shortages of staples and spare parts for machinery. Unemployment is rampant. Some put the estimates as high as 50 percent.

Why? Well, for once, it seems there are some easy answers. In fact, it's only one answer and it's twofold: the U.S. trade embargo and Hanoi's insistence that so much of its budget go into military spending. There is China to the north, of course, relatively bitter foes. Cambodia to the west, hardly a cohesive and formidable foe, even against its own internal insurgents—and there is Thailand, whose real threat to the stability of Vietnam in the '90s is nonexistent.

**FOREIGN INVESTMENT BY REGION**

| Rank | Region | No. of Projects | Total Capital (US$) | Legal Capital (US$) |
|---|---|---|---|---|
| 1 | Ho Chi Minh City | 444 | 4,706,973,933 | 2,130,994,811 |
| 2 | Ha Noi | 193 | 3,028,667,068 | 1,434,873,044 |
| 3 | Dong Nai | 117 | 1,193,386,114 | 497,518,376 |
| 4 | Hai Phong | 38 | 853,165,350 | 335,276,630 |
| 5 | Ba Ria-Vung Tau | 39 | 616,106,999 | 475,880,453 |
| 6 | Da Nang | 34 | 492,868,666 | 208,390,271 |
| 7 | Thanh Hoa | 6 | 420,077,633 | 136,896,733 |
| 8 | Song Be | 45 | 363,180,431 | 170,606,151 |
| 9 | Kien Giang | 3 | 361,676,000 | 136,926,000 |
| 10 | Ha Bac | 6 | 136,022,000 | 56,327,500 |
| 11 | Hay Tay | 15 | 127,426,835 | 73,902,369 |
| 12 | Lam Dong | 23 | 121,653,579 | 92,336,953 |
| 13 | Quang Ninh | 15 | 114,191,542 | 75,745,342 |
| 14 | Long An | 13 | 103,924,758 | 72,626,973 |
| 15 | Khanh Hoa | 16 | 95,369,800 | 59,298,928 |
| 16 | Thua Thien-Hue | 5 | 95,048,000 | 61,598,000 |
| 17 | Tay Ninh | 9 | 63,934,845 | 34,233,890 |
| 18 | Tien Giang | 4 | 59,360,038 | 25,760,038 |

## FOREIGN INVESTMENT BY REGION

| Rank | Region | No. of Projects | Total Capital (US$) | Legal Capital (US$) |
|---|---|---|---|---|
| 19 | Vinh Phu | 8 | 49,581,020 | 28,461,020 |
| 20 | Hai Hung | 11 | 41,635,531 | 24,432,417 |
| 21 | Binh Thuan | 8 | 36,126,700 | 16,087,700 |
| 22 | Binh Dinh | 7 | 30,514,135 | 11,415,040 |
| 23 | Ha Tinh | 7 | 30,260,000 | 17,945,000 |
| 24 | Bac Thai | 4 | 27,205,500 | 11,964,000 |
| 25 | Can Tho | 9 | 24,450,025 | 12,501,025 |
| 26 | Ben Tre | 3 | 23,250,000 | 9,151,700 |
| 27 | Son La | 2 | 20,490,000 | 6.904,000 |
| 28 | Minh Hai | 7 | 16,705,038 | 14,447,636 |
| 29 | Lao Cai | 1 | 12,200,000 | 3,600,000 |
| 30 | Ninh Binh | 2 | 11,750,000 | 9,700,000 |

*Source: SCCI, 6/20/95*

## AUTHOR'S OBSERVATION

*Contrary to popular opinion, it has become less evident that Vietnam can attribute the US economic embargo as the single greatest hinderance to the nation's prosperity. But it still had impact. Although the embargo in all likelihood had little effect for the first decade following the end of the Vietnam War, the breakup of the Eastern Bloc and the collapse of the Soviet Union was a devastating blow to Vietnam's recovery from the war. The embargo prevented loans to Vietnam from the International Monetary Fund, and essentially cut off aid from the West. Although there were moves during the Jimmy Carter administration in 1977 to begin to normalize relations with Hanoi, the U.S embargo wasn't dropped until February 4, 1994. Only a day before, three large block letters were taped over and disguised against the white cement facade of a large computer retailer on Saigon's Ly Tu Trong Street. The day after President Clinton lifted the embargo, workers on scaffolding had unmasked the big logo and were busy painting the letters in a familiar deep blue. They read "IBM," of course.*

But, despite the hardships created by war and international isolation, Vietnam has been a strongly resilient country. Despite the loss of massive economic aid from the former Soviet Union, Vietnam has stayed on its feet. It's dealing with new trading partners, and the relationships have been mutually profitable. Singapore has emerged as Vietnam's largest trading partner—a far cry from Moscow in every sense of the word. Foreign investment has been growing at rates unparalleled outside Asia. By the first quarter of 1993, total foreign investments in the Vietnamese economy totaled more than US$3 billion, more than double the figure of only two years previously. Mid-1995 estimates put the figure at US$6 billion. Money is pouring into Vietnam from Japan, Taiwan, Australia (even though it still steadfastly refuses to "Asianize" itself), Hong Kong, France, Great Britain, and Germany—and now from the U.S. The rewards for Vietnam's trading partners can be astronomical. For instance, Vietnam's Foreign Investment Code, at the time of this writing, permits 100 percent foreign business ownership—astounding for a "communist" country. Foreign businesses are allowed up to 99 percent equity participation in joint ventures.

But if it all seems too good to be true, maybe it is. Foreign businesses are confronted in Vietnam with an essentially nonexistent infrastructure. Many charge that corruption runs rampant in the government, and accountings of how the pies of foreign investment are sliced and where the crumbs fall can be ambiguous if not downright purposefully deceptive.

***Beer trucks have yet to make their debut in Vietnam.***

But the money into Vietnam continues to flow like an aqueduct sourced at a deep snowpack. Tourism, of course, has skyrocketed. In 1989, about 60,000 tourists visited Vietnam, most of whom were overseas Vietnamese living in foreign countries taking advantage of Hanoi's increasingly liberal policies dealing with repatriation and the visiting of relatives inside Vietnam by political and "economic" refugees. Another significant chunk of that figure was the flow of tourists from communist countries, who have more access to communist-controlled tourist destinations than to places like Miami or Rio.

But the figure jumped to nearly 190,000 tourists just one year later, in 1990. Optimistic government officials then predicted that by 1995, the 1991 figure would double. It turned out to be a pessimistic forecast at best. The figure authorities in Hanoi now openly speak of is over 1.4 million. No wonder it's easier to declare a camcorder at customs.

**AUTHOR'S NOTE**

*By the year 2000, Vietnam will need between 12,800 to 17,300 tourist cars and between 47,000 and 63,000 commercial vehicles. If the country decides not to build its own plants, it will have to spend nearly US$1.5 billion to import them. If Vietnam decides to build its own plants, government officials will be looking primarily at the United States, Western Europe and Japan for the necessary technology.*

The problem is a lack of facilities to accommodate all these people. Maybe "facilities" isn't the word. Change that to quality hotel rooms. The number of hotel rooms in Bangkok alone today stands around 30,000. Compare that with less than 12,000 international-standard rooms in the entire country of Vietnam, whose population exceeds that of Thailand's by nearly 20 million.

But these rooms, and thousands more, will come—if for no other reason than there is so much money to be made here. It's believed that northern Vietnam possesses some of Asia's greatest coal deposits. Offshore oil reserves make your head spin. A recent survey estimated that Vietnam's oil reserves are somewhere between two and three billion barrels—more than half a million barrels could be output in a single day in about 10 years from now. With the lifting of the U.S. trade embargo and the recent normalization of relations between Washington and Hanoi, Vietnam is poised to become a huge exporter of oil in the near future.

## AUTHOR'S OBSERVATION

*Besides the high-profile measures the government of Vietnam has made in recent years to lure foreign investors, many of its fledgling and more subtle, recent decrees to placate potential investors tend not to make the headlines. But they're being noticed by companies that stand to make a lot of money in the consumer products sector. For instance, the government has begun a serious crackdown on counterfeit consumer products, including locally-produced and bottled fake Coca-Cola, fake Johnnie Walker Black and Red Label whiskey, Marlboro cigarettes, and counterfeit Lacoste shirts. Around Hanoi, and especially Saigon, it's been commonplace to find electronics outlets peddling cassette players with names suggestive of the real McCoys, brands called "Pensonic," Sonv," and "Toshida." It's called intellectual property rights and, for years, they've been virtually entirely unprotected in major metropolitan areas throughout Southeast Asia. At least in Hanoi, it seems to be changing. The government has promised to be in a position to effectively enforce these rights within the next four years. Granted they have a tough task before them. Hanoi has even established an economics police unit to deal with the problem solely.*

*Vietnam's Patent and Trademark Bureau of the Chamber of Commerce and Industry, along with other state-owned enterprises, acts as the patent attorney for foreign businesses that have registered their invention rights and industrial property in Vietnam. Much of the counterfeit products are available in Vietnam for a fraction of the cost of the originals. Because the Vietnamese have enjoyed greater buying powers over the last few years, there's been a tremendous surge in patent and trademark applications by foreign firms doing or planning to do business in Vietnam. More than 50,000 trademarks have been registered in Vietnam—eighty of them by foreign companies. It's turned out to be an overwhelming amount for the government to process. Last year, the Ministry of Science, Technology and Environment received nearly 8500 applications to register service trademarks, patents, and industrial designs. This was up from 6617 from the previous year. The system has become bottlenecked, a system which has always been marred in red tape.*

*Much of the counterfeit merchandise comes from abroad. "Pensonic" products come from China. And other counterfeits, such as bogus Hennessey cognac smack so much of the original, right down to the seal, it would be impossible to make this product in Vietnam, whose own domestically-produced liquor caps virtually disintegrate after the seal is broken. (If you purchase Vietnamese spirits, be prepared to consume them in one sitting). Additionally, imitation and substandard medications are rampant in Vietnam.*

**AUTHOR'S OBSERVATION**

*To its credit, Vietnam became a member of the Geneva-based World Intellectual Property Organization, an arm of the UN. The country also became affiliated with the International Patent Corporation Treaty. Vietnam was also a participant at the Paris Convention on patents, trademarks and other forms of industrial property protection. After the U.S. embargo was dropped, another 200 U.S. companies applied for patent protection, bringing the number of American applications to nearly 1500. So far, there is no copyright protection for film or literary works in Vietnam. These are areas that will have to be addressed in attracting hundreds of foreign cultural imports.*

## The New Wave of American Investment in Vietnam and Some Tips for Entrepreneurs

The lifting of the trade embargo and the subsequent normalization of ties between the U.S. and Vietnam, has spawned a wave of American business people seeking opportunities in the country. Whereas in 1994, the U.S. ranked 33rd among foreign investors in Vietnam, it leapt to between the 13th and 7th largest investor in the country by the middle of 1995, depending on who you talk to.

The Asia Pacific Chamber of Commerce (APCC) based in Seattle, Washington sent a commission to Vietnam in April 1994 called the "Business Opportunity Mission to Vietnam." Its purpose was to help American entrepreneurs learn Vietnamese business and social customs and how to do business in perhaps the world's fastest growing economy. According to APCC execs, American companies attending the mission included Caterpillar, Clark, Microsoft, Sun Micro Systems, US West and McCaw Cellular (both telecommunications companies), Crate & Barrel, Advanced Technology Labs, and Space Labs (a hospital monitor company).

Official members of the delegation included Senator Patty Murray of Washington, Adlai Stevenson and Paul Cleveland (The U.S. Trade Ambassador).

There were also participants from the American Grocer's Association, the Washington Apple Commission, and officials from Washington State's Department of Agriculture.

Among the many American companies rushing into Vietnam to sign deals are the Texas-based WG Ripley Group (assembly lines for cotton production, a US$2.5 million deal), DuPont (which has opened an office in Ho Chi Minh City and said that Vietnam is now a focal point for its efforts to quadruple sales—to move global sales from 7 percent to 20 percent—in the region by the turn of the century). (Incidentally, DuPont was one of the first

U.S. businesses to open shop in Vietnam after the lifting of the embargo.) DuPont's energy subsidiary, Conoco, has been seeking to obtain offshore oil exploration rights. The company, like a slew of others, is forecasting increasingly sophisticated consumer and industrial markets for electronics, automotive products, electrical goods, construction materials, clothing and crop protection.

Mobil now has a big contract to drill in the South China Sea off southern Vietnam. Chrysler recently opened its first offices and showrooms in Hanoi and Ho Chi Minh City. RJ Reynolds is building a US$21 million factory in Dalat and is starting a 6000 hectare tobacco planting project in nearby Quang Nam-Danang province. Citicorp is here. Delta Airlines will be starting air service soon. Even Baskin Robbins is vending its 31 flavors in HCMC.

Vietnam may become a major importer of U.S. farm products, perhaps procuring as much as US$300 million annually. Vietnam purchased US$213 million worth of food in 1992, the last year statistics are available. About a quarter of the products were purchased from the European Union, Singapore, Japan and Hong Kong.

Because Vietnam is looking at moving toward an economic strategy that would increase its growth rate between 8 percent and 10 percent annually, agricultural imports are likely to skyrocket in coming years, according to a U.S. State Department report. Total agricultural purchases in Vietnam could reach U.S.$1.7 billion annually. Vietnam's interest in American agricultural products include wheat, wheat flour, feed grains, poultry, pork and processed meats, vegetable oils and oil seeds, cotton, and processed fresh fruits.

Businesspeople considering doing business in Vietnam may want to consider that there may be only limited demand for branded consumer products. But assistance with the country's agricultural industry should provide self-starters with boundless opportunities. But remember, you've got some catching up to do. The U.S. currently ranks 13th (at press time) in foreign investment in Vietnam. Investment opportunities flourish. Nearly all of the country's 50 provinces and cities are openly vying for overseas investment.

## AUTHOR'S NOTE

*Hollywood, not one to miss scouting a good location, is also jumping in on the post-embargo feeding fray in Vietnam. The American film "Fields of Fire" will be the first post-embargo American film shot in Vietnam. The film, of course, will be a Vietnam War film, and more than likely feature the rising Vietnamese-American actress Kieu Chinh in the lead role. Production began in May 1994. The film was adapted from the novel of the same name written by the film's director James Webb, who was a lieutenant in the U.S. Army during the war stationed at Quang Nam-Da Nang. Webb also served as secretary of the Navy under the George Bush administration.* Fields of Fire *chronicles the fates of soldiers on both sides of the conflict. The film's primary locations are set in the districts of Duy Xuyen and Dai Loc. Up until now, most movies depicting the war, including Francis Ford Coppola's epic* Apocalypse Now *and* Platoon *used the Philippines, Thailand, Malaysia, and other Southeast Asia locations for shooting.*

In addition, aviation will undoubtedly provide a slew of opportunities for American firms. American aviation companies jumping on the Vietnam bandwagon include United, Continental, Northwest and Delta Airlines; Boeing, and McDonnell-Douglas. Boeing and McDonnell-Douglas are lobbying hard to replace Vietnam Airlines' aging fleet of 20 Soviet-built airlines, which the airline is seeking to do by the end of 1995. Delta, as well, is working with Vietnam Airlines to establish direct links between the United States and Vietnam. Up until this point, travelers have had to endure long layovers in places like Bangkok, Singapore, Hong Kong, or Seoul before boarding flights on different carriers to Vietnam.

## U.S. INVESTMENT IN VIETNAM (IN US$ MILLIONS)

| *SECTORS* | *1994-1995.* | *1998* |
|---|---|---|
| **ENERGY & TRANSPORTATION** | **1062.0** | **2493.0** |
| **ROAD CONSTRUCTION** | **100.0** | **210.0** |
| **TELECOMMUNICATIONS** | **223.5** | **457,5** |
| **OIL & GAS EQUIPMENT** | **113.3** | **11375.5** |
| **AVIATION CONTROL EQUIPMENT** | **87.0** | **195.0** |
| **OIL EXPLORATION** | **25.7** | **41.3** |
| **REFRIGERATION** | **4.5** | **24.0** |
| **COMPUTERS** | **24.5** | **118.8** |
| **AIRPLANE ENGINES** | **200.7** | **750.0** |

## U.S. INVESTMENT IN VIETNAM (IN US$ MILLIONS)

| *SECTORS* | *1994-1995.* | *1998* |
|---|---|---|
| **HOTEL CONSTRUCTION & MANAGEMENT** | **36.1** | **54.8** |
| **AUTOMATIC PRODUCTS** | **33.3** | **65.8** |
| **PHARMACEUTICALS** | **13.3** | **54.0** |
| **AIR SERVICES** | **44.8** | **68.2** |
| **MEDICAL EQUIPMENT** | **3.0** | **9.8** |
| **CHEMICALS** | **25.5** | **110.1** |
| **CONSTRUCTION MATERIALS** | **20.0** | **73.0** |
| **PETRO-CHEMICAL PRODUCTS** | **45.0** | **10.0** |
| **OTHER INDUSTRIAL PRODUCTS** | **60.3** | **138.2** |
| **CONSUMER GOODS** | **390.6** | **1303.3** |
| **AUTOMOBILES** | **30.6** | **57.4** |
| **BANKS & STOCKS** | **21.9** | **68.8** |
| **SHIPPING** | **100.0** | **438.0** |

*Source: U.S.-ASEAN Council*

In the areas of construction, major U.S. companies either seeking to establish contracts in Vietnam or those whose ink has already dried include Fluor Daniel (66th among the largest diversified service companies in the world, according to *Forbes* magazine), and Indochina Partners.

In the north, conditions for conducting and initiating business transactions are far more problematic than in the south. American businesspeople are now jamming airliners headed to Hanoi, and officials in Vietnam are having a difficult time accommodating all the interest American companies are developing in the country's economy. As one observer noted, "The Vietnamese economy still lacks the fundamental preconditions for high, sustainable growth."

In a way, Vietnam is going through a potentially dangerous phase. Central planning has been all but eliminated entirely. But the country has yet to establish a free market system that works within any predictable or regulatory network. The budget deficit continues to widen, currently about seven percent (See "Author's Note" below).

But some of the other numbers sure look good: The gross domestic product expanded by 8 percent in 1993, without any measurable degree of inflation.(Prices rose slightly more than 5 percent.) Nearly one million new jobs were created in the country in 1994 (although countless millions of Vietnamese still remain under- or unemployed). These new workers are helping to construct houses and produce durable goods, efforts that have yielded more progress in the country in the last five years than in the previous half century.

In 1994, projects that have been capitalized comprised more than US$300 million, and experts say that foreign investment in Vietnam doubled to nearly US$4 billion in 1994.

## AUTHOR'S NOTE

*Although the business rush into Vietnam is making people a lot of money and improving the lives of the Vietnamese people, not everyone is happy about it: the communist hardliners in Hanoi. If the pages of the Army's daily newspaper* **Quan Doi Nhan Dan** *are any indication, the trend toward a free market system in Vietnam has a number of high ranking Hanoi officials becoming just a little paranoid. Hanoi's Defense Minister Doan Khue has called for "increased revolutionary vigilance" against those who want to move toward a market economy in order to end communist rule of the country. "Hostile forces are attempting to wipe out socialism and the revolutionary gains of our people," he said. Party ideologues are calling for creating a stable political front where the party's leading role "will hold forever the irreversible gains of the Vietnamese Revolution."*

*The officials claim that those calling for the improvement of Vietnam's human rights efforts are doing so "under the cover of democracy...They are trying to denigrate the Socialist regime," said Doan, who is the fifth ranking member of Hanoi's Politburo. He is perhaps the leading conservative in Vietnam and he fears that the opening of the economy will bring with it corruption, poverty (if there's not enough already) and other "social ills." "The cause of renovation is going well and achieving many advantages," he said, "but the scheming tricks of the enemy against our country, against socialism, remain unchanged. Inside the country there are destabilizing elements which we must not underestimate...We must increase revolutionary vigilance, patriotism and self reliance."*

*Both the police and the military have already voiced their concerns regarding the U.S.-based opposition umbrella movement called the Movement for National Reconciliation and the Construction of Democracy, which is attempting to organize human rights forums in HCMC. Hanoi steadfastly rejects the notions of a multiparty system in Vietnam, and insists on the Party's "democratic"control of the state. According to Vietnamese Prime Minister Vo Van Kiet, in Vietnam, "There are five economic elements, but only one political thought." Of Vietnam's more than 71 million people, only 2.5 million belong to the Communist Party, and even many of those have joined the party simply in the hopes that they will be the first to benefit from Vietnam's expanding economic opportunities.*

Taxation law in Vietnam remains a problem and is generally considered to still be administered mainly by corrupt party officials. The "savings rate," a prime indicator that gleans the mobilization of capital by commercial banks, has risen slightly (to 11 percent of the gross national product) but needs to double, according to the experts, in order for Vietnam to move up to par with the economies of Thailand and Singapore. Additionally, Vietnam's economic growth must be more concurrent with progress in social change, according to government officials. Economic management must match social efforts to reduce or eliminate entirely corruption, drug abuse, prostitution, and especially smuggling, officials say. This disparity could possibly dissuade foreign investors in utilizing the country's vast work force. One has to remember that Vietnam is starting from Ground Zero.

## SOME OF THE U.S. FIRMS DOING BUSINESS IN VIETNAM

| | |
|---|---|
| American International Group | *Insurance* |
| Ashta International, Inc. | *Consultancy* |
| Baker Hughes | *Oil and Gas* |
| Coca Cola | *Soft Drinks* |
| Pepsico | *Soft Drinks* |
| Baker McKenzie | *Lawyers* |
| Carrier | *Air Conditioning Equipment* |
| Caterpillar | *Heavy Equipment Supplies* |
| DeMatteis Development Corp. | *Construction* |
| Connell Bros. | *Commodities* |
| General Electric | *Electrical Equipment* |
| Gemrusa | *Gems/Mining* |
| L.A. Land Resources | *Property* |
| Manolis Co. Asia | *Development and Architecture* |
| Esso/Exxon | *Petroleum* |
| Otis Elevator | *Lifts* |
| Philip Morris | *Tobacco and Food* |
| Spivey International | *Medical Supplies* |
| Vatico | *Consultancy* |
| VIIC | *Consultancy* |
| VINA-USA | *Financial Services for Overseas Vietnamese* |
| South Sea Tours | *Tourism* |
| Vietours Holidays | *Tourism* |
| Bank of America | *Banking* |
| Citibank | *Banking* |
| Russin Vecchi | *Lawyers* |
| American Trading Co. | *Trading* |
| Deloitte Touche Tohmatsu | *Accountants* |
| Digital Equipment Co. | *Computer Technology* |

## SOME OF THE U.S. FIRMS DOING BUSINESS IN VIETNAM

| | |
|---|---|
| Apple Computer | *Computer Technology* |
| American President Lines | *Shipping* |
| Du Pont Far East Inc. | *Chemicals* |
| International Direct Marketing, Inc. | *Marketing* |
| Technomic Consultants | *Consultancy* |
| American Service Co. | *Consultancy* |
| Eastman Kodak | *Photographic Materials & Equipment* |
| IBM | *Computer Technology* |
| Motorola | *Telecommunications* |
| Leo Burnett Co. | *Advertising* |
| White & Case | *Lawyers* |

## The Post Normalization Outlook: A Level Playing Field

What will the normalization of relations between Washington and Hanoi mean for American companies doing—or planning to do—business in Vietnam?

Formal diplomatic ties will put American businesses on the same playing field with companies that have been reaping the fruits of Vietnamese investment for years, according to business people I spoke to in both Saigon and Hanoi. The normalization of political relations between the two countries will boost commercial relations as well. The U.S. government will now be in a position to support its private sector, such as granting import-export credits. The aircraft and oil industries are to be the top beneficiaries of this, as they can now get official support from the U.S. Export-Import Bank and from the Overseas Private Investment Corporation. Vietnam's banking sector will become more strongly developed, as the Vietnamese acquire the advanced technology of U.S. banking.

U.S. exports to Vietnam have surged since the lifting of the embargo. American exports to Vietnam in 1994 topped US$172 million—.03 percent of U.S. total exports that year—up from a scant US$7 million in 1993, according to Vietnam's Trade Ministry. In 1994, Vietnamese exports to the U.S. climbed to US$52 million. Although that figure was only.01 percent of all U.S. imports in 1994, consider that in 1993, not even a mere ton of Vietnamese exports reached U.S. shores.

Vietnam is desperately seeking American technology, and as it now has access to the huge U.S. market for its goods, Vietnam will be in a position to purchase the computer equipment and technology it so direly needs.

Although most American business people in Hanoi and Ho Chi Minh City are welcoming Clinton's decision, some of the smaller American firms that made big gambles by starting operations in Vietnam before even the embargo was lifted are a little worried—but just a little—of the normalization move being premature.

"The next move is most-favored trading nation status," said Ronald Van Wambeke, an American businessman whose construction and infrastructure company Asia Pacific International, Inc. opened a Ho Chi Minh City office eight months prior to the lifting of the embargo. "It's happening a little too quickly. We've been in place a long time and we're poised to make a killing here. And timing is everything. If the most-favored status happens too quickly, there are going to be a lot of cherry (American) bozos coming in here and throwing wrenches into the spokes we've taken years to connect to the wheels of this country."

At press time, there were 115 U.S. representative offices in Vietnam. Fifty-five were involved in trade and investment, while 28 others were doing business in the consultancy, legal and technical arenas.

## What the Businessperson Should Know

Investors in Vietnam should be prepared to expect a lot more red tape than they're used to at home, but also considerably more concessions. The economy is hovering around a double-digit growth rate. Labor is phenomenally cheap, especially compared to labor costs in the U.S. The taxes are low. And there are options for 100 percent foreign ownership of your business.

But remember, Vietnam is a Socialist state. Private enterprise in Vietnam is hardly fully developed. The move toward a free-market economy is still embryonic and is, at best, an experiment. Private businesses are operating under a Socialist political umbrella, deflecting all types of influences that may compromise its integrity. You'll want to grab for the country's economic opportunities, but be prepared for long delays.

You cannot, at the time of this writing, own land in Vietnam. You can lease but can't own. And the land you lease from the government may be claimed at some point in the future by its former owner(s). It could become a sticky litigation problem lasting years. You need to acquire licenses from the Vietnamese State Committee for Cooperation and Investment (SCCI) as well as local and other authorities, a process that can take months, even years, depending on the nature of your business. The structuring of joint ventures can be difficult and time consuming as well.

But there are routes through the yarn ball, many of them.

The most important element is to establish trust with the Vietnamese you contact. The only way you'll get business transacted relatively smoothly is by networking with as many people as possible in Vietnam, both Vietnamese and foreigners who have already established businesses and/or contacts in Vietnam. The better you treat your hosts, the better you will be treated in return. It also pays to know what does and doesn't offend the Vietnamese during formal discussions. Here are some tips.

**1)** If you've made an appointment with a Vietnamese official—government or otherwise—know as much about the person as possible before your first meeting. If possible, get a snapshot of the principal individual before the meeting through a local guide, or other source, so you'll immediately recognize the person you're meeting with.

**2)** If the meeting involves more than one person, go directly to the principal participant upon being introduced and offer your business card. Presenting yourself to an assistant first is considered an insult. Present your cards based upon the chain of command.

**3)** Vietnamese men smoke like a train climbing Pike's Peak. Virtually all men in Vietnam smoke. You will undoubtedly be offered a cigarette. It is important to accept the cigarette, even if you don't smoke. (Many a self-righteous anti-smoker has taken up the habit after spending significant time in Vietnam.) If you don't smoke, simply place the cigarette on the table in front of you. You won't be offered another—not in contempt, but in respect.

**4)** Try not to cross your legs during the meeting, as, in Buddhism, pointing the sole of your foot at someone is a sign of disrespect. However, I've seen an increasing number of men cross their legs in both casual and business environments.

The key to getting things done rapidly in Vietnam is by developing trust and friendship with your Vietnamese contacts. Favors and gifts are also highly appreciated by Vietnamese businesspeople, and will more than likely be reciprocated by means of a smoother and swifter transaction of business.

## The Dong or the Buck?

*In a dramatic and somewhat confusing shift in Vietnam's tourist and business travel economy, as of October 1, 1994, hotels in Vietnam have been required by law to accept only Vietnamese dong in payment for rooms. Whereas the American dollar had previously not only been the preferred currency for hoteliers, many establishments across the country—especially the finer ones—required payment in U.S. currency. The highest Vietnamese monetary note is the 50,000 dong bill, which is about as readily available as a personal meeting with the Pope. Sounds like a lot, but it's worth about five U.S. bucks. That's it, folks. Five dollars. Lines at hotel cashiers' counters were feared to rival the queues at Ticketmaster for Madonna tickets as clerks would be forced to count barrel-loads of dong notes, especially at the higher-ticket hotels.*

*The move is part of the Vietnamese government's effort to replace the U.S. dollar with the dong for most currency transactions. It's scaring some foreign businesses and may send some shivers up the spines of tourists planning to visit Vietnam, as the dollar has remained stable with the dong since the government began opening up the economy in the late 1980s. Foreigners generally have paid for higher-priced goods and services with the dollar during the past seven years. Many experts believe that as much as US$2 billion is floating around the country in U.S. dollar notes. Authorized businesses that have previously accepted or required U.S. dollars in payment are now required to reapply for their licenses. Banks and hotels will be required to set up more currency exchange booths. Airlines are continuing to accept U.S. dollars. Credit cards are still accepted at the time of this writing, but may become more difficult to use. The question is how vigorously the law will eventually be enforced. At press time, in the fall of 1995, the law seems to be largely ignored.*

*Consider this: US$150 in "large" 5000 Vietnamese dong notes is about as thick as this book. That's just for one night in an upscale hotel. Well-heeled tourists planning on visiting Vietnam better pay a visit to a camping shop and get some advice from the grisly-faced, earring-donning youths pricing backpacks.*

### Top 10 Tips for U.S. Investors

**1)** The first step U.S. companies should take is to get a grasp on the legal environment and the market for their products in Vietnam. Companies need to study the legal framework of each specific field they want to invest in.

**2)** Companies must prepare feasibility studies and prepare a list of potential local partners. Feasibility studies should be jointly composed by the company and its local partner.

**3)** The laws in Vietnam are continuously changing and evolving. This presents one of the greatest risks for U.S. investors. U.S. investors should always have contingency plans for changes in laws, especially those pertaining to taxes.

**4)** The gap between the time for obtaining an investment license and the time for projects becoming operational in Vietnam could be a wide one.

**5)** Carefully choose the form of investment. Business in Vietnam can be done as a wholly-owned foreign company, as a joint venture with one or more local partners, or through business cooperation contracts with local companies. The Vietnamese government might prohibit foreign companies from certain types of investments.

**6)** Consider foreign exchange issues. If a company establishes a manufacturing or production facility in Vietnam to produce goods that will be purchased locally, it should consider exporting a percentage of its production to obtain hard currency for the purpose of profit remittance.

**7)** FYI: Most of the foreign loans procured by joint ventures in Vietnam have offshore security.

**8)** In Vietnam, it is extremely difficult to use land use rights as collateral security for a project. Land regulations in Vietnam have yet to be clearly clarified.

**9)** State-owned companies generally have more experience, resources and bigger pools of labor than do the relatively newer private firms.

**10)** Vietnam, at the time of this writing, is most interested in investment in infrastructure projects.

## List of Goods Prohibited to Export and Import

The import of used electronics, electrical equipment, motorcycles and automobiles is prohibited by the government.

**1) Prohibited Exports:** Weapons, ammunition, explosive materials, military equipment, antiques, certain drugs, toxic chemicals, round timber, sawed-up timber, kinds of semi-processed wood products, rattan material, wild and rare animals and plants.

**2) Prohibited Imports:** Weapons, ammunition, explosive materials, military equipment, kinds of drugs, toxic chemicals, reactionary and debauched cultural products, firecrackers, "toys harmful to children's personalities or social order" (I wonder if this includes Barbie dolls and squirt guns), cigarettes (except quantity fixed in personal luggage), used consumer goods (including sewn or weaved goods), under 12-seat automobiles, motorcycles and motor and non-motor tricycles, family-used electronics and electric equipment (except quantity fixed in personal luggage), material that may cause environmental harm or "other inconvenience" (such as used accessories, used tires, abolished products—abolished materials are also classified as prohibited imports—automobiles and vehicles with steering wheels on the right side (including accessories and dismantlements)—except some special vehicles and automobiles having narrow circulation.

## AUTHOR'S NOTE

*In special cases, the import of goods belonging to the above list can be permitted by the Prime Minister with a written statement. The prohibition of export of wild animals to protect the environment is guided by a written statement from both the Ministry of Forestry and the Ministry of Science, Technology and Environment. The government also says that to avoid being "backward" about industry, complete equipment as well as separate machines being used and valued from US$100,000 or more must be checked by the leading offices (Provincial People Committees or Ministries) of the business and the Quality Standard Measurement Office; a license to import will be issued by the Ministry of Commerce. The Ministry of Commerce, the Ministry of Home Affairs and the Customs Office will together approve a concrete list of special vehicles and automobiles addressed under Article II.8. After making an agreement with the Ministry of Commerce and the Ministry of Foreign Affairs, the Customs Office will apply guidelines for the article "Property." It all sounds pretty complicated.*

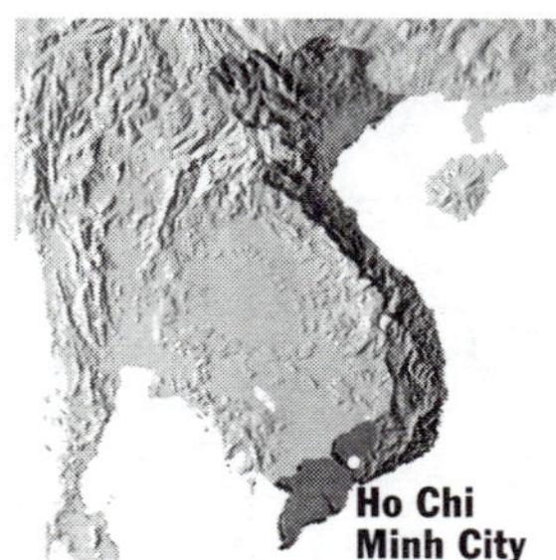


# HO CHI MINH CITY

***Rush hour in central Saigon makes traffic in Los Angeles seem like a Utah interstate highway.***

## HO CHI MINH CITY IN A CAPSULE

*Formerly known as Saigon...Still called Saigon by most...Renamed after reunification in 1975...but central district is still called Saigon...population of about 5 million...Once called Paris of the East because of its French colonial architecture and sidewalk cafes...Much more open than conservative Hanoi to the north...Free enterprise abounds on the streets...City is about 70 km from the South China Sea...Vietnam's economic reforms are most evident in Ho Chi Minh City...Tourism here is booming...Compared with other SE Asian cities, there is little crime—but it's rising rapidly.*

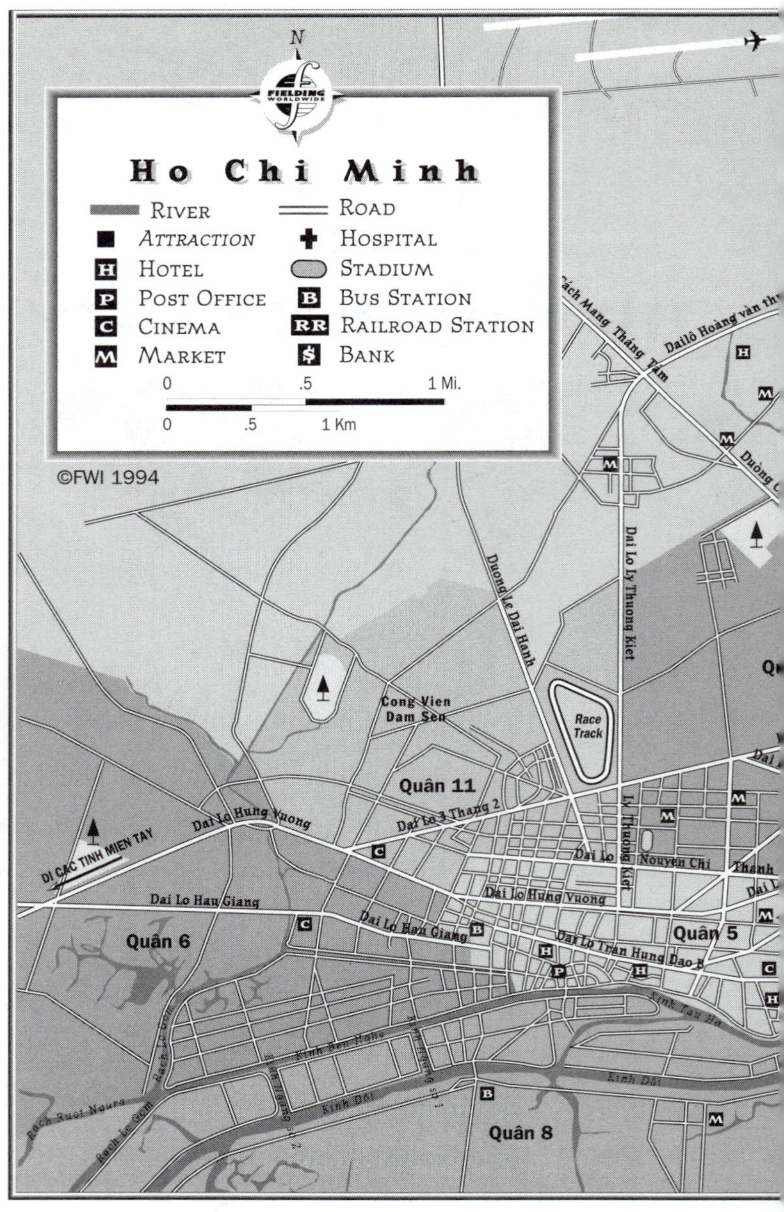

N
FIELDING WORLDWIDE
Ho Chi Minh
River
Road
Attraction
Hospital
Hotel
Stadium
Post Office
Bus Station
Cinema
Railroad Station
Market
Bank
0 .5 1 Mi.
0 .5 1 Km
©FWI 1994
Cách Mang Tháng Tám
Dailô Hoàng vàn th
Duong Le Dai Hanh
Dai Lo Ly Thuong Kiet
Race Track
Cong Vien Dam Sen
Quân 11
Dai Lo 3 Thang 2
Dai Lo Hung Vuong
DI CAC TINH MIEN TAY
Dai Lo Han Giang
Dai Lo Nguyen Chi Thanh
Ly Thuong Kiet
Dai Lo Tran Hung Dao B
Quân 6
Quân 5
Kinh Tau Hu
Kinh Ben Nghe
Rach Lo Gom
Rach Ruot Ngura
Kinh Dôi
Quân 8

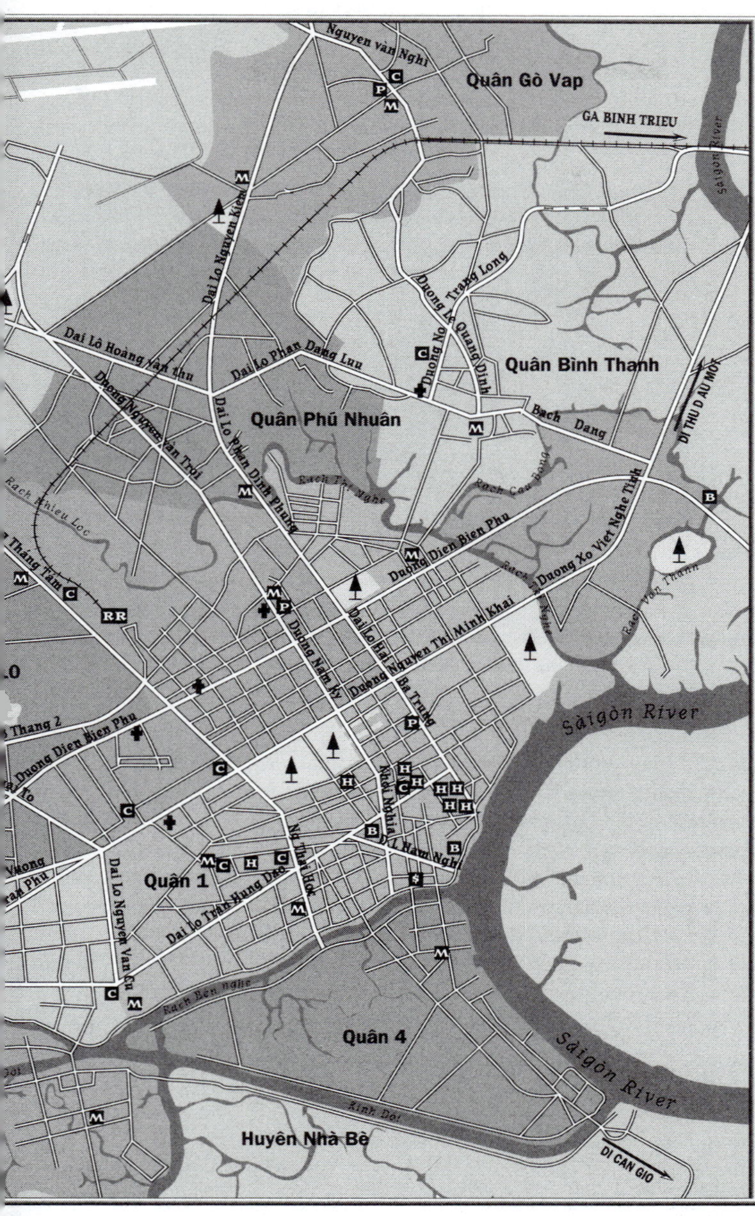
Nguyen vàn Nghi
Quân Gò Vap
GA BINH TRIEU
Saigon River
Dai Lo Nguyen Kiem
Duong Trang Long
Duong No Le Quang Dinh
Dai Lô Hoàng vàn thu
Dai Lo Phan Dang Luu
Quân Bình Thanh
DI THU D AU MOT
Duong Nguyen vàn Troi
Quân Phú Nhuân
Bach Dang
Dai Lo Phan Dinh Phung
Rach Thi Nghe
Rach Cau Bong
Rach Nhieu Loc
Duong Dien Bien Phu
Duong Xo Viet Nghe Tinh
Thang Tam
RR
Duong Nam Ky
Dai Lo Hai Ba Trung
Duong Nguyen Thi Minh Khai
Rach Van Thanh
Thang 2
Duong Dien Bien Phu
Sàigòn River
Khoi Nghia
D.L Ham Nghi
Nu Thai Hok
Quân 1
Dai Lo Tran Hung Dao
Dai Lo Nguyen Van Cu
Rach Ben nghe
Quân 4
Sàigòn River
Kinh Dôi
Huyên Nhà Bè
DI CAN GIO

This is a city that has been called no fewer than seven names through the years, and the latest one, Ho Chi Minh City, is about as embraced by its population as the Marxism that tagged it. People who live here call it Saigon, and people who don't live here call it Saigon. In fact, so many people still call the city Saigon, the government allows the central district to be officially called Saigon.

***The Opera House in central Saigon is the district's social hub on Sunday.***

Like its neighbor to the west, Phnom Penh in Cambodia (although for different reasons), Saigon swelled with refugees from the countryside during the height of the Vietnam War as North Vietnamese forces were toppling the South and closing in on the capital. After the fall of Saigon, the city actually started to resemble Hanoi for a while—with its glum-faced citizenry looking over their shoulders for someone to tout, but instead catching the narrow gaze of the secret police. But all that's changed and it's "Happy Days Again" in some respects for Saigonese, who are starting to come out of the woodwork to service the burgeoning number of Western tourists who have descended upon the city in relative swarms in recent years, and to join foreign companies with their newly-acquired language and technical skills.

There is no doubt that bustling Saigon is the industrial, business, and—many argue—the emerging cultural heart of Vietnam. There are thriving markets, discos and eateries. The ethnic Chinese of Cholon (Hoa) are again exerting their economic might. Before the fall of Saigon, the Hoa controlled more than three quarters of the industry of South Vietnam and nearly half the banks. After 1975, they were persecuted as opportunists by the Vietnamese—but now they're accepted, even encouraged to invest by the government. In fact, Hanoi sees Hoa prosperity as integral in its efforts at moving toward a free market system. Of course, the move toward free enterprise has its inevitable victims. It's estimated that hundreds of thousands of Vietnamese in Saigon alone are unemployed.

In terms of lifestyle, Saigon is like the Southern California of Vietnam. If you're real lucky (or unlucky, depending upon your viewpoint) you might catch a glimpse of a young Saigonese skateboarding along a rutted sidewalk boogying to an old American rock anthem blasting in his headset.

## THE POLLUTION HAZARDS IN HCMC

*Pollution in Ho Chi Minh City is becoming a problem. Respiratory diseases due to pollution are on a marked increase. Asthma cases have risen more than 62% since 1988; bronchitis has jumped more than 45%; sinusitis more than 40%. Pollution in HCMC is primarily caused by industrial waste and motor vehicle exhaust. Thu Duc district is considered the most polluted part of the city. Pollution levels in HCMC are almost twice as high in the dry season than during the rainy season. If you are really sensitive to pollutants, avoid visiting Saigon during the Tet New Year (late January-early February), when the ceaseless detonation of firecrackers causes even the perfectly healthy to want to seek an oxygen tent. On New Year's Eve last February, lead density in the air was 3.5 times higher than the minimum safety limits.*

*It's also worthy to note that sewage and rotting garbage in the city pose a semi-serious hazard. Of the 16,000 cubic meters of garbage and the 2500 tons of manure that are disposed of daily, only about 27% of the garbage and less than 10% of the latter are properly treated. A lot of the trash ends up in the rivers, canals and lakes.*

The people of Saigon are remarkably friendly to Americans, considering the horrific experiences most had to endure just a short generation ago. In fact, once it's gleaned you're not a Russian, you're still likely to be followed down the street by a posse of curious children.

Even during the short period I was away from the metropolis between November 1994 and June 1995, Saigon's changes were vast. New sidewalks now line Tran Hung Dao Street and other major arteries. No more of that Bangkok fear of falling into a 10-foot pit. You can actually get around in high-heels these days.

Elegant new hotels and apartment buildings have sprung up on Le Loi and Nguyen Hue Streets. Two new golf courses opened in the suburbs of Song Be and Thu Duc. Trendy eateries and nightclubs have opened along Thi Sach Street. There are more cars on the roads—and more new motorbikes.

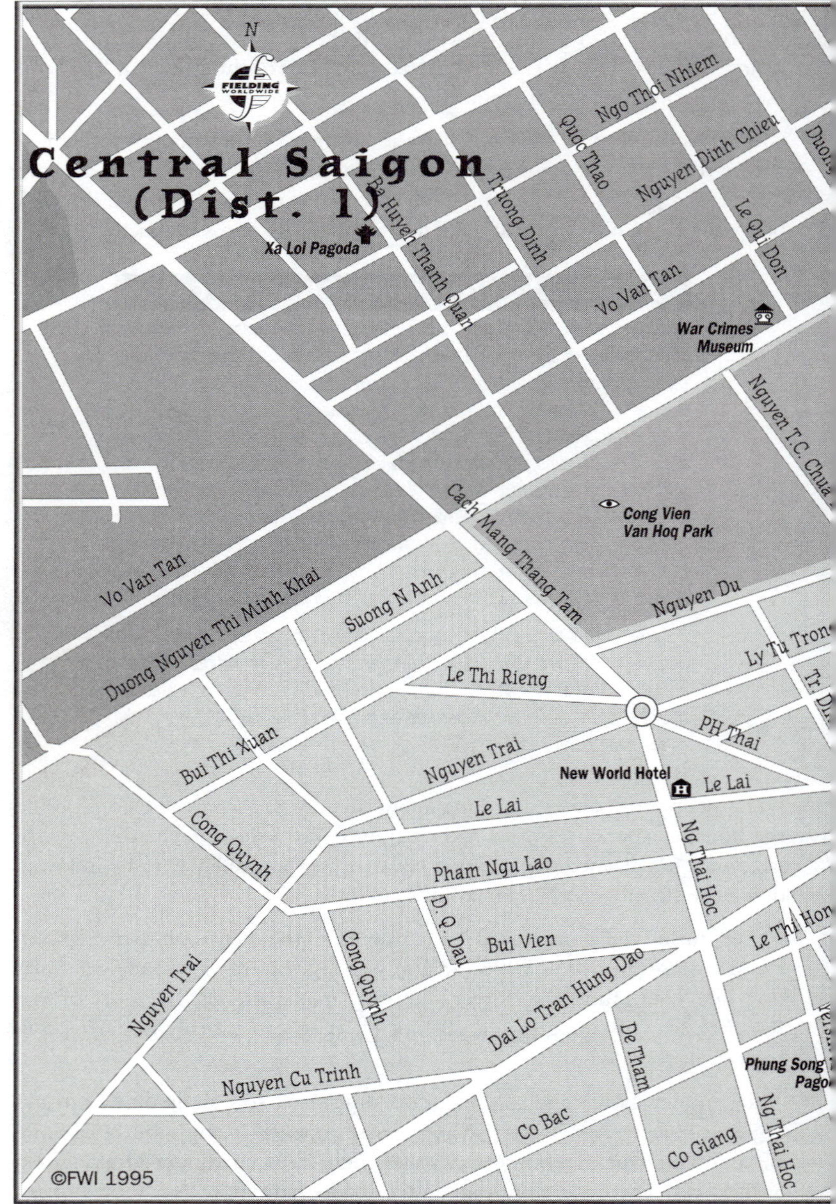
N
FIELDING WORLDWIDE
Central Saigon (Dist. 1)
Xa Loi Pagoda
Ba Huyen Thanh Quan
Truong Dinh
Quoc Thao
Ngo Thoi Nhiem
Nguyen Dinh Chieu
Le Qui Don
Vo Van Tan
War Crimes Museum
Nguyen T.C. Chua
Cach Mang Thang Tam
Cong Vien Van Hoq Park
Vo Van Tan
Duong Nguyen Thi Minh Khai
Suong N Anh
Nguyen Du
Ly Tu Tron
Le Thi Rieng
PH Thai
Bui Thi Xuan
Nguyen Trai
New World Hotel
Le Lai
Le Lai
Cong Quynh
Ng Thai Hoc
Pham Ngu Lao
D. Q. Dau
Bui Vien
Le Thi Hon
Cong Quynh
Dai Lo Tran Hung Dao
Nguyen Trai
De Tham
Phung Song
Nguyen Cu Trinh
Co Bac
Co Giang
Ng Thai Hoc
©FWI 1995

Former U.S. Embassy
General Post Office
Notre Dame Cathedral
Reunification Hall
Municipal Theater
City Hall
Continental Hotel
Phnom Penh Bus Garage
Vietnam Airlines Booking Office
Caravelle Hotel
Saigon Hotel
Revolutionary Museum
Rex Hotel
Bong Sen Hotel
Century Saigon
Mondial Hotel
Orchid Hotel
Majestic Hotel
Asian Hotel
Palace Hotel
Dong Khoi Hotel
Saigon Floating Hotel
Riverside Hotel
New Hotel
Ben Thanh Market
Hai Van Hotel
Ben Thanh Bus Station
Dinner Cruise Boats
Ho Chi Minh Museum
Saigon River
Le Duan
Nguyen Du
Nguyen Binh Khiem
Nguyen Thi Ngan
Duong Nguyen Thi Minh Khai
Hai Ba Trung
Thai Van Lung
Dai Lo
Han Thuyen
Ly Tu Trong
Le Thanh Ton
Nam Ky
Dong Pasteur
Don Dat
Thi Sach
Dong Du
Ton Duc Thang
Nguyen Truc
Dong Khoi
Khoi Nghia
Ole Loi
T. Thiep
Huynh Th. Kang
D.L Ham Nghi
Ton T. Dam
Ho Tung Mau
Nguyen Hue
Nguyen Thai Binh
Pho Duc Chinh
Calmette
Nguyen Cong Tru
B. Chuong Duong
0 .1 .2 Mi
0 100 200 M

This place is changing daily. If you get into town and are a little confused and want to get pointed in the right direction, drop Do Trong Tu, one of the best local guides, a line at *FAX: 84-8-231071.*

## Backpacking in Saigon

*Tay ba lo.* That's the local Vietnamese name for the increasing number of Western backpackers plodding HCMC streets. The Vietnamese know the backpackers have few dong and are mainly interested in Vietnamese culture and sights on a tight budget. *Tay ba lo* range from students to teachers to unemployed sheet metal workers. But the one thing in common they all have in HCMC is where they eat and sleep. Most eat at small food stalls for around 5000 dong and stay in guesthouses in District 1 on Le Lai, Calmette, Pham Ngu Lao, De Tham and Bui Vien Streets. Guesthouses on these avenues cost in the US$5-15 range. If you're lucky, you may be able to get by for as little as US$2-3 a day for accommodations in HCMC.

Getting around by cyclo is cheap, although you must be a shrewd negotiator. Agree on the price beforehand, and make sure that both you and the cyclo driver understand the amount. There is an increasing problem in cities such as HCMC, Hanoi, Danang, Hue, etc., with drivers demanding additional payment after they've dropped you at your destination, saying it was the agreed price. They will not accept the money you give them, nor will they leave, but will instead stand around like a cheated card player, sulking and complaining while a crowd gathers. The point here is to gain sympathy from the bystanders, some of whom may insist you cough up the additional cash. More than likely, though, among the crowd will be an English-speaking Vietnamese who knows precisely the scam the cyclo driver is up to. In all probability, you will find the Vietnamese on your side, and the cyclo driver will end up "losing face." The loss of his face is preferable to the loss of your cash.

Renting a bicycle is also cheap. Many rental shops are on or near the above-mentioned streets. Many bike rental firms will ask for 10,000 dong a day (about US$1), but you can usually get this price down, sometimes to as low as 5000 dong per day. But you should never have to pay more than 10,000 dong per day for a bicycle. Make sure the tires are full before you depart. If you want a motorbike (50cc or under), check out the shops on **Dong Khoi Street** as well as **Lam Son Square**. (I recommend **Kolo Rentals** at *7 Lam Son Square*. The service is extremely friendly, the equipment reliable. Plus if you break down, simply call the shop and they'll arrange for the repair—as well as pay for it.) Remember that renting a motorbike over 50cc requires an international drivers license. In most cases, you will be asked to leave your passport for the duration of your rental. No sweat, GI. Just have a photocopy made to keep on yourself as well as your original visa. This will be appropriate documentation should you be stopped by the police or get into an accident.

Many foreigners can get by in Vietnam for as little as US$500 per month. In HCMC, most backpackers frequent the Sinh Cafe, Pham Ngu Lao Street, where meals can be had for as little as 5000 dong (US$0.50). A bottled soft drink will cost you another 2000 dong. Around the area of De Tham and Pham Ngu Lao Streets there are maybe a dozen restaurants or food stalls with similar prices. Included here are the Lotus Cafe, Kim Cafe, Long Phi, Thang Com Binh Dan and the Saigon Cafe.

### Rooms for Rent

On Pham Ngu Lao Street alone, there are at least 14 guesthouses with 110 rooms for rent. De Tham Street has six guesthouses and 30 rooms. Bui Vien Street features 13 guesthouses with at least 41 rooms at last check in mid-1995. The vast majority of these businesses are unlicensed—some estimates say as high as 85%.

In the sanctioned hostels and hotels in the De Tham area, the price for a double room with fan and private bath runs about US$10 per day, while a room with air conditioning, some furniture and a refrigerator runs at US$15 a day. These are steep rates for a backpacker, but they generally only last during the high season between January and April. During the rainy season, the rates drop, usually from US$10 to eight dollars and from US$15 to $12 a day. Evening arrivals to the area may find comfortable rooms for as little as US$5 a day. Private guesthouses have the luxury of being able to slash their prices when the demand calls for it, but the hotels aren't permitted to do so.

But the high season also brings some great bargains if you really want to get down-and-dirty. The number of backpackers in this small section of HCMC rises to nearly 400 new arrivals a day during the high-season months, and some enterprising homeowners have gotten creative with their use of space. Additional beds and "sedge mats" are laid out in many private homes on the side streets off Pham Ngu Lao and De Tham. Families utilize every square inch of their homes to accommodate the overflow, and travelers will find bargains at these homes for as little as US$1 per night on laid-out sedge mats. Backpackers can share small rooms in these homes for about US$2 per person a day. Floor space is rented out—even closets and furniture.

It's a snap to find these places. Just hang out at Kim Cafe for a BGI or two and the touts will spring from the woodwork. They range from cyclo drivers to chewing gum sellers, who make a 10 percent commission on first-time arrivals and 5 percent on repeat business.

The guesthouses will do your laundry and usually have bicycles and small motorbikes for rent: motorbikes can be had for US$5-6 per day, and bicycles for US$1 a day.

As the De Tahm/Bui Ven area began evolving as a backpackers' haven, the number of coffee shops and cafes proliferated. Formerly, there were only two "in" spots—Kim Cafe and Sinh Cafe. Now, there are no fewer than 15 cafes and coffee shops in the area. Meals typically range in the 10,000 dong (US$1) range and are generally rather tasty, representing the best food bargains found in the city. The service is invariably friendly (with the competition, it has to be) and employees can at least speak restaurant English.

### Guesthouse Tour Services

Many of the guesthouses along De Tham/Bui Ven/Pham Ngu Lao Streets offer tour services in addition to accommodations—or they work in association with operators working in their lobbies.Tours from two to 15 days can be booked—at amazingly low prices. Nearly 10 different itineraries are offered. For instance a 15-day tour of Saigon/Dalat/Nha Trang/Quy Nhon/Hoi An/Danang/Hue/Vinh/Hanoi/Halong Bay ranges from US$220-330, depending on your mode of transportation. Car tours are the most costly, while going via a 24-seat bus can cost as little as US$100 per person. But, beware of these "packages." Like the old saying—you get what you pay for. Travelers have reported being abandoned during the middle of the night. They wake up at some Quy Nhon flea bag only to discover that the guide and driver have split.

### Other Services

Laundries, photo shops, souvenir stores and book "rental" shops have sprung up along the backpacker streets—all of which are not nearly as expensive as similar kiosks and shops found on the more fashionable streets of Nguyen Hue and Dong Khoi. You can get your laundry done on the side streets for as little as 1500 dong an article, depending on the material. T-shirts, film, Chinese-pirated CDs and souvenirs can be had at heavily discounted prices. And, yes, you can even rent books here—for about 4000 dong per day.

## A Word About Shopping in HCMC

Souvenir stores and kiosks abound in Saigon. If you're looking for simple souvenirs for your friends and relatives back home, it's best to find them on the street rather than in the fancy, ornamental and expensive shops that line Le Loi Blvd. and Dong Khoi streets in District 1. (See the "Shopping in Ho Chi Minh City" section in this chapter.) Although the souvenirs aren't as finely crafted as those found in the shops, they are incredibly cheap. Printed T-shirts go for as little as US$1. Small, handcrafted wooden boats run from between US$5–50 dollars. These are incredible bargains. Not to mention the Coke cans that have been crafted into the uncannily realistic shapes of warplanes and helicopters. (These can be had for the remarkable price of about 10,000 a piece!) A lot of it, of course depends upon your ability to bargain. You can also purchase collections of ancient stamps, coins and silk paintings at astoundingly low prices. But remember something: Never pay anything more than 50 percent of the asking price.

### JUNK SHOPPING: 'THE MENEST SOB IN THE VALLEY'

*Take a stroll down Dong Khoi Street and not only will you find the good stuff, but the bad stuff, as well. Numerous vendors offer for sale trinkets they say are spoils from the war–such as Zippo engraved lighters and GI dogtags with shibboleths such as "Yea though I walk through the valley of death I will fear no evil, because I'm the menest SOB in the valley." The bad English invariably gives the items away as fake. But the fake stuff may be what you're looking for. Rolexes from the Vietnam War era may be real or fake. Some are obvious, others dangerously less so, as the asking prices usually start at about US$100 or more. Mont Blanc and Parker fountain pens can be had. Are they fake or real? Or, check out the old Russian box cameras like Praktica, Rolleiflex and Rollei. Interested? Before you buy, shoot a roll of film and have it developed. And mark the camera.*

But remember the bargains are becoming fewer in HCMC, as the number of tourists continues to escalate. Prices for local art and sculpture in both HCMC and Saigon are spiraling. One artist in Hanoi, Nguyen Quan, who only just two short years ago was peddling his art to diplomats and businesspeople looking for cheap souvenirs to bring home, has witnessed his art double and even triple in price—and it continues to ascend at a remarkable rate. "The artists in Vietnam now have the freedom to paint subjects other than peasants, workers and soldiers," he said.

Art in Saigon and Hanoi has taken on distinct Western influences, mostly in the European abstract style. The ban on painting nudes has also been lifted. Paintings that sold for as little as US$300 a year ago are now fetching US$1000 or more. And this is in a country where the per capita annual income hovers around US$200. Private galleries in both HCMC and Hanoi are proliferating to capitalize on the demands of foreign tourists and businesspeople.

Lacquerware is a better bargain in HCMC than in Hanoi, namely because most of it is produced in the Saigon area. You can pick up some of the smaller vases and pots for under a dollar if you bargain hard. More expensive items include four-panel wall hangings that start at about US$40.

Vietnamese silk is generally thinner than Chinese and Thai silk, but the quality can be good. Most prices start at US$14 per two meters.

## Crime in Ho Chi Minh City

*During the past few years, petty theft has surged dramatically in Saigon, particularly in the most touristed areas. One night on Dong Khoi street, I was mugged by a transvestite who relieved me of my US$20 Bangkok Rolex. It was totally professional. She/he posed as a drunken hooker on a dark street and grabbed my arm and crotch. I pushed the lady-boy on her ass and continued my evening stroll, noticing my watch was gone 15 minutes later. A professional hit. Like the Vietnamese who are victims of such crime—and know better—I didn't bother reporting the crime to the police.*

*On another occasion, in broad daylight in the heart of the city's financial district on Nguyen Hue Street, I watched as a gang of youths—both male and female—accosted a shocked Western businessman, stealing his watch and briefcase to the amusement of dozens of onlookers.*

*The Vietnamese themselves will not get involved. Pleas to nearby traffic policemen—who may have witnessed an incident—will invariably fall on deaf ears. "I'm a traffic policeman," is the typical response. "I deal with traffic offenders; I don't chase thieves."*

*Until a few years ago, HCMC police periodically made sweeps of petty street criminals and hookers and hoarded them off to "reeducation camps" in the suburbs. Soon, though, the thugs and prostitutes were back on the streets. The crackdowns are far less frequent these days. And victims who report street crime must supply a photo of themselves and pay US$2 for a crime report, often standing in line with other victims. The thieves are rarely caught.*

*Most street punks operate on motorbikes, where they snatch satchels, purses and briefcases from unsuspecting foreigners as they walk on the streets, ride a cyclo, or ride pillion on other motorbikes. Pickpockets favor hanging around major hotels, such as the Floating Hotel, the Rex and the New World.*

*Dung, the owner of Saigon's best foreign-language newsstand across from the Rex, witnesses daylight street crime frequently. "It's gotten really bad in the last year," he told me. "Robbers don't care about being seen robbing tourists. In fact, they want to be seen. All these kids have been watching Hong Kong and American movies for the last couple of years, and they want to be like the criminals they see on the screen. It's a macho thing to make a broad daylight hit."*

## Crime in Ho Chi Minh City

*The rule of thumb is to stay off the streets after 9 p.m. in Saigon. The police, whose presence on the streets is highly visible during daylight hours, seem to go into hibernation after dark. At any time, if you're wearing a money belt or fanny pack, keep at least one hand on it. And clutch it rather tightly. The same goes for anything else you're carrying. Thugs and ruffians have no scruples, particularly concerning women, the largest victim category of street theft. It pays to be big, or at least act big. The more intimidating you appear, the least likely you are to become a victim. Army boots, a few visits to the gym, and a tight black Megadeath T-shirt can't hurt. If you're strolling, do it with friends. If you're a photographer with a monopod, carry the case with you on the streets. Sure, it's for encasing your monopod–but it looks (and feels) like a billy club. Scares the hell out of the locals.*

*The police do make arrests, but they offer better advice. (Vietnamese crime victims know they have a better chance of recovering their stolen items by waiting at home for a call from the thieves, and offering cash for the return of their papers, valuables and identity cards.) To one Japanese businessman who had his cellular phone swiped, the police simply suggested that he phone his own number and ask how much money the crooks wanted for its return.*

## What to See and Do in Ho Chi Minh City

Places that are must-see in the city generally include the Reunification Palace, formerly the Presidential Palace; the War Museum, which is filled with photographs and memorabilia, including exhibits that depict the horrors of the Vietnam War; the Historical Museum, containing some noteworthy archaeological artifacts and a beautiful bronze Buddha that dates from about the 5th century A.D.; the former U.S. embassies, and the Cu Chi tunnels, which were originally built during Vietnam's battle for independence from the French. The tunnels were greatly enlarged during the war with the U.S. to accommodate the Viet Cong, and contain living quarters, kitchens and surgical areas for the wounded.

**War Crimes Museum (formerly American War Crimes Museum)** ★★

*28 Vo Van Tan, Dist. 3. Located on Vo Van Tan Street near the intersection of Le Qui Don Street.*

*Open daily from 7:30 a.m.–11:45 a.m. and 1:30 p.m.–4:45 p.m.*

This may be the most popular attraction in Saigon. Built on the site of the former Information Service Office of Saigon University, the museum exhibits a slew of photos depicting events of the Vietnam War in general, and alleged and real American atrocities in particular. Many of the shots are absolutely gruesome. Some of the events covered here are the My Lai massacre and the effects of Napalm, Agent Orange, and phosphorous bombs on the Vietnamese people. The museum has been remodeled since my last visit—it seems they've done away with the deformed human fetuses that were once displayed.) Outside the museum is a collection of war materiel, U.S. choppers, and tanks. Here you can see a bunch of downed trainer fighters, light aerial and slow bombers that would hit their targets accurately, but weren't very fast. There's an array of machine guns from both sides of the war;

weapons in poor condition. It's all just a testament to a war that, if one didn't know any better, looks like it may have taken place during the last century.

Americans are depicted as murderers, without any real perspective that war itself is hell, only Americans. You won't see photos here of U.S. GIs giving candy bars to VC children while they sit in Bob Hope's lap. There are a lot of photos depicting carnage all over the place and weapons mounted on pods. Some of the stuff looks pretty bizarre, like microwaves at one of the first Burger Kings. In another room there are many aerial photos depicting bombardment from B-52s—also some evidence here that looks like animal experiments being performed by U.S. scientists—DNA stuff that was conducted by Americans, genetically altering animals to be Robocops trained to destroy the VC.

The worst sight are the photos of babies hideously deformed, the alleged consequences of exposure to Agent Orange. Most of the material here is pure propaganda, but there's a lot to be said for the proportion of it that is correct. Also here are prison and torture cells where VC prisoners were held—cement torture chambers. Scrawled words cover the walls. Above the cells are grid-like floors where the capturers could observe the torture below. The Huey helicopter in the courtyard is in good shape. All in all, despite the fetuses, this is not an unnerving sight. Worth the visit.

**AUTHOR'S NOTE**

*They've seemed to tone down the anti-American rhetoric at this museum in the last year. Phrases and captions such as "M-16 typical of that issued to the imperialist American aggressor troops" have been changed to simply "M-16." The times, they are a changin'.*

### Botanical Gardens

*At the end of Le Duan Blvd., where it meets Nguyen Binh Khiem.*

There were once thousands of species of beautiful orchids and other flowers here, although the war did a lot to dilapidate the place. It's still worth a visit though, if for nothing other than the small zoo on the grounds. The Gardens are 130 years old, while the zoo possesses rare and endangered Vietnamese indigenous animals, as well as some exotic animals from overseas. A couple of big cats, lots of birds and a pair of Komodo dragons donated by the Indonesian government. Admission: 10,000 dong.

### Central Market ★★

*Ben Than Market, at Le Loi and Pham Hong Thai Streets.*

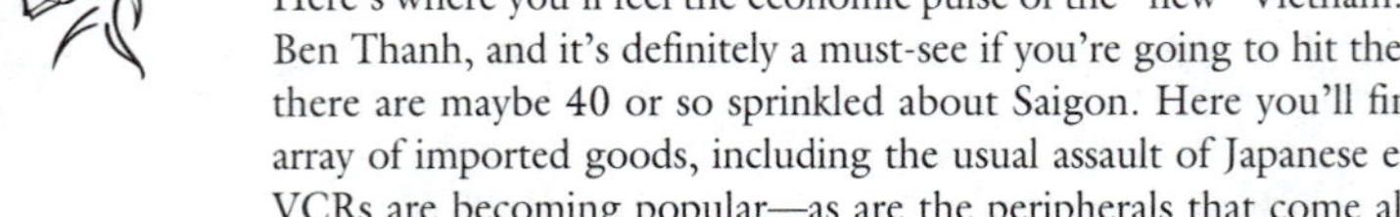

Here's where you'll feel the economic pulse of the "new" Vietnam. This is Saigon's Ben Thanh, and it's definitely a must-see if you're going to hit the market scene—there are maybe 40 or so sprinkled about Saigon. Here you'll find an incredible array of imported goods, including the usual assault of Japanese electronic goods. VCRs are becoming popular—as are the peripherals that come along with them, namely Hong Kong skin flicks.

**Cholon** 

*District 5.*

Talk about the economic pulse of the new Vietnam. This is Saigon's Chinatown, where nearly 400,000 ethnic Chinese are helping to breathe new fire into the Vietnamese economy. There are also pagodas here. The beautiful **Thien Hau Temple** was built in 1825 and is dedicated to the cult of Thien Hau, the goddess of the sea and protector of fishermen. The **Quan Am Pagoda**, built in 1816, has some incredible ceramic illustrations of traditional legends. The **Phuoc An Hoi Quan Pagoda** may be the most elaborately decorated in the city. There's also **Cha Tam Church**, where South Vietnamese President Ngo Dinh Diem fled during his escape in 1963, and the Taoist shrine **Khanh Van Nam Vien Pagoda**. Also check out the produce market of **Binh Tay**.

**Historical Museum** 

*Open 8–11:30 a.m. and 1–4 p.m. Tues.–Fri. Small admission fee.*

This was formerly called the National Museum and is the best place to step back into Vietnam's 4000-year-old history. In addition to the art of the early Chinese and Indonesians, the museum houses artifacts from the Bronze Age and the Dongson period (3500 B.C.–A.D.100). The building was built in 1928 and now also contains items related to the early communist presence in Vietnam. There's a bronze standing Buddha from the 5th century and artifacts from the country's various hilltribes. Also look for Khmer and pre-Angkorean statuary of the Funan period. See if you can get a guide. At last check, none of the labeling was in English.

**Notre Dame Cathedral**

*Opposite the GPO, facing Dong Khoi St.*

Built in 1883 and designed by the French architect Bouvard, this Catholic church (near Tu Do Street) is constructed of granite and red brick. It's quite a magnificent sight in contrast with its surroundings.Tu Do Street was the old red-light district in Saigon.

**Cha Tam Church**

*25 Hoc Lac, on the western end of Tran Hung Dao.*

This is the famous church where South Vietnamese President Ngo Dinh Diem and his brother Ngo Dinh Nhu sought refuge after the 1963 coup attempt at the Presidential Palace. Both Ngos later gave up after realizing they hadn't any political support left and were assassinated a short time after coup leaders picked them up at the church with an armored personnel carrier. The church is worth visiting more for its history than for its architecture. But it's an attractive cathedral, having been built in the early 1900s. Today, its parishioners number in the thousands.

**Reunification Hall (Presidential Palace)**

*Open 7:30–10:30 a.m. and 1–4:30 p.m. Mon.–Sun. There is a US$4 admission charge.*

This is the modern administrative center, located to the southeast of Xo Viet Nghe Tinh Street, where, in a famous photograph, an NVA tank slammed through the gates in April 1975, which symbolically marked the South Vietnamese defeat in the war. The President and the entire South Vietnam cabinet were in the palace at the time and were arrested shortly afterwards. You can tour the former palace in a group.

***Ho Chi Minh City's Reunification Hall was formerly called the Presidential Palace before Saigon fell to the North Vietnamese in 1975.***

**The Rex Hotel**

*141 Nguyen Hue, Dist. 1. Located at the intersection of Nguyen Hue and Le Loi Blvds.*
This was the famous hangout of American officers during the war. It has regained some of its previous glory and now features a number of almost luxurious amenities (at least by Vietnam standards). There's a beauty parlor and an on-site tailor. There are also some respectable business services, such as photocopiers and a fax machine. The place is always packed, so if you're planning a stay, reserve early. Europeans cover the place like bees in a jar of jelly. Rex Regal splendor. If Vietnam is communist you'd never know it. Mahogany and marble all over the place. The breezy rooftop bar's a good place for expensive drinks.

**Ho Chi Minh Museum**

*1 Nguyen Tat Thanh Street.* ☎ *291060.*
*The museum is open on Tues.–Sun (Fri. afternoons only) from 7:30–11:30 a.m. and 1:30–4:30 p.m.*
Chronicles the life and adventures of Uncle Ho, who reportedly made this building his last stop before leaving for France on a freighter in 1911. He wouldn't see Vietnam again for another 30 years. Lots of Ho's personal items are on display here, including clothes and an old American radio he used to listen to. (See "The Ultimate Backpacker: Uncle Ho's Early Years" in the Vietnam Today chapter.) Its seven rooms contain more than 1000 exhibits—there were a mere 400 in 1982. Photos of the young Ho in London and the brick that he used as a heater when he lived in Paris during the early 1920s. The building was constructed between 1862 and 1864

and is characterized by the two dragons on the roof—giving the structure the nickname "Dragon House." The building originally served as the office of the French Royal Shipping Co. It was later converted into a fueling supply base for U.S. ships during the Vietnam War. After reunification in 1975, the building became part of Vietnam's Maritime Transportation Department. The Dragon House didn't become a museum until 1979—although it wasn't opened until January 1, 1982. Admission fee: 8000d.

### Saigon City Hall

*Le Thanh Ton Street at Nguyen Hue, Dist.1.*

This is probably the most photographed building in Saigon. It was formerly the Hotel de Ville and built between 1901 and 1908 by the French. This is a magnificent pastel-yellow building that is now the HCMC People's Committee Building. Getting inside, though—to see its magnificent interior—is a little tricky, as it's not opened to tourists. You may be able to get in with a special appointment through a local travel agent who's connected.

### Military Museum

*Across Nguyen Binh Khiem Street at the corner of Le Duan Blvd.*

Here's an array of Vietnam War-era Soviet and Chinese weapons such as a 57 anti-aircraft gun which supported the Army Corp 4 in the Xuan Loc battle; it was laboriously moved along with the unit to Bien Hoa to liberate that city. There's also an 85 mm gun which was one of the guns of Division 5, Engineering Unit 232, that was used to support the unit as it crossed the Vam Co River to attack Phulam Radar station, a strategic outpost near the capital. Next to that is a 105 mm gun which was one of the guns that was used to stun the ARVN military position northeast of Saigon to support the unit that was attacking the Dong Hu base. Right next to this is a 130 mm gun which was one of the guns of the Nhon Trach battle used to attack Tan Son Nhat on April 29, 1975, which marked the beginning of the victory of the Ho Chi Minh campaign. There's also a 37 mm anti-aircraft gun which belonged to the 7th Anti-Aircraft Regiment of the 7th military zone, which took part in the liberation of Loc Ninh, and later in the liberation of Bien Hoa. There's also an American aircraft, a Cessna A-37, used by the South Vietnamese Air Force. Under Nguyen Thanh Trung's command, five planes left Thanh Son to bomb Tan Son Nhat airport on April 28, 1975. There's also an engineering vehicle and vehicles belonging to various information/propaganda regiments, which don't really bring back a lot of memories other than the truck used by the Beverly Hillbillies. These information units were primarily propaganda units that supported the army units as they moved south. There's also an ARVN armored personnel carrier here, which was captured at Phuoc Long in January 1975. There are also some bulldozers that are only worthy of note because they were supplied by the Cubans, as was engineering aid by Castro advisors. There's an area of destroyed U.S. and South Vietnamese aircraft that clutters some of the grounds of the compound, and it seems nobody has been able to identify the wrecks. Perhaps the most interesting attraction of the museum is the F-5 fighter plane which was flown by the renegade pilot Nguyen Thanh Trung. According to the description, this was the aircraft that bombed the

"Puppet President's Palace" and then landed in a liberated area. It took off with South Vietnamese markings. The plane bombed the palace and then fled the capital. There is also the interesting T-54 tank, Number 848, which was the tank that attacked the Independence Palace at 10:30 a.m., April 1975. Inside, the museum chronicles the history of Vietnamese campaigns ranging from the first Indochina War through the American war. There's an assortment of photos as well as a number of small arms that were used during the wars. The guides here speak relatively decent English, and the photos and maps have English descriptions, although the English is a bit shoddy and not nearly as descriptive as the Vietnamese captions to the museum's artifacts. There's also a large VC and tactical map showing troop movements and firefight sites at American military positions.

**The Former U.S. Embassies**

*39 Nam Nghi Blvd.; Le Duan Blvd. and Mac Dinh Chist.*

The older U.S. embassy is located at *39 Nam Nghi Blvd.* The Americans abandoned it after it was bombed in 1967. They moved to a much more attractive compound at the corner of *Le Duan Blvd. and Mac Dinh Chi Street.* This is the famous structure which Viet Cong guerrillas nearly seized during the Tet Offensive of 1968 and the same building where millions around the world saw on television the rushed rooftop evacuation of hundreds of Americans and Vietnamese as communist forces sped like a torpedo toward central Saigon. Thousands of South Vietnamese, who had been promised evacuation by the U.S. massed outside the embassy gates, repelled by the U.S. Marine guards. U.S. choppers shuttled the lucky passengers between the rooftop and waiting U.S. warships off the coast of Vung Tau. At each corner of the embassy compound, there are concrete pillboxes with explosive shields. The main building is covered with a concrete shield which was to protect it from bombs, grenades and rocket attacks.

**Vinh Nghiem Pagoda**

*339 Nam Ky Khoi Nghia, Dist. 3.*

This is one of the largest pagodas in Saigon. It was built in 1967 in the modern Japanese style. It's an impressive sight, with a stupa reaching up to seven stories, and one of the largest pagodas in Vietnam. The pagoda is 35 meters long, 22 meters wide and 15 meters high. There are a number of wooden carvings, depicting the four sacred animals—unicorn, dragon, tortoise and phoenix, as well as carvings of other famous pagodas. Fantastic bell tower.

**Xa Loi Pagoda**

*Bay Huyen Thanh Quan St. Located near the War Crimes Museum*

This temple was built in 1956 and features a multistory tower which houses a sacred relic of the Lord Buddha. There's a huge bronze-gilded Buddha in the main sanctuary. The pagoda was the site where monks self-immolated themselves in opposition to President Ngo Dinh Diem in the mid–1960s.

**Artex Saigon Orchid Farm**

*5/81 Xa Lo Vong Dai, Thu Duc district, on the Korean Highway.*

Started in 1970, the orchid farm now boasts more than 1000 different types of orchids and around 60,000 plants. A beautiful and relaxing place to kill a Sunday afternoon. This is the largest orchid farm in Vietnam, with orchids indigenous to Vietnam and from abroad. The best time to visit is during the dry season. The only problem is that you need reservations to visit here. You should do it a couple of days in advance. ☎ *240124*.

## Ho Chi Minh City Environs

*Cu Chi Tunnels were remarkably well hidden during the Vietnam War.*

### Cu Chi Tunnels ★

This is a vast network of more than 200 km of underground tunnels in Tay Ninh, a little under 70 km northwest of Saigon. These tunnels were constructed and used by the Viet Cong to conduct operations, sometimes within the perimeters of U.S. military bases, and hide from the enemy. These are thoroughly fascinating subterranean vestibules, where the VC lived, slept, and ate. There are underground hospitals, kitchens and communications centers. There are living areas, sleeping quarters and munitions storage centers. There are even "street" signs under the earth to help guide errant guerrillas and newcomers. When operational, these tunnels amazingly stretched all the way from Saigon to the Cambodian border. What you'll crawl through today are actually widened versions of the originals. Getting access to tunnel areas other than the touristed ones is problematic. You may even get a chance to fire an AK-47 or an M-16 for a U.S. buck a bullet. Fully automatic can be pricey. Admission: 45,000 dong. Buses to Cu Chi leave from the Tay Ninh Bus Station in Tan Binh district. Take Cach Mang Thang all the way out to about one km past where Cach Mang Thang merges with Le Dai Hanh Street. Cars and drivers for hire can be had at the **Phnom Penh Bus Garage** (*155 Nguyen Hue—next to the Rex*). As well, a lot of private owners hang out in the square in front of Reunification Hall. Expect to pay between US$20-30 for a half-day trip out to the tunnels.

### The Iron Triangle (Tam Giac Sat)

This is an area, not far from the Cu Chi Tunnels, that was named by American troops during the war because of their inability to penetrate this Viet Cong stronghold. Although the area isn't far from Saigon, in the forests between Ben Cat, Cu Chi, and Dau Tieng, the region was impenetrable. The "Triangle" served as the base for attacks by the VC on Saigon, in particular the battles during the 1968 Tet lunar New Year as well as bloody battles at Binh Long and Dong Xoai. Now that a greater number of visitors are coming out to the tunnels at Cu Chi, there has developed an interest on the part of tourists to see the Iron Triangle area. To get there, take Highway 13 about 17 km, crossing the Binh Trieu Bridge. You'll arrive at Lai Thieu, a small village known for its handicrafts and lacquerware. You'll also pass Binh Nham and Suoi Don before reaching the town of Thu Dau Mot. From there, on the road to Dau Tieng, you'll see a trail on the left, which is the path to the Iron Triangle. Although altogether void of any cultural, natural or topographical attractions, the region is bound to become popular with returning American veterans of the war. Tours of the area can be arranged through Vietnamtourism and other local operators (see the "Directory" portion of this chapter). You'll visit former battlefields, military bases and villages heavily damaged in the war.

### My Tho ★

In the Mekong Delta, about 70 km southwest of Saigon, this is the former capital of Dinh Tuong province and now the capital of Tien Giang province. This fertile area is home to several interesting temples—including **Vinh Trang Pagoda** and **My Tho Church**. There's also a bustling central market. This area is often included on tours outside of Saigon. (See a more complete description of the area under the My Tho section.)

## Vung Tau Beach

This is a popular beach resort a couple of hours or more (130 km) southeast of Saigon at the mouth of the Saigon River. The front and back beaches are the choice of Vietnamese surf frollickers, while secluded Pineapple Beach features villas and a large statue of Christ overlooking the South China Sea. There are several decent temples here, including the largest one in Vietnam: Niet Ban Tinh Xa. Long Hai is a better beach about 30 km closer to Saigon. (See a more complete description of the area under Vung Tau.)

## Tay Ninh ★

Usually combined with a visit to the Cu Chi tunnels, Tay Ninh is a town about 100 km northwest of Saigon. This is the capital of the Tay Ninh Province, which borders the Cambodian border. Back in the 1970s, Cambodian Khmer Rouge guerrillas, in their campaign of terror against anyone Vietnamese, attacked villages in the province frequently and relentlessly. These attacks were part of the reason the Vietnamese Army invaded Cambodia in late 1978. A few weeks later, in January 1979, Pol Pot's Phnom Penh government collapsed and the Khmer Rouge fled into western Cambodia. Tay Ninh is primarily known for the indigenous religion of Cao Daism and the **Cao Dai Great Temple.** Set inside a complex of schools and other buildings and built between 1933 and 1955, the temple is distinctive for the European influences in its Oriental architecture. It's one of the most intriguing temples in Vietnam, if not all of Southeast Asia. Tay Ninh Province was also the strategic end of the Ho Chi Minh trail during the Vietnam War. (See a more complete description under the Tay Ninh section.)

## Con Dao Island ★★

Thanks to conveniences of modern air travel, it's now possible to reach the relatively unexplored and serene Con Dao Islands, beautiful peaks which rise from the sea much like the islands of Hawaii about 100 miles off the coast of Vung Tau.

About 40 minutes by plane from Ho Chi Minh City and you're there. Con Dao Island has only been accessible for the last couple of years, and a visit to these nearly deserted islands is well worth it, even considering the exorbitant US$200 round-trip airfare from HCMC.

There are miles of deserted beaches and jungle roads and paths to explore. The water is calm and clear here, not like the silty surf of Vung Tau and Long Hai.

The group of islands that make up the Con Daos numbers 14. The largest is Con Dao itself, with a small airstrip that's only manned every couple of days or so when a turboprop plane drops from the sky from HCMC. Con Dao Island is only about 20 square kilometers and its inhabitants number

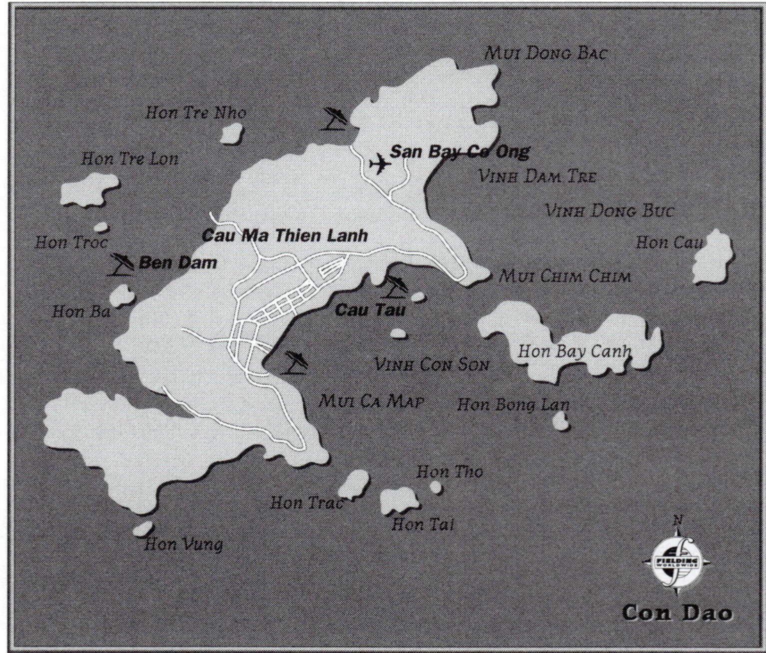


perhaps 2000 or so fishermen and their families. It is a heavily forested island with a number of steep mountains which drop right into the sea, the highest of which reaches 600 meters. Climbing the peaks affords fantastic vistas of the surrounding coral reefs and pristine, white sand beaches.

The island was formerly home to a French prison (built in 1861 and still standing about a kilometer outside the island's main town) for political dissidents and Vietnamese nationalists under French colonial rule of Vietnam. The former South Vietnamese government also used the island as a prison for anti-regime elements. It could house 12,000 inmates.

After touching down at the island's airport, you'll take a minivan or jeep about 13 km into town (where the only accommodations are), most likely without seeing another soul along the way, for 15,000 dong. In town, the only attraction—other than the slow way of life itself—is a house that served as the prison camp warden's home. It's now called **Bao Tang Tong Ho Tinh** and has been turned into a museum. Admission: 5000 dong. The museum depicts the island's prison years and species of plant and animal life found here.Tours are conducted when someone shows up. The assistant director of the museum speaks decent English.

The prison is reachable from town by the Vietnamese version of a *tuk tuk*, a three-wheeled Honda that looks designed to be driven by a circus bear, for a roundtrip fee of about 20,000 dong. At the prison is easy access to the old "tiger cages," where inmates were beaten, tortured and killed by their French and South Vietnamese captors. With little imagination, it's a grisly sight. Near the prison are the graves of and monuments to hundreds—perhaps thousands—of the prisoners who died on this island, including the legendary Vietnamese heroine Vo Thi Sau.

On the southwest side of town are a couple of Buddhist pagodas worth seeing simply for panoramic vistas where they're located.

**Doing It:**

Vasco Co. flies from the domestic terminal at HCMC's Tan Son Nhat Airport directly to Con Dau on Tuesday, Thursday and Saturday at 08:30 using Jetsteam turboprop aircraft. The flight returns the same day at 09:30. The flight takes only about 30–40 minutes, but costs US$200 roundtrip. Book through Vietnam Airlines. Or call *84-8-445999*. The more intrepid can take a small, colorful Vietnamese boat from Vung Tau. The one-way journey costs only about US$20 or less depending on your bargaining skills and takes about 12 hours. Bring plenty of provisions (water and food).

**Where to Stay:**

There are a couple of guesthouses on Con Dau, but you'll first be taken to the island's only hotel, the **Phi Yen** *(☎ 0164-30168)*. There are 10 rooms here, the cheapest being US$20 a night. The hotel also rents boats and jeeps for island excursions. Some of the staff speaks passable English. Cozy place—you'll like it.

**Where to Eat:**

There are a number of stalls with excellent seafood. The best "restaurant" in town is the **Cong Quan Restaurant** *(☎ 30106)*, which is on the ocean next to the pier. Great seafood and cheap.

## Where to Stay in Ho Chi Minh City

### AUTHOR'S NOTE: TELEPHONE PREFIXES

*When dialing telephone numbers in Ho Chi Minh City, the country code is 84. The city code is 8, followed by the local exchange. Numbers listed are local exchanges.*

**Asian Hotel** **US$75**

*146/150 Dong Khoi Street. ☎ 296979. FAX: 297433.*

One restaurant; no charge for children under 12. Service charge and breakfast are included in the tariff.

**Bat Dat Hotel** **US$10**

*238-244 Tran Hung Dao B Blvd. ☎ 555817.*

*117 rooms.*

Recommended by the backpack set. Cheap rooms with air conditioning; cheaper still with fan; Chinese restaurant.

**Caravelle Hotel** **US$50–$180**

*17-23 Lam Son Square, Dist. 1. ☎ 293704/8. FAX: 299746, 296767.*
*115 rooms.*
Not as well kept up on the outside and more run down than its French neighbor the Continental across the square.Very, very French. Once the hangout for journalists during the war and also once owned by the Catholic Church. Recently renovated; 9th floor continental restaurant; conference facilities; foreign exchange counter; Japanese restaurant; disco; coffee shop; air conditioning; IDD; gift shop; gym; sauna; tailor in-house; massage; excellent location. Friendly.

**Chains First Hotel (First Hotel)** **US$65–$125** ★★★

*18 Hoang Viet, Tan Binh Dist. ☎ 441199. FAX: 444282.*
*90 rooms.*
Near the airport; tennis courts; business services; airport shuttle; gift shop; coffee shop; three restaurants; sauna; air-conditioned; refrigerator. Has separate area with rooms with fans.

**Cholon Hotel**

*Su Van Hanh Street. ☎ 357058.*
Popular with visiting Taiwanese; clean rooms; restaurant.

**Century Saigon Hotel** **US$115–$200** ★★★★

*68a Nguyen Hue Blvd. ☎ 293168, 231818. FAX: 292732, 222958.*
Sort of nouveau colonial; big bucks in the first district. Mainly for business travelers. Business center, health club, visa extension assistance service, in-room movies, restaurants and lounges plural. With what the Big Bens people shell out here, this is the definition of "Marksism."

**Continental Hotel** **US$85-170** ★★★★

*132-134 Dong Khoi Street. ☎ 299201, 299255. FAX: 290936.*
*87 rooms.*
This was the setting of Graham Greene's novel *The Quiet American*. Built in 1880, this French colonial building is kept in exquisite shape. It was renovated in 1989. Large, open courtyard. Large rooms with air conditioning; Bamboo Bar; Azur Bar; La Dolce Vita Bar; expensive Italian restaurant; Continental Palace Restaurant serves great Vietnamese fare Good service. Business services.

**Duc Huy Hotel** **US$15**

*422 Hai Ba Trung Street, District 1. ☎ 442937. FAX: 230132.*
This is one of the best bargains in town, for businesspeople as well as for backpackers and other tourists. Opened in April 1994. The rooms are immense and lavishly appointed. Attached bath with hot water. Refrigerator, karaoke and video facilities, meeting rooms, air-conditioned, color TV. Car, motorbike and bicycle rentals. Organized sightseeing tours throughout the country. There are even backpacker tours at "backpacker rates." Hotel, airline and rail bookings. The staff, all English speaking, are extremely friendly. Highly recommended.

**Dong Khoi Hotel**

*12 Ngo Duc Ke Street. ☎ 294046.*
*34 rooms.*
Old French colonial building. Air-conditioned suites with high ceilings. Friendly proprietors; good security. Was being totally renovated at press time, so we'll see what the new rate card looks like.

**Ecumenical Guest House** **US$10–$12**

*15 Tu Xuong, Dist 3. ☎ 222642, 251701. FAX: 231071.*
Perhaps the best bargain I've found in HCMC. They could easily get away charging two times the amount. Modern, clean rooms with air conditioning and private bath. Quiet setting. Breakfast. A deal and a half. Highly recommended.

**Embassy Hotel** **US$60–$100** ★★★

*35 Nguyen Trung Truc, Dist. 1. ☎ 231981. FAX: 231978.*
New hotel in the center of town. Nice rooms with air conditioning, TV, minibar, refrigerator. Business center and restaurant.

**Emperor Hotel** **US$30–$66** ★

*117 Nguyen Dinh Chieu, Dist. 1. ☎ 290811. FAX: 230515.*
Moderate in every respect. Rooms with air conditioning, TV, refrigerator and minibar. Restaurant, conference facilities. But this place doesn't take credit cards at last check.

**Evergreen Hotel** **US$35–$45** ★

*261B Hai Ba Trung, Dist. 1. ☎ 291237. FAX: 291835.*
Close to central location. Brand new hotel that's clean and comfortable, and definitely worth the price. One of the increasing bargains in HCMC as the city is experiencing a hotel glut, and there's something of a price war going on. Spacious rooms with air conditioning, TV, refrigerator, minibar. Friendly service.

**Equatorial** **US$100–$400** ★★★★

*242 Tran Binh Trang, Dist. 5. ☎ 390000. FAX: 390011.*
*334 rooms.*
District 5 is a little out of the way, but maybe these people thought a lot of rich people would enjoy being a little out of the way. At press time, this was indicative of the race to establish the "best" in Saigon.

**Festival Hotel** **US$28–$44** ★

*31 Cao Thang, Dist. 3. ☎ 390704. FAX: 390553.*
Clean and comfortable. Worth the price. Rooms with air conditioning, TV, minibar and refrigerator. Restaurant.

**Hai Van Hotel** **US$14–$25**

*69 Huynh Thuc Khang-Quan 1. ☎ 291274, 230400. FAX: 291275.*
For under US$25, this was one of the best places in town, and no one seems to know about it. But the nearby construction makes for a lot of racket. As well, a new popular disco in the hotel makes the lobby busier than a beehive—and doesn't help with the noise problem. But the staff couldn't be friendlier, perhaps more so than in hotels twice as expensive. Ground floor restaurant serves decent Vietnamese fare. Karaoke club on the second floor. Hot water. No TVs in the rooms.

**Hotel Bongsen** **US$55–$210** ★★★

*117-119-121-123 Dong Khoi Street, Dist. 1. ☎ 291516. FAX: 298076.*
*130 rooms.*

This is actually two hotels: Bongsen I and II, the first being the pricier of the two. Breakfast included and children under six stay free at both. Air conditioning, minibar; private baths with hot water; VCRs; IDD and other business services; sauna; shopping arcade; laundry and valet; photo lab on site; medical staff; travel reservations. Bongsen I is moderate to expensive, Bongsen II inexpensive to moderate.

**Huong Sen** **US$38–$100** ★★

*70 Dong Khoi, Dist. 1. ☎ 291415, 290259. FAX: 290916, 298076.*
*50 rooms.*

Air-conditioned; IDD telephone; TV; hot water; refrigerator; minibar; sauna; coffee shops and restaurants; laundry and valet; cars for hire; express photo services; travel reservations and services. Good location.Great location for business and shopping. Cozy and modern. Rooms with the standard amenities. Restaurant, bar, small business center.

**International Hotel** **US$85–$165** ★★★

*19 Vo Van Tan, Dist. 3. ☎ 290009. FAX: 290066.*

Brand new and luxurious rooms for businesspeople, but I gave it only three stars, because, at press time, there were no computers in the business center. Restaurants, shopping area.

**Kim Do Hotel** **US$119–$479** ★★★★

*133 Nguyen Hue Blvd., Dist. 1. ☎ 225914. FAX: 225913.*
*133 rooms.*

Newly opened by Saigontourist. Mucho dinero. Business center, in-house movies, health club, orchid and rose garden, satellite TV.

**Ky Hoa Hotel** **US$40–$90** ★★

*12 February 3 Street, Dist. 10. ☎ 655037. FAX: 655333.*

Way out of the way, but clean and friendly if you need to be out here. Rooms with air conditioning, minibar & refrigerator, TV, telephone. Restaurant.

**Mekong Travel Hotel** **US$66–$95** ★★★

*243A Hoang Van Thu, Tan Binh Dist. ☎ 442986. FAX: 442981.*

Near the airport if that's where you want to be. Most businesspeople and travelers are settling into the newer hotels closer to downtown. But this place is nice enough. Standard amenities.

**Mercure** **US$95–$230** 

*79 Tran Hung Dao, Dist. 1. ☎ 242525/555/537. FAX: 242533.*

Good location near Ben Thanh market. Shopping arcade, business facilities, great restaurant, conference facilities. Friendly staff.

**Metropole (Binh Minh Hotel)** **US$85–$150** ★★★

*148 Tran Hung Dao, Dist. 1. ☎ 322021/2. FAX: 322019.*

Nice place but the rooms generally have a lousy view, if any. Business and conference facilities, superb restaurant. Rooms with minibar, refrigerator, air conditioning, IDD, TV.

**Majestic Hotel** **US$50** ★★

*1 Dong Khoi Street, Dist 1. ☎ 295515. FAX: 291470.*
*100 plus rooms.*

Once the city's best hotel, a fire ravaged it. Now passable. Some of the rooms have a river view; two restaurants; postal and some business services.

**Mondial Hotel** **US$62–$112** ★★★

*109 Dong Khoi Street, Dist. 1. ☎ 296291 or 296296. FAX: 296324.*
*40 rooms.*

Some rooms with balconies; most have private baths, bar and lounge. Elegant and expensively decorated. Great location in Saigon's 1st District. French restaurant with Continental cuisine.Orchid Lounge; quiet, comfortable. Ornate lobby. Exotic place. There are traditional Vietnamese cultural shows here three times a week.

**New Hotel** **US$25**

*14 Ho Huan Nghiep St., Dist. 1. ☎ 230656, 231343. FAX: 241812.*

Located just off Me Linh Square, this really is a new hotel. The best way to describe it is to say quaint. It's tight and tall, five stories, but it has one of Saigon's only B&B atmospheres. The suites facing the street are impressive and run only about US$65 a night. Cheaper singles run around $25. Friendly staff; fax; laundry, cafe. This is one of the quietest hostelries in the 1st district, yet you're right next to all the action.

**New World Hotel** **US$140–$500** ★★★★

*76 Le Dai, Dist. 1. ☎ 228888. FAX: 230710.*

To date, this is the largest hotel in Saigon and it dominates the downtown skyline. They rushed to get this thing up, and I would've given it 5 stars if it weren't for the reports I've heard about shoddy craftsmanship. Great dining and business facilities. Huge conference center. All the amenities.

**Norfolk Hotel** **US$85–$220** ★★★

*117 Le Thanh Ton, Dist. 1. ☎ 295368. FAX: 293415.*
*45 rooms.*

Located in central Saigon. Usually booked solid. Australian owners/managers. Attached bathroom; air-conditioned; well-furnished; elegant lobby; hot water; color TV with Star satellite network; wetbar; business center with secretarial services; fax; meeting facilities; restaurant; bar; rooftop BBQ.

**Omni Saigon Hotel** **US$150–$800** ★★★★

*215 Nguyen Van Troi Street; Phu Nhuan District. ☎ 449222. FAX: 449200.*
*250 rooms.*

This is an extravagant facility, opened in Feb.'94 near the airport with rooms, suites and longer term apartments. The business services here are outstanding, including fully-serviced satellite offices. Also a ballroom, health club, outdoor swimming pool, IDD, color TV, air-conditioned rooms, minibar, etc., and the full array of capitalist running-dog amenities that would have V.I. Lenin spinning in his formaldehyde.

**Orchid Hotel** **US$50** ★

*29A Don Dat Street. ☎ 231809. FAX: 231811.*
*30 rooms.*

Air-conditioned rooms; bathroom; telephones; refrigerators; bar; restaurant; coffee shop.

**Palace Hotel** **US$40–$145** ★★★

*56-64 Nguyen Hue Blvd., Dist. 1. ☎ 297284, 292860. FAX: 299872, 290457.*

Rooms have bathrooms and hot water; swimming pool; bar; restaurant; great location.

**Rang Dong Hotel** **US$25–$47**

*81 Cach Mang Thang 8, Dist. 1. ☎ 322106.*

Decent location and a clean hotel with great prices. Rooms with air conditioning, hot water, minibar and refrigerator.

**Regent Hotel**

*700 Tran Hung Dao Blvd., Dist 1. ☎ 353548. FAX: 357094.*

Also called the Hotel 700. Located in Cholon. Joint Vietnam/Thai venture.

**Rex Hotel** **US$80–$800** ★★★★

*14 Nguyen Hue Blvd., Dist. 1. ☎ 296042/3. FAX: 291269, 296536.*

*120-plus rooms.*

A favorite of American officers during the war. Enjoying a new life with the opening of tourist and business frontiers in the city. Air-conditioned; color TV; refrigerators with wet bars; three restaurants; IDD telephones; hot water; cassette players; large statuary and topiary; art gallery; dance area; business center; cinema; tailor in-house; large gift shop; tennis court; swimming pool. Expensive as hell. Get there for a drink if nothing else. See description under "What to See and Do in Ho Chi Minh City."

**Riverside Hotel** **US$25–$50**

*19 Ton Duc Thang Street. ☎ 224038. FAX: 298070.*

*34 rooms.*

Rooms have TV; telephone; refrigerator; self-contained bathrooms; business center; bar; restaurant.

**Saigon Floating Hotel** **US$119–$395** ★★★★★

*14 Me Linh Square., Dist 1. Saigon River at Hero Square on the edge of the central city. ☎ 290783. FAX: 290784.*

*200 rooms.*

Towed from Australia's Great Barrier Reef in 1989. The best hotel in Saigon, although many think a few others—such as the New World and the Saigon Omni—have eclipsed it. Floats on the Saigon River; swimming pool; tennis court; ice machines; 24-hour room service; two restaurants; business center; fitness center; saunas; conference room; disco; two bars; cafe; meeting rooms for up to 200 people; gift shop. Rooms have color TV; radio; refrigerator/wet bar; valet service; laundry service; IDD calling. Very Expensive. If it's out of your league, you can watch its lights at night from across the square on the porch of one of the hostess bars while sipping a Tiger Beer with a charming hostess.

**Saigon Hotel** **US$50** ★★

*41-47 Dông Du Street, Dist. 1. ☎ 230-231/2, 241-078, or 299-734. FAX: 84-8-291466*

*105 rooms. 16 deluxe suites.*

Room rates include breakfast, and fruit baskets and newspapers come with the deluxe suites. Children under six stay free. Satellite color TV in the deluxe rooms and suites; IDD; 24-hour service.Minibar; hot water; air conditioning; conference center; bar on the 9th floor and restaurant in the lobby. Also will do air ticket booking. Moderate.

**Saigon Lodge Hotel** **US$78–$305** ★★★

*215 Nam Ky Khoi Nghia, Dist. 3.* ☎ *230112. FAX: 251070.*

Suggested for businesspeople. Close to the business center of District 1. A little expensive. Big rooms with air conditioning, minibar & refrigerator, TV, IDD. Restaurant, bar.

**Saigon Star Hotel** **US$90–$180** ★★★

*204 Nguyen Thi Minh Khai, Dist. 3.* ☎ *230260. FAX: 230255.*

Another hotel catering primarily to business people. Business center, conference facilities.

**Sol Chancery Saigon** **US$107–$180** 

*196 Nguyen Thi Minh Khai, Dist. 3.* ☎ *299152. FAX: 251464.*

A business person's delight. All the rooms are suites, and this is one of the most comfortable and friendly business hotels in town. Recommended restaurant. Gym, sauna, business center. Nice site overlooking the main city park.

**Tan Loc Hotel** **US$50–$110** 

*177 Le Thanh Ton, Dist. 1.* ☎ *230028. FAX: 298360.*

Rooms with air conditioning, satellite TV, IDD, minibar, refrigerator. Nice restaurant.

**Thanh Binh 1 Hotel** **US$30**

*315 Hoang Van Thu, Tan Binh Dist.* ☎ *440984. FAX: 640262.*

A bargain in the boonies. Comfortable rooms with air conditioning, minibar & refrigerator, telephone.

**Victory Hotel** **US$30–$80** 

*14 Vo Van Tan, Dist. 3.* ☎ *231755. FAX: 299604.*

This place has been recently renovated and is one of the best bargains in HCMC. Three-and four-star amenities at budget prices. Recommended. Located just north of District 1's central business district.

**Vien Dong** **US$25–$50** ★

*275A Pham Ngu Lao, Dist. 1.* ☎ *393001.*

Great budget hotel. Rooms with air conditioning, hot water, telephone. Cheers disco is located here.

## Where to Eat in Ho Chi Minh City

Probably the heartiest places to eat in Saigon are at the hundreds of street stalls. For the most part they're safe, excellent and extremely inexpensive—with prices usually less than a dollar. But if you want more ambiance, there are a number of decent establishments in town. The best, and also the most expensive, are found at the better hotels. Here's a look at some of the more than 300 eateries around HCMC.

### INSIDER TIP

*As might be expected, Saigon is experiencing a degree of the "Bangkok Syndrome," an Asian City homogenizing Eastern and Western influences with the pâte of the Chao Phraya River and 30-weight motor oil. Western food is invading the palates of Saigonites like a mozzarella revolution. Four new pizza joints have opened in HCMC, in just the past few months, a couple of them not half bad. Swiss-born Danny Koeppel, sort of the Wolfgang Puck of Indochina, whose credits include more than a year at the internationally-famous Chez Guido at the Continental Hotel, has become something of a consultant to the increasingly popular pizzerias springing up around the city. His new "consultancy" venture is with the new Pizzeria Cappuccino,* 11 Ho Huan Nghiep (off Dong Khoi Street, ☎ 291051). *Because the competition is getting stiffer in Saigon, Koeppel has decided to broaden the offerings. The specialty of the house is pasta, of course. Mozzarella, as well as the anchovies, are shipped from Italy. Koeppel claims to be the first to create "spaghettata," an "island" of pasta surrounded by sauces prepared in minutes for business-people on the run. The homemade bread with a dish of chopped chilies in sauce is delicious. Ho Huan Nghiep Street is known for its bars, and a lot of people come into the eatery without the intention of investing the time in a full sit-down dinner. So try the cheeseburgers if you've got the dong (they run nearly US$4), or even a hot dog; the sausage is imported from Germany. There's also ice cream and, of course, coffee.*

**180 Restaurant** **$$$** ★

*180 Nguyen Van Thu, Dist. 1. ☎ 251673.*

Usually, restaurants names after their addresses in Vietnam are simply glamourized food stalls. Not the case here. Imported American and Australian beef. Wide drink menu; garden villa setting.

**13 Restaurant** **$**

*13 Mac Thi Buoi, Dist. 1.*

Not as fancy as the 180, but highly popular with expats, tourists and locals alike. Cafe-style. Great food, great prices.

**Ashoka** **$$$** ★

*17A-10 Le Thanh Ton, Dist. 1. ☎ 231372.*

North Indian fare. Try the chicken marinated in yogurt or tandoori. The cooking is done in traditional Indian clay ovens. Recommended, but pricey.

**A Nhat** **$$**

*86 Ngo Duc Ke, Dist. 1. ☎ 210494.*

Excellent Vietnamese fare in a French setting. Cafe-style seating.

**Annie's Pizza** **$$**

*57 Nguyen Du, Dist 1. ☎ 392577 (home deliveries) or ☎ 223661 (reservations).*

Popular family-style place for expat and Vietnamese folks. The pizzas and burgers are quite passable. Also pies and sausages. Typical of the new wave of Western fast-food/boutique settings. Also—naturally—with home delivery. Popular.

**Cafe Brodard** **$$**

*131 Dong Khoi Street.* ☎ *225-837.*

A hangout for expats, backpackers and hipsters.

**Buffalo Blues** **$$$** ★

*72A Nguyen Du, Dist. 1.* ☎ *222874.*

Great place for barbeque and jazz, but expensive. Elegant setting.

**Bavaria** **$$**

*20 Le Anh Xuan, Dist. 1.* ☎ *222673.*

Opposite the New World, this is a haunt of German expats and tourists. Don't expect a lot of English spoken, but the schnitzels and wursts are fabulous.

**Cafe Mogambo** **$$** ★

*20 Thi Sach, Dist. 1.* ☎ *251331. FAX: 226031.*

"American" bar and grill. Dark bamboo interior. Western food at Western prices. Filled every night for dinner, entirely by expats.

**Chez Guido** **$$$** ★

*Continental Hotel, 132 Dong Khoi, Dist. 1.* ☎ *299252.*

Expensive Italian cuisine; good portions. All imported ingredients

**Givral Cafe** **$$**

*169 Dong Khoi Street, Dist. 1.*

Like the Brodard, mostly expats and journalists, but better food.

**Harbor View Restaurant** **$$$**

*At the curve where Ton Duc Thang and Ben Chuong Duong Streets meet.*

Lavish eatery right on the riverfront overlooking the harbor. The food (Asian, Vietnamese, and Western) is superb but expensive. This place is frequently rented out for wedding receptions.

**Kim's Cafe** **$**

*De Tham St., Dist. 1.*

The place to be seen for the backpacker set. Reasonable food at rock-bottom prices.

**Krua Thai** **$$**

*2 Thi Sach, Dist. 1.*

The best Thai in Saigon. Excellent green and red curry dishes.

**La Bibliotheque (Madame Dai)** **$$**

*84 Nguyen Du.*

Very good Vietnamese fare and excellent beef.

**La Camargue** **$$$** ★★

*16 Cao Ba Quat, Dist. 1.* ☎ *243148. FAX: 290603.*

Goat's cheese and ratatouille tartelette, roasted whole poussin stuffed with spinach and cheese with garlic and thyme sauce. If this sounds like your kind of evening, this is your place. Bring a wad of cash.

**La Couscoussiere** **$$$** ★

*24 Nguyen Thi Manh Khai, Dist. 1. ☎ 299148.*

Persian, Indian and Arabian fare. Absolutely delicious. Great sausage, lamb, chicken and mixed grill dishes.

**Le Mekong** **$$** ★

*32 Vo Van Tan St., Dist 3. ☎ 291277.*

French fare at great prices.

**Lemon Grass** **$$**

*63 Dong Khoi, Dist. 1. ☎ 298006.*

Vietnamese and Western cuisine in a cafe-style setting.

**Le Pierrot Gourmand** **$$**

*19 Le Thanh Ton, Dist. 1. ☎ 908156.*

French cafe specializing in cakes, pastry and ice cream.

**Lotus Court** **$$$** ★

*Omni Hotel, 251 Nguyen Van Troi, Phu Nhuan Dist. ☎ 449222.*

Beijing Duck prepared by Hong Kong chefs. Get ready to spend a bundle.

**L'Etoile** **$$$** ★

*180 Hai Ba Trung. ☎ 297939.*

Elegant and expensive French and Vietnamese as you're serenaded by guitar music.

**Marina Cafe** **$$** ★

*Saigon Floating Hotel, Dist. 1. ☎ 290783.*

Great lunchtime buffet; the prices aren't too bad. Menu features U.S. steak (during the embargo, the meat was cowjacked, so I was told) and seafood. Probably the best Western food in-country.

**Marine Club** **$$**

*17A/4 Le Thanh Ton, Dist. 1. ☎ 292249.*

Brittany crabs in a setting that's a cross between Long John Silver's and Gilligan's Island.

**Maxim's** **$$$**

*13 Dong Khoi Street, Dist. 1. ☎ 299820.*

Live music, decent food, high prices.

**Napoli** **$$**

*79 Nguyen Hue, Dist. 1. ☎ 225616.*

Small, clean Italian pizzeria in the center of the business district.

**Nha Hang 5 Me Linh** **$$** ★

*Near the statue of Tran Hung Dao.*

Great Vietnamese fare. Even Cobra!

**Nha Hang 51 Nguyen Hue** **$$**

*51 Nguyen Hue Blvd.*

Ditto.

**Nhon Bashi Japanese Restaurant** **$$$** ★

*On the ground floor of the Rex Hotel.*

Excellent Japanese fare but expensive.

**Noodles Restaurant** **$$**

*72 Ngo Duc Ke, Dist. 1.* ☎ *290894.*

As the name suggests, that's what you'll get here, Japanese style. Good tempura.

**Oriental Court** **$$$**

*Saigon Floating Hotel.*

Good Asian cuisine for Western palates.

**Papaya Verte** **$$**

*33A Ben Van Don, Dist. 4.* ☎ *253652.*

French cafe style, a bit out of the way, but worth it for the prices.

**Palace Hotel** **$$$** ★

*15th floor restaurant.*

The best view of Saigon in town.

**Pho Dien Bien** **$** 

*165 Dien Bien Phu, Dist. 1.* ☎ *290286.*

One of the best-kept secrets in Saigon. Not any longer. Local eatery. Great food. Cheap prices.

**Red Rhino** **$$** ★

*8A/1/D2 Don Dat, Dist 1.* ☎ *292216.*

One of the newer and trendier eateries/bars in town. Excellent seafood. Western and Vietnamese dishes. Reasonably priced. Recommended.

**Restaurant A (The Russian Restaurant)** **$$** 

*361/8 Nguyen Dinh Chieu, Dist. 3.* ☎ *359190.*

Azerbaijan-style dishes along with blintzes, borscht, caviar and black bread. For Russian, this is Saigon's best (if not only).

**Restaurant Ami** **$$$** 

*170 Pasteur, Dist. 1.* ☎ *242198.*

Extensive and expensive wine list. Mostly expat clientele. French. Expensive.

**Restaurant Huong Rung** **$$** 

*462 Pham The Hien Street, District 8.* ☎ *55323.*

This is one of the most bizarre dining experiences in HCMC. Eccentric owner Tran Van Kien has created a setting where live pythons, cobras, iguanas, lizards, and all sorts of other reptiles and birds freely roam the environs of this posh and expensive restaurant. While eating such exotic delicacies as cream of goat testicles soup, you may suddenly find a snake slithering into your pants pocket or a turtle traversing your beef satay. This seems to be a popular place with noisy expats drinking vats of Tiger beer.

**Restaurant Vietnam Indochine** **$$$** ★

*173 Nguyen Van Troi, Phu Nhuan Dist.* ☎ *444236.*

Vietnamese with a French twist. Superb and expensive. Opened only recently.

**Rex Garden Restaurant** **$$**

*86 Le Thanh, Dist 1.* ☎ *292186.*

The only place in town with both a tennis court and a tank as backdrops for dining. In back of the Rex. A little pricey and curiously nearly always close to empty.

**Saigon Cafe** **$**

*De Tham Street, Dist 1.*

Backpacker hangout on De Tham.

**Saigon Times Club** **$$$** ★

*37 Nam Ky Khoi Nghia, Dist. 1. ☎ 298676.*

Great Vietnamese. Dark atmosphere. Vietnamese yuppies and live music.

**Saigon Lodge Hotel** **$$** ★

*215 Nam Ky Khoi Nghia, Dist. 3. ☎ 230112.*

For Malaysian, this may be the best in town. Malay Muslim, Chinese and Western dishes.

**Sapa** **$$**

*8A/8 Don Dat, Dist 1. ☎ 295783.*

Swiss and Vietnamese fare. Outdoor setting.

**Sinh Cafe** **$**

*6 Pham Ngu Lao Street.*

A good mingling place for travelers.

**Tex-Mex** **$$**

*24 Le Thanh Ton, Dist. 1. ☎ 295950.*

The bar's the best thing going here. A French attempt at Mexican. Taco Bell authenticity.

**Thuan Tuan** **$$**

*3/6 Nguyen Van Thu, Dist 1. ☎ 244051.*

Specializes in lamb dishes. Small, family-style place.

**Veranda** **$$$** ★

*Saigon Floating Hotel.*

International cuisine.

**Vietnam House** **$$$** ★

*93-95 Dong Khoi Street. ☎ 291623.*

Posh. Expensive Vietnamese cuisine. Live, traditional Vietnamese music performances accompany dinner. Attentive and friendly service. But I've heard that they've re-served food that wasn't eaten by other customers. Maybe a disgruntled former employee.

**Yeebo** **$$**

*97B Ham Nghi, Dist. 1.*

Cantonese and seafood.

## Nightlife in Ho Chi Minh City

Over the last few years, dozens of trendy nightspots have sprung up all over the city. Many of the hipper spots are opening up along District 1's Thi Sach Street. Thi Sach means "beer street" to the Saigonese. It's appropriate. If you're into nightlife, it'll be tough to get bored in Saigon. Imagine saying that 10 years ago. This town is starting to rock.

## Bars

**Apocalypse Now** ★

*2c Thi Sach, District 1.*

This is the hangout for grungers in Saigon. Blaring rock music din in a cavelike setting. This place has been around for a few years but just recently moved to the new location in the expat ghetto around Thi Sach, the East Village of Saigon. Loud tunes, pool table, relatively cheap beer and the recent arrival of "comfort ladies." Does a booming T-shirt business.

**Buffalo Blues** ★

*72A Nguyen Du, Dist. 1. ☎ 222874.*

A spotlessly clean and elegant New Orleans-type jazz club. Once in a while, it gets some out-of-town acts to complement the house band, the Jazz Brothers Band. Frequented by expat businesspeople. Serves Bass Ale and Tennent's Lager. Worth a stop, but it's rather expensive.

**Cay Thung**

*20 Mac Thi Buoi, Dist. 1.*

A good, cheap bar but lacking the "action" of some of HCMC's other venues. Some outdoor tables. Quiet, but a good stop with a date or a few friends.

**Doors Pub** ★

*10 Pham Ngu Lao, Dist 1.*

Not a bar to let your hair down in, but the atmosphere's cozy and they show American movies in the early evening. Cheap prices for beer and other beverages. Serves snacks and light meals.

**Gecko Bar** ★

*74/1A Hai Ba Trung, Dist. 1. ☎ 242754.*

Small bar with a good crowd of regulars. This is the place to go if you miss your Boddington's.

**I Don't Know the Name of This Place** ★★

*Off Cach Mang Thang Tam, about 200 meters from the circle next to the New World Hotel, Dist. 1.*

I really don't know the name of this bustling, loud and get-loose outdoor bar. But it's great. Waiters serve mussels and milk-baskets full of Saigon beer to your table as you're serenaded by beautiful Vietnamese girls in Johnnie Walker T-shirts cooing you into buying a sample drink or three from the bottles they carry around. Almost an all-Vietnamese crowd. The action's loud until only about 9, then the place gets dead quick. Definitely make a stop here and then tell me what the bloody name of the place is!

**Press Club** ★

*Corner of Hai Ba Trung and Le Duan, Dist. 1.*

Semi-outdoor cafe/bar that's a great place to bring a date. Mostly a Vietnamese clientele, mixed with foreigners. Especially cozy when it rains. My only complaint is that the Vietnamese pseudo-techno rock is played way too loud for the ambiance. This is a place for conversation, and the two don't mix. Recommended, though.

Run by the Ho Chi Minh Journalist's Assn. Art exhibits are occasionally presented here.

**Q Bar** 

*Saigon Opera House (Theater) opposite the Caravelle Hotel, Dong Khoi, Dist. 1.*
This is where the movers and shakers retire to martinis and business news in Saigon. Run by an expat New Yorker, the Q Bar is becoming what the Rex and the Caravelle were to expats during the war. Elegant and expensive. Better to be in suit than thongs here.

**Rex Hotel Terrace Bar** 

*141 Nguyen Hue, Dist. 1. ☎ 292185.*
This is the famous rooftop bar of the Rex Hotel where so many American officers nursed cognacs while bitching about Neil Sheehan and Jane Fonda. Sculpted shrubbery and totally outrageous cocktail prices. A single small-pour Johnnie Walker will set you back seven bucks U.S. Worth it only to say you've been there.

**River Bar** 

*5-7 Ho Huan Nghiep, Dist. 1. ☎ 293734.*
A great place for burgers and beer. The music's only okay, but there's a pool table and satellite TV for sports and news freaks.

**Saigon Headlines** 

*Saigon Opera House (Theater), opposite the Continental Hotel, Dist. 1.*
This was the "Q Bar" of Saigon before the Q Bar came around. Low, Moorish ceiling arches (watch your head) separate areas of the bar like caverns in a cave. Now that the full-wallet expat crowd has moved over to the Q Bar, SH has been taken over by Saigonese yuppies. Live music by musical chairs Vietnamese pop performers. Worth a stop if only to see inside.

**Stephanie's**

*14 Don Dat, Dist. 1. ☎ 258471.*
Australian steaks and cold beer. Pool tables upstairs. A good place if you live here, but it can be skipped by tourists in for a night-on-the-town.

**Tex-Mex**

*24 Le Thanh Ton, Dist. 1. ☎ 295950.*
After hearing that a genuine south-of-the-border kind of place with real quesadillas, chile verde burritos and Dos Equis beer had opened in town, I—hailing from close to the border myself—was thrilled. But I was in for a letdown. The place is more French than salsa. More mocking than authentic. I'll just have to wait for the next "hog" run with the boys down to San Felipe.

### Bia Hoi

In addition to the tourists and expat hangouts, no visit to Saigon is complete without a stop at one or more of the hundreds of *bia hoi* (fresh beer) joints in the city. Although more abundant and popular in the north of Vietnam—where the Vietnamese swill some 100,000 liters of the stuff every day—there are plenty of food-stallish *bia hoi* venues in the heart of HCMC.

*Bia hoi* is so fresh and perishable that it has to be consumed within 24 hours of being produced. With less chemical content than bottled beer ( *bia hoi* has a similar alcohol content—but it's the chemicals that usually cause a hangover) *bia hoi* has become the lifeblood of Vietnamese men. *Bia hoi* was only introduced to Vietnam about 30 years ago from Czechoslovakia with the arrival of the Czech *houblom* yeast. You can get drunk on the stuff, but it's not as easy as imbibing bottled or canned beer. Small *bia hoi* stalls can be found throughout the city (and are even more numerous in Hanoi). They're typically sidewalk perches where the owner has thrown out a few stools. They're dirty looking, and the brew attracts flies the way—well, you know. The conditions under which the beverage is consumed naturally keep all the tourists away—grungy-looking stalls and sticky floors strewn with cigarette butts, dried squid, peanut shells, goat meat, snake meat, fish sauce and stray, mangy dogs.

## WHAT TO EAT WITH BIA HOI

*No bia hoi experience is complete without sampling the gourmet cuisine that is served with it. May your taste buds tingle in delight.*

| | |
|---|---|
| **Chan Ga** | *Boiled chicken feet (mmm!)* |
| **Dau Phu** | *Soya cake* |
| **Khoai tay ran** | *Chips* |
| **Lac** | *Peanuts* |
| **Muc** | *Dried squid* |
| **Nem chua** | *Spring rolls* |
| **Nhong** | *Silkworm (plenty of protein!)* |
| **Nom** | *Salad* |
| **Nuoc mam** | *Fish sauce* |
| **Oc** | *Snail (gimmee more!)* |
| **Thit bo xao** | *Fried beef* |
| **Thit cho** | *Dog (Lassie—mmmm!)* |
| **Thit de** | *Goat meat in fish sauce* |
| **Thit ran** | *Snake (chase it quickly)* |

In the south, *bia hoi* is produced by the Saigon and Dong Nai breweries—in the north by the Halida and Hanoi breweries. Vietnamese from all levels of society congregate together when the *bia hoi* barrels are tapped. And they can afford it. *Bia hoi* sells at 2000-3000 dong a glass—a large glass.

*Bia hoi* has been so popular since the mid-'60s, the Vietnamese once had to be rationed the brew. With coupons in hand, they queued at state-run stores waiting for their meager two glasses a day. However, now *bia hoi* is everywhere. But not all the time. The brew is so popular that many stalls run out of their daily supply by mid-day. Most of the stuff is gone by the early evening.

Want to hoist a few?

**Thanh Nha** 

*6 Hai Ba Trung, Dist. 1.*

This is my favorite *bia hoi* stall in Saigon. It's one of the cleaner venues in town (or at least it looks something akin to a bar—i.e., there's a roof over your head). But the flies abound and your hands just may get stuck to the table. It's one of the bigger *bia hoi* stalls around. If you're timid, but have been lured by the above words, this place will make a great introduction.

**Bia Hoi** 

*20-26 Thi Sach, Dist. 1.*

This is my second choice. More foreigners here, who have already gotten their feet wet, literally.

**Bia Hoi Dong Nai** 

*1 Nguyen Sieu, Dist. 1.*

Another popular stall that sees some foreigners from time to time.

**Bia Hoi** 

*79 Nguyen Dinh Chieu, Dist. 3.*

This place is packed all throughout the day. Few foreigners.

**The Garage** 

*90G Tran Quoc Toan, Dist. 3.*

As authentic as they come. You'll be greeted with smiles and back-patting, and the stories of toothless old war vets.

## Nightclubs

**Cheers**

*Vien Dong Hotel, 275 Pham Ngu Lao, Dist.1. ☎ 392116.*

Hostess disco that attracts a large Chinese clientele at times. Cross between a pub and a disco. The karaoke seems more popular than anything else. Private karaoke rooms with English- and Chinese-speaking hostesses.

**Cinta** 

*Saigon Lodge Hotel, 215 Nam Ky Khoi Nghia, Dist. 3. ☎ 230112.*

Depending on the night, you'll find expats, locals or tourists. European, Asian and American DJs at the helm play contemporary Western and Asian pop hits. Popular.

**Down Under Disco**

*Floating Hotel, 1A Me Linh Square, Dist. 1. ☎ 290783.*

Man, are the cocktails expensive here. Come to dance and wear your best threads. The youth of Saigon's elite call this place home, as curious well-heeled tourists gawk and peek—and sometimes dance.

**Hai Van Disco**

*Hai Van Hotel, 69 Huynh Thuc Khang, Dist. 1. ☎ 291274.*

This place, on the third floor of the hotel, gets packed—almost entirely with Vietnamese. But the odd thing about it is its hours. The most popular time to be boogying away to the live music here is 10 a.m. Sunday mornings! Or even more bizarre, at 2 p.m. Monday afternoons! And yet it's closed 11 p.m. Saturday nights. You figure it out.

**Orient Club**

*104 Hai Ba Trung, Dist. 1.* ☎ *222547.*

More popular with locals than with foreigners. This place is dark, the way young Vietnamese couples like it. Mostly Vietnamese "white" pop.

**Saxophone Bar**

*New World Hotel, 76 Le Lai, Dist. 1.* ☎ *228888.*

What you'd expect at a five-star hotel. On Saturday nights, it becomes pretty busy. Mainly Asian clientele dancing to spun music and the occasional international live act.

**Starlight Nightclub & Disco**

*Century Saigon Hotel, 68A Nguyen Hue, Dist. 1.* ☎ *231818.*

Way up on the 11th floor for some great views of Saigon when the action's slow. The disco recently introduced an expat night on Thursdays to attract those who have been staying away.

**Venus Club**

*Saigon Star Hotel, 204 Nguyen Thi Minh Khai, Dist. 3.* ☎ *230260.*

Better for the karaoke than for the disco, which is too small.

## Shopping in Ho Chi Minh City

### Cosmetics & Perfumes

**Angela**

*132 Dong Khoi, Dist. 1.*

Very expensive and specializing in Maybelline and Christian Dior products. Behind the Continental Hotel.

**Fuji Cosmetics**

*96 Nam Ky Khoi Nghia. Dist 1.* ☎ *223100.*

Small little shop in the downtown area with Fuji, Revlon, Max Factor and Chifune products available.

**Paris Beaute**

*127 Le Thanh Ton, Dist. 1.*

Cosmetics shop that specializes in Joseph, Eclat d'Ete, Masculin and Galenie products.

### Sporting Goods, Clothing & Fashion

**Ben Thanh Market**

*At the intersection of Le Loi and Pham Hong Thai, Dist 1.*

Some of the best bargains in Saigon are found here. But be warned that much of the clothing is counterfeit.

**Dung Cu**

*82B Nguyen Thi Minh Khai, Dist. 3.*

All types of sports equipment, from tennis rackets to golf clubs. Sportswear, as well.

**Eskmo**

*82B Nguyen Thi Minh Khai, Dist 3.*
A small, elegant shop for women. European designs.

**Haia**

*68 Ly Tu Trong, Dist. 1. ☎ 295085.*
A wide selection of sports shoes from Reebok, Nike, etc. And some of them are real!

**Khanh Dang Silk & Fashion**

*112 Nguyen Hue, Dist. 1. ☎ 296708.*
One of the best places for silk in HCMC. Everything from suits to T-shirts. Tailored men's silk shirts and trousers, as well as ties. Dresses for women. Material. Recommended.

**Kim Phuong**

*39B Ngo Duc Ke, Dist. 1. ☎ 225665.*
Silk products and tapestries. Beautiful tablecloths.

**Ly Ly**

*229 Ly Tu Trong, Dist. 1.*
Sportswear and swimming attire.

**Minh Doan**

*120 Le Thanh Ton, Dist. 1. ☎ 231687.*
Custom-tailored European styles for men and women.

**Moiselle Collection**

*128C Hai Ba Trung, Dist. 1. ☎ 295579.*
Women's dresses and business suits, all custom-tailored.

**Tropic**

*73A Le Thanh Ton, Dist. 1. ☎ 297542.*
Brand-new silk shop which offers lingerie, embroidery and linen for the home.

### Jewelry

Most jewelry in Saigon is sold along Le Loi and Dong Khoi Streets. Numerous shops offer gold as well as stones. Be warned that items aren't particularly a bargain. Better bargains on gold can be had in Cambodia.

**Alpha**

*163 Dong Khoi, Dist. 1. ☎ 258356.*
Gold and silver items in the heart of the shopping district.

**Saigon Girl**

*176 Ly Tu Trong, Dist. 1.*
Popular with European tourists for clothing as well as jewelry and cosmetics.

### Art

**Hoang Hac**

*73 Ly Tu Trong, Dist. 3. ☎ 223198.*
Large collection of abstract and contemporary oil paintings.

**Tu Do Art Gallery** ★

*142 Dong Khoi, Dist. 1. ☎ 298540.*

This gallery offers the finest selection of oil and lacquer artwork in town, as well as silk prints. Vietnam's most prominent artists are represented here, including Thu Ha, Bui Ngoc Tu and Nguyen Pham. Recommended.

### Food

**Citimart** ★

*235 Nguyen Van Cu, Dist. 5. ☎ 358692.*

The largest and best supermarket in HCMC. Name it and it's here: imported foods, wines, clothing, jewelry, toys, household items.

**Donamart** ★

*63 Ly Tu Trong, Dist. 1. ☎ 244808.*

Big supermarket in central Saigon where most expats do their shopping. Good selection of imported foods as well as other household items. Expensive. Restaurant upstairs.

**Mademoiselle de Paris**

*249 Le Thanh Ton, Dist 1. ☎ 222890.*

French food and wines. Next to Ben Thanh Market.

**Nhu Lan** ★

*66 Ham Nghi, Dist. 1.*

Some say this is the best bakery in town, but it's getting tough to tell these days, with a proliferation of boutique food shops opening in HCMC. Cheeses, meats, breads, cakes, sandwiches.

**Saigon Food Center**

*393b Tran Hung Dao, Dist. 1.*

Brand-new connoisseurs' market that's splashy and expensive. Best bet for pastries, cakes and cheeses. More a series of deserted restaurants and banquet rooms than a market. It doesn't seem to do a roaring business.

**Sana Epicerie** ★

*35 Dong Du, Dist 1.*

A good place to stock up on meats, sausages, wines, champagne, chocolates—and Bass Ale.

**Shop 125** ★

*125 Le Thanh Ton, Dist 1.*

Fancy new establishment offering an array of liquors and soft drinks, as well as food.

**7-Eleven Gesevina**

*16 Nguyen Hue, Dist. 1. ☎ 290046.*

Nice selection of fine foods. Specializes in ice cream and—yes, they have arrived—Slurpees.

## Sports in Ho Chi Minh City

What would have been unheard of 10 years ago is a reality today, as HCMC is beginning to resemble Los Angeles more than Moscow. All types of sporting activities are available today, including golf and even betting on horses.

## Golf Courses

### Golf Vietnam Thu Duc

*An Phu Village, Thu Duc.* ☎ *960756.*

I don't know how they keep the fairways in shape here, but they do. Not a particularly challenging course for the seasoned golfer, it's still a helluvalot of fun to be playing golf in Vietnam. Full, 18-hole course with driving range, clubhouse, 19th hole. You'll need to hire a caddy here. And, yes, you—Joe Public—can call ahead and get a starting time. But be prepared to shell out some cash. Green fees are US$80.

### Song Be Club

*Thuan Giao Commune, Thuan An Dist., Song Be Province.* ☎ *(65) 55800.*

This is perhaps the area's better course, but it's open to members only at press time. 18 holes, par 72, 6647-meter course. Song Be is about 20 km north of HCMC. Get a member to invite you.

## Horse Racing

### Phu Tho Club

*2 Le Dai Hanh, Dist. 11.* ☎ *551205.*

Nice track with a VIP club overlooking the venue. Racing on Saturday and Sunday afternoons, and on twoTuesdays per month. You can place bets here between 1000-50,000d on the first two places (*quinellas*). Long distance cycling events are also held here.

## Gyms & Fitness Centers

### Cu Ta The Hinh Club

*Phan Dinh Phung Stadium Annex, 132 Pasteur, Dist. 3.*

Gym with a less than modern weight training system. But it's still a good place for a heavy workout. Be warned: there's no air conditioning here. You'll fry.

### World Gym

*26 Le Thanh Ton, Dist. 1.* ☎ *295950.*

This is where most of the expats go. Imported, relatively modern weight equipment. Sauna, fitness instruction, custom training programs.

## Directory

### INSIDER TIP: VIETNAM'S BURGEONING MOTORBIKE PROBLEM

*Saigon is one of the most dangerous cities in the world to travel through via car, bicycle, motorbike and motorcycle. To the uninitiated, two-wheeled traffic here is so overwhelmingly intimidating that few Westerners venture into traffic through their own means. And the motorcycle problem in HCMC is only going to get worse. In 1995, there were 2.7 million registered motorbikes on the streets of Vietnam, compared to only 600,000 in 1990. Honda accounts for about 70% of these machines. And more than 400,000 motorbikes and motorcycles are imported into the country each year. Most come from Japan, Taiwan, Korea, Indonesia, Singapore, Thailand, Russia and Germany. But an increasing number of the machines are being smuggled into Vietnam through the Cambodian border. In 1993, 200,000 motorcycles were registered in HCMC alone, bringing the total number of motorbikes in the city to 1,060,000. Motorbike imports reached 350,000 a year in 1995, and will rise to 500,000 annually until the year 2000. This is making congestion virtually unbearable. The number of motorbikes—many dangerously traversing Vietnamese streets—has seriously hampered HCMC's mass transit capabilities. Quite simply, the Vietnamese's increasing ability to purchase motorbikes has far outpaced the government's ability to improve the traffic network. If you have the insane inclination to rent a motorbike in Saigon, remember this important regulation: For any bike you rent over 50cc, you must possess an international driver's license. Vietnamese themselves are not permitted to own or operate a motorcycle more than 175cc, although foreigners are permitted to rent bikes with far greater power (which you'll greatly appreciate on good roads out in the provinces on long journeys). A Vietnamese spotted by the police on a big motorcycle will invariably be pulled over, although foreigners rarely are. (I have been pulled over by the police, however, without violating any Vietnamese law.)*

### Transportation

Ho Chi Minh City is 1710 km from Hanoi, 1071 km from Hue, 965 km from Danang, 445 km from Nha Trang, 340 km from Ha Tien, 300 km from Dalat, 250 from Rach Gia, 165 km from Can Tho, 115 from Vung Tau, 147 from Vinh Long and 72 km from My Tho.

**By air:**

Downtown Ho Chi Minh City is about a 20-minute ride (8 km) from the airport (Tan Son Nhat Airport). It's a relatively modern airport by Southeast Asian standards, but still is far from the likes of Bangkok's Don Muang or Singapore's Changi Airports. But the facilities here are quite a bit better than at Hanoi's Noi Bai Airport. If you do a lot of international traveling, do not let your film, computerized camera, laptop computers, etc., go through the airport's primitive X-Ray machines although they display signs in English saying they are "film safe," which simply means that your equipment won't actually melt or come out the other side as an Egg McMuffin.

There is a branch of the Vietcom Bank here for changing money, as well as Vietnamtourism, Saigontourist and Cuu Long Tourist offices. There is also a post office here. Don't rely on any of the tourist organizations for hotel suggestions if you're on a budget. Instead, just outside the airport, you will find at the taxi stand an acceptable list of accommodations in Saigon with their prices posted. Many backpackers arrive at the airport without any idea as to where they'll be staying, but instead rely on travel guides that often list accommodations that simply don't exist anymore. Remember, hotels in Saigon are generally quite expensive, and if you're only planning on spending US$3–5 a night here, be prepared to share your "room" with various other manifestations of Southeast Asian life forms.

Use the list at the taxi stand to determine where you'll spend at least your first night in HCMC. You should choose a hotel in the US$10–20 range, and one preferably close to District 1 (Downtown Saigon).Get a feel for the city and where other travelers are staying, but don't do this at the bar atop the Rex Hotel. Be sure that all your paperwork is in order, and carry additional passport photos than the required three. Any lapse in presenting the correct documents will send you back to the end of the customs lines, which have become massive waits in recent months with the armies of tourists arriving in Vietnam. If you're an American, at the time of this writing, your visa will not be stamped into your passport, but instead will be a separate document with your picture attached. You'll also need additional photos for your declaration forms. If you don't have the necessary photos, there is a desk behind the customs area where you can have the photos taken. But this can take as long as customs processing itself.

Upon arrival at HCMC airport, assuming everything is kosher, it'll take more than an hour before you're on the street. Outside the airport are numerous touts with license badges attached to their shirts signifying they are official taxi drivers. They will swarm upon you like bees on new lotus blossoms. By taxi, you shouldn't pay any more than US$8 to get to your destination. There are regular international connections to Jakarta, Bangkok, Manila, Kuala Lumpur, Singapore, Vientiane, Moscow, Paris, Frankfurt, and Amsterdam (to list a few) on airlines including Vietnam Airlines, Air France, Philippine Airlines, Garuda Indonesia, Thai, Lao Aviation, SK Air, MAS, Singapore Airlines—and soon on Delta and United.

**By bus:**

The **Mien Tay** terminal (in An Lac, about 10 km west of HCMC) serves the Mekong Delta. To get there, take Hau Giang or Hung Vuong Blvds. west from Cholon. ☎ *255955*). It is quite a distance southwest of town on Hung Vuong Blvd., and serves the Mekong Delta area, including My Tho, Vinh Long, Can Tho, Chau Doc, Rach Gia, Long Xuyen, Long An, Ca Mau, and other delta locations. Buses to points north, including Phan Thiet (6 hours), Vung Tau 3 hours), Dalat (8 hours), Nha Trang (11 hours), Qui Nhon (17 hours), Danang (25 hours) and Hue (29 hours)—as well as other locations—depart from HCMC's **Mien Dong** terminal, which is on the north side of the city on Xo Viet Nghe Tinh Street off National Highway 13 near the Saigon River. Wake up early, as the express buses leave between 5 and 5:30 a.m. Purchase your tickets a day in advance for both terminals.

(Note: Express buses receive priority treatment at ferry crossings and, although I've heard horror stories of tourists waiting an hour or more to cross the two rivers by ferry from HCMC to Can Tho, I've never had to wait more than just a few moments. Automobiles and motorcycles also receive priority treatment at the ferry crossings.) Book your tickets in advance—although, in many instances, you won't need to, as they depart when they are full (first come, first serve). You can also take a bus to Cambodia's Phnom Penh, which leaves from the Phnom Penh Bus Garage at *155 Nguyen Hue Blvd.* You'll need a Cambodian visa; tickets are cheap (about US$5 one way) and the trip takes from 10–12 hours, although I've heard of some taking as few as 8 hours due to a lack of delays at the border.

**By microbus:**

You can also travel by microbus (or minibus), which has become an increasingly popular form of travel for Overseas Vietnamese, Vietnamese, and foreign tourists. However, there never seem to be any permannent departure points for these vehicles. Hotels are the best places to ask about microbus service. There is a microbus office at *39 Nguyen Hue Blvd.* Buses here leave for Dalat, Vung Tau, Nha Trang, Hue, Danang and Qui Nhon. Another office, I was told, is at *89-91 Nguyen Du Street.*

**By train:**

The Saigon railway station (Ga Hoa Hung) is about 2 km from District 1 and has regular daily connections with all points north of Saigon. If you're going anywhere by train for more than eight hours, get a sleeping berth. The trip to Hanoi can take from between 40–50 hours. Ouch! Foreigners are charged extraordinarily more for tickets than are Vietnamese. To get to the dilapidated station, take Cach Mang Thang Tam Street to the turn-off at *132/9.* Or take the roundabout at *Cach Mang Tam Street* and *3 Thang 2 Blvd.* A cyclo ride from the city center should cost between US$.50–1. Train schedules change, so it's nearly pointless to list them here.

**By ferry:**

To get down to the Mekong Delta, go to the ferry landing on Ton Duc Thang Street at the end of Ham Ngi Blvd. To get to Can Tho takes about a day and costs US$1. To Chau Doc, count on another 12 hours and an additional 2000 dong. There are also high speed river **hydrofoils** that make the trip to Vung Tau down the Saigon River from near the Harbor restaurant on Ton Duc Thang and Ham Nghi Streets. It's an exhilarating and fast ride (about 1.5 hours) but expensive (US$10).

**By car:**

Cars with drivers rent for anywhere between US$40–70 a day from HCMC travel agents. However, there are many private operators who hang out in the square next to Reunification Hall and will undercut the tourist and travel agents. To the Cu Chi tunnels, a car can be had for about US$50; although this is only a half-day trip, most of the tourist companies will insist that the minimum car rental period is a full day. Also, some of the larger hotels can provide autos, but filled with five passengers, for as low as US$30 a day. Check around.

Getting around Saigon is easy and cheap. **Cyclos** are the slowest but cheapest form of transportation (the drivers that hang out at the more expensive hotels usually charge more), but you can also rent **bicycles** from numerous hotels and bike rental shops throughout the city for 8000–10,000 dong per day. Negotiate. You can also rent small **motorbikes** such as Honda Cubs and Dreams for as little as US$6 per day. I recommend **Kolo Rentals** at *7 Lam Son Square* (across from the Continental Hotel). ☎ *296499*. They'll rent even larger bikes if you've got the proper international drivers license.If you break down within a 100 km radius, they will provide the necessary repairs free of charge.

### Taxi Services

**Saigon Taxi:** ☎ *448888*

**VINA Taxi:** ☎ *422888, 442170*

**Mai Linh:** ☎ *424242 (lowest rates)*

**Saigon Airport Service Co.:** ☎ *295925*

**Phnom Penh Bus:** ☎ *230754*

### Banks and Moneychangers

**Vietcom Bank** is located across the city, at Nguyen Hue Blvd. across from the Rex, at *123 Dong Khoi Street*, and a large main branch on Ben Chuong Duong and Nam Ky Khoi Nghia Streets. **The Foreign Exchange** bank is located at *101 Nam Ky Khoi Nghia Street* (Vietcom as mentioned above). There is also a Vietcom bank at the airport's international terminal.

Many foreign banks have now opened offices in Saigon. **Bangkok Bank Ltd.** has a branch on Nguyen Hue Blvd about halfway from the Rex to the River. The **Thai Military Bank** is also in Saigon, and banking with them you have the advantage of withdrawing funds directly from the office in Saigon even though your account may be in Thailand. Bangkok Bank offers no such service. Remember, at many banks, you will not be permitted to convert dong into dollars.

You can also change money at hotels, although the rate you may receive is 10,000 for every dollar (if you change small amounts), whereas the official exchange rate is 10,900-11,000 dong to the dollar. Some hotels will offer rates as high as 10,900 dong to the dollar—not bad considering the hotels aren't banks. You can also change money in jewelry and gold shops at favorable rates, but don't change money on the street. At the various markets around HCMC you will be approached by black marketers offering to exchange money. Keep in mind that 50 or so foreign banks have recently opened offices in HCMC, and the number rises daily.

*A portait of Ho Chi Minh dominates Saigon's General Post Office.*

### General Post Office

*2 Cong Xa Paris*, next to the Notre Dame cathedral, open from 7:30 a.m.–10:00 p.m. every day. There are international telephone and fax connections here, although you won't be able to make a collect call overseas without getting a Vietnamese to do it for you.

### TNT International Express

*406 Nguyen Tat Thanh Street.* ☎ *222886* or *225520.*

### DHL Worldwide Express

At the GPO. The major hotels such as the Rex and the Saigon Floating Hotel offer all types of international business services.

### Federal Express

In the GPO buliding, but through a separate entrance on the left hand side of the building near the corner of Hai Ba Trung. International courier Services.

### Foreign Affairs Office

*6 Thai Van Lung Street.* ☎ *223032* or *224124.*

### Immigration Office

*161 Nguyen Du Street.* ☎ *299398.*

### Hospitals

**Cho Ray Hospital.** *Nguyen Chi Thanh Blvd.*

### Airlines

**Vietnam Airlines**

(International Office) *116-118 Nguyen Hue Blvd.* ☎ *292118.* Across from the Rex next to City Hall. (Domestic Office) *15 Dinh Tien Hoang Street.* ☎ *299980.*

**Air France**

*130 Dong Khoi Street.* ☎ *230746.*

**Pacific Airlines**

*27B Nguyen Dinh Chieu Street.* ☎ *200978*

**MAS**

*116 Nguyen Hue Blvd, just above the VN office.* ☎ *292118.*

**Singapore Airlines**

*6 Le Loi Street.* ☎ *231583*

**Cathay Pacific**

*49 Le Thanh Ton Street.* ☎ *223272.*

**KLM Royal Dutch Airlines**

*244 Pasteur Street, Quan 3.* ☎ *231990, 231991. FAX: 231989*

**EVA Air**

*129 Dong Khoi Street.* ☎ *22488. FAX: 223567*

**China Airlines**

*132-134 Dong Khoi Street.* ☎ *251387/9: FAX: 251390*

**Quantas**

*311 Dien Bien Phu Street.* ☎ *396194. FAX: 396199*

**Philippine Airlines**

☎ *292200*

**Thai Airways**

*116 Nguyen Hue Blvd.* ☎ *223365.*

## Tourist Offices

**Saigontourist**

*49 Le Thanh Ton Street.* ☎ *295834. FAX: 224987.*

**Vietnamtourism**

*69-71 Nguyen Hue Blvd.* ☎ *290772. FAX: 290775.*

## Private Tour Operators

**Diethelm Travel**

*International Business Center, 1A Me Linh Square, Dist. 1.* ☎ *294932. FAX: 294747.*
Diethelm is a giant in Southeast Asia, with offices in all major Asian cities.

**Fiditourist**

*71-75 Dong Khoi, Dist. 1.* ☎ *296264. FAX: 223571.*
Package tours and air ticket booking.

**Hung Vai Travel**

*110A Nguyen Hue, Dist. 1.* ☎ *225111.*
Specializes in business, research and investment tours for businesspeople. Visa services, car rentals, ticket booking.

**Mai Linh Tours**

*32 Nguyen Hue, Dist. 1.* ☎ *224491.*
Specializes in tours to the northern part of the country, as well as to Cambodia and Laos.

**Media Service**

*4C Le Thanh Ton, Dist. 1. ☎ 294600. FAX: 295126.*
French company specializing in housing, warehouse rentals.

**Minh Chau**

*39/3 Tran Nhat Duat, Dist. 1. ☎ 442807. FAX: 439471.*
Specialists in Laos and Cambodia. Veterans' tours and Central Highlands trekking. Business introductions.

**Saigon Shipchanco**

*2 Nguyen Hue, Dist 1. ☎ 292424.*
Boat cruises up and down the Saigon river in less than luxurious vessels.

**Superbco**

*110A Nguyen Hue, Dist. 1. ☎ 225111. FAX: 242405.*
One of the best in HCMC. Specializes in all in-country tours and veterans' tours. Comprehensive services.

**T&P Reisen**

*Saigon Business Center, 57 Dong Du, Dist. 1. ☎ 904340. FAX: 298155.*
Caters to German tourists and specializes in Indochina.

**Voiles Vietnam**

*17 Pham Ngoc Thach, Dist. 3. ☎ 296750, 231589. FAX: 231591.*
Specializes in custom junk tours along the Mekong River and Nha Trang. Also offers land services.

### Consulates in Ho Chi Minh City

**Australia**

*The Landmark Bldg., 5B Ton Duc Thang Street, District 1. ☎ 296035.*

**Belgium**

*397B Vo Van Tan, District 3. ☎ 390239.*

**Cambodia**

*41 Phung Khac Hoan Street, District 1. ☎ 294498.*

**China**

*39 Nguyen Thi Minh Khai Street, District 1. ☎ 292457.*

**Cuba**

*23 Phung Khac Hoan Street, District 1 . ☎ 295818, 297350.*

**Czech Republic**

*176 Nguyen Van Thu Street, District 1. ☎ 291475.*

**Denmark**

*23 Phung Khac Khoan, District 1. ☎ 230156*

**France**

*27 Nguyen Thi Minh Khai Street, District 3. ☎ 297231.*

**Germany**

*126 Nguyen Dinh Chieu Street, District 3. ☎ 291967.*

**Hungary**

*22 Phung Khac Hoan Street, District 1. ☎ 290130.*

**India**

*49 Tran Quoc Thao, District 3.* ☎ *294498.*

**Indonesia**

*18 Phung Khac Hoan, District 1.* ☎ *223799.*

**Japan**

*13-17 Nguyen Hue, District 1.* ☎ *291341*

**Korea (South)**

*107 Nguyen Du, District 1.* ☎ *225836*

**Laos**

*181 Hai Ba Trung Street, District 1.* ☎ *299262, 297667.*

**Malaysia**

*53 Nguyen Dinh Chieu Street, District 3.* ☎ *299023.*

**New Zealand**

*455 Nguyen Dinh Chieu, District 3.* ☎ *396227.*

**Poland**

*2b Tran Cao Van Street, District 1.* ☎ *292215, 290114.*

**Russia**

*40 Ba Huyen Thanh Quan Street, District 3.* ☎ *292936/7.*

**Singapore**

*5 Phung Khac Hoan Street, District 1.* ☎ *225173.*

**Sweden**

*4 Dong Khoi Street, District 1.* ☎ *242716.*

**Switzerland**

*270A Bach Dang, Binh Thanh.* ☎ *442568.*

**Thailand**

*77 Tran Quoc Thao, District 3.* ☎ *222637.*

**United Kingdom**

*261 Dien Bien Phu, District 3.* ☎ *298433.*

**United States (liason office)**

*7 Lang Ha, Hanoi.* ☎ *84-4-431500.*

## Important Phone Numbers

**Ambulance**. ☎ *15*

**Emergencies**. ☎ *296485*

**Fire**. ☎ *14*

**Police**. ☎ *13*

**Traffic Police**. ☎ *296449*

## Maps

The best and perhaps the only places to get maps of areas and cities of Vietnam are sidewalk stalls on Le Loi Blvd. opposite the Rex Hotel. Do not rely on obtaining maps on the road, as you will be severely disappointed—even in the major cities. Saigon is the only place in the south where you can obtain maps of various destinations. Don't say we didn't tell you.

### Books, Magazines & Newspapers

There are only a few places in HCMC where foreigners can purchase English-language books and recent magazines and newspapers. The stand with the widest selection is the Lao Dong Shop.

**Lao Dong Shop** ★

*104 Nguyen Hue, Dist. 1. ☎ 251951.*

The best in town. Owner Dung's been doing this for years and has met anyone who's anyone who has ever made it to HCMC. *TIME*, *Newsweek*, *People*, you name it. English-language newspapers from Bangkok, Hong Kong, Singapore are one day late. They also carry the *Asian Wall Street Journal* and the *International Herald Tribune*.

**Khai Minh Bookshop**

*154 Dong Khoi, Dist. 1. ☎ 291439.*

French newspapers and hard-to-find rags about computers, medicine, science, fashion, etc.

**Rex Hotel**

*141 Nguyen Hue, Dist. 1. ☎ 292185.*

There is a stall at the rooftop Terrace Bar with offerings such as the *Financial Times*, *Le Monde*, *Weekly Express*, *Le Figaro*—and a garnishing of pop culture rags, such as *Teen* and *Hot Rod*.

### Photography

There are dozens of film shops along Nguyen Hue Blvd. between the Rex and the Saigon River and on Le Loi. However, the kiosks that formerly lined Nguyen Hue have been torn down. I have no idea what happened to them. Kodak (an American company) recently opened its first lab on the northeastern side of Nguyen Hue Blvd. about halfway between the Rex and the river. A year ago, the majority of shops developed and sold Fuji film only. Kodak had a long way to go to catch up, and they have.

### VIETNAM AIRLINES SCHEDULE TO AND FROM HO CHI MINH CITY

| FROM HO CHI MINH CITY TO: | |
|---|---|
| **Hanoi** | *Flights daily every 30 minutes from 06:30 to 17:30. Flight time 2 hours* |
| **Danang** | *Daily at 07:20, 11:50; Mon./Wed./Sat. at 09:00; Tues./Thur./Fri./Sun. at 13:50. Flight time 1 hour 10 minutes.* |
| **Haiphong** | *Daily at 08:30; Mon./Wed./Sat. at 09:00. Flight time 2 hours.* |
| **Hue** | *Daily at 10:00; daily (except Sat.) at 06:30. Flight time 1 hour 50 minutes.* |
| **Nha Trang** | *Daily at 07:05; Thur./Sun. at 14:40. Flight time 50 minutes.* |

## VIETNAM AIRLINES SCHEDULE TO AND FROM HO CHI MINH CITY

| | |
|---|---|
| **Quy Hhon** | *Daily at 07:00 except Thur./Sun. Flight time 1 hour.* |
| **Dalat** | *Tue./Thur./Sun. at 10:00. Flight time 50 minutes.* |
| **Phu Quoc** | *Tue./Sat. at 11:30. Flight time 50 minutes.* |
| **Buon Ma Thuot** | *Daily at 10:15. Flight time 50 minutes.* |
| **Pleiku** | *Mon./Wed./Fri./Sun. at 11:20. Flight time 1 hour 15 minutes.* |
| **Vinh** | *Mon./Fri. at 11:50. Change planes at Danang. Journey time 4 hours 30 minutes.* |
| **Rach Gia** | *Tue./Sat. at 11:30 via Phu Quoc. Journey time 2 hours.* |
| **Vung Tau** | *6 times a week through Vasco Co. Jetstream aircraft. Continues to Ca Mau.* |
| **Con Dao Islands** | *Tue./Thur./Sat. at 08:30 with Vasco Co. Journey time 45 minutes.* |
| **TO HO CHI MINH CITY FROM:** | |
| **Hanoi** | *Flights daily every 30 minutes from 07:20 to 18:30. Journey time 2 hours.* |
| **Danang** | *Daily at 09:00, 13:50, 16:20. Flight time 1 hour 10 minutes.* |
| **Haiphong** | *Daily at 11:30; Mon./Wed./Sat. at 14:20. Flight time 2 hours.* |
| **Hue** | *Daily (except Sat.) at 08:30; daily (except Tue./Thur. at 16:30; Tue./Thur./Sun. at 13:30. Flight time 1 hour 50 minutes.* |
| **Nha Trang** | *Daily at 08:35 (except Tue./Thur.); Tue./Thur. at 12:30. Thur./Sun. at 16:30. Flight time 50 minutes.* |
| **Quy Nhon** | *Tue./Fri. at 09:00. Flight time 1 hour.* |
| **Dalat** | *Tue./Thur./Sun. at 15:30. Flight time 50 minutes.* |
| **Phu Quoc** | *Tue./Sat. at 15:20. Flight time 50 minutes.* |
| **Buon Ma Thuot** | *Tue./Thur./Sat./Sun. at 12:00; Mon./Wed./Fri. at 16:20. Flight time 50 minutes.* |

## VIETNAM AIRLINES SCHEDULE TO AND FROM HO CHI MINH CITY

| | |
|---|---|
| **Pleiku** | *Mon./Wed./Fri./Sun. at 16:20. Flight time 1 hour 15 minutes.* |
| **Vinh** | *Mon./Fri. at 12:10. Change planes at Danang. Journey time 5 hours 20 minutes.* |
| **Rach Gia** | *Tue./Sat. at 14:10 via Phu Quoc. Journey time 2 hours.* |
| **Vung Tau** | *6 times a week with Vasco Co. Flight originates in Ca Mau.* |
| **Con Dao Islands** | *Tue./Thur./Sat. with Vasco Co. at 09:30. Journey time 45 minutes.* |

*Schedules were current July 1995 but subject to change at short notice. Contact Vietnam Airlines before making travel plans.*

## PACIFIC AIRLINES FLIGHT SCHEDULE

| Route | Days | Departure | Arrival |
|---|---|---|---|
| **HCMC-Hanoi & Hanoi-HCMC** | Every day | | |
| **HCMC-Danang** | Tues-Thurs-Sat | 8:00 a.m. | 9:00 a.m. |
| **Danang-HCMC** | Tues-Thurs-Sat | 10:00 a.m. | 11:00 a.m. |
| **HCMC-Kaohsiung** | Tues-Thurs-Sat | 8:15 a.m. | 12:00 noon |
| **HCMC-Taipei** | Mon & Fri | 8:30 a.m. | 12:30 p.m. |
| **HCMC-Taipei** | Wed | 8:45 a.m. | 12:45 p.m. |

*Effective since August 1, 1995*

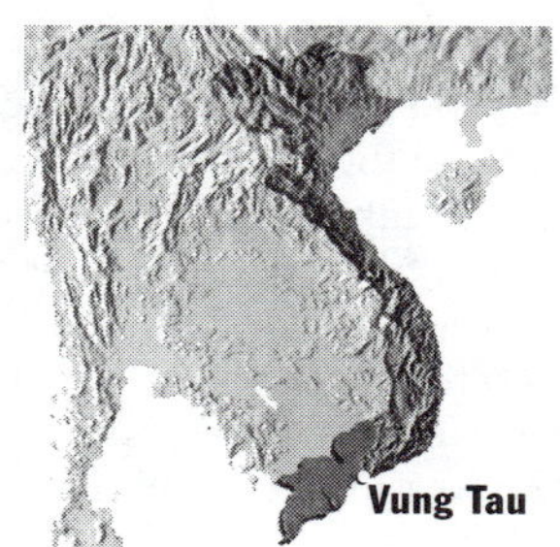


# VUNG TAU

***Beach umbrellas shroud Vung Tau's Paradise Beach.***

## VUNG TAU IN A CAPSULE

*Saigon's closest beach resort, about a three-hour drive from Saigon...Mostly frequented by weekending Saigonese...The beach sees few, but a growing number of foreign tourists...Back and Front Beaches are the least attractive of the resort's beaches...Paradise Beach is the best...For fewer crowds, nearby Long Hai is a better bet...Kiosks and restaurants line Vung Tau's beach-fronts...The drive out from Saigon is over flat terrain and not particularly scenic...But there are a number of decent hotels in town.*

This (along with Long Hai) is the closest beach of any note to Saigon, about 130 km from the city, and where most Saigonese head on out to when the heat becomes too much and they don't mind the two to three hour ride along generally good roads. Frankly, I find the beaches here a disappointment. They're more silty than sandy, and the sea is gray-colored, typical of beaches found at river mouths the world around. (This area is where the Saigon River dumps out into the South China Sea.) The surf is choppy rather than rolling, and not particularly suited for effortless sea bathing—although the body surfer will find the occasional swell to ride in on. Even the drive out to Vung Tau is mainly lacking in any natural beauty. Perhaps Vung Tau is best recommended for Saigon locals and expats with desk jobs who can only get out of town for a day or two.

Vung Tau used to be called Cap Saint Jacques, in honor of the Portuguese patron saint. Before the 17th century, the city was under Khmer rule and the town began to develop as a seaside resort near the beginning of the 20th century. It is a triangular shaped peninsula that juts out into the South China Sea near the mouth of the Saigon River. The beaches are jammed on the weekends, despite the strong currents and high winds that usually buffet the area.

The Thanh Truc Cafe is at about km marker 62 from Vung Tau and makes an excellent roadside rest area for a cool drink about halfway from Saigon. Rubber trees dot the side of the roadway. You pass a former military base that looks just like the former U.S. installations you see all over the south. The strip at Vung Tau is lined with small cafes and bath houses. Not surprisingly, prostitution has spread from one side of the strip to the other, yet the hookers are low-keyed and generally, the beaches make for a suitable family environment. There aren't the roadside "truck stops" that generally characterize some other coastal areas of southern Vietnam beaches, although this is bound to change as tourism increases in the area. Presently one doesn't see a lot of Westerners here, primarily because the beaches aren't particularly good.

To Vung Tau's credit, there is a growing number of very decent hotels appearing in the area. They are primarily frequented by Vietnamese and other Asian tourists, although Westerners are warmly welcomed everywhere.

The beachfront itself is fairly dilapidated, the structures weather beaten. Strangely, most cafes and beachside eateries have seating areas that face the road rather than the beach, which makes for sort of a ridiculous view of nothing really—a couple of hills. The reason for this is that the onshore winds are extremely brisk much of the time, making ocean-facing seating in open-air cafes impossible. Even a full beer would get blown away. Consequently, those who want to swim and frolic in the sea pitch up tents on the beach. Those looking to relax prefer to sit in the cafes, facing roadside.

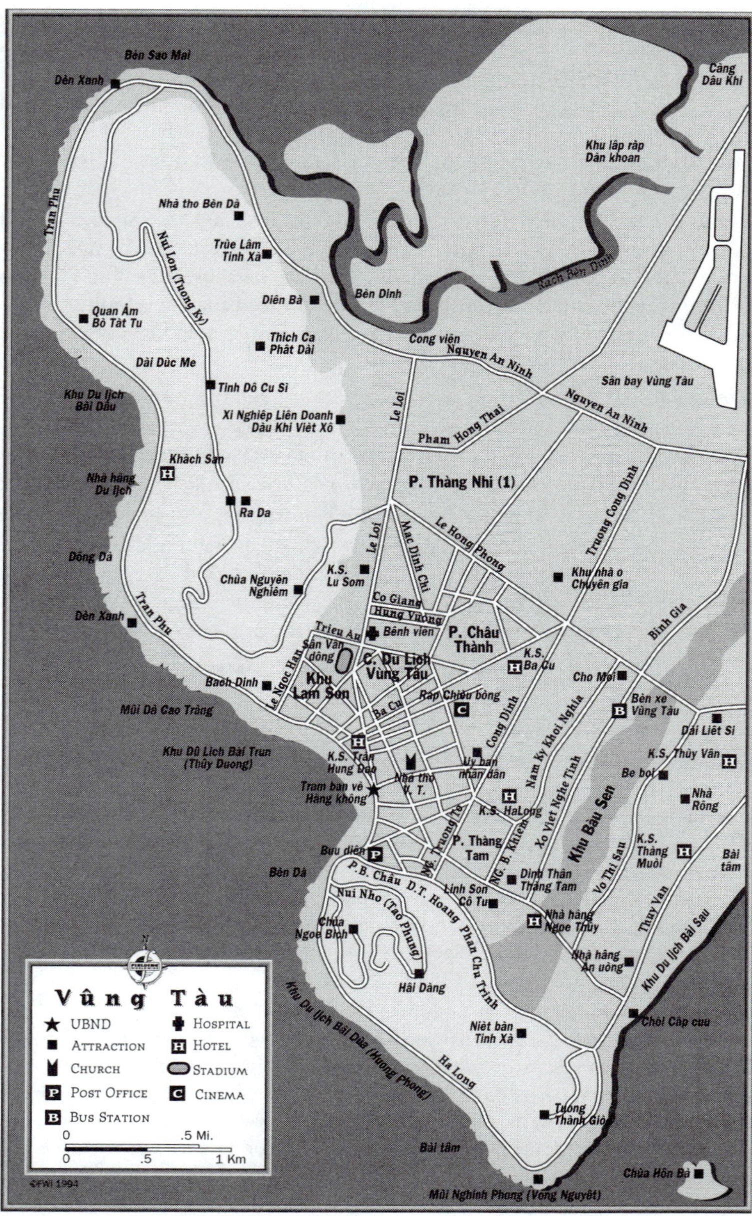
Vûng Tàu
UBND
Attraction
Church
Post Office
Bus Station
Hospital
Hotel
Stadium
Cinema
0 .5 Mi.
0 .5 1 Km
©FWI 1994
Bèn Sao Mai
Dèn Xanh
Càng Dâu Khí
Khu lâp ràp Dàn khoan
Nhà tho Bèn Dà
Trùe Lâm Tinh Xà
Diên Bà
Bèn Dinh
Rach Bèn Dinh
Tran Phu
Nui Lon (Tuong Ky)
Quan Âm Bò Tát Tu
Thích Ca Phât Dài
Cong viên
Nguyen An Ninh
Dài Dúc Me
Tinh Dô Cu Sí
Khu Du lịch Bãi Dâu
Xi Nghiêp Liên Doanh Dâu Khí Viêt Xô
Le Loi
Sân bay Vùng Tàu
Pham Hong Thai
Khách San
Nhà hàng Du lịch
Ra Da
P. Thàng Nhi (1)
Mac Dinh Chi
Le Hong Phong
Truong Cong Dinh
Dông Dà
K.S. Lu Som
Chùa Nguyên Nghiêm
Khu nhà o Chuyên gia
Co Giang
Hung Vuong
Dèn Xanh
Trieu Au
Bènh viên
P. Châu Thành
Binh Gia
Sân Vân dông
C. Du Lịch Vùng Tàu
K.S. Ba Cu
Cho Moi
Bach Dinh
Le Ngoc Han
Khu Lam Son
Ba Cu
Ráp Chiêu bóng
Bèn xe Vùng Tàu
Mûi Dà Cao Trång
Cong Dinh
Nam Ky Khoi Nghia
Dài Liêt Sí
Khu Dû Lich Bãi Trun (Thùy Duong)
K.S. Trân Hung Dao
K.S. Thùy Vân
Uy ban nhân dân
Be boi
Tram ban vé Hàng không
Nhà tho V. T.
Nhà Rông
K.S. HaLong
Xo Viet Nghe Tinh
Khu Bàu Sen
Buu diên
P. Thàng Tam
NG. Truong To
NG. B. Khiem
K.S. Thàng Muôi
Bài tâm
Bèn Dà
P.B. Châu
D.T. Hoang
Phan Chu Trinh
Dinh Thân Thàng Tam
Vo Thi Sau
Linh Son Cô Tu
Nui Nho (Tao Phung)
Nhà hàng Ngoc Thúy
Chùa Ngoc Bình
Thuy Van
Nhà hàng Ân uông
Khu Du lịch Bãi Sau
Hài Dàng
Khu Du lịch Bãi Dùa (Huong Phong)
Niêt bàn Tinh Xà
Chòi Câp cuu
Ha Long
Tuong Thành Giò
Bài tâm
Chùa Hòn Bà
Mûi Nghinh Phong (Vong Nguyêt)

There are two "mountains" in the city (a giant statue of Jesus looks down upon the ocean from one) and they make for good bike riding. In fact, this may be the best activity here, both for the view and the fact that the beach is usually so windy that it feels like being pelted by small weapons fire due to the blowing sand. The big Jesus gives sort of that Rio De Janeiro look with its outstretched arms overlooking the sea.The statue was built in 1974. The best way to get up to it is by a rocky path.

Vung Tau was an area very popular with the Russians during the period when Russians had a great degree of influence here. Here was the headquarters of VIETSOVPETRO, and many Soviet expats used to live in villas around Front Beach, most of which have been razed for the building of hotels for tourists. Many villas also look over Back Beach; they're very attractive and almost Mediterranean in appearance.

Vung Tau is also famous as a departure point for the hundreds of thousands of Vietnamese who fled the country during the latter 1970s through the mid 80s. This may explain why Vung Tau possessed one of the most vast secret police networks after reunification in 1975.

Vung Tau, along with being targeted for tourism, may also become one of Southeast Asia's largest heavy container ports. What will be Vietnam's largest single infrastructure project at US$637 million, a total of eight container wharves will be built. The total handling capacity will be about 60 million tons per year. How this will affect tourism to the area isn't clear.

## What to See and Do in Vung Tau

As you might expect there's not a lot to do here other than swim or look at the rapids-like surf and contemplate swimming. Better yet, take a bike ride around the area.

### Front Beach (Bai Truoc)

*Western edge of town.*

This is commonly referred to as Front Beach, and it's probably the best beach in town, which isn't saying a lot. This is Vietnam's version of Coney Island. Beggars and touts abound. But the shellfish being hawked is excellent. Unfortunately, the beach itself is dirty, rocky, and only acceptable if you close your eyes and dream of being somewhere else. But, all in all, it does make for a nice break from the congestion and hustle & bustle of Saigon.

### Back Beach (Bai Sau)

*2 km south of town.*

This beach is about 2 kilometers south of town and is the area that attracts the most tourists, most of them Saigonese getting out of the city for some fresh air and visiting Asian tourists. You can rent a beach chair and tent for a couple of thousand dong and gaze out at the dangerous surf, which is usually only frolicked in by locals lounging in inner tubes. What the beach has going for it is that it is the only beach in the area with actual sand. Vendors, kiosk proprietors, and a lot of folks carrying strings of dried squid provide the culinary delights. Soda pop and beer are readily available. If you can, get a Vietnamese to do the buying for you; it'll be cheaper. Like other areas in the town, the water can be dangerous for swimming. Sometimes flags will be posted warning of the conditions. A white flag means the water is safe (from what I'm not sure). A red flag means the conditions are unsafe.

**Paradise Beach** ★

*Northern stretch of Back beach.*

This is undoubtedly the best beach in Vung Tau and is the northern stretch of Back Beach. Bright red tents shroud the beach like a Christo exhibition. If you head north on the sand a few hundred meters from the bath house and restaurant, the crowds suddenly vanish and the beach is yours. But I expect a lot more development on the outer reaches of Back Beach in the future. There are a number of decent hotels near here, and good facilities at the beach for dining and souvenir shopping. The bar/restaurant is surprisingly comfortable. Take Le Hong Phong Street and make a left where it intersects with Vo Thi Sau.

**Bai Dau Beach**

*4 km north of central Front Beach.*

There's a pagoda on a hill near here and it's about the only attraction. The beach is nothing special and it's a hike, about 4 km north of town.

**Bai Nghinh Phong**

This is a relatively nice bathing area for Vung Tau. The surf seems more predictable but locals say the swimming can still be quite dangerous, with strong undertows. The few people you do see in the water are rarely swimming but just standing around in the surf getting their street clothes sopping wet.

**Hon Ba**

*Right off Back Beach (Bai Sau)*

This is an impressive looking pagoda on an island only a few hundred yards off the headland, accessible by foot at low tide.

**The Lighthouse**

*Overlooking Bai Truoc Beach*

This offers the best view of the area. It was built just after the turn of the century and rises some 200 km above sea level and can be reached by bicycle, although by foot may be the more attractive alternative. You can also get up to the top from Back Beach, but the roads can be muddy, especially during the wet season.

**Pagodas**

There's the island pagoda of **Hon Ba**, of course, but there are others in Vung Tau worthy of a visit only if pagodas run like heroin through your veins. **Niet Ban Tinh Xa** is easily the most impressive pagoda in Han Ba. It features a giant bronze bell. There is the 1000-year-old **Linh Son Co Tu Pagoda** at *61 Huang Hoa Tham Street*. Also you might want to see the **Whale Dedication Temple**, again not spectacular, but if you've come this far, well...**Thich Ca Phat Dai Park** is where the locals hang out. There's a huge Buddha statue that sits on the side of a hill. There are also a lot of animal and people figurines. Lots of restaurants here as well as a number of souvenir kiosks. The park is on the eastern side of Large Mountain.

**Vung Tau Market**

*North of town on Phan Tru St.*

The market is on seaside Phan Tru Street north of town and was "built" in the beginning of the century. The gardens are a pleasant place to relax.

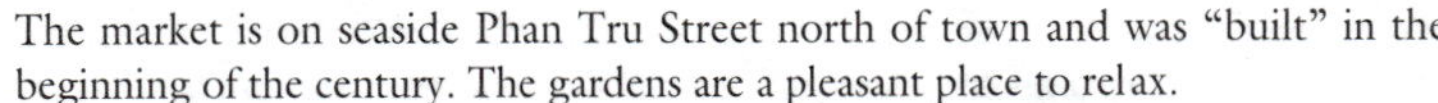

### AUTHOR'S NOTE: TELEPHONE PREFIXES

*When dialing telephone numbers in Vung Tau, the country code is 84. The city code is 64, followed by the local exchange. Numbers listed are local exchanges.*

**Hai Au Hotel 9** **US$45–$85** ★★

*100 Halong Street. ☎ 52278. FAX: 59868.*

*64 rooms.*

This is a small clean place that was only opened about four years ago. Pool, air-conditioned.

**Thang Muoi Hotel** **US$15**

*4-6 Thuy Van Street. ☎ 52665.*

*90 rooms.*

This is an old place on Back Beach and one of the nicer places in the area despite its age. It's a quiet place with a pool, air-conditioning, restaurant and an open courtyard-type area surrounded by the single-story guest units.

**Beautiful Hotel** **US$40–$60** ★★

*100-102 Thuy Van St. ☎ 52177.*

New hotel with comfortable rooms, air conditioning, telephone, minibar. Restaurant. Worth the price.

**The Seabreeze Hotel** **US$50–$80** ★★

*11 Hguyen Trai Street. ☎ 52392, 59856.*

The hotel was opened in 1992 and is Australian-owned and managed. The rooms are expensive by Vietnamese standards but appear to be worth it. Air-conditioned, TV, refrigerator, telephone, fans and clean bathrooms. The more expensive rooms are three room suites. Also a swimming pool and restaurant.

**Canadian Hotel** **US$40–$80** ★★★

*48 Quang Trung Street. ☎ 59852. FAX: 59851.*

This hotel, opened in 1991. It's well-managed and clean—you'd expect it for the prices. Rooms have views of the sea. Restaurant, tennis court, business center, air-conditioned, minibar, disco and a bar.

**Rex Hotel** **US$35–$100** ★★★

*1 Duy Tan Street. ☎ 91766, 52135. FAX: 59862.*

This is a huge structure by Vung Tau standards, nine stories. Restaurant, tennis courts, air-conditioned, disco.

**Hoa Hong La Rose Mini Hotel** **US$20** ★

*39 Durong Thuy Van. ☎ 59455.*

A service oriented inn on the beach with a dining room. Comfortably and tastefully furnished with secure parking. Staff, although their English is limited to nonexistent is extraordinarily friendly.

**New Hotel** **US$35–$60** ★★

*Next door to the Rex at Duy Tan and Quang Trung Streets.*

Just like the New Hotel in Saigon, this is also a new hotel, completed just a couple of years ago. On Front Beach. Good views of the sea.

**International Hotel Hai Dau** **About US$20**

*242 Ba Cu Street. ☎ 52178, 52571.*

Only five years old, this place looks like it could have been used as a fire base by American troops during the war. The amenities, though, belie the trashiness of the place. There's a swimming pool, business center and two restaurants.

**Pacific Hotel** **US$16–$30** ★★

*4 Le Loi Blvd. ☎ 52279.*

The more expensive rooms have a view of the sea. This is a large, drab complex with air-conditioned rooms, refrigerators, hot water, a disco/nightclub, and a decent massage.

**Palace Hotel** **About US$40**

*Nguyen Trai Street near Quang Trung Street. ☎ 52411.*

*105 rooms.*

This is also a sprawling but stale and plain place that at least offers all its rooms with air conditioning, TV, and a refrigerator. It can be tough getting up in the morning in some of the rooms as they have no windows; they almost create a prison-like feel. But there are a couple of restaurants, a "nightclub," a massage parlor and a tennis court.

**Phuong Dong Hotel** **US$50-plus** ★★★

*2 Thuy Van Street-VT. ☎ 52158, 525983.*

This is a new and impressive hotel in Vung Tau, perhaps the town's finest. It sits on the hillside overlooking Back Beach and just above a complex of some of the architecturally attractive Mediterranean style villas in Vung Tau. Service is extremely considerate and the grounds are immaculately kept. Karaoke, massage, and a host of other amenities. It is frequented primarily by visiting businessmen apparently, but the manager, Dinh Van Ha, made it clear that tourist bookings are on the rise.

**Diamond Hotel** **US$15–$20**

*8 Tran Nguyen Han Street. ☎ 95930; FAX: 95930.*

Not much here but a restaurant and a room to watch videos. Rooms with air conditioning.

## INSIDER TIP

*In Bai Dau, there are dozens of guest houses catering to budget tourists, but many of them only accept Vietnamese. These are sometimes nothing more than short-time hooker stops. (If you must, these "ladies" can be had for as little as 40,000 dong, or about US$4. Don't expect a wake-up call.) Although the area itself is not particularly unappealing, the beach along Bai Dau is. Some of the "cement-floor" types might want to try the Nha Nghi My Tho at 47 Tran Phu Street, the Nha Nghi 29 on the beach, the Nha Hang 96 (not on the beach), or the Nha Nghi DK 142, although it's a bit pricier. One thing to remember is that places come and go virtually overnight in this part of the country. Construction of new dwellings is rampant around here, albeit slow. A lot of the older hotels and kiosks appear to be changing their names, or at least recreating their marquees in a grandiose manner to attract customers. Sometimes the addresses of the establishments will be displayed with far more prominence than the actual hotel or restaurant name. So it pays more to know where you are than where you want to be going.*

### Where to Eat in Vung Tau

There are literally dozens of eateries lining the beach along Ha Long, Quang Trung and Thuy Van Streets. Of note on Thuy Van Street along the Back Beach: Thuy Van Cafe, Quan An Binhean Cafe, Don Qui 59, Quai Quan Thuy Tien,Lam Thon Thung, Dai Dung, Nha Hang and Quang Hang. Also try: Thanh Nien, 55 Quang Trung Street.

### Nightlife in Vung Tau

There has been a proliferation of nightclubs and karaoke clubs springing up in and around town. Most of the good hotels have some form of nightlife. Expats have yet to start up beachside reggae bars.

### Directory

#### Banks and Money Changers

**Vietcom Bank**, *27 Tran Hung Dao Blvd.* They will exchange travelers checks and, at last check, issue advances on American issued credit cards.

#### General Post Office

*4 Ha Long Street*, near the Hai Au Hotel.

#### Tourist Office

**Vung Tau Tourism**, *59 Tran Hung Doa Blvd.*

#### Transportation

The bus station is at *52 Nam Ky Khoi Nghia Street*. There are minibuses that depart from Trang Hung Dao Blvd. and Ly Tu Trong Street. The minibuses depart for Saigon as soon as they're filled, usually around every 40 minutes or so and cost about 8000 dong (US$.80). They usually take about three hours, but frequently longer. The regular non-express buses take a lot longer (maybe four hours), but cost only about 2000 dong (US$.20). It may not be necessary, but it's probably a good idea to buy your tickets to

Saigon in advance, even as much as a day. Buses from Saigon for Vung Tau from the Mien Dong Bus Station also leave when they're filled. You can also take a bus to Vung Tau from the station at Nguyen Hue Blvd. These are express buses and usually take about three hours and cost about US$5 return fare. If you want to go by car, ask around, but feel lucky if you can get a ride for less than US$70 round trip for a day excursion. Getting around Vung Tau is best by bicycle, and there are plenty for rent, despite what people might say. Most of the hotels now rent bikes, as do a number of beachside cafes.

# TAY NINH

## TAY NINH IN A CAPSULE

*Headquarters to the Cao Dai Sect, one of the most intriguing religions in Asia, if not the world...features some of the most ornate and intricate religious symbolism in the world...there are elements to the temple that are unique in the world...Cao Daism is an odd blend of both Eastern and Western faiths that were somehow coagulated to form the "perfect religion"...There are elements of Christianity, Buddhism, Confucianism, Hinduism, Taoism, Islam and God knows what else...There was a major conflict between Cao Daism and the South Vietnamese government back in the mid-1950s which ultimately led to the reannexation of Cao Dai territory to the Vietnamese...Tay Ninh itself is nothing special and not worthy of a journey simply for the town itself...It's a typical Vietnamese village with avenues flanked by food stalls, electronics shops, etc....There seems to be emerging an increasing number of petrol stations, though...Before the 17th century, this province, close to the Cambodian border, was under Khmer rule.*

Tay Ninh, the capital of Tay Ninh Province and about 100 km from the capital, is home to the famous and magnificent, if not bizarre, Cao Dai headquarters, a complex of temples and fields including the Cao Dai Great Temple. The excursion is an easy day trip from Saigon and can be done by rented car, bus, or motorcycle. By motorcycle (you can rent one in Saigon with the proper international driving permit for about US$10 per day), the ride is an exhilarating experience, although the countryside isn't all that magnificent. Unless you plan on being at the temple for noon prayer (there are also prayer services at 6 a.m. and 6 p.m.), just getting there might be the highlight of the day, as the roads are well paved and suited for touring by motorcycle (be careful).

Once you get out of Saigon (from District 1, take Cach Mang Thang Tam to Huong Lo and follow the highway past Cu Chi to Go Dau, then take a right), which can take a very long time (the locals insist the entire trip to Tay Ninh takes two hours by car or fast motorbike). It can easily take as long as 3-1/2 hours from central Saigon even at speeds as high as 70 or 80 m.p.h. and drain your nervous system entirely. The highway becomes relatively free of heavy-vehicle traffic outside the sprawling metropolis and you soon become surrounded by rice fields and then, amazingly enough, a few more after that. There are a number of small, pastel yellow pagodas along the route, but few, if any are worth a detour, unless the road starts to become a little too much and you want to prime yourself for the sights of Tay Ninh.

Between 1975 and 1979, Tay Ninh Province was increasingly encroached upon by Cambodian Pol Pot's Khmer Rouge, who invaded villages and reportedly raped women and killed men and children indiscriminately. It was these deeds that gave the Vietnamese government the impetus (or at least a damn good excuse) to invade Cambodia in December of 1978.

The best reasons to visit Tay Ninh, of course, are the Cao Dai temples, particularly the Great Temple, or Holy See. Cao Daism's roots stem from the 1920s in southern Vietnam after the religion's founder, a civil servant named Ngo Van Chieu, received a "visit" from "God," or Cao Dai. Similar to Moses, who descended Mount Sinai with God's gifts of the tablets of the 10 Commandments (not ironically, Cao Dai means "high tower"), Ngo received a message from Cao Dai that the religion was to be based on the "Giant Eye." (The Giant Eye is above each altar in a Cao Dai temple.) In fact, the religion subscribes to five commandments: don't kill anything living, don't practice excessive or extravagant living, do not slander, do not be tempted, and do not covet. This Giant Eye was apparently the manifestation of the vision of a number of lay people, from politicians to poets. Included as saints in the Cao Dai religion are such illustrious luminaries as Winston Churchill, Moses, Joan of Arc, the French writer Victor Hugo, Sun Yat Sen, and Brahma. This helps explains Cao Daism's attempt to merge secular and scientific principles with religious or spiritual devotion. Followers of Cao Daism interpret the "scriptures" through meditation and sort of a séance that contacts the saints utilizing a corbeille-a-bac, an odd wooden planchette.

Their religion became formalized in 1926 and soon developed an almost nationalistic fervor. Within a short time, Cao Daism had tens of thousands of followers.

A year later, Cao Dai convert Le Van Trung staged a religious coup and assumed leadership of the fledgling faith. He built a temple in the village of Long Hoa, near Tay Ninh. Ten years later, the following of Cao Daism had become massive; there were an estimated 4–5 million followers of the sect. It essentially became a political state which, of course, didn't amuse the government. In 1955, when as many as 15 percent of southern Vietnamese were Cao Dais, there was a major confrontation between the religion and the state that ultimately gave the government back control of territory that it had "lost" to the Cao Dais. The South Vietnamese government then conscripted tens of thousands of Cao Dai adherents as soldiers.

After the fall of the south in 1975, Cao Daism all but ceased to exist. Because they refused to support both the Viet Cong and the South Vietnamese forces during the protracted war, they faced especially intense scrutiny and hardship after the Saigon leadership collapsed. Since the relaxation of tensions between the peoples of the north and the south, Cao Daism has reemerged and nearly 1000 Cao Dai temples can be found throughout Vietnam, primarily in the south, receiving the worship of an estimated 2 million adherents to the religion.

Cao Daism has the strongest influence in the province of Tay Ninh and in the Mekong Delta region.

Cao Dais aim to break the cycle of reincarnation by following the five commandments. The principle deities are the Mother Goddess and God. Men and women equally share positions of supreme authority; both men and women become clergy, except at the highest levels. If men and women clergy of the same status are based in the same temple area, the men are bestowed greater authority. Male priests are called "Thanh," while female clergy are referred to as "Huong." Cao Dai temples are built in a fashion where male clergy enter the structures from the right, while the women enter from the left. The same goes for worship; men worship on the right side of the temple while the women do their praying on the left side of the temple.

## INSIDER TIP

*Visitors to the temples should remove both hats and shoes. Similar to Cao Dai clergy, women enter the temple through an entrance on the left, while the men do so on the right–similar to how Cao Dai clergy enter and exit their temples. You'll usually be accompanied by a Cao Dai priest (man or woman), and you will be expected to provide a small donation–the amount entirely up to you. Curiously enough, my guide barely spoke a word of English, and I found that other clergy at the Cao Dai Great Temple weren't exactly fluent in anything but what they seemed to be muttering either. So be prepared. Read the section on Cao Daism in this book (or other more extensive selections, such as Cao Dai Spiritism: A Study of Religion in Vietnamese Society, by Victor Oliver (EL Brill, Leiden, 1976) before visiting the temple. Without doing so, your visit may be virtually meaningless, save for a few snapshots. You will understand none of the artistic depiction of three periods of history that hang on the walls. In the main temple two rows of pink pillars line the aisle, inscribed with dragon figures. These aisles lead up to the main altar, above which is the Giant Eye. Visitors watch the service from a balcony overlooking the cathedral. Plan on staying for the entire service, which lasts about an hour. It would be a disruption as well as an insult to depart earlier. At no time should you walk down the center portion of the nave, although when I inadvertently did I was met with a kindly but "you stupid Hoa Ky" smile from my guide. You may be allowed to take pictures, taking photos of clergy members is forbidden unless they grant you permission, which may mean a small "donation."*

Prayer services—conducted four times daily (6 a.m., 12 noon, 6 p.m., and midnight)—are the best times to visit the temples. Clergy and dignitaries wear ornate red, blue and yellow ceremonial robes and hats, and there are offerings of fruit, flowers, alcohol and tea. During the normal prayer sessions on weekdays, hundreds of clergy members may be present. But there are special Cao Dai holidays where you may actually find yourself among thousands of Cao Dai priests.

Cao Dai priests practice celibacy and vegetarianism. The Cao Dai separate history into three distinct periods or revelations: the first was when the existence of God was revealed to human beings through Laotze and the influences of Taoism, Buddhism, and Confucianism. The second phase involved Sakyamuni Buddha, Jesus Christ, Mohammed, Moses, and Confucius. During the second period, the Cao Dai came to believe that the conduits carrying the divine messages from these individuals had become convoluted and impure.

The new, or third phase, of Cao Daism has its followers believing that the convoluted previous messages have been eliminated through their communication with the spirits. These "spirits" include former Cao Dai leaders as well as an eclectic blend of both lay people and clergy. Many Westerners are spirits the Cao Dai contact frequently. Among them are Shakespeare, Louis Pasteur, and V.I. Lenin (who, curiously enough, didn't appear to inspire the Cao Dai to align themselves with Marxist Viet Cong forces during the war, even though Cao Dai members sided with the French against the Japanese, the Americans against the Viet Minh, and the Viet Minh against the South Vietnamese government). The spirits are communicated with in a number of languages, including French, English, Vietnamese and English. In one ceremony, the priest seals a blank piece of paper in an envelope and places it above the altar. When he takes it down, a message is contained in the envelope.

Although formal Cao Dai seances have been held in temples across the country since 1925, the only "legitimate" seances that reveal divine truth can be conducted at Tay Ninh.

## What to See and Do in Tay Ninh

### Cao Dai Great Temple ★★

*Long Hoa village, 2 km east of Tay Ninh.*

This is the principal temple of the Cao Dai religion and the focal point of the Cao Dai complex called Holy See. Its colorful pastel yellow architecture (which seems to get a new coat of paint hourly by the hordes of workers one sees on scaffolds all the time) is set among a large complex of schools, dormitories, and a "hospital," which utilizes traditional Vietnamese herbal medicine. The main temple consists of an intriguing complex of architectural styles, ranging from Oriental to European. The large front facade features reliefs with depictions of Cao Dai saints. Some have called the building the most impressive structure in the Orient, while others have compared it with Disneyland. If you're impressed with Disneyland, though, you may be disappointed by the lack of rollercoasters at the temple.

The temple is constructed on nine levels, which represent the nine steps to heaven. On each level you will find a pair of columns. There are impressive columns in the nave decorated with dragons. Above the altar, of course, looms the Giant Eye with an eternal flame. The domed ceiling that the columns support represents the heavens.

There is a mural in the entry area displaying the three signatories of the "Third Alliance Between God and Man." There are seven large chairs at the far end of the temple in front of the globe, the largest of which is supposedly "reserved" for the Cao Dai pope, a position that hasn't been filled since the early 1930s. Three of the chairs are for the use of those Cao Dais responsible for the religion's law books. The remaining three chairs represent the seating areas for the leaders of the religion's three branches.

### Cham Temples

*1 km east of Tay Ninh.*

About a kilometer to the east of Tay Ninh are a number of Cham temples.

**Long Hoa Market**

*Middle of town.*

In the middle of Tay Ninh, about a kilometer or two from the Cao Dai complex. Nothing really worth writing home about here; just the basic staples bought by the basic crowds you see in marketplaces all over rural Vietnam. Foodstuffs, fake designer clothes, etc.

### Where to Stay and Eat in Tay Ninh

Near the bridge there are a few places to stay in the US$10-20 range, but Tay Ninh is not an area worth more than just a few hours' visit, which can easily be arranged from Saigon by tour group or rented car. Most visitors combine day tours of Tay Ninh with a visit to the Cu Chi Tunnels, which lie along the route (National Highway 22) to Tay Ninh from Saigon.

For food, your best bets are the numerous food stalls that surround the Long Hoa market. Two restaurants of note are the **Nha Hang So 1**, which is on the western side of the river near the bridge and **Nha Hang Diem Thuy**, located at 30/4 Street. Both restaurants, as are all in Tay Ninh, are extraordinarily cheap, with most meals costing as little as 5000 dong (about US$.50).

## Tay Ninh Environs

### Black Lady Mountain

This is also called Nui Ba Den, and it's located about 15 km from Tay Ninh. I've heard this is the highest peak in southern Vietnam. There are a number of temples on the mountain (the main temple which can be reached in about 45 minutes via a relatively simple hike from the base of the hill), the result of centuries of Khmer, Cham, Vietnamese and Chinese domination of and influence in the area. The term Black Lady Mountain is based on the legend of a young woman named Ly Thi Huong who, despite being wooed by a rich Chinese Mandarin, ended up marrying the man of her dreams. (Another version of the tale has Huong leaping off the side of the mountain in protest of the wealthy Chinese's romantic pursuits.) While the husband was away fighting wars, Huong would make pilgrimages to the summit of Nui Ba Den to visit a magical Buddha statue. One day, as legend has it, there was an attempt by bandits to rape the woman, who, believing death was the more virtuous alternative, threw herself off the face of the edifice. The story became known through her communication with a local monk.

The mountain, which reaches about 900 meters or more above the rice fields was also the setting of intense firefights between the Viet Minh and the French during the first Indochina War, and between the Americans and the Viet Cong during the Vietnam War. Americans heavily defoliated the region during the war, though one can hardly tell today. (If your grandchildren are born resembling cauliflowers, you'll realize that the American defoliation of

Vietnam is a lot like AIDS—you may look verdant on the outside, but something inside is ripping you apart.)

The principal temples of pilgrimage on the mountain are Lang Chang Pagoda and Chua Linh Son Pagoda. Some of the fortune tellers in and around the pagodas speak English.

## Directory

### Travel

The best way to get to Tay Ninh is by minibus or car, the latter which can be had for the US$70–90 range a day, although some private entrepreneurs will offer cars and drivers for as little as $40 a day ($20 per day if you're going only as far as Cu Chi.) Buses leave for Tay Ninh regularly from Saigon via Cu Chi from the Tay Ninh bus station and the Mien Tay bus station in An Loc. They take about three hours, sometimes longer. The other alternative is to rent a motorcycle. Make sure you leave Tay Ninh (if you're not spending the night) by 3 p.m. to avoid the extremely dangerous nighttime traffic, both on treacherous Route 22 and in Saigon, where nighttime motoring is something akin to a circus bumper car ride without electricity. Unless you know what you're doing, it's better to get out to this area with a guide or in a group. Buses back to Saigon leave from the Tay Ninh bus station regularly to the same stations.

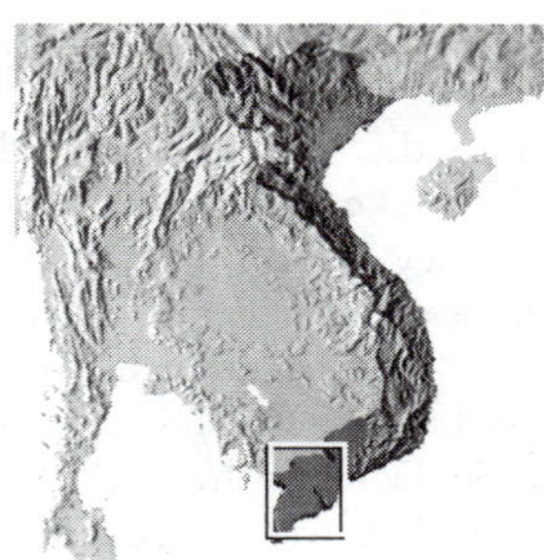

# THE MEKONG DELTA

## THE MEKONG DELTA IN A CAPSULE

**Vi Thanh** *(60 km south of Can Tho) was one of the first "strategic hamlets," a largely unsuccessful attempt by the South Vietnamese government to create artificial urban centers for farming that would be safe from Viet Cong infiltration...* **My Tho** *is the closest delta destination to Saigon...* **Can Tho** *is considered the capital of the Mekong Delta...* **Thot Not** *(40 km upriver from Can Tho on the Bassac River) was where the Trotskyite revolutionary Ta Tu Thau was born...* **Thap Muoi,** *or The Plain of Reeds, at the junction Long An and Dong Thap provinces, is a former Viet Minh and Viet Cong base that neither the French nor the Americans were able to occupy...* **Ca Mau** *(348 km from Ho Chi Minh City, 210 from Vinh Long.) is the biggest city in the Ca Mau peninsula on the Gonh Hoa River. Ca Mau is famous for the U Minh forest, the second largest mangrove swamp in the world. There are many precious and endangered birds and animals...* **Ha Tien** *(340 km from Saigon, 250 km from Vinh Long) is a small town of Kien Giang Province in the Gulf of Thailand, 8 km from the Cambodian border. It has many beautiful beaches, caves and romantic settings. Phu Tu Islet (Father-Son Isle), with its panoramic views, looks like Ha Long Bay in miniature...Stone Cavern...Dong Ho Lake...Cape Nai...Offshore island of* **Phu Quoc** *accessible by air and being developed for tourism.*

This is the richest and the most prolific agricultural region of Vietnam. In fact the majority of all Vietnamese are fed with agricultural products from the Mekong Delta. It's an extremely rural area covering some 67,000 sq. km but, surprisingly it is one of the most densely populated areas of Vietnam, and more than half of the entire region is under cultivation. The only regions of the delta that are to date sparsely cultivated or not cultivated at all are the areas around Minh Hai Province.

The Mekong Delta was formed primarily by mud from the Mekong River spreading in forklike directions out to the South China Sea. The area itself was sparsely populated until the 19th century, when Vietnamese settlers moved slowly down south to take advantage of the newly-formed region's rich agricultural potential. They called the area "Mien-tay," or the "West." Most of the area's geographical, cultural and architectural attractions are, by Vietnamese standards, brand new. Temples that may appear to be hundreds of years old may in fact have been built as recently as the 1930s and 40s. The oldest area of the Delta is Ha Tien, on the southwestern coast at the border of present-day Cambodia. Ha Tien was settled and highly prosperous as early as the start of the 17th century.

Crops grown in the delta include mango, mangosteen, jackfruit, oranges (believe it or not), guava, pepper, durian and pineapple, among others. Also under cultivation are coconut, sugarcane and seafood—if you can call shrimp cultivated. In fact, although the rice yields are lower in the delta than in the north of Vietnam, there is nearly three times as much rice acreage per person as there is in the north. The region is entirely flat and contains a vast network of rivers and waterways that comprise the tributaries of the Mekong River—locally called Song Cuu Long (or the River of the Nine Dragons).

The Mekong's source is high on the Tibetan Plateau, making the river perhaps the mightiest and longest in Asia. It flows nearly 4500 km through China, Laos, Cambodia and Myanmar before finally splitting into both wide and thin branches of waterway in Vietnam's southern region.

In Vietnam, the Mekong splits into two major channels. The river itself moves through Hung Ngu and Vinh Long, where several fingers then branch out on their journeys to the South China Sea.

**INSIDER TIP**

*The Vietnamese government will spend US$9.2 billion each year on improvement of the country's waterways. Investments are also expected to be made to develop modern passenger ships as well as domestic touring vessels.*

The Bassac River, which runs through Long Xuyen and Can Tho is the other main branch. The best time of the year to see the Mekong is in the fall, when the runoff from upriver all through Southeast Asia makes the waterways an incredible sight, as the flow of the river reaches nearly 40,000 cubic meters (compared to 2000 during other times of the year).

**INSIDER TIP**

*There has been increasing interest among independent travelers to creatively find their own ways of exploring the Mekong River. Beware, though, that pirate attacks are not infrequent along this vast stretch of interior waterway. Pirates recently boarded a Cambodian freighter bound for Phnom Penh and beheaded 18 people, including children, and dumped their bodies into the river. Armed with AK-47 rifles and grenade launchers, the pirates escaped before being apprehended by Vietnamese authorities.*

Not surprisingly, because the mighty river's force continues to extend the shoreline of southern Vietnam by as many as 15 meters a year and extend the shorelines at the mouths of the river by about as much as 80 meters a year, the Mekong Delta region is geologically relatively recent in origin. As mentioned, the land of the delta was formed by the silt being pushed down the river from the highlands of China, Myanmar and Laos, and the area—save for the Ha Tien region which was settled in the 17th century—remained virtually unpopulated until the 19th century. Vietnamese settlers moved south into the "Mien-tay." Consequently there is very little of any deep historical significance in the delta. The temples are new, although some appear to be centuries old.

Perhaps the amazing oddity of the Mekong occurs not in Vietnam, but in Cambodia, where, when the river is at flood stage, it drains up the Tonle Sap River, which prevents flooding in the Mekong Delta region and brings Cambodia's Tonle Sap Lake to enormously high levels.

Originally, the delta region belonged to the Cambodians and wasn't settled by the Vietnamese until centuries later (see the Ha Tien chapter). Although most of the region's population is comprised of ethnic Vietnamese, you'll find a number of Khmer descendents living particularly in the lower end of the delta.

## AUTHOR'S OBSERVATION

*The Irrawaddy dolphins of the Mekong River are getting blown out of the water. Literally. The increasing use of explosives by Khmer fishermen to more easily harvest fish from the waters of the Mekong is including in its carnage the slaughter of the Irrawaddy, a rare dolphin that inhabits the waterways of the Mekong in Laos, Cambodia and Vietnam. This is the report from the Bangkok-based Project for Ecological Recovery. According to the report, and travelers visiting the region, the blasting of fish out of the river is on the rise, and has increased steadily in the last 10 years (and even to a greater extent since the signing of the Cambodian Peace Accords in October 1991) occasionally during the high-water rainy season but much more frequently during times of the year when the water levels go down. Many visitors to the region report hearing 10–20 explosions per day in the river.*

The Mekong Delta is a fascinating area to tour, but it is also a monotonous glut of real estate, the topography changing very little, if at all, for thousands of square kilometers. I toured the area by motorcycle and boat, and, frankly, would not have done it any other way simply for the reason that the numerous rest stops I took were the most enjoyable part of my adventure. The people of the delta are truly its attraction, not the topography nor the historical sights. Being invited into families' homes for meals, falling in love with the locals and trading love messages that have to be translated by relatives, these are the real attractions of the delta. At one cafe in the tiny southern delta village of Soc Xoai, I was grilled by a young lady's parents over Vietnamese whiskey and BGI beer about my background and profession in order to gain permission to marry the young woman (which was essentially granted) even though my only request was that myself and the young lady exchange addresses for correspondence purposes.

There are ferry trips across the Bassac and Hau Giang rivers to villages whose inhabitants have rarely—if ever—laid eyes on a Westerner. But keep in mind that traveling the delta below Can Tho isn't easy, and can be quite dangerous. The roads are in dismal shape. I've experienced numerous flat tires and broken clutch cables—many parts of my motorcycle have simply fallen off—due to the harshness of the terrain. At the end of the day, you will be covered in dust, vehicle exhaust and mud if you travel by any other means than by bus or with a tour group in a car or microbus. The water at many hotels in the region may turn out to be nothing more than motivation to remain as dirty as you'll get. Travel by regular bus in the delta below Can Tho is *excruciatingly* uncomfortable for taller Westerners. Nowhere else in the southern half of the country will you have to "rough it" like you will in the Mekong Delta.

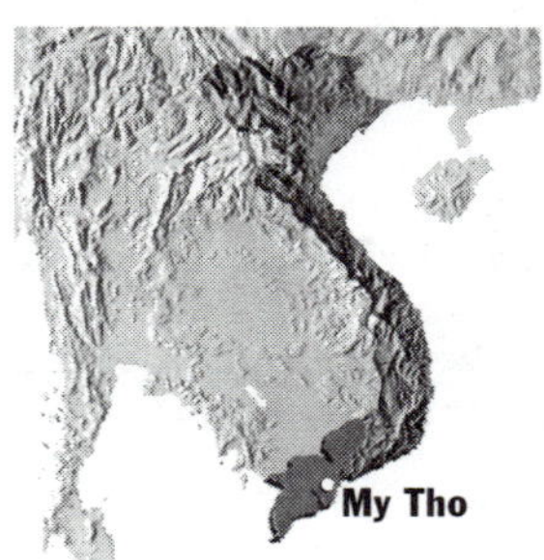


# My Tho

## MY THO IN A CAPULE

*Just 2 hours from Saigon...Capital of Dinh Tuong Province...Under Khmer rule until the 17th century...The French colonized the area in the mid-1800s...A strategic American military base was here in the mid-1960s...Considered the site of the Viet Cong's first major military victory...Makes for an easy day trip from Saigon.*

My Tho, one of the first stops in the Mekong Delta, is only about a two-hour drive from Saigon (about 76 km) and is the capital of Dinh Tuong province (also known as Tien Giang province), with a population of about 100,000. It sits on the banks of the My Tho River, one of the many Mekong River tributaries near the mouths of the Mekong. It was under Cambodian rule until the 17th century and was settled mainly by Chinese after the Nguyen Lords took control of the area later that century. Thai forces subsequently invaded the area but were forced out in 1784. The French took control of the region in the mid-19th century. In the mid-1960s, an important American military base was here.

My Tho is often considered the site of the first Viet Cong victory over ARVN forces, but the fight actually took place in nearby Ap Bac.

Today, My Tho is a relatively prosperous city known for its rice production and fruit orchards. The city itself isn't as drab as Vinh Long. My Tho can easily be seen in a day visit from HCMC, but if you take this kind of excursion, get the most out of it. I especially recommend visiting the nearby islands of Ben Tre and Phung Island, former home of the Coconut Monk—although don't expect a lot of truly magnificent scenery at either. It's the history of the area that makes it worth seeing.

## What to See and Do in My Tho and Environs

### Trung Trac Central Market

*Located on Trung Trac Street near the Bao Dinh channel on the eastern edge of town.*

If you've seen one market, you've seen them all. At least the streets are closed to traffic here. A lot of produce and fruit. I mean a lot. Most of it I'm sure ends up in HCMC. You'll also see a lot more tobacco sold here than in other delta markets. However, this is the best place to get a sample of life in My Tho, as it is the city's most bustling area in an otherwise laid-back environment.

### My Tho Church

*32 Hung Vuong Street.*

This is a big pastel yellow church with twin towers that was built about 100 years ago, making it ancient by Mekong Delta standards. The church serves the city's 8000 or so Catholics, but it's open only about 6 hours a day: very early in the morning (you'll still be in bed), and in the afternoon for about 4 hours. Masses are held twice every day and at least three times on Sunday. The plaques on the wall inside the church are dedicated to Fatima.

### Vinh Trang Pagoda

*60A Nguyen Trung Truc St.*

*Open from 9 a.m.–noon and from 2 to 5 p.m. in the afternoon.*

This is an unimpressive little pagoda that's a little tough to get to without asking for directions. Well, here they are: Cross the bridge at Nguyen Trai Street and then turn left down Nguyen An Ninh Street to the end. Then walk down a dirt path to Nguyen Trung Truc Street. You'll come across a painted bamboo gate on the right. This is the entrance. The actual entrance to the pagoda is through a porcelain gate. Architectural styles range from Chinese to Vietnamese to French colonial (the temple was built in the mid-1800s). I'd simply avoid this place altogether if only for the fact that the animals kept here in the "zoo" live in dismal conditions. It seems the pagoda's lure is not spiritual or architectural, but purely capitalistic. It's sad to watch the microbus loads of tourists gawk at the animals and behave as if they were at Disneyland. The only thing worth seeing here is the portrait of Ho Chi Minh, complete with real beard hairs from Uncle Ho's face.

### Quan Thanh Pagoda

*3-9 Nguyen Trung Truc Street.*

This is a nice restored temple with plaster figures. Otherwise not a lot to see here.

### Con Phung (Phung Island)

This is the island of the Coconut Monk, about 3 km from My Tho. After World War II, the Ong Dao Dua (the Coconut Monk) built a small village on Con Phung and started a new religion, which was a mishmash of Christianity and Buddhism. In its early years it might have reminded you of singer Michael Jackson's ranch in California, with parklike attractions in an attractive setting (although Disneyland's influence seems all too apparent in and around My Tho). The grounds used to contain ornate structures: dragon-wrapped columns and the like, but today, they're run down and musty. The Ong Dao Dua, who was born Nguyen Thanh Nam, was given his moniker because he reputedly ate nothing but coconuts for three years on a stone slab where he also meditated both day and night. Before his monastic life, he was educated in France, married and had a daughter. Later, during his coconut diet, he was persecuted and imprisoned by the various South Vietnamese governments as he sought to reunify Vietnam though a peaceful process. To get out to the island, you can hire a boat at the south end of Trung Trac Street. Prices vary depending on the size of the boat, ranging anywhere from US$3 an hour to US$20 for a round trip and "tour."

**Tan Long Island**

This is worth seeing only because it's a cheap five-minute boat trip from My Tho. Fishing boats cover the palm-lined shores. Take some pictures and then come back.

**Snake Farm** ★

*8 km from My Tho toward Vinh Long.*

Many varieties of snakes, all indigenous to Vietnam, are raised here, from pythons to deadly cobras. The military runs the place and raises the animals for their medicinal qualities. I assure you these snakes have not had the lethal venom removed and the ability of the soldier/snake handlers in dealing with these vicious creatures is a sight in itself. The belief is that the snakes have healing powers in their flesh and glands.These medicines are then bottled and sold to the hordes of tourists who've climbed off the microbuses.

## Where to Stay in My Tho

**AUTHOR'S NOTE: TELEPHONE PREFIXES**

*The following telephone numbers are local exchanges. The country code is 84. The city code is 73.*

**Hotel 43** **US$6–$8**

*43 Ngo Quyen Street. ☎ 73126, 72126.*

*24 rooms.*

The expensive rooms are the doubles with air conditioning, while the cheaper rooms can sleep three and have an attached bath. Service here is some of the friendliest in My Tho. Great value.

**Song Tien Hotel (formerly the Grand Hotel)** **About US$20**

*101 Trung Trac Street. ☎ 712009.*

*35 rooms.*

This is a relatively expensive place that used to have a better reputation as the eight-story Grand Hotel. The staff has been reported to be dishonest. And honestly, the place is overpriced. The upper end-rooms have refrigerators and air conditioning.

**Thanh Binh Hotel** **US$3**

*44 Nguyen Binh Khiem Street.*

*4 rooms.*

Forget it. Like spending the night in a janitor's closet. I wouldn't let them pay me to stay here. In fact, I'm not even sure they still allow foreigners. No fans; no bath.

**Rach Gam** **US$3–$6**

*33 Trung Trac Street.*

This is one of the cheapest accommodations in town and it shows. Backpackers only.

**Lao Dong Hotel** **About US$6**

*Le Loi and 34 Thang 4 Streets.*

This is a relatively new hotel that hasn't yet gotten the opportunity to descend into uncleanliness. And it's cheap. Again, for the backpacker set—but a definite bargain.

## Where to Eat in My Tho

My Tho is known for a couple of specialty dishes, the best being *hu tieu my tho*, a spicy and garnished soup packed with herbs, shrimp, vermicelli, pork and chicken. Find it, or in its various forms, at:

**Restaurant 43**

*43 Ngo Quyen Street.*

Vietnamese, Asian. Inexpensive and good.

**Nha Hang 54**

*54 Trung Trac Street.*

Vietnamese, Asian fare. Ice Cream.

**Nha Hang 52**

*52 Trung Trac Street.*

Vietnamese, Asian. One of the best in town.

## Directory

### Transportation

By **bus** or **car**, My Tho is about 76 km from HCMC and another 70 km from Vinh Long. It's about 180 km to both Rach Gia and Chau Doc, and 275 km from Ha Tien. You can get to My Tho in only a couple of hours from Saigon's Mien Tay Bus Station. The bus station at My Tho is 4 km back on the road toward Saigon and Vinh Long. The station is open from about 4 a.m. to 5 p.m. Take Ap Bac Street to National Highway 1 to get there. There are also buses to Vinh Long, Can Tho, Rach Gia, Chau Doc and other destinations in the delta. Buses generally leave when they are full.

By **boat**, ferries leave to My Tho in the afternoon from Saigon and take about 6-7 hours, sometimes quite a bit longer. They leave from the wharf on Ton Duc Thang Street at the end of Ham Nghi Street. Price about US$1. Transportation around My Tho is by cyclo or by small motorized boats which can be rented from the ferry landing on Trung Trac Street. You can hire a car at Thuan Hung, *130-156 Le Loi*. Note: if you're traveling by car from Saigon to My Tho, remember the road (NH1) splits about 68 kilometers from HCMC. Proceed straight (which is a fork off NH1) to get to My Tho, or turn right to proceed on to Vinh Long. Signs are well marked.

### Tourist Office

Tien Giang Tourism, *66 Hung Vuong Street.* ☎ *72154.*

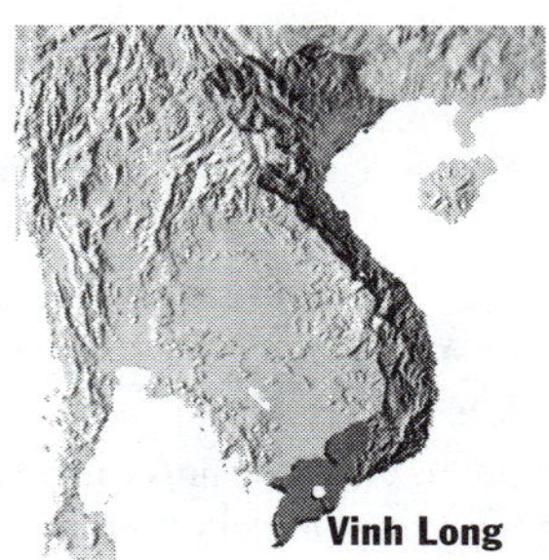


# Vinh Long

## VINH LONG IN A CAPSULE

**Vinh Long**, *(about 135 km southwest of Saigon) is the site of a major temple dedicated to Tong Phuc Hiep, general of the Nguyen Dynasty... It was also the home of Petrus Ky (Truong Vinh Ky), the 19th century spirit who sought to modernize Vietnam.*

About 145 kilometers from Ho Chi Minh City on the Hau River, Vinh Long province occupies a core area of the Mekong Delta. It may be regarded as a microcosm of the entire Mekong Delta due to its primordial prosperity. An Binh Island and Binh Hoa Phuoc Islands dot the huge networks of meandering rivers, bisected by countless arroyos under the dense tropical delta foliage. When you pay a visit to the orchards you can taste ripe fruits you pick from the trees yourself or have friendly conversations with the local people.

Vinh Long (the capital of Vinh Long province) is not the kind of place you'll really want to spend a lot of time in, however, save for taking boat trips along the Co Chien River to visit the orchid-covered islands. There are some decent hotels that have gone up in recent years that make the town a more attractive resting spot in your journey to areas further south and to the west such as Can Tho, Long Xuyen, Rach Gia and Ha Tien. Vinh Long is also the nucleus of the spread of Catholicism in the Mekong Delta region, so you'll come across a couple of cathedrals and a seminary. There's also a Cao Dai church near the second bridge into town coming from both Saigon and My Tho. Vinh Long is about 140 km south of HCMC. The city was also the home of Truong Vinh Ky (Petrus Ky), a legendary figure of the 19th century who sought to bring Vietnam into the "modern" age.

If you visit the islands around Vinh Long, you'll have to hire a boat, the smallest of which can be had for around 10,000–20,000 dong per hour (about US$1–2). The best islands to see are unquestionably An Binh Island

and Binh Hoa Phuoc. The town of Vinh Long itself is rather dreary, but is becoming an increasingly comfortable place to spend the night.

## What to Do and See in Vinh Long and Environs

### The Tong Phuc Hiep Temple

This temple was dedicated to Tong, who was considered a great general during the Nguyen Dynasty. It's worth a few minutes visit.

### Binh Hoa Phuoc and An Binh Islands

Just a short ride across the Mekong (the finger here is called the Co Chien) are islands teeming with tropical fruit plantations, fruit that's eventually trucked or shipped up to HCMC. You could actually spend a few hours out on the river as there are other islands dotting the river, many having never been visited by tourists. Again, though, there are not a lot of sights out here, and the boat ride may be worth it just for the ride itself and the breeze to break up the intense delta heat. For boat info check with the Long Chau Hotel or the Vinh Tra Hotel (addresses below). The boat trip runs about US$30.

## Where to Stay in Vinh Long

**AUTHOR'S NOTE: TELEPHONE PREFIXES**

*The following telephone numbers are local exchanges. The country code is 84. The city code is 70.*

### An Binh Hotel

*3 Hoang Thai Hieu Street. (Some air conditioned rooms).*

### Vinh Tra Hotel — US$12–$35

*1 Thang 5 Street. ☎ 23656.*

*20 rooms.*

Cheapest rooms get you a fan, the more expensive hot water, air conditioning and refrigerator. Hotel offers Mekong River tours, car and microbus rentals, restaurant with Asian and European cuisine and dancing. Hotel overlooks the Mekong.

### Cuu Long Hotel

*Next door to the Cuu Long Restaurant. 1 Thang 5. ☎ 22494.*

### Long Chau Hotel — US$6–$8

*11 Thang 5 Street. ☎ 23611.*

$6 rooms with public toilet. $8 rooms have private bath. The pricier rooms also have air conditioning. Hotel offers river tours, car and microbus rentals. Restaurant featuring Asian and European cuisine. Dancing hall, orchestra and entertainment nightly. This is a hell of a good deal.

## Where to Eat in Vinh Long

### Phuong Thuy Restaurant

*Thang 5 Street, across the street from the Vinh Tra Hotel.*

Excellent seafood at some of the cheapest prices in the delta. There are a number of restaurants serving river fish and seafood specialties along Thang 5 Street. However, the Phuong Thuy may well be the best.

## Directory

### Transportation

Hired motor car or motorcycle is the best way to move between Saigon and Vinh Long, and many tourists will combine a day trip with a visit to nearby My Tho or even Can Tho (about US$70 for the car and another $20 a day for the guide). (Frankly, I don't think a day trip to Vinh Long is worth it. The stop is only reasonable if you're planning an extended trip into the delta.) But if you must travel by bus, buses from HCMC's Mien Tay Station to Vinh Long take between 3-1/2 and 4 hours, as does the return trip from Vinh Long's bus station next to the post office and central market. Buses leave when they're full. There is also bus transport from Vinh Long to other areas in the delta, including My Tho, Can Tho, Rach Gia, Ha Tien and Long Xuyen.

### Tourist Office

Cuu Long Tourism. *1 Thang 5 Street*; ☎ *23616.*

### Post Office

Just behind the bus station on Doan Thi Diem Street.

# Sa Dec

## SA DEC IN A CAPSULE

**Sa Dec,** *about 135 km southwest of Saigon, is the site of the tomb of Nguyen Van Nhon. Two important people, a French military general and the governor of Cochinchina, were assassinated here by a Viet Minh Cao Dai.*

Sa Dec, halfway between Vinh Long and Long Xuyen, is about 135 km from Saigon and is probably most famous for the many flower nurseries that transport fresh flowers daily to Saigon. Ho Chi Minh's father used to spend time here and his grave is located in Sa Dec. Here is also the tomb of Nguyen Van Nhon, the mandarin who helped Emperor Gia Long defeat the Tay Son. Also, the commander of the French Forces in Cochinchina, General Chanson, was assassinated here, as was Thai Lap Thanh, the governor of Cochinchina, in July 1951. The killings were the work of a dissident Viet Minh Cao Dai follower.

Sa Dec is worth a visit for the beautiful nurseries in the area. As well, Ho Chi Minh's father settled here and was buried here.

### Where to Stay and Eat in Sa Dec

Sa Dec isn't worthy of an overnight stop. The few food stalls offer standard Vietnamese fare, but watch where the proprietors crack the ice. If they're doing it on a sidewalk or in the street, avoid it.

### Directory

#### Tourist Office

The tourist office for Dong Thap Province is located at *108 5/A Hung Vuong Street* in Sa Dec. It's called Dong Thap Tourist. ☎ *61430* or *61432*.

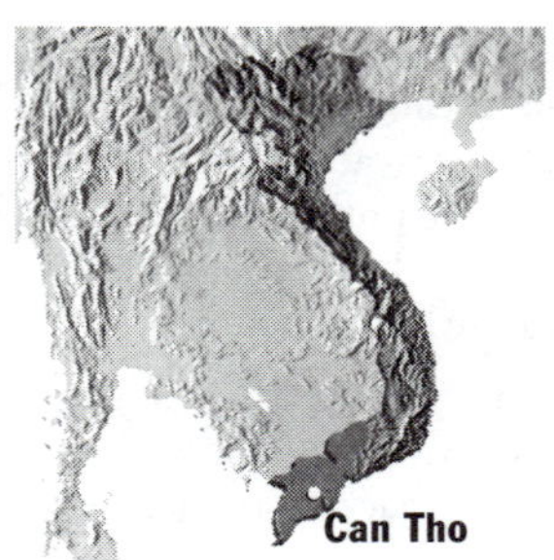


# Can Tho

*This skipper carefully negotiates a narrow canal near Can Tho.*

## CAN THO IN A CAPSULE

**Can Tho** *(170 km southwest of Saigon) is the capital of Can Tho Province and the region's transport center. Since the colonial days, it has been the delta's major center of rice cultivation...There's an important rice research institute here, as well as a university.*

Can Tho (about 170 km south of Saigon), capital of Hau Giang (or Can Tho) Province on the Bassac—or Hau River—is considered to be the Mekong Delta's Capital of the West and is the largest population center in the delta, with more than 200,000 inhabitants. It's probably the cleanest and nicest city to visit in the delta—certainly the city with the best accommodations. Can Tho makes a great base to explore the outlying villages and islands. Canals and rice fields surround this intermittently picturesque city. It also serves as the delta's most important transportation center. Roads and ribbon-thin river tributaries lead to surrounding towns and villages, many of whose inhabitants have rarely seen foreigners.

Can Tho is certainly the political, cultural and economic hub of the Mekong Delta, and many farmers in the surrounding villages possess vast parcels of land (recently given back to the farmers after the communist government seized most private land after 1975) used for agriculture, including tropical fruit, cotton and pepper. Along the canals (that rise to the rims of their banks and then drop like a flushing toilet with the tides) outside Can Tho, visitors will be surprised at the increasing number of tall, modern deco-like structures being erected along the waterways' banks, the result of local prosperity and the money sent back to families by wealthy overseas Vietnamese (Viet Kieu).

In the city's center, along Hai Ba Trung Street on the Can Tho River, is a bustling market and a huge, silver painted statue of Ho Chi Minh in the riverside park that looks like a carved brewery vat. City dwellers and tourists get around by motorcycle cyclos that are unique to the delta; they aren't found anywhere else in Vietnam.

Can Tho is also the site where Nguyen Khoa Nam, commanding general of the 4th Military Region, and his deputy Le Van Hung committed suicide in May 1975 after the fall of South Vietnam to the communists.

## What to See and Do in Can Tho and Environs

**Binh Thuy Temple** 

*3 km west of Can Tho*

Just a few kilometers west of Can Tho, this structure was built in 1852 by Binh Ton and features shrines to the king of longevity. There are some beautiful portraits—and others that are rather amateurish and less flattering—of Vietnamese and Chinese leaders such as Phan Boi Chau, Bui Huu Nghia and Nguyen Hue. Perhaps the most striking features of the temple are the numerous cranes that are built near dragon-wrapped columns. Other figures of cranes and dragons are built of brass that frankly, could use a bit of polishing. There is also a large 150-year-old stuffed tiger. The symbol of the giant cranes reflects the large white birds' visits to the area to be fed marijuana by the locals (as legend has it). Others from Can Tho to Long Xuyen will attest to the birds feeding on the illegal crop each day near sunset on the river's islands. The temple was designated a cultural and historical area by the Hanoi government in 1989.

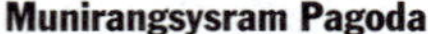

**Munirangsysram Pagoda** 

*36 Hoa Binh Blvd.*

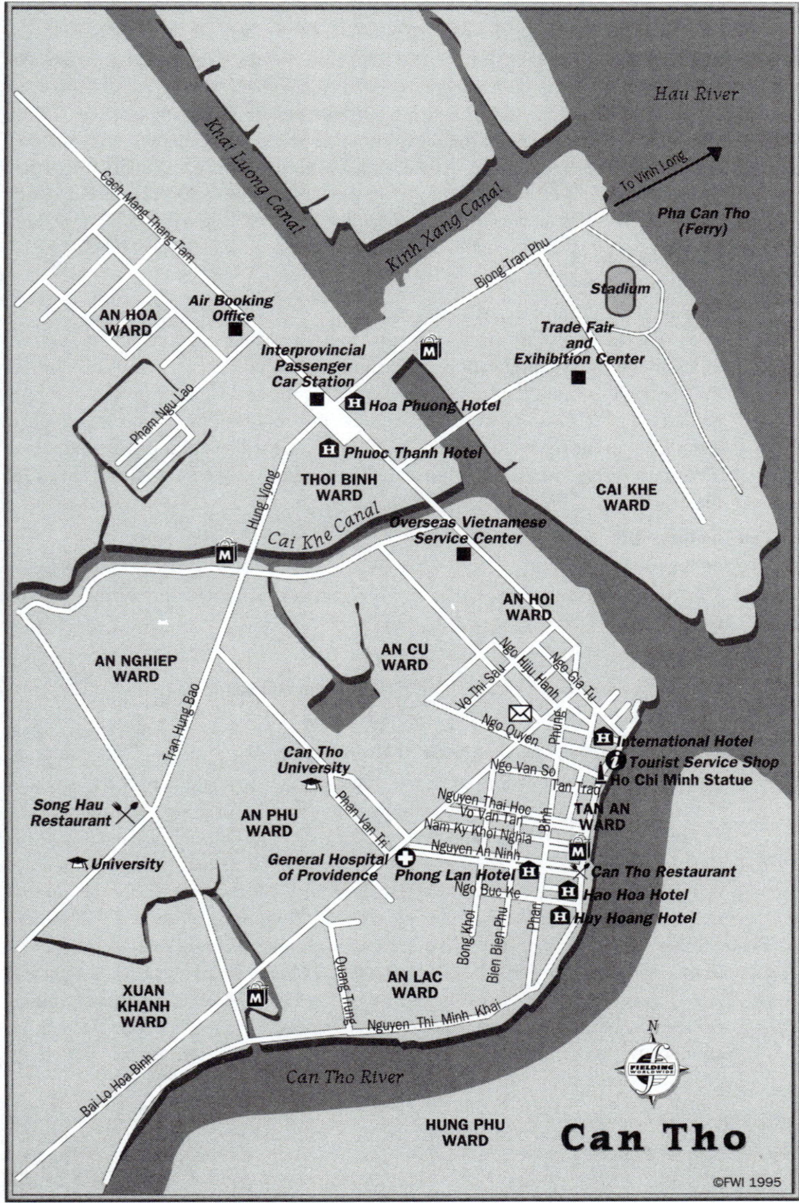
Hau River
To Vinh Long
Pha Can Tho (Ferry)
Khai Luong Canal
Kinh Xang Canal
Cach Mang Thang Tam
Bjong Tran Phu
Stadium
Air Booking Office
AN HOA WARD
Trade Fair and Exihibition Center
Interprovincial Passenger Car Station
Hoa Phuong Hotel
Pham Ngu Lao
Phuoc Thanh Hotel
THOI BINH WARD
CAI KHE WARD
Hung Vuong
Cai Khe Canal
Overseas Vietnamese Service Center
AN HOI WARD
AN CU WARD
AN NGHIEP WARD
Ngo Hiju Hanh
Ngo Gia Tu
Vo Thi Sau
Tran Hung Dao
Ngo Quyen
Phung
International Hotel
Tourist Service Shop
Ho Chi Minh Statue
Can Tho University
Ngo Van So
Tan Trao
Song Hau Restaurant
AN PHU WARD
Phan Van Tri
Nguyen Thai Hoc
Vo Van Tan
Nam Ky Khoi Nghia
Binh
TAN AN WARD
University
General Hospital of Providence
Nguyen An Ninh
Phong Lan Hotel
Can Tho Restaurant
Ngo Duc Ke
Hao Hoa Hotel
Huy Hoang Hotel
Phan
Bong Khoi
Bien Bien Phu
Quang Trung
AN LAC WARD
XUAN KHANH WARD
Nguyen Thi Minh Khai
N
FIELDING WORLDWIDE
Bai Lo Hoa Binh
Can Tho River
HUNG PHU WARD
Can Tho
©FWI 1995

Here is a Khmer Hinayana Buddhist temple that features a 1-1/2-meter tall figure of Siddhartha Gautama, the original Buddha, sitting beneath a bodhi tree. It was built in 1946, at which time more than 200 monks lived at the pagoda. An extremely elderly monk lives here as well as a few much younger monks, youths really. They are extremely friendly and will invite you into their quarters for tea before viewing the inside of the relatively small pagoda. The temple serves the several thousand Khmer Theravada Buddhists who live in the Can Tho area. I felt guilty neglecting to leave a donation, but if the monks were displeased, they didn't show it. Prayers are held early in the morning and in the evening.

**Quan Thanh De Pagoda**

*Le Minh Ngu On Street.*

Also known as Minh Huong Hoi Quan. Built by a Cantonese contingent nearly 75 years ago, this small Chinese pagoda was the house of worship for Can Tho's enormous ethnic Chinese population, who mainly evacuated the city—and Vietnam—in the late 1970s during the Vietnamese government's anti-Chinese persecution program. Quan Cong, as well as administrative mandarin Quan Binh and General Chau Xuong, are in the main dais, while Ong Bon, the Guardian Spirit of Happiness and Virtue are situated to the left of the dais. The Goddess of the Sea (Thien Hau) is on the other side.

**Can Tho University**

*30 Thang 4 Blvd.*

This small university was founded in 1966 and is worth only a brief stop for most visitors.

**Central Market**

Just down the river on Hai Ba Trung street from this statue of Ho, is a busy, cluttered market lined by numerous food stalls.

**The Villages Surrounding Can Tho (Ba Se, O Mon District)** 

These are the real attractions of the city, and if you can get a guide with relatives in the area, the US$20 expense will be more than worth it. All along the main highway to Long Xuyen, are rutted paths that lead deep into the delta's heartland. Small villages line the canals and motorized and oar-propelled boats navigate the sometimes dangerously shallow canals with amazing ingenuity. The best reason for the guide is the opportunity to be invited into his relatives' homes for meals and Vietnamese whiskey, whose distillers have no qualms of beginning their imbibing as early as 10 in the morning. In many of these areas, villagers have never set eyes on foreigners, and wherever you stop you'll be surrounded by dozens of children and women offering coconut milk. If you can go by boat it's better, especially one that can be arranged through a relative of your guide. In one day I had no fewer than five chickens slaughtered in my honor by families scattered along the banks of the canals. I was shown grave sites of family members killed during the war, as well as rich, vast parcels of deep black, rich soil covered with fruit and eucalyptus trees. There are boats for hire in Can Tho that usually rent for around US$2 an hour. They can be found along the river front. You won't have to look hard.

The other way to get out to the villages in O Mon district is to catch a minivan west to O Mon from Can Tho and ask the driver to stop after about 10 km—about halfway to O Mon. At that point, ask any of the numerous locals to bring you back along the arroyos on the back of his motorbike. Most won't hesitate to oblige for US$1-2. Ask to go to Lo Te Ba Se—or show the rider the following: **Rach Xeo De, Ba Se, Xa Tan Thoi, O Mon, Tinh Can Tho.** This means you'd like to go to Xeo De canal, Tan Thoi village, O Mon district, Can Tho province. The rugged ride is a truly remarkable 15 km journey back in time. Few, if any, travelers get back here. Small villages line the slim path deep into the heart of the delta. Canals line the path, where women wash clothes and canoe skippers pole themselves out of the mud as they traverse the ribbon-thin arroyos beneath a canopy of tropical vegetation. When you reach Ba Se, you can dispatch the driver—as there will be many villagers eager to bring you back to the highway after you've finished exploring the region. Ask anyone in Ba Se for a man named Mr. Hai Ky (Ong Hai Ky). Not only will you be treated to a meal, this elderly gentleman will be your proud escort through one of the most colorful experiences you'll have in Vietnam. He'll get one of his sons or nephews to fetch a canoe and bring you along the Mekong's thinnest tributaries. I'm not saying any more. Trust me on this one.

## Where to Stay in Can Tho

### AUTHOR'S NOTE: TELEPHONE PREFIXES

*The following telephone numbers are local exchanges. The country code is 84. The city code is 71.*

**Hotel Song Huong** **US$10–$12**

*101 Nguyen Trai. ☎ 25074.*

*12 rooms.*

Rooms with double or multiple beds. US$6 for a small room with a fan. Restaurant, private toilet. Foreigners accepted and management is quite proficient in English.

**Tay Ho Hotel** **US$7**

*36 Hai Ba Trung Street. ☎ 23392.*

*12 rooms.*

Rooms have two beds with fan and private bath. Foreigners encouraged. Next door is the Mekong Restaurant. Great Vietnamese cuisine at shamefully low prices.

**Tay Do Hotel** **US$4–$5**

*61 Chau Van Liem Street. ☎ 21009.*

*27 rooms (14 double, 13 single).*

This place is quite popular with backpackers. Private bath with the doubles, public toilet for the singles. Fans in all rooms.

**Phong Nha Hotel** **US$4–$5**

*75 Chau Van Liem (Nguyen An Ninh Old). ☎ 21615.*

*24 rooms.*

Singles and doubles both have private baths. Reception friendly. For the price, it's well furnished.

**Hotel Phuong Phu** **US$4–$5**

*79 Chau Van Liem. ☎ 20149.*

*14 rooms.*

One of the best bargains in town for the price. Private rooms with bath. No hot water, of course, but hot water in southern Vietnam is for tea, not bathing in. Electric fan. Currently the hotel is adding more rooms and adding air conditioning.

**Viet Hong Hotel** **US$8–$12**

*55 Phan Dinh Phung Street. ☎ 25831.*

*68 rooms.*

Here's another bargain. Fifty-four of the rooms have electric fans; the balance have air conditioning. Restaurant. The hotel provides tourist services from Can Tho Tourism. They'll also book flights to Phu Quoc Island, which leave on Mondays. For foreigners the cost is US$30 (the cost from Can Tho to Saigon to Can Tho is the same). Get a room on the 5th or 6th floor and you'll get a good view of the surroundings. Of course, you'll have to walk up the stairs.

**Viet Huong Hotel** **About US$10–$15**

*33 Chau Van Liem Street. ☎ 24832.*

Good central location close to the market and the river. A little cramped.

**Khach San Khai**

*83 Chau Van Liem.*

At press time, this place wasn't accepting foreigners, although I expect that to change in the coming months.

**Hotel Hoa Binh** **US$6–$18**

*5 Hoa Binh Street. ☎ 20530, 20536.*

*22 rooms.*

The single rooms at six bucks aren't much, but there is a fan. Rooms with three beds can be had for US$11, and non-air-conditioned doubles for US$8. Check the different rooms. There are a lot of configurations. For instance, 13 of the rooms offer only a public toilet. There is air conditioning offered in nine of the twin bed rooms, which run US$18. Foreigners are welcome and the price includes breakfast.

**Hao Hoa Hotel** **US$10–$15**

*8 Hai Thuong Lang Ong Street. ☎ 24836.*

Small, but it finally is open to foreigners.

**International Hotel** **US$25–$40** ★

*12 Hai Ba Trung Street. ☎ 22079, 22080.*

*40 rooms.*

This is the classiest place in Can Tho without a doubt. You might even be tempted to say that it's up to international standards which, in my opinion, it is. It's well-maintained, modern exterior and interior stand out in distinct contrast with the surrounding environment. Right on the waterfront. Air conditioning, restaurant, friendly service.

**Hau Giang Hotel** **US$23–36** 

*34 Nam Ky Khoi Nghia Street (Can Tho center city).* ☎ *21851, 21189. FAX: 21806. 35 rooms.*

Nicely appointed and friendly staff who know English well. Rooms have private bath, air conditioning, refrigerator, telephone (IDD in the lobby), radio cassette and TV. Hot and cold water systems. Photocopy services, foreign exchange services, car rental service and river tours to orchid-covered islands. Air-conditioned restaurant with 200 seats; Vietnamese, Asian, seafood, Chinese and European dishes. Open from 6 a.m. to 11 p.m. 7 days. Price includes both breakfast and lunch. Dancing hall and karaoke room.

## Where to Eat in Can Tho

**Restaurant Can Tho**

*52 Nguyen Trai Street.* ☎ *22186.*

Vietnamese, Asian, Chinese.

**Restaurant Can Tho**

*27 Chau Van Liem Street.*

Vietnamese, Chinese, European. Romantic setting, nice ambiance.

**Restaurant Hoang Huy**

*65 Phan Dinh Phung, 1st floor.*

Vietnamese.

**Restaurant Rain-Bow**

*54 Nam Ky Khoi Nghia.*

Vietnamese, Asian.

**A Chau Restaurant**

*91 Chau Van Liem Street.* ☎ *22129, 22130.*

Vietnamese, Asian. Prepare for your meal to be served quickly.

**Vinh Loi Restaurant**

*42 Hai Ba Trung Street.*

Soups are the tastiest here. The Vietnamese cuisine is both delicious and a total bargain.

## Directory

### Transportation

Can Tho is 170 km from HCMC, 104 km from My Tho, 115 km from Rach Gia, 35 km from Vinh Long, 115 km from Chau Doc, 62 km from Long Xuyen and 50 km from Sa Dec. By **bus**, you'll leave from HCMC's Mien Tay bus station. Express buses take only about 4 hours to get here and leave HCMC when full. Non-express buses take about 5-6 hours. Can Tho's intercity bus station is located next to the ferry dock on Nguyen Trai and Tran Phu.

There are two ferry crossings—one at Vinh Long and the other at the north side of the Bassac River at Can Tho. Just a note: motorcycles and express buses have priority at the ferry crossings. With a motorcycle, you'll certainly catch the next ferry (two are typically run simultaneously) and probably won't have to wait much more than 15 minutes. Express buses may sometimes wait 30 minutes, but it's rare. Non-express buses frequently wait 30 minutes or more.

**Can Tho Police Dept.**

☎ *270281.*

**Fire Department**

☎ *20170* (An Hoi Quarter, ☎ *21286*).

**Post Office**

*25 Hoa Binh Street.*

**Emergency Medical Services (EMS)**

*213 Hoa Binh;* ☎ *6l: 24644, 24244.*

**Can Tho Tourist Co. (Headquarters)**

*27 Chau Van Liem Street;* ☎ *21804,21853; FAX: 84.71.22719.*

**Can Tho Service Center**

*18 Hai Ba Trung Street;* ☎ *21852; FAX: 84.71.22719*
(In Ho Chi Minh City) *01 Nguyen Tat Thanh Street-4th District;* ☎ *291053.*

## Thot Not (Can Tho Subdistrict)

There's not much here, unless you're moving at night east to Can Tho (about 40 km away) and are extremely tired and want to spend the night at one of the cheapest hotels in Vietnam. The one attraction in this area is **Tan Lap Island**, another area *very rarely* seen by foreigners. You can hire a boat in Thot Not and cross the Hau River for a visit to the orchid-covered island.

### Where to Stay and Eat in Thot Not

**Thot Not Hotel** **US$2.50–$3**

*No address, across the bustling main drag from Thanh Binh Restaurant;* ☎ *51309. 10 rooms.*

This lies on a busy main street lined with cafes, food stalls and small restaurants. The hotel itself is a converted office building that's dirty and musty and sees few foreign travelers. The rooms are relatively clean, but if you've gotten a room with two single beds attached, don't move them apart. The floor will reveal a putrid display of dead cockroaches, rat excrement and used condoms. The public toilet is abhorrent. Don't use it unless you've got a good, high pair of trout fisherman's boots. The water in the showers is like grape vinegar. The manager, though, is eager for business, and is eager to please tourists.

There are numerous food stalls up and down the "strip" in Thot Not with—perhaps not surprisingly—great sea and river food. Most of the proprietors are relatively old and speak both French and English—i.e. they fought or were associated with the South Vietnamese/American efforts to win the Vietnam War. They'll want to practice their English with you and will often trade conversation for libations, and even food. You can have a night on the town here without even having a town to have a night on.

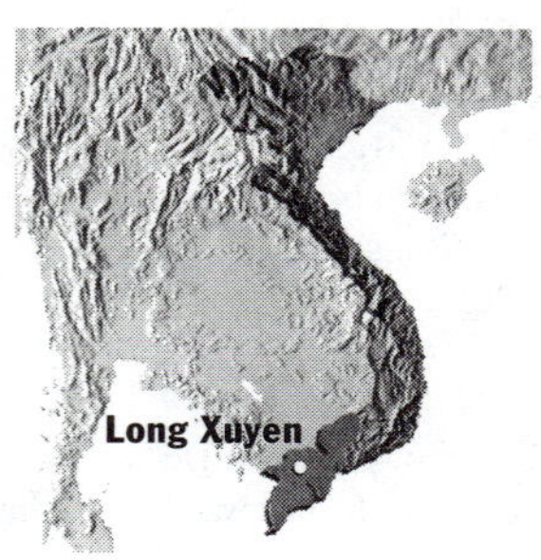


# Long Xuyen

## LONG XUYEN IN A CAPSULE

*Capital of An Giang Province...A grimy city...But marvelous scenery on the other side of the river...The Hoa Hao sect was once very powerful here and had its own army based here...Home to the Hoa Hao University.*

Long Xuyen (about 182 km southwest from Saigon) is the capital of An Giang Province with a population of about 100,000 situated on the west bank of the Bassac River. It's a rather shabby city, as are many in the delta, and seems virtually indistinguishable from Can Tho save for the riverside parks and cafes, of which I couldn't find any in Long Xuyen. It was once a major area of the Hoa Hao sect, an interesting religion without temples nor priests that act as the bond between man and God. But the Hoa Hao people were extremely influential in the area and even possessed their own surprisingly strong and disciplined military force. Today the city is the home of the Hoa Hao University, which was founded in 1970.

My impressions of the provincial capital were redundant with some of the other city centers of the delta: bustling markets, shabby hotels, a river transportation system that takes some asking around to get pointed in the right direction, and small temples and pagodas that are only really worth seeing if you haven't seen some finer examples in other areas of the delta.

There's not a lot to see and do here, and perhaps its greatest attractions are the locations on the other side of the river, many of which have not been seen by foreigners (see next INSIDER TIP).

### What to See and Do in Long Xuyen

**Dinh Than My Phuoc Temple**

*Le Minh Nguy On Street, near the intersection of Huynh Thi Huong Street.*

There's an impressive roof here and the walls near the altar are covered with murals. Worth a quick stop.

**Quan Thanh Pagoda**

*8 Le Minh Nguy On Street.*

This isn't far from Dinh Than My Phuoc Pagoda and is probably more worth the visit. The entrance wall is covered by beautiful murals, and the altar features a figure of Mandarin General Quan Cong as well as other Mandarin leaders including Quan Binh and General Chau Xuong.

**Cao Dai Church**

*Tran Hung Dao St.*

Near the end of Long Xuyen toward Chau Doc on Tran Hung Dao street is a small Cao Dai temple that, again, is really only worth a visit if you haven't already been to Tay Ninh.

**Long Xuyen Catholic Church**

*Center of the triangle formed by Nguyen Hue A, Tran Hung Dao and Hung Vuong Streets.*

This is a huge Catholic church that's an easy landmark in the city and can be seen from several km from outside Long Xuyen. It was finished just prior to reunification of the country in 1975. There's a 50-meter high bell tower and two giant hands clasped together form the spire of the church. This church is reputedly one of the biggest in the delta, if indeed not the largest. Masses are conducted here quite early in the morning (around 4:30 a.m.) and in the evening from 6 to 7 daily. On Sunday, there are three masses.

**Protestant Church of Long Xuyen**

*At 4 Hung Vuong Street.*

This is much smaller than its Catholic cousin close by and is only really worth a visit if you feel compelled to attend service. Services are held every Sunday.

**Cho Moi** ★

*North side of the Bassac River.*

This is the verdant agricultural district on the other side of the Bassac River reached by ferry from the ferry terminal at the base of Nguyen Hue Street. It features bountiful tropical fruit groves of mango, banana, jackfruit, guava, durian and longan. It's worth a few hours' visit.

**My Hoa Hung Memorial House** ★★

*My Hoa Hung village, north side of Bassac River.*

Do you want to visit a fascinating island across the Basac River from Long Xuyen where giant, brilliant white flamingo-like storks arrive by the thousands each evening to munch on marijuana? Do it. As of my first visit, according to both guides and the local villagers, no independent travelers had ever visited the My Hoa Hung village, and this incredible sight of perhaps thousands of snow-white cranes getting trashed on pot. The island is also home to the My Hoa Hung Memorial House, which is where Ton Duc Thang, one of the most well known architects of Vietnamese communism and the Vietnamese labor movement lived from 1888-1906. The memorial house, across the road from Ton's magnificent tropical and eerie hardwood home, features photos of the Viet Minh's—and North Vietnam's—eventual leader at the usual state and formal functions. More interesting are the letters he wrote which are on display in glass cases, as well as his shoes, uniforms, suitcases, spectacles and other clothing items. The memorial house is visited seldomly, and the only Westerners to have seen the area (which have been very few indeed) have arrived via the fledgling Anziang Tourist Agency in Long Xuyen as part of small tour groups crossing the ferry at An Hoa. The place was deserted when I got there. There is no admission fee, but small donations (say 2000 dong) are appreciated. As far as getting out there, forget the tourist agency. (They'll tell you that the storks don't feed on marijuana because it's illegal to grow or possess marijuana in Vietnam. I guess someone's gotta tell that to the storks.) Nothing's marked, so read carefully. If you're coming west from Can Tho continue to Long Xuyen via Lien Tinh Street. Go around the first roundabout in Long Xuyen and continue straight on Lien Tinh. At this point stop and ask someone where Binh Duc Bridge is (it's located along the same route, but you'll need to know EXACTLY where it is!). Just before reaching Binh Duc Bridge, at the last possible meter, there will be a dirt turnoff to the right. Keep going on this path, which flanks the Dra On canal, for about 500 meters to an extremely small ferry landing. On the other side (only bicycles and motorcycles permitted on the ferry) of the river, you'll pass through My Hoa Hung village. You'll then see a bridge off to the right after about 3 km. Make a right over the bridge. The Memory House isn't much farther. Plan your visit to see the stoned storks between 5 and 6 p.m. The ferry to My Hoa Hung village is 700 dong; tack on another 600 dong for a bicycle, or 800 dong for a motorbike. Instead of returning the way you came, continue straight along the dirt road to the An Hoa ferry which runs across the river into downtown Long Xuyen.

## Where to Stay in Long Xuyen

### AUTHOR'S NOTE: TELEPHONE PREFIXES

*The following telephone numbers are local exchanges. The country code is 84. The city code is 76.*

**Long Xuyen Hotel** **US$10–$20**

*17 Nguyen Van Cung Street. ☎ 52927.*

*37 Rooms.*

Newly renovated, at least to an extent, within the last year. Hot water, air conditioning. Cheaper rooms have a fan, no air conditioning. It's run by Angiang Tourism.

**Cuu Long**
**(also called The Mekong Hotel)** **About US$20**

*21 Nguyen Van Cung Street. ☎ 52365.*

*24 rooms.*

Huge rooms here with private bath. Perhaps the best hotel in town. Hot water, air conditioning.

**Tien Thanh Hotel** **US$6–$10**

*240 Tran Hung Dao Street.*

On the road east to Can Tho, several km out of town. Inexpensive.

**Thai Binh** **US$6–$12**

*12 Nguyen Hue Street.* ☎ *52184.*

*24 rooms.*

A good value for the price. The more expensive rooms have air conditioning. Restaurant. Public and private toilet.

**Xuan Phuong Hotel** **US$10–$15**

*68 Nguyen Trai Street.* ☎ *52041.*

This is also not a bad deal. It's a clean hotel, and the more expensive rooms can accommodate four people. Air conditioning.

**Song Hau** **US$6–$10**

*243 Nguyen Luong Duyet Street.* ☎ *52308.*

*26 rooms.*

The cheaper rooms come with fan, while there's air conditioning in the others.

## Where to Eat in Long Xuyen

As in other Mekong Delta destinations, food stalls abound in Long Xuyen, and they're understandably the cheapest places to eat. Most of the small restaurant/cafes can be found along Hai Ba Trung Street, as can the **Long Xuyen Restaurant**, perhaps the best eatery in town, on Hai Ba Trung and Nguyen Trai Streets. Cuisine is Vietnamese, Chinese, and European.

## Directory

### Transportation

Long Xuyen is about 65 km from Can Tho and 126 km from My Tho. The distance to HCMC is about 190 km. **Buses** leave from Saigon's Mien Tay Bus Station. The express bus to HCMC leaves Long Xuyen at 4 a.m. every day. The Long Xuyen bus station is about 1.5 km east of town on Tran Hung Dao Street, not far from the Catholic cathedral. The ride to Saigon takes about 7 hours along generally good roads. Bus connections from Long Xuyen can also be made to Can Tho, Vinh Long, Chau Doc and Rach Gia. It's important to note there are other bus stations around town that can provide more comfortable express bus service to HCMC. An express microbus leaves from near the GPO about 2 a.m. There's also a tourist express bus service (at *93 Nguyen Trai Street)* to HCMC at 4 a.m. each day. It can be confusing to figure out what the best situation is for your own needs, so ask the folks at **Angiang Tourist Office** (*6 Ngo Gia Tu Street*). There are a few private bus companies that offer faster and more comfortable solutions to your transportation needs. Transportation around town is generally via the type of **"cyclo"** which is unique to this part of Vietnam. They are in effect wagons that are pulled by either motorcycle or bicycle. They are the easiest way to get around town.

### Post Office

*101 Tran Hung Dao Street.*

### Banks and Moneychangers

Vietcom Bank is located, *1 Hung Vuong* near the intersection of Hung Vuong and Nguyen Thi Minh Khai Streets. Money can also be changed at reasonable rates at gold and jewelry shops about town, usually about 10,800 dong to the dollar. Many hotels, if they do change money, render 10,000 dong per dollar. But it's gone up at many places in recent months to close to the exchange rate of 10,900 dong per dollar.

### Tourist Office

Angiang Tourist Office is at *6 Ngo Gia Tu Street.* ☎ *52036.*

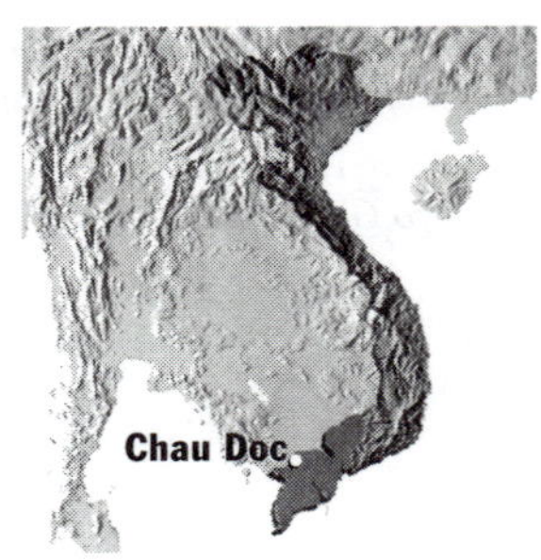


# Chau Doc

## CHAU DOC IN A CAPSULE

*300 km from Saigon, 150 km from Vinh Long...Chau Doc is part of An Giang Province near the Cambodian border...There are many ranges of spectacular mountains, beautiful landscapes and a lot of historical relics...Mount Sam...Ba Chua Xu Temple...Tay An Pagoda...Thoi Knock Hau Mausoleum...Breeding fish rafts on the rivers.*

As is Can Tho, Chau Doc (population about 80,000), is a relatively attractive and clean city for the Mekong Delta and a major commercial center in the western delta—it attracts a lot of French, Vietnamese and particularly Chinese, Taiwanese and Hong Kong tourists. It sits on the west bank of the Bassac River near the Cambodian border and possesses perhaps both the largest Khmer and Cham populations in Vietnam. Until the middle of the 18th century, Chau Doc was under Cambodian rule but was ceded to Lord Nguyen Phuc Khoat after his help in suppressing an uprising in the area. You'll notice that many of the women here, rather than the traditional Vietnamese conical hats, don Khmer scarves on their heads. The area is also home to the Hoa Hao sect, which was founded by Huynh Phu So in 1939 and claims more than a million members, most of whom live in the Chau Doc region.

An interesting and curious feature of Chau Doc are the floating houses in the river. They're not built on stilts, but rather float directly on the river. Fish are raised in nets under the houses and are fed whatever the owners want to feed them. Of course, raising fish this way makes them easier to catch. Perhaps of greater benefit, fishermen don't have to drop explosives into the river to reap their bounty.

## What to See and Do in Chau Doc and Environs

### Chau Doc Church

*459 Lien Tinh Lo 10.*

This is a tiny church that really isn't worth a stop unless, of course, you're Catholic and it's Sunday at 7 a.m.

### Chau Doc Market

This large market stretches along the riverfront on Chi Lang, Le Cong Thanh Bach, Bang Dang and Doc Phu Thu Streets. In addition to an array of fresh produce, you can also find an abundance of goods smuggled into Chau Doc from Thailand via Cambodia.

### Chau Phu Temple

*Gia Long and Bao Ho Thoai Streets.*

This temple was erected in the mid 1920s in honor of Thoai Ngoc Hau. There are both Vietnamese and Chinese influences here, and funeral markers commemorating deceased dignitaries.

### Chau Giang Mosque

*Take the ferry from the Chau Giang ferry terminal and proceed about 25 meters before taking a left and going another 50 meters.*

This attractive mosque features a large dome and arches and is where Chau Doc's Cham Islamic population comes to worship.

### Sam Mountain (Nui Sam) ★

*3 km southwest of town.*

This is perhaps why the Chau Doc area attracts so many tourists. On Sam Mountain there are pagodas and temples that number in the dozens. The mountain was designated as the "Famed Beauty Spot" in 1980 by the Vietnamese Ministry of Culture. Many of the pagodas are set in deep caverns and caves within the mountain. The mountain itself is not a particularly impressive sight from a distance, but its religious and historical significance—as well as the labyrinth of caves makes a visit here well worth the trip. Most of the tourists here flock to the Tay An Pagoda, which is at the base of the mountain, the tomb of Thoai Ngoc Hau, Lady Chua Xu Temple, and the Cavern Pagoda. But that's no reason not to ascend to the top of the mountain, where vistas of the countryside give testimony to the area's agricultural bounty.

### Tay An Pagoda ★

*Base of Sam Mountain.*

Here there are hundreds of wooden carvings of religious figures. There are both Islamic and Hindu elements in the architecture of the pagoda, which was built in the mid 1800s. It was rebuilt in 1958. Tombs of various monks surround the temple, and close to the temple is the statue of Quan Am Thi Kinh (the Guardian Spirit of Mother and Child). Carvings of dragons and lions can be seen above the bilevel roof of Tay An Pagoda as they fight for possession of lotus blossoms, pearls and apricot trees. There are statues in front of the pagoda of a black elephant with two tusks, a white elephant with six tusks.

### The Tomb of Thoai Ngoc Hau

*Sam Mountain.*

Thoai was once a powerful Nguyen lord who served the Nguyen Dynasty. He ordered that his own tomb be built at the base of Sam Mountain and it isn't far from Tay An Pagoda. The steps leading to the platform where the tomb is (and those of his two wives) are made of red stone imported from the eastern and southern portions of Vietnam. There are other less impressive tombs in the area of some of the men who served under Thoai Ngoc Hau.

**Temple of Lady Chua Xu**

*Sam Mountain.*

This inauspicious temple faces Sam Mountain and is also not far from both the tomb of Thoai Ngoc Hau and Tay An Pagoda. It was built in the early 19th century from bamboo and shrubbery but was later reconstructed in the 1970s. Legend has it that the statue of Lady Chua Xu, which now stands at the base of Sam Mountain, was originally at the peak of the hill, but was brought on its way back to Thailand by Siamese warriors in the early part of the 19th century. But they never made it. It was so burdensome, they dumped it by the side of some path. Local villagers then brought the statue back to their town to build a temple for the statue. A young woman in the village, who pronounced herself Lady Chua Xu, instructed 40 virgins to bring the statue down to the base of the hill. After they reached the plain, the statue became too heavy for the women as well, and it was believed by the locals that because the women had stopped carrying the statue out of pure exhaustion, that this was the site where Lady Chua Xu had chosen for a temple to be constructed around it. And that's where it remains today. There's an important festival surrounding the temple from the 23rd to the 26th of each lunar month.

**Cavern Pagoda** ★

*Sam Mountain.*

The upper section of this pagoda, which lies about a third to halfway up the western slope of Sam Mountain, is comprised of two areas: the main sanctuary, where there are statues of Thich Ca Buddha and A Di Da (Buddha of the past). In the back of the cave is a shrine dedicated to the Goddess of Mercy (Quan The Am Bo Tat). The lower area of the pagoda houses the pagoda's monks and also contains two tombs where Thich Hue Thien and a lady named Le Thi Tho are buried.

## Where to Stay in Chau Doc

### AUTHOR'S NOTE: TELEPHONE PREFIXES

*The following telephone numbers are local exchanges. The country code is 84. The city code is 76.*

**Hang Chau Hotel** **US$20–$25** ★

*On the river on Le Loi Street near the ferry terminal.* ☎ *66196.*

This is the best and most expensive hotel in Chau Doc. There's a swimming pool, restaurant and a busy night club. All the rooms come with air conditioning. The more expensive rooms have a great view of the river.

**Thai Binh Hotel**

*37 Nguyen Van Thoai Street.* ☎ *66221.*
*15 rooms.*
Foreigners were previously not allowed to stay here, but this may change by the time you read this.

**Hotel 777** **US$6**

*47 Doc Phu Thu Street.* ☎ *66409.*
A small hotel popular with backpackers. Very Inexpensive.

**My Loc Hotel** **US$10–$15**

*51 Nguyen Van Thoai Street.* ☎ *66455.*
*20 rooms.*
Double rooms with ceiling fans. Some of the rooms have air conditioning. The more expensive rooms sleep up to four guests.

**Chau Doc Hotel** **About US$6–$10**

*17 Doc Phu Thu Street.* ☎ *66484.*
*42 rooms.*
Relatively dismal but with enough life-support systems for backpackers, who seem to fill the place.

**Nha Khach 44 (Guesthouse)** **About US$6**

*44 Doc Phu Thu Street.* ☎ *66540.*
Another popular backpacker's stop. There are doubles and triples here.

## Where to Eat in Chau Doc

The best place undoubtedly is the restaurant at the **Hang Chau Hotel**. There's live entertainment offered here. There's also the **Tourist Restaurant** at the corner of Doc Phu Thu and Phan Ding Phung Streets. Also try **Lam Hung Ky** (*71 Chi Lang Street*).

The cheapest places to eat are at the food stalls that are in and surrounding the Chau Doc market. The river-caught fish is particularly tasty.

## Directory

### Transportation

Chau Doc is about 245 km from HCMC, 118 km from Can Tho, 180 from My Tho, and 96 from Ha Tien. The Chau Doc bus station is on the southeast side of the city on the south side of Le Loi Street, about 1.5 km out of town. **Buses** to Saigon take about 7 hours and arrive at HCMC's Mien Tay bus station. There is supposedly an express bus that leaves for HCMC from in front of Chau Doc Hotel. Buses to Long Xuyen take about 2 hours. There are also connections to other destinations in the delta area, but remember, there is no direct road from Chau Doc to Ha Tien. You'll have to go east nearly to Can Tho (Thot Not) before Highway 1A heads south to Rach Gia. **Ferries** to Saigon often take over 24 hours and leave daily from the wharf at Ton Duc Thang Street (about US$1.20). Ferries, I am told, also ply their way down a series of canals to Ha Tien. Buses to Chau Doc leave from HCMC's Mien Tay station. The principal form of transport around Chau Doc is by **motorized cyclo**.

### Post Office

On the corner of Bao Ho Thoai Street opposite Chau Phu Pagoda. ☎ *94550.*

# Rach Gia

## RACH GIA IN CAPSULE

*Unattractive coastal city on the Gulf of Thailand...But the seafood is great...Considered to be the most prosperous province in Vietnam...One of the two gateways to Phu Quoc Island...Large numbers of ethnic Khmer and Chinese live here.*

Rach Gia, the capital of Kien Giang Province with a population approaching 125,000 people, is a major port city on the Gulf of Thailand at the very bottom of Highway 1A. The flies here outnumber the residents by about five to one (and the prostitutes outnumber the flies). Yet despite its appearance, it's considered to be the center of Vietnam's most prosperous province. Many of the hotels allow prostitutes into guests' rooms, and it is very unlikely one, or perhaps more, won't knock on your door after you've checked into your hotel. Both the hotels and the hookers are the cheapest in all of Vietnam. You'll frequently see men about town with large red circles on their backs and chests. This usually means they've recently been in the company of a massage girl, who performed a flaming alcohol massage by placing the bases of hot glasses on their skin in addition to employing more traditional sexual duties.

The population contains a large number of ethnic Chinese and Khmers. This is one of the oldest population centers in the Mekong Delta, so a number of pagodas and temples in the area are relatively old (if you consider the 18th and 19th centuries old). The city center itself lies on an island between two branches of the Cai Lan River. This is where you'll find most of the hotels, restaurants and shops. Rach Gia is also one of two ports with ferries bound for Phu Quoc Island (Ha Tien being the other).

Rach Gia is a delta boom town—with many goods entering Vietnam here from Thailand and other points in Southeast Asia (many of them smuggled)—and is expected to become even more prosperous in the future as the Vietnamese government continues to open its economy.

**INSIDER TIP**

*The ferry from Rach Gia to Phu Quoc Island (about a 9 hour ride), although it is supposed to leave at about 9 a.m. and around 10 p.m., usually leaves when it is filled with passengers. The round trip costs approximately US$8 (about 80,000 dong) and you can bring a bicycle or motorcycle aboard the ferry for an added surcharge (for a motorcycle, 80,000 dong roundtrip). Warning: If you are traveling in this part of the Mekong Delta by motorcycle and want to bring the machine with you out to Phu Quoc Island, only depart from Rach Gia, and not from Ha Tien (which is much closer to the island with lower fares to match). The boat trip to the island from Ha Tien is aboard a much smaller craft, and even the locals consider the ride a dangerous one. Do not bring a motorcycle from Ha Tien to Phu Quoc by ferry. If you plan on bringing your bike to Phu Quoc, you won't be able to go with it. It will leave on the night ferry. You yourself will then be required to leave by the ferry the next morning. The gamble's yours.*

Despite being directly on the Gulf of Thailand coast, there are no beaches in Rach Gia. There's a dirt road (Tran Hung Dao Street) that leads from the harbor to a small waterside "park" called Hoa Bien Park, which is nothing more than a big dirt patch where you can rent a chair, watch the sea, drink beer (there are a couple of food stalls here) and swat away at the flies.

## What to See and Do in Rach Gia and Environs

### Phat Lon Pagoda

*Just off Quang Trung Street.*

The name means Big Buddha. It's a big Khmer Hinayana Buddhist temple that features figures of the historical Buddha Sakyamuni. Eight small altars are scattered around the exterior of the pagoda. You'll see two curious-looking towers that are used to cremate dead monks. Tombs of other monks surround the temple. The pagoda was constructed 200 years ago. Although the monks that live here at the pagoda are ethnic Khmer, you'll also see ethnic Chinese worshipers. Prayers are held in the wee hours of the morning and in the early evening.

### Nguyen Trung Truc Temple

*18 Nguyen Cong Tru Street.*

Nguyen Trung Truc was the fellow who led the Vietnamese resistance forces against the French colonists in the mid 1800s. He was responsible, at least for the most part, in the destruction of the French warship Espérance, after which he fled to Phu Quoc Island and eluded French capture for a number of years. This infuriated the French so much that they kidnapped his family and took hostage a number of other civilians in 1868. Nguyen gave himself up to the French authorities and then was executed in the Rach Gia marketplace in October of the same year. Although the first temple bearing his name was primitive in structure it has been rebuilt a number of times over the years. On the altar in the main hall is a portrait of Nguyen.

**Pho Minh Pagoda**

*At the corner of Nguyen Van Cu and Co Bac Streets.*

There's a Thai-style Sakyamuni Buddha here that was a gift to the Pagoda by Thai Buddhists in 1971. The small pagoda itself was built in 1967. Close by is the Thich Ca Buddha in the Vietnamese style. There are nuns here that live behind the pagoda. Prayers are held at the practical hours of 3:30 in the morning and also at 6:30 in the evening.

**Ong Bac De Pagoda**

*14 Nguyen Du Street.*

This pagoda has on its main altar a statue of Ong Bac De, a reincarnation of the Emperor of Jade. To the left of the statue is Ong Bon (the Guardian Spirit of Happiness and Vitue), and to the right is the likeness of Quan Cong. The pagoda was built about a hundred years ago by Chinese living in Rach Gia.

**Tam Bao Pagoda**

*The corner of Thich Thien An and Tran Phu Streets.*

Although rebuilt in the early 20th century, the pagoda was originally constructed in the early 1800s. The garden of sculpted trees and bushes depicting dragons and other creatures is quite beautiful. The pagoda is open from 6 a.m. to 8 p.m.

**Rach Gia Museum**

*21 Nguyen Van Troi Street.*

Not a lot here.

**Rach Gia Catholic Church**

*Vinh Thanh Van subdistrict, across the channel from the Vinh Than Van Market.*

This is an unimpressive Catholic church built of red bricks in 1918. It's worth a visit if you're Catholic and don't want to miss mass, which is conducted at 5 a.m. and 5 p.m. on weekdays and at 5 and 7 in the morning and 4 and 5 in the afternoon on Sundays.

**Vinh Thanh Van Market**

*Sprawled along at Bach Dang, Thu Khoa Nghia and Trinh Hoai Streets.*

There's an imported products market close by between Pham Hong Thai and Hoang Hoa Tham Streets.

**Oc Eo**

*10 km from Rach Gia toward Vong.*

Oc Eo is an ancient city near Vong. The village, about 10 km from Rach Gia, was in its prime during the 1st through 6th centuries and was a major commerce center when the area was ruled the empire of Funan. Many archeological discoveries have been made here with relics found representing ancient Malay, Thai, Indonesian and even Roman Empire societies. Many of these artifacts can be seen in HCMC's History and Art Museum and the History Museum in Hanoi. There used to be travel restrictions to Oc Eo but, at the time of this writing, they have been lifted.

**Soc Xoai**

*16 km from Rach Gia toward Ha Tien.*

There is absolutely nothing to do in this small village about 16 km west of Rach Gia on the dilapidated, rutted and chokingly musty highway 9 to Ha Tien (about 90 km to the west) except make a pit stop at the Phuong Mai Cafe on the right side of the highway about halfway through town.

## Where to Stay in Rach Gia

**AUTHOR'S NOTE: TELEPHONE PREFIXES**

*The following telephone numbers are local exchanges. The country code is 84. The city code is 77.*

**Nha Tro Dormitory**

*No address nor phone, but it's located right at the wharf on the gulf where the ferries leave for Phu Quoc Island.*

This may be the best deal in town at US$3 for a double room with fan. Popular with Westerners, I was told, although the only foreigner I saw was Clint Eastwood on a nearby video screen. Fan; no hot water. Public toilet and shower; the water seemed a little dirty and was another reason it's best to visit this part of the world with a crew cut. But if you're going to take the ferry, this is a good place to be, because there really isn't a schedule out to the island. Some leave at 9 at night. Others early in the morning. Stay at this hotel and you'll know at a moment's notice. And you can't beat the price. I stayed in only one hotel in the Mekong Delta that was cheaper. Here is also the Caphe Hung (it closes early) for libation and the Xuan Hai Restaurant next door.

**Nha Khach 77.77** **US$4–$10**

*77.77 Tran Phu Street. ☎ 63375.*

Not much here. Dumpy rooms with public water closest. Inexpensive.

**1-5 Hotel (Khach San 1-5)** **US$5–$20**

*38 Nguyen Hung Son Street. ☎ 62103.*

The biggest problem in what seems to be a nicely decorated hotel is that I couldn't find anyone who could speak English. Rooms have air conditioning, telephone. There's a large parking area if you've come by car. Restaurant with European and Asian dishes. The manager was able to somehow explain that both the receptionists and waitresses were "young." Whether this was for my benefit or yours, I couldn't tell. The business card says the waitresses are "warn careful." Okay. Sounds like a government SIDA (AIDS) brochure. Souvenir shop, tourist cars, barber and beauty shop. Massage available.

**Hoa Binh Hotel** **US$3.50**

*5A Minh Mang Street. ☎ 63115.*

Another cheapie popular with the backpacker set. There are double rooms with a private bath and single rooms with no air conditioning nor hot water. Bargain basement.

## Where to Eat in Rach Gia

**Thien Nga**

*4A Le Loi Street.*

Vietnamese, Asian, and some hybrid European food. Cheap.

**Rach Gia Restaurant**

*Intersection of Ly Tu Trong and Tran Hung Dao Streets on the water.*

Delicious seafood.

**Hai Van Restaurant**

*Khu 16 ha.* ☎ *6305.*

On the rutted dirt road leading to Hoa Bien Park near the harbor. Shrimp, lobster, squid, frog, chicken and fish. Overlooks the water.

In addition, there are numerous food stalls all across the city.

## Directory

### Transportation

Rach Gia is about 250 km from Saigon, 115 km from Can Tho, 180 km from My Tho and 90 km fro Ha Tien. The bus station is on Trung Truc Street south of town. Buses leave regularly for Saigon's Mien Tay station when full. The trip takes about 8 hours. Express buses leave for HCMC from *33/40 Thang 4* street. There are also buses to Can Tho, Long Xuyen, Ha Tien. Buses to other local areas including Soc Xoai, Tan Hiep, Vinh Thuan, Tri Ton, Duong Xuong, Hong Chong, Go Quao and Giong Rieng usually leave the station very early in the morning, between 4 and 5 a.m. Buses leave Saigon's Mien Tay station for Rach Gia regularly. By **air**, VN will get you to Rach Gia via Phu Quoc on Tuesdays and Saturdays at 11:30 a.m. The journey time is two hours. Flights to HCMC leave at 2:10 p.m. the same two days. Cyclos are the best way to get around town.

### Post Office

The general Post office is on Tu Duc Street, near the corner of 207 and Duy Tan Streets.

### Tourist Office

Kien Giang Tourism is at *12 Ly Tu Trong Street.*

### Banks and Moneychangers

Vietcom Bank is next to the post office at *2 Duy Tan Street.*

# Ha Tien

## HA TIEN IN A CAPSULE

*The southwesternmost town in Vietnam...Sits on the Cambodian border...The road leading to the city is in dismal shape, but it's being repaved rapidly...The springboard to Phu Quoc Island...The sight of mass killings by Cambodia's Khmer Rouge in the late 1970s...Has perhaps the most intriguing history of any area in Vietnam...Was once the best link for sea traffic crossing the South China Sea for India.*

Situated in the far southwestern corner of Vietnam on the Cambodian border, Ha Tien, with a population of about 90–100,000, is a seaside anomaly, a mishmash of Khmer, Chinese and Vietnamese (many from the north and other sections of the Mekong Delta) working to construct something reminiscent of roads along the dilapidated dirt paths that connect Ha Tien with the rest of the Mekong Delta.

Although most of the few tourists who venture to this remote corner of Vietnam use Ha Tien as a springboard to nearby Phu Quoc Island, the city of Ha Tien has perhaps the most interesting history of all the regions of southern Vietnam. In 1671, a young Cantonese named Mac Cuu left China's Fukien Province at the age of 17 for the capital of Cambodia, Oudong. There, he impressed the Cambodian monarch King Chey Chettha IV so much, that he was indoctrinated into royal service. He was an aggressive individual capable of attracting vast commerce and exploiting the far away, completely undeveloped reaches of Cambodia. Most of his efforts were in the far southeastern edge of Cambodia in the Ha Tien area, the southern coast of the Cambodian state. Through his vast successes in developing agriculture in the region, the King granted him governorship (Oc Nha) of the region.

Soon, the area that is currently known as Ha Tien became a huge commercial success. Chinese settlers were offered free land. Agriculture flourished in the region, as did the trade in fishing and the distribution of agricultural tools.

Soon, Mac Cuu's "kingdom" without defined borders took on a more formal state-like structure. It became an essentially autonomous state maintaining a precarious existence between neighboring Cambodia, Thailand and Vietnam.

Because of Ha Tien's location as Cambodia's only important port of entry (and the best harbor on Indochina's western peninsula), it attracted the Siamese, who invaded the area in 1708 and essentially ruined the area's prosperity. (Ha Tien had become the strongest link for sea traffic traversing the South China Sea from India.)

Mac Cuu understood that the only way to maintain his "kingdom" was to enlist the aid of more powerful neighbors. So, in 1708, he sent a delegation to the then Vietnamese capital of Hue for a visit with Minh Vuong, southern Vietnam's leader at the time and one of the Nguyen Dynasty's most effective and dynamic Lords, chiefly responsible for expanding Vietnam's empire in the south. Minh liked the idea of essentially annexing territory from the Siamese and Cambodians at virtually no expense without concessions.

When the Siamese invaded the Ha Tien area a short time later, Vietnamese forces quickly drove the aggressors away. Ha Tien was then transformed from a colony of refugees to a full-fledged state, and it regained its prosperity, this time as a southern Vietnamese political state on the southern coast. It remarkably retained a separate identity, even as a province of the Nguyen empire.

Mac Cuu died at 80 in 1735 and is today considered the father of the southern peninsula. His grave, along with those of his family, is located outside the city center and is ornately looked after by the descendents of his family.

Prince Mac Tu Kham, the seventh generation of the family of Mac Cuu, was the last Vietnamese ruler of province—until 1857, when the French decided to annex Ha Tien with the rest of the Mekong Delta. Under French control, pepper plantations were established, but little was done to improve the lives of the region's people.

Much of the recent history of Ha Tien surrounds Khmer Rouge military raids of the city during the savage Cambodian leader Pol Pot's reign of terror, where hundreds of Vietnamese men, women and children were slaughtered by unspeakable means by Khmer Rouge guerrillas. The graves of the Vietnamese victims are scattered at different sites across the town and, by chance, I came across a remote site near the memorial tomb of Mac Cuu, where a sweat-soaked lone man surrounded by a score of children was digging into the claylike earth beside a dirt path. At first I thought he might be digging a latrine or well. I stopped and found out that he was exhuming the remains of his mother and three sisters who had been buried at the site in a single plastic bag 15 years earlier. It is customary for the inhabitants of Ha Tien who had relatives murdered by the Cambodians to exhume the remains of their relatives and have the remains burned and then sealed in a large lacquer pot. I watched in near horror as the man dug and picked his way through four feet of earth, finally reaching a tattered black plastic bag, which he then unceremoniously pulled from the ground as if he were simply removing the roots of a tree. Opening the bag, he sifted through the bones and the still intact clothing his relatives had been wearing the day they were executed. The children, he told me, had been ripped apart alive limb by limb by the guerillas' own hands. On a decayed, crumbling finger of his mother, he pulled off a gold ring, stained brown by the years of its clay earthen environment. The bones of the corpses had become part of the soil and he meticulously separated bone from the earth. The clothes of the woman and the children were then placed back into the grave and set on fire.

***Author helps Ha Tien local exhume the remains of his family, slaughtered by the Khmer Rouge.***

Ha Tien's topographical setting in the Mekong Delta is unlike the rest of the region, and might remind you to a degree of northern Vietnam's Ha Long Bay, with its huge rock formations and caves towering above the seascape.

You'll be disappointed to discover that Ha Tien is one of the more expensive areas to stay and eat in the Mekong Delta. Even Vietnamese nationals are overcharged in many places, and it isn't unusual to pay US$2.50 or so for a meal, about three or four times the rate you'll pay in most places in the delta. Hotels tend to be expensive because fresh water has to be hand carried to each establishment from the city's water tower. Throughout the city, one sees sun-withered men stoically hauling giant drums of fresh water stacked on dilapidated carts. Even in the few hotels that are marginally habitable, the water is often brown and silty, water that you'll eventually be required to bathe in if you decide to spend a few days here. Although it's expensive, I recommend bathing and brushing your teeth with bottled water only.

## What to See and Do in Ha Tien and Environs

**Thach Dong** ★

*3.5 km from town on the Cambodian border.*

This is a massive, cavernous stone temple just a stone's throw from the Cambodian border, where you can watch farmers and other merchants pedal their wares through the border gate from a few locations high in the cave. It's an odd sight, because just on the Vietnamese side of the frontier, formations of Vietnamese police officers can be seen lined up in the style of 18th-century British combat techniques, training in the use of mortars, automatic rifles and small arms—all the weapons pointed toward Cambodia and the flat Khmer countryside (although, admittedly, I didn't see any rounds fired).

It was at Thach Dong where the Khmer Rouge massacred at least 130 people (some of the locals say the number was higher, 162 exactly). Chambers in the grotto feature altars to the Emperor of Jade (Ngoc Hoang) and the Goddess of Mercy (Quan The Am Bo Tat). Some of the more adventurous types might be tempted to make an ascent to the summit of the cave/mountain, but the only route is up a slippery, vertical tunnel which serves as the home to hundreds of bats and, consequently, their droppings. Don't try it.

**Dong Ho** ★

*Ben Tran Hau St.*

Granite hills surround this lagoon from the Gulf of Thailand. It's just east of Ha Tien. The other side of the lagoon is flanked by the To Chau hills.

**Ha Tien Market**

*Just southwest of floating bridge.*

Right in the center of town, left after you cross the floating bridge. It's a bustling place that's worth noting mainly for the smuggled goods you can purchase there from Thailand and Cambodia. And it may be the only market south of HCMC where some of the goods (probably smuggled) can probably be had for cheaper than in Saigon.

**Tam Bao Pagoda**

*328 Phuong Thanh Street.*

Mac Cuu founded this temple in 1730. A statue of the Goddess of Mercy (Quan The Am Bo Tat) can be found in front of the pagoda standing in the middle of a pond surrounded by lotus blossoms. The area surrounding the temple contains the tombs of 16 monks. The bronze statue of the Buddha of the Past (A Di Da Buddha) is inside the temple. Prayers are held in the morning and the afternoon.

### Phu Dung Pagoda

*Off Phuong Thanh Street.*

Founded just a short time after Tam Bao Pagoda by Mac Cuu's second wife, this temple features a statue of nine intricately carved dragons surrounding the newly-born Siddhartha Gautama (Thich Ca Buddha). The bronze statue of the pagoda came from China and is encased in glass. Beside the pagoda the tombs of Nguyen Thi Xuan and other monks are carved into the hillside. (Supposedly Mac Cuu was killed in battle in Thailand and is buried there, although some locals who claim to be of the 8th generation of the family say that his tomb is not in Thailand but on the hillside, as well. The history books indicate there are no longer any living descendents of Mac Cuu.) From the hillside you can look across the bay at the mountain the locals call the "Sleeping Elephant."

Behind the temple is a smaller structure, Dien Ngoc Hoang based on the Taoist Emperor of Jade. Figures beside the emperor include Nam Tao on the right (Taoist God of Happiness and of the Southern Polar Star) and Bac Dao (God of the Northern Polar Star and Longevity) on the left. It is in this area where other unmarked graves contain the victims of Khmer Rouge massacres in the area.

### The Beaches of Ha Tien

*3 km west of town.*

Don't expect the crystal clear waters of Ca Na, Nha Trang or those found farther down the Gulf of Thailand coast, but the water here is calm and extremely warm—hardly refreshing. **Bai No Beach**, one of the best, is about three km west of Ha Tien. It's clean, some snorkeling opportunities and it usually isn't as crowded as **Mui Nai Beach**, which is about 3 km west of town. Mui Nai is usually where the tour micro-buses stop for the afternoon after reaching Ha Tien from Saigon. The beach is small and the sand dark. Women are frequently seen here trying to peddle their recent crab catches. There are two restaurants here, the **Sea Star** and the **Sao Bien** (which also means Sea Star), which are in fact one and the same, but in two different structures. I was disappointed with this beach.

### Phu Quoc Island ★★★

*45 km west of Ha Tien.*

This is a verdant mountainous island with a population of about 50,000 about 45 km in the Gulf of Thailand west of Ha Tien. It's exquisite beaches are becoming quite popular. The island is about 50 km long with an area of 576 sq. km. It provides fantastic fishing for the locals and the water is clear and calm. It's great for swimming and snorkeling and features some of the finest coconut tree-lined beaches in Vietnam, especially in the southern portion of the island. The island lies only about 15 km off the Cambodian coast and, although there's a lot of nasty, verbose talk about sovereignty of the island, it seems that it will remain in Vietnamese control for some time. There are a few ways of getting there, flying in from HCMC the easiest and the most expensive (about US$140 round trip). Or you can take a ferry from either Rach Gia (about 10 hours) or from Ha Tien (about 4 hours, but sometimes as many as 6). The trip from Rach Gia costs 40,000 dong one way per person, and another 40,000 if you bring a motorcycle. Do not attempt to take the ferry from Ha Tien to Phu Quoc with a motorcycle. The police in Ha Tien, as well as some of the locals, say the trip on the small ferry is dangerous enough in itself. The ferries leaving Rach Gia are considerably larger. Also, do not plan on a day trip to the island from Ha Tien. Theoretically, you might board a 9 a.m. ferry (that supposedly only takes 4 hours) and return on the afternoon ferry. But don't try it. You'll have to spend at least one night on the island, and in relatively expensive accommodations. If you do spend some time on the island, I suggest you stay at the **Huong Bien Guest House** *(Duong Dong Town. ☎ 84-77-46050, 46082. US$12-17.).* Vietnam Airlines flies to Phu Quoc Tuesdays and Saturdays at 11:30 a.m. The flight's about 50 minutes. There's a post office in town and a "hospital" just opposite it. The "tourist office" is located at the Huong Bien Guest House.

## THE INDUSTRIALIZATION OF PHU QUOC

*Phu Quoc has an area of 576 square km and is roughly the size of Singapore. There are more than 100 km of beach and thousands of square km of fishing areas. 305,000 tons of sea products are pulled from the Gulf of Thailand each year. By 1995, that figure is expected to climb to 500,000 tons. The island's fish sauce is very popular in Vietnam. There are 80 such fish sauce processing plants on the island which have a capacity of producing 5 million liters of the sauce each year. Pepper is also grown here, but production is down in recent years. However, cashew nut growing areas are increasing rapidly. But to Phu Quoc's credit, the island is investing billions of dong into reforesting 300 hectares that have been denuded within the 370 square km area of forests the island possesses. There is also a boom in industrial products and handicrafts on Phu Quoc. The island now makes some 100 billion dong a year from food processing, building materials and forest products. The Vietnamese government has now permitted Phu Quoc (Kien Giang province) to directly work with foreign companies to build roads, a sea harbor, an export-processing zone, and to install electrical and water supply systems. A total investment of more than US$500 million is planned for such projects. This island is going to change very quickly.*

### Where to Stay in Ha Tien

**INSIDER TIP**

*Although Ha Tien has accommodations that are ridiculously inexpensive, most of the hotels (and the food they serve if they have a restaurant) come with price tags that are the highest in the Mekong Delta. The primary reason is the water, which through the city's water lines is more akin to used radiator antifreeze than anything potable. Fresh water has to be hand carted to the hotels, restaurants, homes, etc., from a storage tank on the edge of town. Most of the water you will find yourself bathing in Ha Tien hostelries is the color of Jamaican Rum. The point is to be careful in Ha Tien. This is not a clean city, and many Vietnamese were surprised that I didn't contract viruses related to the water. Be careful of both what you eat and drink. A good guide is your best source of where to eat and drink in Ha Tien. The following is a list of hotels and eateries I personally experienced, although it is no guarantee that you won't become sick in any of the following places.*

**AUTHOR'S NOTE: TELEPHONE PREFIXES**

*The following telephone numbers are local exchanges. The country code is 84. The city code is 77.*

**To Chau Hotel** **US$5–$6**

*299 Ben Tran Hau. ☎ 52148.*
*7 rooms.*

There are singles and a couple of classes of doubles here. Fans and public water closet. Dirty, but acceptable for Ha Tien, where prices are traditionally higher than in all other areas of the delta.

**Dong Ho Hotel** **US$4–$6**

*Ben Tran Hau Street. ☎ 52141.*
*19 rooms.*

Run of the mill but cheap with a pleasant staff. Fan, public water closet.

**Phuoc Thanh Guesthouse** **US$.50–$2**

This place costs only 5000 dong for Vietnamese for a room and 1500 dong for a dormitory setting. Conditions are dismal here, and the water is as black as Ha Long coal. Public toilet and "shower" that guests also frequently use to urinate in. Don't brush your teeth here or wash yourself unless it's with bottled water. In fact, I'd avoid the place altogether, despite the fact that you can get a room for as little as US$.50.

**Binh Minh Guesthouse** **US$5**

*Duong Du Street. ☎ 52035.*
*8 rooms.*

Standard guest house fare but better than the Phuoc Thanh, and more expensive. Public toilet, no hot water, no air conditioning. Accepts foreigners but staff English is limited.

**Khach San Du Lich** **US$10**

*Cong Ty pu Lich, Kien Giang.* ☎ *52169.*

*18 rooms.*

Ceiling fan, no hot water, but has private Western-style toilets; cafe. Moderate, and probably worth the added cash because they spend more money purifying their water.

## Where to Eat in Ha Tien

There are a number of places to eat in Ha Tien, and you'll find that they're relatively more expensive than elsewhere in the Mekong Delta. After crossing the floating bridge, immediately to your left and right will be a number of semi-outdoor cafes and restaurants. If possible eat at sidewalk stalls, as they tend to be about half as expensive as anything indoors, with or without air conditioning. It is not uncommon to spend US$2.50 a meal at an indoor restaurant, and about half that for food just as palatable as that served in the indoor eateries. Be careful what you ask for at an outdoor stall. They'll promise to serve it but may have to run across the street to have the meal prepared at another restaurant. You'll end up paying more. Eat only what you know the stall or cafe can prepare itself.

Ha Tien reputedly grows coconuts not found elsewhere in the country. Many places serve the exotic coconut milk. If you must eat indoors, perhaps the only place I can recommend is **Xuan Thanh Restaurant** across from the market on Ben Tran Hau street. The food seemed to be prepared in soiled surroundings, but I found it quite good, although Johnny Tu, my guide, was appalled at both the prices and the food, and swore never to return. I guess that means I won't be going back either.

## Directory

### Transportation

Ha Tien is about 92 km from Rach Gia, 96 from Chau Doc, 205 km from Can Tho, and 340 from Saigon. The bus station at Ha Tien is on the southeast side of town, just across the floating bridge on the right hand side of the road. The trip to Saigon takes about 10 hours over some amazingly dismal but rapidly improving roadways. **Buses** arrive at HCMC's Mien Tay Station. They usually leave for Saigon in the wee hours of the morning, so don't plan on sleeping. Buses for Rach Gia leave at least four times daily, the trip taking about 4–5 hours or more depending on the roadwork being done. By fast motorcycle, the trip is much quicker, by at least an hour, as it is by car. But again, the roads in the southern Mekong Delta area are in such disrepair it is unlikely Lewis and Clark would have ventured across them. Currently there is no air service between HCMC and Ha Tien, although you can fly to the island of Phu Quoc from HCMC. Travel into Cambodia, which is terribly tempting, is not permitted. Border police at Ha Tien, although mostly friendly, will turn nasty if you ask too many questions. They say that Khmer Rouge units still operate regularly on the Cambodian side of the border. You can try to get authorization at Ha Tien's immigration police office, but they'll turn you down as well.

# Soc Trang

## SOC TRANG IN A CAPSULE

*About 60 km east of Can Tho...The capital of Soc Trang province...Province population about 1,172,000...65% ethnic Vietnamese, 28% Khmer, 7% Chinese...About 90 Khmer pagodas and 47 Chinese pagodas can be found in the province...Colorful feasts and festivals take place here each year.*

Rather than taking the highway southeast toward the South China Sea, most tourists in the Mekong Delta head northwest to Long Xuyen and Chau Doc or south to Rach Gia and Ha Tien. Soc Trang is an infrequently-visited city by foreigners, mainly because it has few attractions—Although they are growing.

The reason to come here is to see the bizarre Vietnamese Pagoda which is covered with swastikas, Buddha figures (mainly heads) and the statues of animals that cover the grounds. There's also another pagoda here, a Khmer monastery called the Bat Pagoda, where fruit bats live in the trees. They make for good photo opportunities. There are a number of murals here.

But with a little digging, you'll find there are other attractions to the area, as well. Nearly 140 pagodas dot the countryside in the province. There are numerous festivals and traditional feasts, exquisite gardens in the city and, of course, the large influence of Khmer culture in the area.

### What to See and Do in Soc Trang

**Stork Garden of Tan Long Thanh Tri (Vuon Co Tan Long)**

*About 40 km from the city.*

Tens of thousands of white storks make this "garden" their home. The sight of so many of these birds frolicking in the treetops and in the marshes shouldn't be missed.

**Fresh Water Lake (Ho Nuoc Ngot)**

*Center of town.*

This is an attractive little, pine-surrounded lake in town that's a good place to kill a few hot afternoon hours.

**My Phuoc Isle (Cu Lao My Phuoc)**

*In the middle of the Hau River.*

This is an attractive island featuring gardens and fruit trees. The fifth day of the fifth month of the lunar calendar marks the annual Doan Ngo Tet festival—the start of the annual harvest—and the island becomes a focal point. Soc Trang natives return from all over Vietnam to partake in the festivities.

**Tran De Fishing Port (Moo)**

*30 km out of town at the sea.*

This area is being developed, albeit slowly, for tourism. The Tran De estuary flows into the South China Sea from here. There's a quaint fishing port here as well as Mo O Beach, at the mouth of the river. Don't expect an azure sea.

**Museum of Khmer Culture**

*Right in the middle of town.*

Depicts the lives of southern Khmers. A few nice displays here. Attractive and clean as a whistle.

**Moon Worshipping Ceremony** ★

Celebrated on the 15th night of the 10th lunar month, this is a colorful festival dedicated to the moon's role in producing bountiful crops. There's a special offering of flattened rice (*com dep*) to the Man on the Moon. Earlier in the day is the Oc Om Bok Ceremony, when the spectacle of the Ngo Boat Race is held. This is one of the most colorful events in southern Vietnam. Dozens of brightly-clad boat teams row 15-meter canoes in the river while hundreds of revelers on the banks delight to Vietnamese, Khmer and Chinese theater artists.

**Ma Toc Pagoda (The Bat Pagoda)**

Local estimates say that more than 100,000 bats live in the trees around this four-century-old Khmer monastery. Thousands of bats can be seen sleeping upside down on the branches of trees during the daytime. At night, it's creepy.

**Clay Pagoda (Chua Dat Set)**

*Located 1 km from town.*

This is a 200-year-old pagoda filled with animal sculptures and giant candles weighing in at between 100-200 kg. The candles have only been about one-third melted in 20 years of continuous use.

## Where to Stay in Soc Trang

### AUTHOR'S NOTE: TELEPHONE PREFIXES

*The following telephone numbers are local exchanges. The country code is 84. The city code is 79.*

**Tay Nam Hotel** **US$20**

*133 Nguyen Chi Thanh. ☎ 21757.*

One of the two cleanest hotels in Soc Trang. This place even has a tennis court. Rooms with air conditioning, private bath. Restaurant.

**Phong Lan (Orchid) Hotel** **US$20–$35**

*124 Dong Khoi Street.* ☎ *21619.*

The best in town. Rooms with air conditioning, private bath. This is where the tour group set calls it a day. Has one of the best restaurants in town.

## Where to Eat in Soc Trang

Undoubtedly the best place in town is the Orchid Hotel. These guys also do a number of weddings and banquets. Also try:

**Nha Hang Huong Duong (Sunflower Restaurant)**

*Fresh Water Lake.* ☎ *21638.*

Great area for a picnic with food bought at the restaurant.

**Bong Sen (Lotus) Restaurant**

*National Route 1.* ☎ *21344.*

Nice eatery with Vietnamese specialties. Centrally located.

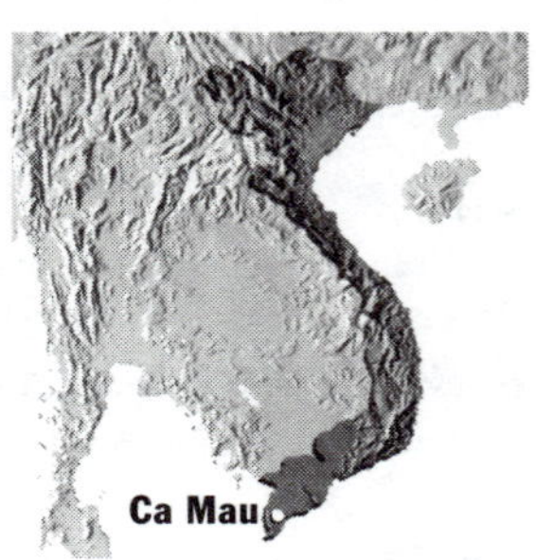


# Ca Mau

## CA MAU IN A CAPSULE

*On the southern edge of the U Minh Forest...Considered the largest mangrove swamps outside the Amazon Basin...Few Westerners visit here...American defoliation during the Vietnam War obliterated the area...Has a zoo that's more like a leper colony...Take medical precautions while visiting this vast swamp.*

Ca Mau on the banks of the Ganh Hao River is 180 km from Can Tho and 350 km from Saigon. It is the largest settlement on the Ca Mau peninsula and is at the southern edge of the U Minh Forest, a giant cajeput swamp that covers approximately 1000 sq. km of Minh Hai and Kien Giang provinces.

Apart from the Amazon basin in South America, the U Minh forest is considered by most to be the largest cajeput (or mangrove) swamp in the world. Aerial defoliation by the Americans during the Vietnam war practically ruined the area. However, nature has its incredible resilience and, today, much of the swamp has regained its beauty (although nearly a quarter of the swamp remains a dank wasteland). Much of the waterfowl have returned to the area, and bees pollinate the mangrove blossoms. However, the area is still being depleted of its natural resources today via shrimp breeding ponds. Locals also use the cajeput in a number of different ways: as charcoal, as a source of timber, and thatch for dwellings.

Ca Mau also features a "zoo," which is a dilapidated, inhumane environment designed for tourism that houses diseased, dismally treated animals that survive (barely) here for the benefit (or the nausea) of the few foreign tourists that visit this area. I'd stay away from it.

Bring your deet and malaria pills (although they might not be effective). Mosquitoes in the mangrove swamps and the town abound. They're especially bothersome at night, and eating at outdoor food stalls can be a miserable experience for this reason alone.

### Where to Stay and Eat in Ca Mau

The **Khach San Sao Mai** on the corner of Duong Ly Bon and Phan Ngoc Hien Streets appears to be nothing more than a whorehouse, as are most of the hotels in Ca Mau. Most of Ca Mau's hotels are on Phan Ngoc Hien Street, as is probably the best hotel in town, **Phuong Nam Hotel** (About US$50). Everything else ranges from around US$7–20, and most of the places are filthy and run down. It's one of the many reasons so few Westerners make it down this far. There is little if any tourism infrastructure in Ca Mau.

On Ly Bon Street can be found a number of roadside food stalls. You'll need nourishment, so eat at them, although the food is nothing to write home about. You should only travel to this area after having spent enough time in Vietnam to become accustomed to eating food stall fare, drinking boiled water, and bathing in rancid water. This is an easy place to get sick, and if your immune system hasn't yet adjusted to rural Vietnam, I'd avoid this area until it has.

### Directory

#### Transportation

Ca Mau is about 350 km from Saigon and 180 km from Can Tho. **Buses** leave for Ca Mau from HCMC's Mien Tay Bus Station and the trip usually takes between 10 and 11 hours by express bus and up to 13 by other buses. The road from Can Tho to Ca Mau is like other roads in the southern delta; they can only peripherally be classified as "roads." Potholes the size of B-52 bomb craters make the trip a roller coaster ride. The long trip by bus from HCMC is unendurable. If you want to go by boat from Saigon, the trip takes well over a day; boats leave for Ca Mau about every other day. Local transport is by water taxi, motorbike, or cyclo. You cannot reach Ca Mau by air.

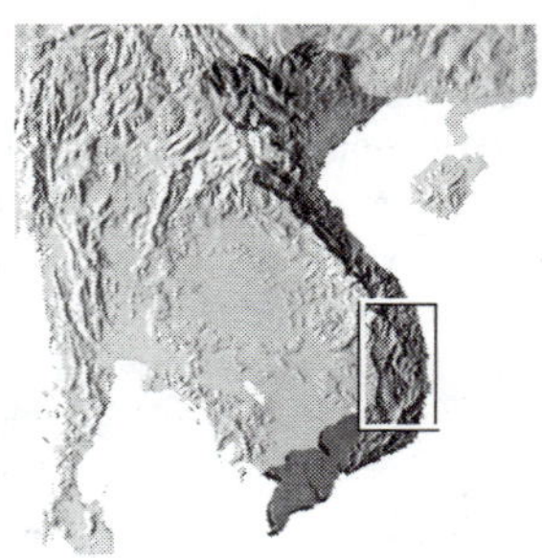

# THE CENTRAL HIGHLANDS

***Vietnam's Central Highlands offer some of the best vistas in the south.***

## THE CENTRAL HIGHLANDS IN A CAPSULE

*Some of the most spectacular mountainous scenery in Vietnam...The hillsides are dotted with hilltribe villages...The southern region of the highlands has Vietnam's best climate, warm days, cool nights...Many of the natural attractions have been somewhat spoiled by overcommercialism...Tourists are fewer and the accommodations sparse in the northern areas such as Pleiku...There was considerable military action in the highlands during the Vietnam War.*

The lush Central Highlands is home to many ethnic groups and famous for spectacular scenery. The area is part of the southern chain of the Truong Son Mountain Range, with a cool climate, beautiful lakes and waterfalls. Although not many people live in the Highlands, the area was considered strategically important during the Vietnam War, and travel restrictions to areas of the Central Highlands exist even today—although they are decreasing.

***A giant rooster crows toward Dalat from the small village of Duc Trong.***

Independent travelers can reach (if they are physically able to) many areas that were once prohibited. Provinces in the Central Highlands consist of Dac Lac, Kon Tum, Lam Dong, and Gia Lai. During the war, a lot of fighting took place around Pleiku, Kon Tum and Buon Ma Thuot. However, Dalat was remarkably spared from the fighting. Supposedly, top military brass on both sides of the conflict used Dalat as a summer retreat, and it's said that officers from opposing armies spent R&R time in villas only a few kilometers from each other.

Although Americans were recently prohibited from visiting the Central Highlands with the exception of touristy Dalat due to the continuing conflict between government forces and FULRO (the United Front for the Struggle of the Oppressed Races. There are even rumors of Reeducation Camps still existing in the area), these restrictions have been almost entirely removed. And where there are the few remaining restricted sites, you know longer need to be guided by Vietnamese Army soldiers. Instead tourism permits can be arranged at provincial tourist offices for a nominal fee of about US$5 (although you'll still have to hire one of their guides and perhaps a vehicle, even if you have your own).

The road leading from Saigon to Dalat is a generally good one (excellent by Vietnamese standards) and scenery is spectacular, particularly between Bao Loc and Dalat. You'll want to stop and take pictures in numerous places, across verdant mountainous vistas as well as the bridge spanning a small section of the Ho Tri An Lake between Bien Hoa and Bao Loc, where floating hootches dot the marshes and lake. The final 20 km to Dalat are almost straight up and, although it's a treacherous ride, the road winds deep through some of the greenest mountainsides you'll ever have a chance to see.

## Hilltribes

The highland areas of Vietnam are considered by most as the most culturally and linguistically numerous and diverse in the entire world. In the southern Central Highlands, there are as many as 35 different tribes, and as many as 50 throughout the country. Some of the ethnic groups possess as few as 500 individuals; the largest may number in the millions. Here's a look at some of the hill people, including those that are in the north:

### Bahnar

Mostly concentrated in the central highland provinces of Gia Lai and Kon Tum, the Bahnar are an ethnic minority group that speak Mon-Khmer. Their population is estimated at about 100,000. After enjoying nearly four centuries of power in the region (15th–18th centuries), the group was nearly wiped out in the 19th century by the Harai and Dedang people. The Bahnar became close with the French, and Christianity (particularly Catholicism) became widespread among the Bahnar. Men and women are considered as equals. Wealth is evenly distributed among a Bahnar family, and marriages can be arranged by the parents of either the man or the woman.

### Koho

These matrilineal people, also called the Kohor, inhabit Lam Dong Province near Dalat on the Lam Dong Plateau. Today's population of around 100,000 live in longhouses in extended family groups. These houses can reach 30 meters in length. Men who marry often live with the family of the wife. Settled agriculture provides the Kohos' subsistence.

### Rhade

This is another matrilineal group that primarily inhabits the Central Highlands. They're also known as the Edeh, and their population is believed to be approximately 170,000. They also befriended the French and Christianity is prevalent in their communities. They are considered to be among the most "modern" of the ethnic hill people. Extended families, like the Koho, also live in longhouses. Inheritance is usually given to the highest ranking female member of the family. Wet rice agriculture is the Rhades' primary form of subsistence, although some communities still practice the more traditional forms of shifting cultivation.

### Gia Rai

Found primarily in the hills in and around Pleiku in the provinces of Gia Lai and Kon Tum, these 260,000 matrilineal people represent the largest ethnic minority in the Central Highlands. They are also known as the Zrai people.

### Sedang

Another Central Highlands tribe, the Sedang (or Xo-dang) number about 100,000 people who live in longhouses in the Gia Lai and Kon Tum province areas. Subsistence is by wet rice cultivation and shifting agriculture. These are a violent people; they have fought both the French and the Viets, and was the group that nearly made the Bahnar extinct in the 19th century.

### Muong

As we move north, we find the Muong who are, numbering at nearly 600,000, one of the largest ethnic minorities in Vietnam. They inhabit the central and northern provinces of Hoa Binh, Son La, Thanh Hoa, Ha Tay, and Nghia Lo provinces. There are many similarities between the Muong and ethnic Vietnamese, both in culture and language. Wealth is inherited through the male line, and their subsistence is through the cultivation of both wet and dry rice. However, unlike the ethnic Vietnamese, the Muong were not confronted with the Chinese and Christian influences that permeated Vietnamese culture. Some Muong still apply a black lacquer to their teeth in their mid-teens to symbolize entry into adulthood.

### Hmong

The Hmong, who can be found in highland areas throughout Vietnam, have a population of about 750,000 people, making them one of the largest groups of ethnic hill people in the country. Originally settling in Vietnam in the 19th century from China, most Hmong can be found near the Chinese border and south to about the 18th parallel. The Hmong are a very isolated people, choosing to live at altitudes far higher than those inhabited by other ethnic hill people. Usually they live some 1500 meters higher then their lower neighbors. Like the Sedang, they are warlike and fought both the French and the Vietnamese. They use slash-and-burn agricultural techniques. There are different groups of the Hmong: the White Hmong, the Flowered Hmong, the Red Hmong and the Black Hmong.

### Nung

These mostly Buddhist people, centered primarily north of Hanoi in the provinces of Ha Bac and Bac Thai, number more than a million people. They subsist on settled agriculture and are known for their bravery in battle. They have been strongly influenced by both the Chinese and the Vietnamese.

### Zao

There are perhaps 400,000 Zao (also called Yao, Dao or Man) people living in the highland areas of northern Vietnam. Most are Buddhists, although some Zao are into Taoism and Confucianism. They usually live in the mountains at between 700-1000 meters high.

### Thai

This is the largest ethnic minority in Vietnam, inhabiting primarily northwest Vietnam, whose numbers exceed 1.4 million. They first came to Vietnam from China during the 4th century. The Thai consist of three groups; the Red Thai *(Thai Do)*, the Back Thai *(Thai Den)* and the White Thai *(Thai Trang)*. The names are based on the color of the tunics worn by the women of each group. They live in the provinces of Lai Chau, Son La, Thanh Hoa, Nghia Lo, Nghe An and Hoa Binh. They use Chinese ideograms for writing and subsist on the cultivation of wet rice.

Other ethnic minority hill people with significant populations include the **Hre**, who number about 80,000 in the provinces of Gia Lai and Kon Tum; the **Mnong**, who number about 65,000 in the provinces of Lam Dong and Dac Lac, and the **Stieng**, who number about 50,000 in the provinces of Dac Lac, Song Be and Lam Dong.

### The Bigfeet of Vietnam

Legend has it that a group of Vietnamese living in Hue were cast under a spell by a "witch doctor," which forced them into the mountains of the Central Highlands in western Quang Binh Province. This "spell" made these people grow hair all over their bodies, similar to apes, and took away their ability to speak. After first establishing settlements in this rugged, mountainous region, they were forced further into the highlands as Vietnamese and other ethnicities migrated into these areas. They made no contact with anyone, but at night would surround the new villages established by the migrating Vietnamese and howl from deep in the forest in remorseful memory of who they once were, and the human capabilities they formerly possessed. Many believe these "monkey people" still exist and torment villages, without being seen, late at night with their baying.

In reality, the legend isn't far from the truth, although it's doubtful they metamorphosed as the result of magic. They're called the Ruc ethnic group and they do indeed inhabit the high jungles of western Quang Binh Province in north-central Vietnam, living by hunting and gathering. By the best estimate, there are only about 200 surviving members of this primitive animal-like tribe. They live in highly remote and mountainous stone caves that are entirely inaccessible. Earlier, the Ruc people had civilized knowledge as well as their own language. They also possessed a concept of the sun and earth and of different species of living animals. But due to scientifically unknown historical events, they were forced to retreat higher and higher into the western mountains near Laos, where they lived totally cut off from the rest of Vietnam's population. The untamed forests, wild animals and severe environment made their lives quite primitive. At night they creep into their caves or primitive huts. In the daytime, the men stalk through the forest and boulders in search of monkeys, deer and bees for food. The men wear only tree bark loin cloths, while the women wear loin cloths of the same material, covering the lower parts of their bodies only. The children do not wear clothes. Fire is created by rubbing black stones together. The fires are kept burning for months and even years. When women give birth, the woman will go deep into the forest and dig a hole where she will bear the child alone. The husband is not allowed to be with his wife, but passes food to her with a long stick. After the birth of the child it is the husband's duty to search the forests for seven white monkeys. Only after the wife has eaten all the monkeys can she return home. This is an important rite for the Ruc, as they believe the practice of giving birth in the forest prepares the newborn child immediately for the severe climate. God decides whether the child will live or die, and the Ruc pray to God by rubbing two bamboo pipes together. The Ruc people are a deeply attached community. For instance, when a water hole is discovered, the person making the find gathers the entire community together to drink at the site. If a man discovers a tree called *nhuc*, he will summon the women and the girls of the community to get the heart wood for food. When a group of men returns to the "village" after a hunt, they share their catch with everyone—and the man who killed the beast severs the head. The rest of the meat is shared by the tribe. There are Ruc festivals, where tribespeople gather around fires to listen to primitive *K Teng* and *T Lenh* songs. These people have been more exposed to the outside "world" in recent years and their customs are changing quickly. Regrettably, the "Bigfeet" of the remote Vietnamese forests will soon start donning Nikes.

***A floating village on Ho Tri An Lake off National Highway 20 near Tan Phu.***

# Bao Loc

***Spectacular Dam Ri Waterfalls outside Bao Loc cascade 40 meters.***

## BAO LOC IN A CAPSULE

*Gateway to the Central Highlands...A good stopover from Saigon to Dalat...Site of some of the most spectacular waterfalls in southern Vietnam...110 km south of Dalat on Highway 20...Surrounded by lush, rolling hillsides supporting coffee and tea plantations...A major center of silk production...Dam Ri waterfalls often bypassed by tourists...Brand new elegant hotel called the Seri.*

Bao Loc (or B'Lao) is 110 km south from Dalat on Highway 20, or Tran Phu Street as the highway is called in town. It makes for a convenient stopover between Saigon and Dalat. The area consists of lush rolling green hills that support a number of coffee, mulberry leaf and tea plantations. Silk production is big in this area. There are also a number of small waterfalls, and one massive one that only a handful of foreigners bother getting out to, the falls at Dam Ri. Listed in few guidebooks, these falls make the waterfalls in Dalat seem like bathroom showers, and they well may be the most spectacular falls in Vietnam. The vast majority of travelers bypass Bao Loc completely. This is bound to change.

### What to See and Do in Bao Loc and Environs

**Dam Ri Waterfalls** ★★★

*Located about 17 km west of Bao Loc.*

There are perhaps the most magnificent waterfalls in Vietnam, in southern Vietnam for sure. More than 40 meters high, the rushing water cascades down a solid rock edifice creating a thunderous cloud of mist and multihued spray. Wonderful photos can be taken from both the summit and the base of the falls. But down below, you'll get wet, so keep your camera dry. The best times of the day to see the falls are in the early morning, where the spray creates spectacular rainbows, or late in the afternoon, when the low sun spills angles of light directly on the rushing water. The best thing about the falls is that few travelers know about them, although now there is a newly-built restaurant at the falls, attracting the tour buses. I saw not a single tourist. Nor are there the floating duck boats and cowboys on ponies with plastic pistols—the blatant, gaudy commercialism—that has taken a lot of the delight out of visiting the falls in the Dalat area. From Bao Loc, you turn west at the post office and then have to make a number of turns on side streets before reaching the road toward the falls, which is flanked by silk, tea and coffee farms. Ask for specific directions at The Bao Loc Hotel or the Seri Hotel. There's the big, but usually empty Dam Ri Restaurant at the admission area. Admission: 10,000 dong for foreigners. Frightful but worth it. Not to be missed.

**Bay Tung Falls**

*23 km south of Bao Loc, off Hwy 20.*

Take Highway 20 seven km south from the Bao Loc Hotel. Then take a trail, 3 km after crossing the Dai Binh River, to the hamlet of Ap Dai Lao in the village of Xa Loc Chau. The trail starts on the right side of the road. You'll walk about 400 meters through tea bushes and coffee trees as well as banana and pineapple groves to reach Suoi Mo, the Stream of Dreaming. There the path goes left through thickets of bamboo. Soon you'll see the Bay Tung Falls and the pools of the Stream of Dreaming. Worth a visit only if you're planning on spending a day or two in Bao Loc—few people do. The falls pale in comparison to the Dam Ri Falls.

**Bao Loc Church**

*In town, north of Bro Loc Hotel.*

Nothing spectacular, but if you're Catholic, you may want to pay a visit. It's located about three hundred meters on Highway 20 north of the Bao Loc Hotel.

**Tea, Silk and Coffee Factories**

*Surrounding hillsides.*

Get a local to show you around some of the factories that produce coffee, tea and silkworms. You can find the factories on Highway 20 south of Bao Loc and also on the well paved road leading to the Dam Ri Falls.

### Where to Stay in Bao Loc

**AUTHOR'S NOTE: TELPEHONE PREFIXES**

*The telephone numbers listed here are local exchanges. The country code is 84. The city codes for both Bao Loc and Dalat are 63.*

**Bao Loc Hotel & Restaurant** **US$5–$20**

*So 11 A Tran Phu-Bao Loc (National Highway 1).* ☎ *4107 or 4268; FAX: 4167.*

*12 rooms.*

There are only two "hotels" in Bao Loc, this one and the more upscale Seri, but I'd suggest, if you're on a budget and only planning to spend the night in Bao Loc, you stay here. It's a pretty big place considering the number of rooms, but the rooms are clean and comfortable—and I didn't see another guest during either visit. Yet the relatively big building, constructed in 1940, has two large, empty restaurants. Everything here seems spacious and empty. But it's clean enough and the staff is pleasant. It's one of those hotels you wonder how it remains in business because of such a small occupancy rate. At the entrance to the hotel, there's a taxidermist's shop—stuffed threatened wildlife cover the driveway to the hotel. Sad.

**Seri Hotel** **US$40–$80** ★★★

*Bao Loc-Lamdoc Province, just off Highway 20 in the center part of town.* ☎ *4150, 4430 or 4065. FAX: 2183.*

*57 rooms.*

*Reservations: Direct or through HCMC, 28 Mac Dinh Chi.* ☎ *298438 or 231375. FAX: 84.8.294086.*

This is a strikingly elegant hotel in a strikingly inelegant city that's a cross between Saigon's Floating Hotel and the Pentagon, and why it would expect to fill its spacious, tastefully decorated rooms is well beyond my comprehension given the lack of attractions in the Bao Loc area. The higher priced rooms are luxurious suites. Singles and doubles, all with TV, hot water, telephone. Restaurant, snack bar, dance hall and Karaoke. It's the kind of place where you'd want to spend at least a few nights but there's no reason to. The staff is especially friendly, well-dressed and surprisingly fluent in English. A shop sells beautiful locally produced silk clothing, but at relatively exorbitant rates. Hotel also offers minibus transportation to tea and coffee plantations, as well as to the area's waterfalls, including the Dam Ri Falls. The falls alone make this hotel worth the visit. Moderate–expensive.

## Where to Eat in Bao Loc

There are a number of food stalls and cafes that line NH20 (Tran Phu Street) through Bao Loc.

**Restaurant Dang Nguyen**

*02b Tran Phu Street.*
Vietnamese, cheap.

**Tram Anh Tra Cafe**

*5 Tran Phu.*
Comfortable, shaded and popular.

**Restaurant Hung Phat and the Hung Phat Cafe**

*Tran Phu Street, across from the Bao Loc Hotel, 20 meters south.*
One of the best restaurants in town with friendly service. There's an outdoor dining area which consists of one-table gazebolike booths. If you happen to get a date in Bao Loc, bring your friend here.

**Dream Cafe**

*Across Tran Phu Street from the Restaurant Hung Phat.*
Nothing to write home about.

**Bao Loc Hotel**

*So 11a Tran Phu Street.*
Usually empty, but vegetable dishes are great. Also Western food.

**Seri Hotel Restaurant**

*Seri Hotel.*
Better then average Vietnamese and Western fare for the area.

**Dam Ri Restaurant**

*Dam Ri Waterfalls.*
New, big and modern establishment; average food.

*A rainbow cuts through the mist at Bao Loc's 40-m-high Dam Ri Waterfalls.*

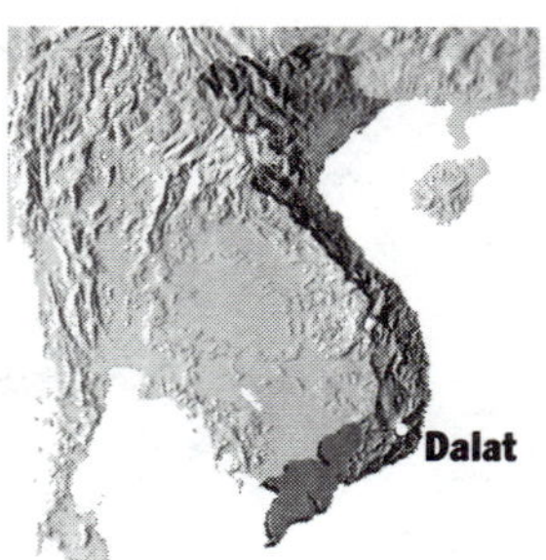


# Dalat

***Dalat's railway station used to serve Saigon via Phan Rang until continuous Viet Cong attacks ruined the track and made the journey impossible.***

## DALAT IN A CAPSULE

*Founded by French scientist Andre Yersin as a French hill resort in 1897...Offers the best climate in Vietnam...a primarily temperate zone with huge tea and coffee plantations as well as silk production facilities...A favorite honeymooning spot for Vietnamese newlyweds...Much of the mountainsides have been heavily deforested in recent years...Very little fighting took place here during the Vietnam War...Montagnard, Da Hoa and Lat hillpeople live in the region...Waterfalls and lakes surround this mountainous area.*

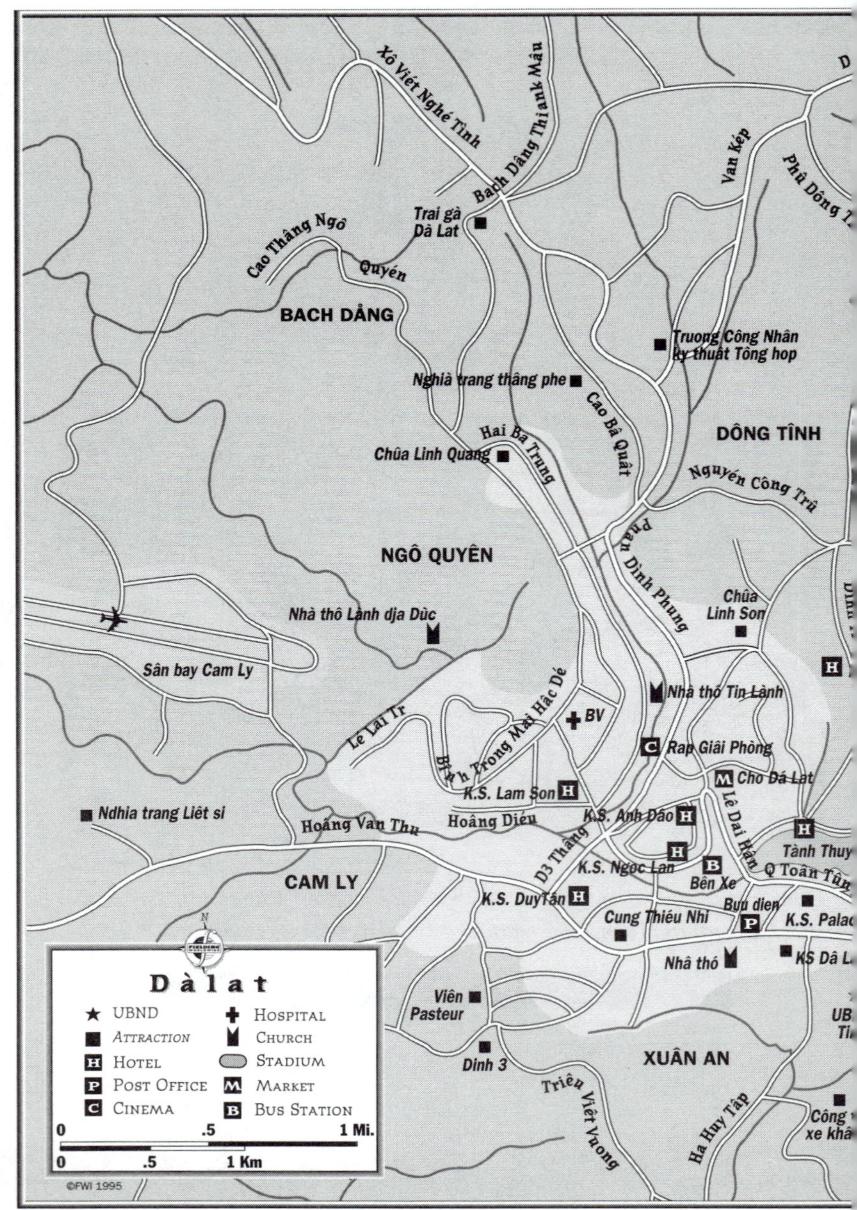

Dàlat
UBND
Attraction
Hotel
Post Office
Cinema
Hospital
Church
Stadium
Market
Bus Station
0 .5 1 Mi.
0 .5 1 Km
©FWI 1995
Xô Viêt Nghê Tinh
Bach Dâng Thiank Mâu
Van Kép
Phù Dông
Trai gà Dà Lat
Cao Thâng Ngô Quyén
BACH DẢNG
Truong Công Nhân ky thuât Tông hop
Nghià trang thâng phe
Cao Bá Quât
Hai Bà Trung
Chùa Linh Quang
DÔNG TÌNH
Nguyén Công Trü
NGÔ QUYÊN
Phan Dinh Phung
Chùa Linh Son
Nhà thô Lành dja Dùc
Sân bay Cam Ly
Nhà thô Tin Lành
BV
Lê Lai Tr
Trong Mai Hâc Dé
Rap Giái Phòng
Cho Dá Lat
K.S. Lam Son
Ndhia trang Liêt si
Hoàng Van Thu
Hoàng Diéu
K.S. Anh Dáo
Lê Dai Hàn
Tành Thuy
D3 Tháng
K.S. Ngọc Lan
Bên Xe
Q Toàn Tü
CAM LY
K.S. DuyTân
Buu dien
Cung Thiéu Nhi
K.S. Palac
Nhâ thó
Viên Pasteur
XUÂN AN
Dinh 3
Triêu Viêt Vuong
Ha Huy Táp

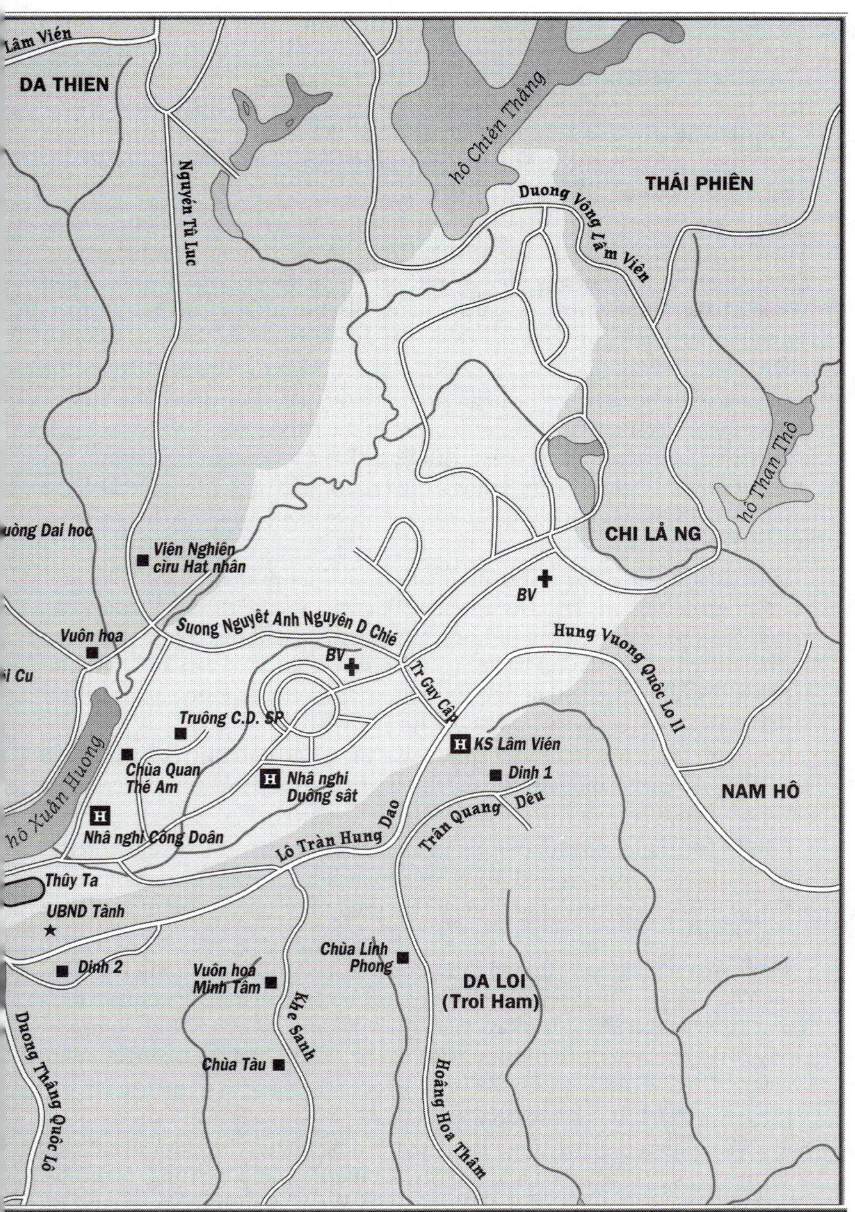
Lâm Viên
DA THIEN
Nguyên Tú Luc
hô Chiên Thång
THÁI PHIÊN
Duong Vông Lâm Viên
hô Than Thô
CHI LẢ NG
uòng Dai hoc
Viên Nghiên
ciru Hat nhân
BV
Vuôn hoa
Suong Nguyêt Anh Nguyên D Chié
BV
Hung Vuong Quôc Lo II
i Cu
Tr Guy Câp
Truông C.D. SP
KS Lâm Viên
Dinh 1
Chùa Quan
Thé Am
Nhâ nghi
Duông sât
NAM HÔ
hô Xuân Huong
Trân Quang Dêu
Nhâ nghi Công Doân
Lô Tràn Hung Dao
Thûy Ta
UBND Tành
Chùa Linh
Phong
Dinh 2
Vuôn hoa
Minh Tâm
DA LOI
(Troi Ham)
Khe Sanh
Duong Thâng Quôc Lô
Chùa Tàu
Hoàng Hoa Thâm

What can you say about Dalat (population about 130,000)? It's certainly one of the most beautiful cities in all of Vietnam and sits atop a mighty plateau at nearly 1500 meters. It features the best climate in Vietnam (warm days and cool nights all year round). Temperatures average here 24 C. (78F.) in the day and 15 C. (60 F.)at night. There is a rainy season from April through November, although even during these months it still rains infrequently and only for a short duration.

The Lang Biang Mountains to the north rise to nearly 2500 meters. They're inhabited by a number of ethnic minorities, including Montagnards, Lat and Da Hoa tribespeople. In the center of the city is pristine Xuan Huong Lake. Around town there are waterfalls, beautiful gardens of temperate flora, deep pine forested valleys, a man-made reservoir, lakes and even a golf course.

Dalat was founded by Frenchman Andre Yersin, who convinced the French government to establish a hill station here in the late 1890s. There was a railway station here that linked Dalat with Phan Rang and Saigon (although it is defunct now). During colonial times, the Frenchmen of Saigon used Dalat as a summer resort to escape the intense heat of Saigon. Much of the architecture is French.

Dalat is still a popular resort destination with more than 2500 villas surrounding the region. Dalat is a more popular resort with the Vietnamese, rather than with Europeans and other Westerners, and the area is a favorite for newlyweds. Caravans of balloon- and streamer-covered cars and minivans traverse the hilly area, and honeymooning couples can be found at practically every attraction site dressed elegantly for photos.

Although Dalat was once well known as a big game hunting resort as late as the 1950s, the wild animals—bears, rhinos, tigers, elephants, and deer—that once roamed these once dense forests have disappeared.

I find Dalat mildly disappointing in a number of ways. Massive deforestation in the area has created bare mountainsides in every direction. This wasn't a result of the war, but instead the result of relentless commercial timber activities.

There was actually very little fighting in and around Dalat during the Vietnam War. In fact, high ranking officers on both sides of the conflict used Dalat villas as retreats not more than a few kilometers apart. But comparatively little remains of the lush environment of the highlands surrounding Dalat.

Dalat has also become overcommercialized. At virtually every attraction in and surrounding the area are dilapidated paddle boats with duck heads that look like a cross between old Soviet submarines and floating bathtubs. "Cowboys" in attire out of the "Wild, Wild West" lead tourists around on ponies in these circuslike environments. There are "zoos" with poorly treated animals, and some unlucky enough to have been stuffed by omnipresent Vietnamese taxidermists and glued to trees and rocks. The sight of these rare and sometimes endangered species is sad. And these poor creatures are everywhere. In shops, at the parks, at the waterfalls, etc. If you care about animals, a visit to Dalat may be extremely depressing.

Thousands of Dalat dwellers were resettled by the new government after 1975 to areas down the plateau outside the city. One such Lat village is 20 km south out of town along Highway 20.

In previous years, you needed a police permit to visit many areas outside of Dalat—and the horror stories abound of corruption and bribery. But when I visited the immigration police station, I was politely told that a permit was only needed to visit Lat Village, about 12 km northwest of town. The permit costs US$5 and could be obtained through Lam Dong Tourism. You'll have to hire a guide through the tourism agency, however. At least it won't be a policeman or soldier.

There also used to be problems with foreigners checking into the few foreigner-permitted hotels. You'd have to file a phenomenal amount of information with the police. This is no longer the case. As in most of Vietnam, travel by foreigners is basically unrestricted in Lam Dong Province.

## What to See and Do in Dalat and Environs

### Xuan Huong Lake

*Central Dalat.*

This is an artificial lake that was created in central Dalat by a dam on the west end of the valley in 1919. The lake itself isn't particularly spectacular but it's surrounded by kiosks and cafes. Rent a bike and take the road that runs around the perimeter of the lake. Many locals swim here, but I'd avoid it, seeing what they toss into it. The lake was named after a controversial 17th-century Vietnamese poet. Unfortunately, this is one of the many water sites in Dalat where you can rent one of those Bozo bathtubs and paddle around for an hour or two.

### Dalat Flower Garden

*Set on the northeast end of the lake.*

These are beautiful gardens were established in 1966 by the South Vietnamese Agricultural Service. After becoming nothing more than a weed patch, the entire gardens were renovated in 1985. Here you can see both tropical and temperate flora, including hydrangeas, orchids, roses, fuchsias, lilies and camellias. How some of the flowers are grown is interesting—orchids are grown inside coconut palm trunks. Admission: 2000 dong.

*Dalat's Cathedral, with its 48-meter-high spire, began construction in the early 1930s but wasn't completed until 1945.*

**Dalat Cathedral**

*Yersin and Tran Phu Streets, next to the Dalat Hotel.*

Built in the early 30s and not finished until 1945, the impressive 48-meter high spire can be seen from all over town. The medieval-style stained glass windows were imported from France and were crafted by Louis Balmet. There are wood carvings of Jesus lining the nave. Masses are conducted every day at 5:15 a.m. and 5:15 p.m., and on Sundays at the ungodly hour of 4:00 a.m. as well as 5:15 a.m., 7 a.m., 8:30 a.m. and 4 p.m. This might be why the pastor seemed a little exhausted during our brief conversation.

**Quan Am Tu Pagoda**

*2 Chien My Street.*

Not a lot here, except for the Buddha with the electric halo around its head. The gardens are nice here, too. Worth a brief stop if you keep stealth from the nice monk, who'll want to keep you there for hours.

**Linh Son Pagoda**

*120 Nguyen Van Troi Street.*

There's a huge gold and bronze bell here. I did not see any women here and was told women weren't allowed by an old man trying to sell me incense. There are two dragons in front of the sanctuary with small ponds on each side of them.

**Su Nu Pagoda**

*1 km south of Le Thai To at 72 Hoang Hoa Tham Street.*

This pagoda is strictly for nuns, although men are allowed to visit. Don't visit here during the lunch hours, you'll offend the praying women, who are all bald headed and wear grey or brown robes. It was built in 1952.

**Domaine de Marie Convent**

*6 Ngo Quyen Street.*

Built in the early 1940s, this convent once housed more than 300 nuns. The few nuns still around today make fruit and spice candies as well as the fruit they grow in an orchard out in back.

**Minh Nguyet Cu Sy Lam Pagoda**

*At the end of Khe Sanh St.*

Built in 1962, this is a Chinese Pagoda just across from the Thien Vuong Pagoda (see below). It is a round structure representing a lotus blossom. The sanctuary is to the right of the main gates after entering the path. Inside the pagoda is a statue of Quan The Am Bo Tat (the Goddess of Mercy). Lotus flowers can be seen all over the gates and the bars on the windows. The pagoda, as is Thien Vuong Pagoda, is very popular with Chinese and Hong Kong visitors. Take off your shoes before entering the pagoda after passing the few stalls that sell vegetable and fruit concoctions.

**Thien Vuong Pagoda** ★

*At the end of Khe Sanh Street.*

This is Chinese and one of the more interesting pagodas in Dalat. At the end of Khe Sanh Street a dirt path rises up a pine-covered hill leading up the pagoda. Souvenir stalls line the path up to the pagoda where there are two large yellow wood-built buildings. In the first building you will not be required to remove your shoes. In this structure is a statue of one of Buddha's protectors, Ho Phap and another statue of Pho Hien, an aide to the A Di Da Buddha (Buddha of the past). In the next building, where you'll be required to remove your shoes, are three huge Buddhas brought over from Hong Kong. These Buddhas are thought to be the largest sandalwood Buddhas in Vietnam. They represent Quan The Am Bo Tat on the right, Sakyamuni (the historical Buddha) in the center, and Dai The Bo Tat on the right. Behind the second building further up on the hill is a giant white Buddha overlooking the valley. The pagoda was built in 1958.

*A large white Buddha at Dalat's Thien Vuong Pagoda overlooks the pine-covered Central Highlands.*

**The Tomb of Nguyen Huu Hao**

*The tomb is atop a 400-meter high hill northwest of Cam Ly Falls.*

Nguyen Huu Hao was the father of Bao Dai's wife, Nam Phuong. Nguyen died in 1939.

**Cam Ly Falls**

*57-59 Hong Ven Thu St.*

Busloads of tourists—that's what you'll find here along with cowboys, plastic guns, and a lot of kids selling chewing gum and cigarettes. A guide here costs US$1 an hour and it ain't worth it, folks. You can adequately tour the small falls in under half an hour on your own quite well, thank you. Animal lovers will cringe at the stuffed jungle animals.

**Valley of Love**

*Five km north of Dalat.*

Given the name by students in the early 1970s who used to hang out here with their lovers, the original name was the Valley of Peace after Emperor Bao Dai decided *that's* what it should be called. Obviously, he was happy by himself. Now the place is a circus, with cowboys and others running around in bunny suits. You can rent those insufferable floating bathtubs here, as well as buy everything from lottery tickets to straw hats. The cowboys are the most annoying aspects of a visit here as well as the chewing gum hawkers. Refreshment stalls abound, as do tourists.

**Dalat (or Crèmailllère) Railway Station** ★

*Five hundred meters east of Xuan Huong Lake and off Quang Trung Street.*

This is a sight not to be missed. About a half dozen ancient train cars and a black steam engine that has to be at least a century old lie on the track next to the pastel yellow railway station. Opened in 1938, the station used to serve Saigon through Phan Rang until continuous Viet Cong attacks on the track made the journey impossible, and the routes were shut down in 1964. However, tourists can now take the "train" about 7 km out of town to Trai Met Village for the ridiculous price of US$10 round trip. The journey's a novelty and pleasant—you pass well-tended, dense vegetable fields—but for 10 bucks?

**Central Market**

*Located at the end of Nguyen Thi Minh Khai Street.*

This is one of the most interesting markets in Vietnam and certainly the best for getting temperate produce and fruit such as strawberries, carrots, plums, avocados, cherries, potatoes, loganberries and apples. Friends in the south will be highly appreciative if you bring back a gift of some of these foods.

**The French District**

*Hoa Binh Square area.*

This is the area around Rap 3/4 cinema that's right off the Universal Studios lot. Move from Vietnam into France in only a few short footsteps.

**Dalat University**

*1 Phu Dong Thien Vuong Street.*

With the aid of New York's Cardinal Spelman, Dalat University opened its doors in 1957 as a Catholic learning institution by Hue Archbishop Ngo Dinh Thuc, who was the older brother of President Diem, assassinated in 1963. When Dalat was "liberated" in 1975, the university shut down but was reopened a couple of years later. Now more than a thousand students study here, from English to agriculture.

***Dalat's Quang Trung Reservoir was created by a dam in 1980.***

**Quang Trung Reservoir** 

*Head down Highway 20 toward Bao Loc. About 5 km from town, turn right down a rutted, dangerous rock and dirt path to the reservoir.*

It was created by a dam in 1980 and, today, about 30 people live on floating houses in the reservoir. It was named after Quang Trung, one of the Tay Son rebellion's great leaders, who was responsible for repressing a vicious Chinese attack in 1789. The reservoir is situated in a deforested valley (there are some recently planted pine trees) beneath a spectacular new Vietnamese pagoda. There's not much to see here and there are only a few visitors, so the child gum and cigarette hawkers are at a minimum. There is one cafe and supposedly small power boats for rent, but I didn't see one on the entire reservoir.

**Truc Lam Thien Vien Pagoda** ★

*Overlooking Quang Trung Reservoir.*

Also called the Bamboo Forest Meditation Center, this is a spectacular new Vietnamese pagoda of 24 hectares high on the bamboo forest hillside overlooking Quang Trung Reservoir. But it's a hike to get up there (150 steps). The brand new domiciles are now home to 52 monks and 45 nuns. The chief monk, Thong Triet (who will not leave the hillside pagoda for at least 3 years) will be more than happy to show you the giant sand and cement Buddha trucked up from Saigon at the altar as well as the one-ton bell that's rung twice a day (at 3 a.m. and 6 p.m.) brought over from Hue. This is a magnificent new structure (built in 1994) with beautiful temperate flora landscaping. Inside the pagoda "giang huong" hardwood covers the ceiling and altar archways. There's also a brand new guesthouse for visiting monks alongside the pagoda. If you're out of shape, a trek up to this pagoda is a day trip.

***"Cowboys" toting plastic six-shooters are typical of Dalat's commercialism.***

**Lake of Sighs** ★

*About 5 km on Phan Chu Trinh Street northeast of Dalat.*

This lake, a natural one that was enlarged by a French-built dam, is supposedly named after girls who were brought here by students at Dalat's military academy. Another story says that it was named after the lovers Hoang Tung and Mai Nuong, who met and fell in love here during the 18th century. Hoang Tung then joined the army to help fight the Chinese, but left Mai Nuong unaware of his new duties and travels. When he left to fight the Chinese, Mai felt that she had been abandoned and drowned herself in the lake. The lake itself is nothing spectacular and largely denuded of its once dense vegetation. There are a few souvenir stands here and the usual stuffed animals. Again, you'll find those cowboys with their little plastic six-shooters looking to bring you around the lake on horseback.

**Datanla Falls**

*200 meters farther down Highway 20 from Quang Trung Reservoir.*

The falls themselves aren't as impressive as some of Dalat's other waterfalls (and pale in comparison with Bao Loc's Dam Ri Falls), but the pleasant thing about them is that they lack the county fairlike environments of Dalat's other attractions. There is only a small viewing area, which is usually full of tourists picnicking. The down side to these falls (again, forgive the pun) is that you've got to be a decathlete to reach them. The walk down the path is steep and long. If you're not in shape, forget it.

**Prenn Falls**

*At the base of Dalat on Highway 20 at the Prenn Restaurant.*

These are perhaps the nicest falls in Dalat, but they're packed with tourists, souvenir touts, mini-sailboats and Vietnamese on horseback dressed like Red Skelton on the set of Mel Brooks' *Blazing Saddles*. At an altitude of 1125 meters, water cascades off a 15 meter edifice into a brown-colored pool the size of a backyard swimming pool in Lubbock where you can rent these tiny toy ships for a "voyage" that's more like an ant crossing a cup of coffee. Kiosks and food stalls abound. The parking area is packed with minibuses. The park around the falls, sprinkled with palm-thatched gazebos was dedicated to Thailand's Queen in 1959. Admission: 5000 dong.

**Prenn Pass** 

*This is the steep stretch of roadway on Highway 20 that leads down from Dalat past Quang Trung Reservoir, Datanla Falls toward Prenn Falls.*

This is a beautiful, but sometimes narrow and dangerous road that's surrounded by tall palms and thick vegetation. Some of the scenery is magnificent. By motorcycle, you'll be tempted to do a Pike's Peak climb in record time. Don't try. The veering minibuses treat the road as if it was their own and use both sides of the road. A collision here and you're in for "dalat" of trouble.

**Duc Trong Village (Quang Hiep)**

*20 km south of Dalat down Highway 20.*

My guide insisted that this small village was Lat Village. To my knowledge, he was wrong. Instead this small agricultural community on the right side of the road is where displaced ethnic Da Hoa were forced to move into the valley by the government after 1975. There's not much here save for the kind villagers and a giant statue of a giant chicken. Here, you'll want to visit Mrs. Nguyen Thi Kim Phung, an English teacher whose knowledge of the relocation of Dalat residents after 1975 is vast and interesting. She'll also want to guide you to the summit of Elephant Mountain, a four-hour, round-trip hike up the heavily deforested peak. Worth a brief visit unless you want to do the hike, which offers spectacular scenery at the summit.

**Lat Village**

*About 12 km north of Dalat.*

Here is the only area around Dalat you'll need a permit to visit, which can be obtained through the Lam Dong Tourist Office for US$5. You'll have to use one of their guides and that'll cost you more. Why you need to obtain a permit to visit these nine small hamlets is a mystery to me. The ethnic Lat, Koho, Ma and Chill tribes that inhabit the area really don't seem like the insurgent types, although many Lat and Montagnard people worked for the Americans during the war. Here, the houses are constructed of thatched roofs built on piles. There are about 300 hectares where the villagers grow rice and produce charcoal. Lat Village also has two Christian churches. It's worth a visit, but the US$30 or so you'll have to spend to make the trip may create some reservations about doing it.

**Lang Bian Mountain** 

*30km north of Dalat.*

These are five volcanic peaks, heavily deforested, and about a four-hour hike from Lat Village. The two highest peaks are called K'Biang and K'Lang. Not so many years ago, tigers, bears, elephants, boars and rhinos roamed the peaks. But not anymore. The hike is worth it for the spectacular views.

**Ankroët Lakes & Falls**

*About 20 km northwest of Dalat.*

The lakes are actually part of a hydroelectric project. Many hilltribes in the area. The falls aren't spectacular, reaching a height of about 15 meters.

**INSIDER TIP**

*There are a number of falls in the Dalat area that require a considerably long and steep hike to reach. Although most tourists in Third-World countries are in generally good shape, others aren't. If you have a heart condition or just plain can't blow out a candle from three feet, I recommend staying at the top, purchasing a souvenir or two and a postcard, and telling your friends at home how beautiful the falls were.*

### Where to Stay in Dalat

Even though tourism in Dalat is exploding it still seems that two of every three hotels in the city will not allow foreigners. If you find yourself in the center of Dalat and are not sure where to stay, it will be a waste of time to roam the streets—which are packed with hotels and mini-hotels (guest houses)—looking for a suitable hotel. You'll get frustrated. Even though the number of foreigners that visit Dalat is increasing rapidly, the overwhelming majority of visitors to Dalat are Vietnamese on holiday. However, on the plus side, the cheaper hotels that once didn't provide hot water now usually do. And you'll want hot water in Dalat, even during the warmer months.

**AUTHOR'S NOTE: TELEPHONE PRFIXES**

*The following telephone numbers are local exchanges. The country code is 84. The city code is 63.*

**Thanh The Hotel** **US$5–$12** 

*118 Phan Dinh Phung Street. ☎ 22180.*

*42 rooms.*

Friendly English speaking staff; comfortable singles and doubles. Private bath, clean rooms. Hot water. Restaurant, cafe. Incredible value for the price, and one of the few hotels on Phan Dinh Phung Street that accepts (and welcomes) foreigners. A similar room in Saigon would go for twice as much money. This makes the Thanh The one of the best values in Dalat. Also, it is enhanced by its central location in the middle of town.

***Dalat's Hang Nga's Guest Home and Art Garden features some of the most bizarre architecture in the country.***

**Thanh Van Hotel** **US$20–$25**

*9/1 Phu Dong Thien Vuong Street. ☎ 22818; FAX: 22782.*
*21 rooms.*

Clean, comfortable rooms, but a little pricey. Price includes breakfast. Restaurant. Private bath. Centrally located. Large, comfortable rooms. Car hire for local tours of the Dalat area.

**Palace 2 Hotel** **US$30–$50** ★

*12 Tran Hung Dao Street. ☎ 22092.*
*28 rooms.*

Hotel has been open for about six years. This place, an elegant structure and built in 1933, was formerly the Governor-General's Residence, and then was used as a guesthouse for dignitaries and for official receptions. Now anyone can stay if you're willing to pay the price, which includes breakfast. The pricier rooms are deluxe suites. There are 19 first-class rooms, seven second class rooms. Rooms are large, almost palatial. Attached bathroom, restaurant, telephone and television in all the rooms as well as IDD services. Organizes area tours via vans, coaches and micro-buses. I found the service here a little too stuffy, although friendly enough.

**Hang Nga's Guest Home and Art Garden** **US$15**

*3 Huynh Thuc Khang. ☎ 22070.*
*12 rooms.*

This is the most bizarre-looking hotel in the Milky Way, a treelike, dripping, sculpted building designed by Dang Viet Nga (who may be the Southeast Asian reincarnation of Salvador Dali) that resembles an outcropping on Uranus. Something right out of a Steven Spielberg flick. Even if you don't stay here, if you're in Dalat, make sure you give this place a visit. They even charge 2000 dong just to go in and see the place. It's right out of Disneyland. However, the rooms are spacious and adorned in a bear cavelike motif with carved dragons and stuffed bears. Big baths. Sitting areas. The lighting is romantic and the place would make a good honeymooners' spot. A giant sculpted giraffe sits next to the complex—it's gotta be 20 meters high. Why it's there and what it has to do with the rest of the hotel's motif is a total mystery.

**Sofitel Dalat Palace Hotel** **US$120–$350** 

*12 Tran Phu. ☎ 25444, 23496.*
*43 rooms.*

This hotel has been thoroughly renovated, and it's taken four years. The building was originally erected in the early 1920s. It is a magnificent, big building with great views of the Xuan Huong Lake. The grounds themselves are beautifully landscaped. The hotel is seeking to get five stars. Whether or not it does, it's still the classiest in town.

**Bao Dai's Summer Palace** **US$30–$40** 

*Biet Dien Quoc Truong.*

This is a beautiful 25-room villa that was constructed for Emperor Bao Dai in 1933. This is now actually a hotel, but the place is a little ambiguous because it closes for "lunch" for a couple of hours during the day and you simply can't get into the place. Even the reception area is closed. I'm not sure what you'll want to do while you wait for the office to reopen about 1:30 p.m. You can also tour the palace/hotel when it is open whether you're staying there or not. Even if you're already a guest I'm still not sure you can get into the structure between 11:30 a.m. and 1:30 p.m. The attractions here are many. There's an engraved glass map of Vietnam that was given to the Emperor during the early'40s by Vietnamese studying in Paris before World War II began really taking its toll on the French people (and others studying there). The palace also features an ornate dining room and Bao Dai's office, which contains some of his books and other personal effects as well as his desk. The "palace" doesn't look really either like a palace or a hotel. Bao Dai spent his enormous amount of money on airplanes while stashing the rest in Swiss and U.S. bank accounts in anticipation of his political demise.

**Savimex Guest House** **US$25**

*11b 34 Street. ☎ 22640.*

This is one of the first hotels you'll run into after cresting the mountain and heading down toward Dalat. Its hillside location offers good views of the mountains and the valleys. Relatively new building. English speaking staff. Hot water, restaurant.

**Cam Do Hotel & Restaurant** **US$7–$20** ★

*81Phan Dinh Phung Street. ☎ 22732.*

Run by Dalat Tourist, this is one of the classier hotels in Dalat and quite a bargain. Price includes breakfast. Friendly, English speaking staff. Elegant lobby. Quite popular with foreigners in the fall. Rooms have private bath and hot water. Restaurant. There are also microbus tours of the Dalat area run by the hotel. Other tourist services. The hotel also provides one-way minibus service to Nha Trang, Phan Rang, and HCMC.

**Mimosa Hotel** **US$7–$20**

*170 Phan Dinh Phung Street. ☎ 22656 or 22180.*

*31 rooms.*

This is a friendly, centrally located hotel located in the heart of Dalat that looks more expensive than it is. Private bath, restaurant in the lobby. You can rent cars here for sight-seeing and the hotel will arrange bus and travel tickets. Mr. Long is the man to talk to about Dalat, especially if you're planning an itinerary within a tight schedule. Popular with backpackers, but I also saw a couple of families here as well.

**Nha Hang Huong Son** **US$25**

*27 Duong 3 Thang 4. ☎ 22124.*

*10 rooms.*

Perhaps overpriced but comfortable. Hot water. Restaurant. Check to see whether they'll allow foreigners. For some reason, there's a disproportionate amount of hotels in Dalat that do not accept foreigners. One employee said yes, the other no.

**Buu Tram Hotel** **US$20–$30**

*138B Phan Dinh Phung Street. ☎ 22887.*

*15 rooms.*

A mostly non-English speaking staff here which at present, doesn't accept foreigners, however, the mamasan said this may change soon. 8 rooms with private bath, 7 with public toilet. Room service.

**Thang Long Mini Hotel and Restaurant** **US$10–$20**

*154 Phan Dinh Phung Street. ☎ 22690.*

This is another one of those places that may or may not accept foreigners. Call in advance.

**Ngoc Lan Hotel** **US$10**

*42 Nguyen Chi Thanh Street. ☎ 22136.*

*25 rooms.*

This is near the southern entrance to Dalat on a hill that overlooks the lake and the bus station. You can decide which is the better view.

**Dalat Hotel** **About US$25**

*7 Phan Tru Street. ☎ 22863.*

*65 rooms.*

A bit run down and the rooms are large, but I think it's too expensive, even though the views are nice. Hot water.

**Anh Dao Hotel** **US$29–$55** ★

*50 Hoa Binh Square, up the hill from the Central Market. ☎ 22384.*

This is a renovated, spotless place with good service. Private bath. Hot water. Restaurant.

**Minh Tam Hotel** **About US$35–$5** ★

*20A Khe Sanh Street (about 3 km out of town). ☎ 22447.*

*17 rooms.*

A bit out of the way but the views of the surrounding forests and valleys are nice. It was built in 1936 as the palace of South Vietnamese President Ngo Dinh Diem's infamous sister-in-law Madame Nhu. It was renovated in the mid 1980s and is especially popular with domestic tourists. All the amenities one would expect for 50 bucks.

**Thuy Tien Hotel** **US$12**

*73 Thang 2 Street. ☎ 22444.*

This hotel is close to both the market and the bus station. A little run down for the price. Hot water, restaurant.

**Nha Khach Com** **US$6**

*48 Phan Dinh Phung Street.*

Out of the way, but cheap. Reasonable rooms.

**Thanh Binh Hotel** **US$7–$26**

*40 Nguyen Thi Minh Khai Street. ☎ 22394 or 22909.*

*42 rooms.*

Near the Central Market and a decent value. Hot water. Attached bath. Restaurant.

**Hai Son Hotel** **US$15–$40**

*1 Nguyen Thi Minh Khai Street. ☎ 22379, FAX: 92889.*

This is a musty, dirty and overpriced place, but the price includes breakfast. Hot water, attached bath. Not worth it.

**VYC Hoa Hung Hotel** **About US$15–$20**

*Lu Gia Street. ☎ 22653.*

*Reservations: Direct or VYC Tourism in HCMC, 180 Nguyen Cu Trinh. ☎ 298707.*

This is away from town but relatively new, clean and friendly. Attached bath, hot water; restaurant.

**Duy Tan Hotel** **About US$20**

*83-3 Thang 2 Street. ☎ 22216.*

Too expensive. Dormitory setting as well as nondescript, private rooms with attached bath. Hot water.

**Triaxco Hotel** **About US$30**

*7 Nguyen Thai Hoc Street. ☎ 22789.*

*8 rooms.*

This overlooks Xuan Huong Lake and some of the rooms have a great view of the lake. But others don't. The rooms vary considerably, so look at a few before deciding (granted the place isn't full, of course). Hot water.

## Where to Eat in Dalat

Dalat has a reputation throughout Vietnam of offering only mediocre food. Of course these are Vietnamese comparing the Vietnamese food of Dalat with that available in other locations. However, most foreign travelers won't be disappointed by the food (particularly vegetarians), especially the Vietnamese food available in Dalat. Most of the hotels have their own restaurants and they are often empty, with a bevy of uniformed waitresses sitting around and not doing much. One reason for this is that food in restaurants is generally more expensive than dishes found in private restaurants or food stalls. One exception would be the Hoang Restaurant at the Thanh The Hotel listed above. The food is good and cheap. Because of Dalat's relatively temperate climate, it is an excellent source of vegetables and is a vegetarian's paradise. There are a number of small restaurants and cafes along Nguyen Thi Minh Khai Street that offer an excellent variety of Vietnamese dishes. Just pick the one that looks the cleanest. And something to remember about eating in Dalat: Restaurants where the prices are included in the menu are generally more expensive than eateries that don't list prices on menus. If the menu has been professionally printed, the same is true. If the menu is handwritten in Vietnamese only (with poor English translations, such as "Freid Eeg"), you'll know you're getting rock-bottom prices.

You may want to avoid the lakeside eateries, which are generally overpriced and serve average food. Backpackers mostly hang out at the Long Hoa and the Hoang Lang Restaurants. Some of the other places to eat:

**Shanghai Restaurant** **$$** ★

*8 Khu Hoa Binh Square.*

Vietnamese, Asian, and European fare including "delicacies" such as goat testicles and beef penis. Interesting.

**Thanh Thuy Restaurant** **$$**

*4 Nguyen Thai Hoc Street. ☎ 22262.*

On the lake beneath the Triaxco Hotel. Vietnamese, Asian, European cuisine. Average but very popular.

**Dang A** **$$**

*82 Phan Dinh Phung Street.*

Vietnamese and exotic Asian fare.

**Cam Do** **$$**

*81 Phan Dinh Phung Street.*

This is typical of the cheap, good food that can be found outside of the hotels, but close by.

**Xuan Huong** **$$**

*Ho Xuan Huong Street. On the west side of the lake overlooking the water.*

Vietnamese, Western dishes.

**Pho Tung** **$$**

*Near the Shanghai Restaurant.*

Excellent bakery, average food.

**My Canh** **$**

*41 Nguyen Thi Minh Khai Street.*

Excellent Chinese fare.

**Thuy Ta** **$$** ★

*Just below the Palace Hotel.*

If not for the food, which is decent, come here for the views of the lake. Breakfast is the best time.

**Long Hoa** **$**

*6-3 Thang 2 Street.*

Western style breakfast, but open all day. Although the morning is the best time to hang out here.

**La Tulipe Rouge** **$$**

*1 Nguyen Thi Minh Khai, between the market and the Hai Son Hotel.*

Vietnamese, Chinese and Western dishes.

**Nhu Hai** **$**

*In front of the Central Market.*

Known for great vegetable dishes.

**Cafe Tung** **$**

*6 Khu Hoa Binh Street.*

Not really a restaurant, but a cafe with a rich history. Artists used to hang out here before 1975.

## Directory

### Transportation

Dalat is about 110 km from Phan Rang, 210 km Nha Trang, 1510 km from Hanoi, 320 km from Saigon, and 110 km from Bao Loc.

**INSIDER TIP**

*Vietnam's Civil Aviation Department is preparing Dalat's Camly airport for more commercial air services. Included in the plan is an upgrade of the airport as well as the railway stations, as well as the number of air routes into Dalat. The airport lies about 4 km from downtown Dalat. Before 1975, it served as an air base.*

**By air:**

There are three flights weekly from Saigon to Dalat (Tuesday, Thursday and Sunday at 10:00 a.m.) and they cost about US$80 round trip aboard a YAK 40. From Dalat to HCMC, there are flights on Tuesday, Thursday and Sunday at 3:30 p.m. You can also fly to Hue on VN on Wednesdays and Saturdays at 10:40 a.m. Flights to Dalat from Hue leave Wednesdays and Saturdays at 1:20 p.m. Flight time is about 40-50 minutes to Saigon and 2 hours to Hue. (Aboard what? A DC-3?).

**By bus:**

Dalat has two bus stations (Dalat Bus Station—the long distance station at the end of Nguyen Thi Minh Khai Street—and the local bus station which is a block north of Rap 3/4 Cinema). From the long distance station, express buses leave for Saigon at about 5 a.m. (11,000 dong, 310 km) and take about 8–9 hours, Nha Trang (8400 dong and 5–6 hours, 205 km), Phan Rang (4,600 dong and 2–3 hours, 100 km), Hue (30,000 dong and a very long time), Danang (27,000 dong, 745 km), Quang Ngai (22,500 dong), Quy Nhon (16,400 dong), and Buon Ma Thuot (17,000 dong, 395 km). Intra-Provincial buses connect Dalat with Bao Loc, Cau Dat, Da Thien, Di Linh, Ta Nun, Ta In and Lac Duong. The fastest way of getting away is by minibus from the local station, however.

**Minibuses** leave for Hanoi (69,000 dong), Hue (40,000 dong), Danang (35,000 dong), Vinh (55,000 dong), Quy Nhon (55,000 dong), and Nha Trang (11,500 dong).There is also hourly minibus service to Saigon for about 18,000 dong. Many hotels offer their own minibus services to Nha Trang, and some offer them even as far as Saigon.

**By car:**

Dalat is about a 6-7 hour trip by a late-model sedan. I did the trip in a little under 5-1/2 hours by large motorcycle, although I do not recommend you try to break that record. The road from Saigon to Dalat is usually quite wide and primarily in excellent shape (by Southeast Asia standards) but, nonetheless, there is a significant amount of pedestrian, ox cart, motorbike, and bicycle traffic—so driving (or riding a motorcycle) is very dangerous. Fortunately, after the fork that splits off NH1 to Dalat, the traffic becomes quite light, except in the villages. There is far less traffic on Highway 20 than on NH1. Be especially careful on the road that ascends from Bao Loc to Dalat through the forested mountains. The road narrows significantly and becomes very steep and winding. Minibuses seem to take great pains to give their passengers the feeling they're on a roller coaster and frequently use the wrong side of the road when negotiating corners at extremely high speeds.

**By train:**

There is no train service presently to Dalat from anywhere but a couple of suburbs, rides which are usually taken on these ancient trains by tourists.

Around town, the best way to get around is on the back of a **motorbike**. You shouldn't have any problem finding someone willing to lend you their services for a day or two. Some will not even require payment. I paid one driver US$7 for two full days of journeying around the Dalat area. You can also travel by **horse cart** or ancient Peugot **taxis**. You can also rent a **bicycle** (if you're in good shape—the terrain is hilly). But you won't find a **cyclo**, because the drivers aren't in good shape.

### Post Office

*14 Tran Phu Street.*

### Banks and Moneychangers

Industrial and Commercial Bank of Vietnam. *46 Hoa Binh Square, above the market.* ☎ *22495.*

### Tourist Offices

Lam Dong Provincial Tourist Office. *12A Tran Phu Street.* ☎ *22125.*

Dalat Tourist. *9 Le Dai Hanh.* ☎ *22479.*

### Immigration Police

Lam Dong Provincial Public Security Immigration Office. *10 Thanh Binh Trong Street.* Hours are between 7:30–11:30 a.m. and 1:30–4:30 p.m.

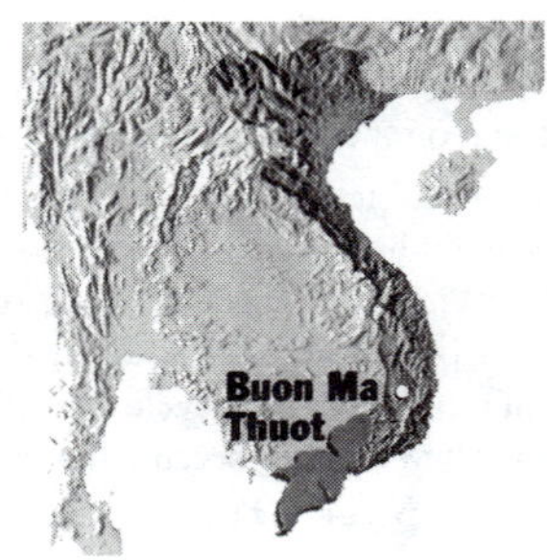


# Buon Ma Thuot

## BUON MA THUOT IN A CAPSULE

*500 meters above sea level...Principal cash crop is coffee...Fell to the North Vietnamese Army on March 11, 1975, 50 days before the war ended...Home to Rhade and M'nong hilltribe people...Population about 67,000...The M'nong are skilled at catching and taming elephants...Many new Chinese arrivals cashing in on the coffee trade.*

Much of this area of the remote central highlands used to be off-limits to foreigners—especially Americans. But this is no longer the case.

Deep within the Central Highlands on the Dac Lac Plateau is the provincial capital of Buon Ma Thuot (population about 67,000 and considered by many as the capital of the Central Highlands), not far from the Cambodian border. This is one of the least accessible areas in Vietnam, although you can get there by car and bus. The bus journey from Saigon can take a grueling 40 hours in the rainy season.

The immigration police in Dalat told me that because of the lengthy and ridiculous road routes to get there, very, very few Westerners make it out to Buon Ma Thuot. Although it is only perhaps 130 km or so as the crow flies northwest from Dalat, to get there by road, you must first take the highway east to the coastal city of Phan Rang (about 110 km), then NH1 north about another 160 km or so, well above Nha Trang (about 35 km), before heading on the road west to Buon Ma Thuot, a dilapidated roadway, for perhaps another 200 km or so. It means a trip from Dalat to Buon Ma Thuot equals well over a whopping 400 km! But you can get there by air. The immigration police in Dalat were unclear, but they said that there already exists a road linking Dalat with Buon Ma Thuot (but that it is for military use only), or that one is being constructed—although, again, it was unclear whether tourists would be allowed to use this route, as Buon Ma Thuot has traditionally been a militarily sensitive area.

But tourists can visit this city. This is an area that was designated a New Economic Zone after the fall of South Vietnam in 1975. Peoples of the Red River region near Hanoi and a significant number of Saigonese were displaced to this area, where villages were created and the forests cleared. The cleared land has yielded little in the form of crops, although the government calls Buon Ma Thuot a "major commercial center." Coffee is the principal crop grown here.

Buon Ma Thuot has the distinction of being the site of the last major battle between NVA and South Vietnamese troops during March 1975 (guess who won?). Then South Vietnamese President Nguyen Van Thieu ordered a withdrawal from the area (in fact the entire Central Highlands) and it was only a short month later before NVA tanks rolled into Saigon.

Today, Buon Ma Thuot's population is ethnically divided, and there is tension with the Rhade minority groups, who have been considered second-class citizens for a number of years.

Buon Ma Thuot shares a similar rainy season with Dalat, but is usually warmer because of its lower elevation.

Along the 250 kilometers from Buon Ma Thuot to Kon Tum there are a number of ethnic minorities, most noticeably the Austronesian tribes Jarai and Raday. Buon Ma Thuot was also home to an American military base during the Vietnam War.

In the center of town is the main square, which features the first NVA tank that entered the city. It's poised on an angled monument.

## What to See and Do in Buon Ma Thuot

### Museum ★

*1 Me Mai Street.*

This is a relatively interesting museum devoted to the ethnography of the Central Highlands. There are displays and artifacts representing Montagnard and Rhade traditions, among the traditions of other ethnic groups. There is earthenware here as well as agricultural tools. There are also displays of traditional Montagnard dress, musical instruments, ancient weapons and other artifacts from more than 30 ethnicities of the Central Highlands. There's also a traditional Rhade house here as well.

### Draylon, Draysap, Drayling and Draynor Waterfalls

These are the several waterfalls that can be found outside town. None are terribly impressive but they rarely see tourists, which makes them that much more delightful to visit. Draysap Falls in particular is a nice area as the falls are surrounded by massive hardwood trees.

**Dac Lap Lake**

Former Emperor Bao Dai used small amounts of money to build a small palace at this lake about 50 km south of Buon Ma Thuot.

**Local Villages** ★★

Foreigners are permitted to visit the local ethnic villages in the vicinity of Buon Ma Thuot, but, at the time of this writing, you need permission from the police to do so. You can visit the Rhade village Buon Tuo—13 km from Buon Ma Thuot. Here there are longhouses where matriarchal Rhade families dwell, although, in many instances, a male will preside over the community. There are also supposedly elephants in the Buon Don area that are captured and trained by the M'nong ethnic group. But there are elephants trained in Buon Don, a M'nong village about 56 km northwest of Buon Ma Thuot. They are captured through the use of domesticated elephants. The M'nong, like the Rhade, are a people whose surnames are passed down through the female rather than male lineage. The M'nong have a lot of animosity against all other ethnicities of the region, including ethnic Vietnamese, although the few Westerners that come to this remote pocket of Vietnam are greeted with great and not unbegrudging curiosity. There is also a 13th-century Cham tower in the area, about 35 km to the north in Ya Liao.

## Where to Stay in Buon Ma Thuot

### AUTHOR'S NOTE: TELEPHONE PREFIXES

*The following phone numbers are local exchanges. The country code is 84. The city code is 50.*

**Thang Loi Hotel** **US$25–$30**

*1-3 Phan Chu Trinh Street.* ☎ *52322.*

This is the largest hotel on Buon Ma Thuot. Dingy but comfortable.

**Tay Nguyen Hotel** **US$20–$30**

*106 Ly Thuong Kiet Street.* ☎ *52250.*

The US$30 rooms have air conditioning. Comfortable. Restaurant.

**Guest House** **US$7–$10**

*42 Ly Thuong Kiet Street.* ☎ *53921.*

Basic and popular with backpackers. Rooms with fan.

**Hong Kong Hotel** **US$10–$15**

*30 Hai Ba Trung Street.* ☎ *52630.*

Basic accommodations. Public toilet.

**Hoang Gia Hotel** **US$6–$10**

*62 Le Hong Phong Street.* ☎ *52161.*

Ditto. Inexpensive.

## Where to Eat in Buon Ma Thuot

Stick to the hotels. Like a number of areas in the Mekong Delta, the folks here don't boil their water. I'd stay away from the food stalls unless you want to spend quite a bit of time in a stall of quite a different variety.

## Directory

### Transportation

Buon Ma Thuot is about 350 km from HCMC, 1430 from Hanoi, 100 km from Dalat as the crow flies, 225 km from Quy Nhon, 665 km from Danang and 190 km from Nha Trang.

**By air:**

VN flies to Buon Ma Thuot daily at 10:15 a.m. from HCMC.

**By bus:**

There is regular bus service to Saigon, Hanoi, Dalat, Nha Trang and most other provincial capitals and major cities.

**By train:**

There is no rail service to or from Buon Ma Thuot.

**By car:**

See the above mileage information.

### Tourist Offices

Dac Lac Tourist Office. *3 Phan Chu Trinh Street.* ☎ *52108.*

### Hospital

*6 Nguyen Du Street.*

### Post Office

*4 Doc Lap Street.*

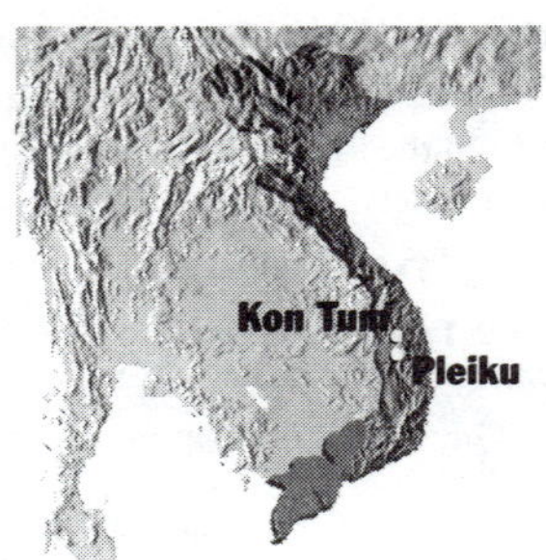


# Pleiku & Kon Tum

Pleiku (with a population of about 40,000 and an elevation of 780 meters) is a market town in the center of a massive and fertile plateau whose red soil is of volcanic origin. Most of the town's inhabitants are from a variety of ethnic origins. Pleiku was also the site of an American base that went through vicious shelling and mortar attacks by the VC during the war in February 1965. The attack was used as justification for the U.S. escalating its military presence in Vietnam (there were about 25,000 U.S. military "advisors" at the time in South Vietnam).

Kon Tum, about 50 km north of Pleiku, is also inhabited primarily by ethnic minority groups. Some of these peoples include the Sedeng, Jarai, Bahnar and Rengao. Kon Tum was the site of massive bombing by American B-52s during the Vietnam War and was essentially leveled by that and the fighting that took place between NVA and ARVN troops in the area in 1972. Kon Tum is extremely remote and should be seen by only the hardiest of travelers. Some government immigration officials told me that permits and fees were required to visit Kon Tum, while others said such documentation and fees were not necessary to see the region.

**INSIDER TIP**

*Although virtually all of Vietnam is open to independent travel, always check with the local immigration police if you want to visit remote, inaccessible areas. The big problem here is that, in many instances, officers within the same province will tell you different stories, especially the farther away you are from the central tourist areas. And, believe me, Pleiku and Kon Tum are off the beaten track.*

### What to See and Do in Pleiku

There is not a tremendous amount to do here; but do see the magnificent **Gia Lai Forest** and **Yali Waterfall**. Also don't miss the elephant village of **Nhon Hoa**, where you may be able to ride an elephant (and that probably depends whether or not you're part of an organized excursion). There are also ethnic dance shows and cultural and folk shows in town.

## INSIDER TIP

*Unfortunately, one of the few ways to visit Pleiku is through one of Saigon-tourist's expensive tours of the area. If you take the tour to Pleiku, you'll have to surrender at least nine days of independent travel time, as the tour will also bring you to sights in Nha Trang, Buon Ma Thuot, Quy Nhon and Dalat, places you can easily reach on your own—and should. The following is the tourist agency's itinerary while stopping in Pleiku: After visiting the hill-tribe museum and Tua Village near Buon Ma Thuot, you'll travel overland and spend the night in Pleiku. Here you'll get an elephant ride in the village of Nhon Hoa and spend the evening seeing cultural and folk shows put on by ethnic minorities. That's it, folks. Even if you're on a tight budget, you might want to consider flying to Pleiku, as the cost is relatively cheap at about US$80 one way from Saigon. From Hanoi, it's about twice as much. The best bet is to fly to Pleiku from Danang for a day or two. The cost is US$80 round trip at last check.*

### Where to Stay in Pleiku

## AUTHOR'S NOTE: TELEPHONE PREFIXES

*The following phone numbers are local exchanges. The country code is 84. The city code is 59.*

**Pleiku Hotel** **US$12**

*124 Le Loi Street.* ☎ *24628.*

Considering you've got little choice in Pleiku, this isn't bad—and it's where most of the backpackers settle in. Clean upon last inspection.

**Yaly Hotel** **US$10–$40**

*89 Hung Vuong Street.* ☎ *24858.*

The best place in town. Rooms with private bath, some with air conditioning. Restaurant. Clean and comfortable.

### Directory

#### Transportation

Pleiku is about 550 km from Saigon, 425 from Nha Trang, 200 km from Buon Ma Thuot and 185 km from Quy Nhon.

**By air:**

VN flies to Pleiku from HCMC on Sundays, Mondays Wednesdays and Fridays at 11:20a.m.; from Hanoi on Fridays at 9:30 a.m., and from Danang on Sundays, Tuesdays and Fridays at 1:35 p.m. From Pleiku, flights depart for HCMC on Sundays, Mondays, Wednesdays and Fridays at 4:20 p.m.

**By bus:**

There are non-express buses that leave from Pleiku to the coastal cities between Nha Trang and Danang. From Saigon, there is express bus service to Pleiku (about 22 hours).

### Airlines

Vietnam Airlines Booking Office. *Yaly Hotel.* ☎ *23834.*

### Post Office

*69 Hung Vuong Street.* ☎ *24006.*

### Hospital

*Tran Hung Dao Street.* ☎ *24125, 24111.*

### Tourist Office

*Tran Phu Street.* ☎ *24271.*

## What to See and Do in Kon Tum

The spectacular 40-meter high **Jrai Li Waterfalls** are perhaps the best reason to visit the region. They can be found about 20 km southwest of Kon Tum.

## Directory

### Transportation

Kon Tum is about 900 km from HCMC, 50 km from Pleiku, 248 from Buon Ma Thuot, 200 km from Quy Nhon, and 435 km from Nha Trang.

**By air:**

You'll have to fly into Pleiku (see the above VN air schedule) and I suggest combining a trip to Kon Tum and Pleiku by flying into Pleiku from Danang.

**By bus:**

Buses leave Kon Tum for Danang, Pleiku and Buon Ma Thuot.

**By car:**

You can rent a car (and driver) to get to Kon Tum. It's worth only a day trip from Pleiku, as Kon Tum has few accommodations for foreign travelers.

# PHAN THIET

***Colorful fishing boats flank the Phan Thiet River.***

## PHAN THIET IN A CAPSULE

*Largest city in Binh Thuan province...About 120 miles northeast of Saigon...Population of 75,000...Clean, casuarina-lined, breezy beaches... Famous in Vietnam for its fish sauce (nuoc mam)...A Cham controlled area until the late 17th Century...Now targeted as major tourist destination.*

Phan Thiet is usually the first stop travelers stay overnight when heading north from Saigon, and the last when heading south from Hue, Danang, or Nha Trang to Saigon. There's not a lot to note here, but the beaches—both Phan Thiet and Mui Ne, 25 km to the east—are clean and expansive and offer a refreshing way to kick back after a hot ride from Saigon. Crossing over the Phan Thiet River on National Highway 1 near the river's mouth at the South China Sea, you'll see row after row of brightly-colored fishing boats tied along both banks. The roads are wide and tree-lined in and outside of Phan Thiet and are usually uncrowded, making sidewalk dining at food stalls comfortable. The enormous width of National Highway 1 leading to Phan Thiet from Saigon was the work of the U.S. Army Corps of Engineers during the Vietnam War. In the effort to widen this central artery between Saigon and Phan Thiet, engineers razed countless buildings, but only partially. It's a bizarre sight to see houses and other structures that appear as if they had gone through a jigsaw. Their owners simply slapped on corrugated metal siding and continued their lives—in half a house. For miles these half-houses flank the highway south of the city.

The north bank of the Phan Thiet River was home to European settlers in the 18th and 19th centuries when Phan Thiet was a relatively bustling port. Prior to European colonization, the city was under Cham control. And this part of Vietnam is still heavily populated with Cham descendents. In fact, even today, the plains and mountains around Phan Thiet possess a population with only about 30 percent ethnic Vietnamese.

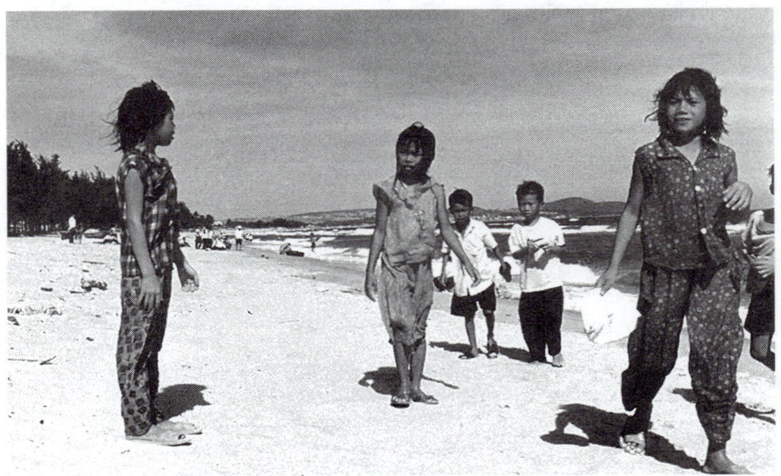

***In Phan Thiet, swimmers don't bother donning bathing suits.***

Phan Thiet is the southernmost city of the former principality of the Cham. Once known as Panduranga, it was once, until the 18th century, entirely left to itself by the Vietnamese because of its inhospitable climate. Slanting from the northeast to the southwest, the region remains relatively free of the monsoons, which, like Ca Na to the north, creates an environment not unlike

Mexico's Baja peninsula. What was originally the coast of Panduranga extended nearly 250 kilometers. Panduranga once reached 100 kilometers west into the valley of the Ndau Nai, which is now referred to as the valley of the Dong Nai River which flowed down to Saigon (then called Raigauv). The Mnong Plateau to the east once served as a natural barrier between Panduranga and Cambodia. The region possessed a number of towns that still exist today: Tanh Linh, Di Linh, Dalat, and Bao Loc.

Today, Phan Thiet is poised to become a hotbed of tourism. The Hai Duong Resort has just opened at Mui Ne Beach, and with it Western-style attractions, such as windsurfing and kayaking. Other resorts are planned for the area as well as an 18-hole golf course. More and more Saigonese are flocking out here on the weekends and bypassing the dirtier Vung Tau area.

The tourist office is located at *82 Trung Trac Street* which is just on the south side of the Phan Thiet River near the bridge.

## What to See and Do in Phan Thiet and Environs

### Phan Thiet Beach

This is about it folks. The beach. Phan Thiet Beach is covered with casuarina pines and isn't your typical palm lined tropical beach, but it's clean and offers some pretty heavy surf, almost the kind of surf you can surf in. But don't get out the board. There are beach chairs for rent in this parklike atmosphere. You can sit and drink for free but you've got to rent a chair. It's a popular place with the locals and, as with the vast majority of Vietnam's beaches, the Vietnamese remain in the protective shade of the pines and coconut palms above the beach, leaving this wide aisle of buttery sand nearly deserted save for occasional bathers. Only the foreigners are stupid enough to lie in the sand nearly naked under a burning sun, the locals muse to themselves.The best way to reach Phan Thiet Beach is to head east at the pointed Victory Monument. You can't miss it. You'll reach the dunes just a few hundred yards later. It's usually pretty windy here.

### Harbor

*South side of town, east of the bridge over the Phan Thiet River.*

Phan Thiet's harbor, which is usually packed with bright, multicolored fishing boats, makes for great photos. Try photographing from the bridge that spans the Ca Ti (Phan Thiet) River.

### Mui Ne Beach

*About 12 miles east of Phan Thiet.*

This is also a nice strip of sand at the end of the Mui Ne peninsula with rising sand dunes and gusty winds. You can get here either by car or bus. Previously, if you were just looking for a beach to relax on, the trip out probably wasn't worth it, as Phan Thiet Beach offers as much in scenery and more in amenities. But that's starting to change, as resorts are beginning to go up along this stretch. Mui Ne is no longer nearly as isolated as it was, which is good news and bad news.

**Vinh Hoa**

*Off NH1 between Phan Thiet and Phan Rang.*

Vinh Hoa is most famous for its mineral water, which is bottled and sold all over Vietnam. It's a small town just off the highway.

## Where to Stay in Phan Thiet

### AUTHOR'S NOTE: TELEPHONE PREFIXES

*The following telephone numbers are local exchanges. The country code is 84. The city code is 62.*

**Phan Thiet Hotel** **US$15–$25**

*40 Trang Hung Dao Street. ☎ 2573.*

This is where you should stay if you're on a budget while staying in Phan Thiet. It's in the center of town, but it's only about a 10-minute walk to the beach. All the rooms have air conditioning, attached bath, and they're generally quite clean. There are doubles and triples in this hotel.

**Khach San 19-4** **About US$15**

*1 Tu Van Tu Street. ☎ 2460.*

This big hotel is just across the street from the bus station and formerly didn't permit foreigners to stay. But this has changed. Air conditioning, restaurant.

**Vinh Thuy Hotel** **US$45** ★

*This expensive hotel is right on the beach on Ton Tuc Thang Street. ☎ 21294 or 22394.*

This is a new structure, built in 1989, although it looks older. And it's expensive. But it's the only choice in town if you want to stay on the beach. Air conditioning, restaurant. Rooms are clean. To get to the hotel follow the directions given above to Phan Thiet Beach. You'll see the multistoried hotel on the left.

**Hai Duong Resort Coco Beach** **US$32–$56** 

*Mui Ne/Phan Thiet Beach. ☎ 23591. FAX: 23590.*

Brand new resort at Phan Thiet/Mui Ne Beach that seems to be poised to become a harbinger of what's to become of this growing area. Comfortable bungalows and villas. 15 villas. Restaurant, bar; private beach with bar. Watersports, including windsurfing, sailing and boat rentals. Mountain bike and moped rentals. Hurry, because these prices won't last long, I'm told.

## Where to Eat in Phan Thiet

Extremely cheap sidewalk foodstalls offering great Vietnamese fare and seafood abound in this port city, but if you must:

**Phan Thiet Hotel** **$$**

*3rd Floor, Phan Thiet Hotel; 40 Tran Hung Dao Street.*

Vietnamese. Relatively expensive.

**Vinh Thuy Hotel** **$$**

*Ton Tuc Thang Street, on the beach.*

Great seafood at moderate-expensive prices.

## Directory

### Transportation

Phan Thiet is about 200 km from HCMC, 248 km from Dalat, and 250 km from Nha Trang.

**By bus:**

From HCMC, buses depart for Phan Thiet at Mien Dong Bus Station. The bus station in Phan Thiet is on Tu Van Tu Street on the northern edge of town. Non-express buses leave here for HCMC, Bien Hoa, Phan Rang, Long Khanh, Phu Cuong, Madagoui, Mui Ne Beach and other destinations. Best to purchase your tickets in advance.

**By train:**

The Reunification Express train runs in both directions up and down the coast from the town of Muong Man, which is about 10 km northwest of Phan Thiet.

**By minivan:**

Minivans leave the Sinh Cafe on Pham Ngu Lao Street, Dist. 1, daily at 7:30 a.m. The price of a one-way ticket is US$10. The journey takes about three hours. This is no day trip.

**Around town:**

Cyclos were the cheapest and only way to get around Phan Thiet. However, bicycles and small motorbikes can be had from some of the hotels these days. About US$1 for the bicycles and about US$6-8 for the mopeds.

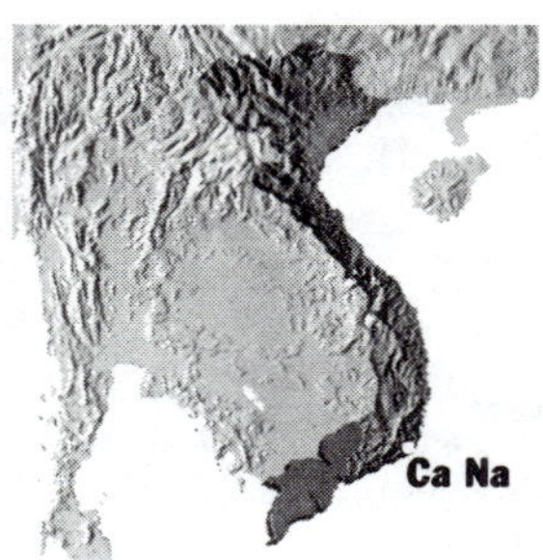


# CA NA

***Former U.S. military turrets dot the beaches around Ca Na.***

## CA NA IN A CAPSULE

*Isolated and arid...a great overnight stop on National Highway 1...Few people, lots of clean, clear ocean...Take panoramic photos from the tiny mountainside pagoda...Terrain is much like Mexico's lower Baja peninsula... Popular stop for tour buses making their way both north and south.*

There's not a helluvalot here, and that's Ca Na's appeal. After a grueling ride over rutted National Highway 1 south from Nha Trang or north from Phan Thiet, Ca Na is what the doctor ordered, as long as you're not expecting a five-star hotel, or even a one-star hostelry for that matter. The accommodations are a little primitive and you'll think the tiny town is a winter destination for migrating flies. But get it out of your mind, snap the tab off a cold one, and enjoy the warm clear waters of this magnificent bay. The seafood in the town's three restaurants is superb and the scenery is some of the most unique in Vietnam. If you didn't hear Vietnamese being spoken around you, you'd swear you were in Baja, Mexico. Cacti poke from the rugged, boulder-strewn mountains that lace this semicircular transparent bay. Casuarina pines tower from the bluffs overlooking the long, deserted beach. There's even a gun turret and bunker left over from the war facing the ocean, defiantly keeping the masses from developing this unique little spike in the South China Sea that will remind you as much of Vietnam as Mazatlan does.

*Arid Ca Na offers Baja California peninsulalike vistas.*

## What to See and Do in Ca Na

There's basically nothing to do here but swim in the warm ocean and enjoy the views. Take a hike up into the mountains. (Be careful. Although the locals say the area has been pretty much depleted of its indigenous fauna, there may be snakes). Take a brief visit up the stairs to the Chinese pagoda resting precariously on the hillside opposite the Hai Son Restaurant and take photos of the clear bay. At night, imbibed new friends that you've made will invite you up into hills to shoot wild animals. Best to decline the offer unless he's got the gun pointed at you.

## Where to Stay and Eat in Ca Na

### Hotels

**Ca Na Hotel** **About US$15**

*National Highway 1. You can't miss it.*
*10 rooms.*

A backpacker's type of place, but the accommodations are sufficient for more upscale visitors. Breezy and desertlike. The Ca Na Hotel looks like a beat-up'50s American motel, but it's right on the beach. The ocean here is very calm and clear, turquoise in hue. The rooms are large and airy and have ocean views. Private toilet but no hot water. Electricity problems. You'll need the mosquito net more for the flies than for the mosquitoes. If you're traveling with a Vietnamese guide, you may get away with paying as little as US$8 a night.

**Hai Son Hotel** **US$15**

*Right next to the Hai Son Restaurant.*
*10 rooms, all facing the sea.*
A small Chinese pagoda overlooks the town perched on the side of a mountain. You can climb a bunch of steps to get up there.

## Restaurants

**Ca Na Quan Restaurant** **$**

*National Highway 1.*
Right on the beach, patio over the water. Excellent seafood, from lobster to urchin to squid. Cheap.

**Nha Hang Hai Son** **$**

*National Highway 1.*
You can rent cars out of this place; great seafood, right down the street from both hotels.

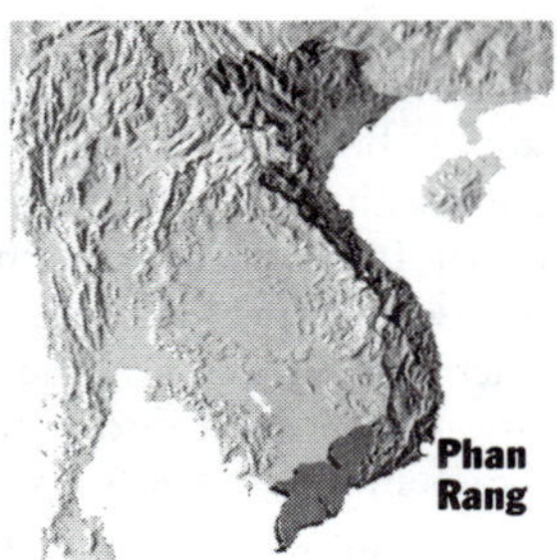


# PHAN RANG

*The four brick Po Klong Garai Cham Towers date from the 13th century.*

Phan Rang (population about 50,000) is sort of a dumpy little nondescript semi-seaside city along the coast a little more than half way between Phan Thiet and Nha Trang. It also serves as the capital of Ninh Thuan Province. Its attractions have nothing to do with the city itself (there are even few hotels for foreigners) but the surrounding Cham towers that rise above the landscape, in particular Po Klong Garai towers, offer magnificent views of the surrounding mountains. And it is this tower complex which is really the only reason you should veer off NH1 through Phan Rang, unless you need to change money or buy table grapes (which are grown here and sent to Saigon).

The climate of Phan Rang itself is relatively dry and arid, although from the Po Klong Garai towers, you can view the arid landscape south toward Ca Na and the more lush mountainside bordering the sea toward Cam Ranh Bay in the north. As well, you can see the concrete remnants of the U.S. airbase called Thanh Son to the north. It was used by Vietnamese Air Force as well as the Soviets until the collapse of that nation. Also you can view from the hill the water tower the Americans built during the war in 1965. Surrounding it are the gun turrets the French built during the First Indochina War. There's a bunch of prickly cacti in the area as well as poinciana trees.

The reason so many towers are in the area is that Phan Rang was once the capital of Champa when it was known as Panduranga. There is still a significant number of Chams that live in the area, and they all seem to be horribly poor, despite the city's trickling trek toward relative economic prosperity.

You'll be tempted to try to find a map of the surroundings identifying sites of Cham towers, but you'll be disappointed. In fact no maps at all (including of Vietnam) are available at any of the newsstands/bookstores in Phan Rang. As I mentioned earlier, buy all the maps you'll need in Saigon or Hanoi. You'll be hard pressed to find any anywhere else.

## What to See and Do in Phan Rang and Environs

**Po Klong Garai Towers** ★★

*About 7 km from Phan Rang off the road toward Dalat.*

This is a spectacular set of four brick Cham towers, highly visible at Thap Cham. To get there take the road to Dalat and turn right onto a dirt road about 2 km past the village Thap Cham. A landmark will be a water tower. When you see it, turn right. The towers are atop a granite, rock-strewn hill called Cho'k Hala Hill just about 200 meters down the road. The biggest of the four towers *(kalan)*—all of which are in remarkably great shape—built as Hindu temples in the 13th century, was constructed in 1306. There's an image of Siva with six arms appearing to be dancing above the entrance. The image itself was reputedly carved in the 12th century, although recently renovated. The pillars surrounding the entrance have detailed inscriptions. Inside it's dark, and the thick incense constantly burning can be overwhelming and make the visit inside a short one, as you'll soon need fresh air. But inside on a raised dais is a lingam featuring a human face, which is said to be that of King Po Klong Garai. It is believed to have been carved in the 16th century. The face is covered with a white dough mask, which is changed during every ceremony. Inside the narrow vestibule is the carving of a bull which was called Nandin, a symbol of agricultural prosperity. There is a tower opposite the kalan's entrance that was originally the main entrance to the kalan. Here there are renovated inscriptions carved into the brick. This definitely is worth a visit if you're passing through Phan Rang. Don't be surprised to find a number of young Vietnamese girls dressed in *ao dais* eager to practice their English with foreign visitors. It was here that I met one such woman who had brought her teacher along to help. The man insisted that the

Vietnam War was lost by the Americans because of a mind-control machine a Vietnamese scientist developed in the early 1960s, giving him the power to redirect American opinion of American involvement in the war. He insisted that the device is still in use today, and that it's thought-control waves are delivered through television. Then he said he spent a year in a Saigon mental hospital. Even though he insisted I give him my address, I have yet to receive one of his ears in the mail.

***Po Nagar Cham Towers were built between the 7th and 12th centuries.***

**Thap Cham Rail Yards**

*About 300 meters southeast of Po Klong Garai, next to the railroad station.*

The main purpose of the yards, built by the French around 1915, is to repair the old railroad engines used by Vietnamese Railways. The Vietnamese are ingenious in their repair methods, as spare parts are made by hand through thoroughly antiquated machinery processes. There was an 85 km-long line between Thap Cham and Dalat, but it was closed in 1964 due to repeated VC sabotaging of the tracks. Chains used to pull the trains up the mountainsides. You can see the steepest mountain along the rail line from the road to Dalat from Phan Rang.

**Po Re Me Cham Tower**

*It's on a rocky hill about 10 km southwest of Phan Rang and 5 km toward the mountains south of Phan Rang off NH1.*

This is more recently constructed than the towers of Po Klong Garai. It can easily be seen from the summit of Cho'k Hala Hill. It was one of the many towers and sanctuaries that encircled the capital, as these towers do in all Cham capitals. It was named for the last Champa ruler King Po Re Mi (1629–1651). Many archeologists believe the structure was built much earlier than the king's reign, perhaps as early as the beginning of the 16th century. Paintings decorate the interior. There are also two statues of the bull Nandin here. There is an excellent life-size image of Siva carved into a relief on a stele. However, this image of Siva has eight arms rather than the six found at Po Klong Garai. There are five figures that are next to the statue—one is a wife of King Po Re Me (Bai Tan Chun). There's another wife of the king, Princess Po Biah Sucih. A third figure was another wife of the king, the Vietnamese princess Po Bia Ut. There are also chapels in the area which possess Hindu influences, but lack the classic Cham style. They are located in the Huu Duc village of Hau Sanh.

**Po Nagar**

*This pagoda is about 15 kilometers east of Phan Rang.*

It's a 19th-century Vietnamese pagoda that celebrates the Goddess Po Nagar. Here there are statues of women and a stone which represents the Mother Goddess.

**Tano Po Riya**

*50 kilometers from Phan Rang at the base of the mountains.*

This is a small chapel in Malam. Ask for directions.

**Po Rayak**

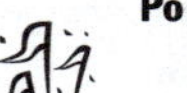

This means God of the Sea and the Rains and rests on the mountain of Cape Padaran. There is a large festival that takes place, in the southern part of the province in March which draws virtually the entire province's population.

**Ninh Chu Beach**

This is a relatively nice stretch of unspoiled and deserted beach (for the most part) sand. About 4 km south of Phan Rang.

**Tuan Tu**

*South on NH1.*

This is a small Muslim Cham village 5 km south of Phan Rang. Go about 250 meters after you cross a large bridge. Here, you'll come across a smaller bridge, after which crossing you'll turn left onto a dirt path. You'll come to a market which is just after a Buddhist pagoda. Turn right on the road at the market for 2 km. You'll then cross two small foot bridges. Depending on the mood of the Provincial Immigration office, you may need a permit to visit here, as well as dishing out fees for a guide, even if you already have one. There is a Cham Mosque. The elected officials of the village can easily be recognized by their ornate costumes, featuring white robes and a turban with long red tassels. The women wear traditional Cham headdress.

## Where to Stay in Phan Rang

**Huu Nghi Hotel** **About US$12–$25**

*1 Hung Vuong Street (just off the road to Thap Cham).* ☎ *22606.*

*20 rooms.*

Some rooms with air conditioning here, but the staff is friendly and they welcome foreigners. The lower priced rooms are a little dingy.

**Phan Rang Hotel** **US$10–$20**

*254 Thong Nhat Street.*

*20 rooms.*

Didn't get a chance to visit here, but I'm told it's the most popular hotel in Phan Rang with foreigners.

**Thong Nhat Hotel** **US$15–$20**

*164 Thong Nhat Street.* ☎ *2515.*

*16 rooms.*

This is a relatively new hotel. Restaurant, hot water, air conditioning in the high-end rooms.

## Where to Eat in Phan Rang

**Huu Nghi** **$**

*1 Hung Vuong Street.*

Great Vietnamese fare.

**Nha Hang 426 (Restaurant)** **$**

*Across the street from the bus station.*

Vietnamese, Asian dishes. A good place to hang out while waiting for your bus.

**Thu Thuy Restaurant** **$**

*Thong Nhat Street.*

Vietnamese, Asian. Delicious and cheap.

**Nha Hang 404 (Restaurant)** **$**

*404 Thang Nhat Street.*

Vietnamese.

## Directory

### Transportation

Phan Rang is about 330 km from Saigon, 105 km from Nha Trang, 110 km from Dalat, and 147 km from Phan Thiet.

**By bus:**

The Intercity Bus Station is opposite *66 Thong Nhat Street*, about 500 meters north of the center of the city. There are regular connections with Saigon, Danang, Nha Trang, Dalat, Ca Na, Cam Ranh Bay, Don Duong, Long Huong, Phan Thiet, Noi Huyen, Song My, Nhi Ha and Phan Ri, to mention some. Buses leave Saigon from Mien Dong Bus Station. The local bus station is at *428 Thong Nhat Street*, south of town.

**By train:**

The station is located at Thap Cham, 5 km west of town and within sight of Po Klong Garai Cham towers. Trains serve all coastal destinations.

**By car:**

From Dalat, the trip takes about 2 hours. From Saigon on NH1, about 7–8 hours.

### Banks and Moneychangers

Foreign Exchange Service. *334 Thong Nhat Street*. There are also a couple of jewelry and gold shops along Thong Nhat Street (which is what NH1 is called going through Phan Rang) that will exchange money, but be prepared to accept a sack of small 2000 dong notes.

### Tourist Office

Ninh Thuan Tourist (in Vietnamese: *Cong Ty Du Lich Ninh Thuan*). Inside the Huu Nghi Hotel.

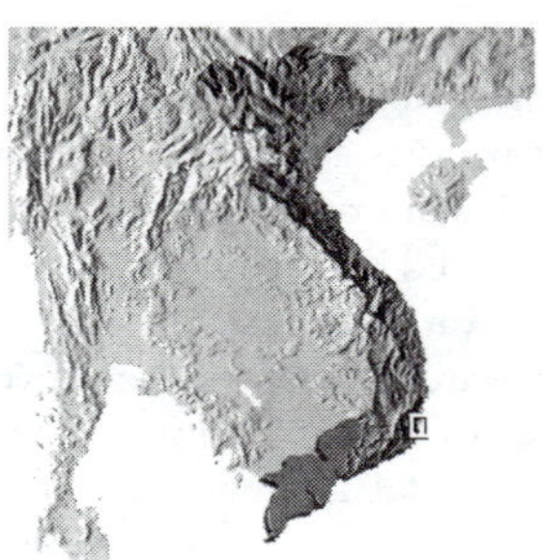

# CAM RANH BAY

***Scenic Cam Ranh Bay has been used as a naval base by several countries, including the Russians, the Japanese, the Americans and the Soviets.***

## CAM RANH BAY IN A CAPSULE

*Hawaii of the Orient...Laid back and lush...This was the site of the largest U.S. naval base in Vietnam during the war...Has been utilized as a naval base for five different nations since 1905...The Russians even managed to maintain a presence here after the Soviet Union collapsed...The area is a major salt production site....A great place to build a summer home and start your own navy.*

Traveling up NH1 from Phan Rang toward Nha Trang lies some of the most beautiful coastal topography in southern Vietnam, much of it in the Cam Ranh Bay area. Salt paddies and small, primitive processing plants dot the roadside—and on both sides of this beautiful natural harbor are towering, lush mountains interrupted by banana plantations, surrounded by dense coconut palm groves. The water here is a crystal-clear sky blue. Perhaps the most disappointing (or rewarding, depending on your viewpoint) aspect of the area is its distinct lack of tourist facilities. This is simply because Cam Ranh Bay has traditionally served as a major naval station for nations including the Russians in 1905, the Japanese during WWII, the Americans during the Vietnam War, and the Soviets again after the Americans left. In fact, even after the fall of the Soviet Union, Russia still managed to maintain a small fleet in Cam Ranh Bay (it was once their largest base outside the Soviet Union)—as a symbolic gesture of defiance if nothing else. Now, in the strangest turn of events, there's talk about the U.S. Navy returning to lease the base—but this time from Hanoi!

In the 1960s, U.S. forces made this area a massive naval institution, and the area has not yet shed it's militarylike milieu. Touring the area today is still difficult—even though the Russians have left. It is still considered militarily sensitive, which is a shame, because there's really nowhere to stay, and it's the kind of environment you could see yourself spending a few days in. The beaches all along the bay are terrific—unspoiled, empty white sand stretches for kilometers.

*Hootches hide behind coconut palms and banana trees south of Cam Ranh.*

### Where to Eat in Cam Ranh Bay

The number of food stalls along NHI approaching Cam Ranh is staggering. Proprietors dart out into the middle of the highway with each approaching vehicle to entice the driver to stop at their eatery. Choose among the dozens that are here. The seafood, including eel, squid, and fresh fish crab is excellent. But be warned. If you're traveling independently without a Vietnamese, you will be charged as much as three times higher than a Vietnamese would, or foreigners traveling with a Vietnamese.

**INSIDER TIP**

*When traveling with a Vietnamese, let this person do all the work for you, in both restaurants and in hotels. Never order or ask for anything yourself. Don't even point at what you want. Tell the Vietnamese guide or friend what your wishes are. If the proprietor has even the slightest indication that you are requesting something yourself, you will be charged more, even if your Vietnamese companion is present. You don't believe me? Go ahead and order that 333 beer, and later see on your bill that it cost 10,000 dong, while it would have cost 5 or 6 thousand dong had your Vietnamese companion ordered it for you.*

# NHA TRANG

***Nha Trang's huge white Buddha was built in 1963.***

## NHA TRANG IN A CAPSULE

*Lazy and beautiful fledgling beach resort city of 200,000 that may one day unfortunately acquire the commercialism and gaudy trappings of Thailand's Pattaya or Bali's Nusa Dua Beach...Offers some of Vietnam's best year-round weather...The beach here is nearly four miles long...Port was established in 1924 and was a popular recreational spot for American sailors during the Vietnam War...The site of some of Vietnam's most magnificent Cham towers...The Po Nagar Cham towers offer spectacular views of the city and harbor, the ocean and islands, and the surrounding verdant mountains.*

Nha Trang (population about 210,000) offers the best combination of clean beaches, clear water and traveler's amenities for the least amount of people than any coastal city in Vietnam. Asked what city travelers would return to after doing a coastal tour of Vietnam, most say Nha Trang. Other than its topographical setting, architecturally it's not a particularly beautiful city. It's not a historical and cultural icon like Hue. It lacks the colorful and heart-wrenching Vietnam War sagas of Danang. It is, though, probably Vietnam's closest answer to a developed tropical resort. Its four miles of beaches are clean and uncrowded, especially outside the city center. The water is usually quite clear, making Nha Trang a diving and watersports destination (although parasailing and jet skis have yet to arrive).

**INSIDER TIP**

*Depending upon whom you believe, Nha Trang is developing a reputation as a turkey shoot for pickpockets and other scam artists. Whether this picture being painted by some guides is accurate or not, the jury's still out. But if you're traveling with a guide, he may warn you that the danger is not from the locals, but from foreigners. You may be advised to stay away from foreigners entirely; even casual greetings should be avoided. Why Nha Trang would be selected over other Vietnamese cities by foreign pickpockets, though, is a mystery to me.*

The clear waters are great for scuba diving and snorkeling, especially off Mieu Island, which can easily be reached by ferry, passenger excursion vessels or small private boats. Unfortunately, this area has the potential of being developed into a major seaside tourist mecca of the likes of Pattaya or Phuket, although this will take some years. The small pockets of tourist areas are packed with foreigners, and rarely do you see any elsewhere in town. The beachside boulevard of Tran Phu is usually virtually empty of traffic and there are a number of hotels lining the street, although they're across the boulevard from the beach, which is coconut palm-lined and features a number of comfortable cafes.

Nha Trang (the name is taken from the Cham word "Yakram," which means bamboo river) also has perhaps Vietnam's best coastal climate, as it can cool down significantly here in the evening. Unlike farther south, the rainy season in Nha Trang runs only from October through early December—and even then, rain usually falls only at night.

There are some magnificent Cham towers (the Cham Po Nagar Complex) which sit high atop a hill on the north bank of the Nha Trang River, near its mouth, offering spectacular views of the city, beaches, the harbor and mountains that reach west far off into the distance. Few tourists visit areas of Nha

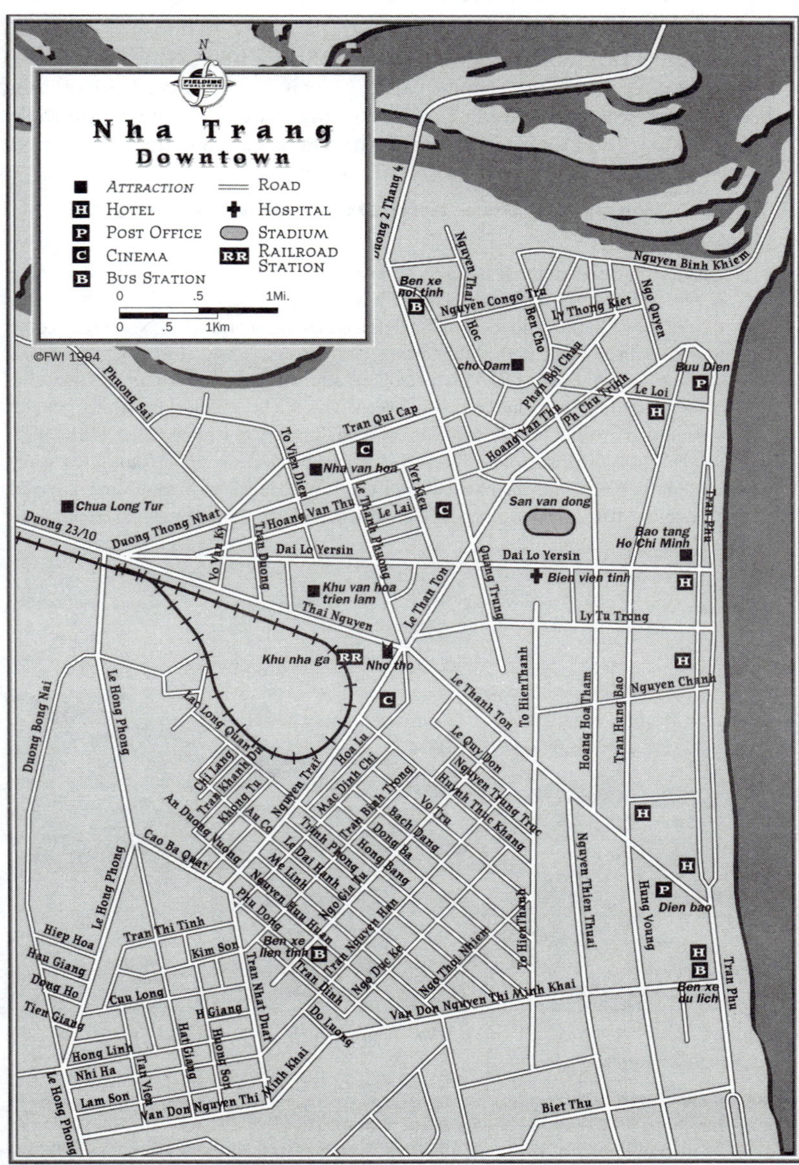
Nha Trang
Downtown
Attraction
Road
Hotel
Hospital
Post Office
Stadium
Cinema
Railroad Station
Bus Station
0 .5 1Mi.
0 .5 1Km
©FWI 1994
Duong 2 Thang 4
Nguyen Thai Hoc
Ben xe noi tinh
Nguyen Congo Tru
Ben Cho
Ly Thong Kiet
Ngo Quyen
Nguyen Binh Khiem
cho Dam
Phan Boi Chau
Buu Dien
Le Loi
Ph Chu Trinh
Hoang Van Thu
Phuong Sai
Tran Qui Cap
To Vien Dien
Nha van hoa
Yet Kieu
Le Thanh Phuong
Chua Long Tur
Hoang Van Thu
Le Lai
San van dong
Tran Phu
Bao tang Ho Chi Minh
Duong 23/10
Duong Thong Nhat
Vo Van Ky
Tran Duong
Dai Lo Yersin
Dai Lo Yersin
Quang Trung
Bien vien tinh
Khu van hoa trien lam
Thai Nguyen
Le Than Ton
Ly Tu Trong
Khu nha ga
Nho tho
Le Thanh Ton
To HienThanh
Hoang Hoa Tham
Tran Hung Bao
Nguyen Chanh
Duong Bong Nai
Le Hong Phong
Lan Long Quan
Le Quy Don
Nguyen Trung Truc
Huynh Thuc Khang
Hoa Lu
Mac Dinh Chi
Tran Binh Trong
Vo Tru
Bach Dang
Chi Lang
Tran Khanh
Khong Tu
Nguyen Trai
An Duong Vuong
Au Co
Trinh Phong
Dong Ba
Hong Bang
Cao Ba Quat
Le Dai Hanh
Me Linh
Ngo Gia Tu
Nguyen Thien Thuai
Hung Vuong
Dien bao
Le Hong Phong
Nguyen Huu Huan
Phu Dong
Tran Nguyen Han
Ngo Thoi Nhiem
To HienThanh
Hiep Hoa
Tran Thi Tinh
Kim Son
Ben xe lien tinh
Ngo Duc Ke
Hau Giang
Dong Ho
Cuu Long
Tran Nhat Duat
Tran Dinh
Van Don Nguyen Thi Minh Khai
Ben xe du lich
Tran Phu
Tien Giang
H Giang
Do Luong
Hai Giang
Huong Son
Hong Linh
Nhi Ha
Tan Viet
Lam Son
Van Don Nguyen Thi Minh Khai
Le Hong Phong
Biet Thu

Trang other than the seaside, except to see the Cham towers, Long Son Pagoda, and the Hon Chong Promontory.

During the Tay Son rebellion in the late 18th century, Nha Trang fell to the rebels after nine bitter days of battle. Now it is a two-tiered city offering both a sleepy seaside community and a bustling city center, which, ironically, offers the best food found in the city. Nha Trang's architecture ranges from French colonial to Chinese to post-1975 Vietnamese.

## What to See and Do in Nha Trang

### The Beaches ★

Nha Trang offers some of the best beaches in all of Vietnam. There is Nha Trang Beach, which runs parallel with Tran Phu Blvd. The coconut-palm lined white sands are dotted with cafes and food stalls. This is where most visitors to Nha Trang come to sun themselves and bathe in the warm, clear waters. As you move down the beach south toward the Bao Dai Villas, strollers, sun worshipers, bathers and souvenir hawkers become fewer and farther between. This is a beautiful, clean stretch of sand surrounded by calm waters that is nearly 6 km long. Hon Chong Beach is actually a few beaches which surround the Hon Chong Promontory. The palm-lined sands are amidst a beautiful sky-blue bay and tall, lush, banana and mango tree-covered mountains that surround the bay. Here is where many of the area's fishermen live.

*Hon Chong Promontory in Nha Trang offers beautiful vistas of the surrounding mountains.*

### Hon Chong Promontory 

*Just north of Nha Trang (about 3.5 km from the city center).*

A tall granite hillside overlooks the small crystal-clear bay where Hon Chong Beach is. You can get here by following *2 Thang 4 Street* past the Po Nagar Cham Towers and turning right on Nguyen Dinh Chieu Street, which leads up the hill to the promontory. There's a decent restaurant and souvenir kiosks at the promontory and a small run-down hotel nearby (Nha Nghi Hon Chong) that's currently closed. From the bluffs of the promontory, you can view the Fairy Mountains, three peaks that are supposed to look like a sleeping fairy (I'll tell you, these Vietnamese!) but look like nothing more than three verdant peaks. Toward Nha Trang, down Hon Chong beach, you can see the small island of Hon Do and its Buddhist temple on top. To the northeast is Tortoise Island. You can also see the two islands of Hon Yen in the distance. The giant rocks of the promontory here are reputed in legend to have been carved by the hands of a giant. A large "handprint" is on one boulder on top of the promontory. Local lore has it that the print was made by a drunk male fairy after he was caught peeking at a female fairy swimming in the buff and then fell down. (Unfortunately, today, the only carving in the rocks is being done by drunk vandals with spray paint cans. Graffiti covers some of the stones.) Although the two fairies eventually married, the male was caught by the gods and sent off to "prison" for his previous voyeurism. After the female could wait no longer for her lover to return, she lay down and turned into Fairy Mountain. I think that Disney could use some of these guys as writers. Admission is 6000 dong per car.

**Gallery**

*20 Tran Phu.*

Vietnamese artists and sculptors works on display and for sale. Oil paintings, lacquer paintings, wood engravings, silk paper paintings, etc. Universal Sciences of Library of Khanh Hoa Province.

**Phong Trung Bay My Thuat Gallery**

*16 Tran Phu. ☎ 22277.*

The various works of several of Vietnamese artists and sculptors. Works for display and sale.

**Pasteur Institute** ★

*Tran Phu Street, across from the beach.*

Andre Yersin, who came to Vietnam from Paris after working for Louis Pasteur and lived for four years in the Central Highlands documenting his experiences, was perhaps the most beloved of all the Frenchmen by the Vietnamese in the late 19th and early 20th centuries. Yersin was the man who "discovered" Dalat and recommended that the French government establish a hill station there. He also was the first to introduce quinine and rubber producing trees to Vietnam. But perhaps he is best known as being the man who discovered the cause of bubonic plague. Yersin founded the Nha Trang institute in 1895 to help research ways of improving Vietnamese hygiene and immune systems. Today, the institute performs the same functions. It develops vaccines and conducts research in microbiology, epidemiology and virology, and develops disease vaccines using primitive equipment. Yersin's library has now been made into a museum. On display here are antiquated research equipment, personal items, and the doctor's books. Open every day from 7:30–11 except Sunday and holidays.

**Po Nagar Cham Towers** 

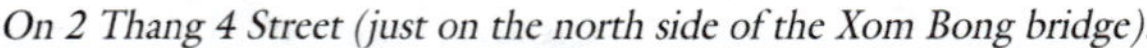
*On 2 Thang 4 Street (just on the north side of the Xom Bong bridge).*

There were once eight magnificent towers on this granite hilltop overlooking the picturesque Nha Trang region, but only four remain today. Po Nagar (locally called Thap Ba) means "Lady of the City," and the towers were built between the 7th and 12th centuries. Well before then, during the 2nd century AD, the area was an important Hindu worshipping hilltop. The largest tower is the 23-meter high Thap Chinh, built in AD 817 by a minister of King Harivarman I named Pangro, which houses the statue of Lady Thien Y-ana (the wife of Prince Bac Hai). Lady Thien Y-ana taught agriculture to the people as well as weaving. The remaining towers were constructed in honor of the gods, the central tower (or Fertility Temple) in honor of Cri Cambhu. The northwest tower was built for Sandhaka (the foster father of Lady Thien Y-ana) and the south tower for Lady Thien Y-ana's daughter, Ganeca.

Some 40 years before the north tower was built, it was raided by Malay corsairs from Sumatra who burned and ransacked the area. A gold mukha-linga was put in the north tower by King Indravarman III in AD 918, although it was later hauled off by raiding Khmer bandits. The mukha-linga was replaced with the stone figure of a shakti of Shiva by King Jaya Indravarman I in AD 965.

The central tower was erected in the 12th century, and is considered the least well-built tower in the complex. Its pyramidal roof possesses no terracing or pilasters.

There's a museum next to the north tower that contains examples of Cham stonework, but relics that hardly rival the magnificent examples of Cham stonework found at the Cham Museum in Danang. The towers are worth a visit if only for the views from the top of the hill. Don't do Nha Trang without seeing them. Admission: 5000 dong.

**Long Son Pagoda** 

*23 Thang 10 Street.*

The Buddha in this temple, founded in the late 19th century, is lit by natural light from behind it. The pagoda itself has been rebuilt a number of times and is now dedicated to the monks and nuns that perished through self-immolation protesting the South Vietnamese Diem regime during the Vietnam War. There are ceramic tile and glass images of dragons on the roof and the entrance to the structure. There are also murals telling of jataka legends covering the upper walls of the pagoda. The principal sanctuary is decorated with dragons wrapped around the columns on both sides of the main altar. Stairs on the right side of the complex head up the hill toward an approximately 10-meter-high white Buddha seated on a lotus blossom. The big Buddha can be seen from many parts of the city.

**Cau Da**

*About 5 km south of Nha Trang.*

This is a tiny, nondescript fishing village best noted for being a good way to get out to Mieu Island, for the Bao Dai Villas and also for the Aquarium. But there are some superb views of Nha Trang from the promontory which is the site of the villas. There's an abundance of souvenir kiosks in Cau Da for tourists while they haggle over private boat fees to the island. Many of the "souvenirs" are stuffed sealife, but you can purchase some fine, polished seashells and seashell jewelry.

**Oceanographic Institute and Aquarium**

*From Nha Trang, go down (south) Tran Phu Blvd. toward the Bao Dai Villas, which becomes To Do Street south of the airport.*

Built in the early 1920s, this is a disappointing display of ocean creatures and plant life in Cau Da. The aquarium's more than 20 tanks contain seahorses, lobsters, turtles and the like. There's a museum of preserved sea creatures behind the aquarium featuring perhaps 60,000 preserved specimens of local sealife. As well, there are stuffed fish and sea birds.

# Nha Trang Environs

## Dai Lanh ★

National Highway 1 passes through the small hamlet of Dai Lanh about 85 km north of Nha Trang. It's a spectacularly scenic location (the lush green mountains descend virtually to the beach), the bay's beach being surrounded by casuarina trees that were, unfortunately, virtually ripped from their roots by the devastating typhoon that hit the central Vietnamese coast in December 1993. I mean this area really took a battering. The palms and casuarina trees, the few that remain, look as if they had been totally defoliated during the war—and many tourists will ask their guides if this was indeed what happened to what is normally an amazingly lush mountain-to-sea hamlet. The beach is of clean, white sand and virtually void of beachgoers. Despite the massive typhoon damage to the flora in the area, Dai Lanh makes for a perfect beach day trip from Nha Trang. The beach touts are few and far between, but they usually offer what you'd want to buy anyway on a hot day, rich local coconut milk and its soft meat to match. There is a restaurant/cafe at the beach (the Dai Lanh Restaurant) as well as an amazingly drab-appearing, unfinished hotel that seems to have been under construction since the Nguyen Dynasty, which will presumably be called the Dai Lanh Hotel. But no one around the area seems to have any idea when or if ever the structure will be completed. It should be, though. Like Ca Na to the south, Dai Lanh has the potential of being one of the most relaxing, remote and commercially undeveloped and least exploited coastal areas in Vietnam. Stop here.

## Mieu Island

The principal village on this island off Nha Trang is Tri Nguyen, a small town that's noted for a fish breeding farm, where dozens of species of sealife are raised in separate compartments. There's one "beach" on the island, Bai Soai, which is really nothing more than where the sea meets a bunch of rocks. If you want to lie out in the sun here, bring a bed. If you want to go swimming, bring hiking boots. Means of reaching the island are discussed in the Cau Da section of this chapter.

### Bamboo Island ★

You'll have to hire a private craft to reach this island, about 3 km off the coast of Nha Trang Beach and the largest isle in the vicinity of Nha Trang. A decent beach is here (Tru Beach) on the northern end of the island.

### Ebony Island

This is just south of Bamboo Island and is noted for its decent snorkeling. Again, you'll have to hire a boat to get out here.

### Salangane Island

These are actually two different isles about 17 km offshore (a 3–4 hour boat ride) where salangane nests are gathered for use in bird's nest soup and for their traditional aphrodisiac qualities. The nests themselves are created from the secretions of salangane birds. The red ones are considered the finest and they're harvested about twice a year. It's believed the virile and promiscuous Emperor Minh Mang who ruled Vietnam in the mid-19th century relied on salangane for his legendary sexual longevity.

### Ba Ho Falls

About 20 km north of Nha Trang and close to the village of Phu Huu is a beautiful set of three waterfalls set amongst a lush forest. You can get there by bus to Ninh Hoa from Nha Trang's local bus station.

### Dien Khanh Citadel

This 17th-century Trinh Dynasty citadel is about 10 km west of Nha Trang and close to the village of Dien Toan. After defeating the Tay Son insurgency, Prince Nguyen Anh, who was later to become Emperor Gia Long, rebuilt the structure in 1793. It's worth only a short visit.

#### Where to Stay in Nha Trang

**AUTHOR'S NOTE: TELEPHONE PREFIXES**

*The following telephone numbers are listed as local exchanges. The country code is 84. The city code is 58.*

**Cau Da Villas (Bao Dai Villas) US$40-plus** 

*Tran Phu Street at Cau Da.* ☎ *, 22449, 22249 or 21124.*

These villas, about 3.5 miles south of town off Tran Phu Street, are the classiest accommodations in town and used to be the estate of the former Emperor Bao Dai. The villas were renovated recently and offer incredible views of the sea, the harbor, and Bamboo and Mieu Islands, although it's a little disappointing when freighters are anchored offshore, as they often are down here. But the villas are an outstanding bargain for the price. The rooms are large, open and airy—with bathrooms to match. All the amenities you'd expect at twice the cost.

**Thuy Duong Hotel & Restaurant** **US$7–$15**

*36 Tran Phu.*
*10 rooms.*

Air conditioning in the cheap rooms. Restaurant. Sort of a lazy place frequented by beer-swilling, but polite, locals. Pool tables in front. Not much going on. I saw no tourists here, but they are accepted.

**Hotel Hoa Hong (Mini Hotel)** **US$15**

*26 Nguyen Thien Thuat. ☎ 22778; FAX: 23842.*

A bit off the beaten track. Not particularly close to the beach, nor the hustle and bustle of the city center. But clean enough. Few tourists.

**Thong Nhat Hotel** **US$12–$27** ★

*18 Tran Phu Street. ☎ 22966 or 22511.*
*86 rooms.*

On the beach strip. Tall, attractive building—the upper floors offer a great view of the islands if you can get a room facing the water. The cheaper price gets you a reasonably comfortable room with two beds, a ceiling fan, and hot water. The splurge price gets you the above plus air conditioning, a refrigerator, telephone and TV. Overall, this is a very nice place for the price.

**Post Hotel** **US$20–$25** ★

*2 Tran Phu Street. ☎ 21181.*
*24 rooms (2 suites).*

Located on the far north end of the Tran Phu strip across the street from the beach. Brand new building and hotel. Opened only a year ago. Friendly, helpful and eager staff—perhaps because they're new. Glamourous white deco building. Clean as a whistle. Get a room on one of the higher floors for a view of the sea. Although it's quiet enough, I'd stay away from the rooms off the lobby if you can. Telephone, refrigerator, TV, air conditioning.

**Duy Tan Hotel (Khach San 24)** **US$11–$30** 

*24 Tran Phu Street. ☎ 22671.*
*83 rooms.*

This building, across Tran Phu from the beach, looks like a toppled ice-cube tray, but it's a popular place. A word of caution. It seems each room has a different price. I counted at least eight different prices, so know what you're getting into. A number of rooms offer separate meeting areas. Restaurant, car rentals, tours, catering, laundry, barber/beauty salon. Photo developing.

**Vien Dong Hotel** **US$7–$50** 

*1 Tran Hung Dao Street. ☎ 21606 or 21608; FAX: 21912.*
*84 rooms (6 suites).*

This is the most happenin' place in town. Just up Tran Hung Dao from the beach, this place is truly a bargain if you take one of the cheaper rooms on the top floor. You'll be able to take advantage of the hotel's amenities which, on a Vietnam scale, make the Vien Dong a full-blown resort. There's a large swimming pool, pool tables, a tennis court, badminton court, and a huge outdoor cafe where traditional Vietnamese dance shows are performed a few times a week. There's a top-shelf gift shop, restaurant, and bicycle rentals. The service is friendly, albeit a little slow. The cheap rooms offer fan, hot water, public WC. The pricier digs come with air conditioning, color TV, telephone (IDD), and refrigerator. This is my choice when in Nha Trang, although it's somewhat sterile, packed with foreigners, and you have to pay to use the pool.

**Hai Au 1 Hotel** **US$15–$20**

*3 Nguyen Chanh. ☎ 22862.*

*21 rooms.*

Tucked away off the beachside drag of Tran Phu, this is a small, unassuming, quiet, and basic hotel that might be just a little overpriced. But the service is friendly and laid-back. Popular with both overseas Vietnamese and Westerners. Air conditioning, hot water.

**Hau Au 2 Hotel** **US$15–$25**

*4 Nguyen Chanh. ☎ 23644.*

*15 rooms.*

This is a more attractive and newer building than its sister up the street. Hot water, air conditioning, restaurant, rest area.

**Khatoco Hotel** **US$30–$60** ★★

*9 Biet Thu Street. ☎ 23724, 23725, or 23723; FAX: 21925.*

*26 rooms.*

This is the classic example of the invasion of capitalism in Vietnam. In the middle of relative squalor with no particular strategic or marketing reason to be there, rises this modern, elegant, dazzling white monolith founded in marble, smoked glass and chrome that looks right off the set of *Miami Vice*. Atop the roof are suspended giant packs of cigarettes produced by the hotel's owners (the Khanh Hoa Tobacco Company). This is truly a bizarre sight, and worth the short walk from the beach just for the chuckle and a snapshot. Opened in April 1993, it has most of the conveniences: guide services, tours, restaurant, air conditioning, refrigerator, international TV, telephone. Very friendly staff. But for the price, make sure you get a view of the water.

**Nha Trang Hotel** **US$8–$20**

*129 Thong Nhat Street. ☎ 22347 or 22224.*

*74 rooms.*

This towering (by Vietnamese standards) seven or eight story hotel is clean and priced right but out of the way unless you have business in the vicinity. Air conditioning.

**Hai Yen Hotel** **US$7–$80** ★

*40 Tran Phu Street. ☎ 22828 or 22974; FAX: 21902.*

*107 rooms.*

This is a popular place across Tran Phu from the beach, and despite its amenities of conference rooms, car rentals, a dancing hall, restaurant, currency exchange, gift shop, and traditional Vietnamese dance performances, the reception—when I visited—ranged from aloof to rude. I don't see what all the fuss is about.

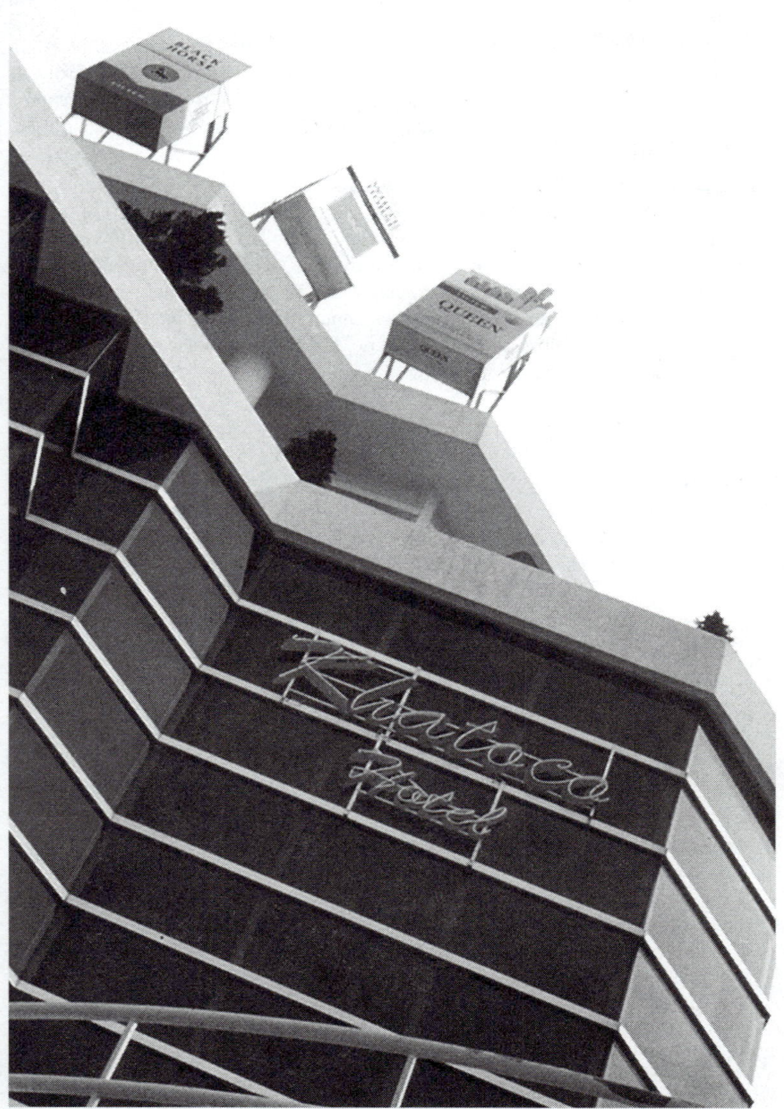


*Nha Trang's Khatoco Hotel leaves no guessing what it's owned by—a giant tobacco monopoly.*

**Hotel La Fregate (Khach San Thang Loi)** **US$20–$38**

*4 Pasteur Street. ☎ 22241 or 22523; FAX: 21905.*

*55 rooms.*

This hotel has undergone a recent renovation and the staff seem as cheerful as the new masonry. Conference hall, large restaurant, cafe, two bars, two banquet rooms, beauty salon/barber, massage and sauna, and gift shop. Also car and bike rentals, boat tours. The upper-end rooms come with refrigerator, hot water, air conditioning, and bathtub. Luxurious for the price.

**The Grand Hotel (Nha Khach 44)** **US$10–$40**

*44 Tran Phu Street; ☎ 22445.*

This yellow French colonial mansion sits right across Tran Phu from the beach and has some breezy, large and elegant rooms. But the cheaper prices put you in a barracks-like annex next to the main building with a fan and a hard, thin mattress. The grounds look more like a boarding school campus than a hotel, but the price—at all levels—includes a full breakfast on the patio. It's relaxing in the early morning sunlight. Beauty salon/barber services.

**Lehoang** **US$8–$16**

*86 Tran Phu; ☎ 24070, 24076.*

*9 rooms.*

On the road just south of town. The $8 rooms are a bargain that would run as high as $12 or more closer to town. Across the road from the beach. Air conditioning, big beds, hot water, individual baths. Nhat Thong is the manager; a real friendly guy. Tell him Fielding sent you and you may get a Vietnamese's rate. Restaurant right next door. Inexpensive.

**Hung Dao Hotel** **US$8–$10** 

*3 Tran Hung Dao Street; ☎ 22246.*

This is where everyone heads when the cheaper rooms at next door's Vien Dong are full. Consequently, this place is full a lot of the time, too. Call in advance. Or better yet, call the Vien Dong in advance. I've heard a rumor about "nasty" elements frequenting this place. Hookers perhaps? Nonetheless, it's an attractive place with a decent location (although not on the beach) and a good restaurant. Bike rentals, too.

**Hai Duong Bungalows**

*Tran Phu Street, about two miles south of town on the beach.*

This place appears to be nothing more than a beachside whore village, for Vietnamese only. As a foreigner, I wasn't allowed to take a "hut." And my inspection of the grounds turned up nothing more accommodating than some drunken Army officers fondling hookers in the bar next to reception. I only mention this place so you'll avoid the temptation to inquire here, because Hai Duong is on the beach and the setting's not bad amid the casuarina trees. If you can get in, I'd like to hear from you.

## Where to Eat in Nha Trang

**Nam Phi Restaurant** **$**

*12 Tran Phu Street.*

Local fare.

**Coco Bar** $

*Tran Phu Street, across from the Pasteur museum on the beach.*
Cafe.

**Dich Vu Du Lich** $

*Thuy Trang, 9a Le Loi.*
Vietnamese, Asian.

**Ninh Hoa** $

*So9 Le Loi.*
Specialty is hash.

**Hoang Yen Guide and Tourist Services Center** $$

*26-28 Tran Phu; ☎ 22961.*
Yes, this is a restaurant. Great seafood.

**Quan An** $

*11 Le Loi.*
Seafood.

**Ninh Hoa** $

*13 Le Loi.*
Vietnamese, Asian.

**Vi Huong** $

*19 Le Loi; ☎ 22872.*
Cuisine of Vietnam.

**Quan Nem** $

*1 Hoang Van Thu.*
Vietnamese.

**Com Phan Dia** $

*33 Le Loi.*
Vietnamese, Asian.

**Khanh Phong** $

*6b Yersin.*
Vietnamese, Asian.

**Cafe Tho** $

*1 Quang Trung.*
Vietnamese, Asian.

**The Second Best Ice Creamery in Vietnam** $$ ★

*58 Quang Trung.*
Yogurt, fruit salad, fruit juice, banana splits galore, soft drinks, sour soft drinks, fruit shakes, coffees, teas, a hodgepodge of stuff. Frequented by Westerners. Very friendly. The woman owner says the name is a takeoff on an ice cream parlor in Saigon called The Best Ice Creamery in Vietnam. But her scheming neighbor, hoping to cash in on some of the success she was seeing next door, suspiciously and less

than fluently renamed her own food stall as the "First Best Offering" store and posted an identical menu alongside the one hanging in The Second Best Ice Creamery. If you're not careful, you'll think the two shops are one and the same and end up getting served by the imposter. But on my visit, First Best Offering was empty and SBICV nearly packed, mostly with dollar-toting foreigners. The owner says she's changing the name to Banana Splits. That'll screw up her neighbor, who'll probably reciprocate with a name change of her own—perhaps to Banana Divides. We'll keep you posted on this, the first corner gas station war in Vietnam since 1975.

**Cafe Vy** **$**

*2 Ly Tu Trong, just right off the main drag by the beach.*

**Cafe Giai Khat** **$**

*Tran Phu.*

Peaceful, bamboo laden setting. Small tables are very private. Nice for couples. Romantic in sort of a grungy way.

**Hai Au Restaurant** **$**

*3 Nguyen Chanh; ☎ 22862.*

Vietnamese specialties. Superb food at cheap prices.

**The Lizard Club and Restaurant** **$$**

*Le Thanh Ton; ☎ 21206.*

**46 Cafe** **$**

*By the Grand Hotel, Tran Phu.*

Standard local fare, nice setting.

**Seamen's Club Restaurant** **$$**

*72-74 Tran Phu, ☎ 22251.*

I'm not sure about this place, whether it's for seamen only or not.

**Dac San Seafood Restaurant** **$$**

*Tran Phu, right on the beach south of town.*

This is a breezy open air cafe and restaurant under a tent on the beach. Good seafood.

**96 Restaurant** **$**

*96 Tran Phu.*

Tasty Vietnamese seafood.

**Kem Cafe** **$**

*Tran Phu.*

Seafood at cheap prices.

**Hanh Green Hat** **$**

*Tran Phu.*

Vietnamese and Western. Popular.

## Directory

### Transportation

Nha Trang is 1300 km from Hanoi, 445 km from Saigon, 240 km from Quy Nhon, 215 km from Dalat, 200 km from Buon Ma Thuot, 410 km to Quang Ngai, 105 km from Phan Rang.

**By air:**

VN has daily flights to Nha Trang from HCMC at 7:05 a.m. Also Thursdays and Sundays at 2:40 p.m. Flights leave daily from Nha Trang to HCMC at 8:35 a.m. (except Tuesdays and Thursdays, when they depart at 12:30 p.m.). Connections to Hanoi are twice a week (Thursday and Sunday) and are extremely expensive (about US$130) one way. Flight schedules are subject to change and the prices will go up soon, as mentioned earlier in this edition).

**By bus:**

The bus station for long-distance travel is located at the intersection of Ngo Gia Tu and Nguyen Huu Huan Streets in the southwest area of town. Express tickets can be purchased at *6A Hoang Hoa Tham Street*, and it's best you buy your tickets in advance. Non-express buses to Saigon cost about 16,000 dong, to Danang 19,000 dong, to Vinh 40,000 dong, Hue 25,000 dong, Quy Nhon 9000 dong, Dalat 8500 dong, and Phan Rang 4000 dong. Express buses to Saigon are about 19,000 dong, Hanoi 55,500 dong, Danang 22,000 dong, Vinh 39,000 dong, Quang Ngai 16,000 dong, Dalat 9400 dong, Vinh 40,000 dong, and Hue 25,000 dong. The local bus station is located across from *115 2 Thang 4 Street*, although there is little reason to travel by local bus.

**Bicycles:**

Bicycles can be rented from most hotels for about 8000 dong a day (they'll try to get 10,000 from you, but just walk away. They'll call you back). A car and driver can be rented for the day from some of the better hotels, such as the Khatoco Hotel, and popular excursions include an afternoon trip to Dai Lanh Beach up the coast about an hour. Cars and microbuses can also be rented at Tourist Car Enterprise, *1 Nguyen Thi Minh Khai Street*. Prices are different everywhere, either for local excursions or long-distance one-way travel.

**Lambrettas**

Lambrettas run to Cau Da from the Central Market.

**By train:**

The train station is located across the street from *26 Thai Nguyen Street*, although you should book in advance at the office at *17 Thai Nguyen Street*. ☎ *22113*.

**Cyclos**

Cyclos are available all over town. If you want to hire a boat, go to the dock at Cau Da, which is 5–6 km south of Nha Trang. From here, you can visit Mieu Island for about US$8–10. (The prices keep going up as tourists don't negotiate properly—so the locals can expect more.) Some boats can be hired for the day—the trips include stops for snorkeling—for as little as US$10 per day. Again, see if you can bargain it down a bit. Ferries also run out to Mieu Island for a pittance.

### Nha Trang Telecommunications Center

*2 Le Loi. Tel: 8458, 21510.; FAX: 84-58-21056*. Fax, phone and telex services are here. There's a post office here, too.

### Central Post Office

*2 Tran Phu Street.*

### TNT International Express

☎ *21043.*

### Hospital

*19 Yersin Street.* ☎ *22168.*

### Banks and Moneychangers

Vietcom Bank. *17 Quang Trung Street*. Will exchange most major currencies and cash travelers' checks. Also will provide cash advances on major U.S. credit cards.

### Tourist Offices

Khanh Hoa Tourism. *1 Trang Hung Dao Street.* ☎ *22753.*

### Airline Offices

Vietnam Airlines. *86 Tran Phu Street.* ☎ *21147.* You can also book at *94 Tran Phu Street.*

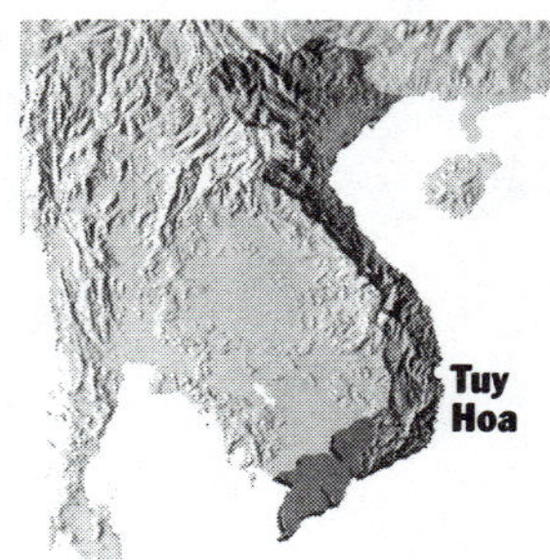


# TUY HOA

## TUY HOA IN A CAPSULE

*The capital of Phu Yen Province, but a small town of only a few thousand inhabitants...This is a good place to break the journey north or south along NH1 only if you're tired...There are no real attractions here.*

Tuy Hoa is a barely noticeable, small town about 100 km south of Quy Nhon. There's little if anything to do here but stop and eat at a food stall or take a cheap hotel room for the night. You virtually could pass through Tuy Hoa without noticing it. It rests on the coast between Quy Nhon and Dai Lanh Beach. Here NH1 passes over a large river. But the beaches in the area aren't worth noting.

Trang Bridge—the longest bridge in southern Vietnam, built in 1954 by the French, at 1100 meters long—is close by.

### Where to Stay in Tuy Hoa

**Huong Sen Hotel** **About US$10**

*NH1, center of town.*

This is a peaceful hotel with a surprisingly good restaurant.

### Directory

### Tourist Office

**Phu Yen Tourist**

*137 Le Thanh Ton Street. ☎ 23353.*

# QUY NHON

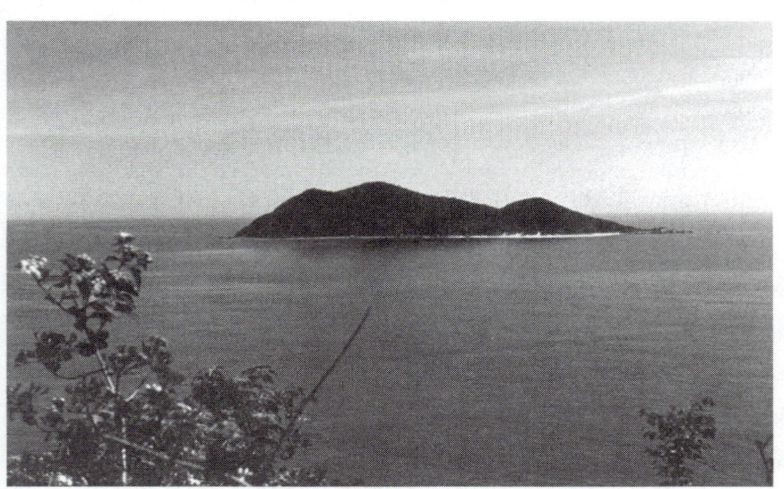

***Enchanting islands flank the coast of Nha Trang and Danang.***

## QUY NHON IN A CAPSULE

*The capital of Binh Dinh Province...A dingy city that experienced a good deal of fighting between the Viet Cong, American and South Korean troops during the Vietnam War...Beaches are some of the worst along the central coast...It makes for a decent overnight stop between Nha Trang and Danang.*

Quy Nhon, the capital of Binh Dinh Province, is a major seaport supporting a population of about 250,000 people. There's not a lot to see and do here, but it does make for a decent night stop on the road between Nha Trang and Danang. In fact, you've got to leave Highway 1 for about 11 km to get here. There are only two hotels of any note, and they both rest on the palm-shaded Quy Nhon Beach, which I found disappointingly grungy and littered (even near the hotels), and the ocean murky and gray (even on a sunny day). Quy Nhon is definitely not a destination, and you really won't find it worth spending even a full day here. The only "attractions" near town are a couple of small Cham towers on the road off NH1 toward town, about 2-3 km from the central area, or the municipal beach, where the breezes can be quite brisk and even chilly toward the evening hours.

The port here used to be internationally recognized during the 17th–19th centuries. The two Hung Thanh towers near here are worth a visit. The larger of the two towers stands at 23 meters tall and they date back to the 13th century. They were once part of a vast Cham complex here that has been largely destroyed. M. Pigneau de Behaine, French missionary and Bishop of Adran, gave protection to defeated Nguyen survivors while his forces were surrounding the city—which was under the control of the Tay Son—in October 1799. Just two years later, the Tay Son fleet was destroyed from offshore by Nguyen Anh.

Quy Nhon itself is an unremarkable and relatively dirty city and was the site of a great deal of fierce fighting during the war between the Viet Cong and a significant number of South Korean troops, as well as ARVN and American forces.

## WHAT WAS THE TAY SON REBELLION?

*The Tay Son Rebellion was a peasant revolt in 1771 that was led by the three Tay Son brothers as the country was leaning toward famine. Sensing unease and kinetic revolt and animosity toward the Nguyen Lords and the Trinh amongst the peasants of this region, the brothers were able to unify the peasantry into a ragtag army that soon became a powerful fighting force.*

*The army soon included others, such as shopkeepers and even intellectuals, who all formed behind the Tay Son brothers. This fighting force soon ruled much of the countryside and cities from as far south as Saigon to Trinh. This is where the Chinese stepped in.*

*Realizing the country was in turmoil, they sent large forces of troops, as many as 200,000, to annex Vietnam in 1788. Quang Trung, the oldest of the three brothers proclaimed himself emperor and fought both the Vietnamese and the Chinese viciously and with significant amounts of success. They attacked the Chinese at Thang Long during the Tet new year and decimated the Chinese forces.*

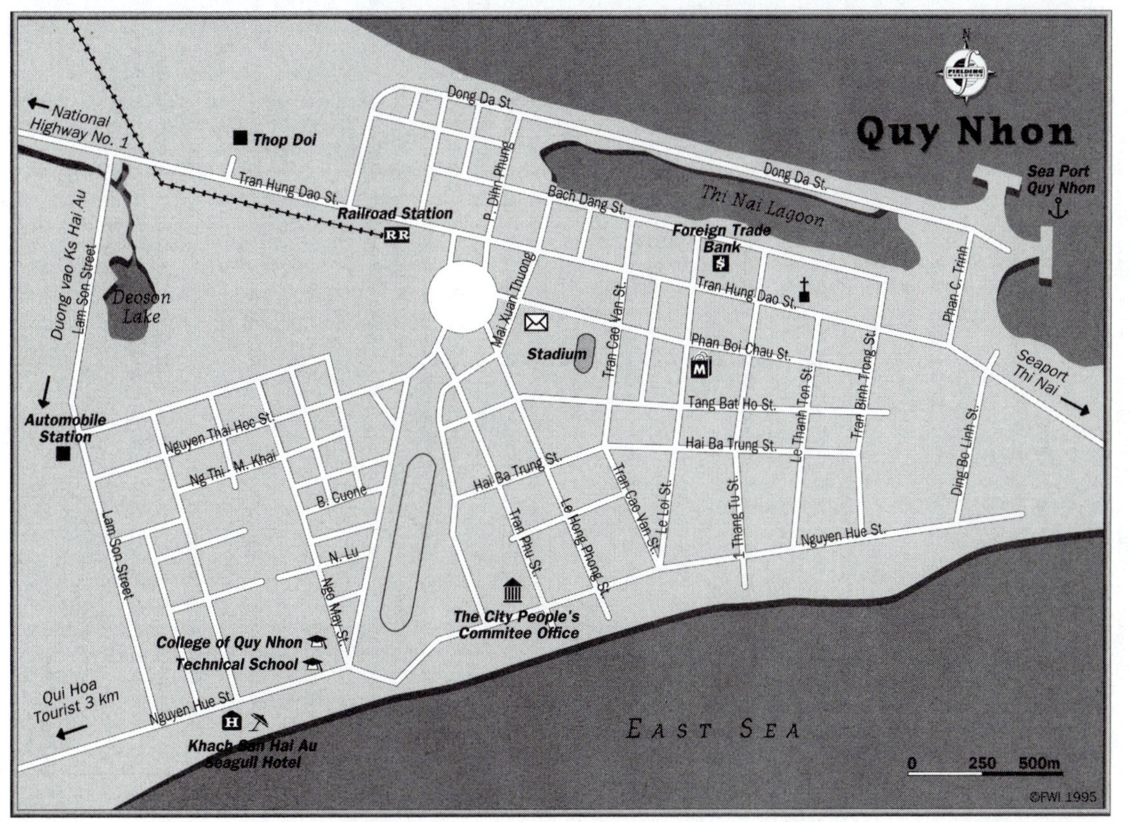
Quy Nhon
Sea Port Quy Nhon
Seaport Thi Nai
Dong Da St.
Thi Nai Lagoon
Foreign Trade Bank
Phan C. Trinh
Ding Bo Linh St.
Tran Binh Trong St.
Le Thanh Ton St.
1 Thang Tu St.
Le Loi St.
Tran Cao Van St.
Tran Hung Dao St.
Phan Boi Chau St.
Tang Bat Ho St.
Hai Ba Trung St.
Nguyen Hue St.
Bach Dang St.
P. Dinh Phung
Mai Xuan Thuong
Stadium
Le Hong Phong St.
Tran Phu St.
The City People's Commitee Office
Railroad Station
RR
Thop Doi
National Highway No. 1
Deoson Lake
Duong vao Ks Hai Au
Lam Son Street
Automobile Station
Nguyen Thai Hoc St.
Ng Thi. M. Khai
B. Cuone
N. Lu
Ngo May St.
College of Quy Nhon
Technical School
Khach San Hai Au
Seagull Hotel
Qui Hoa Tourist 3 km
EAST SEA
0 250 500m
©FWI 1995

## WHAT WAS THE TAY SON REBELLION?

*The Tay Son Battle of Dong Da is considered one of the greatest strategically fought battles in the history of Vietnam. The Tay Son brothers then entertained notions of attacking China. Quang Trung initiated a variety of economic reforms, including land reform, education programs, and less demanding tax structures. He attempted to issue to his followers identity cards with the inscription "The Great Trust of the Empire." But Quang Trung died in 1792 and the movement fell apart to such a degree so as not to be in a position to fend off the newly arriving French forces.*

*Vietnamese Emperor Gia Long then later, in 1802, exhumed the body of the youngest brother and ordered his soldiers to urinate on the corpse while Quang Trung's wife and son watched. Then the corpse was ripped apart by three elephants.*

## What to See and Do in Quy Nhon and Environs

### Thap Doi Cham Towers

Because Quy Nhon was a central Cham area during the Cham Empire, there is a significant amount of the towers scattered about the Quy Nhon area. The two Thap Doi towers, near the edge of town, are perhaps the best examples.

### Quy Nhon's Beaches

As I explained above, the beach areas of Quy Nhon are unimpressive stretches of dirty, dark sand and seriously dim the temptation of swimming in the ocean, which is surprisingly cold. The pictures you send back home won't inspire your friends and family to hop on a jetliner to Vietnam. Probably the "best" corridor of beach is by the Quy Nhon Tourist Hotel (which is most likely due to the hotel being run by Saigon Railway Tourism). Along the west side of the beach, you'll find a number of boats and seaside shacks belonging to local fishermen. Another beach is further west and has fewer people. Its drawback is that part of the beach is flanked by factories and processing plants. Ugh.

### Lon Market

*Phan Boi Street.*
This is the town's central market. It's a relatively new, covered structure where the usual Vietnamese goods and produce can be had.

### Binh Dinh/Xiem Reap/Ratanakiri Zoo

As the name implies, this is a "zoo" with creatures imported from Cambodia, namely from the provinces of Siem Reap and Ratanakiri. Here you can see monkeys, bears and crocodiles on a site near the sea. The conditions here aren't as dismal as in other Vietnamese "zoos."

### Cu Mong Pass ★

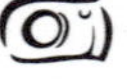

Cu Mong pass is a spectacularly scenic and steeply graded pass south of Quy Nhon that's great for photos but hell on trannies. On the nearly vertical downgrades engineers have cut out ramps for vehicles that have lost their brakes. Shrines with incense burning, dot the roadway here, marking where motorists have fallen victim to the steep grades and ill-prepared vehicles. The Vietnamese believe that they will avoid the same misfortune if they stop at the shrines and pay their respects for the dead drivers/passengers. The Cu Mong Pass represents the point where the Tonkinese prevailed after the fall of the Vijaya in 1471. From the pass, the Chams were able to prevent invasions from both north and south for nearly 150 years until the early 1600s.

**Song Cau**

This stretch of NH1, which hugs the coast, offers spectacular views of the surrounding hillsides. NH1 on the outskirts of the small town, particularly to the north, is flanked by rows of "truck stops," (i.e., brothels) where women wait for long distance truck drivers. Here the girls will sit out on the porches and invite you inside for some tea and some sin.

**Cha Ban** ★

*About 25 km north of Quy Nhon and 5 km from Binh Dinh.*

Here are the ruins of what was once an ancient Cham capital. Cha Ban was the capital of Champa from 1000 until about 1470 when it was variously attacked by the Vietnamese, the Chinese, and the Khmers. The Vietnamese were defeated by the Chams here in 1377, where the Champa king was killed. The Vietnamese then invaded Cha Ban and captured the Cham king and his royal family. This was considered the last great battle of the Chams. Tens of thousands of Chams were killed and taken prisoner. While Cha Ban was under the control of the Tay Son in 1771, the city was ruled by the three Tay Son brothers. Cha Ban was unsuccessfully attacked again in 1793 by the Vietnamese (Nguyen Anh, who later became Emperor Gia Long). But the city fell to the Vietnamese in 1799. The Tay Son then moved to what is now Quy Nhon where they conducted their own siege of Cha Ban. The siege of the city continued until 1801, when Vietnamese General Vu Tinh ran out of provisions. Rather than be defeated, Vu Tinh erected a wooden tower, filled it with gun powder and committed suicide inside by blowing the tower into the sky. The Canh Tien Tower, or Tower of Brass, stands in the middle of the compound.

**Thap Doi**

*About 2 km toward NH1 from the Quy Nhon bus station.*

Head out on Tran Hung Dao Street and turn right onto Thap Doi Street. These four towers don't possess typical Cham architecture, but instead feature pyramid-type roofs and granite doorways. Some of the brickwork is still in evidence on the granite statuary on the peak of the roofs. Torsos of Garudas are on the roofs of the structures.

**Duong Long Cham Towers** ★

*About 10 km from Cha Ban.*

These are referred to as the Towers of Ivory. There are three towers here with ornamentation depicting elephants and snakes. Huge dragons can be found on the corners of the structures. Bas reliefs over the doorways depict dancers, monsters and animals.

**Vinh Son Waterfalls**

*Off Highway 19.*

These unspectacular falls are about 19 km off national Highway 19, which runs between Binh Dinh and Pleiku.

**Quang Trung Museum**

The museum is in Tay Son District, nearly 50 km from Quy Nhon. It's about 5 km from the main route. Ask for directions in Quy Nhon at the Binh Dinh Tourist Company (see Directory). But if you don't want to bother (because they'll try to steer you into an expensive tour of the site), take NH19 toward Pleiku. The museum is dedicated to the middle brother of the three brothers that led the Tay Son Rebellion, Nguyen Hue. Later, in 1789, as Emperor Quang Trang, he led a successful defense against an enormous force of about 200,000 Chinese soldiers. The museum features traditional martial art *binh dinh ho* demonstrations performed with bamboo sticks.

## Where to Stay in Quy Nhon

**AUTHOR'S NOTE: TELEPHONE PREFIXES**

*The following telephone numbers are local exchanges. The country code is 84. The city code id 56.*

**Seagull Hotel (Hai Au Hotel)** **US$8–$25** ★

*48 Nguyen Hue Street. ☎ 21473. FAX: 21926.*

*45 rooms.*

This isn't a bad place save for the suspect staff. It's a beachfront hotel and the rooms on the beach side of the structure offer great views of the ocean and surrounding mountains. The higher up, the better. Restaurant, air conditioning, attached bath. But be careful of the staff. Lock your stuff up. I faxed a single page to the U.S. from here and the desk clerk charged me US$9. I asked to see the rate chart, which I had checked the day before with another staff member. The actual charge per page was 67,000 dong (about US$6.70). So beware. This activity might be indicative of the staff at large; who knows?

**Saigon Hotel** **US$25** ★

*Corner of Dao Duy Tu and Tran Hung Dao Streets.*

This is a fairly new and well appointed hotel that seems designed to entice NH1 travelers to stop by for the night. Restaurant, air conditioning, attached bath. Moderate.

**Quy Nhon Hotel** **US$23–$37** ★

*12 Nguyen Hue Street at Quy Nhon Municipal Beach. ☎ 22401.*

*47 rooms.*

On the beach. Air conditioning, restaurant, attached bath. This place has had a bad reputation for cleanliness, and at these prices, that's the first thing you'd expect in a tourist-class hotel.

**Thanh Binh Hotel** **About US$6–$20**

*17 Ly Thuong Kiet Street. ☎ 22041.*

Overpriced considering the amenities. The cheaper rooms are grimy, while there is air conditioning in the expensive rooms. Private bath. Restaurant.

**Hotel Hai Ha** **US$20–$30**

*1A Tran Binh Trong Street, corner of Hai Ba Trung and Tran Binh Trong Streets. ☎ 21295.*

Ho-hum. It's a small hotel but relatively clean (it should be at these prices). Air conditioning, attached bath.

**Dong Phuong Hotel** **US$8–$15** 

*39-41 Mai Xuan Thuong Street. ☎ 22915.*

*20 Rooms.*

Good location near the center of town and the stadium. Recommended by a lot of travelers. Air conditioning, attached bath.

**The Peace Hotel** **About US$15**

*361 Tran Hung Dao Street. ☎ 22900.*

*64 rooms.*

Clean, comfortable, friendly service. Attached bath.

**Nha Khach Huu Nghi** **About US$7–$8**

*210 Phan Boi Chau Street. ☎ 22152.*

*22 rooms.*

Popular with backpackers. Doubles with private bath.

**Olympic Hotel** **About US$10–$20**

*167 Le Hong Phong Street. ☎ 22375.*

*23 rooms.*

Next to the stadium and popular. Restaurant, attached bath, air conditioning.

## Where to Eat in Quy Nhon

**Dong Phuong Restaurant**

*39-41 Mai Xuan Thuong Street.*

Ground floor of the Dong Phuong Hotel. Vietnamese fare.

**Tu Hai Restaurant**

*On the 3rd floor of the Lon Market, Phan Boi Chau Street.*

Vietnamese, Asian and Western, but bland.

**Ganh Rang Restaurant**

*Nguyen Hue Street, about 3.5 km out of town on the beach, southwest of Municipal Beach.*

This is a great setting, as the restaurant sits on piling above the water. Vietnamese, Asian.

**Vu Hung Restaurant**

*On the roof of the Olympic Hotel, 167 Le Hong Phong Street.*

This is a real restaurant. The food's good and relatively cheap for hotel restaurants.

**Ngoc Lien Restaurant**

*288 Le Hong Phong Street.*

Vietnamese, Asian. Good and cheap.

## Directory

### Transportation

Quy Nhon is about 680 km from HCMC, 410 km from Hue, 305 km from Danang, 240 km from Nha Trang, 225 km from Buon Ma Thuot, 175 km from Quang Ngai.

**By air:**

VN has flights to Quy Nhon from HCMC daily except for Thursdays and Sundays at 7:00 a.m. Flights to HCMC leave Quy Nhon Tuesdays and Fridays at 9 a.m., and Wednesdays and Saturdays at 9:50 a.m. Flights to Hanoi leave Wednesdays and Saturdays at 7:30, with a connection in Danang. Flights to Danang leave at the same time. Into Quy Nhon flights leave Danang Wednesdays and Saturdays at 9:10 a.m.

**By bus:**

The Quy Nhon bus station is 1 km northwest of the town center on Tran Hung Dao Street. Express buses leave at 5 a.m. for Hanoi, Hue, Dalat, Danang, Nha Trang and Saigon, as well as other locations. Tickets should be purchased the day before departure. Non-express buses also leave early in the morning for Bong Son, Nha Trang, Am Lao, An Khe, Dalat, Cam Ranh, Danang, Saigon, Hanoi, Phu My, Hoi An, Pleiku, Vinh Than, Tuy Hoa, Van Canh, and Kon Tum, as well as other destinations.

**By train:**

The train station in Quy Nhon is off the beaten track (express trains do not stop here). The station is 1 km northwest of town on Hoang Hoa Tham Street which is off Tran Hung Dao Street. To catch an express train, you'll have to go to Dieu Tri, which is about 10 km away.

### Post Office

*127 Hai Ba Trung Street*. International calls and faxes can be made from here.

### TNT International Express

☎ *22193* or *22600*.

### Banks and Moneychangers

Vietcom Bank, *148 Tran Hung Dao Street*, on the corner of Le Loi Street.

### Hospital

*102 Nguyen Hue Street*.

### Tourist Office

Binh Dinh Tourism Company, *4 Nguyen Hue Street*. ☎ *22206, 22524*.

### Airline

Vietnam Airlines Booking Office. *2 Ly Thuong Kiet Street*. ☎ *23125*.

# QUANG NGAI

## QUANG NGAI IN A CAPSULE

*Nothing of note in the town itself...gateway to Son My, the site of the My Lai massacre...Great beaches 17 km west of town, although they, also, were the sites of the slaughter of Vietnamese civilians by American troops during the war...Most travelers stop here briefly on their way to Danang.*

Most travelers don't spend a lot of time in Quang Ngai, as it's only about 130 km south of Danang, and it's not even on the coast—the beach is nearly 15 km away. It is a small provincial capital of Quang Ngai Province that lies on the banks of the Tra Khuc River (notice the waterwheels as you pass over the bridge). There's a huge market here and a nice cathedral, but the reason why most travelers stop here is to visit Son My (site of the infamous My Lai massacre), which lies about 13 km from Quang Ngai.

Quang Ngai was formerly a center of French resistance during the First Indochina War, inhabited by a number of Viet Minh. During the Vietnam War, the area was part of the South Vietnamese government's Strategic Hamlet Program, which relocated a number of villagers from here into fortified hamlets. This caused a considerable amount of dissent among the townsfolk, and many became Viet Cong sympathizers. The area was considered by the Americans as a VC stronghold, which precipitated the murderous massacre at My Lai in the Son My Subdistrict. Fighting in the district was intense, and you can still see the rusted, ruined bridges that were destroyed by both the Viet Minh and the Viet Cong. The third bridge that NH1 crosses today looks as if had been erected in a day, which it probably was.

The beaches are great—deserted and immaculate—when you get out to them.

## What to See and Do in Quang Ngai and Environs

### Son My Subdistrict (My Lai)

Thirteen km from Quang Ngai. Turn right just after crossing the bridge at the monument commemorating the My Lai massacre. This is the site of one of the greatest atrocities during the Vietnam War, and perhaps the most heinous military action ever staged by the U.S. American forces thought the hamlet to be a strategic VC stronghold and believed the villagers were not only VC sympathizers, but fighters and saboteurs as well. On March 16, 1968, units of the 23rd Infantry Division (Task Force Barker) were dropped into the village of Son My. Soldiers were dropped into other hamlets as well, including Tu Cong hamlet and Xom Lang sub-hamlet. Two weeks before the massacre, six U.S. soldiers had been killed after coming upon a mine field. The decision was made to search and destroy Son My subdistrict. Lt. William Calley was responsible for investigating the hamlet of My Lai. Nearly 350 civilians died here under his orders. All were unarmed, and most were women and children. The soldiers of Lt. Calley's 1st Platoon shot and bayonetted fleeing villagers and threw grenades into the hootches and family bomb shelters. As the villagers tried to flee their shelters they were shot. Women were raped and sodomized. At no time during the massacre did American troops encounter any resistance. As many as 150 villagers were ordered to line up and were mowed down with machine gun fire. The 2nd and 3rd platoons of Charlie Company (under the commands of Lt. Stephen Brooks and Jeffrey La Cross respectively) were dropped into the zones and "attacked" Tu Cung. Unspeakable crimes were committed here by U.S. troops. Young women were gang raped—one was reportedly then shot in the vagina. Neil Sheehan reported in his marvelous book, *A Bright Shining Lie*, that, "One soldier missed a baby lying on the ground twice with a.45 pistol as his comrades laughed at his marksmanship. He stood over the child and fired a third time. The soldiers beat women with rifle butts and raped some and sodomized others before shooting them." In all, more than 500 civilians were massacred in Son My, most of them in My Lai. To their credit, some of the soldiers refused to take part in the massacre—one shot himself in the foot. But the vast majority of Capt. Ernest Medina's Charlie Company participated in the worst atrocity committed by any American soldiers during any war involving Americans in U.S. history. In all, more than 500 civilians were killed in the turkey shoot, most in My Lai. The story didn't come out for another eight months as action was taken at every level of the American command to cover up the incident. Finally, soldiers returning home told of the incidents at Son My, and an outraged American public demanded action. This was the "action": A number of American soldiers were disciplined, but only one, Lt. Calley, faced a court martial—he was found guilty of the murders of 22 (eventually 109) civilians and sentenced to life imprisonment. He was paroled by President Nixon in 1974. Some action. Some president. There is a memorial to the slaughter in Son My in a park where Xom Lang sub-hamlet once existed. There is a museum and graves of the victims. Permits are no longer required to visit the sites, but expect busloads of tourists.

***This monument in Quang Ngai directs travelers the way to Son My, the site of the My Lai Massacre.***

**Bien Khe Ky (Khe Ky Beach)**

This is a fine, long beach about 17 km from Quang Ngai, and only about 3 km from Son My. This beach was also the site of another massacre by American troops, Bravo Company this time. Near the bridge across Song Kinh Giang, GIs burned down hootches and blasted automatic weapons fire at the fleeing civilians as they ran on the sand toward the sea. Family bomb shelters were annihilated and torched. Women and children were indiscriminately shot. Others were tortured before being killed. As many as 100 civilians were killed in this mass slaughter. Charges against Lt. Thomas Willingham, Bravo Company's leader, were dismissed. These incidents, although there is little left to remind you of the area's history, will sober your visit to this otherwise beautiful length of beach.

## Where to Stay in Quang Ngai

There aren't many places in Quang Ngai where foreigners can stay but this is changing as tourism to My Lai is booming.

**Nha Khach Uy Ban Thi** **About US$20–$40**

*Phan Boi Chau Street.* ☎ *2109.*

Absolutely ridiculous price for this place. Restaurant. Used to be a government guesthouse but foreigners can stay here now. Personally, I'd continue on to Danang or Hoi An.

**Song Tra Hotel** **About US$30**

*Next to the Tra Khuc River bridge.*

Everyone seems to want to cash in on the tourism boon in My Lai. This place is no exception. The service is lacking, especially for the prices. This used to be the only place foreigners could stay in Quang Ngai.

## Where to Eat in Quang Ngai

Food stalls are your best bet in Quang Ngai, but there's a decent restaurant at the Nha Khach Uy Ban Thi hotel, with decent seafood. There are a number of cafes near Khach San So 2, but don't expect much on the menus. Others include:

**Nha Hang 155**

*155 Quang Trung Street.*

Average Vietnamese fare. Cheap, but not as cheap as the surrounding food stalls.

**Tiem An 72 Restaurant**

*72 Nguyen Nghiem Street.*

Vietnamese, Asian. Cheap.

## Directory

### Transportation

Quang Ngai is about halfway between HCMC and Hanoi (840 km from HCMC and 890 km from Hanoi). Other distances are 410 kilometers from Nha Trang, 240 km from Hue, 130 km from Danang, 175 km from Quy Nhon.

**By bus:**

Quang Ngai's bus station is across from *32 Nguyen Nghiem Street*, not far from NH1, which is called Quang Trung Street through Quang Ngai. There is service to Danang, Dalat, Hoi An, Nha Trang, Quy Nhon, Kon Tum, and HCMC.

**By train:**

The railway station is about 3 km west of town. Take Phan Boi Chau Street west from Quang Trung Street. The street name changes to Nguyen Chanh Street, but just keep going. Here you can catch Reunification Express trains either north or south, as the train makes regular stops here.

### Post Office

Located at the intersection of Phan Dinh Phung and Phan Boi Chau Streets.

### Tourist Office

Quang Ngai Tourism, in the Song Tra Hotel. ☎ *2665* or *3870*.

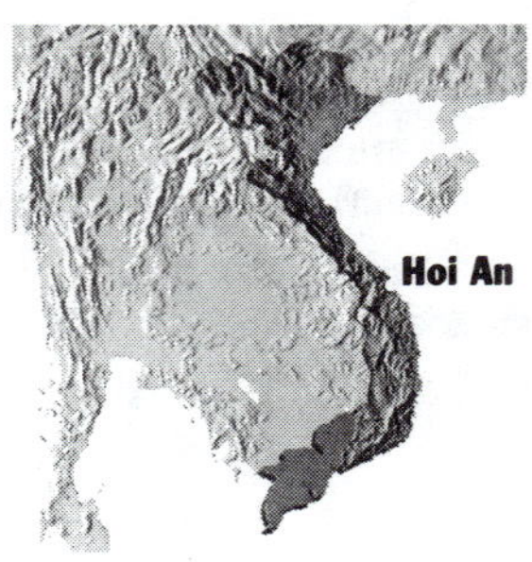


# HOI AN

***The Japanese Covered Bridge in Hoi An was built in 1593.***

## HOI AN IN A CAPSULE

*Perhaps the most unique town in Vietnam...Worth a two-day visit...Ancient seaport that did commerce with dozens of nations, from Europe and even America...Unscathed by the Vietnam War, although there was much damage to the city during the Tay Son Rebellion...Ancient buildings here represent influences from both Asia and the West...Narrow streets flanked by buildings that have remained virtually unchanged for 200 years...Similar in flavor and style to Malaysia's famed port of Malacca...A must-see on the coast.*

Hoi An is a beautiful, ancient Vietnamese town, a little more than 30 km to the south of Danang, that will seem to you like a time machine. It sits on the banks of the Thu Bon River near the South China Sea. It was virtually untouched by the fighting during the Vietnam War (although it was heavily damaged during the Tay Son Rebellion), and it retains its centuries-old Vietnamese, Chinese, Japanese and European architecture. It distinctly reminds me of Malaysia's port at Malacca, with its narrow streets and low, tiled roof houses. The influences are from the Japanese, the Portuguese, the Dutch and the Vietnamese. In the 17th–19th centuries, Hoi An was one of the most important ports in Southeast Asia, and wasn't eclipsed by Danang until the end of the 19th century, when Thu Bon River had silted up to such a degree that major commerce by navigation became problematic as the waters became too shallow.

Hoi An was probably inhabited as early as 2000 years or more ago, and also has the distinction of being, by most accounts, the first place in Vietnam where Christianity was introduced. The French priest Alexandre de Rhodes arrived in the 17th century and later transcribed the Vietnamese language into the Latin-based *quoc ngu* script.

Hoi An was also the site of the first Chinese settlers in southern Vietnam. More than 1500 ethnic Chinese live in Hoi An today. Many Chinese come from all over the southern part of Vietnam to celebrate various Chinese congregational gatherings. Unlike in other parts of Vietnam, there is little friction between ethnic Vietnamese and the Chinese, who have adopted Vietnamese as their first language.

From the 2nd–10th centuries, Hoi An was one of the principal cities in the Champa Kingdom. Archeologists have discovered the bases of numerous Cham towers in the region. Its port was visited by sailors from the Middle East for provisioning. During its heyday, Indian, Dutch, Portuguese, French, Thai, Indonesian, Spanish, American, Japanese, Chinese and Filipino ships came to Hoi An to procure its quality silk, sugar, fabrics, tea, ceramics, pepper, elephant tusks and a slew of other goods.

The Chinese and the Japanese usually stayed in Hoi An for the longest periods of time due to the prevailing winds. In fact, there were "seasons" in which Hoi An experienced the presence of such merchants. Many of the nationalities calling on Hoi An left agents of their respective companies, and this is the reason Hoi An developed it's multinational architectural appearance.

Today, parts of Hoi An look precisely as they did two centuries ago. And although Hoi An today remains largely uncommercialized, don't expect this to continue. Foreign tourists were everywhere during my last visit and the city is gearing up for more. Within a year or two, walking the streets of this quaint town won't be dissimilar to strolling through an American theme park. But get there now, before Disney does.

### What to See and Do in Hoi An and Environs

There are more than a whopping 840 structures in Hoi An that have been deemed as historical structures. They include houses, shops, pagodas, tombs, etc. We can't possibly describe them all but here are a few worth visiting, especially if you've only got a day to spend in Hoi An. (It's actually worth two or more).

**Japanese Covered Bridge** ★★

This is Hoi An's most famous landmark, although there are other structures in town equally if not more compelling. It's located at the west end of Tran Phu Street and connects Tran Phu Street with Nguyen Thi Minh Khai Street. The bridge was reportedly built in the 16th century although there are some experts who think it is much older. It's not a long structure. At the western end of the bridge there are statues of two dogs, and on the east end, two monkeys. Legend has it that the bridge was started in the year of the monkey and finished during the year of the dog. Another tale says that the dogs and monkeys reflect the years that many of Japan's Emperors were born. It was built by the Japanese (although this isn't for certain either) in the same rigid style they built their own bridges—to avoid damage during earthquakes, though there are few in southern Vietnam. It was constructed to link the Japanese quarter of town with the Chinese section. In the 17th century it was the hangout for beggars and the homeless, taking advantage of the hundreds of people who crossed it everyday. During the 20th century the French flattened the bridge's roadway to make it easier to cross by car, but it was restored to its original curvature in 1986. The bridge was once known as the "Faraway People's Bridge," but the name didn't stick. Built on the far side of the bridge is a small pagoda called Chua Cau, where the old Faraway People's Bridge sign hangs.

**Phuoc Kien (or Fukien) Pagoda** 

*46 Tran Phu Street.*

This Chinese pagoda was built around 1690 and then restored and enlarged in 1900. It is typical of the Chinese "dialect associations," or "clans" that were established in the Hoi An area. A hall of worship was also added in 1900. This pagoda is a reflection of the Chinese communities to establish within their dialect associations their own schools, hospitals, places of worship, and cemeteries. In Hoi An, there were four different associations. There was the Fukien, Teochiu, Hainan, and Kwangthung associations. This temple, dedicated Thien Hau Thanh Mau (Goddess of the Sea and Protector Sailors and Fishermen), is a large complex in a compound. Thien Hau is the principal figure at the main altar, dressed in an ornate robe. On the right side after entering the pagoda, you'll see a mural of Thien Hau rescuing a sinking ship. Outside there is a model of an old Chinese war junk.

**Assemby Hall for Maritime Commerce** 

*176 Tran Phu Street.*

Despite the name, this is also a pagoda that was constructed in the early 18th century and was a refuge for Chinese merchants and sailors of all ethnicities. Tien Hau is the deity worshipped here (who else?). The compound is quite beautiful. For a small donation, the monk will write your name and address on a large piece of red paper and glue it to the inside wall of the pagoda. I noticed that there had been quite a few American visitors in recent months.

### Hainan Assembly Hall

*Near the corner of Tran Phu and Hoang Dieu Streets.*

This was built for the Hainan Chinese congregation in 1833. It is dedicated to the 108 merchants from Hainan Island in southern China who were killed after they were mistaken for pirates by forces of Emperor Tu Duc. There are many plaques commemorating the killings inside the hall.

### Ong Hoi Pagoda ★

*24 Tran Phu Street, near the intersection of Nguyen Hue Street.*

These are actually two temples—Chua Quan Cong and Chua Quan Am behind it. They were probably built sometime early in the 16th century. The pagodas are dedicated to Quan Cong and Quan Am, obviously.

### Hoi An Market ★

*Right next to the Ong Hoi Pagoda.*

This is a huge market that extends along the river and Bach Dang Street. At the market area at Tran Phu street, the products are mostly consumer goods, while further down, there is a variety of produce and animal meat.

### Assembly Hall of the Fujian Chinese Congregation ★★

*Opposite 35 Tran Phu Street.*

Dedicated to Tien Hau, this assembly hall eventually became a temple. There's a mural near the entrance that shows Tien Hau crossing the sea with a lantern to rescue a faltering ship. A mural depicting the heads of the six Fujian families that escaped China for Hoi An in the 17th century after the overthrow of the Ming Dynasty is on the opposite wall. One chamber contains a statue of Tien Hau. Near the goddess are two figures, one red and the other green. One could see for a thousand miles; the other could hear things from long distances, and it was their responsibility to inform Tien Hau of ships in trouble. There is a central altar in the last chamber that depicts the six families that fled to Hoi An. Behind the altar is depicted the God of Prosperity. There's also a tall glass dome that contains the figure of Le Huu Trac, a great Vietnamese physician. It is said that married couples without children come here to pray for childbirth.

### Chaozhou Assembly Hall

*Across from 157 Nguyen Duy Hieu Street.*

Woodcarvings on the altar and beams are the attractions at this temple, constructed in 1776 as an assembly hall. There are also carvings of Chinese girls on the doors in front of the altar.

### Chinese All-Community Assembly Hall

*31 Phan Chu Trinh Street.*

This hall is frequented by all members of the Chinese community in Hoi An. Bamboo blinds and hand-woven carpets are also made here. The hall was built in the early 1770s.

### Japanese Tombs 

Sugar cane, crushed sea shells, and boi loi leaves were used to build the tomb of Yajirobei, a Japanese Christian merchant who fled his native land and died here in 1647. The Japanese characters inscribed on the tomb are clearly visible to this day. The tomb faces northeast toward Japan. Getting there is a little difficult: Follow Nguyen Truong Street north to its end and then the sand path which curves left until you reach a junction in the path. Here, turn to the right. At the next junction after about 1 km, take a left, and then another left at the next fork. In the open field, you'll cross over an irrigation channel. Take a right on the other side of it and go up the hill. After about 150 meters, turn left for about 100 meters. The tomb is in the middle of rice fields. In the area is also the tomb of Masai, a Japanese who perished in Hoi An in 1629. There are other Japanese tombs in the area. The best bet is to get a guide if you don't already have one.

### Cao Dai Pagoda

*64-70 Huynh Thuc Khang Street.*

This is a small Cao Dai pagoda near the bus station. It was built in the early 1950s.

### Chuc Thang Pagoda 

At the end of Nguyen Trong Street, turn left on the dirt path for about 500 meters. This pagoda, built around 1454 by a Buddhist monk from China named Minh Hai is by far the oldest pagoda in Hoi An. In the main sanctuary, on the roof, Chinese characters depict the pagoda's construction. There are a few big bells here, one made from stone that's at least 200 years old. On the dais is A Di Da Buddha. On each side of the Buddha are Sakyamuni Buddhas. In front of the shrine is the figurine of Thich Ca as a young boy.

### Phuoc Lam Pagoda

*On the path past Chuc Thanh Pagoda about 350 meters.*

This pagoda was built around the 1750s. Toward the end of the century, the eventual head monk here, An Thiem, who at 18-years-old left monkhood, joined the army in lieu of his brothers and eventually rose to the rank of general. He felt so bad about the number of people he killed, he asked to clean the market in Hoi An for 20 years. He was then asked to enter Phuoc Lam Pagoda as head monk.

### Hoi An Church

*Corner of Nguyen Truong To and Le Hong Phong Streets.*

This is a new structure where Hoi An's European population was buried.

### Tan Ky House ★★★

*101 Nguyen Thai Hoc Street.*

This is one of the three central "monuments" of Hoi An. It is a private house built more than 200 years ago for the worship of ancestors. It's one of the oldest and largest private houses in Hoi An. It was recognized by the government's Ministry of Culture as "an ancient building of high value" in 1985. It's basically unchanged in two centuries and reveals evidence of the period when trade with foreigners in this city was booming. During this time, residents used pulleys to raise goods above the floor. There is a combination of priceless ancient Chinese, Japanese and Vietnamese artwork in the house. The builders of the house had also been involved with constructing royal sites and palaces in Hue. The carpentry in the house represents both Chinese and Japanese influences. The upper reaches of the house reveal 18th-century Japanese architecture. The timber in the house is joined with wooden pegs. The floor is made mostly of brick and flagstone imported from abroad. Many of the decorative works of art and carvings reveal Vietnamese, Chinese and Western influences. Chinese poems are inscribed in mother-of-pearl. The carved wooden balcony is adorned with grape leaves, another European import. Seven generations of the family have lived here. Members of the family, as well as a couple of young hired guides, give one-hour presentations and they charge you 2000 dong.

**77 Tran Phu Street** 

This private house is nearly 300 years old, and it claims to be the oldest private house in Hoi An. Who to believe? There are magnificent carvings in the house on the walls. Around the courtyard balcony, there are ceramic tiles built into the railings. A small fee is charged to visit this home.

**Diep Dong Nguyen House** ★★

*80 Nguyen Thai Hoc Street.*

Built in the late 1800s, this house was constructed for a Chinese merchant, whose family still lives here. The owner has a priceless collection of antiques, including porcelain and furniture, but none are for sale. Some of the items were once on loan to Bao Dai himself. Although there are hours when the house is closed to the public, I just simply knocked on the door and, although I may have spoiled the family's lunch, the owner was more than happy to show me around—without asking for a fee!

**Cua Dai Beach** 

Cua Dai Beach is 5 km from Hoi An, east out on Cua Dai Street, which is what Tran Hung Dao and Phan Dinh Phung Streets become out of town. Although this beautiful stretch of beach has been traditionally deserted, more and more tourists are discovering it. Fortunately Hoi An has so many attractions of its own, still only a handful of tourists make it out to the beach and, once there, don't stay very long. There are souvenir and refreshment kiosks here, but the atmosphere is easy and laid back, and you won't find the hordes of young children hawking chewing gum as you'll find at the nearby Marble Mountains.

**Cham Island** 

About 20 km off Hoi An in the South China Sea. The island is best known for swift's nests, which are exported and eventually find their way into bird's nest soup in other Asian countries. Boats leave Hoi An for Cham Island from the Hoang Van Thu Street dock.

**Cam Kim Island**

This is a nearby island reachable by boat from the Hoang Van Thu Street dock.

## Where to Stay in Hoi An

**AUTHOR'S NOTE: TELEPHONE PREFIXES**

*The following telephone numbers are local exchanges. The country code is 84. The city code is 51.*

**Hotel Hoi An** **About US$20–$50**

*6 Tran Hung Dao Street.* ☎ *61445.*
*16 rooms.*
Beautiful old colonial building. Fans, air conditioning, restaurant, attached bath. Clean. Friendly staff. Air conditioning isn't so important during the winter, and the rooms are essentially the same, so that's what you're paying for with the top-end rooms. Very popular. Most tourists stay here. Especially busy during the summer and at Christmas. Make reservations.

**Guesthouse** **About US$8**

*92 Phan Chu Trinh Street.*
This place is a dump. Only for those who like cement, cockroaches and the like. Shared bath. Very inexpensive.

## Where to Eat in Hoi An

Two specialties in Hoi An are *cao lau*—noodles and croutons with bean sprouts and greens topped with slices of pork. It's mixed with dried rice paper—and Hoi An *loanh thanh*—a delicious wanton soup. There are a number of restaurants offering the same fare up and down Tran Phu Street.

**Cafe des Amis** ★

*52 Rue Bach Dang.*
Superb vegetarian fare at remarkably low prices. No menu and no meat, making it a backpacker's delight. Outspoken owner Nguyen Manh Kim is creating a cult following for the place. A must-do when in Hoi An.

**Cao Lau Restaurant**

*42 Tran Phu Street.*
Delicious cao lau.

**Floating Restaurant**

*Bach Dang and Nguyen Thai Hoc Streets.*
This is a brand new flashy, festive place that sits on the riverfront near the Japanese Covered Bridge. Delicious seafood at reasonable prices. But it's geared for tourists. You can eat more cheaply along Tran Phu Street.

## Directory

### Transportation

Hoi An is about 30 km south of Danang.

**By bus:**

The bus station is about 1 km west of the city center at 74 Huynh Thuc Khang Street. Connections to Danang are constant. If you're on only a day trip, the last bus leaves for Danang at 5 p.m. The ride takes an hour. Van buses leave for Danang, Que Son, Dai Loc, Tra My and Tam Ky.

**By train:**

You'll have to get off the Reunification Express at Danang and find your way south. See the Danang chapter for transport to Hoi An.

**By car:**

If you're traveling north on NH1, the best way is to get off the highway (a sign is posted) about 27 km from Danang. You'll then travel about 10 km to Nguyen Thi Minh Khai street which forks as you get into town. Nguyen Thi Minh Khai Street turns into Tran Phu Street on the other side of the Japanese Covered Bridge. From Danang, there are two routes. You can drive south on Trung Nu Street to the Marble Mountains and then continue south along the Korean Highway for about 20 km. Or you can take NH1 south, the sign posted for Hoi An, but this is a longer trip.

**By boat:**

You can't actually arrive in Hoi An by boat from other destinations, but the docks at Hoang Van Thu Street provide a great way of getting out to see Cam Kim and Cham Islands.

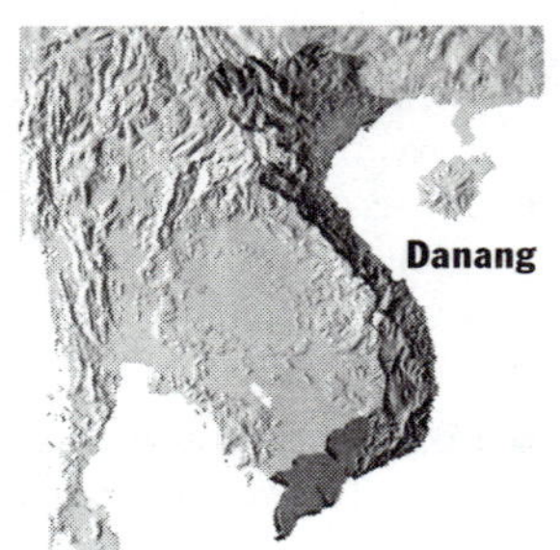


# DANANG

***Linh Ong Pagoda sits high atop the Marble Mountains, a Viet Cong refuge during the war.***

## DANANG IN A CAPSULE

*Fourth largest city in Vietnam...The principal port in the central part of the country...A repository of traditional art objects and architecture from the Cham dynasty, which dates from the 2nd century A.D.... It was here that the French originally landed to begin their "excursion" into Vietnam...A century later, the first U.S. combat troops arrived to begin their Vietnam "excursion"...Danang fell to the Viet Cong in March 1975...It signified South Vietnam's defeat in the war...This is an ancient city with a rich cultural history.*

The Hai Van Pass, a few kilometers to the north of Danang (or the Pass of the Ocean Clouds), is the thin, snaky stretch of roadway that connects Danang and Lang Co Beach. The weather changes dramatically, truly separating the south from the north. Some of the grades are so steep that the road builders had to construct uphill grades on the downslopes for buses and trucks that lose their brakes, which happens with alarming and deadly frequency.

All along the flanks of the pass, shrines mark where vehicles crashed and their occupants met their demise. It is considered good luck for passing motorists to stop and pay their respects to the dead, as it is believed that the life source of the deceased will be absorbed into the spirit of living motorists and thus prevent them from communing with the same fate.

Laboriously, the pass ascends and then drops to the sugary sands of Lang Co Beach. On top, the pass (also once known as the Mandarin Road because it was reserved only for the use of important ancient mandarin VIPs), snakes through 20 km of spectacular jungle mountains and reaches a height of 500 meters. Here are perhaps the most majestic views in Vietnam. Going by train will not give you these views, as the track cuts a swath through the terrain at the base of the mountains along the sea.

Danang (population about 500,000, and originally known as Cho Han—Market of the Han—and later renamed Tourane by the French) has meant a lot of things for a lot of people—in particular, some of the history wrought by the war, some spectacular scenery, and the friendliness of the locals. But Danang is on the threshold of becoming a major destination of "resort" tourists from Europe, Australia and the U.S. who are accustomed to the amenities found in Bali, Phuket, Pattaya and Tahiti. Hordes of foreign tourists wade in the waters off a US$50 a night hotel beside "China Beach," which actually isn't China Beach at all, but a moniker given to a renamed beach by the government tourism authorities because it's more accessible to tourists than the real China Beach.

Most of the informed locals place the actual China Beach (the popular R&R GI resort of the Vietnam War immortalized by a short-lived, U.S. television show) about three miles up the coast. But, regardless, the bogus China Beach of lore made popular by the American TV series of the same name a few years ago has become the natural destination of those who want to impress their friends at home with T-Shirts. "China Beach" today is Hanoi's exploitation of the adventure tourist trade. And it's paying off.

In October 1993, more than 30 international professional surfers, much to the mixed delight/disdain of the local authorities, descended upon "China Beach" in bourgeois day-glo wetsuits for the first international surfing competition to ever have been held in Vietnam. It was a four-day US$60,000

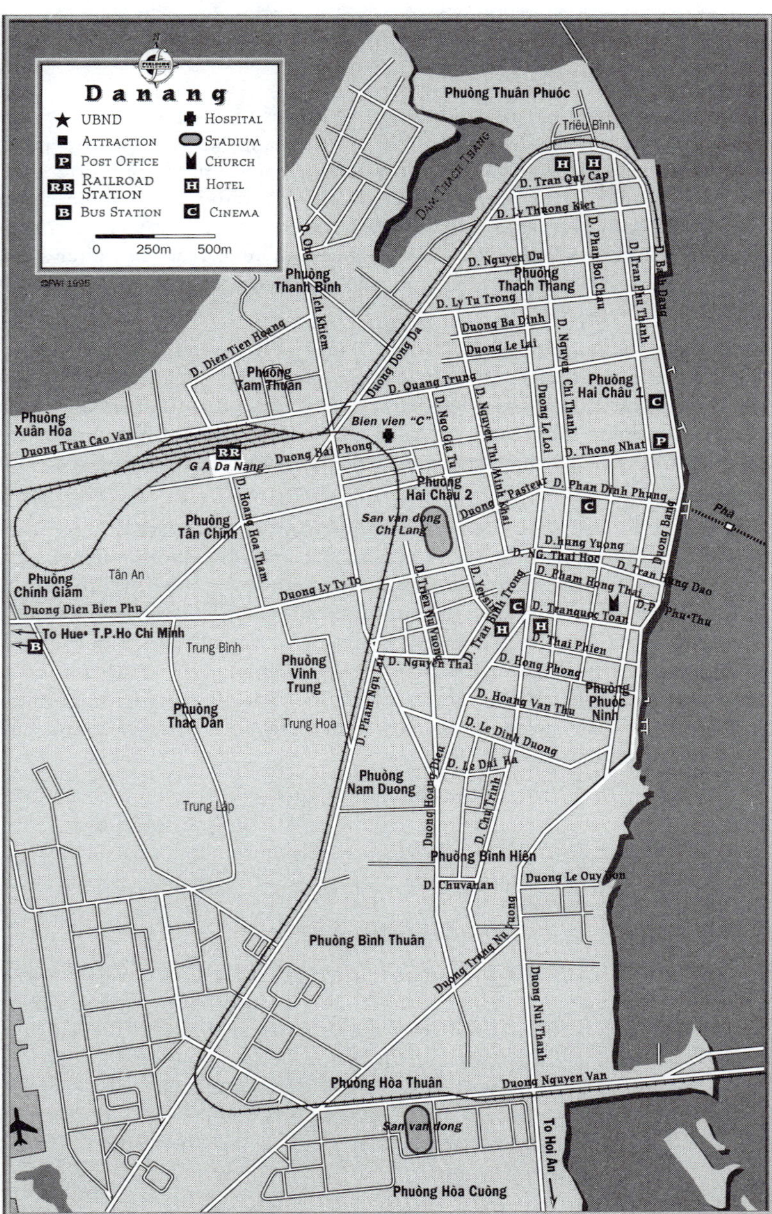
Danang
UBND
Attraction
Post Office
Railroad Station
Bus Station
Hospital
Stadium
Church
Hotel
Cinema
0 250m 500m
©FWI 1995
Phuòng Thuân Phuóc
Triêu Bình
Dam Thach Thang
D. Tran Quy Cap
D. Ly Thuong Kiet
D. Nguyen Du
D. Phan Boi Chau
D. Tran Phu Thanh
D. Bach Dang
Phuòng Thanh Bình
Phuòng Thach Thang
D. Ong Ich Khiem
D. Ly Tu Trong
Duong Ba Dinh
Duong Le Lai
D. Nguyen Chi Thanh
D. Dien Tien Hoang
Duong Dong Da
Phuòng Tam Thuân
D. Quang Trung
Phuòng Hai Châu 1
Phuòng Xuân Hoa
Duong Tran Cao Van
Bien vien "C"
D. Ngo Gia Tu
D. Nguyen Thi Minh Khai
Duong Le Loi
D. Thong Nhat
G A Da Nang
Duong Hai Phong
Phuòng Hai Châu 2
D. Hoang Hoa Tham
Duong Pasteur
D. Phan Dinh Phung
Phà
Phuòng Tân Chính
San van dong Chi Lang
Duong Bang
D.hung Vuong
D. NG. Thai Hoc
D. Tran Hung Dao
Phuòng Chính Giam
Tân An
Duong Ly Ty To
D. Pham Hong Thai
D. Yersin
D. Tran Binh Trong
D. Trieu Nu Vuong
Duong Dien Bien Phu
D. Tranquoc Toan
Phu-Thu
To Hue• T.P.Ho Chi Minh
Trung Bình
D. Thai Phien
Phuòng Vinh Trung
D. Nguyen Thai
D. Hong Phong
D. Pham Ngu Lao
Phuòng Phuóc Ninh
D. Hoang Van Thu
Phuòng Thac Dàn
Trung Hoa
D. Le Dinh Duong
D. Le Dai Ha
Phuòng Nam Duong
Duong Hoang Dieu
D. Chu Trinh
Trung Lâp
Phuòng Bình Hiên
Duong Le Ouy Don
D. Chuvanan
Phuòng Bình Thuân
Duong Trung Nu Vuong
Duong Nui Thanh
Phuòng Hòa Thuân
Duong Nguyen Van
San van dong
To Hoi An
Phuòng Hòa Cuòng

competition called the Saigon Floating Hotel Surf Pro'93, brought to stunning Non Nuoc Beach (the real name for the bogus beach) by Bruce Aitken, director of Sortas Asia.

The entrepreneur had already staged two successful events in Vietnam as a way of promoting surfing and tourism in Vietnam. Surfing has now taken root with the locals, and Vietnam now fields a team of hard-core surfers. Although it's unlikely the perfect wave will ever be found at China Beach, or anywhere else in Vietnam for that matter, the country boasts some 12 "professional" surfers, who took up the sport about nine years ago after some Americans kindly left some boards for the locals; they're all part of the fledgling Danang Surf Club.

Of course, if you're not into surfing, Danang offers a host of other attractions. It serves as an excellent base to make quests to other area sites. There's May Son, about 60 km away, which is considered Vietnam's most impressive Cham site. Some say it's on par with Cambodia's Angkor Wat but, quite frankly, that's usually said by people who haven't had the opportunity to visit Angkor.

When the French took over Danang (Vietnam's fourth largest city), they renamed it Tourane. It then became Thai Pien before adopting the current name. It's located on a peninsula where the Han River flows into the China Sea. It is the last location in Vietnam that really can be considered southern Vietnam, as the weather changes dramatically on the other side of the pass. Danang is also the site where some of the first American Marines landed in 1965 to control the airfield. Shortly after, by 1966, the city had become a strategic American naval and air base, handling both heavy warships and long-range bombers.

After the fall of the south, the communist authorities attempted to reduce the population of Danang by creating agricultural zones outside the city. The policy had little effect in reducing this bustling port's population. Whereas the port was once frequented by ships of Vietnam's socialist allies, today one sees off its shores ships from Taiwan, Singapore and Hong Kong—and soon, no doubt—ships from the U.S.

Danang is one of the most progressive cities in Vietnam in terms of exploiting Vietnam's new free market principles. It is aggressive in attacting foreign investment, and its cultural and geographical isolation from both Hanoi and Saigon virtually make the region relatively autonomous—not unlike Ha Tien in the Mekong Delta during the 17th and 18th centuries. Danang is one of the leaders in Vietnam in economic reforms (attacting foreign investment at a pace faster than both Hanoi and HCMC), and tourism has certainly helped boost the local economy, as more than 100,000 people visited the city in 1994 alone.

***This might not be an example of Vietnam's sandy white beaches, but rocks make for a nice change of pace between Nha Trang and Danang.***

Danang has the stature of perhaps being the most chaotic city in South Vietnam during the war. With both Hue to the north, and Quang Ngai, some 100 km to the south, having fallen to the communists, Danang found itself cut off from the rest of South Vietnam. South Vietnamese troops defected, and on March 29, 1975, truckloads of armed men and women in trucks entered the city and declared it under communist control—without a shot being fired. The only real fighting was between Danang locals and ARVN soldiers battling for space on fleeing aircraft and sea vessels. Two jetliners flew from Saigon to Danang to pick up civilians and soldiers. The scene was utter chaos as soldiers and locals battled one another for space on the planes. Some even attached themselves to the wheelwells of one of the aircraft as the planes took off. They met their deaths as they fell hundreds of feet into the South China Sea, all captured by TV cameras on the second Boeing 727. The only civilians that managed to board the flights were a couple of women and a child.

Danang also contains a beautiful assortment of pagodas, as well as an impressive Cao Dai Temple (which is actually only really impressive if you haven't seen the Cao Dai site at Tay Ninh). The Ho Chi Minh Museum includes a replica of Ho's House. Along Bach Dang Street on the banks of the Han River is the flower market beside the ferry pier.

## What to See and Do in Danang and Environs

**Cham Museum** ★★★

Located where Tran Phu and Le Dinh Duong Streets meet. This houses probably the best collection of Cham art to be found anywhere in the world. There are more than 300 artifacts in the museum, many dating to the 4th century. There are beautiful sculptures reflecting the 1000-year Cham period. The museum was founded by the École Française d'Extrême Orient, a group of French scholars, in 1915 and was expanded in 1935. Check out the magnificent sandstone carvings. Indonesian and Malay influences are seen in the work before the 10th century, while Khmer influences become more apparent in the work after that date. The museum also features the famous 7th-century altar Tra Kieu, which depicts the wedding of Prince Rama.The building itself is worth the visit. The large rooms are airy and each is devoted to a different period of Cham art. There are displays that range from the 4th through the 14th centuries. Cham art can be basically broken down into two periods: before the 10th century, when the art reflected Cham relations with Indonesia and Mahayana Buddhism, and between the 10th and 14th centuries, when continued conflict with both the Cambodians and the Vietnamese created art with significant Khmer influences. The "Mother of the Country" (Uroja, which, in Cham, means the breast of a woman) is the pervasive image in the museum. You'll see a lot of nipples here. There is also the phallic symbol of Shiva. There are dozens of sandstone sculptures and altars, many of which have required surprisingly little renovation, that span a period of more than a thousand years. You'll definitely need a guide here, as the lingas, reliefs, and garudas are only marginally explained (really only the name and date of construction are marked) and only in Vietnamese. Worth a few visits. Open 8–11 a.m. and 1–5 p.m. every day. There is a small admission fee.

**Cao Dai Temple** ★

*35 Hai Phong Street.*

It's the second largest Cao Dai temple in Vietnam, second only to the sect's base in Tay Ninh. There are more than 20,000 Cao Dais in Danang and this is their centerpiece. Women enter on the left, marked "Nu Phai," and men enter the temple on the right, marked "Nam Phai." As in all Cao Dai temples, above the main altar is the image of the Giant Eye, which is the symbol of Cao Daism. What I found most interesting about the temple was the sign hanging in front of the altar on the ceiling which says "Van Giao Nhat Ly." It means that all religions have the same purpose. There are also portraits of Jesus Christ, Mohammed, Buddha and Confucius. I didn't see any pictures of Marilyn Monroe or William Shakespeare, though. The temple was erected in 1956. Prayers are held four times a day.

**Danang Cathedral**

*Located on Tran Phu Street.*

This church serves Danang's Catholic community. Built in 1923 by the French, it's worth a peek for its single-spire, pink sandstone architecture.

**Ho Chi Minh Museum**

*Located on Nguyen Van Troi Street.*

Also called Bao Tang Ho Chi Minh. Here you can see various weaponry of the Vietnam War from the U.S., China and the former Soviet Union. There's also a replica of Ho's Hanoi house on display. Open 7–11 a.m. and 1–4:30 p.m. Tues.–Sun.

**Pho Da Pagoda**

*Across from 293 Phan Chu Trinh Street.*

Not much to see here if you've already seen a lot of pagodas. Built in 1923.

**Phap Lam Pagoda**

*123 Ong Ich Khiem Street.*

The main feature here is the tarnished (at least during my visit) brass statue of Dia Tang, the Chief of Hell. The title would make for an interesting business card, I think.

**Cho Han Market**

*At the corner of Tran Phu and Huong Vuong Streets.*

This is a new market—clean and worth a visit for essentials.

**Cho Con Market**

*At the corner of Ong Ich Khiem Streets.*

A good place for handicrafts and souvenirs.

**Beaches**

One of the best parts of any Danang visit is the beaches, and there are some good ones in the Danang area. The best time to visit Danang's beaches is from April through July, when the surf isn't as dangerous and there are fewer undertows. **China Beach** was an R&R area during the war and was made popular by the U.S. TV series of the same name, although the real China Beach (**My Khe Beach**) is some three miles north. There's a hotel and a number of restaurants in the fake China Beach area. There's also **Nam O Beach**, about 15 km northwest of the city. It's a good place to see the locals' fishing boats. **My Khe Beach** is a little more than 5 km from Danang and one of the better beaches in the area. But watch out for the undertow. **Thanh Binh Beach** in the center of Danang is often packed with locals and can be dirty.

**Marble Mountains** ★★★

These are the beautiful limestone peaks that rise above Danang. About 10 km from the city of Hoi An and only a stone's throw from Bai Non Nuoc are the five craggy peaks of the Marble Mountains (each represents one of the five elements of the universe), the site of numerous guerilla attacks on American troops down below from the nearly inaccessible clifflike edifices overlooking the China Beach area. Because of their relative ruggedness and strategic location overlooking Danang, they were a favorite spot of the VC during the war. The VC could snipe at American troops below virtually uncontested.

A trail of steep stairs cuts into the limestone of the most oft-visited peak (Thuy Son), about 900 if I remember correctly. There are a number of natural caves that were once used as Hindu shrines and then of course later by the Viet Cong in their largely successful attempts to harass American troops below, who were picked off like flies on many occasions. The caves were also used as a hospital during the war for wounded Viet Cong soldiers. Getting up the stairs is difficult, and many older people would be foolish making the attempt. Be prepared for hordes of children touts hawking everything from candy to guided tours. I mean there are hundreds of these little kids; all are flawless in their English, as well as fluent in French, German, Italian and a number of other tongues. Each and every single one of them! As many as a dozen at a time won't leave your side from your ascent of the mountain back to the base. If you're lucky you'll only get away with paying one of them for a guided tour. A few thousand dong should do the trick. It's worth it for two reasons. You get a decent tour, and when the other kids see that you already have someone accompanying you as a guide (although he or she may only be three or four years old) they'll tend to leave you alone.

At the top of the main staircase is the Ong Chon gate, which still reveals bullet holes from the war. Behind that is Linh Ong Pagoda. Then there are the caverns (Tang Chon Dong) which contain a variety of concrete Buddhas. The passage through the rocks and the caves on the mountain can be very narrow and dark, and it's best to carry a flashlight (the childrens' candles do little to help, especially if you're at the back of a group of visitors. But if you can get up to the top, the scenery is spectacular: miles of crystal clear, unspoiled views of the beaches, Cham Island and the surrounding mountains. You can even see the Hai Van Pass through the Truong Son Mountains to the north. Thuy Son is a village in the mountains that sells local handicrafts. The Tam Thai Pagoda has also been carved into the mountains. The name was given to the limestone mountains by the Nguyen Emperor Minh Mang, who obviously wasn't a geologist. The numerous caves and grottoes on the main Marble mountain were formed by chemical treatments. The main temple up here is the Tam Thai Pagoda, which was built in 1825 by Minh Mang. There's a huge statue of the Buddha Sakyamuni (historic Buddha) which is next to Bodhisattva Quan Am (the Goddess of Mercy). There's also another grotto called Huyen Khong Cave. The roof of the cave has five holes poked into the ceiling to allow dim sunlight to filter through. At about 12–2 p.m., the light shines upon the central statue of Sakyamuni. There's also Linh Nham, a vertical cave with an altar inside. Another cave nearby (Hoa Nghiem) contains a Buddha. There's also the spectacular Huyen Khong Cave, which possesses an opening to the sky and contains numerous shrines and inscriptions on the walls. This was the cave the VC used as a field hospital during the war. When finished with your visit, you can descend the mountain through the back staircase, which is a lot easier on the heart and lungs. Cost is 10,000 dong and you should spend at least an hour on Thuy Son. More time does it justice, however.

**Bai Non Nuoc (China Beach)** ★★

The hamlet of Non Nuoc is near the fake China Beach. Accommodations are limited at Bai Non Nuoc to the Non Nuoc Beach Hotel. The 60-room Indochina Beach Hotel is opening in 1995 after renovations. Managed by Majestic International, based in Hong Kong, the hotel's second phase will include about 300 new villas.

**My Son and Dong Duong** 

This is the former site of the Cham's most important cultural, religious and intellectual metropolis back when Tra Kieu was Champa's capital. Although reaching these areas is difficult, they are actually the principal reasons many visitors come to Danang. My Son (which means the Beautiful Mountain) is about 60 km southwest of Danang and it's not an easy journey. To get there, you have to take the road south from Danang about 34 km and cross the Thu Bon River Bridge. About 2 km past the bridge, turn right and follow the tributary of the Thu Bon toward the valley. You'll come across the small village of Tra Kieu after about 7–8 km. Continue to travel upstream for another 28 km to Kim Lam. Turn left for another 6 km. The road here is at times virtually impassable (see INSIDER TIP) during the rainy season. If you're going by car, you'll have to leave it at the end of the "road" and then travel by foot for 8 km on a path that winds through lush hillsides and a lot of brush to reach My Son.

### AUTHOR'S NOTE

*You should definitely have a guide when traveling to My Son. The area was extensively mined during the war, and many of the mines, still quite lethal, remain beside the roads and paths leading around My Son.*

There are more than 70 remarkable Cham monuments in the area, constructed between the 7th and 13th centuries, and it's why many people compare the region with Cambodia's Angkor. (The monuments at My Son are significantly smaller than those found at Angkor in the Cham belief that no grandiose structures should be built.) The small, elegant monuments are surrounded by mountains in a valley with the impressive Cat's Tooth Mountain towering over the basin. There are coffee plantations and clear streams for cooling off.

### INSIDER TIP

*If you do much traveling into the interior from Danang, remember that roads are often washed out between May and October, which is the wet monsoon season in Vietnam. Medical facilities are next to nonexistent; and doctors will, in many instances, demand cash on the spot or they may not take care of you.*

Most of the monuments consist of the classic Cham Tower, which is built high (by Cham standards) to reflect the divinity of the king (Shiva, the founder of the dynasties of Champa). Many of the structures are in incredibly good shape (the bricks were glued together by a vegetable-based cement, according to a number of scientists. Many structures were domed in gold). It's a shame that the remaining buildings aren't in such good shape, the result of incessant B-52 bombing during the war, especially during 1969 (the area was considered a free fire zone at the time). Among those buildings demolished by American sappers was perhaps the most important temple at the site, which was a magnificent tower designated as A1 by French archeologists near the end of the 19th century.

***Cham clergymen rarely see foreigners, and are even less likely to give you permission to photograph them.***

My Son became a major religious area in the 4th century and was bustling until the 13th century. The nearly 1000 years of Cham culture far surpasses religious realms in other Southeast Asia locations. During the early centuries of the dynasties, there was much contact with the Indonesians, as the two empires traded both in commerce and in education. Cham pottery has even been found in Indonesia (Java).

The monuments at My Son were separated into 10 groups (A-K, although, curiously, there are two "A's" and no "I"). The neighboring groups that remain are B, C and D. B and C are two temple enclosures which are about 25 by 25 meters, and lie side by side, although you'll have to use your imagination to distinguish the structures as two separate sanctuaries. Group B is the massive main sanctuary of the southern enclosure. There is a sandstone base and the main building once had eight monolithic columns supporting it.

Temple C is similar to Temple B, more modest in size, measuring 5 by 10 meters but it is a well preserved sanctuary. A small building (C3) is at the southeast corner of the Group C enclosure. Restoration is currently being performed on its interior walls. C7 is in bad shape. C5 and C6 are also being restored.

Temple D is between the Group B and C enclosures and contains six structures. This area is known as the Court of Steles. It's noted for its altars and rows of statues. At the end of the court are two badly demolished buildings. D3 is on the western end where it stands between the gateways to the B and C enclosures.

Dong Duong is about 20 km east of My Son and 60 km south of Danang. In the 9th century, the area emerged as the new center of Cham art after King Indravarman II constructed a big Buddhist monastery here. The towers and reliefs at Dong Duong are more intricate and flamboyant than those at My Son. But only a century later, the Cham art and cultural capital returned to My Son. The new towers built at My Son during the 10th century more reflected those at Dong Duong than those that had been previously built at My Son.

### Lang Co Beach ★★

Lang Co Beach is a kilometers-long stretch of sandy white palm-lined beach that has the only (but significant) misfortune of being located on the north side of the Hai Van Pass, where the climate (much of the year) changes dramatically, from hot and sunny to cold and gray. There are incredible views of Lang Co descending Hai Van Pass from Danang when the mountainous region isn't shrouded in fog, which it usually is. You can walk for kilometers on the beach at Lang Co and not see a sole individual for hours. Train travelers like to stop here for the night simply for its pristine peace and quiet. In fact, there's only one place to stay in Lang Co—Nha Khach Cong Doan—situated up a dirt path off Highway 1. You'll have no problem finding it, just ask someone. It's the only digs in town. The small hotel sits on top of a short path right on the beach and is rather run down. Electricity is only available from about 6 p.m. to 10 p.m. Rooms have as many as four beds and cost as little as US$4-5 if you let a Vietnamese do the negotiating for you, perhaps US$10 if you don't. There's a small restaurant here, but it's a lot easier to simply walk down the hill to NH1 and take advantage of one of the many food stalls lining the highway, where the food is cheaper and company cheerier. The area is a popular rest stop for long distance buses heading both north and south, and passengers in hordes pack the roadside food stalls. It's amazing the small restaurant at the hotel is able to remain in business at all. Another important thing to remember about Lang Co: You can show up at the hotel any time during the winter and expect to get a room. But the small hotel is generally packed with foreigners during the summer months when the weather is better.

## Where to Stay in Danang

**AUTHOR'S NOTE: TELEPHONE PREFIXES**

*The telephone numbers listed here are local exchanges only. The country code is 84. The city code is 51.*

**Danang Hotel** **US$7–$40**

*3 Dong Da Street. ☎ 21179.*

*100 rooms.*

This is one of three hotels bunched together on the northern tip of the peninsula and one of the obligatory checkpoints on the backpacker route. The lower end rooms are dreary, but you get air conditioning for $7 so they're a bargain. Shared bath, but check the toilet and shower before accepting the room. Water pressure seems to vary greatly from room to room. For some reason, this hotel seems to be popular with foreign businessmen. One reason may be the hookers. At any given time, you'll run into Cubans, Indians and, of course, the omnipresent French. Downstairs restaurant is okay. At press time, the hotel was being "rebuilt."

**Marble Mountains Hotel**
**(Ngu Hanh Son Hotel)** **US$8–$40**

*5 Dong Da Street. ☎ 23258 or 23122.*

*60 rooms.*

This is a new hotel next to the Danang Hotel and is far more attractive both inside and out than its neighbor.There are also "flats" available here with a living room, kitchen and two double bed rooms. The hotel offers car rentals and says it can handle visa matters.

**Dong Da Hotel** **US$8–$15**

*7 Dong Da Street. ☎ 42216.*

*68 rooms.*

Next door still is this alternative to the Danang Hotel and the Marble Mountains Hotel. This is, as well, less run down than the Danang Hotel, but a little more expensive for budget travelers. The lower end rooms have a fan, while the others get air conditioning. There is a restaurant.

**Ngan Hang Hotel**

*59 Dong Da. ☎ 21909.*

Inexpensive.

**Orient Hotel (Phuong Dong Hotel)** **US$40–$60** ★★

*93 Phan Chu Trinh Street. ☎ 21266; FAX: 22854.*

The lobby is exquisite in this old structure, and many think the Orient is the best lodging in Danang. TV; refrigerators; good restaurant upstairs.

**Dau Khi Ami Motel**

*7 Quang Trung. ☎ 22582 or 24494; FAX: 25532.*

Inexpensive.

**Pacific Hotel** **US$10–$40**

*92 Phan Chu Trinh Street. ☎ 22137.*

*48 rooms.*

Old building. Basic accommodations; TV; refrigerators; restaurant.

**Bach Dang Hotel** **US$45–$120** ★★★

*50 Bach Dang Street. ☎ 23649 or 23034.*

Situated across Bach Dang Street from the Han River, this may be the nicest place to stay in Danang. There is a restaurant and a nightclub.

**The Fishery Guest House (Nha Khach Thuy San)** **US$15–$20**

*12 Bach Dang Street. ☎ 22612; FAX: 21659.*

*15 rooms.*

This seemed a little overpriced, but there's both a restaurant and a nightclub here and that may be why. Air conditioning, single and double rooms, hot water.

**Phuong Dong Hotel** **US$20–$30**

*93 Phan Chau Trinh Street. ☎ 21266. FAX: 22854.*

Air conditioning; TV; refrigerators; hot water.

**Hai Au Hotel** **US$35–$67** ★★

*215 Tran Phu Street. ☎ 22722. FAX: 22854.*

*40 rooms.*

Situated across the street from the Danang Cathedral. Good location. Air conditioning; telephones; hot water; restaurant; bar; sauna; massage.

**My Khe Guesthouse** **US$30–$35** ★

*My Khe Beach, Bac My An (6 km from Danang). ☎ 36125.*

Neat place facing the beach at My Khe. Recommended.

**INSIDER TIP**

*The American Company DeMatteis Development Corp. plans to construct a 20 hectare seaside resort in Danang. The US$150 million project will include a hotel, offices, shops, an aquarium, corporate villas and an aquarium.*

### Where to Eat in Danang

**Ngoc Anh**

*30 Tran Phu. ☎ 22778.*

Vietnamese, Asian.

**Trieu Chau**

*62 Tran Phu. ☎ 24002.*

Vietnamese.

**Nha HangRestaurant**

*72 Tran Phu.*
Vietnamese.

**Giai Khat**

*187 Tran Phu.*
Vietnamese.

**Tu Do Restaurant** ★★

*172 Tran Phu. ☎ 21869.*
Chinese, European and Vietnamese food served in a large courtyard. The food is good and many claim this to be Danang's best eatery.

**Chin Do**

*174 Tran Phu. ☎ 21846.*
European and Asian specialties as well as Chinese seafood.

**Phuong Nam**

*205 Tran Phu. ☎ 22806.*
Vietnamese.

**Be Thui**

*207 Tran Phu.*
Vietnamese.

**Tien Hung Restaurant**

*190 Tran Phu.*
Vietnamese.

**Christies Harbourside Bar/Grill Restaurant** ★

*9 Bach Bang.*
Hamburgers, pasta, Vietnamese, fish and chips. Located right on the Han River. There's also a duty free shop here.

**Kim Dinh Restaurant**

*7 Bach Dang Street. ☎ 21541.*
Across the street from the Bach Dang Hotel. Vietnamese and Asian. This sits right out over the Han River. Popular with locals.

**Thanh Lich Restaurant** ★

*48 Bach Dang Street.*
Vietnamese, Chinese, and European. Excellent seafood. Right next door to the Bach Dang Hotel.

**Que Huong Restaurant**

*1 Bach Dang Street.*
Vietnamese food, karaoke, cafe.

**Mien Trung Restaurant** ★

*1 Bach Dang Street.*
Vietnamese, Chinese, and European. Expensive.

**Kim Dinh Restaurant**

*7 Bach Dang Street.*

This stretches out over the Han River. Good food, good views.

**Restaurant 72**

*72 Tran Phu Street.*
Great shrimp spring rolls.

**Thanh Lich Restaurant**

*42 Bach Dang Street.*
Vietnamese, Asian. Extensive menu.

## Directory

### Transportation

Danang is 965 km from Saigon, 759 km from Hanoi, 108 km from Hue, 541 km from Nha Trang, 303 km from Quy Nhon, 350 km from the Laos border and 130 km Quang Ngai. Danang has an "international" airport (it has been designated as such to create a better reputation as both a tourist and business destination) located about 3 km from the city. There are regular connections to Saigon and Hanoi (both about US$90) as well as Nha Trang (US$60) and Pleiku (US$30).

There are many examples still standing here of the cement hangars that were built by the Americans during the war, when this was one of the busiest airports in the world. "International" flights (to locations such as Hong Kong, Manila, Paris, Kuala Lumpur, etc.) are always via connections in HCMC or Hanoi; the only difference in the airport being an "international" one is that you can buy a ticket to Bangkok in Danang and not in Nha Trang.

**By air:**

VN flies to Danang. From HCMC, there are daily flights at 7:20 a.m. and 11:50 a.m. Also on Mon./Wed./Sat. at 9 a.m. and Tues./Thur./Fri./Sun. at 1:50 p.m. Flights from Danang to HCMC are daily at 9 a.m., 1:50 p.m. and 4:20 p.m.

**By bus:**

The long distance bus station in Danang is at *8 Dien Bien Phu Street*, about 2 km west of the city. The ticket office is across the street. Here you can get buses to Vinh, Hue, Haiphong, Hanoi and Hong Gai. Next to the Thanh Hotel is a station (*52 Phan Chu Trinh*) where you can get an express bus to Hanoi (about 32,000 dong), Saigon (about 40,000 dong), Nha Trang (about 22,000 dong), Vinh (about 20,000 dong), Dalat (about 32,000 dong), Haiphong (about 34,000 dong), and Buon Ma Thuot (about 27,000 dong). Buses to local destinations such as Hoi An and Marble Mountain leave from opposite *350 Hung Vuong Street*. There is non-express bus service to Trung Phuoc, Hue, Hoi An, Trao Hiep Duc, Tien Phuoc, Ha Tan, Quy Nhon, Thanh My, Que Son, Dong Ha, Giang Ai Nghia, An Hoa, Giao Thuy, Tam Ky, and Kham Duc, among other destinations.

**By train:**

*120 Haiphong Street*, at the intersection with Hoang Hoa Tham Street. Optimistically, it takes about 20 hours to get to Saigon and a little less to Hanoi. The views along the coast are spectacular.

#### Local transportation

Local transportation is by cyclo or rented bicycle. Motorbike riders hang out in front of the Marble Mountains and Danang Hotels and are always available for hire, for either around town or day trips. I paid one to take the 20 km Hai Van Pass over to Lang Co Beach about 40,000 dong. It was too much, as I subsequently learned you can hire a driver for as little as US$5 per day. But you've got to look hard to find one. The Vietnamese know tourist dollars when they see them.

### Post Office

*46 Bach Dang Street at the corner of Le Duan Street;* ☎ *21327.* International telephone and fax services. Faxes can also be transmitted from the Phuong Dong Hotel.

### Tourist Offices

Danang Tourist Office. *48 Bach Dang Street.* ☎ *22226. FAX: 22854.*

Vietnamtourism. *158 Phan Chu Trinh.* ☎ *22990 or 22999. FAX: 22854.*

### TNT International Express

☎ *21685 or 22582.*

### Banks and Moneychangers

Vietcom Bank, *104 Le Loi Street.* ☎ *21024.* Will exchange money and give cash advances on major U.S. credit cards.

### Hospital

Hospital C, *35 Hai Phong Street.* ☎ *22480.*

### Airline Offices

Vietnam Airlines Domestic Booking Office, *3 Yen Bai Street.* ☎ *22808.*

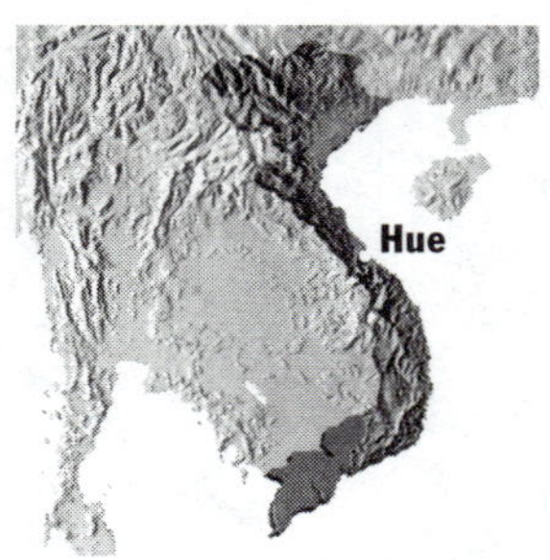


# HUE

***Hue was the capital of Vietnam during the Nguyen Dynasty 1802–1945.***

## HUE IN A CAPSULE

*Hue served as the capital of Vietnam for more than 140 years...it houses ancient temples...Imperial buildings...and French-style edifices...was established in the 17th century...invaded by the French in 1833 and by the Japanese in 1945...was hammered by U.S. forces during the Tet offensive...many historical monuments were destroyed during this military action...but a great many remain.*

The Ancient Capital of Hue (population about 350,000) began to swell with tourism in 1993. Tourism is now the leading generator of hard curren-

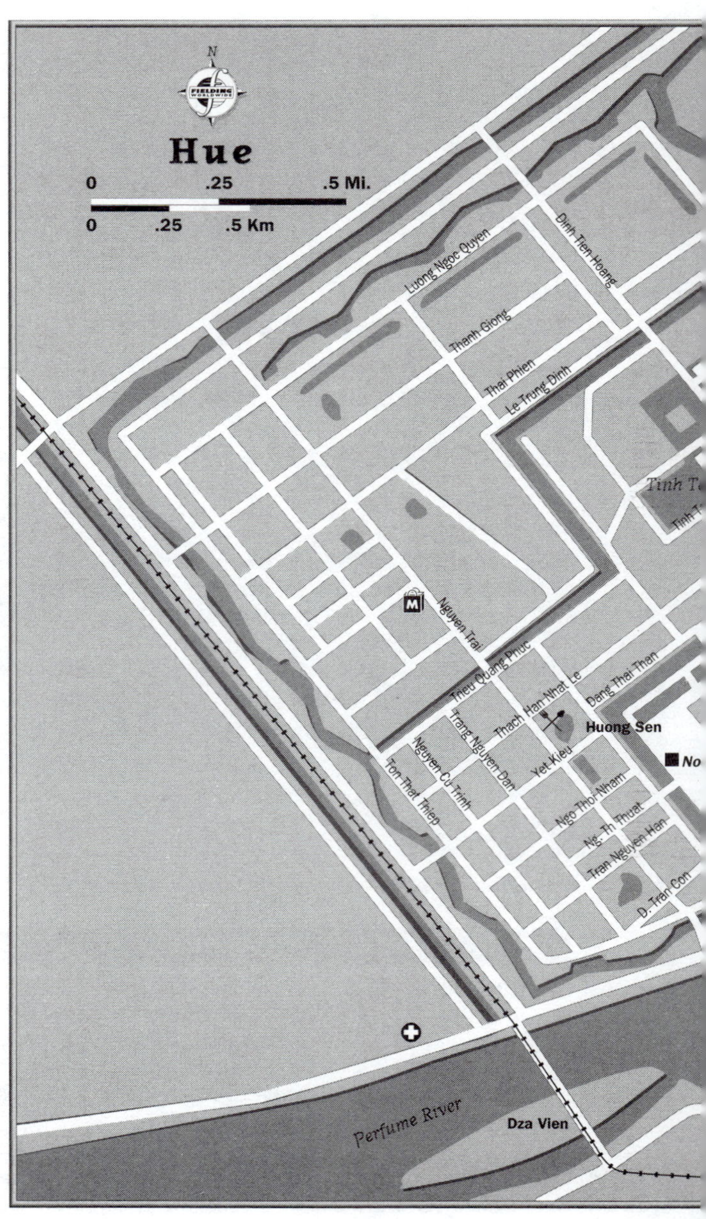

Hue
0 .25 .5 Mi.
0 .25 .5 Km
Luong Ngoc Quyen
Dinh Tien Hoang
Thanh Giong
Thai Phien
Le Trung Dinh
Nguyen Trai
Trieu Quang Phuc
Thach Han Nhat Le
Dang Thai Than
Huong Sen
Trang Nguyen Dan
Nguyen Cu Trinh
Ton That Thiep
Yet Kieu
Ngo Thoi Nham
Ng. Tri Thuat
Tran Nguyen Han
D. Tran Con
Perfume River
Dza Vien

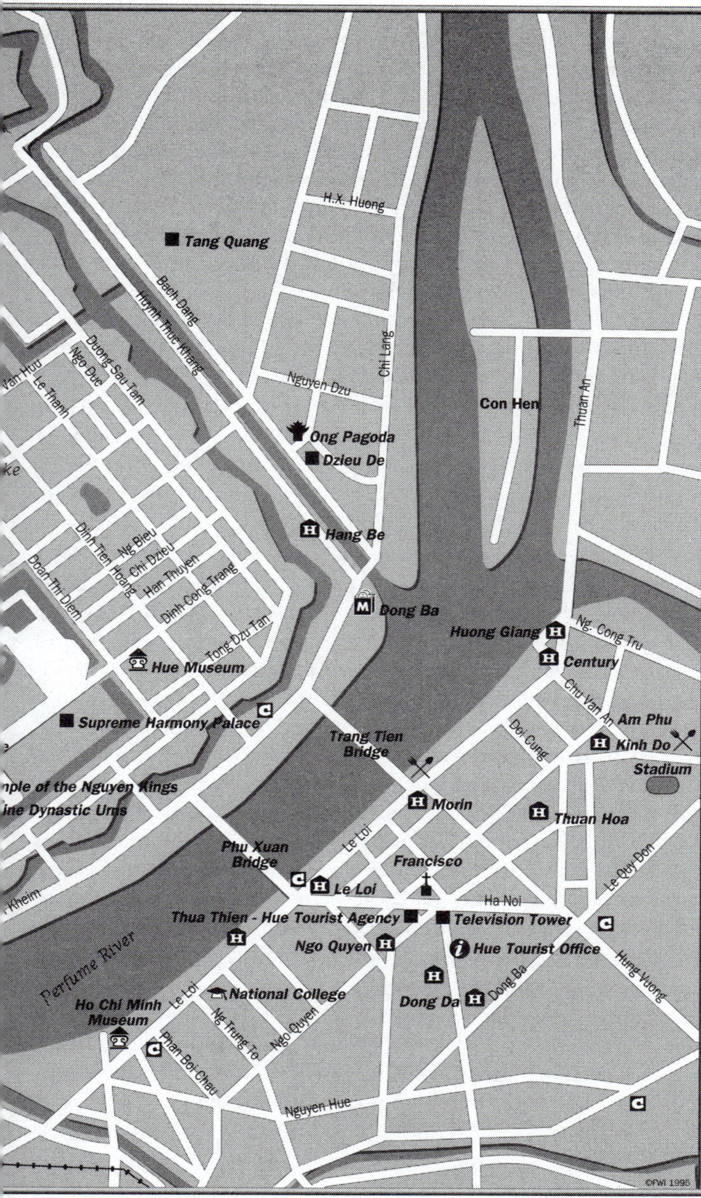
H.X. Huong
Tang Quang
Bach Dang
Huynh Thuc Khang
Duong Sau Tam
Ngo Duc
Le Thanh
Chi Lang
Nguyen Dzu
Con Hen
Thuan An
Ong Pagoda
Dzieu De
Hang Be
Dinh Tien Hoang
Ng Bieu
Chi Dzieu
Han Thuyen
Dinh Cong Trang
Doan Thi Diem
Dong Ba
Huong Giang
Ng. Cong Tru
Tong Dzu Tan
Hue Museum
Century
Chu Van An
Am Phu
Supreme Harmony Palace
Trang Tien Bridge
Doi Cung
Kinh Do
Stadium
Morin
Thuan Hoa
Phu Xuan Bridge
Le Loi
Francisco
Le Quy Don
Ha Noi
Thua Thien - Hue Tourist Agency
Television Tower
Ngo Quyen
Hue Tourist Office
Hung Vuong
Perfume River
Ho Chi Minh Museum
National College
Dong Da
Dong Ba
Ng Trung To
Ngo Quyen
Phan Boi Chau
Nguyen Hue
©FWI 1995

cy in this historic city that was battered during the Vietnam War. Today, thousands of residents make their salaries from tourism. The five principal provincial tourism businesses reaped in more than 32 million dong in 1994. Simply, the city is going through a tourist boom. Tourism in Hue doubled in a single year (from 1992–93). Foreign currency earnings increased threefold. Responding to the surge in tourism, Thua Thien Hue authorities quickly opened the elegant riverside Hotel Hue, which is the first joint-venture hotel to be opened in the city. Since 1975, when there existed only the dilapidated Huong Giang hotel with 47 gutted guest rooms, tourism authorities have opened at least six "luxury" hotels of international standards with 335 rooms (620 beds). And over the last several years, dozens of new hotels have opened up and down the south side of the Perfume River—including the Kinh Do and Dong Ha. The Hoa Hong Hotel on Le Loi Street was the first private hotel to open in the city.

Western visitors in Hue can now find a slew of garden houses and villas as accommodations. Most of the accommodations in the Hue area are enjoying occupancy rates greater than 80 percent, and that's why it's a good bet to book with a particular hotel first rather than simply showing up (although you should always be able to find a room in the city).

By the year 2000 it is predicted that tourism levels will climb to five times higher than their current levels. With the pace of infrastructure developments in the region, this forecast seems reasonable. Officials in the city told me that their predictions will be predicated primarily on the initiation of package tours rather than travel by independent tourists. Hue's Royal Park is being restored and the Tinh Tam Lake. Additionally, under construction is the Bach Ma-Lang Co casino. Visits to the "Nine Underground Bunkers," which depict the atrocities of the South Vietnamese Ngo Dinh Diem regime, are in the works. There are reenactments of ancient and royal ceremonies being devised at various locations. Horsedrawn carriages will soon take tourists to the royal tombs, the mountains and the beaches. As well, re-creations of costumes worn by kings, queens, princes, and princesses are being sewn as fast as possible for staff at all the new hotels. In short, and regrettably to some extent, this city is gearing up to become a "tour" tourist's destination.

Hue is generally cool, rainy and gray (yearly rainfall can total 152 cm or 60 in.). Although the Citadel and the Forbidden Purple City are well worth visiting, the devastation caused by war to these ancient sites makes them essentially unrecognizable, with patches of weeds and occasional deformed rock formations that were once grand splendors of the Nguyen Dynasty now springing from the earth like outcroppings on a moonscape.

Hue (originally called Phu Xuan and built in 1687), during the Nguyen Dynasty, was the cultural, religious and economic capital of Vietnam. Nguyen emperors built the Mandarin Road (Quan Lo) which allowed travelers to remarkably reach Saigon in only two weeks, and Hanoi in under a week. Messengers that were more than two days late were flogged for their tardiness.

***Pedestrian crossings don't need to be marked along national highways because most of the pedestrian users wouldn't recognize one if they saw it.***

In addition to the Vietnam War, Hue has had an extensive history of conflict. There were no fewer than 100 peasant uprisings in the area between 1802 and 1820. Royalty bickered and fought constantly. The French attacked Hue in 1833 and decimated the population to such an extent that the Emperor Hiep Hoa permitted the city to become a protectorate of France. The French divided the population by their spreading of Christianity. Although the French, and later the Japanese, felt it in their best interests to allow the Nguyen Dynasty to continue, there remained perpetual feuding and power scheming among the Nguyen royalty—and its influence on the population dropped to such a degree that the last Nguyen Emperor, Bao Dai, ceded the throne in August 1945.

Even after World War II ended, peace would not come to Hue. The Viet Cong took over the Citadel for 25 days during the Tet Offensive in 1968 and their communist flag defiantly flew from the Citadel's flag pole for more than three weeks. U.S. troops ruthlessly counterattacked, and it was this action which caused much of the damage to the ancient royal sites. The Thai Hoa Palace was decimated. More than 10,000 people died in the bitter fighting in Hue during the Tet Offensive. But with the Americans back in control of the area, peace would still not last long. NVA troops, after taking over the city in 1975, reportedly massacred thousands of civilians, beheading many, making the massacre at My Lai look like a mugging.

For shopping, the most unique item in Hue is a hat called *non bai tho*, which is made from palm and bamboo leaves. Inside the hats are proverbs, poems, and the lyrics to love songs which can only be seen when facing the hat toward the light. Makes for a great gift.

## What to See and Do in Hue

**Citadel** ★

This is a large, moated and walled area that has a perimeter of some 10 km. It was begun in 1804 by Emperor Gia Long. The Citadel used to enclose the entire city. Its seven-meter-high walls were originally built of earth but it was decided in the 1820s to cover them with bricks. This laborious process took thousands of workers and years to complete. Even today, it is used as a military fortress. The most famous gate is the **Ngo Mon Gate**.

**Imperial City** 

This is in the Citadel and was built in the early 19th century and modeled after the Forbidden City in Peking. There are numerous palaces and temples within these walls, as well as towers, a library and a museum. There are also areas for religious ceremonies. The South Gate is the main entrance. The Emperor Gia Long began construction of the city in 1804, and the site eventually encompassed eight different villages and covered six square kms. There are 10 gates that surround the four walls of the citadel. It took more than 20,000 laborers to construct the walls alone. Inside two of the gates are sets of large cannons, four through the **Nhon Gate** and five through the **Quang Duc Gate**. These cannons, made of bronze seized from Tay Son rebels, were cast in 1803. They represent the five natural elements and the four seasons. None of the cannons have ever been fired. Each contains a description of how it was constructed as well as firing instructions which, of course, were never followed. The main gate to the Imperial enclosure, the **Ngo Mon Gate** (built during the reign of Emperor Minh Mang in 1834), could only be used by the emperor. On the top of the gate is the Belvedere of the five Phoenixes. The emperor would appear here during important ceremonial occasions. The last Nguyen Dynasty Emperor Bao Dai formally ended his reign here. A Japanese company is completing the process of renovating the gate, albeit a slow one.

**Forbidden Purple City** 

The imperial family and its entourage were the only individuals permitted to use this royal palace. There were 60 buildings situated in 20 courtyards. "Feminine" affairs happened in the west area of the complex, while the men did their manly things in the east area. Fighting during the Tet offensive ruined the complex. The entire area is a depressing pile of rubble and small vegetableless vegetable gardens. Sadly, the only structures that can still be identified here are the two **Mandarin palaces**, the **Dien Canh Can** and the **Reading Book Palace**, but even these are in dismal shape. Work was started in 1983 to renovate the structures, but not much has been done. There are two large urns at the far side of the **Thai Hoa Palace**, cast in bronze and decorated with animals, birds and plants. On each side of the urns is a pavilion, the **Huu** and **Ta Pavilions**. One is a souvenir shop. The only really surviving buildings are on the west side of the palace, between the walls of the Forbidden Purple City and the outer walls—and many independent visitors miss them altogether. There is the relatively-well preserved **Hien Lam Cac**, where nine large urns made from copper cast in the mid 1830s stand in front of the pavilion. The **Temple of Generations** is next to the urns. This was built in 1821 and features altars of 10 Nguyen Dynasty Emperors. The **Hung Temple** is north of the Temple of Generations. It was built in 1804 in honor of Nguyen Phuc Luan, considered the "Father of the Nguyen Dynasty," and the father of Gia Long. Most blame the American shelling of Hue for the destruction of the Forbidden Purple City, but the complex had been deteriorating over the course of the previous 50 years due to shelling by the French, vandals, natural disasters and termites (not to exonerate the Americans). The only shelling being done here now is the whopping US$4 admission price to get into the Imperial City and Forbidden Purple City.

### The Flag Tower

This is the tall, 37-meter high flagpole between the Nhon and Quang Duc Gates. It was built originally in 1809 and lengthened in 1831. A typhoon knocked it down in 1904; it was rebuilt in 1915 only to be wrecked again in 1947. It was rebuilt in 1949 and that is how it stands today. The VC hung the National Liberation Front flag here for 25 days during the Tet Offensive. A picture of the flag on the pole can be seen in the Ho Chi Minh Museum in Hue.

### Bao Quoc Pagoda

*Bien Phu Street, near the railway line.*

This pagoda was built by the Buddhist monk Giac Phong in the early 18th century. There is a nice stupa behind the pagoda to the left. There are beautiful doors here with Chinese and Sanskrit inscriptions.

### Tu Dam Pagoda

*At the intersection of Dien Bien Phu and Tu Dam Streets.*

This was built in the late 1930s and has the distinction of being the temple where South Vietnamese President Diem sent troops in to silence the residing monks who were reputedly spreading discontent amongst the populace with the South Vietnamese regime.

### Imperial Museum (Museum of Ancient Objects)

*3 Le Truc Street.*

Built in 1845 and restored in 1923, this is a beautiful museum which houses inscribed poems on the walls. Most of the precious artifacts were pillaged during the Vietnam War, but there are many beautiful items here, including lacquerware, ceramics, royal costumes and furniture. In the front courtyard are giant bells and gongs. Admission: 8000 dong. Behind the museum is the **Royal College**, which was moved to this site in 1908 after being built in 1803. This was a school for the sons of princes and high-ranking Mandarins.

## AUTHOR'S NOTE

*The Vietnamese government has invested more than 1 billion dong (US$1 million) into the primary restoration of the Hue Ancient Museum. The Center for Hue Historical Heritage Restoration has copied the design of the museum in order to restore the whole wooden structure of the museum and retile the roof of Hoang Luu Ly and Than Luy Ly tiles. The fence surrounding the museum has been rebuilt to complement the museum's unique architecture. The restoration is a rapid one and should be completed by the time you read this.*

**Thien Mu Pagoda** ★

This is a bizarre sight. Yes, it's a pagoda. But your curiosity is more peaked by something else. It's an old Austin. Yeah, a British car. It was the same car that brought the Buddhist monk Thich Quang Duc to Saigon. There he became the subject of Malcolm Browne's famous photo. It shows the monk immolating himself in 1963. A copy of the photo is pasted on the windshield. Weird.

**Phu Cam Cathedral**

*20 Doan Huu Thrinh Street.*

The cathedral was built in 1963, but wasn't finished until 1975 (although it isn't entirely finished). There are plans to continue the building, which essentially only requires adding a spire to the cathedral. According to reports, this is the eighth church to be built on this site since 1682.

**Tang Tau Lake**

A royal library was formerly on an island in Tan Tau Lake. There is now a small Hinayana pagoda on the island called Ngoc Huong Pagoda.

**Tinh Tam Lake**

This lake is about 500 meters north of the Imperial enclosure and close by to Tang Tau Lake. In the middle of the lake are two islands connected by a bridge. Emperors used to spend lazy afternoons on the lake.

**Gia Long Tomb** ★★

Built between 1814 and 1820, this is a magnificent structure that is unfortunately difficult to visit. There are huge mango trees that surround the tomb. It follows the formula of other royal tombs with a lotus pond surrounding the enclosed compound. Here there is a courtyard with five headless Mandarins. Also there are figurines of horses and elephants. There are steps that lead up to another courtyard where the emperor and his wife are buried. Inscriptions describing the emperor's reign can be found behind the burial area. Gia Long was the first of the Nguyen Dynasty emperors and ruled from 1802–1820, the year he died. He ordered the construction of his tomb in 1814. When the king died, his corpse was washed and clothed in ornate garments. Precious stones and pearls were placed in his mouth. He was then placed in a coffin made of catalpa wood, a type of wood that naturally, through its chemical composition, wards off insects to prevent decomposition.

When a messenger reached the empress a few days later to inform her of Gia Long's death, he found that she, too, was dead—although she could not have known of her husband's death by all accounts. Although Gia Long died on February 3, 1820, he was not actually buried until around May 20. Next to his tomb is a second grave which contains items placed that would be useful to the emperor in his next life. A small donation will be expected at his tomb.

**Khai Dinh Tomb** ★

This was the last monument of the Nguyen dynasty and was constructed between 1920 and 1931. It sits magnificently on the slopes of Chau E Mountain, about 10 km from Hue in Chau Chu village. It has a long staircase flanked by dragons. There are ceiling murals and ceramic frescoes. The emperor reigned over Vietnam from 1916–1925. The tomb looks entirely unlike the other emperors' tombs around Hue. The tomb, combining a gaudy combination of European and Vietnamese influences, has become dilapidated over the years. You have to climb 36 steps to get up to the tomb, where you'll reach the first courtyard, surrounded by two pavilions. The Honor Courtyard is 26 steps farther up the hillside and features depictions of elephants and horses, as well as Mandarin soldiers. Then climb another three sets of stairs to reach the tomb, which is called Thien Dinh. It's divided into three halls and decorated with various murals. The emperor lies beneath the statue of Khai Dinh.

**Minh Mang Tomb** ★★

This complex was built in 1840 by King Minh Mang and is known for its magnificent architecture, military statuaries and elaborate decorations. It is perhaps the most beautiful of Hue's pagodas and tombs. You can get to this location, about 12 km south of Hue by tour boat on the Perfume River or by car.

**Tu Duc Tomb** ★

Seven km from the city, this was once the Royal Palace of Tu Duc, who ruled Hue more than 100 years ago. There are pavilions in a tranquil setting of forested hills and lakes. The tomb was constructed between 1864 and 1867. Tu Duc, who was the longest reigning Emperor (1848–1883), lived a luxurious life. Fifty chefs and 50 stewards presided over the emperor's meals, enough to feed and serve his 104 wives and numerous mistresses (although he never fathered any sons). The tomb is surrounded by a wall; there's a lake inside with a small island where the king constructed replicas of various temples. He used to come here to the surrounding pavilions to relax, hunt animals and recite poetry he composed to his many female companions and listen to music. To the left of the water is the Xung Khiem Pavilion; this was one of the emperor's favorite hangouts. Built on pilings over the lake, it was restored in 1986. The tomb of his Empress Le Thien Anh and adopted son Kien Phuc is to the left of Tu Duc's tomb. Many of the surrounding pavilions are in dire need of restoration, although you can still feel the serenity Tu Duc must have found here. With 104 women, it'd be hard not to. It is rumored that Tu Duc was sterile, and therefore forced to write his own eulogy. The eulogy itself recounts a surprisingly sad life (perhaps because of his sterility). Also, the French took control of Vietnam during his reign, which further saddened the emperor.

**Dong Khanh Tomb**

*Seven km from Hue.*

Built in 1889, this is the tomb of Emperor Dong Khan, the adopted son of Tu Duc. He assumed the throne as a puppet emperor after the French captured Emperor Ham Nhgi, who had fled Hue after the French stormed the palace in 1885. Ham was exiled to Algeria. Dong ruled the dynasty from 1886–1888. The tomb is the smallest of the royal tombs of Hue.

**Trieu Tri Tomb**

*About 7 km from Hue.*

There are conflicting reports as to when this tomb was built. Some say it was constructed in 1848 and other sources say it was constructed between 1864 and 1867. Trieu Tri ruled Vietnam from 1841 to 1847. The tomb is the only emperor's tomb not to be surrounded by a wall.

## Where to Stay in Hue

### AUTHOR'S NOTE: TELEPHONE PREFIXES

*The telephone numbers listed in this chapter are local exchanges. The country code prefix is 84. The city code is 54.*

**Ben Nghe Guest House** **US$7–$12**

*4 Ben Nghe Street. ☎ (84) 54-23687.*

Attached bath; hot water. Rave reviews from backpackers.

**Le Loi Hue (Hue Guest House)** **US$25–$70** ★

*2-5 Le Loi Street. ☎ 24668, 22161, 22155, 22153 or 22323; FAX: 24527.*

This is an interesting-looking compound of several buildings that looks a little bit like a dormitory quad on a college campus. The cheap rooms are a real bargain. The rooms are small but impeccably clean and comfortable. The more expensive doubles are large and airy. Attached bath in all private rooms and "mini-dorm" rooms, accommodating four or more people. There are a number of outdoor cafes downstairs, as well as souvenir stalls. Bicycle rentals. Very comfortable.

**Hue City Tourism Villas** **US$25–$35**

*11, 16, 18 Ly Thuong Kiet Street, and 5 Le Loi Street. ☎ (11) 23753; (16) 23679; (18) 23964; (5) 23945.*

These four properties get mixed reviews from travelers. Basic accommodations; fans; hot water. Inexpensive.

**Century Hotel** **US$88–$95** ★★★

*49 Le Loi Street. ☎ (84) 54-23390. FAX: (84) 54-23399.*

*150 rooms.*

Largest and the newest hotel in Hue. Air conditioning; tennis courts; two restaurants; disco; karaoke; swimming pool; post office; gift shop; TV; telephones; refrigerators; barbers; hairdressers; massage; hot water; all the amenities.

**Huong Giang Hotel** **US$65–$170** ★★★

*51 Le Loi Street. ☎ (84) 54-22122. FAX: (84) 54-23424/23102.*

*42 rooms.*

Built in 1962, but enlarged in 1983. Right on the river. Most rooms offer great views (you better get a great view for a hundred bucks). This is one of the most expensive hotels in town. Whether it's vastly overpriced will depend on your wallet. Friendly staff. Two great restaurants; cafe; large gardens; reception rooms; gift shop; sauna; massage; car and bike rentals; air conditioning; refrigerators; attached bathrooms; hot water with good pressure. The works, if you've got the cash. Great deal if you can afford a lower-priced room. Often full with the well-heeled. If you're on a budget, you'll get a kick out of the "modern" architecture as you pass by on the way to your US$6 guesthouse.

**Kinh Do Hotel** **US$30–$35** ★

*1 Nguyen Thai Hoc Street. ☎ (84) 54-23566/24952; FAX: (84) 54-23858.*

Rooms in three price ranges. Restaurant, bar, sauna, massage, dancing.

**Thuan Hoa Hotel** **About US$25–$70** ★★

*7 Nguyen Tri Phuong Street. ☎ (84) 54-22553/22556; FAX: (84) 54-23858/23036.*

Basic accommodations if a bit overpriced. Air conditioning, restaurant, attached bath.

**Morin Hotel** **About US$20–$40** ★★

*2 Hung Vuong Street. ☎ (84) 54-23866*

*Under construction.*

**Nha Khach Chinh Phu (Gov. Guest House** **About US$20–$40** ★★

*5 Le Loi Street. ☎ (84) 54-22161; FAX: (84) 54-24527.*

This is another recommendation, although it's a bit pricey. Beautiful building on the Perfume River. Large rooms, private bath, air conditioning. Restaurant. Friendly staff and efficient service.

**Royal Hotel** **US$10–$18**

*185B Thuan An Street. ☎ (84) 54-25246/25820.*

11 rooms. Breakfast included. Tell Mr. Ho Dac Dung, director, that Wink & Johnny Tu recommended you to his hotel. We are sure you will get a good rate.

**Nam Giao Hotel** **US$15**

*3B Dien Bien Phu Street. ☎ (84) 54-25736/22140; FAX: (84) 54-25735.*

14 rooms. Breakfast included.

**Von Canh Hotel**

*25 Hung Vuong Street. ☎ (84) 54-24130/25672; FAX: (84) 54-23424/23102.*

**Citadel Hotel**

*9 & 10 Kiem Hue Street. ☎ (84) 54-26249; FAX: (84) 54-26252.*

See Ms. Nguyen Thanh Hoa, the hotel manager and tell her we recommended you, for a good rate.

**Via Da Hotel**

*31 Thuan An Street. ☎ (84) 54-22352/26145/26146.*

See Mr. Nguyen Viet Tro, the director, for a discount.

**A Dong 2 Hotel**

*7 A Doi Cung Street. ☎ (84) 54-22765/22766/22767; FAX: (84) 54-28074.*

**Thien Duong (Paradise) Hotel** **US$15**

*33 Nguyen Thai Hoc Street.* ☎ *(84) 54-25976/25977; FAX: (84) 54-28233.*
Breakfast included.

**Thanh Loi Hotel** **US$15–$20**

*7 Dinh Tien Hoang Street.* ☎ *(84) 54-24803; FAX: (84) 54-25344.*

**Nha Khach 18 Le Loi** **US$10–$15**

*18 Le Loi Street.* ☎ *23720.*
Comfortable for the price. Rooms with air conditioning, hot water. Restaurant.

**Century Riverside** **US$70–$150** ★★★

*49 Le Loi Street.* ☎ *23391.*
This new hotel is what many are calling the best in Hue—and certainly looks a lot better than the Huong Giang. Rooms with air conditioning, hot water, private bath, TV, minibar and refrigerator, telephone. Restaurant, bar. Nice digs.

**Dong Da Hotel** **US$40–$80** ★★

*15 Ly Thuong Kiet.* ☎ *23071.*
Hordes of package guests here. Very comfortable. Rooms with air conditioning, minibar & refrigerator, hot water, TV, telephone. Restaurant, bar, tour services.

## Where to Eat in Hue

The food in Hue is generally very good, and there are a number of specialties unique to Hue. One is a dish of shrimp, pork and bean sprouts filled in a deep-fried egg batter (*banh khoai*). It is served usually with a delicious sesame sauce called *nuoc tuong*. There is also a rice pancake filled with shrimp and herbs called *banh beo*, and a rice pancake with pork called *ram*. The local beer, Huda, is decent but could use some more hops.

**Huong Giang Restaurant**

*51 Le Loi Street.*
Vietnamese and European cuisine. Excellent.

**Ngu Binh Restaurant**

*7 Ly Thuong Kiet Street.*
Food is average. Great place to meet new friends.

**Banh Khoai Thuong Tu** ★

*6 Dinh Tien Hoang Street.*
Excellent Vietnamese.

**Phu Hiep Restaurant** ★

*19 Ho Xuan Huong Street (opposite 53 Nguyen Chi Thanh Street).* ☎ *23560.*
Again, superb Vietnamese fare.

**Song Huong Floating Restaurant** ★

*North of the Trang Tien Bridge on the bank of the Perfume River, near the intersection of Le Loi and Hung Vuong.*
Great Vietnamese fare at low prices.

**Ong Tao Restaurant**

*134 Ngo Duc Ke, on the grounds of the Imperial Palace.*
Vietnamese, Asian, Western. A little pricey but this is a good restaurant.

**Loc Thien**

*6 Dinh Tien Hoang Street.*

Service is friendly, the Vietnamese and Asian fare good. Cheap.

**Pho Restaurant**

*6 Ha Noi Street.*

Vietnamese fare at great prices. The noodle soup *(pho)* is excellent.

## Directory

### Transportation

Hue is 1070 km from Saigon, 654 km from Hanoi, 370 km from Vinh, 108 km from Danang, 165 km from Dong Hoi, 94 km from the Ben Hai River, 56 km from Quang Tri, 72 km from Dong Ha, 152 km from the Laos border, 400 km from the Thai border, and 60 km from A Luoi, which can only be reached by 4-wheel-drive.

**By air:**

VN flies to Hue from Ho Chi Minh City daily at 10 a.m. and daily (except Saturdays) at 6:30 a.m. From Hanoi, flights leave for Hue Sunday–Tuesday and Thursdays and Fridays at 2:30 p.m. Flights from Hue connect to HCMC daily (except Sat.) at 8:30 a.m., daily (except Tues. and Thurs.) at 4:30 p.m., and Tuesdays, Thursdays and Sundays at 1:30 p.m. To Hanoi Sunday-Tuesday and Thursdays and Fridays at 11:30 a.m.

**By bus:**

The An Cuu bus station is at *43 Hung Vuong Street*. This station serves destinations to the south. Buses connect with Lang Co, Quy Nhon, Danang, Buon Ma Thuot, Nha Trang, Dalat and Saigon. They usually leave very early in the morning, about 5 a.m. The bus station serving the north (An Hoa Station), at the northwest corner of the walled city, has connections to Dong Ha, Vinh, Hanoi, Dong Hoi and Khe Sanh. Again, buses usually leave around 5 a.m. Tickets for all destinations can be bought at either station. The local bus station is called Dong Ba (downstream from the Trang Tien Bridge on the river side of Tran Hung Dao Street), and from here non-express buses depart for Dong Ha, Phu Luong, Cho No, An Lo, Bao Vinh, Lang Co, Danang, Thuan An, and Cau Hai.

**By train:**

The train station is at the west end of Le Loi Street and serves all points up and down the coast. It takes about 16 hours to get to Hanoi and 24 hours to Saigon. Book well in advance, especially for sleepers.

**Transport around town:**

Cars with drivers can be hired at Thua Thien Tourism, Hue Tourist Office and Hue City Tourism.

**By bicycle:**

Bicycles are easily rented at most hotels for about 8000-10,000 dong per day. It's the best way of getting around town. Unfortunately, it rains so much in Hue, expect to get wet. Bring a rainsuit.

**By boat:**

There are many ways to rent boats to go up and down the Perfume River. Restaurants can help arrange a boat tour, but they're expensive. Many of the sights in Hue can be reached by boat, including many of the royal tombs, Thuan An Beach, and Thien Mu Pagoda. Also try hiring a boat behind the Dong Ba Market, by the Dap Da Bridge and also the Perfume River Hotel.

## Post Office

*8 Hoang Hoa Tham Street*. You can make international calls and faxes from here.

## Hospital

Hue General Hospital. *16 Le Loi Street. ☎ 22325.*

## Banks and Moneychangers

Industrial and Commercial Bank. *2A Le Quy Don Street*. Open from 7 to 11:30 a.m. and from 1:30 to 4:30 p.m. Monday-Saturday.

## Tourist Offices

**Hue City Tourism**. *18 Le Loi Street*. Can arrange for car rentals, guides and traditional Vietnamese musical performances.

**Hue Tourist Office**. *30 Le Loi Street. ☎ 22369, 22288*. Can arrange for car rentals and guides.

**Hue Tourist Co.** (Hue City Tourism). *9 Ly Thuong Kiet. ☎ 23577.*

## Airline Offices

The booking office for Vietnam Airlines is located at *12 Hanoi Street. ☎ 23249*. There's not much they can do for you here at this primitive, non-computerized office but get you out of Hue. It's staffed by a single employee, so expect to wait a while.

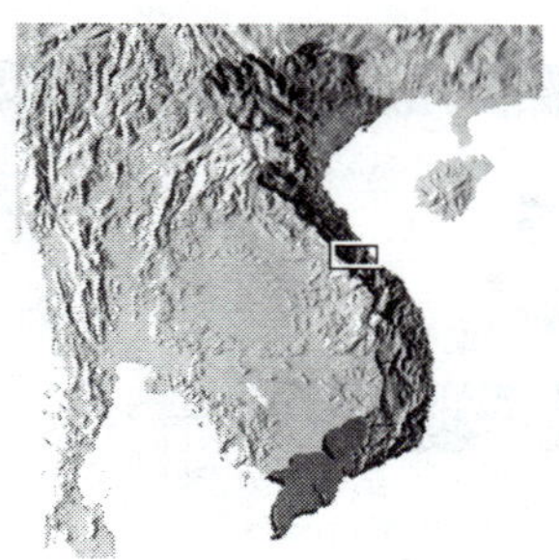

# THE DMZ

## THE DEMILITARIZED ZONE IN A CAPSULE

*The DMZ was the site of the fiercest fighting of the Vietnam War...Tens of thousands of soldiers died here...The siege of Khe Sanh and battles at Hamburger Hill are considered the bloodiest battles of the war...The former DMZ stretched for 5 km in either direction of the Ben Hai River...Thousands of scavengers have been killed since 1975 unearthing old war materiel to sell as scrap metal and souvenirs...The former DMZ was officially created in 1954...It extends along National Highway 9 from the South China Sea to Laos.*

The Demilitarized Zone was the area that extended 5 km both north and south of the Ben Hai river and was the site of some of the bloodiest fighting of the Vietnam War. This was the demarcation line that separated South Vietnam from North Vietnam. The origins of the DMZ were the result of the Potsdam Conference held in Berlin in 1945 (which included representatives of Great Britain, the U.S. and the USSR) that partitioned Vietnam into two separate countries. However, the actual DMZ wasn't established until 1954. What was concluded at the Potsdam conference was that Japanese forces south of the 16th parallel would surrender to the British, while occupying Japanese forces in the north would surrender to the Nationalist Chinese Army led by Chiang Kai Shek.

Eventually, in 1954, the governments of France and of Ho Chi Minh agreed in Geneva to an armistice of sorts that would split the south and north—however, not politically. The demarcation line was to be temporary until general elections could be held in 1956. But when these did not occur, the nation was split in half at the Ben Hai River, also referred to as the 17th parallel.

Fielding
THE DMZ


BEN HAI RIVER
Demarcation between South Vietnam and North Vietnam and the center of the DMZ.
CON THIEN FIREBASE
American base and scene of intense fighting in Sept. 1 967.
NORTH VIETNAM
THE ROCKPILE
U.S. Marine long-range artillery base and lookout station.
Ben Hai River
Dong Ha
DAKRONG BRIDGE
Constructed by the North Vietnamese with Cuban assistance after the "official" withdrawal of American troops.
CAMP CARROLL
U.S. artillery base.
Quang Tri River
LAO BAO
North Vietnamese artillery base.
LANG VAY
U.S. Army Special Forces base overrun by North Vietnamese troops in 1968.
KHE SANH
U.S. Marine base besieged by North Vietnamese troops for 77 days in 1968 as a diversion in preparation for the Tet Offensive.

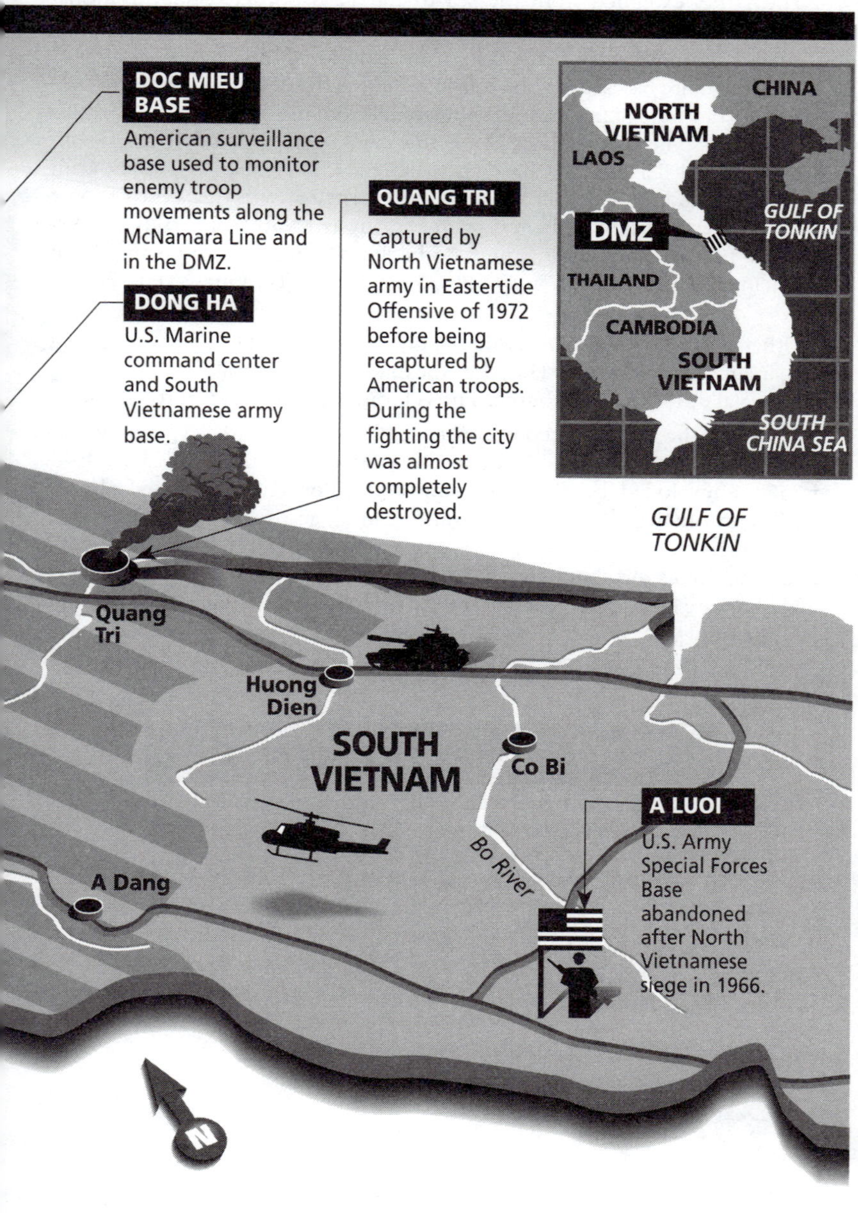

DOC MIEU BASE
American surveillance base used to monitor enemy troop movements along the McNamara Line and in the DMZ.
DONG HA
U.S. Marine command center and South Vietnamese army base.
QUANG TRI
Captured by North Vietnamese army in Eastertide Offensive of 1972 before being recaptured by American troops. During the fighting the city was almost completely destroyed.
CHINA
NORTH VIETNAM
LAOS
DMZ
GULF OF TONKIN
THAILAND
CAMBODIA
SOUTH VIETNAM
SOUTH CHINA SEA
GULF OF TONKIN
Quang Tri
Huong Dien
SOUTH VIETNAM
Co Bi
A LUOI
U.S. Army Special Forces Base abandoned after North Vietnamese siege in 1966.
Bo River
A Dang
N

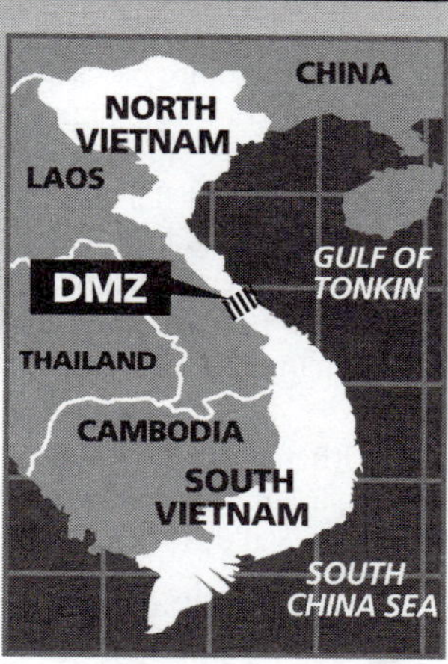

The DMZ extended from the sea to the Laos border. Today National Highway 9 runs along this former border to Laos. As well, the Ho Chi Minh Trail cut across the DMZ, requiring American forces to establish a number of bases and fire bases along the southern side of the demarcation line to prevent the transport of troops and war materiel from moving from the north to the south. Some of the bases along the 17th parallel included Khe Sanh, Camp Carroll, Lang Vay, Cua Viet, Con Thien, Dong Ha, Gio Linh, Cam Lo, Ca Lu, and the Rockpile. Khe Sanh, in particular, was the scene of some of the fiercest fighting of the war, with as many as 10,500 soldiers dying during the two-month siege of the base in the beginning of 1968 by North Vietnamese forces—which was only a decoy for the Tet Offensive in February.

Other areas along the DMZ that experienced bitter fighting were Dong Ha, infamous Hamburger Hill, the Rockpile, Camp Carroll, Quang Tri, the Ashau Valley (where Hamburger Hill is located), Con Thien and Lang Vay.

Although the war has been over for many years, the DMZ remains an extremely dangerous area. Thousands of people have been killed by land mines, unexploded bombs, agonizing and deforming white phosphorus shells and other ordnance that is still spread all across the DMZ. Peasants and farmers still comb the area for scrap metal—aluminum, steel and brass—and other items they hope to sell. They earn only a pittance for these efforts and many are killed each year. It is not wise to touch anything on the ground along Highway 9. In fact it would be deadly, because if the Vietnamese have not already scavenged the materiel it is because they are too frightened to move it.

### A NOTE ABOUT LAND MINES AND UNEXPLODED ORDNANCE

*The Americans recarpeted Vietnam with underground explosives. Even today, scores of Vietnamese and cattle are blown up by land mines and other unexploded ordnance. It seems now that it is the Australians who are trying to remove what's still left, especially in port areas.*

*EXAT is an Australian ordnance disposal firm working with the Vietnamese Army implementing ordnance surveys and clearance services. One contract is with a new cement company on a site near Haiphong heavily bombed by the Americans during the war.*

## A NOTE ABOUT LAND MINES AND UNEXPLODED ORDNANCE

*Another contract is with a mining company in the Central Highlands. Although thousands of bombs near the ground's surface have already been defused by the Vietnamese, more sophisticated clearance operations are required for port expansion, sites of new factories, bridge and road building, and open-cast mining operations.*

*EXAT believes they will achieve a 95% success rate in Vietnam, a figure based on their operations in Kuwait, Afghanistan, Cambodia and Pakistan. Much of EXAT's efforts will be training local demining technicians to utilize the sophisticated equipment required for intense, large-scale demining operations.*

Travel permits to the DMZ area, once required and extremely costly, have largely been removed. But you should only visit the area with a trained, professional guide. The old bases can be visited by either day trips or through Saigontourist's War Veteran Tours or programs offered by other state- and privately-run tour agent (see the War Veterans Tours section).

## A Word About Agent Orange

The debate continues even today regarding the effects of Agent Orange on both the Vietnamese and American war veterans exposed to the chemical. Many "experts," particularly in the U.S., insist that the chemical is essentially harmless and that the higher birth defect rates experienced in the south and central parts of Vietnam are due more to malnutrition than anything else. But consider the following: 72 million liters of chemicals, containing 15 types of poisons, were dropped on 1.7 million hectares of forest during the war. That's nearly 20 percent of the total forest area in southern Vietnam. Of these 72 million liters dropped, 47 million of them were Agent Orange, which contained a blend of 170 kg of dioxin. And this estimate of the total amount of Agent Orange (called Operation Ranch Hand, which lasted from 1961–1971) dropped on Vietnam is considered conservative at best. It is believed that 4600 flying sorties sprayed the herbicide mainly in the following areas: Phuoc Long, Binh Dinh, Thua Thien, Tay Ninh, Long Khanh, Binh Duong, Bien Hoa, Quang Nam, Quang Tri and Kon Tum. There were between 300–700 drops in each of these areas. Nearly 50 percent of the Agent Orange dropped fell in these areas.

Despite protests from around the world and the U.S. government's assurance that the chemical would have no long term effects on the Vietnamese people, American soldiers and foliage in the environment, it became indisputably evident that the chemical would have long-term harmful effects as early as 1970 at an international conference in France of Scientists at Orsay

1964-1975

# BATTLES OF VIETNAM

**AN LOC**

**(Apr 8-Jul 11, 1972)** Capital of Binh Long province which the North Vietnamese laid siege to. The battle ended with the withdrawal of the North Vietnamese from the province.

**OPERATION ATTLEBORO**

**(Sep 14-Nov 24, 1966)** The objective was to find and engage Viet Cong forces near the Cambodian border. The first major battle erupted on October 19th and fighting lasted almost a month.

**OPERATION JUNCTION CITY**

**(Feb 22-May 14 1967)** Combined U.S. and ARVN forces sought to engage Viet Cong forces in Tay Ninh province. This operation resulted in the movement of Viet Cong forces into Cambodia.

**RACH BA**

**(Sep15,1967)** Amphibious assault which was part of Operation Coronado. The objective was to surround and destroy Viet Cong forces in the Mekong Delta.

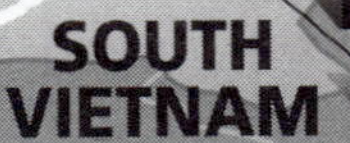

Mekong River
Phnon Penh
CAMBODIA
SOUTH VIETNAM
Saigon
MEKONG DELTA
Bac Lieu

**OPERATION FREQUENT WIND**

**(Mar 11-Apr 30, 1975)** Operation in which the U.S. Navy evacuated remaining Americans and some South Vietnamese before the fall of Saigon.

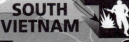

**OPERATION LAM SON**

**(Feb 8-Apr 6, 1971)**
Operation in which South Vietnamese forces with limited American support entered Laos in an attempt to damage the effectiveness of the Ho Chi Minh Trail. Like most other attempts, this attack did little to stop the vast amounts of troops and equipment moving up and down the trail.

**GULF OF TONKIN**

**(Aug. 2, 1964)**
Occurred when U.S. destroyer Maddox, on patrol in the Gulf of Tonkin allegedly, was attacked by North Vietnamese torpedo boats. Resulted in the Aug. 7 Gulf of Tonkin Resolution which gave Lyndon B. Johnson the power to "take all necessary measures to repel an armed attack against the forces of the United States and to prevent further aggression."

**HAMBURGER HILL**

**(May 11-20,1969)**
Nickname for Dong Ap Bia, a hill controlled by the North Vietnamese. During the battle for this hill, heavy casualties were suffered on both sides.

**KHE SANH**

**(Jan 21-Apr 7, 1968)**
Along with attacks on American bases at Con Thien, Loc Ninh, Song Be and Dak To, the North Vietnamese 77-day siege of Khe Sanh was a decoy in preparation for the Tet Offensive.

**OPERATION STARLITE**

**(Aug 2-18, 1965)**
The first major conflict between American and Viet Cong troops. It consisted of an amphibious assault on the Van Tuong Peninsula backed by air support and ground troops designed to surround and destroy the Viet Cong troops there. there.

**MY LAI**

**(Mar 16, 1968)**
Incident in which a company of American troops killed about 500 civilians in and around My Lai in Son My subdistrict.

**IA DRANG**

**(Oct 26-Nov 27, 1965)**
Began when the North Vietnamese attacked the Special Forces camp at Plei Mei. American reinforcements were sent in to repel the attack and then more units were sent in to "search and destroy" North Vietnamese forces in the Ia Drang valley.

University. Regardless, the American military continued to drop the chemical on Vietnam until 1973.

Surveys by scientists have revealed that dioxin is still evident in the blood of the people of Vietnam and in the environment, particularly in the DMZ area and southern Vietnam. For instance, in northern Vietnam, blood tests have shown an average of 2.2 picograms (pg) of dioxin in the blood of the people. (In the U.S., the figure is 5.2 pg per person and in Japan 3.2 pg.). However the levels of dioxin in the blood of southern Vietnamese is staggering. The general figure is between 11.7–14.6 pg per person. Particularly whopping are the amounts of dioxin found in the people of Song Be Province (32 per person!), Bien Hoa (28 pg per person) and Danang (18 pg per person).

An analysis of fat tissue taken from 73 people between 1987 and 1992 revealed that of the 25 people living in areas where the chemical was dropped by U.S. warplanes, 84 percent of them contained large traces of dioxin in their blood. Of the 48 people not living in affected areas, 81 percent also showed high levels of dioxin in their blood. This is essentially conclusive evidence that the dioxins of Agent Orange were and still are spread through the consumption of affected food. In fact, people directly exposed to the dioxin absorb about 25 percent of the pesticide, while those exposed to the chemical indirectly through the consumption of food grown in affected areas absorb 98 percent of the dioxin content!

It is conclusive now, most scientists believe, that exposure to Agent Orange causes fetus damage. Newborn babies today usually have about 0.02 pg of the dioxin in their blood. Death rates of children born in sprayed areas is about 30 percent higher than those born in nonsprayed areas. Most believe that the mother's milk containing the dioxin is the principle cause of the higher death rates. Deformities and abnormalities, such as mental retardation are more prevalent in these areas. Instances of stillbirth, cancer and congenital deformity are also higher in these areas.

Only recently has the U.S. government admitted that Agent Orange and dioxin may cause cancer and skin diseases, as well as nervous, lymphatic and respiratory disorders and diseases such as Hodgkin's Disease. There have also been similar long-term effects on the American soldiers who fought in the affected areas. Of the nearly 40,000 lawsuits filed by American soldiers against the government based on their exposure to Agent Orange, to date only about 470 of them have been settled by most recent accounts. It is believed that as many as 200,000 U.S. soldiers were affected by the chemical.

Today, the Vietnamese are still poisoned by Agent Orange through the food they eat and the soil they till. Scientists hope that the spread and effects of Agent Orange will last only another 5–10 years.

## What to See and Do Around the DMZ

### Ben Hai River

This river, about 20 km north of Dong Ha marks the former border between South Vietnam and North Vietnam. NH1 passes over the river via a dilapidated bridge. During the war the southern half of the bridge was painted yellow, the northern half red. It was destroyed during a U.S. bombing raid in 1967. After the ceasefire agreements in 1973, the rebuilt bridge had two flag towers built. There are decent stretches of beaches on both the south and north sides of where the river empties into the sea.

### Dong Ha

Along National Highway 1 at the intersection of the American-built Highway 9 south of the Ben Hai River. This was the site of a former U.S. Marine command center and later a South Vietnamese Army base. It was fiercely attacked during the spring of 1968 by NVA regulars. Dong Ha is now the capital of Quang Tri Province. Here you can see the **French-built blockhouse** (**Lo Cot Phap**) on Tran Phu Street (about 400 meters of NH1), the perimeter of which can be seen captured war equipment, including tanks. The blockhouse was once used by American and South Vietnamese forces. Near the blockhouse you can stay at the **Dong Ha Hotel** (☎ *361, 24 rooms*). Other hotels in town include the **Buu Dien Tinh Quang Tri Hotel** (on the south side of town, about US$20), **the Ngoai Thuong Hotel** (also near the French blockhouse and very inexpensive), and the **Dong Truong Son Hotel** (about 3 km out from the blockhouse and rather expensive) on Tran Phu Street. There are a slew of roadside restaurants along NH1 in Dong Ha to choose from. There's a decent restaurant next to the Buu Dien Tinh Quang Tri hotel. There is also a restaurant at the Dong Truong Son Hotel.

### Quang Tri

Quang Tri is about 60 km north of Hue and was the site of the Eastertide Offensive in 1972, in which several NVA divisions crossed the DMZ and, using tanks, mortars and heavy artillery, captured both the city and the province. The Americans then carpet-bombed the area with B-52 sorties. South Vietnamese artillery was also employed in the total destruction of the city. In short, the city was leveled in order to retake what was left of it. As a result, there's nothing to see here save for the Quang Tri Memorial and perhaps the ruined citadel, which was formerly an ARVN HQ. There's also another ruined building here that was formerly a Buddhist secondary school, between NH1 and the bus station. If you want, you can visit the bombed-out church where American and VC soldiers fought. It is pockmarked with bullet holes. There are two beaches in the vicinity: Gia Dang Beach and Cua Viet Beach.

### Vinh Moc Tunnels ★

Unlike the tunnels at Cu Chi, these elaborate tunnels used by the VC and NVA troops have not been enlarged to accommodate Western tourists (they average 1.2 meters wide and are only 1.7 meters high) and look exactly as they did in the mid-1960s. There are nearly three kilometers of tunnels here, with at least 12 entrances.

**JAN. 30 - FEB., 1968**

# THE TET OFFENSIVE

Staged during a ceasefire arranged for the Tet Holiday which celebrates the beginning of the lunar new year, the offensive consisted of coordinated attacks by Viet Cong and North Vietnamese troops on major population centers of South Vietnam. The offensive was carried out after diversionary attacks on several American strongholds had absorbed troops and attention. While the North Vietnamese and Viet Cong suffered enormous casualties and were tactically unsuccessful, the offensive raised new questions as to the probability of an American victory over such determined enemy forces. While the offensive encompassed all of South Vietnam, the fighting was particularly fierce in Khe Sanh, Hue and Saigon.

## SAIGON Jan. 31

The capital of South Vietnam, Saigon was an American stronghold and virtually free of conflict except for isolated Viet Cong terrorist attacks. The second wave of the Tet Offensive brought attacks by disguised Viet Cong troops as well as North Vietnamese troops on strategic locations in Saigon such as the American Embassy, the national radio station and the Presidential Palace. These targets were quickly retaken by American and South Vietnamese troops and the false sense of security that Saigon had enjoyed was shattered.

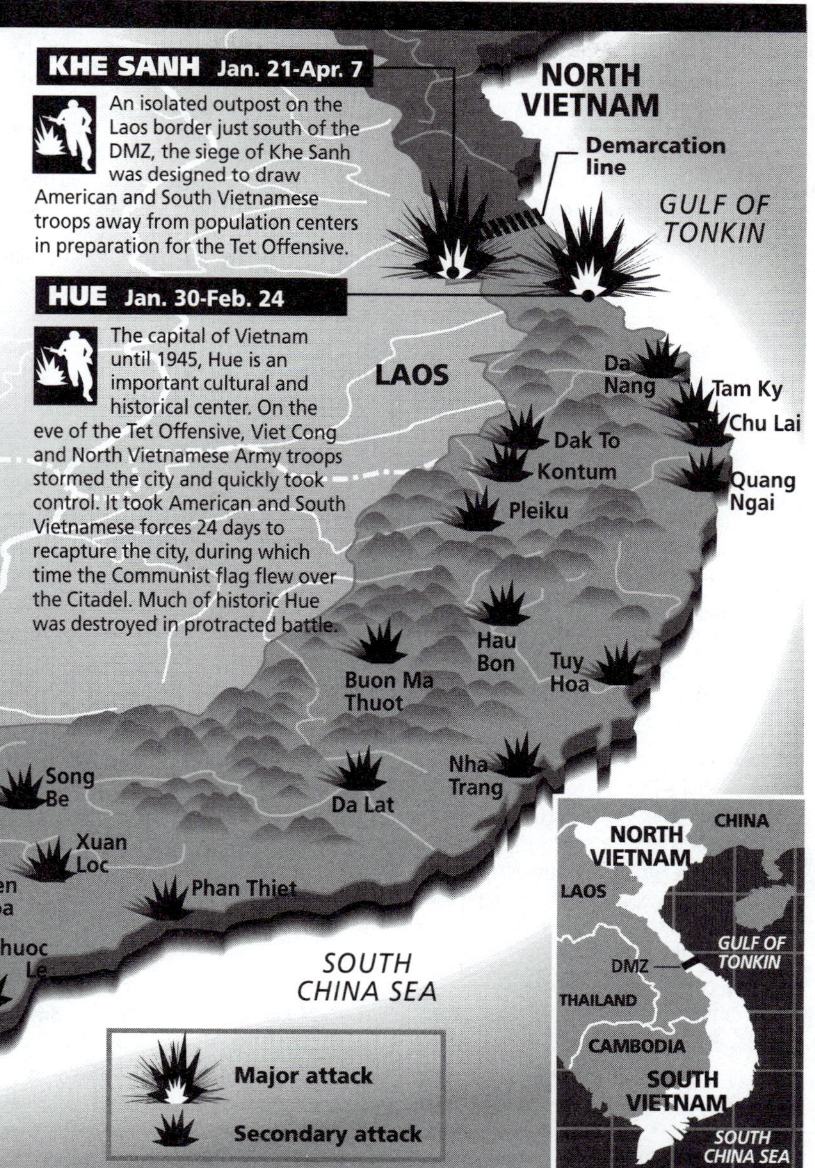
KHE SANH Jan. 21-Apr. 7
An isolated outpost on the Laos border just south of the DMZ, the siege of Khe Sanh was designed to draw American and South Vietnamese troops away from population centers in preparation for the Tet Offensive.
HUE Jan. 30-Feb. 24
The capital of Vietnam until 1945, Hue is an important cultural and historical center. On the eve of the Tet Offensive, Viet Cong and North Vietnamese Army troops stormed the city and quickly took control. It took American and South Vietnamese forces 24 days to recapture the city, during which time the Communist flag flew over the Citadel. Much of historic Hue was destroyed in protracted battle.
NORTH VIETNAM
Demarcation line
GULF OF TONKIN
LAOS
Da Nang
Tam Ky
Chu Lai
Dak To
Kontum
Quang Ngai
Pleiku
Hau Bon
Tuy Hoa
Buon Ma Thuot
Nha Trang
Da Lat
Song Be
Xuan Loc
Bien Hoa
Phan Thiet
Phuoc Le
SOUTH CHINA SEA
Major attack
Secondary attack
CHINA
NORTH VIETNAM
LAOS
GULF OF TONKIN
DMZ
THAILAND
CAMBODIA
SOUTH VIETNAM
SOUTH CHINA SEA

Seven of them are at the beach. The entrances have been covered by shrubs and trees. The tunnels themselves were built on three different levels. Inside the tunnels, there are small chambers where families and soldiers lived. There is even a conference hall that could fit as many as 150 people who would gather for military meetings and social events. (The tunnels themselves usually housed between 2500-3000 people at any given time.) They can easily be visited by tourists, but only with a guide, because it's easy as hell to get lost in these dark, narrow caverns. If you're on the lam and under five feet tall, this would be where the bill collectors definitely wouldn't find you. As well, the government uses poisons to keep away snakes tempted to make the tunnels their home. During the war, the tunnels were bombed, but little damage was inflicted. What the inhabitants feared most were the drilling bombs, which burned their way deep into the earth before exploding. Although electric lighting was added to the tunnels in the early 1970s, bring a flashlight.

**Doc Mieu Base**

Eight km south of the Ben Hai River along NH1. This was the site of "McNamara's Wall," which housed an intricate electronic surveillance site used by the Americans to detect VC and NVA troop movements, as the soldiers would cross electrical wires informing the surveillance station. All around you can see remnants from the war: military uniforms and boots, huge craters leftover from the bombing and shelling, artillery shrapnel and live ammunition rounds. Much has been scavenged by the locals.

**Cua Tung Beach**

Bao Dai used to vacation here, which is on the north side of where the Ben Hai River spills into the South China Sea. Off the coast of Cua Tung Beach is Con Co Island, which can be reached via a three-hour boat ride. Bomb craters of all sizes can be found in the area around the beach. It's a sobering sight.

**Dakrong Bridge**

About 12.5 km to the east past the Khe Sanh bus station. This bridge, which spans over the Dakrong River was built after the "official" withdrawal of American troops. It was constructed by the North Vietnamese with Cuban assistance. The route that heads south from the bridge to A Luoi was once part of the Ho Chi Minh Trail. Although the villagers in the area today are peaceful, they still sling on their backs automatic weapons and assault rifles leftover from the war. It's a little unnerving, but there's little danger for tourists.

**Camp Carroll**

This former U.S. base is 3 km off Highway 9, 24 km east past the Dakrong Bridge and about 36 km east of the Khe Sanh bus station. There's not much today worth visiting here but jackfruit trees, shrubs, and small weapons shells that litter the ground, but this is a historical military site that was established in 1966 and named after a U.S. Marine who was killed during a battle on a nearby ridge. There were giant artillery pieces at the camp, 175mm cannons that could fire volleys as far away as Hue. Today the area is utilized to grow pepper. This was also the site where the

South Vietnamese commander of the base, Lt. Col. Ton That Dinh, deserted and joined the North Vietnamese Army.

### Con Thien Firebase

This was the scene of intense fighting between U.S. and North Vietnamese troops. When the North Vietnamese attacked the firebase in September 1967 as a diversion leading to the upcoming Tet Offensive, the Americans responded by dropping more than 40,000 tons of bombs on the area via fighter bombers and B-52s. In total, there were more than 4000 sorties flown by American war planes. The normally lush and verdant hills surrounding the base were entirely blown apart, making the area look like a desert of craters and rotting wood. The Americans eventually fought off the siege, but at great expense. Even today, the former firebase is too dangerous to visit due to vast amounts of unexploded ordnance in the area.

### The Rockpile

*26 km from Dong Ha toward Khe Sanh.*

This was exactly as the name implies, a giant pile of rocks, which U.S. Marines used as a lookout and long-range artillery camp. Today, local villagers live in stilt houses and subsist on slash-and-burn agriculture.

### Truong Son National Cemetery

This is a cemetery filled with white tombstones of the thousands of North Vietnamese and VC fighters who lost their lives carrying equipment and weaponry down the Ho Chi Minh Trail in the Truong Son Mountains. They were exhumed from where they were originally buried and brought here after the reunification of Vietnam. However, a number of the graves are empty, representing the untold hundreds of thousands of VC and North Vietnamese soldiers missing in action. Above each stone is the inscription *Liet Si*, which translates into "martyr." Disabled veterans maintain this Arlington-type cemetery. The cemetery is divided into five zones, each representing the regions where the soldiers had lived. There is a separate area for decorated heroes and officers.

## THE HO CHI MINH TRAIL

*The famous and vast networks of roads and paths that connected North Vietnam and South Vietnam were used by VC and North Vietnamese Army troops to transport war supplies, primarily to VC strongholds in the south. Many tributaries of the trail were constructed to avoid any one point from being cut off via the constant U.S. bombing of the intricate path.*

*As many as 10 secret roadways were constructed, entirely camouflaged in many places. Defoliants and other chemicals the Americans used to reveal the trail were largely ineffective. More than 300,000 full-time workers and another 200,000 part-time North Vietnamese laborers maintained the trail.*

## THE HO CHI MINH TRAIL

*NVA loss rates along the trail are estimated to be only 10 percent, and perhaps only a third of the machinery and vehicles being transported down the trail were ruined by the Americans. At first, supplies were carried on the backs of men and women on bicycles, but trucks from China and Russia later traversed the route(s). By the end of the Vietnam War, the Ho Chi Minh Trail totaled more than 13,350 km of all-weather roadways.*

*One "trailsman" was reputed to have carried more than 55 tons of supplies down the trail, a distance totalling about 41,000 km—roughly equalling the circumference of the world. Although American bombing did relatively little to ruin the trail and its travelers, the mission of ferrying equipment down the Ho Chi Minh Trail was a damned dangerous one.*

**A Luoi**

60 km west of Hue and about 65 km southeast of the Dakrong Bridge. Here, in 1966, U.S. Army Special Forces units were besieged by the communists and the base here was abandoned. Consequently, it became an important link in the Ho Chi Minh Trail. LZs (landing zones) where bitter fighting took place are located nearby. Included are Hill 1175, Hill 521, Erskine and Razor, and Cunningham LZs. Farther south is Hamburger Hill. This was the site of an incredibly fierce battle in May 1969 and no one seemed to have any reason why it should have taken place, as there was absolutely no strategic advantage of controlling the hill other than "saving face." More than 240 U.S. soldiers died in a week of fighting here that saw possession of the hill change repeatedly. The Americans eventually ceded the area to the North Vietnamese and withdrew.

**Lao Bao**

On top of a Co Roc Mountain, overlooking the Vietnamese town of Lao Bao from the Lao side of the border was a North Vietnamese artillery position near the Tchepone River.

**Lang Vay**

This was an American Army Special Forces camp established in 1962 but overrun by north Vietnamese troops in 1968. The base primarily was composed of South Vietnamese, Bru, and U.S.-trained Montagnard soldiers—as well as a handful of U.S. Green Berets. During the attack more than 300 of the ARVN troops died. Ten of the Americans were killed.

**Khe Sanh** ★

The 77-day siege of Khe Sanh, which started on January 21, 1968, was seen by the American forces as an attempt by the North Vietnamese to create another Dien Bien Phu, when, in actuality, the siege was nothing more than a diversion in preparation for the Tet Offensive. However, as many as 15,000 NVA soldiers lost their lives here, compared to 248 American fatalities (43 of them in a C-123 transport crash). General William Westmoreland, convinced that Khe Sanh was the prime target of NVA forces (reconnaissance revealed that between 20,000-40,000 NVA troops had surrounded the area), had the region carpet-bombed by B-52s and entirely defoliated. More than 100,000 tons of bombs and explosives were dropped by the aircraft. The U.S. Marines at Khe Sanh fired 159,000 shells, including the dreaded white phosphorous type, at NVA positions. Westmoreland would not permit a military humiliation, such as that which occurred to the French at Dien Bien Phu in 1954, to happen to American troops. He even considered the use of tactical nuclear weapons! The area surrounding Khe Sanh was thoroughly leveled. It was a resounding military victory for the Americans (who were able to reopen Highway 9 on April 7, linking the Army with the Marines), but an even greater psychological one for the North Vietnamese—despite their massive losses—as it paved the way to another psychological victory that changed the course of the war: the Tet Offensive, which started a week after the siege of Khe Sanh began. (Westmoreland amazingly continued to believe that Khe Sanh was the primary target, and thought the Tet Offensive was merely a diversion!) After the general's tour of duty was up and he was replaced as Vietnam's military commander-in-chief, American military experts reassessed the significance of Khe Sanh, and forces in the area were silently redeployed after destroying or burying anything of significance. Today villagers inhabit this lush area, many searching for scrap metal and military ordnance, and it's very difficult to believe this was the site of the deadliest battle of the Vietnam War. But all around are shells and remnants of the siege. The area is littered with shell casings. The town of Khe Sanh is set amongst serene hillsides and green fields. Most of the inhabitants here are Bru tribespeople. The thought that comes to mind when visiting here is that the whole affair was an ugly, bloody human travesty. A small (five-room) guesthouse is at Khe Sanh just south of the Khe Sanh Bus Station.

## DMZ Directory

### Dong Ha

#### Transportation

Dong Ha is about 1170 km from Saigon, 617 km from Hanoi, 190 km from Danang, 73 km from Hue, 295 km from Vinh, 40 km from Vinh Moc, 65 km from Khe Sanh, 95 km from Dong Hoi, 22 km from the Ben Hai River, 80 km from the Laos border, and 30 km from the Truong Son National Cemetery. The Dong Ha Bus station is located at the intersection of National Highways 1 and 9. There are connections to surrounding towns, including Quang Tri, Ho Xa, Khe Sanh, Dong Hoi, Lao Bao, Hue and other coastal and interior cities. There is service to Hanoi at least twice a week. The bus leaves at 5 in the morning, stops in Vinh 12 hours later and Hanoi after another 12 hours. Buses south leave for Danang, Con Thien and Ha Tri. The Reunification Express also stops here, with regular connections to the north and south along the Vietnamese coast. The Da Hong Railway station is south of the bus station on NH1 by about a kilometer. Then cross a field to the right of the highway.

#### Tourist Office

Quang Tri Tourism. Dong Truong Son Hotel. ☎ *261*. There are cars and guides available here, but a better situation is making tour arrangements in Hue through Thua Thien-Hue Tourism.

### Quang Tri

#### Transportation

Buses and Citroën Tractions from the Quang Tri Bus Station (Le Duan Street) connect Quang Tri with Hue, Khe Sanh, and Ho Xa.

### Vinh Moc Tunnels

#### Transportation

The best way to get to the tunnels if you're not on a tour is by taking a private car north of the Ben Hai River about 6.5 km to Ho Xa. The tunnels are about 12–13 km from the village.

### Doc Mieu Base

#### Transportation

This is right off NH1 on the right side about 8 km south of the Ben Hai River.

### Cua Tung Beach

#### Transportation

The beach is 8 km on a dirt road to the south of Vinh Moc. If you're headed north, turn right off NH1 exactly 1.2 km north of the Ben Hai River.

### Dakrong Bridge

#### Transportation

Dakrong Bridge is along NH9 13 km east of the Khe Sanh Bus Station.

### Camp Carroll

#### Transportation

To get to Camp Carroll, go about 11–12 km past Cam Lo west on Highway 9 and turn left off NH9 for about 3 km. It's about 25 km east of the Dakrong Bridge and almost 40 km east of the Khe Sanh Bus Station.

### Con Thien Firebase

#### Transportation

Just south of the Ben Hai River, the firebase can be reached from either Cam Lo on Highway 9 or from a turnoff on Highway 1. From Highway 9, Con Thien is about 12 km to the north and 5–6 km from the Truong Son National Cemetery. Con Thien is 7 km east of the Truong Son National Cemetery and 10 km west of NH1. You can reach it by continuing on the road past the cemetery. From the road that connects Cam Lo with the cemetery, you can see the firebase to the east of the road.

### The Rockpile

#### Transportation

To get to The Rockpile, take Highway 9 from Dong Ha for 26 km. The site is off to the right.

### Truong Son National Cemetery

#### Transportation

Thirteen km to the north of Dong Ha, the cemetery is 17 km off of NH1 and 9 km south of the Ben Hai River. A dirt path (only accessible by 4-wheel-drive) connects Cam Lo on Highway 9 with the cemetery. This an 18 km bumpy trip.

## A Luoi

### Transportation

A Luoi is about 60 km west of Hue and about 65 km southeast of the Dakrong Bridge. If you're already in the DMZ, take Highway 9 and go south at the Dakrong Bridge toward the Ashau Valley and Hamburger Hill.

## Lao Bao

### Transportation

Lao Bao is about 80 km from Dong Ha, 150 km from Hue, 18 km west of Khe Sanh and 45 km east of the Lao town of Tchepone along Highway 9, near the Tchepone River marking the Lao border.

## Lang Vay Special Forces Camp

### Transportation

Only 9 km west from the Khe Sanh Bus Station, just off Highway 9 on the southwest side on top of a hill was the Lang Vay Camp. You can also reach it by traveling 7 km toward Khe Sanh from the Lao Bao Market.

## Khe Sanh

### Transportation

The Khe Sanh Bus Station is along Highway 9 less than 1 km from the junction where the northward road veers off toward the former base of Khe Sanh. There is bus service to Hue, Dong Ha, and Lao Bao. Now that the border with Laos is open, the station has become particularly busy and has added new routes in the last year and a half.

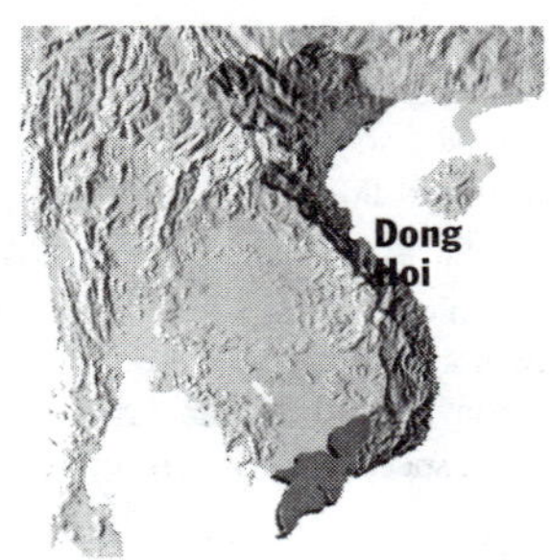


# DONG HOI

## DONG HOI IN A CAPSULE

*The capital of the Quang Binh Province...Inhabitants regularly struggle with the elements, from constant flooding to typhoons...During the Vietnam War, the area was obliterated by the bombing of U.S. war planes...Millions of unexploded devices are still scattered across the area...Some estimates say that a million unexploded bombs have been unearthed since the war...Dong Hoi makes for a good rest stop along NH1.*

Dong Hoi is the capital of the central province of Quang Binh, an area that was obliterated during the Vietnam War due to its proximity to the 17th parallel—the border between South and North Vietnam. Just south of town is the Hien Luong Bridge spanning the Ben Hai River, which split Vietnam in half.

Since the war ended, millions of unexploded bombs and live ordnance have been dug up in the area and, even today inhabitants of the region are inadvertently killed or dismembered by unexploded materiel. The area was also heavily defoliated during the war, and the effects of Agent Orange are probably more in evidence in this region than in any other area of Vietnam, save for the Mekong Delta. Dong Hoi, of anywhere in Vietnam, is one of the best testimonies to the alleged effects of the chemical.

Today, Dong Hoi is a fishing port where numerous significant archeological finds have been made. In the vicinity of Dong Hoi is the Ke Bang Desert, which is the site of perhaps the most extensive and beautiful cave network in the world.

### What to See and Do in Dong Hoi and Environs

**The Ke Bang Desert & The Phong Nha Cave** ★★★★

Ke Bang Desert, which covers more then 10,000 square kilometers from Quang Binh Province in Vietnam to Laos, is the world's largest limestone desert. Geologically evolving over the course of almost three million years, the area has been thinly populated due to harsh living conditions. There are also more than 41,000 hectares of primeval forests where biologists and forestry engineers have discovered rare and threatened species of fauna and flora, such as striped leopards, gayals and 1000-year-old perennial trees.

The people of the region can only reside in the limestone valleys, which are linked with the outside world by tracks clinging on mountains averaging more than 1000 meters in height. Water from rivers and rainstorms is absorbed completely by the limestone, which has created spectacular underground rivers.

The Ke Bang desert really possesses one community, the remote mountainous village of Son Trach, with a population of about 7000. Although only about 50 km from the city of Dong Hoi, the capital Quang Binh Province, and 35 km from the smaller community of Hoan Lao, getting to Son Trach is like getting from Belize to Panama—but around Cape Horn on the tip of South America.

Son Trach's population, an ethnic enclave of Kinh and Arem people, is spread out through the Son Trach Valleys and in the limestone grottos of the Ke Bang Desert. There is so little water during the dry season there is none available for the rice crops, as canals cannot be dug into limestone.

The weather in the Ke Bang Desert is the most unpredictable in Vietnam. It can be hot and sunny one day and cold and rainy the next, regardless of the season.

But the most spectacular elements of the Ke Bang desert are its caves and grottos, a network called Phong Nha. The Phong Nha cave itself is 7729 meters in length. Discoveries of other caves have also been made, such as the 5258-meter-long Toi Cave, Ruc Mon Cave at 2863 meters, Vom Cave at 13,969 meters, Cha Ang Cave at 667 meters, and Ruc Ca Ron Cave at 2800 meters in length. Eventually, scientists expect to find that this circumference of cave networks is the largest and most beautiful in the world. The natural light in Phong Nha gives the cave a cosmic appearance, with its 10-meter high vault ceilings. There are various compartments, some lacking the beautiful natural light found in Phong Nha's first compartment, where water softly drops from the ceilings like from tree leaves after a spring rain. The fourth compartment contains an array of different stalactites, which look like tree trunks made of diamonds. As you move further into the cave it becomes narrower. Conversation should be avoided. Just the resonance of a human voice can cause the frail columns of stalactite to fall from the ceiling.

This is a spectacular place that is essentially unknown to the outside world. After the discovery of a 2 km long cave in Malaysia, the Malaysian government poured huge sums of money into making the cave a tourist attraction. They built roads, and soon 11,000 visitors and scientists visited the site annually, pumping millions of dollars into the local economy. But today, the people of Son Trach remain poor, despite their proximity to one of the world's most magnificent geological sites. To date, there have been but a mere 400-500 visitors to Ke Bang Desert's caves, the majority being geologists. The road to Ke Bang is in dismal condition and there are no plans to improve it. To get out there, take NH1 north to Bo Trach; then head west on the dismal road to Son Trach village. From there, local boats can be hired to go up the Son River to Phong Nha Cave for about US$15 round-trip. The trip to Son Trach takes about three hours, and allow another three or four hours for the round-trip boat ride to the cave.

### Khe Sanh and The Ho Chi Minh Trail

This is a bit of a trip from Dong Hoi, where you'll really want to stop only to see the caves. Travel about 95 km south to Highway 9 toward Laos. Here, you'll be among the most active areas of the Vietnam War. The Ho Chi Minh Trail crosses Route 9. See the Khe Sanh section and the Ho Chi Minh Trail sidebar in the DMZ chapter for more details.

### Beaches

There are a number of sand dunes that line the beaches around Dong Hoi. Kilometers of beach stretch both south and north from the town. The best swimming in the vicinity is **Ly Hoa Beach**. **Nhat Le Beach** lines the mouth of the Nhat Le River.

### Deo Ngang Pass ★

Representing the border between Quang Binh and Ha Tinh Provinces, this is a beautiful pass through the Hoanh Son Mountains which reach from the South China Sea all the way to the Laos border, close to the 18th parallel.

### Cam Xuyen and Ha Tinh

Although these small towns are not really at all in the vicinity of Dong Hoi (Cam Xuyen is about 150 km north of Dong Hoi and Ha Tinh a little farther up the coast), they really aren't worthy of chapters of their own, as they're both essentially attractionless—although a surprising amount of foreigners stay at Cam Xuyen's cheap and only guesthouse.

## Where to Stay in Dong Hoi

The **Hoa Binh Hotel** used to be the only hotel in town allowed to accept foreigners. But also check out **Chuyen Gia**, the **Dong Hoi Hotel** and **Nhat Le Hotel**.

## Directory

### Transportation

Dong Hoi is about 500 km from Hanoi, 200 km from Vinh, 65 km from Hue, 165 km from Hue, and 94 km from Dong Ha. The highway north of Dong Hoi, because it's north of the DMZ, is improving but is not in nearly as good shape as NH1 to the south. There's a ferry crossing 34 km to the north at Cua Gianh. Sometimes it's a long wait.

#### By bus:

Buses from Dong Hoi serve most major coastal provincial capitals, as most buses traveling along NH1 from Saigon to Hanoi or vice versa stop in Dong Hoi.

#### By train:

There are regular connections with Hanoi and Saigon.

### Tourist Offices

The Dong Hoi Tourist Office is located near the Hoa Binh Hotel in the central part of town.

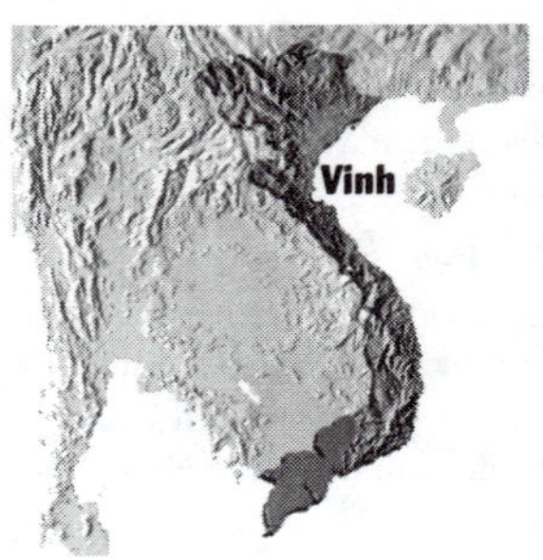


# VINH

## VINH IN A CAPSULE

*Vinh is about halfway between Hue and Hanoi...Perhaps the ugliest city in Vietnam...It is located in one of the poorest provinces in Vietnam...Beggars outnumber the geckos...It was pounded by American shelling during the war and completely destroyed...Rebuilt by the East Germans...Ho Chi Minh was born near here...A good place to exile someone you don't like.*

Annihilated during the Vietnam War by American and South Vietnamese war planes, Vinh is the capital of Nghe Tinh (or Nghe An, depending on who you talk to) Province (one of Vietnam's most populous and poorest provinces) and a major north central Vietnamese industrial and commerce center. Despite its economic importance, because of the climate, its people are the poorest in Vietnam.

The town had the unfortunate geographical position of being located on a narrow coastal plain, where roads and railways were required to pass through. The city was rebuilt by the East Germans after the war and, consequently, Vinh has the distinction of being perhaps the ugliest city in Vietnam. There's little, if anything, of note in the city to see and do. Its only real attractions are the hotel beds to break up the road journey between Hue and Hanoi.

Its weather could use some improvement—hot as hell in the summer and cold and rainy in the winter. But it's under gray skies much of the year. The area is under the constant threat of flooding and typhoons.

But west of Vinh lie thickly forested mountains inhabited by tribespeople and wild creatures alike. The Muong people live here, as well as the Tai, Meo, Khmer and Tho ethnic groups. The jungles are roamed by elephants, tigers, leopards, deer, rhinoceros, gibbons and other monkeys, giant bats and flying squirrels.

Because Vinh is about halfway between Hanoi and Hue, hotel and eatery owners prosper here, but they're about the only ones in the province who do.

The area is known for its insurgent spirit. The Ho Chi Minh Trail was started in this province and Uncle Ho himself was a native of Nghe An province. There were uprisings against the French led by the population here, and communists in the area (members of the Indochinese Communist Party) in the early 1930s staged uprisings and workers' strikes. These uprisings were generally successfully resisted by the French, utilizing fighter planes to disperse unruly demonstrators.

U.S. bombers and warships off the coast obliterated the area between 1964–1972. It is said that fewer than five buildings remained standing here after the Americans left Vietnam in 1973 (some say only two structures were left intact). But this was also the area where the greatest amount of American warplanes were downed in North Vietnam, and naval pilots killed or captured.

Vinh (population about 200,000) is located about 15 km from the coast.

## What to See and Do in Vinh and Environs

### Chua and Sen Villages

The small village of Chua, about 14 km northwest of Vinh, was where Ho Chi Minh was born in 1890. The house is now a sacred shrine, but visitors are welcome. There's a small and unimpressive museum, given the historical significance of this place, close by. Sen village, which is close to Chua, is where Uncle Ho lived starting at the age of six with his highly-educated father. Ho was actually born to relatively wealthy parents; his neighbors were dismally poor. Although Ho's house itself is nothing more than a crude, thatched shack, it was considered upscale for the area.

### Cua Lo Beach

This beach, located about 20 km from Vinh, isn't bad. It's clean and rarely visited, perhaps because the weather here is cold and windy most of the time. There's a modest hotel located here.

### Vinh Central Market

*At the end of Cao Thang Street.*

Despite the amount of people who live here, there is surprisingly little offered, although, like most city markets in Vietnam, it is a bustling, colorful place.

### Restoration Project Clinic

*Nguyen Phong Sac Street near the Children's Hospital.*

A group of California-based war veterans and humanitarians built this structure as a hospital and physical therapy center in 1989. They worked in conjunction with Vietnamese war vets, as well. Nothing of any real interest here. The Nghe Tinh Children's Hospital is also on these grounds.

**Anti-Aircraft Guns**

*Le Hong Phong Street.*

These giant guns are still active and pointed to the sky to fend off an air attack, by whom, I couldn't imagine. Perhaps the Belize Air Force.

**Worker's Cultural Complex**

*Le Mao and Dinh Cong Trang Streets.*

This is Vinh's "community center," a big structure that features a movie and performance theater as well as a dance hall.

## Where to Stay in Vinh

**Vinh Railway Station Hotel** **US$6**

*Le Ninh Street.*

This is right next to the railway station as you might guess it would be. It's a little run down but it's cheap and popular with backpackers.

**Hotel Kim Lien** **US$25–$35** ★

*Quang Trung Street in the middle of town.*

This is the biggest hotel in Vinh and the only one you might cautiously refer to as being up to "international standards." There's hot water, fairly large rooms, air conditioning, restaurant, massage, moneychanging, private bath and a travel agency downstairs. This is the best place in town to rest on the road between Hue and Hanoi.

**Xi Nghiep Dich Vu Hotel** **US$6**

*Le Loi Street near the corner of Nguyen Si Sach Street, east of the railway station.*

The cheapest accommodations in Vinh and popular with backpackers. Don't expect much here but a hard mattress to put your head on.

**Hotel Huu Nghi** **US$20–$25** ★

*Le Loi Street.*

This, like the Kim Lien Hotel, is a decent place for Vinh. The price tag will get you air conditioning, attached bath, restaurant and hot water. Also recommended if you're staying in Vinh.

**Chuyen Gia Giao Te Hotel** **About US$15–$45**

*Thanh Ho Street.* ☎ *4175.*

Vastly overpriced, rather ugly hotel. Air conditioning, attached bath, hot water, restaurant. I'd stay somewhere else in this price range.

**Ben Thuy Hotel** **US$8**

*Nguyen Du Street, just a kilometer from the Lam River toward the middle of Vinh.* ☎ *4892.*

This is another popular place with backpackers, although it's a hike from the train station. No air conditioning, but it does have a small, decent restaurant.

## Where to Eat in Vinh

The best place to eat in town is at the restaurant at the **Hotel Kim Lien**, or perhaps the restaurant at the **Hotel Huu Nghi**. But it's less expensive and equally as filling to eat at one of the many restaurants and food stalls at the Vinh Central Market or near the Railway Station, which has a slew of eateries with dirt-cheap prices.

## Directory

### Transportation

Vinh is about 291 km from Hanoi, 365 km from Hue, 197 km from Dong Hoi, 470 km from Danang, 98 km from the Laos border, and 140 km from Thanh Hoa.

**By air:**

VN flies to Vinh from HCMC Mondays and Fridays at 11:50 a.m. You have to change planes in Danang; the total journey is about 4-1/2 hours. From Vinh to HCMC, flights depart at 12:10 p.m. on Mondays and Fridays, with a change of planes in Danang. The total journey time is about 5-1/2 hours.

**By bus:**

The bus station is on Le Loi Street north of the Central Market by about 1 km. There are express buses that depart for Hanoi, HCMC, Danang and Buon Ma Thuot early in the morning around 5 a.m. There are also express buses that leave for Hanoi at other times of the day as well. Ask at the ticket office (you'd be wise to purchase your tickets in advance). Non-express buses depart for Hanoi, Pleiku, Ba Hai, Ky Anh, Huong Son, Lat, Cau Giat, Hue, Hoa Binh, Yen Thanh, Que Phong, Nghia Dan, Do Luong, Phuc Son and Dung, as well as other destinations.

**By train:**

The Vinh Railway Station is located about 3 km west of the Central Market about 1 km from the intersection of Le Loi and Phan Boi Chau Streets. The Reunification Express stops here. It's about an 8-hour trip to Hanoi, and 35-40 hours to HCMC.

### Post Office

*Nguyen Thi Minh Khai Street, about 280 meters northwest of Dinh Cong Trang Street.* Hours are from 6:30 a.m. to 9 p.m. International and domestic calls and faxes can be made from another office across from the Workers' Cultural Complex (Cong Ty Dien Bao DienThoai) on Dinh Cong Trang Street close to the intersection of Nguyen Thi Minh Khai Street.

### Banks and Moneychangers

Vietcom Bank, *at the corner of Le Loi and Nguyen Si Sach Streets*, can provide advances on American issued credit cards.

### Tourist Office

Vinh Tourist Office. *Quang Trung Street.* ☎ *4629.* The travel agency in the Hotel Kim Lien can book airline flights.

### Hospital

General Hospital. *Le Mao and Tran Phu Streets.*

# NORTH OF VINH

The northern central region of Vietnam contains only one highway, National Highway 1 along the coast. From Vinh to Than Hoa, the road runs at many points right along the coast of the South China Sea through tiny, nondescript villages and towns that offer virtually no amenities to travelers save for a sparse number of roadside cafes and restaurants. The northern provinces in this area are the poorest in Vietnam—the soil isn't good for cultivation and the region experiences havoc with the ravages of flooding and seasonal typhoons. The villagers exist on only a marginal subsistence.

The people of this region did not share in the prosperity the Americans brought to the southern half of the country during the Vietnam War. There is little for the independent traveler to do and see between the 140 km that separate Vinh and Thanh Hoa. By the time you've reached this point, you'll probably have little interest in stopping and exploring these small hamlets.

Some will tell you that the people of north-central Vietnam are not as warm to foreigners (especially Americans) as those in the south. While I do not find this to be entirely correct—indeed, smiles were everywhere—there is more reserve on the part of the people of this region, as they rarely see foreigners. But even the North Vietnamese bear little animosity toward Americans and are generally quite friendly. Keep in mind that very little English is spoken in this area, and that you should carry dong rather than dollars if stopping in small hamlets and towns along NH1. There are few if any places that will change money for you.

## Thanh Hoa

Thanh Hoa is the capital of Thanh Hoa Province (which was the site of the Lam Son Uprising between 1418–1428) and the northernmost point in north-central Vietnam. The 160-meter bridge that spans the Ma River south of Thanh Hoa (Ham Rong Bridge, or "Dragon's Jaw) was an important North Vietnamese military link moving south and was bombed repeatedly by U.S. warplanes during the war. In fact, all around Thanh Hoa are craters left by the bombs of American planes. The North Vietnamese heavily fortified the bridge and the U.S. lost as many as 70 planes during raids on the bridge in the mid-1960s. Finally, in 1972, they were able to take out the bridge using laser-guided bombs, but the NVA quickly erected a pontoon bridge to replace it. There is a big church on the north side of town, the Citadel of Ho, which was built in 1397 when this town was the capital of Vietnam. In Thuan Hoa, you can stay at the Tourist Hotel, at *21A Quang Trung Street* (☎ *298*); the 25B and 25A Hotels along NH1, or the Thanh Hoa Hotel on the west side of NH1 in the middle of town. Rooms are in the US$6–10 range. Near the southern edge of town are a slew of cheap restaurants and cafes. The Reunification Express train does stop here, linking

Thanh Hoa with the rest of the Vietnamese coast. Buses link the provincial capital with a number of coastal towns, including Vinh (140 km), Hue (500 km), and Hanoi (153 km). There are two decent beaches in the area called the Sam Son Beaches, about 15 km southeast of Thanh Hoa. They are mainly frequented by monied Hanoi residents to escape the summer heat. But keep in mind that the weather here is usually cool and damp, and the northerly winds can make a trip to the beaches quite cold. There are some cheap hotels and bungalows here. You can also see the remains of fortifications built here by the NVA to protect the Ham Rong Bridge.

## Ninh Binh

This is the capital of Ninh Binh province on the Day River, about 60 km north of Thanh Hoa. There is little here for the tourist, and it serves as not much more than an overnight spot. It is linked to other coastal communities by both rail and bus service. Perhaps the best reason to come to this region, other than just passing through, is to make the short 10-km trip to the ancient capital of Vietnam in the Truong Son Mountains called **Hoa Lu**. Hoa Lu was built as the new capital of Vietnam in AD 968 and remained so until AD 1010. This was the time of the Dinh and early Le Dynasties. It was selected for its location: in a narrow valley surrounded by limestone mountains with paths that were easily defendable against Chinese invaders. Some say it is like Ha Long Bay without the bay. There are still the remnants of ancient temples in Hoa Lu. Elephants and horses were carved into the stonework.

Although today there is little to see here, this was once an area covering 200 hectares that was dotted with temples and shrines. Hoa Lu was the birthplace of Dinh Bo Linh, the founder of the Dinh Dynasty. There are ruins of the ancient royal citadel here that once covered three square kilometers, and the Dinh Tien Hoang royal temple of the Dinh kings. Inscribed on the pillar in the central temple are the words *Dai Co Viet*, which the name Vietnam was derived from. Inside this temple are statues of Dinh and his sons.

The Vault of Dinh is at the base of Mount Yen. During the 960s, Dinh Bo Linh was able to pacify the area, and even the warring Ngos accepted his dominance of the region. But Dinh Bo Linh's kingdom was wracked with insubordination. He placed a tiger in the center courtyard and announced that anyone who violates his rule will be "boiled and gnawed." But rather than make his oldest blood son, Dinh Lien, the heir to the throne, he chose instead his younger son, Hang Lang. Trouble then dogged the king. Legend says that violent climactic events occurred, and, in 979, Lien ordered an assassin to kill Hang Lang. Just a few months later, a court official named Do Thich murdered both Dinh Bo Linh and Dinh Lien as they lay sleeping in a drunken stupor. Do Thich was caught for his crime, and it's said he was executed and his body fed to the people. Hoa Lu is at the southern edge of the Red River Delta in Truong Yen village. You'll have to take a car from either Hanoi or Ninh Binh to get here.

Near Ninh Binh you can also visit **Bich Dong Pagoda**, a three-hour boat ride on a tributary of the Hoang Long River. Getting there by car is much quicker. The boat ride offers magnificent scenery of limestone caves and surrounding mountains. After getting to the pagoda's landing, there's about a 20 minute walk to reach the pagoda. Also visit **Binh Cach**, 20 km to the north of Ninh Binh. Here are the remains of the citadels of **Bo Co** and **Co Long**. The Chinese army was crushed here by General Tran Gian Dinh in 1408. You can also visit the remains of the **Van Phong Citadel** deep in the nearby Ngo Xa Mountains. The small village of Van Lam possesses the **Bich Dong Grottoes**. They can be reached by boat from Hoa Lu or Binh Dinh. The grottoes have been around since the 10th century, and they were used as hideouts during the First Indochina War by the Viet Minh.

**Ke So** is 34 km northwest of Binh Dinh on the Song Day River. There is a big cathedral here built between 1879 and 1884 by the French monsignor Puginier. **Nam Trang** (35 km north of Ninh Binh) is where Black Flag rebel leader Dinh Kong Trang was born. **Phat Diem** (30 km southeast of Ninh Binh) was a major Catholic center during the French colonial era. The cathedral built here was built of marble, granite and wood. It stands 16 meters high and is 80 meters long. There is also the nearby **Thuan-Dao Church** (built in 1926) which is a strange looking structure. Monsignor Nguyen Ba Tong in Phat Diem was pronounced the first Vietnamese Bishop by the Vatican in 1930. Places to stay in Ninh Binh include the **Hoa Lu Hotel** (about US$15) on the west side of NH1 and the **Ninh Binh Hotel,** also on the west side of NH1 (about US$10). Ninh Binh is a scheduled stop on the Reunification Express train route. Ninh Binh is about 115 km south of Hanoi, 200 km north of Vinh and 60 km north of Thanh Hoa.

## Nam Dinh

Nam Dinh (population about 250,000) is a smoky, ugly gray industrial city about 90 km south of Hanoi. The city is primarily known for its textiles (and lack of tourists). The French built the **Nam Dinh Textile Mill** here in 1899 and it's still up and running. Western missionaries arrived here as early as 1627. Nam Dinh is considered to be the third largest industrial area in the north. There was a giant square citadel here, built in 1804, that faces southeast toward the sea, that was eventually destroyed by the French in 1891 (only the watchtower is marginally intact) after they seized the city in 1882.

Nam Dinh, which was continually attacked by the Chams during the Champa Empire, was designed as sort of a mini-Hanoi, where quarters were built to house areas of tradesmen and craftsmen. For instance, there was a section for cobblers, another for blacksmiths, one for embroiderers, another for goldsmiths, one for coffin makers, and so on. Some of the "sights" of Nam Dinh are outside the city itself, much of them areas of historical rather than architectural interest, as many of the ancient structures have been ruined. **My Loc**, about 2 km north of the city, is where the Tran Dynasty began and was the birthplace of Tran Bich San. All inhabitants of the city were forced to adopt the name Tran to their own names. **Tuc Mac** is 3 km north of the city. Tu Mac's **Den Thien-Truong** (Royal Temple) was built here. Of its many buildings, one, the **Tran Mieu**, was built in 1239. **Den Co Trach** was constructed in 1895, and was a temple dedicated to Tran Hung Dao. **Pho Minh Thu** was the stupa for King Tran Nhan Ton, who ruled the area in the 13th century. It's a 14-story tower built in the early 14th century that was demolished by the Mings and rebuilt in the 15th century. Subsequent restorations took place in the 17th and 18th centuries.

Fifteen km northwest of Nam Dinh is **Yen Do**, where Nguyen Khuyen was born. **Ky Lan Son (The Mountain of the Unicorn)** was home to Le Hoan, who founded the Early Le Dynasty and was its ruler from 980-1005. He was crowned "The King Who Pacified the South" in 981 after driving back an attacking Chinese force. There were also numerous battles with the Chams during his reign. **Chua Dien Linh**, **Doi Son**, and **Doi Dep Pagodas** were built in the 12th century on the hills 46 km northwest of Nam Dinh in Hung Yen Valley. **Phu Giay** is a temple dedicated to the immortal Lieu Hanh about 17 km south of Nam Dinh. Lieu Hanh was the daughter of the Heavenly Emperor, who returned to Earth after he died to make amends for a goblet he broke during a festival. A pilgrimage still arrives here each year on the third day of the third lunar month to celebrate the Pure Light Festival (or the Festival of the Dead, *Thanh Minh*). You might also want to visit the nearby villages of **Dong Dai** (10 km from Nam Dinh), where stands the Phoc Lam Pagoda and stupas of Hung Thien and Hoang Hai; **Van Diem** (20 km north of Nam Dinh) where there is an ancient citadel, and **Doc Bo** (27 km southeast of Nam Dinh), that has a pagoda dedicated to Trieu Viet Vuong, a general who declared himself king of Vietnam in AD 549. In Nam Dinh, you can stay at **Vi Hoang Hotel** *(115 Nguyen Du Street. ☎ 439262)*. The post office is on Ha Huy Tap Street. Ninh Binh Tourist is at the Vi Hoang Hotel.

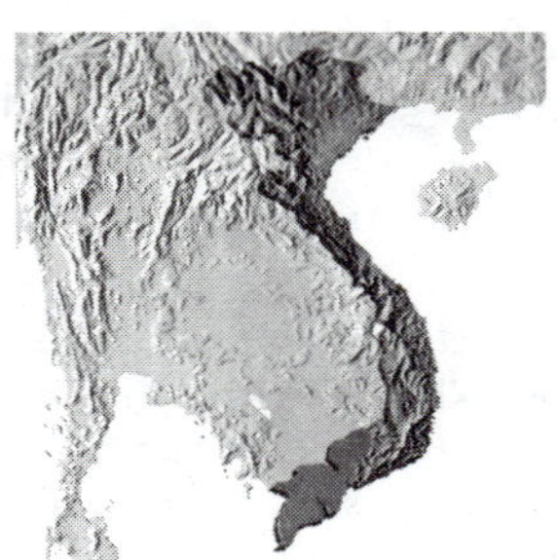

# HANOI & THE NORTH

*Lonely fishing vessels idle on the shores of the Gulf of Tonkin.*

As the border between Vietnam in the north and China becomes increasingly open, a burgeoning amount of travel between the two countries has begun. It has also opened the routes for smugglers. In Lang Son province, which was opened up in January 1994, one can see swarms of Asian travelers carrying on their backs sometimes many times the weight of their bodies. **Dong Dang** has become something of a boom town, and one can see the prosperity in this once shanty town as imported tires, fruit, beer and other consumer items are now offered for sale, lining the streets like a gauntlet of entrepreneurialism. As you head south, you'll notice the rapid construction of multistoried brick and tile buildings as this newly-found prosperity heads south. However, a large degree of this southward-bound caravan of consumer goods has been smuggled into the country or been allowed in through bribery. Be cautious in this region. If you're asked by any traveler to help carry goods that appear too burdensome to the carrier, don't be overcome by your sympathies. Carry only your own belongings on both sides of the border.

The beautiful northern Vietnam region of **Son La** province is getting the gears in motion for tourism. To bolster the local economy, the province has been divided into three separate regions. The first, along Highway 6, will be allocated to developing mulberry silk production, coffee and fruit trees. Son La has installed 4000 mini hydroelectric plants to provide power for lighting and agriculture. The telecommunications network is now in synch with the national grid. Tourism is on the rise in the province, mainly because of the magnificent beauty of the surrounding mountains. To date, though, the roads reaching the province from all areas in the north are in dismal shape, though the views from the rutted path are spectacular.

Road travelers in Vietnam may soon have an easier selection of routes to take to both urban and rural destinations in the north—a four-lane highway linking Bac Ninh (30 km to the north of Hanoi) and Mong Cai, near the Chinese border. As part of the economic triangle that includes Hanoi, Haiphong, and Quang Ninh, the 314-km route is a government infrastructure priority. Additionally, there will also be bridges constructed at Pha Lai (260 meters) and Bai Chay (800 meters), which will replace the present ferries. As well, a new highway has been built from Bac Ninh town to Hanoi's Noi Bai International Airport.The road projects are important as they will connect the Cai Lan port, which is currently under construction in Haiphong with Hanoi and with the Chinese border crossing at Mong Cai.

## Road Wearier: Hanoi to Mong Cai the Hard Way—On Two Wheels

Not a lot of Western tourists have heard of Mong Cai, much less been there. The beaten track in Vietnam's northeast ends at Ha Long, where, after having endured a "grueling" six-hour ride in an air-conditioned microbus, most tourists lather up in the hot showers of the Bai Chay's sprouting caravansaries, wine and dine in relative splendor in the cozy cafes along Bai Chay Street (Ha Long Road) and—the following day—head out in one of the dozens of tourist boats that ply the bay and serpentine through the thousands of rugged grottoes that poke from the sea like the scales of an enormous dragon, which, of course, is what Ha Long Bay is named after.

Sitting under the shade of Carlsberg umbrellas, sipping banana milk shakes, nibbling on prawns and eel prepared by a Paris-trained chef and watching the camcorder-toting middle-aged tourists strolling along the beachside promenade with their bored children, one feels about as adventurous as an accountant moonlighting as a Little League umpire.

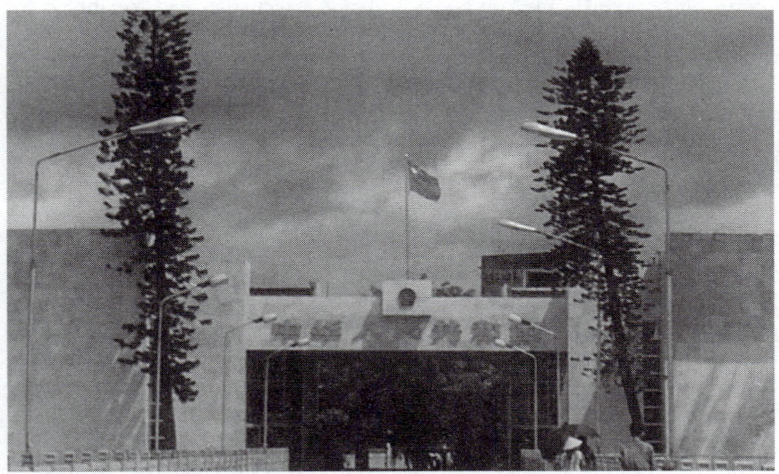

***Chinese border crossing (the Friendship Bridge) at Mong Cai.***

That is what Ha Long Bay has become in just a very, very short time—a natural wonder that's becoming virtually as accessible as Disneyland is to residents of Anaheim. (Yet it may take a few years before pony rides and those quacky duck-shaped paddle boats make their debut here.)

Three years ago, I would not have looked out of place in Ha Long Bay, my tattered attire and exposed skin having become one with the coal-muddied, rutted roads and paths of Cam Pha, Khe Lang, Ha Tu and Dam Ha—much like the locals look themselves.

Instead, tourists in Levis Dockers shorts and "Saigon Vietnam" T-shirts gazed at me in bewilderment as they passed by my cafe table, as I wolfed down my beef noodle soup and a liter of Tiger Beer. Never mind that it was only 9:30 in the morning—I had been on the "road" (actually a congealing tar and granite path sliced frequently by Mother Nature's and Newton's own "above the law" highways) from Tien Yen since 4 a.m. and it seemed to me to be a perfectly reasonable time to ferment and numb the throbbing of my backside and to forget that my soggy feet more resembled a fisherman's catch than a couple of appendages to bipedal on.

My rip-off Reebok rain suit was in shreds; my French army boots like a sea sponge. Photo prints that I had earlier taken and developed in Mong Cai and the border with China's Dong Hung and had inadvertently stashed in my photog's vest had become a slimy, gloss-dripping brick. The Khmer scarf wrapped around my head had become a checkerboard second skin. My motorcycle seemed sculpted from mud. Earlier, it had broken down during a monsoon between Cam Pha and Khe Lang. Mechanics had squabbled for hours over the ignition problem, none coming up with an answer—but at least trying after I said I was Canadian, not American. (After telling a 10-year-old postcard hawker earlier in Hanoi that I was an American, he spat on me and told me that his father kills Americans. I thought it wise to subsequently don a maple leaf and say "eh" a lot while in the north of Vietnam.)

So the tourists gawked at a road-weary, soiled traveler in a place where only a few short years ago, all those who made it here were road-weary and soiled.

### Runway 5

The 100 kilometers on Route 5 between Hanoi and Haiphong are some of the most dangerous in Vietnam. The road is in good enough shape—the pavement smooth and wide. And that perhaps explains its dangers. The more convenient something in Vietnam becomes, the more dangerous the Vietnamese make it. Other rutted, pot-holed thoroughfares in Vietnam work under the same principle as speed bumps in the parking lot of the Federal Building in Hartford—they slow people down. But give the Vietnamese an inch and they'll take a mile—rather quickly, too. As the road to Haiphong is like a 100-km long airport runway, Vietnamese drivers naturally assume that if a Boeing 767 needs to be hurtling along at 170 m.p.h. to reach lift-off speed, their own Toyotas need to be traveling at lift-off speed to reach Haiphong. But an aircraft enjoys the luxury of not having to concern itself with oncoming traffic as it makes its way for the sky. Compound this mechanized anarchy with the throngs of bicyclists and pedestrians and it's no wonder to see people lying dead in the road every 40 klicks. Highway 5 is the ultimate game of chicken. On a motorcycle, it's totally nuts.

But I wouldn't have it any other way.

On one stretch of Route 5, the railroad shares the same bridge with automobiles, although they both can't use it at the same time. Cars queue to take turns crossing the 500 meter span. A motorcycle can use the pedestrian crossing and avoid the wait.

**INSIDER TIP**

*A new stretch of national Route 5 is being constructed through Hai Duong Town. The road has only a distance of 15 km, but it's still 15 km of less dilapidated roadways that are the main infrastructure blight of Vietnam. There will be six traffic lanes, and the road will run over three bridges, in Dong Nieu, Phu Luong and Lai Vu.*

Accidents along this stretch of roadway invariably lead to fisticuffs between the drivers. In Vietnam, there is no car insurance. In Vietnam, a claims adjuster is the man with a stronger right jab.

At Haiphong, after crossing over the first bridge—the river flanked by old French colonial apartment houses, some still partially razed from the B-52 bombings of Haiphong during the Vietnam War—one makes a left to get to the harbor ferry crossing. A few klicks on the other side of the crossing on the road to Hong Gai, I was flagged down by a team of policemen on the roadside. No words were spoken. One policemen simply wrote on an envelope, "40 USD." He nodded at a tiny dent in my gas tank. No check of my passport, visa, nor motorcycle registration. He just wanted 40 bucks because he was quite certain I possessed it. My only traffic infraction was that my net worth was greater than his own. I told him in English that I was indeed rich, but that my capital was liquid, tied up in Microsoft, Pepsi and Barings stocks. He nearly wept over my plight and settled for 100,000 dong. I was on my way.

After another river ferry crossing 10 or 15 km later, and a relatively stable ride for the next 50 km, I was in Bai Chay.

I did the tourist thing, hired a boat, saw the stalagmite caves. The next day it was off to Mong Cai and the far northeastern tip of Vietnam, about 180 km away. The road becomes rutted and grimy as it passes through the coal towns of Cam Pha and Khe Lang. But the last 90 km from Tien Yen to Mong Cai are a motorcyclist's paradise. The smooth road curves and winds its way through rolling tea plantations.Tiny villages dot the roadside every 15 klicks or so. I stopped frequently to photograph Meo hilltribe people. I came across a couple of young men who had killed a large dog and were pulling the hair from its flesh. It would be dinner—or a few. They invited me to the feast. I couldn't do it, thinking of all the unfetched newspapers that would end up in the guy's driveway in about a week.

Occasionally, groups of soldiers wandered in the desolate, jungle-shrouded roadway, apparently going nowhere, and apparently having come from nowhere. Intermittently, the Gulf of Tonkin could be seen shimmering in the distance to the east.

Near Mong Cai, I was stopped again by the police. But this group was far friendlier than the posse that had bilked me near Haiphong. After a simple inspection of my passport, I was permitted to go on.

## The Road Stops Here

Mong Cai is a typical border town and surprisingly large—although it doesn't seem quite as prosperous as Dong Hung, a Free Economic Zone on the Chinese side of the river across from the Vietnamese frontier. The streets of Mong Cai are flanked by an endless gauntlet of gutter-side produce and fruit vendors. Some display their wares in the middle of the streets, not satisfied with the relative anonymity of the sidewalk sellers. There are few foreigners in Mong Cai—a scant trickle of travelers bother to make the journey up here. Because there is no real reason to unless you intend to cross the border into China—or truly want to experience the north of Vietnam. I saw one other foreigner—a British woman—an English teacher from Cao Bang who was on "holiday" with her Vietnamese boyfriend, a man half her height and weight. When they held hands, she seemed to be teaching him to walk.

*Vietnamese smugglers and traders unload their wares in Dong Hung, China.*

## The Border

My goal, of course, was to find a way of getting into China without a visa. I headed for the border gate at 8 p.m. Only a short 50-meter bridge separates the two countries. The Chinese military had occupied the area as well as Lang Son to the northwest during a brief border invasion in 1979. I could clearly see the Chinese border guards playing cards—even spotting the grimace on the face of the officer who was winning. If there had once been tension here between the two communist countries, you'd never know it. The trade between the two cities today is bustling.

The crossing had closed at 4:30. At the Vietnamese gate, I was intercepted by the political officer and an English-speaking immigration captain. Without a visa, they would not let me pass. I had been told earlier in Bai Chay by some residents not to initiate a bribe at this particular border crossing. If they were amenable to my passing, they would bring the subject up themselves.

They didn't.

The next day I tried again and was given the same answer: Vietnamese without a passport are permitted to enter Dong Hung for 24 hours to conduct business. They are issued a small booklet which is stamped. But it was absolutely forbidden for a foreigner without a Chinese visa to enter China. They said it was for my safety. Sure, I could get over there, the officers said—but the Chinese might not let me back.

"Then let me take my chances," I said.

"It's not the trouble *you'll* get into we're worried about," the English-speaking officer replied. Point taken.

Later, a Vietnamese woman told me there was another crossing, but that it was an illegal one used by smugglers a kilometer farther up the river. She took me there. Although this was an "illegal" crossing, it was (perhaps unsurprisingly) manned by Vietnamese police. And I could indeed see why it was illegal. Baskets full of endangered pangolins were being hoisted on a flimsy canoe by Vietnamese smugglers, as well as crates of snakes and other goods whose identity I could only imagine. Again, as the covert frontier post was being supervised by police, I was forbidden from crossing. The Vietnamese were paying the police about 20,000 dong for the "ferry" ride. I was told impolitely to go away—and did.

Later that night, at my hotel room, I was paid an unexpected visit by the English woman, her diminutive Vietnamese boyfriend and another Vietnamese man, who explained that he could get me across the river, but that it would take two days to make the preparations—time that I didn't have, and people I didn't have time for.

## Lost In Faith

I rode 13 kilometers out of town to the beach at Tra Co and then headed north, to where I thought another less conspicuous and more remote crossing could be found. What I found instead was a group of Vietnamese hoeing dirt and digging plant roots from the base of a massive but gutted stone Catholic church in the middle of nowhere, just a few dozen meters from the deserted beach. Young boys and girls as well as old men and women toiled in the searing sun, Christian crosses dangling from their necks. I was told the church had been built by the French in 1914 (others said 1926). A raisin-skinned old man said the North Vietnamese had started tearing the church down during the American War in 1964 to use its stone and wood in the war effort. The Chinese then further ravaged the site during their 1979 invasion and made off with the tower's large iron bell, which they later generously returned at the request of the Bishop of Haiphong.

"We dig and dig and build," the old man said. "No one is paid to do this. We do it for the love of God. But we need money and help. No one knows about us. We are alone. Very alone."

*The Tra Co Cathedral was built in 1914 and gutted by generations of war. The tower, at 45 meters, is about all that is left of the church.*

Indeed, the cathedral is nothing more than a roofless granite shell, it's intricately carved bas relief tower rising 45 meters above the flat, alluvial plain, dominating the landscape for miles. From many kilometers afar, the structure looks like Oz at the end of the yellow brick road. The few Catholics who live here are indeed alone and very poor, bonded by their outcast faith. They work each day reconstructing the church and celebrate mass without a priest in a tiny shed alongside the cathedral. A small wooden cross nailed to the top of the thatched roof lists with the winds from the sea.

The Bishop of Haiphong travels to this remote area "once a month, or maybe once every few months" to celebrate mass, the old man said. In the meantime, they worship Christ in silence in a dilapidated hootch, waiting for someone to help. I was told these people see foreigners as frequently as they do the Bishop of Haiphong.

(To get here, take the road east out of Mong Cai about 5 km and make a left toward the beach at Tra Co. It's the only left—if you've gone as far as the dirt road, you've gone too far. At Tra Co follow the beach road north another 3-4 km. The church is on the left. You can't miss it. The total journey is about 17 km from Mong Cai.)

## A River Runs Over It

The journey back to Hanoi was far more problematic than reaching Mong Cai. Monsoons had swollen the rivers, making the 10 bridges between Mong Cai and Tien Yen impassable. At the first bridge (considered the easiest to pass of the 10 during the monsoons), less than 10 klicks out of town, a mile-long queue of trucks, motorcycles and automobiles waited eight hours for the river to ebb low enough to cross. Young men, charging 20,000 dong a pop to the rider, carried the smaller motorbikes across the torrent using large wooden poles inserted through the wheels (like porters carrying an ancient king), battling the pull of the rushing current like tightrope walkers. My bike was too big and too packed down and gear-laden to be hauled in such a fashion, so I decided to chance a crossing when it was far too dangerous to do so. I had only two options—and neither was particularly attractive: return to Mong Cai and wait out the floods, which might take days, or make a dangerous first-gear crossing in a raging niagara up to my waist, which if I accomplished, might leave me stranded between the first bridge and the even more dangerous crossing 15 km farther—without a town between. I took the precaution of storing up on a couple of day's worth of food and water in anticipation of such a circumstance and barreled through the 90-meter spate. It felt like being terminally caught in the chicane at Willow Springs, but I managed; miraculously the plugs didn't fail. If they had, I would have certainly been washed down river.

It was the same scene at the next crossing. But this was of a much greater distance and the flood waters far higher. Vehicles heading north to Mong Cai stranded on the far side numbered more than 130. The bridge had been closed 12 hours.

I waited two before daring a repeat attempt. Again, success.

## Night Crossing

No such luck at Tien Yen. A 300-meter crossing this time, the river raging over the bridge chest-high. Hours passed. I drank beer with the local cops and lamented to them how damn cold Canada gets in the winter. They laughed and we drank more. They said I should move to Los Angeles. We smoked tobacco in giant bamboo bongs. With the scarf wrapped over my head, one of the cops thought I wasn't Canadian at all, but rather Palestinian, and asked if I knew Yassir Arafat. "Sure, I'm his barber," I said. The cop didn't get it.

Dusk now. Again, the same decision. Cross the rage and reach the only hotel in Tien Yen permitted for foreigners—or sleep on the road next to my bike and the curious cops, and say something silly in my slumber like "I wish I was back in L.A.," or "I think I *will* vote for Robert Dole!"

A night crossing. Perhaps 300 meters. I had just enough of the local suds in my veins to try it. I wasn't the first. I saw a man aboard an old Russian Minsk motorcycle, a giant pig strapped pillion, rip through the roaring current. He was shrouded by the river, engulfed by the rush; the only sight was the white exhaust spewing from the tailpipe into his wake. The squealing of the sow was only a decibel higher than the thunder of the river. Then it, too, became swallowed by the holler of the monster rapids.

I wasn't sure he had made it until I heard cheers from the other side. Hell, if this guy could barge a cheap Russian motorcycle and a 500-lb. hog through Victoria Falls then I could certainly duplicate the feat on an equally cheap Korean motorcycle and a 7-lb. laptop computer.

The bridge, although it couldn't be seen beneath the surging rapids, was straight. If I could just keep the bike upright without steering...

It was like surfing Half Moon Bay under a half moon. My arms struggled to keep the handlebars straight. I actually steered the motorcycle with my feet—not on the ground, but like a tiller on a boat. The water was gushing from right to left. As I was forced left to the abyss, I compensated by dragging my right thigh and calf against the rear wheel, creating more resistance against the tail end of the machine by permitting less water through the rear spokes.

It worked, and I arrived to the other side to even greater applause than the pig received—probably because I was a crazy American...er, Canadian. There's something to be said about being a foreigner in northern Vietnam and getting a bigger hand than a hog.

## Somewhere in the World it's Cocktail Hour

I woke up at 4 a.m. My clothes were still wet. Everything was wet. My ignition and electrical systems failed near Cam Pha two hours later. I had to keep the bike running the final 40 km to Hong Gai over muddy, rutted roads—or risk not getting it started again if the engine cut.

Soaked, muddy and exhausted—yeah, I had a beer at 9:30 in the morning when I got to Ha Long. I had three of them. With jetsetting tourists in spiffy new topsiders sipping mineral water at sidewalk cafes while their guides and tour group leaders bargained for tour boats, I may as well have been in Fort Lauderdale.

Or an accountant umping a Little League game.

**Doing it:**

Unlike in Saigon, it's virtually impossible to rent a bike over 125cc in Hanoi. The authorities are much tighter up here about this, while it is relatively easy to find a larger machine for rent in HCMC. The Vietnamese are not permitted to operate anything larger than 125cc, unless under "special circumstances." Besides, riding a higher-cc machine will only draw more police attention to yourself. I consider myself lucky to have paid only one cop's night out on the town. It easily could have been three or four places where roadside dragnets might have pointed at the nick on my gas tank and demanded BGI money for a month. There are only about 10 places in Hanoi that rent motorcycles to foreigners, and they're hard to find. Machines capable of extended journeys out of Hanoi are even rarer. Best bet is to head on over to the **Memory Cafe (33 Bis)**, *33 Tran Hung Dao Street, Hanoi (☎ 265854)* and have a chat with Nguyen Viet Trung and his stepdaughter, Ha Minh Chau, who will take care of the translation. Great folks. You'll most likely end up on a Bonus 125cc for between US$10–12 a day, depending on how long you take it for. If you can get a Honda out of them, you're in better shape, as many mechanics in the boonies (and believe me, you *will* be in the boonies) have never seen the South Korean-made Bonus machines before. Bring extra spark plugs and a tool kit. Check out the bike carefully. Particularly, check the tires and listen for a valve tap in the cylinder head(s). For a full description of preparing for a motorcycle journey in Vietnam, pick up a copy of *Fielding's Southern Vietnam on 2 Wheels*.

**Getting there:**

Take Highway 5 to Haiphong, about 95 km east of Hanoi. After the second bridge on the edge of western Haiphong, make an immediate left to the harbor ferry. The boat ride will set you back a couple of thousand dong. After another 16 km or so on the road to Hong Gai, there's another ferry—costing 1000 dong. Between the two ferries, you may run into a police roadblock. Keep some extra cash on hand for bribes. Bai Chay/Hong Gai is about 55–60 km from Haiphong. Allow 5–6 hours of daylight to reach the area by motorcycle from Hanoi. Ha Long Bay makes a great place for an overnight or two. From Bai Chay/Hong Gai, continue north about 90 km to Tien Yen. Stop at any one of the small restaurants near the **Thuy Tien Hotel** for lunch and move on. (If you must stay overnight in Tien Yen, the Thuy Tien is the only hotel in town where foreigners are permitted. About 300 meters from the bridge. A nice place at about US$10–20 depending on your bargaining skills.) Nothing to do here. Little to see of any cultural significance. The next 80 km to Mong Cai are the most exhilarating—flat roads, little traffic and few pedestrians. All the kilometers are on a windy mountainous thoroughfare. Let 'er rip here, but keep alert at all times. Remember, the bus drivers also realize there is little traffic on this stretch, and they tend as well to "let 'er rip," using both sides of the road.

**Costs:**

*Motorcycle*: US$10–12 per day. *Fuel*: About US$7–10 round trip. Check oil at each fuel stop. On a Bonus, it's wise to check every 80–100 km. *Ferries*: 6000 dong round trip. *Bridges*: 2000–4000 dong round trip depending on whether they're manned.

**Visas:**

If you want to cross the border into China, you will need a visa. No sneaking across. No day trips without one. They can be had at the Chinese consulate in Haiphong or at the Chinese embassy in Hanoi *(46 Hoang Dieu St. ☎ 25373/7)*. It may be possible to arrange for a visa in Mong Cai through "gentlemen" with friends at the immigration office. If you ask at the border bridge, officials will insist you go first to Hanoi or Haiphong and that such "agents" don't exist. These guys don't have offices, but don't worry, they'll find you. So few foreigners visit Mong Cai, they'll spot you quickly. If you're feeling adventurous and have a couple of days to kill to wait for the "preparations," go for it. See if you can save a pangolin or two.

## What to See and Do in Mong Cai

*The bustling Chinese border town of Dong Hung, as seen from Mong Cai.*

**The Border**

The Chinese border is less than a klick from the center of town. After crossing over the bridge into Mong Cai, hang a left.

• At the first intersection, take another left.

• Where the road Ts after about 100 meters, turn right. This road ends at the bridge that crosses into Dong Hung. Stop and take photos of this bustling Chinese frontier town. If you can find a way to get in, you'll have to change all your money into Chinese yuan, either on the black market or in a bank. Dollars and dong are not accepted. Note that no one, I mean *no one*, in Dong Hung speaks English, including government officials and bank managers. And, as well, virtually no one speaks Vietnamese.

**Tra Co Beach** ★

This is a small beach town about 13 km east of Mong Cai. Take the main road east from Mong Cai, making a left turn after about 10 klicks. The road runs right to the beach. The deserted beach stretches for miles in both directions. The few tourists here are primarily Vietnamese and day-trippers from China who congregate at the beach next to the Tra Co Hotel, about the only place in town. The sand here is less than spectacular, more silt than sand. But it is clean. The sea is generally very rough here. Watch out for dangerous undertows.

**Tra Co Cathedral** ★★

This is certainly the most engaging sight in the Mong Cai area (see the description above). A large old Catholic church that was gutted by the North Vietnamese Army during the Vietnam War and later by invading Chinese forces in 1979. The small Christian community that lives here toils each day at rebuilding the structure, unpaid and unsupported by neither the Bishop in Haiphong nor the Vatican. These believers without a temple toiling under a broiling sun removing weeds and primitively restoring the grand old cathedral are a sight to behold. At their rate of progress, it should only take another century or so to complete. From Tra Co Beach, follow the road north toward the Chinese border along the beach about 3 km to get there.

## Where to Stay in and Around Mong Cai

**Khach San Huei Nghi** **US$15–$25**

*Center of town. ☎ 33.81408. FAX: 33.81144.*

*25 Rooms.*

One of the two tourist hotels in town. Comfortable, clean rooms—that appear straight out of a dollhouse—with air conditioning. Photocopier in the lobby for what it's worth. The reception staff seems a little dizzy. Restaurant.

**Khach San Tra Co** **About US$15**

*Tra Co Beach.*

Soviet block-style hotel on the beach in Tra Co. Clean and friendly. Restaurant. But they're getting some competition. Nearly completed is another hotel a few hundred meters up the beach that looks much more attractive.

### Where to Eat in Mong Cai

Food stalls abound. There are a couple of good restaurants—one on the left side of the traffic triangle after you cross the bridge into town, and a better one on the southern edge of the town. Go around the traffic triangle 180 degrees. Follow the road all the way back (about 50 meters). It's on the right. Funky atmosphere. Large screen TV.

## Lang Son

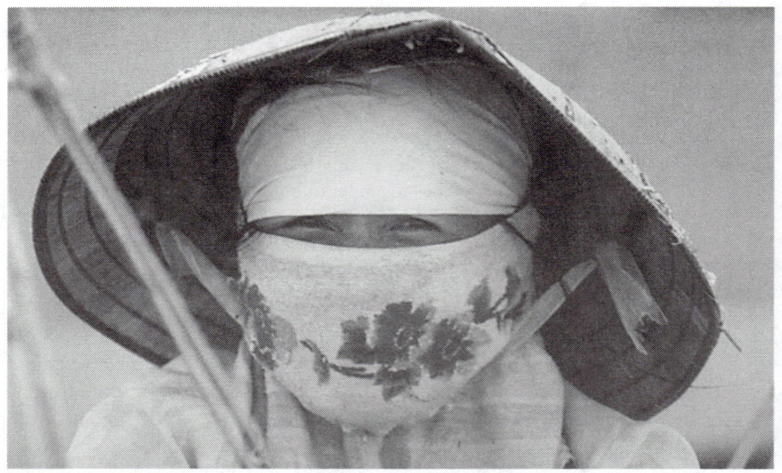

*Produce vendor is well protected from the sun near Lang Son.*

From Mong Cai, you'll have to double back to Tien Yen before you'll be able to get anywhere else in Vietnam.

Lang Son is about 100 km northwest of Tien Yen (150 km from Hanoi) along what at first appears to be a surprisingly acceptable road. But it deteriorates suddenly, and the final 40 km are pure hell on the rump, either on two wheels or four or more.

Lang Son is the capital of Lang Son province and a bustling border town. It is perhaps Vietnam's most important trading outpost with China, and, if you're lucky, you'll be able to cross the border here into China without a Chinese visa for a short stay after taking care of minor details. Since 1992, Vietnam's government has intermittently permitted overland travel for foreigners into China through Lang Son. (In fact, it can also be done from Mong Cai as well, with the proper entry papers.) The number of travelers here has swelled in the last couple of years, namely for this reason—as Lang Son itself isn't particularly an attractive town. (There are some decent caves near Ky Lua district, about 3 km from Lang Son.)

Lang Son, as well as Dong Dang, 20 km to the north, were ravaged during China's 1979 border invasion of northern Vietnam. Today, although there are no longer any signs of tension at the border here, the area is still heavily mined—although it no longer resembles Korea's 38th parallel as it did a few years ago. Chinese and Vietnamese flow across the border to barter and deliver goods, cut business deals, or just get out of their respective countries for an hour or two.

The area is inhabited by a number of ethnic minorities, such as the Dao, Nung, Man and Tho, which makes for another attraction in the area. Nonetheless, most independent travelers come here to cross the border.

In order to cross the border into China, your visa must show Lang Son as an exit point. This can be done at the Foreign Ministry offices in Hanoi and Ho Chi Minh City. If you're without a Chinese visa and just curious how you might be able to get into China for a few hours, the best way is to hook up with a tour packager. Although you won't be traveling independently, Vietnamese guides are usually able to arrange for their flocks to be escorted in and out of China without too much hassle. As in Mong Cai, certain Vietnamese shady-types also have the ability to get you across the border at Dong Dang, but it will cost.

The border itself is at Dong Dang, where there is a 600-km walkway to the Chinese-side "Friendship Gate," that's anything but friendly. Prepare for delays and a number of searches—although these instances are rare when part of a tour.

**Doing it:**

Go yourself, by bus, by train, by Toyota Land Cruiser—or even by motorcycle. The road between Hanoi and Lang Son is in treacherous condition. If you're traveling by motorcycle, it makes far more sense to visit Ha Long Bay first, and then continue directly on to Lang Son via Trot and Son Dong or by way of Tien Yen. If you want to hook up on a tour, I'd contact **Voiles Vietnam**, *17 Pham Ngoc Thach, Dist. 3, HCMC (☎ 84-8-296750, 231589. FAX: 84-8-231591)*—although they may be dropping the Mong Cai leg of the itinerary during the rainy season (between May and October) due to the constant flooding in the region, washing out bridges for hours, even days, at a time

**Getting there:**

It can be done from Hanoi, Ha Long Bay and Tien Yen. By bus, the best bet is from Hanoi. Buses leave from the capital's Long Bien bus station at 6 a.m. It's at least a six-hour ride to hell, as the Hanoi/Lang Son route isn't in nearly as good shape as the roads to the east and northeast. Expect to be jolted, jarred and banged around virtually the entire journey. The cost is about US$6. There are a number of police roadblocks that may or not be functioning, but be prepared to be stopped and perhaps searched by Vietnamese police looking for contraband. If you're doing the trip solo, such as by motorcycle, without a guide, expect to be stopped often and perhaps "fined." By train the journey takes six hours. One leaves Hanoi for Lang Son each morning at 9. If you're going by car, it's necessary that it be of the 4-wheel-drive variety. Nothing else will make it.

### INSIDER TIP

*If you're traveling through Hai Duong, you have to make a point of trying the town's special cuisine, in particular the green bean cake and Tan Cuong Tea. There is an array of green bean cake dealers (you'll see a sign saying Rong Vuong (Golden Dragon) along the street in the town. Bao Hien Restaurant is where the specialty was originally created, using green beans, white sugar, pig fat, shaddock scent and vanilla. There's a lot of protein in the concoction. These cakes can now be found in other areas of Vietnam, but the real thing comes from Hai Duong. The townsfolk consider the preparation of green bean cake an art form. Green bean cakes are often part of wedding meals and engagement ceremonies, and are offered on the altars of ancestors during the Tet holiday in Hanoi and other northern rural areas. Green bean cakes are also offered to visiting foreign businessmen by government representatives at official functions. The authentic green bean cake comes with the trademark Bao Long. The best restaurants for green bean cake in Hai Duong are the Bao Hien Restaurant (now called the Ngoc Bich) and Nguyen Huong Restaurant. Bao Long green bean cakes are now reaching customers at Hanoi's Noi Bai International airport, upscale eateries in Hanoi, the railway station, Quang Ninh Province and Haiphong, just to mention a few of the areas where the delicacy is available. Green bean cake is now just beginning to be exported to foreign countries. The cakes are perhaps northern Vietnam's best representation of the use of its agricultural products. Try some. Absolutely delicious.*

# HAIPHONG

*Haiphong was leveled by American B-52s during the war; some scars still show.*

## HAIPHONG IN A CAPSULE

*A once ugly city that is quickly transforming its image...It was heavily bombed by the Americans during the Vietnam War...This is Vietnam's major port...The city itself offers few attractions...But there remains some nice colonial architecture...The First Indochina War started here with the French bombing of the port in 1946...Thousands of civilians died...During the American War, the U.S. lost more than 300 warplanes here...The nicest areas of the region are Cat Ba Island and Do Son Beach.*

Haiphong, with a population of more than 1.2 million people, is the second largest city in the north and Vietnam's major port. For the most part, much of the area surrounding the city is actually an eyesore—a gray urban sprawl pockmarked with factories and bombed-out buildings, despite massive rebuilding in the city.

Now Greater Haiphong, which sits on the mouth of the Cua Cam River, covers an area more than 1520 square meters. In 1872–1874, when the French took possession of the city, it was nothing more than a small port and market town. With the French in control, Haiphong grew at rocket speed. It soon became a major port, in part, because of its proximity to coal supplies. The French didn't leave until 1955, after their defeat at Dien Bien Phu. In fact, the biggest instigation of the First Indochina War was the 1946 French bombardment of Haiphong's civilian residential areas, an action that killed at least hundreds of civilians; perhaps, by some estimates, as many as 5000 people were killed in the raids. All this happened because a French Navy ship had seized a Vietnamese junk. Vietnamese troops fired on the French ship, which so incensed the French commanders, they decided to bomb the hell out of the city. A month later, the war started.

The Americans pounded Haiphong during the Vietnam War and, in 1972, President Nixon ordered the mining of the city's harbor to prevent the shipment of Soviet-made war equipment that was being moved south. As part of the Paris Peace Agreement the same year, the Americans agreed to help dispose of the mines.

The Vietnamese purportedly downed more than 300 U.S. aircraft from the city's antiaircraft batteries during the war. But the Americans achieved many of their objectives in Haiphong. More than 80 percent of the city's aboveground petrol facilities were destroyed in 1966 in the U.S. effort to prevent these precious supplies from reaching the south—although American intelligence was unable to glean that the North Vietnamese suspected such action would be taken and had moved much of their supplies to underground locations.

Today, there's a resort and even Vietnam's first casino in Haiphong. The hotels, though, are generally overpriced. Surprisingly, much of the old French colonial architecture survived the bombardment, mostly in the downtown area around the **theater square**. A couple of kilometers south of the city center is the **Du Hang Pagoda**, said to have been built in the 1600s. Also check out the numerous street markets near Cau Dat and Tam Bac Streets, as well as the old colonial architecture on Tam Bac Street.

Despite the "resurgence" of the city, it remains a relatively unattractive metropolis. Tourists don't particularly care for it and, apparently, neither do the Vietnamese. Since 1980, massive amounts of Vietnamese have left the city—

and not merely as boat people in search of a new land and economic opportunities, but to other areas in Vietnam itself.

## What to See and Do in Haiphong

*Haiphong retains a remarkable amount of its colonial architecture, despite being leveled during the Vietnam War.*

### The Colonial-Style Architecture

If you're going to spend any time in the city at all, at least check out the old French buildings that remained largely undamaged through both Indochina wars. The best area for seeing the old structures is in the center of the city, particularly where Tran Hung Dao and Quang Trung Streets intersect, which is where an old theater can be found.

### Du Hang Pagoda

*121 Du Hang Street.*

This mildly interesting pagoda was built in the 17th century and has been remodeled many times since. Today, it is being renovated again as you read this. The small pagoda was dedicated to Le Chan, who battled the Chinese alongside the Trung Sisters. There's a courtyard and some impressive Vietnamese-style traditional wood carvings.

### Nghe Pagoda

*51 Ngo Nghe Street.*

This pagoda was also built to honor Le Chan, and was constructed during the early part of the 20th century.

### Dang Hai Flower Village

About 5 km from the city center. All types of tropical and perennial flowers are grown here and sold to countries all over the world. Worth only a brief stop.

### Hang Kenh Tapestry Factory

Wool tapestries are produced at this factory, founded some 66 years ago, and are exported to other nations. Again, worth just a brief stop.

### Hang Kenh Communal House

*Hang Kenh Street.*

This is where you can find an impressive display of about 500 wooden relief sculptures. The area here once belonged to the village of Kenh.

### Other Temples

If you're required to spend some time in Haiphong, you might also want to check out the **Thien Phuc Pagoda**, built in 1551, where there is a statue of Queen Mother Tra Huong; the **Le Chan Temple**, which was built in honor of a military commander of the 1st century and **Linh Quang Pagoda**, which was built in 1709 and possesses many fine wood carvings.

## Haiphong Environs

*Fishing fleet near Yen Hung, Quang Ninh province.*

### Bach Dang River (Cua Cam)

The mouth of the Bach Dang River (also called the Cua Cam River, Cam River or the Haiphong Channel) is about 10 km east of Haiphong. This is where the river flows into the sea. It is actually a maze or network of waterways between Ha Long Bay and Haiphong that has an impressive history. Vietnamese forces prevented the Chinese from landing here to do battle three different times: in AD 938, AD 981, and in 1288 by Tran Hung Dao. Anticipating the Mongol invasion, Tran Hung Dao stopped the Mongols from taking over the region by pounding three stone spikes in the harbor during high tide. The Mongol ships ran into them when they tried to sail away at low tide and sank. The buried remains of the stakes were discovered in 1985 in the nearby district of Yen Hung.

## Do Son Beach

This beach resort, established in 1888 on what is actually an islet (or a series of islets), is 20 km southeast of Haiphong and is popular with the locals. It's not a bad beach but a little dirty due to the hotels that have gone up along the beachfront in recent years. The peninsula is best known for the nine hills called "The Mountain of Nine Dragons," or *Cuu Long*. There's a small temple on Doc Mountain called **Den Ba De Temple**, which is dedicated to a young woman who leapt to her death after spending the night with a man she didn't want to be with.

## Cat Ba National Park ★★★

*30 km to the east of Haiphong and 135 km from Hanoi.* Daily ferries leave for Cat Ba from Haiphong's Ben Bach Dang Street Ferry Terminal, usually early in the morning (however, the schedules are subject to change). Cat Ba Island is the largest island in the Ha Long Bay region. The park represents a small section of the island of Cat Ba that covers a forested area of 120 square km. The total area of Cat Ba is close to 355 square km. The area was declared a national park in 1986 to preserve the island's diverse flora and fauna. The mainly forested park is covered with tropical evergreens, coastal mangrove forests, freshwater swamps and lakes (the biggest being Ech Lake), and surrounded by fine beaches with coral reefs offshore. The principal beaches in the park include Hong Xoai Be, Cai Vieng and Hong Xoai Long beaches. There are reportedly three hotels on the island, although I could only locate one, the Cat Ba Hotel. It's said the other two go by the same name. Don't make plans to meet anyone at the Cat Ba Hotel. There are also two camping villages near the island's fishing village (Cat Ba Town) that attract a horde of both Vietnamese tourists and foreigners alike.

Cat Ba Island also features small waterfalls and grottoes in limestone rock formations (as many as 350 limestone outcroppings). There are high winds at the top of the grottoes and, frankly, sitting on the beach can get a little nippy at any time of the year, although on the rare summer sunny day, nothing beats kicking back on Cat Ba. In fact, there's no real "season" to visit the island, as the winters are cold, drizzly and gray and the summers rattled by typhoons.

Of particular interest have been the discoveries of stone tools and human bones on the island which indicate Cat Ba was inhabited 7000 years ago. Nearly 20 such sites have been found. Today, the island possesses at least a dozen species of mammals, including the rare Francois monkey. There are also deer and wild boar in addition to birds such as hornbills, hawks and cuckoos. Other species stop here on their migration paths. Most of the island's population of 10,000–12,000 people is located in Cat Ba Town. They eke out a living mainly through fishing and rice farming and by growing apples, oranges and cassava. Electricity on the island is limited to only a brief few hours in the evening. Some of the best beaches in Vietnam can be found here, or that's what Hanoi officials would have you believe. And it may be accurate. Cat Ba Island has largely been declared a protected region and, as mentioned, features tropical forests, mangrove swamps, towering dolomite hills, waterfalls, lakes, caves and, of course, gorgeous beaches. There's also a thriving animal population, including, of course, the Francois monkey.

### Where to Stay in Haiphong and Do Son

#### AUTHOR'S NOTE: TELEPHONE PREFIXES

*The following telephone numbers are local exchanges. The country code is 84. The city code is 31.*

**Hotel du Commerce** **US$30–$40** ★★

*62 Dien Bien Phu Street. ☎ 47206 or 47290.*

*40 rooms.*

This French-era hotel has been renovated and is a very comfortable place to stay. All the rooms have air conditioning, attached bath. Restaurant. Hot water, refrigerators. The lower priced rooms are especially a bargain.

**Duyen Hai Hotel** **US$22–$40** ★★

*5 Nguyen Tri Phuong Street. ☎ 47657 or 42157.*

This is also an attractive French colonial style hotel not unlike the Hotel du Commerce, in price, ambiance and service. Air conditioning, hot water, attached bath. Recently renovated.

**Cat Bi Hotel** **US$25–$35**

*30 Tran Phu Street. ☎ 46306.*

The best thing about this hotel is its proximity to the railroad station. Air conditioning, attached bath. Nothing special.

**Hang Hai Hotel** **US$30–$50** ★★

*282 Danang Street. ☎ 48576.*

*38 rooms.*

This is one of the nicest hotels in Haiphong, and if you're spending more than a day or two, this would probably be the best place, even though it's located in a grimy area 3 km from the city center. Large, quiet rooms with air conditioning, refrigerators, telephone, attached bath, hot water. Two restaurants and a disco on the top floor.

**Bach Dang Hotel** **US$12–$40**

*40-42 Dien Bien Phu Street. ☎ 47244.*

All different classes of rooms in this hotel. But it's a little seedy, especially if you're considering the higher priced rooms. Air conditioning, restaurant, attached bath, hot water.

**Hong Bang Hotel** **US$15–$65** ★★

*64 Dien Bien Phu Street.* ☎ *42229.*
*30 rooms.*
Recently renovated. Rooms have attached bath, color TV, air conditioning, refrigerators. Restaurant, massage and sauna. Nice amenities for the price.

**Thang Nam Hotel** **US$15–$20**

*55 Dien Bien Phu Street.* ☎ *42820.*
Average. Rooms have air conditioning, attached bath. There's a restaurant and beauty shop.

**Ben Binh Hotel** **US$25–$50** ★★

*6 Ben Binh Street, across from the ferry dock.* ☎ *42260.*
These are large, attractive and spacious villas. Air conditioning, attached bath, hot water. Friendly service.

**Hoa Binh Hotel** **US$8–$19**

*104 Luong Khanh Thien Street, opposite the railway station.* ☎ *46907.*
The lower priced rooms come with fan; air conditioning in the higher-priced rooms. A convenient and relatively cheap place for backpackers.

**Hai Au Hotel** **US$20–$30**

*Do Son Beach.*
*45 rooms.*
This hotel is run by Haiphong Tourism and is a reasonably good value. Air conditioning, attached bath, hot water, restaurant. There are a slew of hotels strung out along the beach, but this may be the best.

**Hoa Phuong Hotel**

*Right near the Hai Au Hotel on Do Son Beach.*
Also run by Haiphong Tourism. These are villas that were once used by members of the Politburo.

**Ministry of Energy Guest House**
**(Nha Khach Bo Nang Luong)** **About US$20–$35**

*Do Son Beach.*
*100 rooms.*
This is one of the newest hotels at the beach but it doesn't overlook the beach itself. Air conditioning, hot water, balconies with the higher-priced rooms, telephone. A decent deal for foreigners, but the Vietnamese pay half these prices.

**Van Hoa Hotel** **About US$8**

*Do Son Beach, at the tip of the peninsula.*
A favorite among backpackers. Long walk to the beach, however. Bizarre architecture. Rooms have a fan.

## Where to Eat in Haiphong and Do Son

Haiphong has a great many small and cheap restaurants. The most expensive food can be found at the hotel restaurants, the cheapest on the streets. But the seafood in

Haiphong is excellent. At Do Son Beach, try the **Van Hoa Restaurant** at the end of the peninsula in a small park.

## Directory

### Transportation

Haiphong is 100 km southeast of Hanoi on National Highway 5.

**By air:**

VN flights leave HCMC for Haiphong daily at 8:30 a.m. and Mondays, Wednesdays and Saturdays at 9 a.m. From Haiphong, flights depart for HCMC daily at 11:30 a.m., and Mondays, Wednesdays and Saturdays at 2:20 p.m.

**By bus:**

There are regular connections to Hanoi via the minibuses that cruise around the theater area. The trip takes about 2-1/2 hours and costs about 10,000 dong. Buses also depart from Haiphong's bus station in the Thuy Nguyen District, which is on the north bank of the Cua Cam River, for Bai Chay and Ha Long Bay's Hong Gai (about 3 hours). To reach the station, you have to take a ferry to the north bank of the river. Buses leave Hanoi for Haiphong from the Long Bien Bus Station on the east side of the Red River.

**By train:**

This is a more popular means of reaching your destination even though the Reunification Express doesn't stop in Haiphong. There is one train that links Hanoi with Haiphong every day early in the morning. From Haiphong, there are two daily trains to Hanoi.

**By car:**

This is actually a relatively long trip considering the short distance between the two cities. There are a number of bridges that both cars and the train share. If a train is coming, you've got to stop and wait, sometimes for quite a while. This short distance along Highway 5 can take as long as three hours to cover.

**By boat:**

You can also reach Haiphong from Hanoi by boat. The schedule changes often. If you want, you can even go to Saigon by boat from Haiphong. The trip takes 2.5 days. Ferries also leave from the dock on Ben Binh Street for Hong Gai in Ha Long Bay. The trip takes about four hours and costs about US$1. Ferries from Ha Long Bay usually have the same schedules. As I mentioned, boat schedules in the area change frequently, so find out first. You may end up in Haiphong a day or two longer than you anticipated.

### Post Office

*5 Nguyen Tri Phuong Street.* ☎ *42584.* International calls and faxes can be made from here.

### Banks and Moneychangers

Vietcom Bank is located at *11 Hoang Dieu Street*, not far from the Post Office. ☎ *41723.* Will give advances on American-issued credit cards.

### Tourist Offices

Haiphong Tourist. *15 Le Dai Hanh Street.* ☎ *42957.* This is one of the more useful tourist offices in Vietnam for independent travelers. It offers car rentals and boat charters to Ha Long Bay and Cat Ba National Park.

### Hospitals

Vietnam-Czech Friendship Hospital on Nguyen Duc Canh Street or the Traditional Medicine Hospital on Ben Vien Dong Y Street. The best bet, though, is to get yourself back to Hanoi ASAP if you've gotten sick or badly hurt.

There is the Traditional Medicine Hospital on Nguyen Duc Canh Street.

### TNT International Express

☎ *47180.*

### Airlines

Vietnam Airlines Booking Office. *Cat Bi Airport.* ☎ *48309, 45217.*

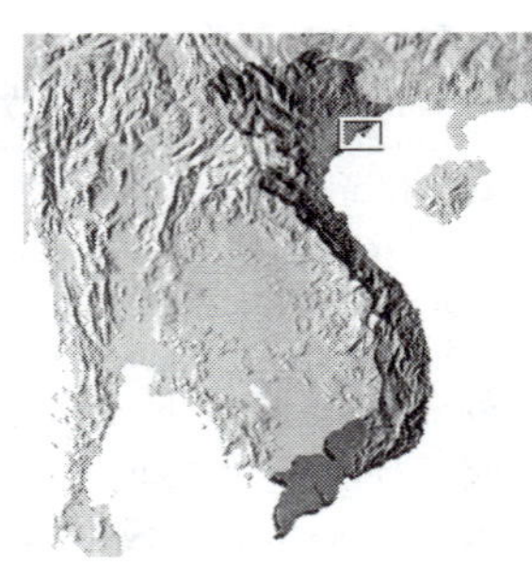

# HA LONG BAY

***Steep grottoes rise hundreds of meters above Ha Long Bay.***

## HA LONG BAY IN A CAPSULE

*165 km from Hanoi to the Bai Chai bus station...Perhaps the most beautiful coastal area of Vietnam...Possesses more than 3000 islands in the bay...Spectacular limestone outcroppings and caves...Stalagmite and stalactite formations perhaps the most beautiful in the world...Huge limestone rock formations appear out of the bay like giant deformed monoliths...Bai Chay and Hong Gai are the major "towns" in the region...Reachable by bus, car or boat.*

Ha Long Bay, 20 km past Haiphong, is targeted for tourism, and it's quickly taking form. The principal towns tourists get to, Bai Chay and Hong Gai (about 55-60 from Haiphong), have sprouted more new hotels in the last year than tulips in a Dutch flower field in April—particularly Bai Chay, which has become practically unrecognizable in a mere eight months. In fact, the "strip" that runs along the beach from Bai Chay to the ferry to Hong Gai is dangerously starting to resemble the beach strips in Thailand's Pattaya and Phuket (Patong Beach). The resemblance is becoming uncanny. Although the hookers and the bar-beers have yet to arrive, can they be far beyond in what is becoming one of Vietnam's biggest tourist attractions?

A mere two years ago, travelers had only a handful of accommodations to choose from when visiting the area. At last count, I registered 62 hotels in Bai Chay alone—most of them reed-thin five- or six-story structures cemented to one another that stretch up the hill on a dirt road (Vuon Dao-Bai Chay Street—or the "patch") from the new Peach Blossom Hotel at the water's edge—engaged in a classic corner gas station price war. Their owners prowl the street, beckoning wary tourists who have strayed past the Ha Long Hotel by mistake. (And just to make sure they don't wander too far past Bai Chay's milestone Ha Long Hotel, the caravansary now has five hotels! Ha Long 1, Ha Long 2, Ha Long 3...You get the idea.)

***Face Island in Ha Long Bay was aptly named.***

Ha Long Bay offers some of Vietnam's most breathtaking scenery, including beautiful limestone formations, sheer edifice cliffs, huge rock arches, peaceful coves and seemingly thousands of limestone islets that rise from the sea like green plaster monsters. If Ha Long Bay was perhaps 1000 km to the south, this would be paradise on Earth. But as it is, the weather here can be horrible—damp, rainy and cold. But catch the area on a good day and you're in for a treat. Boats for hire line the Bai Chay beach area (old day cruisers and overnight boats.) Like the hotels, competition is stiff. Most take groups, usually tour groups vanned up from Hanoi. Independent travelers will find better bargains if they can hitch a ride aboard a boat that's relatively full. But I hopped on a day cruiser as a loner for US$10 for a three-hour ride through the islets, grottoes and caves of the islands of Ha Long. (4 hours does the journey more justice.)

**INSIDER TIP**

*It seems like Ha Long Bay is pretty close to the capital–after all, how long could it take to go a hundred miles? A long darn time.It's a trip that can easily take six hours or more–one way. The trip includes both a river and harbor crossing by ferry, starting at Haiphong. So be warned; it's no day trip.*

Ha Long Bay (the name means "Where the Dragon Descends Into the Sea") is perhaps the most beautiful area in Vietnam. It's only drawback, and it's a major one at that, is that the area is frequently shrouded in a cold, drizzly fog, particularly during the winter months when, frankly, a stay in the area can be a very uncomfortable one.

Myth says that an enormous beast created the bay and outcroppings as it thrashed its way toward the sea to prevent the forward progress of enemy fleets, even though two major battles were fought here in the 10th and 13th centuries. Legend maybe, but there are sailors who even today report sightings of a giant sea beast called the Tarasque. Locals, in their effort to make a few bucks, offer foreigners a chance to sail out in search of the creature.

Ha Long Bay was also the site where, in 1882, French Captain Henri Rivière was beheaded after sending troops into the area to seize the region's vast coal deposits. His head was put on a stick and paraded from village to village. The incident prompted the French government to launch a full-scale effort to turn the country of Vietnam into a colony of France. The two ports of Hong Gai (called the Pointed Peak, about 120 km from Hanoi in Quang Ninh Province) and Cam Pha (150 km east of Hanoi) are areas of vast coal deposits and are mined by the Cai Bao, Mon Duong and Cham peoples. The territory, in Quang Ninh Province, is Vietnam's largest coal-producing region. Archeological evidence suggests an ancient culture in the area dating back to the Neolithic Era (2000) BC following the Bac Son people.

Ha Long Bay is the north's major tourist center; any trip to Vietnam should include a visit to the area on the itinerary. There are magnificent, fragmented limestone outcroppings in this bay which features, by the best estimate, more than 3000 islands. Beautiful Chinese-type sailing junks dot the waters between the outcroppings—many of the islets ascend to heights of 300 meters or more. Many more reach a height of 100 meters. The area appears like a mountain range in the sea. The mountains, consisting of mainly dolomite and limestone, reach for a distance of more than 100 km and cover 1500 square km. The outcropping formations, caves, grottoes, fjords and tunnels possess perhaps the most exotic appearance of any natural wonders in the world. They've been given names founded in wonderment. There is the Isle of Surprise (which is not a surprising name), the Isle of Wonders, and so forth. There are isles named after monkeys, marionettes, toads, turtles and buzzards.

Most foreigners travel to the two principal areas where there is food and accommodations: Bai Chay and Hong Gai on the northern side of the bay. Although some of the more hardy travel to Tra Co next to the Chinese frontier.

## What to See and Do in Ha Long Bay

*Caves cut through the grottoes of Ha Long Bay.*

### Limestone Outcroppings and Grottoes

From Bai Chay and Hong Gai, "junks" (actually small, beat-up—but clean—tour boats) can be rented to see the spectacular caves and grottoes in the bay, some of which possess names such as Fighting Cocks and Customs House Cave. Boats are available all along the beach front in Bai Chay. Expect to pay about US$15-20 for a three-hour cruise of the bay—although better negotiators will get on board for less. English and French speaking guides are available and come with the cost of the boat. Beverages are available on board, but take along food.

Get your guide to bring you to Hang Manh Cave, a giant cave that reaches more than 2 km and offers incredible stalagmite, stalactite and other fantastic rock formations. There is also the Hang Dau Go Grotto, a massive cave of three chambers that can be reached after climbing some slippery steps. In the first hall are scores of stalactites that look like a congregation of small creatures out of a George Lucas film. The cave (translated to the "Cave of Wooden Stakes") derived its name from the famous 13th-century warrior named Tran Hung Dao who used the third chamber of the cave to store pointed stakes which he later pounded into the bed of the Bach Dang River to sink an invading Mongol fleet. Other boats will stop at Deu Island, where visitors can view a rare species of monkey characterized by its red buttocks. The best time for seeing the monkeys is shortly before dusk. At least this is said by the guides, perhaps to entice you to pay for another hour or two.

You should also see Drum Grotto, which is so called because the wind that blows through the stalagmites and stalactites sounds like the faraway beating of drums. Visitors on longer excursions in the bay can also stop at the Grotto of Bo Nau. Those who want to swim, bring along your bathing suits. Some of the islets offer brief stretches of sandy beaches, although they're becoming increasingly crowded as the dozens of day tour boats tend to bring visitors to the same places. But the numerous secluded coves around many of the grottoes offer superb swimming in glassy-smooth, lime-green waters. When it's raining, forget it. And don't try it during the winter, when the bay is ice-cold. It's generally agreed that the only swimming done in the bay in March is by drunken Siberians on holiday.

### Where to Stay in Ha Long Bay

The number of hotels in the area has soared since the end of 1994, and more are being built. Most are mini-hotels, tall and thin hospices that reach six stories. Better to get a room on the lower floors. There aren't any elevators in these places.

**AUTHOR'S NOTE: TELEPHONE PREFIXES**

*Phone numbers are listed as local exchanges. From Hanoi, dial 01.33 before the local exchange. The country code 84. The city code is 33.*

#### Hong Gai

**Hong Gai Floating Hotel** **About US$8**

*Near the ferry dock.*

Very inexpensive. No amenities. A place to lay your head.

**Hai Au Hotel** **About US$10**

*About halfway between the Hong Gai and Bai Chay docks.*

Hot water, when it works. Basic accommodations.

#### Bai Chay

**Bach Dang Hotel** **About US$25**

*Near the ferry dock.* ☎ *46630.*

Comfortable accommodations. One of the better hospices in town. Hot water, private bath.

**Peach Blossom Hotel** **About US$40** ★★

*Corner of Bai Chay and Vuon Dao Streets.*

Brand new hotel that will be called the best in Bai Chay until the high-rise on the hill is finished sometime later in 1995. Typical of what will become a Ha Long hostelry tradition—famous for a day. Each new high-end roadhouse that goes up in this town will have its 15 minutes in the sun—or not much more than a few moments after that—before something else newer and higher (with more Toyota Land Cruisers parked in front) eclipses both the sun and the real reason to "discover" this corner of Vietnam.

**Ha Long Hotel** **US$15–$100** ★★★

*Bai Chay Road. ☎ 46340 (reservations), 46014 (Ha Long 1).*

This was the place for a good night's rest, decent food and an acceptable if not exceptional degree of comfort that "adventurous, but monied" guests used to rely on when coming to Ha Long. But the management must be getting scared of the "other guys." So now there are no fewer then five Ha Long Hotels, all in a community collegelike campus setting—with collegelike campus service. Ha Long 1 fetches the big bucks at about US$50–$100 a night. But even Ha Long 5 won't fit a backpacker's budget at US$15. But all in all, it's not a bad place. Service at the restaurant is slow, but you will eat—at least at breakfast. The top-end isn't a whole lot different than the "proletariat" dormitory. Rooms with air conditioning, private bath, marginally hot water, satellite TV (and TV that has one station on every channel in the cheap rooms). The "V" channel will get here soon, though, I assure you. This place is either the Harvard or Alcatraz of Ha Long.

**Hoang Lan Hotel** **About US$15–$20**

*Vuon Dao Street. ☎ 46318.*

Expensive, but the air conditioning is worth it during the summer. Hot water, private bath. Rooms with color TV, air conditioning, refrigerator.

**Bach Long Hotel** **About US$25**

*☎ 46445.*

*40 rooms.*

This is a good deal, as the rooms are bright, relatively large and clean. Hot water, clean attached bathrooms. Friendly staff. Restaurant.

**Navy Guest House (Nha Khach Hai Quan)** **About US$30**

*☎ 4603.*

*6 rooms.*

These are two colonial mansions overlooking the bay, three rooms in each house. Attached bath, hot water. Moderate.

**Peace Hotel** **US$15–$20**

*Vuon Dao Street. ☎ 46009.*

One of the many new Vuon Dao caravansaries. Clean, comfortable and moderately priced. International telephone and a good view of the bay from some of the rooms.

Rooms with air conditioning, hot water, color TV, refrigerator. Arranges for boat tours of the bay. Accepts major credit cards.

**Hai Trang Hotel** **US$12**

*Vuon Dao Street. ☎ 46094.*

Clean rooms and one of the best deals on Vuon Dao. Rooms with air conditioning, private bath, hot water. Tour boat and car rental service.

**Thu Thuy Mini Hotel** **US$15**

*Vuon Dao Street. ☎ 46295.*

Another good value. Mini, sardine-thin "high-rise." Rooms with air conditioning, hot water, color TV, telephone. Restaurant (sort of).

**Thuon Loi Hotel & Restaurant** **US$15–$20**

*Vuon Dao Street. ☎ 46209.*

Hotel manager Bui Van Hoa is one of the friendliest on the "patch." Clean, comfortable rooms with color TV, air conditioning, hot water, private bath. Excellent food on my visit (Asian, European, seafood). Karaoke and bay excursions. Taxi service.

**Minh Ha Hotel** **US$20**

*Vuon Dao Street. ☎ 46532.*

Reasonable but stretching it a bit as you can find something with the same amenities next door in both directions for a little less. Be nice and Khuat Duy Hai might bring the price down. Rooms with air conditioning, hot water, color TV.

**Nhung Hotel** **US$10–$15**

*Vuon Dao Street. ☎ 46121.*

One of the better bargains. Rooms with air conditioning, hot water, private bath. Boat rentals.

**Tran Tam Mini Hotel** **US$10–$18**

*Just off Vuon Dao Street, 50 meters from Bai Chay Street (Ha Long Road). ☎ 46469.*

Good rooms, good food, good price. Rooms with air conditioning, hot water, TV. Travel services, bay tours.

**Trade Union Guest House** **About US$25**

*Overlooking the beach.*

The biggest building in town and relatively new. Make sure the air conditioning is working during the summer before you choose a room.

**Post Office Hotel (Khach San Buu Dien)**

*2 km on the road back to Hanoi.*

New and comfortable. Attached bath, air conditioning, hot water. Next door are three relatively new hotels managed by Quang Ninh Tourism: the Bach Long, Ha Long, and Hoang Long Hotels. Each are comfortable and in the US$25–40 price range. For those bucks, you get air conditioning, hot water, attached bath and so on. Restaurant. Each of these four hotels are in the moderate price range.

**Van Hai Hotel** **About US$10**

*In the middle of town. ☎ 46403.*

Shared bath. Rooms overlook the sea.

**Bac Long Hotel** **US$5-15**

*Vuon Dao Street.* ☎ *46167.*

Perhaps the cheapest rooms on Vuon Dao Street. Rooms with air conditioning, TV, hot water, private bath, refrigerator, telephone.

Other brand-new mini-hotels are crushed in the Vuon Dao Street area, all offering air conditioning rooms with private bath, hot water and in-room TVs. All are in the US$12–20 range. They include:

**Van Nam Hotel**

*Vuon Dao Street.* ☎ *46593.*

**Viet Hoa Hotel**

*Vuon Dao Street.* ☎ *46035.*

**Minh Cuong Hotel**

*Vuon Dao Street.* ☎ *46086.*

**Minh Minh Hotel**

*Vuon Dao Street.* ☎ *46741.*

**Cam Van Hotel**

*Vuon Dao Street.* ☎ *46675.*

**Than Lich Hotel**

*Vuon Dao Street.* ☎ *46038.*

**Hai Yen Hotel**

*Vuon Dao Street.* ☎ *46126.*

**The Olddaling**

*Vuon Dao Street.*

## Directory

### Transportation

Ha Long Bay is about 165 km from Hanoi, 55 km from Haiphong, and 45 km from Cam Pha.

**By air:**

Hanoi is the closest airport unless you find a way of hiring a seaplane. Or a chopper.

**By helicopter:**

Serving the Hanoi-Ha Long route are now two Russian-made Mi-8 and Mi-17 helicopters that have been taken out of service as search-and-rescue choppers to shuttle tourists back and forth from the bay. The route was inaugurated in July 1995 by Northern Flight Service, a branch of the state-run Vietnam Flight Service Corp. The helicopters can hold up to 24 passengers apiece. The flight from Gia Lam Airport (10 km outside of Hanoi) takes 30 minutes and departs from Hanoi on Sundays. The cost? A whopping US$175 round-trip for foreigners—and only US$68 for Vietnamese nationals. Helicopter flights and tours of the bay are also possible either through Vietnamtourism or Vietnam Airlines. Also try Helijet-VASCO *(15 Ngo Quyen, Hanoi.* ☎ *84-4-266919)* for chopper service out to the bay. And bring your wallet.

**By bus:**

Buses depart Haiphong for Bai Chay from the bus station on the north bank of the Cua Cam River. The trip takes about two hours. The bus station in Bai Chay is on the waterfront road near the Van Hai Hotel. There are also regular connections with Hanoi until the afternoon. The trip takes five to six hours and there are two ferry crossings (where most of the time is spent).You can also make connections to points south.

**By train:**

Budget travelers in Hanoi can take the train to Haiphong in the morning, and then the afternoon ferry to Bai Chay. From Bai Chay you can either return to Haiphong by boat or Hanoi by bus.

**By car:**

This is the best way to get to Ha Long Bay. Go to Bai Chay, spend the night, take a boat tour the next day, and return to Hanoi on the third day. To hire a car and driver from Hanoi will set you back at least US$100 (usually more) for the round trip. The Japanese cars are more expensive to rent than the Russian ones, namely because they're more comfortable. Also expect to pay for the driver's meals and accommodations.

**By boat:**

Getting around the area isn't much fun unless you've got a boat to tour the islands. You won't need to rent a boat yourself as there will be a slew of foreigners as well as Vietnamese also seeking the same trips. Large boats, carrying up to 100 passengers cost between US$12–$20 an hour. But smaller boats holding up to a dozen people can be had for around US$8 an hour. The smaller boats are privately-owned, so you can negotiate.

**By ferry:**

Ferries depart for Hong Gai about three times a day—in the early morning, mid-morning and late afternoon. But these schedules seem to continually change. The one-way trip takes about 3–4 hours and will set you back at least 10,000 dong, and sometimes much more if you're stupid and don't let your independent (i.e., non-Vietnamtourism) guide buy your ticket for you. Ferries for Haiphong leave from the dock at Hong Gai at 6 a.m., 11 a.m. and 4 p.m. (Again, these schedules are subject to change). You can also take a ferry from Hong Gai to Bai Chay that leaves constantly during the day and early evening.

### Tourist Office

Quang Ninh Tourism. *Bai Chay Street in Bai Chay.* ☎ *46351.*

Quang Ninh Tourism & Ship Chandler. *Bai Chay Street in Bai Chay.* ☎ *46405. FAX: 46226.*

### Post Office

Bai Chay opposite the ferry dock. Also at the Post Office Hotel.

### Banks and Moneychangers

Ha Long Hotel in Bai Chay. ☎ *46014.*

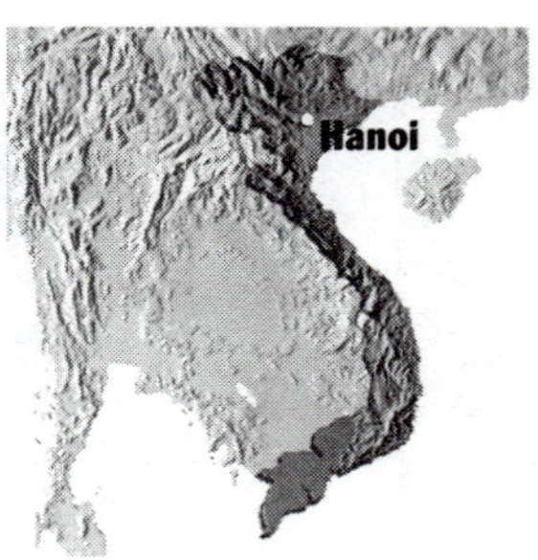


# HANOI

***Hanoi's One Pillar Pagoda was built in 1049 in the image of a lotus blossom.***

## HANOI IN A CAPSULE

*Hanoi is the capital of the Socialist Republic of Vietnam...it's a city of lakes and parks...about 70 km inland from the Gulf of Tonkin...it sits on the banks of the Red River...the streets are tree-lined...trees are uplifting the pavement...it's been a major settlement since A.D. 1010....it became capital of North Vietnam after the Geneva Agreement of 1954...it's not nearly as kinetic and energetic as Saigon...it is inferior in both tourism and infrastructure...was heavily bombed during the Vietnam War...Like Ho Chi Minh City, Hanoi has had more than a half-dozen names over the years.*

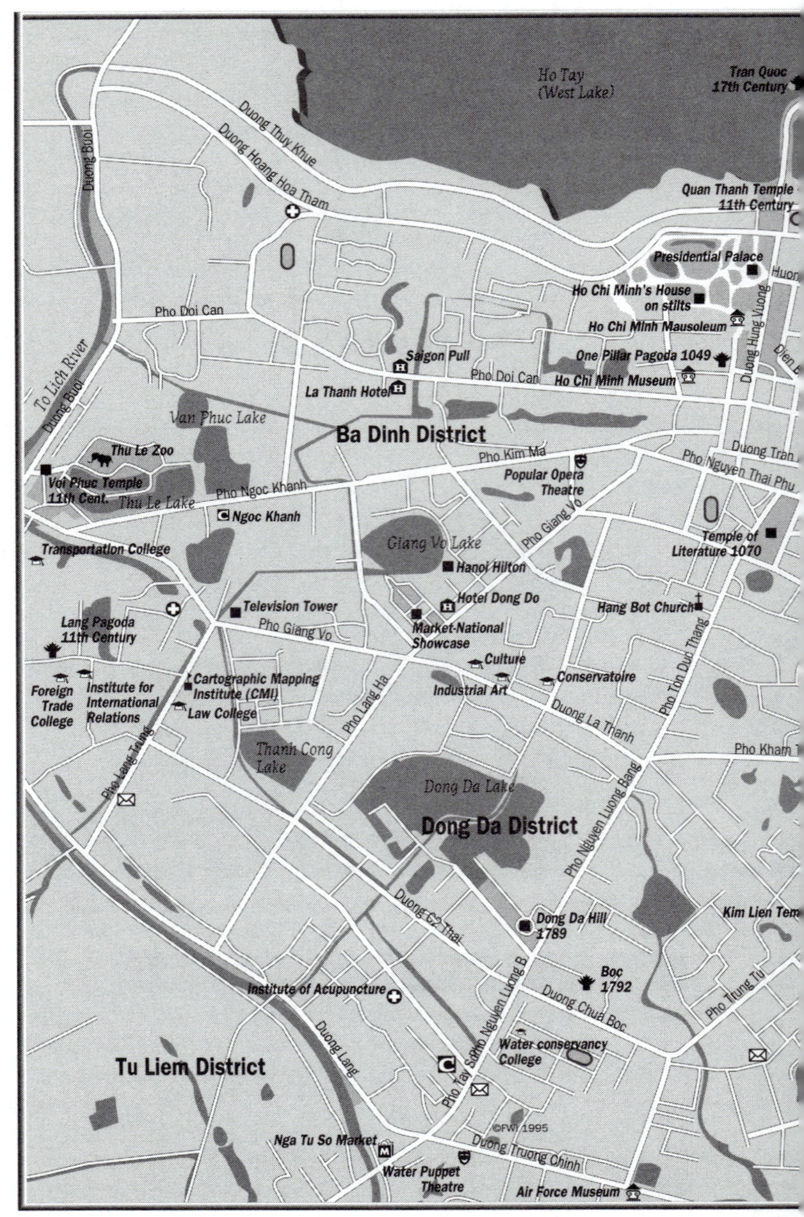

Ho Tay (West Lake)
Tran Quoc 17th Century
Duong Thuy Khue
Duong Hoang Hoa Tham
Duong Buoi
Quan Thanh Temple 11th Century
Presidential Palace
Ho Chi Minh's House on stilts
Ho Chi Minh Mausoleum
Pho Doi Can
One Pillar Pagoda 1049
Ho Chi Minh Museum
Duong Hung Vuong
Saigon Pull
La Thanh Hotel
To Lich River
Van Phuc Lake
Ba Dinh District
Thu Le Zoo
Voi Phuc Temple 11th Cent.
Thu Le Lake
Pho Ngoc Khanh
Ngoc Khanh
Pho Kim Ma
Popular Opera Theatre
Duong Tran
Pho Nguyen Thai Phu
Pho Giang Vo
Giang Vo Lake
Hanoi Hilton
Temple of Literature 1070
Transportation College
Television Tower
Hotel Dong Do
Hang Bot Church
Lang Pagoda 11th Century
Market-National Showcase
Culture
Conservatoire
Industrial Art
Pho Ton Duc Thang
Foreign Trade College
Institute for International Relations
Cartographic Mapping Institute (CMI)
Law College
Pho Lang Ha
Duong La Thanh
Pho Lang Trung
Thanh Cong Lake
Pho Kham Thien
Dong Da Lake
Dong Da District
Pho Nguyen Luong Bang
Duong 62 Thai
Dong Da Hill 1789
Kim Lien Temple
Boc 1792
Duong Chua Boc
Pho Trung Tu
Institute of Acupuncture
Water conservancy College
Duong Lang
Tu Liem District
Pho Tay Son
©FWI 1995
Nga Tu So Market
Duong Truong Chinh
Water Puppet Theatre
Air Force Museum

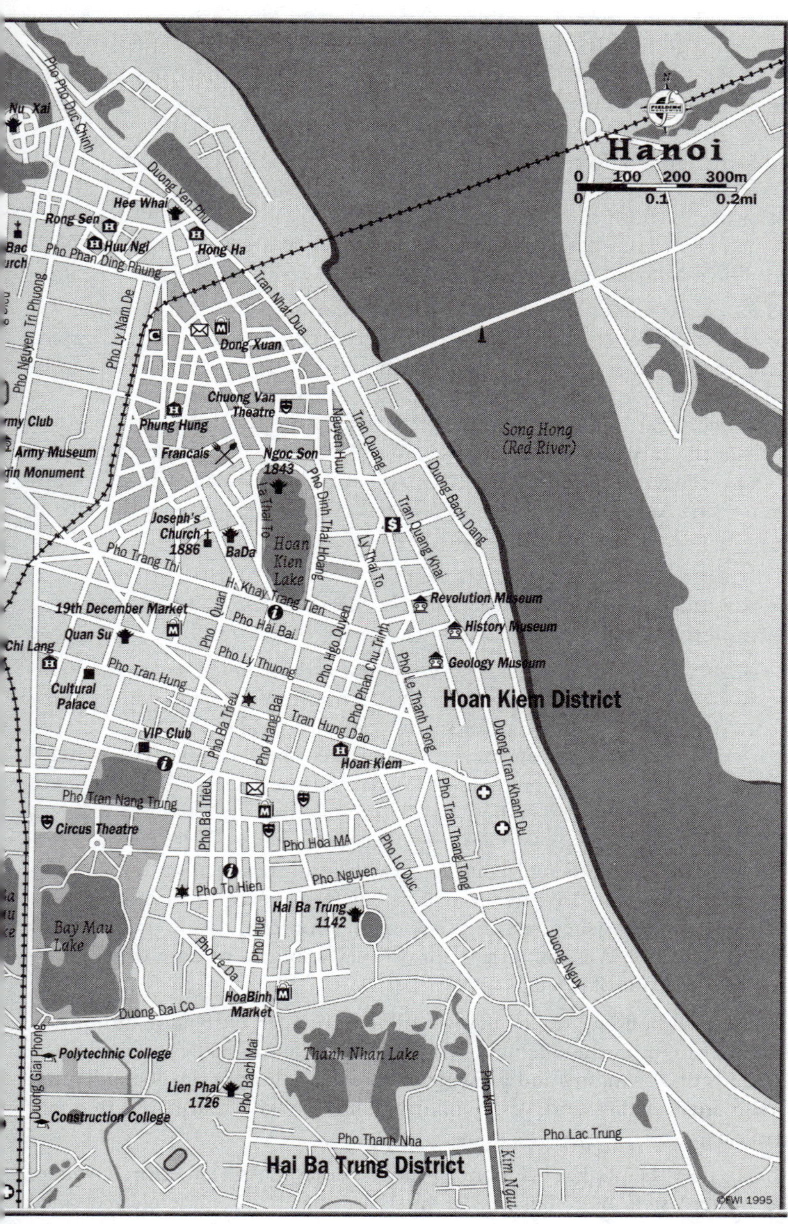

Hanoi
0 100 200 300m
0 0.1 0.2mi
Song Hong (Red River)
Hoan Kiem District
Hai Ba Trung District
Nu Xai
Pho Pho Duc Chinh
Duong Yen Phu
Hee Whai
Rong Sen
Huu Ngi
Hong Ha
Pho Phan Ding Phung
Pho Nguyen Tri Phuong
Pho Ly Nam De
Tran Nhat Dua
Dong Xuan
Chuong Van Theatre
Phung Hung
Army Club
Army Museum
Francais
Ngoc Son 1843
Nguyen Huu
Tran Quang
Duong Bach Dang
Tran Quang Khai
Ly Thai To
Pho Dinh Thai Hoang
Joseph's Church 1886
BaDa
Hoan Kiem Lake
Pho Trang Thi
Khay Trang Tien
Revolution Museum
History Museum
Geology Museum
19th December Market
Quan Su
Chi Lang
Pho Hai Bai
Pho Ly Thuong
Pho Hgo Quyen
Pho Phan Chu Trinh
Pho Le Thanh Tong
Pho Tran Hung
Cultural Palace
Tran Hung Dao
Pho Ba Trieu
Pho Hang Bai
Hoan Kiem
VIP Club
Duong Tran Khanh Du
Pho Tran Nang Trung
Circus Theatre
Pho Tran Thang Tong
Pho Hoa MA
Pho Lo Duc
Pho Nguyen
Pho To Hien
Hai Ba Trung 1142
Bay Mau Lake
Pho Le Da
Pho Hue
Duong Nguy
HoaBinh Market
Duong Dai Co
Duong Giai Phong
Polytechnic College
Thanh Nhan Lake
Lien Phai 1726
Pho Bach Mai
Construction College
Pho Kim
Pho Lac Trung
Pho Thanh Nha
Kim Ngu
©FWI 1995

Although not as popular with tourists as Ho Chi Minh City, and certainly lacking the hustle and bustle of its sister to the south, there's still plenty to see and do in the capital. Some of the sights include the Fine Arts Museum, which houses traditional Vietnamese art as well as European-influenced works; the Water Puppet Theater, Vietnam's humorous version of Punch and Judy; Ho Chi Minh's mausoleum (the Vietnamese hero's body reposes in a glass coffin); the Ho Chi Minh Museum, which opened in 1990 in honor of the 100th anniversary of Ho's birth; and the rubble of what used to be the Hanoi Hilton, the prison where U.S. soldiers were kept (it has been torn down to make way for an actual hotel).

Hanoi was founded in A.D. 1010 at the beginning of the Lu Dynasty; it is the oldest capital city in Southeast Asia. The city was racked by constant bombing from U.S. Air Force B-52 bombers from 1966 to 1972. The center of Hanoi itself doesn't reveal a lot of scars, but the outlying areas do. The French colonial buildings of the capital are in desperate need of renovation—at the very least a coat of paint. But like the big city in the south, Hanoi's people are extremely friendly and seem to bear few ill feelings toward Westerners, Americans in particular. In fact, you can almost call this city of more than three million charming.

Whereas movement of Westerners in the city was once strictly controlled, tourists today move about Hanoi freely. Bicycles can be hired, and even sights off the beaten track are within easy reach of the traveler.

Perhaps what is most interesting about the city is the enormous changes the war ultimately has brought to the architecture of the capital. Many Hanoi dwelling owners are tearing down their properties and rebuilding in such a way that seriously threatens the character of the capital. These building owners are evidently preparing for what they believe will be a deluge of American customers descending on the capital after the embargo is lifted. Residents are tearing down centuries' old structures as well as ramshackle wooden dwellings and replacing them with multistoried mini-hotels complete with expensive TV satellite dishes. There seems to be little regard for style in these new structures, and they neither conform to any traditional or modern Asian or Western style—nor do they conform to each other. They look odd and out of place.

These new building trends haven't gone unnoticed by Hanoi authorities, who are caught in the dilemma of preserving tradition while faced with the demands of a changing and growing economy so thoroughly dependent on foreign investment—and, yes, buildings that look like six-story inverted railroad cars.

Up to now, Hanoi has been one of the few cities in Asia left entirely void of the western-style boxy business architecture that has completely redefined urban areas like Bangkok, Manila, and Kuala Lumpur. There are two very unique historical areas: the ancient city of Hanoi near Hoan Kiem Lake that was settled in the 11th century, and the large French Quarter that was built by the French during their reign in the region from 1880–1930.The French Quarter is really quite attractive, with its tree-lined streets and small French-style houses. Old Hanoi, or the ancient city, is an old network of narrow alleys with dilapidated, crumbling houses set on nearly 40 streets named after the original craftsmen and artisans who settled the area: Gold Street, Baker Street, etc.

Urban planners in Hanoi, not eager to see either area become infected by modernization, are seeking to zone areas specifically for the development of business and residential centers that will become necessary as the Vietnamese economy expands. But the problem is which areas to earmark.

Although independent travel has become extraordinarily easy throughout Vietnam, the government is still somewhat wary of travelers straying from the traditional, government approved sights (many of which are drab and, quite frankly, boring). This is evident by the fact that Hanoi was, until recently, one of 10 localities in the country where tourist offices administer entire tourist establishments and other tourist activities in the area. Now a slew of private tour agents are operating, and it is easy to move about the city and its environs quite easily on your own, usually with no hassle from the authorities.

Hanoi has a lot of interesting things to see besides the formaldehyde immersed corpse of Ho Chi Minh. The capital has a history of more than 1000 years. Ho Guam (Restored Sword Lake) features water that has been dyed with green ink! There are the golden buffalo in the West Lake (Ho Tay). There's the bronze-casting village of Ngu Xa, the snake village Le Mat, and the flower villages of Ngoc Ha and Nhat Tan.

Besides the hundreds of pagodas and temples in the city (if you're not already entirely "pagodaed"-out) there are more than 35 ancient streets blooming with the same lotus flowers that have existed here for centuries.

But remember that tourism infrastructure in Hanoi is still substandard, well below amenities offered in HCMC. There were only a total of about 2000 hotel rooms in the city at the end of 1994, and only about a quarter of these were considered worthy of "international standards." Roads are in dilapidated condition, except in central Hanoi. Electricity and the water supply continue to be unpredictable. (Foreign-invested joint projects with Vietnamese firms, however, are changing these conditions, but at a tortoiselike rate.)

Hanoi is looking for ways to improve its tourist industry. It's predicted, since the inception of the new laws pertaining to foreign investment, that by

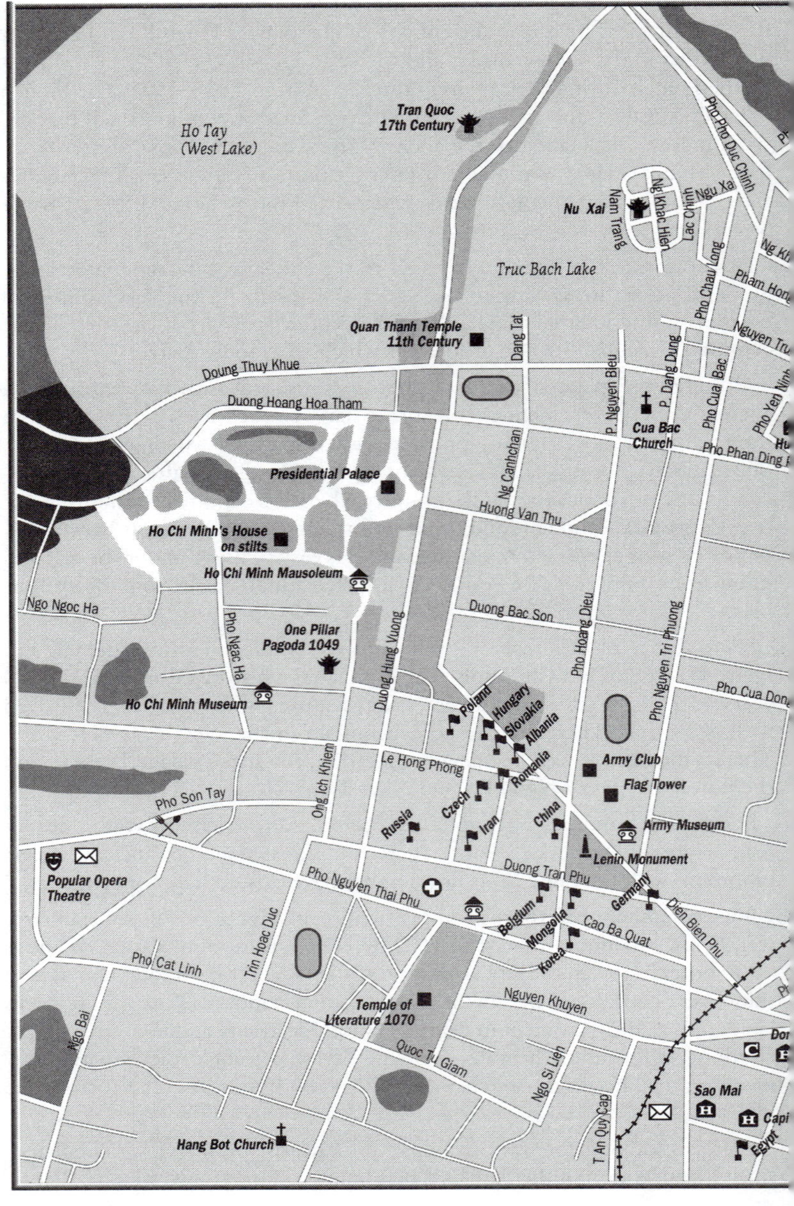
Ho Tay
(West Lake)
Tran Quoc
17th Century
Nu Xai
Nam Trang
Ng Khac Hieu
Lac Chinh
Ngu Xa
Pho Pho Duc Chinh
Truc Bach Lake
Pho Chau Long
Pham Hong
Nguyen Tru
Quan Thanh Temple
11th Century
Dang Tat
P. Dang Dung
Pho Cua Bac
Pho Yen Ninh
Doung Thuy Khue
Duong Hoang Hoa Tham
P. Nguyen Bieu
Cua Bac
Church
Pho Phan Ding
Presidential Palace
Ng Canhchan
Huong Van Thu
Ho Chi Minh's House
on stilts
Ho Chi Minh Mausoleum
Ngo Ngoc Ha
Duong Bac Son
Pho Ngac Ha
One Pillar
Pagoda 1049
Duong Hung Vuong
Pho Hoang Dieu
Pho Nguyen Tri Phuong
Pho Cua Don
Ho Chi Minh Museum
Poland
Hungary
Slovakia
Albania
Romania
Army Club
Flag Tower
Le Hong Phong
Ong Ich Khiem
Czech
Russia
Iran
China
Army Museum
Pho Son Tay
Lenin Monument
Duong Tran Phu
Popular Opera
Theatre
Pho Nguyen Thai Phu
Germany
Dien Bien Phu
Belgium
Mongolia
Cao Ba Quat
Korea
Trin Hoac Duc
Pho Cat Linh
Temple of
Literature 1070
Nguyen Khuyen
Ngo Bai
Quoc Tu Giam
Ngo Si Lien
T An Quy Cap
Sao Mai
Hang Bot Church
Egypt

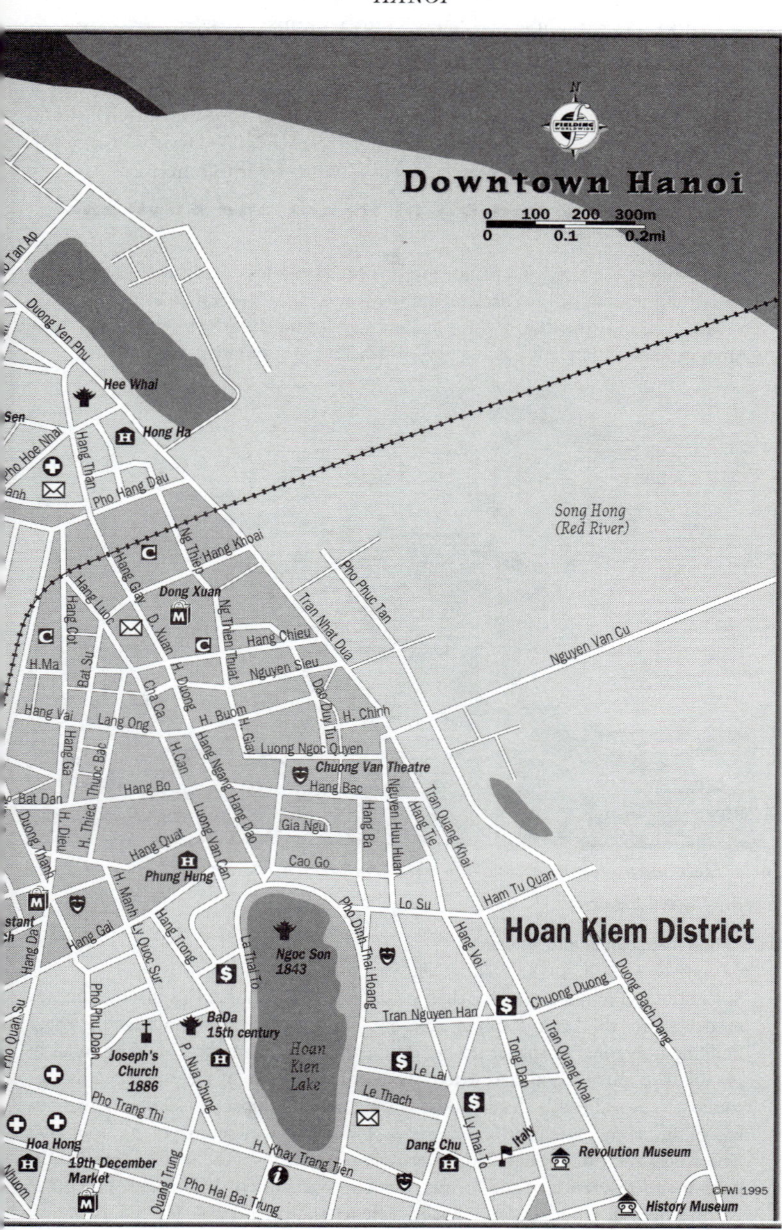
Downtown Hanoi
0 100 200 300m
0 0.1 0.2mi
Song Hong (Red River)
Hoan Kiem District
Duong Yen Phu
Hee Whai
Hong Ha
Hang Than
Pho Hang Dau
Hang Khoai
Ng Thiep
Hang Giay
Hang Luoc
Hang Cot
Dong Xuan
Ng Thien Thuat
Hang Chieu
Nguyen Sieu
Tran Nhat Dua
Pho Phuc Tan
Nguyen Van Cu
H.Ma
Bat Su
D. Xuan
H. Duong
Dao Duy Tu
H. Chinh
Hang Vai
Lang Ong
Cha Ca
H. Buom
H. Giai
Luong Ngoc Quyen
Chuong Van Theatre
Hang Bac
Hang Ga
Thuoc Bac
H.Can
Hang Ngang Hang Dao
Hang Bo
Bat Dan
Nguyen Huu Huan
Hang Tre
Tran Quang Khai
Hang Ba
Gia Ngu
Cao Go
Duong Thanh
H. Dieu
H. Thiec
Hang Quat
Luong Van Can
Phung Hung
Ham Tu Quan
Lo Su
Pho Dinh Thai Hoang
Hang Voi
H. Manh
Hang Gai
Ly Quoc Su
Hang Trong
La Thai To
Ngoc Son 1843
Duong Bach Dang
Chuong Duong
Tran Nguyen Han
Pho Phu Doan
BaDa 15th century
Joseph's Church 1886
P. Nua Chung
Hoan Kien Lake
Le Lai
Le Thach
Tong Dan
Tran Quang Khai
Pho Trang Thi
Hoa Hong
19th December Market
Quang Trung
H. Khay Trang Tien
Pho Hai Bai Trung
Dang Chu
Ly Thai To
Italy
Revolution Museum
History Museum
©FWI 1995

the year 2000, Hanoi will be attracting US$10 billion in foreign investment capital. Hanoi predicts that in order for the region to become an area of mass tourism that per capita income will need to increase to US$1000 by the year 2000. By then the capital expects to have nearly 20 hotels of international standards. Equally as important, infrastructure projects—largely consisting of decent roadways to the provinces—will have to be implemented.

## What to See and Do in Hanoi and Environs

### Army Museum

If you want to see tanks and planes and grenades and shells, this is the place. Better to see this museum before checking out the War Crimes Museum in Saigon. It's not as shocking and sobering. However, here you'll find the wreckage of B-52s and American fighter jets, such as F-111s—if this kind of stuff fascinates you.

***Uncle Ho's mausoleum, where Ho rests embalmed, despite his request to be cremated after his death.***

### Ho Chi Minh Mausoleum and Museum 

*Open 7:30–11:30 a.m. Tues.–Thurs. and Sat.–Sun.*

Somehow you're not surprised when your guide tells you that this mausoleum was modeled after the Lenin tomb in Moscow. The structure itself is a huge imposing building polygonal in shape. It's no doubt the best-maintained building in all of Hanoi. The inner chamber is where the embalmed body of Ho rests; guards surround it. The old man's an eery-looking sight, and his impact on all of our lives this half of the century is felt through the glass. From the mausoleum, you can tour **Ho's house** near the Communist Party guesthouse— which was the former **presidential palace** and residence of the former French governors of Indochina. When the North's quest for independence finally came to fruition in 1954, Ho refused to live

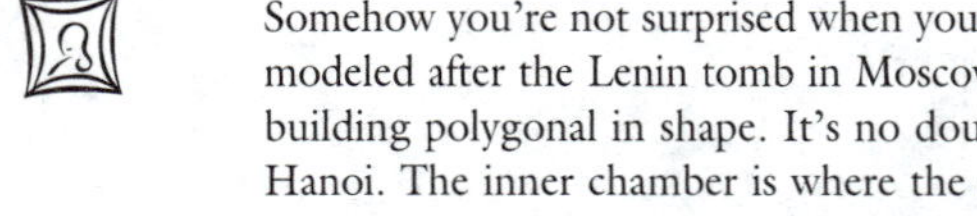

in the palace, opting instead for the electrician's meager house on the palace grounds; he claimed the palace belonged to the people.

**Hanoi Hilton**

*Off of Hai Ba Trung Street.*

This is the morbidly humorous name given to the grisly, forboding Hanoi prison structure that housed U.S. POWs, namely American flyers, during the Vietnam War. Prisoners were tortured here up until at least 1969. Some were held seven years or longer. This was a dark, eery sight before it was razed for the construction of a new hotel. If you hurry, you can still peer through portions of the surrounding wall and look at the rubble.

**National Arts Museum** ★

*Open 8–12 and 1–4 p.m. Tues.–Sun.*

Vietnamese sculpture is exhibited in this small museum located next to the Van Mieu, Vietnam's first university. The museum also features bronze drums and modern Vietnamese painting.

**National History Museum** ★

*Open 8–12 and 1–4 p.m. Tues.–Sun. There is an admission fee.*

This is actually a great place to visit, especially after seeing all the other sights and coming to the conclusion that the Vietnamese must love to yawn. This is Vietnam's leading museum and the center for cultural and historical research. Granted it's tough to know exactly what you're looking at if you don't read Vietnamese or don't have a guide, but the exhibits here are impressive. It's all designed so you can walk though the different periods of Vietnamese history. There are some beautiful bronze Dongson drums and funeral urns, Nguyen Dynasty pieces, models of ancient cities, weapons from the Tay Son revolt, and much more. If you're lucky, you may even get a private tour from one of the museum's curators.

**Old Hanoi (The French Quarter)** ★★

Check out the old quarter of Hanoi, a maze of narrow back alleys with shops selling antiques, flowers and handicrafts. This area is located in Central Hanoi, and was once located in the southeast part of the city as part of the royal plan for placing foreigners. But the quarter's location was far from the city center (down the Red River, susceptible to pollutants spilled into the river, near cemeteries and a leper colony). When the French took the city in 1882, they moved into the area south of Hoan Kiem, between the former area and the Ambassador Pagoda. This is where they built their new city. In 1884, the first permanent houses were built, replacing the huts that existed in the area at the time. But in order to do so, they had to ruin numerous monuments that stood in the area at the time. The Museum of Mines, which is now called the Museum of the Revolution, is on Tong Dan Street, behind the Opera. So is the History Museum. The style of the two buildings contrast with their surroundings. The Museum of History, especially, is built in a neo-Vietnamese style. St. Joseph's Cathedral is between the French and Vietnamese Quarters. It was built in the mid-1880s at the site formerly occupied by Bao Thien Pagoda by Monsignor Puginier. There are two large towers on the cathedral which was built in the neo-gothic style. According to the local Catholic population, this is the highest seat

Southeast Hanoi
0 100 200 300m
0 0.1 0.2mi
Hang Bot Church
Capital
Dong Loi
Hoa Hong
19th December Market
Egypt
Australia
Quan Su
Quan Su 17th Century
Cuba
Tho Nhuom
Chi Lang
Cultural Palace
Pho Tran Hung Dao
Iraq
Cambodia
India
Phan Boi Chau
Pho Yet Kieu
Pho Tran Binh Trong
Duong Le Duan
T An Quy Cap
Pho Nguyen Du
VIP Club
Quang Trung
Pho Kham Thien
Ng. Thuong Hien
Korea
Pho Tran Nang Trung
Circus Theatre
Nguyen Dinh Chieu
Nguyen Binh Khiem
Canadian
Pho 325
Philippines
Nicaragua
Palestine
Thailand
Bay Mau Lake
Kim Lien Temple
Van Hg III
Pho Le Dai Hanh
Pho Kim Lien
Pho Trung Tu
Duong Dai Co Viet
Polytechnic College
Duong Giai Phong
Pho Phuong Mai
Construction College

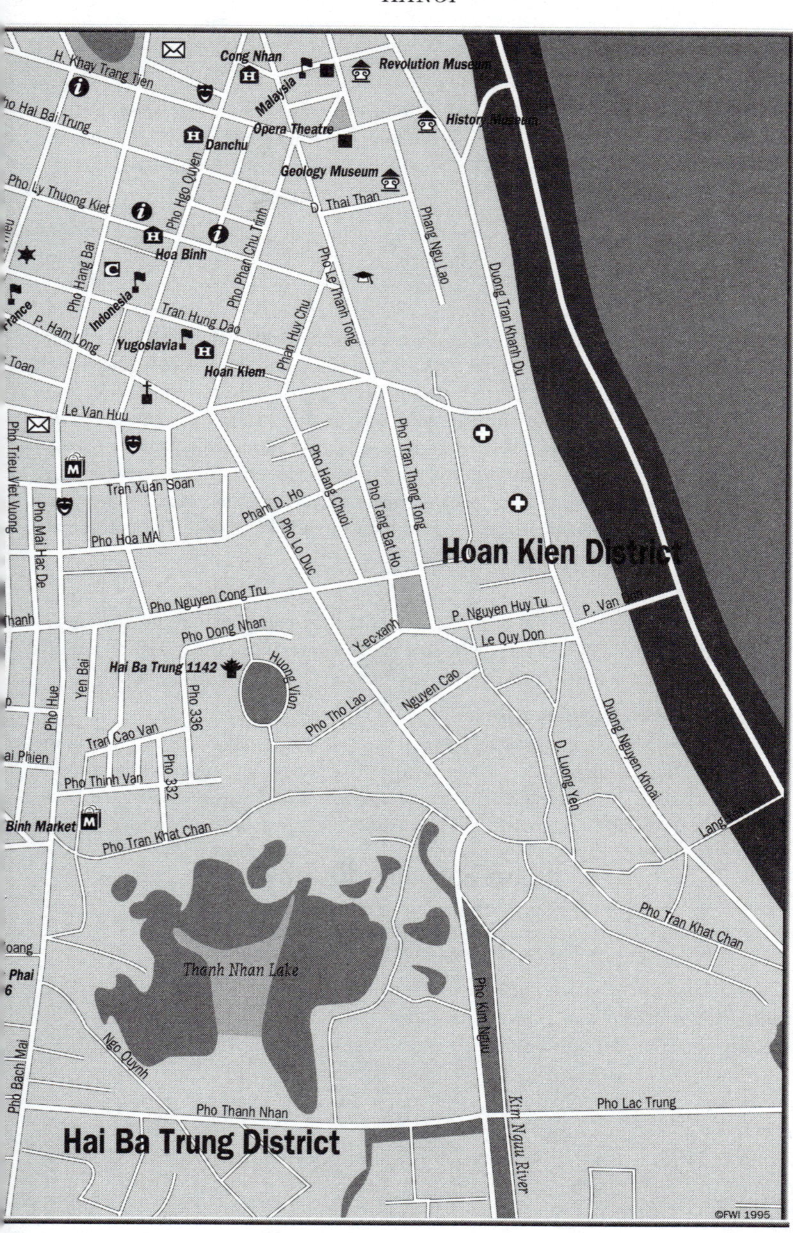

H. Khay Trang Tien
Cong Nhan
Malaysia
Revolution Museum
History Museum
Opera Theatre
Danchu
Geology Museum
D. Thai Than
Pho Ly Thuong Kiet
Pho Ngo Quyen
Hoa Binh
Pho Phan Chu Trinh
Pho Le Thanh Tong
Phang Ngu Lao
Duong Tran Khanh Du
Pho Hang Bai
Indonesia
Tran Hung Dao
P. Ham Long
Yugoslavia
Hoan Kiem
Phan Huy Chu
Le Van Huu
Pho Trieu Viet Vuong
Tran Xuan Soan
Pho Hang Chuoi
Pho Tran Thang Tong
Pho Tang Bat Ho
Pham D. Ho
Pho Lo Duc
Pho Mai Hac De
Pho Hoa MA
Hoan Kien District
Pho Nguyen Cong Tru
P. Nguyen Huy Tu
P. Van Don
Pho Dong Nhan
Y-ec-xanh
Le Quy Don
Hai Ba Trung 1142
Huong Vion
Yen Bai
Pho 336
Pho Hue
Nguyen Cao
Pho Tho Lao
Duong Nguyen Khoai
D. Luong Yen
Tran Cao Van
Pho Thinh Van
Pho 332
Binh Market
Pho Tran Khat Chan
Lang
Thanh Nhan Lake
Pho Kim Nguu
Ngo Quynh
Pho Bach Mai
Pho Thanh Nhan
Pho Lac Trung
Kim Nguu River
Hai Ba Trung District
©FWI 1995

of Vietnam's Catholics. When the communists took control of the city, the size of the congregation dwindled, but has now again grown with the relaxing of religious restrictions. Vietnam is second only to the Philippines in Asia in its number of Catholics. The Ambassador Pagoda is at *73 Quan Su Street*. This was formerly a reception house for visiting Buddhist ambassadors. The main temple is in front, while the rear is dedicated to the monk who cured Emperor Ly Thanh Tong of a disease.

**Botanical Garden**

In the 15th century, King Le Thanh Tong ordered a ring built on an earthen mount so he could better view martial arts demonstrations. After Le died, a temple was built in his honor. For centuries the area was a peaceful sanctuary from the densely populated city. In 1890, the French moved the local residents away and created the Botanical and Zoological Park, which was later named simply the Botanical Garden. The native bamboo and banana trees, as well the rattan trees were replaced with perennial plants and trees. They created ponds and small hills and, after a short time, the garden became luxuriantly green. Today, many of the trees and plants are imported from Africa, as well as vegetables and flowers from temperate zones. During the first part of the 20th century, the French began bringing in cages for lions, tigers and bears—as well as for leopards, goats, deer, elephants, peacocks and pheasants. Now it's a popular attraction for both tourists and locals alike. It's a great place to spend a hot summer afternoon.

**Quan Su Pagoda**

Built in the late 1930s this pagoda is on a site that once served as the quarters for visiting Buddhist VIPs. Some of the Buddha sculptures inside the temple are exquisite. This place is usually packed with wayfarers.

**Temple of Literature (Van Mieu Pagoda)** ★★★

This is the biggest temple attraction in Hanoi. It was founded in 1070 during the reign of Ly Thanh Tong. It is dedicated to Confucious and purportedly modeled after a temple in Shantung, China. There are courtyards, a big bronze bell, and multistoried roofs in the complex. The courtyards feature beautifully carved stelae.

## Hanoi Environs Nearby

### ★Tay Phuong Pagoda

Three km from the first left turn at the 34th km marker of Highway 11A from Hanoi. Its initial name was Sung Phuc Pagoda and then it became Hoanh Son Thien Lam Tu before acquiring its current name. It's located in the Thach Xa commune in the Thach That district of Ha Tay Province. On the horizontal board at the pagoda's gate are written four hieroglyphs, *Tay Phuong Co To* (meaning the West Ancient Pagoda). It was built on a 50-meter tall mountain that locals say looks like a hook. They say that viewing it from a distance, the mountain and the surrounding hills remind them of a buffalo herd. Cau Lau is the herd's leader turning his head back for a drink of water from a lotus pond. After climbing 239 laterite paved steps, you reach the pagoda's gate. There is a main temple and a temple behind it which represent three treasures: Buddha, his law, and the bonze (the Buddhist Trinity). Each building features two roof layers. The upper layer is formed by tile with fig leaf reliefs. The bottom layer is paved with square tiles, painted in the five colors of a monk's robe. The surrounding wall of the pagoda is constructed of Bat Trang bricks. The wooden supporting pillars are on bases of blue limestone and decorated with lotus petal ornaments. The roof edges are carved in the form of rolled leaves. On top of the roofs are small figurines. The curved corners of the roofs also feature carved flower, dragon and phoenix reliefs. Its architecture is outstanding, true sculptural art. All over the pagoda are carved mulberry and fig tree leaves, lotus, chrysanthemums, dragons and tiger heads. There's a collection of 76 statues at the pagoda, red lacquered, carved out of jact-tree wood and trimmed with gold. The statues bear only Vietnamese inscriptions, and each has its own facial expression. These sculptures are perhaps unparalleled in Vietnam. Perhaps the most famous is the statue of Tuyet Son. Intricate lines are cut deeply into his face. His thin body and solitary appearance are designed to elicit remorse and loneliness. According to ancient inscriptions on the pagoda, it was restored in 1632. A three-sector upper temple and a back temple with a 20-sector corridor were also added. Four years later a giant bell was cast and the statues carved. The pagoda was again rebuilt during the Tay Son period in 1794. Definitely worth the visit.

## Thay Pagoda

This pagoda is in Ha Tay Province about 40 km southwest of Hanoi. This is also known as the Master's Pagoda and is dedicated to the historical Thich Ca Buddha (Sakyamuni) as well as to the 18 monks that achieved Nirvana.The monks are on the central altar. There is also a statue of the 12th century monk the pagoda was named after, Tu Dao Hanh. As well, there is a statue of King Ly Nhan Tong, who was reincarnated from Tu Dao Hanh. There's also a stage here where puppet shows are performed during festivals. There are some magnificent caves in the area. The annual festival here is held for three days during the third lunar month.

## Den Hai Ba Trung (Temple)

This temple, well south of Hanoi, was dedicated to the heroines of an aborted revolt against the Chinese in AD 40-43. It was built in 1142 and restored in both the 19th and 20th centuries. Once a year, legend has it, the two sisters return to the temple and walk around it. There's a stone relief depicting the battle, probably carved in the late 15th century.

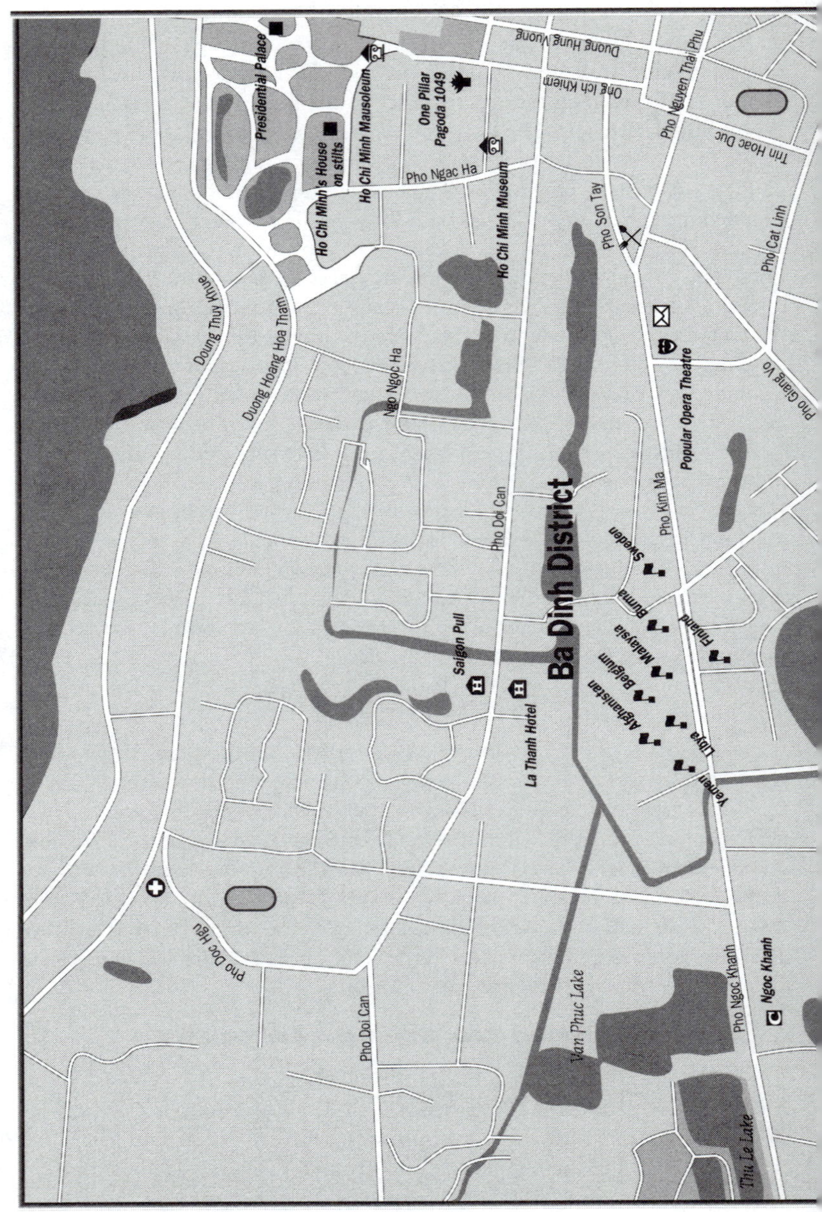

Presidential Palace
Ho Chi Minh's House on stilts
Ho Chi Minh Mausoleum
One Pillar Pagoda 1049
Ho Chi Minh Museum
Pho Ngac Ha
Duong Hung Vuong
Ong Ich Khiem
Pho Nguyen Thai Phu
Tinh Hoac Duc
Pho Son Tay
Pho Cat Linh
Pho Giang Vo
Popular Opera Theatre
Pho Kim Ma
Doung Thuy Khue
Duong Hoang Hoa Tham
Ngo Ngoc Ha
Pho Doi Can
Ba Dinh District
Sweden
Burma
Malaysia
Belgium
Afghanistan
Finland
Libya
Yemen
Saigon Pull
La Thanh Hotel
Pho Doc Ngu
Pho Doi Can
Van Phuc Lake
Pho Ngoc Khanh
Ngoc Khanh
Thu Le Lake

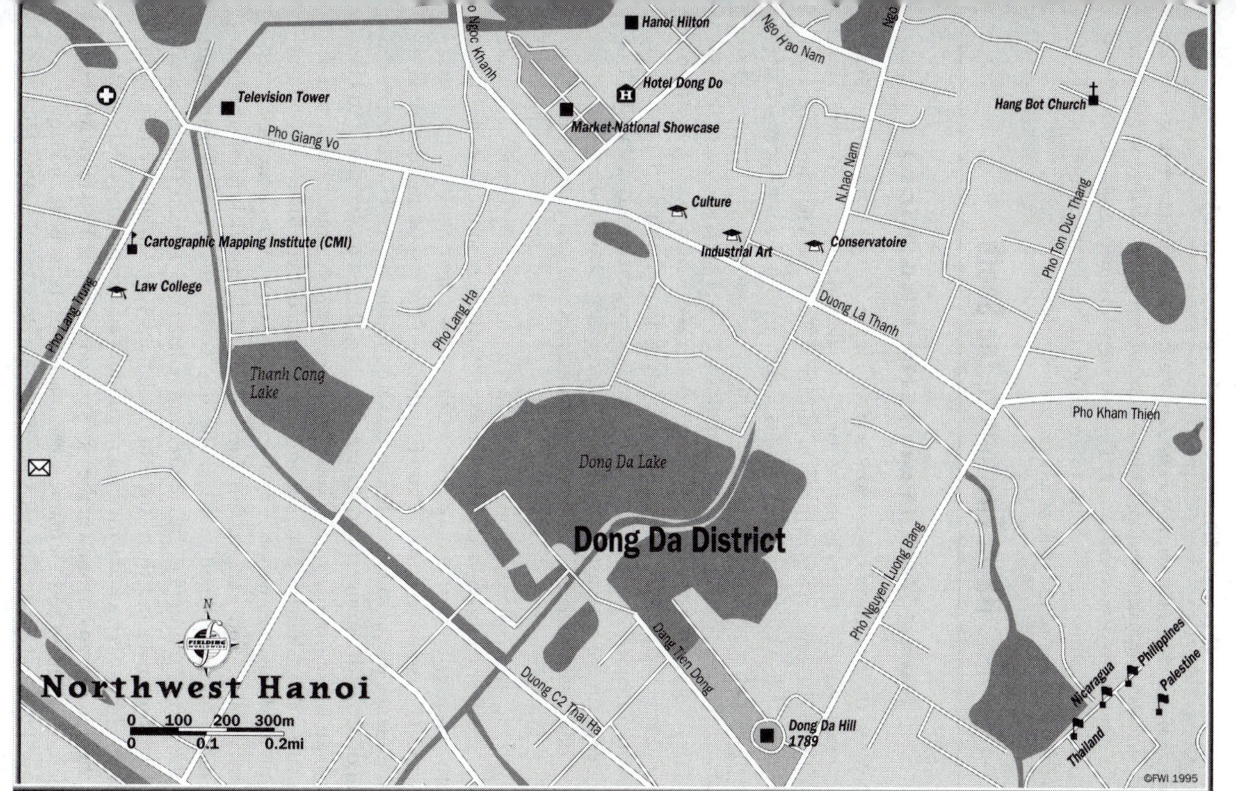
Hanoi Hilton
Ngo Hao Nam
Television Tower
Hotel Dong Do
Hang Bot Church
Market-National Showcase
Pho Giang Vo
N.hao Nam
Culture
Pho Ton Duc Thang
Cartographic Mapping Institute (CMI)
Industrial Art
Conservatoire
Law College
Pho Lang Trung
Pho Lang Ha
Duong La Thanh
Thanh Cong Lake
Pho Kham Thien
Dong Da Lake
Dong Da District
Pho Nguyen Luong Bang
Dang Tien Dong
Philippines
Palestine
Nicaragua
N
Northwest Hanoi
0 100 200 300m
0 0.1 0.2mi
Duong C2 Thai Ha
Dong Da Hill 1789
Thailand
©FWI 1995

### Chua Lien Phai (Pagoda)

*Bach Mai Street, 2 km south of Petic Lac.* Built during the Ly Dynasty in the early 1730s, it was restored in 1884. There are many interesting stupas here and a nine-story octagonal tower. There weren't many pagodas built of this style for the tombs of the laity. Interestingly enough, the temple was built over the remains of the wife of an actor from Saigon.

## Hanoi Environs to the South

### Hung Yen (Formerly Pho Hien)

Next to the Red River 60 km southeast of Hanoi, this historic town with its rich multicultural influences makes for an excellent day or half-day trip. During the 17th century, a number of different cities in Vietnam prospered through trade with other Asian nations as well as with the Europeans. Hung Yen was such a place, and brings to mind cities such as Hoi An, south of Danang. Because of its superb geographic location, Pho Hien was developed and thriving as early as the 15th century, and was once considered Vietnam's second largest commercial center. In the late 16th and early 17th centuries it became a major foreign trade center. The Japanese had quite an amount of influence on the area during the early 17th century. Shortly after, ships from the Philippines, Malaysia, Portugal, England, Holland and France came in to call at Pho Hien. But the Chinese, who had arrived centuries earlier, still played the strongest economic role in the region, especially in the handicraft area. The first Europeans to arrive were the Portuguese in the first part of the 16th century. Long term business relationships lasted between the Portuguese and businessmen from Pho Hien through the rest of the century. British influence began to be felt in the area around the 1670s. However, by the end of the 17th century, European traders were forced to abandon Pho Hien through a magistrate's order, and commerce was performed only with the Japanese and Chinese. Many of the goods traded were for royalty and include gold, bronze, weapons and gunpowder, silver, herbal medicine, textiles, jewelry, and ceramic products. Exported material from the area included silk and painted wood handicrafts. Today, there are still many signs of the past on Pho Hien. Its architecture reflects the Tonkin Delta, China's Fukien Province, and there are other buildings with strong Western influences. The city is packed with ancient antiques and architectural relics. Many of these items can be found in the city's pagodas and the Pho Hien Museum. There are Chinese and Vietnamese ceramic goods, brass bells and laquerware items. Even today, ancient relics are still being discovered in Pho Hien.

## Cuc Phuong National Park

This is quite a trip, as it's about 150 km south of Hanoi and west of Nam Dinh. Set amidst deeply cut limestone mountains, this national park covers more than 25,000 hectares. It is an important archeological site discovered in 1974 in the Hang Dang (Bat) and Con Mong (Animal) grottoes. There have been numerous discoveries here of prehistoric tools and artifacts. This park is home to thousands of different species of endangered and exotic tropical wildlife. A nature preserve was established here in 1962.

## Kiep Bac Pagoda

This is 60 km from Hanoi and about 30 km from Bac Ninh. This recently restored pagoda (founded in the early 1300s) was built to honor the Tran Quoc Tuan, the famous general who aided Tran Hung Dao in defeating more than a quarter-million Mongol soldiers in the mid 1280s.

## Hoa Binh

Hoa Binh is 74 km southwest of Hanoi and the capital of Hoa Binh province. The city, famous for its hill tribes and a large dam on the Song Da River (which created the Song Da Reservoir) can be visited from Hanoi in a day trip. There is a major hydro-electric operation at the dam that generates electricity for much of the north of the country, in fact enough to keep Hanoi from experiencing the constant power failures that put HCMC in the dark. This is also home to members of Muong hill people as well as the Thai. Although there have been problems with foreigners visiting the dam in the past, these obstructions have been largely removed. The tourist office (Hoa Binh Tourism) is located only about 10 km from Hanoi in Ha Dong, at *24 Tran Hung Dao Street.*

## Perfume Pagoda ★

Located about 60 km southwest of Hanoi in Hoa Binh Province, this is a complex of pagodas constructed into the sides of the limestone cliffs of Huong Tich Mountain. Here is found **Huong Tich Chu Pagoda** (Pagoda of the Perfumed Vestige), **Giai Oan Chu Pagoda** (Pagoda of Purgatory), and **Thien Chu** (Pagoda Leading to Heaven). This region experiences a great number of pilgrims who come here to fish, hike, explore caves and go boating. There is a festival that begins during the second lunar month and concludes the last week of the third lunar month.

## Keo Pagoda

Keo Pagoda is 10 km from the town of Thai Binh in Thai Binh Province, close to Thai Bac. There's a beautiful wood-carved bell at this pagoda, which was built to honor Buddha and the monk Khong Minh Khong who cured Emperor Ly Than Ton of leprosy. It was constructed in the 12th century.

There's a dike nearby that makes for good photo opportunities of the pagoda grounds.

## Hanoi Environs to the North & East

### Buc Thap Pagoda

In Ha Bac Province and nearby Van Phuc Pagoda, about 28 km northeast of Hanoi. This pagoda is perhaps best known for its stone four-story stupa dedicated to the monk Chuyet Cong. The exact date of its construction isn't known, however it was built either before or during the 17th century.

### Van Phuc Pagoda

About 28 km northeast from Hanoi. This pagoda was built in 1037 and is surrounded by lush hills.

## Hanoi Environs to the North & West

### Tam Dao Hill Station ★

About 85 km northwest of Hanoi. In 1907 this hill station (some call it Dalat of the north) was founded by the French so that monied colonists could make summer retreats to this elevation of 935 meters to escape the heat of the Red River Delta. This is a beautiful, lush mountainous area featuring giant fern trees about two hours by car from Hanoi. Few foreign tourists reach this hill station, unlike Dalat, so that Tam Dao has yet to suffer from duck paddle boats and Vietnamese cowboys dressed like Roy Rogers that plague Dalat.

Tam Dao Mountain features three summits. Each is about 1200 meters in height. The highest is 1265 meters. They're easily seen from Tam Dao. The hills are teeming with rare animals and plants. The area is also home to a number of hilltribe people. Although the buildings in Tam Dao are somewhat dilapidated, this makes for a beautiful excursion from Hanoi. The summertime is the best time of the year to come here. It gets quite cold up here in the winter. You can stay at the **Tam Dao Hotel** (virtually all foreigners do). The tourist office is located in the hotel. ☎ *306* for both.

### Vinh Yen

Vinh Yen is about 60 km northwest of Hanoi. It's a tiny village cut off from most everything (even though it's on the main road!) that sees few, if any, foreigners. It lies between the Song River and the Tam Dao Mountains. It was the site of battles during the First Indochina War. It has the distinction of being the first place in Vietnam where napalm was used (not by the Americans, but by the French). The attacks killed and wounded thousands of Viet

Minh soldiers. The French General who engineered the strategy, Gen. de Lattre, was called the Fire General by the locals.

## Son Tay

About 40 km northwest of Hanoi. Son Tay is located at the end of the delta region around Hanoi. There's a small citadel in the middle of the complex which was fortified in 1822, but captured in 1883 by French Admiral Courbet.

## A Hung Hoa

A Hung Hoa is 66 km from Hanoi upriver. There's a famous citadel here (at least for the architecture of its watchtower) that used to stand watch over the Song River. Here the topography descends into the valley where the Lo and Black rivers flow. The local population depends on the river for its livelihood, and the inhabitants here tend to be less friendly to foreigners. Legend has it that this was the area where the Hong Bang Dynasty started in 2880 BC and ended in 258 BC. It was part of the Van Long Kingdom. Its capital was Bach Hach (then called Phong Chau), about 80 km from Hanoi to the northwest in Vinh Phu Province. The site of the Hong Bang kings' temple, Den Hung, is close to here in the Nung Hills (80 km west of Hanoi). The temple, the ruins of which are still precariously standing, dates back to the Ly Dynasty. There is the tomb of the mythical leader Hung Huy Vuong in front of the temple.

## Tuyen Quang

Tuyen Quang is located 165 km northwest of Hanoi in Ha Tuyen Province. Tuyen Quang faces Yen Bay from the banks of the Lo River. It was a strategic hamlet for the Nguyen on the path to Yunnan. From 1884-1885, the town was occupied by the French and then was occupied by the Chinese. The Second National Congress of the Vietnamese Communist Party was held here in 1951 in honor of the start-up of the Worker's Party.

## Binh Son

Binh Son is 85 km west of Hanoi on the Lo River. There's an 11-story tower here dating from at least the 11th century. When archeologists were working to restore the tower in 1979, they discovered a "blueprint" (inscribed on a brick) of the temple that dates back to the 8th century. Between Vinh Yen and Tuyen Quang is the village of Thien Khe, which is the site of numerous Buddhist rock paintings. Fifteen km before reaching Tuyen Quang is the former Binh Ca Fortress. It was built in the early 16th century by Vu Cong Mat, a famous general. The walls around the fortress are still visible.

### Tan Trao

Tan Trao is situated 150 km from Hanoi, northwest in Ha Tuyen Province. This town has the distinction of once being the capital of revolutionary Vietnam. Ho Chi Minh organized a mass upheaval here in May 1945. Most of the mandates of the Communist Party were drawn up here. Also in Tan Trao, the Central Committee of the National Liberation was elected. Uncle Ho was elected president.

## Hanoi Environs to the East

The Dong Trieu Ridge and the surrounding area are historically extremely significant in Vietnamese history, particularly to scholars of the country. The ridge averages 500–1000 meters high and borders northern Vietnam with China. During the Cham and Mongol invasions of the 14th century, Tran Dynasty rulers used the area as a hideout and sanctuary. The following areas are extremely remote and rarely, if ever see Western tourists. If you want to visit these areas, as well as the remote areas described earlier in the west, it's extremely important you find a good (a very good) private guide in Hanoi. You should not rely on Vietnamtourism to provide much help in reaching many of these destinations. These communities and sites are well off the beaten track and many are inaccessible by vehicle. Only the hardiest of travelers should attempt visiting these sites. Don't expect any accommodations or decent food and water. Bring your own from Hanoi.

### Dong Trieu

Dong Trieu in Quang Ninh Province is 85 km east of Hanoi. This is an important coal mining area. There are vast deposits in the vicinity. The Trans virtually worshipped the surrounding area at the base of Nui Yen Tu. About 4 km away is the village of Ha Loi where there is the Quynh Lam Pagoda, which dates from the Tran Dynasty. There's a giant bell here. Almost 4 km to the north lies the village of Yen Sinh and a temple and tombs of Tran rulers of the 14th century.

### Kiep Bac

Kiep Bac is located 60 km northeast of Hanoi. This "quaint" village is north of Hai Duong by about 15 km on the eastern border of the Dong Trieu Ridge, above the Hom Hills. Refuge was taken in the hills here by Prince General Hung Dao, better known as Than Quoc Tuan, in 1285 after being defeated by the Mongolians from Loang Son. The prince then regrouped his forces here and later attacked and beat the Mongols in 1289. After his death in 1300 he was buried in a pagoda that was built here earlier in his honor. Hung Doa is considered a national hero in Vietnam. After his death soldiers used to come to the pagoda when war was pending for luck and signs of the battle's outcome. If a soldier's sword was heard to be removed from its sheath, it meant that the battle would be lost. Pregnant women also came to the temple to pray to the spirits for a safe delivery of the child.

## Hai Duong

Hai Duong is in Hai Duong Province, 60 km east of Hanoi. This was a strategic location on the road from Hanoi to Ha Long Bay, as it is located near the summit of the delta in Thai Binh. Today, you can view the remains of a fort that was built here in 1804 by the Nguyen Dynasty.

## Nui Yen Tu

Nui Yen Tu is 45 km east of Hanoi. Here there are many pagodas in the surrounding hills that were constructed by Tan rulers, who used Nui Yen Tu as a retreat. It's damned difficult to get here, but once you reach the area, the views of Ha Long Bay are magnificent.

## Mao Khe

About 8 km east of Dong Trieu. This is the most eastern point of the Co Bang Hills. The Dong Trieu Ridge begins here.

## Con Son

Con Son is 80 km northeast of Hanoi, and 30 km north of Hai Duong. The village offers gorgeous views of the surrounding hillsides. Nguyen Trai, the trusted advisor and aide to Le Loi used this location as a retreat.

## Where to Stay in Hanoi

It wasn't that long ago that one could stroll down the tree-shaded streets of Hanoi and run into nothing more than a few cyclo drivers clamoring for a fare in this sleepy, slow-paced capital. Although it has a long way to go to catch up with the hustle and bustle of Saigon, some pretty good hotels have been springing out of the concrete recently. Sidewalk cafes, nightclubs, and restaurants seem to be opening like barbers at a heavy metal concert. It is said that each week a new hotel opens its doors in Hanoi, most to cater to the hordes of businesspeople converging on the capital in recent years. Even so, the current hotel scheme is still hard pressed to meet the demand, and it can be difficult to find a hotel room in Hanoi at any time of the year. Building more hotels in the capital has been problematic at best due to the government's increasing involvement in the integrity of the structures being razed to make room for the new hotels (see section on architecture). At present, it seems that most new structures are being being born from exisiting ones, although I've seen a good many exceptions to this "rule."

Construction of the US$30 million Ever Fortune Plaza in Hanoi opposite the United Nations compound and the Australian and Egyptian embassies started during the third quarter of 1994 and will be completed by the end of 1996. The hotel and office plaza will feature a five-story base structure and a 16-floor, 242-room hotel tower. The base area will include offices, restaurants, a bar, meeting rooms and a ballroom. Roof-top swimming facilities will be available as well as a health and beauty center. The new structure will tower high over the opposite seven-story Saigon Hotel on the opposite corner.

Also, an American company (New York-based DeMatteis Development Corp.) will build a 14-story tower on the southern bank of Hanoi's West Lake, an area that will cover 4000 square meters. The building will include office and retail space as well as a restaurant, health club, conference facilities and a movie theatre. DeMatteis hopes to build a number of movie theatres throughout Vietnam. The following establishments are already in operation.

### AUTHOR'S NOTE: TELEPHONE PREFIXES

*The following telephone numbers are local exchanges. The country code is 84. The city code is 4.*

**Army Guest House, Army Hotel** **US$50–$120** ★★

*33C Pham Ngu Lao. ☎ 252896. FAX: 259276.*

These two hostelries are run by the defense ministry and are surprisingly clean and well run considering the ominous sounding monikers.*Just 2 blocks from the municipal theatre, and just down the street from the museum of history on Pham Ngu Lao Street*, these two establishments offer 84 rooms with modern facilities, including satellite TV and IDD at moderate prices. Both are popular with ExPats.

**The Dong Loi** **US$45–$70**

*Ly Thuong Kiet Street and Le Duan Street, close to the Hanoi Railway Station. 94 Ly Thuong Kiet Street. ☎ 255721. FAX: 267999.*

This hotel is operated by the Hanoi Tourist Services Company (Torseco). It offers old world charm at moderate prices. Built in the 1930s, this 30-room stucco structure features a spiral staircase and wrought iron banisters as well as molded ceilings and art nouveau light fixtures.

**Hoa Binh Hotel** **US$96–$184** 

*Ngo Quyen Street and the corner of Ly Thuong Kiet. 27 Ly Thuong Kiet. ☎ 253315. FAX: 269818.*

This place has been around since 1923 and it has an excellent location which ensures a steady stream of both tourists and businesspeople alike.The top floor bar offer an excellent view of the city and the tree-lined boulevards below of central Hanoi. Hanoi Tourism runs the place and is in the process of renovating a number of the rooms; at the last count, there were 112—42 are still open during the renovation into a three-star caravansary.

**Thang Loi Hotel** **US$76–$140** 

*Yen Phu, West Lake. ☎ 268211/5. FAX: 252800.*

Hanoi Tourism runs seven hotels in the Hanoi area in addition to the Metropole. It is the biggest hotel operator in the region. Many consider the Thang Loi to be the flagship hotel which was built as a gift from Cuba in 1975. There are a number of new lakeside bungalows built from bamboo bringing the existing amount of rooms to 175. They're all on beautifully landscaped grounds on a small peninsula jutting out into the West Lake. There is a swimming pool and a tennis court. Although the hotel is several kilometers from the city center, you won't mind unless your business brings you into central Hanoi frequently. Tourists will relish the rest and relaxation the Thang Loi affords.

**Tay Ho Palace** **US$64–$120** ★★

*Quang An, Tu Liem.* ☎ *232381. FAX: 232390.*

This hotel also borders the lake, and it takes quite a drive to get there. It's a modern building flanked by lotus paddies, but the service leaves a bit to be desired for an international standard hotel. I'd avoid it. Expensive.

**Boss Hotel** **US$60–$80**

*60 Nguyen Du Street.* ☎ *252690. FAX: 257634.*

*15 rooms.*

This is a lot closer to the center of Hanoi and faces Thien Quang Lake. It's a small and modern hotel, and its VIP lounge is one of the more popular discos in town. Air conditioning, TV, telephone, refrigerators, hot water.

**Hanoi Hotel** **US$169–$390** ★★★★

*D8 Giang Vo Street, Ba Binh District.* ☎ *252240/270. FAX: 259209.*

*76 rooms.*

Hong Kong built and owned, it is managed by the foreign partner Ever Universal Company, and is distinctively Hong Kong in taste and styling, and perhaps even in snotty attitude according to a number of visitors. It's a bit cramped but the 10-year-old structure was recently renovated at a cost of about US$6 million. The structure is 11 stories high and features a huge Chinese restaurant, a business center, nightclub and karaoke. Soon there will be a tennis court overlooking the Giang Vo Lake. Its luxury suites are in the neighborhood of US$300 per night.

**Trang An Hotel** **US$40** ★

*58 Hang Gai Street.* ☎ *268982, 261135. FAX: 84-4-258511.*

Comfortable and cozy, one of Hanoi's skinny highrises (6 stories) with charm and a guesthouse feel. Service extremely friendly. Here, you truly feel like guest. Close to the lake in the city center. Artwork and antiques cover the lobby. Completely renovated. Rooms large and cool with modern air conditioning. Hot water, bath tub, satellite TV, minibar and refrigerator. Great little rooftop restaurant where breakfast is free. Bar. Car rentals, travel reservations and ticketing, tourist guides. No elevator, so the rooms on the top floors require a huff and a puff to get to. But worth it. Recommended.

**Heritage Hotel** **US$105–$120** ★★★

*80 Giang Vo.* ☎ *351414. FAX: 351458, 343882.*

This is on the same street as the Hanoi Hotel and is under Singaporean management. This is a favorite among foreign businesspeople, and I'm told this is Hanoi's only completely new hotel, although I find this hard to believe. The 41-room structure is run by Singapore's Orient Vacation and a Vietnamese local partner Coal Company No. 3. There is a nightclub with karaoke booths, and a restaurant offering a full range of Southeast Asian cuisine.

**The Dong Do** **About US$50–$75** ★★

*Giang Vo Street. Close to Giang Vo Lake. ☎ 343021. FAX: 334228.*

On the top floor is the Sunset Bar, which is run by a Finn and his Vietnamese wife. It's popular with Expats. They claim to have the longest bar in Hanoi. When you've imbibed too much, proprietors can usually get away with such claims. The drink list here includes more than 100 concoctions. Try half of them and you'll be convinced the Finn's claim to the longest bar in Hanoi is absolutely correct, especially when you're trying to find the toilet. Rooms with air conditioning, telephone, minibar.

**Binh Minh Hotel** **US$50**

*27 Ly Thai To Street. ☎ 266441. FAX: 257725.*

*43 rooms.*

Air conditioning, telephones, hot water. Good location.

**Bong Sen Hotel** **US$50**

*34 Hang Bun Street. ☎ 254017.*

*26 rooms.*

Open since 1991 with air conditioned rooms, TV, refrigerator, attached bathrooms.

**Dan Chu Hotel** **US$65–$130** ★★★

*29 Trang Tien Street. ☎ 253323. FAX: 266786.*

A 100-year-old building and it shows. Friendly service. Air conditioning, telephone, TV, dining room, lounge bar. Excellent location.

**Friendship Hotel** **US$45–$60**

*23 Quan Thanh Street. ☎ 253182.*

Singles and doubles. Bar, giftshop.

**Hong Ha Hotel** **US$40**

*78 Yen Phu Street. ☎ 253688.*

*30 rooms.*

North of the railway bridge. Air conditioning, telephones, TV, hot water, refrigerators. Not a bad deal.

**Ho Tay Villa** **US$35–$80** ★

*Quang An, Tu Liem. ☎ 252393. FAX: 232126.*

On the banks of West Lake. Comfortable and clean. Rooms with air conditioning, TV, minibar & refrigerator.

**Hoa Linh Hotel** **US$50**

*35 Hang Bo Street. ☎ 250034. FAX: 243886.*

Air travel booking, car rentals and city tours. Rooms with air conditioning, TV, refrigerator. Good deal.

**Kim Lien Hotel** **US$50–$75** ★★

*Kim Lien A, Dong Da District. ☎ 524930. FAX: 524919.*

Rooms with air conditioning, satellite color TV, minibar, refrigerator. Conference facilities. Great restaurant if you don't feel like going out.

**Melody Hotel** **US$40–$60** ★

*17 Hang Duong. ☎ 263029. FAX: 243746.*

Charming place in a decent location. Rooms with air conditioning, hot water, mninbar and refrigerator.

**Hotel Sofitel Metropole** **US$180–$400** ★★★★★

*15 Ngo Quyen Street. ☎ 266919. FAX: 266920.*
*109 rooms (16 suites).*
*Reservations: ☎ (800) 221-4542 in the U.S.*

Totally renovated. This is the grande dame of Hanoi's hotels. It was first opened in 1910 and was beginning to show signs of aging before US$9 million was pumped into renovations back in 1989. The original hardwood floors remain as do the original shuttered windows. Expats and tourists alike congregate here to share news, read the news and take all this luxury in. All the rooms have air conditioning, attached bathrooms, IDD telephones, satellite TV, private safe deposit boxes. Bar, restaurant with French and Asian cuisine with chefs from China and France, live music—traditional Vietnamese, classical, American jazz. Airport shuttle. A new renovation and expansion, costing some US$34 million, has added 135 rooms and 6000 square meters of office space. Architects were careful to preserve the integrity of the structure, including retaining the hardwood floors in the bedrooms and the shuttered French windows. Sooner or later, most visitors to the capital end up here, not necessarily to stay, but at least to sample the fine food created by both French and Vietnamese chefs. This is the only five-star experience in Hanoi. The hotel also features live music, including jazz, traditional Vietnamese music, as well as classical and contemporary. The French, Vietnamese and Chinese chefs make their own pastries, patés, and ice cream. The hotel's wine selection is the most extensive in Vietnam.Typically, the hotel runs at 95 percent occupancy and you should book at least a month in advance.

**Queen Hotel** **US$40–$70** ★

*189 Giai Phong. ☎ 641238. FAX: 641237.*

Comfortable hotel with the usual amenities in this price range. The drawback is that it's a bit far south of the city center. Restaurant.

**Rose Hotel**

*20 Phan Boi Chau Street. ☎ 254438. FAX: 254437.*

Near the railway station. Singles and doubles. Moderate.

**Saigon Hotel** **US$79–$149** ★★★

*80 Ly Thuong Kiet. ☎ 269499. FAX: 266631.*

Relaxing rooftop terrace. Sauna, massage. Rooms with air conditioning, color satellite TV, refrigerator, minibar. Restaurant.

**Spring Song Hotel** **US$50–$80** ★★

*27 Mai Hoc De. ☎ 229169. FAX: 229162.*
*27 rooms.*

Relaxing atmosphere. Rooms with color satellite TV, IDD telephone. Hey, there's even an elevator here. Unheard of in Hanoi! Good Asian and European fare in the restaurant. Music performances.

**Thuy Tien (Narcissus) Hotel** **US$45–$180** ★★★

*1C Tong Dan. ☎ 244775/7. FAX: 244784.*
*60 rooms.*

This place has been getting good reviews. All the amenities for the price range. Restaurant, bar. Spacious rooms with air conditioning, TV, minibar & refrigerator.

**Thang Long Hotel** **US$50–$100**

*Giang Vo. ☎ 252270.*

Drab 10-story structure near Giang Vo, with service to match. Air conditioning, TV, two restaurant, shop, bar.

**Trang Tien Hotel** **US$10–$20**

*35 Trang Tien Street.*

Basic guesthouse fare, but popular with the backpacker set. Restaurant downstairs. A good place to trade trail stories.

There are also a ton of mini-hotels in Hanoi (the numbers change daily), the type that the government has discouraged due to the decimating of historic architecture. But not ones to turn down hard currency, the government has allowed these establishments to proliferate as if it were rebuilding the city after a war, which in many ways it still is. According to Vietnamtourism, there are more than 80 such guesthouses, although I suspect the number has gone up substantially in the last two years. Among the better mini-hotels are the **Bac Nam Hotel**, just a few blocks from the Metropole on Ngo Nguyen Street. There's also the **Phu Gia Hotel** on Hang Trong Street which overlooks Hoan Kiem Lake in the center of the city. The **Trang An Hotel** on Hang Gai Street has been getting good reviews. The narrow, wedding-cake-like building is squeezed between shops in the 36 historic streets section of the city.

## Where to Eat in Hanoi

### INSIDER TIP

*Where in Hanoi can you order a plate of bangers and mash and a pint of Bass? Amidst the faded pastel architecture of the capital's Old Quarter, try the Emerald* (53 Hang Luoc Street, ☎ 259258*). This is one of the newest eateries and drinking establishments in Hanoi, an authentic Irish pub. There's also Guinness and a variety of Scottish malts. The proprietors–Steven, Patrick, and David–go by the acronym SPUD and decided to create their home away from home about a year ago. The interior is graced with Gaelic motifs and glasses hang in brass rail holders over a dark wood counter. The pub offers hamburgers, chili con carne, soups, fries, fish pie, shepherds's pie, and a chicken and mushroom-stuffed pie that some folks complain is too stuffed. The big disappointment is the price of the Bass, which runs US$6 a pint. The owners say it's because the stuff has to go through hell and back, and worse–the Malacca Strait–before it reaches Hanoi.*

**A Restaurant** **$**

*Thang Long Hotel.*

One of two of perhaps the most creatively named eateries in Tomorrowland. Basic Vietnamese fare. The place seats hundreds. **B Restaurant** is a lot smaller and has a menu in English. Hooray.

**A Little Italian** **$$**

*81 Thu Nhuom. ☎ 258167.*

Excellent Italian fare. Best for pizza and spaghetti.

**The Pear Tree** **$$$**

*78 Tho Nhuom. ☎ 257812.*

Australian run with an Aussie atmosphere. Expats gather here to soak up the suds and munch on shrimp.

**Indochine** **$$$** ★

*16 NamNgu. ☎ 245097.*

Expensive and fashionable. One of the trendiest eateries in Hanoi. Popular with expat hipsters and yuppies and an increasing number of their Vietnamese counterparts.

**Restaurant 22** **$$$**

*22 Hang Can. ☎ 267160.*

Superb Vietnamese and French.

**Restaurant 75** **$**

*75 Tran Quoc Toan. ☎ 265619.*

Vietnamese cuisine. Excellent and inexpensive. Popular with the locals.

**Bodega Cafe** **$$**

*57 Trang Tien Street.*

For good pastries.

**Dan Chu Hotel Restaurant** **$$**

*29 Tran Tien St. ☎ 253323.*

Cheery atmosphere, average food. Menus in three languages.

**Darling Cafe** **$**

*33 Hang Quat Street.*

Decent Western food, cheap. Popular with backpackers.

**Hoa Binh Hotel Restaurant** **$**

*Hoa Binh Hotel.*

This is good, cheap food.

**Piano Restaurant** **$$$**

*50 Hang Vai Street. ☎ 232423.*

Features some imported wines and beers; good shrimp and crab; live music.

**Restaurant 202** **$$**

*202A Pho Hue Street. ☎ 259487.*

This used to be the best restaurant in Hanoi before all the trendy joints started opening up in the last couple of years. Still highly recommended. Both Vietnamese and Western food, but specializes in the latter.

**Rose Restaurant** **$$**

*15 Tran Quoe Tian Street. ☎ 254400.*

This place is usually quite crowded. Both Asian and Western cuisine.

**Sophia Restaurant** **$$**

*6 Hang Bai Street. ☎ 255069.*

There's a cafe downstairs and restaurant upstairs. Average.

**Mekki-Lan Anh** **$$$**

*9A Da Tuong. ☎ 267552.*

Known for its Algerian cuisine of all things. Also Vietnamese and French fare.

**Club Opera** **$$$**

*59 Ly Thai To. ☎ 268802.*

Vietnamese and Western food at very French prices. Oo-la-la.

**Galleon Steakhouse** **$$$**

*50 Tran Quoc Toan. ☎ 228611.*

Steaks and crepes at outrageous prices but delicious.

**Hot Rock Cafe** **$$**

*11A1 Giang Vo. ☎ 245661.*

It's only a matter of time before the Hard Rock people hire lawyers.

**Le Loft** **$$$**

*17 Trang Tien. ☎ 250625.*

Vietnamese and French. Expensive.

**The Pastry & Yoghurt Shop** **$$**

*252 Hang Bong. ☎ 250216.*

More a cafe rather than a place for a full sit-down meal. The name says it all.

**Mother's Pride** **$$**

*53 Ba Trieu. ☎ 228055.*

Superb Malaysian-style cafe. Satay, the works.

**Cherry Blossom Inn** **$$**

*18 La Thai Tu. ☎ 266377.*

If you're into Japanese, this is the place. Packed with Japanese tourists.

**Sunset Pub** **$$**

*On the roof of the Dong Do Hotel. 10 Giang Vo. ☎ 351382.*

Great burgers; passable pizza.

**Le Coq D'Or** **$$$**

*130 Le Duan. ☎ 524713.*

Packed with the French movers and shakers of Hanoi. If you're anyone else, you'll feel out of place.

**Le Bistro** **$$$**

*35 Tran Hung Dao Street. ☎ 266136.*

French and Vietnamese. Expensive.

**Marriott's Cook House** **$$$**

*65 Ngo Hue. ☎ 226634.*

Excellent Chinese, Vietnamese and European fare.

**The Emerald** **$$**

*53 Hang Luoc. ☎ 259285.*

British-style pub and ale house serving Brit pies, stews and fish & chips.

**Gala International** **$$**

*33 Nghi Tam. ☎ 234290.*

Local and European dishes. Karaoke.

**Balance Bar** **$$**

*25C Phan Dinh Phung. ☎ 230048.*

European cuisine in a relaxing setting.

**Little Dream Snack Bar & Gallery** **$$$**

*9 Pham Su Manh.* ☎ *243922.*

Dine to classical music as you're surrounded by original oil paintings. Not popular with backpackers.

**L'Elegant** **$$$**

*33 Pho Hue.* ☎ *261639.*

Vietnamese the French way.

**Cafe de Paris** **$$$**

*16A Nguyen Cong Tu.* ☎ *212701.*

Parisian to the max. Expensive.

**Five Royal Fish** **$$**

*16 Le Thai To.* ☎ *244368.*

Great setting. Vietnamese and Western cuisine.

**Viet Hoa** **$$**

*119 Hue.* ☎ *266918.*

Great Vietnamese.

**La Terrazza** **$$$**

*49 Nghi Tam Road (West Lake).* ☎ *238049.*

Home-made pasta and other Italian specialties. Excellent.

**Poppy** **$$**

*1 Ngoc Khanh.* ☎ *349069.*

A hangout for Swiss expats and tourists. Good Swiss cuisine, including sausages, racelette and fondue.

**The Pear Tree** **$$$**

*78 Tho Nhuom.* ☎ *257812.*

Western cuisine, Italian coffee and fresh cakes.

**Lucky Restaurant** **$$**

*49 Quan Thanh.* ☎ *432888.*

Chinese, specializing in Hainanese chicken rice.

**The First Restaurant** **$$**

*12 Trang Thi.* ☎ *240060.*

Shanghai specialties. Gathering place for Chinese businessmen. Just opened.

**The Green Bamboo** **$** ★

*42 Nha Trung Street.* ☎ *268752.*

Opened in Jan. '94. It was hip while it was undiscovered, but now it's a favorite among backpackers. January 1994 was a long time ago. Now just another brick in the wall—although still worth it. Music, outdoor dining, cheap prices in the heart of Hanoi.

## Nightlife in Hanoi

Hanoi has always been considered a little more tame than its cousin to the south, Ho Chi Minh City, but the scene is changing rapidly. Although it's still a little tougher to find the constellations and hip clubs in the capital that abound in Saigon, the underground is beginning to surface. If you don't like to get to bed until the wee hours you might want to consider checking out the following:

## Bars

**Apocalypse Now** ★

☎ *244302.*

This is exactly like it's sister bar in Saigon. Manufactured seediness with great music. At press time, the bar was relocating, just as the one in Saigon did a short time ago. Expect much of the same when Hanoi's version reopens. Backpackers, rockers and young expats trying to find a job or buy T-shirts.

**Sunset Pub** ★

*Dong Do Hotel.* ☎ *351382.*

Live music on Thursdays and Saturdays. Boasts the longest bar in Hanoi. You can drink yourself from here to Haiphong. Serves pizza that's not half bad.

**Green Bamboo**

*42 Nha Chung.* ☎ *268752.*

Backpackers and young locals hang here. It's above the restaurant. Cheap drinks and a quiet atmosphere. On my visit a loud American was tying to tell a young Vietnamese that shuttlecock isn't a real man's game.

**Bar Le Club**

*Hotel Metropole. 15 Ngo Quyen.* ☎ *266919.*

Forget this place unless you've got a wad of cash and a pressed linen suit handy. Best for business people. Nothing more than a very expensive bar in a very expensive hotel. Do not get drunk here. Well-heeled customers nurse their drinks as they might a glass of gasoline.

**The Blue Bar**

*57 Ly Thai To.* ☎ *249247.*

As the name implies, you walk around in this place feeling like you're under a black light—or that at any moment Willy Dixon and Albert Collins will walk in and sit down with a couple of dobros. But, alas, it's more boring here than that. Karaoke, bad music and warm beer. But as I always drink mine with ice, it didn't matter. Mainly expat crowd. Large outdoor area with a pool table.

**The White Bar**

*15 Nguyen Dinh Chieu.* ☎ *228380.*

No relation to the Blue Bar. Stays open all night and attracts Hanoi's expat boozers. Reminds me a little of Bangkok's Thermae Cafe, but without the hookers.

**Balance Bar**

*25C Phan Dinh Phung.* ☎ *230048.*

Decent music and predominantly thirsty Vietnamese customers. The bar says it offers at least 1000 types of drinks. The only one who will get a chance to test this claim is the chief engineer on the reconstruction of National Highway 1.

**The Polite Pub**

*5 Bao Khanh.* ☎ *250959.*

This place is very polite indeed. If you've found a local partner, it's a great place to bring her/him—as neither of you will be offended or distracted by anything. Sterile but cozy.

**The Gold Cock** ★

*5 Bao Khanh.* ☎ *259499.*

Right next door to the Polite Pub. This is one of the most happenin' watering holes in town and anything but polite, although for no particular reason. But on the weekends it's packed with tourists, expats and Vietnamese. It gets loud in here. A good place to imbibe until 3 a.m.

**The Pear Tree**

*78 Tho Nhuom.* ☎ *257812.*

Open until midnight. I kinda liked this place, although at three bucks for a beer, it's a little steep. Satellite TV and a couple of pool tables for amusement between swills. Expats and some locals.

**The Pub**

*52 Ly Thuong Kiet.* ☎ *243054.*

Usually full with expats, this is a quiet bar and good place to bring a friend for a relaxing brew and a game of darts. There's not a lot of action here. Two bar areas with a tree between them that rises up above the roof. Closing time at 2 a.m.

**The Billabong Bar** ★★

*Australian Embassy. 62 Ly Thuong Kiet.*

This place is classic Aussie and highly popular with well-heeled expats. All the great Australian beers here. But dress well and don't get too loud unless an Aussie drinking buddy gets loud first. At press time, the club was accepting only members and their guests.

## Nightclubs/Discos

**The Lakeside**

*West Lake.*

Some of the best music and dancing in Hanoi. But be prepared to sweat. There's no air conditioning here and the place gets packed with Hanoi groovsters.

**Music City**

*Near the Bach Mai Hospital.*

Large upstairs club at around 2000 square meters. There's a dance floor here but not a lot of people use it. The lighting is a little brash and that may be the reason why. Great sound system, but you better be into the squealing of recorded Vietnamese pop.

**The Top(Disco) Club**

*Thuyen Quang Lake.* ☎ *226641.*

Nobody ever seems to be in this dark, moody venue, although the music is good and the sound system makes for decent grooving.

**My Lan Hotel**

Barry Manilow does Guns n' Roses here. Small. Pass it by.

**Queen Bee** 

*42 Lang Ha. ☎ 352612.*

One of the coolest spots in town, or at least it's well on the way. Huge dance floor and Hanoi's version of a grunge-punk crowd. There's live music here, which is its best appeal. Some of the music rocks, by even Western standards. But the heavy stuff comes in spurts, separated by corny pop foot-tappers. The place is usually packed with well-dressed Hanoi hipster youths with earrings, but is attracting a growing number of Westerners. Great dance floor which is always jammed. Get ready to sweat your ass off if you decide to actually dance to this stuff. Tough to get local ladies to dance with you if you're a foreigner.

**Chessboard Hotel**

This place rocks when there's a decent band on the bill. There used to be a US$15 cover charge here, but it was dropped after customers began dropping off. Although the music can get loud here, not a lot of dancing goes on. Low-key atmosphere. A place where I don't feel out of place not wearing white. It was the first place in Hanoi I felt at home in "naked chick on an Indian motorcycle" T-shirt.

**Royal Palace Nightclub**

*20 Hang Tre. ☎ 244233.*

Live music, but usually performed by Filipino bands that come across more like Barry Manilow doing Guns 'n Roses.

**The VIP Club** ★

*62 Nguyen Du. ☎ 269167.*

Tiny venue. Hot and sweaty. This place was formerly the only joint in town where foreigners could let their hair down.

## Shopping in Hanoi

### Lacquerware & Souvenirs

**The Souvenir Shop**

*30A Ly Thuong Kiet.*

Top-quality handicrafts, including a wide range of lacquerware, stone carvings, woodwork, textiles & fabrics, paintings and ceramics. Definitely worth checking out.

A number of other lacquerware and souvenir shops can be found at **3**, **13**, **17**, **19**, and **21**, **Hang Khay**. These shops offer traditional Vietnamese handicrafts as well as watches and clocks from Germany, Russia and France.

### Clothing & Fashion

It is pretty difficult to find top-quality Western-made clothing, although it is available. But you didn't come to Vietnam for Levis. Vietnamese silk is among the best in the world. The best places for silk in Hanoi are along Hang Gai Street (Thread Street).

**Khai Silk**

*96 Hang Gai. ☎ 254237. FAX: 245150.*

Exquisite raw and refined silk, either in material or apparel form. Tailors on site to create either Vietnamese or Western styles. Recommended.

**Kenly Silk**

*102 Hang Gai.* ☎ *267236. FAX: 252496.*
Great place for embroidery, lace and silk.

Van Can Street is a good area for purchasing traditional Vietnamese **ao dai** dresses. For Western styles, try the following:

**The Leather Boutique**

*53A Hang Bai.*
Western clothes, leather goods and shoes.

**Verve Boutique**

*18 Hang Bai.*
This is also a good place for Western fashions, although some of the styles are dated.

## Gourmet Foods

It seems that every potato chip and soda stall in the city are now carrying expensive imported foods, wines and liquors. You won't have any problem finding them. Two of the better centers you might want to check out:

**The Food Shop**

*3 Hom Market, Pho Hue.* ☎ *227557.*
Imported canned and dry foods, as well as French cheeses and expensive imported wines.

**Hanoi Minimart**

*72 Tran Xuan Soan (2nd floor of Hom Market).* ☎ *229714/5.*
This is one of Hanoi's rare American-style supermarkets, offering a wide variety of the stuff you're used to getting back at Ralph's, Albertson's or Piggly Wiggly. Expensive, and the place gets jammed aisle-to-aisle with expats and the newly-affluent locals.

## Lingerie & Cosmetics

**Cho Hom (Hon Market)**

*Pho Hue.*
This area contains a number of kiosks offering an array of Western-made and other international products. But you'll pay the price.

## Musical Instruments

**Hanoi Music Center**

*42 Nha Chung.*
Here is offered a large variety of pianos, violins, guitars and other instruments, as well as modern sound equipment. Really the only place in town if you're looking to replace that guitar that got smashed up on the flight from HCMC.

Another store at *11 Hang Non* offers a dazzling selection of classical Vietnamese instruments.

## Sports in Hanoi

### Health Clubs/Gyms

Catching on to the Western fad of body-beautiful, numerous health clubs and gyms have opened up in Hanoi in recent years and months. There may be as many as 40 gyms/

health centers in the capital, the crux of them frequented by locals only. However, a growing number cater to expats and tourists, at incredibly low prices. The ladies' centers offer the most hi-tech equipment, while the men typically go for the traditional free weights. Most of the men's gyms are stocked with relatively primitive equipment. Keep in mind that most of these places aren't Gold's Gym in Redondo Beach. Vietnamese men traditionally work out barefooted or in sandals—many exercise in their street clothes (some in suit trousers and wingtips!). In clubs catering to foreigners and locals alike of both sexes, it would be prudent for Western women to forego thong leotards in favor of baggier gym wear. (However, the Barbie cutie-pie workout fashions made popular by Jane Fonda in the early 80s are just starting to catch on here, namely leggings, spandex, lipstick and nail polish in the hue of the spandex, and big hair.) As well, most of the clubs do not offer medical advice nor guidance on diet to help the body building process. Keeping in shape in Hanoi is at your own risk.

**Army Club**

*19 Hoang Dieu. ☎ 233751.*

*US$8.40 per month.*

Women only. There's a cold shower here. The club accepts locals and foreigners alike.

**Eva Club**

*3rd floor, Hom Market. ☎ 226374.*

*US$9 per month.*

Women only. Multi-gym with saunas and a steam bath. Locals and foreigners are both welcomed.

**Hoan Kiem Fitness Club** ★

*41 Nha Chung. ☎ 285530. US$7 for men per month.*

*US$12 for women. US$30 for foreigners.*

A clip-joint. The excuse for the heavy foreigners' tag is that the club is responsible in the event of an accident. A case of the pre-ASEAN Vietnam blues. Upscale; there's a swimming pool and even a disco here to flaunt those new flanks. Hot and cold shower.

**Khuc Hao Club**

*18 Le Hong Phong.*

*US$4 a month for locals. US$8.20 for foreigners.*

Men and women welcome, foreigners and locals alike. Another clip-joint. But you're probably used to price discrimination by now.

**October 10th Club**

*115 Quan Thanh. ☎ 259559.*

*US$4 for men per month. US$5 for women.*

Pretty basic. Don't expect any LCDs on your T-cell count here.

**Que Lam Fitness Club**

*Dong Da district cultural house. ☎ 525278.*

*US$3 per month for men. US$5 for women.*

This is a bargain for a multi-gym.

## Directory

### AUTHOR'S NOTE

*Hanoi will invest close to US$500 million to upgrade Hanoi International Airport's facilities, as nearly 10 million travelers are expected to pass through the airport in the near future. Additionally, 10 tube lines for incoming aircraft are expected to be built. The total airport area will increase to 50,000 square meters, including a three-story terminal building. Take-off areas, runways, and technical stations are also anticipated to be improved.*

### Transportation

Hanoi is 1710 km from Saigon, 765 km from Danang, 660 km from Hue, 420 km from Dien Bien Phu, 165 km from Ha Long Bay, 153 km from Thanh Hoa, 103 km from Haiphong, and 90 km from Ninh Binh.

**By air:**

Hanoi's airport, Noi Bai Airport is about 50 km from the center of Hanoi and is about an hour's drive by microbus (the new bridge has cut this down to 40 minutes or less), the cheapest and fastest way of reaching the city center, although there are local buses that pick up passengers at the airport's domestic terminal. Expect to pay about US$.60 for the bus ride and at least US$4 for a microbus ride that brings passengers to their destinations in Hanoi and then ends up at the Vietnam Airlines offices at *60 Nguyen Du Street* or *1 Quang Trung Street*. Be duly warned that coming into Hanoi by air is an absolute pain in the ass. The airport itself resembles a warehouse, and the wait for your baggage can take some time indeed. Incoming planes park well away from the terminal, and there is only one baggage conveyor belt in the domestic terminal, sometimes handling luggage from three or four different aircraft. Microbuses also depart for the airport many times during the day, but contact the VN office for the exact schedules, as they change and are infrequently adhered to. Microbuses tend to leave when full no matter what time they are scheduled to depart. International passengers can arrange to depart for the airport at the VN office located at *1 Quang Trung Street*. Again, buses leave when they are full. But remember to buy a ticket for the microbus a day in advance. By taxi, the hour trip will set you back at least US$10 and I've talked with people who have paid as much as US$20-35 for the ride. You can arrange for a taxi to meet you at your hotel or you can hire one at the VN office for the airport. If you're negotiating with a taxi driver, it's better to do it in dong, and be sure the rate agreed upon is for either the car itself or your own personal fare if you're being joined by other passengers. **Touts:** After flying into Noi Bai Airport, you will be greeted by throngs of taxi touts asking US$25 for the one-way trip downtown. These fares can usually be bargained down to US$10-15.

Flights leave from HCMC to Hanoi daily every 30 minutes from 6:30 a.m. to 5:30 p.m. Flights from Hanoi to HCMC depart every 30 minutes from 7:20 a.m. to 6:30 p.m.

**Note:** Much less English is spoken in the north, and this is particularly frustrating at the airport, where few, if any transportation directors have the ability to say many more than just a few words. They certainly know the meaning of $ signs, however. Conditions are a little more modern at the international terminal, but certainly not up to international standards

See "Author's Note" above on the proposed expansion of the airport's facilities. Also see the VN timetable found earlier in this edition for selected international and domestic routes and schedules on Vietnam Airlines.

**By train:**

Trains leave daily for Saigon from Hanoi's Ga Hanoi train station, about a 15 minute cyclo ride from the city center. Expect a 50-hour train ride to Saigon from Hanoi.(See the railway timetable earlier in this edition.)

**By bus:**

Hanoi has four "bus stations." One station *5 Le Thong Street* has two buses a day which depart for Ha Long Bay. The trip takes about 5 hours. They leave early in the morning, around 7–9 a.m. The Kim Ma station on Nguyen Thai Hoc street services the northwest of Vietnam., including Son Tay, Hat Lot, Phu To, Trung Ha, Moc Chau, Bat Bat, Da Chong, Son La, Yen Bai, and Hoa Binh. Kim Lien station is on the southwest edge of Thien Quang Lake and serves destinations in the south, including Vinh, Hue, Danang, Quy Nhon, Ninh Binh, Nam Dinh, Cam Ranh, Nha Trang, and Saigon to mention a few. Again, buses leave early in the morning. The fountain at the northern tip of Hoan Kiem Lake has microbuses that leave regularly for Haiphong.

Transportation around town is usually done by conventional **cyclo**. But their charges to foreigners are usually outrageous. Agree upon a price and put it in writing is the suggestion of many travelers, as the scam in Saigon whereby cyclo drivers claim to be cheated at the end of the ride is an even worse problem in Hanoi. Hiring a bicycle (for about US$1 per day) is the best way of seeing the sights of Hanoi. They can be rented from a number of hotels and bike rental shops across Hanoi.

| LAND DISTANCES FROM HANOI | |
|---|---|
| **Ba Be Lakes** | *240 km* |
| **Bac Giang** | *52 km* |
| **Bac Ninh** | *30 km* |
| **Bach Thong** | *160 km* |
| **Cam Pha** | *190 km* |
| **Cao Bang** | *272 km* |
| **Da Bac** | *105 km* |
| **Danang** | *765 km* |
| **Dien Bien Phu** | *420 km* |

| LAND DISTANCES FROM HANOI | |
|---|---|
| **Ha Dong** | *10 km* |
| **Ha Giang** | *345 km* |
| **Hai Duong** | *56 km* |
| **Haiphong** | *95 km* |
| **Hong Gai/Bai Chay** | *165 km* |
| **Ho Chi Minh City** | *1720 km* |
| **Hue** | *660 km* |
| **Lai Chau** | *490 km* |
| **Lang Son** | *150 km* |
| **Nam Dinh** | *90 km* |
| **Ninh Binh** | *43 km* |
| **Phat Diem** | *120 km* |
| **Son La** | *308 km* |
| **Tam Dao** | *85 km* |
| **Thai Binh** | *110 km* |
| **Thai Nguyen** | *80 km* |
| **Thanh Hoa** | *150 km* |
| **Tuyen Quang** | *165 km* |
| **Viet Tri** | *290 km* |
| **Yen Bai** | *180 km* |

### General Post Office

*85 Dinh Tien Hoang Street*. The International Post Office is next door at *87 Dinh Tien Hoang Street*.

### International Telephone, Fax Services

The necessary international communications services can be found at the International Post Office or at *66-68 Trang Tien Street* and *66 Luong Van Can Street*. All of Hanoi's upscale hotels also offer fax and IDD services. Expect to pay US$7–8 for the first page when faxing to the States and slightly less than that for additional pages. IDD phone calls can be done at a rate of about US$5 for the first minute and slightly less than that for subsequent minutes.

### TNT International Express Office

*3 Hang Khay Street.* ☎ *257615; FAX: 255829.*

## Immigration Police Station

*89 Tran Hung Dao Street.*

## Hospitals & Emergencies

**Bach Mai Hospital**

*Giai Phong Rd. ☎ 253731, 522004.*

**K Hospital**

*43 Quan Su Street. ☎ 252143.*

**Asia Emergency Assistance**

*4 Tran Hung Dao Street, 4th floor. ☎ 213555*

**Dr. Kot Rafi**

*Van Phuc A2, Room 101/102. ☎ 430748. Mobile: 019-041919.*

**French Embassy**

*57 Tran Hung Dao. ☎ 252719*

**Swedish Clinic**

*Van Phuc area. ☎ 252464.*

## Tourist Offices

**Vietnamtourism**

*54 Nguyen Du Street. ☎ 255963; FAX: 252707.*
*30A Ly Thuong Kiet. ☎ 264154, 257532.*

**Hanoi Tourism Service Co. (TOSERCO)**

*1 Trang Tien Street. ☎ 250876; FAX: 259209.*
*25 Tran Dung Dao Street. ☎ 254347*
*94 Ly Thuong Kiet. ☎ 255721, 267957.*

**Oscan Enterprises**

*60 Ngyuen Du Street. ☎ 52690; FAX: 57634.*

**Vung Tau International Tourist Services**

*136 Hang Trong Street. ☎ 252739.*

## Banks and Moneychangers

**Bank of Foreign Trade**. *49-49 Ly Thai To Street*. This bank, like others in Vietnam, will not change dong back into dollars. On the black market you can change dong back into US dollars. Locations are usually found on Trang Tien Street.

## Airline Offices

**Vietnam Airlines**

*International address: 1 Quang Trung Street. ☎ 253842, 250888, 254440.*
*Domestic address: 60 Nguyen Du Street. ☎ 255194.*

**Singapore Airlines**

*15 Ngo Quyen Street at the Hotel Sofitel Metropole.*

**Air France**

*1 Ba Trieu Street. ☎ 253484; FAX: 266694.*

**Thai Airways**

*1c Quang Trung Street. ☎ 266893; FAX: 267394.*

Note: These are also the offices for **Cathay Pacific** and **Malaysian Airlines**.

## Useful Taxi Numbers

**Hanoi Taxi**

☎ *265252, 535252.*

Metered. US$25-35 one-way to the airport. Local: US$2 for the first 2 km and US$0.67 per km after that.

**Thang Long Taxi**

☎ *265241.*

**Fujicab**

☎ *255452.*

Unmetered. US$35 one-way to the airport.

**Taxi PT**

☎ *533171.*

Metered. US$20-25 one-way to the airport. Local: US$1.5 for the first 2 km and US$0.40 per km after that.

**Red Taxi**

☎ *353686.*

A new fleet of metered taxis. Prices comparable with Hanoi taxi.

## Embassies in Hanoi

**Afganistan**

*D1 Van Phuc Quarter.*
☎ *253249.*

**Algeria**

*15 Phan Chu Trinh Street.*
☎ *253865.*

**Australia**

*66 Ly Thuong Kiet Street.*
☎ *252763.*

**Belgium**

*D1 Vann Phuc Quarter, Rooms-105-108.*
☎ *252263.*

**Bulgaria**

*358 Street, Van Phuc Quarter.*
☎ *257923.*

**Cambodia**

*71A Tran Hung Dao Street.*
☎ *253789.*

**Canada**

*39 Nguyen Dinh Chieu Street.*
☎ *265840.*

**China**

*46 Hoang Dieu Street.*
☎ *253737.*

**Cuba**

*65 Ly Thuong Kiet Street.*
☎ *254775.*

**Czech and Slovakia**

*6 Le Hong Phong Street.*
☎ *254335.*

**Egypt**

*85 Ly Thuong Kiet Street.*
☎ *252944.*

**Finland**

*b3b Giang Vo Quarter.*
☎ *256754.*

**France**

*49 Ba Trieu Street.*
☎ *252719.*

**Germany**

*29 Tran Phu Street.*
☎ *252836.*

**Hungary**

*47 Dien Bien Phu Street.*
☎ *253353.*

**India**

*58-60 Tran Hung Doa Street.*
☎ *253409.*

**Indonesia**

*50 Ngo Quyen Street.*
☎ *253353.*

**Iran**

*54 Tran Phu Street.*
☎ *232068.*

**Iraq**

*66 Tran Hung Dao Street.*
☎ *254141.*

**Italy**

*9 Le Phing Hieu Street.*
☎ *256246.*

**Japan**

*E3\Trung Tu Quarter.*
☎ *L 257902.*

**Democratic Peoples' Republic of Korea**

*25 Cao Ba Quat Street.*
☎ *253008.*

**Korea (Republic of)**

*60 Nguyen Du Street.*
☎ *269161.*

**Laos**

*22 Tran Binh Trong Street.*
☎ *254576.*

**Libya**

*A3 Van Phuc Quarter.*
☎ *253371.*

**Malaysia**

*A3 Van Phuc Quarter.*
☎ *253371.*

**Mongolia**

*39 Tran Phu Street.*
☎ *253009.*

**Myanmar**

*A3 Van Phuc Quarter.*
☎ *253369.*

**Palestine**

*E4b Trung Tu Quarter.*
☎ *254013.*

**Philippines**

*E1 Trung Tu Center, Rm. 305-308.*
☎ *257-948.*

**Poland**

*3 Chua Mot Cot Street.*
☎ *252027.*

**Romania**

*5 Le Hong P`hong Street.*
☎ *252014.*

**The Russia Federation**

*58 Tran Phu Street.*
☎ *254632.*

**Singapore**

*BVan Phuc Quarter, Rms. 301-302.*
☎ *233966.*

**Sweden**

*2-358 Street, Van Phuc Center.*
☎ *254824.*

**Switzerland**

*77b Kim Ma Street.*
☎ *232019.*

**Thailand**

*63-65 Hoang Dieu Street.*
☎ *253092.*

**United Kingdom**

*16 Ly Thuong Kiet Street.*
☎ *252510.*

**Yugoslavia**

*47 Tran Phu Street.*
☎ *252343.*

# DIEN BIEN PHU

*Meo hilltribe woman.*

## DIEN BIEN PHU IN A CAPSULE

*Famous site of the French defeat to Viet Minh forces in May 1954...The battle marked the end to French colonial rule of northern Vietnam...Extremely remote near the Laos border...Transportation by ground is long, tedious, and treacherous...Can now be reached by twice-weekly flights from Hanoi...Spectacular scenery in the Muong Thanh Valley...15 km from the Laos border.*

Dien Bien Phu, the site in Northern Vietnam which marked the astounding and tactically brilliant defeat of French forces by Vietnamese patriots on May 6, 1954, has become another hot tourist destination. Not surprisingly, it has become particularly popular with French tourists.

Dien Bien Phu, about 15 km from the Laos border, is a highly inaccessible area 420 km west of Hanoi and has, up to now, been only reached after an exhausting 15–17 hour road trip by 4-wheel-drive. If you choose to go by 4-wheel-drive, the trip is perilous, especially along the 40-km pass known as "Where Heaven and Earth Meet," a path that reaches 1000 meters into the sky. It is the only "thoroughfare" that links Lai Chau province in northern Vietnam with the rest of the country.

It was here, across Pha Din, that the Vietnamese cut a path and painfully moved their supplies toward Dien Bien Phu in 1954.

Myth has it that a Meo king once lived in the mountain with a bevy of beautiful women, both Meo and Thai girls. His son fell in love with one of the Thai girls and the woman was mercilessly beaten and punished by the king. After fleeing into the forest to study magic, the prince was finally able to liberate the Thai girl from the clutches of his cruel father. But because there was no path in the mountains to flee, the couple decided to "fly" to heaven. The young prince carried the woman on his back up to Pha Din, where they encountered cold weather and were unable to continue further. As the story goes, they couldn't find the gate to heaven so they embraced each other and turned to stone.

But it was the battle between French and Viet Minh forces that put the location on the map. The day before the Geneva Conference on Indochina was to begin on May 7, 1954, 55,000 Viet Minh forces decisively overran the French unit stationed at Dien Bien Phu. It was a remarkable battle. Gen. Henri Navarre, commander of the French forces in Indochina, deployed 12 battalions during the early months of 1954 to gain and hold control of the Muong Thanh Valley. The French believed the Viet Minh would use the valley as an alley into Laos, where they would seize the Lao capital of Luang Phubang. The high command thought the area to be impregnable.

The French forces were then besieged for 57 days by the Viet Minh, who overcame incredible obstacles to ferry soldiers and supplies to the area (nearly 200,000 porters were employed to carry the equipment) over impossibly steep mountainsides, and attacked on May 6, 1954. The French soldiers, nearly a third of whom were ethnic Vietnamese, were routed by a Viet Minh force under the leadership of Gen. Vo Nguyen Giap estimated at five or six times stronger than the French. The weaponry was carried by hand through jungles and over mountains and then camouflaged in strategically-located sites overlooking the valley.

The first assault on the compound failed. But the Viet Minh then shelled the French encampment continuously for nearly two months and dug a network of trenches and tunnels that were undetected by the French and allowed the Viet Minh to harass the French units unchecked. As the situation became more perilous for the French, the French high command parachuted a half-dozen battalions into Dien Bien Phu to fortify the compound. But a combination of bad weather and the constant bombardment by Viet Minh artillery pieces made attempts at reinforcing Dien Bien Phu largely ineffective.

The French consorted with the Americans. The Americans, of course, wanted to carpet-bomb the valley. (Was it John Foster Dulles' idea to use tactical nuclear weapons in the struggle?) They didn't. On May 6, the Viet Minh attacked the French garrison in force and killed or captured all 13,000 Frenchmen and Vietnamese defending the valley, despite the loss of nearly 25,000 soldiers of their own units. But the battle was decisive and catastrophic, and it signified the beginning of the entire French Vietnam. Interestingly enough, the night before the attack, the Viet Minh played a recording of the song "Song of the Partisans," which was the theme of the French Resistance during WWII. There was a unit of French paratroopers that continued to defend the valley for another 24 hours but, they, too, were overran.

On July 20, 1954, the French asked for peace and Vietnam was divided into the communist north and the capitalist south at the 17th parallel. Terms set up at the conference included the honorable burial of all forces from both sides killed in the battle. But when South Vietnamese President Ngo Dinh Diem urinated over dead Viet Minh soldiers in the south as a symbolic gesture, Ho Chi Minh decided to let the French lay where they died. During the course of the nine-year war between the French and the Vietnamese, as many as one million civilians died, about a quarter million Viet Minh perished, and nearly 95,000 French troops died.

Today, at the site, rusted French artillery guns and tanks litter the valley. There is a museum dedicated to the battle as well as a hotel to accommodate the increasing number of tourists wishing to visit the area. Additionally, the headquarters of French Col. Christian de Castries has been recreated. There is a monument to the Viet Minh killed at the former French position called "Elaine."

Today, Route 6 from Hanoi to Pha Din, which passes through the villages of Hoa Binh, Moc Chau and Son La, is crowded with vehicles. Highway 6 ends at Tuan Giao. You then have to head southwest for 90 or so kilometers to reach the battlefield at Dien Bien Phu.

Of course, there are easier ways. By air. But it's on-and-off with Vietnam Airlines. The carrier inaugurated flight service to the historic battle site, spurred mostly by French tourist demand to visit the area, in 1994 after years of not serving the desolate location. But as of late summer 1995, these flights were no longer. However, they may again resume by the time you read this. In 1994, the one-hour flights from Hanoi left twice weekly on ATR-72 aircraft, each Tuesday and Friday. You may want to check with Vietnam Airlines once you get in-country. In Hanoi, contact ☎ *250888*; in Danang *21130*, or in Saigon ☎ *292118*, *230697*, or *299910*.

## Dien Bien Phu Environs

### Son La

Son La is the capital of Son La Province on the Laos border. Hmong, Black Thai, Muong and White Thai hillpeople live in this heavily mountainous and forested region. Only early in the 20th century was the area annexed by Vietnam; it had been an independent "state" prior to this time, ruled primarily by the Black Thais. This area is within an extremely mountainous area and is highly inaccessible. The road from Hanoi is in treacherous condition, and it worsens even still after Ha Dong and Hoa Binh as it turns north. There is a prison here built at the turn of the century, which is the town's only attraction. Other than that, it serves as not much more than a stopping off point for travelers on their way to Dien Bien Phu. Son La is about two thirds of the way between Hanoi and Dien Bien Phu. It was the site of a surprisingly successful uprising against the French by the Thai people, who took control over the town for a brief period. When the French regrouped and recaptured Son La, their revenge on the ethnic minorities of the town was savage. There is a small guesthouse here where most travelers between Hanoi and Dien Phu stay, going in both directions. Bring your own food and water. Buses leave for Son La from Hanoi's Kim Ma Station, near the intersection of Giang Vo and Nguyen Thai Hoc Streets.

### Lao Cai

The border into China is now open, and that's the main reason travelers head to Lao Cai. Most are headed for China's city of **Kunming**, capital of Yunnan Province. The scenery around the area is magnificent. Most of the townsfolk have never seen Westerners, although this is changing rapidly. But you will be followed by hordes of villagers wherever you go.

Lao Cai is on the Chinese border, 346 km northwest of Hanoi and 40 km northeast of Sa Pa, at the termination of the rail line. This was a former Black Flag capital after the Black Flags drove out the Yellow Flags. The Black Flag leader, known in Vietnam as Luu Vinh Phuoc, was the former Taipang army general who battled the Manchus. Lao Cai was the last station in Vietnam on the French-built train line to Yunnan in the early 20th century. It cost the French perhaps hundreds of lives to build the train line in this rugged area. In 1979, the Chinese took control of Lao Cai.

If you decide to stay in Lao Cai, there is reportedly a hotel being built for visiting foreigners, but you may end up spending the night in the house of a villager. A gift to the host would be appropriate, preferably cash. Twenty or 30 thousand dong should do it. There is a hotel in Pho Lo near the railway station (see Hanoi's "Directory"), but it's run down and dilapidated. You can get to Pho Lo by train from Hanoi and, although it continues on to Lao Cai, it is usually reserved for freight. But with the border being open, there have been reports of Westerners reaching Lao Cai by train. Even so, you can change trains at Pho Lo and reach a small village about 10 km from Lao Cai. You can get to Lao Cai by motorbike. Lao Cai is also the gateway to Sa Pa, a magnificent, scenic small town about 30 km from Lao Cai. (See the chapter SA PA.)

## Directory

### Transportation

Dien Bien Phu is 420 km west of Hanoi, 345 km from Hoa Binh and 110 km from San La.

**By air:**

VN, up until 1995, flew to Dien Bien Phu from Hanoi on Tuesdays and Fridays. At press time, these flights had been cancelled.

**By bus:**

This is an extremely arduous and lengthy trip although the scenery is spectacular. The road is in horrendous condition. When it rains, buses and other vehicles can get stuck in the mud for hours. Buses do leave for Dien Bien Phu from Hanoi but terminate in Son La. I don't recommend getting to Dien Bien Phu by bus.

**By 4-wheel-drive:**

This also is an arduous drive (but far more comfortable than by bus) that takes two full days, but it is a beautiful drive, especially as it nears Dien Bien Phu through hill-tribe villages in the mountains. The best way to do it is by renting a Russian jeep or Toyota Land Cruiser (which is far more comfortable) and sharing the costs with three or four other people. Count on at least 5–6 days for the roundtrip journey. There are some incredibly cheap bargain tours out to Dien Bien Phu from Hanoi. I recommend getting in touch with the **Memory Cafe**, *33 Tran Hung Dao Street*,

*Hanoi.* ☎ *(84-4) 265854.* The reports coming back to me about these folks have thus far been stellar.

***Author's motorcycle endured the rutted roads of the north—barely.***

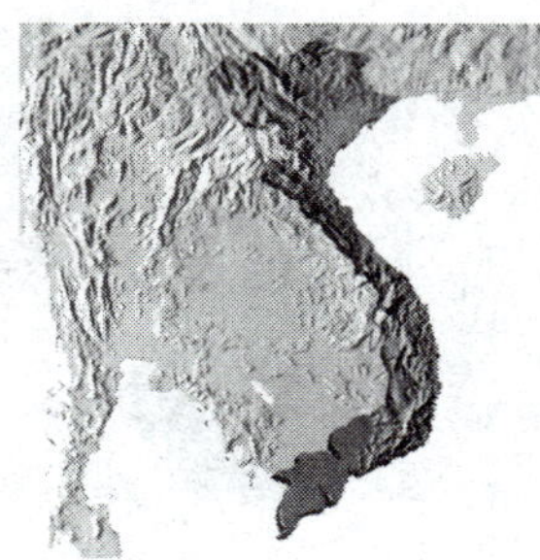

# THE CHAY AND HONG RIVERS

These are areas where there was a strong colonial presence, and the French influence in the region is evident everywhere. The French called Hoang Lien Mountains the Tonkin (or Tonkinese) Alps. There are two valleys that parallel the Chay and Hong Rivers which form a topographical pass to China's Yunnan and the provincial capitals of Kunming and Dali.

The area was a strategic trade route, although access was difficult, between Burma and Sichuan. It became a stronghold of Pon Yi refugees who fled Guizhou and now populate the upper valleys. Vietnam's Hoang Lien Son Province is considered to possess the highest mountains in Vietnam. Tourists in the region are few, and only recently have foreigners been allowed basically unrestricted access to the region. Visits to the area will elicit intense curiosity amongst the ethnic hill people, and now that the border to China is open, the inhabitants of this area will be seeing more foreigners, although I dare say that there won't be many, as the following villages are highly inaccessible from Hanoi. But where there's a will, there's a way. If you haven't drawn up your own will, you might consider doing so before visiting the far north of Vietnam.

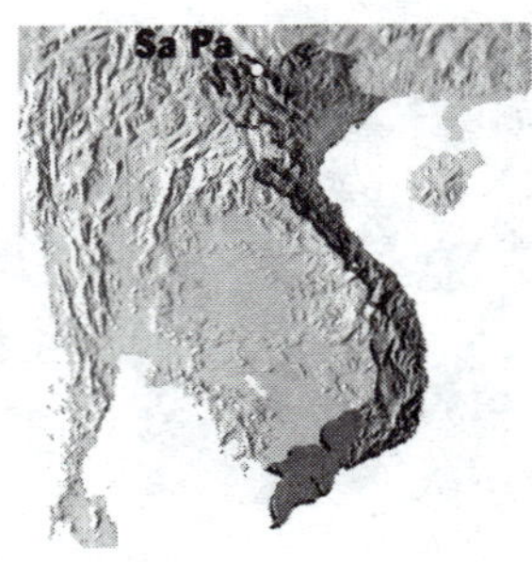


# SA PA

## SA PA IN A CAPSULE

*Not easily reached; in fact, it can be treacherous...Sees few tourists but the numbers are growing...Unbelievable mountain scenery...Still retains many French cultural and architectural influences...Has been under the control of at least four different countries over the centuries...Unlike other Vietnamese hill towns, different ethnicities cohabitate peacefully here.*

Sa Pa is nearly 1600 meters above sea level in the northern province of Lao Cai, 30 km from the border city and provincial capital of Lao Cai. It is known for spectacular scenery (the craggy hills around the area are called the Tonkinese Alps—at least by tourists—and Vietnam's highest mountain, Phan Si Pan, stretching to more than 3100 meters, is in the area) and the amazing hillpeople called the Hmong. Other ethnic minorities in the region are the White Thai people.

The town has changed hands so many times over the generations, it's difficult to count. It has been under Japanese, French, Chinese, and Vietnamese control at various times in its history. It was most recently rebuilt by the Vietnamese, although the French legacy survives in the form of spacious villas. The place was devastated and pillaged by the Chinese in 1979, and all that remains of the Catholic church are crumbling walls and a statue of Notre Dame De France, which has been haphazardly restored. The remaining chunks of the statue are held together by pieces of brick.

More ruins of the Chinese aggression include the remains of a fort that stands on an isolated hill overlooking the Sa Pa Valley. The countryside is broken up by rice terraces surrounded by the clay and thatch houses of ethnic Hmong. These people wear intricately embroidered collars and dark blue outfits fitted with sashes. They also don bizarre-looking black Chinese umbrellas. Many can be seen carrying wicker baskets on their backs carrying produce, firewood and clothing for trade at the marketplace, which is becoming a main tourist attraction.

The French influence is still evident among the Hmong, many of whom still wear Christian crosses around their necks. The Hmong people welcome the presence of Western tourists who have increasingly become the villagers best customers of items ranging from hats, handbags, bracelets, and sashes to locally-produced medicines, produce, and liquor—a potent, locally-produced libation that'll knock you on your ass.

Unlike a number of other ethnic minorities in Vietnam, the Hmong speak Vietnamese (it's a little more bothersome trying to communicate with the White Thais).

Sa Pa is not easily reached. It's better to do it from Lao Cai by horse than any mechanized means (although horses have been replaced by Hondas in recent years). Some of the roadway is under construction, but the ride is a fitful one—the road is hideously rutted and cratered. Lao Cai itself is accessible by train from Hanoi—an 11-hour ride—and cars or motorbikes can be hired for the final leg to Sa Pa, which even at less than 30 km, can take a couple of hours.

**INSIDER TIP**

*The Hmong are a friendly and warm people, but most will not tolerate having their pictures taken. Instead, use your camera for photos of the verdant countryside. In Sa Pa, if you find yourself surrounded by hordes of curious townsfolk and want to be alone, simply take out your camera. They'll react the way most people react to a skunk–they'll flee. You'll find yourself quite alone rather instantly.*

## What to See and Do in Sa Pa

**Sa Pa Market**

The market at Sa Pa is the principal tourist attraction. Here, all kinds of locally-made handicrafts, clothes, jewelry, and ornaments can be purchased at prices you'll have to bargain for. Despite the Hmong people's friendliness, they are shrewd negotiators. Chances are they'll make out better than you did. But who else on your block back in Indiana will have a genuine Hmong beaded collar?

## Where to Stay and Eat in Sa Pa

Currently there are five guest houses in Sa Pa, none of which exceed minimum accommodation standards—two of them close in the winter time, when temperatures can dip below freezing. But this is expected to change as the number of tourists to the region increases. The best bets in town these days are:

**Agriculture & Forestry Guest House** **US$6–$12**

*US$6–12.*

**Auberge Hotel** **US$10**

☎ *84-20-71243*
*US$10.*
The name's a little redundant, but Proprietor Trung is one of the guys in Sa Pa that you'll want to get to know, especially if you want to stay at his popular "auberge" in town. His rooms are the best in Sa Pa, although there are not that many of them. He's got a good scorecard of finding travelers digs somewhere else in the event the Auberge is booked. He's sought out. You might want to call ahead, although it's no guarantee that you'll get a room.

Eating is at your own risk. There are no "restaurants" (if you've found one, let me know!) in the town. There are food stalls, but be careful of the cutlery and make sure that any water you consume is either purified or has been boiled. Put simply, Sa Pa is off the beaten track—way off it.

## Sa Pa Environs

Of course, there's **Phan Si Pan**, Vietnam's highest peak. It is part of the Hoang Lien Mountains (the Tonkinese Alps), and is accessible by foot from Sa Pa. At present, few foreigners attempt to climb the peak, but the number is growing, as are the number of "guides" in both Sa Pa and Lao Cai who will offer you their services by either car or motorbike (a 4-wheel-drive is the best alternative). Also within walking or driving distance of Sa Pa are the **Thac Bac** (Silver Falls) and **Cau May** (Cloud Bridge) which spans the Muong Hoa River.

### Yen Bai

Yen Bai is located about 155 km northwest of Hanoi. This is at the base of the delta. In February 1930, a Vietnamese "army" started an uprising here against the French colonial authorities based on the initiative of the Vietnamese Nationalist Party of Vietnam (Quoc Dan Dang).

### Phan Si Pan

Phan Si Pan is 395 km northwest of Hanoi. This area is the site of Vietnam's tallest mountain, at 3143 meters high. The mountain is climbable, but best done in December. There are tremendously steep slopes, and the wind and rain here make the ascent a treacherous affair. For the fittest of the fit (as well as experienced climbers) an ascent of Phan Si Pan is a minimum five-day roundtrip trek from Sa Pa. There has been some talk about organized treks up Phan Si Pan, but they have yet to develop. For information about a trek up Phan Si Pan, or to get advice if you're planning on going solo, contact:

**Samifana Indochina**

*21 Phan Dinh Phung, Hanoi.* ☎ *(84-4) 281516.*
This is an adventure travel ground operator that specializes in treks, mountain bike trips and tours for Vietnam veterans. Recommended.

# PACKAGE TOURS

## Fielding Worldwide Vietnam Tour Programs

As a special service to our readers, Fielding Worldwide has by contract associated itself with a select number of Vietnamese tour operators, those we feel our discerning readers will get the most from. If a tour package is the route you decide to embark on for either a brief or extended stay, the following programs come heavily recommended by travelers to Vietnam.

Fielding programs range from exotic scuba diving adventures aboard old French sailing junks to custom-designed visits to former battlefields and bases for Vietnam War veterans.

Compare our prices. No other tour packager to Vietnam in America comes close to the value Fielding offers. Through other tour operators, you're dealing with sometimes two or three "middle men." Of course, you're not informed of that. Fielding/VIVA USA tours cut out the middle guys. We work directly with selected Vietnamese ground operators. The following tours do not include international air fare. For comparison purposes, add to the price schedules return air fare to Vietnam (which typically runs about US$1200) and then compare our prices with those of similar itineraries offered by other U.S.-based tour packagers. The Fielding difference is clear.

To book a Fielding tour of Vietnam is the easiest possible way of getting the most out of your Vietnam adventure without the hassles associated with trying to book tours once you're inside Vietnam. And remember, group bookings usually include significant discounts.

To book a Fielding Vietnam tour is a snap. Simply call Fielding/VIVA USA toll free ☎ *(800) 360-8482.*

We'll take care of the rest. It's that easy.

Remember, all tour prices and itineraries listed are subject to change without notice. Call us if you have any questions.

Note: Where noted, price schedules for the following Fielding/VIVA USA tours are based on hotel class accommodations. Class A price schedules are for accommodations in the US$90–120 range. Class B schedules are for accommodations in the US$50–70 range. Class C schedules denote accommodations in the US$30–45 range.

### Traveler's Insurance

It is strongly recommended that you purchase your own traveler's insurance in your own country, as insurance provided by the Vietnamese Bao Viet Co. (the state insurance company that most Vietnamese tour companies are covered through) provides a minimum amount of coverage, usually not exceeding US$10,000. Fielding Worldwide, Inc. assumes absolutely no legal liability nor financial responsibility in the event of death, accident, illness or injury while participants are enroute to or from and during any of the Vietnamese tour packages mentioned below.

Additionally, you can, for a cost of US$12 for your entire stay in Vietnam, purchase International SOS Assistance. SOS is an organization that provides prompt assistance in the event of an emergency situation while in Vietnam. SOS must be purchased prior to the start of your tour through either Fielding or our associate tour company in Vietnam. SOS members receive the SOS Tourist Program Card which identifies you as eligible for the organization's benefits. The card lists 24-hour contact numbers in Vietnam and Singapore. The card should be carried by you at all times.

In Vietnam, SOS has been approved by the National Administration of Tourism to carry out the evacuation and repatriation of foreign tourists. SOS can provide assistance and send medical teams to the most remote parts of Vietnam. Services available include 24-hour medical consultation and evaluation, referral to doctors and hospitals, emergency medical evacuation, post evacuation medical expenses (hospitalization and medical fees incurred by the member after evacuation will be borne by SOS up to US$10,000), medically supervised repatriation, hospital admittance deposits (any required hospital admittance fee deposit up to US$2500 will be guaranteed if you are without immediate means of payment), return of dependent children, dispatch of doctors and medicine, companion visit assistance, repatriation of mortal remains, interpreter access and referral, 24-hour emergency message transmission, and legal assistance.

But, again, remember, SOS is not an insurance policy in the traditional sense. Any serious medical problem abroad should be covered by insurance you've purchased in your country. It's wise to purchase SOS if your stay in Vietnam will last more than a few days and/or you plan to travel to areas other than major urban centers. Fielding still strongly recommends you acquire your own personal travel insurance.

Cancellation penalties differ with the tour companies. While some tour companies offer complete or nearly complete refunds in the event of a cancellation, others levy large cancellation fees. It would be wise to check with Fielding or the Vietnamese tour company regarding refunds in the event of cancellation.

When booking a tour offered through *Fielding's Vietnam*, always refer to the full tour number, each of which begins with the letter "F."

Our representative in Vietnam, *Fielding's Vietnam* author Wink Dulles, will also periodically be available in Ho Chi Minh City for assistance in making your stay in Vietnam as adventurous and/or as relaxing as possible. The choices in Vietnam are yours, thanks to Fielding.

## "Song Saigon" Cruises Off Nha Trang

Off the idyllic and easily accessible coastal city of Nha Trang, countless tropical islands dot the emerald blue South China Sea with precipitous rocks, coconut palm-lined bright sandy beaches, sand dunes, and an undersea world teeming with brightly-colored coral reefs and an array of electric-hued sea life–plus an incredibly diverse environment of flora and fauna. Giant angelfish, white-tip sharks, batfish sweetlips, damselfish, moorish idols, rays, pastel gorgonias, sea fans, sponges, morays, grouper, fighting shrimp and lobsters inhabit these crystal-clear waters. Steep walls of underwater canyons are carpeted with colorful nudibranches, Christmas tree worms and hard and soft corals—not to mention the number of historical wreck sites, in short, a diver's paradise.

If you're not a diver, you can stroll on untouched, isolated islands of Hon Ho and Hon Cha La, home to thousands of sea swallows. Discover Bamboo Island and the beautiful natural harbor of Vung Coco as well as the primitive villages of Hon Lon Island.

All this and much more are yours through voyages aboard the "Song Saigon," a remarkable and luxurious 30-meter long traditional junk that has been appointed to give 10 passengers the adventure and pampering of a lifetime.

"Song Saigon" has been regally fitted with five air-conditioned, two-person cabins, three bathrooms, a sitting and dining room equipped with video and audio cassette equipment and tapes. On the wide back deck, under the braided palm roof, there are deck mattresses, hammocks and large hardwood tables for meals, including American-style breakfasts and the best Vietnamese food off the coast of Vietnam.

Two cruise packages are offered–one for divers and one for nondivers–with weekly departures from Nha Trang.

### F/V-VV1 Departure from Nha Trang aboard the junk "Song Saigon." (4 days - 3 nights)

**Day 1** *Transfer from hotel or airport in Nha Trang to Cauda Pier for embarkation at 8 a.m. Sailing between the rocky islands to the south of Nha Trang, including Hon Mun and Hon Mot, where local fishermen can be observed netting their catches. Anchorage at Bich Dam. Bathing, snorkeling. Visit to local fishing village. Discover the pristine beaches on the north side of Hon Tre Island. Dinner and night aboard.*

**Day 2** *Navigation to the northern islands of Hon Don and Hon Cha La, where thousands of sea swallows nest. Then on to Hon Lon and the pass of Lach Cua Be to enter the crystalline waters of the natural port of Vung Coco. Anchorage, with dinner and night aboard.*

**Day 3** *Sunning and bathing. Meet the inhabitants of Vung Coco. Then set sail for the Hon My Giang peninsula and the magnificent bay of Cay Ban, which teems with rich varieties of coral and tropical sealife. The colorful fishing boats you'll see leave for Nha Trang once a week for food supply. You'll see Ghe Thung, round canoes made from braided bamboo, traditional island families in their huts in the palm-lined shade. Bathing at the beach, snorkeling, village visiting. Dinner and night aboard.*

**Day 4** *After breakfast the junk anchors beneath the green heights of Hon Thi, the monkey island. These mysterious monkeys welcome visitors by leaping from hidden places in the trees into the clear water of a small creek. Then a sail by Tortoise Island and entry into the Song Cai River by canoe past the fishing boats to the Po Nagar Cham Towers of Nha Trang. Lunch aboard and sailing in Nha Trang Bay near the Bao Dai Villas. Leave the "Song Saigon" for transfer back to hotel*

**Price Schedule:**

*US$665*

*Supplement Cabin Single: US$479*

*Note: Price includes full-boarding cruise, double cabin accommodation, services, excursions, air-conditioned transportation from hotel or airport to junk, French- and English-speaking guides. The price does not include personal expenses, insurance and extra beverages.*

### F/V-VV2 Diving Cruise on "Song Saigon" from Nha Trang (4 days - 3 nights)

*This itinerary is similar to the one above but is reserved for certified divers only. The land excursions are in the function of the dive program. There will be two or three dives a day led by NAUI instructor Christian.*

## F/V-VV2 Diving Cruise on "Song Saigon" from Nha Trang (4 days - 3 nights)

**Price Schedule:**

*US$865*

*Supplemental Cabin Single: US$479*

*Note: Price includes full-boarding cruise, double cabin accommodation, services, excursions, air-conditioned transportation from airport or hotel to the junk, 2-3 dives per day, all heavy equipment (tank and weight system), air and the assistance of an NAUI instructor. The price does not include personal expenses, insurance and extra drinks. Supplemental diving equipment can be rented.*

## F/V-VV3 Departure from Nha Trang aboard the junk "Song Saigon" (2 days - 1 night)

**Day 1** *Transfer from hotel or airport in Nha Trang to Cauda Pier for embarkation at 8 a.m. Sailing between the rocky islands to the south of Nha Trang, including Hon Mun and Hon Mot, where local fishermen can be observed netting their catches. Anchorage at Bich Dam. Bathing, snorkeling. Visit to local fishing village. Discover the pristine beaches on the north side of Hon Tre Island. Dinner and night aboard.*

**Day 2** *After breakfast, the junk anchors beneath the green heights of Hon Thi, the monkey island. These mysterious monkeys welcome visitors by leaping from hidden places in the trees into the clear water of a small creek. Then a sail by Tortoise Island and entry into the Song Cai River by canoe past the fishing boats to the Po Nagar Cham Towers of Nha Trang. Lunch aboard and sailing in Nha Trang Bay under the Cap Mui Chut near the Bao Dai Villas. Leave the "Song Saigon" at Cau Da village for transfer back to hotel.*

**Price Schedule:**

*US$280*

*Supplement Cabin Single: US$200*

*Note: Price includes full-boarding cruise, double cabin accommodation, services, excursions, air-conditioned transportation from hotel or airport to junk, French- and English-speaking guides. The price does not include personal expenses, insurance and extra beverages.*

## F/V-VV4 Diving Cruise on "Song Saigon" from Nha Trang (2 days - 1 night)

*This itinerary is similar to the one above but is reserved for certified divers only. The land excursions are in the function of the dive program. There will be two or three dives a day led by NAUI instructor Christian near Khanh Hoa.*

## F/V-VV4 Diving Cruise on "Song Saigon" from Nha Trang (2 days - 1 night)

**Price Schedule:**

*US$380*

*Supplement Cabin Single: US$200*

*Note: Price includes full-boarding cruise, double cabin accommodation, services, excursions, air-conditioned transportation from airport or hotel to the junk, 2-3 dives per day, all heavy equipment (tank and weight system), air and the assistance of a NAUI instructor. The price does not include personal expenses, insurance and extra drinks. Supplemental diving equipment can be rented.*

### "Song Saigon" Cruises of the Mekong Delta and Cambodia

From November–April three cruise programs are offered, one to and from Cambodia via the Mekong Delta in Vietnam, one from Phnom Penh, Cambodia to Ho Chi Minh City and the other exploring Vietnam's Mekong Delta by junk.

### Visa Applications and Passing Port Formalities

To get the Vietnam exit visa and the Cambodia entry visa via the Mekong River, our Vietnamese ground operator must receive three (3) passport photos and three (3) copies of your passport at least 15 days before the beginning of the cruise. Passengers must arrive in HCMC at least two working days prior to the cruise. The Vietnam entry visa can be obtained at the same time.

Coming from Cambodia into Vietnam via the Mekong River, Vietnamese entry visas are obtained at the Embassy of Vietnam in Phnom Penh. Two (2) passport photos and one (1) copy of your passport must arrive at Voiles Vietnam at least 15 days before the beginning of the cruise. Passengers must arrive in Phnom Penh at least two working days prior to the departure of the cruise.

## F/V-VV5 HCMC/My Tho/Phnom Penh (7 days - 6 nights)

**Day 1** *Leave HCMC by air-conditioned van for My Tho. Embark on the junk "Song Saigon." Sail to My Luan, a small village at the junction of a number of canals. Junk anchors. By small boat a visit to a Chinese brick factory with dome-shaped stoves. Tour of the village. Return to junk for dinner.*

**Day 2** *Sail through narrow arroyos and bamboo farms. Anchorage off Sa Dec. Visits to a Chinese pagoda adorned with Chinese paintings amid old sampans and the bustling central market. Then by boat to a Cao Dai temple and towers offering fantastic vistas of the delta. Return to junk. Dinner and night aboard.*

## F/V-VV5 HCMC/My Tho/Phnom Penh (7 days - 6 nights)

**Day 3** *Sail up the Mekong. Anchorage in Cao Lanh Province. Disembark and stroll through village. Visits to a Buddhist monastery and a small sugar processing workshop. Dinner and night aboard the junk.*

**Day 4** *Leave for Hong Ngu, the last village of any significance before the border with Cambodia. Received by family for meal of local delicacies. Boat trip in the floating markets. Dinner and night aboard the junk.*

**Day 5** *Visit a small shipyard on the way to Vinh Xuong port. Dinner and night aboard junk.*

**Day 6** *After border formalities, the junk is in Cambodia. The population becomes less dense, cultivating fertile riverside land. Pass pagoda beneath a canopy of sugar palms. At sunset, we reach Phnom Penh's Royal Palace. Anchor in Phnom Penh for the night.*

**Day 7** *During breakfast, junk sails up the Tonle Sap River at Phnom Penh. Disembark at 10 a.m.*

**Price Schedule:**

*US$1300*

*Supplement cabin single: US$845*

*Note: Price includes full-boarding cruise, services, excursions, air-conditioned transportation, guide, visa application and port formalities. Not included are personal expenses, insurance and extra drinks.*

## F/V-VV6 Phnom Penh/My Tho/HCMC (6 days - 5 nights)

**Day 1** *Meet at port in Phnom Penh and embark on the "Song Saigon." Set sail down the delta passing the Royal Palace, locals cultivating the Mekong region and a pagoda beneath sugar palms. Anchor at Koom San Nar border area at sunset. Dinner and night aboard junk.*

**Day 2** *After border formalities, junk moves into the Mekong Delta. Observe small shipyard on the river's bank. Sail on to Hong Ngu. Small boat trip to the floating markets. Family receives passengers for meal of local delicacies. Dinner and night aboard junk.*

**Day 3** *After breakfast, junk sets sail for Sa Dec. Visit to the central market and Cao Dai temple and towers for a magnificent panorama of the delta. Dinner and overnight aboard junk near Sa Dec.*

**Day 4** *Sail on to Vinh Long in the heart of the delta. Observe markets and sampans loaded with produce. Visit Chinese Pagoda with remarkable ink inscriptions. Return to junk. Anchor at the village of My Luan at the junction of numerous canals. Through narrow arroyos, gardens and bamboo farms are visited under a vault of palms. Dinner and overnight aboard junk at My Luan.*

## F/V-VV6 Phnom Penh/My Tho/HCMC (6 days - 5 nights)

**Day 5** *After breakfast, a visit to a Chinese brick factory with dome-shaped stoves. Tour the village and return to the junk. Junk anchors at sugar processing workshop. Dinner and overnight aboard junk.*

**Day 6** *Breakfast. Arrive at My Tho. Junk anchors among brightly colored fishing boats. Disembark junk for air-conditioned car ride to HCMC.*

**Price Schedule:**

*US$1100*

*Supplement Cabin Single: US$740*

*Note: Price includes full-boarding cruise, services, excursions, air-conditioned transportation, guide, visa application and port formalities. Not included are personal expenses, insurance and extra drinks.*

## F/V-VV7 HCMC/My Tho/Vinh Long/Sa Dec/HCMC (3 days- 2 nights)

**Day 1** *Morning departure from HCMC by air-conditioned van to My Tho. Embark on the junk "Song Saigon." Sail the Mekong to My Luan, a small fishing village at the junction of a number of canals. The junk anchors and guests travel by small boat to visit a Chinese brick factory with dome-shaped stoves. Tour of the village. Dinner and overnight aboard the junk.*

**Day 2** *Traveling through narrow arroyos under palm vaults, guests will visit bountiful gardens and bamboo farms. Sailing on the junk with anchorage at Vinh Long. Lunch aboard. By small boat, visits to the floating market and a Chinese pagoda with elaborate ink inscriptions. Sail on to Sa Dec. Dinner and overnight.*

**Day 3** *Market tour of Sa Dec. Visit to a Cao Dai temple through a flotilla of old ferries and sampans. The towers of the temple offer magnificent vistas of the Mekong Delta. Lunch aboard the junk. Disembark and return to HCMC via the My Thuan ferry and local buses.*

**Price Schedule:**

*US$470*

*Supplement Cabin Single: US$350*

*Note: Price includes full-boarding cruise, services, excursions, air-conditioned transportation, guide, visa application and port formalities. Not included are personal expenses, insurance and extra drinks.*

## F/V-VV8 HCMC/Sa Dec/Vinh Long/My Tho/HCMC (3 days - 2 nights)

**Day 1** *Leave HCMC by air-conditioned van along the banks of the Mekong to the ferry at My Thuan. Cross to Sa Dec. Embarkation on the junk "Song Saigon." Lunch aboard. Visit to a Cao Dai temple through a flotilla of old ferries and sampans. The towers of the temple offer magnificent vistas of the Mekong Delta. Sail to Vinh Long. Dinner and overnight aboard.*

**Day 2** *Anchorage at Vinh Long. Breakfast aboard. Tour bustling Vinh Long. By small boat, visits to the floating market and a Chinese pagoda with elaborate ink inscriptions. Lunch aboard. Sail to My Luan, a small fishing village at the junction of a number of canals. The junk anchors and guests travel by small boat to visit a Chinese brick factory with dome-shaped stoves. Tour of the village. Dinner and overnight aboard the junk.*

**Day 3** *Traveling through narrow arroyos under thick palm vaults, guests will visit bountiful gardens and bamboo farms. Return to junk and have lunch while sailing on to My Tho, where the junk anchors amongst colorful fishing boats and sampans. Disembark and take van back to HCMC.*

**Price Schedule:**

*US$470*
*Supplement Cabin Single: US$350*
*Note: Price includes full-boarding cruise, services, excursions, air-conditioned transportation, guide, visa application and port formalities. Not included are personal expenses, insurance and extra drinks.*

# Overland Tours

### General Information

1) Charges include transportation, hotel accommodations (based on double occupancy), gourmet meals, entrance fees and guide/interpreter assistance.

2) Charges do not include laundry, taxi for personal use, mail, faxes, long-distance calls, airport taxes, medical and personal travel insurance and all other expenses of a purely personal nature.

3) Superbco Tours shall not be responsible for any personal injury, damage, property loss, burglary, accidental delays and other factors beyond the company's control.

4) Tour itineraries, prices and modes of transportation as described are subject to change without prior notice.

5) Superbco reserves the right to substitute hotels and means of transportation regarding the tours if such changes are necessary due to prior unforeseen circumstances.

## F/V-DT1 HCMC/Dalat/HCMC (4 days - 3 nights)

**Day 1** *Airport transfer and/or meeting guests at the hotel. Leave for Dalat. Lunch at Bao Loc restaurant. Then a visit to Prenn Waterfalls. Continue to Dalat. Check in at the hotel. Dinner. Free evening.*

**Day 2** *Breakfast. Then visits to the Flower Garden, Valley of Love and LiSon Pagoda. Lunch. Then visits to Cam Ly Waterfall, Bao Dai's Palace, and the Dalat Market. Dinner. Free evening.*

**Day 3** *Breakfast. Hiking tour to Lang Bian mountains. Lunch. Visit to a Chinese pagoda and a stroll around beautiful Xuan Huong Lake. Dinner. Free evening.*

**Day 4** *Breakfast. Leave for HCMC. Lunch at a Bao Loc restaurant. Then on to HCMC. Check in at the hotel. Tour concludes.*

| | | |
|---|---|---|
| *1 Person:US$590 ea.* | *5 Person:US$277 ea.* | *9 Person:US$242 ea.* |
| *2 Person:US$386 ea.* | *6 Person:US$261 ea.* | *10 Person:US$236 ea.* |
| *3 Person:US$318 ea.* | *7 Person:US$259 ea.* | *11 Person:US$231 ea.* |
| *4 Person:US$284 ea.* | *8 Person:US$249 ea.* | *12 Person:US$227 ea.* |

## F/V-DT2 HCMC/Vung Tau/HCMC (3 days - 2 nights)

**Day 1** *Meeting of guests at Ho Chi Minh City's TSN Airport. Transfer to the luxurious Saigon Floating Hotel.*

**Day 2** *Breakfast. Leave for Vung Tau, the Saigon area's premier beach resort. Check-in at the Rex Hotel. Sunbathing, swimming. Lunch. Visits to Gautama Buddha Statue and the White Palace. Then leisure and swimming at Bai Dua Beach.*

**Day 3** *Breakfast. Swimming and sunbathing. Return to HCMC for dinner and overnight.*

**Day 4** *Breakfast. Transfer to TSN Airport and the seeing off of guests.*

| | | |
|---|---|---|
| *1 Person:US$745 ea.* | *5 Person:US$504 ea.* | *9 Person:US$477 ea.* |
| *2 Person:US$590 ea.* | *6 Person:US$492 ea.* | *10 Person:US$473 ea.* |
| *3 Person:US$538 ea.* | *7 Person:US$490 ea.* | *11 Person:US$470 ea.* |
| *4 Person:US$512 ea.* | *8 Person:US$483 ea.* | *12 Person:US$467 ea.* |

## F/V-DT3 HCMC/Cu Chi/Tay Ninh/MyTho/HCMC (5 days - 4 nights)

**Day 1** *Guests are met at the airport. Transfer to hotel. Free to explore HCMC.*

**Day 2** *Breakfast. Leave for My Tho in the Mekong Delta. Boating excursion along the Mekong River. Lunch. A visit to Vinh Trang Pagoda. Back to HCMC.*

## F/V-DT3 HCMC/Cu Chi/Tay Ninh/ MyTho/HCMC (5 days - 4 nights)

**Day 3** *Breakfast. Visit to the famed Cu Chi tunnels. Then on to the Cao Dai capital of Tay Ninh. Visit Cao Dai Pagoda. Lunch at "Cay Mai" restaurant. Back to HCMC.*

**Day 4** *Day tour of HCMC, visiting the Museum of History, Vinh Nghiem Pagoda, Thong Nhat Conference Hall, the War Crimes Museum and Ben Thanh Market.*

**Day 5** *Breakfast. Transfer to TSN Airport. End of the tour.*

| | | |
|---|---|---|
| 1 Person:US$541 ea. | 5 Person:US$317 ea. | 9 Person:US$292 ea. |
| 2 Person:US$396 ea. | 6 Person:US$306 ea. | 10 Person:US$288 ea. |
| 3 Person:US$348 ea. | 7 Person:US$304 ea. | 11 Person:US$285 ea. |
| 4 Person:US$324 ea. | 8 Person:US$297 ea. | 12 Person:US$282 ea. |

## F/V-DT4 Hanoi/Ha Long/Haiphong/Hue/ Danang/HCMC (8 days - 7 nights)

**Day 1** *Meeting of guests at Noi Bai Airport, with transfer to Saigon Hotel.*

**Day 2** *A half-day city tour of Hanoi before leaving for Ha Long Bay, where you'll check in at the Ha Long I Hotel.*

**Day 3** *Cruising tour of Ha Long Bay. Check in at the Peace Hotel. Evening free.*

**Day 4** *Return to Hanoi. Check-in at Saigon Hotel. Evening free.*

**Day 5** *Transfer to airport and flight to Hue. Visits to Tu Duc Mausoleum and the Museum of Hue. Check-in at Century Hotel.*

**Day 6** *Leave for Danang. Visit to the Marble Mountains. Check-in at Hai Au Hotel.*

**Day 7** *Fly to HCMC. Half-day city tour. Check-in at the Majestic Hotel.*

**Day 8** *Transfer to Saigon's TSN Airport. End of tour.*

| | | |
|---|---|---|
| 1 Person:US$1165 ea. | 5 Person:US$786 ea. | 9 Person:US$744 ea. |
| 2 Person:US$920 ea. | 6 Person:US$768 ea. | 10 Person:US$737 ea. |
| 3 Person:US$838 ea. | 7 Person:US$764 ea. | 11 Person:US$731 ea. |
| 4 Person:US$797 ea. | 8 Person:US$753 ea. | 12 Person:US$727 ea. |

## F/V-DT5 HCMC/Vung Tau/Dalat/HCMC (8 days - 7 nights)

**Day 1** *Meeting of guests at TSN Airport. Transfer to the Floating Hotel.*

**Day 2** *Breakfast. Departure for Vung Tau. Check-in at the Rex Hotel. Swimming and sunbathing. Lunch. Visits to Gautama Buddha Statue and White Palace. Swimming and sunbathing at Bai Dua Beach. Dinner.*

## F/V-DT5 HCMC/Vung Tau/Dalat/HCMC (8 days - 7 nights)

**Day 3** *Breakfast. Leave for Dalat. Lunch at Bao Loc restaurant. Visit to Dam Ri Waterfall. Continue to Dalat. Check-in at Anh Dao Hotel.*

**Day 4** *Breakfast and visits to the Valley of Love and Linh Son Pagoda. Lunch. Visit Cam Ly Waterfalls and Bao Dai's Summer Palace.*

**Day 5** *Breakfast. Visits to the Dalat Market and ethnic villages.*

**Day 6** *Breakfast. Leave for HCMC.*

**Day 7** *Half-day city tour of HCMC. Rest of the day free.*

**Day 8** *Breakfast and transfer to TSN Airport. Guests will be seen off. End of tour.*

| | | |
|---|---|---|
| *1 Person:US$1348 ea.* | *5 Person:US$874 ea.* | *9 Person:US$822 ea.* |
| *2 Person:US$1042 ea.* | *6 Person:US$851 ea.* | *10 Person:US$813 ea.* |
| *3 Person:US$940 ea.* | *7 Person:US$846 ea.* | *11 Person:US$806 ea.* |
| *4 Person:US$889 ea.* | *8 Person:US$832 ea.* | *12 Person:US$800 ea.* |

## F/V-DT6 Hanoi/Ha Long Bay/Haiphong/Danang/Quy Nhon/Nha Trang/Dalat/HCMC (13 days - 12 nights)

**Day 1** *Meeting of guests at Noi Bai Airport. Transfer to Saigon Hotel. Visits to Ngoc Son Temple and the Fine Arts Museum.*

**Day 2** *Visits to Ho Chi Minh's Mausoleum and Quan Thanh Temple. Leave for Ha Long Bay. Check-in at the Ha Long 1 Hotel.*

**Day 3** *Cruising tour of Ha Long Bay. Overnight on Peace Island.*

**Day 4** *Depart for Haiphong with a visit to Cat Ba Island. Check-in at Huu Nghi Hotel.*

**Day 5** *Breakfast and departure for Hanoi. Check-in at the Saigon Hotel. Evening free.*

**Day 6** *Transfer to airport for flight to Danang. Then transfer to Hue. Visits to Thien Mu Pagoda and Tu Duc Mausoleum. Check-in at the Century Hotel.*

**Day 7** *Leave for Danang. Half-day city tour and then check-in at Hai Au Hotel.*

**Day 8** *Leave for Quy Nhon. Check-in at Quy Nhon Hotel.*

**Day 9** *Leave for Nha Trang. Check-in at Hai Yen Hotel. Visits to the Oceanographic Institute and Hon Chong Beach for swimming and sunbathing.*

**Day 10** *Leave for Dalat with a visit to the Prenn Waterfalls on the way. On to Dalat. Check-in at Anh Dao Hotel.*

**Day 11** *Visits to Linh Son Pagoda, Bao Dai's Summer Palace, and the Dalat Market for shopping before departure to HCMC. Check-in at the Majestic Hotel.*

## F/V-DT6 Hanoi/Ha Long Bay/Haiphong/ Danang/Quy Nhon/Nha Trang/ Dalat/HCMC (13 days - 12 nights)

**Day 12** *Visits to Thong Nhat Conference Hall, Vinh Nghiem Pagoda, Nha Rong Wharf and the Lacquerware Factory. Shopping at Ben Thanh Market. Rest of the day free.*

**Day 13** *Check-out and transfer to TSN Airport. End of the tour.*

| | | |
|---|---|---|
| *1 Person:US$1920 ea.* | *5 Person:US$1082 ea.* | *9 Person:US$989 ea.* |
| *2 Person:US$1377 ea.* | *6 Person:US$1041 ea.* | *10 Person:US$974 ea.* |
| *3 Person:US$1196 ea.* | *7 Person:US$1034 ea.* | *11 Person:US$961 ea.* |
| *4 Person:US$1106 ea.* | *8 Person:US$1009 ea.* | *12 Person:US$951 ea.* |

## F/V-DT7 Hunting Tour in Dalat (6 days - 5 nights)

**Day 1** *Meeting of guests at Saigon's TSN Airport. Transfer to hotel for check-in before a city tour of HCMC. Rest of the day free.*

**Day 2** *Leave for Dalat. Lunch at Bao Loc restaurant. On to Dalat. Check-in at Ngoc Lan or Duy Tan Hotels. Dinner. At 7 p.m., leave for Tuyen Lam Lake where canoes will take guests to the hunting area. Return to hotel at midnight.*

**Day 3** *Breakfast. Morning free. Half-day city tour of Dalat. Dinner at the hotel. Depart for Da Nhim Lake at 5 p.m., entering the hunting area by canoe. Return to the hotel the next morning.*

**Day 4** *Breakfast. Morning free. Visit Dalat Market. Dancing at 10 p.m.*

**Day 5** *Breakfast. Leave for HCMC. Lunch at Bao Loc restaurant with regional specialties. City tour of HCMC. Evening free.*

**Day 6** *Breakfast and transfer to airport. End of tour.*

| | | |
|---|---|---|
| *1 Person:US$1119 ea.* | *5 Person:US$538 ea.* | *9 Person:US$476 ea.* |
| *2 Person:US$732 ea.* | *6 Person:US$508 ea.* | *10 Person:US$463 ea.* |
| *3 Person:US$603 ea.* | *7 Person:US$496 ea.* | *11 Person:US$452 ea.* |
| *4 Person:US$540 ea.* | *8 Person:US$477 ea.* | *12 Person:US$443 ea.* |

## F/V-DT8 The Golfer's Tour. HCMC/Dalat/ HCMC (5 days - 4 nights)

**Day 1** *Meeting of guests at TSN Airport. Transfer to hotel. City tour of HCMC.*

**Day 2** *Breakfast and departure for Dalat. Lunch at Bao Loc restaurant. On to Dalat. Check-in at Anh Dao, Ngoc Lan or Duy Tan Hotels. Dinner. Free evening.*

**Day 3** *Breakfast and transfer to the golf course. Lunch. City tour.*

## F/V-DT8 The Golfer's Tour. HCMC/Dalat/HCMC (5 days - 4 nights)

**Day 4** *Breakfast before checking out for HCMC. Stops at Prenn Waterfalls and Bao Loc for lunch. Visit Dam Ri Waterfalls. On to HCMC. Check-in at the hotel. Free evening.*

**Day 5** *Breakfast before check-out. Shopping and then transfer to TSN Airport for send-off. End of tour.*

| | | |
|---|---|---|
| *1 Person:US$1065 ea.* | *5 Person:US$703 ea.* | *9 Person:US$663 ea.* |
| *2 Person:US$831 ea.* | *6 Person:US$685 ea.* | *10 Person:US$656 ea.* |
| *3 Person:US$753 ea.* | *7 Person:US$681 ea.* | *11 Person:US$651 ea.* |
| *4 Person:US$714 ea.* | *8 Person:US$671 ea.* | *12 Person:US$646 ea.* |

## F/V-DT9 HCMC/Nha Trang/Danang/Hue/Hanoi/Ha Long Bay (12 days - 11 nights)

**Day 1** *Meeting of guests at HCMC's TSN Airport. Transfer to hotel. Lunch. Half-day city tour.*

**Day 2** *Breakfast. Leave for Nha Trang. Check-in at the hotel. Lunch. Rest of the day free for sight-seeing and entertainment.*

**Day 3** *Breakfast before visiting and bathing in the Mineral Stream of Truong Xuan (Long Youth). Lunch at Ninh Hoa. Visits to Hon Chong Beach, Po Nagar Cham Temple and Long Tu Pagoda. Swimming and sunbathing. Shopping. Dinner. Evening free.*

**Day 4** *Breakfast. Leave for Danang. Lunch and then a city tour of Danang.*

**Day 5** *Swimming and sunbathing at China Beach. Lunch. Leave for Hue. Check-in at the hotel. Rest of the day free.*

**Day 6** *Breakfast. Visits to Tu Duc Mausoleum and the Hue Museum. Rest of the day free for sight-seeing and entertainment.*

**Day 7** *Breakfast. Transfer to airport for flight to Hanoi. Check-in at the hotel. Rest of the day free.*

**Day 8** *Breakfast. Half-day city tour of Hanoi. Lunch. Leave for Ha Long Bay. Check-in at the hotel. Rest of the day free.*

**Day 9** *A cruising tour on Ha Long Bay. Overnight stay on Peace Island.*

**Day 10** *Leave for Hanoi. Check-in at the hotel.*

**Day 11** *Transfer to airport for flight to HCMC. Check-in at the hotel. Rest of the day free.*

## F/V-DT9 HCMC/Nha Trang/Danang/Hue/Hanoi/Ha Long Bay (12 days - 11 nights)

**Day 12** *Breakfast. Transfer to TSN Airport. Seeing off of guests. End of the tour.*

| | | |
|---|---|---|
| *1 Person:US$1809 ea.* | *5 Person:US$1114 ea.* | *9 Person:US$1037 ea.* |
| *2 Person:US$1357 ea.* | *6 Person:US$1079 ea.* | *10 Person:US$1024 ea.* |
| *3 Person:US$1207 ea.* | *7 Person:US$1074 ea.* | *11 Person:US$1013 ea.* |
| *4 Person:US$1132 ea.* | *8 Person:US$1053 ea.* | *12 Person:US$1004 ea.* |

## F/V-DT10 HCMC/Vung Tau/Dalat/Nha Trang/HCMC/Tay Ninh (9 days - 8 nights)

**Day 1** *Meeting of guests at TSN Airport. Transfer and check-in at the Saigon Hotel. City tour with visits to Giac Lam Pagoda, the HCMC Zoo and Ben Thanh Market. Dinner. Evening free.*

**Day 2** *Breakfast. Leave for Vung Tau. Check-in at the Song Hong Hotel. Sea swimming and sunbathing. Lunch. Visits to the White Palace, Village of Fishers and Niet Ban Tinh Xa Pagoda. Swimming and sunbathing. Dinner. Evening free.*

**Day 3** *Breakfast. Leave for Dalat. Photo stops along the way. Visits to Dam Ri Waterfalls in Bao Loc and silkworm reeling factories. Lunch in Bao Loc. On to Dalat with stops at tea and coffee plantations as well as ethnic group villages. Check-in at Anh Doa Hotel. Dinner. Evening free.*

**Day 4** *Breakfast. Visits to the Railway Station, the Flower Garden and the Valley of Love. Lunch. Visits to Bao Dai's Palace, Linh Son or Linh Phong Pagoda and the Cathedral.*

**Day 5** *Breakfast. Leave for Nha Trang. Stops at Prenn Waterfalls and Ngoan Muc Pass. Visit Cham temple. Check-in at Nha Trang Hotel. Rest of the day free.*

**Day 6** *Breakfast. Visits to the Oceanographic Institute and Tri Nguyen Aquarium. Lunch. Visits to Po Nagar Cham Temple, Hon Chong Beach and Long Son Pagoda. Dinner. Evening free.*

**Day 7** *Breakfast. Visiting and bathing in the Mineral Stream of Truong Xuan (Long Youth). Lunch at Ninh Hoa. Back to Nha Trang. Sea swimming, sunbathing and additional visits to Po Nagar Temple and Long Tu Pagoda. Shopping. Dinner. Evening free.*

**Day 8** *Breakfast and check-out. Leave for HCMC. Check-in at the hotel. Dinner. Evening free.*

## F/V-DT10 HCMC/Vung Tau/Dalat/ Nha Trang/HCMC/Tay Ninh (9 days - 8 nights)

**Day 9** *Breakfast. Shopping. Lunch. Transfer to the airport. End of tour.*

*1 Person: US$1126 ea.*
*2 Person: US$769 ea.*
*3 Person: US$650 ea.*
*4 Person: US$591 ea.*
*5 Person: US$577 ea.*
*6 Person: US$549 ea.*
*7 Person: US$546 ea.*
*8 Person: US$529 ea.*
*9 Person: US$516 ea.*
*10 Person: US$506 ea.*
*11 Person: US$497 ea.*
*12 Person: US$490 ea.*

## F/V-DT11 HCMC/Vung Tau/Dalat/ Nha Trang/HCMC (10 days - 9 nights)

**Day 1** *Meeting of guests at TSN Airport. Transfer and check-in at the hotel. Dinner. Evening free.*

**Day 2** *Breakfast. Visit to Cu Chi Tunnels. Lunch. Depart for Vung Tau. Check-in at the hotel. Dinner. Evening free.*

**Day 3** *Breakfast. Visits to the White Palace, the Reclining Buddha Temple, the Whale Shrine, the New Market and Front Beach. Dinner. Evening free.*

**Day 4** *Breakfast. Leave for Dalat. Sight-seeing stops at Suoi Tien (Fairy Stream) and Suoi Ba Co (Three Spinster Stream). Lunch in Bao Loc. Stop at Prenn Waterfalls. On to Dalat. Check-in at the hotel. Dinner. Evening free.*

**Day 5** *Breakfast. Visits to Domaine de Marie, Linh Son Pagoda, the Valley of Love and Bao Dai's Palace. Lunch. Visits to Cam Ly Waterfalls, Chinese Pagoda, the Mayor's Palace and Xuan Huong Lake. Rest of the day free.*

**Day 6** *Breakfast. Visits to Tuyen Lam Lake and Datanla Waterfalls. Lunch. Visits to the Lake of Sighs, Twin Tomb Pine Hill and the Garden of Orchids. Dinner. Coffee at Thuyta.*

**Day 7** *Breakfast. Check-out. Visit Dalat Market. Leave for Nha Trang. Visits to Da Nhim Hydro-Electric Dam and the Cham Tower in Phan Rang. Lunch. On to Nha Trang. Check-in at the hotel. Evening free.*

**Day 8** *Breakfast. Visiting and bathing in the Mineral Stream of Truong Xuan (Long Youth). Lunch in Ninh Hoa. Back to Nha Trang. Visits to Hon Chong Beach, Po Nagar Cham Temple and Long Tu Pagoda. Sea swimming and sunbathing. Shopping. Dinner. Strolling along the beach.*

**Day 9** *Breakfast. Leave for HCMC. Check-in at the hotel. Dinner. Evening free.*

## F/V-DT11 HCMC/Vung Tau/Dalat/ Nha Trang/HCMC (10 days - 9 nights)

**Day 10** *Breakfast. Shopping. Lunch. Transfer to TSN Airport for departure and send-off. End of the tour.*

| | | |
|---|---|---|
| *1 Person:US$1201 ea.* | *5 Person:US$631 ea.* | *9 Person:US$567 ea.* |
| *2 Person:US$831 ea.* | *6 Person:US$602 ea.* | *10 Person:US$557 ea.* |
| *3 Person:US$707 ea.* | *7 Person:US$598 ea.* | *11 Person:US$548 ea.* |
| *4 Person:US$645 ea.* | *8 Person:US$581 ea.* | *12 Person:US$540 ea.* |

## F/V-1 HCMC/Vung Tau/ HCMC (3 days - 2 nights)

**Day 1** *Arrive at TSN Airport. Transfer to hotel. Afternoon city tour with visits to Nha Rong Wharf and Thien Hau Temple in Chinatown. Overnight in HCMC.*

**Day 2** *Day trip to Vung Tau. Visits to Nirvada Retreat and Buddhist Shrine and the White Palace. Swimming and sunbathing. Return to and overnight in HCMC.*

**Day 3** *Leisure in HCMC before check-out. Transfer to TSN airport for departure.*

**Price schedule:**

*1 Person:US$260*
*2-3:US$215*
*4-8:US$137*
*9-14:US$122*

## F/V-S2 HCMC/Cu Chi/HCMC (3 days - 2 nights)

**Day 1** *Arrival at TSN Airport. Transfer to hotel. Afternoon city tour with stops at Nha Rong Wharf and Thien Hau Temple in Chinatown. Overnight in HCMC.*

**Day 2** *Morning excursion to the Cu Chi Tunnels. Afternoon visits to Reunification Hall, lacquer-ware workshop, Vinh Nghiem Pagoda or Historical Museum and Giac Lam Pagoda. Over-night in HCMC.*

**Day 3** *Leisure before check-out. Transfer to TSN airport for departure.*

**Price Schedule:**

*1 person:US$260*
*2-3:US$215*

## F/V-S3 HCMC/Cu Chi/Vung Tau/HCMC (4 days - 3 nights)

**Day 1** *Arrive at TSN Airport. Transfer to hotel. Afternoon city tour with a stop at Thien Hau Temple in Chinatown. Overnight in HCMC.*

**Day2** *Morning excursion to Cu Chi Tunnels. Afternoon visits to Reunification Hall, lacquerware workshop and Vinh Nghiem Pagoda. Overnight in HCMC.*

**Day 3** *Day trip to Vung Tau for swimming and sunbathing with a visit to Nirvada Retreat and Buddhist Shrine. Overnight in Vung Tau.*

**Day 4** *Free morning before check-out. Back to HCMC for transfer to airport for departure.*

**Price Schedule:**

*1 Person:US$395*
*2-3:US$313*
*4-8:US$237*
*9-15:US$212*

## F/V-S4 HCMC/My Tho/Vung Tau/HCMC (4 days - 3 nights)

**Day 1** *Arrival at TSN Airport. Transfer to hotel. Afternoon city tour with stops at Nha Rong Wharf and Thien Hau Temple in Chinatown. Overnight in HCMC.*

**Day 2** *Day trip to My Tho with visits to the Orchard Garden and Vinh Trang Pagoda. Overnight in HCMC.*

**Day 3** *Day trip to Vung Tau for sunbathing and swimming, as well as a visit to Nirvada Retreat and Buddhist Shrine. Overnight in Vung Tau.*

**Day 4** *Free morning before check-out. Back to HCMC for transfer to airport for departure.*

**Price Schedule:**

*1 Person:US$405*
*2-3:US$313*
*4-8:US$227*
*9-15:US$202*

## F/V-S5 HCMC/Tay Ninh/Cu Chi/Vung Tau/HCMC (4 days - 3 nights)

**Day 1** *Arrive at TSN Airport. Transfer to hotel. Afternoon city tour with a stop at Thien Hau Temple in Chinatown. Overnight in HCMC.*

**Day 2** *Morning excursion to Cu Chi Tunnels. Afternoon visits to Reunification Hall, lacquerware workshop and Vinh Nghiem Pagoda. Overnight in HCMC.*

## F/V-S5 HCMC/Tay Ninh/Cu Chi/Vung Tau/HCMC (4 days - 3 nights)

**Day 3** *Day trip to Cu Chi Tunnels and Tay Ninh. Visit to Cao Dai Holy Temple. Overnight in HCMC.*

**Day 4** *Day trip to Vung Tau for sunbathing and swimming, as well as a visit to Nirvada Retreat and Buddhist Shrine. Overnight in Vung Tau.*

**Day 5** *Free morning before check-out. Back to HCMC for transfer to airport for departure.*

**Price Schedule:**

*1 Person:US$520*
*2-3:US$445*
*4-8:US$316*
*9-15:US$293*

## F/V-S6 HCMC/Vung Tau/Dalat/HCMC (6 days - 5 nights)

**Day 1** *Arrival at TSN Airport. Transfer to hotel. Afternoon city tour with stops at Nha Rong Wharf and Thien Hau Temple in Chinatown. Overnight in HCMC.*

**Day 2** *Day trip to Vung Tau. Visits to Nirvada Retreat and Buddhist Shrine and the White Palace. Swimming and sunbathing. Return to and overnight in HCMC.*

**Day 3** *Morning excursion to Dalat. Lunch enroute with a stop at Suoi Tien (Fairy Stream) and Prenn Waterfalls. Overnight in Dalat.*

**Day 4** *Full day of sight-seeing, with stops at the Valley of Love, Lake of Sighs, the Flower Garden and Bao Dai's Palace.*

**Day 5** *Return to HCMC. Lunch enroute. Overnight in HCMC.*

**Day 6** *Leisure before check-out. Transfer to TSN Airport for departure.*

**Price Schedule:**

*1 Person:US$735*
*2-3:US$588*
*4-8:US$410*
*9-15:US$366*

## F/V-S7 HCMC/My Tho/Dalat/HCMC (6 days - 5 nights)

**Day 1** *Arrival at TSN Airport. Transfer to hotel. Afternoon city tour with stops at Nha Rong Wharf and Thien Hau Temple in Chinatown. Overnight in HCMC.*

**Day 2** *Day trip to My Tho with visits to the Orchard Garden and Vinh Trang Pagoda. Overnight in HCMC.*

**Day 3** *Leave for Dalat. Lunch enroute with stops at Suoi Tien (Fairy Stream) and Prenn Waterfalls. Evening free. Overnight in Dalat.*

**Day 4** *Full day of sight-seeing, with stops at the Valley of Love, Lake of Sighs and Bao Dai's Palace. Overnight in Dalat.*

**Day 5** *Return to HCMC. Lunch enroute. Overnight in HCMC.*

**Day 6** *Leisure before check-out. Transfer to TSN Airport for departure.*

**Price Schedule:**

*1 Person:US$640*
*2-3:US$572*
*4-8:US$362*
*9-15:US$343*

## F/V-S8 HCMC/Cu Chi/Nha Trang/Dalat/HCMC (7 days - 6 nights)

**Day 1** *Arrival at TSN Airport. Transfer to hotel. Afternoon city tour with stops at Nha Rong Wharf and Thien Hau Temple in Chinatown. Overnight in HCMC.*

**Day 2** *Morning excursion to Cu Chi Tunnels. Afternoon visits to Reunification Hall, lacquerware workshop and Vinh Nghiem Pagoda. Overnight in HCMC.*

**Day 3** *Leave for Dalat. Lunch enroute with stops at Suoi Tien (Fairy Stream) and Prenn Waterfalls. Evening free. Overnight in Dalat.*

**Day 4** *Sight-seeing at the Valley of Love, Lake of Sighs and Bao Dai's Palace. Leave for Nha Trang in the afternoon.*

**Day 5** *Full day of sight-seeing in Nha Trang, with stops at Po Nagar Cham Towers, Overlapping Rocks and Long Son Pagoda. Sunbathing and sea swimming. Overnight in Nha Trang.*

**Day 6** *Return to HCMC. Lunch enroute. Overnight in HCMC.*

**Day 7** *Leisure before check-out. Transfer to TSN Airport for departure.*

## F/V-S8 HCMC/Cu Chi/Nha Trang/Dalat/HCMC (7 days - 6 nights)

**Price Schedule:**

*1 Person:US$820*
*2-3:US$712*
*4-8:US$657*
*9-15:US$627*

## F/V-S9 HCMC/Cu Chi/Danang/Hue/Hanoi/ Ha Long (10 days - 9 nights)

**Day 1** *Arrival at TSN Airport. Transfer to hotel. Afternoon city tour with stops at Nha Rong Wharf and Thien Hau Temple in Chinatown. Overnight in HCMC.*

**Day 2** *Morning excursion to Cu Chi Tunnels. Afternoon visits to Reunification Hall, lacquerware workshop and Vinh Nghiem Pagoda. Overnight in HCMC.*

**Day 3** *Fly to Danang; transfer to hotel. Visits to Cham Museum, Marble Mountains and China Beach. Overnight in Danang.*

**Day 4** *Leave for Hue via spectacular Hai Van Pass. Afternoon visits to Tu Duc and Khai Dinh Mausoleums. Overnight in Hue.*

**Day 5** *Morning cruise on the Perfume River to Thien Mu Pagoda, with later stops at the Museum of Royal Relics and the Imperial Citadel. Return to Danang for overnight.*

**Day 6** *Flight to Hanoi, with transfer to hotel. Afternoon city tour with stops at the Historical Museum, Quan Thanh Temple, Ambassador Pagoda and the Literature Temple. Overnight in Hanoi.*

**Day 7** *Visit to Ho Chi Minh's Mausoleum. Leave for Ha Long Bay for overnight stay.*

**Day 8** *Boat cruise on Ha Long Bay. Afternoon return to Hanoi. Overnight in Hanoi.*

**Day 9** *Day trip to Hoa Binh with a visit to a Muong ethnic village. Late afternoon return to Hanoi.*

**Day 10** *Leisure before check-out. Transfer to airport for departure.*

**Price Schedule:**

*1 Person:US$1850*
*2-3:US$1292*
*4-8:US$860*
*9-15:US$703*

## F/V-S10 HCMC/Cu Chi/Nha Trang/Buon Me Thuot/Quy Nhon/Danang/Hue/HCMC (12 days - 11 nights)

**Day 1** *Arrival at TSN Airport. Transfer to hotel. Afternoon city tour with stop at Thien Hau Temple in Chinatown. Overnight in HCMC.*

**Day 2** *Morning excursion to Cu Chi Tunnels. Afternoon visits to Reunification Hall, lacquerware workshop and Vinh Nghiem Pagoda. Overnight in HCMC.*

**Day 3** *Leave for Nha Trang with lunch enroute. Overnight in Nha Trang.*

**Day 4** *Full day of sight-seeing in Nha Trang, with stops at Po Nagar Cham Towers, Overlapping Rocks and Long Son Pagoda. Sunbathing and sea swimming. Overnight in Nha Trang.*

**Day 5** *Leave for Buon Me Thuot. Afternoon visits to the New Economic Zone and Drong Ksack Waterfalls. Overnight in Buon Me Thuoc.*

**Day 6** *Leave for Quy Nhon. Picnic or lunch enroute. Overnight in Quy Nhon.*

**Day 7** *Leave for Danang. Visits to the Cham Museum and the Marble Mountains. Overnight in Danang.*

**Day 8** *Leave for Hue via Hai Van Pass. Afternoon visits to Tu Duc and Khai Dinh Mausoleums. Overnight in Hue.*

**Day 9** *Morning excursion to Imperial Citadel and Tinh Tam Lake. Afternoon boat trip on the Perfume River to Thien Mu Pagoda and Minh Mang Tomb. Overnight in Hue.*

**Day 10** *Return to Nha Trang. Overnight in Nha Trang. Free evening.*

**Day 11** *Leave for HCMC. Overnight in HCMC. Free evening.*

**Day 12** *Leisure before hotel check-out. Transfer to TSN Airport for departure.*

**Price Schedule:**

*1 Person:US$3175*
*2-3:US$1680*
*4-8:US$979*

## F/V-S11 HCMC/Cu Chi/Nha Trang/Hue/HCMC (10 days - 9 nights)

**Day 1** *Arrival at TSN Airport. Transfer to hotel. Afternoon city tour with stop at Thien Hau Temple in Chinatown. Overnight in HCMC.*

**Day 2** *Morning excursion to Cu Chi Tunnels. Afternoon visits to Reunification Hall, lacquerware workshop and Vinh Nghiem Pagoda. Overnight in HCMC.*

**Day 3** *Leave for Nha Trang with lunch enroute. Overnight in Nha Trang.*

**Day 4** *Visits to Long Son Pagoda, Po Nagar Cham Towers and Overlapping Rocks. Overnight in Nha Trang.*

## F/V-S11 HCMC/Cu Chi/Nha Trang/Hue/HCMC (10 days - 9 nights)

**Day 5** *Flight to Danang. City tour with stops including the Cham Museum. Overnight in Danang.*

**Day 6** *Visits to the Marble Mountains and China Beach. Afternoon departure for Hue. Overnight in Hue.*

**Day 7** *Boat trip on Perfume River to Thien Mu Pagoda. Also visits to the Museum of Royal Relics and the Imperial Citadel. Overnight in Hue.*

**Day 8** *Visits to Tu Duc and Khai Dinh Mausoleums. Afternoon return to Danang. Overnight in Danang.*

**Day 9** *Flight back to HCMC. Rest of the day free.*

**Day 10** *Transfer to airport for departure.*

**Price Schedule:**

*1 Person:US$1285*
*2-3:US$980*
*4-8:US$674*
*9-15:US$493*

## F/V-S12-CAMBODIA HCMC/Tay Ninh/Mekong Delta/HCMC/Cambodia/HCMC (10 days - 9 nights)

**Day 1** *Arrival at TSN Airport. Transfer to hotel. Afternoon city tour with stop at Thien Hau Temple in Chinatown. Overnight in HCMC.*

**Day 2** *Morning visit to the War Crimes Museum. Afternoon visits to Reunification Hall, lacquerware workshop and Vinh Nghiem Pagoda. Overnight in HCMC.*

**Day 3** *Day trip to Cu Chi Tunnels and Tay Ninh, with a visit to the Cao Dai Holy Temple. Overnight in HCMC.*

**Day 4** *Day trip to My Tho. Boat trip to Phung Island or the Island of the Coconut Monk. Then visits to the Orchard Gardens and Vinh Trang Pagoda. Overnight in HCMC.*

**Day 5** *Flight to Phnom Penh, Cambodia. Visa delivery at the airport. Transfer to hotel. Full day city tour with stops at the National Museum, Genocidal Toul Sleng Museum, the Killing Fields and Wat Phnom. Overnight in Phnom Penh.*

**Day 6** *Morning flight to Siem Reap. Full-day tour of the Angkor temple complex. Overnight in Siem Reap.*

**Day 7** *Full day of sight-seeing in the Siem Reap area.*

**Day 8** *Further excursions of the Angkor complex or an optional tour to Bateay Srei. P.M. return to Phnom Penh. Transfer to hotel and overnight.*

## F/V-S12-CAMBODIA HCMC/Tay Ninh/Mekong Delta/HCMC/Cambodia/HCMC (10 days - 9 nights)

**Day 9** *Flight to HCMC. Transfer to hotel. Free day. Overnight in HCMC.*

**Day 10** *Leisure before check-out. Transfer to TSN Airport for departure.*

**Price Schedule:**

*1 Person:US$1569*
*2-3:US$1253*
*4-8:US$1144*
*9-14:US$1059*

## F/V-S13-CAMBODIA HCMC/Cu Chi/Tay Ninh/Vung Tau/HCMC/Cambodia/HCMC (9 days - 8 nights)

**Day 1** *Arrival at TSN Airport. Transfer to hotel. Afternoon city tour with stop at Thien Hau Temple in Chinatown. Overnight in HCMC.*

**Day 2** *Day trip to Cu Chi Tunnels and Tay Ninh, with a visit to the Cao Dai Holy Temple. Overnight in HCMC.*

**Day 3** *Day trip to Vung Tau for swimming and sunbathing, with visit to Nirvada Retreat and Buddhist Shrine. Overnight in HCMC.*

**Day 4** *Flight to Phnom Penh, Cambodia. Visa delivery at the airport. Transfer to hotel. Full day city tour with stops at the National Museum, Genocidal Toul Sleng Museum, the Killing Fields and Wat Phnom. Overnight in Phnom Penh.*

**Day 5** *Morning flight to Siem Reap. Full-day tour of the Angkor temple complex. Overnight in Siem Reap.*

**Day 6** *Full day of sight-seeing in the Siem Reap area. Overnight in Siem Reap.*

**Day 7** *Further excursions of the Angkor complex or an optional tour to Bateay Srei. P.M. return to Phnom Penh. Transfer to hotel and overnight.*

**Day 8** *Flight to HCMC. Transfer to hotel. Free day. Overnight in HCMC.*

**Day 9** *Leisure before check-out. Transfer to TSN Airport for departure.*

**Price Schedule:**

*1 Person:US$1569*
*2-3:US$1253*
*4-8:US$1144*
*9-14:US$1059*

## F/V-V14 HCMC (2 days - 1 night)

**Day 1** *Arrival at TSN Airport. Transfer to hotel. Half-day city tour with stops at Independence Palace, Historical Museum, Thien Hau Pagoda and Chinatown. Also a traditional Vietnamese music show.*

**Day 2** *Shopping. Transfer to the airport.*

**Price Schedule:**

*1 Person:(A) US$215, (B) US$180, (C) US$155*

*2:(A) US$160, (B) US$135, (C) US$125*

*3-6:(A) US$145, (B) US$120, (C) US$110*

*7-10:(A) US$135, (B) US$120, (C) US$100*

*11-14:(A) US$130, (B) US$105, (C) US$95*

*15 and up:(A) US$125, (B) US$100, (C) US$90*

*Single room request:(A) US$45, (B) US$30, (C) US$15*

## F/V-V14 HCMC/Cu Chi Tunnels (3 days - 2 nights)

**Day 1** *Arrival at TSN Airport. Transfer to hotel. Half-day city tour with stops at Independence Palace, Historical Museum, Thien Hau Pagoda and Chinatown. Also a traditional Vietnamese music show.*

**Day 2** *Morning visit to the Cu Chi Tunnels. Afternoon city tour of HCMC with stops in Chinatown and the War Museum.*

**Day 3** *Shopping and transfer to the airport.*

**Price Schedule:**

*1 Person:(A) US$335, (B) US$275, (C) US$225*

*2:(A) US$245, (B) US$195, (C) US$175*

*3-6:(A) US$225, (B) US$175, (C) US$155*

*7-10:(A) US$210, (B) US$160, (C) US$140*

*11-14:(A) US$200, (B) US$150, (C) US$130*

*15 and up:(A) US$190, (B) US$140, (C) US$120*

*Single room request:(A) US$90, (B) US$60, (C) US$30*

## F/V-V15 HCMC/Vung Tau (3 days - 2 nights)

**Day 1** *Arrival at TSN Airport. Transfer to hotel. Half-day city tour with stops at Independence Palace, Historical Museum, Thien Hau Pagoda and Chinatown. Also a traditional Vietnamese music show.*

**Day 2** *Travel to Vung Tau Beach. Sun and seabathing as well visits to pagodas and the White Palace. Return to and overnight in HCMC.*

**Day 3** *Shopping and transfer to the airport.*

**Price Schedule:**

*1 Person:(A) US$345, (B) US$275, (C) US$235*

*2:(A) US$255, (B) US$205, (C) US$185*

*3-6:(A) US$235, (B) US$185, (C) US$165*

*7-10:(A) US$220, (B) US$170, (C) US$150*

*11-14:(A) US$210, (B) US$160, (C) US$140*

*15 and up:(A) US$200, (B) US$150, (C) US$130*

*Single room request:(A) US$90, (B) US$60, (C) US$30*

## F/V-V16 Hanoi (3 days - 2 nights)

**Day 1** *Arrival at Noi Bai Airport and transfer to hotel. City tour with stops at The Literature Temple and Quan Thanh Temple. Dinner and overnight in Hanoi.*

**Day 2** *City tour with stops at Ho Chi Minh's Mausoleum, Ho Chi Minh Museum, the One-Pillar Pagoda, Hoan Kiem Lake, the Fine Arts Museum, West Lake and the Old Town area of Hanoi. Dinner and overnight in Hanoi.*

**Day 3** *Transfer to airport for departure.*

**Price Schedule:**

*1 Person:(A) US$410, (B) US$340, (C) US$300*

*2:(A) US$320, (B) US$270, (C) US$230*

*3-6:(A) US$290, (B) US$240, (C) US$200*

*7-10:(A) US$270, (B) US$220, (C) US$180*

*11-14:(A) US$260, (B) US$210, (C) US$170*

*15 and up:(A) US$250, (B) US$200, (C) US$160*

*Single room request:(A) US$90, (B) US$60, (C) US$30*

## F/V-V17 HCMC/Vung Tau/Cu Chi (4 days - 3 nights)

**Day 1** *Arrival at TSN Airport. Transfer to hotel. Half-day city tour with stops at Independence Palace, Historical Museum, Thien Hau Pagoda and Chinatown. Also a traditional Vietnamese music show.*

**Day 2** *Morning visit to Cu Chi Tunnels. Afternoon return to HCMC for a city tour with stops at a lacquerware product center and the War Museum. Dinner and overnight in HCMC.*

**Day 3** *Morning travel to Vung Tau. Sun and seabathing as well visits to pagodas and the White Palace. Return to and overnight in HCMC.*

**Day 4** *Transfer to airport for departure.*

**Price Schedule:**

*1 Person:(A) US$485, (B) US$380, (C) US$ 320*

*2:(A) US$355, (B) US$280, (C) US$250*

*3-6:(A) US$325, (B) US$250, (C) US$220*

*7-10:(A) US$305, (B) US$230, (C) US$200*

*11-14:(A) US$295, (B) US$220, (C) US$190*

*15 and up:(A) US$285, (B) US$210, (C) US$180*

*Single room request:(A) US$135, (B) US$90, (C) US$45*

## F/V-V18 HCMC/Cu Chi/Mekong Delta (4 days - 3 nights)

**Day 1** *Arrival at TSN Airport. Transfer to hotel. Half-day city tour with stops at the Independence Palace and the Historical Museum. Dinner and overnight in HCMC.*

**Day 2** *Morning visit to Cu Chi Tunnels. Afternoon return to HCMC with a half-day city tour. Stops at pagodas, Chinatown, the War Museum and a traditional Vietnamese music show. Dinner and overnight in HCMC.*

**Day 3** *Travel to My Tho for a boat cruise along the Mekong River. Visits to Vinh Trang Pagoda and the Dong Tam Snake Farm. Return to HCMC for dinner and overnight.*

**Day 4** *Shopping and transfer to the airport for departure.*

**Price Schedule:**

*1 Person:(A) US$485, (B) US$380, (C) US$320*

*2:(A) US$355, (B) US$ 280, (C) US$250*

*3-6:(A) US$325, (B) US$250, (C) US$220*

*7-10:(A) US$305, (B) US$230, (C) US$200*

## F/V-V18 HCMC/Cu Chi/Mekong Delta (4 days - 3 nights)

*11-14:(A) US$295, (B) US$220, (C) US$190*

*15 and up:(A) US$285, (B) US$210, (C) US$180*

*Single room request:(A) US$135, (B) US$90, (C) US$45*

## F/V-V19 HCMC/Mekong Delta/Floating Market/Cu Chi (5 days - 4 nights)

**Day 1** *Arrival at TSN Airport. Transfer to hotel. Half-day city tour with stops at the Independence Palace and the Historical Museum. Vietnamese traditional music show, dinner and overnight in HCMC.*

**Day 2** *Morning visit to the Cu Chi Tunnels. Afternoon HCMC tour with stops including the War Museum. Dinner and overnight in HCMC.*

**Day 3** *Trip to the Mekong Delta with visits to the Khmer Museum and Bat Pagoda. Overnight in Can Tho with a Cailong (Vietnamese traditional music) show.*

**Day 4** *Boat cruise on the Mekong Delta with a visit to Phung Hiep Floating Market on the river. Experience the delicacies of the region's exotic tropical fruit. Return to and overnight in HCMC.*

**Day 5** *Shopping and transfer to the airport for departure.*

**Price Schedule:**

*1 Person:(A) US$640, (B) US$510, (C) US$420*

*2:(A) US$510, (B) US$370, (C) US$330*

*3-6:(A) US$470, (B) 330, (C) US$290*

*7-10:(A) US$ 440, (B) US$330, (C) US$290*

*11-14:(A) US$420, (B) US$280, (C) US$240*

*15 and up:(A) US$410, (B) US$270, (C) US$230*

*Single room request:(A) US$180, (B) US$115, (C) US$55*

## F/V-V20 HCMC/Dalat/Cu Chi (5 days - 4 nights)

**Day 1** *Arrival at TSN Airport. Transfer to hotel. Half-day city tour with stops at the Independence Palace and the Historical Museum. Dinner and overnight in HCMC.*

**Day 2** *Morning visit to the Cu Chi Tunnels. Afternoon return to HCMC with visits to a lacquerware center, Chinatown and the War Museum. Dinner and overnight in HCMC.*

## F/V-V20 HCMC/Dalat/Cu Chi (5 days - 4 nights)

**Days 3 & 4** *Travel to Dalat by road. Visits to Prenn, Datala, Camly and Dam Ri Waterfalls as well as the Minhy Tam Flower Garden, the Valley of Love, Linh Son Pagoda and Xuan Huong and Tuyen Lam lakes. Return to HCMC during the afternoon of Day 4. Dinner and overnight.*

**Day 5** *Shopping and transfer to the airport for departure.*

**Price Schedule:**

*1 Person:(A) US$660, (B) US$520, (C) US$440*

*2:(A) US$520, (B) US$390, (C) US$350*

*3-6:(A) US$450, (B) US$350, (C) U$310*

*7-10:(A) US$420, (B) US$320, (C) US$280*

*11-14:(A) US$400, (B) US$300, (C) US$260*

*15 and up:(A) US$390, (B) US$290, (C) US$250*

*Single room request:(A) US$180, (B) US$115, (C) US$55*

## F/V-V21 HCMC/Phan Rang/Nha Trang (5 days - 4 nights)

**Day 1** *Arrival at TSN Airport. Transfer to hotel. Half-day city tour with stops at Independence Palace, Historical Museum, and the War Museum. Dinner and overnight in HCMC.*

**Days 2 & 3** *Travel via air-conditioned car or van to Nha Trang. Sea and sunbathing and visits to the Husband's Rock, Tri Nguyen Aquarium, Po Nagar Cham Towers and the Marine Biological Research Institute. Dinner and overnight in Nha Trang.*

**Day 4** *Visit Cham towers in Phan Rang and the beaches of Ca Na. Return to HCMC.*

**Day 5** *Shopping and transfer to airport.*

**Price Schedule:**

*1 Person:(A) US$660, (B) US$520, (C) US$440*

*2:(A) US$520, (B) US$390, (C) US$350*

*3-6:(A) US$450, (B) US$350, (C) U$310*

*7-10:(A) US$420, (B) US$320, (C) US$280*

*11-14:(A) US$400, (B) US$300, (C) US$260*

*15 and up:(A) US$390, (B) US$290, (C) US$250*

*Single room request:(A) US$180, (B) US$115, (C) US$55*

## F/V-V22 HCMC/Hanoi (5 days - 4 nights)

**Day 1** *Arrival at TSN Airport. Transfer to hotel. Half-day city tour with stops at Independence Palace, Historical Museum, and the War Museum. Dinner and overnight in HCMC.*

**Day 2** *Morning visit to the Cu Chi Tunnels. Afternoon visits to HCMC's pagodas, Chinatown and the War Museum. Dinner and overnight in HCMC.*

**Day 3** *Fly to Hanoi. Transfer to hotel. City tour of West Lake and Tran Quoc Pagoda. Dinner and overnight in Hanoi.*

**Day 4** *Hanoi city tour with stops at Ho Chi Minh's Mausoleum, 1- Pillar Pagoda, Literature Temple, Hoan Kiem Lake, the Fine Arts Museum and the Old Town area of Hanoi.*

**Day 5** *Shopping and transfer to airport.*

**Price Schedule:**

*1 Person:(A) US$850, (B) US$710, (C) US$630*

*2:(A) US$660, (B) US$560, (C) US$520*

*3-6:(A) US$610, (B) US$510, (C) US$470*

*7-10:(A) US$590, (B) US$490, (C) US$450*

*11-14:(A) US$570, (B) US$470, (C) US$430*

*15 and up:(A) US$550, (B) US$450, (C) US$410*

*Single room request:(A) US$180, (B) US$115, (C) US$55*

## F/V-V23 Hanoi/Ha Long Bay (5 days - 4 nights)

**Day 1** *Arrival at Noi Bai Airport. Transfer to hotel. Half-day city tour with stops at the Literature Temple and Quan Thanh Temple. Dinner and overnight.*

**Day 2** *City tour with stops at Ho Chi Minh's Mausoleum, 1-Pillar Pagoda, Hoan Kiem Lake, the Fine Arts Museum, West Lake and the Old Town section of Hanoi. Dinner and overnight.*

**Day 3** *Morning departure for Ha Long Bay with a general visit of the bay area. Dinner and overnight at Ha Long.*

**Day 4** *Boat cruising on Ha Long Bay with an afternoon return to Hanoi. Dinner and overnight.*

**Day 5** *Breakfast and transfer to airport for departure.*

**Price Schedule:**

*1 Person:(A) US$750, (B) US$610, (C) US$530*

*2:(A) US$560, (B) US$460, (C) US$420*

*3-6:(A) US$520, (B) US$420, (C) US$380*

*7-10:(A) US$500, (B) US$400, (C) US$360*

## F/V-V23 Hanoi/Ha Long Bay (5 days - 4 nights)

*11-14:(A) US$480, (B) US$380, (C) US$340*

*15 and up:(A) US$460, (B) US$360, (C) US$320*

*Single room request:(A) US$180, (B) US$115, (C) US$55*

## F/V-V24 HCMC/Nha Trang/Dalat/HCMC (6 days - 5 nights)

**Day 1** *Arrival at TSN Airport. Transfer to hotel. Half-day city tour with stops at Independence Palace, the Historical Museum and the War Museum. Traditional Vietnamese music show. Dinner and overnight.*

**Day 2** *Travel to Nha Trang. Dinner and overnight.*

**Day 3** *City tour and visits to Prenn Datala, Camly, Damry Waterfalls. Also Gougah, Linh Son Pagoda, Bao Dai's Palace, Minh Tam Flower Garden, Xuan Huong Lake and the Valley of Love.*

**Day 4** *Travel to Dalat. City tour with stops at Bao Dai's Palace, Minh Tam Flower Garden and Xuan Huong Lake. Dinner and overnight.*

**Day 5** *Dalat city tour with stops at the Prenn, Datala, Camly and Dam Ri Waterfalls. Also Gougah and Linh Son Pagoda. Afternoon return to HCMC. Dinner and overnight.*

**Day 6** *Shopping and transfer to the airport.*

**Price Schedule:**

*1 Person:(A) US$820, (B) US$645, (C) US$545*

*2:(A) US$590, (B) US$465, (C) US$425*

*3-6:(A) US$550, (B) US$425, (C) US$375*

*7-10:(A) US$515, (B) US$390, (C) US$340*

*11-14:(A) US$495, (B) US$370, (C) US$320*

*15 and up:(A) US$485, (B) US$360, (C) US$310*

*Single room request:(A) US$200, (B) US$140, (C) US$70*

## F/V-V25 HCMC/Danang/Hue/HCMC (7 days - 6 nights)

**Day 1** *Arrival at TSN Airport. Transfer to hotel. Half-day city tour with stops at Independence Palace, the Historical Museum and the War Museum. Traditional Vietnamese music show. Dinner and overnight.*

**Day 2** *Fly to Danang. City tour and stops at China Beach and the Marble Mountains, including Ngu Hanh. Dinner and overnight.*

## F/V-V25 HCMC/Danang/Hue/HCMC (7 days - 6 nights)

**Day 3** *Visit to the ancient town of Hoi An and the Cham Sculpture Museum. Car trip to Hue. Dinner and overnight.*

**Day 4** *Morning city tour with stops at Tu Duc's, Khai Dinh's and Minh Mang's Mausoleums. Also the Hue Citadel. Afternoon boat trip on the Huong River with a stop at Thien Mu Pagoda. Dinner and overnight.*

**Day 5** *Fly back to HCMC. Visit to the Cu Chi Tunnels. Dinner and overnight in HCMC.*

**Day 6** *Visit to the Mekong Delta with a boat cruise on the Mekong River. Visits to Vinh Trang Pagoda and the Dong Tam Snake Farm. Dinner and overnight in HCMC.*

**Day 7** *Shopping and transfer to the airport.*

**Price Schedule:**

*1 Person:(A) US$1090, (B) US$885, (C) US$765*

*2:(A) US$830, (B) US$680, (C) US$620*

*3-6:(A) US$780, (B) US$630, (C) US$570*

*7-10:(A) US$750, (B) US$600, (C) US$540*

*11-14:(A) US$720, (B) US$570, (C) US$510*

*15 and up:(A) US$700, (B) US$550, (C) US$490*

*Single room request:(A) US$230, (B) US$160, (C) US$80*

## F/V-V26 HCMC/Hanoi/Ha Long Bay (7 days - 6 nights)

**Day 1** *Arrival at TSN Airport. Transfer to hotel. Half-day city tour with stops at Independence Palace, the Historical Museum and the War Museum. Traditional Vietnamese music show. Dinner and overnight.*

**Day 2** *Visit to either the Cu Chi Tunnels or the Mekong Delta. Shopping. Dinner and overnight in HCMC.*

**Day 3** *Fly to Hanoi. Transfer to hotel. City tour with stops at West Lake and Tran Quoc Pagoda. Dinner and overnight.*

**Day 4** *City tour with stops at Ho Chi Minh's Mausoleum, 1-Pillar Pagoda, Hoan Kiem Lake, the Fine Arts Museum, West Lake and the Old Town section of Hanoi. Dinner and overnight.*

**Day 5** *Trip to Haiphong and Ha Long Bay. City tour of Haiphong. Dinner and overnight.*

**Day 6** *Boat cruise on Ha Long Bay in the morning. Afternoon return to Hanoi. Dinner and overnight.*

**Day 7** *Transfer to the airport for departure.*

## F/V-V26 HCMC/Hanoi/Ha Long Bay (7 days - 6 nights)

**Price Schedule:**

*1 Person:(A) US$1140, (B) US$930, (C) US$810*

*2:(A) US$870, (B) US$720, (C) US$660*

*3-6:(A) US$820, (B) US$670, (C) US$610*

*7-10:(A) US$790, (B) US$640, (C) US$580*

*11-14:(A) US$760, (B) US$610, (C) US$550*

*15 and up:(A) US$740, (B) US$590, (C) US$530*

*Single room request:(A) US$230, (B) US$160, (C) US$80*

## F/V-V27 HCMC/Nha Trang/Dalat/HCMC (7 days - 6 nights)

**Day 1** *Arrival at TSN Airport. Transfer to hotel. Half-day city tour with stops at Independence Palace, the Historical Museum and the War Museum. Traditional Vietnamese music show. Dinner and overnight.*

**Day 2** *Morning visit to the Cu Chi Tunnels. Afternoon city tour with stops at a lacquerware product center, the War Museum and Chinatown. Dinner and overnight in HCMC.*

**Days 3 & 4** *Travel to Dalat. Hotel check-in. City tour and visits to Prenn Datala, Camly, Damry Waterfalls. Also Gougah, Linh Son Pagoda, Bao Dai's Palace, Minh Tam Flower Garden, Xuan Huong Lake and the Valley of Love. Leave for Nha Trang in the afternoon of Day 4. Dinner and overnight in Nha Trang.*

**Day 5** *Sea and sunbathing as well as visits to Husband's Rock, Tri Nguyen Aquarium, Po Nagar Cham Towers and the Marine Biological Research Institute. Dinner and overnight.*

**Day 6** *Return to HCMC, visiting Cham towers on the way back. Dinner and overnight in HCMC.*

**Day 7** *Shopping and transfer to the airport.*

**Price Schedule:**

*1 Person:(A) US$950, (B) US$740, (C) US$620*

*2:(A) US$710, (B) US$560, (C) US$500*

*3-6:(A) US$650, (B) US$500, (C) US$440*

*7-10:(A) US$610, (B) US$460, (C) US$400*

*11-14:(A) US$580, (B) US$430, (C) US$370*

*15 and up:(A) US$565, (B) US$415, (C) US$355*

*Single room request:(A) US$230, (B) US$160, (C) US$80*

## F/V-V28 HCMC/Danang/Hue/Hanoi (8 days - 7 nights)

**Day 1** *Arrival at TSN Airport. Transfer to hotel. Half-day city tour with stops at Independence Palace, the Historical Museum and the War Museum. Traditional Vietnamese music show. Dinner and overnight.*

**Day 2** *Morning visit to the Cu Chi Tunnels. Afternoon HCMC city tour with stops at a lacquerware product center, the War Museum, Chinatown and various significant pagodas.. Dinner and overnight in HCMC.*

**Day 3** *Fly to Danang. City tour and visits to China Beach and the Marble Mountain Ngu Hanh. Dinner and overnight.*

**Day 4** *Visits to Hoi An and the Cham Sculpture Museum. Travel to Hue. Hotel check-in. Dinner and overnight in Hue.*

**Day 5** *City tour with visits to the Hue Citadel and the mausoleums of Tu Duc, Khai Dinh and Minh Mang. Afternoon boat trip on the Huong river with a stop at Thien Mu Pagoda. Dinner and overnight in Hue.*

**Day 6** *Fly to Hanoi and hotel check-in. General city tour with stops at the Temple of Literature and Hoan Kiem Lake. Dinner and overnight.*

**Day 7** *City tour with stops at Ho Chi Minh's Mausoleum, West Lake, 1-Pillar Pagoda, Tran Quoc Pagoda, the Fine Arts Museum and the Old Town area. of Hanoi. Dinner and overnight.*

**Day 8** *Shopping and transfer to airport.*

**Price Schedule:**

*1 Person:(A) US$1250, (B) US$1000, (C) US$870*

*2:(A) US$970, (B) US$800, (C) US$730*

*3-6:(A) US$880, (B) US$710, (C) US$640*

*7-10:(A) US$840, (B) US$670, (C) US$600*

*11-14:(A) US$810, (B) US$640, (C) US$570*

*15 and up:(A) US$780, (B) US$610, (C) US$540*

*Single room request:(A) US$270, (B) US$180, (C) US$90*

## F/V-V29 HCMC/Dalat/Nha Trang/ Danang/Hue/HCMC (9 days - 8 nights)

**Day 1** *Arrival at TSN Airport. Transfer to hotel. Half-day city tour with stops at Independence Palace, the Historical Museum and the War Museum. Traditional Vietnamese music show. Dinner and overnight.*

**Day 2** *Morning visit to the Cu Chi Tunnels and then travel to Dalat. Check-in at the hotel. Dinner and overnight.*

**Day 3** *City tour and visits to Prenn Datala, Camly, Damry Waterfalls. Also Gougah, Linh Son Pagoda, Bao Dai's Palace, Minh Tam Flower Garden, Xuan Huong Lake and the Valley of Love. Dinner and overnight in Dalat.*

**Day 4** *Travel to Nha Trang. Hotel check-in. Sea and sunbathing as well as visits to Husband's Rock, Tri Nguyen Aquarium, Po Nagar Cham Towers and the Marine Biological Research Institute. Dinner and overnight.*

**Day 5** *Travel to Danang observing the remarkable scenery. Dinner and overnight.*

**Day 6** *Visits to the ancient town of Hoi An and the Cham Sculpture Museum. Car travel to Hue. Hotel check-in, dinner and overnight.*

**Day 7** *City tour of Hue with visits to the Hue Citadel and the mausoleums of Tu Duc, Khai Dinh and Minh Mang. Afternoon boat trip on the Huong river with a stop at Thien Mu Pagoda. Dinner and overnight in Hue.*

**Day 8** *Fly back to HCMC. Dinner and overnight.*

**Day 9** *Shopping and transfer to airport.*

**Price Schedule:**

*1 Person:(A) US$1380, (B) US$1100, (C) US$940*

*2:(A) US$1080, (B) US$880, (C) US$800*

*3-6:(A) US$980, (B) US$780, (C) US$700*

*7-10:(A) US$940, (B) US$740, (C) US$660*

*11-14:(A) US$910, (B) US$710, (C) US$630*

*15 and up:(A) US$880, (B) US$680, (C) US$600*

*Single room request:(A) US$300, (B) US$195, (C) US$100*

## F/V-V30 HCMC/Mekong Delta/ Danang/Hue/Hanoi (9 days - 8 nights)

**Day 1** *Arrival at TSN Airport. Transfer to hotel. Half-day city tour with stops at Independence Palace, the Historical Museum and the War Museum. Traditional Vietnamese music show. Dinner and overnight.*

**Day 2** *Morning visit to the Cu Chi Tunnels. Afternoon HCMC city tour with stops at a lacquerware product center, the War Museum, Chinatown and various significant pagodas. Dinner and overnight in HCMC.*

**Day 3** *Visit to the Mekong Delta. Boat cruise on the Mekong River and visits to Vinh Trang Pagoda and the Dong Tam Snake Farm. Return to HCMC. Dinner and overnight.*

**Day 4** *Fly to Danang. City tour and stops at China Beach and the Marble Mountain of Ngu Hanh. Dinner and overnight in Danang.*

**Day 5** *Visits to the ancient town of Hoi An and the Cham Sculpture Museum. Car travel to Hue. Hotel check-in, dinner and overnight.*

**Day 6** *City tour of Hue with visits to the Hue Citadel and the mausoleums of Tu Duc, Khai Dinh and Minh Mang. Afternoon boat trip on the Huong river with a stop at Thien Mu Pagoda. Dinner and overnight in Hue.*

**Day 7** *Fly to Hanoi. Transfer to hotel. Visits to West Lake and Tran Quoc Pagoda. Dinner and overnight.*

**Day 8** *City tour with stops at Ho Chi Minh's Mausoleum, West Lake, 1-Pillar Pagoda, Hoan Kiem Lake, the Fine Arts Museum and the Old Town area. of Hanoi. Dinner and overnight.*

**Day 9** *Shopping and transfer to the airport.*

**Price Schedule:**

*1 Person:(A) US$1420, (B) US$1140, (C) US$980*

*2:(A) US$1120, (B) US$920, (C) US$830*

*3-6:(A) US$1010, (B) US$810, (C) US$730*

*7-10:(A) US$960, (B) US$760, (C) US$680*

*11-14:(A) US$930, (B) US$730, (C) US$650*

*15 and up:(A) US$900, (B) US$700, (C) US$620*

*Single room request:(A) US$300, (B) US$195, (C) US$100*

## F/V-V31 HCMC/Danang/Hue/Hanoi/Ha Long Bay (11 days - 10 nights)

**Day 1** *Arrival at TSN Airport. Transfer to hotel. Half-day city tour with stops at Independence Palace, the Historical Museum and the War Museum. Traditional Vietnamese music show. Dinner and overnight.*

**Day 2** *Morning visit to the Cu Chi Tunnels. Afternoon HCMC city tour with stops at a lacquerware product center, the War Museum, Chinatown and various significant pagodas. Dinner and overnight in HCMC.*

**Day 3** *Visit to the Mekong Delta. Boat cruise on the Mekong River and visits to Vinh Trang Pagoda and the Dong Tam Snake Farm. Return to HCMC. Dinner and overnight.*

**Day 4** *Fly to Danang. City tour and stops at China Beach and the Marble Mountain of Ngu Hanh. Dinner and overnight in Danang.*

**Day 5** *Visits to the ancient town of Hoi An and the Cham Sculpture Museum. Car travel to Hue. Hotel check-in, dinner and overnight.*

**Day 6** *City tour of Hue with visits to the Hue Citadel and the mausoleums of Tu Duc, Khai Dinh and Minh Mang. Afternoon boat trip on the Huong river with a stop at Thien Mu Pagoda. Dinner and overnight in Hue.*

**Day 7** *Fly to Hanoi. Transfer to hotel. Visits to West Lake and Tran Quoc Pagoda. Dinner and overnight.*

**Day 8** *City tour with stops at Ho Chi Minh's Mausoleum, West Lake, 1-Pillar Pagoda, Hoan Kiem Lake, the Fine Arts Museum and the Old Town area. of Hanoi. Dinner and overnight.*

**Day 9** *Trip to Ha Long Bay. Visits to Yen Lap Lake and Hon Gai Town.*

**Day 10** *Boat cruise on Ha Long Bay. Return to Hanoi. Dinner and overnight.*

**Day 11** *Shopping and transfer to the airport.*

**Price Schedule:**

*1 Person:(A) US$1750, (B) US$1400, (C) US$1200*

*2:(A) US$1340, (B) US$1090, (C) US$990*

*3-6:(A) US$1210, (B) US$960, (C) US$860*

*7-10:(A) US$1160, (B) US$900, (C) US$810*

*11-14:(A) US$1130, (B) US$880, (C) US$780*

*15 and up:(A) US$1080, (B) US$850, (C) US$750*

*Single room request:(A) US$360, (B) US$220, (C) US$120*

## F/V-V32 HCMC/Mekong Delta/Dalat/ Nha Trang/Danang/Hue/Hanoi/ Ha Long Bay/Hanoi (15 days - 14 nights)

**Day 1** *Arrival at TSN Airport. Transfer to hotel. Half-day city tour with stops at Independence Palace, the Historical Museum and the War Museum. Traditional Vietnamese music show. Dinner and overnight.*

**Day 2** *Morning visit to the Cu Chi Tunnels. Afternoon HCMC city tour with stops at a lacquerware product center, the War Museum, Chinatown and various significant pagodas. Dinner and overnight in HCMC.*

**Day 3** *Visit to the Mekong Delta. Boat cruise on the Mekong River and visits to Vinh Trang Pagoda and the Dong Tam Snake Farm. Return to HCMC. Dinner and overnight.*

**Day 4** *Trip to Dalat. Hotel check-in and general city tour. Dinner and overnight.*

**Day 5** *City tour and visits to Prenn Datala, Camly, Damry Waterfalls. Also Gougah, Linh Son Pagoda, Bao Dai's Palace, Minh Tam Flower Garden, Xuan Huong Lake and the Valley of Love. Dinner and overnight in Dalat.*

**Day 6** *Travel to Nha Trang. Hotel check-in. Sea and sunbathing as well as visits to Husband's Rock, Tri Nguyen Aquarium, Po Nagar Cham Towers and the Marine Biological Research Institute. Dinner and overnight.*

**Day 7** *Trip to Quy Nhon. Visit to Quang Trung King's House. Dinner and overnight.*

**Day 8** *Trip to Danang. Dinner and overnight.*

**Day 9** *Visits to the Cham Sculpture Museum, the ancient town of Hoi An, China Beach and Ngu Hanh Marble Mountain. Car trip to Hue. Hotel check-in, dinner and overnight.*

**Day 10** *City tour of Hue with visits to the Hue Citadel and the mausoleums of Tu Duc, Khai Dinh and Minh Mang. Afternoon boat trip on the Huong river with a stop at Thien Mu Pagoda. Dinner and overnight in Hue.*

**Day 11** *Fly to Hanoi. Transfer to hotel. Visits to West Lake and Tran Quoc Pagoda. Dinner and overnight.*

**Day 12** *City tour with stops at Ho Chi Minh's Mausoleum, West Lake, 1-Pillar Pagoda, Hoan Kiem Lake, the Fine Arts Museum, Nghi Tam Flower Garden, Dong Xuan Market and the Old Town area. of Hanoi. Dinner and overnight.*

**Day 13** *Trip to Ha Long Bay. Visits to Yen Lap Lake and Hon Gai Town.*

**Day 14** *Boat cruise on Ha Long Bay. Return to Hanoi. Dinner and overnight.*

**Day 15** *Shopping and transfer to the airport.*

**Price Schedule:**

*1 Person:(A) US$2370, (B) US$1880, (C) US$1600*

*2:(A) US$1800, (B) US$1440, (C) US$1290*

## F/V-V32 HCMC/Mekong Delta/Dalat/ Nha Trang/Danang/Hue/Hanoi/ Ha Long Bay/Hanoi (15 days - 14 nights)

*3-6:(A) US$1620, (B) US$1270, (C) US$1130*

*7-10:(A) US$1560, (B) US$1210, (C) US$1070*

*11-14:(A) US$1510, (B) US$1160, (C) US$1020*

*15 and up:(A) US$1470, (B) US$1120, (C) US$980*

*Single room request:(A) US$480, (B) US$280, (C) US$160*

## F/V-V33 HCMC/Nha Trang/ Buon Me Thuot/Pleiku/Kontum (8 days - 7 nights)

**Day 1** *Arrival at TSN Airport. Transfer to hotel. Half-day city tour with stops at the Historical Museum and a water puppet show, as well Independence Palace or Chinatown with a stop at Gia Clam Pagoda.*

**Day 2** *Breakfast. Then drive to Nha Trang with a stopover at Ca Na Beach for lunch. Arrive in Nha Trang. Hotel check-in. Dinner.*

**Day 3** *Breakfast and seabathing in the morning. Then visits to Po Nagar Cham Towers, Tri Nguyen Aquarium by boat, the Institute of Marine Research and Hon Chong Promontory. Dinner and overnight in Nha Trang.*

**Day 4** *Breakfast. Drive to Buon Me Thuot with visits to the hot springs Duc My, the Eaphe War Monument, Draystrap Waterfalls and forests in the western highlands. Hotel check-in. Dinner.*

**Day 5** *Breakfast. Drive to Nhon Hoa for a visit to an elephant village. Then on to Pleiku and a visit to a Bana ethnic minority village. Local music and dance. Dinner and overnight in Pleiku.*

**Day 6** *Breakfast. Drive to Quy Nhon. Visits to an ethnic minority convent and Quang Trung King's Museum. Hotel check-in and dinner.*

**Day 7** *Breakfast. Flight back to HCMC. Visit to Cu Chi Tunnels. Return to HCMC for hotel check-in and dinner.*

**Day 8** *Breakfast. Shopping. Departure from TSN Airport.*

**Price Schedule:**

*1 Person:US$1100* *7-10:US$580*

*2:US$900* *11-15:US$520*

## F/V-V33 HCMC/Nha Trang/ Buon Me Thuot/Pleiku/Kontum (8 days - 7 nights)

*3-6:US$690* *16 and up:US$490*

*Note: Prices include deluxe hotel accommodations (based on double occupancy), meals, transportation and transfers, domestic airfare, tour guide, boat cruising fees and visa assistance. Prices do not include international airfares, personal expenses, airport tax, insurance (an optional US$1.50 per day policy can be purchased, but it is recommended you carry your own travelers' insurance) and visa fee.*

## F/V-SS34 Ho Chi Minh City/Mekong Delta/ Cu Chi/Tay Ninh/Danang/Hue/ Ha Long/Hanoi

**Day 1** *Arrival in HCMC (Formerly Saigon). Welcome ceremony before transferring to the hotel. City tour and "get-acquainted" dinner with the guide.*

**Day 2** *City tour: Chinatown, the Lam Son lacquerware workshop, the Presidential Palace and the Saigon markets. Traditional Vietnamese dinner in a Vietnamese family's home.*

**Day 3** *Transfer to My Tho. Visit to the Vinh Trang Pagoda and farmers' villages. Boat cruise on the Mekong River. Visit to tropical fruit orchards and the Snake Farm. Return to HCMC.*

**Day 4** *Transfer to Tay Ninh for a visit to the Cao Dai's Holy See Temple. Excursion of the Tunnels of Cu Chi. Return to HCMC.*

**Day 5** *Flight to Danang. Visit to the Marble Mountains and China Beach. Transfer to Hoi An (one of the most important trading ports in Southeast Asia during the 17th Century) for a city tour. Overnight in Danang.*

**Day 6** *Transfer to Hue. Visit to the Tu Duc and Khai Dinh Shrines and the Imperial Citadel. "King's Night" and overnight.*

**Day 7** *Visit to the Royal Relics Museum and the Dong Ba Market. Afternoon sampan cruise on the Perfume River ending at the Thien Mu Pagoda.*

**Day 8** *Flight to Hanoi. City tour: One Pillar Pagoda, Ho Chi Minh Mausoleum, Temple of Literature and the Old French Quarter. Water Puppet Show or traditional opera performance in the evening.*

**Day 9** *Transfer to Ha Long. Visit to Haiphong. Overnight in Ha Long.*

**Day 10** *Boat excursion of Ha Long Bay. Lunch on the boat. Return to Hanoi.*

**Day 11** *At leisure before transferring to the airport for departure.*

**Price Schedule:**

*U.S. $ / Person (Double Occupancy)*
*Class A: $2190, Class B: $1990, Class C: $1650*

## F/V-SS35 Hanoi/Hoa Binh/Son La/ Dien Bien Phu/Hanoi

**Day 1** *Arrival in Hanoi. Welcome ceremony before transferring to the hotel. City tour and "get-acquainted" dinner with the guide.*

**Day 2** *Morning city tour: One Pillar Pagoda, Ho Chi Minh Mausoleum, Temple of Literature. Afternoon transfer to Hoa Binh. Meeting with the Muong minority in their village. Overnight in Hoa Binh.*

**Day 3** *Transfer to Son La.*

**Day 4** *Transfer to Dien Bien Phu.*

**Day 5** *Full-day visit to Dien Bien Phu and its historical sites.*

**Day 6** *Return to Son La. Encounter with the H'mong tribe.*

**Day 7** *Return to Hanoi. Shopping at the 36 Guilds. Water Puppet Show or traditional opera performance in the evening.*

**Day 8** *At leisure before transferring to the airport for departure.*

**Price Schedule:**

*U.S. $ / Person (Double Occupancy)*
*Class A: $1650, Class B: $1450, Class C: $1200*

## F/V-SS36 Ho Chi Minh City/My Tho/ Ho Chi Minh City

**Day 1** *Arrival in HCMC (formerly Saigon). Welcome ceremony before transferring to the hotel. City tour and "get-acquainted" dinner with the guide.*

**Day 2** *Visit to the Cu Chi Tunnels. Afternoon city tour: Chinatown, the Lam Son lacquerware workshop and the Presidential Palace. Traditional Vietnamese dinner in a Vietnamese family's home.*

**Day 3** *Transfer to My Tho. Visit to the Vinh Trang Pagoda and farmers' villages. Boat cruise on the Mekong River. Visit to tropical fruit orchards and the Snake Farm. Return to HCMC.*

**Day 4** *At leisure before transferring to the airport for departure.*

**Price Schedule:**

*U.S. $ / Person (Double Occupancy)*
*Class A: $800, Class B: $700, Class C: $600*

## F/V-SS37 Ho Chi Minh City/Can Tho/ Long Xuyen/Rach Gia/Ha Tien/ Ho Chi Minh City

**Day 1** *Arrival in HCMC (formerly Saigon). Welcome ceremony before transferring to the hotel. City tour and "get-acquainted" dinner with the guide.*

**Day 2** *Transfer to Can Tho. City tour: Central Market, Can Tho University.*

**Day 3** *Transfer to Long Xuyen. Visit to Chau Doc and the Holy Lady Temple.*

**Day 4** *Transfer to Rach Gia. City tour.*

**Day 5** *Transfer to Ha Tien. City tour featuring the Tam Bao Pagoda and the Thach Dong "Stone" Cavern.*

**Day 6** *Transfer back to Vinh Long. Boat cruise on the Mekong River and visit to the Bonsai Garden.*

**Day 7** *Return to HCMC. City tour: Chinatown, the Lam Son lacquerware workshop, the Presidential Palace and the Saigon markets. Traditional Vietnamese dinner in a Vietnamese family's home.*

**Day 8** *At leisure before transferring to the airport for departure.*

**Price Schedule:**

*U.S. $ / Person (Double Occupancy)*
*Class A: $1600, Class B: $1400, Class C: $1200*

## F/V-SS38 Ho Chi Minh City/Soc Trang/ Can Tho/Chau Doc/Dong Thap/ Ho Chi Minh City

**Day 1** *Arrival in HCMC (formerly Saigon). Welcome ceremony before transferring to the hotel. City tour and "get-acquainted" dinner with the guide.*

**Day 2** *Visit to the Cu Chi Tunnels. Afternoon city tour: Chinatown, the Lam Son lacquerware workshop and the Presidential Palace. Traditional Vietnamese dinner in a Vietnamese family's home.*

**Day 3** *Transfer to My Tho. Visit to the Vinh Trang Pagoda, farmers' villages, tropical fruit orchards and the Snake Farm. Transfer to Vinh Long.*

**Day 4** *Boat cruise on the Mekong River and visit to the Bonsai Garden.*

**Day 5** *Transfer to Soc Trang. Visit to the Kmer "Bat Temple" before transferring to Can Tho. City tour: Central Market, Can Tho University.*

**Day 6** *Transfer to Chau Doc. Afternoon on your own.*

**Day 7** *Visit to the local fishermen's floating houses, the Ba Chua Xu Temple and the Sam Mountain.*

## F/V-SS38 Ho Chi Minh City/Soc Trang/ Can Tho/Chau Doc/Dong Thap/ Ho Chi Minh City

**Day 8** *Leave for Dong Thap. Visit to the central market and to the Bonsai Garden.*

**Day 9** *Boat cruise on the Mekong River and visit to Tram Chim.*

**Day 10** *Return to HCMC. Visit to the local markets and shopping.*

**Day 11** *At leisure before transferring to the airport for departure.*

**Price Schedule:**

*U.S. $ / Person (Double Occupancy)*
*Class A: $2190, Class B: $1990, Class C: $1650*

## F/V-SS39 Ho Chi Minh City/Ha Long/Hanoi

**Day 1** *Arrival in HCMC (formerly Saigon). Welcome ceremony before transferring to the hotel. City tour and "get-acquainted" dinner with the guide.*

**Day 2** *Visit to the Cu Chi Tunnels. Afternoon city tour: Chinatown, the Lam Son lacquerware workshop and the Presidential Palace. Traditional Vietnamese dinner in a Vietnamese family's home.*

**Day 3** *Flight to Hanoi. City tour: One Pillar Pagoda, Ho Chi Minh Mausoleum, Temple of Literature and the Old French Quarter. Water Puppet Show or traditional opera performance in the evening.*

**Day 4** *Transfer to Ha Long. Visit to Haiphong. Overnight in Ha Long.*

**Day 5** *Boat excursion of Ha Long Bay. Lunch on the boat. Return to Hanoi.*

**Day 6** *At leisure before transferring to the airport for departure.*

**Price Schedule:**

*U.S. $ / Person (Double Occupancy)*
*Class A: $1190, Class B: $1080, Class C: $990*

## F/V-SS40 Ho Chi Minh City/Hanoi/Nam Dinh/ Hoa Lu/Ha Long/Hanoi

**Day 1** *Arrival in HCMC (formerly Saigon). Welcome ceremony before transferring to the hotel. City tour and "get-acquainted" dinner with the guide.*

**Day 2** *Visit to the Cu Chi Tunnels. Afternoon city tour: Chinatown, the Lam Son lacquerware workshop and the Presidential Palace. Traditional Vietnamese dinner in a Vietnamese family's home.*

**F/V-SS40 Ho Chi Minh City/Hanoi/Nam Dinh/Hoa Lu/Ha Long/Hanoi**

**Day 3** *Flight to Hanoi. City tour: One Pillar Pagoda, Ho Chi Minh Mausoleum, Temple of Literature and the Old French Quarter. Water Puppet Show or traditional opera performance in the evening.*

**Day 4** *Transfer to Nam Dinh. Visit to Tran King's Temple, Minh and Co Le Temple. Transfer to Hoa Lu.*

**Day 5** *Visit to Phat Diem Cathedral in Luu Phuong. Boat excursion of the underground river of Tam Coc and visit to the Bich Dong Temple.*

**Day 6** *Transfer to Ha Long. Visit to Haiphong. Overnight in Ha Long.*

**Day 7** *Boat excursion of Ha Long Bay. Lunch on the boat. Return to Hanoi.*

**Day 8** *At leisure before transferring to the airport for departure.*

**Price Schedule:**

*U.S. $ / Person (Double Occupancy)*
*Class A: $1580, Class B: $1380, Class C: $1190*

## Vietnam Veterans' Tours

These tour programs are designed to allow Vietnam War veterans to visit sites in Vietnam where their former units were based, areas of military activity and former battlefields. These tours are designed specifically for Fielding readers who are veterans of the Vietnam conflict, as well as for family members and relatives of those who returned home and those who didn't. These tours are not advertised to the general public. Many of these areas cannot be visited by means of any other program than through Fielding/VIVA USA packages. Clients will have the opportunity to meet with and reminisce with former soldiers of Viet Cong, ARVN and NVA units.

The tours below are exclusive programs for Fielding readers, both American and otherwise, who served in Vietnam and wish to return to these areas for a number of personal reasons. Fielding/Superbco veterans' tours can take you back to the "Ho Bo Secret Zone," the "Iron Triangle," the Cu Chi Tunnels or to the Tay Ninh Forest, where "Operation Junction City" took place. You can revisit the former Dong Tam base at My Tho in the Mekong Delta or Quang Tri in the former DMZ—even more remote former battlefields in the Central Highlands and farther north.

Additionally, at your request, more specialized tours can be arranged—where you can attend seminars and embark on personal fact-finding trips. You can visit with former field commanders and officers of both sides of the conflict, as well as the different Vietnamese ethnic groups that were involved in the war—all in the spirit of friendship and hospitality.

## F/V-SVET1 HCMC/Lai Khe/An Loc/Cu Chi (7 days - 6 nights)

*This tour has been arranged for veterans of the U.S. 1st Infantry Division (The Big Red One), attached elements of the U.S. 101st Airborne Division, 1st Cavalry Division and the 11th Armored Cavalry Brigade to visit locations of former military action and to visit places of interest and historical significance in HCMC.*

**Price Schedule:**

*1 Person: US$965*
*2-3:US$883*
*4-8:US$637*
*9-14:US$546*

## F/V-SVET2 HCMC/Tay Ninh/Dong Pan/Cu Chi (6 days - 5 nights)

*This tour has been arranged for veterans of the U.S. 25th Infantry Division, 3rd Brigade, the 82nd Airborne Division and their coordinated units, and the 1st Philippine Civic Action Group.*

**Price Schedule:**

*1 Person:US$998*
*2-3:US$937*
*4-8:US$660*
*9-14:US$568*

## F/V-SVET3 HCMC/Nui Dat/Long Tan/Vung Tau/ Cu Chi (7 days - 6 nights)

*This tour has been primarily designed for veterans of the Royal Australian Regiment, the New Zealand "V Force" and the Royal Thai Army Regiment.*

**Price Schedule:**

*1 Person:US$782*
*2-3:US$731*
*4-8:US$527*
*9-14:US$452*

## F/V-SVET4 HCMC/Rach Kien/Tan An/Dong Tam (My Tho)/Cu Chi (7 days - 6 nights)

*Specifically designed for veterans of the U.S. 9th Infantry Division and those who saw action in the Mekong Delta.*

**Price Schedule:**

*1 Person:US$998*
*2-3:US$925*
*4-8:US$643*
*9-14:US$550*

## F/V-SVET5 HCMC/Nha Trang/Quang Ngai/Quang Nam/Danang/Hue/Quang Tri/Cu Chi (12 days - 11 nights)

*This tour has been designed for former members of the U.S. 1st and 3rd Marine Corps Divisions and the U.S. 101st Airborne Division to revisit the northern provinces of the central part of Vietnam where a significant amount of fighting occurred.*

**Price Schedule:**

*1 Person:US$2143*
*2-3:US$1843*
*4-8:US$1235*
*9-14:US$1204*

## F/V-SVET6 HCMC/An Khe/Pleiku/Kontum/Cu Chi (10 days - 9 nights)

*This tour has been formatted for veterans of the U.S. 1st Cavalry Division, 4th Infantry Division and the 173rd Airborne Brigade to visit the principle areas of fighting in the Central Highlands area.*

**Price Schedule:**

*1 Person:US$1758*
*2-3:US$1417*
*4-8:US$935*
*9-14:US$765*

## F/V-SVET7 HCMC/Nha Trang/Quy Nhon/Quang Ngai (11 days - 10 nights)

*This tour has been specifically designed for veterans of the Republic of Korea Capital Division "Tigers," the 9th Infantry Division, Division "White Horse" and the 2nd Marine Corps Brigade "Blue Dragons" to visit central areas of Vietnam where their units were based and saw action.*

**Price Schedule:**

*1 Person:US$1282*
*2-3:US$1176*
*4-8:US$873*
*9-14:US$775*

## FV-VVET8 HCMC/Cu Chi/Nha Trang/Quy Nhon/ Quang Ngai/Quang Nam/Hue (12 days - 11 nights)

**Day 1** *Arrival at TSN Airport. Transfer to hotel. Half-day city tour with a visit to the Army Museum and other areas of interest in HCMC. Dinner.*

**Day 2** *Breakfast. Visit to the Cu Chi Tunnels. Lunch. Return to HCMC. Water puppet show and a visit to the Historical Museum. Dinner.*

**Day 3** *Breakfast. Trip to Nha Trang with a stopover at Ca Na Beach. Lunch. Arrival in Nha Trang and hotel check-in. Dinner.*

**Day 4** *Breakfast. Seabathing. City tour with stops at Po Nagar Cham Towers, Tri Nguyen Aquarium. Lunch. Then on to the Institute of Marine Research and Hon Chong Promontory. Dinner.*

**Day 5** *Breakfast. Trip to Quy Nhon. Lunch on the way. Of particular interest to Korean veterans will be Phu Cat Airport, Korean camps, Lo Boi Church, and the Korean-Cuong De High School. U.S. vets will get a chance to visit Cho Cat, Trang Pass, De Duc Airport and Hoang Dieu in Hoai Nhon Quy Nhon. Check-in at Quy Nhon hotel. Dinner.*

**Day 6** *Breakfast. Trip to Quang Ngai. Check-in at the hotel. Lunch. Visit the 1968 massacre site of Son My (My Lai). Dinner.*

**Day 7** *Breakfast. Trip to Danang. Visit to U.S. military base Chu Lai. Lunch. Arrival in Danang. Hotel check-in. Visit to Cham Museum. Dinner.*

**Day 8** *Breakfast. Visit to Hoi An and continue to Hue via the Hai Van Pass. Arrival and hotel check-in at Hue. Leisure. Dinner.*

**Day 9** *Breakfast. City tour with visits to the mausoleums of Khai Dinh, Tu Duc and Minh Mang. Boat cruise on the Huong River. Visit to Thien Mu Pagoda. Dinner.*

**Day 10** *Breakfast and transfer to airport for flight back to HCMC. Boat cruising and island hopping along the Mekong River in the Mekong Delta. Dinner.*

## FV-VVET8 HCMC/Cu Chi/Nha Trang/Quy Nhon/ Quang Ngai/Quang Nam/Hue (12 days - 11 nights)

**Day 11** *Breakfast. Shopping. Free time. Lunch. Dinner.*

**Day 12** *Breakfast. Transfer to TSN Airport for departure.*

**Price Schedule:**

| | |
|---|---|
| *1 Person:US$1600* | *7-10:US$870* |
| *2:US$1300* | *11-15:US$800* |
| *3-6:US$1000* | *16 and up:US$730* |

*Note: Prices include deluxe hotel accommodations (double occupancy), meals, entrance fees and boat cruises, transportation and transfers, tour guide, domestic airfare and visa assistance. Prices do not include international airfares, personal expenses, airport tax, insurance (an optional US$1.50 per day policy can be purchased, but it is recommended you carry your own travelers' insurance) and visa fee.*

## FV-VVET9 HCMC/Lai Khe/Binh Long/Cu Chi (7 days - 6 nights)

*This tour has been designed for veterans of the U.S. 101st Airborne Division, 11th Armored Cavalry Brigade and the 173rd Airborne Brigade to revisit former battle sites, camps, bases and areas of historical significance.*

**Day 1** *Arrival at TSN Airport. Transfer to hotel. City tour of HCMC. Dinner.*

**Day 2** *Breakfast and continued city tour with stops in Chinatown, Thien Hau Pagoda and Phu Tho Hoa War Vestige Site. Lunch. Then stops at the Army Museum of South Vietnam East Zone and Independence Palace. Dinner.*

**Day 3** *Breakfast. Visits to the Ben Suc area (the Iron Triangle) and Dau Tieng. Lunch. Visit to An Tay village and nearby areas. Dinner. Overnight in Thu Dau.*

**Day 4** *Breakfast. Visits to Lai Khe base and the former battlefield at Bau Bang. Lunch in Bau Bang restaurant. Visits to the An Loc and Soc Xiem areas with a stop at a rubber plantation. Dinner and overnight at Soc Xiem Bungalow.*

**Day 5** *Breakfast. Visits to Bong Trang and Nha Do battlefields. Lunch in Thu Dau Mot. Visit to a lacquerware and ceramics factory. Return to HCMC. Dinner and overnight in HCMC.*

**Day 6** *Breakfast. Visit to Cu Chi Tunnels. Lunch. Return to HCMC. Shopping, dinner and overnight in HCMC.*

**Day 7** *Breakfast. Shopping. Transfer to airport for departure.*

**Price Schedule:**

| | |
|---|---|
| *1 Perso:nUS$940* | *7-10:US$500* |
| *2:US$750* | *11-15:US$450* |
| *3-6:US$590* | *16 and up:US$420* |

## FV-VVET9 HCMC/Lai Khe/Binh Long/Cu Chi (7 days - 6 nights)

*Note: Prices include deluxe hotel accommodations (double occupancy), meals, entrance fees and boat cruises, transportation and transfers, tour guide, domestic airfare and visa assistance. Prices do not include international airfares, personal expenses, airport tax, insurance (an optional US$1.50 per day policy can be purchased, but it is recommended you carry your own travelers' insurance) and visa fee.*

## F/V-SSVET10 Ho Chi Minh City/Danang/Hue/Quang Tri/Khe Sanh/Ho Chi Minh City

**Day 1** *Arrival in HCMC (formerly Saigon). Welcome ceremony before transferring to the hotel. City tour and "get-acquainted" dinner with the guide.*

**Day 2** *Flight to Danang. Transfer to Quang Tri and visit to the Quang Tri Citadel. Transfer to Dong Ha and overnight.*

**Day 3** *Visit to the Ben Hai River (the former demarcation line between South and North Vietnam) and the Tunnels of Vinh Moc. Visit to the Doc Mieu Base (Mc Namara's Electronic Fence), Camp Carroll, The Rockpile, Khe Sanh Combat base, Ashau - Aluoi Valleys and Hamburger Hill. Transfer to Hue and overnight.*

**Day 4** *Visit to the Tu Duc and Khai Dinh Shrines, the Imperial Citadel and Thien Mu Pagoda. Coach transfer to Danang and overnight.*

**Day 5** *Visit to the Marble Mountains and China Beach. Transfer to Hoi An (one of the most important trading ports in Southeast Asia during the 17th Century) for a city tour. Overnight in Danang.*

**Day 6** *Flight to HCMC. Sightseeing tour: the former South Vietnam Presidential Palace, the War Museum, the former U.S. Embassy and Chinatown. Visit to the Cu Chi Tunnels. Traditional Vietnamese dinner in a Vietnamese family's home in Saigon.*

**Day 7** *At leisure before transferring to the airport for departure.*

**Price Schedule:**

*U.S. $ / Person (Double Occupancy)*
*Class A: $1550, Class B: $1380, Class C: $1190*

## Scuba Diving Tours

### F/V-SS1S — Ho Chi Minh City/Nha Trang/Dalat/Vung Tau/Ho Chi Minh City

**Day 1** *Arrival in HCMC (formerly Saigon). Welcome ceremony before transferring to the hotel. City tour and "get-acquainted" dinner with the guide.*

**Day 2** *Visit to the Cu Chi Tunnels. Afternoon city tour: Chinatown, the Lam Son lacquerware workshop and the Presidential Palace. Traditional Vietnamese dinner in a Vietnamese family's home.*

**Day 3** *Transfer to Nha Trang. Scuba-diving activities in the afternoon.*

**Day 4** *Early morning fishing expedition with local fishermen. Afternoon visit to the Tri Nguyen Aquarium and the Oceanography Institute.*

**Day 5** *Transfer to Dalat. Visit to the Datanla Waterfall and the Orchid Market.*

**Day 6** *City tour: Cam Ly Waterfall, Flower Garden, Prenn Waterfall, Whisper Lake and Love Valley.*

**Day 7** *Transfer to HCMC in the morning. Afternoon visit to the local markets.*

**Day 8** *Transfer to Vung Tau. Scuba-diving activities. Return to HCMC.*

**Day 9** *At leisure before transferring to the airport for departure.*

**Price Schedule:**

*U.S. $ / Person (Double Occupancy)*
*Class A: $1780, Class B: $1650, Class C: $1350*

## Bicycle Tours

### F/V-V1B — HCMC/Dalat/Nha Trang/Tuy Hoa/Quy Nhon/Quangai/Hue/Hanoi/Ha Long Bay (20 days - 19 nights)

*This tour covers virtually the entire country of Vietnam, and will bring you through diverse flora and fauna, climates and cultures. You should be in pretty good shape for this one. However, we provide trucks and vans for the weary. Although bicycles of touring quality can be obtained in Vietnam, they're few and far between. We suggest you pack your own set of wheels. Accommodations are of international standards.*

**Day 1** *Arrival at TSN Airport. Transfer to hotel. Tour of Chinatown with a stop at Thien Hau Pagoda. Dinner. Evening free.*

**Day 2** *Breakfast. City tour with visits to Reunification Hall, Historical Museum and the War Museum. Lunch. Then visits to the Lacquerware and Handicrafts Center and Giac Lam Pagoda. Dinner. Evening free.*

**Day 3** *Breakfast. Excursion to Cu Chi Tunnels. Lunch. Back to HCMC to prepare for the next day's departure. Dinner.*

## F/V-V1B HCMC/Dalat/Nha Trang/Tuy Hoa/Quy Nhon/Quangai/Hue/Hanoi/Ha Long Bay (20 days - 19 nights)

**Day 4** *Breakfast. Bicycle to Bao Loc toward the Central Highlands. Lunch on the way. Check-in at Bao Loc hotel. Dinner.*

**Day 5** *Breakfast. Bicycle to Dalat. Check-in at the hotel. Lunch. City tour with stops at Xuan Huong Lake, Tuyen Lam Lake and the Valley of Love. Dinner.*

**Day 6** *Breakfast. Cycle via magnificent mountain scenery to Phan Rang. Lunch and a stop at the Cham Towers. Arrival in Phan Rang. Hotel check-in. Dinner.*

**Day 7** *Breakfast. Cycle up the coast to the beautiful beach resort of Nha Trang. Lunch on the way. Arrival and hotel check-in. Rest of the day free. Dinner.*

**Day 8** *Breakfast and city tour of Nha Trang, with stops at the Po Nagar Cham Towers and Tri Nguyen Aquarium. Lunch. Then stops at the Marine Institute and the Hon Chong Promontory. Dinner.*

**Day 9** *Breakfast. Cycle via a spectacular pass to Tuy Hoa. Lunch at Dai Lanh Beach. Arrival and check-in at the hotel. Dinner.*

**Day 10** *Breakfast. Cycle to Quy Nhon via the Cu Mong Pass. Lunch on the way. Arrival and hotel check-in. Dinner.*

**Day 11** *Breakfast. Cycle to Sahuynh. Lunch on the way. Arrival. Sunbathing and sea swimming. Dinner.*

**Day 12** *Breakfast. Cycle to Quan Gai. Arrival and hotel check-in. Visits to a famous war relic in Son My village and My Khe Beach. Dinner.*

**Day 13** *Breakfast. Cycle to Danang. Lunch on the way. Stop to visit the historical town of Hoi An. Arrival in Danang and hotel check-in. Dinner.*

**Day 14** *Breakfast and a visit to the Cham Museum. Cycle to Hue via the spectacular Hai Van Pass. Lunch on the way. Hotel check-in and dinner.*

**Day 15** *Breakfast and city tour of Hue, with stops at the mausoleums of Minh Mang, Tu Duc and Khai Dinh. Lunch. A boat cruise on the Perfume River to Thien Mu Pagoda. Dinner.*

**Day 16** *Breakfast. Trip by train to Hanoi. Lunch, dinner and overnight on the train.*

**Day 17** *Morning arrival in Hanoi. Transfer to hotel. Breakfast and a city tour with stops at the Temple of Literature, Ho Chi Minh's Mausoleum, the 1-Pillar Pagoda, West Lake and Ho Guam Lake. Dinner.*

**Day 18** *Breakfast. Trip by bus to Ha Long Bay. Visit to Haiphong. Lunch. Arrival in Ha Long. Hotel check-in. Leisure. Dinner.*

**Day 19** *Breakfast and a boat cruise on Ha Long Bay with a seafood lunch. Afternoon departure to Hanoi. Hotel check-in and dinner.*

**Day 20** *Breakfast. Shopping. Transfer to airport for departure.*

## F/V-V1B HCMC/Dalat/Nha Trang/Tuy Hoa/Quy Nhon/Quangai/Hue/Hanoi/Ha Long Bay (20 days - 19 nights)

**Price Schedule:**

*5-8 PersonsUS$1400* *16 and upUS$1150*

*9-15US$1250*

*Note: Customers can also choose an opposite itinerary from north to south, with departure from HCMC. Prices include international standard hotel accommodations, meals, entrance fees and boat cruises, transportation and transfers, train ticket, foreign language speaking guides, visa assistance and sightseeing tours. Prices do not include international airfares, personal expenses, airport tax and insurance. However, customers may purchase insurance before the start of the trip through Bao Viet at a cost of US$1.50 per day. However, Fielding strongly recommends you purchase your own travelers' insurance before embarking on a tour in Vietnam.*

## F/V-SS2B Ho Chi Minh City/Dalat/Phan Rang/ Nha Trang/Tuy Hoa/Qui Nhon/Sa Huynh/ Quang Ngai/Danang/Hue/Hanoi

**Day 1** *Arrival in HCMC (formerly Saigon). Welcome ceremony before transferring to the hotel. City tour and "get-acquainted" dinner with the guide.*

**Day 2** *Visit to the Cu Chi Tunnels. Afternoon city tour: Chinatown, the Lam Son lacquerware workshop and the Presidential Palace. Traditional Vietnamese dinner in a Vietnamese family's home.*

**Day 3** *Transfer to Dalat. Visit to the Prenn waterfall. Check in the hotel.*

**Day 4** *Cycle to the Lat village and encounter with hilltribes. Afternoon return to Dalat for city tour: Flower Garden, Whisper Lake, Cam Ly Waterfall.*

**Day 5** *Cycle to Phan Rang. Picnic en route. Mid-afternoon arrival. Transfer to the hotel.*

**Day 6** *Cycle to Nha Trang. Picnic en route. Mid-afternoon arrival. Transfer to the hotel.*

**Day 7** *Cycle to Tuy Hoa. Picnic en route. Mid-afternoon arrival. Transfer to the hotel.*

**Day 8** *Cycle to Qui Nhon. Picnic en route. Mid-afternoon arrival. Transfer to the hotel.*

**Day 9** *Cycle to Sa Huynh. Picnic en route. Mid-afternoon arrival. Transfer to the hotel.*

**Day 10** *Cycle to Quang Ngai. Picnic en route. Mid-afternoon arrival. Transfer to the hotel.*

**Day 11** *Cycle to Danang. Picnic en route. Mid-afternoon arrival. Transfer to the hotel.*

**Day 12** *Early morning arrival in Danang. Visit to the Marble Mountains and China Beach. Transfer to Hoi An (one of the most important trading ports in Southeast Asia during the 17th Century) for a city tour. Overnight in Danang.*

**Day 13** *Cycle to Hue. Picnic en route. Mid-afternoon arrival. Transfer to the hotel.*

## F/V-SS2B Ho Chi Minh City/Dalat/Phan Rang/ Nha Trang/Tuy Hoa/Qui Nhon/Sa Huynh/ Quang Ngai/Danang/Hue/Hanoi

**Day 14** *Visit to the Tu Duc and Khai Dinh Shrines and the Imperial Citadel. Afternoon sampan cruise on the Perfume River ending at the Thien Mu Pagoda. "King's Night" and overnight.*

**Day 15** *Morning at leisure. Afternoon train transfer to Hanoi. Dinner and overnight on the train.*

**Day 16** *Early morning arrival in Hanoi. City tour: One Pillar Pagoda, Ho Chi Minh Mausoleum, Temple of Literature and the Old French Quarter. Water Puppet Show or traditional opera performance in the evening.*

**Day 17** *At leisure before transferring to the airport for departure.*

**Price Schedule:**

*U.S. $ / Person (Double Occupancy)*
*Class A: $3400, Class B: $3050, Class C: $2550*

# Trekking Tours

## F/V-SS1T Hanoi/Hoa Binh/Hanoi

**Day 1** *Arrival in Hanoi. Welcome ceremony before transferring to the hotel. City tour and "get-acquainted" dinner with the guide.*

**Day 2** *Transfer to Hoa Binh. Overnight.*

**Day 3** *Transfer to Pa Co. Trekking to Hang Kia. Overnight in a H'Mong village.*

**Day 4** *Trekking to Bao La. Overnight in a Thai village. (15 kms)*

**Day 5** *Trekking to Ban Lac. Overnight in a Thai village. (15 kms)*

**Day 6** *Trekking to Bac Son. Overnight in a Thai village. (15 kms)*

**Day 7** *Trekking to Lung Van. Overnight in a Muong village. (15 kms)*

**Day 8** *Trekking to Cho Lo. Transfer back to Hoa Binh. Overnight in Hoa Binh.*

**Day 9** *Transfer to Hanoi. City tour: One Pillar Pagoda, Ho Chi Minh Mausoleum, Temple of Literature. Water Puppet Show or traditional opera performance in the evening.*

**Day 10** *At leisure before transferring to the airport for departure.*

**Price Schedule:**

*U.S. $ / Person (Double Occupancy)*
*Class A: $2050, Class B: $1850, Class C: $1500*

## Photo Safaris

**F/V-V1P** **Hanoi/Tam Dao/Cuc Phuong/HCMC/ Cat Tien/Bao Loc/Dalat/Tam Nong (18 days - 17 nights)**

**Day 1** *Arrival at Noi Bai Airport. Pick-up and drive to Tam Dao Hill Station. Dinner and overnight at Tam Dao Hotel.*

**Day 2** *Breakfast. Full day of bird and wildlife watching in Tam Dao Forest. Dinner. Overnight at Tam Dao Hotel.*

**Day 3** *A full repeat of the previous day's activities.*

**Day 4** *Breakfast. Drive to Cuc Phuong National Jungle Park. Lunch. Extensive excursion into the jungle. Dinner and overnight in Cuc Phuong or nearest hotel.*

**Day 5** *Breakfast. Full day of nature watching in Cuc Phuong National Park. Lunch. Dinner and overnight in the park or at the nearest hotel.*

**Day 6** *Breakfast. Bird and wildlife watching in the morning. Back to Hanoi. Lunch on the way. Hotel check-in and city tour. Dinner.*

**Day 7** *Transfer and flight to HCMC. Drive to Nam Cat Tien National Jungle Park. Excursions into the jungle. Dinner and overnight at National Park Headquarters.*

**Day 8** *Breakfast. Full day of nature watching in Nam Cat Tien National Park. Dinner and overnight at the park's headquarters.*

**Day 9** *Breakfast. Nature watching in the morning. Drive to Bao Loc. Visit to Dam Ri Waterfalls. Hotel check-in. Dinner.*

**Day 10** *Breakfast. Visit to Deo Nui San in Di Linh. Lunch. Drive to Dalat. Dinner and overnight in Dalat.*

**Day 11** *Breakfast. Full day of bird and nature watching on Mt. Liang Biang. Dinner and overnight.*

**Day 12** *Breakfast. Boat cruise to Tuyen Lake for a full day of bird and nature watching in the forest near the lake. Dinner and overnight in Dalat hotel.*

**Day 13** *Same itinerary as Day ll.*

**Day 14** *Breakfast. Drive to HCMC. Hotel check-in. Half-day city tour with stops at the Historical Museum, a water puppet show and Ben Thanh Market. Dinner and overnight.*

**Day 15** *Breakfast. Drive to Tam Nong National Park. Lunch. Then a boat excursion through the jungle. Dinner and overnight in Tam Nong National Park Headquarters.*

**Day 16** *Breakfast. Full day of bird and nature watching in Tam Nong National Park. Dinner and overnight at the park's headquarters.*

**Day 17** *Breakfast. Bird and nature watching in the morning. Lunch. Return to HCMC. Hotel check-in and dinner.*

## F/V-V1P Hanoi/Tam Dao/Cuc Phuong/HCMC/Cat Tien/Bao Loc/Dalat/Tam Nong (18 days - 17 nights)

**Day 18** *Breakfast. Birdwatching in the HCMC area. Transfer to airport for departure.*

**Price Schedule:**

| | |
|---|---|
| *1 Person:US$2500* | *7-10:US$1200* |
| *2:US$1900* | *11-15:US$1050* |
| *3-6:US$1500* | *16 and up:US$1000* |

*Note: Prices include deluxe hotel accommodations (based on double occupancy), meals, transportation and transfers, domestic airfare, tour guide, boat cruising fees and visa assistance. Prices do not include international airfares, personal expenses, airport tax, insurance (an optional US$1.50 per day policy can be purchased, but it is recommended you carry your own travelers' insurance) and visa fee.*

# Hilltribe Tours

## F/V-SS1H Ho Chi Minh City/Dac Lac/Buon Me Thuot/Ho Chi Minh City

**Day 1** *Arrival in HCMC (formerly Saigon). Welcome ceremony before transferring to the hotel. City tour and "get-acquainted" dinner with the guide.*

**Day 2** *Flight to Buon Me Thuot. City tour. Overnight.*

**Day 3** *Visit to the Krong Bong District, the D'Sap and Virgin Gia Long waterfalls. Hiking expedition to the Chu Kty village. Evening tribal party with the Ede tribe.*

**Day 4** *Excursion of the Lak Lake on piraguas and elephant-back ride to M'nong villages. Evening tribal party with the locals (music, dance, food). Overnight in the tribal village.*

**Day 5** *Boat excursion on Krong Ana River and Eao Don Lake.*

**Day 6** *Visit to the Don Village and the "Elephant Hunters" cemetery.*

**Day 7** *Morning at leisure in Buon Me Thuot before transferring to the airport for departure to HCMC.*

**Day 8** *Visit to the Cu Chi Tunnels. Afternoon city tour: Chinatown, the Lam Son lacquerware workshop and the Presidential Palace. Traditional Vietnamese dinner in a Vietnamese family's home.*

**Day 9** *At leisure before transferring to the airport for departure.*

**Price Schedule:**

*U.S. $ / Person (Double Occupancy)*
*Class A: $1800, Class B: $1600, Class C: $1400*

## Business Tours

### F/V-SS1BT Ho Chi Minh City/Danang/Hue/Hanoi

**Day 1** *Arrival in HCMC (formerly Saigon). Welcome ceremony before transferring to the hotel. City tour and "get-acquainted" dinner with the guide.*

**Day 2** *Visit to manufacturing factories and meeting with the managing staff: Thanh Cong Textile Factory, Thang Loi Textile Factory and Legamex.*

**Day 3** *Morning meeting with the State Committee for Cooperation and Investment (SCCI) and the Department of Foreign Economic Relations. Afternoon visit to the main locations of investment: Linh Trung and Tan Thuan Export Processing Zone.*

**Day 4** *Morning flight to Danang. Meeting with The People's Committee of the Quang Nam Danang Province. Afternoon visit to some potential development sites: graphite mining, glass processing, wood processing, China Beach resorts.*

**Day 5** *Transfer to Hue. Visit to local businesses and sightseeing tour.*

**Day 6** *Flight to Hanoi. Meeting with the State Committee for Cooperation and Investment, the Ministries of Finance, Power, Communication & Transportation.*

**Day 7** *Meeting with the Ministries of Construction, Commerce & Tourism, Culture & Information, Foreign Trade and Commerce. Visit to potential investment sites.*

**Day 8** *At leisure before transferring to the airport for departure.*

**Price Schedule:**

*U.S. $ / Person (Double Occupancy)*
*Class A: $1980, Class B: $1700, Class C: $1580*

## Train Tours

### F/VSS1TT Ho Chi Minh City/Nha Trang/Danang/Hue/Hanoi

**Day 1** *Arrival in HCMC (formerly Saigon). Welcome ceremony before transferring to the hotel. City tour and "get-acquainted" dinner with the guide.*

**Day 2** *City tour: Chinatown, the Lam Son lacquerware workshop, the Presidential Palace and the Saigon markets. Traditional Vietnamese dinner in a Vietnamese family's home.*

**Day 3** *Transfer to Tay Ninh for a visit to the Cao Dai's Holy See Temple. Excursion of the Tunnels of Cu Chi. Return to HCMC and overnight.*

**Day 4** *Early morning departure to Nha Trang on the "Reunification Train." Lunch on the train and late afternoon arrival in Nha Trang.*

**Day 5** *Morning boat excursions to islands and visit to the Tri Nguyen Aquarium. Afternoon visit to the Po Nagar Cham site and the Linh Son Pagoda. Late afternoon train departure to Danang. Dinner and overnight on the train.*

## F/VSS1TT Ho Chi Minh City/Nha Trang/ Danang/Hue/Hanoi

**Day 6** *Early morning arrival in Danang. Visit to the Marble Mountains and China Beach. Transfer to Hoi An (one of the most important trading ports in Southeast Asia during the 17th Century) for a city tour. Overnight in Danang.*

**Day 7** *Early morning train departure to Hue. Lunch on the train. Afternoon visit to the Tu Duc and Khai Dinh Shrines and the Imperial Citadel. "King's Night" and overnight.*

**Day 8** *Visit to the Royal Relics Museum and the Dong Ba Market. Afternoon sampan cruise on the Perfume River ending at the Thien Mu Pagoda.*

**Day 9** *Morning at leisure. Train departure to Hanoi. Dinner and overnight on the train.*

**Day 10** *Early morning arrival in Hanoi. City tour: One Pillar Pagoda, Ho Chi Minh Mausoleum, Temple of Literature and the Old French Quarter. Water Puppet Show or traditional opera performance in the evening.*

**Day 11** *Excursion to the Chua Huong Pagoda. Boat cruise. Return to Hanoi and overnight.*

**Day 12** *At leisure before transferring to the airport for departure.*

**Price Schedule:**

*U.S. $ / Person (Double Occupancy)*
*Class A: $2390, Class B: $2150, Class C: $1800*

# MAJOR ROAD ROUTES OF SOUTHERN VIETNAM

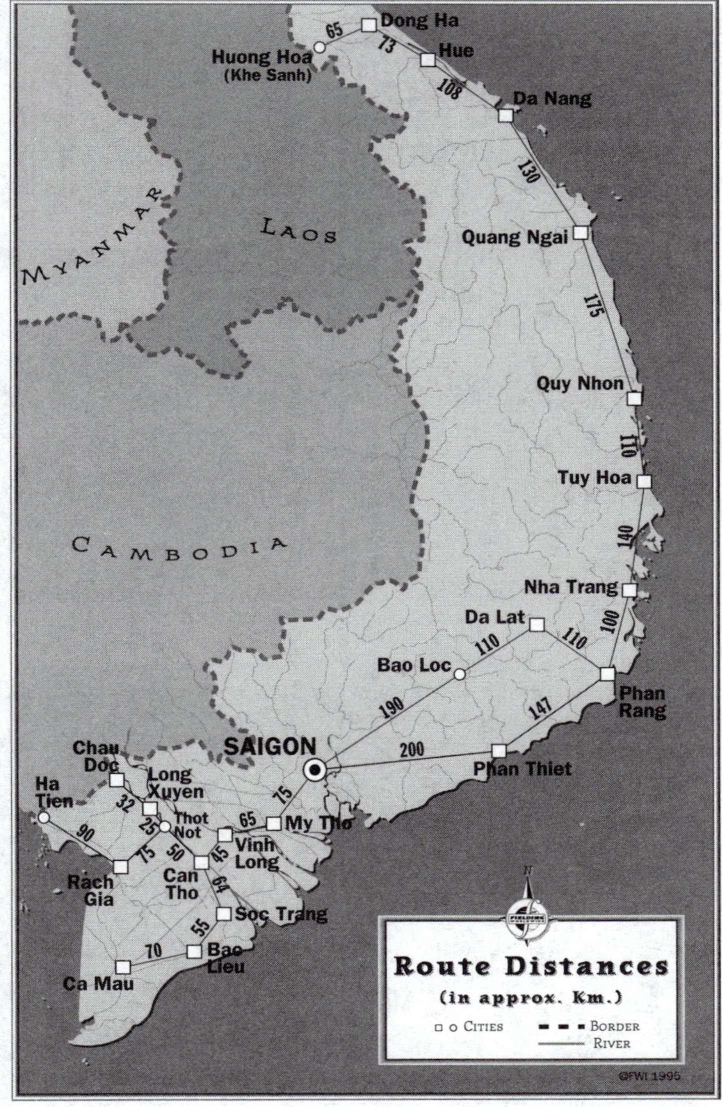

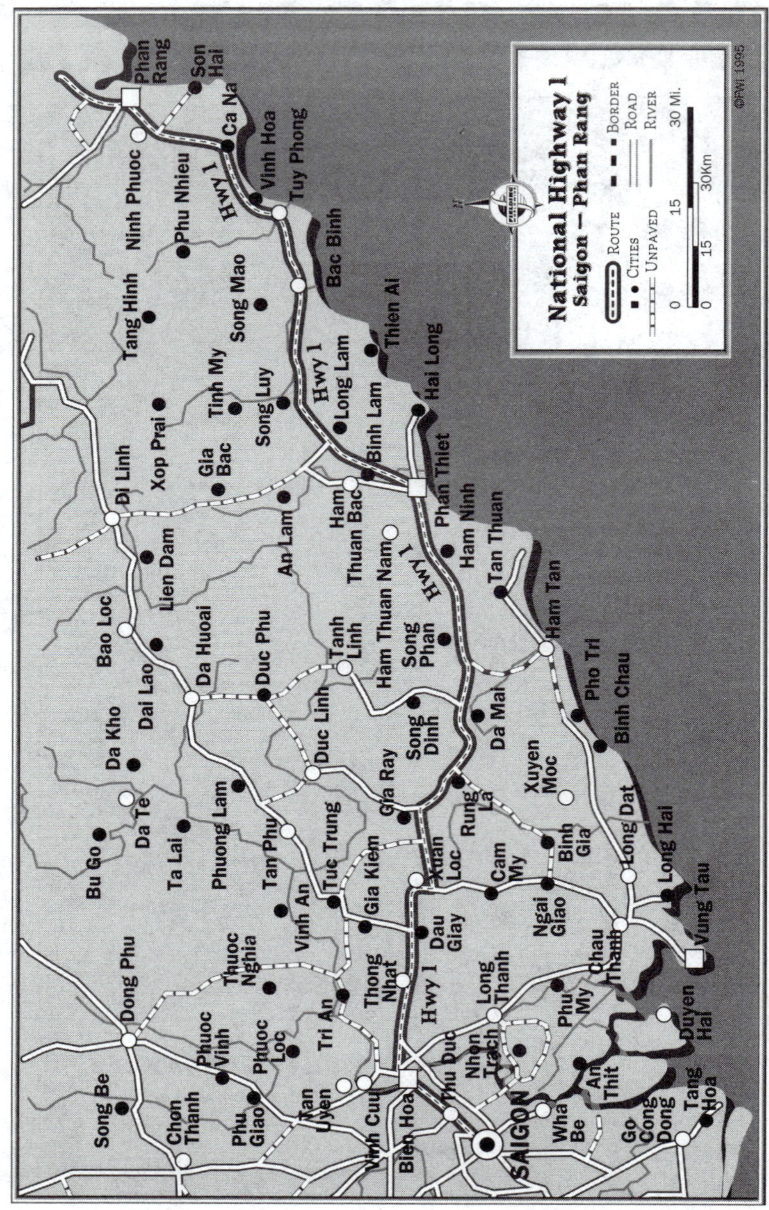
National Highway 1
Saigon — Phan Rang
Route
Cities
Unpaved
Border
Road
River
0 15 30 Mi.
0 15 30Km
©FWI 1995
Hwy 1
Phan Rang
Son Hai
Ca Na
Vinh Hoa
Tuy Phong
Ninh Phuoc
Phu Nhieu
Bac Binh
Tang Hinh
Song Mao
Thien Ai
Tinh My
Song Luy
Long Lam
Hai Long
Xop Prai
Gia Bac
Binh Lam
Di Linh
Phan Thiet
Ham Thuan Bac
An Lam
Ham Ninh
Tan Thuan
Lien Dam
Ham Thuan Nam
Bao Loc
Da Huoai
Duc Phu
Tanh Linh
Song Phan
Ham Tan
Pho Tri
Dai Lao
Da Kho
Duc Linh
Song Dinh
Da Mai
Binh Chau
Da Te
Phuong Lam
Gia Ray
Xuyen Moc
Long Dat
Bu Go
Ta Lai
Tan Phu
Tuc Trung
Rung La
Binh Gia
Long Hai
Gia Kiem
Xuan Loc
Cam My
Vinh An
Ngai Giao
Vung Tau
Dong Phu
Thuoc Nghia
Dau Giay
Thong Nhat
Chau Thanh
Long Thanh
Phu My
Tri An
Phuoc Vinh
Phuoc Loc
Duyen Hai
Song Be
Nhon Trach
Phu Duc
An Thit
Chon Thanh
Phu Giao
Tan Uyen
Vinh Cuu
Bien Hoa
SAIGON
Nha Be
Go Cong Dong
Tang Hoa

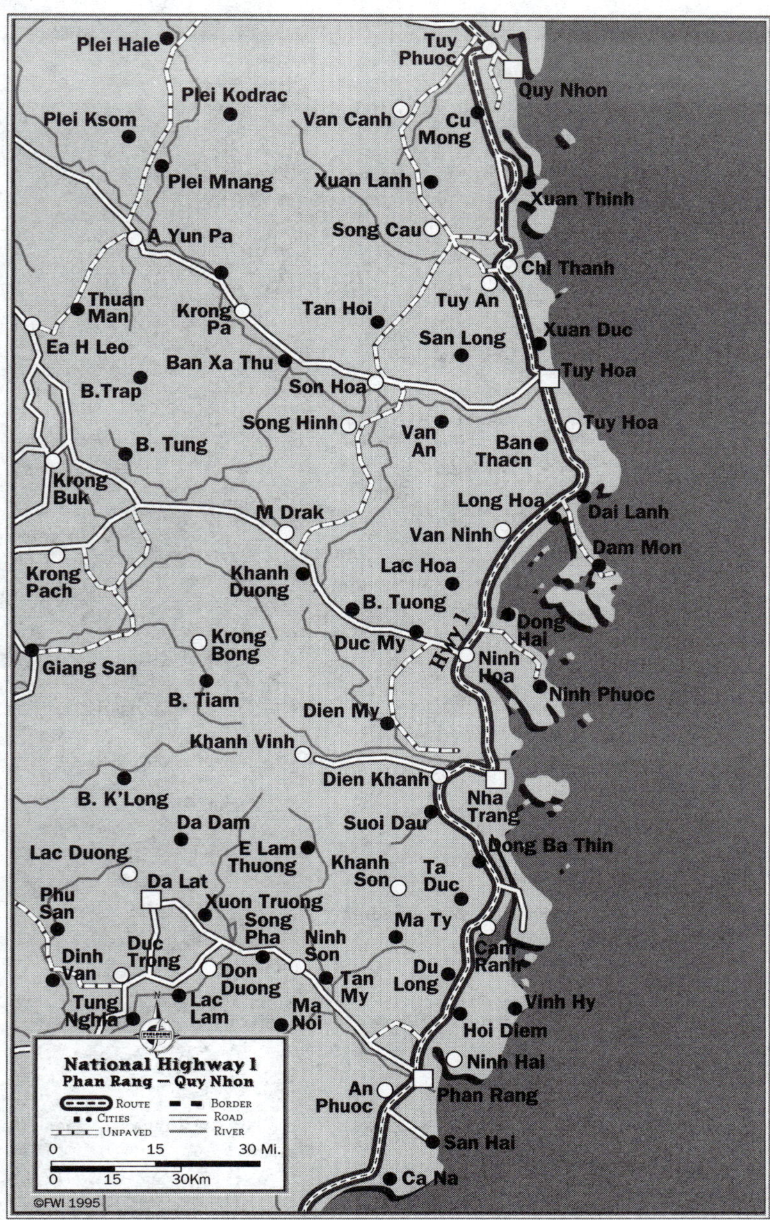
Plei Hale
Tuy Phuoc
Quy Nhon
Plei Kodrac
Plei Ksom
Van Canh
Cu Mong
Plei Mnang
Xuan Lanh
Xuan Thinh
A Yun Pa
Song Cau
Chi Thanh
Thuan Man
Krong Pa
Tan Hoi
Tuy An
Ea H Leo
San Long
Xuan Duc
Ban Xa Thu
B.Trap
Son Hoa
Tuy Hoa
Song Hinh
Van An
Tuy Hoa
B. Tung
Ban Thacn
Krong Buk
Long Hoa
Dai Lanh
M Drak
Van Ninh
Dam Mon
Krong Pach
Khanh Duong
Lac Hoa
B. Tuong
Dong Hai
Hwy 1
Krong Bong
Duc My
Ninh Hoa
Giang San
B. Tiam
Ninh Phuoc
Dien My
Khanh Vinh
Dien Khanh
Nha Trang
B. K'Long
Da Dam
Suoi Dau
Dong Ba Thin
Lac Duong
E Lam Thuong
Khanh Son
Ta Duc
Da Lat
Phu San
Xuon Truong
Song Pha
Ma Ty
Ninh Son
Cam Ranh
Dinh Van
Duc Trong
Don Duong
Tan My
Du Long
Vinh Hy
Tung Nghia
Lac Lam
Ma Noi
Hoi Diem
National Highway 1
Phan Rang — Quy Nhon
Ninh Hai
An Phuoc
Phan Rang
Route
Border
Cities
Road
Unpaved
River
0 15 30 Mi.
0 15 30Km
San Hai
Ca Na
©FWI 1995

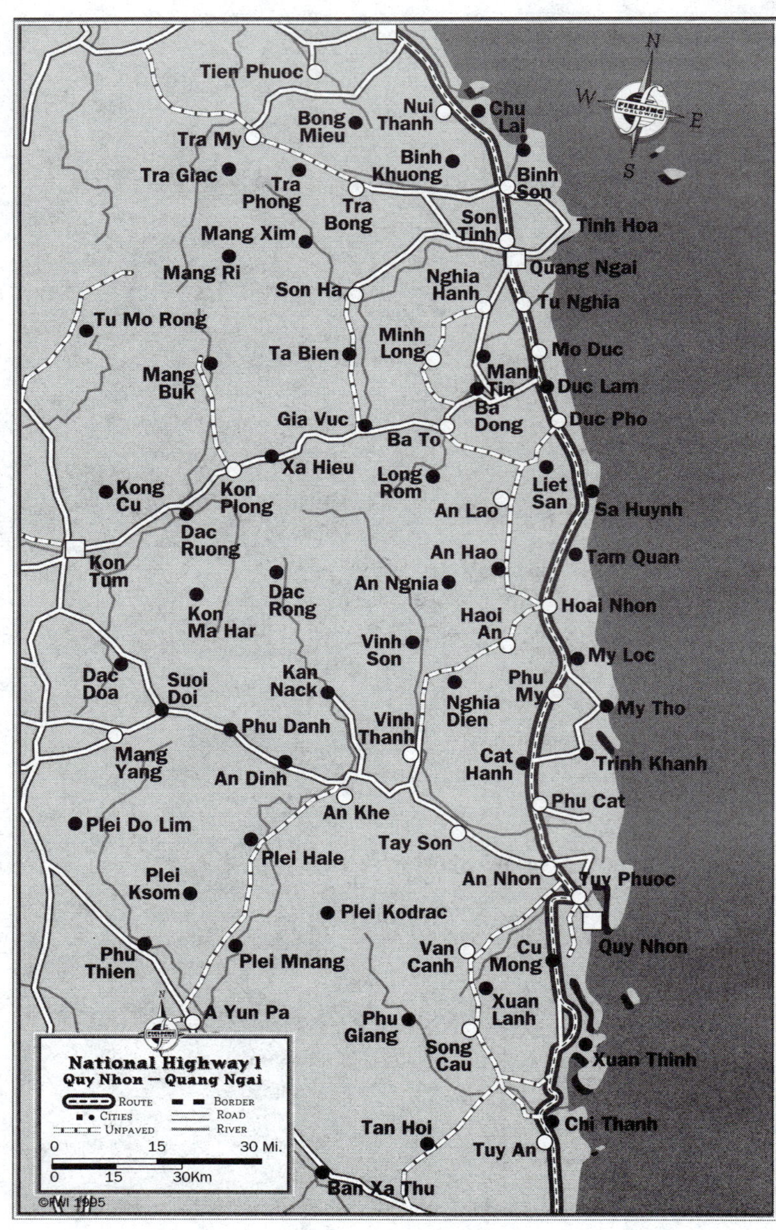
Tien Phuoc
Nui Thanh
Chu Lai
Bong Mieu
Tra My
Binh Khuong
Tra Giac
Tra Phong
Tra Bong
Binh Son
Son Tinh
Tinh Hoa
Mang Xim
Mang Ri
Quang Ngai
Son Ha
Nghia Hanh
Tu Nghia
Tu Mo Rong
Minh Long
Mo Duc
Ta Bien
Mang Buk
Manh Tin
Duc Lam
Ba Dong
Gia Vuc
Duc Pho
Ba To
Xa Hieu
Long Rom
Liet San
Kong Cu
Kon Plong
An Lao
Sa Huynh
Dac Ruong
Kon Tum
An Hao
Tam Quan
An Ngnia
Dac Rong
Kon Ma Har
Haoi An
Hoai Nhon
Vinh Son
My Loc
Dac Doa
Suoi Doi
Kan Nack
Phu My
Nghia Dien
My Tho
Phu Danh
Vinh Thanh
Mang Yang
Cat Hanh
Trinh Khanh
An Dinh
An Khe
Phu Cat
Plei Do Lim
Tay Son
Plei Hale
An Nhon
Tuy Phuoc
Plei Ksom
Plei Kodrac
Quy Nhon
Phu Thien
Van Canh
Cu Mong
Plei Mnang
Xuan Lanh
A Yun Pa
Phu Giang
Song Cau
Xuan Thinh
Tan Hoi
Chi Thanh
Tuy An
Ban Xa Thu
N
W
E
S
National Highway I
Quy Nhon — Quang Ngai
Route
Border
Cities
Road
Unpaved
River
0 15 30 Mi.
0 15 30Km
©FWI 1995

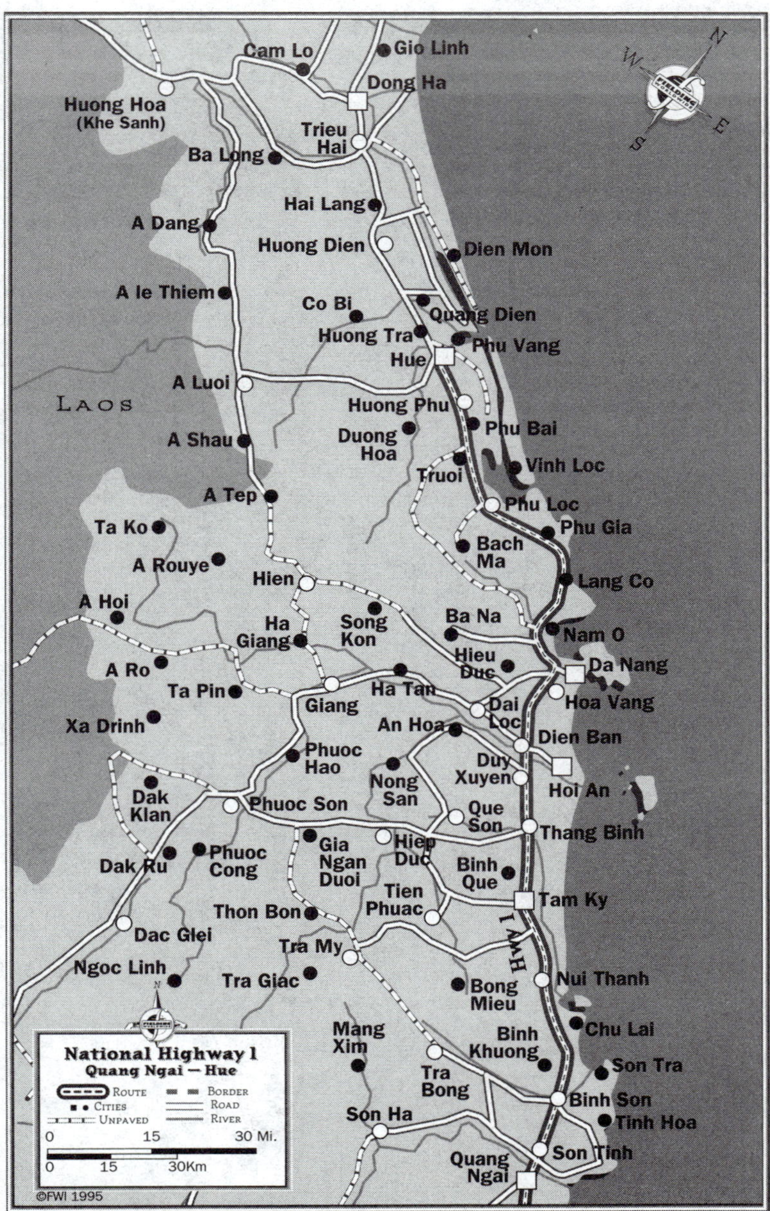
Cam Lo
Gio Linh
Dong Ha
Huong Hoa
(Khe Sanh)
Trieu
Hai
Ba Long
Hai Lang
A Dang
Huong Dien
Dien Mon
A le Thiem
Co Bi
Quang Dien
Huong Tra
Phu Vang
Hue
A Luoi
Laos
Huong Phu
Phu Bai
A Shau
Duong
Hoa
Vinh Loc
Truoi
A Tep
Phu Loc
Phu Gia
Ta Ko
Bach
Ma
A Rouye
Lang Co
Hien
A Hoi
Ba Na
Ha
Giang
Song
Kon
Nam O
Hieu
Duc
Da Nang
A Ro
Ta Pin
Giang
Ha Tan
Hoa Vang
Dai
Loc
Xa Drinh
An Hoa
Dien Ban
Phuoc
Hao
Duy
Xuyen
Nong
San
Hoi An
Dak
Klan
Phuoc Son
Que
Son
Thang Binh
Gia
Ngan
Duoi
Hiep
Duc
Dak Ru
Phuoc
Cong
Binh
Que
Tien
Phuac
Tam Ky
Thon Bon
HWY 1
Dac Glei
Tra My
Nui Thanh
Ngoc Linh
Tra Giac
Bong
Mieu
Chu Lai
Mang
Xim
Binh
Khuong
Son Tra
Tra
Bong
Binh Son
Son Ha
Tinh Hoa
Son Tinh
Quang
Ngai
N
E
S
W
National Highway 1
Quang Ngai — Hue
Route
Border
Cities
Road
Unpaved
River
0 15 30 Mi.
0 15 30Km
©FWI 1995

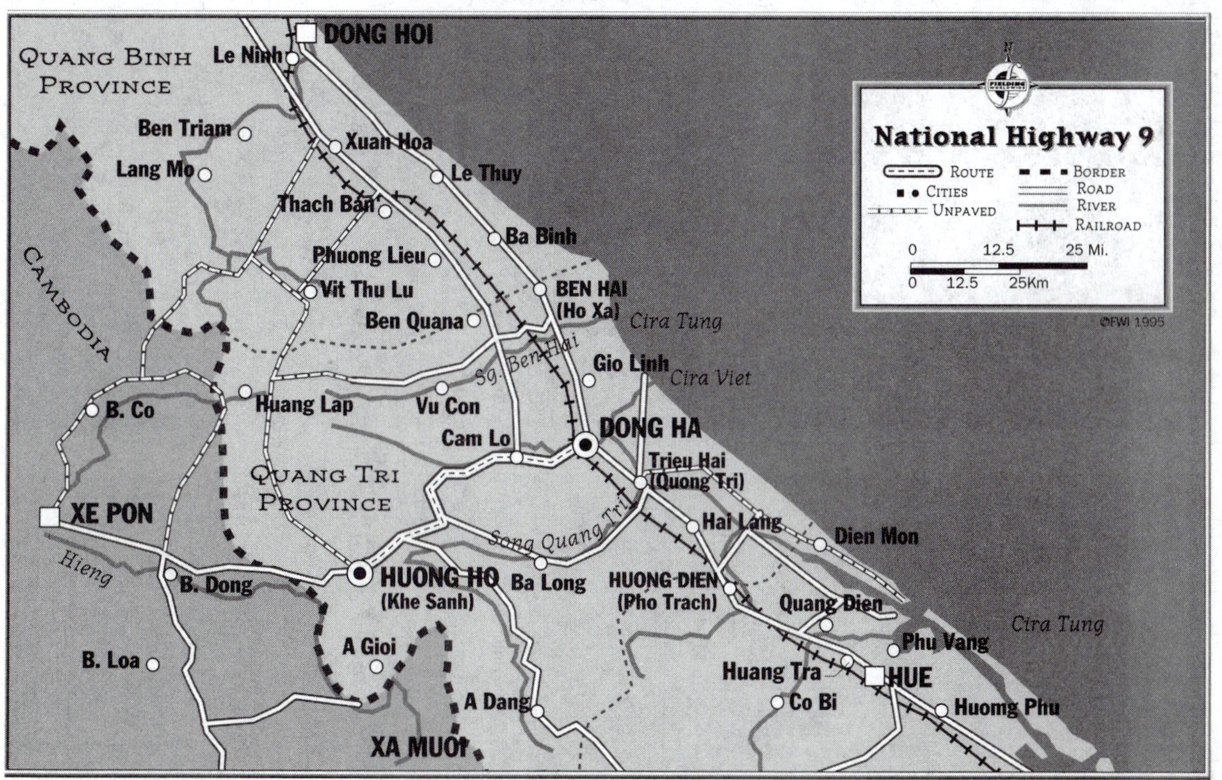
National Highway 9
Route
Cities
Unpaved
Border
Road
River
Railroad
0 12.5 25 Mi.
0 12.5 25Km
©FWI 1995
DONG HOI
Quang Binh Province
Le Ninh
Ben Triam
Xuan Hoa
Lang Mo
Le Thuy
Thach Ban
Ba Binh
Phuong Lieu
Cambodia
Vit Thu Lu
BEN HAI (Ho Xa)
Ben Quana
Cira Tung
Sg. Ben Hai
Gio Linh
Cira Viet
B. Co
Huang Lap
Vu Con
DONG HA
Cam Lo
Trieu Hai (Quong Tri)
Quang Tri Province
XE PON
Hai Lang
Dien Mon
Song Quang Tri
Hieng
B. Dong
HUONG HO (Khe Sanh)
Ba Long
HUONG DIEN (Pho Trach)
Quang Dien
Cira Tung
A Gioi
Phu Vang
B. Loa
Huang Tra
HUE
A Dang
Co Bi
Huomg Phu
XA MUOI

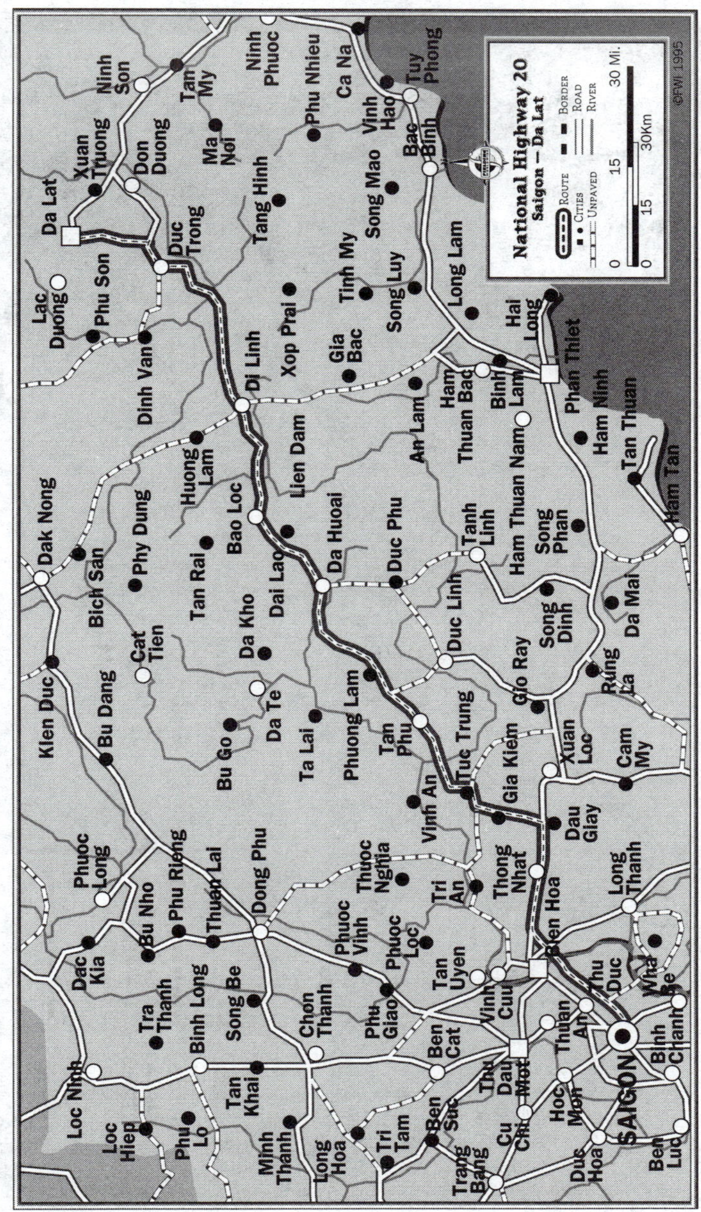
National Highway 20
Saigon — Da Lat
Route
Cities
Unpaved
Border
Road
River
0 15 30 Mi.
0 15 30Km
©FWI 1995
Da Lat
Xuan Truong
Ninh Son
Tam My
Ninh Phuoc
Phu Nhieu
Ca Na
Tuy Phong
Vinh Hao
Bac Binh
Ma Noi
Don Duong
Duc Trong
Tang Hinh
Song Mao
Lac Duong
Phu Son
Dinh Van
Di Linh
Xop Prai
Gia Bac
Tinh My
Song Luy
Long Lam
Hai Long
Phan Thiet
Ham Thuan Bac
Binh Lam
An Lam
Lien Dam
Huong Lam
Dak Nong
Phy Dung
Bao Loc
Ham Thuan Nam
Ham Ninh
Tan Thuan
Ham Tan
Bich San
Tan Rai
Dai Lao
Da Huoai
Duc Phu
Tanh Linh
Song Phan
Da Mai
Song Dinh
Duc Linh
Da Kho
Cat Tien
Kien Duc
Bu Dang
Da Te
Bu Go
Ta Lai
Phuong Lam
Tan Phu
Tuc Trung
Gia Kiem
Gio Ray
Rung La
Xuan Loc
Cam My
Dau Giay
Vinh An
Phuoc Long
Phu Rieng
Thuan Lai
Dong Phu
Bu Nho
Thuoc Nghia
Tri An
Thong Nhat
Long Thanh
Bien Hoa
Phuoc Vinh
Phuoc Loc
Tan Uyen
Dac Kia
Tra Thanh
Binh Long
Song Be
Chon Thanh
Phu Giao
Ben Cat
Vinh Cuu
Thu Duc
Nha Be
Thuan An
SAIGON
Binh Chanh
Loc Ninh
Tan Khai
Thu Dau Mot
Hoc Mon
Loc Hiep
Phu Lo
Minh Thanh
Long Hoa
Tri Tam
Ben Suc
Cu Chi
Trang Bang
Duc Hoa
Ben Luc

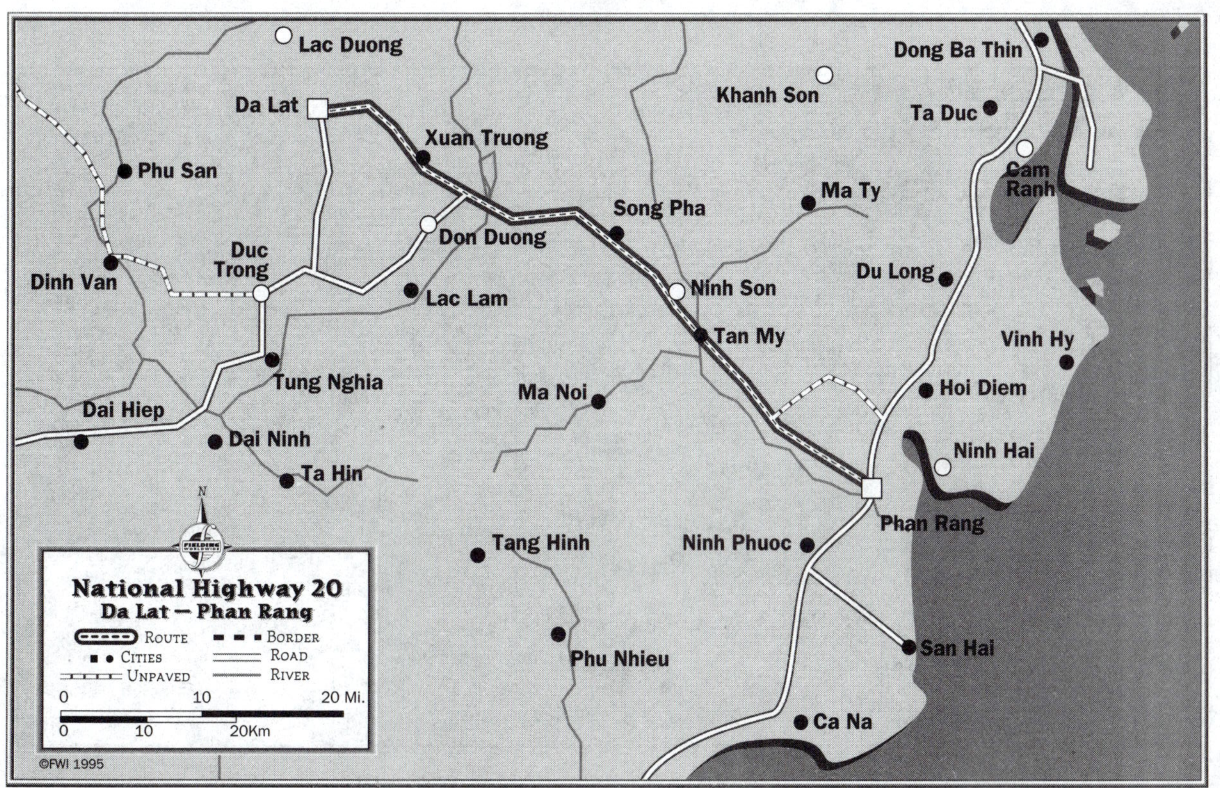
Lac Duong
Da Lat
Xuan Truong
Phu San
Song Pha
Don Duong
Duc Trong
Dinh Van
Lac Lam
Ninh Son
Tan My
Tung Nghia
Ma Noi
Dai Hiep
Dai Ninh
Ta Hin
Khanh Son
Dong Ba Thin
Ta Duc
Cam Ranh
Ma Ty
Du Long
Vinh Hy
Hoi Diem
Ninh Hai
Phan Rang
Tang Hinh
Ninh Phuoc
San Hai
Phu Nhieu
Ca Na
National Highway 20
Da Lat – Phan Rang
Route
Border
Cities
Road
Unpaved
River
0
10
20 Mi.
0
10
20Km
©FWI 1995

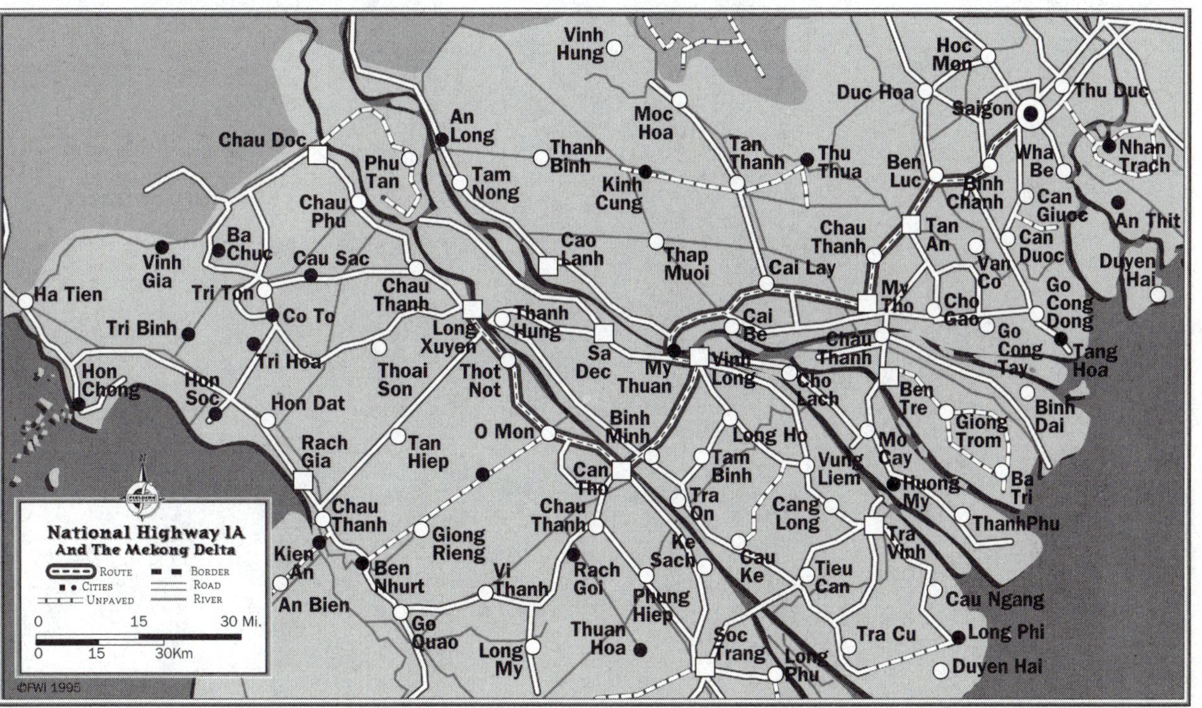
Vinh Hung
Hoc Mon
Duc Hoa
Thu Duc
Saigon
Moc Hoa
An Long
Chau Doc
Thanh Binh
Tan Thanh
Thu Thua
Ben Luc
Wha Be
Nhan Trach
Phu Tan
Tam Nong
Kinh Cung
Binh Chanh
Can Giuoc
An Thit
Chau Phu
Chau Thanh
Tan An
Can Duoc
Cao Lanh
Thap Muoi
Van Co
Duyen Hai
Ba Chuc
Vinh Gia
Cau Sac
Cai Lay
My Tho
Go Cong Dong
Ha Tien
Tri Ton
Chau Thanh
Cho Gao
Co To
Thanh Hung
Cai Be
Go Cong Tay
Tri Binh
Long Xuyen
Sa Dec
Chau Thanh
Tang Hoa
Tri Hoa
Vinh Long
Hon Chong
Hon Soc
Thoai Son
Thot Not
My Thuan
Cho Lach
Ben Tre
Binh Dai
Hon Dat
Binh Minh
Giong Trom
O Mon
Long Ho
Mo Cay
Rach Gia
Tan Hiep
Tam Binh
Vung Liem
Can Tho
Huong My
Ba Tri
Chau Thanh
Tra On
Chau Thanh
Cang Long
ThanhPhu
Giong Rieng
Tra Vinh
Ke Sach
Kien An
Ben Nhurt
Vi Thanh
Rach Goi
Cau Ke
Tieu Can
Phung Hiep
Cau Ngang
An Bien
Go Quao
Thuan Hoa
Tra Cu
Long Phi
Long My
Soc Trang
Long Phu
Duyen Hai
National Highway 1A
And The Mekong Delta
Route
Cities
Unpaved
Border
Road
River
0 15 30 Mi.
0 15 30Km
©FWI 1995

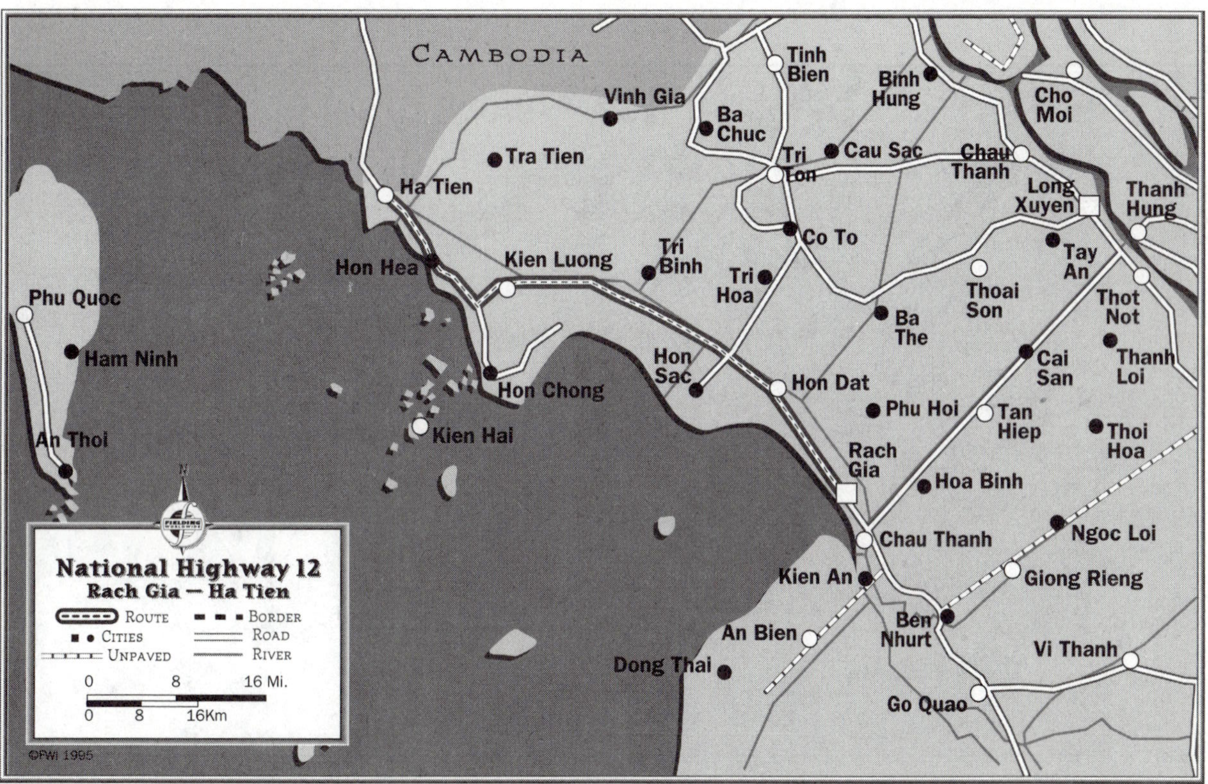
CAMBODIA
Vinh Gia
Tinh Bien
Binh Hung
Cho Moi
Ba Chuc
Tra Tien
Tri Ton
Cau Sac
Chau Thanh
Ha Tien
Long Xuyen
Thanh Hung
Co To
Tay An
Hon Hea
Kien Luong
Tri Binh
Tri Hoa
Thoai Son
Thot Not
Phu Quoc
Ba The
Ham Ninh
Cai San
Thanh Loi
Hon Sac
Hon Dat
Hon Chong
Phu Hoi
Tan Hiep
Thoi Hoa
An Thoi
Kien Hai
Rach Gia
Hoa Binh
Chau Thanh
Ngoc Loi
Kien An
Giong Rieng
Ben Nhurt
An Bien
Vi Thanh
Dong Thai
Go Quao
National Highway 12
Rach Gia — Ha Tien
Route
Border
Cities
Road
Unpaved
River
0
8
16 Mi.
0
8
16Km
©PWI 1995

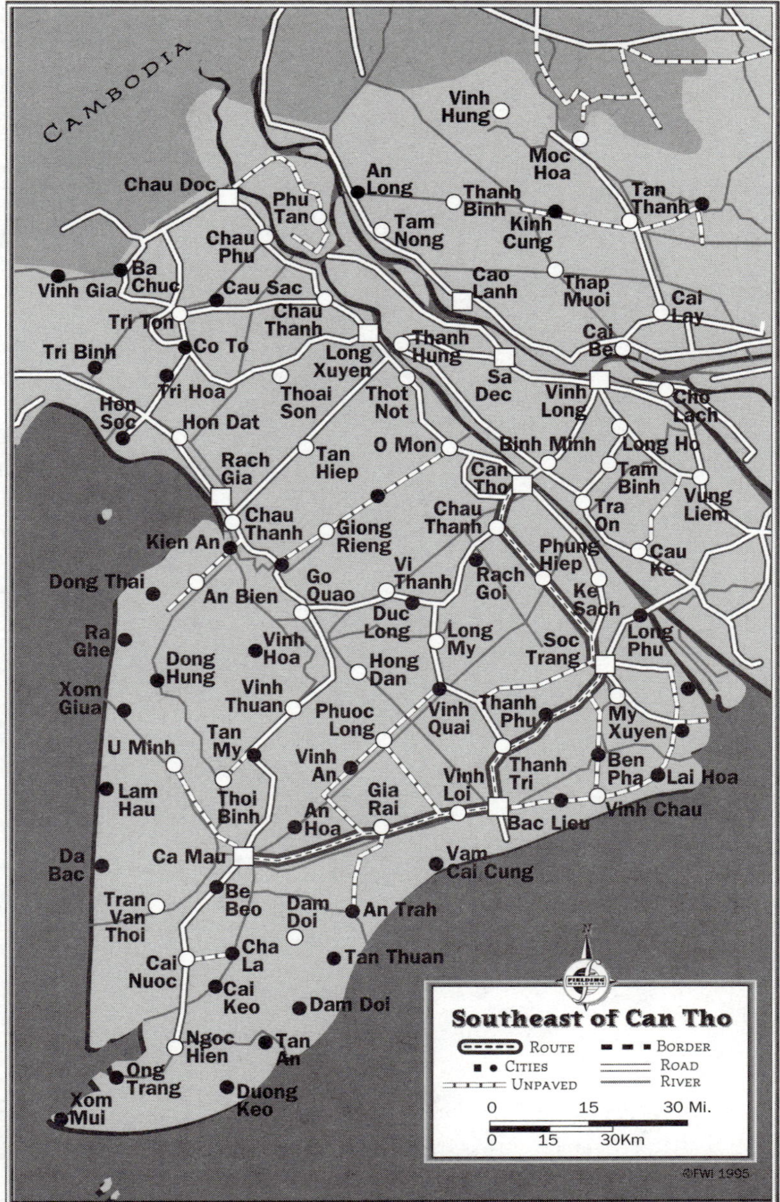
CAMBODIA
Vinh Hung
Moc Hoa
An Long
Chau Doc
Phu Tan
Thanh Binh
Tan Thanh
Kinh Cung
Tam Nong
Chau Phu
Ba Chuc
Vinh Gia
Cau Sac
Cao Lanh
Thap Muoi
Cai Lay
Tri Ton
Chau Thanh
Cai Be
Co To
Thanh Hung
Tri Binh
Long Xuyen
Sa Dec
Tri Hoa
Vinh Long
Cho Lach
Hon Soc
Thoai Son
Thot Not
Hon Dat
O Mon
Binh Minh
Long Ho
Tan Hiep
Can Tho
Tam Binh
Rach Gia
Vung Liem
Tra On
Chau Thanh
Chau Thanh
Giong Rieng
Kien An
Cau Ke
Phung Hiep
Dong Thai
Vi Thanh
Rach Goi
Go Quao
An Bien
Ke Sach
Duc Long
Long Phu
Ra Ghe
Long My
Soc Trang
Vinh Hoa
Hong Dan
Dong Hung
Xom Giua
Vinh Thuan
Thanh Phu
My Xuyen
Phuoc Long
Vinh Quai
Tan My
U Minh
Ben Pha
Vinh An
Thanh Tri
Lai Hoa
Lam Hau
Thoi Binh
Gia Rai
Vinh Loi
Vinh Chau
An Hoa
Bac Lieu
Da Bac
Ca Mau
Vam Cai Cung
Be Beo
Tran Van Thoi
Dam Doi
An Trah
Cha La
Tan Thuan
Cai Nuoc
Cai Keo
Dam Doi
Ngoc Hien
Tan An
Ong Trang
Duong Keo
Xom Mui
N
FIELDING WORLDWIDE
Southeast of Can Tho
ROUTE
BORDER
CITIES
ROAD
UNPAVED
RIVER
0 15 30 Mi.
0 15 30Km
©FWI 1995

# INDEX

## E



## F



## G



## H

## I



## K



## L

## Y



## Z

# Order Your Guide to Travel and Adventure

| Title | ISBN | Price |
|---|---|---|
| Fielding's Alaska Cruises/Inside Passage | 1-56952-068-2 | $17.95 |
| Fielding's Amazon | 1-56952-000-3 | $16.95 |
| Fielding's Australia '96 | 1-56952-097-6 | $16.95 |
| Fielding's Bahamas '96 | 1-56952-081-X | $15.95 |
| Fielding's Belgium '96 | 1-56952-078-X | $16.95 |
| Fielding's Bermuda '96 | 1-56952-082-8 | $15.95 |
| Fielding's Borneo | 1-56952-026-7 | $18.95 |
| Fielding's Brazil | 1-56952-027-5 | $18.95 |
| Fielding's Britain '96 | 1-56952-083-6 | $16.95 |
| Fielding's Budget Europe '96 | 1-56952-084-4 | $17.95 |
| Fielding's Caribbean '96 | 1-56952-085-2 | $18.95 |
| Fielding's Caribbean Cruises '96 | 1-56952-070-4 | $18.95 |
| Fielding's Eastern Caribbean '96 | 1-56952-071-2 | $17.95 |
| Fielding's Europe '96 | 1-56952-087-9 | $18.95 |
| Fielding's European Cruises '96 | 1-56952-074-7 | $17.95 |
| Fielding's Far East '95/96 | 1-56952-032-1 | $18.95 |
| Fielding's France | 1-56952-033-X | $16.95 |
| Fielding's Freewheelin' USA | 1-56952-067-4 | $17.95 |
| Fielding's Hawaii '96 | 1-56952-090-9 | $17.95 |
| Fielding's Holland '96 | 1-56952-086-0 | $16.95 |
| Fielding's Italy '96 | 1-56952-091-7 | $17.95 |
| Fielding's Guide to Kenya's Best Hotels, Lodges & Homestays | 1-56952-038-0 | $17.95 |
| Fielding's Las Vegas Agenda | 1-56952-075-5 | $14.95 |
| Fielding's London Agenda | 1-56952-039-9 | $14.95 |
| Fielding's Los Angeles Agenda | 1-56952-040-2 | $14.95 |
| Fielding's Malaysia and Singapore | 1-56952-041-0 | $17.95 |
| Fielding's Mexico | 1-56952-092-5 | $18.95 |
| Fielding's New York Agenda | 1-56952-044-5 | $12.95 |
| Fielding's New Zealand | 1-56952-101-8 | $16.95 |
| Fielding's Paris Agenda | 1-56952-045-3 | $14.95 |
| Fielding's Portugal '96 | 1-56952-102-6 | $16.95 |
| Fielding's Rome Agenda | 1-56952-077-1 | $14.95 |
| Fielding's San Diego Agenda | 1-56952-088-7 | $14.95 |
| Fielding's Scandinavia | 1-56952-103-4 | $16.95 |
| Fielding's Southeast Asia '96 | 1-56952-065-8 | $18.95 |
| Fielding's Southern Vietnam on Two Wheels | 1-56952-064-X | $15.95 |
| Fielding's Spain | 1-56952-094-1 | $17.95 |
| Fielding's Guide to Thailand Including Cambodia, Laos, Myanmar | 1-56952-069-0 | $18.95 |
| Fielding's Vacation Places Rated | 1-56952-062-3 | $19.95 |
| Fielding's Vietnam | 1-56952-095-X | $17.95 |
| Fielding's Western Caribbean '96 | 1-56952-072-0 | $15.95 |
| Fielding's Guide to the World's Most Dangerous Places | 1-56952-031-3 | $19.95 |
| Fielding's Worldwide Cruises '96 | 1-56952-073-9 | $18.95 |
| The Indiana Jones Survival Guide | 1-56952-076-3 | $18.95 |

To place an order: call toll-free 1-800-FW-2-GUIDE
(VISA, MasterCard and American Express accepted)
or send your check or money order to:
Fielding Worldwide, Inc., 308 S. Catalina Avenue, Redondo Beach, CA 90277
add $2.00 per book for shipping & handling (sorry, no COD's), allow 2–6 weeks for delivery

# Order Your Guide to Travel and Adventure

| Title | ISBN | Price |
|---|---|---|
| Fielding's Alaska Cruises/Inside Passage | 1-56952-068-2 | $17.95 |
| Fielding's Amazon | 1-56952-000-3 | $16.95 |
| Fielding's Australia '96 | 1-56952-097-6 | $16.95 |
| Fielding's Bahamas '96 | 1-56952-081-X | $15.95 |
| Fielding's Belgium '96 | 1-56952-078-X | $16.95 |
| Fielding's Bermuda '96 | 1-56952-082-8 | $15.95 |
| Fielding's Borneo | 1-56952-026-7 | $18.95 |
| Fielding's Brazil | 1-56952-027-5 | $18.95 |
| Fielding's Britain '96 | 1-56952-083-6 | $16.95 |
| Fielding's Budget Europe '96 | 1-56952-084-4 | $17.95 |
| Fielding's Caribbean '96 | 1-56952-085-2 | $18.95 |
| Fielding's Caribbean Cruises '96 | 1-56952-070-4 | $18.95 |
| Fielding's Eastern Caribbean '96 | 1-56952-071-2 | $17.95 |
| Fielding's Europe '96 | 1-56952-087-9 | $18.95 |
| Fielding's European Cruises '96 | 1-56952-074-7 | $17.95 |
| Fielding's Far East '95/96 | 1-56952-032-1 | $18.95 |
| Fielding's France | 1-56952-033-X | $16.95 |
| Fielding's Freewheelin' USA | 1-56952-067-4 | $17.95 |
| Fielding's Hawaii '96 | 1-56952-090-9 | $17.95 |
| Fielding's Holland '96 | 1-56952-086-0 | $16.95 |
| Fielding's Italy '96 | 1-56952-091-7 | $17.95 |
| Fielding's Guide to Kenya's Best Hotels, Lodges & Homestays | 1-56952-038-0 | $17.95 |
| Fielding's Las Vegas Agenda | 1-56952-075-5 | $14.95 |
| Fielding's London Agenda | 1-56952-039-9 | $14.95 |
| Fielding's Los Angeles Agenda | 1-56952-040-2 | $14.95 |
| Fielding's Malaysia and Singapore | 1-56952-041-0 | $17.95 |
| Fielding's Mexico | 1-56952-092-5 | $18.95 |
| Fielding's New York Agenda | 1-56952-044-5 | $12.95 |
| Fielding's New Zealand | 1-56952-101-8 | $16.95 |
| Fielding's Paris Agenda | 1-56952-045-3 | $14.95 |
| Fielding's Portugal '96 | 1-56952-102-6 | $16.95 |
| Fielding's Rome Agenda | 1-56952-077-1 | $14.95 |
| Fielding's San Diego Agenda | 1-56952-088-7 | $14.95 |
| Fielding's Scandinavia | 1-56952-103-4 | $16.95 |
| Fielding's Southeast Asia '96 | 1-56952-065-8 | $18.95 |
| Fielding's Southern Vietnam on Two Wheels | 1-56952-064-X | $15.95 |
| Fielding's Spain | 1-56952-094-1 | $17.95 |
| Fielding's Guide to Thailand Including Cambodia, Laos, Myanmar | 1-56952-069-0 | $18.95 |
| Fielding's Vacation Places Rated | 1-56952-062-3 | $19.95 |
| Fielding's Vietnam | 1-56952-095-X | $17.95 |
| Fielding's Western Caribbean '96 | 1-56952-072-0 | $15.95 |
| Fielding's Guide to the World's Most Dangerous Places | 1-56952-031-3 | $19.95 |
| Fielding's Worldwide Cruises '96 | 1-56952-073-9 | $18.95 |
| The Indiana Jones Survival Guide | 1-56952-076-3 | $18.95 |

To place an order: call toll-free 1-800-FW-2-GUIDE
(VISA, MasterCard and American Express accepted)
or send your check or money order to:
Fielding Worldwide, Inc., 308 S. Catalina Avenue, Redondo Beach, CA 90277
add $2.00 per book for shipping & handling (sorry, no COD's), allow 2–6 weeks for delivery

# Favorite People, Places & Experiences

ADDRESS: NOTES:

Name

Address

Telephone

Name

Address

Telephone

Name

Address

Telephone

Name

Address

Telephone

Name

Address

Telephone

## Favorite People, Places & Experiences

| ADDRESS: | NOTES: |
|---|---|

Name

Address

Telephone

Name

Address

Telephone

Name

Address

Telephone

Name

Address

Name

Address

Telephone

*Name*

Address

Telephone